From the Pages of
The Brothers Karamazov

"He is haunted by a great, unsolved doubt. He is one of those who don't want millions, but an answer to their questions."

(page 82)

"All we Karamazovs are such insects, and, angel as you are, that insect lives in you, too, and will stir up a tempest in your blood."

(page 106)

"I have a longing for life, and I go on living in spite of logic. Though I may not believe in the order of the universe, yet I love the sticky little leaves as they open in spring. I love the blue sky, I love some people, whom one loves you know sometimes without knowing why."

(page 214)

"For any one to love a man, he must be hidden, for as soon as he shows his face, love is gone."

(page 219)

"A beast can never be so cruel as a man, so artistically cruel."   (page 221)

"In every man, of course, a demon lies hidden—the demon of rage, the demon of lustful heat at the screams of the tortured victim, the demon of lawlessness let off the chain, the demon of diseases that follow on vice."

(page 224)

"Sometimes even if he has to do it alone, and his conduct seems to be crazy, a man must set an example, and so draw men's souls out of their solitude, and spur them to some act of brotherly love, that the great idea may not die."

(page 280)

And what follows from this right of multiplication of desires? In the rich, isolation and spiritual suicide; in the poor, envy and murder; for they have been given rights, but have not been shown the means of satisfying their wants. . . . Interpreting freedom as the multiplication and rapid satisfaction of desires, men distort their own nature, for many senseless and foolish desires and habits and ridiculous fancies are fostered in them. . . . They have succeeded in accumulating a greater mass of objects, but the joy in the world has grown less.

(page 289)

Kiss the earth and love it with an unceasing, consuming love. Love all men, love everything. Seek that rapture and ecstasy.

(page 296)

Fathers and teachers, I ponder "What is hell?" I maintain that it is the suffering of being unable to love.

(page 297)

"I'll confess all my infernal wickedness, but to put you to shame, and you'll be surprised yourself at the depth of ignominy to which a medley of human passions can sink."
(pages 451–452)

"And, besides, who isn't suffering from aberration, nowadays?—you, I, all of us are in a state of aberration, and there are ever so many examples of it: a man sits singing a song, suddenly something annoys him, he takes a pistol and shoots the first person he comes across, and no one blames him for it."
(page 528)

"Suffering is life. Without suffering what would be the pleasure of it? It would be transformed into an endless church service; it would be holy, but tedious."
(page 584)

"My father has been murdered and they pretend they are horrified. . . . They all desire the death of their fathers."
(page 625)

"But *beyond*—I don't know whether Karamazov wondered at that moment 'What lies beyond,' and whether Karamazov could, like Hamlet, wonder 'What lies beyond.' No, gentlemen of the jury, they have their Hamlets, but we still have our Karamazovs!"
(page 650)

"Gentlemen of the jury, what is a father—a real father? What is the meaning of that great word? What is the great idea in that name?" (page 672)

"You must know that there is nothing higher and stronger and more wholesome and good for life in the future than some good memory. . . . Even that may sometime be the means of saving us."
(page 700)

"Dear friends, don't be afraid of life! How good life is when one does something good and just!"
(page 701)

THE BROTHERS KARAMAZOV

Fyodor Dostoevsky

With an Introduction and Notes
by Maire Jaanus

Translated by Constance Garnett

George Stade
Consulting Editorial Director

BARNES & NOBLE CLASSICS
NEW YORK

B

BARNES & NOBLE CLASSICS
NEW YORK

Published by Barnes & Noble Books
122 Fifth Avenue
New York, NY 10011

www.barnesandnoble.com/classics

The Brothers Karamazov—in Russian, *Bratya Karamazov*—was first published
between 1879 and 1880.
Constance Garnett's translation first appeared in 1912.

Published in 2004 by Barnes & Noble Classics with new Introduction,
Notes, Biography, Chronology, List of Characters, Inspired By, Comments &
Questions, and For Further Reading.

Introduction, Notes, List of Characters, and For Further Reading
Copyright © 2004 by Maire Jaanus.

Note on Fyodor Dostoevsky, The World of Fyodor Dostoevsky
and *The Brothers Karamazov*, Inspired by *The Brothers Karamazov*,
and Comments & Questions
Copyright © 2004 by Barnes & Noble, Inc.

The Brothers Karamazov
ISBN 978-1-59308-045-7
LC Control Number 2004100523

Produced and published in conjunction with:
Fine Creative Media, Inc.
322 Eighth Avenue
New York, NY 10001

Michael J. Fine, President and Publisher

Printed in the United States of America

QM

25   27   29   30   28   26

Fyodor Dostoevsky

Fyodor Mikhailovich Dostoevsky was born in Moscow on October 30, 1821. His mother died when he was fifteen, and his father, a former army surgeon, sent him and his older brother, Mikhail, to preparatory school in St. Petersburg. Fyodor continued his education at the St. Petersburg Academy of Military Engineers and graduated as a lieutenant in 1843. After serving as a military engineer and inheriting some money from his father's estate, he retired from the army and decided instead to devote himself to writing.

Dostoevsky won immediate recognition with the 1846 publication of his first work of fiction, a short novel titled *Poor Folk*. The important Russian critic Vissarion Grigorievich Belinsky praised his work and introduced him into the literary circles of St. Petersburg. Over the next few years Dostoevsky published several stories, including "The Double" and "White Nights." He also became involved with a progressive group known as the Petrashevsky Circle, headed by the charismatic utopian socialist Mikhail Petrashevsky. In 1849 Tsar Nicholas I ordered the arrest of all the members of the group, including Dostoevsky. He was kept in solitary confinement for eight months while the charges against him were investigated and then, along with other members of Petrashevsky's group, was sentenced to death by firing squad. At the last minute Nicholas commuted the sentence to penal servitude in Siberia for four years, and then service in the Russian Army. This near-execution haunts much of Dostoevsky's subsequent writing.

The ten years Dostoevsky spent in prison and then in exile in Siberia had a profound effect on him. By the time he returned to St. Petersburg in 1859, he had rejected his radical ideas and acquired a new respect for the religious ideas and ideals of the Russian people. He had never been an atheist, but his Christianity was now closer to the Orthodox faith. While in exile he had also married.

Dostoevsky quickly resumed his literary career in St. Petersburg. He and his brother Mikhail founded two journals, *Vremya* (1861–1863) and *Epokha* (1864–1865). Dostoevsky published many of his well-known post-Siberian works in these journals, including *The House of the Dead*, an account of his prison experiences, and the dark, complex novella "Notes from Underground."

The next several years of Dostoevsky's life were marked by the deaths of his wife, Maria, and his brother Mikhail. He began to gamble compulsively on his trips abroad, and he suffered from bouts of epilepsy. In 1866, while dictating his novel *The Gambler* to meet a deadline, he met a young stenographer, Anna Snitkina, and the two married a year later. Over the next fifteen years Dostoevsky produced his finest works, including the novels *Crime and Punishment* (1866), *The Idiot* (1868), *The Possessed*

(1871–1872), and *The Brothers Karamazov* (1879–1880). His novels are perceptive psychological studies that examine man's struggle with such elemental issues as good and evil, life and death, belief and reason. Fyodor Mikhailovich Dostoevsky died from a lung hemorrhage on January 28, 1881, in St. Petersburg at the age of fifty-nine.

TABLE OF CONTENTS

The World of Fyodor Dostoevsky and The Brothers Karamazov

1821   Fyodor Mikhailovich Dostoevsky is born on October 30 in Moscow. The second of seven children, he grows up in a middle-class household run by his father, a former army surgeon and strict family man.

1833   Aleksandr Pushkin's novel in verse *Eugene Onegin* is published.

1836   Pushkin's story "The Queen of Spades" is published.

1837   Fyodor's mother dies. He and his older brother Mikhail are sent to a preparatory school in St. Petersburg.

1838   Dostoevsky begins his tenure at the St. Petersburg Academy of Military Engineers, where he studies until 1843. He becomes acquainted with the works of such writers as Byron, Corneille, Dickens, Goethe, Gogol, Homer, Hugo, Pushkin, Racine, Rousseau, Shakespeare, and Schiller.

1839   Dostoevsky's father is, according to rumor, murdered on his country estate, presumably by his own serfs.

1842   Part 1 of Nikolai Gogol's novel *Dead Souls* is published.

1843   Dostoevsky graduates from the Academy as a lieutenant, but instead of pursuing a career in the army, resolves to dedicate his life to writing.

1844   His first published work appears, a Russian translation of Honoré de Balzac's 1833 novel *Eugénie Grandet*. Dostoevsky begins work on his first novel, *Poor Folk*.

1845   On the basis of *Poor Folk*, Dostoevsky wins the friendship and acclaim of Russia's premier literary critic, Vissarion Grigorievich Belinsky, author of the scathingly critical "Letter to Gogol" (1847).

1846   *Poor Folk* and "The Double" are published. "The Double" is the first work in which Dostoevsky writes about the psychology of the split self. Dostoevsky meets the utopian socialist M. V. Butashevich-Petrashevsky.

1847   Dostoevsky publishes numerous short stories, including "A Weak Heart," "Polzunkov," and "The Landlady."

1848   He publishes the short story "White Nights." The *Communist Manifesto*, by Karl Marx and Friedrich Engels, is published. Revolutions break out in France, Germany, Hungary, Italy, and Poland.

1849   Dostoevsky is arrested for his participation in the socialist Petrashevsky Circle. He first spends eight months in solitary confinement and is then condemned to death by firing squad. Tsar Nicholas I commutes his sentence to penal servitude in Siberia, but orders this to be announced only at the last minute.

1850   Dostoevsky begins his four-year internment at Omsk in western Siberia. His experiences there will influence many of his later works. While imprisoned he abandons the radical ideas of his youth and becomes more deeply religious; his only book in prison is a copy of the Bible.

1852   Part 2 of Gogol's *Dead Souls* is published.

1853   The Crimean War breaks out, the cause being a dispute between Russia and France over the Palestinian holy places.

1854   Still exiled in Siberia, Dostoevsky begins four years of compulsory military service.

1857   He marries the widow Maria Dmitrievna Isaeva.

1859   Dostoevsky and Maria are allowed to return to St. Petersburg.

1861   He and his brother Mikhail establish *Vremia* (Time); this year and the next the journal publishes Dostoevsky's *The House of the Dead*, a work based on his experiences in Siberia.

1862   Dostoevsky travels to England, France, Germany, Italy, and Switzerland, a trip that engenders in him an anti-European outlook. He gambles heavily at resorts abroad, losing money.

1863   Dostoevsky makes a second trip to Europe and arranges to meet Apollinaria Suslova in Paris; he had published a story by her in *Vremia* the previous year. The two have an affair.

1863   The progressive Nikolai Chernyshevsky publishes the utopian novel *What Is to Be Done?*, which Dostoevsky will react against a year later in "Notes from Underground." *Vremia* is banned for printing a potentially subversive article regarding the Polish rebellion.

1864   Dostoevsky and his brother Mikhail establish *Epokha* (Epoch), the short-lived successor to *Vremia*; the journal publishes "Notes from Underground," the first of Dostoevsky's masterworks. Dostoevsky's wife, Maria, dies from tuberculosis. His brother Mikhail dies three months later.

1865   Burdened with debt, Dostoevsky embarks on another failed gambling spree in Europe. He proposes to Apollinaria Suslova without success.

1866   *Crime and Punishment* starts serial publication at the beginning of the year. Dostoevsky interrupts the writing in October in order to work on *The Gambler*; he is forced to meet the contract deadline for that book in order to retain the rights to his published works, including *Crime and Punishment*. He dictates *The Gambler* to a stenographer, Anna Grigorievna Snitkina, over the course of a month. He and Anna, who is twenty-five years his junior, become romantically involved.

1867   Dostoevsky marries Anna Snitkina, the alliance is one of the most fortunate events of his life. To avoid financial ruin, the two live abroad for the next four years, in Geneva, Florence, Vienna, Prague, and finally Dresden. Dostoevsky's epilepsy worsens. He begins work on his novel *The Idiot*, in which the protagonist is an epileptic. The first three of what will be six volumes of Leo Tol-stoy's *War and Peace* appear in print in December, bound in yellow covers.

1868   *The Idiot* is published in installments this year and next. The fourth volume of *War and Peace* appears in March.

1869   The final volumes of Tolstoy's *War and Peace* are published: the fifth in February and the sixth in December.

1871   Dostoevsky and his wife return to St. Petersburg. Serialization of his novel *The Possessed* begins.

1873   Dostoevsky becomes editor of the conservative weekly *Grazh-danin* (The Citizen); "The Diary of a Writer" becomes a regular and popular feature of the weekly.

1875   Tolstoy begins publishing *Anna Karenina*.

1876   *The Diary of a Writer* is published as a monojournal—that is, it was written and edited entirely by Dostoevsky; in it he publishes "The Meek One."

1877   "The Dream of a Ridiculous Man" is published in *The Diary of a Writer*.

1879   Serialization begins in another journal of *The Brothers Karama-zov*, widely considered Dostoevsky's greatest novel.

1880   Six months before his death, Dostoevsky delivers his famous speech on Pushkin at the dedication of the Pushkin memorial in Moscow.

1881   Dostoevsky dies from a lung hemorrhage on January 28 in St. Petersburg. His epitaph, also the epigraph to *The Brothers Kara-mazov*, is from the Bible (John 12:24); it reads, "Verily, verily, I say unto you, Except a corn of wheat fall into the ground and die, it abideth alone: but if it die, it bringeth forth much fruit" (King James Version).

1886   German philosopher Friedrich Nietzsche publishes *Beyond Good and Evil*, which was greatly influenced by *The Possessed*.

1912   Constance Garnett begins her translations of the works of Dosto-evsky, introducing his writings to the English-reading world.

Introduction

> Man is a mystery. It needs to be unravelled, and if you spend your whole life unravelling it, don't say that you've wasted time. I am studying that mystery because I want to be a human being.
> —Fyodor Dostoevsky, in a letter to his brother,
> M. M. Dostoevsky, August 16, 1839

The Brothers Karamazov is an encounter with passion. For Dostoevsky the passions are the most mysterious dimension of the human being, and, therefore, this is the dimension that obsesses and compels him. It is the source of his art. Against any Enlightenment trust in reason, against any Hegelian faith in consciousness and its development, against any demand for a final meaning, Dostoevsky persists in pointing to an impassable joy as well as a blocked darkness and muteness at the core of our being. Consciousness tries to be deterministic, to predict and to control; but the passions are unpredictable, random, and accidental. Thus in Dostoevsky's novels sudden, grand epiphanies of rapture and despair arise out of a narrative that is classical, linear, and realistic, with a plot that is one of the most logical ever constructed. At moments these flashings of bliss and anxiety seem, in their intensity, to destroy the narrative and to stop its motion. They are instances of Dostoevsky's desire to grasp something beyond the limits of reason, knowledge, and language. They are his reaching beyond realism or what we ordinarily acknowledge as reality into infinitude and silence.

At these moments, Dostoevsky attempts to answer what he calls the eternal questions: What is heaven and what is hell? What pleasure or pain do these grand original metaphors represent within the psychic human domain? He is not only interested in the theological answer to these questions, but in an existential and psychological answer. What conditions make for a psychic heaven or hell in the here and now? What could give Ivan those two seconds of senseless, useless, speechless joy that he so desperately desires and for which he would give a "quadrillion quadrillions" (p. 625)? What do we finally really believe in? What gives us conviction? That which makes us happy or sad, Dostoevsky answers, that which both our body and emotions confirm as solid and true: our deepest pleasures and pains.

These incidences of sheer, sublime excess are the deeply original, poetic core of Dostoevsky, the place from which this author is truly each time born. At such moments of acute joy and pain, his characters, as well as we his readers, depart from a mundane chronology of limited beginnings, middles, and ends, and move into an open and infinite time and space. We leave the obsessiveness and anxiety of finite time that culminates in endings and death, and enter into eternity. In such heightened moments of passion—such as Alyosha's ecstatic dream of Zossima at the marriage in Cana of Galilee, Zossima's conversion, or Ivan's delirious dialogue with the devil—the subject escapes from the body, from the field of narcissism, sexuality, and sexual rivalry, in which nearly everyone but Alyosha and Zossima struggle, to a wider field of death or love, extending beyond the confines of sexuality and language.

Parricide, Smerdyakov, and Hysteria

The passion for a father murder is at the heart of this novel. That Dostoevsky takes up this great passion links him on the one hand to Greek tragedy and Sophocles' *Oedipus Rex*, and on the other to psychoanalysis and Freud's *Totem and Taboo*. Parricide and regicide are motivated by a desire to destroy something foundational—all law, representation, and order, or the fundamental gift of the father that makes these possible: language. Smerdyakov, the father murderer in act, ultimately turns taciturn and mute. Ivan cries to him, "Speak, please, speak" (p. 569); but ultimately Smerdyakov refuses. Rather than submit to the law that demands giving an account, narrating, speaking, and being judged by others, Smerdyakov escapes by suicide. He returns to the solitude of his languageless body.

The languageless body was once with the mother, who is aligned with the bodily and sensuous. The father function is to separate us from this natural, speechless union with the mother by the introduction of language. From this perspective, therefore, the father murder, insofar as it is a desire to stay with or to have the mother, is an attempt to avoid the splitting of our being that the acquisition of language demands. The refusal of this division into, on the one hand, a living organism in nature and, on the other, a dead and abstract system of language and symbolic means, inevitably signals a rebellion as well against subsequent divisions, such as the sexual. The sexual division pits a predominantly phallic father against a more generally sensuous and erotic mother. Dostoevsky intuits these foundational psychoanalytic insights in that he does not entirely condemn the murder of the father: In the climactic trial scene, he introduces a systematic questioning of the very right of a father to that name if he is not loving toward his children or, in essence, not at all motherly. Who is a father? Who has right to that name? asks the defense attorney. Can an unloving, irresponsible father be called a father? Did Dmitri kill a father or just a man? Was this parricide or homicide? In a bold move, Dostoevsky goes beyond the inviolability of the father and his unquestioned position of dominance, opening up a space for femininity and the mother. From the perspective of our century, this is a radical gesture on Dostoevsky's part, one that aligns Dostoevsky and his "hero" Alyosha on the side of the feminine, equality, and the law of love.

The retention of the value of love and unreasoning nature that the mother represents introduces doubt and indecisiveness into all the decisions as well as the actions of the Karamazov brothers. How should one act or reason: according to the laws of the mother or those of the father? Should one punish or forgive? Should one impose the law or give way to loving trust, charity, and hope? None of the characters seem to know what to do with the passions aroused by the contradictions between their bodies and their ideas or how to handle, manipulate, or take care of the forces of desire, love, and hate that impel them. Thus, the ultimate source of the characters' symptoms and pathologies, their renown and excruciating doubts and inner conflicts, is the general, unavoidable trauma of the knotting of a living body to a dead, abstract system of language. This knotting introduces an intense desire for unity and resolution, and at the same time, it makes such unity impossible. In intangible language all things seem possible; but given the gap between language and concrete reality and language's essential distance from any actualization, language brings us up against impotence. Dostoevsky's characters all rebel against such impotence and impossibility, though in very different ways. None knows how to heal the symptom and the division that each lives with. The ferocity of their desire for a unity, an answer, produces various kinds of beliefs as well as fantasies and fictions. These beliefs are the sutures for the fundamental rupture that the human being is of nature by culture, of instinctual life by intuitions and visionary images, and of mere belief by reason.

Alyosha escapes the rupture by belief. He seeks the dream of divine love to which the hysteria of his mother, produced in reaction to the father's cruel phallic excesses, directed him early on. Ivan is broken by his inexorable contradictions and forced into the nightmare of madness. Dmitri tries to deal with his division in various very physical and concrete ways, which makes him capable of both brutally humiliating a father in front of his child and weeping for a hungry and freezing baby in a dream. The final hope for a resolution lies for him in an ethical sexuality that mutes the phallic sexuality belonging to the father with the desire for love and union with the object of love (the mother substitute) that is on the side of the mother. Thus, entwined with the narrative, which calls to account the arbitrary character of phallocentrism and paternal authority, is a narrative of a purely sexual rivalry between a father and a son that expands into a dialogue elaborating the conflicts between sex and love. Consequently, the father murder represents a perverse attempt to stop the fundamental hysterical split from which Dostoevsky himself and all of his characters suffer. The hysterical side of Dostoevsky seeks an enjoyment beyond the phallic and beyond the law of the father; but it is also this hysterical side that enables him to question this very desire and to be his century's greatest interrogator of the historical progress of humankind and of its sciences and laws.

In his essay "Dostoevsky and Parricide" (in Wasiolek, *"The Brothers Karamazov" and the Critics*; see "For Further Reading"), in which he calls *The Brothers Karamazov* "the most magnificent novel ever written," Freud interprets Dostoevsky's epilepsy as a neurotic symptom of hysteria. He tells us that even as a child Dostoevsky had strange attacks of a sense of imminent death and melancholy, that before going to sleep he used to leave little notes about saying that if he seemed dead, he was not to be buried for five days. Freud says the meaning of the deathlike attack Dostoevsky apparently feared is identification with a dead person or someone we wish dead, and that in the latter case the attack has the value of a punishment. We can add that the young Dostoevsky's notes connect writing with death and the hope of succor from an other. Writing is a communication between the dead and the living, a defense against the fear of death, and a reassurance that one is still alive.

The same fundamental anxiety and incertitude about life and death that prevented Dostoevsky as a child from relaxing and sleeping runs through the veins of this novel and through every one of his characters. It is an unstillable anxiety and ambivalence about the truth of our existence and about what we can or dare to believe. Until his death Dostoevsky himself remained torn and divided between atheism and belief, albeit the central issue of this novel is not belief or disbelief in God, but belief or disbelief in one's fellow human being.

Dostoevsky's hysterical dividedness assures that the novel's discourse as a whole, as well as that of its narrator, is never a master discourse. No answer or resolution is ever imposed. The extremes of bliss and cruelty are represented as matched. Bliss does not redeem cruelty. Both exist, but apart. The saint does not triumph over the murderer. The saint's body stinks. The law punishes the wrong man. Reason proves futile against radical evil. The seemingly idiotic, useless, and gratuitous act of love matches the idiotic, gratuitous act of murder. One is as unwarranted and as uncaused as the other, yet for each and from each a chain of cause and effect can be created. Dostoevsky's argument is like that of the defense, who says, "Oh, I admit that the chain of evidence—the coincidences—are really suggestive. But examine all these facts separately, regardless of their connection," and nothing is proven (p. 667). On the basis of the facts, one can argue that Dmitri committed the crime as well as that he did not. Similarly, it is possible to argue that God exists or that He does not. We are predisposed one way or another, and we arrange the facts to meet our basic expectations or desire. It all boils down to belief, to whether or how each brother does or does not believe that Dmitri is the murderer. There is seemingly no basis for the decision, no proof. The image of the trial is an image of the failure and inadequacy of our judgment, and as such it indirectly supports Zossima's argument for nonjudgment. Maintaining the hysterical tension of a split forces the reader to choose, and Dostoevsky's sense is that we are reluctant to assume the responsibility of choice; we would much rather that some necessity of logic or passion force us to choose one way or another. Then, at least, we are not responsible. However, even if Dostoevsky's hysteria prevents his commitment to a belief, one can say that he continues to believe in believing rather than in disbelieving.

In terms of conception rather than action, however, the real father murderer is Ivan, for the idea of the father murder is his. He is the one who conceives the idea—his is the vision of a godless and masterless society where all would be equal, though he understands that godlessness would also mean lawlessness. It is this idea of lawlessness, that all is permitted, that captivates Smerdyakov's mind because it is the very key to his own existence. Ivan becomes Smerdyakov's "law," his father, his god. "I put my whole trust in you, as in God Almighty," he says to Ivan (p. 552). He believes in Ivan's words. Ivan's words are his law: "It was following your words I did it," he tells Ivan (p. 567). (The Latin words *lex* for "law" and *lexis* for "speech" are related.) Smerdyakov is the word of Ivan made flesh: "It was done in a most natural way, following your very words" (p. 569). Smerdyakov's cold-blooded portrayal of his unreasonable reasoning and act of murder as "most natural" infinitely distances his "confession" from the tormented one Zossima receives from a mysterious visitor who murdered the widow he loved out of jealous passion.

The Grand Inquisitor believes men need authority and the word. Ivan was the first ever to give Smerdyakov a sense of a paternal voice or commandment, a word in which he could believe and which struck him as true: lawlessness. Ivan's idea suddenly makes sense of his senseless life: He was conceived and born because "all is permitted"; a fundamental lawless, senseless, and violent sexuality was the cause of his coming into being. Smerdyakov's motivation for murder is, therefore, not "revenge or greed" as the prosecutor says, for then we would understand him; it is actually his belief in an idea, in a lawless law that at once awakens and perverts his mind. What Smerdyakov, however, as a pervert lacks is a sense of the distance between words and acts, wishes and deeds, and thus he thinks Ivan wants his wish for the murder enacted.

Smerdyakov's being is not only porous to Ivan's words but also affectively attuned to Ivan's innermost wishes for his father's death. However, he executes Ivan's unconscious wish for the death of his father, not only because he is able to identify with it, but because he believes in the death of a father whose law and power are in truth utter lawlessness, violence, and profound indifference to anyone on earth but himself. It is not easy for him to kill; he does so in fear and trembling. Being the coward that he is, he has to force himself to do it. And it is because he is so fearful that he thinks about it so much and takes so many precautions. What he really wants, above all, is Ivan's protection and closeness. Thus Smerdyakov reveals the deepest roots of Ivan's unconscious reality, but he does so because Ivan's trauma is his own reality and deepest truth as well. He thinks Ivan guessed that the murder would occur and left in order to protect himself. He thinks Ivan's departure was a signal to him that he could go ahead unhindered with the murder. His fear, his cowardice, and his current suffering over Ivan's rejection of his act are his bit of humanity. When Smerdyakov ceases to believe in Ivan, he learns that he is alone. The other, whom he imagined as his likeness, throws him away. This entails a loss of himself as a subject that precipitates his suicide. Smerdyakov kills himself because he has lost the only bond he ever formed; because he has also lost the self it was so difficult for him to become, the murderer; and because he can with this suicide escape being once more subjected to Ivan and used by him. With his escape, he can defeat and frustrate Ivan's desire for truth: There is no evidence at the trial. Suicide is his revenge upon Ivan.

Human law cannot reach or punish a belief; it can only judge and punish an act. Smerdyakov escapes the law, and its judgment and punishment, by his suicide. If he allowed himself to be condemned by human law, then his own belief that all things are lawful would be seen to be condemned as wrong. And he wants to be right. He wants to be the embodiment of the truth of lawlessness, which he at core is. Illegitimacy and illegality are his identity and his legacy. He wants to establish proof of lawlessness, which is the truth of his very life, even at the cost of his own life; or at least he wants to do this in the eyes of Ivan, for whom he now feels "contempt," "repulsion," and "insane hatred" (pp. 566–567). "Well, kill me. Kill me now.... You won't dare do that even! ... You won't dare to do anything, you, who used to be so bold!" (p. 575). With death he escapes being accountable or wrong. There is nothing to contradict his belief. Suicide is a final affirmation of "everything is lawful."

In his suicide note, Smerdyakov writes, "I destroy myself of my own will and inclination so as to throw no blame on any one" (p. 647). He puts a stop to himself by himself, by death. He becomes his own law. We like to say that he went insane and dismiss him. But what if to kill an other or himself is his desire? What if suicide is his inclination and his will, or even his satisfaction? He wants to kill himself. He abdicates speaking, and then being. Maybe his is a rebellion against the coming into existence of human life as such, a preference of death over life? We don't know. Smerdyakov ends in the same muteness that Christ does.

Smerdyakov's purpose in the novel is to assert the prereflective, inaccessible, foundationless darkness and mystery in humankind, without which there would be no need for salvation or love. He is a testimony against the existence of love. He is the void that fills with hatred. His negative transcendence and sublimation occurs through the "sacrifice" of himself—his life and his body—for himself, not for another. Christ's suicide is for the other; Smerdyakov's is against the other, against Ivan. He kills himself to defy another and to uphold the truth of the lack of law and a "beyond" of the law that is not love but death. If the Karamazov force is the human being as the unbounded, the volcanic force ever ready to erupt, the only thing that can stop a Karamazov is something that is equally unbounded and beyond any law. There are only three such things: love, life, and death. Smerdyakov ultimately arrests and binds himself through death. Death is his end, the ultimate master to whom he surrenders, as well as the infinity, albeit negative, to which he aspires. He escapes the law and himself into the unboundedness and "freedom" of death.

The prosecutor, in the name of Russia, presses for the punishment of the parricide; otherwise law and the authority of the father are undermined, and by extension, so are the order of society and civilization. Society has to kill those who have no respect for life. The defense argues that the father-son bond has to be love, not law. The defense asks for charity, arguing that the law has always to allow for exceptions (petitions, pardons, exemptions), because otherwise the law is impossible and totalitarian.

By the end of his three dramatic visits to Smerdyakov, Ivan has come to understand the utter uselessness of his mind. He will not be able to prove that Smerdyakov is the murderer although he knows this to be true. From this follows the hallucinatory scene of self-confrontation and Ivan's indictment of his own reason: It is Ivan in hell, judging, condemning, and damning his own most precious gift. Momentarily he apprehends all that his intellect has always fought: his own desire not to be intellectual, not to think, but simply to believe and to have joy; his knowledge that the intellect cannot answer any of the eternal questions and that he knows, in fact, nothing beyond the boundary of death; his perception that life is not logical, deterministic, or necessary but utterly accidental and contingent in a way that escapes rational ordering, apprehension, and control. The scene of delirium is an uncurbed examination of the limits of the mind and of language.

Ivan is in pain. His fundamental identity has always been closely tied to his very thought processes and dependent on his chain of words and ideas, and now it proves to be utterly precarious because such a chain does not give him a real being—one located in his own body and emotions. When his faith in this chain breaks, he loses himself as a subject and falls into a void of ignorance and stupidity: "Why, why is everything so stupid?" (p. 626) he cries the moment before he is carried out of the court, his mind broken and screaming. Stupidity is the intellectual's opposite and his death. Stupidity is what everyone flees, except Dostoevsky and his intellectual hero, Ivan. Smerdyakov's stupidity, in the broadest sense, represents the very center of what neither Ivan nor symbolic means can get at: a stubborn impossibility, a wall, a barrier at the heart of life. Smerdyakov's subtle death drive and his fundamental incomprehension and misrecognition of everything are at the center of the novel, though this center is perforce inaccessible. He is marginal, almost hidden, though he emerges as the "clarification" of, even as "the answer" to, Ivan's questions and as the proof of the truth that something fundamentally against life and love, something deadly and evil exists, even if it cannot be grasped.

Ivan, who in his intellectual arrogance and emotional coldness, his sense of personal freedom and autonomy and lack of appreciation for others has never had to acknowledge his relationship to anyone, finds himself responsible for a fellow man he despises. He discovers that his pride in his independence is an illusion. There are no clearly defined borders between himself and Smerdyakov. The boundaries are not fixed; instead they shift and overlap. For Ivan, it is tragic to have to say: I am the other of the murderer or I am the murderer. He is forced to recognize another in an excruciating bond not of love but of hatred. Ivan has in fact acted as irresponsibly as his father and Dmitri, though Ivan's is an intellectual irresponsibility whereas the father's is a basic biological one, an amorality that makes him oblivious even to the fact that his sensuality has begotten him children, and Dmitri's is that of a physical and temperamental lack of control over his violence. Dmitri's body governs his mind. Against all of them Zossima preaches the doctrine of responsibility to one's fellow man.

The Silence of Love and Christ's Kiss

There is Smerdyakov's stubborn muteness of passionate hatred and murderous anger, but there is also the muteness of love. The silent Christ who appears in Ivan's Grand Inquisitor's tale "speaks" only in signs. He responds to the Grand Inquisitor's virulent harangue and indictment of him with a single bodily gesture of acceptance, tolerance, understanding, and compassion. "The kiss glows in his heart, but the old man adheres to his idea" (p. 243). Muteness is beyond language. Where is it then? It is in a domain of irrational knowledge that comes by way of pathos and bodily affects and not by the working through of concepts. The Grand Inquisitor represents belief in the intellect, in the law, in order and authority. He represents the logic of death, both perceptual and actual. Yet his knowledge, like all knowledge, is never free of doubt, otherwise this ninety-year-old man would not need to justify himself and claim his righteousness once again. Like every intellectual, the Grand Inquisitor is reiterating his convictions precisely because all remains doubtful and uncertain. The mind's binary system of language continually produces negations and contraries. ("Doubt," from the Latin *dubitare*, means, precisely, to hesitate in the face of two possibilities.)

The Grand Inquisitor claims to know human nature. He believes that the devil solved the enigma of human nature with the three questions he posed to Christ in the desert. At the same time the devil proved his "absolute and eternal" (p. 234) intelligence. Given that we now know the mystery of man and know mankind as rationally and scientifically analyzable, the Grand Inquisitor also believes that mankind is now predictable and that therefore we can proceed to build a state, organized on the basis of this knowledge, that would provide humans with at least some security, peace, and happiness. Christ is wrong to have refused and contradicted the devil. He did not love mankind; He came only for the elect; He is undemocratic; He left mankind freedom and choice, which makes humans suffer; He had no compassion; He was mad; He failed utterly to understand humans; He burdened them with doubt, choice, and the responsibility to become human and to humanize their society collectively, tasks to which humans are not equal and which cause them great anxiety. The Grand Inquisitor says he also went into the wilderness, but that he "awakened and would not serve madness" (pp. 240–241). He is an atheist, and though in his state miracles will be staged and belief in God upheld, he knows that after life there is only death. Man is not ever beyond man, as Christ believed. Man on the contrary is "weak, vicious, worthless and rebellious" (p. 235), and, therefore, in need of authority and direction, or a benign totalitarian or communist state.

Every human wants first of all to live—that is, to have bodily and material security (food, shelter, and clothing) that guarantee self-preservation.

That there are some humans, like Gandhi and other freedom fighters and heroes, who can oppose their natural survival instincts does not count for the Grand Inquisitor because they are only the rare elect. Secondly, according to the Grand Inquisitor, man wants peace and security in his mind; he wants to be doubt-free and certain about what he believes, what he thinks, and what he does; he wants a guarantee that what he thinks and does is right. If there is agreement, or even better universal assent, then he is assured. Men war for that assent and for the dominance of their beliefs. Humans cannot tolerate uncertainty or doubt in their minds or conscience. They want a secure and doubt-free mental and ethical existence. Finally, humans want something to live for. In essence what they want is simply to live more, to live eternally; they want immortality. They want not only to live in a secure and safe way, bodily and mentally, but to do so forever. Thus they require some proof of eternity to still their anxiety, and this too the Grand Inquisitor will provide. His state robs humans of freedom and the right to the pursuit of truth, but it liberates them from doubt, anxiety, fear, competition, and war. Humans will surrender their freedom for the sake of their more urgent needs for survival and safety. The only ones who will know the truth are a few, like the Grand Inquisitor himself, who will have to bear the burden of the deception for the sake of the happiness of the majority. The Grand Inquisitor sees mankind as limited, closed, and finished, whereas Christ represents mankind as something unlimited, open, and unfinished. In a sense, the Grand Inquisitor claims for himself the place of Christ: He is the suffering one, the tragic figure, the moral masochist, the one on the cross, bearing the weakness and deficiencies of mankind in order to provide them with some moderate happiness. The Grand Inquisitor suffers; he lacks belief in human beings; his knowledge is motivated by a deficiency of joy.

The Grand Inquisitor is a figure born of Ivan's own pain. Ivan cannot grasp how God and such horrible sufferings as there are in the world can coexist. He says it is not God he rejects but the world God created. Ivan's torment is the cruelty, sadism, and indifference that he sees as the fundamental symptom of his world. He believes in the reality of this senseless suffering, and he refuses to accept that there is an ultimate significance or sense to it. The agony of a child torn apart by hunting dogs, set on him by a sadistic landlord, before his mother's eyes, is a torture that for Ivan could never be made good, not even in a paradise that would reunite this mother and son, healed. The existential horror they endured is real, as paradise would be, but one has nothing to do with the other; one cannot undo the other. That there is a miracle called love that could provide us with so inconceivable a healing is a hope to which Ivan cannot yield his reality-embedded mind. He proceeds to create a figure, the Grand Inquisitor, who after a lifetime of thinking has figured out how the world without God and immortality could be organized so as to provide some minimal, utilitarian happiness for the majority.

"Hell . . . is the suffering of being unable to love" (p. 297). For Dostoevsky love is the only state of being that allows us to experience eternity, for love is a pleasure that connects us to timelessness. Sex is a defense against love. Why? Because it limits love. Sex has a beginning, a middle, and an end. Sex is finitude; love is infinitude. Sex is intense pleasure; love is bliss. It is a difference that Dmitri discovers. It is the secret of Christ's kiss.

Christ was a figure of tremendous importance to Dostoevsky. He wrote that even if it were proven that Christ is outside the truth, he "would prefer to remain with Christ rather than with the truth" (letter to Natalya Fonvizina, January/February 1854, in Dostoevsky, *Complete Letters: Vol. 1*, p. 195). Ivan almost consents to something similar that Alyosha says, namely that one must "love life more than the meaning of it" and "love it, regardless of logic" (p. 214). In Ivan's conception, Christ is a radiant, feminine, and romantic figure, reminiscent of Ernest Renan's biography of Christ and William Holman Hunt's painting *The Light of the World*. His gesture of the kiss points to the heart, to love, and to human desire, which is ever for what we do not have, but which is central to our aliveness, to our very feeling of being alive. And this aliveness that love gives is, as Dostoevsky says, more important than the truth.

Dostoevsky is seemingly trying to move the Russian soul from an autocratic, autonomous, and isolated Christ, who is separate from the world and, as the son of God, identical with God's "I" ("I am I"—that is, I am one with the original "I," or Oneness) toward a more modern, historical, and realistic Christ, who lives in the world and whose main difference from other humans lies in his greater serenity and rapture and his greater capacity to embrace everyone. He comes among mankind to say not "I am I," but "I am and I love" (p. 297). He has the irresistible power of beauty, grace, and gentleness: "The sun of love burns in His Heart, light and power shine from His eyes, and their radiance, shed on the people, stirs their hearts with responsive love" (p. 230). He celebrates coexistence, not divine or Cartesian autonomy ("I think therefore I am"). His love is unconditional, and it is not qualified by a demand to obey the laws and the commandments.

Thus he is not the Pantocrator, the ruler of the world who appears on Byzantine icons with all the traditional symbols of knowledge, authority, and power. He is instead the power of love, freedom, tenderness, and nonjudgment. He is not concerned with learning, wisdom, power, or ideas. As in Hunt's painting, he is associated with nature, trees, leaves, and flowers; with the symbols of the open door, lamplight, and moonlight; and with a new dawn, a new age, and a new type of human being. Like Zossima, his only teaching is the love of everything: "Love every leaf, every ray of God's light. Love the animals, love the plants, love everything" (p. 293). And if we do, then we can feel, as does Zossima, such "sweetness" and "youthful gladness," and "such bliss in my heart as I had never known before in my life." We will see that "life is heaven" (p. 276).

For Zossima the true guilt of mankind lies not in our crimes but in our failure to commit acts of love. We don't believe in love: That is the greatest human flaw, not our disbelief in God. We do not trust that others love or that we ourselves love. We have never even tried to build a civilization on love, on our desire for a vaster, more asexual eroticism. We think belief is just a desire, like the Freudian wish, and therefore a fiction. But belief has effects; it leads to striving and development. Belief could develop our passional nature. We have not yet begun to explore the potential productivity of an eroticism that is not the focused eroticism of the Freudian sexual body. Dostoevsky is concerned with the differences between sexual, phallic love and the more general, asexual eroticism that we are capable of. With Dmitri he is exploring how sexual and asexual love are allied. What finally is of value? What finally matters in having lived? Is it not love? Dostoevsky's eros is a broad and passionate love of all of life. Zossima teaches that even if there is no one left to love and you are alone, bow down: "Kiss the earth and love it with an unceasing, consuming love. Love all men, love everything. Seek that rapture and ecstasy" (p. 296). Zossima sees the need for us to increase our capacity not to think, but to love. Love changes one more than knowledge does. Love is more powerful than thought: That is Zossima's thesis.

In a sense, one can say that this, Dostoevsky's last novel, is about love and nothing but love. Love unbinds us; it gives us a sense of infinitude and eternity. But that is precisely why love for Zossima must, in fact, be bound. It cannot go flying off into nowhere in the imagination; it must be bound by acts of love, by what Zossima calls active love. Active love means that love has to become joined to an action, a gesture, or a deed. One must give an onion or a pound of nuts, put a pillow under someone's head, or help a freezing peasant out of the snow. Active love is more than a feeling or a thought; it is a concrete action.

The Grand Inquisitor and Ivan doubt that love exists or that it is a source of agency or power. Indeed, love does not "exist"; rather, there is the possibility of creating it. Active love is as much such a creation as is a poem. It is poetry of small, wordless gestures and signs. Once one begins to practice active love, one can potentially acquire faith. As we advance in love, we "grow surer of the reality of God and of the immortality of [the] soul" (p. 60). Belief, however, can be maintained or restored only by doing the creative work active love requires. Belief is born secondarily to the experience of love. Dostoevsky knows that for modern human beings there can be no belief without experience, and that the only earthly experience that can lead to belief in Christ or God is active love. In love one abandons all judgment, all logic of good and evil, of beautiful and ugly. Real love, which for Zossima is nonjudgmental love, makes one naturally ethical because the happiness of loving and being loved is so great that one is naturally good. There's no other conceivable path.

When love does exist, it feels like our nature. Markel (Zossima's elder brother), Zossima, and Alyosha are characters who have discovered their nature; they have discovered: "I am and I love." Alyosha is Dostoevsky's main example of the practice of active love. Alyosha, as the narrator tells us, is his hero about whom he hoped to write a second volume. Like Zossima, Alyosha listens impartially and mostly silently to the traumas and sufferings of others. His position is similar to that of the psychoanalyst in that his being is a clearing in which others can appear and become visible; he has space for others because his own ego is not in the way. They appear as Lise does—as hysterical, cruel, weak; and yet Alyosha simply accepts this, as does Zossima. Unlike the Grand Inquisitor, Alyosha and Zossima do not see the other as in need of correction or as tragic. Neither do they think that the Grand Inquisitor's radically de-idealized vision of humans is wrong; contrary to him, however, although they see the same human condition that he does, they let it be. They refuse to judge the other, the fellow human being. Dostoevsky seems to understand, as Freud did, that judgment (or the superego) is a castrating agency and that it severs one from infinitude. Thus Zossima preaches that we should not judge. He teaches a radical detachment from judgment, a positive unwillingness to judge: "Remember particularly that you cannot be a judge of any one" (p. 295).

Alyosha is constantly subjected to the confessions and disclosures of others because he lets others in. He is the character with the loosest ego boundaries. Lise says that she at times despised him because he is not a master. He who loves is not a master. Love contradicts the idea of mastership and of singleness. Love is, therefore, the only sane practice, the only sane language. It presupposes the "I" and the "You." Love thus also allows the human function of language as communication and creation to emerge. Alyosha is testimony to the fact that human existence, which is an existence in language, is by that fact always a relationship to an other, a passionate, speaking coexistence. Ideally this coexistence is love and belief in another, but it can also be hatred. Alyosha is Dostoevsky's neo-subject, a new kind of human being, born of love and of the recognition of the other, beyond any master-slave or power relationship.

For some readers, Alyosha remains an unreal and unconvincing character, with whom they cannot identify and whom they cannot love because he is so borderless, so lacking in a strong ego. Indeed, Alyosha is not confined to his ego. Whenever we see Alyosha we see and feel others. He is both himself and the other. For this he evokes disrespect in Lise, for example, who asks him: "Alyosha, why is it I don't respect you? . . . If I respected you, I shouldn't talk to you without shame, should I?" (p. 530). The person we respect is someone autonomous and masterly, with his own boundaries and opinions, to whom we can and cannot say certain things because we know they will react and give us arguments. Alyosha accepts everything. He listens; he lets others flow through him. He sets up no barriers. He insists on no strict boundaries between the "I" and an opponent, "you." He is a new kind of egoless subject. But if I am the other, does this not mean that I am not myself? Does it not mean some self-loss? We dread any self-loss; but Zossima calls it a gift we should welcome because it frees us from doubt and it is our chance for rebirth. "If you attain to perfect self-forgetfulness in the love of your neighbour, then you will believe without doubt, and no doubt can possibly enter your soul. This has been tried. This is certain" (p. 60). For Zossima, self-forgetfulness, liberation from our own ego and its clamorous demands, is the gift that love gives us. Love brings a voiding of our ego, which allows us to fill it anew. Unless, however, your loving attains to this void or self-emptiness, you have no chance for renewal. This is what Christ meant when he said unless you die, you cannot be reborn or begin anew.

The answer to the Grand Inquisitor's vision of control and punishment is Alyosha's and Zossima's vision of free self-punishment and their faith in love. One cannot experience guilt toward someone one does not love. Alyosha believes in the deepest sense that everyone who loves or who has been loved can experience guilt and thereby save himself. And this is why he speaks of memory. Memories give weight and content to the self. The best memories are those that include others. If a child has loved, it is saved. Acts of love and hate of others may be forgotten by the recipient, but the law is: You remember your own acts of love or lovelessness, and that is why the little boy, Ilusha, is tormented by the memory of the dog that he thinks must have died in agony because Smerdyakov told him to feed it a piece of bread with a pin in it.

Alyosha is not a master and neither is Zossima. The Grand Inquisitor, however, believes that he must be a master, even against his own will and desire for happiness. He is a tragic master. For Ivan and his Grand Inquisitor, love, like many other things, is unsubstantial, an unreality; and they both want reality. Indoctrinated as we all are into reality by realism and science, we forget that we could not understand reality without an understanding of unreality. The consequence of the occlusion of this dimension is despair. And the consequence of not believing that the disposition to love actually exists in human beings is having to believe instead in mankind's radical evil or bad nature, and by extension in a curb on man's freedom, in a strong state and a strong law, in rule and punishment. If human nature is bad, we need strict law and government. Dostoevsky understood this and therefore argued against the Grand Inquisitor's totalitarian state for a law of love and charity and belief—a law that believes in the efficacy of love because love fulfills human desire. Such a law is the first impulse at birth and therefore our deepest desire. It is the potential of the ethical impulse in mankind. Love automatically entails a self-forgetting, a self-renunciation, a self-sacrifice that is at the core of ethics. When we give up on love, when we no longer want love, because we come to believe that the other doesn't want to give it to us, is unable to give it to us, or, more awful, actually hates us, we die or we kill ourselves as Smerdyakov does. We turn to the only other beyond: death.

The Eternal Questions, Humanism, and the Beyond

Dostoevsky's characters are concerned with infinitude. They refuse to live without infinitude or without a Hamlet-like concern with the eternal questions. A maddening lack of satisfaction sustains desire in this novel—sexual desire, intellectual desire, and spiritual desire, along with all the more mundane desires for money and power. And all these desires are blocked by impossibility, by the finite. One can choose to live only in the finite, but then, according to Kierkegaard and Dostoevsky, one is in despair. To find joy, one has at that boundary of the finite to choose belief and love. Even a fragmented and muddled being like Dmitri understands that although mankind is conflicted because of too many choices between good and evil, and too broad—"Yes, man is broad, too broad, indeed. I'd have him narrower" (p. 107)—if you whittle him down you lose freedom and ethical accountability, and Dmitri's major question concerns ethics. "What is ethics?" he asks (p. 537), and what is the right thing for me to do? If you reduce the human being, you also lose desire and love. Then you create the hell that is "the suffering of being unable to love," to connect, to reach for the impossible.

Modern bureaucratization and technologization aggravate the rupture between us and infinity. This infinity that it was still possible to grasp through religion or philosophy in Dostoevsky's era is today only maintained by psychoanalysis via the passions, via that which is bodily and seemingly a product of the body and yet not bodily: that is, via the body's demand for its own beyond. Thus now we can grasp infinity only by a transcendence of our sexual reality toward death or toward love. It is the transcendence that Dmitri is at the end striving for with Grushenka. He feels perturbed and changed by his affective experience with her. She has become for him the unexpected event, an encounter with a love that is beyond phallic sexuality.

Dostoevsky does not consider the questions of ethics, epistemology, and subjectivity without considering their founding in the passions, in human desire and fantasies and their attendant modes of enjoyment. He also knows that paradoxically our enjoyment can be a resistance to joy, a desire for unhappiness. Thus Dmitri has said, "There's no living without joy" (p. 330), but Dostoevsky puts Lise into the novel to contradict him: She says, "I don't want to be happy" (p. 531). The conscious, commonsense idea that everyone wants to be happy becomes thereby more thorny and complex, as does everything having to do with the human passions in Dostoevsky. It was Marx who investigated the grounding of culture in economic labor, work, and production, and similarly it is Dostoevsky who investigates the grounding of the thinking and speaking subject in the work, movement, and productions of the emotions and the passions.

The Brothers Karamazov energizes and taxes the intellect; it calls on the reader to think about and to answer the "eternal questions": What is human happiness? Is there a God? What is despair (or Hell)? What is a father? What is the law and how should it operate? When does one forgive? Why is there cruelty? What is ethics? Why do we suffer? How can we face and comfort each other over death and loss? It is because he asks the eternal questions that Dostoevsky is above all a humanist, someone deeply interested in the possibilities and limits of the human condition, someone who wonders where we are going, what our purpose is. The humanist reminds us of the needs and dimensions of the human, what Dostoevsky calls mankind's broadness. We have no boundaries; we bring into the world a sense of something beyond anything in reality or anything graspable. And this dimension is so much a part of mankind that if it is destroyed his being is destroyed. What supports this beyond is freedom, love, belief, and language. Without these things, there cannot be a true subject.

There are intellectually taxing sections in the novel that may make some feel Dostoevsky is just beyond their head; but that is because Dostoevsky understood that the human condition as such is beyond our head. Who understands life, its purpose or meaning, given that it empirically concludes in death? Who understands love or death? Life, love, and death are issues that are beyond our logic and comprehension. They permanently and profoundly disturb our existence. The corpse is the ultimate fear and challenge to our courage and the body that is desired is the ultimate object of strife, contest, and war.

The main question of the novel—it was perhaps the most passionate question of the nineteenth century—is: What can bind and constrain or what can best guide these passions? Love or law? Not law because, for one, humans transgress it, and, for another, it is not commensurate with human and interhuman complexity or the mystery of human nature. The magnificent extended court scene at the end of the novel proves that law is not enough. An innocent human being, Dmitri, is sentenced for a murder he has not committed, but only desired.

Thus Dostoevsky belongs among those humanists who have seen that there is for us always a beyond, a more, an absolute, a purity, an excess. Not to live in some way for this beyond (even if it is death) or to accept it is to be not fully human. To reduce ourselves to a life without desire for a beyond is partly to dehumanize ourselves. The beyond is freedom and uncertainty, and it is inherently traumatic. The novel's very trajectory is toward a trauma, the trauma of murder and death, the trauma of injustice and incorrect deductions, the trauma of the perverse mind and act of Smerdyakov.

Dostoevsky belongs both to the Enlightenment and to Romanticism. What stands out about his work is, on the one hand, an intensity, ferocity, and agony of thinking unequaled in literature. It is a thinking beyond the limits of reason, into madness. This is the Enlightenment stretched to extremity. On the other hand, there is in his work a domain of the passions that operates without conscious thinking and judging, a more romantic region of fear and of love, a domain of the feminine that points to the future, to new and different ways of dying and living.

Maire Jaanus is Professor of English at Barnard College, Columbia University. She is the author of *Georg Trakl* (1974), *Literature and Negation* (1979), *She* (a novel, 1984), and numerous articles; an associate editor of *Literature and Psychology*; and coeditor of *Reading Seminars I and II: Lacan's Return to Freud* (1996), *Reading Seminar XI: Lacan's Four Fundamental Concepts* (1995), and *Lacan in the German-Speaking World* (2004).

List of Characters

Russian middle names are patronymics; that is, they are derived from the father's first name, with a suffix that indicates the gender of the child. Russian speakers use the first name and patronymic together when they wish to refer to someone formally (for example, Alexey Fyodorovitch). Family members and close friends use diminutives—shortened versions of the first name—to refer to one another affectionately (for example, Alyosha). In this list, diminutives and nicknames appear in parentheses after full names.

Alexey Fyodorovitch Karamazov (Alyosha): Third son of Fyodor Karamazov and the protagonist of the novel.

Dmitri Fyodorovitch Karamazov (Mitya, Mityenka): Eldest son of Fyodor Karamazov.

Ivan Fyodorovitch Karamazov (Vanka): Middle son of Fyodor Karamazov.

Fyodor Pavlovitch Karamazov: Patriarch of the Karamazov family.

Agrafena Alexandrovna Svyetlov (Grusha, Grushenka): Brought to town by Samsonov, Grushenka becomes a wellspring of romantic intrigue for the men in the town, including Fyodor and Dmitri.

Pavel Fyodorovitch Smerdyakov: Epileptic son of Fyodor Karamazov and Lizaveta Smerdyastchaya, raised by Grigory Vassilyevitch and his wife Marfa.

Zossima: Elder at the monastery who mentors Alyosha.

Katerina Ivanovna Verkhovtsev (Katya): Dmitri's fiancée; he leaves her when he falls for Grushenka.

Madame Hohlakov: Wealthy townswoman.

Lise Hohlakov: Madame Hohlakov's daughter; she is engaged to Alyosha for a brief period.

Mihail Ospovitch Rakitin (Misha): Seminary student who secretly hates Alyosha.

Pyotr Alexandrovitch Miüsov: Cousin of Fyodor Karamazov's first wife and a wealthy landowner; for a short period of time he serves as Dmitri's guardian.

Pyotr Ilyitch Perhotin: Young official and a friend of Dmitri.

Kuzma Kuzmitch Samsonov: Merchant who brings Grushenka to town.

Lizaveta Smerdyastchaya: Young townswoman who is retarded; she is often referred to as "Stinking Lizaveta."

Fetyukovitch: Lawyer who represents Dmitri.

Ippolit Kirillovitch: Prosecutor in Dmitri's case.

Father Ferapont: Monk who despises Zossima.

Nikolay Ivanovitch Krassotkin (Kolya): Young boy who becomes friends with Alyosha after the illness of Ilusha.

Ilusha Snegiryov: Son of a military captain who becomes friends with Alyosha; he eventually becomes very ill.

Grigory Vassilyevitch: Servant of Fyodor Karamazov who raises Smerdyakov.

THE BROTHERS KARAMAZOV

Dedicated to
Anna Grigorievna Dostoevsky[1]

"Verily, verily, I say unto you, except a corn of wheat fall into the ground and die, it abideth alone: but if it die, it bringeth forth much fruit."

John 12:24

From the Author

I N BEGINNING the life story of my hero, Alexey Fyodorovitch Karamazov, I find myself in somewhat of a quandary. Namely, although I call
Alexey Fyodorovitch my hero, I myself know that he is by no means a
great man, and hence I foresee such unavoidable questions as these:
"What is so remarkable about your Alexey Fyodorovitch, that you have
chosen him as your hero? What has he accomplished? What is he known
for, and by whom? Why should I, the reader, spend time learning the facts
of his life?"

The last question is the most fateful, for to it I can only answer: "Perhaps you will see for yourself from the novel." Well, suppose you read the
novel, and fail to see, and so do not agree to the remarkability of my
Alexey Fyodorovitch? I say this because unhappily I anticipate it. For me
he is remarkable, but I doubt strongly whether I shall succeed in proving
this to the reader. The fact is, if you please, that he is a protagonist, but a
protagonist vague and undefined. And, in truth, in times such as ours it
would be strange to require clarity of people. One thing, I dare say, is fairly
certain: this man is odd, even eccentric. But oddness and eccentricity interfere with rather than help in the uniting of the strands and in the finding of some sort of common meaning in the general confusion. In most
cases the eccentric is a particularity, a separate element. Isn't that so?

Now, if you do not agree with this last thesis, and answer, "It isn't so," or
"It isn't always so," then I, if you please, might become encouraged about
the significance of my hero, Alexey Fyodorovitch. For not only is an eccentric "not always" a particularity and a separate element, but, on the
contrary, it happens sometimes that such a person, I dare say, carries
within himself the very heart of the universal, and the rest of the men of
his epoch have for some reason been temporarily torn from it, as if by a
gust of wind. . . .

Still, I should not have plunged into these eternally uninteresting and
confused explanations and should have begun quite simply, without introduction: "If they like it, they will read it"; but the trouble is that I have two
tales, and only one life story. The main narrative is the second—it is the action of my hero in our day, at the very present time. The first tale takes
place thirteen years ago, and it is hardly even a novel, but only a period in
my hero's early youth. I cannot do without this first tale, because much in
the second tale would be unintelligible without it. But in this way my original difficulty is rendered still more complicated: if I, that is, the biogra-
pher himself, find that even one tale would perhaps be superfluous for
such a modest and undefined hero, how ever can I appear with two, and
how from my point of view can I justify such presumption?

Finding myself lost in the solution of these questions, I decide to bypass
them with no solution at all. Of course, the astute reader has long since

guessed that from the very first I was leading up to this, and was vexed with me for wasting fruitless words and precious time. To this, I shall answer explicitly: I was spending fruitless words and precious time, first, out of courtesy, and second, out of shrewdness: "Still," the reader might say, "he has forewarned us of something." Indeed, I am actually glad that my book has of itself split into two narratives, "with essential unity of the whole": having become acquainted with the first tale, the reader will then decide for himself whether it is worth his while to attempt the second. Of course, one is not bound by anything—the book can be abandoned at the second page of the first tale, never to be opened again. But then, you know, there are those considerate readers who have a compulsion to read to the end, so as not to be mistaken in their impartial judgment; such, for example, are all the Russian critics. It is before this type of person that my heart somehow becomes lighter: despite all their careful exactness and conscientiousness, I nevertheless give them a perfectly legitimate pretext to abandon the tale at the novel's first episode. Well, there is the whole foreword. I completely agree that it is needless, but since it has already been written, let it stand.

And now to the matter at hand.

Contents

PART ONE

BOOK ONE

THE HISTORY OF A FAMILY

1

FYODOR PAVLOVITCH KARAMAZOV

ALEXEY FYODOROVITCH KARAMAZOV was the third son of Fyodor Pavlovitch Karamazov, a landowner well known in our district in his own day, and still remembered among us owing to his gloomy and tragic death, which happened thirteen years ago, and which I shall describe in its proper place. For the present I will only say that this "landowner"—for so we used to call him, although he hardly spent a day of his life on his own estate—was a strange type, yet one pretty frequently to be met with, a type abject and vicious and at the same time senseless. But he was one of those senseless persons who are very well capable of looking after their wordly affairs, and, apparently, after nothing else. Fyodor Pavlovitch, for instance, began with next to nothing; his estate was of the smallest; he ran to dine at other men's tables, and fastened on them as a toady, yet at his death it appeared that he had a hundred thousand roubles in hard cash. At the same time, he was all his life one of the most senseless, fantastical fellows in the whole district. I repeat, it was not stupidity—the majority of these fantastical fellows are shrewd and intelligent enough—but just senselessness, and a peculiar national form of it.

He was married twice, and had three sons, the eldest, Dmitri, by his first wife, and two, Ivan and Alexey, by his second. Fyodor Pavlovitch's first wife, Adelaïda Ivanovna, belonged to a fairly rich and distinguished noble family, also landowners in our district, the Miüsovs. How it came to pass that an heiress, who was also a beauty, and moreover one of those vigorous, intelligent girls, so common in this generation, but sometimes also to be found in the last, could have married such a worthless puny weakling, as we all called him, I won't attempt to explain. I knew a young lady of the last "romantic" generation who after some years of an enigmatic passion for a gentleman, whom she might quite easily have married at any moment, invented insuperable obstacles to their union, and ended by throwing herself one stormy night into a rather deep and rapid river from a high bank, almost a precipice, and so perished, entirely to satisfy her own caprice, and to be like Shakespeare's Ophelia.* Indeed, if this precipice, a chosen and favourite spot of hers, had been less picturesque, if there had been a prosaic flat bank in its place, most likely the suicide would never have taken place. This is a fact, and probably there have been not a few

---

*Female protagonist of Shakespeare's *Hamlet*, who was driven to madness and suicide.

15

similar instances in the last two or three generations. Adelaïda Ivanovna Miüsov's action was similarly, no doubt, an echo of other people's ideas, and was due to the irritation caused by lack of mental freedom. She wanted, perhaps, to show her feminine independence, to override class distinctions and the despotism of her family. And a pliable imagination persuaded her, we must suppose, for a brief moment, that Fyodor Pavlovitch, in spite of his parasitic position, was one of the bold and ironical spirits of that progressive epoch, though he was, in fact, an ill-natured buffoon and nothing more. What gave the marriage piquancy was that it was preceded by an elopement, and this greatly captivated Adelaïda Ivanovna's fancy. Fyodor Pavlovitch's position at the time made him specially eager for any such enterprise, for he was passionately anxious to make a career in one way or another. To attach himself to a good family and obtain a dowry was an alluring prospect. As for mutual love it did not exist apparently, either in the bride or in him, in spite of Adelaïda Ivanovna's beauty. This was, perhaps, a unique case of the kind in the life of Fyodor Pavlovitch, who was always of a voluptuous temper, and ready to run after any petticoat on the slightest encouragement. She seems to have been the only woman who made no particular appeal to his senses.

Immediately after the elopement Adelaïda Ivanovna discerned in a flash that she had no feeling for her husband but contempt. The marriage accordingly showed itself in its true colours with extraordinary rapidity. Although the family accepted the event pretty quickly and apportioned the runaway bride her dowry, the husband and wife began to lead a most disorderly life, and there were everlasting scenes between them. It was said that the young wife showed incomparably more generosity and dignity than Fyodor Pavlovitch, who, as is now known, got hold of all her money up to twenty-five thousand roubles as soon as she received it, so that those thousands were lost to her for ever. The little village and the rather fine town house which formed part of her dowry he did his utmost for a long time to transfer to his name, by means of some deed of conveyance. He would probably have succeeded, merely from her moral fatigue and desire to get rid of him, and from the contempt and loathing he aroused by his persistent and shameless importunity. But, fortunately, Adelaïda Ivanovna's family intervened and circumvented his greediness. It is known for a fact that frequent fights took place between the husband and wife, but rumour had it that Fyodor Pavlovitch did not beat his wife but was beaten by her, for she was a hot-tempered, bold, dark-browed, impatient woman, possessed of remarkable physical strength. Finally, she left the house and ran away from Fyodor Pavlovitch with a destitute divinity student, leaving Mitya, a child of three years old, in her husband's hands. Immediately Fyodor Pavlovitch introduced a regular harem into the house, and abandoned himself to orgies of drunkenness. In the intervals he used to drive all over the province, complaining tearfully to each and all of Adelaïda Ivanovna's having left him, going into details too disgraceful for a husband to mention in regard to his own married life. What seemed to gratify him and flatter his self-love most was to play the ridiculous part of the injured husband, and to parade his woes with embellishments.

"One would think that you'd got a promotion, Fyodor Pavlovitch, you seem so pleased in spite of your sorrow," scoffers said to him. Many even added that he was glad of a new comic part in which to play the buffoon, and that it was simply to make it funnier that he pretended to be unaware of his ludicrous position. But, who knows, it may have been simplicity. At last he succeeded in getting on the track of his runaway wife. The poor woman turned out to be in Petersburg, where she had gone with her divinity student, and where she had thrown herself into a life of complete emancipation. Fyodor Pavlovitch at once began bustling about, making preparations to go to Petersburg, with what object he could not himself have said. He would perhaps have really gone; but having determined to do so he felt at once entitled to fortify himself for the journey by another bout of reckless drinking. And just at that time his wife's family received the news of her death in Petersburg. She had died quite suddenly in a garret, according to one story, of typhus, or as another version had it, of starvation. Fyodor Pavlovitch was drunk when he heard of his wife's death, and the story is that he ran out into the street and began shouting with joy, raising his hands to Heaven: "Lord, now lettest Thou Thy servant depart in peace,"[1] but others say he wept without restraint like a little child, so much so that people were sorry for him, in spite of the repulsion he inspired. It is quite possible that both versions were true, that he rejoiced at his release, and at the same time wept for her who released him. As a general rule, people, even the wicked, are much more naïve and simple-hearted than we suppose. And we ourselves are, too.

2

HE GETS RID OF HIS ELDEST SON

YOU can easily imagine what a father such a man could be and how he would bring up his children. His behaviour as a father was exactly what might be expected. He completely abandoned the child of his marriage with Adelaïda Ivanovna, not from malice, nor because of his matrimonial grievances, but simply because he forgot him. While he was wearying every one with his tears and complaints, and turning his house into a sink of debauchery, a faithful servant of the family, Grigory, took the three-year-old Mitya into his care. If he hadn't looked after him there would have been no one even to change the baby's little shirt.

It happened moreover that the child's relations on his mother's side forgot him too at first. His grandfather was no longer living, his widow, Mitya's grandmother, had moved to Moscow, and was seriously ill, while his daughters were married, so that Mitya remained for almost a whole year in old Grigory's charge and lived with him in the servant's cottage. But if his father had remembered him (he could not, indeed, have been altogether unaware of his existence) he would have sent him back to the cottage, as the child would only have been in the way of his debaucheries. But a cousin of Mitya's mother, Pyotr Alexandrovitch Miüsov, happened to return from Paris. He lived for many years afterwards abroad, but was at that time quite a young man, and distinguished among the Miüsovs as a man of enlightened ideas and of European culture, who had been in the capitals and abroad. Towards the end of his life he became a Liberal of the type common in the forties and fifties. In the course of his career he had come into contact with many of the most Liberal men of his epoch, both in Russia and abroad. He had known Proudhon and Bakunin* personally, and in his declining years was very fond of describing the three days of the Paris Revolution of February, 1848, hinting that he himself had almost taken part in the fighting on the barricades. This was one of the most grateful recollections of his youth. He had an independent property of about a thousand souls, to reckon in the old style. His splendid estate lay on the outskirts of our little town and bordered on the lands of our famous monastery, with which Pyotr Alexandrovitch began an endless lawsuit, almost as soon as he came into the estate, concerning the rights of fishing in the river or wood-cutting in the forest, I don't know exactly which. He regarded it as his duty as a citizen and a man of culture to open an attack upon the "clericals." Hearing all about Adelaïda Ivanovna, whom he, of course, remembered, and in whom he had at one time been interested, and learning of the existence of Mitya, he intervened, in spite of all his youthful indignation and contempt for Fyodor Pavlovitch. He made the latter's acquaintance for the first time, and told him directly that he wished to undertake the child's education. He used long afterwards to tell as a characteristic touch, that when he began to speak of Mitya, Fyodor Pavlovitch looked for some time as though he did not understand what child he was talking about, and even as though he was surprised to hear that he had a little son in the house. The story may have been exaggerated, yet it must have been something like the truth.

Fyodor Pavlovitch was all his life fond of acting, of suddenly playing an unexpected part, sometimes without any motive for doing so, and even to his own direct disadvantage, as, for instance, in the present case. This habit, however, is characteristic of a very great number of people, some of them very clever ones, not like Fyodor Pavlovitch. Pyotr Alexandrovitch carried the business through vigorously, and was appointed, with Fyodor Pavlovitch, joint guardian of the child, who had a small property, a house

---

*Pierre-Joseph Proudhon (1809–1865), French socialist; Mikhail Aleksandrovich Bakunin (1814–1876), Russian anarchist.

and land, left him by his mother. Mitya did, in fact, pass into this cousin's keeping, but as the latter had no family of his own, and after securing the revenues of his estates was in haste to return at once to Paris, he left the boy in charge of one of his cousins, a lady living in Moscow. It came to pass that, settling permanently in Paris he, too, forgot the child, especially when the revolution of February broke out making an impression on his mind that he remembered all the rest of his life. The Moscow lady died, and Mitya passed into the care of one of her married daughters. I believe he changed his home a fourth time later on. I won't enlarge upon that now, as I shall have much to tell later of Fyodor Pavlovitch's first-born, and must confine myself now to the most essential facts about him, without which I could not begin my story.

In the first place, this Mitya, or rather Dmitri Fyodorovitch, was the only one of Fyodor Pavlovitch's three sons who grew up in the belief that he had property, and that he would be independent on coming of age. He spent an irregular boyhood and youth. He did not finish his studies at the gymnasium, he got into a military school, then went to the Caucasus, was promoted, fought a duel, and was degraded to the ranks, earned promotion again, led a wild life, and spent a good deal of money. He did not begin to receive any income from Fyodor Pavlovitch until he came of age, and until then got into debt. He saw and knew his father, Fyodor Pavlovitch, for the first time on coming of age, when he visited our neighbourhood on purpose to settle with him about his property. He seems not to have liked his father. He did not stay long with him, and made haste to get away, having only succeeded in obtaining a sum of money, and entering into an agreement for future payments from the estate, of the revenues and value of which he was unable (a fact worthy of note) upon this occasion, to get a statement from his father. Fyodor Pavlovitch remarked for the first time then (this, too, should be noted) that Mitya had a vague and exaggerated idea of his property. Fyodor Pavlovitch was very well satisfied with this, as it fell in with his own designs. He gathered only that the young man was frivolous, unruly, of violent passions, impatient, and dissipated, and that if he could only obtain ready money he would be satisfied, although only, of course, for a short time. So Fyodor Pavlovitch began to take advantage of this fact, sending him from time to time small doles, instalments. In the end, when four years later, Mitya, losing patience, came a second time to our little town to settle up once for all with his father, it turned out to his amazement that he had nothing, that it was difficult to get an account even, that he had received the whole value of his property in sums of money from Fyodor Pavlovitch, and was perhaps even in debt to him, that by various agreements into which he had, of his own desire, entered at various previous dates, he had no right to expect anything more, and so on, and so on. The young man was overwhelmed, suspected deceit and cheating, and was almost beside himself. And, indeed, this circumstance led to the catastrophe, the account of which forms the subject of my first introductory story, or rather the external side of it. But before I pass to that story I must say a little of Fyodor Pavlovitch's other two sons, and of their origin.

3

THE SECOND MARRIAGE
AND THE SECOND FAMILY

Very shortly after getting his four-year old Mitya off his hands Fyodor Pavlovitch married a second time. His second marriage lasted eight years. He took this second wife, Sofya Ivanovna, also a very young girl, from another province, where he had gone upon some small piece of business in company with a Jew. Though Fyodor Pavlovitch was a drunkard and a vicious debauchee he never neglected investing his capital, and managed his business affairs very successfully, though, no doubt, not over scrupulously. Sofya Ivanovna was the daughter of an obscure deacon, and was left from childhood an orphan without relations. She grew up in the house of a general's widow, a wealthy old lady of good position, who was at once her benefactress and tormentor. I do not know the details, but I have only heard that the orphan girl, a meek and gentle creature, was once cut down from a halter in which she was hanging from a nail in the loft, so terrible were her sufferings from the caprice and everlasting nagging of this old woman, who was apparently not bad-hearted but had become an insufferable tyrant through idleness.

Fyodor Pavlovitch made her an offer; inquiries were made about him and he was refused. But again, as in his first marriage, he proposed an elopement to the orphan girl. There is very little doubt that she would not on any account have married him if she had known a little more about him in time. But she lived in another province; besides what could a little girl of sixteen know about it, except that she would be better at the bottom of the river than remaining with her benefactress. So the poor child exchanged a benefactress for a benefactor. Fyodor Pavlovitch did not get a penny this time, for the general's widow was furious. She gave them nothing and cursed them both. But he had not reckoned on a dowry; what allured him was the remarkable beauty of the innocent girl, above all her innocent appearance, which had a peculiar attraction for a vicious profligate, who had hitherto admired only the coarser types of feminine beauty.

"Those innocent eyes slit my soul up like a razor," he used to say afterwards, with his loathsome snigger. In a man so depraved this might, of course, mean no more than sensual attraction. As he had received no dowry with his wife, and had, so to speak, taken her "from the halter," he did not stand on ceremony with her. Making her feel that she had "wronged" him, he took advantage of her phenomenal meekness and submissiveness to trample on the elementary decencies of marriage. He gathered loose women into his house, and carried on orgies of debauchery in his wife's presence.

To show what a pass things had come to, I may mention that Grigory, the gloomy, stupid, obstinate, argumentative servant, who had always hated his first mistress, Adelaïda Ivanovna, took the side of his new mistress. He championed her cause, abusing Fyodor Pavlovitch in a manner little befitting a servant, and, on one occasion broke up the revels and drove all the disorderly women out of the house. In the end this unhappy young woman, kept in terror from her childhood, fell into that kind of nervous disease which is most frequently found in peasant women who are said to be "possessed by devils." At times after terrible fits of hysterics she even lost her reason. Yet she bore Fyodor Pavlovitch two sons, Ivan and Alexey, the eldest in the first year of marriage and the second three years later. When she died, little Alexey was in his fourth year, and, strange as it seems, I know that he remembered his mother all his life, like a dream, of course. At her death almost exactly the same thing happened to the two little boys as to their elder brother, Mitya. They were completely forgotten and abandoned by their father. They were looked after by the same Grigory and lived in his cottage, where they were found by the tyrannical old lady who had brought up their mother. She was still alive, and had not, all those eight years, forgotten the insult done her. All that time she was obtaining exact information as to her Sofya's manner of life, and hearing of her illness and hideous surroundings she declared aloud two or three times to her retainers:

"It serves her right. God has punished her for her ingratitude."

Exactly three months after Sofya Ivanovna's death the general's widow suddenly appeared in our town, and went straight to Fyodor Pavlovitch's house. She spent only half an hour in the town but she did a great deal. It was evening. Fyodor Pavlovitch, whom she had not seen for those eight years, came in to her drunk. The story is that instantly upon seeing him, without any sort of explanation, she gave him two good, resounding slaps of the face, seized him by a tuft of hair, and shook him three times up and down. Then, without a word, she went straight to the cottage to the two boys. Seeing, at the first glance, that they were unwashed and in dirty linen, she promptly gave Grigory, too, a box on the ear, and announcing that she would carry off both the children she wrapped them just as they were in a rug, put them in the carriage, and drove off to her own town. Grigory accepted the blow like a devoted slave, without a word, and when he escorted the old lady to her carriage he made her a low bow and pronounced impressively that, "God would repay her for the orphans." "You are a blockhead all the same," the old lady shouted to him as she drove away.

Fyodor Pavlovitch, thinking it over, decided that it was a good thing, and did not refuse the general's widow his formal consent to any proposition in regard to his children's education. As for the slaps she had given him, he drove all over the town telling the story.

It happened that the old lady died soon after this, but she left the boys in her will a thousand roubles each "for their instruction, and so that all be spent on them exclusively, with the condition that it be so portioned out as to last till they are twenty-one, for it is more than adequate provision for such children. If other people think fit to throw away their money, let them." I have not read the will myself, but I heard there was something queer of the sort, very whimsically expressed. The principal heir, Yefim Petrovitch Polenov, the Marshal of Nobility of the province, turned out, however, to be an honest man. Writing to Fyodor Pavlovitch, and discerning at once that he could extract nothing from him for his children's education (though the latter never directly refused but only procrastinated as he always did in such cases, and was, indeed, at times effusively sentimental), Yefim Petrovitch took a personal interest in the orphans. He became especially fond of the younger, Alexey, who lived for a long while as one of his family. I beg the reader to note this from the beginning. And to Yefim Petrovitch, a man of a generosity and humanity rarely to be met with, the young people were more indebted for their education and bringing up than to any one. He kept the two thousand roubles left to them by the general's widow intact, so that by the time they came of age their portions had been doubled by the accumulation of interest. He educated them both at his own expense, and certainly spent far more than a thousand roubles upon each of them. I won't enter into a detailed account of their boyhood and youth, but will only mention a few of the most important events. Of the elder, Ivan, I will only say that he grew into a somewhat morose and reserved, though far from timid boy. At ten years old he had realised that they were living not in their own home but on other people's charity, and that their father was a man of whom it was disgraceful to speak. This boy began very early, almost in his infancy (so they say at least), to show a brilliant and unusual aptitude for learning. I don't know precisely why, but he left the family of Yefim Petrovitch when he was hardly thirteen, entering a Moscow gymnasium, and boarding with an experienced and celebrated teacher, an old friend of Yefim Petrovitch. Ivan used to declare afterwards that this was all due to the "ardour for good works" of Yefim Petrovitch, who was captivated by the idea that the boy's genius should be trained by a teacher of genius. But neither Yefim Petrovitch nor this teacher was living when the young man finished at the gymnasium and entered the university. As Yefim Petrovitch had made no provision for the payment of the tyrannical old lady's legacy, which had grown from one thousand to two, it was delayed, owing to formalities inevitable in Russia, and the young man was in great straits for the first two years at the university, as he was forced to keep himself all the time he was studying. It must be noted that he did not even attempt to communicate with his father, perhaps from pride, from contempt for him, or perhaps from his cool common sense, which told him that from such a father he would get no real assistance. However that may have been, the young man was by no means despondent and succeeded in getting work, at first giving sixpenny lessons and afterwards getting paragraphs on street incidents into the newspapers under the signature of "Eye-Witness." These paragraphs, it was said, were so interesting and piquant that they were soon taken. This alone showed the young man's practical and intellectual superiority over the masses of needy and unfortunate students of both sexes who hang about the offices of the newspapers and journals, unable to think of anything better than everlasting entreaties for copying and translations from the French. Having once got into touch with the editors Ivan Fyodorovitch always kept up his connection with them, and in his latter years at the university he published brilliant reviews of books upon various special subjects, so that he became well known in literary circles. But only in his last year he suddenly succeeded in attracting the attention of a far wider circle of readers, so that a great many people noticed and remembered him. It was rather a curious incident. When he had just left the university and was preparing to go abroad upon his two thousand roubles Ivan Fyodorovitch published in one of the more important journals a strange article, which attracted general notice, on a subject of which he might have been supposed to know nothing, as he was a student of natural science. The article dealt with a subject which was being debated everywhere at the time—the position of the ecclesiastical courts.[2] After discussing several opinions on the subject he went on to explain his own view. What was most striking about the article was its tone, and its unexpected conclusion. Many of the Church party regarded him unquestioningly as on their side. And yet not only the secularists but even atheists joined them in their applause. Finally some sagacious persons opined that the article was nothing but an impudent satirical burlesque. I mention this incident particularly because this article penetrated into the famous monastery in our neighbourhood, where the inmates, being particularly interested in the question of the ecclesiastical courts, were completely bewildered by it. Learning the author's name, they were interested in his being a native of the town and the son of "that Fyodor Pavlovitch." And just then it was that the author himself made his appearance among us.

Why Ivan Fyodorovitch had come amongst us I remember asking myself at the time with a certain uneasiness. This fateful visit, which was the first step leading to so many consequences, I never fully explained to myself. It seemed strange on the face of it that a young man so learned, so proud, and apparently so cautious, should suddenly visit such an infamous house and a father who had ignored him all his life, hardly knew him, never thought of him, and would not under any circumstances have given him money, though he was always afraid that his sons Ivan and Alexey would also come to ask him for it. And here the young man was staying in the house of such a father, had been living with him for two months, and they were on the best possible terms. This last fact was a special cause of wonder to many others as well as to me. Pyotr Alexandrovitch Miüsov, of whom we have spoken already, the cousin of Fyodor Pavlovitch's first wife, happened to be in the neighbourhood again on a visit to his estate. He had come from Paris, which was his permanent home. I remember that he was more surprised than any one when he made the acquaintance of the young man, who interested him extremely, and with whom he sometimes argued and not without an inner pang compared himself in acquirements.

"He is proud," he used to say, "he will never be in want of pence; he has got money enough to go abroad now. What does he want here? Every one can see that he hasn't come for money, for his father would never give him any. He has no taste for drink and dissipation, and yet his father can't do without him. They get on so well together!"

That was the truth; the young man had an unmistakable influence over his father, who positively appeared to be behaving more decently and even seemed at times ready to obey his son, though often extremely and even spitefully perverse.

It was only later that we learned that Ivan had come partly at the request of, and in the interests of, his elder brother, Dmitri, whom he saw for the first time on this very visit, though he had before leaving Moscow been in correspondence with him about an important matter of more concern to Dmitri than himself. What that business was the reader will learn fully in due time. Yet even when I did know of this special circumstance I still felt Ivan Fyodorovitch to be an enigmatic figure, and thought his visit rather mysterious.

I may add that Ivan appeared at the time in the light of a mediator between his father and his elder brother Dmitri, who was in open quarrel with his father and even planning to bring an action against him.

The family, I repeat, was now united for the first time, and some of its members met for the first time in their lives. The younger brother, Alexey, had been a year already among us, having been the first of the three to arrive. It is of that brother Alexey I find it most difficult to speak in this introduction. Yet I must give some preliminary account of him, if only to explain one queer fact, which is that I have to introduce my hero to the reader wearing the cassock of a novice. Yes, he had been for the last year in our monastery, and seemed willing to be cloistered there for the rest of his life.

4

THE THIRD SON, ALYOSHA

He was only twenty, his brother Ivan was in his twenty-fourth year at the time, while their elder brother Dmitri was twenty-seven. First of all, I must explain that this young man, Alyosha, was not a fanatic, and, in my opinion, at least, was not even a mystic. I may as well give my full opinion from the beginning. He was simply an early lover of humanity, and that he adopted the monastic life was simply because at that time it struck him, so to say, as the ideal escape for his soul struggling from the darkness of worldly wickedness to the light of love. And the reason this life struck him in this way was that he found in it at that time, as he thought, an extraordinary being, our celebrated elder, Zossima, to whom he became attached with all the warm first love of his ardent heart. But I do not dispute that he was very strange even at that time, and had been so indeed from his cradle. I have mentioned already, by the way, that though he lost his mother in his fourth year he remembered her all his life—her face, her caresses, "as though she stood living before me." Such memories may persist, as every one knows, from an even earlier age, even from two years old, but scarcely standing out through a whole lifetime like spots of light out of darkness, like a corner torn out of a huge picture, which has all faded and disappeared except that fragment. That is how it was with him. He remembered one still summer evening, an open window, the slanting rays of the setting sun (that he recalled most vividly of all); in a corner of the room the holy image, before it a lighted lamp, and on her knees before the image his mother, sobbing hysterically with cries and moans, snatching him up in both arms, squeezing him close till it hurt, and praying for him to the Mother of God, holding him out in both arms to the image as though to put him under the Mother's protection . . . and suddenly a nurse runs in and snatches him from her in terror. That was the picture! And Alyosha remembered his mother's face at that minute. He used to say that it was frenzied but beautiful as he remembered. But he rarely cared to speak of this memory to any one. In his childhood and youth he was by no means expansive, and talked little indeed, but not from shyness or a sullen unsociability; quite the contrary, from something different, from a sort of inner preoccupation entirely personal and unconcerned with other people, but so important to him that he seemed, as it were, to forget others on account of it. But he was fond of people: he seemed throughout his life to put implicit trust in people: yet no one ever looked on him as a simpleton or naïve person. There was something about him which made one feel at once (and it was so all his life afterwards) that he did not care to be a judge of others—that he would never take it upon himself to criticise and would never condemn any one for anything. He seemed, indeed, to accept everything without the least condemnation though often grieving bitterly: and this was so much so that no one could surprise or frighten him even in his earliest youth. Coming at twenty to his father's house, which was a very sink of filthy debauchery, he, chaste and pure as he was, simply withdrew in silence when to look on was unbearable, but without the slightest sign of contempt or condemnation. His father, who had once been in a dependent position, and so was sensitive and ready to take offence, met him at first with distrust and sullenness. "He does not say much," he used to say, "and thinks the more." But soon, within a fortnight indeed, he took to embracing him and kissing him terribly often, with drunken tears, with sottish sentimentality, yet he evidently felt a real and deep affection for him, such as he had never been capable of feeling for any one before.

Every one, indeed, loved this young man wherever he went, and it was so from his earliest childhood. When he entered the household of his patron and benefactor, Yefim Petrovitch Polenov, he gained the hearts of all the family, so that they looked on him quite as their own child. Yet he entered the house at such a tender age that he could not have acted from design nor artfulness in winning affection. So that the gift of making himself loved directly and unconsciously was inherent in him, in his very nature so to speak. It was the same at school, though he seemed to be just one of those children who are distrusted, sometimes ridiculed, and even disliked by their schoolfellows. He was dreamy, for instance, and rather solitary. From his earliest childhood he was fond of creeping into a corner to read, and yet he was a general favourite all the while he was at school. He was rarely playful or merry, but any one could see at the first glance that this was not from any sullenness. On the contrary he was bright and good-tempered. He never tried to show off among his schoolfellows. Perhaps because of this, he was never afraid of any one, yet the boys immediately understood that he was not proud of his fearlessness and seemed to be un-aware that he was bold and courageous. He never resented an insult. It would happen that an hour after the offence he would address the of-fender or answer some question with as trustful and candid an expression as though nothing had happened between them. And it was not that he seemed to have forgotten or intentionally forgiven the affront, but simply that he did not regard it as an affront, and this completely conquered and captivated the boys. He had one characteristic which made all his schoolfel-lows from the bottom class to the top want to mock at him, not from mal-ice but because it amused them. This characteristic was a wild fanatical modesty and chastity. He could not bear to hear certain words and certain conversations about women. There are "certain" words and conversations unhappily impossible to eradicate in schools. Boys pure in mind and heart, almost children, are fond of talking in school among themselves, and even aloud, of things, pictures, and images of which even soldiers would some-times hesitate to speak. More than that, much that soldiers have no knowl-edge or conception of is familiar to quite young children of our intellectual and higher classes. There is no moral depravity, no real corrupt inner cyni-cism in it, but there is the appearance of it, and it is often looked upon among them as something refined, subtle, daring, and worthy of imitation. Seeing that Alyosha Karamazov put his fingers in his ears when they talked of "that," they used sometimes to crowd round him, pull his hands away, and shout nastiness into both ears, while he struggled, slipped to the floor, tried to hide himself without uttering one word of abuse, enduring their insults in silence. But at last they left him alone and gave up taunting him with being a "regular girl," and what's more they looked upon it with compassion as a weakness. He was always one of the best in the class but was never first.

At the time of Yefim Petrovitch's death Alyosha had two more years to complete at the provincial gymnasium. The inconsolable widow went al-most immediately after his death for a long visit to Italy with her whole family, which consisted only of women and girls. Alyosha went to live in the house of two distant relations of Yefim Petrovitch, ladies whom he had never seen before. On what terms he lived with them he did not know himself. It was very characteristic of him, indeed, that he never cared at whose expense he was living. In that respect he was a striking contrast to his elder brother Ivan, who struggled with poverty for his first two years in the university, maintained himself by his own efforts, and had from childhood been bitterly conscious of living at the expense of his benefactor. But this strange trait in Alyosha's character must not, I think, be criticised too severely, for at the slightest acquaintance with him any one would have perceived that Alyosha was one of those youths, almost of the type of religious enthusiast, who, if they were suddenly to come into possession of a large fortune, would not hesitate to give it away for the asking, either for good works or perhaps to a clever rogue. In general he seemed scarcely to know the value of money, not, of course, in a literal sense. When he was given pocket-money, which he never asked for, he was either terribly careless of it so that it was gone in a moment, or he kept it for weeks together, not knowing what to do with it.

In later years Pyotr Alexandrovitch Miüsov, a man very sensitive on the score of money and bourgeois honesty, pronounced the following judgment, after getting to know Alyosha:

"Here is perhaps the one man in the world whom you might leave alone without a penny, in the centre of an unknown town of a million inhabitants, and he would not come to harm, he would not die of cold and hunger, for he would be fed and sheltered at once; and if he were not, he would find a shelter for himself, and it would cost him no effort or humiliation. And to shelter him would be no burden, but, on the contrary, would probably be looked on as a pleasure."

He did not finish his studies at the gymnasium. A year before the end of the course he suddenly announced to the ladies that he was going to see his father about a plan which had occurred to him. They were sorry and unwilling to let him go. The journey was not an expensive one, and the ladies would not let him pawn his watch, a parting present from his benefactor's family. They provided him liberally with money and even fitted him out with new clothes and linen. But he returned half the money they gave him, saying that he intended to go third class. On his arrival in the town he made no answer to his father's first inquiry why he had come before completing his studies, and seemed, so they say, unusually thoughtful. It soon became apparent that he was looking for his mother's tomb. He practically acknowledged at the time that that was the only object of his visit. But it can hardly have been the whole reason of it. It is more probable that he himself did not understand and could not explain what had suddenly arisen in his soul, and drawn him irresistibly into a new, unknown, but inevitable path. Fyodor Pavlovitch could not show him where his second wife was buried, for he had never visited her grave since he had thrown earth upon her coffin, and in the course of years had entirely forgotten where she was buried.

Fyodor Pavlovitch, by the way, had for some time previously not been living in our town. Three or four years after his wife's death he had gone to the south of Russia and finally turned up in Odessa, where he spent several years. He made the acquaintance at first, in his own words, "of a lot of low Jews, Jewesses, and Jewkins," and ended by being received by "Jews high and low alike." It may be presumed that at this period he developed a peculiar faculty for making and hoarding money. He finally returned to our town only three years before Alyosha's arrival. His former acquaintances found him looking terribly aged, although he was by no means an old man. He behaved not exactly with more dignity but with more effrontery. The former buffoon showed an insolent propensity for making buffoons of others. His depravity with women was not simply what it used to be, but even more revolting. In a short time he opened a great number of new taverns in the district. It was evident that he had perhaps a hundred thousand roubles or not much less. Many of the inhabitants of the town and district were soon in his debt, and, of course, had given good security. Of late, too, he looked somehow bloated and seemed more irresponsible, more uneven, had sunk into a sort of incoherence, used to begin one thing and go on with another, as though he were letting himself go altogether. He was more and more frequently drunk. And, if it had not been for the same servant Grigory, who by that time had aged considerably too, and used to look after him sometimes almost like a tutor, Fyodor Pavlovitch might have got into terrible scrapes. Alyosha's arrival seemed to affect even his moral side, as though something had awakened in this prematurely old man which had long been dead in his soul.

"Do you know," he used often to say, looking at Alyosha, "that you are like her, 'the crazy woman'"—that was what he used to call his dead wife, Alyosha's mother. Grigory it was who pointed out the "crazy woman's" grave to Alyosha. He took him to our town cemetery and showed him in a remote corner a cast-iron tomb-stone, cheap but decently kept, on which were inscribed the name and age of the deceased and the date of her death, and below a four-lined verse, such as are commonly used on old-fashioned middle-class tombs. To Alyosha's amazement this tomb turned out to be Grigory's doing. He had put it up on the poor "crazy woman's" grave at his own expense, after Fyodor Pavlovitch, whom he had often pestered about the grave, had gone to Odessa, abandoning the grave and all his memories. Alyosha showed no particular emotion at the sight of his mother's grave. He only listened to Grigory's minute and solemn account of the erection of the tomb; he stood with bowed head and walked away without uttering a word. It was perhaps a year before he visited the cemetery again. But this little episode was not without an influence upon Fyodor Pavlovitch—and a very original one. He suddenly took a thousand roubles to our monastery to pay for requiems for the soul of his wife; but not for the second, Alyosha's mother, the "crazy woman," but for the first, Adelaïda Ivanovna, who used to thrash him. In the evening of the same day he got drunk and abused the monks to Alyosha. He himself was far from being religious; he had probably never put a penny candle before the image of a saint. Strange impulses of sudden feeling and sudden thought are common in such types.

I have mentioned already that he looked bloated. His countenance at this time bore traces of something that testified unmistakably to the life he had led. Besides the long fleshy bags under his little, always insolent, suspicious, and ironical eyes; besides the multitude of deep wrinkles in his little fat face, the Adam's apple hung below his sharp chin like a great, fleshy goitre, which gave him a peculiar, repulsive, sensual appearance; add to that a long rapacious mouth with full lips, between which could be seen little stumps of black decayed teeth. He slobbered every time he began to speak. He was fond indeed of making fun of his own face, though, I believe, he was well satisfied with it. He used particularly to point to his nose, which was not very large, but very delicate and conspicuously aquiline. "A regular Roman nose," he used to say, "with my goitre I've quite the countenance of an ancient Roman patrician of the decadent period." He seemed proud of it.

Not long after visiting his mother's grave Alyosha suddenly announced that he wanted to enter the monastery, and that the monks were willing to receive him as a novice. He explained that this was his strong desire, and that he was solemnly asking his consent as his father. The old man knew that the elder Zossima, who was living in the monastery hermitage, had made a special impression upon his "gentle boy."

"That is the most honest monk among them, of course," he observed, after listening in thoughtful silence to Alyosha, and seeming scarcely surprised at his request. "H'm! . . . So that's where you want to be, my gentle boy?"

He was half drunk, and suddenly he grinned his slow half-drunken grin, which was not without a certain cunning and tipsy slyness. "H'm! . . . I had a presentiment that you would end in something like this. Would you believe it? You were making straight for it. Well, to be sure you have your own two thousand. That's a dowry for you. And I'll never desert you, my angel. And I'll pay what's wanted for you there, if they ask for it. But, of course, if they don't ask, why should we worry them? What do you say? You know, you spend money like a canary, two grains a week. H'm! . . . Do you know that near one monastery there's a place outside the town where every baby knows there are none but 'the monks' wives' living, as they are called. Thirty women, I believe. I have been there myself. You know, it's interesting in its own way, of course, as a variety. The worst of it is it's awfully Russian. There are no French women there. Of course they could get them fast enough, they have plenty of money. If they get to hear of it they'll come along. Well, there's nothing of that sort here, no 'monks' wives,' and two hundred monks. They're honest. They keep the fasts. I admit it . . . H'm! . . . So you want to be a monk? And do you know I'm sorry to lose you, Alyosha; would you believe it, I've really grown fond of you? Well, it's a good opportunity. You'll pray for us sinners; we have sinned too much here. I've always been thinking who would pray for me, and whether there's any one in the world to do it. My dear boy, I'm awfully stupid about that. You wouldn't believe it. Awfully. You see, however stupid I am about it,

I keep thinking, I keep thinking—from time to time, of course, not all the while. It's impossible, I think, for the devils to forget to drag me down to hell with their hooks when I die. Then I wonder—hooks? Where would they get them? What of? Iron hooks? Where do they forge them? Have they a foundry there of some sort? The monks in the monastery probably believe that there's a ceiling in hell, for instance. Now I'm ready to believe in hell, but without a ceiling. It makes it more refined, more enlightened, more Lutheran that is. And, after all, what does it matter whether it has a ceiling or hasn't? But, do you know, there's a damnable question involved in it? If there's no ceiling there can be no hooks, and if there are no hooks it all breaks down, which is unlikely again, for then there would be none to drag me down to hell, and if they don't drag me down what justice is there in the world? *Il faudrait les inventer,** those hooks, on purpose for me alone, for, if you only knew, Alyosha, what a blackguard I am."

"But there are no hooks there," said Alyosha, looking gently and seriously at his father.

"Yes, yes, only the shadows of hooks. I know, I know. That's how a Frenchman described hell. *'J'ai vu l'ombre d'un cocher qui avec l'ombre d'une brosse frottait l'ombre d'une carosse.'*[3] How do you know there are no hooks, darling? When you've lived with the monks you'll sing a different tune. But go and get at the truth there, and then come and tell me. Anyway it's easier going to the other world if one knows what there is there. Besides, it will be more seemly for you with the monks than here with me, with a drunken old man and young harlots . . . though you're like an angel, nothing touches you. And I daresay nothing will touch you there. That's why I let you go, because I hope for that. You've got all your wits about you. You will burn and you will burn out; you will be healed and come back again. And I will wait for you. I feel that you're the only creature in the world who has not condemned me. My dear boy, I feel it, you know. I can't help feeling it."

And he even began blubbering. He was sentimental. He was wicked and sentimental.

---

*It would be necessary to invent them (French).

5

ELDERS

SOME of my readers may imagine that my young man was a sickly, ecstatic, poorly developed creature, a pale, consumptive dreamer. On the
contrary, Alyosha was at this time a well-grown, red-cheeked, clear-
eyed lad of nineteen, radiant with health. He was very handsome, too, grace-
ful, moderately tall, with hair of a dark brown, with a regular, rather long,
oval-shaped face, and wide-set dark grey, shining eyes; he was very thoughtful, and apparently very serene. I shall be told, perhaps, that red cheeks are
not incompatible with fanaticism and mysticism; but I fancy that Alyosha
was more of a realist than any one. Oh! no doubt, in the monastery he fully
believed in miracles, but, to my thinking, miracles are never a stumbling-
block to the realist. It is not miracles that dispose realists to belief. The genuine realist, if he is an unbeliever, will always find strength and ability to
disbelieve in the miraculous, and if he is confronted with a miracle as an irrefutable fact he would rather disbelieve his own senses than admit the fact.
Even if he admits it, he admits it as a fact of nature till then unrecognised by
him. Faith does not, in the realist, spring from the miracle but the miracle
from faith. If the realist once believes, then he is bound by his very realism
to admit the miraculous also. The Apostle Thomas said that he would not
believe till he saw, but when he did see he said, "My Lord and my God!"*
Was it the miracle forced him to believe? Most likely not, but he believed
solely because he desired to believe and possibly he fully believed in his secret heart even when he said, "I do not believe till I see."

I shall be told, perhaps, that Alyosha was stupid, undeveloped, had not
finished his studies, and so on. That he did not finish his studies is true, but
to say that he was stupid or dull would be a great injustice. I'll simply repeat what I have said above. He entered upon this path only because, at
that time, it alone struck his imagination and presented itself to him as offering an ideal means of escape for his soul from darkness to light. Add to
that that he was to some extent a youth of our last epoch—that is, honest
in nature, desiring the truth, seeking for it and believing in it, and seeking
to serve it at once with all the strength of his soul, seeking for immediate
action, and ready to sacrifice everything, life itself, for it. Though these
young men unhappily fail to understand that the sacrifice of life is, in many
cases, the easiest of all sacrifices, and that to sacrifice, for instance, five or

---

*See the Bible, John 20:25–28. Hereafter all references to the Bible will
note book, chapter, and verse only.

six years of their seething youth to hard and tedious study, if only to multiply ten-fold their powers of serving the truth and the cause they have set
before them as their goal—such a sacrifice is utterly beyond the strength
of many of them. The path Alyosha chose was a path going in the opposite
direction, but he chose it with the same thirst for swift achievement. As
soon as he reflected seriously he was convinced of the existence of God
and immortality, and at once he instinctively said to himself: "I want to live
for immortality, and I will accept no compromise." In the same way, if he had
decided that God and immortality did not exist, he would at once have become an atheist and a socialist. For socialism is not merely the labour
question, it is before all things the atheistic question, the question of the
form taken by atheism to-day, the question of the tower of Babel built
without God, not to mount to Heaven from earth but to set up Heaven on
earth. Alyosha would have found it strange and impossible to go on living
as before. It is written: "Give all that thou hast to the poor and follow Me,
if thou wouldst be perfect."*

Alyosha said to himself: "I can't give two roubles instead of 'all,' and
only go to mass instead of 'following Him.'" Perhaps his memories of
childhood brought back our monastery, to which his mother may have
taken him to mass. Perhaps the slanting sunlight and the holy image to
which his poor "crazy" mother had held him up still acted upon his imagination. Brooding on these things he may have come to us perhaps only to
see whether here he could sacrifice all or only "two roubles," and in the
monastery he met this elder. I must digress to explain what an "elder" is in
Russian monasteries, and I am sorry that I do not feel very competent to
do so. I will try, however, to give a superficial account of it in a few words.
Authorities on the subject assert that the institution of "elders" is of recent date, not more than a hundred years old in our monasteries, though in
the orthodox East, especially in Sinai and Athos, it has existed over a thousand years. It is maintained that it existed in ancient times in Russia also,
but through the calamities which overtook Russia—the Tatars, civil war,
the interruption of relations with the East after the destruction of Constantinople[4]—this institution fell into oblivion. It was revived among us
towards the end of last century by one of the great "ascetics," as they
called him, Païssy Velitchkovsky,[5] and his disciples. But to this day it exists
in few monasteries only, and has sometimes been almost persecuted as an
innovation in Russia. It flourished especially in the celebrated Kozelski
Optin Monastery. When and how it was introduced into our monastery I
cannot say. There had already been three such elders and Zossima was the
last of them. But he was almost dying of weakness and disease, and they
had no one to take his place. The question for our monastery was an important one, for it had not been distinguished by anything in particular till
then: they had neither relics of saints, nor wonder-working ikons, nor glorious traditions, nor historical exploits. It had flourished and been glorious

*See Mark 10:21.

all over Russia through its elders, to see and hear whom pilgrims had flocked for thousands of miles from all parts.

What was such an elder? An elder was one who took your soul, your will, into his soul and his will. When you choose an elder, you renounce your own will and yield it to him in complete submission, complete self-abnegation. This novitiate, this terrible school of abnegation, is undertaken voluntarily, in the hope of self-conquest, of self-mastery, in order, after a life of obedience, to attain perfect freedom, that is, from self; to escape the lot of those who have lived their whole life without finding their true selves in themselves. This institution of elders is not founded on theory, but was established in the East from the practice of a thousand years. The obligations due to an elder are not the ordinary "obedience" which has always existed in our Russian monasteries. The obligation involves confession to the elder by all who have submitted themselves to him, and to the indissoluble bond between him and them.

The story is told, for instance, that in the early days of Christianity one such novice, failing to fulfil some command laid upon him by his elder, left his monastery in Syria and went to Egypt. There, after great exploits he was found worthy at last to suffer torture and a martyr's death for the faith. When the Church, regarding him as a saint, was burying him, suddenly, at the deacon's exhortation, "Depart all ye unbaptized," the coffin containing the martyr's body left its place and was cast forth from the church, and this took place three times. And only at last they learnt that this holy man had broken his vow of obedience and left his elder, and, therefore, could not be forgiven without the elder's absolution in spite of his great deeds. Only after this could the funeral take place. This, of course, is only an old legend. But here is a recent instance.

A monk was suddenly commanded by his elder to quit Athos, which he loved as a sacred place and a haven of refuge, and to go, first to Jerusalem to do homage to the Holy Places and then to go to the north to Siberia: "There is the place for thee and not here." The monk overwhelmed with sorrow went to the Œcumenical Patriarch at Constantinople and besought him to release him from his obedience. But the Patriarch replied that not only was he unable to release him, but there was not and could not be on earth a power which could release him except the elder who had himself laid that duty upon him. In this way the elders are endowed in certain cases with unbounded and inexplicable authority. That is why in many of our monasteries the institution was at first resisted almost to persecution. Meantime the elders immediately began to be highly esteemed among the people. Masses of the ignorant people as well as men of distinction flocked, for instance, to the elders of our monastery to confess their doubts, their sins, and their sufferings, and ask for counsel and admonition. Seeing this, the opponents of the elders declared that the sacrament of confession was being arbitrarily and frivolously degraded, though the continual opening of the heart to the elder by the monk or the layman had nothing of the character of the sacrament. In the end, however, the institution of elders has been retained and is becoming established in Russian monasteries. It is true, perhaps, that this instrument which had stood the test of a thousand years for the moral regeneration of a man from slavery to freedom and to moral perfectibility may be a two-edged weapon and it may lead some not to humility and complete self-control but to the most Satanic pride, that is, to bondage and not to freedom.

The elder Zossima was sixty-five. He came of a family of landowners, had been in the army in early youth, and served in the Caucasus as an officer. He had, no doubt, impressed Alyosha by some peculiar quality of his soul. Alyosha lived in the cell of the elder, who was very fond of him and let him wait upon him. It must be noted that Alyosha was bound by no obligation and could go where he pleased and be absent for whole days. Though he wore the monastic dress it was voluntarily, not to be different from others. No doubt he liked to do so. Possibly his youthful imagination was deeply stirred by the power and fame of his elder. It was said that so many people had for years past come to confess their sins to Father Zossima and to entreat him for words of advice and healing, that he had acquired the keenest intuition and could tell from an unknown face what a new comer wanted, and what was the suffering on his conscience. He sometimes astounded and almost alarmed his visitors by his knowledge of their secrets before they had spoken a word.

Alyosha noticed that many, almost all, went in to the elder for the first time with apprehension and uneasiness, but came out with bright and happy faces. Alyosha was particularly struck by the fact that Father Zossima was not at all stern. On the contrary, he was always almost gay. The monks used to say that he was more drawn to those who were more sinful, and the greater the sinner the more he loved him. There were, no doubt, up to the end of his life, among the monks some who hated and envied him, but they were few in number and they were silent, though among them were some of great dignity in the monastery, one, for instance, of the older monks distinguished for his strict keeping of fasts and vows of silence. But the majority were on Father Zossima's side and very many of them loved him with all their hearts, warmly and sincerely. Some were almost fanatically devoted to him, and declared, though not quite aloud, that he was a saint, that there could be no doubt of it, and, seeing that his end was near, they anticipated miracles and great glory to the monastery in the immediate future from his relics. Alyosha had unquestioning faith in the miraculous power of the elder, just as he had unquestioning faith in the story of the coffin that flew out of the church. He saw many who came with sick children or relatives and besought the elder to lay hands on them and to pray over them, return shortly after—some the next day—and, falling in tears at the elder's feet, thank him for healing their sick.

Whether they had really been healed or were simply better in the natural course of the disease was a question which did not exist for Alyosha, for he fully believed in the spiritual power of his teacher and rejoiced in his fame, in his glory, as though it were his own triumph. His heart throbbed, and he beamed, as it were, all over when the elder came out to the gates of the hermitage into the waiting crowd of pilgrims of the humbler class who had flocked from all parts of Russia on purpose to see the elder and obtain his blessing. They fell down before him, wept, kissed his feet, kissed the earth on which he stood, and wailed, while the women held up their children to him and brought him the sick "possessed with devils." The elder spoke to them, read a brief prayer over them, blessed them, and dismissed them. Of late he had become so weak through attacks of illness that he was sometimes unable to leave his cell, and the pilgrims waited for him to come out for several days. Alyosha did not wonder why they loved him so, why they fell down before him and wept with emotion merely at seeing his face. Oh! he understood that for the humble soul of the Russian peasant, worn out by grief and toil, and still more by the everlasting injustice and everlasting sin, his own and the world's, it was the greatest need and comfort to find some one or something holy to fall down before and worship.

"Among us there is sin, injustice, and temptation, but yet, somewhere on earth there is some one holy and exalted. He has the truth; he knows the truth; so it is not dead upon the earth; so it will come one day to us, too, and rule over all the earth according to the promise."

Alyosha knew that this was just how the people felt and even reasoned. He understood it, but that the elder Zossima was this saint and custodian of God's truth—of that he had no more doubt than the weeping peasants and the sick women who held out their children to the elder. The conviction that after his death the elder would bring extraordinary glory to the monastery was even stronger in Alyosha than in any one there, and, of late a kind of deep flame of inner ecstasy burnt more and more strongly in his heart. He was not at all troubled at this elder's standing as a solitary example before him.

"No matter. He is holy. He carries in his heart the secret of renewal for all: that power which will, at last, establish truth on the earth, and all men will be holy and love one another, and there will be no more rich nor poor, no exalted nor humbled, but all will be as the children of God, and the true Kingdom of Christ will come." That was the dream in Alyosha's heart.

The arrival of his two brothers, whom he had not known till then, seemed to make a great impression on Alyosha. He more quickly made friends with his half-brother Dmitri (though he arrived later) than with his own brother Ivan. He was extremely interested in his brother Ivan, but when the latter had been two months in the town, though they had met fairly often, they were still not intimate. Alyosha was naturally silent, and he seemed to be expecting something, ashamed about something, while his brother Ivan, though Alyosha noticed at first that he looked long and curiously at him, seemed soon to have left off thinking of him. Alyosha noticed it with some embarrassment. He ascribed his brother's indifference at first to the disparity of their age and education. But he also wondered whether the absence of curiosity and sympathy in Ivan might be due to some other cause entirely unknown to him. He kept fancying that Ivan was absorbed in something—something inward and important—that he was striving towards some goal, perhaps very hard to attain, and that that was why he had no thought for him. Alyosha wondered, too, whether there was not some contempt on the part of the learned atheist for him—a foolish novice. He knew for certain that his brother was an atheist. He could not take offence at this contempt, if it existed; yet, with an uneasy embarrassment which he did not himself understand, he waited for his brother to come nearer to him. Dmitri used to speak of Ivan with the deepest respect and with a peculiar earnestness. From him Alyosha learnt all the details of the important affair which had of late formed such a close and remarkable bond between the two elder brothers. Dmitri's enthusiastic references to Ivan were the more striking in Alyosha's eyes since Dmitri was, compared with Ivan, almost uneducated, and the two brothers were such a contrast in personality and character that it would be difficult to find two men more unlike.

It was at this time that the meeting, or, rather gathering of the members of this inharmonious family took place in the cell of the elder who had such an extraordinary influence on Alyosha. The pretext for this gathering was a false one. It was at this time that the discord between Dmitri and his father seemed at its acutest stage and their relations had become insufferably strained. Fyodor Pavlovitch seems to have been the first to suggest, apparently in joke, that they should all meet in Father Zossima's cell, and that, without appealing to his direct intervention, they might more decently come to an understanding under the conciliating influence of the elder's presence. Dmitri, who had never seen the elder, naturally supposed that his father was trying to intimidate him, but, as he secretly blamed himself for his outbursts of temper with his father on several recent occasions, he accepted the challenge. It must be noted that he was not, like Ivan, staying with his father, but living apart at the other end of the town. It happened that Pyotr Alexandrovitch Miüsov, who was staying in the district at the time, caught eagerly at the idea. A Liberal of the forties and fifties, a freethinker and atheist, he may have been led on by boredom or the hope of frivolous diversion. He was suddenly seized with the desire to see the monastery and the holy man. As his lawsuit with the monastery still dragged on, he made it the pretext for seeing the Superior, in order to attempt to settle it amicably. A visitor coming with such laudible intentions might be received with more attention and consideration than if he came from simple curiosity. Influences from within the monastery were brought to bear on the elder, who of late had scarcely left his cell, and had been forced by illness to deny even his ordinary visitors. In the end he consented to see them, and the day was fixed.

"Who has made me a judge over them?"* was all he said, smilingly, to Alyosha.

Alyosha was much perturbed when he heard of the proposed visit. Of all the wrangling, quarrelsome party, Dmitri was the only one who could regard the interview seriously. All the others would come from frivolous

---

*See Luke 12:14.

motives, perhaps insulting to the elder. Alyosha was well aware of that. Ivan and Miüsov would come from curiosity, perhaps of the coarsest kind, while his father might be contemplating some piece of buffoonery. Though he said nothing, Alyosha thoroughly understood his father. The boy, I repeat, was far from being so simple as every one thought him. He awaited the day with a heavy heart. No doubt he was always pondering in his mind how the family discord could be ended. But his chief anxiety concerned the elder. He trembled for him, for his glory, and dreaded any affront to him, especially the refined, courteous irony of Miüsov and the supercilious half-utterances of the highly educated Ivan. He even wanted to venture on warning the elder, telling him something about them, but, on second thoughts, said nothing. He only sent word the day before, through a friend, to his brother Dmitri, that he loved him and expected him to keep his promise. Dmitri wondered, for he could not remember what he had promised, but he answered by letter that he would do his utmost not to let himself be provoked "by vileness," but that, although he had a deep respect for the elder and for his brother Ivan, he was convinced that the meeting was either a trap for him or an unworthy farce.

"Nevertheless I would rather bite out my tongue than be lacking in respect to the sainted man whom you reverence so highly," he wrote in conclusion. Alyosha was not greatly cheered by the letter.

BOOK TWO

AN UNFORTUNATE GATHERING

1

THEY ARRIVE AT THE MONASTERY

IT was a warm, bright day at the end of August. The interview with the elder had been fixed for half-past eleven, immediately after late mass. Our visitors did not take part in the service, but arrived just as it was over. First an elegant open carriage, drawn by two valuable horses, drove up with Miüsov and a distant relative of his, a young man of twenty, called Pyotr Fomitch Kalganov. This young man was preparing to enter the university. Miüsov, with whom he was staying for the time, was trying to persuade him to go abroad to the university of Zürich or Jena. The young man was still undecided. He was thoughtful and absent-minded. He was nice-looking, strongly built, and rather tall. There was a strange fixity in his gaze at times. Like all very absent-minded people he would sometimes stare at a person without seeing him. He was silent and rather awkward, but sometimes, when he was alone with any one he became talkative and effusive, and would laugh at anything or nothing. But his animation vanished as quickly as it appeared. He was always well and even elaborately dressed; he had already some independent fortune and expectations of much more. He was a friend of Alyosha's.

In an ancient, jolting, but roomy, hired carriage, with a pair of old pinkish-grey horses, a long way behind Miüsov's carriage, came Fyodor Pavlovitch, with his son Ivan. Dmitri was late, though he had been informed of the time the evening before. The visitors left their carriage at the hotel, outside the precincts, and went to the gates of the monastery on foot. Except Fyodor Pavlovitch, none of the party had ever seen the monastery, and Miüsov had probably not even been to church for thirty years. He looked about him with curiosity, together with assumed ease. But, except the church and the domestic buildings, though these too were ordinary enough, he found nothing of interest in the interior of the monastery. The last of the worshippers were coming out of the church, bareheaded and crossing themselves. Among the humbler people were a few of higher rank—two or three ladies and a very old general. They were all staying at the hotel. Our visitors were at once surrounded by beggars, but none of them gave them anything, except young Kalganov, who took a ten-kopeck piece out of his purse, and, nervous and embarrassed—God knows why!—hurriedly gave it to an old woman, saying: "Divide it equally." None of his companions made any remark upon it, so that he had no reason to be embarrassed; but, perceiving this, he was even more overcome.

It was strange that their arrival did not seem expected, and that they were not received with special honour, though one of them had recently made a donation of a thousand roubles, while another was a very wealthy and highly cultured landowner, upon whom all in the monastery were in a sense dependent, as a decision of the lawsuit might at any moment put their fishing rights in his hands. Yet no official personage met them.

Miüsov looked absent-mindedly at the tombstones round the church, and was on the point of saying that the dead buried here must have paid a pretty penny for the right of lying in this "holy place," but refrained. His liberal irony was rapidly changing almost into anger.

"Who the devil is there to ask in this imbecile place? We must find out, for time is passing," he observed suddenly, as though speaking to himself.

All at once there came up a bald-headed, elderly man with ingratiating little eyes, wearing a full, summer overcoat. Lifting his hat, he introduced himself with a honeyed lisp as Maximov, a landowner of Tula. He at once entered into our visitors' difficulty.

"Father Zossima lives in the hermitage, apart, four hundred paces from the monastery, the other side of the copse."

"I know it's the other side of the copse," observed Fyodor Pavlovitch, "but we don't remember the way. It is a long time since we've been here."

"This way, by this gate, and straight across the copse . . . the copse. Come with me, won't you? I'll show you. I have to go . . . I am going myself. This way, this way."

They came out of the gate and turned towards the copse. Maximov, a man of sixty, ran rather than walked, turning sideways to stare at them all, with an incredible degree of nervous curiosity. His eyes looked starting out of his head.

"You see, we have come to the elder upon business of our own," observed Miüsov severely. "That personage has granted us an audience so to speak, and so, though we thank you for showing us the way, we cannot ask you to company us."

"I've been there. I've been already; *un chevalier parfait*,"* and Maximov snapped his fingers in the air.

"Who is a *chevalier*?" asked Miüsov.

"The elder, the splendid elder, the elder! The honour and glory of the monastery, Zossima. Such an elder!"

But his incoherent talk was cut short by a very pale, wan-looking monk of medium height, wearing a monk's cap, who overtook them. Fyodor Pavlovitch and Miüsov stopped.

The monk, with an extremely courteous, profound bow, announced:

"The Father Superior invites all of you gentlemen to dine with him after your visit to the hermitage. At one o'clock, not later. And you also," he added, addressing Maximov.

"That I certainly will, without fail," cried Fyodor Pavlovitch, hugely delighted at the invitation. "And, believe me, we've all given our word to behave properly here. . . . And you, Pyotr Alexandrovitch, will you go, too?"

---

*A perfect knight (French).

"Yes, of course. What have I come for but to study all the customs here? The only obstacle to me is your company. . . ."

"Yes, Dmitri Fyodorovitch is non-existent as yet."

"It would be a capital thing if he didn't turn up. Do you suppose I like all this business, and in your company, too? So we will come to dinner. Thank the Father Superior," he said to the monk.

"No, it is my duty now to conduct you to the elder," answered the monk.

"If so I'll go straight to the Father Superior—to the Father Superior," babbled Maximov.

"The Father Superior is engaged just now. But as you please——" the monk hesitated.

"Impertinent old man!" Miüsov observed aloud, while Maximov ran back to the monastery.

"He's like Von Sohn,"* Fyodor Pavlovitch said suddenly.

"Is that all you can think of? . . . In what way is he like Von Sohn? Have you ever seen Von Sohn?"

"I've seen his portrait. It's not the features, but something indefinable. He's a second Von Sohn. I can always tell from the physiognomy."

"Ah, I dare say you are a connoisseur in that. But, look here, Fyodor Pavlovitch, you said just now that we had given our word to behave properly. Remember it. I advise you to control yourself. But, if you begin to play the fool I don't intend to be associated with you here. . . . You see what a man he is"—he turned to the monk—"I'm afraid to go among decent people with him." A fine smile, not without a certain slyness, came on to the pale, bloodless lips of the monk, but he made no reply, and was evidently silent from a sense of his own dignity. Miüsov frowned more than ever.

"Oh, devil take them all! An outer show elaborated through centuries, and nothing but charlatanism and nonsense underneath," flashed through Miüsov's mind.

"Here's the hermitage. We've arrived," cried Fyodor Pavlovitch. "The gates are shut."

And he repeatedly made the sign of the cross to the saints painted above and on the sides of the gates.

"When you go to Rome you must do as the Romans do. Here in this hermitage there are twenty-five saints being saved. They look at one another, and eat cabbages. And not one woman goes in at this gate. That's what is remarkable. And that really is so. But I did hear that the elder receives ladies," he remarked suddenly to the monk.

"Women of the people are here too now, lying in the portico there waiting. But for ladies of higher rank two rooms have been built adjoining the portico, but outside the precincts—you can see the windows—and the elder goes out to them by an inner passage when he is well enough. They

*Reference to an actual homicide case tried in St. Petersburg in 1870; see also page 87.

are always outside the precincts. There is a Harkov lady, Madame Hohlakov, waiting there now with her sick daughter. Probably he has promised to come out to her, though of late he has been so weak that he has hardly shown himself even to the people."

"So then there are loopholes, after all, to creep out of the hermitage to the ladies. Don't suppose, holy father, that I mean any harm. But do you know that at Athos not only the visits of women are not allowed, but no creature of the female sex—no hens, nor turkey-hens, nor cows."

"Fyodor Pavlovitch, I warn you I shall go back and leave you here. They'll turn you out when I'm gone."

"But I'm not interfering with you, Pyotr Alexandrovitch. Look," he cried suddenly, stepping within the precincts, "what a vale of roses they live in!"

Though there were no roses now, there were numbers of rare and beautiful autumn flowers growing wherever there was space for them, and evidently tended by a skilful hand; there were flower-beds round the church, and between the tombs; and the one-storied wooden house where the elder lived was also surrounded with flowers.

"And was it like this in the time of the last elder, Varsonofy? He didn't care for such elegance. They say he used to jump up and thrash even ladies with a stick," observed Fyodor Pavlovitch, as he went up the steps.

"The elder Varsonofy did sometimes seem rather strange, but a great deal that's told is foolishness. He never thrashed any one," answered the monk. "Now, gentlemen, if you will wait a minute I will announce you."

"Fyodor Pavlovitch, for the last time, your compact, do you hear? Behave properly or I will pay you out!" Miüsov had time to mutter again.

"I can't think why you are so agitated," Fyodor Pavlovitch observed sarcastically. "Are you uneasy about your sins? They say he can tell by one's eyes what one has come about. And what a lot you think of their opinion! you, a Parisian, and so advanced. I'm surprised at you."

But Miüsov had no time to reply to this sarcasm. They were asked to come in. He walked in, somewhat irritated.

"Now, I know myself, I am annoyed, I shall lose my temper and begin to quarrel—and lower myself and my ideas," he reflected.

2

THE OLD BUFFOON

THEY entered the room almost at the same moment that the elder came in from his bedroom. There were already in the cell, awaiting the elder, two monks of the hermitage, one the Father Librarian, and the other Father Païssy, a very learned man, so they said, in delicate health, though not old. There was also a tall young man, who looked about two and twenty, standing in the corner throughout the interview. He had a broad, fresh face, and clever, observant, narrow brown eyes, and was wearing ordinary dress. He was a divinity student, living under the protection of the monastery. His expression was one of unquestioning, but self-respecting, reverence. Being in a subordinate and dependent position, and so not on an equality with the guest, he did not greet them with a bow.

Father Zossima was accompanied by a novice, and by Alyosha. The two monks rose and greeted him with a very deep bow, touching the ground with their fingers; then kissed his hand. Blessing them, the elder replied with as deep a reverence to them, and asked their blessing. The whole ceremony was performed very seriously and with an appearance of feeling, not like an everyday rite. But Miüsov fancied that it was all done with intentional impressiveness. He stood in front of the other visitors. He ought—he had reflected upon it the evening before—from simple politeness, since it was the custom here, to have gone up to receive the elder's blessing, even if he did not kiss his hand. But when he saw all this bowing and kissing on the part of the monks he instantly changed his mind. With dignified gravity he made a rather deep, conventional bow, and moved away to a chair. Fyodor Pavlovitch did the same, mimicking Miüsov like an ape. Ivan bowed with great dignity and courtesy, but he too kept his hands at his sides, while Kalganov was so confused that he did not bow at all. The elder let fall the hand raised to bless them, and bowing to them again, asked them all to sit down. The blood rushed to Alyosha's cheeks. He was ashamed. His forebodings were coming true.

Father Zossima sat down on a very old-fashioned mahogany sofa, covered with leather, and made his visitors sit down in a row along the opposite wall on four mahogany chairs, covered with shabby black leather. The monks sat, one at the door and the other at the window. The divinity student, the novice, and Alyosha remained standing. The cell was not very large and had a faded look. It contained nothing but the most necessary furniture, of coarse and poor quality. There were two pots of flowers in the window, and a number of holy pictures in the corner. Before one huge ancient ikon of the Virgin a lamp was burning. Near it were two other holy pictures in shining settings, and, next them, carved cherubims, china eggs, a Catholic cross of ivory, with a Mater Dolorosa embracing it, and several foreign engravings from the great Italian artists of past centuries. Next to these costly and artistic engravings were several of the roughest Russian prints of saints and martyrs, such as are sold for a few farthings at all the fairs. On the other walls were portraits of Russian bishops, past and present.

Miüsov took a cursory glance at all these "conventional" surroundings and bent an intent look upon the elder. He had a high opinion of his own insight, a weakness excusable in him as he was fifty, an age at which a clever man of the world of established position can hardly help taking himself rather seriously. At the first moment he did not like Zossima. There was, indeed, something in the elder's face which many people besides Miüsov might not have liked. He was a short, bent, little man, with very weak legs, and though he was only sixty-five, he looked at least ten years older. His face was very thin and covered with a network of fine wrinkles, particularly numerous about his eyes, which were small, light-coloured, quick, and shining like two bright points. He had a sprinkling of grey hair about his temples. His pointed beard was small and scanty, and his lips, which smiled frequently, were as thin as two threads. His nose was not long, but sharp, like a bird's beak.

"To all appearances a malicious soul, full of petty pride," thought Miüsov. He felt altogether dissatisfied with his position.

A cheap little clock on the wall struck twelve hurriedly, and served to begin the conversation.

"Precisely to our time," cried Fyodor Pavlovitch, "but no sign of my son, Dmitri. I apologise for him, sacred elder!" (Alyosha shuddered all over at "sacred elder.") "I am always punctual myself, minute for minute, remembering that punctuality is the courtesy of kings. . . ."

"But you are not a king, anyway," Miüsov muttered, losing his self-restraint at once.

"Yes; that's true. I'm not a king, and, would you believe it, Pyotr Alexandrovitch, I was aware of that myself. But, there! I always say the wrong thing. Your reverence," he cried, with sudden pathos, "you behold before you a buffoon in earnest! I introduce myself as such. It's an old habit, alas! And if I sometimes talk nonsense out of place it's with an object, with the object of amusing people and making myself agreeable. One must be agreeable, mustn't one? I was seven years ago in a little town where I had business, and I made friends with some merchants there. We went to the captain of police because we had to see him about something, and to ask him to dine with us. He was a tall, fat, fair, sulky man, the most dangerous type in such cases. It's their liver. I went straight up to him, and with the ease of a man of the world, you know, 'Mr. Ispravnik,' said I, 'be our Napravnik.'[1] 'What do you mean by Napravnik?' said he. I saw, at the first half-second, that it had misfired. He stood there so glum. 'I wanted to make a joke,' said I, 'for the general diversion, as Mr. Napravnik is our well-known Russian orchestra conductor and what we need for the harmony of our undertaking is some one of that sort.' And I explained my comparison very reasonably, didn't I? 'Excuse me,' said he, 'I am an Is-pravnik, and I do not allow puns to be made on my calling.' He turned and walked away. I followed him, shouting, 'Yes, yes, you are an Ispravnik, not a Napravnik.' 'No,' he said, 'since you called me a Napravnik, I am one.' And would you believe it, it ruined our business! And I'm always like that, always like that. Always injuring myself with my politeness. Once, many years ago, I said to an influential person: 'Your wife is a ticklish lady,' in an honourable sense, of the moral qualities, so to speak. But he asked me, 'Why, have you tickled her?' I thought I'd be polite, so I couldn't help say-ing 'Yes,' and he gave me a fine tickling on the spot. Only that happened long ago, so I'm not ashamed to tell the story. I'm always injuring myself like that."

"You're doing it now," muttered Miüsov, with disgust.

Father Zossima scrutinised them both in silence.

"Am I? Would you believe it, I was aware of that, too, Pyotr Alexan-drovitch, and let me tell you, indeed, I foresaw I should as soon as I began to speak. And do you know I foresaw, too, that you'd be the first to remark on it. The minute I see my joke isn't coming off, your reverence, both my cheeks feel as though they were drawn down to the lower jaw and there is almost a spasm in them. That's been so since I was young, when I had to make jokes for my living in noblemen's families. I am an inveterate buf-foon, and have been from my birth up, your reverence, it's as though it were a craze in me. I daresay it's a devil within me. But only a little one. A more serious one would have chosen another lodging. But not your soul, Pyotr Alexandrovitch: you're not a lodging worth having either. But I do believe—I believe in God, though I have had doubts of late. But now I sit and await words of wisdom. I'm like the philosopher, Diderot, your rever-ence. Did you ever hear, most Holy Father, how Diderot went to see the Metropolitan Platon, in the time of the Empress Catherine?[2] He went in and said straight out, 'There is no God.' To which the great Bishop lifted up his finger and answered, 'The fool has said in his heart there is no God.'* And he fell down at his feet on the spot. 'I believe,' he cried, 'and will be christened. And so he was. Princess Dashkov was his godmother, and Potyomkin his godfather.' "[3]

"Fyodor Pavlovitch, this is unbearable! You know you're telling lies and that that stupid anecdote isn't true. Why are you playing the fool?" cried Miüsov in a shaking voice.

"I suspected all my life that it wasn't true," Fyodor Pavlovitch cried with conviction. "But I'll tell you the whole truth, gentlemen. Great elder! Forgive me, the last thing about Diderot's christening I made up just now. I never thought of it before. I made it up to add piquancy. I play the fool, Pyotr Alexandrovitch, to make myself agreeable. Though I really don't know myself, sometimes, what I do it for. And as for Diderot, I heard as far as 'the fool hath said in his heart' twenty times from the gentry about here

---

*See Psalms 14:1.

when I was young. I heard your aunt, Pyotr Alexandrovitch, tell the story.
They all believe to this day that the infidel Diderot came to dispute about
God with the Metropolitan Platon. . . ."

Miüsov got up, forgetting himself in his impatience. He was furious, and
conscious of being ridiculous.

What was taking place in the cell was really incredible. For forty or fifty
years past, from the times of former elders, no visitors had entered that
cell without feelings of the profoundest veneration. Almost every one admitted to the cell felt that a great favour was being shown him. Many
remained kneeling during the whole visit. Of those visitors, many had been
men of high rank and learning, some even freethinkers, attracted by curiosity, but all without exception had shown the profoundest reverence
and delicacy, for here there was no question of money, but only, on the one
side love and kindness, and on the other penitence and eager desire to decide some spiritual problem or crisis. So that such buffoonery amazed and
bewildered the spectators, or at least some of them. The monks, with unchanged countenances, waited, with earnest attention, to hear what the
elder would say, but seemed on the point of standing up, like Miüsov.
Alyosha stood, with hanging head, on the verge of tears. What seemed to
him strangest of all was that his brother Ivan, on whom alone he had
rested his hopes, and who alone had such influence on his father that he
could have stopped him, sat now quite unmoved, with downcast eyes, apparently waiting with interest to see how it would end, as though he had
nothing to do with it. Alyosha did not dare to look at Rakitin, the divinity
student, whom he knew almost intimately. He alone in the monastery
knew Rakitin's thoughts.

"Forgive me," began Miüsov, addressing Father Zossima, "for perhaps I
seem to be taking part in this shameful foolery. I made a mistake in believing that even a man like Fyodor Pavlovitch would understand what
was due on a visit to so honoured a personage. I did not suppose I should
have to apologise simply for having come with him. . . ."

Pyotr Alexandrovitch could say no more, and was about to leave the
room, overwhelmed with confusion.

"Don't distress yourself, I beg." The elder got on to his feeble legs, and
taking Pyotr Alexandrovitch by both hands, made him sit down again. "I
beg you not to disturb yourself. I particularly beg you to be my guest."
And with a bow he went back and sat down again on his little sofa.

"Great elder, speak! Do I annoy you by my vivacity?" Fyodor
Pavlovitch cried suddenly, clutching the arms of his chair in both hands, as
though ready to leap up from it if the answer were unfavourable.

"I earnestly beg you, too, not to disturb yourself, and not to be uneasy,"
the elder said impressively. "Do not trouble. Make yourself quite at home.
And, above all, do not be so ashamed of yourself, for that is at the root of
it all."

"Quite at home? To be my natural self? Oh, that is much too much,
but I accept it with grateful joy. Do you know, blessed father, you'd better
not invite me to be my natural self. Don't risk it. . . . I will not go so far as

that myself. I warn you for your own sake. Well, the rest is still plunged in the mists of uncertainty, though there are people who'd be pleased to describe me for you. I mean that for you, Pyotr Alexandrovitch. But as for you, holy being, let me tell you, I am brimming over with ecstasy."

He got up, and throwing up his hands, declaimed, "Blessed be the womb that bare thee, and the paps that gave thee suck"*—the paps especially. When you said just now, 'Don't be so ashamed of yourself for that is at the root of it all,' you pierced right through me by that remark, and read me to the core. Indeed, I always feel when I meet people that I am lower than all, and that they all take me for a buffoon. So I say, 'Let me really play the buffoon. I am not afraid of your opinion, for you are every one of you worse than I am.' That is why I am a buffoon. It is from shame, great elder, from shame; it's simply over-sensitiveness that makes me rowdy. If I had only been sure that every one would accept me as the kindest and wisest of men, oh, Lord, what a good man I should have been then! Teacher!" he fell suddenly on his knees, "what must I do to gain eternal life?"†

It was difficult even now to decide whether he was joking or really moved.

Father Zossima, lifting his eyes, looked at him, and said with a smile:

"You have known for a long time what you must do. You have sense enough: don't give way to drunkenness and incontinence of speech; don't give way to sensual lust; and, above all, to the love of money. And close your taverns. If you can't close all, at least two or three. And, above all—don't lie."

"You mean about Diderot?"

"No, not about Diderot. Above all, don't lie to yourself. The man who lies to himself and listens to his own lie comes to such a pass that he cannot distinguish the truth within him, or around him, and so loses all respect for himself and for others. And having no respect he ceases to love, and in order to occupy and distract himself without love he gives way to passions and coarse pleasures, and sinks to bestiality in his vices, all from continual lying to other men and to himself. The man who lies to himself can be more easily offended than any one. You know it is sometimes very pleasant to take offence, isn't it? A man may know that nobody has insulted him, but that he has invented the insult for himself, has lied and exaggerated to make it picturesque, has caught at a word and made a mountain out of a molehill—he knows that himself, yet he will be the first to take offence, and will revel in his resentment till he feels great pleasure in it, and so pass to genuine vindictiveness. But get up, sit down, I beg you. All this, too, is deceitful posturing. . . ."

"Blessed man! Give me your hand to kiss."

Fyodor Pavlovitch skipped up, and imprinted a rapid kiss on the elder's thin hand. "It is, it is pleasant to take offence. You said that so well, as I never heard it before. Yes, I have been all my life talking offence, to please

---

*See Luke 11:27.
†See Luke 10:25.

myself, taking offence on æsthetic grounds, for it is not so much pleasant as distinguished sometimes to be insulted—that you had forgotten, great elder, it is distinguished! I shall make a note of that. But I have been lying, lying positively my whole life long, every day and hour of it. Of a truth, I am a lie, and the father of lies.* Though I believe I am not the father of lies. I am getting mixed in my texts. Say, the son of lies, and that will be enough. Only . . . my angel . . . I may sometimes talk about Diderot! Diderot will do no harm, though sometimes a word will do harm. Great elder, by the way, I was forgetting, though I had been meaning for the last two years to come here on purpose to ask and to find out something. Only to tell Pyotr Alexandrovitch not to interrupt me. Here is my question: Is it true, great Father, that the story is told somewhere in the 'Lives of the Saints' of a holy saint martyred for his faith who, when his head was cut off at last, stood up, picked up his head, and, 'courteously kissing it,' walked a long way, carrying it in his hands. Is that true or not, honoured Father?"

"No, it is untrue," said the elder.

"There is nothing of the kind in all the lives of the saints. What saint do you say the story is told of?" asked the Father Librarian.

"I do not know what saint. I do not know, and can't tell. I was deceived. I was told the story. I had heard it, and do you know who told it? Pyotr Alexandrovitch Miüsov here, who was so angry just now about Diderot. He it was who told the story."

"I have never told it you, I never speak to you at all."

"It is true you did not tell me, but you told it when I was present. It was three years ago. I mentioned it because by that ridiculous story you shook my faith, Pyotr Alexandrovitch. You knew nothing of it, but I went home with my faith shaken, and I have been getting more and more shaken ever since. Yes, Pyotr Alexandrovitch, you were the cause of a great fall. That was not a Diderot!"

Fyodor Pavlovitch got excited and pathetic, though it was perfectly clear to every one by now that he was playing a part again. Yet Miüsov was stung by his words.

"What nonsense, and it is all nonsense," he muttered. "I may really have told it, some time or other . . . but not to you. I was told it myself. I heard it in Paris from a Frenchman. He told me it was read at our mass from the 'Lives of the Saints' . . . he was a very learned man who had made a special study of Russian statistics and had lived a long time in Russia. . . . I have not read the 'Lives of the Saints' myself, and I am not going to read them . . . all sorts of things are said at dinner—we were dining then."

"Yes, you were dining then, and so I lost my faith!" said Fyodor Pavlovitch, mimicking him.

"What do I care for your faith?" Miüsov was on the point of shouting, but he suddenly checked himself, and said with contempt, "You defile everything you touch."

---

*See John 8:44.

The elder suddenly rose from his seat. "Excuse me gentlemen, for leaving you a few minutes," he said, addressing all his guests. "I have visitors awaiting me who arrived before you. But don't you tell lies all the same," he added, turning to Fyodor Pavlovitch with a good-humoured face. He went out of the cell. Alyosha and the novice flew to escort him down the steps. Alyosha was breathless: he was glad to get away, but he was glad, too, that the elder was good-humoured and not offended. Father Zossima was going towards the portico to bless the people waiting for him there. But Fyodor Pavlovitch persisted in stopping him at the door of the cell.

"Blessed man!" he cried, with feeling. "Allow me to kiss your hand once more. Yes, with you I could still talk, I could still get on. Do you think I always lie and play the fool like this? Believe me, I have been acting like this all the time on purpose to try you. I have been testing you all the time to see whether I could get on with you. Is there room for my humility beside your pride? I am ready to give you a testimonial that one can get on with you! But now, I'll be quiet; I will keep quiet all the time. I'll sit in a chair and hold my tongue. Now it is for you to speak, Pyotr Alexandrovitch. You are the principal person left now—for ten minutes."

3

PEASANT WOMEN WHO HAVE FAITH

NEAR the wooden portico below, built on to the outer wall of the precinct, there was a crowd of about twenty peasant women. They had been told that the elder was at last coming out, and they had gathered together in anticipation. Two ladies, Madame Hohlakov and her daughter, had also come out into the portico to wait for the elder, but in a separate part of it set aside for women of rank.

Madame Hohlakov was a wealthy lady, still young and attractive, and always dressed with taste. She was rather pale, and had lively black eyes. She was not more than thirty-three, and had been five years a widow. Her daughter, a girl of fourteen, was partially paralysed. The poor child had not been able to walk for the last six months, and was wheeled about in a long reclining chair. She had a charming little face, rather thin from illness, but full of gaiety. There was a gleam of mischief in her big dark eyes with their long lashes. Her mother had been intending to take her abroad ever since the spring, but they had been detained all the summer by business connected with their estate. They had been staying a week in our town, where they had come more for purposes of business than devotion, but had visited

Father Zossima once already, three days before. Though they knew that the elder scarcely saw any one, they had now suddenly turned up again, and urgently entreated "the happiness of looking once again on the great healer."

The mother was sitting on a chair by the side of her daughter's invalid carriage, and two paces from her stood an old monk, not one of our monastery, but a visitor from an obscure religious house in the far north. He too sought the elder's blessing.

But Father Zossima, on entering the portico, went first straight to the peasants who were crowded at the foot of the three steps that led up into the portico. Father Zossima stood on the top step, put on his stole, and began blessing the women who thronged about him. One crazy woman was led up to him. As soon as she caught sight of the elder she began shrieking and writhing as though in the pains of childbirth. Laying the stole on her forehead, he read a short prayer over her, and she was at once soothed and quieted.

I do not know how it may be now, but in my childhood I often happened to see and hear these "possessed" women in the villages and monasteries. They used to be brought to mass; they would squeal and bark like a dog so that they were heard all over the church. But when the sacrament was carried in and they were led up to it, at once the "possession" ceased, and the sick women were always soothed for a time. I was greatly impressed and amazed at this as a child; but then I heard from country neighbours and from my town teachers that the whole illness was simulated to avoid work, and that it could always be cured by suitable severity; various anecdotes were told to confirm this. But later on I learnt with astonishment from medical specialists that there is no pretence about it, that it is a terrible illness to which women are subject, specially prevalent among us in Russia, and that it is due to the hard lot of the peasant women. It is a disease, I was told, arising from exhausting toil too soon after hard, abnormal and unassisted labour in childbirth, and from the hopeless misery, from beatings, and so on, which some women were not able to endure like others. The strange and instant healing of the frantic and struggling woman as soon as she was led up to the holy sacrament, which had been explained to me as due to malingering and the trickery of the "clericals," arose probably in the most natural manner. Both the women who supported her and the invalid herself fully believed as a truth beyond question that the evil spirit in possession of her could not hold out if the sick woman were brought to the sacrament and made to bow down before it. And so, with a nervous and psychically deranged woman, a sort of convulsion of the whole organism always took place, and was bound to take place, at the moment of bowing down to the sacrament, aroused by the expectation of the miracle of healing and the implicit belief that it would come to pass; and it did come to pass, though only for a moment. It was exactly the same now as soon as the elder touched the sick woman with the stole.

Many of the women in the crowd were moved to tears of ecstasy by the effect of the moment: some strove to kiss the hem of his garment, others cried out in sing-song voices.

He blessed them all and talked with some of them. The "possessed" woman he knew already. She came from a village only six versts from the monastery, and had been brought to him before.

"But here is one from afar." He pointed to a woman by no means old but very thin and wasted, with a face not merely sunburnt but almost blackened by exposure. She was kneeling and gazing with a fixed stare at the elder; there was something almost frenzied in her eyes.

"From afar off, Father, from afar off! From two hundred miles from here. From afar off, Father, from afar off!" the woman began in a sing-song voice as though she were chanting a dirge, swaying her head from side to side with her cheek resting in her hand.

There is silent and long-suffering sorrow to be met with among the peasantry. It withdraws into itself and is still. But there is a grief that breaks out, and from that minute it bursts into tears and finds vent in wailing. This is particularly common with women. But it is no lighter a grief than the silent. Lamentations comfort only by lacerating the heart still more. Such grief does not desire consolation. It feeds on the sense of its hopelessness. Lamentations spring only from the constant craving to re-open the wound.

"You are of the tradesman class?" said Father Zossima, looking curiously at her.

"Townfolk we are, Father, townfolk. Yet we are peasants though we live in the town. I have come to see you, oh Father! We heard of you, Father, we heard of you. I have buried my little son, and I have come on a pilgrimage. I have been in three monasteries, but they told me, 'Go, Nastasya, go to them'—that is to you. I have come; I was yesterday at the service, and to-day I have come to you."

"What are you weeping for?"

"It's my little son I'm grieving for, Father. He was three years old—three years all but three months. For my little boy, Father, I'm in anguish, for my little boy. He was the last one left. We had four, my Nikita and I, and now we've no children, our dear ones have all gone. I buried the first three without grieving overmuch, and now I have buried the last I can't forget him. He seems always standing before me. He never leaves me. He has withered my heart. I look at his little clothes, his little shirt, his little boots, and I wail. I lay out all that is left of him, all his little things. I look at them and wail. I say to Nikita, my husband, let me go on a pilgrimage, master. He is a driver. We're not poor people, Father, not poor; he drives our own horse. It's all our own, the horse and the carriage. And what good is it all to us now? My Nikita has begun drinking while I am away. He's sure to. It used to be so before. As soon as I turn my back he gives way to it. But now I don't think about him. It's three months since I left home. I've forgotten him. I've forgotten everything. I don't want to remember. And what would our life be now together? I've done with him, I've done. I've done with them all. I don't care to look upon my house and my goods. I don't care to see anything at all."

"Listen, mother," said the elder. "Once in olden times a holy saint saw in the Temple a mother like you weeping for her little one, her only one, whom God had taken. 'Knowest thou not,' said the saint to her, 'how bold these little ones are before the throne of God? Verily there are none bolder than they in the Kingdom of Heaven.' 'Thou didst give us life, oh Lord,' they say, 'and scarcely had we looked upon it when Thou didst take it back again.' And so boldly they ask and ask again that God gives them at once the rank of angels. 'Therefore,' said the saint, 'thou too, oh mother, rejoice and weep not, for thy little one is with the Lord in the fellowship of the angels.' That's what the saint said to the weeping mother of old. He was a great saint and he could not have spoken falsely. Therefore you too, mother, know that your little one is surely before the throne of God, is rejoicing and happy, and praying to God for you, and therefore weep not, but rejoice."

The woman listened to him, looking down with her cheek in her hand. She sighed deeply.

"My Nikita tried to comfort me with the same words as you. 'Foolish one,' he said, 'why weep? Our son is no doubt singing with the angels before God.' He says that to me, but he weeps himself. I see that he cries like me. 'I know, Nikita,' said I. 'Where could he be if not with the Lord God? Only, here with us now he is not as he used to sit beside us before.' And if only I could look upon him one little time, if only I could peep at him one little time, without going up to him, without speaking, if I could be hidden in a corner and only see him for one little minute, hear him playing in the yard, calling in his little voice, 'Mammy, where are you?' If only I could hear him pattering with his little feet about the room just once, only once; for so often, so often I remember how he used to run to me and shout and laugh, if only I could hear his little feet I should know him! But he's gone, Father, he's gone, and I shall never hear him again. Here's his little sash, but him I shall never see or hear now."

She drew out of her bosom her boy's little embroidered sash, and as soon as she looked at it she began shaking with sobs, hiding her eyes with her fingers through which the tears flowed in a sudden stream.

"It is Rachel of old," said the elder, "weeping for her children, and will not be comforted because they are not.* Such is the lot set on earth for you mothers. Be not comforted. Consolation is not what you need. Weep and be not consoled, but weep. Only every time that you weep be sure to remember that your little son is one of the angels of God, that he looks down from there at you and sees you, and rejoices at your tears, and points at them to the Lord God; and a long while yet will you keep that great mother's grief. But it will turn in the end into quiet joy, and your bitter tears will be only tears of tender sorrow that purifies the heart and delivers it from sin. And I shall pray for the peace of your child's soul. What was his name?"

"Alexey, Father."

"A sweet name. After Alexey, the man of God?"[4]

---

*See Matthew 2:18.

"Yes, Father."

"What a saint he was! I will remember him, mother, and your grief in my prayers, and I will pray for your husband's health. It is a sin for you to leave him. Your little one will see from heaven that you have forsaken his father, and will weep over you. Why do you trouble his happiness? He is living, for the soul lives for ever, and though he is not in the house he is near you, unseen. How can he go into the house when you say that the house is hateful to you? To whom is he to go if he find you not together, his father and mother? He comes to you in dreams now, and you grieve. But then he will send you gentle dreams. Go to your husband, mother; go this very day."

"I will go, Father, at your word. I will go. You've gone straight to my heart. My Nikita, my Nikita, you are waiting for me," the woman began in a sing-song voice; but the elder had already turned away to a very old woman, dressed like a dweller in the town, not like a pilgrim. Her eyes showed that she had come with an object, and in order to say something. She said she was the widow of a non-commissioned officer, and lived close by in the town. Her son Vasenka was in the commissariat service, and had gone to Irkutsk in Siberia. He had written twice from there, but now a year had passed since he had written. She did inquire about him, but she did not know the proper place to inquire.

"Only the other day Stepanida Ilyinishna—she's a rich merchant's wife—said to me. 'You go, Prohorovna, and put your son's name down for prayer in the church, and pray for the peace of his soul as though he were dead. His soul will be troubled,' she said, 'and he will write you a letter.' And Stepanida Ilyinishna told me it was a certain thing which had been many times tried. Only I am in doubt. . . . Oh, you light of ours! is it true or false, and would it be right?"

"Don't think of it. It's shameful to ask the question. How is it possible to pray for the peace of a living soul? And his own mother too! It's a great sin, akin to sorcery. Only for your ignorance it is forgiven you. Better pray to the Queen of Heaven, our swift defence and help, for his good health, and that she may forgive you for your error. And another thing I will tell you, Prohorovna. Either he will soon come back to you, your son, or he will be sure to send a letter. Go, and henceforward be in peace. Your son is alive, I tell you."

"Dear Father, God reward you, our benefactor, who prays for all of us and for our sins!"

But the elder had already noticed in the crowd two glowing eyes fixed upon him. An exhausted, consumptive-looking, though young peasant woman was gazing at him in silence. Her eyes besought him, but she seemed afraid to approach.

"What is it, my child?"

"Absolve my soul, Father," she articulated softly and slowly, sank on her knees and bowed down at his feet. "I have sinned, Father. I am afraid of my sin."

The elder sat down on the lower step. The woman crept closer to him, still on her knees.

"I am a widow these three years," she began in a half-whisper, with a sort of shudder. "I had a hard life with my husband. He was an old man. He used to beat me cruelly. He lay ill; I thought looking at him, if he were to get well, if he were to get up again, what then? And then the thought came to me——"

"Stay!" said the elder, and he put his ear close to her lips.

The woman went on in a low whisper, so that it was almost impossible to catch anything. She had soon done.

"Three years ago?" asked the elder.

"Three years. At first I didn't think about it, but now I've begun to be ill, and the thought never leaves me."

"Have you come from far?"

"Over three hundred miles away."

"Have you told it in confession?"

"I have confessed it. Twice I have confessed it."

"Have you been admitted to Communion?"

"Yes. I am afraid. I am afraid to die."

"Fear nothing and never be afraid; and don't fret. If only your penitence fail not, God will forgive all. There is no sin, and there can be no sin on all the earth, which the Lord will not forgive to the truly repentant! Man cannot commit a sin so great as to exhaust the infinite love of God. Can there be a sin which could exceed the love of God? Think only of repentance, continual repentance, but dismiss fear altogether. Believe that God loves you as you cannot conceive; that He loves you with your sin, in your sin. It has been said of old that over one repentant sinner there is more joy in heaven than over ten righteous men.* Go, and fear not. Be not bitter against men. Be not angry if you are wronged. Forgive the dead man in your heart what wrong he did you. Be reconciled with him in truth. If you are penitent, you love. And if you love you are of God. All things are atoned for, all things are saved by love. If I, a sinner, even as you are, am tender with you and have pity on you, how much more will God. Love is such a priceless treasure that you can redeem the whole world by it, and expiate not only your own sins but the sins of others."

He signed her three times with the cross, took from his own neck a little ikon and put it upon her. She bowed down to the earth without speaking.

He got up and looked cheerfully at a healthy peasant woman with a tiny baby in her arms.

"From Vyshegorye, dear Father."

"Five miles you have dragged yourself with the baby. What do you want?"

"I've come to look at you. I have been to you before—or have you forgotten? You've no great memory if you've forgotten me. They told us you were ill. Thinks I, I'll go and see him for myself. Now I see you, and you're not ill! You'll live another twenty years. God bless you! There are plenty to pray for you; how should you be ill?"

---

*See Luke 15:7.

"I thank you for all, daughter."

"By the way, I have a thing to ask, not a great one. Here are sixty kopecks. Give them, dear Father, to some one poorer than me. I thought as I came along, better give through him. He'll know whom to give to."

"Thanks, my dear, thanks! You are a good woman. I love you. I will do so certainly. Is that your little girl?"

"My little girl, Father, Lizaveta."

"May the Lord bless you both, you and your babe Lizaveta! You have gladdened my heart, mother. Farewell, dear children, farewell, dear ones."

He blessed them all and bowed low to them.

4

A LADY OF LITTLE FAITH

A VISITOR looking on the scene of his conversation with the peasants and his blessing them shed silent tears and wiped them away with her handkerchief. She was a sentimental society lady of genuinely good disposition in many respects. When the elder went up to her at last she met him enthusiastically.

"Ah, what I have been feeling, looking on at this touching scene! . . ." She could not go on for emotion. "Oh, I understand the people's love for you. I love the people myself. I want to love them. And who could help loving them, our splendid Russian people, so simple in their greatness!"

"How is your daughter's health? You wanted to talk to me again?"

"Oh, I have been urgently begging for it, I have prayed for it! I was ready to fall on my knees and kneel for three days at your windows until you let me in. We have come, great healer, to express our ardent gratitude. You have healed my Lise,* healed her completely, merely by praying over her last Thursday and laying your hands upon her. We have hastened here to kiss those hands, to pour out our feelings and our homage."

"What do you mean by healed? But she is still lying down in her chair."

"But her night fevers have entirely ceased ever since Thursday," said the lady with nervous haste. "And that's not all. Her legs are stronger. This morning she got up well; she had slept all night. Look at her rosy cheeks, her bright eyes! She used to be always crying, but now she laughs and is gay and happy. This morning she insisted on my letting her stand up, and

---

*French form of Liza.

she stood up for a whole minute without any support. She wagers that in a fortnight she'll be dancing a quadrille. I've called in Doctor Herzenstube. He shrugged his shoulders and said, 'I am amazed; I can make nothing of it.' And would you have us not come here to disturb you, not fly here to thank you? Lise, thank him—thank him!"

Lise's pretty little laughing face became suddenly serious. She rose in her chair as far as she could and, looking at the elder, clasped her hands before him, but could not restrain herself and broke into laughter.

"It's at him," she said, pointing to Alyosha, with childish vexation at herself for not being able to repress her mirth.

If any one had looked at Alyosha standing a step behind the elder, he could have caught a quick flush crimsoning his cheeks in an instant. His eyes shone and he looked down.

"She has a message for you, Alexey Fyodorovitch. How are you?" the mother went on, holding out her exquisitely gloved hand to Alyosha.

The elder turned round and all at once looked attentively at Alyosha. The latter went nearer to Lise and, smiling in a strangely awkward way, held out his hand to her too. Lise assumed an important air.

"Katerina Ivanovna has sent you this through me." She handed him a little note. "She particularly begs you to go and see her as soon as possible; that you will not fail her, but will be sure to come."

"She asks me to go and see her? Me? What for?" Alyosha muttered in great astonishment. His face at once looked anxious.

"Oh, it's all to do with Dmitri Fyodorovitch and—what has happened lately," the mother explained hurriedly. "Katerina Ivanovna has made up her mind, but she must see you about it. . . . Why, of course, I can't say. But she wants to see you at once. And you will go to her, of course. It is a Christian duty."

"I have only seen her once," Alyosha protested with the same perplexity.

"Oh, she is such a lofty, incomparable creature! If only for her suffering . . . Think what she has gone through, what she is enduring now! Think what awaits her! It's all terrible, terrible!"

"Very well, I will come," Alyosha decided, after rapidly scanning the brief, enigmatic note, which consisted of an urgent entreaty that he would come, without any sort of explanation.

"Oh, how sweet and generous that would be of you!" cried Lise with sudden animation. "I told mamma you'd be sure not to go. I said you were saving your soul. How splendid you are! I've always thought you were splendid. How glad I am to tell you so!"

"Lise!" said her mother impressively, though she smiled after she had said it.

"You have quite forgotten us, Alexey Fyodorovitch," she said; "you never come to see us. Yet Lise has told me twice that she is never happy except with you."

Alyosha raised his downcast eyes and again flushed, and again smiled without knowing why. But the elder was no longer watching him. He had begun talking to a monk who, as mentioned before, had been awaiting his entrance by Lise's chair. He was evidently a monk of the humblest, that is of the peasant, class, of a narrow outlook, but a true believer, and, in his own way, a stubborn one. He announced that he had come from the 'far north, from Obdorsk, from Saint Sylvester, and was a member of a poor monastery, consisting of only ten monks. The elder gave him his blessing and invited him to come to his cell whenever he liked.

"How can you presume to do such deeds?" the monk asked suddenly, pointing solemnly and significantly at Lise. He was referring to her "healing."

"It's too early, of course, to speak of that. Relief is not complete cure, and may proceed from different causes. But if there has been any healing, it is by no power but God's will. It's all from God. Visit me, Father," he added to the monk. "It's not often I can see visitors, I am ill, and I know that my days are numbered."

"Oh, no, no! God will not take you from us. You will live a long, long time yet," cried the lady. "And in what way are you ill? You look so well, so gay and happy."

"I am extraordinarily better to-day. But I know that it's only for a moment. I understand my disease now thoroughly. If I seem so happy to you, you could never say anything that would please me so much. For men are made for happiness, and any one who is completely happy has a right to say to himself, 'I am doing God's will on earth.' All the righteous, all the saints, all the holy martyrs were happy."

"Oh, how you speak! What bold and lofty words!" cried the lady. "You seem to pierce with your words. And yet—happiness, happiness—where is it? Who can say of himself that he is happy? Oh, since you have been so good as to let us see you once more to-day, let me tell you what I could not utter last time, what I dared not say, all I am suffering and have been for so long! I am suffering! Forgive me! I am suffering!"

And in a rush of fervent feeling she clasped her hands before him.

"From what specially?"

"I suffer . . . from lack of faith."

"Lack of faith in God?"

"Oh, no, no! I dare not even think of that. But the future life—it is such an enigma! And no one, no one can solve it. Listen! You are a healer, you are deeply versed in the human soul, and of course I dare not expect you to believe me entirely, but I assure you on my word of honour that I am not speaking lightly now. The thought of the life beyond the grave distracts me to anguish, to terror. And I don't know to whom to appeal, and have not dared to all my life. And now I am so bold as to ask you. Oh, God! What will you think of me now?"

She clasped her hands.

"Don't distress yourself about my opinion of you," said the elder. "I quite believe in the sincerity of your suffering."

"Oh, how thankful I am to you! You see, I shut my eyes and ask myself if every one has faith, where did it come from? And then they do say that it all comes from terror at the menacing phenomena of nature, and that none of it's real. And I say to myself, 'What if I've been believing all my life, and when I come to die there's nothing but the burdocks growing on my grave?'* as I read in some author. It's awful! How—how can I get back my faith? But I only believed when I was a little child, mechanically, without thinking of anything. How, how is one to prove it? I have come now to lay my soul before you and to ask you about it. If I let this chance slip, no one all my life will answer me. How can I prove it? How can I convince myself? Oh, how unhappy I am! I stand and look about me and see that scarcely any one else cares; no one troubles his head about it, and I'm the only one who can't stand it. It's deadly—deadly!"

"No doubt. But there's no proving it, though you can be convinced of it."

"How?"

"By the experience of active love. Strive to love your neighbour actively and indefatigably. In as far as you advance in love you will grow surer of the reality of God and of the immortality of your soul. If you attain to perfect self-forgetfulness in the love of your neighbour, then you will believe without doubt, and no doubt can possibly enter your soul. This has been tried. This is certain."

"In active love? There's another question—and such a question! You see, I so love humanity that—would you believe it?—I often dream of forsaking all that I have, leaving Lise, and becoming a sister of mercy. I close my eyes and think and dream, and at that moment I feel full of strength to overcome all obstacles. No wounds, no festering sores could at that moment frighten me. I would bind them up and wash them with my own hands. I would nurse the afflicted. I would be ready to kiss such wounds."

"It is much, and well that your mind is full of such dreams and not others. Sometime, unawares, you may do a good deed in reality."

"Yes. But could I endure such a life for long?" the lady went on fervently, almost frantically. "That's the chief question—that's my most agonising question. I shut my eyes and ask myself, 'Would you persevere long on that path? And if the patient whose wounds you are washing did not meet you with gratitude, but worried you with his whims, without valuing or remarking your charitable services, began abusing you and rudely commanding you, and complaining to the superior authorities of you (which often happens when people are in great suffering)—what then? Would you persevere in your love, or not?' And do you know, I came with horror to the conclusion that, if anything could dissipate my love to humanity, it would be ingratitude. In short, I am a hired servant, I expect my payment at once—that is, praise, and the repayment of love with love. Otherwise I am incapable of loving any one."

She was in a very paroxysm of self-castigation, and, concluding, she looked with defiant resolution at the elder.

"It's just the same story as a doctor once told me," observed the elder. "He was a man getting on in years, and undoubtedly clever. He spoke as

---

*Quotation from the character Bazarov in Ivan Turgenev's *Fathers and Sons* (1862).

frankly as you, though in jest, in bitter jest. 'I love humanity,' he said, 'but I wonder at myself. The more I love humanity in general, the less I love man in particular. In my dreams,' he said, 'I have often come to making enthusiastic schemes for the service of humanity, and perhaps I might actually have faced crucifixion if it had been suddenly necessary; and yet I am incapable of living in the same room with any one for two days together, as I know by experience. As soon as any one is near me, his personality disturbs my self-complacency and restricts my freedom. In twenty-four hours I begin to hate the best of men: one because he's too long over his dinner; another because he has a cold and keeps on blowing his nose. I become hostile to people the moment they come close to me. But it has always happened that the more I detest men individually the more ardent becomes my love for humanity.' "

"But what's to be done? What can one do in such a case? Must one despair?"

"No. It is enough that you are distressed at it. Do what you can, and it will be reckoned unto you. Much is done already in you since you can so deeply and sincerely know yourself. If you have been talking to me so sincerely, simply to gain approbation for your frankness, as you did from me just now, then of course you will not attain to anything in the achievement of real love; it will all get no further than dreams, and your whole life will slip away like a phantom. In that case you will naturally cease to think of the future life too, and will of yourself grow calmer after a fashion in the end."

"You have crushed me! Only now, as you speak, I understand that I was really only seeking your approbation for my sincerity when I told you I could not endure ingratitude. You have revealed me to myself. You have seen through me and explained me to myself!"

"Are you speaking the truth? Well, now, after such a confession, I believe that you are sincere and good at heart. If you do not attain happiness, always remember that you are on the right road, and try not to leave it. Above all, avoid falsehood, every kind of falsehood, especially falseness to yourself. Watch over your own deceitfulness and look into it every hour, every minute. Avoid being scornful, both to others and to yourself. What seems to you bad within you will grow purer from the very fact of your observing it in yourself. Avoid fear, too, though fear is only the consequence of every sort of falsehood. Never be frightened at your own faint-heartedness in attaining love. Don't be frightened overmuch even at your evil actions. I am sorry I can say nothing more consoling to you, for love in action is a harsh and dreadful thing compared with love in dreams. Love in dreams is greedy for immediate action, rapidly performed and in the sight of all. Men will even give their lives if only the ordeal does not last long but is soon over, with all looking on and applauding as though on the stage. But active love is labour and fortitude, and for some people too, perhaps, a complete science. But I predict that just when you see with horror that in spite of all your efforts you are getting further from your goal instead of nearer to it—at that very moment I predict that you will reach it and behold clearly the miraculous power of the Lord who has been all the time

loving and mysteriously guiding you. Forgive me for not being able to stay
longer with you. They are waiting for me. Good-bye."

The lady was weeping.

"Lise, Lise! Bless her—bless her!" she cried, starting up suddenly.

"She does not deserve to be loved. I have seen her naughtiness all
along," the elder said jestingly. "Why have you been laughing at Alexey?"

Lise had in fact been occupied in mocking at him all the time. She had
noticed before that Alyosha was shy and tried not to look at her, and she
found this extremely amusing. She waited intently to catch his eye. Alyosha,
unable to endure her persistent stare, was irresistibly and suddenly drawn to
glance at her, and at once she smiled triumphantly in his face. Alyosha was
even more disconcerted and vexed. At last he turned away from her altogether and hid behind the elder's back. After a few minutes, drawn by the
same irresistible force, he turned again to see whether he was being looked
at or not, and found Lise almost hanging out of her chair to peep sideways
at him, eagerly waiting for him to look. Catching his eye, she laughed so that
the elder could not help saying, "Why do you make fun of him like that,
naughty girl?"

Lise suddenly and quite unexpectedly blushed. Her eyes flashed and
her face became quite serious. She began speaking quickly and nervously
in a warm and resentful voice:

"Why has he forgotten everything, then? He used to carry me about
when I was little. We used to play together. He used to come to teach me
to read, do you know. Two years ago, when he went away, he said that he
would never forget me, that we were friends for ever, for ever, for ever!
And now he's afraid of me all at once. Am I going to eat him? Why doesn't
he want to come near me? Why doesn't he talk? Why won't he come and
see us? It's not that you won't let him. We know that he goes everywhere.
It's not good manners for me to invite him. He ought to have thought of it
first, if he hasn't forgotten me. No, now he's saving his soul! Why have you
put that long gown on him? If he runs he'll fall."

And suddenly she hid her face in her hand and went off into irresistible, prolonged, nervous, inaudible laughter. The elder listened to her
with a smile, and blessed her tenderly. As she kissed his hand she suddenly
pressed it to her eyes and began crying.

"Don't be angry with me. I'm silly and good for nothing . . . and perhaps Alyosha's right, quite right, in not wanting to come and see such a
ridiculous girl."

"I will certainly send him," said the elder.

5

SO BE IT! SO BE IT!

THE elder's absence from his cell had lasted for about twenty-five minutes. It was more than half-past twelve, but Dmitri, on whose account they had all met there, had still not appeared. But he seemed almost to be forgotten, and when the elder entered the cell again, he found his guests engaged in eager conversation. Ivan and the two monks took the leading share in it. Miüsov, too, was trying to take a part, and apparently very eagerly, in the conversation. But he was unsuccessful in this also. He was evidently in the background, and his remarks were treated with neglect, which increased his irritability. He had had intellectual encounters with Ivan before and he could not endure a certain carelessness Ivan showed him.

"Hitherto at least I have stood in the front ranks of all that is progressive in Europe, and here the new generation positively ignores us," he thought.

Fyodor Pavlovitch, who had given his word to sit still and be quiet, had actually been quiet for some time, but he watched his neighbour Miüsov with an ironical little smile, obviously enjoying his discomfiture. He had been waiting for some time to pay off old scores, and now he could not let the opportunity slip. Bending over his shoulder he began teasing him again in a whisper.

"Why didn't you go away just now, after the 'courteously kissing'? Why did you consent to remain in such unseemly company? It was because you felt insulted and aggrieved, and you remained to vindicate yourself by showing off your intelligence. Now you won't go till you've displayed your intellect to them."

"You again? . . . On the contrary, I'm just going."

"You'll be the last, the last of all to go!" Fyodor Pavlovitch delivered him another thrust, almost at the moment of Father Zossima's return.

The discussion died down for a moment, but the elder, seating himself in his former place, looked at them all as though cordially inviting them to go on. Alyosha, who knew every expression of his face, saw that he was fearfully exhausted and making a great effort. Of late he had been liable to fainting fits from exhaustion. His face had the pallor that was common before such attacks, and his lips were white. But he evidently did not want to break up the party. He seemed to have some special object of his own in keeping them. What object? Alyosha watched him intently.

"We are discussing this gentleman's most interesting article," said Father Iosif, the librarian, addressing the elder, and indicating Ivan. "He brings forward much that is new, but I think the argument cuts both ways. It is an article written in answer to a book by an ecclesiastical authority on the question of the ecclesiastical court, and the scope of its jurisdiction."

"I'm sorry I have not read your article, but I've heard of it," said the elder, looking keenly and intently at Ivan.

"He takes up a most interesting position," continued the Father Librarian. "As far as Church jurisdiction is concerned he is apparently quite opposed to the separation of Church from State."

"That's interesting. But in what sense?" Father Zossima asked Ivan.

The latter, at last, answered him, not condescendingly, as Alyosha had feared, but with modesty and reserve, with evident goodwill and apparently without the slightest *arrièrepensée.**

"I start from the position that this confusion of elements, that is, of the essential principles of Church and State, will, of course, go on for ever, in spite of the fact that it is impossible for them to mingle, and that the confusion of these elements cannot lead to any consistent or even normal results, for there is falsity at the very foundation of it. Compromise between the Church and State in such questions as, for instance, jurisdiction, is, to my thinking, impossible in any real sense. My clerical opponent maintains that the Church holds a precise and defined position in the State. I maintain, on the contrary, that the Church ought to include the whole State, and not simply to occupy a corner in it, and, if this is, for some reason, impossible at present, then it ought, in reality, to be set up as the direct and chief aim of the future development of Christian society!"

"Perfectly true," Father Païssy, the silent and learned monk, assented with fervour and decision.

"The purest Ultramontanism!"[5] cried Miüsov impatiently, crossing and recrossing his legs.

"Oh, well, we have no mountains," cried Father Iosif, and turning to the elder he continued, "observe the answer he makes to the following 'fundamental and essential' propositions of his opponent, who is, you must note, an ecclesiastic. First, that 'no social organisation can or ought to arrogate to itself power to dispose of the civic and political rights of its members.' Secondly, that 'criminal and civil jurisdiction ought not to belong to the Church, and is inconsistent with its nature, both as a divine institution and as an organisation of men for religious objects,' and, finally, in the third place, 'the Church is a kingdom not of this world.'"

"A most unworthy play upon words for an ecclesiastic!" Father Païssy could not refrain from breaking in again. "I have read the book which you have answered," he added, addressing Ivan, "and was astounded at the words 'the Church is a kingdom not of this world.'† If it is not of this world, then it cannot exist on earth at all. In the Gospel, the words 'not of this world,' are not used in that sense. To play with such words is indefensible.

---

*Ulterior motive (French).
†See John 18:36.

Our Lord Jesus Christ came to set up the Church upon earth. The Kingdom of Heaven, of course, is not of this world, but in Heaven; but it is only entered through the Church which has been founded and established upon earth. And so a frivolous play upon words in such a connection is unpardonable and improper. The Church is, in truth, a kingdom and ordained to rule, and in the end must undoubtedly become the kingdom ruling over all the earth. For that we have the divine promise."

He ceased speaking suddenly, as though checking himself. After listening attentively and respectfully Ivan went on, addressing the elder with perfect composure and as before with ready cordiality:

"The whole point of my article lies in the fact that during the first three centuries Christianity only existed on earth in the Church and was nothing but the Church. When the pagan Roman Empire desired to become Christian, it inevitably happened that, by becoming Christian, it included the Church but remained a pagan State in very many of its departments. In reality this was bound to happen. But Rome as a State retained too much of the pagan civilisation and culture, as, for example, in the very objects and fundamental principles of the State. The Christian Church entering into the State could, of course, surrender no part of its fundamental principles—the rock on which it stands—and could pursue no other aims than those which have been ordained and revealed by God Himself, and among them that of drawing the whole world and, therefore the ancient pagan State itself, into the Church. In that way (that is, with a view to the future) it is not the Church that should seek a definite position in the State, like 'every social organisation,' or as 'an organisation of men for religious purposes' (as my opponent calls the Church) but, on the contrary, every earthly State should be, in the end, completely transformed into the Church and should become nothing else but a Church, rejecting every purpose incongruous with the aims of the Church. All this will not degrade it in any way or take from its honour and glory as a great State, nor from the glory of its rulers, but only turns it from a false, still pagan, and mistaken path to the true and rightful path, which alone leads to the eternal goal. This is why the author of the book 'On the Foundations of Church Jurisdiction' would have judged correctly if, in seeking and laying down those foundations, he had looked upon them as only a temporary compromise inevitable in our sinful and imperfect days. But as soon as the author ventures to declare that the foundations which he predicates now, part of which Father Iosif just enumerated, are the permanent, essential, and eternal foundations, he is going directly against the Church and its sacred and eternal vocation. That is the gist of my article."

"That is, in brief," Father Païssy began again, laying stress on each word, "according to certain theories only too clearly formulated in the nineteenth century, the Church ought to be transformed into the State, as though this would be an advance from a lower to a higher form, so as to disappear into it, making way for science, for the spirit of the age, and civilisation. And if the Church resists and is unwilling, some corner will be set apart for her in the State, and even that under control—and this will be so everywhere in all modern European countries. But Russian hopes and conceptions demand not that the Church should pass as from a lower into a higher type into the State, but, on the contrary, that the State should end by being worthy to become only the Church and nothing else. So be it! So be it!"

"Well, I confess you've reassured me somewhat," Miüsov said smiling, again crossing his legs. "So far as I understand then, the realisation of such an ideal is infinitely remote, at the second coming of Christ. That's as you please. It's a beautiful Utopian dream of the abolition of war, diplomacy, banks, and so on—something after the fashion of socialism, indeed. But I imagined that it was all meant seriously, and that the Church might be *now* going to try criminals, and sentence them to beating, prison, and even death."

"But if there were none but the ecclesiastical court, the Church would not even now sentence a criminal to prison or to death. Crime and the way of regarding it would inevitably change, not all at once of course, but fairly soon," Ivan replied calmly, without flinching.

"Are you serious?" Miüsov glanced keenly at him.

"If everything became the Church, the Church would exclude all the criminal and disobedient, and would not cut off their heads," Ivan went on. "I ask you, what would become of the excluded? He would be cut off then not only from men, as now, but from Christ. By his crime he would have transgressed not only against men but against the Church of Christ. This is so even now, of course, strictly speaking, but it is not clearly enunciated, and very, very often the criminal of to-day compromises with his conscience: 'I steal,' he says, 'but I don't go against Church. I'm not an enemy of Christ.' That's what the criminal of to-day is continually saying to himself, but when the Church takes the place of the State it will be difficult for him, in opposition to the Church all over the world, to say: 'All men are mistaken, all in error, all mankind are the false Church. I, a thief and murderer, am the only true Christian Church?' It will be very difficult to say this to himself; it requires a rare combination of unusual circumstances. Now, on the other side, take the Church's own view of crime: is it not bound to renounce the present almost pagan attitude, and to change from a mechanical cutting off of its tainted member for the preservation of Society, as at present, into completely and honestly adopting the idea of the regeneration of the man, of his reformation and salvation?"

"What do you mean? I fail to understand again," Miüsov interrupted. "Some sort of dream again. Something shapeless and even incomprehensible. What is excommunication? What sort of exclusion? I suspect you are simply amusing yourself, Ivan Fyodorovitch."

"Yes, but you know, in reality it is so now," said the elder suddenly, and all turned to him at once. "If it were not for the Church of Christ there would be nothing to restrain the criminal from evil-doing, no real chastisement for it afterwards; none, that is, but the mechanical punishment spoken of just now, which in the majority of cases only embitters the heart; and not the real punishment, the only effectual one, the only deterrent and softening one, which lies in the recognition of sin by conscience."

"How is that, may one inquire?" asked Miüsov, with lively curiosity.

"Why," began the elder, "all these sentences to exile with hard labour, and formerly with flogging also, reform no one, and what's more, deter hardly a single criminal, and the number of crimes does not diminish but is continually on the increase. You must admit that. Consequently the security of society is not preserved, for, although the obnoxious member is mechanically cut off and sent far away out of sight, another criminal always comes to take his place at once, and often two of them. If anything does preserve society, even in our time, and does regenerate and transform the criminal, it is only the law of Christ speaking in his conscience. It is only by recognising his wrong-doing as a son of a Christian society—that is, of the Church—that he recognises his sin against society—that is, against the Church. So that it is only against the Church, and not against the State, that the criminal of to-day can recognise that he has sinned. If society, as a Church, had jurisdiction then it would know whom to bring back from exclusion and to re-unite to itself. Now the Church having no real jurisdiction, but only the power of moral condemnation, withdraws of her own accord from punishing the criminal actively. She does not excommunicate him but simply persists in fatherly exhortation of him. What is more, the Church even tries to preserve all Christian communion with the criminal. She admits him to church services, to the holy sacrament, gives him alms, and treats him more as a captive than as a convict. And what would become of the criminal, O Lord, if even the Christian society—that is, the Church—were to reject him even as the civil law rejects him and cuts him off? What would become of him if the Church punished him with her excommunication as the direct consequence of the secular law? There could be no more terrible despair, at least for a Russian criminal, for Russian criminals still have faith. Though, who knows, perhaps then a fearful thing would happen, perhaps the despairing heart of the criminal would lose its faith and then what would become of him? But the Church, like a tender, loving mother, holds aloof from active punishment herself, as the sinner is too severely punished already by the civil law, and there must be at least some one to have pity on him. The Church holds aloof, above all, because its judgment is the only one that contains the truth, and therefore cannot practically and morally be united to any other judgment even as a temporary compromise. She can enter into no compact about that. The foreign criminal, they say, rarely repents, for the very doctrines of to-day confirm him in the idea that his crime is not a crime, but only a reaction against an unjustly oppressive force. Society cuts him off completely by a force that triumphs over him mechanically and (so at least they say of themselves in Europe) accompanies this exclusion with hatred, forgetfulness, and the most profound indifference as to the ultimate fate of the erring brother. In this way, it all takes place without the compassionate intervention of the Church, for in many cases there are no churches there at all, for though ecclesiastics and splendid church buildings remain, the churches themselves have long ago striven to pass from Church into State and to disappear in it completely. So it seems at least in Lutheran countries. As for Rome, it was proclaimed a State instead of a Church a thousand years ago. And so the criminal is no longer conscious of being a member of the Church and sinks into despair. If he returns to society, often it is with such hatred that society itself instinctively cuts him off. You can judge for yourself how it must end. In many cases it would seem to be the same with us, but the difference is that besides the established law courts we have the Church too, which always keeps up relations with the criminal as a dear and still precious son. And besides that, there is still preserved, though only in thought, the judgment of the Church, which though no longer existing in practice is still living as a dream for the future, and is, no doubt, instinctively recognised by the criminal in his soul. What was said here just now is true too, that is, that if the jurisdiction of the Church were introduced in practice in its full force, that is, if the whole of the society were changed into the Church, not only the judgment of the Church would have influence on the reformation of the criminal such as it never has now, but possibly also the crimes themselves would be incredibly diminished. And there can be no doubt that the Church would look upon the criminal and the crime of the future in many cases quite differently and would succeed in restoring the excluded, in restraining those who plan evil, and in regenerating the fallen. It is true," said Father Zossima, with a smile, "the Christian society now is not ready and is only resting on some seven righteous men, but as they are never lacking, it will continue still unshaken in expectation of its complete transformation from a society almost heathen in character into a single universal and all-powerful Church. So be it, so be it. Even though at the end of the ages, for it is ordained to come to pass! And there is no need to be troubled about times and seasons, for the secret of the times and seasons is in the wisdom of God,* in His foresight, and His love. And what in human reckoning seems still afar off, may by the Divine ordinance be close at hand, on the eve of its appearance. And so be it, so be it!"

"So be it, so be it!" Father Païssy repeated austerely and reverently.

"Strange, extremely strange!" Miüsov pronounced, not so much with heat as with latent indignation.

"What strikes you as so strange?" Father Iosif inquired cautiously.

"Why, it's beyond anything!" cried Miüsov, suddenly breaking out, "the State is eliminated and the Church is raised to the position of the State. It's not simply Ultramontanism, it's arch-ultramontanism! It's beyond the dreams of Pope Gregory the Seventh!"†

"You are completely misunderstanding it," said Father Païssy sternly, "understand the Church is not to be transformed into the State. That is Rome and its dream. That is the third temptation of the devil.‡ On the contrary, the State is transformed into the Church, will ascend and become a

---

*See Acts 1:7.
†Pope Gregory VII (1073–1085) worked to achieve supremacy of the papacy over both church and state.
‡See Matthew 4:1–11.

Church over the whole world—which is the complete opposite of Ultra-montanism and Rome, and your interpretation, and is only the glorious destiny ordained for the Orthodox Church. This star will arise in the east!"

Miüsov was significantly silent. His whole figure expressed extraordinary personal dignity. A supercilious and condescending smile played on his lips. Alyosha watched it all with a throbbing heart. The whole conversation stirred him profoundly. He glanced casually at Rakitin, who was standing immovable in his place by the door listening and watching intently though with downcast eyes. But from the colour in his cheeks Alyosha guessed that Rakitin was probably no less excited, and he knew what caused his excitement.

"Allow me to tell you one little anecdote, gentlemen," Miüsov said impressively, with a peculiarly majestic air. "Some years ago, soon after the *coup d'état* of December,* I happened to be calling in Paris on an extremely influential personage in the Government, and I met a very interesting man in his house. This individual was not precisely a detective but was a sort of superintendent of a whole regiment of political detectives—a rather powerful position in its own way. I was prompted by curiosity to seize the opportunity of conversation with him. And as he had not come as a visitor but as a subordinate official bringing a special report, and as he saw the reception given me by his chief he deigned to speak with some openness, to a certain extent only, of course. He was rather courteous than open, as Frenchmen know how to be courteous, especially to a foreigner. But I thoroughly understood him. The subject was the socialist revolutionaries who were at that time persecuted. I will quote only one most curious remark dropped by this person. 'We are not particularly afraid,' said he, 'of all these socialists, anarchists, infidels, and revolutionists; we keep watch on them and know all their goings on. But there are a few peculiar men among them who believe in God and are Christians, but at the same time are socialists. Those are the people we are most afraid of. They are dreadful people! The socialist who is a Christian is more to be dreaded than a socialist who is an atheist.' The words struck me at the time, and now they have suddenly come back to me here, gentlemen."

"You apply them to us, and look upon us as socialists?" Father Païssy asked directly, without beating about the bush.

But before Pyotr Alexandrovitch could think what to answer, the door opened, and the guest so long expected, Dmitri Fyodorovitch, came in. They had, in fact, given up expecting him, and his sudden appearance caused some surprise for a moment.

---

*Reference to the coup d'état of December 2, 1851, which established the power of Louis Napoléon Bonaparte, future emperor of France.

6

WHY IS SUCH A MAN ALIVE?

DMITRI FYODOROVITCH, a young man of eight and twenty, of medium height and agreeable countenance, looked older than his years. He was muscular, and showed signs of considerable physical strength. Yet there was something not healthy in his face. It was rather thin, his cheeks were hollow, and there was an unhealthy sallowness in their colour. His rather large, prominent, dark eyes had an expression of firm determination, and yet there was a vague look in them, too. Even when he was excited and talking irritably, his eyes somehow did not follow his mood, but betrayed something else, sometimes quite incongruous with what was passing. "It's hard to tell what he's thinking," those who talked to him sometimes declared. People who saw something pensive and sullen in his eyes were startled by his sudden laugh, which bore witness to mirthful and light-hearted thoughts at the very time when his eyes were so gloomy. A certain strained look in his face was easy to understand at this moment. Every one knew, or had heard of the extremely restless and dissipated life which he had been leading of late, as well as of the violent anger to which he had been roused in his quarrels with his father. There were several stories current in the town about it. It is true that he was irascible by nature, "of an unstable and unbalanced mind," as our justice of the peace, Katchalnikov, happily described him.

He was stylishly and irreproachably dressed in a carefully buttoned frock-coat. He wore black gloves and carried a top hat. Having only lately left the army, he still had moustaches and no beard. His dark brown hair was cropped short, and combed forward on his temples. He had the long determined stride of a military man. He stood still for a moment on the threshold, and glancing at the whole party went straight up to the elder, guessing him to be their host. He made him a low bow, and asked his blessing. Father Zossima, rising in his chair, blessed him. Dmitri kissed his hand respectfully, and with intense feeling, almost anger, he said:

"Be so generous as to forgive me for having kept you waiting so long, but Smerdyakov, the valet sent me by my father, in reply to my inquiries, told me twice over that the appointment was for one. Now I suddenly learn——"

"Don't disturb yourself," interposed the elder. "No matter. You are a little late. It's of no consequence. . . ."

"I'm extremely obliged to you, and expected no less from your goodness."

Saying this, Dmitri bowed once more. Then, turning suddenly towards his father, made him, too, a similarly low and respectful bow. He had evidently considered it beforehand, and made this bow in all seriousness, thinking it his duty to show his respect and good intentions.

Although Fyodor Pavlovitch was taken unawares, he was equal to the occasion. In response to Dmitri's bow he jumped up from his chair and made his son a bow as low in return. His face was suddenly solemn and impressive, which gave him a positively malignant look. Dmitri bowed generally to all present, and without a word walked to the window with his long, resolute stride, sat down on the only empty chair, near Father Païssy, and, bending forward, prepared to listen to the conversation he had interrupted.

Dmitri's entrance had taken no more than two minutes, and the conversation was resumed. But this time Miüsov thought it unnecessary to reply to Father Païssy's persistent and almost irritable question.

"Allow me to withdraw from this discussion," he observed with a certain well-bred nonchalance. "It's a subtle question, too. Here Ivan Fyodorovitch is smiling at us. He must have something interesting to say about that also. Ask him."

"Nothing special, except one little remark," Ivan replied at once. "European Liberals in general, and even our liberal dilettanti, often mix up the final results of socialism with those of Christianity. This wild notion is, of course, a characteristic feature. But it's not only Liberals and dilettanti who mix up socialism and Christianity, but, in many cases, it appears, the police—the foreign police, of course—do the same. Your Paris anecdote is rather to the point, Pyotr Alexandrovitch."

"I ask your permission to drop this subject altogether," Miüsov repeated. "I will tell you instead, gentlemen, another interesting and rather characteristic anecdote of Ivan Fyodorovitch himself. Only five days ago, in a gathering here, principally of ladies, he solemnly declared in argument that there was nothing in the whole world to make men love their neighbours. That there was no law of nature that men should love mankind, and that, if there had been any love on earth hitherto, it was not owing to a natural law, but simply because men have believed in immortality. Ivan Fyodorovitch added in parenthesis that the whole natural law lies in that faith, and that if you were to destroy in mankind the belief in immortality, not only love but every living force maintaining the life of the world would at once be dried up. Moreover, nothing then would be immoral, everything would be lawful, even cannibalism. That's not all. He ended by asserting that for every individual, like ourselves, who does not believe in God or immortality, the moral law of nature must immediately be changed into the exact contrary of the former religious law, and that egoism, even to crime, must become, not only lawful but even recognised as the inevitable, the most rational, even honourable outcome of his position. From this paradox, gentlemen, you can judge of the rest of our eccentric and paradoxical friend Ivan Fyodorovitch's theories."

"Excuse me," Dmitri cried suddenly, "if I've heard aright: crime must not only be permitted but even recognised as the inevitable and the most rational outcome of his position for every infidel! Is that so or not?"

"Quite so," said Father Païssy.

"I'll remember it."

Having uttered these words Dmitri ceased speaking as suddenly as he had begun. Every one looked at him with curiosity.

"Is that really your conviction as to the consequences of the disappearance of the faith in immortality?" the elder asked Ivan suddenly.

"Yes. That was my contention. There is no virtue if there is no immortality."

"You are blessed in believing that, or else most unhappy."

"Why unhappy?" Ivan asked smiling.

"Because, in all probability you don't believe yourself in the immortality of your soul, nor in what you have written yourself in your article on Church jurisdiction."

"Perhaps you are right! . . . But I wasn't altogether joking," Ivan suddenly and strangely confessed, flushing quickly.

"You were not altogether joking. That's true. The question is still fretting your heart, and not answered. But the martyr likes sometimes to divert himself with his despair, as it were driven to it by despair itself. Meanwhile, in your despair, you, too, divert yourself with magazine articles, and discussions in society, though you don't believe your own arguments, and with an aching heart mock at them inwardly. . . . That question you have not answered, and it is your great grief, for it clamours for an answer."

"But can it be answered by me? Answered in the affirmative?" Ivan went on asking strangely, still looking at the elder with the same inexplicable smile.

"If it can't be decided in the affirmative, it will never be decided in the negative. You know that that is the peculiarity of your heart, and all its suffering is due to it. But thank the Creator who has given you a lofty heart capable of such suffering; of thinking and seeking higher things, for our dwelling is in the heavens. God grant that your heart will attain the answer on earth, and may God bless your path."

The elder raised his hand and would have made the sign of the cross over Ivan from where he stood. But the latter rose from his seat, went up to him, received his blessing, and kissing his hand went back to his place in silence. His face looked firm and earnest. This action and all the preceding conversation, which was so surprising from Ivan, impressed every one by its strangeness and a certain solemnity, so that all were silent for a moment, and there was a look almost of apprehension in Alyosha's face. But Miüsov suddenly shrugged his shoulders. And at the same moment Fyodor Pavlovitch jumped up from his seat.

"Most pious and holy elder," he cried pointing to Ivan, "that is my son, flesh of my flesh, the dearest of my flesh! He is my most dutiful Karl Moor, so to speak, while this son who has just come in, Dmitri, against whom I am seeking justice from you, is the undutiful Franz Moor—they are both out of Schiller's *Robbers,* and so I am the reigning Count von Moor![6] Judge and save us! We need not only your prayers but your prophecies!"

"Speak without buffoonery, and don't begin by insulting the members of your family," answered the elder, in a faint, exhausted voice. He was obviously getting more and more fatigued, and his strength was failing.

"An unseemly farce which I foresaw when I came here!" cried Dmitri indignantly. He too leapt up. "Forgive it, reverend Father," he added, addressing the elder. "I am not a cultivated man, and I don't even know how to address you properly, but you have been deceived and you have been too good-natured in letting us meet here. All my father wants is a scandal. Why he wants it only he can tell. He always has some motive. But I believe I know why——"

"They all blame me, all of them!" cried Fyodor Pavlovitch in his turn. "Pyotr Alexandrovitch here blames me too. You have been blaming me, Pyotr Alexandrovitch, you have!" he turned suddenly to Miüsov, although the latter was not dreaming of interrupting him. "They all accuse me of having hidden the children's money in my boots, and cheated them, but isn't there a court of law? There they will reckon out for you, Dmitri Fyodorovitch, from your notes, your letters, and your agreements, how much money you had, how much you have spent, and how much you have left. Why does Pyotr Alexandrovitch refuse to pass judgment? Dmitri is not a stranger to him. Because they are all against me, while Dmitri Fyodorovitch is in debt to me, and not a little, but some thousands of which I have documentary proof. The whole town is echoing with his debaucheries. And where he was stationed before, he several times spent a thousand or two for the seduction of some respectable girl; we know all about that, Dmitri Fyodorovitch, in its most secret details. I'll prove it. . . . Would you believe it, holy Father, he has captivated the heart of the most honourable of young ladies of good family and fortune, daughter of a gallant colonel, formerly his superior officer, who had received many honours and had the Anna Order on his breast. He compromised the girl by his promise of marriage, now she is an orphan and here; she is betrothed to him, yet before her very eyes he is dancing attendance on a certain enchantress. And although this enchantress has lived in, so to speak, civil marriage with a respectable man, yet she is of an independent character, an unapproachable fortress for everybody, just like a legal wife—for she is virtuous, yes, holy Father, she is virtuous. Dmitri Fyodorovitch wants to open this fortress with a golden key, and that's why he is insolent to me now, trying to get money from me, though he had wasted thousands on this enchantress already. He's continually borrowing money for the purpose. From whom do you think? Shall I say, Mitya?"

"Be silent!" cried Dmitri, "wait till I'm gone. Don't dare in my presence to asperse the good name of an honourable girl! That you should utter a word about her is an outrage, and I won't permit it!"

He was breathless.

"Mitya! Mitya!" cried Fyodor Pavlovitch hysterically, squeezing out a tear. "And is your father's blessing nothing to you? If I curse you, what then?"

"Shameless hypocrite!" exclaimed Dmitri furiously.

"He says that to his father! his father! What would he be with others? Gentlemen, only fancy; there's a poor but honourable man living here, burdened with a numerous family, a captain who got into trouble and was discharged from the army, but not publicly, not by court-martial, with no slur on his honour. And three weeks ago, Dmitri seized him by the beard in a tavern, dragged him out into the street and beat him publicly, and all because he is an agent in a little business of mine."

"It's all a lie! Outwardly it's the truth, but inwardly, a lie!" Dmitri was trembling with rage. "Father, I don't justify my action. Yes, I confess it publicly, I behaved like a brute to that captain, and I regret it now, and I'm disgusted with myself for my brutal rage. But this captain, this agent of yours, went to that lady whom you call an enchantress, and suggested to her from you, that she should take I.O.U.s of mine which were in your possession, and should sue me for the money so as to get me into prison by means of them, if I persisted in claiming an account from you of my property. Now you reproach me for having a weakness for that lady when you yourself incited her to captivate me! She told me so to my face. . . . She told me the story and laughed at you. . . . You wanted to put me in prison because you are jealous of me with her, because you'd begun to force your attentions upon her; and I know all about that, too; she laughed at you for that as well—you hear—she laughed at you as she described it. So here you have this man, this father who reproaches his profligate son! Gentlemen, forgive my anger, but I foresaw that this crafty old man had only brought you together to create a scandal. I had come to forgive him if he held out his hand; to forgive him, and ask forgiveness! But as he has just this minute insulted not only me, but an honourable young lady for whom I feel such reverence that I dare not take her name in vain, I have made up my mind to show up his game, though he is my father. . . ."

He could not go on. His eyes were glittering and he breathed with difficulty. But every one in the cell was stirred. All except Father Zossima got up from their seats uneasily. The monks looked austere but waited for guidance from the elder. He sat still, pale, not from excitement but from the weakness of disease. An imploring smile lighted up his face; from time to time he raised his hand, as though to check the storm, and, of course, a gesture from him would have been enough to end the scene; but he seemed to be waiting for something and watched them intently as though trying to make out something which was not perfectly clear to him. At last Miüsov felt completely humiliated and disgraced.

"We are all to blame for this scandalous scene," he said hotly. "But I did not foresee it when I came, though I knew with whom I had to deal. This must be stopped at once! Believe me, your reverence, I had no precise knowledge of the details that have just come to light, I was unwilling to believe them, and I learn for the first time. . . . A father is jealous of his son's relations with a woman of loose behaviour and intrigues with the creature to get his son into prison! This is the company in which I have been forced to be present! I was deceived. I declare to you all that I was as much deceived as any one."

"Dmitri Fyodorovitch," yelled Fyodor Pavlovitch suddenly, in an unnatural voice, "if you were not my son I would challenge you this instant to a duel . . . with pistols, at three paces . . . across a handkerchief," he ended, stamping with both feet.

With old liars who have been acting all their lives there are moments when they enter so completely into their part that they tremble or shed tears of emotion in earnest, although at that very moment or a second later, they are able to whisper to themselves, "You know you are lying, you shameless old sinner! You're acting now, in spite of your 'holy' wrath."

Dmitri frowned painfully, and looked with unutterable contempt at his father.

"I thought . . . I thought," he said, in a soft and, as it were, controlled voice, "that I was coming to my native place with the angel of my heart, my betrothed, to cherish his old age, and I find nothing but a depraved profligate, a despicable clown!"

"A duel!" yelled the old wretch again, breathless and spluttering at each syllable. "And you, Pyotr Alexandrovitch Miüsov, let me tell you that there has never been in all your family a loftier, and more honest—you hear—more honest woman than this 'creature,' as you have dared to call her! And you, Dmitri Fyodorovitch, have abandoned your betrothed for that 'creature,' so you must yourself have thought that your betrothed couldn't hold a candle to her. That's the woman called a 'creature'!"

"Shameful!" broke from Father Iosif.

"Shameful and disgraceful!" Kalganov, flushing crimson, cried in a boyish voice, trembling with emotion. He had been silent till that moment.

"Why is such a man alive?" Dmitri, beside himself with rage, growled in a hollow voice, hunching up his shoulders till he looked almost deformed. "Tell me, can he be allowed to go on defiling the earth?" He looked round at every one and pointed at the old man. He spoke evenly and deliberately.

"Listen, listen, monks, to the parricide!" cried Fyodor Pavlovitch, rushing up to Father Iosif. "That's the answer to your 'shameful!' What is shameful? That 'creature,' that 'woman of loose behaviour' is perhaps holier than you are yourselves, you monks who are seeking salvation! She fell perhaps in her youth, ruined by her environment. But she loved much, and Christ himself forgave the woman 'who loved much.' "*

"It was not for such love Christ forgave her," broke impatiently from the gentle Father Iosif.

"Yes, it was for such, monks, it was! You save your souls here, eating cabbage, and think you are the righteous. You eat a gudgeon a day, and you think you bribe God with gudgeon."

"This is unendurable!" was heard on all sides in the cell.

But this unseemly scene was cut short in a most unexpected way. Father Zossima rose suddenly from his seat. Almost distracted with anxiety for

---

*See Luke 7:47.

the elder and every one else, Alyosha succeeded, however, in supporting him by the arm. Father Zossima moved towards Dmitri and reaching him sank on his knees before him. Alyosha thought that he had fallen from weakness, but this was not so. The elder distinctly and deliberately bowed down at Dmitri's feet till his forehead touched the floor. Alyosha was so astounded that he failed to assist him when he got up again. There was a faint smile on his lips.

"Good-bye! Forgive me, all of you!" he said, bowing on all sides to his guests.

Dmitri stood for a few moments in amazement. Bowing down to him— what did it mean? Suddenly he cried aloud, "Oh God!" hid his face in his hands and rushed out of the room. All the guests flocked out after him, in their confusion not saying good-bye, or bowing to their host. Only the monks went up to him again for a blessing.

"What did it mean, falling at his feet, like that? Was it symbolic or what?" said Fyodor Pavlovitch, suddenly quieted and trying to reopen conversation without venturing to address anybody in particular. They were all passing out of the precincts of the hermitage at the moment.

"I can't answer for a madhouse and for madmen," Miüsov answered at once ill-humouredly, "but I will spare myself your company, Fyodor Pavlovitch, and, trust me, for ever. Where's that monk?"

"That monk," that is, the monk who had invited them to dine with the Superior, did not keep them waiting. He met them as soon as they came down the steps from the elder's cell, as though he had been waiting for them all the time.

"Reverend Father, kindly do me a favour. Convey my deepest respect to the Father Superior, apologise for me personally, Miüsov, to his reverence, telling him that I deeply regret that owing to unforeseen circumstances I am unable to have the honour of being present at his table, greatly as I should desire to do so," Miüsov said irritably to the monk.

"And that unforeseen circumstance, of course, is myself," Fyodor Pavlovitch cut in immediately. "Do you hear, Father; this gentleman doesn't want to remain in my company or else he'd come at once. And you shall go, Pyotr Alexandrovitch, pray go to the Father Superior and good appetite to you. I will decline, and not you. Home, home, I'll eat at home, I don't feel equal to it here, Pyotr Alexandrovitch, my amiable relative."

"I am not your relative and never have been, you contemptible man!"

"I said it on purpose to madden you, because you always disclaim the relationship, though you really are a relation in spite of your shuffling. I'll prove it by the church calendar. As for you, Ivan, stay if you like. I'll send the horses for you later. Propriety requires you to go to the Father Superior, Pyotr Alexandrovitch, to apologise for the disturbance we've been making. . . ."

"Is it true that you are going home? Aren't you lying?"

"Pyotr Alexandrovitch! How could I dare after what's happened! Forgive me, gentlemen, I was carried away! And upset besides! And, indeed, I am ashamed. Gentlemen, one man has the heart of Alexander of Macedon and another the heart of the little dog Fido. Mine is that of the little dog Fido. I am abashed! After such an escapade how can I go to dinner, to gobble up the monastery's sauces. I am ashamed, I can't. You must excuse me!"

"The devil only knows, what if he deceives us," thought Miüsov, still hesitating, and watching the retreating buffoon with distrustful eyes. The latter turned round, and noticing that Miüsov was watching him, waved him a kiss.

"Well, are you coming to the Superior?" Miüsov asked Ivan abruptly.

"Why not? I was especially invited yesterday."

"Unfortunately I feel myself compelled to go to this confounded dinner," said Miüsov with the same irritability, regardless of the fact that the monk was listening. "We ought, at least, to apologise for the disturbance, and explain that it was not our doing. What do you think?"

"Yes, we must explain that it wasn't our doing. Besides, father won't be there," observed Ivan.

"Well, I should hope not! Confound this dinner!"

They all walked on, however. The monk listened in silence. On the road through the copse he made one observation however—that the Father Superior had been waiting a long time, and that they were more than half an hour late. He received no answer. Miüsov looked with hatred at Ivan.

"Here he is, going to the dinner as though nothing had happened," he thought. "A brazen face, and the conscience of a Karamazov!"

7

A YOUNG MAN BENT ON A CAREER

ALYOSHA helped Father Zossima to his bedroom and seated him on his bed. It was a little room furnished with the bare necessities. There was a narrow iron bedstead, with a strip of felt for a mattress. In the corner, under the ikons, was a reading-desk with a cross and the Gospel lying on it. The elder sank exhausted on the bed. His eyes glittered and he breathed hard. He looked intently at Alyosha, as though considering something.

"Go, my dear boy, go. Porfiry is enough for me. Make haste, you are needed there, go and wait at the Father Superior's table."

"Let me stay here," Alyosha entreated.

"You are more needed there. There is no peace there. You will wait, and be of service. If evil spirits rise up, repeat a prayer. And remember, my son (the elder liked to call him that), this is not the place for you in the future. When it is God's will to call me, leave the monastery. Go away for good."

Alyosha started.

"What is it? This is not your place for the time. I bless you for great service in the world. Yours will be a long pilgrimage. And you will have to take a wife, too. You will have to bear *all* before you come back. There will be much to do. But I don't doubt of you, and so I send you forth. Christ is with you. Do not abandon Him and He will not abandon you. You will see great sorrow, and in that sorrow you will be happy. This is my last message to you: in sorrow seek happiness. Work, work unceasingly. Remember my words, for although I shall talk with you again, not only my days but my hours are numbered."

Alyosha's face again betrayed strong emotion. The corners of his mouth quivered.

"What is it again?" Father Zossima asked, smiling gently. "The worldly may follow the dead with tears, but here we rejoice over the father who is departing. We rejoice and pray for him. Leave me, I must pray. Go, and make haste. Be near your brothers. And not near one only, but near both."

Father Zossima raised his hand to bless him. Alyosha could make no protest, though he had a great longing to remain. He longed, moreover, to ask the significance of his bowing to Dmitri, the question was on the tip of his tongue, but he dared not ask it. He knew that the elder would have explained it unasked if he had thought fit. But evidently it was not his will. That action had made a terrible impression on Alyosha; he believed blindly in its mysterious significance. Mysterious, and perhaps awful.

As he hastened out of the hermitage precincts to reach the monastery in time to serve at the Father Superior's dinner he felt a sudden pang at his heart, and stopped short. He seemed to hear again Father Zossima's words, foretelling his approaching end. What he had foretold so exactly must infallibly come to pass. Alyosha believed that implicitly. But how could he be left without him? How could he live without seeing and hearing him? Where should he go? He had told him not to weep, and to leave the monastery. Good God! It was long since Alyosha had known such anguish. He hurried through the copse that divided the monastery from the hermitage, and unable to bear the burden of his thoughts, he gazed at the ancient pines beside the path. He had not far to go—about five hundred paces. He expected to meet no one at that hour, but at the first turn of the path he noticed Rakitin. He was waiting for some one.

"Are you waiting for me?" asked Alyosha, overtaking him.

"Yes," grinned Rakitin. "You are hurrying to the Father Superior, I know; he has a banquet. There's not been such a banquet since the Superior entertained the Bishop and General Pahatov, do you remember? I shan't be there, but you go and hand the sauces. Tell me one thing Alexey, what does that vision mean? That's what I want to ask you."

"What vision?"

"That bowing to your brother, Dmitri. And didn't he tap the ground with his forehead, too!"

"You speak of Father Zossima?"

"Yes of Father Zossima."

"Tapped the ground?"

"Ah, an irreverent expression! Well, what of it? Anyway, what does that vison mean?"

"I don't know what it means, Misha."

"I knew he wouldn't explain it to you! There's nothing wonderful about it, of course, only the usual holy mummery. But there was an object in the performance. All the pious people in the town will talk about it and spread the story through the province, wondering what it meant. To my thinking the old man really has a keen nose; he sniffed a crime. Your house stinks of it."

"What crime?"

Rakitin evidently had something he was eager to speak of.

"It'll be in your family, this crime. Between your brothers and your rich old father. So Father Zossima flopped down to be ready for what may turn up. If something happens later on, it'll be: 'Ah, the holy man foresaw it, prophesied it!' though it's a poor sort of prophecy, flopping like that. 'Ah, but it was symbolic,' they'll say, 'an allegory,' and the devil knows what all! It'll be remembered to his glory: 'He predicted the crime and marked the criminal!' That's always the way with these crazy fanatics; they cross themselves at the tavern and throw stones at the temple. Like your elder, he takes a stick to a just man and falls at the feet of a murderer."

"What crime? What murderer? What do you mean?"

Alyosha stopped dead. Rakitin stopped, too.

"What murderer? As though you didn't know! I'll bet you've thought of it before. That's interesting, too, by the way. Listen, Alyosha, you always speak the truth, though you're always between too stools. Have you thought of it or not? Answer."

"I have," answered Alyosha in a low voice. Even Rakitin was taken aback.

"What? Have you really?" he cried.

"I . . . I've not exactly thought of it," muttered Alyosha, "but directly you began speaking so strangely, I fancied I had thought of it myself."

"You see? (And how well you expressed it!) Looking at your father and your brother Mitya to-day you thought of a crime. Then I'm not mistaken?"

"But wait, wait a minute," Alyosha broke in uneasily, "What has led you to see all this? Why does it interest you? That's the first question."

"Two questions, disconnected, but natural. I'll deal with them separately. What led me to see it? I shouldn't have seen it, if I hadn't suddenly understood your brother Dmitri, seen right into the very heart of him all at once. I caught the whole man from one trait. These very honest but passionate people have a line which mustn't be crossed. If it were, he'd run at your father with a knife. But your father's a drunken and abandoned old sinner, who can never draw the line—if they both let themselves go, they'll both come to grief."

"No, Misha, no. If that's all, you've reassured me! It won't come to that."

"But why are you trembling? Let me tell you; he may be honest—your Mitya (he is stupid, but honest) but he's—a sensualist. That's the very definition and inner essence of him. It's your father who handed him on his low sensuality. Do you know, I simply wonder at you, Alyosha, how you can have kept your purity. You're a Karamazov too, you know! In your family sensuality is carried to a disease. But now, these three sensualists are watching one another, with their knives in their belts. The three of them are knocking their heads together, and you may be the fourth."

"You are mistaken about that woman. Dmitri—despises her," said Alyosha, with a sort of shudder.

"Grushenka? No, brother, he doesn't despise her. Since he has openly abandoned his betrothed for her, he doesn't despise her. There's something here, my dear boy, that you don't understand yet. A man will fall in love with some beauty, with a woman's body, or even with a part of a woman's body (a sensualist can understand that) and he'll abandon his own children for her, sell his father and mother, and his country, Russia, too. If he's honest, he'll steal; if he's humane, he'll murder; if he's faithful, he'll deceive. Pushkin, the poet of women's feet, sung of their feet in his verse.* Others don't sing their praises, but they can't look at their feet without a thrill— and it's not only their feet. Contempt's no help here, brother, even if he did despise Grushenka. He does, but he can't tear himself away."

"I understand that," Alyosha jerked out suddenly.

"Really? Well, I daresay you do understand since you blurt it out at the first word," said Rakitin, malignantly. "That escaped you unawares, and the confession's the more precious. So it's a familiar subject; you've thought about it already, about sensuality, I mean! Oh, you virgin soul! You're a quiet one, Alyosha, you're a saint, I know, but the devil only knows what you've thought about, and what you know already! You are pure, but you've been down into the depths. . . . I've been watching you a long time. You're a Karamazov yourself; you're a thorough Karamazov— no doubt birth and selection have something to answer for. You're a sensualist from your father, a crazy saint from your mother. Why do you tremble? Is it true, then? Do you know, Grushenka has been begging me to bring you along. 'I'll pull off his cassock,' she says. You can't think how she keeps begging me to bring you. I wondered why she took such an interest in you. Do you know, she's an extraordinary woman too!"

"Thank her and say I'm not coming," said Alyosha, with a strained smile. "Finish what you were saying, Misha. I'll tell you my idea after."

"There's nothing to finish. It's all clear. It's the same old tune, brother. If even you are a sensualist at heart what of your brother, Ivan? He's a Karamazov, too. What is at the root of all you Karamazovs is that you're all sensual, grasping and crazy! Your brother Ivan writes theological articles in joke, for some idiotic, unknown motive of his own, though he's an

---

*Reference to the poetry of Aleksandr Pushkin (1799–1837).

atheist, and he admits it's a fraud himself—that's your brother Ivan. He's trying to get Mitya's betrothed for himself, and I fancy he'll succeed, too. And what's more it's with Mitya's consent. For Mitya will surrender his betrothed to him to be rid of her, and escape to Grushenka. And he's ready to do that in spite of all his nobility and disinterestedness. Observe that. Those are the most fatal people! Who the devil can make you out? He recognises his vileness and goes on with it! Let me tell you, too, the old man, your father is standing in Mitya's way now. He has suddenly gone crazy over Grushenka. His mouth waters at the sight of her. It's simply on her account he made that scene in the cell just now, simply because Miüsov called her an 'abandoned creature.' He's worse than a tom cat in love. At first she was only employed by him in connection with his taverns and in some other shady business, but now he has suddenly realised all she is and has gone wild about her. He keeps pestering her with his offers, not honourable ones, of course. And they'll come into collision, the precious father and son, on that path! But Grushenka favours neither of them, she's still playing with them, and teasing them both, considering which she can get most out of. For though she could filch a lot of money from the papa he wouldn't marry her, and maybe he'll turn stingy in the end, and keep his purse shut. That's where Mitya's value comes in, he has no money, but he's ready to marry her. Yes, ready to marry her! to abandon his betrothed, a rare beauty, Katerina Ivanovna who's rich, and the daughter of a colonel, and to marry Grushenka, who has been the mistress of a dissolute old merchant, Samsonov, a coarse, uneducated, provincial mayor. Some murderous conflict may well come to pass from all this, and that's what your brother Ivan is waiting for. It would suit him down to the ground. He'll carry off Katerina Ivanovna, for whom he is languishing, and pocket her dowry of sixty thousand. That's very alluring to start with, for a man of no consequence and a beggar. And, take note, he won't be wronging Mitya, but doing him the greatest service. For I know as a fact that Mitya only last week when he was with some gipsy girls drunk in a tavern, cried out aloud that he was unworthy of his betrothed, Katya, but that his brother Ivan, he was the man who deserved her. And Katerina Ivanovna will not in the end refuse such a fascinating man as Ivan. She's hesitating between the two of them already. And how has that Ivan won you all, so that you all worship him? He is laughing at you, and enjoying himself at your expense."

"How do you know? How can you speak so confidently?" Alyosha asked sharply, frowning.

"Why do you ask, and are frightened at my answer? It shows that you know I'm speaking the truth."

"You don't like Ivan. Ivan wouldn't be tempted by money."

"Really? And the beauty of Katerina Ivanovna? It's not only the money, though a fortune of sixty thousand is an attraction."

"Ivan is above that. He wouldn't make up to any one for thousands. It is not money, it's not comfort Ivan is seeking. Perhaps it's suffering he is seeking?"

"What wild dream now? Oh, you—aristocrats!"

"Ah, Misha, he has a stormy spirit. His mind is in bondage. He is haunted by a great, unsolved doubt. He is one of those who don't want millions, but an answer to their questions."

"That's plagiarism, Alyosha. You're quoting your elder's phrases. Ah, Ivan has set you a problem!" cried Rakitin, with undisguised malice. His face changed, and his lips twitched. "And the problem's a stupid one. It is no good guessing it. Rack your brains—you'll understand it. His article is absurd and ridiculous. And did you hear his stupid theory just now: if there's no immortality of the soul, then there's no virtue, and everything is lawful? (And by the way, do you remember how your brother Mitya cried out: 'I will remember!') An attractive theory for scoundrels!—(I'm being abusive, that's stupid.) Not for scoundrels, but for pedantic poseurs, 'haunted by profound, unsolved doubts.' He's showing off, and what it all comes to is, 'on the one hand we cannot but admit' and 'on the other it must be confessed!' His whole theory is a fraud! Humanity will find in itself the power to live for virtue even without believing in immortality. It will find it in love for freedom, for equality, for fraternity."

Rakitin could hardly restrain himself in his heat, but, suddenly, as though remembering something he stopped short.

"Well, that's enough," he said, with a still more crooked smile. "Why are you laughing? Do you think I'm a vulgar fool?"

"No, I never dreamed of thinking you a vulgar fool. You are clever but . . . never mind, I was silly to smile. I understand your getting hot about it, Misha. I guess from your warmth that you are not indifferent to Katerina Ivanovna yourself; I've suspected that for a long time, brother, that's why you don't like my brother Ivan. Are you jealous of him?"

"And jealous of her money, too? Won't you add that?"

"I'll say nothing about money. I am not going to insult you."

"I believe it, since you say so, but confound you, and your brother Ivan with you. Don't you understand that one might very well dislike him, apart from Katerina Ivanovna? And why the devil should I like him? He condescends to abuse me, you know. Why haven't I a right to abuse him?"

"I never heard of his saying anything about you, good or bad. He doesn't speak of you at all."

"But I heard that the day before yesterday at Katerina Ivanovna's he was abusing me for all he was worth—you see what an interest he takes in your humble servant. And which is the jealous one after that, brother, I can't say. He was so good as to express the opinion that, if I don't go in for the career of an archimandrite in the immediate future and don't become a monk I shall be sure to go to Petersburg and get on to some solid magazine as a reviewer, that I shall write for the next ten years, and in the end become the owner of the magazine, and bring it out on the liberal and atheistic side, with a socialistic tinge, with a tiny gloss of socialism, but keeping a sharp look-out all the time, that is, keeping in with both sides and hoodwinking the fools. According to your brother's account, the tinge of socialism won't hinder me from laying by the proceeds and investing them under the guidance of some Jew, till at the end of my career I build a great house

in Petersburg and move my publishing offices to it, and let out the upper
storeys to lodgers. He has even chosen the place for it, near the new stone
bridge across the Neva, which they say is to be built in Petersburg."

"Ah, Misha, that's just what will really happen, every word of it," cried
Alyosha, unable to restrain a good-humoured smile.

"You are pleased to be sarcastic, too, Alexey Fyodorovitch."

"No, no, I'm joking, forgive me. I've something quite different in my
mind. But, excuse me, who can have told you all this? You can't have been
at Katerina Ivanovna's yourself when he was talking about you?"

"I wasn't there, but Dmitri Fyodorovitch was; and I heard him tell it with
my own ears; if you want to know, he didn't tell me, but I overheard him, un-
intentionally, of course, for I was sitting in Grushenka's bedroom and I
couldn't go away because Dmitri Fyodorovitch was in the next room."

"Oh yes, I'd forgotten she was a relation of yours."

"A relation! That Grushenka a relation of mine!" cried Rakitin, turning
crimson. "Are you mad? You're out of your mind!"

"Why, isn't she a relation of yours? I heard so."

"Where can you have heard it? You Karamazovs brag of being an ancient, noble family, though your father used to run about playing the buffoon at other men's tables, and was only admitted to the kitchen as a
favour. I may be only a priest's son, and dirt in the eyes of noblemen like
you, but don't insult me so lightly and wantonly. I have a sense of honour,
too, Alexey Fyodorovitch, I couldn't be a relation of Grushenka, a common harlot. I beg you to understand that!"

Rakitin was intensely irritated.

"Forgive me, for goodness' sake, I had no idea . . . besides . . . how can
you call her a harlot? Is she . . . that sort of woman?" Alyosha flushed suddenly. "I tell you again, I heard that she was a relation of yours. You often
go to see her, and you told me yourself you're not her lover. I never
dreamed that you of all people had such contempt for her! Does she really
deserve it?"

"I may have reasons of my own for visiting her. That's not your business. But as for relationship, your brother, or even your father is more
likely to make her yours, than mine. Well, here we are. You'd better go to
the kitchen. Hullo! what's wrong, what is it? Are we late? They can't have
finished dinner so soon! Have the Karamazovs been making trouble
again? No doubt they have. Here's your father and your brother Ivan after
him. They've broken out from the Father Superior's. And look, Father
Isidor's shouting out something after them from the steps. And your father's shouting and waving his arms. I expect he's swearing. Bah, and there
goes Miüsov driving away in his carriage. You see, he's going. And there's
old Maximov running!—there must have been a row. There can't have
been any dinner. Surely they've not been beating the Father Superior! Or
have they, perhaps, been beaten? It would serve them right!"

There was reason for Rakitin's exclamations. There had been a scandalous, an unprecedented scene. It had all come from the impulse of a
moment.

8

THE SCANDALOUS SCENE

Mıŭsov, as a man of breeding and delicacy, could not but feel some inward qualms, when he reached the Father Superior's with Ivan: he felt ashamed of having lost his temper. He felt that he ought to have disdained that despicable wretch, Fyodor Pavlovitch, too much to have been upset by him in Father Zossima's cell, and so to have forgotten himself. "The monks were not to blame, in any case," he reflected, on the steps. "And if they're decent people here (and the Father Superior, I understand, is a nobleman) why not be friendly and courteous with them? I won't argue, I'll fall in with everything, I'll win them by politeness, and . . . and . . . show them that I've nothing to do with that Æsop,* that buffoon, that Pierrot, and have merely been taken in over this affair, just as they have."

He determined to drop his litigation with the monastery, and relinquish his claims to the wood-cutting and fishery rights at once. He was the more ready to do this because the rights had become much less valuable, and he had indeed the vaguest idea where the wood and river in question were.

These excellent intentions were strengthened when he entered the Father Superior's dining-room, though, strictly speaking, it was not a dining-room, for the Father Superior had only two rooms altogether; they were, however, much larger and more comfortable than Father Zossima's. But there was no great luxury about the furnishing of these rooms either. The furniture was of mahogany, covered with leather, in the old-fashioned style of 1820; the floor was not even stained, but everything was shining with cleanliness, and there were many choice flowers in the windows; the most sumptuous thing in the room at the moment was, of course, the beautifully decorated table. The cloth was clean, the service shone; there were three kinds of well-baked bread, two bottles of wine, two of excellent mead, and a large glass jug of kvass†—both the latter made in the monastery, and famous in the neighbourhood. There was no vodka. Rakitin related afterwards that there were five dishes: fish-soup made of sterlets, served with little fish patties; then boiled fish served in a special way; then salmon cutlets, ice pudding and compôte, and finally, blanc-mange. Rakitin found out about all these good things, for he could not resist peeping into the kitchen, where he already had a footing. He had a footing

---

*Reputed Greek author of *Aesop's Fables* (sixth century B.C.).
†Russian fermented drink made from rye or barley.

everywhere, and got information about everything. He was of an uneasy and envious temper. He was well aware of his own considerable abilities, and nervously exaggerated them in his self-conceit. He knew he would play a prominent part of some sort, but Alyosha, who was attached to him, was distressed to see that his friend Rakitin was dishonourable, and quite unconscious of being so himself, considering, on the contrary, that because he would not steal money left on the table he was a man of the highest integrity. Neither Alyosha nor any one else could have influenced him in that.

Rakitin, of course, was a person of too little consequence to be invited to the dinner, to which Father Iosif, Father Païssy, and one other monk were the only inmates of the monastery invited. They were already waiting when Miüsov, Kalganov, and Ivan arrived. The other guest, Maximov, stood a little aside, waiting also. The Father Superior stepped into the middle of the room to receive his guests. He was a tall, thin, but still vigorous old man, with black hair streaked with grey, and a long, grave, ascetic face. He bowed to his guests in silence. But this time they approached to receive his blessing. Miüsov even tried to kiss his hand, but the Father Superior drew it back in time to avoid the salute. But Ivan and Kalganov went through the ceremony in the most simple-hearted and complete manner, kissing his hand as peasants do.

"We must apologise most humbly, your reverence," began Miüsov, simpering affably, and speaking in a dignified and respectful tone. "Pardon us for having come alone without the gentleman you invited, Fyodor Pavlovitch. He felt obliged to decline the honour of your hospitality, and not without reason. In the reverend Father Zossima's cell he was carried away by the unhappy dissension with his son, and let fall words which were quite out of keeping . . . in fact, quite unseemly . . . as (he glanced at the monks) your reverence is, no doubt, already aware. And therefore, recognising that he had been to blame, he felt sincere regret and shame, and begged me, and his son Ivan Fyodorovitch, to convey to you his apologies and regrets. In brief, he hopes and desires to make amends later. He asks your blessing, and begs you to forget what has taken place."

As he uttered the last word of his tirade, Miüsov completely recovered his self-complacency, and all traces of his former irritation disappeared. He fully and sincerely loved humanity again.

The Father Superior listened to him with dignity, and, with a slight bend of the head, replied:

"I sincerely deplore his absence. Perhaps at our table he might have learnt to like us, and we him. Pray be seated, gentlemen."

He stood before the holy image, and began to say grace, aloud. All bent their heads reverently, and Maximov clasped his hands before him, with peculiar fervour.

It was at this moment that Fyodor Pavlovitch played his last prank. It must be noted that he really had meant to go home, and really had felt the impossibility of going to dine with the Father Superior as though nothing had happened, after his disgraceful behaviour in the elder's cell. Not that he was so very much ashamed of himself—quite the contrary perhaps. But still he felt it would be unseemly to go to dinner. Yet his creaking carriage had hardly been brought to the steps of the hotel, and he had hardly got into it, when he suddenly stopped short. He remembered his own words at the elder's: "I always feel when I meet people that I am lower than all, and that they all take me for a buffoon; so I say let me play the buffoon, for you are, every one of you, stupider and lower than I." He longed to revenge himself on every one for his own unseemliness. He suddenly recalled how he had once in the past been asked, "Why do you hate so and so, so much?" And he had answered them, with his shameless impudence, "I'll tell you. He had done me no harm. But I played him a dirty trick, and ever since I have hated him."

Remembering that now, he smiled quietly and malignantly, hesitating for a moment. His eyes gleamed, and his lips positively quivered. "Well, since I have begun, I may as well go on," he decided. His predominant sensation at that moment might be expressed in the following words, "Well, there is no rehabilitating myself now. So let me shame them for all I am worth. I will show them I don't care what they think—that's all!"

He told the coachman to wait, while with rapid steps he returned to the monastery and straight to the Father Superior's. He had no clear idea what he would do, but he knew that he could not control himself, and that a touch might drive him to the utmost limits of obscenity, but only to obscenity, to nothing criminal, nothing for which he could be legally punished. In the last resort, he could always restrain himself, and had marvelled indeed at himself, on that score, sometimes. He appeared in the Father Superior's dining-room, at the moment when the prayer was over, and all were moving to the table. Standing in the doorway, he scanned the company, and laughing his prolonged, impudent, malicious chuckle, looked them all boldly in the face. "They thought I had gone, and here I am again," he cried to the whole room.

For one moment every one stared at him without a word; and at once every one felt that something revolting, grotesque, positively scandalous, was about to happen. Miüsov passed immediately from the most benevolent frame of mind to the most savage. All the feelings that had subsided and died down in his heart revived instantly.

"No! this I cannot endure!" he cried. "I absolutely cannot! and . . . I certainly cannot!"

The blood rushed to his head. He positively stammered; but he was beyond thinking of style, and he seized his hat.

"What is it he cannot?" cried Fyodor Pavlovitch, "that he absolutely cannot and certainly cannot? Your reverence, am I to come in or not? Will you receive me as your guest?"

"You are welcome with all my heart," answered the Superior. "Gentlemen!" he added, "I venture to beg you most earnestly to lay aside your dissensions, and to be united in love and family harmony—with prayer to the Lord at our humble table."

"No, no, it is impossible!" cried Miüsov, beside himself.

"Well, if it is impossible for Pyotr Alexandrovitch, it is impossible for me, and I won't stop. That is why I came. I will keep with Pyotr Alexandrovitch everywhere now. If you will go away, Pyotr Alexandrovitch, I will go away too, if you remain, I will remain. You stung him by what you said about family harmony, Father Superior, he does not admit he is my relation. That's right, isn't it, Von Sohn? Here's Von Sohn. How are you, Von Sohn?"

"Do you mean me?" muttered Maximov, puzzled.

"Of course I mean you," cried Fyodor Pavlovitch. "Who else? The Father Superior could not be Von Sohn."

"But I am not Von Sohn either. I am Maximov."

"No, you are Von Sohn. Your reverence, do you know who Von Sohn was? It was a famous murder case. He was killed in a house of harlotry. I believed that is what such places are called among you—he was killed and robbed, and in spite of his venerable age, he was nailed up in a box and sent from Petersburg to Moscow in the luggage van, and while they were nailing him up, the harlots sang songs and played the harp, that is to say, the piano. So this is that very Von Sohn. He has risen from the dead, hasn't he, Von Sohn?"

"What is happening? What's this?" voices were heard in the group of monks.

"Let us go," cried Miüsov, addressing Kalganov.

"No, excuse me," Fyodor Pavlovitch broke in shrilly, taking another step into the room. "Allow me to finish. There in the cell you blamed me for behaving disrespectfully just because I spoke of eating gudgeon, Pyotr Alexandrovitch. Miüsov, my relation, prefers to have *plus de noblesse que de sincerité* in his words, but I prefer in mine *plus de sincerité que de noblesse,** and—damn the noblesse! That's right, isn't it, Von Sohn? Allow me, Father Superior, though I am a buffoon and play the buffoon, yet I am the soul of honour, and I want to speak my mind. Yes, I am the soul of honour, while in Pyotr Alexandrovitch there is wounded vanity and nothing else. I came here, perhaps, to have a look and speak my mind. My son, Alexey, is here, being saved. I am his father; I care for his welfare, and it is my duty to care. While I've been playing the fool, I have been listening and having a look on the sly; and now I want to give you the last act of the performance. You know how things are with us? As a thing falls, so it lies. As a thing once has fallen, so it must lie for ever. Not a bit of it! I want to get up again. Holy Father, I am indignant with you. Confession is a great sacrament, before which I am ready to bow down reverently; but there in the cell, they all kneel down and confess aloud. Can it be right to confess aloud? It was ordained by the holy fathers to confess in secret: then only your confession will be a mystery, and so it was of old. But how can I explain to him before every one that I did this and that . . . well, you understand what—sometimes it would not be proper to talk about it—so it is

---

*More nobility than sincerity . . . more sincerity than nobility (French).

really a scandal! No, fathers, one might be carried along with you to the Flagellants,* I dare say ... at the first opportunity I shall write to the Synod, and I shall take my son, Alexey, home."

We must note here that Fyodor Pavlovitch knew where to look for the weak spot. There had been at one time malicious rumours which had even reached the Archbishop (not only regarding our monastery, but in others where the institution of elders existed) that too much respect was paid to the elders, even to the detriment of the authority of the Superior, that the elders abused the sacrament of confession and so on and so on—absurd charges which had died away of themselves everywhere. But the spirit of folly, which had caught up Fyodor Pavlovitch, and was bearing him on the current of his own nerves into lower and lower depths of ignominy, prompted him with this old slander. Fyodor Pavlovitch did not understand a word of it, and he could not even put it sensibly, for on this occasion no one had been kneeling and confessing aloud in the elder's cell, so that he could not have seen anything of the kind. He was only speaking from confused memory of old slanders. But as soon as he had uttered his foolish tirade, he felt he had been talking absurd nonsense, and at once longed to prove to his audience and above all to himself, that he had not been talking nonsense. And, though he knew perfectly well that with each word he would be adding more and more absurdity, he could not restrain himself, and plunged forward blindly.

"How disgraceful!" cried Pyotr Alexandrovitch.

"Pardon me!" said the Father Superior. "It was said of old 'Many have begun to speak against me and have uttered evil sayings about me. And hearing it I have said to myself: it is the correction of the Lord and He has sent it to heal my vain soul.' And so we humbly thank you, honoured guest!" and he made Fyodor Pavlovitch a low bow.

"Tut—tut—tut—sanctimoniousness and stock phrases! Old phrases and old gestures. The old lies and formal prostrations. We know all about them. A kiss on the lips and a dagger in the heart, as in Schiller's *Robbers*. I don't like falsehood, fathers, I want the truth. But the truth is not to be found in eating gudgeon and that I proclaim aloud! Father monks, why do you fast! Why do you expect reward in heaven for that? Why, for reward like that I will come and fast too! No, saintly monk, you try being virtuous in the world, do good to society, without shutting yourself up in a monastery at other people's expense, and without expecting a reward up aloft for it—you'll find that a bit harder. I can talk sense, too, Father Superior. What have they got here?" He went up to the table. "Old port wine, mead brewed by the Eliseyev Brothers.† Fie, fie, fathers! That is something beyond gudgeon. Look at the bottles the fathers have brought out, he! he! he! And who has provided it all? The Russian peasant, the labourer, brings here the farthing earned by his horny hand, wringing it

---

*Religious sect whose followers practiced self-flagellation.
†St. Petersburg's most famous provisioner.

from his family and the tax-gatherer! You bleed the people, you know, holy fathers."

"This is too disgraceful!" said Father Iosif.

Father Païssy kept obstinately silent. Miüsov rushed from the room, and Kalganov after him.

"Well, Father, I will follow Pyotr Alexandrovitch! I am not coming to see you again. You may beg me on your knees, I shan't come. I sent you a thousand roubles, so you have more. I am taking my revenge for my youth, for all the humiliation I endured." He thumped the table with his fist in a paroxysm of simulated feeling. "This monastery has played a great part in my life! It has cost me many bitter tears. You used to set my wife, the crazy one, against me. You cursed me with 'bell and book,' you spread stories about me all over the place. Enough, fathers! This is the age of Liberalism, the age of steamers and railways. Neither a thousand, nor a hundred roubles, no, nor a hundred farthings will you get out of me!"

It must be noted again that our monastery never had played any great part in his life, and he never had shed a bitter tear owing to it. But he was so carried away by his simulated emotion, that he was for one moment almost believing it himself. He was so touched he was almost weeping. But at that very instant, he felt that it was time to draw back.

The Father Superior bowed his head at his malicious lie, and again spoke impressively:

"It is written again, 'Bear circumspectly and gladly dishonour that cometh upon thee by no act of thine own, be not confounded and hate not him who hath dishonoured thee.' And so will we."

"Tut, tut, tut! Bethinking thyself and the rest of the rigmarole. Bethink yourselves, fathers, I will go. But I will take my son, Alexey, away from here for ever, on my parental authority. Ivan Fyodorovitch, my most dutiful son, permit me to order you to follow me. Von Sohn, what have you to stay for? Come and see me now in the town. It is fun there. It is only one short verst, instead of lenten oil, I will give you sucking-pig and kasha. We will have dinner with some brandy and liqueur to it, . . . I've cloudberry wine. Hey, Von Sohn, don't lose your chance." He went out, shouting and gesticulating.

It was that moment Rakitin saw him and pointed him out to Alyosha.

"Alexey!" his father shouted, from far off, catching sight of him. "You come home to me to-day, for good, and bring your pillow and mattress, and leave no trace behind."

Alyosha stood rooted to the spot, watching the scene in silence. Meanwhile, Fyodor Pavlovitch had got into the carriage and Ivan was about to follow him in grim silence without even turning to say good-bye to Alyosha. But at this point another almost incredible scene of grotesque buffoonery gave the finishing touch to the episode. Maximov suddenly appeared by the side of the carriage. He ran up, panting, afraid of being too late. Rakitin and Alyosha saw him running. He was in such a hurry that in his impatience he put his foot on the step on which Ivan's left foot was still resting, and clutching the carriage he kept trying to jump in. "I am going with you!" he kept shouting, laughing a thin mirthful laugh with a look of reckless glee in his face. "Take me, too."

"There!" cried Fyodor Pavlovitch, delighted. "Did I not say he was Von Sohn. It is Von Sohn himself, risen from the dead. Why, how did you tear yourself away? What did you *vonsohn* there? And how could you get away from the dinner? You must be a brazen-faced fellow! I am that myself, but I am surprised at you, brother! Jump in, jump in! Let him pass, Ivan. It will be fun. He can lie somewhere at our feet. Will you lie at our feet, Von Sohn? Or perch on the box with the coachman. Skip on to the box, Von Sohn!"

But Ivan, who had by now taken his seat, without a word gave Maximov a violent punch in the breast and sent him flying. It was quite by chance he did not fall.

"Drive on!" Ivan shouted angrily to the coachman.

"Why, what are you doing, what are you about? Why did you do that?" Fyodor Pavlovitch protested.

But the carriage had already driven away. Ivan made no reply.

"Well, you are a fellow," Fyodor Pavlovitch said again.

After a pause of two minutes, looking askance at his son, "Why, it was you got up all this monastery business. You urged it, you approved of it. Why are you angry now?"

"You've talked rot enough. You might rest a bit now," Ivan snapped sullenly.

Fyodor Pavlovitch was silent again for two minutes.

"A drop of brandy would be nice now," he observed sententiously, but Ivan made no response.

"You shall have some, too, when we get home."

Ivan was still silent.

Fyodor Pavlovitch waited another two minutes.

"But I shall take Alyosha away from the monastery, though you will dislike it so much, most honoured Karl von Moor."

Ivan shrugged his shoulders contemptuously, and turning away stared at the road. And they did not speak again all the way home.

BOOK THREE

THE SENSUALISTS

1

IN THE SERVANTS' QUARTERS

THE Karamazovs' house was far from being in the centre of the town, but it was not quite outside it. It was a pleasant-looking old house of two storeys, painted grey, with a red iron roof. It was roomy and snug, and might still last many years. There were all sorts of unexpected little cupboards and closets and staircases. There were rats in it, but Fyodor Pavlovitch did not altogether dislike them. "One doesn't feel so solitary when one's left alone in the even," he used to say. It was his habit to send the servants away to the lodge for the night and to lock himself up alone. The lodge was a roomy and solid building in the yard. Fyodor Pavlovitch used to have the cooking done there, although there was a kitchen in the house; he did not like the smell of cooking, and, winter and summer alike, the dishes were carried in across the courtyard. The house was built for a large family; there was room for five times as many, with their servants. But at the time of our story there was no one living in the house but Fyodor Pavlovitch and his son Ivan. And in the lodge there were only three servants: old Grigory, and his old wife Marfa, and a young man called Smerdyakov. Of these three we must say a few words. Of old Grigory we have said something already. He was firm and determined and went blindly and obstinately for his object, if once he had been brought by any reasons (and they were often very illogical ones) to believe that it was immutably right. He was honest and incorruptible. His wife, Marfa Ignatyevna, had obeyed her husband's will implicitly all her life, yet she had pestered him terribly after the emancipation of the serfs.* She was set on leaving Fyodor Pavlovitch and opening a little shop in Moscow with their small savings. But Grigory decided then, once for all, that "the woman's talking nonsense, for every woman is dishonest," and that they ought not to leave their old master, whatever he might be, for "that was now their duty."

"Do you understand what duty is?" he asked Marfa Ignatyevna.

"I understand what duty means, Grigory Vassilyevitch, but why it's our duty to stay here I never shall understand," Marfa answered firmly.

"Well, don't understand then. But so it shall be. And you hold your tongue."

And so it was. They did not go away, and Fyodor Pavlovitch promised them a small sum for wages, and paid it regularly. Grigory knew, too, that he had an indisputable influence over his master. It was true, and he was

---

*Serfdom was abolished in Russia in 1861.

aware of it. Fyodor Pavlovitch was an obstinate and cunning buffoon, yet, though his will was strong enough "in some of the affairs of life," as he expressed it, he found himself, to his surprise, extremely feeble in facing certain other emergencies. He knew his weaknesses and was afraid of them. There are positions in which one has to keep a sharp look-out. And that's not easy without a trustworthy man, and Grigory was a most trustworthy man. Many times in the course of his life Fyodor Pavlovitch had only just escaped a sound thrashing through Grigory's intervention, and on each occasion the old servant gave him a good lecture. But it wasn't only thrashings that Fyodor Pavlovitch was afraid of. There were graver occasions, and very subtle and complicated ones, when Fyodor Pavlovitch could not have explained the extraordinary craving for some one faithful and devoted, which sometimes unaccountably came upon him all in a moment. It was almost a morbid condition. Corrupt and often cruel in his lust, like some noxious insect, Fyodor Pavlovitch was sometimes, in moments of drunkenness, overcome by superstitious terror and a moral convulsion which took an almost physical form. "My soul's simply quaking in my throat at those times," he used to say. At such moments he liked to feel that there was near at hand, in the lodge if not in the room, a strong, faithful man, virtuous and unlike himself, who had seen all his debauchery and knew all his secrets, but was ready in his devotion to overlook all that, not to oppose him, above all, not to reproach him or threaten him with anything, either in this world or in the next, and, in case of need, to defend him—from whom? From somebody unknown, but terrible and dangerous. What he needed was to feel that there was *another* man, an old and tried friend, that he might call him in his sick moments merely to look at his face, or, perhaps, exchange some quite irrelevant words with him. And if the old servant were not angry, he felt comforted, and if he were angry, he was more dejected. It happened even (very rarely however) that Fyodor Pavlovitch went at night to the lodge to wake Grigory and fetch him for a moment. When the old man came, Fyodor Pavlovitch would begin talking about the most trivial matters, and would soon let him go again, sometimes even with a jest. And after he had gone, Fyodor Pavlovitch would get into bed with a curse and sleep the sleep of the just. Something of the same sort had happened to Fyodor Pavlovitch on Alyosha's arrival. Alyosha "pierced his heart" by "living with him, seeing everything and blaming nothing." Moreover, Alyosha brought with him something his father had never known before: a complete absence of contempt for him and an invariable kindness, a perfectly natural unaffected devotion to the old man who deserved it so little. All this was a complete surprise to the old profligate, who had dropped all family ties. It was a new and surprising experience for him, who had till then loved nothing but "evil." When Alyosha had left him, he confessed to himself that he had learnt something he had not till then been willing to learn.

I have mentioned already that Grigory had detested Adelaïda Ivanovna, the first wife of Fyodor Pavlovitch and the mother of Dmitri, and that he had, on the contrary, protected Sofya Ivanovna, the poor "crazy woman" against his master and any one who chanced to speak ill or lightly of her. His sympathy for the unhappy wife had become something sacred to him, so that even now, twenty years after, he could not bear a slighting allusion to her from any one, and would at once check the offender. Externally, Grigory was cold, dignified and taciturn, and spoke, weighing his words, without frivolity. It was impossible to tell at first sight whether he loved his meek, obedient wife; but he really did love her, and she knew it.

Marfa Ignatyevna was by no means foolish; she was probably, indeed, cleverer than her husband, or, at least, more prudent than he in worldly affairs, and yet she had given in to him in everything without question or complaint ever since her marriage, and respected him for his spiritual superiority. It was remarkable how little they spoke to one another in the course of their lives, and only of the most necessary daily affairs. The grave and dignified Grigory thought over all his cares and duties alone, so that Marfa Ignatyevna had long grown used to knowing that he did not need her advice. She felt that her husband respected her silence, and took it as a sign of her good sense. He had never beaten her but once, and then only slightly. Once during the year after Fyodor Pavlovitch's marriage with Adelaïda Ivanovna, the village girls and women—at that time serfs—were called together before the house to sing and dance. They were beginning "In the Green Meadows," when Marfa, at that time a young woman, skipped forward and danced "the Russian Dance," not in the village fashion, but as she had danced it when she was a servant in the service of the rich Miüsov family, in their private theatre where the actors were taught to dance by a dancing master from Moscow. Grigory saw how his wife danced, and, an hour later, at home in their cottage he gave her a lesson, pulling her hair a little. But there it ended: the beating was never repeated, and Marfa Ignatyevna gave up dancing.

God had not blessed them with children. One child was born but it died. Grigory was fond of children, and was not ashamed of showing it. When Adelaïda Ivanovna had run away, Grigory took Dmitri, then a child of three years old, combed his hair and washed him in a tub with his own hands, and looked after him for almost a year. Afterwards he had looked after Ivan and Alyosha, for which the general's widow had rewarded him with a slap in the face; but I have already related all that. The only happiness his own child had brought him had been in the anticipation of its birth. When it was born, he was overwhelmed with grief and horror. The baby had six fingers. Grigory was so crushed by this, that he was not only silent till the day of the christening, but kept away in the garden. It was spring, and he spent three days digging the kitchen garden. The third day was fixed for christening the boy: meantime Grigory had reached a conclusion. Going into the cottage where the clergy were assembled and the visitors had arrived, including Fyodor Pavlovitch, who was to stand godfather, he suddenly announced that the baby "ought not to be christened at all." He announced this quietly, briefly, forcing out his words, and gazing with dull intentness at the priest.

"Why not?" asked the priest with good-humoured surprise.

"Because it's a dragon," muttered Grigory.

"A dragon? What dragon?"

Grigory did not speak for some time. "It's a confusion of nature," he muttered vaguely, but firmly, and obviously unwilling to say more.

They laughed, and of course christened the poor baby. Grigory prayed earnestly at the font, but his opinion of the newborn child remained unchanged. Yet he did not interfere in any way. As long as the sickly infant lived he scarcely looked at it, tried indeed not to notice it, and for the most part kept out of the cottage. But when, at the end of a fortnight, the baby died of thrush, he himself laid the child in its little coffin, looked at it in profound grief, and when they were filling up the shallow little grave he fell on his knees and bowed down to the earth. He did not for years afterwards mention his child, nor did Marfa speak of the baby before him, and, even if Grigory were not present, she never spoke of it above a whisper. Marfa observed that, from the day of the burial, he devoted himself to "religion," and took to reading the "Lives of the Saints," for the most part sitting alone and in silence, and always putting on his big, round, silver-rimmed spectacles. He rarely read aloud, only perhaps in Lent. He was fond of the book of Job, and had somehow got hold of a copy of the sayings and sermons of "the God-fearing Father Isaac the Syrian," which he read persistently for years together, understanding very little of it, but perhaps prizing and loving it the more for that. Of late he had begun to listen to the doctrines of the sect of Flagellants settled in the neighbourhood. He was evidently shaken by them, but judged it unfitting to go over to the new faith. His habit of theological reading gave him an expression of still greater gravity.

He was perhaps predisposed to mysticism. And the birth of his deformed child, and its death, had, as though by special design, been accompanied by another strange and marvellous event, which, as he said later, had left a "stamp" upon his soul. It happened that, on the very night after the burial of his child, Marfa was awakened by the wail of a new-born baby. She was frightened and waked her husband. He listened and said he thought it was more like some one groaning, "it might be a woman." He got up and dressed. It was a rather warm night in May. As he went down the steps, he distinctly heard groans coming from the garden. But the gate from the yard into the garden was locked at night, and there was no other way of entering it, for it was enclosed all round by a strong, high fence. Going back into the house, Grigory lighted a lantern, took the garden key, and taking no notice of the hysterical fears of his wife, who was still persuaded that she heard a child crying, and that it was her own baby crying and calling for her, went into the garden in silence. There he heard at once that the groans came from the bath-house that stood near the garden gate, and that they were groans of a woman. Opening the door of the bath-house, he saw a sight which petrified him. An idiot girl, who wandered about the streets and was known to the whole town by the nickname of Lizaveta Smerdyastchaya (Stinking Lizaveta),* had got into the bath-house and had just given birth to a child. She lay dying with the baby beside her. She said nothing, for she had never been able to speak. But her story needs a chapter to itself.

2

LIZAVETA

THERE was one circumstance which struck Grigory particularly, and confirmed a very unpleasant and revolting suspicion. This Lizaveta was a dwarfish creature, "not five foot within a wee bit," as many of the pious old women said pathetically about her, after her death. Her broad, healthy, red face had a look of blank idiocy and the fixed stare in her eyes was unpleasant, in spite of their meek expression. She wandered about, summer and winter alike, barefooted, wearing nothing but a hempen smock. Her coarse, almost black hair curled like lamb's wool, and formed a sort of huge cap on her head. It was always crusted with mud, and had leaves, bits of stick, and shavings clinging to it, as she always slept on the ground and in the dirt. Her father, a homeless, sickly drunkard, called Ilya, had lost everything and lived many years as a workman with some well-to-do tradespeople. Her mother had long been dead. Spiteful and diseased, Ilya used to beat Lizaveta inhumanly whenever she returned to him. But she rarely did so, for every one in the town was ready to look after her as being an idiot, and so specially dear to God. Ilya's employers and many others in the town, especially of the tradespeople, tried to clothe her better, and always rigged her out with high boots and a sheepskin coat for the winter. But, although she allowed them to dress her up without resisting, she usually went away, preferably to the cathedral porch, and taking off all that had been given her—kerchief, sheepskin, skirt or boots—she left them there and walked away barefoot in her smock as before. It happened on one occasion that a new governor of the province, making a tour of inspection in our town, saw Lizaveta, and was wounded in his tenderest susceptibilities. And though he was told she was an idiot, he pronounced that for a young woman of twenty to wander about in nothing but a smock was

---

Smerdyashchaya is the present active feminine form of *smerdet'*, an obsolete verb meaning "to stink" in Russian.

a breach of the proprieties, and must not occur again. But the governor went his way, and Lizaveta was left as she was. At last her father died, which made her even more acceptable in the eyes of the religious persons of the town, as an orphan. In fact, every one seemed to like her; even the boys did not tease her, and the boys of our town, especially the schoolboys, are a mischievous set. She would walk into strange houses, and no one drove her away. Every one was kind to her and gave her something. If she were given a copper, she would take it, and at once drop it in the alms-jug of the church or prison. If she were given a roll or bun in the market, she would hand it to the first child she met. Sometimes she would stop one of the richest ladies in the town and give it to her, and the lady would be pleased to take it. She herself never tasted anything but black bread and water. If she went into an expensive shop, where there were costly goods or money lying about, no one kept watch on her, for they knew that if she saw thousands of roubles overlooked by them, she would not have touched a farthing. She scarcely ever went to church. She slept either in the church porch or climbed over a hurdle (there are many hurdles instead of fences to this day in our town) into a kitchen garden. She used at least once a week to turn up "at home," that is at the house of her father's former employers, and in the winter went there every night, and slept either in the passage or the cowhouse. People were amazed that she could stand such a life, but she was accustomed to it, and, although she was so tiny, she was of a robust constitution. Some of the townspeople declared that she did all this only from pride, but that is hardly credible. She could hardly speak, and only from time to time uttered an inarticulate grunt. How could she have been proud?

It happened one clear, warm, moonlight night in September (many years ago) five or six drunken revellers were returning from the club at a very late hour, according to our provincial notions. They passed through the "back-way," which led between the back gardens of the houses, with hurdles on either side. This way leads out on to the bridge over the long, stinking pool which we were accustomed to call a river. Among the nettles and burdocks under the hurdle our revellers saw Lizaveta asleep. They stopped to look at her, laughing, and began jesting with unbridled licentiousness. It occurred to one young gentleman to make the whimsical inquiry whether any one could possibly look upon such an animal as a woman, and so forth. . . . They all pronounced with lofty repugnance that it was impossible. But Fyodor Pavlovitch, who was among them, sprang forward and declared that it was by no means impossible, and that, indeed, there was a certain piquancy about it, and so on. . . . It is true that at that time he was overdoing his part as a buffoon. He liked to put himself forward and entertain the company, ostensibly on equal terms, of course, though in reality he was on a servile footing with them. It was just at the time when he had received the news of his first wife's death in Petersburg, and, with crape upon his hat, was drinking and behaving so shamelessly that even the most reckless among us were shocked at the sight of him. The revellers, of course, laughed at this unexpected opinion; and one of them even began challenging him to act upon it. The others repelled the idea even more emphatically, although still with the utmost hilarity, and at last they went on their way. Later on, Fyodor Pavlovitch swore that he had gone with them, and perhaps it was so, no one knows for certain, and no one ever knew. But five or six months later, all the town was talking, with intense and sincere indignation, of Lizaveta's condition, and trying to find out who was the miscreant who had wronged her. Then suddenly a terrible rumour was all over the town that this miscreant was no other than Fyodor Pavlovitch. Who set the rumour going? Of that drunken band five had left the town and the only one still among us was an elderly and much respected civil councillor, the father of grown-up daughters, who could hardly have spread the tale, even if there had been any foundation for it. But rumour pointed straight at Fyodor Pavlovitch, and persisted in pointing at him. Of course this was no great grievance to him: he would not have troubled to contradict a set of tradespeople. In those days he was proud, and did not condescend to talk except in his own circle of the officials and nobles, whom he entertained so well.

At the time, Grigory stood up for his master vigorously. He provoked quarrels and altercations in defence of him and succeeded in bringing some people round to his side. "It's the wench's own fault," he asserted, and the culprit was Karp, a dangerous convict, who had escaped from prison and whose name was well known to us, as he had hidden in our town. This conjecture sounded plausible, for it was remembered that Karp had been in the neighbourhood just at that time in the autumn, and had robbed three people. But this affair and all the talk about it did not estrange popular sympathy from the poor idiot. She was better looked after than ever. A well-to-do merchant's widow named Kondratyev arranged to take her into her house at the end of April, meaning not to let her go out until after the confinement. They kept a constant watch over her, but in spite of their vigilance she escaped on the very last day, and made her way into Fyodor Pavlovitch's garden. How, in her condition, she managed to climb over the high, strong fence remained a mystery. Some maintained that she must have been lifted over by somebody; others hinted at something more uncanny. The most likely explanation is that it happened naturally—that Lizaveta, accustomed to clambering over hurdles to sleep in gardens, had somehow managed to climb this fence, in spite of her condition, and had leapt down, injuring herself.

Grigory rushed to Marfa and sent her to Lizaveta, while he ran to fetch an old midwife who lived close by. They saved the baby, but Lizaveta died at dawn. Grigory took the baby, brought it home, and making his wife sit down, put it on her lap. "A child of God—an orphan is akin to all," he said, "and to us above others. Our little lost one has sent us this, who has come from the devil's son and a holy innocent. Nurse him and weep no more."

So Marfa brought up the child. He was christened Pavel, to which people were not slow in adding Fyodorovitch (son of Fyodor). Fyodor Pavlovitch did not object to any of this, and thought it amusing, though he persisted vigorously in denying his responsibility. The townspeople were pleased at his adopting the foundling. Later on, Fyodor Pavlovitch invented a surname for the child, calling him Smerdyakov, after his mother's nickname.

So this Smerdyakov became Fyodor Pavlovitch's second servant, and was living in the lodge with Grigory and Marfa at the time our story begins. He was employed as cook. I ought to say something of this Smerdyakov, but I am ashamed of keeping my readers' attention so long occupied with these common menials, and I will go back to my story, hoping to say more of Smerdyakov in the course of it.

3

THE CONFESSION OF A PASSIONATE HEART—IN VERSE

ALYOSHA remained for some time irresolute after hearing the command his father shouted to him from the carriage. But in spite of his uneasiness he did not stand still. That was not his way. He went at once to the kitchen to find out what his father had been doing above. Then he set off, trusting that on the way he would find some answer to the doubt tormenting him. I hasten to add that his father's shouts, commanding him to return home "with his mattress and pillow" did not frighten him in the least. He understood perfectly that those peremptory shouts were merely "a flourish" to produce an effect. In the same way a tradesman in our town who was celebrating his name-day with a party of friends, getting angry at being refused more vodka, smashed up his own crockery and furniture and tore his own and his wife's clothes, and finally broke his windows, all for the sake of effect. Next day, of course, when he was sober, he regretted the broken cups and saucers. Alyosha knew that his father would let him go back to the monastery next day, possibly even that evening. Moreover, he was fully persuaded that his father might hurt any one else, but would not hurt him. Alyosha was certain that no one in the whole world ever would want to hurt him, and, what is more, he knew that no one could hurt him. This was for him an axiom, assumed once for all without question, and he went his way without hesitation, relying on it.

But at that moment an anxiety of a different sort disturbed him, and worried him the more because he could not formulate it. It was the fear of a woman, of Katerina Ivanovna, who had so urgently entreated him in the note handed to him by Madame Hohlakov to come and see her about something. This request and the necessity of going had at once aroused an uneasy feeling in his heart, and this feeling had grown more and more painful all the morning in spite of the scenes at the hermitage and at the Father Superior's. He was not uneasy because he did not know what she would speak of and what he must answer. And he was not afraid of her simply as a woman. Though he knew little of women, he had spent his life, from early childhood till he entered the monastery, entirely with women. He was afraid of that woman, Katerina Ivanovna. He had been afraid of her from the first time he saw her. He had only seen her two or three times, and had only chanced to say a few words to her. He thought of her as a beautiful, proud, imperious girl. It was not her beauty which troubled him, but something else. And the vagueness of his apprehension increased the apprehension itself. The girl's aims were of the noblest, he knew that. She was trying to save his brother Dmitri simply through generosity, though he had already behaved badly to her. Yet, although Alyosha recognised and did justice to all these fine and generous sentiments, a shiver began to run down his back as soon as he drew near her house.

He reflected that he would not find Ivan, who was so intimate a friend, with her, for Ivan was certainly now with his father. Dmitri he was even more certain not to find there, and he had a foreboding of the reason. And so his conversation would be with her alone. He had a great longing to run and see his brother Dmitri before that fateful interview. Without showing him the letter, he could talk to him about it. But Dmitri lived a long way off, and he was sure to be away from home too. Standing still for a minute, he reached a final decision. Crossing himself with a rapid and accustomed gesture, and at once smiling, he turned resolutely in the direction of his terrible lady.

He knew her house. If he went by the High Street and then across the market-place, it was a long way round. Though our town is small, it is scattered, and the houses are far apart. And meanwhile his father was expecting him, and perhaps had not yet forgotten his command. He might be unreasonable, and so he had to make haste to get there and back. So he decided to take a short cut by the back-way, for he knew every inch of the ground. This meant skirting fences, climbing over hurdles, and crossing other people's back-yards, where every one he met knew him and greeted him. In this way he could reach the High Street in half the time.

He had to pass the garden adjoining his father's, and belonging to a little tumbledown house with four windows. The owner of this house, as Alyosha knew, was a bedridden old woman, living with her daughter, who had been a genteel maid-servant in generals' families in Petersburg. Now she had been at home a year, looking after her sick mother. She always dressed up in fine clothes, though her old mother and she had sunk into such poverty that they went every day to Fyodor Pavlovitch's kitchen for soup and bread, which Marfa gave readily. Yet, though the young woman came up for soup, she had never sold any of her dresses, and one of these even had a long train—a fact which Alyosha had learned from Rakitin, who always knew everything that was going on in the town. He had forgotten it as soon as he heard it, but now, on reaching the garden, he remembered the dress with the train, raised his head, which had been bowed in thought, and came upon something quite unexpected.

Over the hurdle in the garden, Dmitri, mounted on something, was leaning forward, gesticulating violently, beckoning to him, obviously afraid to utter a word for fear of being overheard. Alyosha ran up to the hurdle.

"It's a good thing you looked up. I was nearly shouting to you," Mitya said in a joyful, hurried whisper. "Climb in here quickly! How splendid that you've come! I was just thinking of you!"

Alyosha was delighted too, but he did not know how to get over the hurdle. Mitya put his powerful hand under his elbow to help him jump. Tucking up his cassock, Alyosha leapt over the hurdle with the agility of a bare-legged street urchin.

"Well done! Now come along," said Mitya in an enthusiastic whisper.

"Where?" whispered Alyosha, looking about him and finding himself in a deserted garden with no one near but themselves. The garden was small, but the house was at least fifty paces away.

"There's no one here. Why do you whisper?" asked Alyosha.

"Why do I whisper? Deuce take it!" cried Dmitri at the top of his voice. "You see what silly tricks nature plays one. I am here in secret, and on the watch. I'll explain later on, but, knowing it's a secret, I began whispering like a fool, when there's no need. Let us go. Over there. Till then be quiet. I want to kiss you.

> Glory to God in the world,
> Glory to God in me . . .*

I was just repeating that, sitting here, before you came."

The garden was about three acres in extent, and planted with trees only along the fence at the four sides. There were apple-trees, maples, limes and birch-trees. The middle of the garden was an empty grass space, from which several hundredweight of hay was carried in the summer. The garden was let out for a few roubles for the summer. There were also plantations of raspberries and currants and gooseberries laid out along the sides; a kitchen garden had been planted lately near the house.

Dmitri led his brother to the most secluded corner of the garden. There, in a thicket of lime-trees and old bushes of black currant, elder, snow-ball-tree, and lilac, there stood a tumbledown green summer-house, blackened with age. Its walls were of lattice-work, but there was still a roof which could give shelter. God knows when this summer-house was built. There was a tradition that it had been put up some fifty years before by a retired colonel called Von Schmidt, who owned the house at that time. It was all in decay, the floor was rotting, the planks were loose, the woodwork smelled musty. In the summer-house there was a green wooden table fixed in the ground, and round it were some green benches upon which it

---

*Dmitri's own verse.

was still possible to sit. Alyosha had at once observed his brother's exhilarated condition, and on entering the arbour he saw half a bottle of brandy and a wineglass on the table.

"That's brandy," Mitya laughed. "I see your look: 'He's drinking again!' Distrust the apparition.

> Distrust the worthless, lying crowd,
> And lay aside thy doubts.*

I'm not drinking, I'm only 'indulging,' as that pig, your Rakitin, says. He'll be a civil councillor one day, but he'll always talk about 'indulging.' Sit down. I could take you in my arms, Alyosha, and press you to my bosom till I crush you, for in the whole world—in reality—in re-al-i-ty—(can you take it in?) I love no one but you!"

He uttered the last words in a sort of exaltation.

"No one but you and one 'jade' I have fallen in love with, to my ruin. But being in love doesn't mean loving. You may be in love with a woman and yet hate her. Remember that! I can talk about it gaily still. Sit down here by the table and I'll sit beside you and look at you, and go on talking. You shall keep quiet and I'll go on talking, for the time has come. But on reflection, you know, I'd better speak quietly, for here—here—you can never tell what ears are listening. I will explain everything, as they say, 'the story will be continued.' Why have I been longing for you? Why have I been thirsting for you all these days, and just now? (It's five days since I've cast anchor here.) Because it's only to you I can tell everything; because I must, because I need you, because to-morrow I shall fly from the clouds, because to-morrow life is ending and beginning. Have you ever felt, have you ever dreamt of falling down a precipice into a pit? That's just how I'm falling, but not in a dream. And I'm not afraid, and don't you be afraid. At least, I am afraid, but I enjoy it. It's not enjoyment though, but ecstasy. Damn it all, whatever it is! A strong spirit, a weak spirit, a womanish spirit—whatever it is! Let us praise nature; you see what sunshine, how clear the sky is, the leaves are all green, it's still summer; four o'clock in the afternoon and the stillness! Where were you going?"

"I was going to father's, but I meant to go to Katerina Ivanovna's first."

"To her, and to father! Oo! what a coincidence! Why was I waiting for you? Hungering and thirsting for you in every cranny of my soul and even in my ribs? Why, to send you to father and to her, Katerina Ivanovna, so as to have done with her and with father. To send an angel. I might have sent any one, but I wanted to send an angel. And here you are on your way to see father and her."

"Did you really mean to send me?" cried Alyosha with a distressed expression.

---

*From "When from the Darkness of Delusion" (1846), a poem about a redeemed prostitute, by Russian poet Nikolai Nekrasov.

"Stay! You knew it! And I see you understand it all at once. But be quiet, be quiet for a time. Don't be sorry, and don't cry."

Dmitri stood up, thought a moment, and put his finger to his forehead.

"She's asked you, written to you a letter or something, that's why you're going to her? You wouldn't be going except for that?"

"Here is her note." Alyosha took it out of his pocket. Mitya looked through it quickly.

"And you were going the back-way! Oh, gods, I thank you for sending him by the back-way, and he came to me like the golden fish to the silly old fishermen in the fable![1] Listen, Alyosha, listen, brother! Now I mean to tell you everything, for I must tell some one. An angel in heaven I've told already; but I want to tell an angel on earth. You are an angel on earth. You will hear and judge and forgive. And that's what I need, that some one above me should forgive. Listen! If two people break away from everything on earth and fly off into the unknown, or at least one of them, and before flying off or going to ruin he comes to some one else and says, 'Do this for me'—some favour never asked before that could only be asked on one's deathbed—would that other refuse, if he were a friend or a brother?"

"I will do it, but tell me what it is, and make haste," said Alyosha.

"Make haste! H'm! . . . Don't be in a hurry, Alyosha, you hurry and worry yourself. There's no need to hurry now. Now the world has taken a new turning. Ah, Alyosha, what a pity you can't understand ecstasy. But what am I saying to him? As though you didn't understand it. What an ass I am, what am I saying: 'Be noble, oh, man!'[*] who says that?"

Alyosha made up his mind to wait. He felt that, perhaps, indeed, his work lay here. Mitya sank into thought for a moment, with his elbow on the table and his head in his hand. Both were silent.

"Alyosha," said Mitya, "you're the only one who won't laugh. I should like to begin—my confession—with Schiller's 'Hymn to Joy,' An die Freude![†] I don't know German, I only know it's called that. Don't think I'm talking nonsense because I'm drunk. I'm not a bit drunk. Brandy's all very well, but I need two bottles to make me drunk:

> Silenus with his rosy phiz
> Upon his stumbling ass.[‡]

But I've not drunk a quarter of a bottle, and I'm not Silenus. I'm not Silenus, though I am strong,[§] for I've made a decision once for all. Forgive

---

[*]Echoes lines from the German poet Johann Wolfgang von Goethe's 1783 poem "Das Göttliche" ("The Divine").

[†]Dmitri refers to Friedrich von Schiller's 1785 poem "An die Freude" ("Ode to Joy").

[‡]Lines from A. N. Maikov's poem "Bas-relief" (1842).

[§]Referenced word is "strong" (in context: "I'm not Silenus, though I am strong"). In Russian "Silen" (translator's note).

me the pun; you'll have to forgive me a lot more than puns to-day. Don't be uneasy. I'm not spinning it out. I'm talking sense, and I'll come to the point in a minute. I won't keep you in suspense. Stay, how does it go?"

He raised his head, thought a minute, and began with enthusiasm:

> "Wild and fearful in his cavern
> Hid the naked troglodyte,
> And the homeless nomad wandered
> Laying waste the fertile plain.
> Menacing with spear and arrow
> In the woods the hunter strayed. . . .
> Woe to all poor wretches stranded
> On those cruel and hostile shores!

> "From the peak of high Olympus
> Came the mother Ceres down,
> Seeking in those savage regions
> Her lost daughter Proserpine.
> But the Goddess found no refuge,
> Found no kindly welcome there,
> And no temple bearing witness
> To the worship of the gods.

> "From the fields and from the vineyards
> Came no fruits to deck the feats,
> Only flesh of blood-stained victims
> Smouldered on the altar-fires,
> And where'er the grieving goddess
> Turns her melancholy gaze,
> Sunk in vilest degradation
> Man his loathesomeness displays."*

Mitya broke into sobs and seized Alyosha's hand.

"My dear, my dear, in degradation, in degradation now, too. There's a terrible amount of suffering for man on earth, a terrible lot of trouble. Don't think I'm only a brute in an officer's uniform, wallowing in dirt and drink. I hardly think of anything but of that degraded man—if only I'm not lying. I pray God I'm not lying and showing off. I think about that man because I am that man myself.

> Would he purge his soul from vileness
> And attain to light and worth,
> He must turn and cling forever
> To his ancient Mother Earth.†

---

*From Schiller's 1798 poem "Das Eleusische Fest" ("The Eleusinian Festival").
†From "The Eleusinian Festival."

But the difficulty is how am I to cling for ever to Mother Earth. I don't kiss
her. I don't cleave her bosom. Am I to become a peasant or a shepherd? I
go on and I don't know whether I'm going to shame or to light and joy.
That's the trouble, for everything in the world is a riddle! And whenever
I've happened to sink into the vilest degradation (and it's always been
happening) I always read that poem about Ceres and man. Has it reformed me? Never! For I'm a Karamazov. For when I do leap into the pit,
I go headlong with my heels up, and am pleased to be falling in that degrading attitude, and pride myself upon it. And in the very depths of that
degradation I begin a hymn of praise. Let me be accursed. Let me be vile
and base, only let me kiss the hem of the veil in which my God is
shrouded. Though I may be following the devil, I am Thy son, O Lord, and
I love Thee, and I feel the joy without which the world cannot stand.

> Joy everlasting fostereth
> The soul of all creation,
> It is her secret ferment fires
> The cup of life with flame.
> 'Tis at her beck the grass hath turned
> Each blade towards the light
> And solar systems have evolved
> From chaos and dark night,
> Filling the realms of boundless space
> Beyond the sage's sight.
>
> At bounteous nature's kindly breast,
> All things that breathe drink Joy,
> And birds and beasts and creeping things
> All follow where She leads.
> Her gifts to man are friends in need,
> The wreath, the foaming must,
> To angels—vision of God's throne,
> To insects—sensual lust.*

But enough poetry! I am in tears; let me cry. It may be foolishness that
every one would laugh at. But you won't laugh. Your eyes are shining, too.
Enough poetry. I want to tell you now about the insects to whom God
gave 'sensual lust.'

> To insects—sensual lust.

I am that insect, brother, and it is said of me especially. All we Karamazovs
are such insects, and, angel as you are, that insect lives in you, too,
and will stir up a tempest in your blood. Tempests, because sensual lust is

---

*From Schiller's "Ode to Joy."

a tempest—worse than a tempest! Beauty is a terrible and awful thing! It is terrible because it has not been fathomed and never can be fathomed, for God sets us nothing but riddles. Here the boundaries meet and all contradictions exist side by side. I am not a cultivated man, brother, but I've thought a lot about this. It's terrible what mysteries there are! Too many riddles weigh men down on earth. We must solve them as we can, and try to keep a dry skin in the water. Beauty! I can't endure the thought that a man of lofty mind and heart begins with the ideal of the Madonna and ends with the ideal of Sodom. What's still more awful is that a man with the ideal of Sodom in his soul does not renounce the ideal of the Madonna, and his heart may be on fire with that ideal, genuinely on fire, just as in his days of youth and innocence. Yes, man is broad, too broad, indeed. I'd have him narrower. The devil only knows what to make of it! What to the mind is shameful is beauty and nothing else to the heart. Is there beauty in Sodom? Believe me, that for the immense mass of mankind beauty is found in Sodom. Did you know that secret? The awful thing is that beauty is mysterious as well as terrible. God and the devil are fighting there and the battlefield is the heart of man. But a man always talks of his own ache. Listen, now to come to facts."

4

THE CONFESSION OF A PASSIONATE HEART—IN ANECDOTE

I WAS leading a wild life then. Father said just now that I spent several thousand roubles in seducing young girls. That's a swinish invention, and there was nothing of the sort. And if there was, I didn't need money simply for *that*. With me money is an accessory, the overflow of my heart, the framework. To-day she would be my lady, to-morrow a wench out of the streets in her place. I entertained them both. I threw away money by the handful on music, rioting, and gipsies. Sometimes I gave it to the ladies, too, for they'll take it greedily, that must be admitted, and be pleased and thankful for it. Ladies used to be fond of me: not all of them, but it happened, it happened. But I always liked side-paths, little dark back-alleys behind the main road—there one finds adventures and surprises, and precious metal in the dirt. I am speaking figuratively, brother. In the town I was in, there were no such back-alleys in the literal sense, but morally there were. If you were like me, you'd know what that means. I loved vice, I loved the ignominy of vice. I loved cruelty; am I not a bug, am I not a noxious insect? In fact a Karamazov! Once we went, a whole lot of us, for a picnic, in seven sledges. It was dark, it was winter, and I began squeezing a girl's hand, and forced her to kiss me. She was the daughter of an official, a sweet, gentle, submissive creature. She allowed me, she allowed me much in the dark. She thought, poor thing, that I should come next day to make her an offer (I was looked upon as a good match, too). But I didn't say a word to her for five months. I used to see her in a corner at dances (we were always having dances), her eyes watching me. I saw how they glowed with fire—a fire of gentle indignation. This game only tickled that insect lust I cherished in my soul. Five months later she married an official and left the town, still angry, and still, perhaps, in love with me. Now they live happily. Observe that I told no one. I didn't boast of it. Though I'm full of low desires, and love what's low, I'm not dishonourable. You're blushing; your eyes flashed. Enough of this filth with you. And all this was nothing much—wayside blossoms *à la* Paul de Kock*—though the cruel insect had already grown strong in my soul. I've a perfect album of reminiscences, brother. God bless them, the darlings. I tried to break it off without quarrelling. And I never gave them away. I never bragged of one of them. But that's enough. You can't suppose I brought you here simply to talk of such nonsense. No, I'm going to tell you something more curious; and don't be surprised that I'm glad to tell you, instead of being ashamed."

"You say that because I blushed," Alyosha said suddenly. "I wasn't blushing at what you were saying or at what you've done. I blushed because I am the same as you are."

"You? Come, that's going a little too far!"

"No, it's not too far," said Alyosha warmly (obviously the idea was not a new one). "The ladder's the same. I'm at the bottom step, and you're above, somewhere about the thirteenth. That's how I see it. But it's all the same. Absolutely the same in kind. Any one on the bottom step is bound to go up to the top one."

"Then one ought not to step on at all."

"Any one who can help it had better not."

"But can you?"

"I think not."

"Hush, Alyosha, hush, darling! I could kiss your hand, you touch me so. That rogue Grushenka has an eye for men. She told me once that she'd devour you one day. There, there, I won't! From this field of corruption fouled by flies, let's pass to my tragedy, also befouled by flies, that is by every sort of vileness. Although the old man told lies about my seducing innocence, there really was something of the sort in my tragedy, though it was only once, and then it did not come off. The old man who has reproached me with what never happened does not even know of this fact; I never told any one about it. You're the first, except Ivan, of course—Ivan knows everything. He knew about it long before you. But Ivan's a tomb."

---

*Charles-Paul de Kock (1793–1871), popular French writer of romances.

"Ivan's a tomb?"

"Yes."

Alyosha listened with great attention.

"I was lieutenant in a line regiment, but still I was under supervision, like a kind of convict. Yet I was awfully well received in the little town. I spent money right and left. I was thought to be rich; I thought so myself. But I must have pleased them in other ways as well. Although they shook their heads over me, they liked me. My colonel, who was an old man, took a sudden dislike to me. He was always down upon me, but I had powerful friends, and, moreover, all the town was on my side, so he couldn't do me much harm. I was in fault myself for refusing to treat him with proper respect. I was proud. This obstinate old fellow, who was really a very good sort, kind-hearted and hospitable, had had two wives, both dead. His first wife, who was of a humble family, left a daughter as unpretentious as herself. She was a young woman of four and twenty when I was there, and was living with her father and an aunt, her mother's sister. The aunt was simple and illiterate; the niece was simple but lively. I like to say nice things about people. I never knew a woman of more charming character than Agafya—fancy, her name was Agafya Ivanovna! And she wasn't bad-looking either, in the Russian style: tall, stout, with a full figure, and beautiful eyes, though a rather coarse face. She had not married, although she had had two suitors. She refused them, but was as cheerful as ever. I was intimate with her, not in 'that' way, it was pure friendship. I have often been friendly with women quite innocently. I used to talk to her with shocking frankness, and she only laughed. Many women like such freedom, and she was a girl too, which made it very amusing. Another thing, one could never think of her as a young lady. She and her aunt lived in her father's house with a sort of voluntary humility, not putting themselves on an equality with other people. She was a general favourite, and of use to every one, for she was a clever dressmaker. She had a talent for it. She gave her services freely without asking for payment, but if any one offered her payment, she didn't refuse. The colonel, of course, was a very different matter. He was one of the chief personages in the district. He kept open house, entertained the whole town, gave suppers and dances. At the time I arrived and joined the battalion, all the town was talking of the expected return of the colonel's second daughter, a great beauty, who had just left a fashionable school in the capital. This second daughter is Katerina Ivanovna, and she was the child of the second wife, who belonged to a distinguished general's family; although, as I learnt on good authority, she, too, brought the colonel no money. She had connections, and that was all. There may have been expectations, but they had come to nothing.

"Yet, when the young lady came from boarding-school on a visit, the whole town revived. Our most distinguished ladies—two 'Excellencies' and a colonel's wife—and all the rest following their lead, at once took her up and gave entertainments in her honour. She was the belle of the balls and picnics, and they got up *tableaux vivants* in aid of distressed governesses. I took no notice, I went on as wildly as before, and one of my exploits at the

time set all the town talking. I saw her eyes taking my measure one evening at the battery commander's, but I didn't go up to her, as though I disdained her acquaintance. I did go up and speak to her at an evening party
not long after. She scarcely looked at me, and compressed her lips scornfully. 'Wait a bit. I'll have my revenge,' thought I. I behaved like an awful
fool on many occasions at that time, and I was conscious of it myself. What
made it worse was that I felt that 'Katenka' was not an innocent boarding-
school miss, but a person of character, proud and really high-principled;
above all, she had education and intellect, and I had neither. You think I
meant to make her an offer? No, I simply wanted to revenge myself, because I was such a hero and she didn't seem to feel it.

"Meanwhile, I spent my time in drink and riot, till the lieutenant-colonel put me under arrest for three days. Just at that time father sent me six
thousand roubles in return for my sending him a deed giving up all claims
upon him—settling our accounts, so to speak, and saying that I wouldn't
expect anything more. I didn't understand a word of it at the time. Until I
came here, Alyosha, till the last few days, indeed, perhaps even now, I
haven't been able to make head or tail of my money affairs with father. But
never mind that, we'll talk of it later.

"Just as I received the money, I got a letter from a friend telling me
something that interested me immensely. The authorities, I learnt, were
dissatisfied with our lieutenant-colonel. He was suspected of irregularities;
in fact, his enemies were preparing a surprise for him. And then the commander of the division arrived, and kicked up the devil of a shindy. Shortly
afterwards he was ordered to retire. I won't tell you how it all happened.
He had enemies certainly. Suddenly there was a marked coolness in the
town towards him and all his family. His friends all turned their backs on
him. Then I took my first step. I met Agafya Ivanovna, with whom I'd always kept up a friendship, and said, 'Do you know there's a deficit of 4500
roubles of government money in your father's accounts?'

" 'What do you mean? What makes you say so? The general was here
not long ago, and everything was all right.'

" 'Then it was, but now it isn't.'

"She was terribly scared.

" 'Don't frighten me!' she said. 'Who told you so?'

" 'Don't be uneasy,' I said, 'I won't tell any one. You know I'm as silent
as the tomb. I only wanted, in view of "possibilities," to add, that when they
demanded that 4500 roubles from your father, and he can't produce it,
he'll be tried, and made to serve as a common soldier in his old age, unless
you like to send me your young lady secretly. I've just had money paid me.
I'll give her four thousand, if you like, and keep the secret religiously.'

" 'Ah, you scoundrel!' that's what she said. 'You wicked scoundrel! How
dare you!'

"She went away furiously indignant, while I shouted after her once
more that the secret should be kept sacred. Those two simple creatures,
Agafya and her aunt, I may as well say at once, behaved like perfect angels
all through this business. They genuinely adored their 'Katya,' and thought

her far above them, and waited on her, hand and foot. But Agafya told her of our conversation. I found that out afterwards. She didn't keep it back, and of course that was all I wanted.

"Suddenly the new major arrived to take command of the battalion. The old lieutenant-colonel was taken ill at once, couldn't leave his room for two days, and didn't hand over the government money. Dr. Kravchenko declared that he really was ill. But I knew for a fact, and had known for a long time, that for the last four years the money had never been in his hands except when the Commander made his visits of inspection. He used to lend it to a trustworthy person, a merchant of our town called Trifonov, an old widower, with a big beard and gold-rimmed spectacles. He used to go to the fair, do a profitable business with the money, and return the whole sum to the colonel, bringing with it a present from the fair, as well as interest on the loan. But this time (I heard all about it quite by chance from Trifonov's son and heir, a drivelling youth and one of the most vicious in the world)—this time, I say, Trifonov brought nothing back from the fair. The lieutenant-colonel flew to him. 'I've never received any money from you, and couldn't possibly have received any.' That was all the answer he got. So now our lieutenant-colonel is confined to the house, with a towel round his head, while they're all three busy putting ice on it. All at once an orderly arrives on the scene with the book and the order to 'hand over the battalion money immediately, within two hours.' He signed the book (I saw the signature in the book afterwards), stood up, saying he would put on his uniform, ran to his bedroom, loaded his double-barreled gun with a service bullet, took the boot off his right foot, fixed the gun against his chest, and began feeling for the trigger with his foot. But Agafya, remembering what I had told her, had her suspicions. She stole up and peeped into the room just in time. She rushed in, flung herself upon him from behind, threw her arms round him, and the gun went off, hit the ceiling, but hurt no one. The others ran in, took away the gun, and held him by the arms. I heard all about this afterwards. I was at home, it was getting dusk, and I was just preparing to go out. I had dressed, brushed my hair, scented my handkerchief, and taken up my cap, when suddenly the door opened, and facing me in the room stood Katerina Ivanovna.

"It's strange how things happen sometimes. No one had seen her in the street, so that no one knew of it in the town. I lodged with two decrepit old ladies, who looked after me. They were most obliging old things, ready to do anything for me, and at my request were as silent afterward as two cast-iron posts. Of course I grasped the position at once. She walked in and looked straight at me, her dark eyes determined, even defiant, but on her lips and round her mouth I saw uncertainty.

" 'My sister told me,' she began, 'that you would give me 4500 roubles if I came to you for it—myself. I have come . . . give me the money!'

"She couldn't keep it up. She was breathless, frightened, her voice failed her, and the corners of her mouth and the lines round it quivered. Alyosha, are you listening, or are you asleep?"

"Mitya, I know you will tell the whole truth," said Alyosha in agitation.

"I am telling it. If I tell the whole truth just as it happened I shan't spare myself. My first idea was a—Karamazov one. Once I was bitten by a centipede, brother, and laid up a fortnight with fever from it. Well, I felt a centipede biting at my heart then—a noxious insect, you understand? I looked her up and down. You've seen her? She's a beauty. But she was beautiful in another way then. At that moment she was beautiful because she was noble, and I was a scoundrel; she in all the grandeur of her generosity and sacrifice for her father, and I—a bug! And, scoundrel as I was, she was altogether at my mercy, body and soul. She was hemmed in. I tell you frankly, that thought, that venomous thought, so possessed my heart that I almost swooned with suspense. It seemed as if there could be no resisting it; as though I should act like a bug, like a venomous spider, without a spark of pity. I could scarcely breathe. Understand, I should have gone next day to ask for her hand, so that it might end honourably, so to speak, and that nobody would or could know. For though I'm a man of base desires, I'm honest. And at that very second some voice seemed to whisper in my ear, 'But when you come to-morrow to make your proposal, that girl won't even see you; she'll order her coachman to kick you out of the yard. "Publish it through all the town," she would say, "I'm not afraid of you."' I looked at the young lady, my voice had not deceived me. That is how it would be, not a doubt of it. I could see from her face now that I should be turned out of the house. My spite was roused. I longed to play her the nastiest swinish cad's trick: to look at her with a sneer, and on the spot where she stood before me to stun her with a tone of voice that only a shopman could use.

"'Four thousand! What do you mean? I was joking. You've been counting your chickens too easily, madam. Two hundred, if you like, with all my heart. But four thousand is not a sum to throw away on such frivolity. You've put yourself out to no purpose.'

"I should have lost the game, of course. She'd have run away. But it would have been an infernal revenge. It would have been worth it all. I'd have howled with regret all the rest of my life, only to have played that trick. Would you believe it, it has never happened to me with any other woman, not one, to look at her at such a moment with hatred. But, on my oath, I looked at her for three seconds, or five perhaps, with fearful hatred—that hate which is only a hair's-breath from love, from the maddest love!

"I went to the window, put my forehead against the frozen pane, and I remember the ice burnt my forehead like fire. I did not keep her long, don't be afraid. I turned round, went up to the table, opened the drawer and took out a banknote for five thousand roubles (it was lying in a French dictionary). Then I showed it her in silence, folded it, handed it to her, opened the door into the passage, and, stepping back, made her a deep bow, a most respectful, a most impressive bow, believe me! She shuddered all over, gazed at me for a second, turned horribly pale—white as a sheet, in fact—and all at once, not impetuously but softly, gently, bowed down to my feet—not a boarding-house curtsey, but a Russian bow, with her forehead to the floor. She jumped up and ran away. I was wearing my sword.

I drew it and nearly stabbed myself with it on the spot; why, I don't know. It would have been frightfully stupid, of course. I suppose it was from delight. Can you understand that one might kill oneself from delight? But I didn't stab myself. I only kissed my sword and put it back in the scabbard—which there was no need to have told you, by the way. And I fancy that in telling you about my inner conflict I have laid it on rather thick to glorify myself. But let it pass, and to hell with all who pry into the human heart! Well, so much for that 'adventure' with Katerina Ivanovna. So now Ivan knows of it, and you—no one else."

Dmitri got up, took a step or two in his excitement, pulled out his handkerchief and mopped his forehead, then sat down again, not in the same place as before, but on the opposite side, so that Alyosha had to turn quite round to face him.

5

THE CONFESSION OF A PASSIONATE HEART—"HEELS UP"

Now," said Alyosha, "I understand the first half."

"You understand the first half. That half is a drama, and it was played out there. The second half is a tragedy, and it is being acted here."

"And I understand nothing of that second half so far," said Alyosha.

"And I? Do you suppose I understand it?"

"Stop, Dmitri. There's one important question. Tell me, you were betrothed, you are betrothed still?"

"We weren't betrothed at once, not for three months after that adventure. The next day I told myself that the incident was closed, concluded, that there would be no sequel. It seemed to me caddish to make her an offer. On her side she gave no sign of life for the six weeks that she remained in the town; except, indeed, for one action. The day after her visit the maidservant slipped round with an envelope addressed to me. I tore it open; it contained the change out of the banknote. Only 4500 was needed, but there was a discount of about 200 on changing it. She only sent me about 260 roubles, I don't remember exactly, but not a note, not a word of explanation. I searched the packet for a pencil mark—n-nothing! Well, I spent the rest of the money on such an orgy that the new major was obliged to reprimand me.

"Well, the lieutenant-colonel produced the battalion money, to the astonishment of every one, for nobody believed that he had the money untouched. He'd no sooner paid it than he fell ill, took to his bed, and, three weeks later, softening of the brain set in, and he died five days afterwards. He was buried with military honours, for he had not had time to receive his discharge. Ten days after his funeral, Katerina Ivanovna, with her aunt and sister, went to Moscow. And, behold, on the very day they went away (I hadn't seen them, didn't see them off or take leave) I received a tiny note, a sheet of thin blue paper, and on it only one line in pencil: 'I will write to you. Wait. K.' And that was all.

"I'll explain the rest now, in two words. In Moscow their fortunes changed with the swiftness of lightning and the unexpectedness of an Arabian fairy tale. That general's widow, their nearest relation, suddenly lost the two nieces who were her heiresses and next-of-kin—both died in the same week of small-pox. The old lady, prostrated with grief, welcomed Katya as a daughter, as her one hope, clutched at her, altered her will in Katya's favour. But that concerned the future. Meanwhile she gave her, for present use, eighty thousand roubles, as a marriage portion, to do what she liked with. She was an hysterical woman. I saw something of her in Moscow, later.

"Well, suddenly I received by post four thousand five hundred roubles. I was speechless with surprise, as you may suppose. Three days later came the promised letter. I have it with me now. I always keep it, and shall keep it till I die. Shall I show you? You must read it. She offers to be my wife, offers herself to me. 'I love you madly,' she says, 'even if you don't love me, never mind. Be my husband. Don't be afraid. I won't hamper you in any way. I will be your chattel. I will be the carpet under your feet. I want to love you for ever. I want to save you from yourself.' Alyosha, I am not worthy to repeat those lines in my vulgar words and in my vulgar tone, my everlastingly vulgar tone, that I can never cure myself of. That letter stabs me even now. Do you think I don't mind—that I don't mind still? I wrote her an answer at once, as it was impossible for me to go to Moscow. I wrote to her with tears. One thing I shall be ashamed of for ever. I referred to her being rich and having a dowry while I was only a stuck-up beggar! I mentioned money! I ought to have borne it in silence, but it slipped from my pen. Then I wrote at once to Ivan, and told him all I could about it in a letter of six pages, and sent him to her. Why do you look like that? Why are you staring at me? Yes, Ivan fell in love with her; he's in love with her still. I know that. I did a stupid thing, in the world's opinion; but perhaps that one stupid thing may be the saving of us all now. Oo! Don't you see what a lot she thinks of Ivan, how she respects him? When she compares us, do you suppose she can love a man like me, especially after all that has happened here?"

"But I'm convinced that she does love a man like you, and not a man like him."

"She loves her own *virtue*, not me." The words broke involuntarily, and almost malignantly, from Dmitri. He laughed, but a minute later his eyes gleamed, he flushed crimson and struck the table violently with his fist.

"I swear, Alyosha," he cried, with intense and genuine anger at himself; "you may not believe me, but as God is holy, and as Christ is God, I swear that though I smiled at her lofty sentiments just now, I know that I am a million times baser in soul than she, and that these lofty sentiments of hers are as sincere as a heavenly angel's. That's the tragedy of it—that I know that for certain. What if any one does show off a bit? Don't I do it myself? And yet I'm sincere, I'm sincere. As for Ivan, I can understand how he must be cursing nature now—with his intellect, too! To see the preference given—to whom, to what? To a monster who, though he is betrothed and all eyes are fixed on him, can't restrain his debaucheries—and before the very eyes of his betrothed! And a man like me is preferred, while he is rejected. And why? Because a girl wants to sacrifice her life and destiny out of gratitude. It's ridiculous! I've never said a word of this to Ivan, and Ivan of course has never dropped a hint of the sort to me. But destiny will be accomplished, and the best man will hold his ground while the undeserving one will vanish into his back-alley for ever—his filthy back-alley, his beloved back-alley, where he is at home and where he will sink in filth and stench at his own free will and with enjoyment. I've been talking foolishly. I've no words left. I use them at random, but it will be as I have said. I shall drown in the back-alley, and she will marry Ivan."

"Stop, Dmitri," Alyosha interrupted again with great anxiety.

"There's one thing you haven't made clear yet: you are still betrothed all the same, aren't you? How can you break off the engagement if she, your betrothed, doesn't want to?"

"Yes, formally and solemnly betrothed. It was all done on my arrival in Moscow, with great ceremony, with ikons, all in fine style. The general's wife blessed us, and—would you believe it?—congratulated Katya. 'You've made a good choice,' she said, 'I see right through him.' And, would you believe it, she didn't like Ivan, and hardly greeted him? I had a lot of talk with Katya in Moscow. I told her about myself—sincerely, honourably. She listened to everything.

> There was sweet confusion.
> There were tender words.*

Though there were proud words, too. She wrung out of me a mighty promise to reform. I gave my promise, and here——"

"What?"

"Why, I called to you and brought you out here to-day, this very day—remember it—to send you—this very day again—to Katerina Ivanovna, and——"

"What?"

"To tell her that I shall never come to see her again. Say 'He sends you his compliments.' "

"But is that possible?"

"That's just the reason I'm sending you, in my place, because it's impossible. And, how could I tell her myself?"

---

*The source of these lines is unidentified.

"And where are you going?"

"To the back-alley."

"To Grushenka then!" Alyosha exclaimed mournfully, clasping his hands. "Can Rakitin really have told the truth? I thought that you had just visited her, and that was all."

"Can a betrothed man pay such visits? Is such a thing possible and with such a betrothed, and before the eyes of all the world? Confound it, I have some honour! As soon as I began visiting Grushenka, I ceased to be betrothed, and to be an honest man. I understand that. Why do you look at me? You see, I went in the first place to beat her. I had heard, and I know for a fact now, that that captain, father's agent, had given Grushenka an I. O. U. of mine for her to sue me for payment, so as to put an end to me. They wanted to scare me. I went to beat her. I had had a glimpse of her before. She doesn't strike one at first sight. I knew about her old merchant, who's lying ill now, paralysed; but he's leaving her a decent little sum. I knew, too, that she was fond of money, that she hoarded it, and lent it at a wicked rate of interest, that she's a merciless cheat and swindler. I went to beat her, and I stayed. The storm broke,—it struck me down like the plague. I'm plague-stricken still, and I know that everything is over, that there will never be anything more for me. The cycle of the ages is accomplished. That's my position. And though I'm a beggar, as fate would have it, I had three thousand just then in my pocket. I drove with Grushenka to Mokroe, a place twenty-five versts from here. I got gipsies there and champagne and made all the peasants there drunk on it, and all the women and girls. I sent the thousands flying. In three days' time I was stripped bare, but a hero. Do you suppose the hero had gained his end? Not a sign of it from her. I tell you that rogue, Grushenka, has a supple curve all over her body. You can see it in her little foot, even in her little toe. I saw it, and kissed it, but that was all I swear! 'I'll marry you if you like,' she said, 'you're a beggar you know. Say that you won't beat me, and will let me do anything I choose, and perhaps I will marry you.' She laughed, and she's laughing still!"

Dmitri leapt up with a sort of fury. He seemed all at once as though he were drunk. His eyes became suddenly bloodshot.

"And do you really mean to marry her?"

"At once, if she will. And if she won't, I shall stay all the same. I'll be the porter at her gate. Alyosha!" he cried. He stopped short before him, and taking him by the shoulders began shaking him violently, "Do you know, you innocent boy, that this is all delirium, senseless delirium, for there's a tragedy here. Let me tell you, Alexey, that I may be a low man, with low and degraded passions, but a thief and a pickpocket Dmitri Karamazov never can be. Well, then; let me tell you that I am a thief and a pickpocket. That very morning, just before I went to beat Grushenka, Katerina Ivanovna sent for me, and in strict secrecy (why I don't know, I suppose she had some reason) asked me to go to the chief town of the province and to post three thousand roubles to Agafya Ivanovna in Moscow, so that nothing should be known of it in the town here. So I had that three thousand roubles in my pocket when I went to see Grushenka, and it was that money we spent at Mokroe. Afterwards I pretended I had been to the town, but did not show her the post office receipt. I said I had sent the money and would bring the receipt, and so far I haven't brought it. I've forgotten it. Now what do you think you're going to her to-day to say. 'He sends his compliments,' and she'll ask you, 'What about the money? You might still have said to her, 'He's a degraded sensualist, and a low creature, with uncontrolled passions. He didn't send your money then, but wasted it, because, like a low brute, he couldn't control himself.' But still you might have added, 'He isn't a thief though. Here is your three thousand; he sends it back. Send it yourself to Agafya Ivanovna. But he told me to say "he sends his compliments."' But, as it is, she will ask, 'But where is the money?'"

"Mitya, you are unhappy, yes! But not as unhappy as you think. Don't worry yourself to death with despair."

"What, do you suppose I'd shoot myself because I can't get three thousand to pay back? That's just it. I shan't shoot myself. I haven't the strength now. Afterwards, perhaps. But now I'm going to Grushenka. I don't care what happens."

"And what then?"

"I'll be her husband if she deigns to have me, and when lovers come, I'll go into the next room. I'll clean her friends' goloshes, blow up their samovar, run their errands."

"Katerina Ivanovna will understand it all," Alyosha said solemnly. "She'll understand how great this trouble is and will forgive. She has a lofty mind, and no one could be more unhappy than you. She'll see that for herself."

"She won't forgive everything," said Dmitri, with a grin. "There's something in it, brother, that no woman could forgive. Do you know what would be the best thing to do?"

"What?"

"Pay back the three thousand."

"Where can we get it from? I say, I have two thousand. Ivan will give you another thousand—that makes three. Take it and pay it back."

"And when would you get it, your three thousand? You're not of age, besides, and you must—you absolutely must—take my farewell to her to-day, with the money or without it, for I can't drag on any longer, things have come to such a pass. To-morrow is too late. I shall send you to father."

"To father?"

"Yes, to father first. Ask him for three thousand."

"But, Mitya, he won't give it."

"As though he would! I know he won't. Do you know the meaning of despair, Alexey?"

"Yes."

"Listen. Legally he owes me nothing. I've had it all from him, I know that. But morally he owes me something, doesn't he? You know he started with twenty-eight thousand of my mother's money and made a hundred thousand with it. Let him give me back only three out of the twenty-eight thousand, and he'll draw my soul out of hell, and it will atone for many of his sins. For that three thousand—I give you my solemn word—I'll make an end of everything, and he shall hear nothing more of me. For the last time I give him the chance to be a father. Tell him God Himself sends him this chance."

"Mitya, he won't give it for anything."

"I know he won't. I know it perfectly well. Now, especially. That's not all. I know something more. Now, only a few days ago, perhaps only yes-terday he found out for the first time *in earnest* (underline *in earnest*) that Grushenka is really perhaps not joking, and really means to marry me. He knows her nature; he knows the cat. And do you suppose he's going to give me money to help to bring that about when he's crazy about her him-self? And that's not all, either. I can tell you more than that. I know that for the last five days he has had three thousand drawn out of the bank, changed into notes of a hundred roubles, packed into a large envelope, sealed with five seals, and tied across with red tape. You see how well I know all about it! On the envelope is written: 'To my angel, Grushenka, when she will come to me.' He scrawled it himself in silence and in secret, and no one knows that the money's there except the valet, Smerdyakov, whom he trusts like himself. So now he has been expecting Grushenka for the last three or four days; he hopes she'll come for the money. He has sent her word of it, and she has sent him word that perhaps she'll come. And if she does go to the old man, can I marry her after that? You understand now why I'm here in secret and what I'm on the watch for."

"For her?"

"Yes, for her. Foma has a room in the house of these sluts here. Foma comes from our parts; he was a soldier in our regiment. He does jobs for them. He's watchman at night and goes grouse shooting in the day-time; and that's how he lives. I've established myself in his room. Neither he nor the women of the house know the secret—that is, that I am on the watch here."

"No one but Smerdyakov knows, then?"

"No one else. He will let me know if she goes to the old man."

"It was he told you about the money, then?"

"Yes. It's a dead secret. Even Ivan doesn't know about the money, or anything. The old man is sending Ivan to Tchermashnya on a two or three days' journey. A purchaser has turned up for the copse; he'll give eight thousand for the timber. So the old man keeps asking Ivan to help him by going to arrange it. It will take him two or three days. That's what the old man wants, so that Grushenka can come while he's away."

"Then he's expecting Grushenka to-day?"

"No, she won't come to-day; there are signs. She's certain not to come," cried Mitya suddenly. "Smerdyakov thinks so, too. Father's drinking now. He's sitting at table with Ivan. Go to him, Alyosha, and ask for the three thousand."

"Mitya, dear, what's the matter with you?" cried Alyosha, jumping up from his place, and looking keenly at his brother's frenzied face. For one moment the thought struck him that Dmitri was mad.

"What is it? I'm not insane," said Dmitri, looking intently and earnestly at him. "No fear. I am sending you to father, and I know what I'm saying. I believe in miracles."

"In miracles?"

"In a miracle of Divine Providence. God knows my heart. He sees my despair. He sees the whole picture. Surely He won't let something awful happen. Alyosha. I believe in miracles. Go!"

"I am going. Tell me, will you wait for me here?"

"Yes. I know it will take some time. You can't go at him point blank. He's drunk now. I'll wait three hours—four, five, six, seven. Only remember you must go to Katerina Ivanovna to-day, if it has to be at midnight, *with the money or without the money,* and say, 'He sends his compliments to you.' I want you to say that verse to her: 'He sends his compliments to you.' "

"Mitya! And what if Grushenka comes to-day—if not to-day, to-mor-row, or the next day?"

"Grushenka? I shall see her. I shall rush out and prevent it."

"And if——?"

"If there's an if, it will be murder. I couldn't endure it."

"Who will be murdered?"

"The old man. I shan't kill her."

"Brother, what are you saying?"

"Oh, I don't know. . . . I don't know. Perhaps I shan't kill him, and per-haps I shall. I'm afraid that he will suddenly become so loathsome to me with his face at that moment. I hate his ugly throat, his nose, his eyes, his shameless snigger. I feel a physical repulsion. That's what I'm afraid of. That's what may be too much for me."

"I'll go, Mitya. I believe that God will order things for the best, that nothing awful may happen."

"And I will sit and wait for the miracle. And if it doesn't come to pass——"

Alyosha went thoughtfully towards his father's house.

6

SMERDYAKOV

H E did in fact find his father still at table. Though there was a dining-room in the house, the table was laid as usual in the drawing-room, which was the largest room, and furnished with old-fashioned os-tentation. The furniture was white and very old, upholstered in old, red, silky material. In the spaces between the windows there were mirrors in elaborate white and gilt frames, of old-fashioned carving. On the walls, covered with white paper, which was torn in many places, there hung two large portraits—one of some prince who had been governor of the district thirty years before, and the other of some bishop, also long since dead. In the corner opposite the door there were several ikons, before which a lamp was lighted at nightfall . . . not so much for devotional purposes as to light the room. Fyodor Pavlovitch used to go to bed very late, at three or four o'clock in the morning, and would wander about the room at night or sit in an armchair, thinking. This had become a habit with him. He often slept quite alone in the house, sending his servants to the lodge; but usually Smerdyakov remained on a bench in the hall.

When Alyosha came in, dinner was over, but coffee and preserves had been served. Fyodor Pavlovitch liked sweet things with brandy after dinner. Ivan was also at table, sipping coffee. The servants, Grigory and Smerdyakov, were standing by. Both the gentlemen and the servants seemed in singularly good spirits. Fyodor Pavlovitch was roaring with laughter. Before he entered the room, Alyosha heard the shrill laugh he knew so well, and could tell from the sound of it that his father had only reached the good-humoured stage, and was far from being completely drunk.

"Here he is! Here he is!" yelled Fyodor Pavlovitch, highly delighted at seeing Alyosha. "Join us. Sit down. Coffee is a lenten dish, but it's hot and good. I don't offer you brandy, you're keeping the fast. But would you like some? No; I'd better give you some of our famous liqueur. Smerdyakov, go to the cupboard, the second shelf on the right. Here are the keys. Look sharp!"

Alyosha began refusing the liqueur.

"Never mind. If you won't have it, we will," said Fyodor Pavlovitch, beaming. "But stay—have you dined?"

"Yes," answered Alyosha, who had in truth only eaten a piece of bread and drunk a glass of kvass in the Father Superior's kitchen. "Though I shall be pleased to have some hot coffee."

"Bravo, my darling! He'll have some coffee. Does it want warming? No, it's boiling. It's capital coffee: Smerdyakov's making. My Smerdyakov's an artist at coffee and at fish patties, and at fish soup, too. You must come one day and have some fish soup. Let me know beforehand. . . . But, stay; didn't I tell you this morning to come home with your mattress and pillow and all? Have you brought your mattress? He, he, he!"

"No, I haven't," said Alyosha, smiling, too.

"Ah, but you were frightened, you were frightened this morning, weren't you? There, my darling, I couldn't do anything to vex you. Do you know, Ivan, I can't resist the way he looks one straight in the face and laughs? It makes me laugh all over. I'm so fond of him. Alyosha, let me give you my blessing—a father's blessing."

Alyosha rose, but Fyodor Pavlovitch had already changed his mind.

"No, no," he said, "I'll just make the sign of the cross over you, for now. Sit still. Now we've a treat for you, in your own line, too. It'll make you laugh. Balaam's ass has begun talking to us here*—and how he talks! How he talks!"

Balaam's ass, it appeared, was the valet, Smerdyakov. He was a young man of about four and twenty, remarkably unsociable and taciturn. Not that he was shy or bashful. On the contrary, he was conceited and seemed to despise everybody.

But we must pause to say a few words about him now. He was brought up by Grigory and Marfa, but the boy grew up "with no sense of gratitude," as Grigory expressed it; he was an unfriendly boy, and seemed to look at the world mistrustfully. In his childhood he was very fond of hanging cats, and burying them with great ceremony. He used to dress up in a sheet as though it were a surplice, and sang, and waved some object over the dead cat as though it were a censer. All this he did on the sly, with the greatest secrecy. Grigory caught him once at this diversion and gave him a sound beating. He shrank into a corner and sulked there for a week. "He doesn't care for you or me, the monster," Grigory used to say to Marfa, "and he doesn't care for any one. Are you a human being?" he said, addressing the boy directly. "You're not a human being. You grew from the mildew in the bath-house.† That's what you are." Smerdyakov, it appeared afterwards, could never forgive him those words. Grigory taught him to read and write, and when he was twelve years old, began teaching him the Scriptures. But this teaching came to nothing. At the second or third lesson the boy suddenly grinned.

"What's that for?" asked Grigory, looking at him threateningly from under his spectacles.

"Oh, nothing. God created light on the first day, and the sun, moon, and stars on the fourth day.‡ Where did the light come from on the first day?"

Grigory was thunderstruck. The boy looked sarcastically at his teacher. There was something positively condescending in his expression. Grigory could not restrain himself. "I'll show you where!" he cried, and gave the boy a violent slap on the cheek. The boy took the slap without a word, but withdrew into his corner again for some days. A week later he had his first attack of the disease to which he was subject all the rest of his life— epilepsy. When Fyodor Pavlovitch heard of it, his attitude to the boy seemed changed at once. Till then he had taken no notice of him, though he never scolded him, and always gave him a kopeck when he met him. Sometimes, when he was in good humour, he would send the boy something sweet from his table. But as soon as he heard of his illness, he showed an active interest in him, sent for a doctor, and tried remedies, but the disease turned out to be incurable. The fits occurred, on an average, once

---

*See Numbers 22:21–33, in which Balaam's ass finally speaks to save its master.
†A proverbial expression in Russia (translator's note).
‡See Genesis 1:3–5, 14–19.

a month, but at various intervals. The fits varied too, in violence: some were light and some were very severe. Fyodor Pavlovitch strictly forbade Grigory to use corporal punishment to the boy, and began allowing him to come upstairs to him. He forbade him to be taught anything whatever for a time, too. One day when the boy was about fifteen, Fyodor Pavlovitch noticed him lingering by the bookcase, and reading the titles through the glass. Fyodor Pavlovitch had a fair number of books—over a hundred—but no one ever saw him reading. He at once gave Smerdyakov the key of the bookcase. "Come, read. You shall be my librarian. You'll be better sitting reading than hanging about the courtyard. Come, read this," and Fyodor Pavlovitch gave him "Evenings in a Cottage near Dikanka."*

He read a little, but didn't like it. He did not once smile, and ended by frowning.

"Why? Isn't it funny?" asked Fyodor Pavlovitch.

Smerdyakov did not speak.

"Answer, stupid!"

"It's all untrue," mumbled the boy, with a grin.

"Then go to the devil! You have the soul of a lackey. Stay, here's Smaragdov's 'Universal History.'† That's all true. Read that."

But Smerdyakov did not get through ten pages of Smaragdov. He thought it dull. So the bookcase was closed again.

Shortly afterwards Marfa and Grigory reported to Fyodor Pavlovitch that Smerdyakov was gradually beginning to show an extraordinary fastidiousness. He would sit before his soup, take up his spoon and look into the soup, bend over it, examine it, take a spoonful and hold it to the light.

"What is it? A beetle?" Grigory would ask.

"A fly, perhaps," observed Marfa.

The squeamish youth never answered, but he did the same with his bread, his meat, and everything he ate. He would hold a piece on his fork to the light, scrutinise it microscopically, and only after long deliberation decide to put it in his mouth.

"Ach! What fine gentlemen's airs!" Grigory muttered, looking at him.

When Fyodor Pavlovitch heard of this development in Smerdyakov he determined to make him his cook, and sent him to Moscow to be trained. He spent some years there and came back remarkably changed in appearance. He looked extraordinarily old for his age. His face had grown wrinkled, yellow, and strangely emasculate. In character he seemed almost exactly the same as before he went away. He was just as unsociable, and showed not the slightest inclination for any companionship. In Moscow, too, as we heard afterwards, he had always been silent. Moscow itself had little interest for him; he saw very little there, and took scarcely any notice of anything. He went once to the theatre, but returned silent and displeased with it. On the other hand, he came back to us from Moscow well dressed, in a clean coat and

---

*First collection of short stories (1831–1832) by the Russian author Nikolai Gogol.
†Reference to a history textbook by S. N. Smaragdov used in the lower schools.

clean linen. He brushed his clothes most scrupulously twice a day invariably, and was very fond of cleaning his smart calf boots with a special English polish, so that they shone like mirrors. He turned out a first-rate cook. Fyodor Pavlovitch paid him a salary, almost the whole of which Smerdyakov spent on clothes, pomade, perfumes, and such things. But he seemed to have as much contempt for the female sex as for men; he was discreet, almost unapproachable, with them. Fyodor Pavlovitch began to regard him rather differently. His fits were becoming more frequent, and on the days he was ill Marfa cooked, which did not suit Fyodor Pavlovitch at all.

"Why are your fits getting worse?" asked Fyodor Pavlovitch, looking askance at his new cook. "Would you like to get married? Shall I find you a wife?"

But Smerdyakov turned pale with anger, and made no reply. Fyodor Pavlovitch left him with an impatient gesture. The great thing was that he had absolute confidence in his honesty. It happened once, when Fyodor Pavlovitch was drunk, that he dropped in the muddy courtyard three hundred-rouble notes which he had only just received. He only missed them next day, and was just hastening to search his pockets when he saw the notes lying on the table. Where had they come from? Smerdyakov had picked them up and brought them in the day before.

"Well, my lad, I've never met any one like you," Fyodor Pavlovitch said shortly, and gave him ten roubles. We may add that he not only believed in his honesty, but had, for some reason, a liking for him, although the young man looked as morosely at him as at every one and was always silent. He rarely spoke. If it had occurred to any one to wonder at the time what the young man was interested in, and what was in his mind, it would have been impossible to tell by looking at him. Yet he used sometimes to stop suddenly in the house, or even in the yard or street, and would stand still for ten minutes, lost in thought. A physiognomist studying his face would have said that there was no thought in it, no reflection, but only a sort of contemplation. There is a remarkable picture by the painter Kramskoy, called "Contemplation."[2] There is a forest in winter, and on a roadway through the forest, in absolute solitude, stands a peasant in a torn kaftan and bark shoes. He stands, as it were, lost in thought. Yet he is not thinking; he is "contemplating." If any one touched him he would start and look at one as though awakening and bewildered. It's true he would come to himself immediately; but if he were asked what he had been thinking about, he would remember nothing. Yet probably he has hidden within himself, the impression which had dominated him during the period of contemplation. Those impressions are dear to him and no doubt he hoards them imperceptibly, and even unconsciously. How and why, of course, he does not know either. He may suddenly, after hoarding impressions for many years, abandon everything and go off to Jerusalem on a pilgrimage for his soul's salvation, or perhaps he will suddenly set fire to his native village, and perhaps do both. There are a good many "contemplatives" among the peasantry. Well, Smerdyakov was probably one of them, and he probably was greedily hoarding up his impressions, hardly knowing why.

7

THE CONTROVERSY

BUT Balaam's ass had suddenly spoken. The subject was a strange one. Grigory had gone in the morning to make purchases, and had heard from the shopkeeper Lukyanov the story of a Russian soldier which had appeared in the newspaper of that day. This soldier had been taken prisoner in some remote part of Asia, and was threatened with an immediate agonising death if he did not renounce Christianity and follow Islam. He refused to deny his faith, and was tortured, flayed alive, and died, praising and glorifying Christ. Grigory had related the story at table. Fyodor Pavlovitch always liked, over the dessert after dinner, to laugh and talk, if only with Grigory. This afternoon he was in a particularly good-humoured and expansive mood. Sipping his brandy and listening to the story, he observed that they ought to make a saint of a soldier like that, and to take his skin to some monastery. "That would make the people flock, and bring the money in."

Grigory frowned, seeing that Fyodor Pavlovitch was by no means touched, but, as usual, was beginning to scoff. At that moment, Smerdyakov, who was standing by the door, smiled. Smerdyakov often waited at table towards the end of dinner, and since Ivan's arrival in our town he had done so every day.

"What are you grinning at?" asked Fyodor Pavlovitch, catching the smile instantly, and knowing that it referred to Grigory.

"Well, my opinion is," Smerdyakov began suddenly and unexpectedly in a loud voice, "that if that laudable soldier's exploit was so very great there would have been, to my thinking, no sin in it if he had on such an emergency renounced, so to speak, the name of Christ and his own christening, to save by that same his life, for good deeds, by which, in the course of years to expiate his cowardice."

"How could it not be a sin? You're talking nonsense. For that you'll go straight to hell and be roasted there like mutton," put in Fyodor Pavlovitch.

It was at this point that Alyosha came in, and Fyodor Pavlovitch, as we have seen, was highly delighted at his appearance.

"We're on your subject, your subject," he chuckled gleefully, making Alyosha sit down to listen.

"As for mutton, that's not so, and there'll be nothing there for this, and there shouldn't be either, if it's according to justice," Smerdyakov maintained stoutly.

"How do you mean 'according to justice'?" Fyodor Pavlovitch cried still more gaily, nudging Alyosha with his knee.

"He's a rascal, that's what he is!" burst from Grigory. He looked Smerdyakov wrathfully in the face.

"As for being a rascal, wait a little, Grigory Vassilyevitch," answered Smerdyakov with perfect composure. "You'd better consider yourself that, once I am taken prisoner by the enemies of the Christian race, and they demand from me to curse the name of God and to renounce my holy christening, I am fully entitled to act by my own reason, since there would be no sin in it."

"But you've said that before. Don't waste words. Prove it," cried Fyodor Pavlovitch.

"Soup maker!" muttered Grigory contemptuously.

"As for being a soup maker, wait a bit, too, and consider for yourself, Grigory Vassilyevitch, without abusing me. For as soon as I say to those enemies, 'No, I'm not a Christian, and I curse my true God,' then at once, by God's high judgment, I become immediately and specially anathema accursed, and am cut off from the Holy Church, exactly as though I were a heathen, so that at that very instant, not only when I say it aloud, but when I think of saying it, before a quarter of a second has passed, I am cut off. Is that so or not, Grigory Vassilyevitch?"

He addressed Grigory with obvious satisfaction, though he was really answering Fyodor Pavlovitch's questions, and was well aware of it, and intentionally pretending that Grigory had asked the questions.

"Ivan," cried Fyodor Pavlovitch suddenly, "stoop down for me to whisper. He's got this all up for your benefit. He wants you to praise him. Praise him."

Ivan listened with perfect seriousness to his father's excited whisper.

"Stay, Smerdyakov, be quiet a minute," cried Fyodor Pavlovitch once more. "Ivan, your ear again."

Ivan bent down again with a perfectly grave face.

"I love you as I do Alyosha. Don't think I don't love you. Some brandy?"

"Yes." "But you're rather drunk yourself," thought Ivan, looking steadily at his father.

He was watching Smerdyakov with great curiosity.

"You're anathema accursed, as it is," Grigory suddenly burst out, "and how dare you argue, you rascal, after that, if. . . ."

"Don't scold him, Grigory, don't scold him," Fyodor Pavlovitch cut him short.

"You should wait, Grigory Vassilyevitch, if only a short time, and listen, for I haven't finished all I had to say. For at the very moment I become accursed, at that same highest moment, I become exactly like a heathen, and my christening is taken off me and becomes of no avail. Isn't that so?"

"Make haste and finish, my boy," Fyodor Pavlovitch urged him, sipping from his wine-glass with relish.

"And if I've ceased to be a Christian, then I told no lie to the enemy when they asked whether I was a Christian or not a Christian, seeing I had already been relieved by God Himself of my Christianity by reason of the thought alone, before I had time to utter a word to the enemy. And if

I have already been discharged, in what manner and with what sort of justice can I be held responsible as a Christian in the other world for having denied Christ, when, through the very thought alone, before denying Him I had been relieved from my christening? If I'm no longer a Christian, then I can't renounce Christ, for I've nothing then to renounce. Who will hold an unclean Tatar responsible, Grigory Vassilyevitch, even in heaven, for not having been born a Christian? And who would punish him for that, considering that you can't take two skins off one ox? For God Almighty Himself, even if He did make the Tatar responsible, when he dies would give him the smallest possible punishment, I imagine (since he must be punished) judging that he is not to blame if he has come into the world an unclean heathen, from heathen parents. The Lord God can't surely take a Tatar and say he was a Christian? That would mean that the Almighty would tell a real untruth. And can the Lord of Heaven and Earth tell a lie, even in one word?"

Grigory was thunderstruck and looked at the orator, his eyes nearly starting out of his head. Though he did not clearly understand what was said, he had caught something in this rigmarole, and stood, looking like a man who has just hit his head against a wall. Fyodor Pavlovitch emptied his glass and went off into his shrill laugh.

"Alyosha! Alyosha! What do you say to that! Ah, you casuist! He must have been with the Jesuits somewhere, Ivan. Oh, you stinking Jesuit, who taught you? But you're talking nonsense, you casuist, nonsense, nonsense, nonsense. Don't cry, Grigory, we'll reduce him to smoke and ashes in a moment. Tell me this, oh, ass; you may be right before your enemies, but you have renounced your faith all the same in your own heart, and you say yourself that in that very hour you became anathema accursed. And if once you're anathema they won't pat you on the head for it in hell. What do you say to that, my fine Jesuit?"

"There is no doubt that I have renounced it in my own heart, but there was no special sin in that. Or if there was sin, it was the most ordinary."

"How's that the most ordinary?"

"You lie, accursed one!" hissed Grigory.

"Consider yourself, Grigory Vassilyevitch," Smerdyakov went on, staid and unruffled, conscious of his triumph, but, as it were, generous to the vanquished foe. "Consider yourself, Grigory Vassilyevitch; it is said in the Scripture that if you have faith, even as a mustard seed, and bid a mountain move into the sea, it will move without the least delay at your bidding.* Well, Grigory Vassilyevitch, if I'm without faith and you have so great a faith that you are continually swearing at me, you try yourself telling this mountain, not to move into the sea for that's a long way off, but even to our stinking little river which runs at the bottom of the garden. You'll see for yourself that it won't budge, but will remain just where it is however much you shout at it, and that shows, Grigory Vassilyevitch, that

---

*See Matthew 17:20 and 21:21.

you haven't faith in the proper manner, and only abuse others about it. Again, taking into consideration that no one in our day, not only you, but actually no one, from the highest person to the lowest peasant can shove mountains into the sea—except perhaps some one man in the world, or, at most, two, and they most likely are saving their souls in secret somewhere in the Egyptian desert, so you wouldn't find them—if so it be, if all the rest have no faith, will God curse all the rest? that is, the population of the whole earth, except about two hermits in the desert, and in His well-known mercy will He not forgive one of them? And so I'm persuaded that though I may once have doubted, I shall be forgiven if I shed tears of repentance."

"Stay!" cried Fyodor Pavlovitch, in a transport of delight. "So you do suppose there are two who can move mountains? Ivan, make a note of it, write it down. There you have the Russian all over!"

"You're quite right in saying it's characteristic of the people's faith," Ivan assented, with an approving smile.

"You agree. Then it must be so, if you agree. It's true, isn't it, Alyosha? That's the Russian faith all over, isn't it?"

"No, Smerdyakov has not the Russian faith at all," said Alyosha firmly and gravely.

"I'm not talking about his faith. I mean those two in the desert, only that idea. Surely that's Russian, isn't it?"

"Yes, that's purely Russian," said Alyosha smiling.

"Your words are worth a gold piece, oh, ass, and I'll give it to you today. But as to the rest you talk nonsense, nonsense, nonsense. Let me tell you, stupid, that we here are all of little faith, only from carelessness, because we haven't time; things are too much for us, and, in the second place, the Lord God has given us so little time, only twenty-four hours in the day, so that one hasn't even time to get sleep enough, much less to repent of one's sins. While you have denied your faith to your enemies when you'd nothing else to think about but to show your faith! So I consider, brother, that it constitutes a sin."

"Constitute a sin it may, but consider yourself, Grigory Vassilyevitch, that it only extenuates it, if it does constitute. If I had believed then in very truth, as I ought to have believed, then it really would have been sinful if I had not faced tortures for my faith, and had gone over to the pagan Mohammedan faith. But, of course, it wouldn't have come to torture then, because I should only have had to say at that instant to the mountain 'move and crush the tormentor,' and it would have moved and at the very instant have crushed him like a black-bettle, and I should have walked away as though nothing had happened, praising and glorifying God. But, suppose at that very moment I had tried all that, and cried to that mountain, 'Crush these tormentors,' and it hadn't crushed them, how could I have helped doubting, pray, at such a time, and at such a dread hour of mortal terror? And apart from that, I should know already that I could not attain to the fulness of the Kingdom of Heaven (for since the mountain had not moved at my word, they could not think very much of my faith up aloft, and there could be no very great reward awaiting me in the world to come). So why should I let them flay the skin off me as well, and to no good purpose? For, even though they had flayed my skin half off my back, even then the mountain would not have moved at my word or at my cry. And at such a moment not only doubt might come over one but one might lose one's reason from fear, so that one would not be able to think at all. And, therefore, how should I be particularly to blame if not seeing my advantage or reward there or here, I should, at least, save my skin. And so trusting fully in the grace of the Lord I should cherish the hope that I might be altogether forgiven."

8

OVER THE BRANDY

THE controversy was over. But strange to say Fyodor Pavlovitch, who had been so gay, suddenly began frowning. He frowned and gulped brandy, and it was already a glass too much.

"Get along with you, Jesuits!" he cried to the servants. "Go away, Smerdyakov. I'll send you the gold piece I promised you to-day, but be off! Don't cry, Grigory. Go to Marfa. She'll comfort you and put you to bed. The rascals won't let us sit in peace after dinner," he snapped peevishly, as the servants promptly withdrew at his word.

"Smerdyakov always pokes himself in now, after dinner. It's you he's so interested in. What have you done to fascinate him?" he added to Ivan.

"Nothing whatever," answered Ivan. "He's pleased to have a high opinion of me; he's a lackey and a mean soul. Raw material for revolution, however, when the time comes."

"For revolution?"

"There will be others and better ones. But there will be some like him as well. His kind will come first, and better ones after."

"And when will the time come?"

"The rocket will go off and fizzle out, perhaps. The peasants are not very fond of listening to these soup makers, so far."

"Ah, brother, but a Balaam's ass like that thinks and thinks, and the devil knows where he gets to."

"He's storing up ideas," said Ivan, smiling.

"You see, I know he can't bear me, nor any one else, even you, though you fancy that he has a high opinion of you. Worse still with Alyosha, he despises Alyosha. But he doesn't steal, that's one thing, and he's not a gossip, he holds his tongue, and doesn't wash our dirty linen in public. He makes capital fish pasties too. But, damn him, is he worth talking about so much?"

"Of course he isn't."

"And as for the ideas he may be hatching, the Russian peasant, generally speaking, needs thrashing. That I've always maintained. Our peasants are swindlers, and don't deserve to be pitied, and it's a good thing they're still flogged sometimes. Russia is rich in birches. If they destroyed the forests, it would be the ruin of Russia. I stand up for the clever people. We've left off thrashing the peasants, we've grown so clever, but they go on thrashing themselves. And a good thing too. 'For with what measure ye mete it shall be measured to you again,'* or how does it go? Anyhow, it will be measured. But Russia's all swinishness. My dear, if you only knew how I hate Russia. . . . That is, not Russia, but all this vice! But maybe I mean Russia. *Tout cela c'est de la cochonnerie*†. . . . Do you know what I like? I like wit."

"You've had another glass. That's enough."

"Wait a bit. I'll have one more, and then another, and then I'll stop. No, stay, you interrupted me. At Mokroe I was talking to an old man, and he told me: 'There's nothing we like so much as sentencing girls to be thrashed, and we always give the lads the job of thrashing them. And the girl he has thrashed to-day, the young man will ask in marriage to-morrow. So it quite suits the girls, too,' he said. There's a set of de Sades for you![3] But it's clever, anyway. Shall we go over and have a look at it, eh? Alyosha, are you blushing? Don't be bashful, child. I'm sorry I didn't stay to dinner at the Superior's and tell the monks about the girls at Mokroe. Alyosha, don't be angry that I offended your Superior this morning. I lost my temper. If there is a God, if He exists, then, of course, I'm to blame, and I shall have to answer for it. But if there isn't a God at all, what do they deserve, your fathers? It's not enough to cut their heads off, for they keep back progress. Would you believe it, Ivan, that that lacerates my sentiments? No, you don't believe it as I see from your eyes. You believe what people say, that I'm nothing but a buffoon. Alyosha, do you believe that I'm nothing but a buffoon?"

"No, I don't believe it."

"And I believe you don't, and that you speak the truth. You look sincere and you speak sincerely. But not Ivan. Ivan's supercilious. . . . I'd make an end of your monks, though, all the same. I'd take all that mystic stuff and suppress it, once for all, all over Russia, so as to bring all the fools to reason. And the gold and the silver that would flow into the mint!"

"But why suppress it?" asked Ivan.

"That Truth may prevail. That's why."

"Well, if Truth were to prevail, you know, you'd be the first to be robbed and suppressed."

---

*See Matthew 7:2.

†That's all swinishness (French).

"Ah! I daresay you're right. Ah, I'm an ass!" burst out Fyodor Pavlovitch, striking himself lightly on the forehead.

"Well, your monastery may stand then, Alyosha, if that's how it is. And we clever people will sit snug and enjoy our brandy. You know, Ivan, it must have been so ordained by the Almighty Himself. Ivan, speak, is there a God or not? Stay, speak the truth, speak seriously. Why are you laughing again?"

"I'm laughing that you should have made a clever remark just now about Smerdyakov's belief in the existence of two saints who could move mountains."

"Why, am I like him now, then?"

"Very much."

"Well, that shows I'm a Russian, too, and I have a Russian characteristic. And you may be caught in the same way, though you are a philosopher. Shall I catch you? What do you bet that I'll catch you to-morrow. Speak, all the same, is there a God, or not? Only, be serious. I want you to be serious now."

"No, there is no God."

"Alyosha, is there a God?"

"There is."

"Ivan, and is there immortality of some sort, just a little, just a tiny bit?"

"There is no immortality either."

"None at all?"

"None at all."

"There's absolute nothingness then. Perhaps there is just something? Anything is better than nothing!"

"Absolute nothingness."

"Alyosha, is there immortality?"

"There is."

"God and immortality?"

"God and immortality. In God is immortality."

"H'm! It's more likely Ivan's right. Good Lord! to think what faith, what force of all kinds, man has lavished for nothing, on that dream, and for how many thousand years. Who is it laughing at man? Ivan! For the last time, once for all, is there a God or not? I ask for the last time?"

"And for the last time there is not."

"Who is laughing at mankind, Ivan?"

"It must be the devil," said Ivan, smiling.

"And the devil? Does he exist?"

"No, there's no devil either."

"It's a pity. Damn it all, what wouldn't I do to the man who first invented God! Hanging on a bitter aspen tree would be too good for him."

"There would have been no civilisation if they hadn't invented God."

"Wouldn't there have been? Without God?"

"No. And there would have been no brandy either. But I must take your brandy away from you, anyway."

"Stop, stop, stop, dear boy, one more little glass. I've hurt Alyosha's feelings. You're not angry with me, Alyosha? My dear little Alexey!"

"No, I am not angry. I know your thoughts. Your heart is better than your head."

"My heart better than my head, is it? Oh Lord! And that from you. Ivan, do you love Alyosha?"

"Yes."

"You must love him" (Fyodor Pavlovitch was by this time very drunk). "Listen, Alyosha, I was rude to your elder this morning. But I was excited. But there's wit in that elder, don't you think, Ivan?"

"Very likely."

"There is, there is. *Il y a du Piron là dedans.*[4] He's a Jesuit, a Russian one, that is. As he's an honourable person there's a hidden indignation boiling within him at having to pretend and affect holiness."

"But, of course, he believes in God."

"Not a bit of it. Didn't you know? Why, he tells every one of himself. That is, not every one, but all the clever people who come to him. He said straight out to Governor Schultz not long ago: 'Credo, but I don't know in what.'"

"Really?"

"He really did. But I respect him. There's something of Mephistopheles* about him, or rather of 'The hero of our time.' . . . Arbenin, or what's his name?[5] . . . You see, he's a sensualist. He's such a sensualist that I should be afraid for my daughter or my wife if she went to confess to him. You know, when he begins telling stories. . . . The year before last he invited us to tea, tea with liqueur (the ladies send him liqueur) and began telling us about old times till we nearly split our sides. . . . Especially how he once cured a paralysed woman. 'If my legs were not bad I know a dance I could dance you,' he said. What do you say to that? 'I've plenty of tricks in my time,' said he. He did Demidov, the merchant, out of sixty-thousand."

"What, he stole it?"

"He brought him the money as a man he could trust, saying, 'Take care of it for me, friend, there'll be a police search at my place to-morrow.' And he kept it. 'You have given it to the Church,' he declared. I said to him: 'You're a scoundrel,' I said. 'No,' said he, 'I'm not a scoundrel, but I'm broad-minded.' But that wasn't he, that was some one else. I've muddled him with some one else . . . without noticing it. Come, another glass and that's enough. Take away the bottle, Ivan. I've been telling lies. Why didn't you stop me, Ivan, and tell me I was lying?"

"I knew you'd stop of yourself."

"That's a lie. You did it from spite, from simple spite against me. You despise me. You have come to me and despised me in my own house."

"Well, I'm going away. You've had too much brandy."

"I've begged you for Christ's sake to go to Tchermashnya for a day or two, and you don't go."

"I'll go to-morrow if you're so set upon it."

*Personification of the devil, popularized in Goethe's dramatic poem *Faust* (1808, 1832).

"You won't go. You want to keep an eye on me. That's what you want, spiteful fellow. That's why you won't go."

The old man persisted. He had reached that state of drunkenness when the drunkard who has till then been inoffensive tries to pick a quarrel and to assert himself.

"Why are you looking at me? Why do you look like that? Your eyes look at me and say, 'You ugly drunkard!' Your eyes are mistrustful. They're contemptuous.... You've come here with some design. Alyosha, here, looks at me and his eyes shine. Alyosha doesn't despise me. Alexey, you mustn't love Ivan."

"Don't be ill-tempered with my brother. Leave off attacking him," Alyosha said emphatically.

"Oh, all right. Ugh, my head aches. Take away the brandy, Ivan. It's the third time I've told you."

He mused, and suddenly a slow, cunning grin spread over his face.

"Don't be angry with a feeble old man, Ivan. I know you don't love me, but don't be angry all the same. You've nothing to love me for. You go to Tchermashnya. I'll come to you myself and bring you a present. I'll show you a little wench there. I've had my eye on her a long time. She's still running about bare-foot. Don't be afraid of bare-footed wenches—don't despise them—they're pearls!"

And he kissed his hand with a smack.

"To my thinking," he revived at once, seeming to grow sober the instant he touched on his favourite topic. "To my thinking ... Ah, you boys! You children, little sucking-pigs, to my thinking ... I never thought a woman ugly in my life—that's been my rule! Can you understand that? How could you understand it? You've milk in your veins, not blood. You're not out of your shells yet. My rule has been that you can always find something devilishly interesting in every woman that you wouldn't find in any other. Only, one must know how to find it, that's the point! That's a talent! To my mind there are no ugly women. The very fact that she is a woman is half the battle ... but how could you understand that? Even in *vielles filles*,* even in them you may discover something that makes you simply wonder that men have been such fools as to let them grow old without noticing them. Bare-footed girls or unattractive ones, you must take by surprise. Didn't you know that? You must astound them till they're fascinated, upset, ashamed that such a gentleman should fall in love with such a little slut. It's a jolly good thing that there always are and will be masters and slaves in the world, so there always will be a little maid-of-all-work and her master, and you know, that's all that's needed for happiness. Stay ... listen, Alyosha, I always used to surprise your mother, but in a different way. I paid no attention to her at all, but all at once, when the minute came, I'd be all devotion to her, crawl on my knees, kiss her feet, and I always, always—I remember it as

---

*Old maids (French).

though it were to-day—reduced her to that tinkling, quiet, nervous queer little laugh. It was peculiar to her. I knew her attacks always used to begin like that, the next day she would begin shrieking hysterically, and that this little laugh was not a sign of delight, but it made a very good counterfeit. That's the great thing, to know how to take every one. Once Belyavsky—he was a handsome fellow, and rich—used to like to come here and hang about her—suddenly gave me a slap in the face in her presence. And she—such a mild sheep—why, I thought she would have knocked me down for that blow. How she set on me! 'You're beaten, beaten now,' she said, 'You've taken a blow from him. You have been trying to sell me to him,' she said. . . . 'And how dared he strike you in my presence! Don't dare come near me again, never, never! Run at once, challenge him to a duel!' . . . I took her to the monastery then to bring her to her senses. The holy Fathers prayed her back to reason. But I swear, by God, Alyosha, I never insulted the poor crazy girl! Only once, perhaps, in the first year; then she was very fond of praying. She used to keep the feasts of Our Lady particularly and used to turn me out of her room then. I'll knock that mysticism out of her, thought I! 'Here,' said I, 'you see your holy image. Here it is. Here I take it down. You believe it's miraculous, but here, I'll spit on it directly and nothing will happen to me for it!' . . . When she saw it, good Lord! I thought she would kill me. But she only jumped up, wrung her hands, then suddenly hid her face in them, began trembling all over and fell on the floor . . . fell all of a heap. Alyosha, Alyosha, what's the matter?"

The old man jumped up in alarm. From the time he had begun speaking about his mother, a change had gradually come over Alyosha's face. He flushed crimson, his eyes glowed, his lips quivered. The old sot had gone spluttering on, noticing nothing, till the moment when something very strange happened to Alyosha. Precisely what he was describing in the crazy woman was suddenly repeated with Alyosha. He jumped up from his seat exactly as his mother was said to have done, wrung his hands, hid his face in them, and fell back in his chair, shaking all over in an hysterical paroxysm of sudden violent, silent weeping. His extraordinary resemblance to his mother particularly impressed the old man.

"Ivan, Ivan! Water, quickly! It's like her, exactly as she used to be then, his mother. Spurt some water on him from your mouth, that's what I used to do to her. He's upset about his mother, his mother," he muttered to Ivan.

"But she was my mother, too, I believe, his mother. Was she not?" said Ivan, with uncontrolled anger and contempt. The old man shrank before his flashing eyes. But something very strange had happened, though only for a second; it seemed really to have escaped the old man's mind that Alyosha's mother actually was the mother of Ivan too.

"Your mother?" he muttered, not understanding, "What do you mean? What mother are you talking about? Was she? . . . Why, damn it! of course she was yours too! Damn it! My mind has never been so darkened before. Excuse me, why, I was thinking Ivan . . . He, he, he!" He stopped. A broad, drunken, half senseless grin overspread his face.

At that moment a fearful noise and clamour was heard in the hall, there were violent shouts, the door was flung open, and Dmitri burst into the room. The old man rushed to Ivan in terror.

"He'll kill me! He'll kill me! Don't let him get at me!" he screamed, clinging to the skirt of Ivan's coat.

9

THE SENSUALISTS

GRIGORY and Smerdyakov ran into the room after Dmitri. They had been struggling with him in the passage, refusing to admit him, acting on instructions given them by Fyodor Pavlovitch some days before. Taking advantage of the fact that Dmitri stopped a moment on entering the room to look about him, Grigory ran round the table, closed the double doors on the opposite side of the room leading to the inner apartments, and stood before the closed doors, stretching wide his arms, prepared to defend the entrance, so to speak, with the last drop of his blood. Seeing this, Dmitri uttered a scream rather than a shout and rushed at Grigory.

"Then she's there! She's hidden there! Out of the way, scoundrel!"

He tried to pull Grigory away, but the old servant pushed him back. Beside himself with fury, Dmitri struck out, and hit Grigory with all his might. The old man fell like a log, and Dmitri, leaping over him broke in the door. Smerdyakov remained pale and trembling at the other end of the room, huddling close to Fyodor Pavlovitch.

"She's here!" shouted Dmitri. "I saw her turn towards the house just now, but I couldn't catch her. Where is she? Where is she?"

That shout, "She's here!" produced an indescribable effect on Fyodor Pavlovitch. All his terror left him.

"Hold him! Hold him!" he cried, and dashed after Dmitri. Meanwhile Grigory had got up from the floor, but still seemed stunned. Ivan and Alyosha ran after their father. In the third room something was heard to fall on the floor with a ringing crash: it was a large glass vase—not an expensive one—on a marble pedestal which Dmitri had upset as he ran past it.

"At him!" shouted the old man. "Help!"

Ivan and Alyosha caught the old man and were forcibly bringing him back.

"Why do you run after him? He'll murder you outright," Ivan cried wrathfully at his father.

"Ivan! Alyosha! She must be here. Grushenka's here. He said he saw her himself, running."

He was choking. He was not expecting Grushenka at the time, and the sudden news that she was here made him beside himself. He was trembling all over. He seemed frantic.

"But you've seen for yourself that she hasn't come," cried Ivan.

"But she may have come by that other entrance."

"You know that entrance is locked, and you have the key."

Dmitri suddenly reappeared in the drawing-room. He had, of course, found the other entrance locked, and the key actually was in Fyodor Pavlovitch's pocket. The windows of all the rooms were also closed so Grushenka could not have come in anywhere nor have run out anywhere.

"Hold him!" shrieked Fyodor Pavlovitch, as soon as he saw him again. "He's been stealing money in my bedroom." And tearing himself from Ivan he rushed again at Dmitri. But Dmitri threw up both hands and suddenly clutched the old man by the two tufts of hair that remained on his temples, tugged at them, and flung him with a crash on the floor. He kicked him two or three times with his heel in the face. The old man moaned shrilly. Ivan, though not so strong as Dmitri, threw his arms round him, and with all his might pulled him away. Alyosha helped him with his slender strength, holding Dmitri in front.

"Madman! You've killed him!" cried Ivan.

"Serve him right!" shouted Dmitri breathlessly. "If I haven't killed him, I'll come again and kill him. You can't protect him!"

"Dmitri! Go away at once!" cried Alyosha commandingly.

"Alexey! You tell me. It's only you I can believe; was she here just now, or not? I saw her myself creeping this way by the fence from the lane. I shouted, she ran away."

"I swear she's not been here, and no one expected her."

"But I saw her. . . . So she must . . . I'll find out at once where she is. . . . Good-bye, Alexey! Not a word to Æsop about the money now. But go to Katerina Ivanovna at once and be sure to say, 'He sends his compliments to you!' Compliments, his compliments! Just compliments and farewell! Describe the scene to her."

Meanwhile Ivan and Grigory had raised the old man and seated him in an armchair. His face was covered with blood, but he was conscious and listened greedily to Dmitri's cries. He was still fancying that Grushenka really was somewhere in the house. Dmitri looked at him with hatred as he went out.

"I don't repent shedding your blood!" he cried. "Beware, old man, beware of your dream, for I have my dream, too. I curse you, and disown you altogether."

He ran out of the room.

"She's here. She must be here. Smerdyakov! Smerdyakov!" the old man wheezed, scarcely audibly, beckoning to him with his finger.

"No, she's not here, you old lunatic!" Ivan shouted at him angrily. "Here, he's fainting! Water! A towel! Make haste, Smerdyakov!"

Smerdyakov ran for water. At last they got the old man undressed, and put him to bed. They wrapped a wet towel round his head. Exhausted by the brandy, by his violent emotion, and the blows he had received, he shut his eyes and fell asleep as soon as his head touched the pillow. Ivan and Alyosha went back to the drawing-room. Smerdyakov removed the fragments of the broken vase, while Grigory stood by the table looking gloomily at the floor.

"Shouldn't you put a wet bandage on your head and go to bed, too?" Alyosha said to him. "We'll look after him. My brother gave you a terrible blow—on the head."

"He's insulted me!" Grigory articulated gloomily and distinctly.

"He's 'insulted' his father, not only you," observed Ivan with a forced smile.

"I used to wash him in his tub. He's insulted me," repeated Grigory.

"Damn it all, if I hadn't gulled him away perhaps he'd have murdered him. It wouldn't take much to do for Æsop, would it?" whispered Ivan to Alyosha.

"God forbid!" cried Alyosha.

"Why should He forbid?" Ivan went on in the same whisper, with a malignant grimace. "One reptile will devour the other. And serve them both right, too."

Alyosha shuddered.

"Of course I won't let him be murdered as I didn't just now. Stay here, Alyosha, I'll go for a turn in the yard. My head's begun to ache."

Alyosha went to his father's bedroom and sat by his bedside behind the screen for about an hour. The old man suddenly opened his eyes and gazed for a long while at Alyosha, evidently remembering and meditating. All at once his face betrayed extraordinary excitement.

"Alyosha," he whispered apprehensively, "where's Ivan?"

"In the yard. He's got a headache. He's on the watch."

"Give me that looking-glass. It stands over there. Give it me."

Alyosha gave him a little round folding looking-glass which stood on the chest of drawers. The old man looked at himself in it; his nose was considerably swollen, and on the left side of his forehead there was a rather large crimson bruise.

"What does Ivan say? Alyosha, my dear, my only son, I'm afraid of Ivan. I'm more afraid of Ivan than the other. You're the only one I'm not afraid of. . . ."

"Don't be afraid of Ivan either. He is angry, but he'll defend you."

"Alyosha, and what of the other? He's run to Grushenka. My angel, tell me the truth, was she here just now or not?"

"No one has seen her. It was a mistake. She has not been here."

"You know Mitya wants to marry her, to marry her."

"She won't marry him."

"She won't. She won't. She won't. She won't on any account!"

The old man fairly fluttered with joy, as though nothing more comforting could have been said to him. In his delight he seized Alyosha's hand and pressed it warmly to his heart. Tears positively glittered in his eyes.

"That image of the Mother of God of which I was telling you just now," he said. "Take it home and keep it for yourself. And I'll let you go back to the monastery. . . . I was joking this morning, don't be angry with me. My head aches, Alyosha. . . . Alyosha, comfort my heart. Be an angel and tell me the truth!"

"You're still asking whether she has been here or not?" Alyosha said sorrowfully.

"No, no, no. I believe you. I'll tell you what it is: you go to Grushenka yourself, or see her somehow; make haste and ask her; see for yourself, which she means to choose, him or me? Eh? What? can you?"

"If I see her I'll ask her," Alyosha muttered embarrassed.

"No, she won't tell you," the old man interrupted, "she's a rogue. She'll begin kissing you and say that it's you she wants. She's a deceitful, shameless hussy. You mustn't go to her, you mustn't!"

"No, father, and it wouldn't be suitable, it wouldn't be right at all."

"Where was he sending you just now? He shouted 'Go' as he ran away."

"To Katerina Ivanovna."

"For money? To ask her for money?"

"No. Not for money."

"He's no money; not a farthing. I'll settle down for the night, and think things over, and you can go. Perhaps you'll meet her. . . . Only be sure to come to me to-morrow in the morning. Be sure to. I have a word to say to you to-morrow. Will you come?"

"Yes."

"When you come, pretend you've come of your own accord to ask after me. Don't tell any one I told you to. Don't say a word to Ivan."

"Very well."

"Good-bye, my angel. You stood up for me, just now. I shall never forget it. I've a word to say to you to-morrow—but I must think about it."

"And how do you feel now?"

"I shall get up to-morrow and go out, perfectly well, perfectly well!"

Crossing the yard Alyosha found Ivan sitting on the bench at the gateway. He was sitting writing something in pencil in his note-book. Alyosha told Ivan that their father had waked up, was conscious, and had let him go back to sleep at the monastery.

"Alyosha, I should be very glad to meet you to-morrow morning," said Ivan cordially, standing up. His cordiality was a complete surprise to Alyosha.

"I shall be at the Hohlakovs' to-morrow," answered Alyosha, "I may be at Katerina Ivanovna's, too, if I don't find her now."

"But you're going to her now, anyway? For that 'compliments and farewell,'" said Ivan smiling. Alyosha was disconcerted.

"I think I quite understand his exclamations just now, and part of what went before. Dmitri has asked you to go to her and say that he—well, in fact—takes his leave of her?"

"Brother, how will all this horror end between father and Dmitri?" exclaimed Alyosha.

"One can't tell for certain. Perhaps in nothing: it may all fizzle out. That woman is a beast. In any case we must keep the old man indoors and not let Dmitri in the house."

"Brother, let me ask one thing more: has any man a right to look at other men and decide which is worthy to live?"

"Why bring in the question of worth? The matter is most often decided in men's hearts on other grounds much more natural. And as for rights— who has not the right to wish?"

"Not for another man's death?"

"What even if for another man's death? Why lie to oneself since all men live so and perhaps cannot help living so. Are you referring to what I said just now—that one reptile will devour the other? In that case let me ask you, do you think me like Dmitri capable of shedding Æsop's blood, murdering him, eh?"

"What are you saying, Ivan? Such an idea never crossed my mind. I don't think Dmitri is capable of it, either."

"Thanks, if only for that," smiled Ivan. "Be sure, I should always defend him. But in my wishes I reserve myself full latitude in this case. Good-bye till to-morrow. Don't condemn me, and don't look on me as a villain," he added with a smile.

They shook hands warmly as they had never done before. Alyosha felt that his brother had taken the first step towards him, and that he had certainly done this with some definite motive.

10

BOTH TOGETHER

ALYOSHA left his father's house feeling even more exhausted and dejected in spirit than when he had entered it. His mind too seemed shattered and unhinged, while he felt that he was afraid to put together the disjointed fragments and form a general idea from all the agonising and conflicting experiences of the day. He felt something bordering upon despair, which he had never known till then. Towering like a mountain above all the rest stood the fatal insoluble question: How would things end between his father and his brother Dmitri with this terrible woman? Now he had himself been a witness of it, he had been present and seen them face to face. Yet only his brother Dmitri could be made unhappy, terribly, completely unhappy: there was trouble awaiting him. It appeared too that there were other people concerned, far more so than Alyosha could have supposed before. There was something positively mysterious in it, too. Ivan had made a step towards him, which was what Alyosha had been long desiring. Yet now he felt for some reason that he was frightened at it. And these women? Strange to say, that morning he had set out for Katerina Ivanovna's in the greatest embarrassment; now he felt nothing of the kind. On the contrary, he was hastening there as though expecting to find guidance from her. Yet to give her this message was obviously more difficult than before. The matter of the three thousand was decided irrevocably, and Dmitri, feeling himself dishonoured and losing his last hope, might sink to any depth. He had, moreover, told him to describe to Katerina Ivanovna the scene which had just taken place with his father.

It was by now seven o'clock, and it was getting dark as Alyosha entered the very spacious and convenient house in the High Street occupied by Katerina Ivanovna. Alyosha knew that she lived with two aunts. One of them, a woman of little education, was that aunt of her half-sister Agafya Ivanovna who had looked after her in her father's house when she came from boarding-school. The other aunt was a Moscow lady of style and consequence, though in straitened circumstances. It was said that they both gave way in everything to Katerina Ivanovna, and that she only kept them with her as chaperones. Katerina Ivanovna herself gave way to no one but her benefactress, the General's widow, who had been kept by illness in Moscow, and to whom she was obliged to write twice a week a full account of all her doings.

When Alyosha entered the hall and asked the maid who opened the door to him to take his name up, it was evident that they were already aware of his arrival. Possibly he had been noticed from the window. At least, Alyosha heard a noise, caught the sound of flying footsteps and rustling skirts. Two or three women perhaps had run out of the room.

Alyosha thought it strange that his arrival should cause such excitement. He was conducted however to the drawing-room at once. It was a large room, elegantly and amply furnished, not at all in provincial style. There were many sofas, lounges, settees, big and little tables. There were pictures on the walls, vases and lamps on the tables, masses of flowers, and even an aquarium in the window. It was twilight and rather dark. Alyosha made out a silk mantle thrown down on the sofa, where people had evidently just been sitting; and on a table in front of the sofa were two unfinished cups of chocolate, cakes, a glass saucer with blue raisins, and another with sweetmeats. Alyosha saw that he had interrupted visitors, and frowned. But at that instant the portière was raised, and with rapid, hurrying footsteps Katerina Ivanovna came in, holding out both hands to Alyosha with a radiant smile of delight. At the same instant a servant brought in two lighted candles and set them on the table.

"Thank God! At last you have come too! I've been simply praying for you all day! Sit down."

Alyosha had been struck by Katerina Ivanovna's beauty when, three weeks before, Dmitri had first brought him, at Katerina Ivanovna's special request, to be introduced to her. There had been no conversation between them at that interview, however. Supposing Alyosha to be very shy, Katerina Ivanovna had talked all the time to Dmitri to spare him. Alyosha had been silent, but he had seen a great deal very clearly. He was struck by the imperiousness, proud ease, and self-confidence, of the haughty girl. And all that was certain, Alyosha felt that he was not exaggerating it. He thought her great glowing black eyes were very fine, especially with her pale, even rather sallow, longish face. But in those eyes and in the lines of her exquisite lips there was something with which his brother might well be passionately in love, but which perhaps could not be loved for long. He expressed this thought almost plainly to Dmitri when, after the visit, his brother besought and insisted that he should not conceal his impressions on seeing his betrothed.

"You'll be happy with her, but perhaps—not tranquilly happy."

"Quite so, brother. Such people remain always the same. They don't yield to fate. So you think I shan't love her for ever."

"No; perhaps you will love her for ever. But perhaps you won't always be happy with her."

Alyosha had given his opinion at the time, blushing, and angry with himself for having yielded to his brother's entreaties and put such "foolish" ideas into words. For his opinion had struck him as awfully foolish immediately after he had uttered it. He felt ashamed too of having given so confident an opinion about a woman. It was with the more amazement that he felt now, at the first glance at Katerina Ivanovna as she ran in to him, that he had perhaps been utterly mistaken. This time her face was beaming with spontaneous good-natured kindliness, and direct warmhearted sincerity. The "pride and haughtiness," which had struck Alyosha so much before, was only betrayed now in a frank, generous energy and a sort of bright strong faith in herself. Alyosha realised at the first glance, at the first word, that all the tragedy of her position in relation to the man she loved so dearly was no secret to her; that she perhaps already knew everything, positively everything. And yet, in spite of that, there was such brightness in her face, such faith in the future. Alyosha felt at once that he had gravely wronged her in his thoughts. He was conquered and captivated immediately. Besides all this, he noticed at her first words that she was in great excitement, an excitement perhaps quite exceptional and almost approaching ecstasy.

"I was so eager to see you, because I can learn from you the whole truth—from you and no one else."

"I have come," muttered Alyosha confusedly, "I—he sent me."

"Ah, he sent you! I foresaw that. Now I know everything—everything!" cried Katerina Ivanovna, her eyes flashing. "Wait a moment, Alexey Fyodorovitch, I'll tell you why I've been so longing to see you. You see, I know perhaps far more than you do yourself, and there's no need for you to tell me anything. I'll tell you what I want from you. I want to know your own last impression of him. I want you to tell me most directly, plainly, coarsely even (oh, as coarsely as you like!), what you thought of him just now and of his position after your meeting with him to-day. That will perhaps be better than if I had a personal explanation with him, as he does not want to come to me.

Do you understand what I want from you? Now, tell me simply, tell me every word of the message he sent you with (I knew he would send you)."

"He told me to give you his compliments—and to say that he would never come again—but to give you his compliments."

"His compliments? Was that what he said—his own expression?"

"Yes."

"Accidentally perhaps he made a mistake in the word, perhaps he did not use the right word?"

"No; he told me precisely to repeat that word. He begged me two or three times not to forget to say so."

Katerina Ivanovna flushed hotly.

"Help me now, Alexey Fyodorovitch. Now I really need your help. I'll tell you what I think, and you must simply say whether it's right or not. Listen! If he had sent me his compliments in passing, without insisting on your repeating the words, without emphasising them, that would be the end of everything! But if he particularly insisted on those words, if he particularly told you not to forget to repeat them to me, then perhaps he was in excitement, beside himself. He had made his decision and was frightened at it. He wasn't walking away from me with a resolute step, but leaping headlong. The emphasis on that phrase may have been simply bravado."

"Yes, yes!" cried Alyosha warmly. "I believe that is it."

"And, if so, he's not altogether lost. I can still save him. Stay! Did he not tell you anything about money—about three thousand roubles?"

"He did speak about it, and it's that more than anything that's crushing him. He said he had lost his honour and that nothing matters now," Alyosha answered warmly, feeling a rush of hope in his heart and believing that there really might be a way of escape and salvation for his brother. "But do you know about the money?" he added, and suddenly broke off.

"I've known of it a long time; I telegraphed to Moscow to inquire, and heard long ago that the money had not arrived. He hadn't sent the money, but I said nothing. Last week I learnt that he was still in need of money. My only object in all this was that he should know to whom to turn, and who was his true friend. No, he won't recognise that I am his truest friend; he won't know me, and looks on me merely as a woman. I've been tormented all the week, trying to think how to prevent him from being ashamed to face me because he spent that three thousand. Let him feel ashamed of himself, let him be ashamed of other people's knowing, but not of my knowing. He can tell God everything without shame. Why is it he still does not understand how much I am ready to bear for his sake? Why, why doesn't he know me"? How dare he not know me after all that has happened? I want to save him for ever. Let him forget me as his betrothed. And here he fears that he is dishonoured in my eyes. Why, he wasn't afraid to be open with you, Alexey Fyodorovitch. How is it that I don't deserve the same?"

The last words she uttered in tears. Tears gushed from her eyes.

"I must tell you," Alyosha began, his voice trembling too, "what happened just now between him and my father."

And he described the whole scene, how Dmitri had sent him to get the money, how he had broken in, knocked his father down, and after that had again specially and emphatically begged him to take his compliments and farewell. "He went to that woman," Alyosha added softly.

"And do you suppose that I can't put up with that woman? Does he think I can't? But he won't marry her," she suddenly laughed nervously. "Could such a passion last for ever in a Karamazov? It's passion, not love. He won't marry her because she won't marry him." Again Katerina Ivanovna laughed strangely.

"He may marry her," said Alyosha mournfully, looking down.

"He won't marry her, I tell you. That girl is an angel. Do you know that? Do you know that?" Katerina Ivanovna exclaimed suddenly with extraordinary warmth. "She is one of the most fantastic of fantastic creatures. I know how bewitching she is, but I know too that she is kind, firm and noble. Why do you look at me like that, Alexey Fyodorovitch? Perhaps you are wondering at my words, perhaps you don't believe me? Agrafena Alexandrovna, my angel!" she cried suddenly to some one, peeping into the next room, "come in to us. This is a friend. This is Alyosha. He knows all about our affairs. Show yourself to him."

"I've only been waiting behind the curtain for you to call me," said a soft, one might even say sugary, feminine voice.

The portière was raised and Grushenka herself, smiling and beaming, came up to the table. A violent revulsion passed over Alyosha. He fixed his eyes on her and could not take them off. Here she was, that awful woman, the "beast," as Ivan had called her half an hour before. And yet one would have thought the creature standing before him most simple and ordinary, a good-natured, kind woman, handsome certainly, but so like other handsome ordinary women! It is true she was very, very good-looking with that Russian beauty so passionately loved by many men. She was a rather tall woman, though a little shorter than Katerina Ivanovna, who was exceptionally tall. She had a full figure, with soft, as it were, noiseless, movements, softened to a peculiar over-sweetness, like her voice. She moved, not like Katerina Ivanovna, with a vigorous, bold step, but noiselessly. Her feet made absolutely no sound on the floor. She sank softly into a low chair, softly rustling her sumptuous black silk dress, and delicately nestling her milk-white neck and broad shoulders in a costly black cashmere shawl. She was twenty-two years old, and her face looked exactly that age. She was very white in the face, with a pale pink tint on her cheeks. The modelling of her face might be said to be too broad, and the lower jaw was set a trifle forward. Her upper lip was thin, but the slightly prominent lower lip was at least twice as full, and looked pouting. But her magnificent, abundant dark brown hair, her sable-coloured eye-brows and charming grey-blue eyes with their long lashes would have made the most indifferent person, meeting her casually in a crowd in the street, stop at the sight of her face and remember it long after. What struck Alyosha most in that face was its expression of child-like good-nature. There was a child-like look in her eyes, a look of childish delight. She came up to the table, beaming with delight and seeming to expect something with childish, impatient, and confiding curiosity. The light in her eyes gladdened the soul—Alyosha felt that. There was something else in her which he could not understand, or would not have been able to define, and which yet perhaps unconsciously affected him. It was that softness, that voluptuousness of her bodily movements, that catlike noiselessness. Yet it was a vigorous, ample body. Under the shawl could be seen full broad shoulders, a high, still quite girlish bosom. Her figure suggested the lines of the Venus of Milo, though already in somewhat exaggerated proportions. That could be divined. Connoisseurs of Russian beauty could have foretold with certainty that this fresh, still youthful, beauty would lose its harmony by the age of thirty, would "spread"; that the face would become puffy, and that wrinkles would very soon appear upon her forehead and round the eyes; the complexion would grow coarse and red perhaps—in fact, that it was the beauty of the moment, the fleeting beauty which is so often met with in Russian women. Alyosha, of course, did not think of this; but though he was fascinated, yet he wondered with an unpleasant sensation, and as it were regretfully, why she drawled in that way and could not speak naturally. She did so evidently feeling there was a charm in the exaggerated, honeyed modulation of the syllables. It was, of course, only a bad, underbred habit that showed bad education and a false idea of good manners. And yet this intonation and manner of speaking impressed Alyosha as almost incredibly incongruous with the childishly simple and happy expression of her face, the soft, babyish joy in her eyes. Katerina Ivanovna at once made her sit down in an armchair facing Alyosha, and ecstatically kissed her several times on her smiling lips. She seemed quite in love with her.

"This is the first time we've met, Alexey Fyodorovitch," she said rapturously. "I wanted to know her, to see her. I wanted to go to her, but I'd no sooner expressed the wish than she came to me. I knew we should settle everything together—everything. My heart told me so—I was begged not to take the step, but I foresaw it would be a way out of the difficulty, and I was not mistaken. Grushenka has explained everything to me, told me all she means to do. She flew here like an angel of goodness and brought us peace and joy."

"You did not disdain me, sweet, excellent young lady," drawled Grushenka in her sing-song voice, still with the same charming smile of delight.

"Don't dare to speak to me like that, you sorceress, you witch! Disdain you! Here I must kiss your lower lip once more. It looks as though it were swollen, and now it will be more so, and more and more. Look how she laughs, Alexey Fyodorovitch! It does one's heart good to see the angel."

Alyosha flushed, and faint, imperceptible shivers kept running down him.

"You make so much of me, dear young lady, and perhaps I am not at all worthy of your kindness."

"Not worthy! She's not worthy of it!" Katerina Ivanovna cried again with the same warmth. "You know, Alexey Fyodorovitch, we're fanciful, we're self-willed, but proudest of the proud in our little heart. We're noble, we're generous, Alexey Fyodorovitch, let me tell you. We have only been unfortunate. We were too ready to make every sacrifice for an unworthy, perhaps, or fickle man. There was one man—one, an officer too, we loved him, we sacrificed everything to him. That was long ago, five years ago, and he has forgotten us, he has married. Now he is a widower, he has written, he is coming here, and, do you know, we've loved him, none but him, all this time, and we've loved him all our life! He will come, and Grushenka will be happy again. For the last five years she's been wretched. But who can reproach her, who can boast of her favour? Only that bedridden old merchant, but he is more like her father, her friend, her protector. He found her then in despair, in agony, deserted by the man she loved. She was ready to drown herself then, but the old merchant saved her—saved her!"

"You defend me very kindly, dear young lady. You are in a great hurry about everything," Grushenka drawled again.

"Defend you! Is it for me to defend you? Should I dare to defend you? Grushenka, angel, give me your hand. Look at that charming soft little hand, Alexey Fyodorovitch! Look at it! It has brought me happiness and has lifted me up, and I'm going to kiss it, outside and inside, here, here, here!"

And three times she kissed the certainly charming, though rather fat, hand of Grushenka in a sort of rapture. She held out her hand with a charming musical, nervous little laugh, watched the "sweet young lady," and obviously liked having her hand kissed.

"Perhaps there's rather too much rapture," thought Alyosha, He blushed. He felt a peculiar uneasiness at heart the whole time.

"You won't make me blush, dear young lady, kissing my hand like this before Alexey Fyodorovitch."

"Do you really think I meant to make you blush?" said Katerina Ivanovna, somewhat surprised. "Ah, my dear, how little you understand me!"

"Yes, and you too perhaps quite misunderstand me, dear young lady. Maybe I'm not so good as I seem to you. I've a bad heart; I will have my own way, I fascinated poor Dmitri Fyodorovitch that day simply for fun."

"But now you'll save him. You've given me your word. You'll explain it all to him. You'll break to him that you have long loved another man, who is now offering you his hand."

"Oh, no! I didn't give you my word to do that. It was you kept talking about that. I didn't give you my word."

"Then I didn't quite understand you," said Katerina Ivanovna slowly, turning a little pale. "You promised. . . ."

"Oh no, angel lady, I've promised nothing." Grushenka interrupted softly and evenly, still with the same gay and simple expression. "You see at once, dear young lady, what a wilful wretch I am compared with you. If I want to do a thing I do it. I may have made you some promise just now. But now again I'm thinking: I may take to Mitya again. I liked him very much once—liked him for almost a whole hour. Now maybe I shall go and tell him to stay with me from this day forward. You see, I'm so changeable."

"Just now you said—something quite different," Katerina Ivanovna whispered faintly.

"Ah, just now! But, you know, I'm such a soft-hearted, silly creature. Only think what he's gone through on my account! What if when I go home I feel sorry for him? What then?"

"I never expected——"

"Ah, young lady, how good and generous you are compared with me! Now perhaps you won't care for a silly creature like me, now you know my character. Give me your sweet little hand, angelic lady," she said tenderly, and with a sort of reverence took Katerina Ivanovna's hand.

"Here, dear young lady, I'll take your hand and kiss it as you did mine. You kissed mine three times, but I ought to kiss yours three hundred times to be even with you. Well, but let that pass. And then it shall be as God wills. Perhaps I shall be your slave entirely and want to do your bidding like a slave. Let it be as God wills, without any agreements and promises. What a sweet hand—what a sweet hand you have! You sweet young lady, you incredible beauty!"

She slowly raised the hands to her lips, with the strange object indeed of "being even" with her in kisses.

Katerina Ivanovna did not take her hand away. She listened with timid hope to the last words, though Grushenka's promise to do her bidding like a slave was very strangely expressed. She looked intently into her eyes; she still saw in those eyes the same simple-hearted, confiding expression, the same bright gaiety.

"She's perhaps too naïve," thought Katerina Ivanovna, with a gleam of hope.

Grushenka meanwhile seemed enthusiastic over the "sweet hand." She raised it deliberately to her lips. But she held it for two or three minutes near her lips, as though reconsidering something.

"Do you know, angel lady," she suddenly drawled in an even more soft and sugary voice, "do you know, after all, I think I won't kiss your hand?" And she laughed a little merry laugh.

"As you please. What's the matter with you?" said Katerina Ivanovna, starting suddenly.

"So that you may be left to remember that you kissed my hand, but I didn't kiss yours."

There was a sudden gleam in her eyes. She looked with awful intentness at Katerina Ivanovna.

"Insolent creature!" cried Katerina Ivanovna, as though suddenly grasping something. She flushed all over and leapt up from her seat.

Grushenka too got up, but without haste.

"So I shall tell Mitya how you kissed my hand, but I didn't kiss yours at all. And how he will laugh!"

"Vile slut! Go away!"

"Ah, for shame, young lady! Ah, for shame! That's unbecoming for you, dear young lady, a word like that."

"Go away! You're a creature for sale!" screamed Katerina Ivanovna. Every feature was working in her utterly distorted face.

"For sale indeed! You used to visit gentlemen in the dusk for money once; you brought your beauty for sale. You see, I know."

Katerina Ivanovna shrieked, and would have rushed at her, but Alyosha held her with all his strength.

"Not a step, not a word! Don't speak, don't answer her. She'll go away — she'll go at once."

At that instant Katerina Ivanovna's two aunts ran in at her cry, and with them a maid-servant. All hurried to her.

"I will go away," said Grushenka, taking up her mantle from the sofa. "Alyosha, darling, see me home!"

"Go away—go away, make haste!" cried Alyosha, clasping his hands imploringly.

"Dear little Alyosha, see me home! I've got a pretty little story to tell you on the way. I got up this scene for your benefit, Alyosha. See me home, dear, you'll be glad of it afterwards."

Alyosha turned away, wringing his hands. Grushenka ran out of the house, laughing musically.

Katerina Ivanovna went into a fit of hysterics. She sobbed, and was shaken with convulsions. Every one fussed round her.

"I warned you," said the elder of her aunts. "I tried to prevent your doing this. You're too impulsive. How could you do such a thing? You don't know these creatures, and they say she's worse than any of them. You are too self-willed."

"She's a tigress!" yelled Katerina Ivanovna. "Why did you hold me, Alexey Fyodorovitch! I'd have beaten her—beaten her!"

She could not control herself before Alyosha; perhaps she did not care to, indeed.

"She ought to be flogged in public on a scaffold!"

Alyosha withdrew towards the door.

"But, my God!" cried Katerina Ivanovna, clasping her hands. "He! He! He could be so dishonourable, so inhuman! Why, he told that creature what happened on that fatal, accursed day! 'You brought your beauty for sale, dear young lady.' She knows it! Your brother's a scoundrel, Alexey Fyodorovitch."

Alyosha wanted to say something, but he couldn't find a word. His heart ached.

"Go away, Alexey Fyodorovitch! It's shameful, it's awful for me! To-morrow, I beg you on my knees, come to-morrow. Don't condemn me. Forgive me. I don't know what I shall do with myself now!"

Alyosha walked out into the street reeling. He could have wept as she did. Suddenly he was overtaken by the maid.

"The young lady forgot to give you this letter from Madame Hohlakov; it's been left with us since dinner-time."

Alyosha took the little pink envelope mechanically and put it, almost unconsciously, into his pocket.

11

ANOTHER REPUTATION RUINED

I T was not much more than three-quarters of a mile from the town to the monastery. Alyosha walked quickly along the road, at that hour deserted. It was almost night, and too dark to see anything clearly at thirty paces ahead. There were cross-roads half-way. A figure came into sight under a solitary willow at the cross-roads. As soon as Alyosha reached the cross-roads the figure moved out and rushed at him, shouting savagely:

"Your money or your life!"*

"So it's you, Mitya," cried Alyosha, in surprise, violently startled however.

"Ha, ha, ha! You didn't expect me? I wondered where to wait for you. By her house? There are three ways from it, and I might have missed you. At last I thought of waiting here, for you had to pass here, there's no other way to the monastery. Come, tell me the truth. Crush me like a beetle. But what's the matter?"

"Nothing, brother—it's the fright you gave me. Oh, Dmitri! Father's blood just now." (Alyosha began to cry, he had been on the verge of tears for a long time, and now something seemed to snap in his soul.) "You almost killed him—cursed him—and now—here—you're making jokes— 'Your money or your life.' "

"Well, what of that? It's not seemly—is that it? Not suitable in my position?"

"No—I only——"

"Stay. Look at the night. You see what a dark night, what clouds, what a wind has risen. I hid here under the willow waiting for you. And as God's above, I suddenly thought, why go on in misery any longer, what is there to wait for? Here I have a willow, a handkerchief, a shirt, I can twist them into a rope in a minute, and braces besides, and why go on burdening the earth, dishonouring it with my vile presence. And then I heard you coming—Heavens, it was as though something flew down to me suddenly. So there is a man, then, whom I love. Here he is, that man, my dear little brother, whom I love more than any one in the world, the only one I love in the world. And I loved you so much, so much at that moment that I thought, 'I'll fall on his neck at once.' Then a stupid idea struck me, to have a joke with you and scare you. I shouted, like a fool, 'your money!' Forgive my foolery—it was only nonsense, and there's nothing unseemly in my

---

*Quotation from Schiller's 1782 play *The Robbers* (act 1, scene 2).

soul. . . . Damn it all, tell me what's happened. What did she say? Strike me, crush me, don't spare me! Was she furious?"

"No, not that. . . . There was nothing like that, Mitya. There—I found them both there."

"Both? Whom?"

"Grushenka at Katerina Ivanovna's."

Dmitri was struck dumb.

"Impossible!" he cried. "You're raving! Grushenka with her?"

Alyosha described all that had happened from the moment he went in to Katerina Ivanovna's. He was ten minutes telling his story. He can't be said to have told it fluently and consecutively, but he seemed to make it clear, not omitting any word or action of significance, and vividly describing, often in one word, his own sensations. Dmitri listened in silence, gazing at him with a terrible fixed stare, but it was clear to Alyosha that he understood it all, and had grasped every point. But as the story went on, his face became not merely gloomy, but menacing. He scowled, he clenched his teeth, and his fixed stare became still more rigid, more concentrated, more terrible, when suddenly, with incredible rapidity, his wrathful, savage face changed, his tightly compressed lips parted, and Dmitri Fyodorovitch broke into uncontrolled, spontaneous laughter. He literally shook with laughter. For a long time he could not speak.

"So she wouldn't kiss her hand! So she didn't kiss it; so she ran away!" he kept exclaiming with hysterical delight; insolent delight it might have been called, if it had not been so spontaneous. "So the other one called her tigress! And a tigress she is! So she ought to be flogged on a scaffold! Yes, yes, so she ought. That's just what I think; she ought to have been long ago. It's like this, brother, let her be punished, but I must get better first. I understand the queen of impudence. That's her all over! You saw her all over in that hand-kissing, the she-devil! She's the queen of all she-devils you can imagine in the world! She's magnificent in her own line! So she ran home? I'll go—ah—I'll run to her! Alyosha, don't blame me, I agree that hanging is too good for her."

"But Katerina Ivanovna!" exclaimed Alyosha sorrowfully.

"I see her, too! I see right through her, as I've never done before! It's a regular discovery of the four continents of the world, that is, of the five![6] What a thing to do! That's just like Katya, who was not afraid to face a coarse, unmannerly officer and risk a deadly insult on a generous impulse to save her father! But the pride, the recklessness, the defiance of fate, the unbounded defiance! You say that aunt tried to stop her? That aunt, you know, is overbearing, herself. She's the sister of the general's widow in Moscow, and even more stuck-up than she. But her husband was caught stealing government money. He lost everything, his estate and all, and the proud wife had to lower her colours, and hasn't raised them since. So she tried to prevent Katya, but she wouldn't listen to her! She thinks she can overcome everything, that everything will give way to her. She thought she could bewitch Grushenka if she liked, and she believed it herself; she plays a part to herself, and whose fault is it? Do you think she kissed Grushenka's hand first, on purpose, with a motive? No, she really was fascinated by Grushenka, that's to say, not by Grushenka, but by her own dream, her own delusion—because it was *her* dream, *her* delusion! Alyosha, darling, how did you escape from them, those women? Did you pick up your cassock and run? Ha, ha, ha!"

"Brother, you don't seem to have noticed how you've insulted Katerina Ivanovna by telling Grushenka about that day. And she flung it in her face just now that she had gone to gentlemen in secret to sell her beauty! Brother, what could be worse than that insult?"

What worried Alyosha more than anything was that, incredible as it seemed, his brother appeared pleased at Katerina Ivanovna's humiliation.

"Bah!" Dmitri frowned fiercely, and struck his forehead with his hand. He only now realised it, though Alyosha had just told him of the insult, and Katerina Ivanovna's cry: "Your brother is a scoundrel!"

"Yes, perhaps, I really did tell Grushenka about that 'fatal day,' as Katya calls it. Yes, I did tell her, I remember! It was that time at Mokroe. I was drunk, the gipsies were singing. . . . But I was sobbing. I was sobbing then, kneeling and praying to Katya's image, and Grushenka understood it. She understood it all then. I remember, she cried herself. . . . Damn it all! But it's bound to be so now. . . . Then she cried, but now the 'dagger in the heart'! That's how women are."

He looked down and sank into thought.

"Yes, I am a scoundrel, a thorough scoundrel!" he said suddenly, in a gloomy voice. "It doesn't matter whether I cried or not, I'm a scoundrel! Tell her I accept the name, if that's any comfort. Come, that's enough. Good-bye. It's no use talking! It's not amusing. You go your way and I mine. And I don't want to see you again except as a last resource. Good-bye, Alexey!"

He warmly pressed Alyosha's hand, and still looking down, without raising his head, as though tearing himself away, turned rapidly towards the town.

Alyosha looked after him, unable to believe he would go away so abruptly.

"Stay, Alexey, one more confession to you alone!" cried Dmitri, suddenly turning back. "Look at me, Look at me well. You see here, here—there's terrible disgrace in store for me." (As he said "here," Dmitri struck his chest with his fist with a strange air, as though the dishonour lay precisely on his chest, in some spot, in a pocket, perhaps, or hanging round his neck.) "You know me now, a scoundrel, an avowed scoundrel, but let me tell you that I've never done anything before and never shall again, anything that can compare in baseness with the dishonour which I bear now at this very minute on my breast, here, here, which will come to pass, though I'm perfectly free to stop it. I can stop it or carry it through, note that. Well, let me tell you, I shall carry it through. I shan't stop it. I told you everything just now, but I didn't tell you this, because even I had not brass enough for it. I can still pull up; if I do, I can give back the full half of my lost honour to-morrow. But I shan't pull up. I shall carry out my base plan, and you can bear witness that I told you so beforehand. Darkness and destruction! No need to explain. You'll find out in due time. The filthy back-alley and the she-devil. Good-bye. Don't pray for me, I'm not worth it. And there's no need, no need at all . . . I don't need it! Away!"

And he suddenly retreated, this time finally. Alyosha went towards the monastery.

"What? I shall never see him again! What is he saying?" he wondered wildly. "Why, I shall certainly see him to-morrow. I shall look him up. I shall make a point of it. What does he mean?"

He went round the monastery and crossed the pine-wood to the hermitage. The door was opened to him, though no one was admitted at that hour. There was a tremor in his heart as he went into Father Zossima's cell.

"Why, why, had he gone forth? Why had he sent him into the world? Here was peace. Here was holiness. But there was confusion, there was darkness in which one lost one's way and went astray at once. . . ."

In the cell he found the novice Porfiry and Father Païssy, who came every hour to inquire after Father Zossima. Alyosha learnt with alarm that he was getting worse and worse. Even his usual discourse with the brothers could not take place that day. As a rule every evening after service the monks flocked into Father Zossima's cell, and all confessed aloud their sins of the day, their sinful thoughts and temptations; even their disputes, if there had been any. Some confessed kneeling. The elder absolved, reconciled, exhorted, imposed penance, blessed, and dismissed them. It was against this general "confession" that the opponents of "elders" protested, maintaining that it was a profanation of the sacrament of confession, almost a sacrilege, though this was quite a different thing. They even represented to the diocesan authorities that such confessions attained no good object, but actually to a large extent led to sin and temptation. Many of the brothers disliked going to the elder, and went against their own will because every one went, and for fear they should be accused of pride and rebellious ideas. People said that some of the monks agreed beforehand, saying, "I'll confess I lost my temper with you this morning, and you confirm it," simply in order to have something to say. Alyosha knew that this actually happened sometimes. He knew, too, that there were among the monks some who deeply resented the fact that letters from relations were habitually taken to the elder, to be opened and read by him before those to whom they were addressed.

It was assumed, of course, that all this was done freely, and in good faith, by way of voluntary submission and salutary guidance. But, in fact, there was sometimes no little insincerity, and much that was false and strained in this practice. Yet the older and more experienced of the monks adhered to their opinion, arguing that "for those who have come within these walls sincerely seeking salvation, such obedience and sacrifice will certainly be salutary and of great benefit; those, on the other hand, who find it irksome, and repine, are no true monks, and have made a mistake in entering the monastery—their proper place is in the world. Even in the temple one cannot be safe from sin and the devil. So it was no good taking it too much into account."

"He is weaker, a drowsiness has come over him," Father Païssy whispered to Alyosha, as he blessed him. "It's difficult to rouse him. And he must not be roused. He waked up for five minutes, sent his blessing to the brothers, and begged their prayers for him at night. He intends to take the sacrament again in the morning. He remembered you, Alexey. He asked whether you had gone away, and was told that you were in the town. 'I blessed him for that work,' he said, 'his place is there, not here, for awhile.' Those were his words about you. He remembered you lovingly, with anxiety; do you understand how he honoured you? But how is it that he has decided that you shall spend some time in the world? He must have foreseen something in your destiny! Understand, Alexey, that if you return to the world, it must be to do the duty laid upon you by your elder, and not for frivolous vanity and worldly pleasures."

Father Païssy went out. Alyosha had no doubt that Father Zossima was dying, though he might live another day or two. Alyosha firmly and ardently resolved that in spite of his promises to his father, the Hohlakovs, and Katerina Ivanovna, he would not leave the monastery next day, but would remain with his elder to the end. His heart glowed with love, and he reproached himself bitterly for having been able for one instant to forget him whom he had left in the monastery on his deathbed, and whom he honoured above every one in the world. He went into Father Zossima's bedroom, knelt down, and bowed to the ground before the elder, who slept quietly without stirring, with regular, hardly audible breathing and a peaceful face.

Alyosha returned to the other room, where Father Zossima had received his guests in the morning. Taking off his boots, he lay down on the hard, narrow, leathern sofa, which he had long used as a bed, bringing nothing but a pillow. The mattress, about which his father had shouted to him that morning, he had long forgotten to lay on. He took off his cassock, which he used as a covering. But before going to bed, he fell on his knees and prayed a long time. In his fervent prayer he did not beseech God to lighten his darkness but only thirsted for the joyous emotion, which always visited his soul after the praise and adoration, of which his evening prayer usually consisted. That joy always brought him light untroubled sleep. As he was praying, he suddenly felt in his pocket the little pink note the servant had handed him as he left Katerina Ivanovna's. He was disturbed, but finished his prayer. Then, after some hesitation, he opened the envelope. In it was a letter to him, signed by Lise, the young daughter of Madame Hohlakov, who had laughed at him before the elder in the morning.

"Alexey Fyodorovitch," she wrote, "I am writing to you without any one's knowledge, even mamma's, and I know how wrong it is. But I cannot live without telling you the feeling that has sprung up in my heart, and this no one but us two must know for a time. But how am I to say what I want so much to tell you? Paper, they say, does not blush, but I assure you it's not true and that it's blushing just as I am now, all over. Dear Alyosha, I love you, I've loved you from my childhood, since our Moscow days, when you were very different from what you are now, and I shall love you all my life. My heart has chosen you, to unite our lives, and pass them together till our old age. Of course, on condition that you will leave the monastery. As for our age we will wait for the time fixed by the law. By that time I shall certainly be quite strong, I shall be walking and dancing. There can be no doubt of that.

"You see how I've thought of everything. There's only one thing I can't imagine: what you'll think of me when you read this? I'm always laughing and being naughty. I made you angry this morning, but I assure you before I took up my pen, I prayed before the Image of the Mother of God, and now I'm praying, and almost crying.

"My secret is in your hands. When you come to-morrow, I don't know how I shall look at you. Ah, Alexey Fyodorovitch, what if I can't restrain myself like a silly and laugh when I look at you as I did to-day? You'll think I'm a nasty girl making fun of you, and you won't believe my letter. And so I beg you, dear one, if you've any pity for me, when you come to-morrow, don't look me straight in the face, for if I meet your eyes, it will be sure to make me laugh, especially, as you'll be in that long gown. I feel cold all over when I think of it, so when you come, don't look at me at all for a time, look at mamma or at the window. . . .

"Here I've written you a love-letter. Oh, dear, what have I done? Alyosha, don't despise me, and if I've done something very horrid and wounded you, forgive me. Now the secret of my reputation, ruined perhaps for ever, is in your hands.

"I shall certainly cry to-day. Good-bye till our meeting, our *awful* meeting.—LISE.

"P.S.—Alyosha! You must, must, must come!—LISE."

Alyosha read the note in amazement, read it through twice, thought a little, and suddenly laughed a soft, sweet laugh. He started. That laugh seemed to him sinful. But a minute later he laughed again just as softly and happily. He slowly replaced the note in the envelope, crossed himself and lay down. The agitation in his heart passed at once. "God have mercy upon all of them, have all these unhappy and turbulent souls in Thy keeping, and set them in the right path. All ways are Thine. Save them according to Thy wisdom. Thou art love. Thou wilt send joy to all!" Alyosha murmured crossing himself, and falling into peaceful sleep.

PART TWO

BOOK FOUR

LACERATIONS

1

FATHER FERAPONT

ALYOSHA was roused early, before daybreak. Father Zossima woke up feeling very weak, though he wanted to get out of bed and sit up in a chair. His mind was quite clear; his face looked very tired, yet bright and almost joyful. It wore an expression of gaiety, kindness and cordiality. "Maybe I shall not live through the coming day," he said to Alyosha. Then he desired to confess and take the sacrament at once. He always confessed to Father Païssy. After taking the communion, the service of extreme unction followed. The monks assembled and the cell was gradually filled up by the inmates of the hermitage. Meantime it was daylight. People began coming from the monastery. After the service was over the elder desired to kiss and take leave of every one. As the cell was so small the earlier visitors withdrew to make room for others. Alyosha stood beside the elder, who was seated again in his arm-chair. He talked as much as he could. Though his voice was weak, it was fairly steady.

"I've been teaching you so many years, and therefore I've been talking aloud so many years, that I've got into the habit of talking, and so much so that it's almost more difficult for me to hold my tongue than to talk, even now, in spite of my weakness, dear fathers and brothers," he jested, looking with emotion at the group round him.

Alyosha remembered afterwards something of what he said to them. But though he spoke out distinctly and his voice was fairly steady, his speech was somewhat disconnected. He spoke of many things, he seemed anxious before the moment of death to say everything he had not said in his life, and not simply for the sake of instructing them, but as though thirsting to share with all men and all creation his joy and ecstasy, and once more in his life to open his whole heart.

"Love one another, Fathers," said Father Zossima, as far as Alyosha could remember afterwards. "Love God's people. Because we have come here and shut ourselves within these walls, we are no holier than those that are outside, but on the contrary, from the very fact of coming here, each of us has confessed to himself that he is worse than others, than all men on earth. . . . And the longer the monk lives in his seclusion, the more keenly he must recognise that. Else he would have had no reason to come here. When he realises that he is not only worse than others, but that he is responsible to all men for all and everything, for all human sins, national and individual, only then the aim of our seclusion is attained. For know, dear ones, that every one of us is undoubtedly responsible for all men and everything on earth, not merely through the general sinfulness of creation, but each one personally for all mankind and every individual man. This knowledge is the crown of life for the monk and for every man. For monks are not a special sort of men, but only what all men ought to be. Only through that knowledge, our heart grows soft with infinite, universal, inexhaustible love. Then every one of you will have the power to win over the whole world by love and to wash away the sins of the world with your tears. . . . Each of you keep watch over your heart and confess your sins to yourself unceasingly. Be not afraid of your sins, even when perceiving them, if only there be penitence, but make no conditions with God. Again I say, Be not proud. Be proud neither to the little nor to the great. Hate not those who reject you, who insult you, who abuse and slander you. Hate not the atheists, the teachers of evil, the materialists—and I mean not only the good ones—for there are many good ones among them, especially in our day—hate not even the wicked ones. Remember them in your prayers thus: Save, O Lord, all those who have none to pray for them, save too all those who will not pray. And add: It is not in pride that I make this prayer, O Lord, for I am lower than all men. . . . Love God's people, let not strangers draw away the flock, for if you slumber in your slothfulness and disdainful pride, or worse still, in covetousness, they will come from all sides and draw away your flock. Expound the Gospel to the people unceasingly . . . be not extortionate. . . . Do not love gold and silver, do not hoard them. . . . Have faith. Cling to the banner and raise it on high."

But the elder spoke more disconnectedly than Alyosha reported his words afterwards. Sometimes he broke off altogether, as though to take breath and recover his strength, but he was in a sort of ecstasy. They heard him with emotion, though many wondered at his words and found them obscure. . . . Afterwards all remembered those words.

When Alyosha happened for a moment to leave the cell, he was struck by the general excitement and suspense in the monks who were crowding about it. This anticipation showed itself in some by anxiety, in others by devout solemnity. All were expecting that some marvel would happen immediately after the elder's death. Their suspense was, from one point of view, almost frivolous, but even the most austere of the monks were affected by it. Father Païssy's face looked the gravest of all.

Alyosha was mysteriously summoned by a monk to see Rakitin, who had arrived from town with a singular letter for him from Madame Hohlakov. In it she informed Alyosha of a strange and very opportune incident. It appeared that among the women who had come on the previous day to receive Father Zossima's blessing, there had been an old woman from the town, a sergeant's widow, called Prohorovna. She had inquired whether she might pray for the rest of the soul of her son, Vassenka, who had gone to Irkutsk, and had sent her no news for over a year. To which Father Zossima had answered sternly, forbidding her to do so, and saying that to pray for the living as though they were dead was a kind of sorcery. He afterwards forgave her on account of her ignorance, and added "as though reading the book of the future" (this was Madame Hohlakov's expression) words of comfort: "that her son Vassya was certainly alive and he would either come himself very shortly or send a letter, and that she was to go home and expect him." And "would you believe it," exclaimed Madame Hohlakov enthusiastically, "the prophecy has been fulfilled literally indeed, and more than that." Scarcely had the old woman reached home when they gave her a letter from Siberia which had been awaiting her. But that was not all; in the letter written on the road from Ekaterinburg, Vassya informed his mother that he was returning to Russia with an official, and that three weeks after her receiving the letter he hoped "to embrace his mother."

Madame Hohlakov warmly entreated Alyosha to report this new "miracle of prediction" to the Superior and all the brotherhood. "All, all, ought to know of it!" she concluded. The letter had been written in haste, the excitement of the writer was apparent in every line of it. But Alyosha had no need to tell the monks, for all knew of it already. Rakitin had commissioned the monk who brought his message "to inform most respectfully his reverence Father Païssy, that he, Rakitin, has a matter to speak of with him, of such gravity that he dare not defer it for a moment, and humbly begs forgiveness for his presumption." As the monk had given the message to Father Païssy before that to Alyosha, the latter found after reading the letter, there was nothing left for him to do but to hand it to Father Païssy in confirmation of the story.

And even that austere and cautious man, though he frowned as he read the news of the "miracle," could not completely restrain some inner emotion. His eyes gleamed, and a grave and solemn smile came into his lips.

"We shall see greater things!" broke from him.

"We shall see greater things, greater things yet!" the monks around repeated.

But Father Païssy, frowning again, begged all of them at least for a time, not to speak of the matter "till it be more fully confirmed, seeing there is so much credulity among those of this world, and indeed this might well have chanced naturally," he added, prudently, as it were to satisfy his conscience, though scarcely believing his own disavowal, a fact his listeners very clearly perceived.

Within the hour the "miracle" was of course known to the whole monastery, and many visitors who had come for the mass. No one seemed more impressed by it than the monk who had come the day before from St. Sylvester, from the little monastery of Obdorsk in the far North. It was he who had been standing near Madame Hohlakov the previous day and had asked Father Zossima earnestly, referring to the "healing" of the lady's daughter, "how can you presume to do such things?"

He was now somewhat puzzled and did not know whom to believe. The evening before he had visited Father Ferapont in his cell apart, behind the apiary, and had been greatly impressed and overawed by the visit. This Father Ferapont was that aged monk so devout in fasting and observing silence who has been mentioned already, as antagonistic to Father Zossima and the whole institution of "elders," which he regarded as a pernicious and frivolous innovation. He was a very formidable opponent, although from his practice of silence he scarcely spoke a word to any one. What made him formidable was that a number of monks fully shared his feeling, and many of the visitors looked upon him as a great saint and ascetic, although they had no doubt that he was crazy. But it was just his craziness attracted them.

Father Ferapont never went to see the elder. Though he lived in the hermitage they did not worry him to keep its regulations, and this too because he behaved as though he were crazy. He was seventy-five or more, and he lived in a corner beyond the apiary in an old decaying wooden cell which had been built long ago for another great ascetic, Father Iona, who had lived to be a hundred and five, and of whose saintly doings many curious stories were still extant in the monastery and the neighbourhood.

Father Ferapont had succeeded in getting himself installed in this same solitary cell seven years previously. It was simply a peasant's hut, though it looked like a chapel, for it contained an extraordinary number of ikons with lamps perpetually burning before them—which men brought to the monastery as offerings to God. Father Ferapont had been appointed to look after them and keep the lamps burning. It was said (and indeed it was true) that he ate only two pounds of bread in three days. The beekeeper, who lived close by the apiary, used to bring him the bread every three days, and even to this man who waited upon him, Father Ferapont rarely uttered a word. The four pounds of bread, together with the sacrament bread, regularly sent him on Sundays after the late mass by the Father Superior, made up his weekly rations. The water in his jug was changed every day. He rarely appeared at mass. Visitors who came to do him homage saw him sometimes kneeling all day long at prayer without looking round. If he addressed them, he was brief, abrupt, strange, and almost always rude. On very rare occasions, however, he would talk to visitors, but for the most part he would utter some one strange saying which was a complete riddle, and no entreaties would induce him to pronounce a word in explanation. He was not a priest, but a simple monk. There was a strange belief, chiefly however among the most ignorant, that Father Ferapont had communication with heavenly spirits and would only converse with them, and so was silent with men.

The monk from Obdorsk, having been directed to the apiary by the beekeeper, who was also a very silent and surly monk, went to the corner where Father Ferapont's cell stood. "Maybe he will speak as you are a stranger and maybe you'll get nothing out of him," the beekeeper had warned him. The monk, as he related afterwards, approached in the utmost apprehension. It was rather late in the evening. Father Ferapont was sitting at the door of his cell on a low bench. A huge old elm was lightly rustling overhead. There was an evening freshness in the air. The monk from Obdorsk bowed down before the saint and asked his blessing.

"Do you want me to bow down to you, monk?" said Father Ferapont. "Get up!"

The monk got up.

"Blessing, be blessed! Sit beside me. Where have you come from?"

What most struck the poor monk was the fact that in spite of his strict fasting and great age, Father Ferapont still looked a vigorous old man. He was tall, held himself erect, and had a thin, but fresh and healthy face. There was no doubt he still had considerable strength. He was of athletic build. In spite of his great age he was not even quite grey, and still had very thick hair and a full beard, both of which had once been black. His eyes were grey, large and luminous, but strikingly prominent. He spoke with a broad accent. He was dressed in a peasant's long reddish coat of coarse convict cloth (as it used to be called) and had a stout rope round his waist. His throat and chest were bare. Beneath his coat, his shirt of the coarsest linen showed almost black with dirt, not having been changed for months. They said that he wore irons weighing thirty pounds under his coat. His stockingless feet were thrust in old slippers almost dropping to pieces.

"From the little Obdorsk monastery, from St. Sylvester," the monk answered humbly, whilst his keen and inquisitive, but rather frightened little eyes kept watch on the hermit.

"I have been at your Sylvester's. I used to stay there. Is Sylvester well?"

The monk hesitated.

"You are a senseless lot! How do you keep the fasts?"

"Our dietary is according to the ancient conventual rules. During Lent there are no meals provided for Monday, Wednesday, and Friday. For Tuesday and Thursday we have white bread, stewed fruit with honey, wild berries, or salt cabbage and wholemeal stirabout. On Saturday white cabbage soup, noodles with peas, kasha, all with hemp oil. On weekdays we have dried fish and kasha with the cabbage soup. From Monday till Saturday evening, six whole days in Holy Week,* nothing is cooked, and we have only bread and water, and that sparingly; if possible not taking food every day, just the same as is ordered for first week in Lent. On Good Friday nothing is eaten. In the same way on the Saturday we have to fast till three o'clock, and then take a little bread and water and drink a single cup of wine. On Holy Thursday we drink wine and have something cooked without oil or not cooked at all. Inasmuch as the Laodicean council† lays down for Holy Thursday: 'it is unseemly by remitting the fast on the Holy Thursday to dishonour the whole of Lent!' This is how we keep the fast. But what is that compared with you, holy Father," added the monk, growing more confident, "for all the year round, even at Easter, you take nothing but bread and water, and what we should eat in two days lasts you full seven. It's truly marvellous—your great abstinence."

"And mushrooms?" asked Father Ferapont, suddenly.

"Mushrooms?" repeated the surprised monk.

*The last week of Lent, between Palm Sunday and Easter.
†The fourth-century Council of Laodicea established many tenets of the Christian ecclesiastical canon.

"Yes. I can give up their bread, not needing it at all, and go away into the forest and live there on the mushrooms or the berries, but they can't give up their bread here, wherefore they are in bondage to the devil. Nowadays the unclean deny that there is need of such fasting. Haughty and unclean is their judgment."

"Och, true," sighed the monk.

"And have you seen devils among them?" asked Ferapont.

"Among them? Among whom?" asked the monk, timidly.

"I went to the Father Superior on Trinity Sunday last year, I haven't been since. I saw a devil sitting on one man's chest hiding under his cassock, only his horns poked out; another had one peeping out of his pocket with such sharp eyes, he was afraid of me; another settled in the unclean belly of one, another was hanging round a man's neck, and so he was carrying him about without seeing him."

"You—can see spirits?" the monk inquired.

"I tell you I can see, I can see through them. When I was coming out from the Superior's I saw one hiding from me behind the door, and a big one, a yard and a half or more high, with a thick long grey tail, and the tip of his tail was in the crack of the door and I was quick and slammed the door, pinching his tail in it. He squealed and began to struggle, and I made the sign of the cross over him three times. And he died on the spot like a crushed spider. He must have rotted there in the corner and be stinking, but they don't see, they don't smell it. It's a year since I have been there. I reveal it to you, as you are a stranger."

"Your words are terrible! But, holy and blessed Father," said the monk, growing bolder and bolder, "is it true, as they noise abroad even to distant lands about you, that you are in continual communication with the Holy Ghost?"

"He does fly down at times."

"How does he fly down? In what form?"

"As a bird."

"The Holy Ghost in the form of a dove?"*

"There's the Holy Ghost and there's the Holy Spirit. The Holy Spirit can appear as other birds—sometimes as a swallow, sometimes a goldfinch and sometimes as a blue-tit."

"How do you know him from an ordinary tit?"

"He speaks."

"How does he speak, in what language?"

"Human language."

"And what does he tell you?"

"Why, to-day he told me that a fool would visit me and would ask me unseemly questions. You want to know too much, monk."

---

*At Christ's baptism, the Holy Spirit appeared in the form of a dove (see Matthew 3:16).

"Terrible are your words, most holy and blessed Father," the monk shook his head. But there was a doubtful look in his frightened little eyes.

"Do you see this tree?" asked Father Ferapont, after a pause.

"I do, blessed Father."

"You think it's an elm, but for me it has another shape."

"What sort of shape?" inquired the monk, after a pause of vain expectation.

"It happens at night. You see those two branches? In the night it is Christ holding out His arms to me and seeking me with those arms, I see it clearly and tremble. It's terrible, terrible!"

"What is there terrible if it's Christ Himself?"

"Why, He'll snatch me up and carry me away."

"Alive?"

"In the spirit and glory of Elijah, haven't you heard? He will take me in His arms and bear me away."

Though the monk returned to the cell he was sharing with one of the brothers, in considerable perplexity of mind, he still cherished at heart a greater reverence for Father Ferapont than for Father Zossima. He was strongly in favour of fasting, and it was not strange that one who kept so rigid a fast as Father Ferapont should "see marvels." His words seemed certainly queer, but God only could tell what was hidden in those words, and were not worse words and acts commonly seen in those who have sacrificed their intellects for the glory of God? The pinching of the devil's tail he was ready and eager to believe, and not only in the figurative sense. Besides he had, before visiting the monastery, a strong prejudice against the institution of "elders," which he only knew of by hearsay and believed to be a pernicious innovation. Before he had been long at the monastery, he had detected the secret murmurings of some shallow brothers who disliked the institution. He was, besides, a meddlesome, inquisitive man, who poked his nose into everything. This was why the news of the fresh "miracle" performed by Father Zossima reduced him to extreme perplexity. Alyosha remembered afterwards how their inquisitive guest from Obdorsk had been continually flitting to and fro from one group to another, listening and asking questions among the monks that were crowding within and without the elder's cell. But he did not pay much attention to him at the time, and only recollected it afterwards.

He had no thought to spare for it indeed, for when Father Zossima, feeling tired again, had gone back to bed, he thought of Alyosha as he was closing his eyes, and sent for him. Alyosha ran at once. There was no one else in the cell but Father Païssy, Father Iosif, and the novice Porfiry. The elder, opening his weary eyes and looking intently at Alyosha, asked him suddenly:

"Are your people expecting you, my son?"

Alyosha hesitated.

"Haven't they need of you? Didn't you promise some one yesterday to see them to-day?"

"I did promise—to my father—my brothers—others too."

"You see, you must go. Don't grieve. Be sure I shall not die without your being by to hear my last word. To you I will say that word, my son, it will be my last gift to you. To you, dear son, because you love me. But now go to keep your promise."

Alyosha immediately obeyed, though it was hard to go. But the promise that he should hear his last word on earth, that it should be the last gift to him, Alyosha, sent a thrill of rapture through his soul. He made haste that he might finish what he had to do in the town and return quickly. Father Païssy, too, uttered some words of exhortation which moved and surprised him greatly. He spoke as they left the cell together.

"Remember, young man, unceasingly," Father Païssy began, without preface, "that the science of this world, which has become a great power, has, especially in the last century, analysed everything divine handed down to us in the holy books. After this cruel analysis the learned of this world have nothing left of all that was sacred of old. But they have only analysed the parts and overlooked the whole, and indeed their blindness is marvellous. Yet the whole still stands steadfast before their eyes, and the gates of hell shall not prevail against it. Has it not lasted nineteen centuries, is it not still a living, a moving power in the individual soul and in the masses of people? It is still as strong and living even in the souls of atheists, who have destroyed everything! For even those who have renounced Christianity and attack it, in their inmost being still follow the Christian ideal, for hitherto neither their subtlety nor the ardour of their hearts has been able to create a higher ideal of man and of virtue than the ideal given by Christ of old. When it has been attempted, the result has been only grotesque. Remember this especially, young man, since you are being sent into the world by your departing elder. Maybe, remembering this great day, you will not forget my words, uttered from the heart for your guidance, seeing you are young, and the temptations of the world are great and beyond your strength to endure. Well, now go, my orphan."

With these words Father Païssy blessed him. As Alyosha left the monastery and thought them over, he suddenly realised that he had met a new and unexpected friend, a warmly loving teacher, in this austere monk who had hitherto treated him sternly. It was as though Father Zossima had bequeathed him to him at his death, and "perhaps that's just what had passed between them," Alyosha thought suddenly. The philosophic reflections he had just heard so unexpectedly testified to the warmth of Father Païssy's heart. He was in haste to arm the boy's mind for conflict with temptation and to guard the young soul left in his charge with the strongest defence he could imagine.

2

AT HIS FATHER'S

First of all, Alyosha went to his father. On the way he remembered that his father had insisted the day before that he should come without his brother Ivan seeing him. "Why so?" Alyosha wondered suddenly. "Even if my father has something to say to me alone, why should I go in unseen? Most likely in his excitement yesterday he meant to say something different," he decided.

Yet he was very glad when Marfa Ignatyevna, who opened the garden gate to him (Grigory, it appeared, was ill in bed in the lodge), told him in answer to his question that Ivan Fyodorovitch had gone out two hours ago.

"And my father?"

"He is up, taking his coffee," Marfa answered somewhat drily.

Alyosha went in. The old man was sitting alone at the table, wearing slippers and a little old overcoat. He was amusing himself by looking through some accounts, rather inattentively however. He was quite alone in the house, for Smerdyakov too had gone out marketing. Though he had got up early and was trying to put a bold face on it, he looked tired and weak. His forehead, upon which huge purple bruises had come out during the night, was bandaged with a red handkerchief; his nose too had swollen terribly in the night, and some smaller bruises covered it in patches, giving his whole face a peculiarly spiteful and irritable look. The old man was aware of this, and turned a hostile glance on Alyosha as he came in.

"The coffee is cold," he cried harshly; "I won't offer you any. I've ordered nothing but a Lenten fish soup to-day, and I don't invite any one to share it. Why have you come?"

"To find out how you are," said Alyosha.

"Yes. Besides, I told you to come yesterday. It's all of no consequence. You need not have troubled. But I knew you'd come poking in directly."

He said this with almost hostile feeling. At the same time he got up and looked anxiously in the looking-glass (perhaps for the fortieth time that morning) at his nose. He began, too, binding his red handkerchief more becomingly on his forehead.

"Red's better. It's just like the hospital in a white one," he observed sententiously. "Well, how are things over there? How is your elder?"

"He is very bad; he may die to-day," answered Alyosha. But his father had not listened, and had forgotten his own question at once.

"Ivan's gone out," he said suddenly. "He is doing his utmost to carry off Mitya's betrothed. That's what he is staying here for," he added maliciously, and, twisting his mouth, looked at Alyosha.

"Surely he did not tell you so?" asked Alyosha.

"Yes, he did, long ago. Would you believe it, he told me three weeks ago? You don't suppose he too came to murder me, do you? He must have had some object in coming."

"What do you mean? Why do you say such things?" said Alyosha, troubled.

"He doesn't ask for money, it's true, but yet he won't get a farthing from me. I intend living as long as possible, you may as well know, my dear Alexey Fyodorovitch, and so I need every farthing, and the longer I live, the more I shall need it," he continued, pacing from one corner of the room to the other, keeping his hands in the pockets of his loose greasy overcoat made of yellow cotton material. "I can still pass for a man at five and fifty, but I want to pass for one for another twenty years. As I get older, you know, I shan't be a pretty object. The wenches won't come to me of their own accord, so I shall want my money. So I am saving up more and more, simply for myself, my dear son Alexey Fyodorovitch. You may as well know. For I mean to go on in my sins to the end, let me tell you. For sin is sweet; all abuse it, but all men live in it, only others do it on the sly, and I openly. And so all the other sinners fall upon me for being so simple. And your paradise, Alexey Fyodorovitch, is not to my taste, let me tell you that; and it's not the proper place for a gentleman, your paradise, even if it exists. I believe that I fall asleep and don't wake up again, and that's all. You can pray for my soul if you like. And if you don't want to, don't, damn you! That's my philosophy. Ivan talked well here yesterday, though we were all drunk. Ivan is a conceited coxcomb, but he has no particular learning . . . nor education either. He sits silent and smiles at one without speaking—that's what pulls him through."

Alyosha listened to him in silence.

"Why won't he talk to me? If he does speak, he gives himself airs. Your Ivan is a scoundrel! And I'll marry Grushenka in a minute if I want to. For if you've money, Alexey Fyodorovitch, you have only to want a thing and you can have it. That's what Ivan is afraid of, he is on the watch to prevent me getting married and that's why he is egging on Mitya to marry Grushenka himself. He hopes to keep me from Grushenka by that (as though I should leave him my money if I don't marry her!). Besides if Mitya marries Grushenka, Ivan will carry off his rich betrothed, that's what he's reckoning on! He is a scoundrel, your Ivan!"

"How cross you are. It's because of yesterday; you had better lie down," said Alyosha.

"There! you say that," the old man observed suddenly, as though it had struck him for the first time, "and I am not angry with you. But if Ivan said it, I should be angry with him. It is only with you I have good moments, else you know I am an ill-natured man."

"You are not ill-natured, but distorted," said Alyosha with a smile.

"Listen. I meant this morning to get that ruffian Mitya locked up and I don't know now what I shall decide about it. Of course in these fashionable days fathers and mothers are looked upon as a prejudice, but even now the law does not allow you to drag your old father about by the hair, to kick him in the face in his own house, and brag of murdering him outright—all in the presence of witnesses. If I liked, I could crush him and could have him locked up at once for what he did yesterday."

"Then you don't mean to take proceedings?"

"Ivan has dissuaded me. I shouldn't care about Ivan, but there's another thing."

And bending down to Alyosha, he went on in a confidential half-whisper.

"If I send the ruffian to prison, she'll hear of it and run to see him at once. But if she hears that he has beaten me, a weak old man, within an inch of my life, she may give him up and come to me. . . . For that's her way, everything by contraries. I know her through and through! Won't you have a drop of brandy? Take some cold coffee and I'll pour a quarter of a glass of brandy into it, it's delicious, my boy."

"No, thank you. I'll take that roll with me if I may," said Alyosha, and taking a halfpenny French roll he put it in the pocket of his cassock. "And you'd better not have brandy, either," he suggested apprehensively, looking into the old man's face.

"You are quite right, it irritates my nerves instead of soothing them. Only one little glass. I'll get it out of the cupboard."

He unlocked the cupboard, poured out a glass, drank it, then locked the cupboard and put the key back in his pocket.

"That's enough. One glass won't kill me."

"You see you are in a better humour now," said Alyosha smiling.

"Um! I love you even without the brandy, but with scoundrels I am a scoundrel. Ivan is not going to Tchermashnya—why is that? He wants to spy how much I give Grushenka if she comes. They are all scoundrels! But I don't recognise Ivan, I don't know him at all. Where does he come from? He is not one of us in soul. As though I'd leave him anything! I shan't leave a will at all, you may as well know. And I'll crush Mitya like a beetle. I squash black beetles at night with my slipper; they squelch when you tread on them. And your Mitya will squelch too. *Your* Mitya, for you love him. Yes, you love him and I am not afraid of your loving him. But if Ivan loved him I should be afraid for myself at his loving him. But Ivan loves nobody. Ivan is not one of us. People like Ivan are not our sort, my boy. They are like a cloud of dust. When the wind blows, the dust will be gone . . . I had a silly idea in my head when I told you to come to-day; I wanted to find out from you about Mitya. If I were to hand him over a thousand or maybe two now, would the beggarly wretch agree to take himself off altogether for five years or, better still, thirty-five, and without Grushenka, and give her up once for all, eh?"

"I—I'll ask him," muttered Alyosha. "If you would give him three thousand, perhaps he——"

"That's nonsense! You needn't ask him now, no need! I've changed my mind. It was a nonsensical idea of mine. I won't give him anything, not a penny, I want my money myself," cried the old man, waving his hand. "I'll crush him like a beetle without it. Don't say anything to him or else he will begin hoping. There's nothing for you to do here, you needn't stay. Is that betrothed of his, Katerina Ivanovna, whom he has kept so carefully hidden from me all this time, going to marry him or not? You went to see her yesterday, I believe?"

"Nothing will induce her to abandon him."

"There you see how dearly these fine young ladies love a rake and a scoundrel. They are poor creatures I tell you, those pale young ladies, very different from ... Ah, if I had his youth and the looks I had then (for I was better-looking than he at eight and twenty) I'd have been a conquering hero just as he is. He is a low cad! But he shan't have Grushenka, anyway, he shan't! I'll crush him!"

His anger had returned with the last words.

"You can go. There's nothing for you to do here to-day," he snapped harshly.

Alyosha went up to say good-bye to him, and kissed him on the shoulder.

"What's that for?" the old man was a little surprised. "We shall see each other again, or do you think we shan't?"

"Not at all, I didn't mean anything."

"Nor did I, I did not mean anything," said the old man, looking at him. "Listen, listen," he shouted after him, "make haste and come again and I'll have a fish soup for you, a fine one, not like to-day. Be sure to come! Come to-morrow, do you hear, to-morrow!"

And as soon as Alyosha had gone out of the door, he went to the cupboard again and poured out another half-glass.

"I won't have more!" he muttered, clearing his throat, and again he locked the cupboard and put the key in his pocket. Then he went into his bedroom, lay down on the bed, exhausted, and in one minute he was asleep.

3

A MEETING WITH THE SCHOOLBOYS

THANK goodness he did not ask me about Grushenka," thought Alyosha, as he left his father's house and turned towards Madame Hohlakov's, "or I might have to tell him of my meeting with Grushenka yesterday."

Alyosha felt painfully that since yesterday both combatants had renewed their energies, and that their hearts had grown hard again. "Father is spiteful and angry, he's made some plan and will stick to it. And what of

Dmitri? He too will be harder than yesterday, he too must be spiteful and angry, and he too, no doubt, has made some plan. Oh, I must succeed in finding him to-day, whatever happens."

But Alyosha had not long to meditate. An incident occurred on the road, which, though apparently of little consequence, made a great impression on him. Just after he had crossed the square and turned the corner coming out into Mihailovsky Street, which is divided by a small ditch from the High Street (our whole town is intersected by ditches), he saw a group of schoolboys between the ages of nine and twelve, at the bridge. They were going home from school, some with their bags on their shoulders, others with leather satchels slung across them, some in short jackets, others in little overcoats. Some even had those high boots with creases round the ankles, such as little boys spoilt by rich fathers love to wear. The whole group was talking eagerly about something, apparently holding a council. Alyosha had never from his Moscow days been able to pass children without taking notice of them, and although he was particularly fond of children of three or thereabout, he liked schoolboys of ten and eleven too. And so, anxious as he was to-day, he wanted at once to turn aside to talk to them. He looked into their excited rosy faces, and noticed at once that all the boys had stones in their hands. Behind the ditch some thirty paces away, there was another schoolboy standing by a fence. He too had a satchel at his side. He was about ten years old, pale, delicate-looking and with sparkling black eyes. He kept an attentive and anxious watch on the other six, obviously his schoolfellows with whom he had just come out of school, but with whom he had evidently had a feud.

Alyosha went up and addressing a fair, curly-headed, rosy boy in a black jacket observed:

"When I used to wear a satchel like yours, I always used to carry it on my left side, so as to have my right hand free, but you've got yours on your right side. So it will be awkward for you to get at it."

Alyosha had no art or premeditation in beginning with this practical remark. But it is the only way for a grown-up person to get at once into confidential relations with a child, or still more with a group of children. One must begin in a serious businesslike way so as to be on a perfectly equal footing. Alyosha understood it by instinct.

"But he is left-handed," another, a fine healthy-looking boy of eleven, answered promptly. All the others stared at Alyosha.

"He even throws stones with his left hand," observed a third.

At that instant a stone flew into the group, but only just grazed the left-handed boy, though it was well and vigorously thrown by the boy standing the other side of the ditch.

"Give it him, hit him back, Smurov," they all shouted. But Smurov, the left-handed boy, needed no telling, and at once revenged himself; he threw a stone, but it missed the boy and hit the ground. The boy on the other side of the ditch, the pocket of whose coat was visibly bulging with stones, flung another stone at the group; this time it flew straight at Alyosha and hit him painfully on the shoulder.

"He aimed it at you, he meant it for you. You are Karamazov, Karamazov!" the boys shouted laughing, "Come, all throw at him at once!" and six
stones flew at the boy. One struck the boy on the head and he fell down,
but at once leapt up and began ferociously returning their fire. Both sides
threw stones incessantly. Many of the group had their pockets full too.

"What are you about! Aren't you ashamed? Six against one! Why, you'll
kill him," cried Alyosha.

He ran forward and met the flying stones to screen the solitary boy.
Three or four ceased throwing for a minute.

"He began first!" cried a boy in a red shirt in an angry childish voice.
"He is a beast, he stabbed Krassotkin in class the other day with a
penknife. It bled. Krassotkin wouldn't tell tales, but he must be thrashed."

"But what for? I suppose you tease him."

"There, he sent a stone in your back again, he knows you," cried the children. "It's you he is throwing at now, not us. Come, all of you, at him again,
don't miss, Smurov!" and again a fire of stones, and a very vicious one, began. The boy the other side of the ditch was hit in the chest; he screamed,
began to cry and ran away uphill towards Mihailovsky Street. They all
shouted: "Aha, he is funking, he is running away. Wisp of tow!"

"You don't know what a beast he is, Karamazov, killing is too good for
him," said the boy in the jacket, with flashing eyes. He seemed to be the
eldest.

"What's wrong with him?" asked Alyosha, "is he a tell-tale or what?"

The boys looked at one another as though derisively.

"Are you going that way, to Mihailovsky?" the same boy went on. "Catch
him up . . . You see he's stopped again, he is waiting and looking at you."

"He is looking at you," the other boys chimed in.

"You ask him, does he like a dishevelled wisp of tow. Do you hear, ask
him that!"

There was a general burst of laughter. Alyosha looked at them, and they
at him.

"Don't go near him, he'll hurt you," cried Smurov in a warning voice.

"I shan't ask him about the wisp of tow, for I expect you tease him with
that question somehow. But I'll find out from him why you hate him so."

"Find out then, find out," cried the boys laughing.

Alyosha crossed the bridge and walked uphill by the fence, straight towards the boy.

"You'd better look out," the boys called after him; "he won't be afraid
of you. He will stab you in a minute, on the sly, as he did Krassotkin."

The boy waited for him without budging. Coming up to him, Alyosha
saw facing him a child of about nine years old. He was an undersized
weakly boy with a thin long pale face, with large dark eyes that gazed at
him vindictively. He was dressed in a rather shabby old overcoat, which he
had monstrously outgrown. His bare arms stuck out beyond his sleeves.
There was a large patch on the right knee of his trousers, and in his right
boot just at the toe there was a big hole in the leather, carefully blackened
with ink. Both the pockets of his great coat were weighed down with

stones. Alyosha stopped two steps in front of him, looking inquiringly at him. The boy, seeing at once from Alyosha's eyes that he wouldn't beat him, became less defiant, and addressed him first.

"I am alone, and there are six of them. I'll beat them all, alone!" he said suddenly, with flashing eyes.

"I think one of the stones must have hurt you badly," observed Alyosha.

"But I hit Smurov on the head!" cried the boy.

"They told me that you know me, and that you threw a stone at me on purpose," said Alyosha.

The boy looked darkly at him.

"I don't know you. Do you know me?" Alyosha continued.

"Let me alone!" the boy cried irritably, but he did not move, as though he were expecting something, and again there was a vindictive light in his eyes.

"Very well, I am going," said Alyosha; "only I don't know you and I don't tease you. They told me how they tease you, but I don't want to tease you. Good-bye!"

"Monk in silk trousers!" cried the boy, following Alyosha with the same vindictive and defiant expression, and he threw himself into an attitude of defence, feeling sure that now Alyosha would fall upon him; but Alyosha turned, looked at him, and walked away. He had not gone three steps before the biggest stone the boy had in his pocket hit him a painful blow in the back.

"So you'll hit a man from behind! They tell the truth, then, when they say that you attack on the sly," said Alyosha, turning round again. This time the boy threw a stone savagely right into Alyosha's face; but Alyosha just had time to guard himself, and the stone struck him on the elbow.

"Aren't you ashamed? What have I done to you?" he cried.

The boy waited in silent defiance, certain that now Alyosha would attack him. Seeing that even now he would not, his rage was like a little wild beast's; he flew at Alyosha himself, and before Alyosha had time to move, the spiteful child had seized his left hand with both of his and bit his middle finger. He fixed his teeth in it and it was ten seconds before he let go. Alyosha cried out with pain and pulled his finger away with all his might. The child let go at last and retreated to his former distance. Alyosha's finger had been badly bitten to the bone, close to the nail; it began to bleed. Alyosha took out his handkerchief and bound it tightly round his injured hand. He was a full minute bandaging it. The boy stood waiting all the time. At last Alyosha raised his gentle eyes and looked at him.

"Very well," he said, "you see how badly you've bitten me. That's enough, isn't it? Now tell me what have I done to you?"

The boy stared in amazement.

"Though I don't know you and it's the first time I've seen you," Alyosha went on with the same serenity, "yet I must have done something to you—you wouldn't have hurt me like this for nothing. So what have I done? How have I wronged you, tell me?"

Instead of answering, the boy broke into a loud tearful wail and ran away. Alyosha walked slowly after him towards Mihailovsky Street, and for a long time he saw the child running in the distance as fast as ever, not turning his head, and no doubt still keeping up his tearful wail. He made up his mind to find him out as soon as he had time, and to solve this mystery. Just now he had not the time.

4

AT THE HOHLAKOVS'

ALYOSHA soon reached Madame Hohlakov's house, a handsome stone house of two storeys, one of the finest in our town. Though Madame Hohlakov spent most of her time in another province where she had an estate, or in Moscow, where she had a house of her own, yet she had a house in our town too, inherited from her forefathers. The estate in our district was the largest of her three estates, yet she had been very little in our province before this time. She ran out to Alyosha in the hall.

"Did you get my letter about the new miracle?" She spoke rapidly and nervously.

"Yes."

"Did you show it to every one? He restored the son to his mother!"

"He is dying to-day," said Alyosha.

"I have heard, I know, oh, how I long to talk to you, to you, or some one about all this. No, to you, to you! And how sorry I am I can't see him! The whole town is in excitement, they are all suspense. But now—do you know Katerina Ivanovna is here now?"

"Ah, that's lucky," cried Alyosha. "Then I shall see her here. She told me yesterday to be sure to come and see her to-day."

"I know, I know all. I've heard exactly what happened yesterday—and the atrocious behaviour of that—creature. *C'est tragique,* and if I'd been in her place I don't know what I should have done. And your brother Dmitri Fyodorovitch, what do you think of him?—my goodness! Alexey Fyodorovitch, I am forgetting, only fancy; your brother is in there with her, not that dreadful brother who was so shocking yesterday, but the other, Ivan Fyodorovitch, he is sitting with her talking; they are having a serious conversation. If you could only imagine what's passing between them now—it's awful, I tell you it's lacerating; it's like some incredible tale of horror. They are ruining their lives for no reason any one can see. They both recognise it and revel in it. I've been watching for you! I've been thirsting for you! It's too much for me, that's the worst of it. I'll tell you all about it presently, but now I must speak of something else, the most important thing—I had quite forgotten what's most important. Tell me; why has Lise been in hysterics? As soon as she heard you were here, she began to be hysterical!"

"*Maman,* it's you who are hysterical now, not I." Lise's voice carolled through a tiny crack of the door at the side. Her voice sounded as though she wanted to laugh, but was doing her utmost to control it. Alyosha at once noticed the crack, and no doubt Lise was peeping through it, but that he could not see.

"And no wonder, Lise, no wonder . . . your caprices will make me hysterical too. But she is so ill, Alexey Fyodorovitch, she has been so ill all night, feverish and moaning! I could hardly wait for the morning and for Herzenstube to come. He says that he can make nothing of it, that we must wait. Herzenstube always comes and says that he can make nothing of it. As soon as you approached the house, she screamed, fell into hysterics, and insisted on being wheeled back into this room here."

"Mamma, I didn't know he had come. It wasn't on his account I wanted to be wheeled into this room."

"That's not true, Lise, Yulia ran to tell you that Alexey Fyodorovitch was coming. She was on the look-out for you."

"My darling mamma, it's not at all clever of you. But if you want to make up for it and say something very clever, dear mamma, you'd better tell our honoured visitor, Alexey Fyodorovitch, that he has shown his want of wit by venturing to us after what happened yesterday and although every one is laughing at him."

"Lise, you go too far. I declare I shall have to be severe. Who laughs at him? I am so glad he has come, I need him, I can't do without him. Oh, Alexey Fyodorovitch, I am exceedingly unhappy!"

"But what's the matter with you, mamma, darling?"

"Ah, your caprices, Lise, your fidgetiness, your illness, that awful night of fever, that awful everlasting Herzenstube, everlasting, everlasting, that's the worst of it! Everything, in fact, everything. . . . Even that miracle, too! Oh, how it has upset me, how it has shattered me, that miracle, dear Alexey Fyodorovitch! And that tragedy in the drawing-room, it's more than I can bear, I warn you. I can't bear it. A comedy, perhaps, not a tragedy. Tell me, will Father Zossima live till to-morrow, will he? Oh, my God! What is happening to me? Every minute I close my eyes and see that it's all nonsense, all nonsense."

"I should be very grateful," Alyosha interrupted suddenly, "if you could give me a clean rag to bind up my finger with. I have hurt it, and it's very painful."

Alyosha unbound his bitten finger. The handkerchief was soaked with blood. Madame Hohlakov screamed and shut her eyes.

"Good heavens, what a wound, how awful!"

But as soon as Lise saw Alyosha's finger through the crack, she flung the door wide open.

"Come, come here," she cried, imperiously. "No nonsense now! Good heavens, why did you stand there saying nothing about it all this time? He might have bled to death, mamma! How did you do it? Water, water! You must wash it first of all, simply hold it in cold water to stop the pain, and keep it there, keep it there. . . . Make haste, mamma, some water in a slop basin. But do make haste," she finished nervously. She was quite frightened at the sight of Alyosha's wound.

"Shouldn't we send for Herzenstube?" cried Madame Hohlakov.

"Mamma, you'll be the death of me. Your Herzenstube will come and say that he can make nothing of it! Water, water! Mamma, for goodness' sake go yourself and hurry Yulia, she is such a slowcoach and never can come quickly! Make haste, mamma, or I shall die."

"Why, it's nothing much," cried Alyosha, frightened at this alarm.

Yulia ran in with water and Alyosha put his finger in it.

"Some lint, mamma, for mercy's sake, bring some lint and that muddy caustic lotion for wounds, what's it called? We've got some. You know where the bottle is, mamma; it's in your bedroom in the right-hand cupboard, there's a big bottle of it there with the lint."

"I'll bring everything in a minute, Lise, only don't scream and don't fuss. You see how bravely Alexey Fyodorovitch bears it. Where did you get such a dreadful wound, Alexey Fyodorovitch?"

Madame Hohlakov hastened away. This was all Lise was waiting for.

"First of all, answer the question, where did you get hurt like this?" she asked Alyosha, quickly. "And then I'll talk to you about something quite different. Well?"

Instinctively feeling that the time of her mother's absence was precious for her, Alyosha hastened to tell her of his enigmatic meeting with the schoolboys in the fewest words possible. Lise clasped her hands at his story.

"How can you, and in that dress too, associate with schoolboys!" she cried angrily, as though she had a right to control him. "You are nothing but a boy yourself if you can do that, a perfect boy! But you must find out for me about that horrid boy and tell me all about it, for there's some mystery in it. Now for the second thing, but first a question: does the pain prevent you talking about utterly unimportant things, but talking sensibly?"

"Of course not, and I don't feel much pain now."

"That's because your finger is in the water. It must be changed directly for it will get warm in a minute. Yulia, bring some ice from the cellar and another basin of water. Now she is gone, I can speak; will you give me the letter I sent you yesterday, dear Alexey Fyodorovitch—be quick for mamma will be back in a minute and I don't want——"

"I haven't got the letter."

"That's not true, you have. I knew you would say that. You've got it in that pocket. I've been regretting that joke all night. Give me back the letter at once, give it me."

"I've left it at home."

"But you can't consider me as a child, a little girl, after that silly joke! I beg your pardon for that silliness, but you must bring me the letter, if you really haven't got it—bring it to-day, you must, you must."

"To-day, I can't possibly, for I am going back to the monastery and I shan't come and see you for the next two days—three or four perhaps—for Father Zossima——"

"Four days, what nonsense! Listen. Did you laugh at me very much?"

"I didn't laugh at all."

"Why not?"

"Because I believed all you said."

"You are insulting me!"

"Not at all. As soon as I read it, I thought that all that would come to pass, for as soon as Father Zossima dies, I am to leave the monastery. Then I shall go back and finish my studies, and when you reach the legal age we will be married. I shall love you. Though I haven't had time to think about it, I believe I couldn't find a better wife than you, and Father Zossima tells me I must marry."

"But I am a cripple, wheeled about in a chair," laughed Lise, flushing crimson.

"I'll wheel you about myself, but I'm sure you'll get well by then."

"But you are mad," said Lise, nervously, "to make all this nonsense out of a joke! Here's mamma, very *à propos,* perhaps. Mamma, how slow you always are, how can you be so long! And here's Yulia with the ice!"

"Oh, Lise, don't scream, above all things don't scream. That scream drives me . . . How can I help it when you put the lint in another place. I've been hunting and hunting—I do believe you did it on purpose."

"But I couldn't tell that he would come with a bad finger, or else perhaps I might have done it on purpose. My darling mamma, you begin to say really witty things."

"Never mind my being witty, but I must say you show nice feeling for Alexey Fyodorovitch's sufferings! Oh, my dear Alexey Fyodorovitch, what's killing me is no one thing in particular, not Herzenstube, but everything together, that's what is too much for me."

"That's enough, mamma, enough about Herzenstube," Lise laughed gaily. "Make haste with the lint and the lotion, mamma. That's simply Goulard's water, Alexey Fyodorovitch, I remember the name now, but it's a splendid lotion. Would you believe it, mamma, on the way here he had a fight with the boys in the street, and it was a boy bit his finger, isn't he a child, a child himself? Is he fit to be married after that? For only fancy, he wants to be married, mamma. Just think of him married, wouldn't it be funny, wouldn't it be awful?"

And Lise kept laughing her thin hysterical giggle, looking slyly at Alyosha.

"But why married, Lise? What makes you talk of such a thing? It's quite out of place—and perhaps the boy was rabid."

"Why, mamma! As though there were rabid boys!"

"Why not, Lise, as though I had said something stupid! Your boy might have been bitten by a mad dog and he would become mad and bite any one near him. How well she has bandaged it, Alexey Fyodorovitch. I couldn't have done it. Do you still feel the pain?"

"It's nothing much now."

"You don't feel afraid of water?" asked Lise.

"Come, that's enough, Lise, perhaps I really was rather too quick talking of the boy being rabid, and you pounced upon it at once. Katerina Ivanovna has only just heard that you are here, Alexey Fyodorovitch, she simply rushed at me, she's dying to see you, dying!"

"Ach, mamma, go to them yourself. He can't go just now, he is in too much pain."

"Not at all, I can go quite well," said Alyosha.

"What! You are going away? Is that what you say?"

"Well, when I've seen them, I'll come back here and we can talk as much as you like. But I should like to see Katerina Ivanovna at once, for I am very anxious to be back at the monastery as soon as I can."

"Mamma, take him away quickly. Alexey Fyodorovitch, don't trouble to come and see me afterwards, but go straight back to your monastery and a good riddance. I want to sleep, I didn't sleep all night."

"Ah, Lise, you are only making fun, but how I wish you would sleep!" cried Madame Hohlakov.

"I don't know what I've done. . . . I'll stay another three minutes, five if you like," muttered Alyosha.

"Even five! Do take him away quickly, mamma, he is a monster."

"Lise, you are crazy. Let us go, Alexey Fyodorovitch, she is too capricious to-day. I am afraid to cross her. Oh, the trouble one has with nervous girls! Perhaps she really will be able to sleep after seeing you. How quickly you have made her sleepy, and how fortunate it is."

"Ah, mamma, how sweetly you talk. I must kiss you for it, mamma."

"And I kiss you too, Lise. Listen, Alexey Fyodorovitch," Madame Hohlakov began mysteriously and importantly, speaking in a rapid whisper. "I don't want to suggest anything, I don't want to lift the veil, you will see for yourself what's going on. It's appalling. It's the most fantastic farce. She loves your brother, Ivan, and she is doing her utmost to persuade herself she loves your brother, Dmitri. It's appalling! I'll go in with you, and if they don't turn me out, I'll stay to the end."

5

A LACERATION IN THE DRAWING-ROOM

BUT in the drawing-room the conversation was already over. Katerina Ivanovna was greatly excited, though she looked resolute. At the moment Alyosha and Madame Hohlakov entered, Ivan Fyodorovitch stood up to take leave. His face was rather pale, and Alyosha looked at him anxiously. For this moment was to solve a doubt, a harassing enigma which had for some time haunted Alyosha. During the preceding month it had been several times suggested to him that his brother Ivan was in love with Katerina Ivanovna, and, what was more, that he meant "to carry her off" from Dmitri. Until quite lately the idea seemed to Alyosha monstrous, though it worried him extremely. He loved both his brothers, and dreaded such rivalry between them. Meantime, Dmitri had said outright on the previous day that he was glad that Ivan was his rival, and that it was a great assistance to him, Dmitri. In what way did it assist him? To marry Grushenka? But that Alyosha considered the worst thing possible. Besides all this, Alyosha had till the evening before implicitly believed that Katerina Ivanovna had a steadfast and passionate love for Dmitri; but he had only believed it till the evening before. He had fancied, too, that she was incapable of loving a man like Ivan, and that she did love Dmitri, and loved him just as he was, in spite of all the strangeness of such a passion.

But during yesterday's scene with Grushenka another idea had struck him. The word "lacerating," which Madame Hohlakov had just uttered, almost made him start, because half waking up towards daybreak that night he had cried out, "Laceration, laceration," probably applying it to his dream. He had been dreaming all night of the previous day's scene at Katerina Ivanovna's. Now Alyosha was impressed by Madame Hohlakov's blunt and persistent assertion that Katerina Ivanovna was in love with Ivan, and only deceived herself through some sort of pose, from "self-laceration," and tortured herself by her pretended love for Dmitri from some fancied duty of gratitude. "Yes," he thought, "perhaps the whole truth lies in those words." But in that case what was Ivan's position? Alyosha felt instinctively that a character like Katerina Ivanovna's must dominate, and she could only dominate some one like Dmitri, and never a man like Ivan. For Dmitri might at last submit to her domination "to his own happiness" (which was what Alyosha would have desired), but Ivan—no, Ivan could not submit to her, and such submission would not give him happiness. Alyosha could not help believing that of Ivan. And now all these doubts and reflections flitted through his mind as he entered the drawing-room. Another idea, too, forced itself upon him: "What if she loved neither of them—neither Ivan nor Dmitri?"

It must be noted that Alyosha felt as it were ashamed of his own thoughts and blamed himself when they kept recurring to him during the last month. "What do I know about love and women and how can I decide such questions?" he thought reproachfully, after such doubts and surmises. And yet it was impossible not to think about it. He felt instinctively that this rivalry was of immense importance in his brothers' lives and that a great deal depended upon it.

"One reptile will devour the other," Ivan had pronounced the day before, speaking in anger of his father and Dmitri. So Ivan looked upon Dmitri as a reptile, and perhaps had long done so. Was it perhaps since he had known Katerina Ivanovna? That phrase had, of course, escaped Ivan unawares yesterday, but that only made it more important. If he felt like that, what chance was there of peace? Were there not, on the contrary, new grounds for hatred and hostility in their family? And with which of them was Alyosha to sympathise? And what was he to wish for each of them? He loved them both, but what could he desire for each in the midst of these conflicting interests? He might go quite astray in this maze, and Alyosha's heart could not endure uncertainty, because his love was always of an active character. He was incapable of passive love. If he loved any one, he set to work at once to help him. And to do so he must know what he was aiming at; he must know for certain what was best for each, and having ascertained this it was natural for him to help them both. But instead of a definite aim, he found nothing but uncertainty and perplexity on all sides. "It was lacerating," as was said just now. But what could he understand even in this "laceration"? He did not understand the first word in this perplexing maze.

Seeing Alyosha, Katerina Ivanovna said quickly and joyfully to Ivan, who had already got up to go, "A minute! Stay another minute! I want to hear the opinion of this person here whom I trust absolutely. Don't go away," she added, addressing Madame Hohlakov. She made Alyosha sit down beside her, and Madame Hohlakov sat opposite, by Ivan.

"You are all my friends here, all I have in the world, my dear friends," she began warmly, in a voice which quivered with genuine tears of suffering, and Alyosha's heart warmed to her at once. "You, Alexey Fyodorovitch, were witness yesterday of that abominable scene, and saw what I did. You did not see it, Ivan Fyodorovitch, he did. What he thought of me yesterday I don't know. I only know one thing, that if it were repeated today, this minute, I should express the same feelings again as yesterday— the same feelings, the same words, the same actions. You remember my actions, Alexey Fyodorovitch; you checked me in one of them" ... (as she said that, she flushed and her eyes shone). "I must tell you that I can't get over it. Listen, Alexey Fyodorovitch. I don't even know whether I still love *him*. I feel *pity* for him, and that is a poor sign of love. If I loved him, if I still loved him, perhaps I shouldn't be sorry for him now, but should hate him."

Her voice quivered, and tears glittered on her eyelashes. Alyosha shuddered inwardly. "That girl is truthful and sincere," he thought, "and she does not love Dmitri any more."

"That's true, that's true," cried Madame Hohlakov.

"Wait, dear. I haven't told you the chief, the final decision I came to during the night. I feel that perhaps my decision is a terrible one—for me, but I foresee that nothing will induce me to change it—nothing. It will be so all my life. My dear, kind, ever-faithful and generous adviser, the one friend I have in the world, Ivan Fyodorovitch, with his deep insight into the heart, approves and commends my decision. He knows it."

"Yes, I approve of it," Ivan assented, in a subdued but firm voice.

"But I should like Alyosha, too (Ah! Alexey Fyodorovitch, forgive my calling you simply Alyosha), I should like Alexey Fyodorovitch, too, to tell me before my two friends whether I am right. I feel instinctively that you, Alyosha, my dear brother (for you are a dear brother to me)," she said again ecstatically, taking his cold hand in her hot one, "I foresee that your decision, your approval, will bring me peace, in spite of all my sufferings, for, after your words, I shall be calm and submit—I feel that."

"I don't know what you are asking me," said Alyosha, flushing. "I only know that I love you and at this moment wish for your happiness more than my own! . . . But I know nothing about such affairs," something impelled him to add hurriedly.

"In such affairs, Alexey Fyodorovitch, in such affairs, the chief thing is honour and duty and something higher—I don't know what—but higher perhaps even than duty. I am conscious of this irresistible feeling in my heart, and it compels me irresistibly. But it may all be put in two words. I've already decided, even if he marries that—creature (she began solemnly), whom I never, never can forgive, *even then I will not abandon him*. Henceforward I will never, never abandon him!" she cried, breaking into a sort of pale, hysterical ecstasy. "Not that I would run after him continually, get in his way and worry him. Oh, no! I will go away to another town—where you like—but I will watch over him all my life—I will watch over him all my life unceasingly. When he becomes unhappy with that woman, and that is bound to happen quite soon, let him come to me and he will find a friend, a sister. . . . Only a sister, of course, and so for ever; but he will learn at least that that sister is really his sister, who loves him and has sacrificed all her life to him. I will gain my point. I will insist on his knowing me and confiding entirely in me, without reserve," she cried, in a sort of frenzy. "I will be a god to whom he can pray—and that, at least, he owes me for his treachery and for what I suffered yesterday through him. And let him see that all my life I will be true to him and the promise I gave him, in spite of his being untrue and betraying me. I will—I will become nothing but a means for his happiness, or—how shall I say?—an instrument, a machine for his happiness, and that for my whole life, my whole life, and that he may see that all his life! That's my decision. Ivan Fyodorovitch fully approves me."

She was breathless. She had perhaps intended to express her idea with more dignity, art and naturalness, but her speech was too hurried and crude. It was full of youthful impulsiveness, it betrayed that she was still smarting from yesterday's insult, and that her pride craved satisfaction. She felt this herself. Her face suddenly darkened, an unpleasant look came into her eyes. Alyosha at once saw it and felt a pang of sympathy. His brother Ivan made it worse by adding:

"I've only expressed my own view," he said. "From any one else, this would have been affected and overstrained, but from you—no. Any other woman would have been wrong, but you are right. I don't know how to explain it, but I see that you are absolutely genuine and, therefore, you are right."

"But that's only for the moment. And what does this moment stand for? Nothing but yesterday's insult." Madame Hohlakov obviously had not intended to interfere, but she could not refrain from this very just comment.

"Quite so, quite so," cried Ivan, with peculiar eagerness, obviously annoyed at being interrupted, "in any one else this moment would be only due to yesterday's impression and would be only a moment. But with Katerina Ivanovna's character, that moment will last all her life. What for any one else would be only a promise is for her an everlasting, burdensome, grim perhaps, but unflagging duty. And she will be sustained by the feeling of this duty being fulfilled. Your life, Katerina Ivanovna, will henceforth be spent in painful brooding over your own feelings, your own heroism, and your own suffering; but in the end that suffering will be softened and will pass into sweet contemplation of the fulfilment of a bold and proud design. Yes, proud it certainly is, and desperate in any case, but a triumph for you. And the consciousness of it will at last be a source of complete satisfaction and will make you resigned to everything else."

This was unmistakably said with some malice and obviously with intention; even perhaps with no desire to conceal that he spoke ironically and with intention.

"Oh, dear, how mistaken it all is!" Madame Hohlakov cried again.

"Alexey Fyodorovitch, you speak. I want dreadfully to know what you will say!" cried Katerina Ivanovna, and burst into tears. Alyosha got up from the sofa.

"It's nothing, nothing!" she went on through her tears. "I'm upset, I didn't sleep last night. But by the side of two such friends as you and your brother I still feel strong—for I know—you two will never desert me."

"Unluckily I am obliged to return to Moscow—perhaps to-morrow—and to leave you for a long time—And, unluckily, it's unavoidable," Ivan said suddenly.

"To-morrow—to Moscow!" her face was suddenly contorted; "but—but, dear me, how fortunate," she cried in a voice suddenly changed. In one instant there was no trace left of her tears. She underwent an instantaneous transformation, which amazed Alyosha. Instead of a poor, insulted girl, weeping in a sort of "laceration," he saw a woman completely self-possessed and even exceedingly pleased, as though something agreeable had just happened.

"Oh, not fortunate that I am losing you, of course not," she corrected herself suddenly, with a charming society smile. "Such a friend as you are could not suppose that. I am only too unhappy at losing you." She rushed impulsively at Ivan, and seizing both his hands, pressed them warmly. "But what is fortunate is that you will be able in Moscow to see auntie and Agafya and to tell them all the horror of my present position. You can speak with complete openness to Agafya, but spare dear auntie. You will know how to do that. You can't think how wretched I was yesterday and this morning, wondering how I could write them that dreadful letter—for one can never tell such things in a letter. . . . Now it will be easy for me to write, for you will see them and explain everything. Oh, how glad I am! But I am only glad of that, believe me. Of course, no one can take your place. . . . I will run at once to write the letter," she finished suddenly, and took a step as though to go out of the room.

"And what about Alyosha and his opinion, which you were so desperately anxious to hear?" cried Madame Hohlakov. There was a sarcastic, angry note in her voice.

"I had not forgotten that," cried Katerina Ivanovna, coming to a sudden standstill, "and why are you so antagonistic at such a moment?" she added, with warm and bitter reproachfulness. "What I said, I repeat. I must have his opinion. More than that, I must have his decision! As he says, so it shall be. You see how anxious I am for your words, Alexey Fyodorovitch. . . . But what's the matter?"

"I couldn't have believed it. I can't understand it!" Alyosha cried suddenly in distress.

"What? What?"

"He is going to Moscow, and you cry out that you are glad. You said that on purpose! And you begin explaining that you are not glad of that but sorry to be—losing a friend. But that was acting, too—you were playing a part—as in a theatre!"

"In a theatre? What? What do you mean?" exclaimed Katerina Ivanovna, profoundly astonished, flushing crimson, and frowning.

"Though you assure him you are sorry to lose a friend in him, you persist in telling him to his face that it's fortunate he is going," said Alyosha breathlessly. He was standing at the table and did not sit down.

"What are you talking about? I don't understand?"

"I don't understand myself. . . . I seemed to see in a flush . . . I know I am not saying it properly, but I'll say it all the same," Alyosha went on in the same shaking and broken voice. "What I see is that perhaps you don't love Dmitri at all . . . and never have, from the beginning. . . . And Dmitri, too, has never loved you . . . and only esteems you. . . . I really don't know how I dare to say all this, but somebody must tell the truth . . . for nobody here will tell the truth."

"What truth?" cried Katerina Ivanovna, and there was an hysterical ring in her voice.

"I'll tell you," Alyosha went on with desperate haste, as though he were jumping from the top of a house. "Call Dmitri; I will fetch him—and let him come here and take your hand and take Ivan's and join your hands. For you're torturing Ivan, simply because you love him—and torturing him, because you love Dmitri through 'self-laceration'—with an unreal love—because you've persuaded yourself."

Alyosha broke off and was silent.

"You . . . you . . . you are a little religious idiot—that's what you are!" Katerina Ivanovna snapped. Her face was white and her lips were moving with anger.

Ivan suddenly laughed and got up. His hat was in his hand.

"You are mistaken, my good Alyosha," he said, with an expression Alyosha had never seen in his face before—an expression of youthful sincerity and strong, irresistibly frank feeling. "Katerina Ivanovna has never cared for me! She has known all the time that I cared for her—though I never said a word of my love to her—she knew, but she didn't care for me. I have never been her friend either, not for one moment; she is too proud to need my friendship. She kept me at her side as a means of revenge. She revenged with me and on me all the insults which she has been continually receiving from Dmitri ever since their first meeting. For even that first meeting has rankled in her heart as an insult—that's what her heart is like! She has talked to me of nothing but her love for him. I am going now; but, believe me, Katerina Ivanovna, you really love him. And the more he insults you, the more you love him—that's your 'laceration.' You love him just as he is; you love him for insulting you. If he reformed, you'd give him up at once and cease to love him. But you need him so as to contemplate continually your heroic fidelity and to reproach him for infidelity. And it all comes from your pride. Oh, there's a great deal of humiliation and self-abasement about it, but it all comes from pride. . . . I am too young and I've loved you too much. I know that I ought not to say this, that it would be more dignified on my part simply to leave you, and it would be less offensive for you. But I am going far away, and shall never come back. . . . It is for ever. I don't want to sit beside a 'laceration'. . . . But I don't know how to speak now. I've said everything. . . . Good-bye Katerina Ivanovna; you can't be angry with me, for I am a hundred times more severely punished than you, if only by the fact that I shall never see you again. Good-bye! I don't want your hand. You have tortured me too deliberately for me to be able to forgive you at this moment. I shall forgive you later, but now I don't want your hand. 'Den Dank, Dame, begehr ich nicht,' "* he added, with a forced smile, showing, however, that he could read Schiller, and read him till he knew him by heart—which Alyosha would never have believed. He went out of the room without saying good-bye even to his hostess, Madame Hohlakov. Alyosha clasped his hands.

"Ivan!" he cried desperately after him. "Come back, Ivan! No, nothing will induce him to come back now!" he cried again, regretfully realising it;

---

*"This thanks, my lady, I do not desire" (German), a quotation from Schiller's 1797 poem "Der Handschuh" ("The Glove").

"but it's my fault, my fault. I began it! Ivan spoke angrily, wrongly. Unjustly and angrily. He must come back here, come back," Alyosha kept exclaiming frantically.

Katerina Ivanovna went suddenly into the next room.

"You have done no harm. You behaved beautifully, like an angel," Madame Hohlakov whispered rapidly and ecstatically to Alyosha. "I will do my utmost to prevent Ivan Fyodorovitch from going."

Her face beamed with delight, to the great distress of Alyosha, but Katerina Ivanovna suddenly returned. She had two hundred-rouble notes in her hand.

"I have a great favour to ask of you, Alexey Fyodorovitch," she began, addressing Alyosha with an apparently calm and even voice, as though nothing had happened. "A week—yes, I think it was a week ago—Dmitri Fyodorovitch was guilty of a hasty and unjust action—a very ugly action. There is a low tavern here and in it he met that discharged officer, that captain, whom your father used to employ in some business. Dmitri Fyodorovitch somehow lost his temper with this captain, seized him by the beard and dragged him out into the street and for some distance along it, in that insulting fashion. And I am told that his son, a boy, quite a child, who is at the school here, saw it and ran beside them crying and begging for his father, appealing to every one to defend him, while every one laughed. You must forgive me, Alexey Fyodorovitch, I cannot think without indignation of that disgraceful action of *his* . . . one of those actions of which only Dmitri Fyodorovitch would be capable in his anger . . . and in his passions! I can't describe it even. . . . I can't find my words. I've made inquiries about his victim, and find he is quite a poor man. His name is Snegiryov. He did something wrong in the army and was discharged. I can't tell you what. And now he has sunk into terrible destitution, with his family—an unhappy family of sick children, and, I believe, an insane wife. He has been living here a long time; he used to work as a copying clerk, but now he is getting nothing. I thought if you . . . that is I thought . . . I don't know. I am so confused. You see, I wanted to ask you, my dear Alexey Fyodorovitch, to go to him, to find some excuse to go to them—I mean to that captain—oh, goodness, how badly I explain it!—and delicately, carefully, as only you know how to (Alyosha blushed), manage to give him this assistance, these two hundred roubles. He will be sure to take it. . . . I mean, persuade him to take it. . . . Or, rather, what do I mean? You see it's not by way of compensation to prevent him from taking proceedings (for I believe he meant to), but simply a token of sympathy, of a desire to assist him from me, Dmitri Fyodorovitch's betrothed, not from himself. . . . But you know. . . . I would go myself, but you'll know how to do it ever so much better. He lives in Lake Street, in the house of a woman called Kalmikov. . . . For God's sake, Alexey Fyodorovitch do it for me, and now . . . now I am rather . . . tired. Good-bye!"

She turned so quickly and disappeared behind the portière that Alyosha had not time to utter a word, though he wanted to speak. He longed to beg her pardon, to blame himself, to say something, for his heart was full and he could not bear to go out of the room without it. But Madame Hohlakov took him by the hand and drew him along with her. In the hall she stopped him again as before.

"She is proud, she is struggling with herself; but kind, charming, generous," she exclaimed, in a half-whisper. "Oh, how I love her, especially sometimes, and how glad I am again of everything! Dear Alexey Fyodorovitch, you didn't know, but I must tell you, that we all, all—both her aunts, I and all of us, Lise, even—have been hoping and praying for nothing for the last month but that she may give up your favourite Dmitri, who takes no notice of her and does not care for her, and may marry Ivan Fyodorovitch—such an excellent and cultivated young man, who loves her more than anything in the world. We are in a regular plot to bring it about, and I am even staying on here perhaps on that account."

"But she has been crying—she has been wounded again," cried Alyosha.

"Never trust a woman's tears, Alexey Fyodorovitch. I am never for the women in such cases. I am always on the side of the men."

"Mamma, you are spoiling him," Lise's little voice cried from behind the door.

"No, it was all my fault. I am horribly to blame," Alyosha repeated unconsoled, hiding his face in his hands in an agony of remorse for his indiscretion.

"Quite the contrary; you behaved like an angel, like an angel. I am ready to say so a thousand times over."

"Mamma, how has he behaved like an angel?" Lise's voice was heard again.

"I somehow fancied all at once," Alyosha went on as though he had not heard Lise, "that she loved Ivan, and so I said that stupid thing. . . . What will happen now?"

"To whom, to whom?" cried Lise. "Mamma, you really want to be the death of me. I ask you and you don't answer."

At the moment the maid ran in.

"Katerina Ivanovna is ill. . . . She is crying, struggling . . . hysterics."

"What is the matter?" cried Lise, in a tone of real anxiety. "Mamma, I shall be having hysterics, and not she!"

"Lise, for mercy's sake, don't scream, don't persecute me. At your age one can't know everything that grown-up people know. I'll come and tell you everything you ought to know. Oh, mercy on us! I am coming, I am coming. . . . Hysterics is a good sign, Alexey Fyodorovitch; it's an excellent thing that she is hysterical. That's just as it ought to be. In such cases I am always against the woman, against all these feminine tears and hysterics. Run and say, Yulia, that I'll fly to her. As for Ivan Fyodorovitch's going away like that, it's her own fault. But he won't go away. Lise, for mercy's sake, don't scream! Oh, yes; you are not screaming. It's I am screaming. Forgive your mamma; but I am delighted, delighted, delighted! Did you notice, Alexey Fyodorovitch, how young, how young Ivan Fyodorovitch was just now when he went out, when he said all that and went out? I thought he was so learned, such a *savant,* and all of a sudden he behaved so warmly, openly, and youthfully, with such youthful inexperience, and it was all so fine, like you. . . . And the way he repeated that German verse, it was just like you! But I must fly, I must fly! Alexey Fyodorovitch, make haste to carry out her commission, and then make haste back. Lise, do you want anything now? For mercy's sake, don't keep Alexey Fyodorovitch a minute. He will come back to you at once."

Madame Hohlakov at last ran off. Before leaving, Alyosha would have opened the door to see Lise.

"On no account," cried Lise. "On no account now. Speak through the door. How have you come to be an angel? That's the only thing I want to know."

"For an awful piece of stupidity, Lise! Good-bye!"

"Don't dare to go away like that!" Lise was beginning.

"Lise, I have a real sorrow! I'll be back directly, but I have a great, great sorrow!"

And he ran out of the room.

6

A LACERATION IN THE COTTAGE

HE certainly was really grieved in a way he had seldom been before. He had rushed in like a fool, and meddled in what? In a love-affair. "But what do I know about it? What can I tell about such things?" he repeated to himself for the hundredth time, flushing crimson. "Oh, being ashamed would be nothing; shame is only the punishment I deserve. The trouble is I shall certainly have caused more unhappiness. . . . And Father Zossima sent me to reconcile and bring them together. Is this the way to bring them together?" Then he suddenly remembered how he had tried to join their hands, and he felt fearfully ashamed again. "Though I acted quite sincerely, I must be more sensible in the future," he concluded suddenly, and did not even smile at his conclusion.

Katerina Ivanovna's commission took him to Lake Street, and his brother Dmitri lived close by, in a turning out of Lake Street. Alyosha decided to go to him in any case before going to the captain, though he had a presentiment that he would not find his brother. He suspected that he would intentionally keep out of his way now, but he must find him anyhow. Time was passing: the thought of his dying elder had not left Alyosha for one minute from the time he set off from the monastery.

There was one point which interested him particularly about Katerina Ivanovna's commission; when she had mentioned the captain's son, the little schoolboy who had run beside his father crying, the idea had at once struck Alyosha that this must be the schoolboy who had bitten his finger when he, Alyosha, asked him what he had done to hurt him. Now Alyosha felt practically certain of this, though he could not have said why. Thinking of another subject was a relief, and he resolved to think no more about the "mischief" he had done, and not to torture himself with remorse, but to do what he had to do, let come what would. At that thought he was completely comforted. Turning to the street where Dmitri lodged, he felt hungry, and taking out of his pocket the roll he had brought from his father's, he ate it. It made him feel stronger.

Dmitri was not at home. The people of the house, an old cabinetmaker, his son, and his old wife, looked with positive suspicion at Alyosha. "He hasn't slept here for the last three nights. Maybe he has gone away," the old man said in answer to Alyosha's persistent inquiries. Alyosha saw that he was answering in accordance with instructions. When he asked whether he were not at Grushenka's or in hiding at Foma's (Alyosha spoke so freely on purpose), all three looked at him in alarm. "They are fond of him, they are doing their best for him," thought Alyosha. "That's good."

At last he found the house in Lake Street. It was a decrepit little house, sunk on one side, with three windows looking into the street, and with a muddy yard, in the middle of which stood a solitary cow. He crossed the yard and found the door opening into the passage. On the left of the passage lived the old woman of the house with her old daughter. Both seemed to be deaf. In answer to his repeated inquiry for the captain, one of them at last understood that he was asking for their lodgers, and pointed to a door across the passage. The captain's lodging turned out to be a simple cottage room. Alyosha had his hand on the iron latch to open the door, when he was struck by the strange hush within. Yet he knew from Katerina Ivanovna's words that the man had a family. "Either they are all asleep or perhaps they have heard me coming and are waiting for me to open the door. I'd better knock first," and he knocked. An answer came, but not at once, after an interval of perhaps ten seconds.

"Who's there?" shouted some one in a loud and very angry voice.

Then Alyosha opened the door and crossed the threshold. He found himself in a regular peasant's room. Though it was large, it was cumbered up with domestic belongings of all sorts, and there were several people in it. On the left was a large Russian stove. From the stove to the window on the left was a string running across the room, and on it there were rags hanging. There was a bedstead against the wall on each side, right and left, covered with knitted quilts. On the one on the left was a pyramid of four print-covered pillows, each smaller than the one beneath. On the other there was only one very small pillow. The opposite corner was screened off by a curtain or a sheet hung on a string. Behind this curtain could be seen a bed made up on a bench and a chair. The rough square table of plain wood had been moved into the middle window. The three windows, which consisted each of four tiny greenish mildewy panes, gave little light, and were close shut, so that the room was not very light and rather stuffy. On the table was a frying-pan with the remains of some fried eggs, a half-eaten piece of bread, and a small bottle with a few drops of vodka.

A woman of genteel appearance, wearing a cotton gown, was sitting on a chair by the bed on the left. Her face was thin and yellow, and her sunken cheeks betrayed at the first glance that she was ill. But what struck Alyosha most was the expression in the poor woman's eyes—a look of surprised inquiry and yet of haughty pride. And while he was talking to her husband, her big brown eyes moved from one speaker to the other with the same haughty and questioning expression. Beside her at the window stood a young girl, rather plain, with scanty reddish hair, poorly but very neatly dressed. She looked disdainfully at Alyosha as he came in. Beside the other bed was sitting another female figure. She was a very sad sight, a young girl of about twenty, but hunchback and crippled "with withered legs," as Alyosha was told afterwards. Her crutches stood in the corner close by. The strikingly beautiful and gentle eyes of this poor girl looked with mild serenity at Alyosha. A man of forty-five was sitting at the table, finishing the fried eggs. He was spare, small and weakly built. He had reddish hair and a scanty light-coloured beard, very much like a wisp of tow (this comparison and the phrase "a wisp of tow" flashed at once into Alyosha's mind for some reason, he remembered it afterwards). It was obviously this gentleman who had shouted to him, as there was no other man in the room. But when Alyosha went in, he leapt up from the bench on which he was sitting, and, hastily wiping his mouth with a ragged napkin, darted up to Alyosha.

"It's a monk come to beg for the monastery. A nice place to come to!" the girl standing in the left corner said aloud. The man spun round instantly towards her and answered her in an excited and breaking voice.

"No, Varvara, you are wrong. Allow me to ask," he turned again to Alyosha, "what has brought you to—our retreat?"

Alyosha looked attentively at him. It was the first time he had seen him. There was something angular, flurried and irritable about him. Though he had obviously just been drinking, he was not drunk. There was extraordinary impudence in his expression, and yet, strange to say, at the same time there was fear. He looked like a man who had long been kept in subjection and had submitted to it, and now had suddenly turned and was trying to assert himself. Or, better still, like a man who wants dreadfully to hit you but is horribly afraid you will hit him. In his words and in the intonation of his shrill voice there was a sort of crazy humour, at times spiteful and at times cringing, and continually shifting from one tone to another. The question about "our retreat" he had asked as it were quivering all over, rolling his eyes, and skipping up so close to Alyosha that he instinctively drew back a step. He was dressed in a very shabby dark cotton coat, patched and spotted. He wore checked trousers of an extremely light colour, long out of fashion, and of very thin material. They were so crumpled and so short that he looked as though he had grown out of them like a boy.

"I am Alexey Karamazov," Alyosha began in reply.

"I quite understand that, sir," the gentleman snapped out at once to assure him that he knew who he was already. "I am Captain Snegiryov, sir, but I am still desirous to know precisely what has led you——"

"Oh, I've come for nothing special. I wanted to have a word with you—if only you allow me."

"In that case, here is a chair, sir; kindly be seated. That's what they used to say in the old comedies, 'kindly be seated,' " and with a rapid gesture he seized an empty chair (it was a rough wooden chair, not upholstered) and set it for him almost in the middle of the room; then, taking another similar chair for himself, he sat down facing Alyosha, so close to him that their knees almost touched.

"Nikolay Ilyitch Snegiryov, sir, formerly a captain in the Russian infantry, put to shame for his vices, but still a captain. Though I might not be one now for the way I talk; for the last half of my life I've learnt to say 'sir.' It's a word you use when you've come down in the world."

"That's very true," smiled Alyosba. "But is it used involuntarily or on purpose?"

"As God's above, it's involuntary, and I usen't to use it! I didn't use the word 'sir' all my life, but as soon as I sank into low water I began to say 'sir.' It's the work of a higher power. I see you are interested in contemporary questions, but how can I have excited your curiosity, living as I do in surroundings impossible for the exercise of hospitality?"

"I've come—about that business."

"About what business?" the captain interrupted impatiently.

"About your meeting with my brother Dmitri Fyodorovitch," Alyosha blurted out awkwardly.

"What meeting, sir? You don't mean that meeting? About my 'wisp of tow,' then?" He moved closer so that his knees positively knocked against Alyosha. His lips were strangely compressed like a thread.

"What wisp of tow?" muttered Alyosha.

"He is come to complain of me, father!" cried a voice familiar to Alyosha—the voice of the schoolboy—from behind the curtain. "I bit his finger just now." The curtain was pulled, and Alyosha saw his assailant lying on a little bed made up on the bench and the chair in the corner under the ikons. The boy lay covered by his coat and an old wadded quilt. He was evidently unwell, and, judging by his glittering eyes, he was in a fever. He looked at Alyosha without fear, as though he felt he was at home and could not be touched.

"What! Did he bite your finger?" The captain jumped up from his chair. "Was it your finger he bit?"

"Yes. He was throwing stones with other schoolboys. There were six of them against him alone. I went up to him, and he threw a stone at me and then another at my head. I asked him what I had done to him. And then he rushed at me and bit my finger badly, I don't know why."

"I'll thrash him, sir, at once—this minute!" The captain jumped up from his seat.

"But I am not complaining at all, I am simply telling you. . . . I don't want him to be thrashed. Besides, he seems to be ill."

"And do you suppose I'd thrash him? That I'd take my Ilusha and thrash him before you for your satisfaction? Would you like it done at once, sir?" said the captain, suddenly turning to Alyosha, as though he were going to attack him. "I am sorry about your finger, sir; but instead of thrashing Ilusha, would you like me to chop off my four fingers with this knife here before your eyes to satisfy your just wrath? I should think four fingers would be enough to satisfy your thirst for vengeance. You won't ask for the fifth one too?" He stopped short with a catch in his throat. Every feature in his face was twitching and working; he looked extremely defiant. He was in a sort of frenzy.

"I think I understand it all now," said Alyosha gently and sorrowfully, still keeping his seat. "So your boy is a good boy, he loves his father, and he attacked me as the brother of your assailant. . . . Now I understand it," he repeated thoughtfully. "But my brother Dmitri Fyodorovitch regrets his action, I know that, and if only it is possible for him to come to you, or better still, to meet you in that same place, he will ask your forgiveness before every one—if you wish it."

"After pulling out my beard, you mean, he will ask my forgiveness? And he thinks that will be a satisfactory finish, doesn't he?"

"Oh, no! On the contrary, he will do anything you like and in any way you like."

"So if I were to ask his highness to go down on his knees before me in that very tavern—'The Metropolis' it's called—or in the market-place, he would do it?"

"Yes, he would even go down on his knees."

"You've pierced me to the heart, sir. Touched me to tears and pierced me to the heart! I am only too sensible of your brother's generosity. Allow me to introduce my family, my two daughters and my son—my litter. If I die, who will care for them, and while I live who but they will care for a wretch like me? That's a great thing the Lord has ordained for every man of my sort, sir. For there must be some one able to love even a man like me."

"Ah, that's perfectly true!" exclaimed Alyosha.

"Oh, do leave off playing the fool! Some idiot comes in, and you put us to shame!" cried the girl by the window, suddenly turning to her father with a disdainful and contemptuous air.

"Wait a little, Varvara!" cried her father, speaking peremptorily but looking at her quite approvingly. "That's her character," he said, addressing Alyosha again.

> "And in all nature there was naught
>   That could find favour in his eyes*

---

*Quotation from Pushkin's poem "Demon" (1823).

or rather in the feminine: that could find favour in her eyes. But now let me present you to my wife, Arina Petrovna. She is crippled, she is forty-three; she can move, but very little. She is of humble origin. Arina Petrovna, compose your countenance. This is Alexey Fyodorovitch Karamazov. Get up, Alexey Fyodorovitch." He took him by the hand and with unexpected force pulled him up. "You must stand up to be introduced to a lady. It's not the Karamazov, mamma, who . . . h'm . . . etcetera, but his brother, radiant with modest virtues. Come Arina Petrovna, come, mamma, first your hand to be kissed."

And he kissed his wife's hand respectfully and even tenderly. The girl at the window turned her back indignantly on the scene; an expression of extraordinary cordiality came over the haughtily inquiring face of the woman.

"Good morning! Sit down, Mr. Tchernomazov,"[1] she said.

"Karamazov, mamma, Karamazov (we are of humble origin)," he whispered again.

"Well, Karamazov, or whatever it is, but I always think of Tchernomazov. . . . Sit down. Why has he pulled you up? He calls me crippled but I am not, only my legs are swollen like barrels, and I am shrivelled up myself. Once I used to be so fat, but now it's as though I had swallowed a needle."

"We are of humble origin," the captain muttered again.

"Oh, father, father!" the hunchback girl, who had till then been silent on her chair, said suddenly, as she hid her eyes in her handkerchief.

"Buffoon!" blurted out the girl at the window.

"Have you heard our news?" said the mother, pointing at her daughters. "It's like clouds coming over; the clouds pass and we have music again. When we were with the army, we used to have many such guests. I don't mean to make any comparisons; every one to their taste. The deacon's wife used to come then and say, 'Alexandr Alexandrovitch is a man of the noblest heart, but Nastasya Petrovna,' she would say, 'is of the brood of hell.' 'Well,' I said, 'that's a matter of taste; but you are a little spitfire.' 'And you want keeping in your place,' says she. 'You black sword,' said I, 'who asked you to teach me?' 'But my breath,' says she, 'is clean, and yours is unclean.' 'You ask all the officers whether my breath is unclean.' And ever since then I had it in my mind. Not long ago I was sitting here as I am now, when I saw that very General come in who came here for Easter, and I asked him: 'Your Excellency,' said I, 'can a lady's breath be unpleasant?' 'Yes,' he answered; 'you ought to open a window-pane or open the door, for the air is not fresh here.' And they all go on like that! And what is my breath to them? The dead smell worse still! 'I won't spoil the air,' said I, 'I'll order some slippers and go away.' My darlings, don't blame your own mother! Nikolay Ilyitch, how is it I can't please you? There's only Ilusha who comes home from school and loves me. Yesterday he brought me an apple. Forgive your own mother—forgive a poor lonely creature! Why has my breath become unpleasant to you?"

And the poor mad woman broke into sobs, and tears streamed down her cheeks. The captain rushed up to her.

"Mamma, mamma, my dear, give over! You are not lonely. Every one loves you, every one adores you." He began kissing both her hands again and tenderly stroking her face; taking the dinner-napkin, he began wiping away her tears. Alyosha fancied that he too had tears in his eyes. "There, you see, you hear?" he turned with a sort of fury to Alyosha, pointing to the poor imbecile.

"I see and hear," muttered Alyosha.

"Father, father, how can you—with him! Let him alone!" cried the boy, sitting up in his bed and gazing at his father with glowing eyes.

"Do give over fooling, showing off your silly antics which never lead to anything!" shouted Varvara, stamping her foot with passion.

"Your anger is quite just this time, Varvara, and I'll make haste to satisfy you. Come, put on your cap, Alexey Fyodorovitch, and I'll put on mine. We will go out. I have a word to say to you in earnest, but not within these walls. This girl sitting here is my daughter Nina; I forgot to introduce her to you. She is a heavenly angel incarnate . . . who has flown down to us mortals, . . . if you can understand."

"There he is shaking all over, as though he is in convulsions!" Varvara went on indignantly.

"And she there stamping her foot at me and calling me a fool just now, she is a heavenly angel incarnate too, and she has good reason to call me so. Come along, Alexey Fyodorovitch, we must make an end."

And, snatching Alyosha's hand, he drew him out of the room into the street.

7

AND IN THE OPEN AIR

"THE air is fresh, but in my apartment it is not so in any sense of the word. Let us walk slowly, sir. I should be glad of your kind interest."

"I too have something important to say to you," observed Alyosha, "only I don't know how to begin."

"To be sure you must have business with me. You would never have looked in upon me without some object. Unless you come simply to complain of the boy, and that's hardly likely. And, by the way, about the boy: I could not explain to you in there, but here I will describe that scene to you. My tow was thicker a week ago—I mean my beard. That's the nickname they give to my beard, the schoolboys most of all. Well, your brother Dmitri Fyodorovitch was pulling me by my beard, I'd done nothing, he was in a towering rage and happened to come upon me. He dragged me out of the tavern into the market-place; at that moment the boys were coming out of school, and with them Ilusha. As soon as he saw me in such a state he rushed up to me. 'Father,' he cried, 'father!' He caught hold of me, hugged me, tried to pull me away, crying to my assailant, 'Let go, let go, it's my father, forgive him!'—yes, he actually cried 'forgive him.' He clutched at that hand, that very hand, in his little hands and kissed it. . . . I remember his little face at that moment, I haven't forgotten it and I never shall!"

"I swear," cried Alyosha, "that my brother will express his most deep and sincere regret, even if he has to go down on his knees in that same market-place. . . . I'll make him or he is no brother of mine!"

"Aha, then it's only a suggestion! And it does not come from him but simply from the generosity of your own warm heart. You should have said so. No, in that case allow me to tell you of your brother's highly chivalrous soldierly generosity, for he did give expression to it at the time. He left off dragging me by my beard and released me: 'You are an officer,' he said, 'and I am an officer, if you can find a decent man to be your second send me your challenge. I will give you satisfaction, though you are a scoundrel.' That's what he said. A chivalrous spirit indeed; I retired with Ilusha, and that scene is a family record imprinted for ever on Ilusha's soul. No, it's not for us to claim the privileges of noblemen. Judge for yourself. You've just been in our mansion, what did you see here? Three ladies, one a cripple and weak-minded, another a cripple and hunchback and the third not crippled but far too clever. She is a student, dying to get back to Petersburg, to work for the emancipation of the Russian woman on the banks of the Neva. I won't speak of Ilusha, he is only nine. I am alone in the world, and if I die, what will become of all of them, I simply ask you that. And if I challenge him and he kills me on the spot, what then? What will become of them? And worse still, if he doesn't kill me but only cripples me: I couldn't work, but I should still be a mouth to feed. Who would feed it and who would feed them all? Must I take Ilusha from school and send him to beg in the streets? That's what it means for me to challenge him to a duel. It's silly talk and nothing else."

"He will beg your forgiveness, he will bow down at your feet in the middle of the market-place," cried Alyosha again, with glowing eyes.

"I did think of prosecuting him," the captain went on, "but look in our code, could I get much compensation for a personal injury? And then Agrafena Alexandrovna* sent for me and shouted at me: 'Don't dare to dream of it! If you proceed against him, I'll publish it to all the world that he beat you for your dishonesty, and then you will be prosecuted.' I call God to witness whose was the dishonesty and by whose commands I acted, wasn't it by her own and Fyodor Pavlovitch's? 'And what's more,' she went on, 'I'll dismiss you for good and you'll never earn another penny from me. I'll speak to my merchant too (that's what she calls her old man) and he will dismiss you!' And if he dismisses me, what can I earn then

---

*Grushenka (translator's note).

from any one? Those two are all I have to look to, for your Fyodor Pavlovitch has not only given over employing me, for another reason, but he means to make use of papers I've signed to go to law against me. And so I kept quiet, and you have seen our retreat. But now let me ask you: did Ilusha hurt your finger much? I didn't like to go into it in our mansion before him."

"Yes, very much, and he was in a great fury. He was avenging you on me as a Karamazov, I see that now. But if only you had seen how he was throwing stones at his school-fellows! It's very dangerous. They might kill him. They are children and stupid. A stone may be thrown and break somebody's head."

"That's just what has happened. He has been bruised by a stone to-day. Not on the head but on the chest, just above the heart. He came home crying and groaning and now he is ill."

"And you know he attacks them first. He is bitter against them on your account. They say he stabbed a boy called Krassotkin with a pen-knife not long ago."

"I've heard about that too, it's dangerous. Krassotkin is an official here, we may hear more about it."

"I would advise you," Alyosha went on warmly, "not to send him to school at all for a time till he is calmer . . . and his anger is passed."

"Anger!" the captain repeated, "that's just what it is. He is a little creature, but it's a mighty anger. You don't know all, sir. Let me tell you more. Since that incident all the boys have been teasing him about the 'wisp of tow.' Schoolboys are a merciless race, individually they are angels, but together, especially in schools, they are often merciless. Their teasing has stirred up a gallant spirit in Ilusha. An ordinary boy, a weak son, would have submitted, have felt ashamed of his father, sir, but he stood up for his father against them all. For his father and for truth and justice. For what he suffered when he kissed your brother's hand and cried to him 'forgive father, forgive him,'—that only God knows—and I, his father. For our children—not your children, but ours—the children of the poor gentlemen looked down upon by every one—know what justice means, sir, even at nine years old. How should the rich know? They don't explore such depths once in their lives. But at that moment in the square when he kissed his hand, at that moment my Ilusha had grasped all that justice means. That truth entered into him and crushed him for ever, sir," the captain said hotly again with a sort of frenzy, and he struck his right fist against his left palm as though he wanted to show how "the truth" crushed Ilusha. "That very day, sir, he fell ill with fever and was delirious all night. All that day he hardly said a word to me, but I noticed he kept watching me from the corner, though he turned to the window and pretended to be learning his lessons. But I could see his mind was not on his lessons. Next day I got drunk to forget my troubles, sinful man as I am, and I don't remember much. Mamma began crying, too—I am very fond of mamma—well, I spent my last penny drowning my troubles. Don't despise me for that, sir, in Russia men who drink are the best. The best men amongst us are the greatest drunkards. I lay down and I don't remember about Ilusha, though all that day the boys had been jeering at him at school. 'Wisp of tow,' they shouted, 'your father was pulled out of the tavern by his wisp of tow, you ran by and begged forgiveness.'

"On the third day when he came back from school, I saw he looked pale and wretched. 'What is it?' I asked. He wouldn't answer. Well, there's no talking in our mansion without mamma and the girls taking part in it. What's more the girls had heard about it the very first day. Varvara had begun snarling. 'You fools and buffoons, can you ever do anything rational?' 'Quite so,' I said, 'can we ever do anything rational?' For the time I turned it off like that. So in the evening I took the boy out for a walk, for you must know we go for a walk every evening, always the same way, along which we are going now—from our gate to that great stone which lies alone in the road under the hurdle, which marks the beginning of the town pasture. A beautiful and lonely spot, sir. Ilusha and I walked along hand in hand as usual. He has a little hand, his fingers are thin and cold—he suffers with his chest, you know. 'Father,' said he, 'father!' 'Well?' said I. I saw his eyes flashing. 'Father, how he treated you then!' 'It can't be helped, Ilusha,' I said. 'Don't forgive him, father, don't forgive him! At school they say that he has paid you ten roubles for it.' 'No, Ilusha,' said I, 'I would not take money from him for anything.' Then he began trembling all over, took my hand in both his and kissed it again, 'Father,' he said, 'father, challenge him to a duel, at school they say you are a coward and won't challenge him, and that you'll accept ten roubles from him.' 'I can't challenge him to a duel, Ilusha,' I answered. And I told briefly what I've just told you. He listened. 'Father,' he said, 'anyway don't forgive it. When I grow up I'll call him out myself and kill him.' His eyes shone and glowed. And of course I am his father, and I had to put in a word: 'It's a sin to kill,' I said, 'even in a duel.' 'Father,' he said, 'when I grow up, I'll knock him down, knock the sword out of his hand, I'll fall on him, wave my sword over him and say: "I could kill you, but I forgive you, so there!"' You see what the workings of his little mind have been during these two days; he must have been planning that vengeance all day, and raving about it at night.

"But he began to come home from school badly beaten, I found out about it the day before yesterday, and you are right, I won't send him to that school any more. I heard that he was standing up against all the class alone and defying them all, that his heart was full of resentment, of bitterness—I was alarmed about him. We went for another walk. 'Father,' he asked, 'are the rich people stronger than any one else on earth?' 'Yes, Ilusha,' I said, 'there are no people on earth stronger than the rich.' 'Father,' he said, 'I will get rich, I will become an officer and conquer everybody. The Tsar will reward me, I will come back here and then no one will dare.' . . . Then he was silent and his lips still kept trembling, 'Father,' he said, 'what a horrid town this is.' 'Yes, Ilusha,' I said, 'it isn't a very nice town.' 'Father, let us move into another town, a nice one,' he said, 'where people don't know about us.' 'We will move, we will, Ilusha,' said I, 'only I must save up for it.' I was glad to be able to turn his mind from painful thoughts, and we began to dream of how we would move to another town, how we would buy a horse and cart. 'We will put mamma and your sisters inside, we will cover them up and we'll walk, you shall have a lift now and then, and I'll walk beside, for we must take care of our horse, we can't all ride. That's how we'll go.' He was enchanted at that, most of all at the thought of having a horse and driving him. For of course a Russian boy is born among horses. We chattered a long while. Thank God, I thought, I have diverted his mind and comforted him.

"That was the day before yesterday, in the evening, but last night everything was changed. He had gone to school in the morning, he came back depressed, terribly depressed. In the evening I took him by the hand and we went for a walk; he would not talk. There was a wind blowing and no sun, and a feeling of autumn; twilight was coming on. We walked along, both of us depressed. 'Well, my boy,' said I, 'how about our setting off on our travels?' I thought I might bring him back to our talk of the day before. He didn't answer, but I felt his fingers trembling in my hand. Ah, I thought, it's a bad job; there's something fresh. We had reached the stone where we are now. I sat down on the stone. And in the air there were lots of kites flapping and whirling. There were as many as thirty in sight. Of course, it's just the season for the kites. 'Look, Ilusha,' said I, 'it's time we got out our last year's kite again. I'll mend it, where have you put it away?' My boy made no answer. He looked away and turned sideways to me. And then a gust of wind blew up the sand. He suddenly fell on me, threw both his little arms round my neck and held me tight. You know, when children are silent and proud, and try to keep back their tears when they are in great trouble and suddenly break down, their tears fall in streams. With those warm streams of tears, he suddenly wetted my face. He sobbed and shook as though he were in convulsions, and squeezed up against me as I sat on the stone. 'Father,' he kept crying, 'dear father, how he insulted you!' And I sobbed too. We sat shaking in each other's arms. 'Ilusha,' I said to him, 'Ilusha darling.' No one saw us then. God alone saw us, I hope he will record it to my credit. You must thank your brother, Alexey Fyodorovitch. No, sir, I won't thrash my boy for your satisfaction."

He had gone back to his original tone of resentful buffoonery. Alyosha felt though that he trusted him, and that if there had been some one else in his, Alyosha's place, the man would not have spoken so openly and would not have told what he had just told. This encouraged Alyosha whose heart was trembling on the verge of tears.

"Ah, how I would like to make friends with your boy!" he cried, "If you could arrange it——"

"Certainly, sir," muttered the captain.

"But now listen to something quite different!" Alyosha went on. "I have a message for you. That same brother of mine, Dmitri, has insulted his betrothed, too, a noble-hearted girl of whom you have probably heard. I have a right to tell you of her wrong; I ought to do so, in fact, for hearing of the insult done to you and learning all about your unfortunate position, she commissioned me at once—just now—to bring you this help from her—but only from her alone, not from Dmitri, who has abandoned her. Nor from me, his brother, nor from any one else, but from her, only from her! She entreats you to accept her help. . . . You have both been insulted by the same man. She thought of you only when she had just received a similar insult from him—similar in its cruelty, I mean. She comes like a sister to help a brother in misfortune. . . . She told me to persuade you to take these two hundred roubles from her, as from a sister, knowing that you are in such need. No one will know of it, it can give rise to no unjust slander. There are the two hundred roubles, and I swear you must take them unless—unless all men are to be enemies on earth! But there are brothers even on earth. . . . You have a generous heart, . . . you must see that, you must," and Alyosha held out two new rainbow-coloured hundred-rouble notes.

They were both standing at the time by the great stone close to the fence, and there was no one near. The notes seemed to produce a tremendous impression on the captain. He started, but at first only from astonishment. Such an outcome of their conversation was the last thing he expected. Nothing could have been further from his dreams than help from any one—and such a sum!

He took the notes, and for a minute he was almost unable to answer, quite a new expression came into his face.

"That for me? So much money—two hundred roubles! Good heavens! Why, I haven't seen so much money for the last four years! Mercy on us! And she says she is a sister. . . . And is that the truth?"

"I swear that all I told you is the truth," cried Alyosha.

The captain flushed red.

"Listen, my dear, listen. If I take it, I shan't be behaving like a scoundrel? In your eyes, Alexey Fyodorovitch, I shan't be a scoundrel? No, Alexey Fyodorovitch, listen, listen," he hurried, touching Alyosha with both his hands, "You are persuading me to take it, saying that it's a sister sends it, but inwardly, in your heart won't you feel contempt for me if I take it, eh?"

"No, no, on my salvation I swear I shan't! And no one will ever know but me—I, you and she, and one other lady, her great friend."

"Never mind the lady! Listen, Alexey Fyodorovitch, at a moment like this you must listen, for you can't understand what these two hundred roubles mean to me now." The poor fellow went on rising gradually into a sort of incoherent, almost wild enthusiasm. He was thrown off his balance and talked extremely fast, as though afraid he would not be allowed to say all he had to say.

"Besides it's being honestly acquired from a 'sister,' so highly respected and revered, do you know that now I can look after mamma and Nina, my hunchback angel daughter? Doctor Herzenstube came to me in the kindness of his heart and was examining them both for a whole hour. 'I can make nothing of it,' said he, but he prescribed a mineral water which is kept at a chemist's here. He said it would be sure to do her good, and he ordered baths, too, with some medicine in them. The mineral water costs thirty kopecks, and she'd need to drink forty bottles perhaps; so I took the prescription and laid it on the shelf under the ikons, and there it lies. And he ordered hot baths for Nina with something dissolved in them, morning and evening. But how can we carry out such a cure in our mansion, without servants, without help, without a bath, and without water? Nina is rheumatic all over, I don't think I told you that. All her right side aches at night, she is in agony, and, would you believe it, the angel bears it without groaning for fear of waking us. We eat what we can get, and she'll only take the leavings, what you'd scarcely give to a dog. 'I am not worth it, I am taking it from you, I am a burden on you,' that's what her angel eyes try to express. We wait on her, but she doesn't like it. 'I am a useless cripple, no good to any one.' As though she were not worth it, when she is the saving of all of us with her angelic sweetness. Without her, without her gentle word it would be hell among us! She softens even Varvara. And don't judge Varvara harshly either, she is an angel too, she, too, has suffered wrong. She came to us for the summer, and she brought sixteen roubles she had earned by lessons and saved up, to go back with to Petersburg in September, that is now. But we took her money and lived on it, so now she has nothing to go back with. Though indeed she couldn't go back, for she has to work for us like a slave. She is like an overdriven horse with all of us on her back. She waits on us all, mends and washes, sweeps the floor, puts mamma to bed. And mamma is capricious and tearful and insane! And now I can get a servant with this money, you understand, Alexey Fyodorovitch, I can get medicines for the dear creatures, I can send my student to Petersburg, I can buy beef, I can feed them properly. Good Lord, but it's a dream!"

Alyosha was delighted that he had brought him such happiness and that the poor fellow had consented to be made happy.

"Stay, Alexey Fyodorovitch, stay," the captain began to talk with frenzied rapidity carried away by a new day-dream. "Do you know that Ilusha and I will perhaps really carry out our dream. We will buy a horse and cart, a black horse, he insists on its being black, and we will set off as we pretended the other day. I have an old friend, a lawyer in K. province, and I heard through a trustworthy man that if I were to go he'd give me a place as clerk in his office, so, who knows, maybe he would. So I'd just put mamma and Nina in the cart, and Ilusha could drive, and I'd walk, I'd walk. . . . Why, if I only succeed in getting one debt paid that's owing me, I should have perhaps enough for that too!"

"There would be enough!" cried Alyosha. "Katerina Ivanovna will send you as much more as you need, and you know, I have money too, take what you want, as you would from a brother, from a friend, you can give it back later. . . . (You'll get rich, you'll get rich!) And you know you couldn't have a better idea than to move to another province! It would be the saving of you, especially of your boy—and you ought to go quickly, before the winter, before the cold. You must write to us when you are there, and we will always be brothers. . . . No, it's not a dream!"

Alyosha could have hugged him, he was so pleased. But glancing at him he stopped short. The man was standing with his neck outstretched and his lips protruding, with a pale and frenzied face. His lips were moving as though trying to articulate something; no sound came, but still his lips moved. It was uncanny.

"What is it?" asked Alyosha, startled.

"Alexey Fyodorovitch . . . I . . . you," muttered the captain, faltering, looking at him with a strange, wild, fixed stare, and an air of desperate resolution. At the same time there was a sort of grin on his lips. "I . . . you, sir . . . wouldn't you like me to show you a little trick I know?" he murmured, suddenly, in a firm rapid whisper, his voice no longer faltering.

"What trick?"

"A pretty trick," whispered the captain. His mouth was twisted on the left side, his left eye was screwed up. He still stared at Alyosha.

"What trick?" Alyosha cried, now thoroughly alarmed.

"Why, look," squealed the captain suddenly, and showing him the two notes which he had been holding by one corner between his thumb and forefinger during the conversation, he crumpled them up savagely and squeezed them tight in his right hand. "Do you see, do you see?" he shrieked, pale and infuriated. And suddenly flinging up his hand, he threw the crumpled notes on the sand. "Do you see?" he shrieked again, pointing to them. "Look there!"

And with wild fury he began trampling them under his heel, gasping and exclaiming as he did so:

"So much for your money! So much for your money! So much for your money! So much for your money!"

Suddenly he darted back and drew himself up before Alyosha, and his whole figure expressed unutterable pride.

Tell those who sent you that the wisp of tow does not sell his honour," he cried, raising his arm in the air. Then he turned quickly and began to run; but he had not run five steps before he turned completely round and kissed his hand to Alyosha. He ran another five paces and then turned round for the last time. This time his face was not contorted with laughter, but quivering all over with tears. In a tearful, faltering, sobbing voice he cried:

"What should I say to my boy if I took money from you for our shame?"

And then he ran on without turning. Alyosha looked after him, inexpressibly grieved. Oh, he saw that till the very last moment the man had not known he would crumple up and fling away the notes. He did not turn back. Alyosha knew he would not. He would not follow him and call him back, he knew why. When he was out of sight, Alyosha picked up the two notes. They were very much crushed and crumpled, and had been pressed into the sand, but were uninjured and even rustled like new ones when Alyosha unfolded them. After smoothing them out, he folded them up, put them in his pocket and went to Katerina Ivanovna to report on the success of her commission.

BOOK FIVE

PRO AND CONTRA

1

THE ENGAGEMENT

MADAME HOHLAKOV was again the first to meet Alyosha. She was flustered; something important had happened. Katerina Ivanovna's hysterics had ended in a fainting fit, and then "a terrible, awful weakness had followed, she lay with her eyes turned up and was delirious. Now she was in a fever. They had sent for Herzenstube; they had sent for the aunts. The aunts were already here, but Herzenstube had not yet come. They were all sitting in her room, waiting. She was unconscious now, and what if it turned to brain fever!"

Madame Hohlakov looked gravely alarmed. "This is serious, serious," she added at every word, as though nothing that had happened to her before had been serious. Alyosha listened with distress, and was beginning to describe his adventures, but she interrupted him at the first words. She had not time to listen. She begged him to sit with Lise and wait for her there.

"Lise," she whispered almost in his ear, "Lise has greatly surprised me just now, dear Alexey Fyodorvitch. She touched me, too, and, so my heart forgives her everything. Only fancy, as soon as you had gone, she began to be truly remorseful for having laughed at you to-day and yesterday, though she was not laughing at you, but only joking. But she was seriously sorry for it, almost ready to cry, so that I was quite surprised. She has never been really sorry for laughing at me, but has only made a joke of it. And you know she is laughing at me every minute. But this time she was in earnest. She thinks a great deal of your opinion, Alexey Fyodorovitch, and don't take offence or be wounded by her if you can help it. I am never hard upon her, for she's such a clever little thing—would you believe it? She said just now that you were a friend of her childhood, 'the greatest friend of her childhood'—just think of that—'greatest friend'—and what about me? She has very strong feelings and memories, and, what's more, she uses these phrases, most unexpected words, which come out all of a sudden when you least expect them. She spoke lately about a pine-tree, for instance: there used to be a pine-tree standing in our garden in her early childhood. Very likely it's standing there still; so there's no need to speak in the past tense. Pine-trees are not like people, Alexey Fyodorovitch, they don't change quickly. 'Mamma,' she said, 'I remember this pine-tree as in a dream,' only she said something so original about it that I can't repeat it. Besides, I've forgotten it. Well, good-bye! I am so worried I feel I shall go out of my mind. Ah! Alexey Fyodorovitch, I've been out of my mind twice in my life. Go to Lise, cheer her up, as you always can so charmingly. Lise," she cried, going to her door, "here I've brought you Alexey Fyodorovitch, whom you insulted so. He is not at all angry, I assure you; on the contrary, he is surprised that you could suppose so."

"*Merci*, maman. Come in, Alexey Fyodorovitch."

Alyosha went in. Lise looked rather embarrassed, and at once flushed crimson. She was evidently ashamed of something, and, as people always do in such cases, she began immediately talking of other things, as though they were of absorbing interest to her at the moment.

"Mamma has just told me all about the two hundred roubles, Alexey Fyodorovitch, and your taking them to that poor officer . . . and she told me all the awful story of how he had been insulted . . . and you know, although mamma muddles things . . . she always rushes from one thing to another . . . I cried when I heard. Well, did you give him the money and how is that poor man getting on?"

"The fact is I didn't give it to him, and it's a long story," answered Alyosha, as though he, too, could think of nothing but his regret at having failed, yet Lise saw perfectly well that he, too, looked away, and that he, too, was trying to talk of other things.

Alyosha sat down to the table and began to tell his story, but at the first words he lost his embarrassment and gained the whole of Lise's attention as well. He spoke with deep feeling, under the influence of the strong impression he had just received, and he succeeded in telling his story well and circumstantially. In old days in Moscow he had been fond of coming to Lise and describing to her what had just happened to him, what he had read, or what he remembered of his childhood. Sometimes they had made day-dreams and woven whole romances together—generally cheerful and amusing ones. Now they both felt suddenly transported to the old days in Moscow, two years before. Lise was extremely touched by his story. Alyosha described Ilusha with warm feeling. When he finished describing how the luckless man trampled on the money, Lise could not help clasping her hands and crying out:

"So you didn't give him the money! So you let him run away! Oh, dear, you ought to have run after him!"

"No, Lise; it's better I didn't run after him," said Alyosha, getting up from his chair and walking thoughtfully across the room.

"How so? How is it better? Now they are without food and their case is hopeless."

"Not hopeless, for the two hundred roubles will still come to them. He'll take the money to-morrow. To-morrow he will be sure to take it," said Alyosha, pacing up and down, pondering. "You see, Lise," he went on, stopping suddenly before her, "I made one blunder, but that, even that, is all for the best."

"What blunder, and why is it for the best?"

"I'll tell you. He is a man of weak and timorous character; he has suffered so much and is very good-natured. I keep wondering why he took offence so suddenly, for I assure you, up to the last minute, he did not know that he was going to trample on the notes. And I think now that there was a great deal to offend him . . . and it could not have been otherwise in his position. . . . To begin with, he was sore at having been so glad of the money in my presence and not having concealed it from me. If he had been pleased, but not so much; if he had not shown it: if he had begun affecting scruples and difficulties, as other people do when they take money, he might still endure to take it. But he was too genuinely delighted, and that was mortifying. Ah, Lise, he is a good and truthful man—that's the worst of the whole business. All the while he talked, his voice was so weak, so broken, he talked so fast, so fast, he kept laughing such a laugh, or perhaps he was crying—yes, I am sure he was crying, he was so delighted—and he talked about his daughters—and about the situation he could get in another town. . . . And when he had poured out his heart, he felt ashamed at having shown me his inmost soul like that. So he began to hate me at once. He is one of those awfully sensitive poor people. What had made him feel most ashamed was that he had given in too soon and accepted me as a friend, you see. At first he almost flew at me and tried to intimidate me, but as soon as he saw the money he had begun embracing me; he kept touching me with his hands. This must have been how he came to feel it all so humiliating, and then I made that blunder, a very important one. I suddenly said to him that if he had not money enough to move to another town, we would give it to him, and, indeed, I myself would give him as much as he wanted out of my own money. That struck him all at once. Why, he thought, did I put myself forward to help him? You know, Lise, it's awfully hard for a man who has been injured, when other people look at him as though they were his benefactors. . . . I've heard that; Father Zossima told me so. I don't know how to put it, but I have often seen it myself. And I feel like that myself, too. And the worst of it was that though he did not know, up to the very last minute, that he would trample on the notes, he had a kind of presentiment of it, I am sure of that. That's just what made him so ecstatic, that he had that presentiment. . . . And though it's so dreadful, it's all for the best. In fact, I believe nothing better could have happened."

"Why, why could nothing better have happened?" cried Lise, looking with great surprise at Alyosha.

"Because if he had taken the money, in an hour after getting home, he would be crying with mortification, that's just what would have happened. And most likely he would have come to me early to-morrow, and perhaps have flung the notes at me and trampled upon them as he did just now. But now he has gone home awfully proud and triumphant, though he knows he has 'ruined himself.' So now nothing could be easier than to make him accept the two hundred roubles by to-morrow, for he has already vindicated his honour, tossed away the money, and trampled it under foot. . . . He couldn't know when he did it that I should bring it to him again to-morrow, and yet he is in terrible need of that money. Though he is proud of himself now, yet even to-day he'll be thinking what a help he has lost. He will think of it more than ever at night, will dream of it, and by to-morrow morning he may be ready to run to me to ask forgiveness. It's just then that I'll appear. 'Here, you are a proud man,' I shall say: 'you have shown it; but now take the money and forgive us!' And then he will take it!"

Alyosha was carried away with joy as he uttered the last words. "And then he will take it!" Lise clapped her hands.

"Ah, that's true! I understand that perfectly now. Ah, Alyosha, how do you know all this? So young and yet he knows what's in the heart. . . . I should never have worked it out."

"The great thing now is to persuade him that he is on an equal footing with us, in spite of his taking money from us," Alyosha went on in his excitement, "and not only on an equal, but even on a higher footing."

"On a higher footing is charming, Alexey Fyodorovitch; but go on, go on!"

"You mean there isn't such an expression as 'on a higher footing'; but that doesn't matter because——"

"Oh, no, of course it doesn't matter. Forgive me, Alyosha, dear. . . . You know, I scarcely respected you till now—that is I respected you but on an equal footing; but now I shall begin to respect you on a higher footing. Don't be angry, dear, at my joking," she put in at once, with strong feeling. "I am absurd and small, but you, you! Listen, Alexey Fyodorovitch. Isn't there in all our analysis—I mean your analysis. . . . No, better call it ours—aren't we showing contempt for him, for that poor man—in analysing his soul like this, as it were, from above, eh? In deciding so certainly that he will take the money?"

"No, Lise, it's not contempt," Alyosha answered, as though he had prepared himself for the question. "I was thinking of that on the way here. How can it be contempt when we are all like him, when we are all just the same as he is. For you know we are just the same, no better. If we are better, we should have been just the same in his place. . . . I don't know about you, Lise, but I consider that I have a sordid soul in many ways, and his soul is not sordid; on the contrary, full of fine feeling. . . . No, Lise, I have no contempt for him. Do you know, Lise, my elder told me once to care for most people exactly as one would for children, and for some of them as one would for the sick in hospitals."

"Ah, Alexey Fyodorovitch, dear, let us care for people as we would for the sick!"

"Let us, Lise; I am ready. Though I am not altogether ready in myself. I am sometimes very impatient and at other times I don't see things. It's different with you."

"Ah, I don't believe it! Alexey Fyodorovitch, how happy I am."

"I am so glad you say so, Lise."

"Alexey Fyodorovitch, you are wonderfully good, but you are sometimes sort of formal. . . . And yet you are not a bit formal really. Go to the door, open it gently, and see whether mamma is listening," said Lise, in a nervous, hurried whisper.

Alyosha went, opened the door, and reported that no one was listening.

"Come here, Alexey Fyodorovitch," Lise went on, flushing redder and redder. "Give me your hand—that's right. I have to make a great confession, I didn't write to you yesterday in joke, but in earnest," and she hid her eyes with her hand. It was evident that she was greatly ashamed of the confession.

Suddenly she snatched his hand and impulsively kissed it three times.

"Ah, Lise, what a good thing!" cried Alyosha joyfully. "You know, I was perfectly sure you were in earnest."

"Sure? Upon my word!" She put aside his hand, but did not leave go of it, blushing hotly, and laughing a little happy laugh. "I kiss his hand and he says, 'What a good thing.'"

But her reproach was undeserved, Alyosha, too, was greatly overcome.

"I should like to please you always, Lise, but I don't know how to do it," he muttered, blushing too.

"Alyosha, dear, you are cold and rude. Do you see? He has chosen me as his wife and is quite settled about it. He is sure I was in earnest. What a thing to say! Why, that's impertinence—that's what it is."

"Why was it wrong of me to feel sure?" Alyosha asked, laughing suddenly.

"Ah, Alyosha, on the contrary, it was delightfully right," cried Lise, looking tenderly and happily at him.

Alyosha stood still, holding her hand in his. Suddenly he stooped down and kissed her on her lips.

"Oh, what are you doing?" cried Lise. Alyosha was terribly abashed.

"Oh, forgive me if I shouldn't. . . . Perhaps I'm awfully stupid. . . . You said I was cold, so I kissed you. . . . But I see it was stupid."

Lise laughed, and hid her face in her hands. "And in that dress!" she ejaculated in the midst of her mirth. But she suddenly ceased laughing and became serious, almost stern.

"Alyosha, we must put off kissing. We are not ready for that yet, and we shall have a long time to wait," she ended suddenly. "Tell me rather why you who are so clever, so intellectual, so observant, choose a little idiot, an invalid like me? Ah, Alyosha, I am awfully happy for I don't deserve you a bit."

"You do, Lise. I shall be leaving the monastery altogether in a few days. If I go into the world, I must marry. I know that. *He* told me to marry, too. Whom could I marry better than you—and who would have me except you? I have been thinking it over. In the first place, you've known me from a child and you've a great many qualities I haven't. You are more light-hearted than I am; above all, you are more innocent than I am. I have been brought into contact with many, many things already. . . . Ah, you don't know, but I, too, am a Karamazov. What does it matter if you do laugh and make jokes, and at me, too? Go on laughing. I am so glad you do. You laugh like a little child, but you think like a martyr."

"Like a martyr? How?"

"Yes, Lise, your question just now: whether we weren't showing contempt for that poor man by dissecting his soul—that was the question of a sufferer. . . . You see, I don't know how to express it, but any one who thinks of such questions is capable of suffering. Sitting in your invalid chair you must have thought over many things already."

"Alyosha, give me your hand. Why are you taking it away?" murmured Lise in a failing voice, weak with happiness. "Listen, Alyosha. What will you wear when you come out of the monastery? What sort of suit? Don't laugh, don't be angry, it's very, very important to me."

"I haven't thought about the suit, Lise; but I'll wear whatever you like."

"I should like you to have a dark blue velvet coat, a white piqué waistcoat, and a soft grey felt hat. . . . Tell me, did you believe that I didn't care for you when I said I didn't mean what I wrote?"

"No, I didn't believe it."

"Oh, you insupportable person, you are incorrigible."

"You see, I knew that you—seemed to care for me, but I pretended to believe that you didn't care for me to make it—easier for you."

"That makes it worse! Worse and better than all! Alyosha, I am awfully fond of you. Just before you came this morning, I tried my fortune. I decided I would ask you for my letter, and if you brought it out calmly and gave it to me (as might have been expected from you) it would mean that you did not love me at all, that you felt nothing, and were simply a stupid boy, good for nothing, and that I am ruined. But you left the letter at home and that cheered me. You left it behind on purpose, so as not to give it back, because you knew I would ask for it? That was it, wasn't it?"

"Ah, Lise, it was not so a bit. The letter is with me now, and it was this morning, in this pocket. Here it is."

Alyosha pulled the letter out laughing, and showed it her at a distance.

"But I am not going to give it to you. Look at it from here."

"Why, then you told a lie? You, a monk, told a lie!"

"I told a lie if you like," Alyosha laughed, too. "I told a lie so as not to give you back the letter. It's very precious to me," he added suddenly, with strong feeling, and again he flushed.

"It always will be, and I won't give it up to any one!"

Lise looked at him joyfully. "Alyosha," she murmured again, "look at the door. Isn't mamma listening?"

"Very well, Lise, I'll look; but wouldn't it be better not to look? Why suspect your mother of such meanness?"

"What meanness? As for her spying on her daughter, it's her right, it's not meanness!" cried Lise, firing up. "You may be sure, Alexey Fyodorovitch, that when I am a mother, if I have a daughter like myself I shall certainly spy on her!"

"Really, Lise? That's not right."

"Oh, my goodness! What has meanness to do with it? If she were listening to some ordinary worldly conversation, it would be meanness, but when her own daughter is shut up with a young man . . . Listen, Alyosha, do you know I shall spy upon you as soon as we are married, and let me tell you I shall open all your letters and read them, so you may as well be prepared."

"Yes, of course, if so—" muttered Alyosha, "only it's not right."

"Ah, how contemptuous! Alyosha, dear, we don't quarrel the very first day. I'd better tell you the whole truth. Of course, it's very wrong to spy on people, and, of course, I am not right and you are, only I shall spy on you all the same."

"Do, then; you won't find out anything," laughed Alyosha.

"And Alyosha, will you give in to me? We must decide that too."

"I shall be delighted to, Lise, and certain to, only not in the most important things. Even if you don't agree with me, I shall do my duty in the most important things."

"That's right; but let me tell you I am ready to give in to you not only in the most important matters, but in everything. And I am ready to vow to do so now—in everything, and for all my life!" cried Lise fervently, "and I'll do it gladly, gladly! What's more I'll swear never to spy on you, never once, never to read one of your letters. For you are right and I am not. And though I shall be awfully tempted to spy, I know that I won't do it since you consider it dishonourable. You are my conscience now. . . . Listen, Alexey Fyodorovitch, why have you been so sad lately—both yesterday and to-day? I know you have a lot of anxiety and trouble, but I see you have some special grief besides, some secret one, perhaps?"

"Yes, Lise, I have a secret one, too," answered Alyosha mournfully. "I see you love me, since you guessed that."

"What grief? What about? Can you tell me?" asked Lise with timid entreaty.

"I'll tell you later, Lise—afterwards," said Alyosha, confused. "Now you wouldn't understand it perhaps—and perhaps I couldn't explain it."

"I know your brothers and your father are worrying you, too?"

"Yes, my brothers too," murmured Alyosha, pondering.

"I don't like your brother Ivan, Alyosha," said Lise suddenly.

He noticed this remark with some surprise, but did not answer it.

"My brothers are destroying themselves," he went on, "my father, too. And they are destroying others with them. It's 'the primitive force of the Karamazovs,' as Father Païssy said the other day, a crude, unbridled, earthly force. Does the spirit of God move above that force? Even that I don't know. I only know that I, too, am a Karamazov. . . . Me a monk, a monk! Am I a monk, Lise? You said just now that I was."

"Yes, I did."

"And perhaps I don't even believe in God."

"You don't believe? What is the matter?" said Lise quietly and gently. But Alyosha did not answer. There was something too mysterious, too subjective in these last words of his, perhaps obscure to himself, but yet torturing him.

"And now on the top of it all, my friend, the best man in the world is going, is leaving the earth! If you knew, Lise, how bound up in soul I am with him! And then I shall be left alone. . . . I shall come to you, Lise. . . . For the future we will be together."

"Yes, together, together! Henceforward we shall be always together, all our lives! Listen, kiss me, I allow you."

Alyosha kissed her.

"Come, now go. Christ be with you!" and she made the sign of the cross over him. "Make haste back to *him* while he is alive. I see I've kept you cruelly. I'll pray to-day for him and you. Alyosha, we shall be happy! Shall we be happy, shall we?"

"I believe we shall, Lise."

Alyosha thought it better not to go in to Madame Hohlakov and was going out of the house without saying good-bye to her. But no sooner had he opened the door than he found Madame Hohlakov standing before him. From the first word Alyosha guessed that she had been waiting on purpose to meet him.

"Alexey Fyodorovitch, this is awful. This is all childish nonsense and ridiculous. I trust you won't dream. . . . It's foolishness, nothing but foolishness!" she said, attacking him at once.

"Only don't tell her that," said Alyosha, "or she will be upset, and that's bad for her now."

"Sensible advice from a sensible young man. Am I to understand that you only agreed with her from compassion for her invalid state, because you didn't want to irritate her by contradiction?"

"Oh no, not at all. I was quite serious in what I said," Alyosha declared stoutly.

"To be serious about it is impossible, unthinkable, and in the first place I shall never be at home to you again, and I shall take her away, you may be sure of that."

"But why?" asked Alyosha. "It's all so far off. We may have to wait another year and a half."

"Ah, Alexey Fyodorovitch, that's true, of course, and you'll have time to quarrel and separate a thousand times in a year and a half. But I am so unhappy! Though it's such nonsense, it's a great blow to me. I feel like Famusov in the last scene of *Sorrow from Wit*.[1] You are Tchatsky and she is Sofya, and, only fancy, I've run down to meet you on the stairs, and in the play the fatal scene takes place on the staircase. I heard it all; I almost dropped. So this is the explanation of her dreadful night and her hysterics of late! It means love to the daughter but death to the mother. I might as well be in my grave at once. And a more serious matter still, what is this letter she has written? Show it me at once, at once!"

"No, there's no need. Tell me, how is Katerina Ivanovna now? I must know."

"She still lies in delirium; she has not regained consciousness. Her aunts are here; but they do nothing but sigh and give themselves airs. Herzenstube came, and he was so alarmed that I didn't know what to do for him. I nearly sent for a doctor to look after him. He was driven home in my carriage. And on the top of it all, you and this letter! It's true nothing can happen for a year and a half. In the name of all that's holy, in the name of your dying elder, show me that letter, Alexey Fyodorovitch. I'm her mother. Hold it in your hand, if you like, and I will read it so."

"No, I won't show it to you. Even if she sanctioned it, I wouldn't. I am coming to-morrow, and if you like, we can talk over many things, but now good-bye!"

And Alyosha ran downstairs and into the street.

2

SMERDYAKOV WITH A GUITAR

H<small>E</small> had no time to lose indeed. Even while he was saying good-bye to Lise, the thought had struck him that he must attempt some stratagem to find his brother Dmitri, who was evidently keeping out of his way. It was getting late, nearly three o'clock. Alyosha's whole soul turned to the monastery, to his dying saint, but the necessity of seeing Dmitri outweighed everything. The conviction that a great inevitable catastrophe was about to happen grew stronger in Alyosha's mind with every hour. What that catastrophe was, and what he would say at that moment to his brother, he could perhaps not have said definitely. "Even if my benefactor must die without me, anyway I won't have to reproach myself all my life with the thought that I might have saved something and did not, but passed by and hastened home. If I do as I intend, I shall be following his great precept."

His plan was to catch his brother Dmitri unawares, to climb over the fence, as he had the day before, get into the garden and sit in the summer-house. If Dmitri were not there, thought Alyosha, he would not announce himself to Foma or the women of the house, but would remain hidden in the summer-house, even if he had to wait there till evening. If, as before, Dmitri were lying in wait for Grushenka to come, he would be very likely to come to the summer-house. Alyosha did not, however, give much thought to the details of his plan, but resolved to act upon it, even if it meant not getting back to the monastery that day.

Everything happened without hindrance, he climbed over the hurdle almost in the same spot as the day before, and stole into the summer-house unseen. He did not want to be noticed. The women of the house and Foma too, if he were here, might be loyal to his brother and obey his instructions, and so refuse to let Alyosha come into the garden, or might warn Dmitri that he was being sought and inquired for.

There was no one in the summer-house. Alyosha sat down and began to wait. He looked round the summer-house, which somehow struck him as a great deal more ancient than before. Though the day was just as fine as yesterday, it seemed a wretched little place this time. There was a circle on the table, left no doubt from the glass of brandy having been spilt the day before. Foolish and irrelevant ideas strayed about his mind, as they always do in a time of tedious waiting. He wondered, for instance, why he had sat down precisely in the same place as before, why not in the other seat. At last he felt very depressed—depressed by suspense and uncertainty. But he had not sat there more than a quarter of an hour, when he suddenly heard the thrum of a guitar somewhere quite close. People were sitting, or had only just sat down, somewhere in the bushes not more than twenty paces away. Alyosha suddenly recollected that on coming out of the summer-house the day before, he had caught a glimpse of an old green low garden-seat among the bushes on the left, by the fence. The people must be sitting on it now. Who were they?

A man's voice suddenly began singing in a sugary falsetto, accompanying himself on the guitar:

> With invincible force
> I am bound to my dear.
> Oh, Lord, have mercy
> On her and on me!
> On her and on me!
> On her and on me![2]

The voice ceased. It was a lackey's tenor and a lackey's song. Another voice, a woman's, suddenly asked insinuatingly and bashfully, though with mincing affectation:

"Why haven't you been to see us for so long, Pavel Fyodorovitch? Why do you always look down upon us?"

"Not at all," answered a man's voice politely, but with emphatic dignity. It was clear that the man had the best of the position, and that the woman was making advances. "I believe the man must be Smerdyakov," thought Alyosha, "from his voice. And the lady must be the daughter of the house here, who has come from Moscow, the one who wears the dress with a tail and goes to Marfa for soup."

"I am awfully fond of verses of all kinds, if they rhyme," the woman's voice continued, "Why don't you go on?"

The man sang again:

> What do I care for royal wealth
> If but my dear one be in health?
> Lord have mercy
> On her and on me!
> On her and on me!
> On her and on me!

"It was even better last time," observed the woman's voice. "You sang 'If my darling be in health'; it sounded more tender. I suppose you've forgotten to-day."

"Poetry is rubbish!" said Smerdyakov curtly.

"Oh, no! I am very fond of poetry."

"So far as it's poetry, it's essential rubbish. Consider yourself, who ever talks in rhyme? And if we were all to talk in rhyme, even though it were decreed by government, we shouldn't say much, should we? Poetry is no good, Marya Kondratyevna."

"How clever you are! How is it you've gone so deep into everything?" The woman's voice was more and more insinuating.

"I could have done better than that. I could have known more than that, if it had not been for my destiny from my childhood up. I would have shot a man in a duel if he called me names because I am descended from a filthy beggar and have no father. And they used to throw it in my teeth in Moscow. It had reached them from here, thanks to Grigory Vassilyevitch. Grigory Vassilyevitch blames me for rebelling against my birth, but I would have sanctioned their killing me before I was born that I might not have come into the world at all. They used to say in the market, and your mamma too, with great lack of delicacy, set off telling me that her hair was like a mat on her head, and that she was short of five foot by a wee bit. Why talk of a wee bit while she might have said 'a little bit,' like every one else? She wanted to make it touching, a regular peasant's feeling. Can a Russian peasant be said to feel, in comparison with an educated man? He can't be said to have feeling at all, in his ignorance. From my childhood up when I hear 'a wee bit,' I am ready to burst with rage. I hate all Russia, Marya Kondratyevna."

"If you'd been a cadet in the army, or a young hussar, you wouldn't have talked like that, but would have drawn your sabre to defend all Russia."

"I don't want to be a hussar, Marya Kondratyevna, and, what's more, I should like to abolish all soldiers."

"And when an enemy comes, who is going to defend us?"

"There's no need of defence. In 1812 there was a great invasion of Russia by Napoleon, first Emperor of the French, father of the present one,* and it would have been a good thing if they had conquered us. A clever nation would have conquered a very stupid one and annexed it. We should have had quite different institutions."

"Are they so much better in their own country than we are? I wouldn't change a dandy I know of for three young Englishmen," observed Marya Kondratyevna tenderly, doubtless accompanying her words with a most languishing glance.

"That's as one prefers."

"But you are just like a foreigner—just like a most gentlemanly foreigner. I tell you that, though it makes me bashful."

"If you care to know, the folks there and ours here are just alike in their vice. They are swindlers, only there the scoundrel wears polished boots and here he grovels in filth and sees no harm in it. The Russian people want thrashing, as Fyodor Pavlovitch said very truly yesterday, though he is mad, and all his children."

"You said yourself you had such a respect for Ivan Fyodorovitch."

"But he said I was a stinking lackey. He thinks that I might be unruly. He is mistaken there. If I had a certain sum in my pocket, I would have left

---

*Napoléon III, emperor of the French from 1852 to 1870, was actually the nephew of Napoléon I.

here long ago. Dmitri Fyodorovitch is lower than any lackey in his behaviour, in his mind, and in his poverty. He doesn't know how to do anything, and yet he is respected by everyone. I may be only a soup maker, but with luck I could open a café restaurant in Petrovka,* in Moscow, for my cookery is something special, and there's no one in Moscow except the foreigners, whose cookery is anything special. Dmitri Fyodorovitch is a beggar, but if he were to challenge the son of the first count in the country, he'd fight him. Though in what way is he better than I am? For he is ever so much stupider than I am. Look at the money he has wasted without any need!"

"It must be lovely, a duel," Marya Kondratyevna observed suddenly.

"How so?"

"It must be so dreadful and so brave, especially when young officers with pistols in their hands pop at one another for the sake of some lady. A perfect picture! Ah, if only girls were allowed to look on, I'd give anything to see one!"

"It's all very well when you are firing at some one, but when he is firing straight in your mug, you must feel pretty silly. You'd be glad to run away, Marya Kondratyevna."

"You don't mean you would run away?" But Smerdyakov did not deign to reply. After a moment's silence the guitar tinkled again, and he sang again in the same falsetto:

> Whatever you may say,
> I shall go far away.
> Life will be bright and gay
> In the city far away.
> I shall not grieve,
> I shall not grieve at all,
> I don't intend to grieve at all.

Then something unexpected happened. Alyosha suddenly sneezed. They were silent. Alyosha got up and walked towards them. He found Smerdyakov dressed up and wearing polished boots, his hair pomaded, and perhaps curled. The guitar lay on the garden-seat. His companion was the daughter of the house, wearing a light blue dress with a train two yards long. She was young and would not have been bad-looking, but that her face was so round and terribly freckled.

"Will my brother Dmitri soon be back?" asked Alyosha with as much composure as he could.

Smerdyakov got up slowly; Marya Kondratyevna rose too.

"How am I to know about Dmitri Fyodorovitch? It's not as if I were his keeper," answered Smerdyakov quietly, distinctly, and superciliously.

"But I simply asked whether you do know?" Alyosha explained.

"I know nothing of his whereabouts and don't want to."

---

*Street in central Moscow.

"But my brother told me that you let him know all that goes on in the house, and promised to let him know when Agrafena Alexandrovna comes."

Smerdyakov turned a deliberate, unmoved glance upon him.

"And how did you get in this time, since the gate was bolted an hour ago?" he asked, looking at Alyosha.

"I came in from the back-alley, over the fence, and went straight to the summer-house. I hope you'll forgive me," he added, addressing Marya Kondratyevna. "I was in a hurry to find my brother."

"Ach, as though we could take it amiss in you!" drawled Marya Kondratyevna, flattered by Alyosha's apology. "For Dmitri Fyodorovitch often goes to the summer-house in that way. We don't know he is here and he is sitting in the summer-house."

"I am very anxious to find him, or to learn from you where he is now. Believe me, it's on business of great importance to him."

"He never tells us," lisped Marya Kondratyevna.

"Though I used to come here as a friend," Smerdyakov began again, "Dmitri Fyodorovitch has pestered me in a merciless way even here by his incessant questions about the master. 'What news?' he'll ask. 'What's going on in there now? Who's coming and going?' and can't I tell him something more. Twice already he's threatened me with death."

"With death?" Alyosha exclaimed in surprise.

"Do you suppose he'd think much of that, with his temper, which you had a chance of observing yourself yesterday? He says if I let Agrafena Alexandrovna in and she passes the night there, I'll be the first to suffer for it. I am terribly afraid of him, and if I were not even more afraid of doing so, I ought to let the police know. God only knows what he might not do!"

"His honour said to him the other day, 'I'll pound you in a mortar!'" added Marya Kondratyevna.

"Oh, if it's pounding in a mortar, it may be only talk," observed Alyosha. "If I could meet him, I might speak to him about that too."

"Well the only thing I can tell you is this," said Smerdyakov, as though thinking better of it; "I am here as an old friend and neighbour, and it would be odd if I didn't come. On the other hand, Ivan Fyodorovitch sent me first thing this morning to your brother's lodging in Lake Street, without a letter, but with a message to Dmitri Fyodorovitch to go to dine with him at the restaurant here, in the market-place. I went, but didn't find Dmitri Fyodorovitch at home, though it was eight o'clock. 'He's been here, but he is quite gone,' those were the very words of his landlady. It's as though there was an understanding between them. Perhaps at this moment he is in the restaurant with Ivan Fyodorovitch, for Ivan Fyodorovitch has not been home to dinner and Fyodor Pavlovitch dined alone an hour ago, and is gone to lie down. But I beg you most particularly not to speak of me and of what I have told you, for he'd kill me for nothing at all."

"Brother Ivan invited Dmitri to the restaurant to-day?" repeated Alyosha quickly.

"That's so."

"The Metropolis tavern in the market-place?"

"The very same."

"That's quite likely," cried Alyosha, much excited. "Thank you, Smerdyakov; that's important. I'll go there at once."

"Don't betray me," Smerdyakov called after him.

"Oh, no, I'll go to the tavern as though by chance. Don't be anxious."

"But wait a minute, I'll open the gate to you," cried Marya Kondratyevna.

"No; it's a short cut, I'll get over the fence again."

What he had heard threw Alyosha into great agitation. He ran to the tavern. It was impossible for him to go into the tavern in his monastic dress, but he could inquire at the entrance for his brothers and call them down. But just as he reached the tavern, a window was flung open, and his brother Ivan called down to him from it.

"Alyosha, can't you come up here to me? I shall be awfully grateful."

"To be sure I can, only I don't quite know whether in this dress . . ."

"But I am in a room apart. Come up the steps; I'll run down to meet you."

A minute later Alyosha was sitting beside his brother. Ivan was alone dining.

3

THE BROTHERS MAKE FRIENDS

IVAN was not, however, in a separate room, but only in a place shut off by a screen, so that it was unseen by other people in the room. It was the first room from the entrance with a buffet along the wall. Waiters were continually darting to and fro in it. The only customer in the room was an old retired military man drinking tea in a corner. But there was the usual bustle going on in the other rooms of the tavern; there were shouts for the waiters, the sound of popping corks, the click of billiard balls, the drone of the organ. Alyosha knew that Ivan did not usually visit this tavern and disliked taverns in general. So he must have come here, he reflected, simply to meet Dmitri by arrangement. Yet Dmitri was not there.

"Shall I order you fish, or anything, you don't live on tea alone, I suppose," cried Ivan, apparently delighted at having got hold of Alyosha. He had finished dinner and was drinking tea.

"Let me have soup, and tea afterwards, I am hungry," said Alyosha gaily.

"And cherry jam? They have it here. You remember how you used to love cherry jam when you were little?"

"You remember that? Let me have jam too, I like it still."

Ivan ran for the waiter and ordered soup, jam and tea.

"I remember everything, Alyosha, I remember you till you were eleven, I was nearly fifteen. There's such a difference between fifteen and eleven that brothers are never companions at those ages. I don't know whether I was fond of you even. When I went away to Moscow for the first few years I never thought of you at all. Then, when you came to Moscow yourself, we only met once somewhere, I believe. And now I've been here more than three months, and so far we have scarcely said a word to each other. To-morrow I am going away, and I was just thinking as I sat here how I could see you to say good-bye and just then you passed."

"Were you very anxious to see me then?"

"Very, I want to get to know you once for all, and I want you to know me. And then to say good-bye. I believe it's always best to get to know people just before leaving them. I've noticed how you've been looking at me these three months. There has been a continual look of expectation in your eyes, and I can't endure that. That's how it is I've kept away from you. But in the end I have learned to respect you. The little man stands firm, I thought. Though I am laughing, I am serious. You do stand firm, don't you? I like people who are firm like that whatever it is they stand by, even if they are such little fellows as you. Your expectant eyes ceased to annoy me, I grew fond of them in the end, those expectant eyes. You seem to love me for some reason, Alyosha?"

"I do love you, Ivan. Dmitri says of you—Ivan is a tomb! I say of you, Ivan is a riddle. You are a riddle to me even now. But I understand something in you, and I did not understand it till this morning."

"What's that?" laughed Ivan.

"You won't be angry?" Alyosha laughed too.

"Well?"

"That you are just as young as other young men of three and twenty, that you are just a young and fresh and nice boy, green in fact! Now, have I insulted you dreadfully?"

"On the contrary, I am struck by a coincidence," cried Ivan, warmly and good-humouredly. "Would you believe it that ever since that scene with her, I have thought of nothing else but my youthful greenness, and just as though you guessed that, you begin about it. Do you know I've been sitting here thinking to myself: that if I didn't believe in life, if I lost faith in the woman I love, lost faith in the order of things, were convinced in fact that everything is a disorderly, damnable, and perhaps devil-ridden chaos, if I were struck by every horror of man's disillusionment—still I should want to live and, having once tasted of the cup, I would not turn away from it till I had drained it! At thirty though, I shall be sure to leave the cup, even if I've not emptied it, and turn away—where I don't know. But till I am thirty, I know that my youth will triumph over everything—every disillusionment, every disgust with life. I've asked myself many times whether there is in the world any despair that would overcome this frantic and perhaps unseemly thirst for life in me, and I've come to the conclusion that there isn't, that is till I am thirty, and then I shall lose it of myself I fancy. Some drivelling consumptive moralists—and poets especially—often call that thirst for life base. It's a feature of the Karamazovs it's true, that thirst for life regardless of everything; you have it no doubt too, but why is it base? The centripetal force on our planet is still fearfully strong, Alyosha. I have a longing for life, and I go on living in spite of logic. Though I may not believe in the order of the universe, yet I love the sticky little leaves as they open in spring.* I love the blue sky, I love some people, whom one loves you know sometimes without knowing why. I love some great deeds done by men, though I've long ceased perhaps to have faith in them, yet from old habit one's heart prizes them. Here they have brought the soup for you, eat it, it will do you good. It's first-rate soup, they know how to make it here. I want to travel in Europe, Alyosha, I shall set off from here. And yet I know that I am only going to a grave-yard, but it's a most precious grave-yard, that's what it is! Precious are the dead that lie there, every stone over them speaks of such burning life in the past, of such passionate faith in their work, their truth, their struggle and their science, that I know I shall fall on the ground and kiss those stones and weep over them; though I'm convinced in my heart that it's long been nothing but a grave-yard. And I shall not weep from despair, but simply because I shall be happy in my tears, I shall steep my soul in my emotion. I love the sticky leaves in spring, the blue sky—that's all it is. It's not a matter of intellect or logic, it's loving with one's inside, with one's stomach. One loves the first strength of one's youth. Do you understand anything of my tirade, Alyosha?" Ivan laughed suddenly.

"I understand too well, Ivan. One longs to love with one's inside, with one's stomach. You said that so well and I am awfully glad that you have such a longing for life," cried Alyosha. "I think every one should love life above everything in the world."

"Love life more than the meaning of it?"

"Certainly, love it, regardless of logic as you say, it must be regardless of logic, and it's only then one will understand the meaning of it. I have thought so a long time. Half your work is done, Ivan, you love life, now you've only to try to do the second half and you are saved."

"You are trying to save me, but perhaps I am not lost! And what does your second half mean?"

"Why, one has to raise up one's dead, who perhaps have not died after all. Come, let me have tea. I am so glad of our talk, Ivan."

"I see you are feeling inspired. I am awfully fond of such *professions de foi*† from such—novices. You are a steadfast person, Alexey. Is it true that you mean to leave the monastery?"

---

*The phrase "sticky little leaves" comes from a Pushkin poem, "Chill Winds Still Blow" (1828).
†Professions of faith (French).

"Yes, my elder sends me out into the world."

"We shall see each other then in the world. We shall meet before I am thirty, when I shall begin to turn aside from the cup. Father doesn't want to turn aside from his cup till he is seventy, he dreams of hanging on to eighty in fact, so he says. He means it only too seriously, though he is a buffoon. He stands on a firm rock, too, he stands on his sensuality—though after we are thirty, indeed, there may be nothing else to stand on. . . . But to hang on to seventy is nasty, better only to thirty; one might retain 'a shadow of nobility'* by deceiving oneself. Have you seen Dmitri to-day?"

"No, but I saw Smerdyakov," and Alyosha rapidly, though minutely, described his meeting with Smerdyakov. Ivan began listening anxiously and questioned him.

"But he begged me not to tell Dmitri that he had told me about him," added Alyosha. Ivan frowned and pondered.

"Are you frowning on Smerdyakov's account?" asked Alyosha.

"Yes, on his account. Damn him, I certainly did want to see Dmitri, but now there's no need," said Ivan reluctantly.

"But are you really going so soon, brother?"

"Yes."

"What of Dmitri and father? how will it end?" asked Alyosha anxiously.

"You are always harping upon it! What have I to do with it? Am I my brother Dmitri's keeper?" Ivan snapped irritably, but then he suddenly smiled bitterly. "Cain's answer about his murdered brother, wasn't it? Perhaps that's what you're thinking at this moment? Well, damn it all, I can't stay here to be their keeper, can I? I've finished what I had to do, and I am going. Do you imagine I am jealous of Dmitri, that I've been trying to steal his beautiful Katerina Ivanovna for the last three months. Nonsense, I had business of my own. I finished it. I am going. I finished it just now, you were witness."

"At Katerina Ivanovna's?"

"Yes, and I've released myself once for all. And after all, what have I to do with Dmitri? Dmitri doesn't come in. I had my own business to settle with Katerina Ivanovna. You know, on the contrary, that Dmitri behaved as though there was an understanding between us. I didn't ask him to do it, but he solemnly handed her over to me and gave us his blessing. It's all too funny. Ah, Alyosha, if you only knew how light my heart is now! Would you believe it, I sat here eating my dinner and was nearly ordering champagne to celebrate my first hour of freedom. Tfoo! It's been going on nearly six months, and all at once I've thrown it off. I could never have guessed even yesterday, how easy it would be to put an end to it if I wanted."

"You are speaking of your love, Ivan?"

"Of my love, if you like. I fell in love with the young lady, I worried myself over her and she worried me. I sat watching over her . . . and all at once it's collapsed! I spoke this morning with inspiration, but I went away

---

*Quotation from a Pushkin epigram (1825).

and roared with laughter. Would you believe it? Yes, it's the literal truth."

"You seem very merry about it now," observed Alyosha, looking into his face, which had suddenly grown brighter.

"But how could I tell that I didn't care for her a bit! Ha-ha! It appears after all I didn't. And yet how she attracted me! How attractive she was just now when I made my speech! And do you know she attracts me awfully even now, yet how easy it is to leave her. Do you think I am boasting?"

"No, only perhaps it wasn't love."

"Alyosha," laughed Ivan, "don't make reflections about love, it's unseemly for you. How you rushed into the discussion this morning! I've forgotten to kiss you for it. . . . But how she tormented me! It certainly was sitting by a 'laceration.' Ah, she knew how I loved her! She loved me and not Dmitri," Ivan insisted gaily. "Her feeling for Dmitri was simply a self-laceration. All I told her just now was perfectly true, but the worst of it is, it may take her fifteen or twenty years to find out that she doesn't care for Dmitri, and loves me whom she torments, and perhaps she may never find it out at all, in spite of her lesson to-day. Well, it's better so; I can simply go away for good. By the way, how is she now? What happened after I departed?"

Alyosha told him she had been hysterical, and that she was now, he heard, unconscious and delirious.

"Isn't Madame Hohlakov laying it on?"

"I think not."

"I must find out. Nobody dies of hysterics though. They don't matter. God gave woman hysterics as a relief. I won't go to her at all. Why push myself forward again?"

"But you told her that she had never cared for you."

"I did that on purpose. Alyosha, shall I call for some champagne? Let us drink to my freedom. Ah, if only you knew how glad I am!"

"No, brother, we had better not drink," said Alyosha suddenly. "Besides I feel somehow depressed."

"Yes, you've been depressed a long time, I've noticed it."

"Have you settled to go to-morrow morning then?"

"Morning? I didn't say I should go in the morning. . . . But perhaps it may be the morning. Would you believe it, I dined here to-day only to avoid dining with the old man, I loathe him so. I should have left long ago, so far as he is concerned. But why are you so worried about my going away? We've plenty of time before I go, an eternity!"

"If you are going away to-morrow, what do you mean by an eternity?"

"But what does it matter to us?" laughed Ivan, "we've time enough for our talk, for what brought us here. Why do you look so surprised? Answer: why have we met here? To talk of my love for Katerina Ivanovna, of the old man and Dmitri? of foreign travel? of the fatal position of Russia? of the Emperor Napoleon? Is that it?"

"No."

"Then you know what for. It's different for other people; but we in our green youth have to settle the eternal questions first of all. That's what we care about. Young Russia is talking about nothing but the eternal questions now. Just when the old folks are all taken up with practical questions. Why have you been looking at me in expectation for the last three months? To ask me 'what do you believe, or don't you believe at all?' That's what your eyes have been meaning for these three months, haven't they?"

"Perhaps so," smiled Alyosha. "You are not laughing at me, now, Ivan?"

"Me laughing! I don't want to wound my little brother who has been watching me with such expectation for three months. Alyosha, look straight at me! Of course I am just such a little boy as you are, only not a novice. And what have Russian boys been doing up till now, some of them, I mean? In this stinking tavern, for instance, here, they meet and sit down in a corner. They've never met in their lives before and, when they go out of the tavern, they won't meet again for forty years. And what do they talk about in that momentary halt in the tavern? Of the eternal questions, of the existence of God and immortality. And those who do not believe in God talk of socialism or anarchism, of the transformation of all humanity on a new pattern, so that it all comes to the same, they're the same questions turned inside out. And masses, masses of the most original Russian boys do nothing but talk of the eternal questions! Isn't it so?"

"Yes, for real Russians the questions of God's existence and of immortality, or, as you say, the same questions turned inside out, come first and foremost, of course, and so they should," said Alyosha, still watching his brother with the same gentle and inquiring smile.

"Well, Alyosha, it's sometimes very unwise to be a Russian at all, but anything stupider than the way Russian boys spend their time one can hardly imagine. But there's one Russian boy called Alyosha I am awfully fond of."

"How nicely you put that in!" Alyosha laughed suddenly.

"Well, tell me where to begin, give your orders. The existence of God, eh?"

"Begin where you like. You declared yesterday at father's that there was no God." Alyosha looked searchingly at his brother.

"I said that yesterday at dinner on purpose to tease you and I saw your eyes glow. But now I've no objection to discussing with you, and I say so very seriously. I want to be friends with you, Alyosha, for I have no friends and want to try it. Well, only fancy, perhaps I too accept God," laughed Ivan, "that's a surprise for you, isn't it?"

"Yes, of course, if you are not joking now."

"Joking? I was told at the elder's yesterday that I was joking. You know, dear boy, there was an old sinner in the eighteenth century who declared that, if there were no God, he would have to be invented. *S'il n'existait pas Dieu, il faudrait l'inventer.*[3] And man has actually invented God. And what's strange, what would be marvellous, is not that God should really exist; the marvel is that such an idea, the idea of the necessity of God, could enter the head of such a savage, vicious beast as man. So holy it is, so touching, so wise and so great a credit it does to man. As for me, I've long resolved not to think whether man created God or God man. And I won't go through all the axioms laid down by Russian boys on that subject, all derived from European hypotheses; for what's a hypothesis there, is an axiom with the Russian boys, and not only with the boys but with their teachers too, for our Russian professors are often just the same boys themselves. And so I omit all the hypotheses. For what are we aiming at now? I am trying to explain as quickly as possible my essential nature, that is what manner of man I am, what I believe in, and for what I hope, that's it, isn't it? And therefore I tell you that I accept God simply. But you must note this: if God exists and if He really did create the world, then, as we all know, He created it according to the geometry of Euclid and the human mind with the conception of only three dimensions in space. Yet there have been and still are geometricians and philosophers, and even some of the most distinguished, who doubt whether the whole universe, or to speak more widely the whole of being, was only created in Euclid's geometry;* they even dare to dream that two parallel lines, which according to Euclid can never meet on earth, may meet somewhere in infinity. I have come to the conclusion that, since I can't understand even that, I can't expect to understand about God. I acknowledge humbly that I have no faculty for settling such questions, I have a Euclidian, earthly mind, and how could I solve problems that are not of this world? And I advise you never to think about it either, my dear Alyosha, especially about God, whether He exists or not. All such questions are utterly inappropriate for a mind created with an idea of only three dimensions. And so I accept God and am glad to, and what's more I accept His wisdom, His purpose—which are utterly beyond our ken; I believe in the underlying order and the meaning of life; I believe in the eternal harmony in which they say we shall one day be blended. I believe in the Word to Which the universe is striving, and Which Itself was "with God," and Which Itself is God and so on, and so on, to infinity.†️ There are all sorts of phrases for it. I seem to be on the right path, don't I? Yet would you believe it, in the final result I don't accept this world of God's, and, although I know it exists, I don't accept it at all. It's not that I don't accept God, you must understand, it's the world created by Him I don't and cannot accept. Let me make it plain. I believe like a child that suffering will be healed and made up for, that all the humiliating absurdity of human contradictions will vanish like a pitiful mirage, like the despicable fabrication of the impotent and infinitely small Euclidian mind of man, that in the world's finale, at the moment of eternal harmony, something so precious will come to pass that it will suffice for all hearts, for the comforting of all resentments, for the atonement of all the crimes of humanity, of all the blood they've shed; that it will make it not only possible to forgive but to justify all that has happened with men—but though all that may

---

*Russian mathematician N. I. Lobachevsky presented his non-Euclidean geometry in 1826 (Euclid was an important Greek mathematician from the third century B.C.)
†See John 1:1–2.

come to pass, I don't accept it. I won't accept it. Even if parallel lines do meet and I see it myself, I shall see it and say that they've met, but still I won't accept it. That's what's at the root of me, Alyosha; that's my creed. I am in earnest in what I say. I began our talk as stupidly as I could on purpose, but I've led up to my confession, for that's all you want. You didn't want to hear about God, but only to know what the brother you love lives by. And so I've told you."

Ivan concluded his long tirade with marked and unexpected feeling.

"And why did you begin 'as stupidly as you could'?" asked Alyosha, looking dreamily at him.

"To begin with, for the sake of being Russian. Russian conversations on such subjects are always carried on inconceivably stupidly. And secondly, the stupider one is, the closer one is to reality. The stupider one is, the clearer one is. Stupidity is brief and artless, while intelligence wriggles and hides itself. Intelligence is a knave, but stupidity is honest and straight-forward. I've led the conversation to my despair, and the more stupidly I have presented it, the better for me."

"You will explain why you don't accept the world?" said Alyosha.

"To be sure I will, it's not a secret, that's what I've been leading up to. Dear little brother, I don't want to corrupt you or to turn you from your stronghold, perhaps I want to be healed by you." Ivan smiled suddenly quite like a little gentle child. Alyosha had never seen such a smile on his face before.

4

REBELLION

I MUST make you one confession," Ivan began. "I could never under-stand how one can love one's neighbours. It's just one's neighbours, to my mind, that one can't love, though one might love those at a distance. I once read somewhere of John the Merciful, a saint, that when a hungry, frozen beggar came to him, he took him into his bed, held him in his arms, and began breathing into his mouth, which was putrid and loathsome from some awful disease.[4] I am convinced that he did that from 'self-laceration,' from the self-laceration of falsity, for the sake of the charity imposed by duty, as a penance laid on him. For any one to love a man, he must be hid-den, for as soon as he shows his face, love is gone."

"Father Zossima has talked of that more than once," observed Alyosha, "he, too, said that the face of a man often hinders many people not practised in love, from loving him. But yet there's a great deal of love in mankind, and almost Christ-like love. I know that myself, Ivan."

"Well, I know nothing of it so far, and can't understand it, and the innumerable mass of mankind are with me there. The question is, whether that's due to men's bad qualities or whether it's inherent in their nature. To my thinking, Christ-like love for men is a miracle impossible on earth. He was God. But we are not gods. Suppose I, for instance, suffer intensely. Another can never know how much I suffer, because he is another and not I. And what's more, a man is rarely ready to admit another's suffering (as though it were a distinction). Why won't he admit it, do you think? Because I smell unpleasant, because I have a stupid face, because I once trod on his foot. Besides there is suffering and suffering; degrading, humiliating suffering such as humbles me—hunger, for instance,—my benefactor will perhaps allow me; but when you come to higher suffering—for an idea, for instance—he will very rarely admit that, perhaps because my face strikes him as not at all what he fancies a man should have who suffers for an idea. And so he deprives me instantly of his favour, and not at all from badness of heart. Beggars, especially genteel beggars, ought never to show themselves, but to ask for charity through the newspapers. One can love one's neighbours in the abstract, or even at a distance, but at close quarters it's almost impossible. If it were as on the stage, in the ballet, where if beggars come in, they wear silken rags and tattered lace and beg for alms dancing gracefully, then one might like looking at them. But even then we should not love them. But enough of that. I simply wanted to show you my point of view. I meant to speak of the suffering of mankind generally, but we had better confine ourselves to the sufferings of the children. That reduces the scope of my argument to a tenth of what it would be. Still we'd better keep to the children, though it does weaken my case. But, in the first place, children can be loved even at close quarters, even when they are dirty, even when they are ugly (I fancy, though, children never are ugly). The second reason why I won't speak of grown-up people is that, besides being disgusting and unworthy of love, they have a compensation—they've eaten the apple and know good and evil, and they have become 'like gods.'* They go on eating it still. But the children haven't eaten anything, and are so far innocent. Are you fond of children, Alyosha? I know you are, and you will understand why I prefer to speak of them. If they, too, suffer horribly on earth, they must suffer for their fathers' sins, they must be punished for their fathers, who have eaten the apple; but that reasoning is of the other world and is incomprehensible for the heart of man here on earth. The innocent must not suffer for another's sins, and especially such innocents! You may be surprised at me, Alyosha, but I am awfully fond of children, too. And observe, cruel people, the violent, the rapacious, the Karamazovs are sometimes very fond of children. Children while they are quite little—up to seven, for instance—are so remote from grown-up people;

---

*See Genesis 3:5.

they are different creatures, as it were, of a different species. I knew a criminal in prison who had, in the course of his career as a burglar, murdered whole families, including several children. But when he was in prison, he had a strange affection for them. He spent all his time at his window, watching the children playing in the prison yard. He trained one little boy to come up to his window and made great friends with him. . . . You don't know why I am telling you all this, Alyosha? My head aches and I am sad."

"You speak with a strange air," observed Alyosha uneasily, "as though you were not quite yourself."

"By the way, a Bulgarian I met lately in Moscow," Ivan went on, seeming not to hear his brother's words, "told me about the crimes committed by Turks and Circassians in all parts of Bulgaria through fear of a general rising of the Slavs. They burn villages, murder, outrage women and children, they nail their prisoners by the ears to the fences, leave them so till morning, and in the morning they hang them—all sorts of things you can't imagine. People talk sometimes of bestial cruelty, but that's a great injustice and insult to the beasts; a beast can never be so cruel as a man, so artistically cruel. The tiger only tears and gnaws, that's all he can do. He would never think of nailing people by the ears, even if he were able to do it. These Turks took a pleasure in torturing children, too; cutting the unborn child from the mother's womb, and tossing babies up in the air and catching them on the points of their bayonets before their mother's eyes. Doing it before the mother's eyes was what gave zest to the amusement. Here is another scene that I thought very interesting. Imagine a trembling mother with her baby in her arms, a circle of invading Turks around her. They've planned a diversion; they pet the baby, laugh to make it laugh. They succeed, the baby laughs. At that moment a Turk points a pistol four inches from the baby's face. The baby laughs with glee, holds out its little hands to the pistol, and he pulls the trigger in the baby's face and blows out its brains. Artistic, wasn't it? By the way, Turks are particularly fond of sweet things, they say."

"Brother, what are you driving at?" asked Alyosha.

"I think if the devil doesn't exist, but man has created him, he has created him in his own image and likeness."

"Just as he did God, then?" observed Alyosha.

" 'It's wonderful how you can turn words,' as Polonius says in *Hamlet*,"* laughed Ivan. "You turn my words against me. Well, I am glad. Yours must be a fine God, if man created Him in His image and likeness.† You asked just now what I was driving at. You see, I am fond of collecting certain facts, and, would you believe, I even copy anecdotes of a certain sort from newspapers and books, and I've already got a fine collection. The Turks, of course, have gone into it, but they are foreigners. I have specimens from home that are even better than the Turks. You know we prefer beating—rods and scourges—that's our national institution. Nailing ears is unthinkable for

---

*From a Russian translation of *Hamlet* (act I, scene 3).
†See Genesis 1:26.

us, for we are, after all, Europeans. But the rod and the scourge we have always with us and they cannot be taken from us. Abroad now they scarcely do any beating. Manners are more humane, or laws have been passed, so that they don't dare to flog men now. But they make up for it in another way just as national as ours. And so national that it would be practically impossible among us, though I believe we are being inoculated with it, since the religious movement began in our aristocracy. I have a charming pamphlet, translated from the French, describing how, quite recently, five years ago, a murderer, Richard, was executed—a young man, I believe, of three and twenty, who repented and was converted to the Christian faith at the very scaffold. This Richard was an illegitimate child who was given as a child of six by his parents to some shepherds on the Swiss mountains. They brought him up to work for them. He grew up like a little wild beast among them. The shepherds taught him nothing, and scarcely fed or clothed him, but sent him out at seven to herd the flock in cold and wet, and no one hesitated or scrupled to treat him so. Quite the contrary, they thought they had every right, for Richard had been given to them as a chattel, and they did not even see the necessity of feeding him. Richard himself describes how in those years, like the Prodigal Son in the Gospel, he longed to eat of the mash given to the pigs, which were fattened for sale. But they wouldn't even give him that, and beat him when he stole from the pigs. And that was how he spent all his childhood and his youth, till he grew up and was strong enough to go away and be a thief. The savage began to earn his living as a day labourer in Geneva. He drank what he earned, he lived like a brute, and finished by killing and robbing an old man. He was caught, tried, and condemned to death. They are not sentimentalists there. And in prison he was immediately surrounded by pastors, members of Christian brotherhoods, philanthropic ladies, and the like. They taught him to read and write in prison, and expounded the Gospel to him. They exhorted him, worked upon him, drummed at him incessantly, till at last he solemnly confessed his crime. He was converted. He wrote to the court himself that he was a monster, but that in the end God had vouchsafed him light and shown grace. All Geneva was in excitement about him—all philanthropic and religious Geneva. All the aristocratic and well-bred society of the town rushed to the prison, kissed Richard and embraced him; 'You are our brother, you have found grace.' And Richard does nothing but weep with emotion, 'Yes, I've found grace! All my youth and childhood I was glad of pigs' food, but now even I have found grace. I am dying in the Lord.' 'Yes, Richard, die in the Lord; you have shed blood and must die. Though it's not your fault that you knew not the Lord, when you coveted the pigs' food and were beaten for stealing it (which was very wrong of you, for stealing is forbidden); but you've shed blood and you must die.' And on the last day, Richard, perfectly limp, did nothing but cry and repeat every minute: 'This is my happiest day. I am going to the Lord.' 'Yes,' cry the pastors and the judges and philanthropic ladies. 'This is the happiest day of your life, for you are going to the Lord!' They all walk or drive to the scaffold in procession behind the prison van. At the scaffold they call to

Richard: 'Die, brother, die in the Lord, for even thou hast found grace!'
And so, covered with his brothers' kisses, Richard is dragged on to the scaffold, and led to the guillotine. And they chopped off his head in brotherly fashion, because he had found grace. Yes, that's characteristic. That pamphlet is translated into Russian by some Russian philanthropists of aristocratic rank and evangelical aspirations, and has been distributed gratis for the enlightenment of the people. The case of Richard is interesting because it's national. Though to us it's absurd to cut off a man's head, because he has become our brother and has found grace, yet we have our own specialty, which is all but worse. Our historical pastime is the direct satisfaction of inflicting pain. There are lines in Nekrassov describing how a peasant lashes a horse on the eyes, 'on its meek eyes,'* every one must have seen it. It's peculiarly Russian. He describes how a feeble little nag had foundered under too heavy a load and cannot move. The peasant beats it, beats it savagely, beats it at last not knowing what he is doing in the intoxication of cruelty, thrashes it mercilessly over and over again. 'However weak you are, you must pull, if you die for it.' The nag strains, and then he begins lashing the poor defenceless creature on its weeping, on its 'meek eyes.' The frantic beast tugs and draws the load, trembling all over, gasping for breath, moving sideways, with a sort of unnatural spasmodic action—it's awful in Nekrassov. But that's only a horse, and God has given horses to be beaten. So the Tatars have taught us, and they left us the knout as a remembrance of it. But men, too, can be beaten. A well-educated, cultured gentleman and his wife beat their own child with a birch-rod, a girl of seven. I have an exact account of it. The papa was glad that the birch was covered with twigs. 'It stings more,' said he, and so he began stinging his daughter. I know for a fact there are people who at every blow are worked up to sensuality, to literal sensuality, which increases progressively at every blow they inflict. They beat for a minute, for five minutes, for ten minutes, more often and more savagely. The child screams. At last the child cannot scream, it gasps, 'Daddy! daddy!' By some diabolical unseemly chance the case was brought into court. A counsel is engaged. The Russian people have long called a barrister 'a conscience for hire.' The counsel protests in his client's defence. 'It's such a simple thing,' he says, 'an every-day domestic event. A father corrects his child. To our shame be it said, it is brought into court.' The jury, convinced by him, gives a favourable verdict. The public roars with delight that the torturer is acquitted. Ah, pity I wasn't there! I would have proposed to raise a subscription in his honour! . . . Charming pictures.

"But I've still better things about children. I've collected a great, great deal about Russian children, Alyosha. There was a little girl of five who was hated by her father and mother, 'most worthy and respectable people, of good education and breeding.' You see, I must repeat again, it is a peculiar characteristic of many people, this love of torturing children, and children only. To all other types of humanity these torturers behave mildly

---

*Line from Nikolai Nekrasov's poem "Before Twilight" (1859).

and benevolently, like cultivated and humane Europeans; but they are very fond of tormenting children, even fond of children themselves in that sense. It's just their defencelessness that tempts the tormentor, just the angelic confidence of the child who has no refuge and no appeal, that sets his vile blood on fire. In every man, of course, a demon lies hidden—the demon of rage, the demon of lustful heat at the screams of the tortured victim, the demon of lawlessness let off the chain, the demon of diseases that follow on vice, gout, kidney disease, and so on.

"This poor child of five was subjected to every possible torture by those cultivated parents. They beat her, thrashed her, kicked her for no reason till her body was one bruise. Then, they went to greater refinements of cruelty—shut her up all night in the cold and frost in a privy, and because she didn't ask to be taken up at night (as though a child of five sleeping its angelic, sound sleep could be trained to wake and ask), they smeared her face and filled her mouth with excrement, and it was her mother, her mother did this.[5] And that mother could sleep, hearing the poor child's groans! Can you understand why a little creature, who can't even understand what's done to her, should beat her little aching heart with her tiny fist in the dark and the cold, and weep her meek unresentful tears to dear, kind God to protect her? Do you understand that, friend and brother, you pious and humble novice? Do you understand why this infamy must be and is permitted? Without it, I am told, man could not have existed on earth, for he could not have known good and evil. Why should he know that diabolical good and evil when it costs so much? Why, the whole world of knowledge is not worth that child's prayer to 'dear, kind God'! I say nothing of the sufferings of grown-up people, they have eaten the apple, damn them, and the devil take them all! But these little ones! I am making you suffer, Alyosha, you are not yourself. I'll leave off if you like."

"Never mind. I want to suffer too," muttered Alyosha.

"One picture, only one more, because it's so curious, so characteristic, and I have only just read it in some collection of Russian antiquities. I've forgotten the name.[6] I must look it up. It was in the darkest days of serf-dom at the beginning of the century, and long live the Liberator of the People!* There was in those days a general of aristocratic connections, the owner of great estates, one of those men—somewhat exceptional, I believe, even then—who, retiring from the service into a life of leisure, are convinced that they've earned absolute power over the lives of their subjects. There were such men then. So our general, settled on his property of two thousand souls, lives in pomp, and domineers over his poor neighbours as though they were dependents and buffoons. He has kennels of hundreds of hounds and nearly a hundred dog-boys—all mounted, and in uniform. One day a serf boy, a little child of eight, threw a stone in play and hurt the paw of the general's favourite hound. 'Why is my favourite dog lame?' He

---

*Reference to Czar Alexander II (1855–1881), who liberated the serfs in 1861 and carried out many other reforms.

is told that the boy threw a stone that hurt the dog's paw. 'So you did it.' The general looked the child up and down. 'Take him.' He was taken— taken from his mother and kept shut up all night. Early that morning the general comes out on horseback, with the hounds, his dependents, dog- boys, and huntsmen, all mounted around him in full hunting parade. The servants are summoned for their edification, and in front of them all stands the mother of the child. The child is brought from the lock-up. It's a gloomy, cold, foggy autumn day, a capital day for hunting. The general or- ders the child to be undressed; the child is stripped naked. He shivers, numb with terror, not daring to cry. . . . 'Make him run,' commands the general. 'Run! run!' shout the dog-boys. The boy runs. . . . 'At him!' yells the general, and he sets the whole pack of hounds on the child. The hounds catch him, and tear him to pieces before his mother's eyes! . . . I believe the general was afterwards declared incapable of administering his estates. Well—what did he deserve? To be shot? To be shot for the satisfaction of our moral feelings? Speak, Alyosha!"

"To be shot," murmured Alyosha, lifting his eyes to Ivan with a pale, twisted smile.

"Bravo!" cried Ivan delighted. "If even you say so . . . You're a pretty monk! So there is a little devil sitting in your heart, Alyosha Karamazov!"

"What I said was absurd, but——"

"That's just the point, that 'but'!" cried Ivan. "Let me tell you, novice, that the absurd is only too necessary on earth. The world stands on ab- surdities, and perhaps nothing would have come to pass in it without them. We know what we know!"

"What do you know?"

"I understand nothing," Ivan went on, as though in delirium. "I don't want to understand anything now. I want to stick to the fact. I made up my mind long ago not to understand. If I try to understand anything, I shall be false to the fact and I have determined to stick to the fact."

"Why are you trying me?" Alyosha cried, with sudden distress. "Will you say what you mean at last?"

"Of course, I will; that's what I've been leading up to. You are dear to me, I don't want to let you go, and I won't give you up to your Zossima."

Ivan for a minute was silent, his face became all at once very sad.

"Listen! I took the case of children only to make my case clearer. Of the other tears of humanity with which the earth is soaked from its crust to its centre, I will say nothing. I have narrowed my subject on purpose. I am a bug, and I recognise in all humility that I cannot understand why the world is arranged as it is. Men are themselves to blame, I suppose; they were given paradise, they wanted freedom, and stole fire from heaven,* though they knew they would become unhappy, so there is no need to pity them. With my pitiful, earthly, Euclidian understanding, all I know is that there is

---

*In Greek mythology, the Titan Prometheus stole fire from heaven and gave it to humans.

suffering and that there are none guilty; that cause follows effect, simply and directly; that everything flows and finds its level—but that's only Euclidian nonsense, I know that, and I can't consent to live by it! What comfort is to me that there are none guilty and that cause follows effect simply and directly, and that I know it—I must have justice, or I will destroy myself. And not justice in some remote infinite time and space, but here on earth, and that I could see myself. I have believed in it. I want to see it, and if I am dead by then, let me rise again, for if it all happens without me, it will be too unfair. Surely I haven't suffered, simply that I, my crimes and my sufferings, may manure the soil of the future harmony for somebody else. I want to see with my own eyes the hind lie down with the lion* and the victim rise up and embrace his murderer. I want to be there when every one suddenly understands what it has all been for. All the religions of the world are built on this longing, and I am a believer. But then there are the children, and what am I to do about them? That's a question I can't answer. For the hundredth time I repeat, there are numbers of questions, but I've only taken the children, because in their case what I mean is so unanswerably clear. Listen! If all must suffer to pay for the eternal harmony, what have children to do with it, tell me, please? It's beyond all comprehension why they should suffer, and why they should pay for the harmony. Why should they, too, furnish material to enrich the soil for the harmony of the future? I understand solidarity in sin among men. I understand solidarity in retribution, too; but there can be no such solidarity with children. And if it is really true that they must share responsibility for all their fathers' crimes, such a truth is not of this world and is beyond my comprehension. Some jester will say, perhaps, that the child would have grown up and have sinned, but you see he didn't grow up, he was torn to pieces by the dogs, at eight years old. Oh, Alyosha, I am not blaspheming! I understand, of course, what an upheaval of the universe it will be, when everything in heaven and earth blends in one hymn of praise and everything that lives and has lived cries aloud: 'Thou art just, O Lord, for Thy ways are revealed.'† When the mother embraces the fiend who threw her child to the dogs, and all three cry aloud with tears, 'Thou are just, O Lord!' then, of course, the crown of knowledge will be reached and all will be made clear. But what pulls me up here is that I can't accept that harmony. And while I am on earth, I make haste to take my own measures. You see, Alyosha, perhaps it really may happen that if I live to that moment, or rise again to see it, I, too, perhaps, may cry aloud with the rest, looking at the mother embracing the child's torturer, 'Thou art just, O Lord!' but I don't want to cry aloud then. While there is still time, I hasten to protect myself and so I renounce the higher harmony altogether. It's not worth the tears of that one tortured child who beat itself on the breast with its little fist and prayed in its stinking outhouse, with its unexpiated tears to 'dear, kind God'! It's not worth it, because those tears are unatoned for. They must be

*See the Bible, Isaiah 11:6.
†See Revelation 15:3.

atoned for, or there can be no harmony. But how? How are you going to atone for them? Is it possible? By their being avenged? But what do I care for avenging them? What do I care for a hell for oppressors? What good can hell do, since those children have already been tortured? And what becomes of harmony, if there is hell? I want to forgive. I want to embrace. I don't want more suffering. And if the sufferings of children go to swell the sum of sufferings which was necessary to pay for truth, then I protest that the truth is not worth such a price. I don't want the mother to embrace the oppressor who threw her son to the dogs! She dare not forgive him! Let her forgive him for herself, if she will, let her forgive the torturer for the immeasurable suffering of her mother's heart. But the sufferings of her tortured child she has no right to forgive; she dare not forgive the torturer, even if the child were to forgive him! And if that is so, if they dare not forgive, what becomes of harmony? Is there in the whole world a being who would have the right to forgive and could forgive? I don't want harmony. From love for humanity I don't want it. I would rather be left with the unavenged suffering. I would rather remain with my unavenged suffering and unsatisfied indignation, *even if I were wrong*. Besides, too high a price is asked for harmony; it's beyond our means to pay so much to enter on it. And so I hasten to give back my entrance ticket,* and if I am an honest man I am bound to give it back as soon as possible. And that I am doing. It's not God that I don't accept, Alyosha, only I most respectfully return Him the ticket."

"That's rebellion," murmured Alyosha, looking down.

"Rebellion? I am sorry you call it that," said Ivan earnestly. "One can hardly live in rebellion, and I want to live. Tell me yourself, I challenge you—answer. Imagine that you are creating a fabric of human destiny with the object of making men happy in the end, giving them peace and rest at last, but that it was essential and inevitable to torture to death only one tiny creature—that baby beating its breast with its fist, for instance—and to found that edifice on its unavenged tears, would you consent to be the architect on those conditions? Tell me, and tell the truth."

"No, I wouldn't consent," said Alyosha softly.

"And can you admit the idea that men for whom you are building it would agree to accept their happiness on the foundation of the unexpiated blood of a little victim? And accepting it would remain happy for ever?"

"No, I can't admit it. Brother," said Alyosha suddenly, with flashing eyes, "you said just now, is there a being in the whole world who would have the right to forgive and could forgive? But there is a Being and He can forgive everything, all and for all, because He gave His innocent blood for all and everything. You have forgotten Him, and on Him is built the edifice, and it is to Him they cry aloud, 'Thou art just, O Lord, for Thy ways are revealed!'"

"Ah! the One without sin† and His blood! No, I have not forgotten

---

*Reference to Schiller's 1784 poem "Resignation."
†That is, Christ (the expression comes from an Orthodox hymn of the Resurrection).

Him; on the contrary I've been wondering all the time how it was you did not bring Him in before, for usually all arguments on your side put Him in the foreground. Do you know, Alyosha—don't laugh! I made a poem about a year ago. If you can waste another ten minutes on me, I'll tell it to you."

"You wrote a poem?"

"Oh, no, I didn't write it," laughed Ivan, "and I've never written two lines of poetry in my life. But I made up this poem in prose and I remembered it. I was carried away when I made it up. You will be my first reader—that is, listener. Why should an author forego even one listener?" smiled Ivan. "Shall I tell it to you?"

"I am all attention," said Alyosha.

"My poem is called 'The Grand Inquisitor'; it's a ridiculous thing, but I want to tell it to you."

5

THE GRAND INQUISITOR

EVEN this must have a preface—that is, a literary preface," laughed Ivan, "and I am a poor hand at making one. You see, my action takes place in the sixteenth century, and at that time, as you probably learnt at school, it was customary in poetry to bring down heavenly powers on earth. Not to speak of Dante, in France, clerks, as well as the monks in the monasteries, used to give regular performances in which the Madonna, the saints, the angels, Christ, and God Himself were brought on the stage. In those days it was done in all simplicity. In Victor Hugo's 'Notre Dame de Paris' an edifying and gratuitous spectacle was provided for the people in the Hotel de Ville of Paris in the reign of Louis XI. in honour of the birth of the dauphin. It was called *Le bon jugement de la très sainte et gracieuse Vierge Marie*,* and she appears herself on the stage and pronounces her *bon jugement*. Similar plays, chiefly from the Old Testament, were occasionally performed in Moscow too, up to the times of Peter the Great.†
But besides plays there were all sorts of legends and ballads scattered about the world, in which the saints and angels and all the powers of Heaven took

---

*The Compassionate Judgment of the Very Holy and Gracious Virgin Mary (French).

†Peter I, czar of Russia (1682–1725).

part when required. In our monasteries the monks busied themselves in translating, copying, and even composing such poems—and even under the Tatars. There is, for instance, one such poem (of course, from the Greek), 'The Wanderings of Our Lady through Hell,' with descriptions as bold as Dante's. Our Lady visits Hell, and the Archangel Michael leads her through the torments. She sees the sinners and their punishment. There she sees among others one noteworthy set of sinners in a burning lake; some of them sink to the bottom of the lake so that they can't swim out, and 'these God forgets'—an expression of extraordinary depth and force. And so Our Lady, shocked and weeping, falls before the throne of God and begs for mercy for all in Hell—for all she has seen there, and indiscriminately. Her conversation with God is immensely interesting. She beseeches Him, she will not desist, and when God points to the hands and feet of her Son, nailed to the Cross, and asks, 'How can I forgive His tormentors?' she bids all the saints, all the martyrs, all the angels and archangels to fall down with her and pray for mercy on all without distinction. It ends by her winning from God a respite of suffering every year from Good Friday till Trinity day, and the sinners at once raise a cry of thankfulness from Hell, chanting, 'Thou art just, O Lord, in this judgment.'[7] Well, my poem would have been of that kind if it had appeared at that time. He comes on the scene in my poem, but He says nothing, only appears and passes on. Fifteen centuries have passed since He promised to come in His glory, fifteen centuries since His prophet wrote, 'Behold, I come quickly'; 'Of that day and that hour knoweth no man, neither the Son, but the Father,'* as He Himself predicted on earth. But humanity awaits him with the same faith and with the same love. Oh, with greater faith, for it is fifteen centuries since man has ceased to see signs from Heaven.

> No signs from Heaven come to-day
> To add to what the heart doth say.[†]

There was nothing left but faith in what the heart doth say. It is true there were many miracles in those days. There were saints who performed miraculous cures; some holy people, according to their biographies, were visited by the Queen of Heaven herself. But the devil did not slumber, and doubts were already arising among men of the truth of these miracles. And just then there appeared in the north of Germany a terrible new heresy.[8] 'A huge star like to a torch' (that is, to a church) 'fell on the sources of the waters and they became bitter.'[‡] These heretics began blasphemously denying miracles. But those who remained faithful were all the more ardent in their faith. The tears of humanity rose up to Him as before, awaiting His

---

*Quotations from Revelation 3:11 and Mark 13:32.
†From Schiller's 1801 poem "Sehn sucht" ("Longing").
‡See Revelation 8:10–11.

coming, loved Him, hoped for Him, yearned to suffer and die for Him as before. And so many ages mankind had prayed with faith and fervour, 'O Lord our God, hasten Thy coming,' so many ages called upon Him, that in His infinite mercy He deigned to come down to His servants. Before that day He had come down, He had visited some holy men, martyrs and hermits, as is written in their 'Lives.' Among us, Tyutchev, with absolute faith in the truth of his words, bore witness that

> Bearing the Cross, in slavish dress
> Weary and worn, the Heavenly King
> Our mother, Russia, came to bless,
> And through our land went wandering.*

And that certainly was so, I assure you.

"And behold, He deigned to appear for a moment to the people, to the tortured, suffering people, sunk in iniquity, but loving Him like children. My story is laid in Spain, in Seville, in the most terrible time of the Inquisition, when fires were lighted every day to the glory of God, and 'in the splendid *auto da fé* the wicked heretics were burnt.'⁹ Oh, of course, this was not the coming in which He will appear according to His promise at the end of time in all His heavenly glory, and which will be sudden 'as lightning flashing from east to west.'† No, He visited His children only for a moment, and there where the flames were crackling round the heretics. In His infinite mercy He came once more among men in that human shape in which He walked among men for three years fifteen centuries ago. He came down to the 'hot pavement'‡ of the southern town in which on the day before almost a hundred heretics had, *ad majorem gloriam Dei,*§ been burnt by the cardinal, the Grand Inquisitor, in a magnificent *auto da fé,* in the presence of the king, the court, the knights, the cardinals, the most charming ladies of the court, and the whole population of Seville.

"He came softly, unobserved, and yet, strange to say, every one recognised Him. That might be one of the best passages in the poem. I mean, why they recognised Him. The people are irresistibly drawn to Him, they surround Him, they flock about Him, follow Him. He moves silently in their midst with a gentle smile of infinite compassion. The sun of love burns in His heart, light and power shine from His eyes, and their radiance, shed on the people, stirs their hearts with responsive love. He holds out His hands to them, blesses them, and a healing virtue comes from contact with Him, even with His garments. An old man in the crowd, blind from childhood, cries out, 'O Lord, heal me and I shall see Thee!' and, as it

---

*Quotation from Russian poet F. I. Tyutchev's lyric "These Poor Villages" (1855).
†See Matthew 24:27.
‡From A. I. Polezhayev's poem "Coriolanus" (1857).
§"To the greater glory of God" (Latin), motto of the Jesuits.

were, scales fall from his eyes and the blind man sees Him. The crowd weeps and kisses the earth under His feet. Children throw flowers before Him, sing, and cry hosannah. 'It is He—it is He!' all repeat. 'It must be He, it can be no one but Him!' He stops at the steps of the Seville cathedral at the moment when the weeping mourners are bringing in a little open white coffin. In it lies a child of seven, the only daughter of a prominent citizen. The dead child lies hidden in flowers. 'He will raise your child,' the crowd shouts to the weeping mother. The priest, coming to meet the coffin, looks perplexed, and frowns, but the mother of the dead child throws herself at His feet with a wail. 'If it is Thou, raise my child!' she cries, holding out her hands to Him. The procession halts, the coffin is laid on the steps at His feet. He looks with compassion, and His lips once more softly pronounce, 'Maiden, arise!' and the maiden arises.* The little girl sits up in the coffin and looks round, smiling with wide-open wondering eyes, holding a bunch of white roses they had put in her hand.

"There are cries, sobs, confusion among the people, and at that moment the cardinal himself, the Grand Inquisitor, passes by the cathedral. He is an old man, almost ninety, tall and erect, with a withered face and sunken eyes, in which there is still a gleam of light. He is not dressed in his gorgeous cardinal's robes, as he was the day before, when he was burning the enemies of the Roman Church—at that moment he was wearing his coarse, old, monk's cassock. At a distance behind him come his gloomy assistants and slaves and the 'holy guard.' He stops at the sight of the crowd and watches it from a distance. He sees everything; he sees them set the coffin down at His feet, sees the child rise up, and his face darkens. He knits his thick grey brows and his eyes gleam with a sinister fire. He holds out his finger and bids the guards take Him. And such is his power, so completely are the people cowed into submission and trembling obedience to him, that the crowd immediately make way for the guards, and in the midst of deathlike silence they lay hands on Him and lead Him away. The crowd instantly bows down to the earth, like one man, before the old inquisitor. He blesses the people in silence and passes on. The guards lead their prisoner to the close, gloomy vaulted prison in the ancient palace of the Holy Inquisition and shut Him in it. The day passes and is followed by the dark, burning 'breathless' night of Seville. The air is 'fragrant with laurel and lemon.'† In the pitch darkness the iron door of the prison is suddenly opened and the Grand Inquisitor himself comes in with a light in his hand. He is alone; the door is closed at once behind him. He stands in the doorway and for a minute or two gazes into His face. At last he goes up slowly, sets the light on the table and speaks.

" 'Is it Thou? Thou?' but receiving no answer, he adds at once, 'Don't answer, be silent. What canst Thou say, indeed? I know too well what Thou

---

*See Mark 5:41–42.

†Quotation from Pushkin's play *The Stone Guest* (1826–1830), a recasting of the Don Juan legend.

wouldst say. And Thou hast no right to add anything to what Thou hadst
said of old. Why, then, art Thou come to hinder us? For Thou hast come to
hinder us, and Thou knowest that. But dost Thou know what will be to-
morrow? I know not who Thou art and care not to know whether it is Thou
or only a semblance of Him, but to-morrow I shall condemn Thee and burn
Thee at the stake as the worst of heretics. And the very people who have
to-day kissed Thy feet, to-morrow at the faintest sign from me will rush to
heap up the embers of Thy fire. Knowest Thou that? Yes, maybe Thou knowest it,' he added with thoughtful penetration, never for a moment taking
his eyes off the Prisoner."

"I don't quite understand, Ivan. What does it mean?" Alyosha, who had
been listening in silence, said with a smile. "Is it simply a wild fantasy, or a
mistake on the part of the old man—some impossible *quid pro quo*?"*

"Take it as the last," said Ivan, laughing, "if you are so corrupted by
modern realism and can't stand anything fantastic. If you like it to be a
case of mistaken identity, let it be so. It is true," he went on, laughing, "the
old man was ninety, and he might well be crazy over his set idea. He might
have been struck by the appearance of the Prisoner. It might, in fact, be
simply his ravings, the delusion of an old man of ninety, over-excited by
the *auto da fé* of a hundred heretics the day before. But does it matter to
us after all whether it was a mistake of identity or a wild fantasy? All that
matters is that the old man should speak out, should speak openly of what
he has thought in silence for ninety years."

"And the Prisoner too is silent? Does He look at him and not say a
word?"

"That's inevitable in any case," Ivan laughed again. "The old man has
told Him He hasn't the right to add anything to what He has said of old.
One may say it is the most fundamental feature of Roman Catholicism, in
my opinion at least. 'All has been given by Thee to the Pope,' they say, 'and
all, therefore, is still in the Pope's hands, and there is no need for Thee to
come now at all. Thou must not meddle for the time, at least.' That's how
they speak and write too—the Jesuits, at any rate. I have read it myself in
the works of their theologians. 'Hast Thou the right to reveal to us one of the
mysteries of that world from which Thou hast come?' my old man asks Him,
and answers the question for Him. 'No, Thou hast not; that Thou mayest
not add to what has been said of old, and mayest not take from men the
freedom which Thou didst exalt when Thou wast on earth. Whatsoever
Thou revealest anew will encroach on men's freedom of faith; for it will be
manifest as a miracle, and the freedom of their faith was dearer to Thee
than anything in those days fifteen hundred years ago. Didst Thou not often say then, "I will make you free"?† But now Thou has seen these "free"
men,' the old man adds suddenly, with a pensive smile. 'Yes, we've paid
dearly for it,' he goes on, looking sternly at Him, 'but at last we have

*Literally, one for another (Latin); mistaken identity.
†See John 8:31–33.

completed that work in Thy name. For fifteen centuries we have been wrestling with Thy freedom, but now it is ended and over for good. Dost Thou not believe that it's over for good? Thou lookest meekly at me and deignest not even to be wroth with me. But let me tell Thee that now, to-day, people are more persuaded than ever that they have perfect freedom, yet they have brought their freedom to us and laid it humbly at our feet. But that has been our doing. Was this what Thou didst? Was this Thy freedom?' "

"I don't understand again," Alyosha broke in. "Is he ironical, is he jesting?"

"Not a bit of it! He claims it as a merit for himself and his Church that at last they have vanquished freedom and have done so to make men happy. 'For now' (he is speaking of the Inquisition, of course) 'for the first time it has become possible to think of the happiness of men. Man was created a rebel; and how can rebels be happy? Thou wast warned,' he says to Him. 'Thou hast had no lack of admonitions and warnings, but Thou didst not listen to those warnings; Thou didst reject the only way by which men might be made happy. But, fortunately, departing Thou didst hand on the work to us. Thou has promised, Thou hast established by Thy word, Thou has given to us the right to bind and to unbind,* and now, of course, Thou canst not think of taking it away. Why, then, hast Thou come to hinder us?' "

"And what's the meaning of 'no lack of admonitions and warnings'?" asked Alyosha.

"Why, that's the chief part of what the old man must say."

" 'The wise and dread Spirit, the Spirit of self-destruction and non-existence,' the old man goes on, 'the great Spirit talked with Thee in the wilderness, and we are told in the books that he "tempted" Thee.† Is that so? And could anything truer be said than what he revealed to Thee in three questions and what Thou didst reject, and what in the books is called "the temptation"? And yet if there has ever been on earth a real stupendous miracle, it took place on that day, on the day of the three temptations. The statement of those three questions was itself the miracle. If it were possible to imagine simply for the sake of argument that those three questions of the dread spirit had perished utterly from the books, and that we had to restore them and to invent them anew, and to do so had gathered together all the wise men of the earth—rulers, chief priests, learned men, philosophers, poets—and had set them the task to invent three questions, such as would not only fit the occasion, but express in three words, three human phrases, the whole future history of the world and of humanity— dost Thou believe that all the wisdom of the earth united could have invented anything in depth and force equal to the three questions which were actually put to Thee then by the wise and mighty Spirit in the wilderness? From those questions alone, from the miracle of their statement, we can see that we have here to do not with the fleeting human intelligence,

---

*See Matthew 16:19.
†See Matthew 4:1–11.

but with the absolute and eternal. For in those three questions the whole subsequent history of mankind is, as it were, brought together into one whole, and foretold, and in them are united all the unsolved historical contradictions of human nature. At the time it could not be so clear, since the future was unknown; but now that fifteen hundred years have passed, we see that everything in those three questions was so justly divined and foretold, and has been so truly fulfilled, that nothing can be added to them or taken from them.

" 'Judge Thyself who was right—Thou or he who questioned Thee then? Remember the first question; its meaning, in other words, was this: "Thou wouldst go into the world, and art going with empty hands, with some promise of freedom which men in their simplicity and their natural unruliness cannot even understand, which they fear and dread—for nothing has ever been more insupportable for a man and a human society than freedom. But seest Thou these stones in this parched and barren wilderness? Turn them into bread, and mankind will run after Thee like a flock of sheep, grateful and obedient, though for ever trembling, lest Thou withdraw Thy hand and deny them Thy bread." But Thou wouldst not deprive man of freedom and didst reject the offer, thinking, what is that freedom worth, if obedience is bought with bread? Thou didst reply that man lives not by bread alone. But dost Thou know that for the sake of that earthly bread the spirit of the earth will rise up against Thee and will strive with Thee and overcome Thee, and all will follow him, crying. "Who can compare with this beast? He has given us fire from heaven!"* Dost Thou know that the ages will pass, and humanity will proclaim by the lips of their sages that there is no crime, and therefore no sin; there is only hunger? "Feed men, and then ask of them virtue!" that's what they'll write on the banner, which they will raise against Thee, and with which they will destroy Thy temple. Where Thy temple stood will rise a new building; the terrible tower of Babel will be built again,† and though, like the one of old, it will not be finished, yet Thou mightest have prevented that new tower and have cut short the sufferings of men for a thousand years; for they will come back to us after a thousand years of agony with their tower. They will seek us again, hidden underground in the catacombs, for we shall be again persecuted and tortured. They will find us and cry to us, "Feed us, for those who have promised us fire from heaven haven't given it!" And then we shall finish building their tower, for he finishes the building who feeds them. And we alone shall feed them in Thy name, declaring falsely that it is in Thy name. Oh, never, never can they feed themselves without us! No science will give them bread so long as they remain free. In the end they will lay their freedom at our feet, and say to us, "Make us your slaves, but feed us." They will understand themselves, at last, that freedom and bread enough for all are inconceivable together, for never, never will they be

---

*See Revelation 13:4, 13.
†See Genesis 11:1–9.

able to share between them! They will be convinced, too, that they can never be free, for they are weak, vicious, worthless and rebellious. Thou didst promise them the bread of Heaven, but, I repeat again, can it compare with earthly bread in the eyes of the weak, ever sinful and ignoble race of man? And if for the sake of the bread of Heaven thousands and tens of thousands shall follow Thee, what is to become of the millions and tens of thousands of millions of creatures who will not have the strength to forego the earthly bread for the sake of the heavenly? Or dost Thou care only for the tens of thousands of the great and strong, while the millions, numerous as the sands of the sea, who are weak but love Thee, must exist only for the sake of the great and strong? No, we care for the weak too. They are sinful and rebellious, but in the end they too will become obedient. They will marvel at us and look on us as gods, because we are ready to endure the freedom which they have found so dreadful and to rule over them—so awful it will seem to them to be free. But we shall tell them that we are Thy servants and rule them in Thy name. We shall deceive them again, for we will not let Thee come to us again. That deception will be our suffering, for we shall be forced to lie.

" 'This is the significance of the first question in the wilderness, and this is what Thou hast rejected for the sake of that freedom which Thou hast exalted above everything. Yet in this question lies hid the great secret of this world. Choosing "bread," Thou wouldst have satisfied the universal and everlasting craving of humanity—to find some one to worship. So long as man remains free he strives for nothing so incessantly and so painfully as to find some one to worship. But man seeks to worship what is established beyond dispute, so that all men would agree at once to worship it. For these pitiful creatures are concerned not only to find what one or the other can worship, but to find something that all would believe in and worship; what is essential is that all may be *together* in it. This craving for *community* of worship is the chief misery of every man individually and of all humanity from the beginning of time. For the sake of common worship they've slain each other with the sword. They have set up gods and challenged one another, "Put away your gods and come and worship ours, or we will kill you and your gods!" And so it will be to the end of the world, even when gods disappear from the earth; they will fall down before idols just the same. Thou didst know, Thou couldst not but have known, this fundamental secret of human nature, but Thou didst reject the one infallible banner which was offered Thee to make all men bow down to Thee alone—the banner of earthly bread; and Thou hast rejected it for the sake of freedom and the bread of Heaven. Behold what Thou didst further. And all again in the name of freedom! I tell Thee that man is tormented by no greater anxiety than to find some one quickly to whom he can hand over that gift of freedom with which the ill-fated creature is born. But only one who can appease their conscience can take over their freedom. In bread there was offered Thee an invincible banner; give bread, and man will worship Thee, for nothing is more certain than bread. But if some one else gains possession of his conscience—oh! then he will cast away Thy bread and follow after him who has ensnared his conscience. In that Thou wast right. For the secret of man's being is not only to live but to have something to live for. Without a stable conception of the object of life, man would not consent to go on living, and would rather destroy himself than remain on earth, though he had bread in abundance. That is true. But what happened? Instead of taking men's freedom from them, Thou didst make it greater than ever! Didst Thou forget that man prefers peace, and even death, to freedom of choice in the knowledge of good and evil? Nothing is more seductive for man than his freedom of conscience, but nothing is a greater cause of suffering. And behold, instead of giving a firm foundation for setting the conscience of man at rest for ever, Thou didst choose all that is exceptional, vague and enigmatic; Thou didst choose what was utterly beyond the strength of men, acting as though Thou didst not love them at all—Thou who didst come to give Thy life for them! Instead of taking possession of men's freedom, Thou didst increase it, and burdened the spiritual kingdom of mankind with its sufferings for ever. Thou didst desire man's free love, that he should follow Thee freely, enticed and taken captive by Thee. In place of the rigid ancient law, man must hereafter with free heart decide for himself what is good and what is evil, having only Thy image before him as his guide. But didst Thou not know he would at last reject even Thy image and Thy truth, if he is weighed down with the fearful burden of free choice? They will cry aloud at last that the truth is not in Thee, for they could not have been left in greater confusion and suffering than Thou hast caused, laying upon them so many cares and unanswerable problems.

" 'So that, in truth, Thou didst Thyself lay the foundation for the destruction of Thy kingdom, and no one is more to blame for it. Yet what was offered Thee? There are three powers, three powers alone, able to conquer and to hold captive for ever the conscience of these impotent rebels for their happiness—those forces are miracle, mystery and authority. Thou hast rejected all three and hast set the example for doing so. When the wise and dread spirit set Thee on the pinnacle of the temple and said to Thee, "If Thou wouldst know whether Thou art the Son of God then cast Thyself down, for it is written: the angels shall hold him up lest he fall and bruise himself, and Thou shalt know then whether Thou art the Son of God and shalt prove then how great is Thy faith in Thy Father."* But Thou didst refuse and wouldst not cast Thyself down. Oh! of course, Thou didst proudly and well like God; but the weak, unruly race of men, are they gods? Oh, Thou didst know then that in taking one step, in making one movement to cast Thyself down, Thou wouldst be tempting God and have lost all Thy faith in Him, and wouldst have been dashed to pieces against that earth which Thou didst come to save. And the wise spirit that tempted Thee would have rejoiced. But I ask again, are there many like Thee? And couldst Thou believe for one moment that men, too, could face such a temptation? Is the nature of men such, that they can reject miracle, and at the great moments

*See Matthew 4:6.

of their life, the moments of their deepest, most agonising spiritual difficulties, cling only to the free verdict of the heart? Oh, Thou didst know that
Thy deed would be recorded in books, would be handed down to remote
times and the utmost ends of the earth, and Thou didst hope that man, following Thee, would cling to God and not ask for a miracle. But Thou didst
not know that when man rejects miracle he rejects God too; for man seeks
not so much God as the miraculous. And as man cannot bear to be without
the miraculous, he will create new miracles of his own for himself, and will
worship deeds of sorcery and witchcraft, though he might be a hundred
times over a rebel, heretic and infidel. Thou didst not come down from the
Cross when they shouted to Thee, mocking and reviling Thee, "Come down
from the cross and we will believe that Thou art He."* Thou didst not come
down, for again Thou wouldst not enslave man by a miracle, and didst crave
faith given freely, not based on miracle. Thou didst crave for free love and
not the base raptures of the slave before the might that has overawed him
for ever. But Thou didst think too highly of men therein, for they are slaves,
of course, though rebellious by nature. Look round and judge; fifteen centuries have passed, look upon them. Whom hast Thou raised up to Thyself?
I swear, man is weaker and baser by nature than Thou hast believed him!
Can he, can he do what Thou didst? By showing him so much respect, Thou
didst, as it were, cease to feel for him, for Thou didst ask far too much from
him—Thou who hast loved him more than Thyself! Respecting him less,
Thou wouldst have asked less of him. That would have been more like love,
for his burden would have been lighter. He is weak and vile. What though
he is everywhere now rebelling against our power, and proud of his rebellion? It is the pride of a child and a schoolboy. They are little children rioting and barring out the teacher at school. But their childish delight will end;
it will cost them dear. They will cast down temples and drench the earth
with blood. But they will see at last, the foolish children, that, though they
are rebels, they are impotent rebels, unable to keep up their own rebellion.
Bathed in their foolish tears, they will recognise at last that He who created
them rebels must have meant to mock at them. They will say this in despair,
and their utterance will be a blasphemy which will make them more unhappy still, for man's nature cannot bear blasphemy, and in the end always
avenges it on itself. And so unrest, confusion and unhappiness—that is the
present lot of man after Thou didst bear so much for their freedom! Thy
great prophet tells in vision and in image, that he saw all those who took
part in the first resurrection and that there were of each tribe twelve thousand.† But if there were so many of them, they must have been not men but
gods. They had borne Thy cross, they had endured scores of years in the
barren, hungry wilderness, living upon locusts and roots‡—and Thou
mayest indeed point with pride at those children of freedom, of free love,

---

*See Matthew 27:42.
†See Revelation 7:4–8; the "great prophet" is Saint John.
‡See Matthew 3:4.

of free and splendid sacrifice for Thy name. But remember that they were only some thousands; and what of the rest? And how are the other weak ones to blame, because they could not endure what the strong have endured? How is the weak soul to blame that it is unable to receive such terrible gifts? Canst Thou have simply come to the elect and for the elect? But if so, it is a mystery and we cannot understand it. And if it is a mystery, we too have a right to preach a mystery, and to teach them that it's not the free judgment of their hearts, not love that matters, but a mystery which they must follow blindly, even against their conscience. So we have done. We have corrected Thy work and have founded it upon *miracle, mystery* and *authority*. And men rejoiced that they were again led like sheep, and that the terrible gift that had brought them such suffering, was, at last, lifted from their hearts. Were we right teaching them this? Speak! Did we not love mankind, so meekly acknowledging their feebleness, lovingly lightening their burden, and permitting their weak nature even sin with our sanction? Why hast Thou come now to hinder us? And why dost Thou look silently and searchingly at me with Thy mild eyes? Be angry. I don't want Thy love, for I love Thee not. And what use is it for me to hide anything from Thee? Don't I know to Whom I am speaking? All that I can say is known to Thee already. And is it for me to conceal from Thee our mystery? Perhaps it is Thy will to hear it from my lips. Listen, then. We are not working with Thee, but with *him*—that is our mystery. It's long—eight centuries—since we have been on *his* side and not on Thine. Just eight centuries ago, we took from him what Thou didst reject with scorn,[10] that last gift he offered Thee, showing Thee all the kingdoms of the earth. We took from him Rome and the sword of Cæsar, and proclaimed ourselves sole rulers of the earth, though hitherto we have not been able to complete our work. But whose fault is that? Oh, the work is only beginning, but it has begun. It has long to await completion and the earth has yet much to suffer, but we shall triumph and shall be Cæsars, and then we shall plan the universal happiness of man. But Thou mightest have taken even then the sword of Cæsar. Why didst Thou reject that last gift? Hadst Thou accepted that last counsel of the mighty spirit, Thou wouldst have accomplished all that man seeks on earth—that is, some one to worship, some one to keep his conscience, and some means of uniting all in one unanimous and harmonious ant-heap, for the craving for universal unity is the third and last anguish of men. Mankind as a whole has always striven to organise a universal state. There have been many great nations with great histories, but the more highly they were developed the more unhappy they were, for they felt more acutely than other people the craving for worldwide union. The great conquerors, Timours and Ghenghis-Khans,* whirled like hurricanes over the face of the earth striving to subdue its people, and they too were but the unconscious expression of the same craving for universal

---

*Timur, or Tamerlane (1336–1405), was a Turkic conqueror; Genghis Khan (c.1162–1227) was a Mongol conqueror.

unity. Hadst Thou taken the world and Cæsar's purple, Thou wouldst have founded the universal state and have given universal peace. For who can rule men if not he who holds their conscience and their bread in his hands. We have taken the sword of Cæsar, and in taking it, of course, have rejected Thee and followed *him*. Oh, ages are yet to come of the confusion of free thought, of their science and cannibalism. For having begun to build their tower of Babel without us, they will end, of course, with cannibalism. But then the beast will crawl to us and lick our feet and spatter them with tears of blood. And we shall sit upon the beast and raise the cup, and on it will be written, "Mystery."* But then, and only then, the reign of peace and happiness will come for men. Thou art proud of Thine elect, but Thou hast only the elect, while we give rest to all. And besides, how many of those elect, those mighty ones who could become elect, have grown weary waiting for Thee, and have transferred and will transfer the powers of their spirit and the warmth of their heart to the other camp, and end by raising their *free* banner against Thee. Thou didst Thyself lift up that banner. But with us all will be happy and will no more rebel nor destroy one another as under Thy freedom. Oh, we shall persuade them that they will only become free when they renounce their freedom to us and submit to us. And shall we be right or shall we be lying? They will be convinced that we are right, for they will remember the horrors of slavery and confusion to which Thy freedom brought them. Freedom, free thought and science, will lead them into such straits and will bring them face to face with such marvels and insoluble mysteries, that some of them, the fierce and rebellious, will destroy themselves, others, rebellious but weak, will destroy one another, while the rest, weak and unhappy, will crawl fawning to our feet and whine to us: "Yes, you were right, you alone possess His mystery, and we come back to you, save us from ourselves!"

" 'Receiving bread from us, they will see clearly that we take the bread made by their hands from them, to give it to them, without any miracle. They will see that we do not change the stones to bread, but in truth they will be more thankful for taking it from our hands than for the bread itself! For they will remember only too well that in old days, without our help, even the bread they made turned to stones in their hands, while since they have come back to us, the very stones have turned to bread in their hands. Too, too well they know the value of complete submission! And until men know that, they will be unhappy. Who is most to blame for their not knowing it, speak? Who scattered the flock and sent it astray on unknown paths? But the flock will come together again and will submit once more, and then it will be once for all. Then we shall give them the quiet humble happiness of weak creatures such as they are by nature. Oh, we shall persuade them at last not to be proud, for Thou didst lift them up and thereby taught them to be proud. We shall show them that they are weak, that they are only pitiful children, but that childlike happiness is the sweetest of all. They will

---

*See Revelation 13 and 17.

become timid and will look to us and huddle close to us in fear, as chicks to the hen. They will marvel at us and will be awe-stricken before us, and will be proud at our being so powerful and clever, that we have been able to subdue such a turbulent flock of thousands of millions. They will tremble impotently before our wrath, their minds will grow fearful, they will be quick to shed tears like women and children, but they will be just as ready at a sign from us to pass to laughter and rejoicing, to happy mirth and childish song. Yes, we shall set them to work, but in their leisure hours we shall make their life like a child's game, with children's songs and innocent dance. Oh, we shall allow them even sin, they are weak and helpless, and they will love us like children because we allow them to sin. We shall tell them that every sin will be expiated, if it is done with our permission, that we allow them to sin because we love them, and the punishment for these sins we take upon ourselves. And we shall take it upon ourselves, and they will adore us as their saviours who have taken on themselves their sins before God. And they will have no secrets from us. We shall allow or forbid them to live with their wives and mistresses, to have or not to have children—according to whether they have been obedient or disobedient—and they will submit to us gladly and cheerfully. The most painful secrets of their conscience, all, all they will bring to us, and we shall have an answer for all. And they will be glad to believe our answer, for it will save them from the great anxiety and terrible agony they endure at present in making a free decision for themselves. And all will be happy, all the millions of creatures except the hundred thousand who rule over them. For only we, we who guard the mystery, shall be unhappy. There will be thousands of millions of happy babes, and a hundred thousand sufferers who have taken upon themselves the curse of the knowledge of good and evil. Peacefully they will die, peacefully they will expire in Thy name, and beyond the grave they will find nothing but death. But we shall keep the secret, and for their happiness we shall allure them with the reward of heaven and eternity. Though if there were anything in the other world, it certainly would not be for such as they. It is prophesied that Thou wilt come again in victory, Thou wilt come with Thy chosen, the proud and strong, but we will say that they have only saved themselves, but we have saved all. We are told that the harlot who sits upon the beast, and holds in her hands the *mystery,* shall be put to shame, that the weak will rise up again and will rend her royal purple and will strip naked her loathsome body.* But then I will stand up and point out to Thee the thousand millions of happy children who have known no sin. And we who have taken their sins upon us for their happiness will stand up before Thee and say: "Judge us if Thou canst and darest." Know that I fear Thee not. Know that I too have been in the wilderness, I too have lived on roots and locusts, I too prized the freedom with which Thou hast blessed men, and I too was striving to stand among Thy elect, among the strong and powerful, thirsting "to make up the

---

*See Revelation 17:16.

number."* But I awakened and would not serve madness. I turned back and joined the ranks of those *who have corrected Thy work.* I left the proud and went back to the humble, for the happiness of the humble. What I say to Thee will come to pass, and our dominion will be built up. I repeat, to-morrow Thou shalt see that obedient flock who at a sign from me will hasten to heap up the hot cinders about the pile on which I shall burn Thee for coming to hinder us. For if any one has ever deserved our fires, it is Thou. To-morrow I shall burn Thee. Dixi.' "†

Ivan stopped. He was carried away as he talked and spoke with excitement; when he had finished, he suddenly smiled.

Alyosha had listened in silence; towards the end he was greatly moved and seemed several times on the point of interrupting, but restrained himself. Now his words came with a rush.

"But . . . that's absurd!" he cried, flushing. "Your poem is in praise of Jesus, not in blame of Him—as you meant it to be. And who will believe you about freedom? Is that the way to understand it? That's not the idea of it in the Orthodox Church. . . . That's Rome, and not even the whole of Rome, it's false—those are the worst of the Catholics, the Inquisitors, the Jesuits! . . . And there could not be such a fantastic creature as your Inquisitor. What are these sins of mankind they take on themselves? Who are these keepers of the mystery who have taken some curse upon themselves for the happiness of mankind? When have they been seen? We know the Jesuits, they are spoken ill of, but surely they are not what you describe? They are not that at all, not at all. . . . They are simply the Romish army for the earthly sovereignty of the world in the future, with the Pontiff of Rome for Emperor . . . that's their ideal, but there's no sort of mystery or lofty melancholy about it. . . . It's simple lust of power, of filthy earthly gain, of domination—something like a universal serfdom with them as masters—that's all they stand for. They don't even believe in God perhaps. Your suffering inquisitor is a mere fantasy."

"Stay, stay," laughed Ivan, "how hot you are! A fantasy you say, let it be so! Of course it's a fantasy. But allow me to say: do you really think that the Roman Catholic movement of the last centuries is actually nothing but the lust of power, of filthy earthly gain? Is that Father Païssy's teaching?"

"No, no, on the contrary, Father Païssy did once say something rather the same as you . . . but of course it's not the same, not a bit the same," Alyosha hastily corrected himself.

"A precious admission, in spite of your 'not a bit the same.' I ask you why your Jesuits and Inquisitors have united simply for vile material gain? Why can there not be among them one martyr oppressed by great sorrow and loving humanity? You see, only suppose that there was one such man among all those who desire nothing but filthy material gain—if there's only one like my old inquisitor, who had himself eaten roots in the desert

---

*See Revelation 6:11.

†I have spoken (Latin).

and made frenzied efforts to subdue his flesh to make himself free and perfect. But yet all his life he loved humanity, and suddenly his eyes were opened, and he saw that it is no great moral blessedness to attain perfection and freedom, if at the same time one gains the conviction that millions of God's creatures have been created as a mockery, that they will never be capable of using their freedom, that these poor rebels can never turn into giants to complete the tower, that it was not for such geese that the great idealist dreamt his dream of harmony. Seeing all that he turned back and joined—the clever people. Surely that could have happened?"

"Joined whom, what clever people?" cried Alyosha, completely carried away. "They have no such great cleverness and no mysteries and - secrets. . . . Perhaps nothing but Atheism, that's all their secret. Your inquisitor does not believe in God, that's his secret!"

"What if it is so! At last you have guessed it. It's perfectly true that that's the whole secret, but isn't that suffering, at least for a man like that, who has wasted his whole life in the desert and yet could not shake off his incurable love of humanity? In his old age he reached the clear conviction that nothing but the advice of the great dread spirit could build up any tolerable sort of life for the feeble, unruly 'incomplete, empirical creatures created in jest.' And so, convinced of this, he sees that he must follow the council of the wise spirit, the dread spirit of death and destruction, and therefore accept lying and deception, and lead men consciously to death and destruction, and yet deceive them all the way so that they may not notice where they are being led, that the poor blind creatures may at least on the way think themselves happy. And note, the deception is in the name of Him in Whose ideal the old man had so fervently believed all his life long. Is not that tragic? And if only one such stood at the head of the whole army 'filled with the lust of power only for the sake of filthy gain'—would not one such be enough to make a tragedy? More than that, one such standing at the head is enough to create the actual leading idea of the Roman Church with all its armies and Jesuits, its highest idea. I tell you frankly that I firmly believe that there has always been such a man among those who stood at the head of the movement. Who knows, there may have been some such even among the Roman Popes. Who knows, perhaps the spirit of that accursed old man who loves mankind so obstinately in his own way, is to be found even now in a whole multitude of such old men, existing not by chance but by agreement, as a secret league formed long ago for the guarding of the mystery, to guard it from the weak and the unhappy, so as to make them happy. No doubt it is so, and so it must be indeed. I fancy that even among the Masons there's something of the same mystery at the bottom,[11] and that that's why the Catholics so detest the Masons as their rivals breaking up the unity of the idea, while it is so essential that there should be one flock and one shepherd. . . . But from the way I defend my idea I might be an author impatient of your criticism. Enough of it."

"You are perhaps a Mason yourself!" broke suddenly from Alyosha. "You don't believe in God," he added, speaking this time very sorrowfully.

He fancied besides that his brother was looking at him ironically. "How does your poem end?" he asked, suddenly looking down. "Or was it the end?"

"I meant to end it like this. When the Inquisitor ceased speaking he waited some time for his Prisoner to answer him. His silence weighed down upon him. He saw that the Prisoner had listened intently all the time, looking gently in his face and evidently not wishing to reply. The old man longed for Him to say something, however bitter and terrible. But He suddenly approached the old man in silence and softly kissed him on his bloodless aged lips. That was all his answer. The old man shuddered. His lips moved. He went to the door, opened it, and said to Him: 'Go, and come no more.... Come not at all, never, never!' And he let Him out into the dark alleys of the town. The Prisoner went away."

"And the old man?"

"The kiss glows in his heart, but the old man adheres to his idea."

"And you with him, you too?" cried Alyosha, mournfully.

Ivan laughed.

"Why, it's all nonsense, Alyosha. It's only a senseless poem of a senseless student, who could never write two lines of verse. Why do you take it so seriously? Surely you don't suppose I am going straight off to the Jesuits, to join the men who are correcting His work? Good Lord, it's no business of mine. I told you, all I want is to live on to thirty, and then ... dash the cup to the ground!"

"But the little sticky leaves, and the precious tombs, and the blue sky, and the woman you love! How will you live, how will you love them?" Alyosha cried sorrowfully. "With such a hell in your heart and your head, how can you? No, that's just what you are going away for, to join them ... if not, you will kill yourself, you can't endure it!"

"There is a strength to endure everything," Ivan said with a cold smile.

"What strength?"

"The strength of the Karamazovs—the strength of the Karamazov baseness."

"To sink into debauchery, to stifle your soul with corruption, yes?"

"Possibly even that ... only perhaps till I am thirty I shall escape it, and then."

"How will you escape it? By what will you escape it? That's impossible with your ideas."

"In the Karamazov way, again."

" 'Everything is lawful,' you mean? Everything is lawful, is that it?"

Ivan scowled, and all at once turned strangely pale.

"Ah, you've caught up yesterday's phrase, which so offended Miüsov—and which Dmitri pounced upon so naïvely and paraphrased!" he smiled queerly. "Yes, if you like, 'everything is lawful' since the word has been said. I won't deny it. And Mitya's version isn't bad."

Alyosha looked at him in silence.

"I thought that going away from here I have you at least," Ivan said suddenly, with unexpected feeling; "but now I see that there is no place for me even in your heart, my dear hermit. The formula, 'all is lawful,' I won't renounce—will you renounce me for that, yes?"

Alyosha got up, went to him and softly kissed him on the lips.

"That's plagiarism," cried Ivan, highly delighted. "You stole that from my poem. Thank you though. Get up, Alyosha, it's time we were going, both of us."

They went out, but stopped when they reached the entrance of the restaurant.

"Listen, Alyosha," Ivan began in a resolute voice, "if I am really able to care for the sticky little leaves I shall only love them, remembering you. It's enough for me that you are somewhere here, and I shan't lose my desire for life yet. Is that enough for you? Take it as a declaration of love if you like. And now you go to the right and I to the left. And it's enough, do you hear, enough. I mean even if I don't go away to-morrow (I think I certainly shall go) and we meet again, don't say a word more on these subjects. I beg that particularly. And about Dmitri too, I ask you specially never speak to me again," he added, with sudden irritation; "it's all exhausted, it has all been said over and over again, hasn't it? And I'll make you one promise in return for it. When at thirty, I want to 'dash the cup to the ground,' wherever I may be I'll come to have one more talk with you, even though it were from America, you may be sure of that. I'll come on purpose. It will be very interesting to have a look at you, to see what you'll be by that time. It's rather a solemn promise, you see. And we really may be parting for seven years or ten. Come, go now to your Pater Seraphicus,[12] he is dying. If he dies without you, you will be angry with me for having kept you. Good-bye, kiss me once more; that's right, now go."

Ivan turned suddenly and went his way without looking back. It was just as Dmitri had left Alyosha the day before, though the parting had been very different. The strange resemblance flashed like an arrow through Alyosha's mind in the distress and dejection of that moment. He waited a little, looking after his brother. He suddenly noticed that Ivan swayed as he walked and that his right shoulder looked lower than his left. He had never noticed it before. But all at once he turned too, and almost ran to the monastery. It was nearly dark, and he felt almost frightened; something new was growing up in him for which he could not account. The wind had risen again as on the previous evening, and the ancient pines murmured gloomily about him when he entered the hermitage copse. He almost ran. "Pater Seraphicus—he got that name from somewhere—where from?" Alyosha wondered. "Ivan, poor Ivan, and when shall I see you again? . . . Here is the hermitage. Yes, yes, that he is, Pater Seraphicus, he will save me—from him and for ever!"

Several times afterwards he wondered how he could on leaving Ivan so completely forget his brother Dmitri, though he had that morning, only a few hours before, so firmly resolved to find him and not to give up doing so, even should he be unable to return to the monastery that night.

6

FOR AWHILE A VERY OBSCURE ONE

AND Ivan, on parting from Alyosha, went home to Fyodor Pav-lovitch's house. But, strange to say, he was overcome by insuffer-able depression, which grew greater at every step he took towards the house. There was nothing strange in his being depressed; what was strange was that Ivan could not have said what was the cause of it. He had often been depressed before, and there was nothing surprising at his feeling so at such a moment, when he had broken off with everything that had brought him here, and was preparing that day to make a new start and enter upon a new, unknown future. He would again be as solitary as ever, and though he had great hopes, and great—too great—expectations from life, he could not have given any definite account of his hopes, his expectations, or even his desires.

Yet at that moment, though the apprehension of the new and unknown certainly found place in his heart, what was worrying him was something quite different. "Is it loathing for my father's house?" he wondered. "Quite likely; I am so sick of it; and though it's the last time I shall cross its hateful threshold, still I loathe it. . . . No, it's not that either. Is it the parting with Alyosha and the conversation I had with him? For so many years I've been silent with the whole world and not deigned to speak, and all of a sudden I reel off a rigmarole like that." It certainly might have been the youthful vexation of youthful inexperience and vanity—vexation at having failed to express himself, especially with such a being as Alyosha, on whom his heart had certainly been reckoning. No doubt that came in, that vexation, it must have done indeed; but yet that was not it, that was not it either. "I feel sick with depression and yet I can't tell what I want. Better not think, perhaps."

Ivan tried "not to think," but that, too, was no use. What made his depression so vexatious and irritating was that it had a kind of casual, external character—he felt that. Some person or thing seemed to be standing out somewhere, just as something will sometimes obtrude itself upon the eye, and though one may be so busy with work or conversation that for a long time one does not notice it, yet it irritates and almost torments one till at last one realises, and removes the offending object, often quite a trifling and ridiculous one—some article left about in the wrong place, a handkerchief on the floor, a book not replaced on the shelf, and so on.

At last, feeling very cross and ill-humoured, Ivan arrived home, and suddenly, about fifteen paces from the garden gate, he guessed what was fretting and worrying him.

On a bench in the gateway the valet Smerdyakov was sitting, enjoying the coolness of the evening, and at the first glance at him Ivan knew that the valet Smerdyakov was on his mind, and that it was this man that his soul loathed. It all dawned upon him suddenly and became clear. Just before, when Alyosha had been telling him of his meeting with Smerdyakov, he had felt a sudden twinge of gloom and loathing, which had immediately stirred responsive anger in his heart. Afterwards, as he talked, Smerdyakov had been forgotten for the time; but still he had been in his mind, and as soon as Ivan parted from Alyosha and was walking home, the forgotten sensation began to obtrude itself again. "Is it possible that a miserable, contemptible creature like that can worry me so much?" he wondered, with insufferable irritation.

It was true that Ivan had come of late to feel an intense dislike for the man, especially during the last few days. He had even begun to notice in himself a growing feeling that was almost of hatred for the creature. Perhaps this hatred was accentuated by the fact that when Ivan first came to the neighbourhood he had felt quite differently. Then he had taken a marked interest in Smerdyakov, and had even thought him very original. He had encouraged him to talk to him, although he had always wondered at a certain incoherence, or rather restlessness, in his mind, and could not understand what it was that so continually and insistently worked upon the brain of "the contemplative." They discussed philosophical questions and even how there could have been light on the first day when the sun, moon, and stars were only created on the fourth day, and how that was to be understood. But Ivan soon saw that, though the sun, moon, and stars might be an interesting subject, yet that it was quite secondary to Smerdyakov, and that he was looking for something altogether different. In one way and another, he began to betray a boundless vanity, and a wounded vanity, too, and that Ivan disliked. It had first given rise to his aversion. Later on, there had been trouble in the house. Grushenka had come on the scene, and there had been the scandals with his brother Dmitri—they discussed that, too. But though Smerdyakov always talked of that with great excitement, it was impossible to discover what he desired to come of it. There was, in fact, something surprising in the illogicality and incoherence of some of his desires, accidentally betrayed and always vaguely expressed. Smerdyakov was always inquiring, putting certain indirect but obviously premeditated questions, but what his object was he did not explain, and usually at the most important moment he would break off and relapse into silence or pass to another subject. But what finally irritated Ivan most and confirmed his dislike for him was the peculiar revolting familiarity which Smerdyakov began to show more and more markedly. Not that he forgot himself and was rude; on the contrary, he always spoke very respectfully, yet he had obviously begun to consider—goodness knows why!—that there was some sort of understanding between him and Ivan Fyodorovitch. He always spoke in a tone that suggested that those two had some kind of compact, some secret between them, that had at some time been expressed on both sides, only known to them and beyond the comprehension of those around them. But for a long while Ivan did not recognise the real cause of his growing dislike and he had only lately realised what was at the root of it.

With a feeling of disgust and irritation he tried to pass in at the gate without speaking or looking at Smerdyakov. But Smerdyakov rose from the bench, and from that action alone, Ivan knew instantly that he wanted particularly to talk to him. Ivan looked at him and stopped, and the fact that he did stop, instead of passing by, as he meant to the minute before, drove him to fury. With anger and repulsion he looked at Smerdyakov's emasculate, sickly face, with the little curls combed forward on his forehead. His left eye winked and grinned as though to say, "Where are you going? You won't pass by; you see that we two clever people have something to say to each other."

Ivan shook. "Get away, miserable idiot. What have I to do with you?" was on the tip of his tongue, but to his profound astonishment he heard himself say, "Is my father still asleep, or has he waked?"

He asked the question softly and meekly, to his own surprise, and at once, again to his own surprise, sat down on the bench. For an instant he felt almost frightened; he remembered it afterwards. Smerdyakov stood facing him, his hands behind his back, looking at him with assurance and almost severity.

"His honour is still asleep," he articulated deliberately ("You were the first to speak, not I," he seemed to say). "I am surprised at you, sir," he added, after a pause, dropping his eyes affectedly, setting his right foot forward, and playing with the tip of his polished boot.

"Why are you surprised at me?" Ivan asked abruptly and sullenly, doing his utmost to restrain himself, and suddenly realising, with disgust, that he was feeling intense curiosity and would not, on any account, have gone away without satisfying it.

"Why don't you go to Tchermashnya, sir?" Smerdyakov suddenly raised his eyes and smiled familiarly. "Why I smile you must understand of yourself, if you are a clever man," his screwed up left eye seemed to say.

"Why should I go to Tchermashnya?" Ivan asked in surprise.

Smerdyakov was silent again.

"Fyodor Pavlovitch himself has so begged you to," he said at last, slowly and apparently attaching no significance to his answer. "I put you off with a secondary reason," he seemed to suggest, "simply to say something."

"Damn you! Speak out what you want!" Ivan cried angrily at last, passing from meekness to violence.

Smerdyakov drew his right foot up to his left, pulled himself up, but still looked at him with the same serenity and the same little smile.

"Substantially nothing—but just by way of conversation."

Another silence followed. They did not speak for nearly a minute. Ivan knew that he ought to get up and show anger, and Smerdyakov stood before him and seemed to be waiting as though to see whether he would be angry or not. So at least it seemed to Ivan. At last he moved to get up. Smerdyakov seemed to seize the moment.

"I'm in an awful position, Ivan Fyodorovitch. I don't know how to help myself," he said resolutely and distinctly, and at his last word he sighed. Ivan Fyodorovitch sat down again.

"They are both utterly crazy, they are no better than little children," Smerdyakov went on. "I am speaking of your parent and your brother Dmitri Fyodorovitch. Here Fyodor Pavlovitch will get up directly and begin worrying me every minute, 'Has she come? Why hasn't she come?' and so on up till midnight and even after midnight. And if Agrafena Alexandrovna doesn't come (for very likely she does not mean to come at all) then he will be at me again to-morrow morning, 'Why hasn't she come? When will she come?'—as though I were to blame for it. On the other side it's no better. As soon as it gets dark, or even before, your brother will appear with his gun in his hands: 'Look out, you rogue, you soup maker. If you miss her and don't let me know she's been—I'll kill you before any one.' When the night's over, in the morning, he, too, like Fyodor Pavlovitch, begins worrying me to death. 'Why hasn't she come? Will she come soon?' And he, too, thinks me to blame because his lady hasn't come. And every day and every hour they get angrier and angrier, so that I sometimes think I shall kill myself in a fright. I can't depend upon them, sir."

"And why have you meddled? Why did you begin to spy for Dmitri Fyodorovitch?" said Ivan irritably.

"How could I help meddling? Though, indeed, I haven't meddled at all, if you want to know the truth of the matter. I kept quiet from the very beginning, not daring to answer; but he pitched on me to be his servant. He has had only one thing to say since: 'I'll kill you, you scoundrel, if you miss her.' I feel certain, sir, that I shall have a long fit to-morrow."

"What do you mean by 'a long fit'?"

"A long fit, lasting a long time—several hours, or perhaps a day or two. Once it went on for three days. I fell from the garret that time. The struggling ceased and then began again, and for three days I couldn't come back to my senses. Fyodor Pavlovitch sent for Herzenstube, the doctor here, and he put ice on my head and tried another remedy, too. . . . I might have died."

"But they say one can't tell with epilepsy when a fit is coming. What makes you say you will have one to-morrow?" Ivan inquired, with a peculiar, irritable curiosity.

"That's just so. You can't tell beforehand."

"Besides you fell from the garret then."

"I climb up to the garret every day. I might fall from the garret again to-morrow. And, if not, I might fall down the cellar steps. I have to go into the cellar every day, too."

Ivan took a long look at him.

"You are talking nonsense, I see, and I don't quite understand you," he said softly, but with a sort of menace. "Do you mean to pretend to be ill to-morrow for three days, eh?"

Smerdyakov, who was looking at the ground again, and playing with the toe of his right foot, set the foot down, moved the left one forward, and, grinning, articulated:

"If I were able to play such a trick, that is, pretend to have a fit—and it would not be difficult for a man accustomed to them—I should have a perfect right to use such a means to save myself from death. For even if Agrafena Alexandrovna comes to see his father while I am ill, his honour can't blame a sick man for not telling him. He'd be ashamed to."

"Hang it all!" Ivan cried, his face working with anger, "Why are you always in such a funk for your life? All my brother Dmitri's threats are only hasty words and mean nothing. He won't kill you; it's not you he'll kill!"

"He'd kill me first of all, like a fly. But even more than that, I am afraid I shall be taken for an accomplice of his when he does something crazy to his father."

"Why should you be taken for an accomplice?"

"They'll think I am an accomplice, because I let him know the signals as a great secret."

"What signals? Whom did you tell? Confound you, speak more plainly."

"I'm bound to admit the fact," Smerdyakov drawled with pedantic composure, "that I have a secret with Fyodor Pavlovitch in this business. As you know yourself (if only you do know it) he has for several days past locked himself in as soon as night or evening comes on. Of late you've been going upstairs to your room early every evening, and yesterday you did not come down at all, and so perhaps you don't know how carefully he has begun to lock himself in at night, and even if Grigory Vassilyevitch comes to the door he won't open to him till he hears his voice. But Grigory Vassilyevitch does not come, because I wait upon him alone in his room now. That's the arrangement he made himself ever since this to-do with Agrafena Alexandrovna began. But at night, by his orders, I go away to the lodge so that I don't get to sleep till midnight, but am on the watch, getting up and walking about the yard, waiting for Agrafena Alexandrovna to come. For the last few days he's been perfectly frantic expecting her. What he argues is, she is afraid of him, Dmitri Fyodorovitch (Mitya, as he calls him) 'and so,' says he, 'she'll come the back-way, late at night, to me. You look out for her,' says he, 'till midnight and later; and if she does come, you run up and knock at my door or at the window from the garden. Knock at first twice, rather gently, and then three times more quickly, then,' says he, 'I shall understand at once that she has come, and will open the door to you quietly.' Another signal he gave me in case anything unexpected happens. At first, two knocks, and then, after an interval, another much louder. Then he will understand that something has happened suddenly and that I must see him, and he will open to me so that I can go and speak to him. That's all in case Agrafena Alexandrovna can't come herself, but sends a message. Besides, Dmitri Fyodorovitch might come, too, so I must let him know he is near. His honour is awfully afraid of Dmitri Fyodorovitch, so that even if Agrafena Alexandrovna had come and were locked in with him, and Dmitri Fyodorovitch were to turn up anywhere near at the time, I should be bound to let him know at once, knocking three times. So that the first signal of five knocks means Agrafena Alexandrovna has come, while the second signals of three knocks means 'something important to tell you.' His honour has shown me them several times and explained them. And as in the whole universe no one knows of these signals but myself and his honour, so he'd open the door without the slightest hesitation and without calling out (he is awfully afraid of calling out aloud). Well, those signals are known to Dmitri Fyodorovitch too, now."

"How are they known? Did you tell him? How dared you tell him?"

"It was through fright I did it. How could I dare to keep it back from him? Dmitri Fyodorovitch kept persisting every day, 'You are deceiving me, you are hiding something from me! I'll break both your legs for you.' So I told him those secret signals that he might see my slavish devotion, and might be satisfied that I was not deceiving him, but was telling him all I could."

"If you think that he'll make use of those signals and try to get in, don't let him in."

"But if I should be laid up with a fit, how can I prevent him coming in then, even if I dared prevent him, knowing how desperate he is?"

"Hang it! How can you be so sure you are going to have a fit, confound you? Are you laughing at me?"

"How could I dare laugh at you, and I am in no laughing humour with this fear on me? I feel I am going to have a fit. I have a presentiment. Fright alone will bring it on."

"Confound it! If you are laid up, Grigory will be on the watch. Let Grigory know beforehand; he will be sure not to let him in."

"I should never dare to tell Grigory Vassilyevitch about the signals without orders from my master. And as for Grigory Vassilyevitch hearing him and not admitting him, he has been ill ever since yesterday, and Marfa Ignatyevna intends to give him medicine to-morrow. They've just arranged it. It's a very strange remedy of hers. Marfa Ignatyevna knows of a preparation and always keeps it. It's a strong thing made from some herb. She has the secret of it, and she always gives it to Grigory Vassilyevitch three times a year when his lumbago's so bad he is almost paralysed by it. Then she takes a towel, wets it with the stuff, and rubs his whole back for half an hour till it's quite red and swollen, and what's left in the bottle she gives him to drink with a special prayer; but not quite all, for on such occasions she leaves some for herself, and drinks it herself. And as they never take strong drink, I assure you they both drop asleep at once and sleep sound a very long time. And when Grigory Vassilyevitch wakes up he is perfectly well after it, but Marfa Ignatyevna always has a headache from it. So, if Marfa Ignatyevna carries out her intention to-morrow, they won't hear anything and hinder Dmitri Fyodorovitch. They'll be asleep."

"What a rigmarole! And it all seems to happen at once, as though it were planned. You'll have a fit and they'll both be unconscious," cried Ivan. "But aren't you trying to arrange it so?" broke from him suddenly, and he frowned threateningly.

"How could I? . . . And why should I, when it all depends on Dmitri Fyodorovitch and his plans? . . . If he means to do anything he'll do it; but if not, I shan't be thrusting him upon his father."

"And why should he go to father, especially on the sly, if, as you say yourself Agrafena Alexandrovna won't come at all?" Ivan went on, turning white with anger. "You say that yourself, and all the while I've been here, I've felt sure it was all the old man's fancy, and the creature won't come to him. Why should Dmitri break in on him if she doesn't come? Speak, I want to know what you are thinking!"

"You know yourself why he'll come. What's the use of what I think? His honour will come simply because he is in a rage or suspicious on account of my illness perhaps, and he'll dash in, as he did yesterday through impatience to search the rooms, to see whether she hasn't escaped him on the sly. He is perfectly well aware, too, that Fyodor Pavlovitch has a big envelope with three thousand roubles in it, tied up with ribbon and sealed with three seals. On it is written in his own hand, 'To my angel Grushenka, if she will come,' to which he added three days later, 'for my little chicken.' There's no knowing what that might do."

"Nonsense!" cried Ivan, almost beside himself. "Dmitri won't come to steal money and kill my father to do it. He might have killed him yesterday on account of Grushenka, like the frantic, savage fool he is, but he won't steal."

"He is in very great need of money now—the greatest need, Ivan Fyodorovitch. You don't know in what need he is," Smerdyakov explained, with perfect composure and remarkable distinctness. "He looks on that three thousand as his own, too. He said so to me himself. 'My father still owes me just three thousand,' he said. And besides that, consider, Ivan Fyodorovitch, there is something else perfectly true. It's as good as certain, so to say, that Agrafena Alexandrovna will force him, if only she cares to, to marry her— the master himself, I mean Fyodor Pavlovitch—if only she cares to, and of course she may care to. All I've said is that she won't come, but maybe she's looking for more than that—I mean to be mistress here. I know myself that Samsonov, her merchant, was laughing with her about it, telling her quite openly that it would not be at all a stupid thing to do. And she's got plenty of sense. She wouldn't marry a beggar like Dmitri Fyodorovitch. So, taking that into consideration, Ivan Fyodorovitch, reflect that then neither Dmitri Fyodorovitch nor yourself and your brother, Alexey Fyodorovitch, would have anything after the master's death, not a rouble, for Agrafena Alexandrovna would marry him simply to get hold of the whole, all the money there is. But if your father were to die now, there'd be some forty thousand for sure, even for Dmitri Fyodorovitch whom he hates so, for he's made no will. . . . Dmitri Fyodorovitch knows all that very well."

A sort of shudder passed over Ivan's face. He suddenly flushed.

"Then why on earth," he suddenly interrupted Smerdyakov, "do you advise me to go to Tchermashnya? What did you mean by that? If I go away, you see what will happen here." Ivan drew his breath with difficulty.

"Precisely so," said Smerdyakov, softly and reasonably, watching Ivan intently, however.

"What do you mean by 'precisely so'?" Ivan questioned him, with a menacing light in his eyes, restraining himself with difficulty.

"I spoke because I felt sorry for you. If I were in your place I should simply throw it all up . . . rather than stay on in such a position," answered Smerdyakov, with the most candid air looking at Ivan's flashing eyes. They were both silent.

"You seem to be a perfect idiot, and what's more . . . an awful scoundrel, too." Ivan rose suddenly from the bench. He was about to pass straight through the gate, but he stopped short and turned to Smerdyakov. Something strange followed. Ivan, in a sudden paroxysm, bit his lip, clenched his fists, and, in another minute, would have flung himself on Smerdyakov. The latter, anyway, noticed it at the same moment, started, and shrank back. But the moment passed without mischief to Smerdyakov, and Ivan turned in silence, as it seemed in perplexity, to the gate.

"I am going away to Moscow to-morrow, if you care to know—early to-morrow morning. That's all!" he suddenly said aloud angrily, and wondered himself afterwards what need there was to say this then to Smerdyakov.

"That's the best thing you can do," he responded, as though he had expected to hear it; "except that you can always be telegraphed for from Moscow, if anything should happen here."

Ivan stopped again, and again turned quickly to Smerdyakov. But a change had passed over him, too. All his familiarity and carelessness had completely disappeared. His face expressed attention and expectation, intent but timid and cringing.

"Haven't you something more to say—something to add?" could be read in the intent gaze he fixed on Ivan.

"And couldn't I be sent for from Tchermashnya, too—in case anything happened?" Ivan shouted suddenly, for some unknown reason raising his voice.

"From Tchermashnya, too . . . you could be sent for," Smerdyakov muttered, almost in a whisper, looking disconcerted, but gazing intently into Ivan's eyes.

"Only Moscow is further and Tchermashnya is nearer. Is it to save my spending money on the fare, or to save my going so far out of my way, that you insist on Tchermashnya?"

"Precisely so . . ." muttered Smerdyakov, with a breaking voice. He looked at Ivan with a revolting smile, and again made ready to draw back. But to his astonishment Ivan broke into a laugh, and went through the gate still laughing. Any one who had seen his face at that moment would have known that he was not laughing from lightness of heart, and he could not have explained himself what he was feeling at that instant. He moved and walked as though in a nervous frenzy.

7

"IT'S ALWAYS WORTH WHILE SPEAKING TO A CLEVER MAN"

AND in the same nervous frenzy, too, he spoke. Meeting Fyodor Pavlovitch in the drawing-room directly he went in, he shouted to him, waving his hands, "I am going upstairs to my room, not in to you. Good-bye!" and passed by, trying not even to look at his father. Very possibly the old man was too hateful to him at that moment; but such an unceremonious display of hostility was a surprise even to Fyodor Pavlovitch. And the old man evidently wanted to tell him something at once and had come to meet him in the drawing-room on purpose. Receiving this amiable greeting, he stood still in silence and with an ironical air watched his son going upstairs, till he passed out of sight.

"What's the matter with him?" he promptly asked Smerdyakov, who had followed Ivan.

"Angry about something. Who can tell?" the valet muttered evasively.

"Confound him! Let him be angry then. Bring in the samovar, and get along with you. Look sharp! No news?"

Then followed a series of questions such as Smerdyakov had just complained of to Ivan, all relating to his expected visitor, and these questions we will omit. Half an hour later the house was locked, and the crazy old man was wandering alone through the rooms in excited expectation of hearing every minute the five knocks agreed upon. Now and then he peered out into the darkness, seeing nothing.

It was very late, but Ivan was still awake and reflecting. He sat up late that night, till two o'clock. But we will not give an account of his thoughts, and this is not the place to look into that soul—its turn will come. And even if one tried, it would be very hard to give an account of them, for there were no thoughts in his brain, but something very vague, and, above all, intense excitement. He felt himself that he had lost his bearings. He was fretted, too, by all sorts of strange and almost surprising desires; for instance, after midnight he suddenly had an intense irresistible inclination to go down, open the door, go to the lodge and beat Smerdyakov. But if he had been asked why, he could not have given any exact reason, except perhaps that he loathed the valet as one who had insulted him more gravely than any one in the world. On the other hand, he was more than once that night overcome by a sort of inexplicable humiliating terror, which he felt positively paralysed his physical powers. His head ached and he was giddy. A feeling of hatred was rankling in his heart, as though he meant to avenge himself on some one. He even hated Alyosha, recalling the conversation he had just had with him. At moments he hated himself intensely. Of Katerina Ivanovna he almost forgot to think, and wondered greatly at this afterwards, especially as he remembered perfectly that when he had protested so valiantly to Katerina Ivanovna that he would go away next day to Moscow, something had whispered in his heart, "That's nonsense, you are not going, and it won't be so easy to tear yourself away as you are boasting now."

Remembering that night long afterwards, Ivan recalled with peculiar repulsion how he had suddenly got up from the sofa and stealthily, as though he were afraid of being watched, had opened the door, gone out on the staircase and listened to Fyodor Pavlovitch stirring down below, had listened a long while—some five minutes—with a sort of strange curiosity, holding his breath while his heart throbbed. And why he had done all this, why he was listening, he could not have said. That "action" all his life afterwards he called "infamous," and at the bottom of his heart, he thought of it as the basest action of his life. For Fyodor Pavlovitch himself he felt no hatred at that moment, but was simply intensely curious to know how he was walking down there below and what he must be doing now. He wondered and imagined how he must be peeping out of the dark windows and stopping in the middle of the room, listening, listening—for some one to knock. Ivan went out on to the stairs twice to listen like this.

About two o'clock when everything was quiet, and even Fyodor Pavlovitch had gone to bed, Ivan had got into bed, firmly resolved to fall asleep at once, as he felt fearfully exhausted. And he did fall asleep at once, and slept soundly without dreams, but waked early, at seven o'clock, when it was broad daylight. Opening his eyes, he was surprised to feel himself extraordinarily vigorous. He jumped up at once and dressed quickly; then dragged out his trunk and began packing immediately. His linen had come back from the laundress the previous morning. Ivan positively smiled at the thought that everything was helping his sudden departure. And his departure certainly was sudden. Though Ivan had said the day before (to Katerina Ivanovna, Alyosha, and Smerdyakov) that he was leaving next day, yet he remembered that he had no thought of departure when he went to bed, or, at least, had not dreamed that his first act in the morning would be to pack his trunk. At last his trunk and bag were ready. It was about nine o'clock when Marfa Ignatyevna came in with her usual inquiry, "Where will your honour take your tea, in your own room or downstairs?" He looked almost cheerful, but there was about him, about his words and gestures, something hurried and scattered. Greeting his father affably, and even inquiring specially after his health, though he did not wait to hear his answer to the end, he announced that he was starting off in an hour to return to Moscow for good, and begged him to send for the horses. His father heard this announcement with no sign of surprise, and forgot in an unmannerly way to show regret at losing him. Instead of doing so, he flew into a great flutter at the recollection of some important business of his own.

"What a fellow you are! Not to tell me yesterday! Never mind; we'll manage it all the same. Do me a great service, my dear boy. Go to

Tchermashnya on the way. It's only to turn to the left from the station at Volovya, only another twelve versts and you come to Tchermashnya."

"I'm sorry, I can't. It's eighty versts to the railway and the train starts for Moscow at seven o'clock to-night. I can only just catch it."

"You'll catch it to-morrow or the day after, but to-day turn off to Tchermashnya. It won't put you out much to humour your father! If I hadn't had something to keep me here, I would have run over myself long ago, for I've some business there in a hurry. But here I . . . it's not the time for me to go now. . . . You see, I've two pieces of copse land there. The Maslovs, an old merchant and his son, will give eight thousand for the timber. But last year I just missed a purchaser who would have given twelve. There's no getting any one about here to buy it. The Maslovs have it all their own way. One has to take what they'll give, for no one here dare bid against them. The priest at Ilyinskoe wrote to me last Thursday that a merchant called Gorstkin, a man I know, had turned up. What makes him valuable is that he is not from these parts, so he is not afraid of the Maslovs. He says he will give me eleven thousand for the copse. Do you hear? But he'll only be here, the priest writes, for a week altogether, so you must go at once and make a bargain with him."

"Well, you write to the priest; he'll make the bargain."

"He can't do it. He has no eye for business. He is a perfect treasure, I'd give him twenty thousand to take care of for me without a receipt; but he has no eye for business, he is a perfect child, a crow could deceive him. And yet he is a learned man, would you believe it? This Gorstkin looks like a peasant, he wears a blue kaftan, but he is a regular rogue. That's the common complaint. He is a liar. Sometimes he tells such lies that you wonder why he is doing it. He told me the year before last that his wife was dead and that he had married another, and would you believe it, there was not a word of truth in it? His wife has never died at all, she is alive to this day and gives him a beating twice a week. So what you have to find out is whether he is lying or speaking the truth, when he says he wants to buy it and would give eleven thousand."

"I shall be no use in such a business. I have no eye either."

"Stay, wait a bit! You will be of use, for I will tell you the signs by which you can judge about Gorstkin. I've done business with him a long time. You see, you must watch his beard; he has a nasty, thin, red beard. If his beard shakes when he talks and he gets cross, its all right, he is saying what he means, he wants to do business. But if he strokes his beard with his left hand and grins—he is trying to cheat you. Don't watch his eyes, you won't find out anything from his eyes, he is a deep one, a rogue—but watch his beard! I'll give you a note and you show it to him. He's called Gorstkin, though his real name is Lyagavy;* but don't call him so, he will be offended. If you come to an understanding with him, and see it's all right, write here at once. You need only write: 'He's not lying.' Stand out for eleven thousand;

---

*i.e., setter dog (translator's note).

one thousand you can knock off, but not more. Just think! there's a difference between eight thousand and eleven thousand. It's as good as picking up three thousand; it's not so easy to find a purchaser, and I'm in desperate need of money. Only let me know it's serious, and I'll run over and fix it up. I'll snatch the time somehow. But what's the good of my galloping over, if it's all a notion of the priest's? Come, will you go?"

"Oh, I can't spare the time. You must excuse me."

"Come, you might oblige your father. I shan't forget it. You've no heart, any of you—that's what it is! What's a day or two to you? Where are you going now—to Venice? Your Venice will keep another two days. I would have sent Alyosha, but what use is Alyosha in a thing like that? I send you just because you are a clever fellow. Do you suppose I don't see that? You know nothing about timber, but you've got an eye. All that is wanted is to see whether the man is in earnest. I tell you, watch his beard—if his beard shakes you know he is in earnest."

"You force me to go to that damned Tchermashnya yourself, then?" cried Ivan, with a malignant smile.

Fyodor Pavlovitch did not catch, or would not catch, the malignancy, but he caught the smile.

"Then you'll go, you'll go? I'll scribble the note for you at once."

"I don't know whether I shall go. I don't know. I'll decide on the way."

"Nonsense! Decide at once. My dear fellow, decide! If you settle the matter, write me a line; give it to the priest and he'll send it on to me at once. And I won't delay you more than that. You can go to Venice. The priest will give you horses back to Volovya station."

The old man was quite delighted. He wrote the note, and sent for the horses. A light lunch was brought in, with brandy. When Fyodor Pavlovitch was pleased, he usually became expansive, but to-day he seemed to restrain himself. Of Dmitri, for instance, he did not say a word. He was quite unmoved by the parting, and seemed, in fact, at a loss for something to say. Ivan noticed this particularly. "He must be bored with me," he thought. Only when accompanying his son out on to the steps, the old man began to fuss about. He would have kissed him, but Ivan made haste to hold out his hand, obviously avoiding the kiss. His father saw it at once, and instantly pulled himself up.

"Well, good luck to you, good luck to you!" he repeated from the steps. "You'll come again some time or other? Mind you do come. I shall always be glad to see you. Well, Christ be with you!"

Ivan got into the carriage.

"Good-bye, Ivan! Don't be too hard on me!" the father called for the last time.

The whole household came out to take leave—Smerdyakov, Marfa and Grigory. Ivan gave them ten roubles each. When he had seated himself in the carriage, Smerdyakov jumped up to arrange the rug.

"You see . . . I am going to Tchermashnya," broke suddenly from Ivan. Again, as the day before, the words seemed to drop of themselves, and he laughed, too, a peculiar, nervous laugh. He remembered it long after.

"It's a true saying then, that 'it's always worth while speaking to a clever man,'" answered Smerdyakov firmly, looking significantly at Ivan.

The carriage rolled away. Nothing was clear in Ivan's soul, but he looked eagerly around him at the fields, at the hills, at the trees, at a flock of geese flying high overhead in the bright sky. And all of a sudden he felt very happy. He tried to talk to the driver, and he felt intensely interested in an answer the peasant made him; but a minute later he realised that he was not catching anything, and that he had not really even taken in the peasant's answer. He was silent, and it was pleasant even so. The air was fresh, pure and cool, the sky bright. The images of Alyosha and Katerina Ivanovna floated into his mind. But he softly smiled, blew softly on the friendly phantoms, and they flew away. "There's plenty of time for them," he thought. They reached the station quickly, changed horses, and galloped to Volovya. "Why is it worth while speaking to a clever man? What did he mean by that?" The thought seemed suddenly to clutch at his breathing. "And why did I tell him I was going to Tchermashnya?" They reached Volovya Station. Ivan got out of the carriage, and the drivers stood round him bargaining over the journey of twelve versts to Tchermashnya. He told them to harness the horses. He went into the station house, looked round, glanced at the overseer's wife, and suddenly went back to the entrance.

"I won't go to Tchermashnya. Am I too late to reach the railway by seven, brothers?"

"We shall just do it. Shall we get the carriage out?"

"At once. Will any one of you be going to the town to-morrow?"

"To be sure. Mitri here will."

"Can you do me a service, Mitri? Go to my father's, to Fyodor Pavlovitch Karamazov, and tell him I haven't gone to Tchermashnya. Can you?"

"Of course I can. I've known Fyodor Pavlovitch a long time."

"And here's something for you, for I daresay he won't give you anything," said Ivan, laughing gaily.

"You may depend on it he won't." Mitri laughed too. "Thank you, sir, I'll be sure to do it."

At seven o'clock Ivan got into the train and set off for Moscow. "Away with the past. I've done with the old world for ever, and may I have no news, no echo, from it. To a new life, new places, and no looking back!" But instead of delight his soul was filled with such gloom, and his heart ached with such anguish, as he had never known in his life before. He was thinking all the night. The train flew on, and only at daybreak, when he was approaching Moscow, he suddenly roused himself from his meditation.

"I am a scoundrel," he whispered to himself.

Fyodor Pavlovitch remained well satisfied at having seen his son off. For two hours afterwards he felt almost happy, and sat drinking brandy. But suddenly something happened which was very annoying and unpleasant for every one in the house, and completely upset Fyodor Pavlovitch's equanimity at once. Smerdyakov went to the cellar for something and fell down from the top of the steps. Fortunately, Marfa Ignatyevna was in the yard and heard him in time. She did not see the fall, but heard his

scream—the strange, peculiar scream, long familiar to her—the scream of
the epileptic falling in a fit. They could not tell whether the fit had come on
him at the moment he was descending the steps, so that he must have
fallen unconscious, or whether it was the fall and the shock that had
caused the fit in Smerdyakov, who was known to be liable to them. They
found him at the bottom of the cellar steps, writhing in convulsions and
foaming at the mouth. It was thought at first that he must have broken
something—an arm or a leg—and hurt himself, but "God had preserved
him," as Marfa Ignatyevna expressed it—nothing of the kind had happened. But it was difficult to get him out of the cellar. They asked the
neighbours to help and managed it somehow. Fyodor Pavlovitch himself
was present at the whole ceremony. He helped, evidently alarmed and upset. The sick man did not regain consciousness; the convulsions ceased for
a time, but then began again, and every one concluded that the same thing
would happen, as had happened a year before, when he accidentally fell
from the garret. They remembered that ice had been put on his head then.
There was still ice in the cellar, and Marfa Ignatyevna had some brought
up. In the evening, Fyodor Pavlovitch sent for Doctor Herzenstube, who
arrived at once. He was a most estimable old man, and the most careful
and conscientious doctor in the province. After careful examination, he
concluded that the fit was a very violent one and might have serious consequences; that meanwhile he, Herzenstube, did not fully understand it,
but that by to-morrow morning, if the present remedies were unavailing,
he would venture to try something else. The invalid was taken to the lodge,
to a room next to Grigory's and Marfa Ignatyevna's.

Then Fyodor Pavlovitch had one misfortune after another to put up
with that day. Marfa Ignatyevna cooked the dinner, and the soup, compared with Smerdyakov's, was no "better than dish water," and the fowl
was so dried up that it was impossible to masticate it. To her master's bitter, though deserved, reproaches, Marfa Ignatyevna replied that the fowl
was a very old one to begin with, and that she had never been trained as a
cook. In the evening there was another trouble in store for Fyodor
Pavlovitch; he was informed that Grigory, who had not been well for the
last three days, was completely laid up by his lumbago. Fyodor Pavlovitch
finished his tea as early as possible and locked himself up alone in the
house. He was in terrible excitement and suspense. That evening he reckoned on Grushenka's coming almost as a certainty. He had received from
Smerdyakov that morning an assurance "that she had promised to come
without fail." The incorrigible old man's heart throbbed with excitement;
he paced up and down his empty rooms listening. He had to be on the alert.
Dmitri might be on the watch for her somewhere, and when she knocked
on the window (Smerdyakov had informed him two days before that he
had told her where and how to knock) the door must be opened at once.
She must not be a second in the passage, for fear—which God forbid!—
that she should be frightened and run away. Fyodor Pavlovitch had much
to think of, but never had his heart been steeped in such voluptuous hopes.
This time he could say almost certainly that she would come!

BOOK SIX

THE RUSSIAN MONK

1

FATHER ZOSSIMA AND HIS VISITORS

WHEN with an anxious and aching heart Alyosha went into his elder's cell, he stood still almost astonished. Instead of a sick man at his last gasp, perhaps unconscious, as he had feared to find him, he saw him sitting up in his chair and, though weak and exhausted, his face was bright and cheerful, he was surrounded by visitors and engaged in a quiet and joyful conversation. But he had only got up from his bed a quarter of an hour before Alyosha's arrival; his visitors had gathered together in his cell earlier, waiting for him to wake, having received a most confident assurance from Father Païssy that "the teacher would get up, and as he had himself promised in the morning, converse once more with those dear to his heart." This promise and indeed every word of the dying elder's Father Païssy put implicit trust in. If he had seen him unconscious, if he had seen him breathe his last, and yet had his promise that he would rise up and say good-bye to him, he would not have believed perhaps even in death, but would still have expected the dead man to recover and fulfil his promise. In the morning as he lay down to sleep, Father Zossima had told him positively: "I shall not die without the delight of another conversation with you, beloved of my heart. I shall look once more on your dear faces and pour out my heart to you once again." The monks, who had gathered for this probably last conversation with Father Zossima, had all been his devoted friends for many years. There were four of them; Father Iosif and Father Païssy, Father Mihail, the warden of the hermitage, a man not very old and far from being learned. He was of humble origin, of strong will and steadfast faith, of austere appearance, but of deep tenderness, though he obviously concealed it as though he were almost ashamed of it. The fourth, Father Anfim, was a very old and humble little monk of the poorest peasant class. He was almost illiterate, and very quiet, scarcely speaking to any one. He was the humblest of the humble, and looked as though he had been frightened by something great and awful beyond the scope of his intelligence. Father Zossima had a great affection for this timorous man, and always treated him with marked respect, though perhaps there was no one he had known to whom he had said less, in spite of the fact that he had spent years wandering about holy Russia with him. That was very long ago, forty years before, when Father Zossima first began his life as a monk in a poor and little monastery at Kostroma, and when, shortly after, he had accompanied Father Anfim on his pilgrimage to collect alms for their poor monastery.

The whole party were in the bedroom which, as we mentioned before,

was very small, so that there was scarcely room for the four of them (in ad-
dition to Porfiry, the novice, who stood) to sit round Father Zossima on
chairs brought from the sitting-room. It was already beginning to get dark,
the room was lighted up by the lamps and the candles before the ikons.

Seeing Alyosha standing embarrassed in the doorway, Father Zossima
smiled at him joyfully and held out his hand.

"Welcome, my quiet one, welcome, my dear, here you are too. I knew
you would come."

Alyosha went up to him, bowed down before him to the ground and
wept. Something surged up from his heart, his soul was quivering, he
wanted to sob.

"Come, don't weep over me yet," Father Zossima smiled, laying his
right hand on his head. "You see I am sitting up talking; maybe I shall live
another twenty years yet, as that dear good woman from Vishegorye, with
her little Lizabeta in her arms, wished me yesterday. God bless the mother
and the little girl Lizabeta," he crossed himself. "Porfiry, did you take her
offering where I told you?"

He meant the sixty kopecks brought him the day before by the good-
humoured woman to be given "to some one poorer than me." Such offerings, always of money gained by personal toil, are made by way of penance
voluntarily undertaken. The elder had sent Porfiry the evening before to a
widow, whose house had been burnt down lately, and who after the fire
had gone with her children begging alms. Porfiry hastened "to reply that
he had given the money, as he had been instructed, from an unknown
benefactress."

"Get up, my dear boy," the elder went on to Alyosha. "Let me look at
you. Have you been home and seen your brother?" It seemed strange to
Alyosha that he asked so confidently and precisely, about one of his brothers only—but which one? Then perhaps he had sent him out both yesterday and to-day for the sake of that brother.

"I have seen one of my brothers," answered Alyosha.

"I mean the elder one, to whom I bowed down."

"I only saw him yesterday and could not find him to-day," said Alyosha.

"Make haste to find him, go again to-morrow and make haste, leave
everything and make haste. Perhaps you may still have time to prevent
something terrible. I bowed down yesterday to the great suffering in store
for him."

He was suddenly silent and seemed to be pondering. The words were
strange. Father Iosif, who had witnessed the scene yesterday, exchanged
glances with Father Païssy. Alyosha could not resist asking:

"Father and teacher," he began, his voice trembling with extreme emotion, "your words are too obscure. . . . What is this suffering in store for
him?"

"Don't inquire. I seemed to see something terrible yesterday . . . as
though his whole future were expressed in his eyes. A look came into his
eyes—so that I was instantly horror-stricken at what that man is preparing
for himself. Once or twice in my life I've seen such a look in a man's

face . . . reflecting as it were his future fate, and that fate, alas, came to pass. I sent you to him, Alexey, for I thought your brotherly face would help him. But everything and all our fates are from the Lord. 'Except a corn of wheat fall into the ground and die, it abideth alone; but if it die, it bringeth forth much fruit.' Remember that. You, Alexey, I've many times silently blessed for your face, know that," added the elder with a gentle smile. "This is what I think of you, you will go forth from these walls, but will live like a monk in the world. You will have many enemies, but even your foes will love you. Life will bring you many misfortunes, but you will find your happiness in them, and will bless life and will make others bless it—which is what matters most. Well, that is your character. Fathers and teachers," he addressed his friends with a tender smile, "I have never till to-day told even him why the face of this youth is so dear to me. Now I will tell you. His face has been as it were a remembrance and a prophecy for me. At the dawn of my life when I was a child I had an elder brother who died before my eyes at seventeen. And later on in the course of my life I gradually became convinced that that brother had been for a guidance and a sign from on high for me. For had he not come into my life, I should never perhaps, so I fancy at least, have become a monk and entered on this precious path. He appeared first to me in my childhood and here at the end of my pilgrimage, he seems to have come to me over again. It is marvellous, fathers and teachers, that Alexey, who has some, though not a great, resemblance in face, seems to me so like him spiritually, that many times I have taken him for that young man, my brother, mysteriously come back to me at the end of my pilgrimage, as a reminder and an inspiration. So that I positively wondered at so strange a dream in myself. Do you hear this, Porfiry?" he turned to the novice who waited on him. "Many times I've seen in your face as it were a look of mortification that I love Alexey more than you. Now you know why that was so, but I love you too, know that, and many times I grieved at your mortification. I should like to tell you, dear friends, of that youth, my brother, for there has been no presence in my life more precious, more significant and touching. My heart is full of tenderness, and I look at my whole life at this moment as though living through it again."

Here I must observe that this last conversation of Father Zossima with the friends who visited him on the last day of his life had been partly preserved in writing. Alexey Fyodorovitch Karamazov wrote it down from memory, some time after his elder's death. But whether this was only the conversation that took place then, or whether he added to it his notes of parts of former conversations with his teacher, I cannot determine. In his account, Father Zossima's talk goes on without interruption, as though he told his life to his friends in the form of a story, though there is no doubt, from other accounts of it, that the conversation that evening was general. Though the guests did not interrupt Father Zossima much, yet they too talked, perhaps even told something themselves. Besides, Father Zossima could not have carried on an uninterrupted narrative, for he was sometimes gasping for breath, his voice failed him, and he even lay down to rest

on his bed, though he did not fall asleep and his visitors did not leave their
seats. Once or twice the conversation was interrupted by Father Païssy's
reading the Gospel. It is worthy of note, too, that no one of them supposed
that he would die that night, for on that evening of his life after his deep
sleep in the day he seemed suddenly to have found new strength, which
kept him up through this long conversation. It was like a last effort of love
which gave him marvellous energy; only for a little time, however, for his
life was cut short immediately. . . . But of that later. I will only add now
that I have preferred to confine myself to the account given by Alexey Fyodorovitch Karamazov. It will be shorter and not so fatiguing, though of
course, as I must repeat, Alyosha took a great deal from previous conversations and added them to it.

Notes of the Life of the deceased Priest and Monk, the Elder Zossima, taken from his own words by Alexey Fyodorovitch Karamazov.

Biographical Notes

(a) Father Zossima's Brother

Beloved fathers and teachers, I was born in a distant province in the
north, in the town of V. My father was a gentleman by birth, but of no
great consequence or position. He died when I was only two years old, and
I don't remember him at all. He left my mother a small house built of
wood, and a fortune, not large, but sufficient to keep her and her children
in comfort. There were two of us, my elder brother Markel and I. He was
eight years older than I was, of hasty, irritable temperament, but kind-
hearted and never ironical. He was remarkably silent, especially at home
with me, his mother, and the servants. He did well at school, but did not get
on with his schoolfellows, though he never quarrelled, at least so my
mother has told me. Six months before his death, when he was seventeen,
he made friends with a political exile who had been banished from
Moscow to our town for freethinking, and led a solitary existence there.
He was a good scholar who had gained distinction in philosophy in the
university. Something made him take a fancy to Markel, and he used to
ask him to see him. The young man would spend whole evenings with him
during that winter, till the exile was summoned to Petersburg to take up
his post again at his own request, as he had powerful friends.
    It was the beginning of Lent, and Markel would not fast, he was rude and
laughed at it. "That's all silly twaddle and there is no God," he said, horrifying my mother, the servants, and me too. For though I was only nine, I too
was aghast at hearing such words. We had four servants, all serfs. I remember my mother selling one of the four, the cook Afimya, who was lame and
elderly, for sixty paper roubles, and hiring a free servant to take her place.
    In the sixth week in Lent, my brother, who was never strong and
had a tendency to consumption, was taken ill. He was tall but thin and

delicate-looking, and of very pleasing countenance. I suppose he caught cold, anyway the doctor, who came, soon whispered to my mother that it was galloping consumption, that he would not live through the spring. My mother began weeping, and careful not to alarm my brother she entreated him to go to church, to confess and take the sacrament, as he was still able to move about. This made him angry, and he said something profane about the church. He grew thoughtful, however; he guessed at once that he was seriously ill, and that that was why his mother was begging him to confess and take the sacrament. He had been aware, indeed, for a long time past, that he was far from well, and had a year before coolly observed at dinner to our mother and me, "My life won't be long among you, I may not live another year," which seemed now like a prophecy.

Three days passed and Holy Week had come. And on Tuesday morning my brother began going to church. "I am doing this simply for your sake, mother, to please and comfort you," he said. My mother wept with joy and grief, "his end must be near," she thought, "if there's such a change in him." But he was not able to go to church long, he took to his bed, so he had to confess and take the sacrament at home.

It was a late Easter, and the days were bright, fine, and full of fragrance. I remember he used to cough all night and sleep badly, but in the morning he dressed and tried to sit up in an arm-chair. That's how I remember him sitting, sweet and gentle, smiling, his face bright and joyous, in spite of his illness. A marvellous change passed over him, his spirit seemed transformed. The old nurse would come in and say, "Let me light the lamp before the holy image, my dear." And once he would not have allowed it and would have blown it out.

"Light it, light it, dear, I was a wretch to have prevented you doing it. You are praying when you light the lamp, and I am praying when I rejoice seeing you. So we are praying to the same God."

Those words seemed strange to us, and mother would go to her room and weep, but when she went in to him she wiped her eyes and looked cheerful. "Mother, don't weep, darling," he would say, "I've long to live yet, long to rejoice with you, and life is glad and joyful."

"Ah, dear boy, how can you talk of joy when you lie feverish at night, coughing as though you would tear yourself to pieces."

"Don't cry, mother," he would answer, "life is paradise, and we are all in paradise, but we won't see it, if we would, we should have heaven on earth the next day."

Every one wondered at his words, he spoke so strangely and positively; we were all touched and wept. Friends came to see us. "Dear ones," he would say to them, "what have I done that you should love me so, how can you love any one like me, and how was it I did not know, I did not appreciate it before?"

When the servants came in to him he would say continually, "Dear, kind people, why are you doing so much for me, do I deserve to be waited on? If it were God's will for me to live, I would wait on you, for all men should wait on one another."

Mother shook her head as she listened. "My darling, it's your illness makes you talk like that."

"Mother darling," he would say, "there must be servants and masters, but if so I will be the servant of my servants, the same as they are to me. And another thing, mother, every one of us has sinned against all men, and I more than any."

Mother positively smiled at that, smiled through her tears. "Why, how could you have sinned against all men, more than all? Robbers and murderers have done that, but what sin have you committed yet, that you hold yourself more guilty than all?"

"Mother, little heart of mine," he said (he had begun using such strange caressing words at that time), "little heart of mine, my joy, believe me, every one is really responsible to all men for all men and for everything. I don't know how to explain it to you, but I feel it is so, painfully even. And how is it we went on then living, getting angry and not knowing?"

So he would get up every day, more and more sweet and joyous and full of love. When the doctor, an old German called Eisenschmidt, came: "Well, doctor, have I another day in this world?" he would ask, joking.

"You'll live many days yet," the doctor would answer, "and months and years too."

"Months and years!" he would exclaim. "Why reckon the days? One day is enough for a man to know all happiness. My dear ones, why do we quarrel, try to outshine each other and keep grudges against each other? Let's go straight into the garden, walk and play there, love, appreciate, and kiss each other, and glorify life."

"Your son cannot last long," the doctor told my mother, as she accompanied him to the door. "The disease is affecting his brain."

The windows of his room looked out into the garden, and our garden was a shady one, with old trees in it which were coming into bud. The first birds of spring were flitting in the branches, chirruping and singing at the windows. And looking at them and admiring them, he began suddenly begging their forgiveness too, "Birds of heaven, happy birds, forgive me, for I have sinned against you too." None of us could understand that at the time, but he shed tears of joy. "Yes," he said, "there was such a glory of God all about me; birds, trees, meadows, sky, only I lived in shame and dishonoured it all and did not notice the beauty and glory."

"You take too many sins on yourself," mother used to say, weeping.

"Mother, darling, it's for joy, not for grief I am crying. Though I can't explain it to you, I like to humble myself before them, for I don't know how to love them enough. If I have sinned against every one, yet all forgive me, too, and that's heaven. Am I not in heaven now?"

And there was a great deal more I don't remember. I remember I went once into his room when there was no one else there. It was a bright evening, the sun was setting, and the whole room was lighted up. He beckoned me, and I went up to him. He put his hands on my shoulders and looked into my face tenderly, lovingly; he said nothing for a minute, only looked at me like that.

"Well," he said, "run and play now, enjoy life for me too."

I went out then and ran to play. And many times in my life afterwards I remembered even with tears how he told me to enjoy life for him too. There were many other marvellous and beautiful sayings of his, though we did not understand them at the time. He died the third week after Easter. He was fully conscious though he could not talk; up to his last hour he did not change. He looked happy, his eyes beamed and sought us, he smiled at us, beckoned us. There was a great deal of talk even in the town about his death. I was impressed by all this at the time, but not too much so, though I cried a great deal at his funeral. I was young then, a child, but a lasting impression, a hidden feeling of it all, remained in my heart, ready to rise up and respond when the time came. So indeed it happened.

(b) Of the Holy Scriptures in the life of Father Zossima

I was left alone with my mother. Her friends began advising her to send me to Petersburg as other parents did. "You have only one son now," they said, "and have a fair income, and you will be depriving him perhaps of a brilliant career if you keep him here." They suggested I should be sent to Petersburg to the Cadet Corps, that I might afterwards enter the Imperial Guard. My mother hesitated for a long time, it was awful to part with her only child, but she made up her mind to it at last, though not without many tears, believing she was acting for my happiness. She brought me to Petersburg and put me into the Cadet Corps, and I never saw her again. For she too died three years afterwards. She spent those three years mourning and grieving for both of us.

From the house of my childhood I have brought nothing but precious memories, for there are no memories more precious than those of early childhood in one's first home. And that is almost always so if there is any love and harmony in the family at all. Indeed, precious memories may remain even of a bad home, if only the heart knows how to find what is precious. With my memories of home I count, too, my memories of the Bible, which, child as I was, I was very eager to read at home. I had a book of Scripture history then with excellent pictures, called "A Hundred and Four Stories from the Old and New Testament,"[1] and I learned to read from it. I have it lying on my shelf now, I keep it as a precious relic of the past. But even before I learned to read, I remember first being moved to devotional feeling at eight years old. My mother took me alone to mass (I don't remember where my brother was at the time) on the Monday before Easter. It was a fine day, and I remember to-day, as though I saw it now, how the incense rose from the censer and softly floated upwards and, overhead in the cupola, mingled in rising waves with the sunlight that streamed in at the little window. I was stirred by the sight, and for the first time in my life I consciously received the seed of God's word in my heart. A youth came out into the middle of the church carrying a big book, so large that at the time I fancied he could scarcely carry it. He laid it on the reading desk, opened it, and began reading, and suddenly for the first time I understood something read in the church of God. In the land of Uz, there lived a man,[2] righteous and God-fearing, and he had great wealth, so many camels, so many sheep and asses, and his children feasted, and he loved them very much and prayed for them. "It may be that my sons have sinned in their feasting." Now the devil came before the Lord together with the sons of God, and said to the Lord that he had gone up and down the earth and under the earth. "And hast thou considered my servant Job?" God asked of him. And God boasted to the devil, pointing to his great and holy servant. And the devil laughed at God's words. "Give him over to me and Thou wilt see that Thy servant will murmur against Thee and curse Thy name." And God gave up the just man He loved so, to the devil. And the devil smote his children and his cattle and scattered his wealth, all of a sudden like a thunderbolt from heaven. And Job rent his mantle and fell down upon the ground and cried aloud, "Naked came I out of my mother's womb, and naked shall I return into the earth; the Lord gave and the Lord has taken away. Blessed be the name of the Lord for ever and ever."

Fathers and teachers, forgive my tears now, for all my childhood rises up again before me, and I breathe now as I breathed then, with the breast of a little child of eight, and I feel as I did then, awe and wonder and gladness. The camels at that time caught my imagination, and Satan, who talked like that with God, and God who gave His servant up to destruction, and His servant crying out: "Blessed be Thy name although Thou dost punish me," and then the soft and sweet singing in the Church: "Let my prayer rise up before Thee," and again incense from the priest's censer and the kneeling and the prayer. Ever since then—only yesterday I took it up—I've never been able to read that sacred tale without tears. And how much that is great, mysterious and unfathomable there is in it! Afterwards I heard the words of mockery and blame, proud words, "How could God give up the most loved of His saints for the diversion of the devil, take from him his children, smite him with sore boils so that he cleansed the corruption from his sores with a potsherd—and for no object except to boast to the devil! 'See what My saint can suffer for My sake.'" But the greatness of it lies just in the fact that it is a mystery—that the passing earthly show and the eternal verity are brought together in it. In the face of the earthly truth, the eternal truth is accomplished. The Creator, just as on the first days of creation He ended each day with praise: "that is good that I have created," looks upon Job and again praises His creation. And Job praising the Lord, serves not only Him but all His creation for generations and generations, and for ever and ever, since for that he was ordained. Good heavens, what a book it is, and what lessons there are in it! What a book the Bible is, what a miracle, what strength is given with it to man. It is like a mould cast of the world and man and human nature, everything is there, and a law for everything for all the ages. And what mysteries are solved and revealed; God raises Job again, gives him wealth again. Many years pass by, and he has other children and loves them. But how could he love those new ones when those first children are no more, when he has lost them? Remembering them, how could he be fully happy with those new ones, however dear the new ones might be? But he could, he could. It's the great mystery of human life that old grief passes gradually into quiet tender joy. The mild serenity of age takes the place of the riotous blood of youth. I bless the rising sun each day, and, as before, my heart sings to meet it, but now I love even more its setting, its long slanting rays and the soft tender gentle memories that come with them, the dear images from the whole of my long happy life—and over all the Divine Truth, softening, reconciling, forgiving! My life is ending, I know that well, but every day that is left me I feel how my earthly life is in touch with a new infinite, unknown, but approaching life, the nearness of which sets my soul quivering with rapture, my mind glowing and my heart weeping with joy.

Friends and teachers, I have heard more than once, and of late one may hear it more often, that the priests, and above all the village priests, are complaining on all sides of their miserable income and their humiliating lot. They plainly state, even in print—I've read it myself—that they are unable to teach the Scriptures to the people because of the smallness of their means, and if Lutherans and heretics come and lead the flock astray, they let them lead them astray because they have so little to live upon. May the Lord increase the sustenance that is so precious to them, for their complaint is just, too. But of a truth I say, if any one is to blame in the matter, half the fault is ours. For he may be short of time, he may say truly that he is overwhelmed all the while with work and services, but still it's not all the time, even he has an hour a week to remember God. And he does not work the whole year round. Let him gather round him once a week, some hour in the evening, if only the children at first—the fathers will hear of it and they too will begin to come. There's no need to build halls for this, let him take them into his own cottage. They won't spoil his cottage, they would only be there one hour. Let him open that book and begin reading it without grand words or superciliousness, without condescension to them, but gently and kindly, being glad that he is reading to them and that they are listening with attention, loving the words himself, only stopping from time to time to explain words that are not understood by the peasants. Don't be anxious, they will understand everything, the orthodox heart will understand all! Let him read them about Abraham and Sarah, about Isaac and Rebecca, of how Jacob went to Laban and wrestled with the Lord in his dream and said, "This place is holy"*—and he will impress the devout mind of the peasant. Let him read, especially to the children, how the brothers sold Joseph, the tender boy, the dreamer and prophet, into bondage, and told their father that a wild beast had devoured him, and showed him his blood-stained clothes. Let him read them how the brothers afterwards journeyed into Egypt for corn, and Joseph, already a greater ruler, unrecognised by them, tormented them, accused them, kept his brother Benjamin, and all through love: "I love you, and loving you I torment you."† For he remembered all his life

---

*See Genesis 11–35.
†See Genesis 37–50.

how they had sold him to the merchants in the burning desert by the well, and how, wringing his hands, he had wept and besought his brothers not to sell him as a slave in a strange land. And how, seeing them again after many years, he loved them beyond measure, but he harassed and tormented them in love. He left them at last not able to bear the suffering of his heart, flung himself on his bed and wept. Then, wiping his tears away he went out to them joyful and told them, "Brothers, I am your brother Joseph!" Let him read them further how happy old Jacob was on learning that his darling boy was still alive, and how he went to Egypt leaving his own country, and died in a foreign land, bequeathing his great prophecy that had lain mysteriously hidden in his meek and timid heart all his life, that from his offspring, from Judah, will come the great hope of the world, the Messiah and Saviour.*

Fathers and teachers, forgive me and don't be angry, that like a little child I've been babbling of what you know long ago, and can teach me a hundred times more skilfully. I only speak from rapture, and forgive my tears, for I love the Bible. Let him too weep, the priest of God, and be sure that the hearts of his listeners will throb in response. Only a little tiny seed is needed—drop it into the heart of the peasant and it won't die, it will live in his soul all his life, it will be hidden in the midst of his darkness and sin, like a bright spot, like a great reminder. And there's no need of much teaching or explanation, he will understand it all simply. Do you suppose that the peasants don't understand? Try reading them the touching story of the fair Esther and the haughty Vashti; or the miraculous story of Jonah in the whale. Don't forget either the parables of Our Lord, choose especially from the Gospel of St. Luke (that is what I did) and then from the Acts of the Apostles the conversion of St. Paul† (that you mustn't leave out on any account), and from the Lives of the Saints, for instance, the life of Alexey, the man of God and, greatest of all, the happy martyr and the seer of God, Mary of Egypt[3]–and you will penetrate their hearts with these simple tales. Give one hour a week to it in spite of your poverty, only one little hour. And you will see for yourself that our people are gracious and grateful, and will repay you a hundredfold. Mindful of the kindness of their priest and the moving words they have heard from him, they will of their own accord help him in his fields and in his house, and will treat him with more respect than before—so that it will even increase his worldly well-being too. The thing is so simple that sometimes one is even afraid to put it into words, for fear of being laughed at, and yet how true it is! One who does not believe in God will not believe in God's people. He who believes in God's people will see His Holiness too, even though he had not believed in it till then. Only the people and their future spiritual power will convert our atheists, who have torn themselves away from their native soil.

And what is the use of Christ's words, unless we set an example? The

---

*See Genesis 49:10.
†See Acts 13:16–41.

people are lost without the word of God, for their souls are athirst for the Word and for all that is good.

In my youth, long ago, nearly forty years ago, I travelled all over Russia with Father Anfim, collecting funds for our monastery, and we stayed one night on the bank of a great navigable river with some fishermen. A good-looking peasant lad, about eighteen, joined us; he had to hurry back next morning to pull a merchant's barge along the bank. I noticed him looking straight before him with clear and tender eyes. It was a bright, warm, still, July night, a cool mist rose from the broad river, we could hear the plash of a fish, the birds were still, all was hushed and beautiful, everything praying to God. Only we two were not sleeping, the lad and I, and we talked of the beauty of this world of God's and of the great mystery of it. Every blade of grass, every insect, ant, and golden bee, all so marvellously know their path, though they have not intelligence, they bear witness to the mystery of God and continually accomplish it themselves. I saw the dear lad's heart was moved. He told me that he loved the forest and the forest birds. He was a bird-catcher, knew the note of each of them, could call each bird. "I know nothing better than to be in the forest," said he, "though all things are good."

"Truly," I answered him, "all things are good and fair, because all is truth. Look," said I, "at the horse, that great beast that is so near to man; or the lowly, pensive ox, which feeds him and works for him; look at their faces, what meekness, what devotion to man, who often beats them mercilessly. What gentleness, what confidence and what beauty! It's touching to know that there's no sin in them, for all, all except man, is sinless, and Christ has been with them before us."

"Why," asked the boy, "is Christ with them too?"

"It cannot but be so," said I, "since the Word is for all. All creation and all creatures, every leaf is striving to the Word, singing glory to God, weeping to Christ, unconsciously accomplishing this by the mystery of their sinless life. Yonder," said I, "in the forest wanders the dreadful bear, fierce and menacing, and yet innocent in it." And I told him how once a bear came to a great saint who had taken refuge in a tiny cell in the wood. And the great saint pitied him, went up to him without fear and gave him a piece of bread. "Go along," said he, "Christ be with you," and the savage beast walked away meekly and obediently, doing no harm.[4] And the lad was delighted that the bear had walked away without hurting the saint, and that Christ was with him too. "Ah," said he, "how good that is, how good and beautiful is all God's work!" He sat musing softly and sweetly. I saw he understood. And he slept beside me a light and sinless sleep. May God bless youth! And I prayed for him as I went to sleep. Lord, send peace and light to Thy people!

2

NOTES ON THE LIFE OF THE DECEASED PRIEST AND MONK, THE ELDER ZOSSIMA, TAKEN FROM HIS OWN WORDS BY ALEXEY FYODOROVITCH KARAMAZOV

(c) Recollections of Father Zossima's youth before he became a monk. The duel

I SPENT a long time, almost eight years, in the military cadet school at Petersburg, and in the novelty of any surroundings there, many of my childish impressions grew dimmer, though I forgot nothing. I picked up so many new habits and opinions that I was transformed into a cruel, absurd, almost savage creature. A surface polish of courtesy and society manners I did acquire together with the French language.

But we all, myself included, looked upon the soldiers in our service as cattle. I was perhaps worse than the rest in that respect, for I was so much more impressionable than my companions. By the time we left the school as officers, we were ready to lay down our lives for the honour of the regiment, but no one of us had any knowledge of the real meaning of honour, and if any one had known it, he would have been the first to ridicule it. Drunkenness, debauchery and devilry were what we almost prided ourselves on. I don't say that we were bad by nature, all these young men were good fellows, but they behaved badly, and I worst of all. What made it worse for me was that I had come into my own money, and so I flung myself into a life of pleasure, and plunged headlong into all the recklessness of youth.

I was fond of reading, yet strange to say, the Bible was the one book I never opened at that time, though I always carried it about with me, and I was never separated from it; in very truth I was keeping that book "for the day and the hour, for the month and the year,"* though I knew it not.

After four years of this life, I chanced to be in the town of K. where our regiment was stationed at the time. We found the people of the town hospitable, rich and fond of entertainments. I met with a cordial reception everywhere, as I was of a lively temperament and was known to be well off, which always goes a long way in the world. And then a circumstance happened which was the beginning of it all.

I formed an attachment to a beautiful and intelligent young girl of noble and lofty character, the daughter of people much respected. They were well-to-do people of influence and position. They always gave me a cordial and friendly reception. I fancied that the young lady looked on me with

---

*See Revelation 9:15.

favour and my heart was aflame at such an idea. Later on I saw and fully realised that I perhaps was not so passionately in love with her at all, but only recognised the elevation of her mind and character, which I could not indeed have helped doing. I was prevented, however, from making her an offer at the time by my selfishness, I was loth to part with the allurements of my free and licentious bachelor life in the heyday of my youth, and with my pockets full of money. I did drop some hint as to my feelings however, though I put off taking any decisive step for a time. Then, all of a sudden, we were ordered off for two months to another district.

On my return two months later, I found the young lady already married to a rich neighbouring landowner, a very amiable man, still young though older than I was, connected with the best Petersburg society, which I was not, and of excellent education, which I also was not. I was so overwhelmed at this unexpected circumstance that my mind was positively clouded. The worst of it all was that, as I learned then, the young landowner had been a long while betrothed to her, and I had met him indeed many times in her house, but blinded by my conceit I had noticed nothing. And this particularly mortified me; almost everybody had known all about it, while I knew nothing. I was filled with sudden irrepressible fury. With flushed face I began recalling how often I had been on the point of declaring my love to her, and as she had not attempted to stop me or to warn me, she must, I concluded, have been laughing at me all the time. Later on, of course, I reflected and remembered that she had been very far from laughing at me; on the contrary, she used to turn off any love-making on my part with a jest and begin talking of other subjects; but at that moment I was incapable of reflecting and was all eagerness for revenge. I am surprised to remember that my wrath and revengeful feelings were extremely repugnant to my own nature, for being of an easy temper, I found it difficult to be angry with any one for long, and so I had to work myself up artificially and became at last revolting and absurd.

I waited for an opportunity and succeeded in insulting my "rival" in the presence of a large company. I insulted him on a perfectly extraneous pretext, jeering at his opinion upon an important public event—it was in the year 1826*—and my jeer was, so people said, clever and effective. Then I forced him to ask for an explanation, and behaved so rudely that he accepted my challenge in spite of the vast inequality between us, as I was younger, a person of no consequence, and of inferior rank. I learned afterwards for a fact that it was from a jealous feeling on his side also that my challenge was accepted; he had been rather jealous of me on his wife's account before their marriage; he fancied now that if he submitted to be insulted by me and refused to accept any challenge, and if she heard of it, she might begin to despise him and waver in her love for him. I soon found

---

*Probably the public event was the Decabrist plot against the Tsar, of December 1825, in which the most distinguished men in Russia were concerned (translator's note).

a second in a comrade, an ensign of our regiment. In those days though duels were severely punished, yet duelling was a kind of fashion among the officers—so strong and deeply rooted will a brutal prejudice sometimes be.

It was the end of June, and our meeting was to take place at seven o'clock the next day on the outskirts of the town—and then something happened that in very truth was the turning-point of my life. In the evening, returning home in a savage and brutal humour, I flew into a rage with my orderly Afanasy, and gave him two blows in the face with all my might, so that it was covered with blood. He had not long been in my service and I had struck him before, but never with such ferocious cruelty. And, believe me, though it's forty years ago, I recall it now with shame and pain. I went to bed and slept for about three hours; when I waked up the day was breaking. I got up—I did not want to sleep any more—I went to the window—opened it, it looked out upon the garden; I saw the sun rising; it was warm and beautiful, the birds were singing.

What's the meaning of it, I thought, I feel in my heart as it were something vile and shameful? Is it because I am going to shed blood? No, I thought, I feel it's not that. Can it be that I am afraid of death, afraid of being killed? No, that's not it, that's not it at all. . . . And all at once I knew what it was: it was because I had beaten Afanasy the evening before! It all rose before my mind, it all was as it were repeated over again; he stood before me and I was beating him straight on the face and he was holding his arms stiffly down, his head erect, his eyes fixed upon me as though on parade. He staggered at every blow and did not even dare to raise his hands to protect himself. That is what a man has been brought to, and that was a man beating a fellow creature! What a crime! It was as though a sharp dagger had pierced me right through. I stood as if I were struck dumb, while the sun was shining, the leaves were rejoicing and the birds were trilling the praise of God. . . . I hid my face in my hands, fell on my bed and broke into a storm of tears. And then I remembered my brother Markel and what he said on his deathbed to his servants: "My dear ones, why do you wait on me, why do you love me, am I worth your waiting on me?"

Yes, am I worth it? flashed through my mind. After all what am I worth, that another man, a fellow creature, made in the likeness and image of God, should serve me? For the first time in my life this question forced itself upon me. He had said, "Mother, my little heart, in truth we are each responsible to all for all, it's only that men don't know this. If they knew it, the world would be a paradise at once."

"God, can that too be false?" I thought as I wept, "in truth perhaps, I am more than all others responsible for all, a greater sinner than all men in the world. And all at once the whole truth in its full light appeared to me: what was I going to do? I was going to kill a good, clever, noble man, who had done me no wrong, and by depriving his wife of happiness for the rest of her life, I should be torturing and killing her too. I lay thus in my bed with my face in the pillow, heedless how the time was passing. Suddenly my second, the ensign, came in with the pistols to fetch me.

"Ah," said he, "it's a good thing you are up already, it's time we were off, come along!"

I did not know what to do and hurried to and fro undecided; we went out to the carriage, however.

"Wait here a minute," I said to him. "I'll be back directly, I have forgotten my purse."

And I ran back alone, straight to Afanasy's little room.

"Afanasy," I said, "I gave you two blows on the face yesterday, forgive me," I said.

He started as though he were frightened, and looked at me; and I saw that it was not enough, and on the spot, in my full officer's uniform, I dropped at his feet and bowed my head to the ground.

"Forgive me," I said.

Then he was completely aghast.

"Your honour . . . sir, what are you doing? Am I worth it?"

And he burst out crying as I had done before, hid his face in his hands, turned to the window and shook all over with his sobs. I flew out to my comrade and jumped into the carriage.

"Ready," I cried. "Have you ever seen a conqueror?" I asked him. "Here is one before you."

I was in ecstasy, laughing and talking all the way, I don't remember what about.

He looked at me. "Well, brother, you are a plucky fellow, you'll keep up the honour of the uniform, I can see."

So we reached the place and found them there, waiting for us. We were placed twelve paces apart; he had the first shot. I stood gaily, looking him full in the face; I did not twitch an eyelash. I looked lovingly at him, for I knew what I would do. His shot just grazed my cheek and ear.

"Thank God," I cried, "no man has been killed," and I seized my pistol, turned back and flung it far away into the wood.

"That's the place for you," I cried.

I turned to my adversary.

"Forgive me, young fool that I am, sir," I said, "for my unprovoked insult to you and for forcing you to fire at me. I am ten times worse than you and more, maybe. Tell that to the person whom you hold dearest in the world."

I had no sooner said this than they all three shouted at me.

"Upon my word," cried my adversary, annoyed, "if you did not want to fight, why did not you let me alone?"

"Yesterday I was a fool, to-day I know better," I answered him gaily.

"As to yesterday, I believe you, but as for to-day, it is difficult to agree with your opinion," said he.

"Bravo," I cried, clapping my hands. "I agree with you there too, I have deserved it!"

"Will you shoot, sir, or not?"

"No, I won't," I said, "if you like, fire at me again, but it would be better for you not to fire."

The seconds, especially mine, were shouting too: "Can you disgrace the

regiment like this, facing your antagonist and begging his forgiveness! If
I'd only known this!"

I stood facing them all, not laughing now.

"Gentlemen," I said, "is it really so wonderful in these days to find a
man who can repent of his stupidity and publicly confess his wrongdoing?"

"But not in a duel," cried my second again.

"That's what's so strange," I said. "For I ought to have owned my fault
as soon as I got here, before he had fired a shot, before leading him into a
great and deadly sin; but we have made our life so grotesque, that to act in
that way would have been almost impossible, for only after I have faced his
shot at the distance of twelve paces could my words have any significance
for him, and if I had spoken before, he would have said 'he is a coward, the
sight of the pistols has frightened him, no use to listen to him.' Gentlemen,"
I cried suddenly, speaking straight from my heart, "look around you at the
gifts of God, the clear sky, the pure air, the tender grass, the birds; nature is
beautiful and sinless, and we, only we, are sinful and foolish, and we don't
understand that life is heaven, for we have only to understand that and it will
at once be fulfilled in all its beauty, we shall embrace each other and weep."

I would have said more but I could not; my voice broke with the sweetness and youthful gladness of it, and there was such bliss in my heart as I
had never known before in my life.

"All this is rational and edifying," said my antagonist, "and in any case
you are an original person."

"You may laugh," I said to him, laughing too, "but afterwards you will
approve of me."

"Oh, I am ready to approve of you now," said he; "will you shake hands,
for I believe you are genuinely sincere."

"No," I said, "not now, later on when I have grown worthier and deserve your esteem, then shake hands and you will do well."

We went home, my second upbraiding me all the way, while I kissed
him. All my comrades heard of the affair at once and gathered together to
pass judgment on me the same day.

"He has disgraced the uniform," they said; "let him resign his commission."

Some stood up for me: "He faced the shot," they said.

"Yes, but he was afraid of his other shot and begged for forgiveness."

"If he had been afraid of being shot, he would have shot his own pistol
first before asking forgiveness, while he flung it loaded into the forest. No,
there's something else in this, something original."

I enjoyed listening and looking at them. "My dear friends and comrades," said I, "don't worry about my resigning my commission, for I have
done so already. I have sent in my papers this morning and as soon as I get
my discharge I shall go into a monastery—it's with that object I am leaving the regiment."

When I had said this every one of them burst out laughing.

"You should have told us of that first, that explains everything, we can't
judge a monk."

They laughed and could not stop themselves, and not scornfully, but kindly and merrily. They all felt friendly to me at once, even those who had been sternest in their censure, and all the following month, before my discharge came, they could not make enough of me. "Ah, you monk," they would say. And every one said something kind to me, they began trying to dissuade me, even to pity me: "What are you doing to yourself?"

"No," they would say, "he is a brave fellow, he faced fire and could have fired his own pistol too, but he had a dream the night before that he should become a monk, that's why he did it."

It was the same thing with the society of the town. Till then I had been kindly received, but had not been the object of special attention, and now all came to know me at once and invited me; they laughed at me, but they loved me. I may mention that although everybody talked openly of our duel, the authorities took no notice of it, because my antagonist was a near relation of our general, and as there had been no bloodshed and no serious consequences, and as I resigned my commission, they took it as a joke. And I began then to speak aloud and fearlessly, regardless of their laughter, for it was always kindly and not spiteful laughter. These conversations mostly look place in the evenings, in the company of ladies; women particularly liked listening to me then and they made the men listen.

"But how can I possibly be responsible for all?" every one would laugh in my face. "Can I, for instance, be responsible for you?"

"You may well not know it," I would answer, "since the whole world has long been going on a different line, since we consider the veriest lies as truth and demand the same lies from others. Here I have for once in my life acted sincerely and, well, you all look upon me as a madman. Though you are friendly to me, yet, you see, you all laugh at me."

"But how can we help being friendly to you?" said my hostess, laughing. The room was full of people. All of a sudden the young lady rose, on whose account the duel had been fought and whom only lately I had intended to be my future wife. I had not noticed her coming into the room. She got up, came to me and held out her hand.

"Let me tell you," she said, "that I am the first not to laugh at you, but on the contrary I thank you with tears and express my respect for you for your action then."

Her husband too came up and then they all approached me and almost kissed me. My heart was filled with joy, but my attention was especially caught by a middle-aged man who came up to me with the others. I knew him by name already, but had never made his acquaintance nor exchanged a word with him till that evening.

(d) The mysterious visitor

He had long been an official in the town; he was in a prominent position, respected by all, rich and had a reputation for benevolence. He subscribed considerable sums to the almshouse and the orphan asylum; he was very charitable, too, in secret, a fact which only became known after his death. He was a man of about fifty, almost stern in appearance and not much given to conversation. He had been married about ten years and his wife, who was still young, had borne him three children. Well, I was sitting alone in my room the following evening, when my door suddenly opened and this gentleman walked in.

I must mention, by the way, that I was no longer living in my former quarters. As soon as I resigned my commission, I took rooms with an old lady, the widow of a government clerk. My landlady's servant waited upon me, for I had moved into her rooms simply because on my return from the duel I had sent Afanasy back to the regiment, as I felt ashamed to look him in the face after my last interview with him. So prone is the man of the world to be ashamed of any righteous action.

"I have," said my visitor, "with great interest listened to you speaking in different houses the last few days and I wanted at last to make your personal acquaintance, so as to talk to you more intimately. Can you, dear sir, grant me this favour?"

"I can, with the greatest pleasure and I shall look upon it as an honour." I said this, though I felt almost dismayed, so greatly was I impressed from the first moment by the appearance of this man. For though other people had listened to me with interest and attentions, no one had come to me before with such a serious, stern and concentrated expression. And now he had come to see me in my rooms. He sat down.

"You are, I see, a man of great strength of character," he said; "as you have dared to serve the truth, even when by doing so you risked incurring the contempt of all."

"Your praise is, perhaps, excessive," I replied.

"No, it's not excessive," he answered; "believe me, such a course of action is far more difficult than you think. It is that which has impressed me, and it is only on that account that I have come to you," he continued. "Tell me, please, that is if you are not annoyed by my perhaps unseemly curiosity, what were your exact sensations, if you can recall them, at the moment when you made up your mind to ask forgiveness at the duel. Do not think my question frivolous; on the contrary, I have in asking the question a secret motive of my own, which I will perhaps explain to you later on, if it is God's will that we should become more intimately acquainted."

All the while he was speaking, I was looking at him straight into the face and I felt all at once a complete trust in him and great curiosity on my side also, for I felt that there was some strange secret in his soul.

"You ask what were my exact sensations at the moment when I asked my opponent's forgiveness," I answered; "but I had better tell you from the beginning what I have not yet told any one else." And I described all that had passed between Afanasy and me, and how I had bowed down to the ground at his feet. "From that you can see for yourself," I concluded, "that at the time of the duel it was easier for me, for I had made a beginning already at home, and when once I had started on the road, to go further along it was far from being difficult, but became a source of joy and happiness."

I liked the way he looked at me as he listened. "All that," he said, "is exceedingly interesting, I will come to see you again and again."

And from that time forth he came to see me nearly every evening. And we should have become greater friends, if only he had ever talked of himself. But about himself he scarcely ever said a word, yet continually asked me about myself. In spite of that I became very fond of him and spoke with perfect frankness to him about all my feelings; for, thought I, what need have I to know his secrets, since I can see without that that he is a good man. Moreover, though he is such a serious man and my senior, he comes to see a youngster like me and treats me as his equal. And I learned a great deal that was profitable from him, for he was a man of lofty mind.

"That life is heaven," he said to me suddenly, "that I have long been thinking about;" and all at once he added, "I think of nothing else indeed." He looked at me and smiled. "I am more convinced of it than you are, I will tell you later why."

I listened to him and thought that he evidently wanted to tell me something.

"Heaven," he went on, "lies hidden within all of us—here it lies hidden in me now, and if I will it, it will be revealed to me to-morrow and for all time."

I looked at him; he was speaking with great emotion and gazing mysteriously at me, as if he were questioning me.

"And that we are all responsible to all for all, apart from our own sins, you were quite right in thinking that, and it is wonderful how you could comprehend it in all its significance at once. And in very truth, so soon as men understand that, the Kingdom of Heaven will be for them not a dream, but a living reality."

"And when," I cried out to him bitterly, "when will that come to pass? and will it ever come to pass? Is not it simply a dream of ours?"

"What then, you don't believe it," he said. "You preach it and don't believe it yourself. Believe me, this dream, as you call it, will come to pass without doubt; it will come, but not now, for every process has its law. It's a spiritual, psychological process. To transform the world, to recreate it afresh, men must turn into another path psychologically. Until you have become really, in actual fact, a brother to every one, brotherhood will not come to pass. No sort of scientific teaching, no kind of common interest, will ever teach men to share property and privileges with equal consideration for all. Every one will think his share too small and they will be always envying, complaining and attacking one another. You ask when it will come to pass; it will come to pass, but first we have to go through the period of isolation."

"What do you mean by isolation?" I asked him.

"Why, the isolation that prevails everywhere, above all in our age—it has not fully developed, it has not reached its limit yet. For every one strives to keep his individuality as apart as possible, wishes to secure the greatest possible fulness of life for himself; but meantime all his efforts result not in attaining fulness of life but self-destruction, for instead of self-realisation he ends by arriving at complete solitude. All mankind in our age have split up into units, they all keep apart, each in his own groove; each one holds aloof, hides himself and hides what he has, from the rest, and he ends by being repelled by others and repelling them. He heaps up riches by himself and thinks, 'how strong I am now and how secure,' and in his madness he does not understand that the more he heaps up, the more he sinks into self-destructive impotence. For he is accustomed to rely upon himself alone and to cut himself off from the whole; he has trained himself not to believe in the help of others, in men and in humanity, and only trembles for fear he should lose his money and the privileges that he has won for himself. Everywhere in these days men have, in their mockery, ceased to understand that the true security is to be found in social solidarity rather than in isolated individual effort. But this terrible individualism must inevitably have an end, and all will suddenly understand how unnaturally they are separated from one another. It will be the spirit of the time, and people will marvel that they have sat so long in darkness without seeing the light. And then the sign of the Son of Man will be seen in the heavens.* . . . But, until then, we must keep the banner flying. Sometimes even if he has to do it alone, and his conduct seems to be crazy, a man must set an example, and so draw men's souls out of their solitude, and spur them to some act of brotherly love, that the great idea may not die."

Our evenings, one after another, were spent in such stirring and fervent talk. I gave up society and visited my neighbours much less frequently. Besides, my vogue was somewhat over. I say this, not as blame, for they still loved me and treated me good-humouredly, but there's no denying that fashion is a great power in society. I began to regard my mysterious visitor with admiration, for besides enjoying his intelligence, I began to perceive that he was brooding over some plan in his heart, and was preparing himself perhaps for a great deed. Perhaps he liked my not showing curiosity about his secret, not seeking to discover it by direct question nor by insinuation. But I noticed at last, that he seemed to show signs of wanting to tell me something. This had become quite evident, indeed, about a month after he first began to visit me.

"Do you know," he said to me once, "that people are very inquisitive about us in the town and wonder why I come to see you so often. But let them wonder, for *soon all will be explained*."

Sometimes an extraordinary agitation would come over him, and almost always on such occasions he would get up and go away. Sometimes he would fix a long piercing look upon me, and I thought "he will say something directly now." But he would suddenly begin talking of something ordinary and familiar. He often complained of headache too.

One day, quite unexpectedly indeed, after he had been talking with great fervour a long time, I saw him suddenly turn pale, and his face worked convulsively, while he stared persistently at me.

---

*See Matthew 24:30.

"What's the matter?" I said; "do you feel ill?"—he had just been complaining of headache.

"I ... do you know ... I murdered some one."

He said this and smiled with a face as white as chalk. "Why is it he is smiling?" The thought flashed through my mind before I realised anything else. I too turned pale.

"What are you saying?" I cried.

"You see," he said, with a pale smile, "how much it has cost me to say the first word. Now I have said it, I feel I've taken the first step and shall go on."

For a long while I could not believe him, and I did not believe him at that time, but only after he had been to see me three days running and told me all about it. I thought he was mad, but ended by being convinced, to my great grief and amazement. His crime was a great and terrible one.

Fourteen years before, he had murdered the widow of a landowner, a wealthy and handsome young woman who had a house in our town. He fell passionately in love with her, declared his feeling and tried to persuade her to marry him. But she had already given her heart to another man, an officer of noble birth and high rank in the service, who was at that time away at the front, though she was expecting him soon to return. She refused his offer and begged him not to come and see her. After he had ceased to visit her, he took advantage of his knowledge of the house to enter at night through the garden by the roof, at great risk of discovery. But as often happens, a crime committed with extraordinary audacity is more successful than others.

Entering the garret through the skylight, he went down the ladder, knowing that the door at the bottom of it was sometimes, through the negligence of the servants, left unlocked. He hoped to find it so, and so it was. He made his way in the dark to her bedroom, where a light was burning. As though on purpose, both her maids had gone off to a birthday-party in the same street, without asking leave. The other servants slept in the servants' quarters or in the kitchen on the ground-floor. His passion flamed up at the sight of her asleep, and then vindictive, jealous anger took possession of his heart, and like a drunken man, beside himself, he thrust a knife into her heart, so that she did not even cry out. Then with devilish and criminal cunning he contrived that suspicion should fall on the servants. He was so base as to take her purse, to open her chest with keys from under her pillow, and to take some things from it, doing it all as it might have been done by an ignorant servant, leaving valuable papers and taking only money. He took some of the larger gold things, but left smaller articles that were ten times as valuable. He took with him, too, some things for himself as remembrances, but of that later. Having done this awful deed, he returned by the way he had come.

Neither the next day, when the alarm was raised, nor at any time after in his life, did any one dream of suspecting that he was the criminal. No one indeed knew of his love for her, for he was always reserved and silent and had no friend to whom he would have opened his heart. He was looked upon simply as an acquaintance, and not a very intimate one, of the murdered woman, as for the previous fortnight he had not even visited her. A serf of hers called Pyotr was once suspected, and every circumstance confirmed the suspicion. The man knew—indeed his mistress did not conceal the fact—that having to send one of her serfs as a recruit she had decided to send him, as he had no relations and his conduct was unsatisfactory. People had heard him angrily threatening to murder her when he was drunk in a tavern. Two days before her death, he had run away, staying no one knew where in the town. The day after the murder, he was found on the road leading out of the town, dead drunk, with a knife in his pocket and his right hand happened to be stained with blood. He declared that his nose had been bleeding, but no one believed him. The maids confessed that they had gone to a party and that the street-door had been left open till they returned. And a number of similar details came to light, throwing suspicion on the innocent servant.

They arrested him, and he was tried for the murder; but a week after the arrest, the prisoner fell sick of a fever and died unconscious in the hospital. There the matter ended and the judges and the authorities and every one in the town remained convinced that the crime had been committed by no one but the servant who had died in the hospital. And after that the punishment began.

My mysterious visitor, now my friend, told me that at first he was not in the least troubled by pangs of conscience. He was miserable a long time, but not for that reason; only from regret that he had killed the woman he loved, that she was no more, that in killing her he had killed his love, while the fire of passion was still in his veins. But of the innocent blood he had shed, of the murder of a fellow creature, he scarcely thought. The thought that his victim might have become the wife of another man was insupportable to him, and so, for a long time, he was convinced in his conscience that he could not have acted otherwise.

At first he was worried at the arrest of the servant, but his illness and death soon set his mind at rest, for the man's death was apparently (so he reflected at the time) not owing to his arrest or his fright, but a chill he had taken on the day he ran away, when he had lain all night dead drunk on the damp ground. The theft of the money and other things troubled him little, for he argued that the theft had not been committed for gain but to avert suspicion. The sum stolen was small, and he shortly afterwards subscribed the whole of it, and much more, towards the funds for maintaining an almshouse in the town. He did this on purpose to set his conscience at rest about the theft, and it's a remarkable fact that for a long time he really was at peace—he told me this himself. He entered then upon a career of great activity in the service, volunteered for a difficult and laborious duty, which occupied him two years, and being a man of strong will almost forgot the past. Whenever he recalled it, he tried not to think of it at all. He became active in philanthropy too, founded and helped to maintain many institutions in the town, did a good deal in the two capitals, and in both Moscow and Petersburg was elected a member of philanthropic societies.

At last, however, he began brooding over the past, and the strain of it was too much for him. Then he was attracted by a fine and intelligent girl and soon after married her, hoping that marriage would dispel his lonely depression, and that by entering on a new life and scrupulously doing his duty to his wife and children, he would escape from old memories altogether. But the very opposite of what he expected happened. He began, even in the first month of his marriage, to be continually fretted by the thought, "My wife loves me—but what if she knew?" When she first told him that she would soon bear him a child, he was troubled. "I am giving life, but I have taken life." Children came. "How dare I love them, teach and educate them, how can I talk to them of virtue? I have shed blood." They were splendid children, he longed to caress them; "and I can't look at their innocent candid faces, I am unworthy."

At last he began to be bitterly and ominously haunted by the blood of his murdered victim, by the young life he had destroyed, by the blood that cried out for vengeance. He had begun to have awful dreams. But, being a man of fortitude, he bore his suffering a long time, thinking: "I shall expiate everything by this secret agony." But that hope, too, was vain; the longer it went on, the more intense was his suffering.

He was respected in society for his active benevolence, though every one was overawed by his stern and gloomy character. But the more he was respected, the more intolerable it was for him. He confessed to me that he had thoughts of killing himself. But he began to be haunted by another idea—an idea which he had at first regarded as impossible and unthinkable, though at last it got such a hold on his heart that he could not shake it off. He dreamed of rising up, going out and confessing in the face of all men that he had committed murder. For three years this dream had pursued him, haunting him in different forms. At last he believed with his whole heart that if he confessed his crime, he would heal his soul and would be at peace for ever. But this belief filled his heart with terror, for how could he carry it out? And then came what happened at my duel.

"Looking at you, I have made up my mind."

I looked at him.

"Is it possible," I cried, clasping my hands, "that such a trivial incident could give rise to such a resolution in you?"

"My resolution has been growing for the last three years," he answered, "and your story only gave the last touch to it. Looking at you, I reproached myself and envied you," he said this to me almost sullenly.

"But you won't be believed," I observed; "it's fourteen years ago."

"I have proofs, great proofs. I shall show them."

Then I cried and kissed him.

"Tell me one thing, one thing," he said (as though it all depended upon me), "my wife, my children! My wife may die of grief, and though my children won't lose their rank and property, they'll be a convict's children and for ever! And what a memory, what a memory of me I shall leave in their hearts!"

I said nothing.

"And to part from them, to leave them for ever? It's for ever, you know, for ever!"

I sat still and repeated a silent prayer. I got up at last, I felt afraid.

"Well?" He looked at me.

"Go!" said I, "confess. Everything passes, only the truth remains. Your children will understand, when they grow up, the nobility of your resolution."

He left me that time as though he had made up his mind. Yet for more than a fortnight afterwards, he came to me every evening, still preparing himself, still unable to bring himself to the point. He made my heart ache. One day he would come determined and say fervently:

"I know it will be heaven for me, heaven, the moment I confess. Fourteen years I've been in hell. I want to suffer. I will take my punishment and begin to live. You can pass through the world doing wrong, but there's no turning back. Now I dare not love my neighbour nor even my own children. Good God, my children will understand, perhaps, what my punishment has cost me and will not condemn me! God is not in strength but in truth."

"All will understand your sacrifice," I said to him, "if not at once, they will understand later; for you have served truth, the higher truth, not of the earth."

And he would go away seeming comforted, but next day he would come again, bitter, pale, sarcastic.

"Every time I come to you, you look at me so inquisitively as though to say, 'he has still not confessed!' Wait a bit, don't despise me too much. It's not such an easy thing to do, as you would think. Perhaps I shall not do it at all. You won't go and inform against me then, will you?"

And far from looking at him with indiscreet curiosity, I was afraid to look at him at all. I was quite ill from anxiety, and my heart was full of tears. I could not sleep at night.

"I have just come from my wife," he went on. "Do you understand what the word 'wife' means? When I went out, the children called to me, 'Good-bye, father, make haste back to read "The Children's Magazine" with us.' No, you don't understand that! No one is wise from another man's woe."

His eyes were glittering, his lips were twitching. Suddenly he struck the table with his fist so that everything on it danced—it was the first time he had done such a thing, he was such a mild man.

"But need I?" he exclaimed, "must I? No one has been condemned, no one has been sent to Siberia in my place, the man died of fever. And I've been punished by my sufferings for the blood I shed. And I shan't be believed, they won't believe my proofs. Need I confess, need I? I am ready to go on suffering all my life for the blood I have shed, if only my wife and children may be spared. Will it be just to ruin them with me? Aren't we making a mistake? What is right in this case? And will people recognise it, will they appreciate it, will they respect it?"

"Good Lord!" I thought to myself, "he is thinking of other people's respect at such a moment!" And I felt so sorry for him then, that I believe I would have shared his fate if it could have comforted him. I saw he was beside himself. I was aghast, realising with my heart as well as my mind what such a resolution meant.

"Decide my fate!" he exclaimed again.

"Go and confess," I whispered to him. My voice failed me, but I whispered it firmly. I took up the New Testament from the table, the Russian translation,* and showed him the Gospel of St. John, ch. xii. verse 24:

"Verily, verily, I say unto you, except a corn of wheat fall into the ground and die, it abideth alone: but if it die, it bringeth forth much fruit."

I had just been reading that verse when he came in. He read it.

"That's true," he said, but he smiled bitterly. "It's terrible the things you find in those books," he said, after a pause. "It's easy enough to thrust them upon one. And who wrote them? Can they have been written by men?"

"The Holy Spirit wrote them," said I.

"It's easy for you to prate," he smiled again, this time almost with hatred.

I took the book again, opened it in another place and showed him the Epistle to the Hebrews, ch. x. verse 31. He read:

"It is a fearful thing to fall into the hands of the living God."

He read it and simply flung down the book. He was trembling all over.

"An awful text," he said. "There's no denying you've picked out fitting ones." He rose from the chair. "Well!" he said, "Good-bye, perhaps I shan't come again . . . we shall meet in heaven. So I have been for fourteen years 'in the hands of the living God,' that's how one must think of those fourteen years. To-morrow I will beseech those hands to let me go."

I wanted to take him in my arms and kiss him, but I did not dare—his face was contorted and sombre. He went away.

"Good God," I thought, "what has he gone to face!" I fell on my knees before the ikon and wept for him before the Holy Mother of God, our swift defender and helper. I was half an hour praying in tears, and it was late, about midnight. Suddenly I saw the door open and he came in again. I was surprised.

"Where have you been?" I asked him.

"I think," he said, "I've forgotten something . . . my handkerchief, I think. . . . Well, even if I've not forgotten anything, let me stay a little."

He sat down. I stood over him.

"You sit down, too," said he.

I sat down. We sat still for two minutes; he looked intently at me and suddenly smiled—I remembered that—then he got up, embraced me warmly and kissed me.

"Remember," he said, "how I came to you a second time. Do you hear, remember it!"

And he went out.

"To-morrow," I thought.

And so it was. I did not know that evening that the next day was his

---

*This Russian translation appeared in the early nineteenth century; the language of the Russian Orthodox Church is Old Slavonic.

birthday. I had not been out for the last few days so I had no chance of hearing it from any one. On that day he always had a great gathering, every one in the town went to it. It was the same this time. After dinner he walked into the middle of the room, with a paper in his hand—a formal declaration to the chief of his department who was present. This declaration he read aloud to the whole assembly. It contained a full account of the crime, in every detail.

"I cut myself off from men as a monster. God has visited me," he said in conclusion. "I want to suffer for my sin!"

Then he brought out and laid on the table all the things he had been keeping for fourteen years, that he thought would prove his crime, the jewels belonging to the murdered woman which he had stolen to divert suspicion, a cross and a locket taken from her neck with a portrait of her betrothed in the locket, her notebook and two letters; one from her betrothed, telling her that he would soon be with her, and her unfinished answer left on the table to be sent off next day. He carried off these two letters—what for? Why had he kept them for fourteen years afterwards instead of destroying them as evidence against him?

And this is what happened: every one was amazed and horrified, every one refused to believe it and thought that he was deranged, though all listened with intense curiosity. A few days later it was fully decided and agreed in every house that the unhappy man was mad. The legal authorities could not refuse to take the case up, but they too dropped it. Though the trinkets and letters made them ponder, they decided that even if they did turn out to be authentic, no charge could be based on those alone. Besides, she might have given him those things as a friend, or asked him to take care of them for her. I heard afterwards, however, that the genuineness of the things was proved by the friends and relations of the murdered woman, and that there was no doubt about them. Yet nothing was destined to come of it, after all.

Five days later, all had heard that he was ill and that his life was in danger. The nature of his illness I can't explain, they said it was an affection of the heart. But it became known that the doctors had been induced by his wife to investigate his mental condition also, and had come to the conclusion that it was a case of insanity. I betrayed nothing, though people ran to question me. But when I wanted to visit him, I was for a long while forbidden to do so, above all by his wife.

"It's you who have caused his illness," she said to me; "he was always gloomy, but for the last year people noticed that he was peculiarly excited and did strange things, and now you have been the ruin of him. Your preaching has brought him to this; for the last month he was always with you."

Indeed, not only his wife but the whole town were down upon me and blamed me. "It's all your doing," they said. I was silent and indeed rejoiced at heart, for I saw plainly God's mercy to the man who had turned against himself and punished himself. I could not believe in his insanity.

They let me see him at last, he insisted upon saying good-bye to me. I went in to him and saw at once, that not only his days, but his hours were numbered. He was weak, yellow, his hands trembled, he gasped for breath, but his face was full of tender and happy feeling.

"It is done!" he said. "I've long been yearning to see you, why didn't you come?"

I did not tell him that they would not let me see him.

"God has had pity on me and is calling me to Himself. I know I am dying, but I feel joy and peace for the first time after so many years. There was heaven in my heart from the moment I had done what I had to do. Now I dare to love my children and to kiss them. Neither my wife nor the judges, nor any one has believed it. My children will never believe it either. I see in that God's mercy to them. I shall die, and my name will be without a stain for them. And now I feel God near, my heart rejoices as in Heaven. . . . I have done my duty."

He could not speak, he gasped for breath, he pressed my hand warmly, looking fervently at me. We did not talk for long, his wife kept peeping in at us. But he had time to whisper to me:

"Do you remember how I came back to you that second time, at midnight? I told you to remember it. You know what I came back for? I came to kill you!"

I started.

"I went out from you then into the darkness, I wandered about the streets, struggling with myself. And suddenly I hated you so that I could hardly bear it. Now, I thought, he is all that binds me, and he is my judge. I can't refuse to face my punishment to-morrow, for he knows all. It was not that I was afraid you would betray me (I never even thought of that) but I thought, 'How can I look him in the face if I don't confess?' And if you had been at the other end of the earth, but alive, it would have been all the same, the thought was unendurable that you were alive knowing everything and condemning me. I hated you as though you were the cause, as though you were to blame for everything. I came back to you then, remembering that you had a dagger lying on your table. I sat down and asked you to sit down, and for a whole minute I pondered. If I had killed you, I should have been ruined by that murder even if I had not confessed the other. But I didn't think about that at all, and I didn't want to think of it at that moment. I only hated you and longed to revenge myself on you for everything. The Lord vanquished the devil in my heart. But let me tell you, you were never nearer death."

A week later he died. The whole town followed him to the grave. The chief priest made a speech full of feeling. All lamented the terrible illness that had cut short his days. But all the town was up in arms against me after the funeral, and people even refused to see me. Some, at first a few and afterwards more, began indeed to believe in the truth of his story, and they visited me and questioned me with great interest and eagerness, for man loves to see the downfall and disgrace of the righteous. But I held my tongue, and very shortly after, I left the town, and five months later by God's grace I entered upon the safe and blessed path, praising the unseen finger which had guided me so clearly to it. But I remember in my prayer to this day, the servant of God, Mihail, who suffered so greatly.

3

CONVERSATIONS AND EXHORTATIONS OF FATHER ZOSSIMA

(e) The Russian monk and his possible significance

FATHERS and teachers, what is the monk? In the cultivated world the word is nowadays pronounced by some people with a jeer, and by others it is used as a term of abuse, and this contempt for the monk is growing. It is true, alas, it is true, that there are many sluggards, gluttons, profligates and insolent beggars among monks. Educated people point to these; "You are idlers, useless members of society, you live on the labour of others, you are shameless beggars." And yet how many meek and humble monks there are, yearning for solitude and fervent prayer in peace. These are less noticed, or passed over in silence. And how surprised men would be if I were to say that from these meek monks, who yearn for solitary prayer, the salvation of Russia will come perhaps once more. For they are in truth made ready in peace and quiet "for the day and the hour, the month and the year." Meanwhile, in their solitude, they keep the image of Christ fair and undefiled, in the purity of God's truth, from the times of the Fathers of old, the Apostles and the martyrs. And when the time comes they will show it to the tottering creeds of the world. That is a great thought. That star will rise out of the East.*

That is my view of the monk, and is it false? is it too proud? Look at the worldly and all who set themselves up above the people of God, has not God's image and His truth been distorted in them? They have science; but in science there is nothing but what is the object of sense. The spiritual world, the higher part of man's being is rejected altogether, dismissed with a sort of triumph, even with hatred. The world has proclaimed the reign of freedom, especially of late, but what do we see in this freedom of theirs? Nothing but slavery and self-destruction! For the world says:

"You have desires and so satisfy them, for you have the same rights as the most rich and powerful. Don't be afraid of satisfying them and even

*See Matthew 2:2.

multiply your desires." That is the modern doctrine of the world. In that they see freedom. And what follows from this right of multiplication of desires? In the rich, isolation and spiritual suicide; in the poor, envy and murder; for they have been given rights, but have not been shown the means of satisfying their wants. They maintain that the world is getting more and more united, more and more bound together in brotherly community, as it overcomes distance and sets thoughts flying through the air.

Alas, put no faith in such a bond of union. Interpreting freedom as the multiplication and rapid satisfaction of desires, men distort their own nature, for many senseless and foolish desires and habits and ridiculous fancies are fostered in them. They live only for mutual envy, for luxury and ostentation. To have dinners, visits, carriages, rank and slaves to wait on one is looked upon as a necessity, for which life, honour and human feeling are sacrificed, and men even commit suicide if they are unable to satisfy it. We see the same thing among those who are not rich, while the poor drown their unsatisfied need and their envy in drunkenness. But soon they will drink blood instead of wine, they are being led on to it. I ask you is such a man free? I knew one "champion of freedom" who told me himself that, when he was deprived of tobacco in prison, he was so wretched at the privation that he almost went and betrayed his cause for the sake of getting tobacco again! And such a man says, "I am fighting for the cause of humanity."

How can such a one fight, what is he fit for? He is capable perhaps of some action quickly over, but he cannot hold out long. And it's no wonder that instead of gaining freedom they have sunk into slavery, and instead of serving the cause of brotherly love and the union of humanity have fallen, on the contrary, into dissension and isolation, as my mysterious visitor and teacher said to me in my youth. And therefore the idea of the service of humanity, of brotherly love and the solidarity of mankind, is more and more dying out in the world, and indeed this idea is sometimes treated with derision. For how can a man shake off his habits, what can become of him if he is in such bondage to the habit of satisfying the innumerable desires he has created for himself? He is isolated, and what concern has he with the rest of humanity? They have succeeded in accumulating a greater mass of objects, but the joy in the world has grown less.

The monastic way is very different. Obedience, fasting and prayer are laughed at, yet only through them lies the way to real, true freedom. I cut off my superfluous and unnecessary desires, I subdue my proud and wanton will and chastise it with obedience, and with God's help I attain freedom of spirit and with it spiritual joy. Which is most capable of conceiving a great idea and serving it—the rich man in his isolation or the man who has freed himself from the tyranny of material things and habits? The monk is reproached for his solitude, "You have secluded yourself within the walls of the monastery for your own salvation, and have forgotten the brotherly service of humanity!" But we shall see which will be most zealous in the cause of brotherly love. For it is not we, but they, who are in isolation, though they don't see that. Of old, leaders of the people came from

among us, and why should they not again? The same meek and humble ascetics will rise up and go out to work for the great cause. The salvation of
Russia comes from the people. And the Russian monk has always been on
the side of the people. We are isolated only if the people are isolated. The
people believe as we do, and an unbelieving reformer will never do anything in Russia, even if he is sincere in heart and a genius. Remember that!
The people will meet the atheist and overcome him, and Russia will be
one and orthodox. Take care of the peasant and guard his heart. Go on
educating him quietly. That's your duty as monks, for the peasant has God
in his heart.

(f) Of masters and servants, and of whether it is possible for them to be brothers in the spirit

Of course, I don't deny that there is sin in the peasants too. And the fire
of corruption is spreading visibly, hourly, working from above downwards.
The spirit of isolation is coming upon the people too. Moneylenders and
devourers of the commune are rising up. Already the merchant grows
more and more eager for rank, and strives to show himself cultured though
he has not a trace of culture, and to this end meanly despises his old traditions, and is even ashamed of the faith of his fathers. He visits princes,
though he is only a peasant corrupted. The peasants are rotting in drunkenness and cannot shake off the habit. And what cruelty to their wives, to
their children even! All from drunkenness! I've seen in the factories children of nine years old, frail, rickety, bent and already depraved. The stuffy
workshop, the din of machinery, work all day long, the vile language and
the drink, the drink—is that what a little child's heart needs? He needs
sunshine, childish play, good examples all about him, and at least a little
love. There must be no more of this, monks, no more torturing of children,
rise up and preach that, make haste, make haste!

But God will save Russia, for though the peasants are corrupted and
cannot renounce their filthy sin, yet they know it is cursed by God and that
they do wrong in sinning. So that our people still believe in righteousness,
have faith in God and weep tears of devotion.

It is different with the upper classes. They, following science, want to
base justice on reason alone, but not with Christ, as before, and they have
already proclaimed that there is no crime, that there is no sin. And that's
consistent, for if you have no God what is the meaning of crime? In Europe
the people are already rising up against the rich with violence, and the
leaders of the people are everywhere leading them to bloodshed, and
teaching them that their wrath is righteous. But their "wrath is accursed,
for it is cruel."* But God will save Russia as He has saved her many times.
Salvation will come from the people, from their faith and their meekness.

Fathers and teachers, watch over the people's faith and this will not be

---

*See Genesis 49:7.

a dream. I've been struck all my life in our great people by their dignity, their true and seemly dignity. I've seen it myself, I can testify to it, I've seen it and marvelled at it, I've seen it in spite of the degraded sins and poverty-stricken appearance of our peasantry. They are not servile, and even after two centuries of serfdom, they are free in manner and bearing, yet without insolence, and not revengeful and not envious. "You are rich and noble, you are clever and talented, well be so, God bless you. I respect you, but I know that I too am a man. By the very fact that I respect you without envy I prove my dignity as a man."

In truth if they don't say this (for they don't know how to say this yet) that is how they act. I have seen it myself, I have known it myself, and, would you believe it, the poorer our Russian peasant is, the more notice-able is that serene goodness, for the rich among them are for the most part corrupted already, and much of that is due to our carelessness and indifference. But God will save His people, for Russia is great in her humility. I dream of seeing, and seem to see clearly already, our future. It will come to pass, that even the most corrupt of our rich will end by being ashamed of his riches before the poor, and the poor, seeing his humility, will under-stand and give way before him, will respond joyfully and kindly to his honourable shame. Believe me that it will end in that; things are moving to that. Equality is to be found only in the spiritual dignity of man, and that will only be understood among us. If we were brothers, there would be fra-ternity, but before that, they will never agree about the division of wealth. We preserve the image of Christ, and it will shine forth like a precious di-amond to the whole world. So may it be, so may it be!

Fathers and teachers, a touching incident befell me once. In my wander-ings I met in the town of K. my old orderly, Afanasy. It was eight years since I had parted from him. He chanced to see me in the market-place, recog-nised me, ran up to me, and how delighted he was, he simply pounced on me: "Master dear, is it you? is it really you I see?" He took me home with him.

He was no longer in the army, he was married and already had two lit-tle children. He and his wife earned their living as costermongers in the market-place. His room was poor, but bright and clean. He made me sit down, set the samovar, sent for his wife, as though my appearance were a festival, for them. He brought me his children; "Bless them, father."

"Is it for me to bless them, I am only a humble monk. I will pray for them. And for you, Afanasy Pavlovitch, I have prayed every day since that day, for it all came from you," said I. And I explained that to him as well as I could. And what do you think? The man kept gazing at me and could not believe that I, his former master, an officer, was now before him in such a guise and position; it made him shed tears.

"Why are you weeping?" said I, "better rejoice over me, dear friend, whom I can never forget, for my path is a glad and joyful one."

He did not say much, but kept sighing and shaking his head over me tenderly.

"What has become of your fortune?" he asked.

"I gave it to the monastery," I answered; "we live in common."

After tea I began saying good-bye, and suddenly he brought out half a rouble as an offering to the monastery, and another half-rouble I saw him thrusting hurriedly into my hand: "That's for you in your wanderings, it may be of use to you, father."

I took his half-rouble, bowed to him and his wife, and went out rejoicing. And on my way I thought: "Here we are both now, he at home and I on the road, sighing and shaking our heads, no doubt, and yet smiling joyfully in the gladness of our hearts, remembering how God brought about our meeting."

I have never seen him again since then. I had been his master and he my servant, but now when we exchanged a loving kiss with softened hearts, there was a great human bond between us. I have thought a great deal about that, and now what I think is this: is it so inconceivable that that grand and simple-hearted unity might in due time become universal among the Russian people? I believe that it will come to pass and that the time is at hand.

And of servants I will add this, in old days when I was young I was often angry with servants; "the cook had served something too hot, the orderly had not brushed my clothes." But what taught me better then was a thought of my dear brother's, which I had heard from him in childhood: "Am I worth it, that another should serve me and be ordered about by me in his poverty and ignorance?" And I wondered at the time that such simple and self-evident ideas should be so slow to occur to our minds.

It is impossible that there should be no servants in the world, but act so that your servant may be freer in spirit than if he were not a servant. And why cannot I be a servant to my servant and even let him see it, and that without any pride on my part or any mistrust on his? Why should not my servant be like my own kindred, so that I may take him into my family and rejoice in doing so? Even now this can be done, but it will lead to the grand unity of men in the future, when a man will not seek servants for himself, or desire to turn his fellow creatures into servants as he does now, but on the contrary, will long with his whole heart to be the servant of all, as the Gospel teaches.*

And can it be a dream, that in the end man will find his joy only in deeds of light and mercy, and not in cruel pleasures as now, in gluttony, fornication, ostentation, boasting and envious rivalry of one with the other? I firmly believe that it is not and that the time is at hand. People laugh and ask: "When will that time come and does it look like coming?" I believe that with Christ's help we shall accomplish this great thing. And how many ideas there have been on earth in the history of man which were unthinkable ten years before they appeared? Yet when their destined hour had come, they came forth and spread over the whole earth. So it will be with us, and our people will shine forth in the world, and all men will say: "The stone which the builders rejected has become the corner-stone of the building."†

---

*See Matthew 20:25–27, 23:11; Mark 9:35, 10:43–44.
†See Matthew 21:42.

And we may ask the scornful themselves: if our hope is a dream, when will you build up your edifice and order things justly by your intellect alone, without Christ? If they declare that it is they who are advancing towards unity, only the most simple-hearted among them believe it, so that one may positively marvel at such simplicity. Of a truth, they have more fantastic dreams than we. They aim at justice, but, denying Christ, they will end by flooding the earth with blood, for blood cries out for blood, and he that taketh up the sword shall perish by the sword.* And if it were not for Christ's covenant, they would slaughter one another down to the last two men on earth. And those two last men would not be able to restrain each other in their pride, and the one would slay the other and then himself. And that would come to pass, were it not for the promise of Christ that for the sake of the humble and meek the days shall be shortened.

While I was still wearing an officer's uniform after my duel, I talked about servants in general society, and I remember every one was amazed at me; "What!" they asked, "are we to make our servants sit down on the sofa and offer them tea?" And I answered them: "Why not, sometimes at least." Every one laughed. Their question was frivolous and my answer was not clear; but the thought in it was to some extent right.

(g) Of prayer, of love, and of contact with other worlds

Young man, be not forgetful of prayer. Every time you pray, if your prayer is sincere, there will be new feeling and new meaning in it, which will give you fresh courage, and you will understand that prayer is an education. Remember too, every day, and whenever you can, repeat to yourself, "Lord, have mercy on all who appear before Thee to-day." For every hour and every moment thousands of men leave life on this earth, and their souls appear before God. And how many of them depart in solitude, unknown, sad, dejected, that no one mourns for them or even knows whether they have lived or not. And behold, from the other end of the earth perhaps, your prayer for their rest will rise up to God though you knew them not nor they you. How touching it must be to a soul standing in dread before the Lord to feel at that instant that, for him too, there is one to pray, that there is a fellow creature left on earth to love him too. And God will look on you both more graciously, for if you have had so much pity on him, how much more will He have pity Who is infinitely more loving and merciful than you. And He will forgive him for your sake.

Brothers, have no fear of men's sin. Love a man even in his sin, for that is the semblance of Divine Love and is the highest love on earth. Love all God's creation, the whole and every grain of sand in it. Love every leaf, every ray of God's light. Love the animals, love the plants, love everything. If you love everything, you will perceive the divine mystery in things. Once you perceive it, you will begin to comprehend it better every day. And you

---

*See Matthew 26:52.

will come at last to love the whole world with an all-embracing love. Love the animals: God has given them the rudiments of thought and joy untroubled. Do not trouble it, don't harass them, don't deprive them of their happiness, don't work against God's intent. Man, do not pride yourself on superiority to the animals; they are without sin, and you, with your greatness, defile the earth by your appearance on it, and leave the traces of your foulness after you—alas, it is true of almost every one of us! Love children especially, for they too are sinless like the angels; they live to soften and purify our hearts and as it were to guide us. Woe to him who offends a child! Father Anfim taught me to love children. The kind, silent man used often on our wanderings to spend the farthings given us on sweets and cakes for the children. He could not pass by a child without emotion, that's the nature of the man.

At some thoughts one stands perplexed, especially at the sight of men's sin, and wonders whether one should use force or humble love. Always decide to use humble love. If you resolve on that once for all, you may subdue the whole world. Loving humility is marvellously strong, the strongest of all things and there is nothing else like it.

Every day and every hour, every minute, walk round yourself and watch yourself, and see that your image is a seemly one. You pass by a little child, you pass by, spiteful, with ugly words, with wrathful heart; you may not have noticed the child, but he has seen you, and your image, unseemly and ignoble, may remain in his defenceless heart. You don't know it, but you may have sown an evil seed in him and it may grow, and all because you were not careful before the child, because you did not foster in yourself a careful, actively benevolent love. Brothers, love is a teacher; but one must know how to acquire it, for it is hard to acquire, it is dearly bought, it is won slowly by long labour. For we must love not only occasionally, for a moment, but for ever. Every one can love occasionally, even the wicked can.

My brother asked the birds to forgive him; that sounds senseless, but it is right; for all is like an ocean, all is flowing and blending; a touch in one place sets up movement at the other end of the earth. It may be senseless to beg forgiveness of the birds, but birds would be happier at your side—a little happier, anyway—and children and all animals, if you yourself were nobler than you are now. It's all like an ocean, I tell you. Then you would pray to the birds too, consumed by an all-embracing love, in a sort of transport, and pray that they too will forgive you your sin. Treasure this ecstasy, however senseless it may seem to men.

My friends, pray to God for gladness. Be glad as children, as the birds of heaven. And let not the sin of men confound you in your doings. Fear not that it will wear away your work and hinder its being accomplished. Do not say, "Sin is mighty, wickedness is mighty, evil environment is mighty, and we are lonely and helpless, and evil environment is wearing us away and hindering our good work from being done." Fly from that dejection, children! There is only one means of salvation, then take yourself and make yourself responsible for all men's sins, that is the truth, you know, friends, for as soon as you sincerely make yourself responsible for everything and for all men, you will see at once that it is really so, and that you are to blame for every one and for all things. But throwing your own indolence and impotence on others you will end by sharing the pride of Satan and murmuring against God.

Of the pride of Satan what I think is this: it is hard for us on earth to comprehend it, and therefore it is so easy to fall into error and to share it, even imagining that we are doing something grand and fine. Indeed many of the strongest feelings and movements of our nature we cannot comprehend on earth. Let not that be a stumbling-block, and think not that it may serve as a justification to you for anything. For the Eternal Judge asks of you what you can comprehend and not what you cannot. You will know that yourself hereafter, for you will behold all things truly then and will not dispute them. On earth, indeed, we are as it were astray, and if it were not for the precious image of Christ before us, we should be undone and altogether lost, as was the human race before the flood. Much on earth is hidden from us, but to make up for that we have been given a precious mystic sense of our living bond with the other world, with the higher heavenly world, and the roots of our thoughts and feelings are not here but in other worlds. That is why the philosophers say that we cannot apprehend the reality of things on earth.

God took seeds from different worlds and sowed them on this earth, and His garden grew up and everything came up that could come up, but what grows lives and is alive only through the feeling of its contact with other mysterious worlds. If that feeling grows weak or is destroyed in you, the heavenly growth will die away in you. Then you will be indifferent to life and even grow to hate it. That's what I think.

(h) Can a man judge his fellow creatures? Faith to the end

Remember particularly that you cannot be a judge of any one. For no one can judge a criminal, until he recognises that he is just such a criminal as the man standing before him, and that he perhaps is more than all men to blame for that crime. When he understands that, he will be able to be a judge.* Though that sounds absurd, it is true. If I had been righteous myself, perhaps there would have been no criminal standing before me. If you can take upon yourself the crime of the criminal your heart is judging, take it at once, suffer for him yourself, and let him go without reproach. And even if the law itself makes you his judge, act in the same spirit so far as possible, for he will go away and condemn himself more bitterly than you have done. If, after your kiss, he goes away untouched, mocking at you, do not let that be a stumbling-block to you. It shows his time has not yet come, but it will come in due course. And if it come not, no matter; if not he, then another in his place will understand and suffer, and judge and condemn himself, and the truth will be fulfilled. Believe

---

*See Matthew 7:1–5.

that, believe it without doubt; for in that lies all the hope and faith of the saints.

Work without ceasing. If you remember in the night as you go to sleep, "I have not done what I ought to have done," rise up at once and do it. If the people around you are spiteful and callous and will not hear you, fall down before them and beg their forgiveness; for in truth you are to blame for their not wanting to hear you. And if you cannot speak to them in their bitterness, serve them in silence and in humility, never losing hope. If all men abandon you and even drive you away by force, then when you are left alone fall on the earth and kiss it, water it with your tears and it will bring forth fruit even though no one has seen or heard you in your solitude. Believe to the end, even if all men went astray and you were left the only one faithful; bring your offering even then and praise God in your loneliness. And if two of you are gathered together—then there is a whole world, a world of living love. Embrace each other tenderly and praise God, for if only in you two His truth has been fulfilled.

If you sin yourself and grieve even unto death for your sins or for your sudden sin, then rejoice for others, rejoice for the righteous man, rejoice that if you have sinned, he is righteous and has not sinned.

If the evil doing of men moves you to indignation and overwhelming distress, even to a desire for vengeance on the evil-doers, shun above all things that feeling. Go at once and seek suffering for yourself, as though you were yourself guilty of that wrong. Accept that suffering and bear it and your heart will find comfort, and you will understand that you too are guilty, for you might have been a light to the evil-doers, even as the one man sinless, and you were not a light to them. If you had been a light, you would have lightened the path for others too and the evil-doer might perhaps have been saved by your light from his sin. And even though your light was shining, yet you see men were not saved by it, hold firm and doubt not the power of the heavenly light. Believe that if they were not saved, they will be saved hereafter. And if they are not saved hereafter, then their sons will be saved, for your light will not die even when you are dead. The righteous man departs, but his light remains. Men are always saved after the death of the deliverer. Men reject their prophets and slay them, but they love their martyrs and honour those whom they have slain. You are working for the whole, you are acting for the future. Seek no reward, for great is your reward on this earth: the spiritual joy which is only vouchsafed to the righteous man. Fear not the great nor the mighty, but be wise and ever serene. Know the measure, know the times, study that. When you are left alone, pray. Love to throw yourself on the earth and kiss it. Kiss the earth and love it with an unceasing, consuming love. Love all men, love everything. Seek that rapture and ecstasy. Water the earth with the tears of your joy and love those tears. Don't be ashamed of that ecstasy, prize it, for it is a gift of God and a great one; it is not given to many but only to the elect.

(i) Of hell and hell fire, a mystic reflection

Fathers and teachers, I ponder "What is hell?" I maintain that it is the suffering of being unable to love.* Once in infinite existence, immeasurable in time and space, a spiritual creature was given on his coming to earth, the power of saying, "I am and I love." Once, only once, there was given him a moment of active *living* love and for that was earthly life given him, and with it times and seasons. And that happy creature rejected the priceless gift, prized it and loved it not, scorned it and remained callous. Such a one, having left the earth, sees Abraham's bosom and talks with Abraham as we are told in the parable of the rich man and Lazarus,† and beholds heaven and can go up to the Lord. But that is just his torment, to rise up to the Lord without ever having loved, to be brought close to those who have loved when he has despised their love. For he sees clearly and says to himself, "Now I have understanding and though I now thirst to love, there will be nothing great, no sacrifice in my love, for my earthly life is over, and Abraham will not come even with a drop of living water (that is the gift of earthly, active life) to cool the fiery thirst of spiritual love which burns in me now, though I despised it on earth; there is no more life for me and will be no more time!‡ Even though I would gladly give my life for others, it can never be, for that life is passed which can be sacrificed for love, and now there is a gulf fixed between that life and this existence."

They talk of hell fire in the material sense. I don't go into that mystery and I shun it. But I think if there were fire in material sense, they would be glad of it, for, I imagine, that in material agony, their still greater spiritual agony would be forgotten for a moment. Moreover, that spiritual agony cannot be taken from them, for that suffering is not external but within them. And if it could be taken from them, I think it would be bitterer still for the unhappy creatures. For even if the righteous in Paradise forgave them, beholding their torments, and called them up to heaven in their infinite love, they would only multiply their torments, for they would arouse in them still more keenly a flaming thirst for responsive, active and grateful love which is now impossible. In the timidity of my heart I imagine, however, that the very recognition of this impossibility would serve at last to console them. For accepting the love of the righteous together with the impossibility of repaying it, by this submissiveness and the effect of this humility, they will attain at last, as it were, to a certain semblance of that active love which they scorned in life, to something like its outward expression. . . . I am sorry, friends and brothers, that I cannot express this clearly. But woe to those who have slain themselves on earth, woe to the suicides! I believe that there can be none more miserable than they. They tell us that it is a sin to pray for them and outwardly the Church, as it were, renounces them, but in my secret heart

---

*Allusion to Homily 84 of Saint Isaac the Syrian (died c.700).
†See Luke 16:19–31.
‡See Revelation 10:6.

I believe that we may pray even for them.[5] Love can never be an offence to Christ. For such as those I have prayed inwardly all my life, I confess it, fathers and teachers, and even now I pray for them every day.

Oh, there are some who remain proud and fierce even in hell, in spite of their certain knowledge and contemplation of the absolute truth; there are some fearful ones who have given themselves over to Satan and his proud spirit entirely. For such, hell is voluntary and ever consuming; they are tortured by their own choice. For they have cursed themselves, cursing God and life. They live upon their vindictive pride like a starving man in the desert sucking blood out of his own body. But they are never satisfied, and they refuse forgiveness, they curse God Who calls them. They cannot behold the living God without hatred, and they cry out that the God of life should be annihilated, that God should destroy Himself and His own creation. And they will burn in the fire of their own wrath for ever and yearn for death and annihilation. But they will not attain to death. . . .

Here Alexey Fyodorovitch Karamazov's manuscript ends. I repeat, it is incomplete and fragmentary. Biographical details, for instance, cover only Father Zossima's earliest youth. Of his teaching and opinions we find brought together sayings evidently uttered on very different occasions. His utterances during the last few hours have not been kept separate from the rest, but their general character can be gathered from what we have in Alexey Fyodorovitch's manuscript.

The elder's death came in the end quite unexpectedly. For although those who were gathered about him that last evening realised that his death was approaching, yet it was difficult to imagine that it would come so suddenly. On the contrary, his friends, as I observed already, seeing him that night apparently so cheerful and talkative, were convinced that there was at least a temporary change for the better in his condition. Even five minutes before his death, they said afterwards wonderingly, it was impossible to foresee it. He seemed suddenly to feel an acute pain in his chest, he turned pale and pressed his hands to his heart. All rose from their seats and hastened to him. But though suffering, he still looked at them with a smile, sank slowly from his chair on to his knees, then bowed his face to the ground, stretched out his arms and as though in joyful ecstasy, praying and kissing the ground, quietly and joyfully gave up his soul to God.

The news of his death spread at once through the hermitage and reached the monastery. The nearest friends of the deceased and those whose duty it was from their position began to lay out the corpse according to the ancient ritual, and all the monks gathered together in the church. And before dawn the news of the death reached the town. By the morning all the town was talking of the event, and crowds were flocking from the town to the monastery. But this subject will be treated in the next book; I will only add here that before a day had passed something happened so unexpected, so strange, upsetting, and bewildering in its effect on the monks and the townspeople, that after all these years, that day of general suspense is still vividly remembered in the town.

PART THREE

BOOK SEVEN

ALYOSHA

1

THE BREATH OF CORRUPTION

T HE body of Father Zossima was prepared for burial according to the established ritual. As is well known, the bodies of dead monks and hermits are not washed. In the words of the Church Ritual: "If any one of the monks depart in the Lord, the monk designated (that is, whose office it is) shall wipe the body with warm water, making first the sign of the cross with a sponge on the forehead of the deceased, on the breast, on the hands and feet and on the knees, and that is enough." All this was done by Father Païssy, who then clothed the deceased in his monastic garb and wrapped him in his cloak, which was, according to custom, somewhat slit to allow of its being folded about him in the form of a cross. On his head he put a hood with an eight-cornered cross. The hood was left open and the dead man's face was covered with black gauze. In his hands was put an ikon of the Saviour. Towards morning he was put in the coffin which had been made ready long before. It was decided to leave the coffin all day in the cell, in the larger room in which the elder used to receive his visitors and fellow monks. As the deceased was a priest and monk of the strictest rule, the Gospel, not the Psalter, had to be read over his body by monks in holy orders. The reading was begun by Father Iosif immediately after the requiem service. Father Païssy desired later on to read the Gospel all day and night over his dead friend, but for the present he, as well as the Father Superintendent of the Hermitage, was very busy and occupied, for something extraordinary, and unheard of, even "unseemly" excitement and impatient expectation began to be apparent in the monks, and the visitors from the monastery hostels, and the crowds of people flocking from the town. And as time went on, this grew more and more marked. Both the Superintendent and Father Païssy did their utmost to calm the general bustle and agitation.

When it was fully daylight, some people began bringing their sick, in most cases children, with them from the town—as though they had been waiting expressly for this moment to do so, evidently persuaded that the dead elder's remains had a power of healing, which would be immediately made manifest in accordance with their faith. It was only then apparent how unquestionably every one in our town had accepted Father Zossima during his lifetime as a great saint. And those who came were far from being all of the humbler classes.

This intense expectation on the part of believers displayed with such haste, such openness, even with impatience and almost insistence, impressed Father Païssy as unseemly. Though he had long foreseen something of the sort, the actual manifestation of the feeling was beyond anything he had looked for. When he came across any of the monks who displayed this excitement, Father Païssy began to reprove them. "Such immediate expectation of something extraordinary," he said, "shows a levity, possible to worldly people but unseemly in us."

But little attention was paid him and Father Païssy noticed it uneasily. Yet he himself (if the whole truth must be told), secretly at the bottom of his heart, cherished almost the same hopes and could not but be aware of it, though he was indignant at the too impatient expectation around him, and saw in it light-mindedness and vanity. Nevertheless, it was particularly unpleasant to him to meet certain persons, whose presence aroused in him great misgivings. In the crowd in the dead man's cell he noticed with inward aversion (for which he immediately reproached himself) the presence of Rakitin and of the monk from Obdorsk, who was still staying in the monastery. Of both of them Father Païssy felt for some reason suddenly suspicious—though, indeed, he might well have felt the same about others.

The monk from Obdorsk was conspicuous as the most fussy in the excited crowd. He was to be seen everywhere; everywhere he was asking questions, everywhere he was listening, on all sides he was whispering with a peculiar, mysterious air. His expression showed the greatest impatience and even a sort of irritation.

As for Rakitin, he, as appeared later, had come so early to the hermitage at the special request of Madame Hohlakov. As soon as that good-hearted but weak-minded woman, who could not herself have been admitted to the hermitage, waked and heard of the death of Father Zossima, she was overtaken with such intense curiosity that she promptly despatched Rakitin to the hermitage, to keep a careful look-out and report to her by letter every half-hour or so *"everything that takes place."* She regarded Rakitin as a most religious and devout young man. He was particularly clever in getting round people and assuming whatever part he thought most to their taste, if he detected the slightest advantage to himself from doing so.

It was a bright, clear day and many of the visitors were thronging about the tombs, which were particularly numerous round the church and scattered here and there about the hermitage. As he walked round the hermitage, Father Païssy remembered Alyosha and that he had not seen him for some time, not since the night. And he had no sooner thought of him than he at once noticed him in the furthest corner of the hermitage garden, sitting on the tombstone of a monk who had been famous long ago for his saintliness. He sat with his back to the hermitage and his face to the wall, and seemed to be hiding behind the tombstone. Going up to him, Father Païssy saw that he was weeping quietly but bitterly, with his face hidden in his hands and that his whole frame was shaking with sobs. Father Païssy stood over him for a little.

"Enough, dear son, enough, dear," he pronounced with feeling at last. "Why do you weep? Rejoice and weep not. Don't you know that this is the greatest of his days? Think only where he is now, at this moment!"

Alyosha glanced at him, uncovering his face, which was swollen with crying like a child's, but turned away at once without uttering a word and hid his face in his hands again.

"Maybe it is well," said Father Païssy thoughtfully; "weep if you must, Christ has sent you those tears."

"Your touching tears are but a relief to your spirit and will serve to gladden your dear heart," he added to himself, walking away from Alyosha, and thinking lovingly of him. He moved away quickly, however, for he felt that he too might weep looking at him.

Meanwhile the time was passing; the monastery services and the requiems for the dead followed in their due course. Father Païssy again took Father Iosif's place by the coffin and began reading the Gospel. But before three o'clock in the afternoon that something took place to which I alluded at the end of the last book, something so unexpected by all of us and so contrary to the general hope, that, I repeat, this trivial incident has been minutely remembered to this day in our town and all the surrounding neighbourhood. I may add here, for myself personally, that I feel it almost repulsive to recall that event which caused such frivolous agitation and was such a stumbling-block to many, though in reality it was the most natural and trivial matter. I should, of course, have omitted all mention of it in my story, if it had not exerted a very strong influence on the heart and soul of the chief, *though future,* hero of my story, Alyosha, forming a crisis and turning-point in his spiritual development, giving a shock to his intellect, which finally strengthened it for the rest of his life and gave it a definite aim.

And so, to return to our story. When before dawn they laid Father Zossima's body in the coffin and brought it into the front room, the question of opening the windows was raised among those who were around the coffin. But this suggestion made casually by some one was unanswered and almost unnoticed. Some of those present may perhaps have inwardly noticed it, only to reflect that the anticipation of decay and corruption from the body of such a saint was an actual absurdity, calling for compassion (if not a smile) for the lack of faith and the frivolity it implied. For they expected something quite different.

And, behold, soon after midday there were signs of something, at first only observed in silence by those who came in and out and were evidently each afraid to communicate the thought in his mind. But by three o'clock those signs had become so clear and unmistakable, that the news swiftly reached all the monks and visitors in the hermitage, promptly penetrated to the monastery, throwing all the monks into amazement, and finally, in the shortest possible time, spread to the town, exciting every one in it, believers and unbelievers alike. The unbelievers rejoiced, and as for the believers some of them rejoiced even more than the unbelievers, for "men love the downfall and disgrace of the righteous," as the deceased elder had said in one of his exhortations.

The fact is that a smell of decomposition began to come from the coffin, growing gradually more marked, and by three o'clock it was quite unmistakable. In all the past history of our monastery, no such scandal could be recalled, and in no other circumstances could such a scandal have been possible, as showed itself in unseemly disorder immediately after this discovery among the very monks themselves. Afterwards, even many years afterwards, some sensible monks were amazed and horrified, when they recalled that day, that the scandal could have reached such proportions. For in the past, monks of very holy life had died, God-fearing old men, whose saintliness was acknowledged by all, yet from their humble coffins, too, the breath of corruption had come, naturally, as from all dead bodies, but that had caused no scandal nor even the slightest excitement. Of course there had been, in former times, saints in the monastery whose memory was carefully preserved and whose relics, according to tradition, showed no signs of corruption. This fact was regarded by the monks as touching and mysterious, and the tradition of it was cherished as something blessed and miraculous, and as a promise, by God's grace, of still greater glory from their tombs in the future.

One such, whose memory was particularly cherished, was an old monk, Job, who had died seventy years before at the age of a hundred and five. He had been a celebrated ascetic, rigid in fasting and silence, and his tomb was pointed out to all visitors on their arrival with peculiar respect and mysterious hints of great hopes connected with it. (That was the very tomb on which Father Païssy had found Alyosha sitting in the morning.) Another memory cherished in the monastery was that of the famous Father Varsonofy, who was only recently dead and had preceded Father Zossima in the eldership. He was reverenced during his lifetime as a crazy saint by all the pilgrims to the monastery. There was a tradition that both of these had laid in their coffins as though alive, that they had shown no signs of decomposition when they were buried and that there had been a holy light in their faces. And some people even insisted that a sweet fragrance came from their bodies.

Yet, in spite of these edifying memories, it would be difficult to explain the frivolity, absurdity and malice that were manifested beside the coffin of Father Zossima. It is my private opinion that several different causes were simultaneously at work, one of which was the deeply rooted hostility to the institution of elders as a pernicious innovation, an antipathy hidden deep in the hearts of many of the monks. Even more powerful was jealousy of the dead man's saintliness, so firmly established during his lifetime that it was almost a forbidden thing to question it. For though the late elder had won over many hearts, more by love than by miracles, and had gathered round him a mass of loving adherents, none the less, in fact, rather the more on that account he had awakened jealousy and so had come to have bitter enemies, secret and open, not only in the monastery but in the world outside it. He did no one any harm, but "Why do they think him so saintly?" And that question alone gradually repeated gave rise at last to an intense, insatiable hatred of him. That I believe was why many people were extremely delighted at the smell of decomposition which came so quickly, for not a day had passed since his death. At the same time there were some among those who had been hitherto reverently devoted to the elder, who were almost mortified and personally affronted by this incident. This was how the thing happened.

As soon as signs of decomposition had begun to appear, the whole aspect of the monks betrayed their secret motives in entering the cell. They went in, stayed a little while and hastened out to confirm the news to the crowd of other monks waiting outside. Some of the latter shook their heads mournfully, but others did not even care to conceal the delight, which gleamed unmistakably in their malignant eyes. And now no one reproached them for it, no one raised his voice in protest, which was strange, for the majority of the monks had been devoted to the dead elder. But it seemed as though God had in this case let the minority get the upper hand for a time.

Visitors from outside, particularly of the educated class, soon went into the cell, too, with the same spying intent. Of the peasantry few went into the cell, though there were crowds of them at the gates of the hermitage. After three o'clock the rush of worldly visitors was greatly increased and this was no doubt owing to the shocking news. People were attracted who would not otherwise have come on that day and had not intended to come, and among them were some personages of high standing. But external decorum was still preserved and Father Païssy, with a stern face, continued firmly and distinctly reading aloud the Gospel, apparently not noticing what was taking place around him, though he had, in fact, observed something unusual long before. But at last the murmurs, first subdued but gradually louder and more confident, reached even him. "It shows God's judgment is not as man's," Father Païssy heard suddenly. The first to give utterance to this sentiment was a layman, an elderly official from the town, known to be a man of great piety. But he only repeated aloud what the monks had long been whispering. They had long before formulated this damning conclusion, and the worst of it was that a sort of triumphant satisfaction at that conclusion became more and more apparent every moment. Soon they began to lay aside even external decorum and almost seemed to feel they had a sort of right to discard it.

"And for what reason can *this* have happened," some of the monks said, at first with a show of regret; "he had a small frame and his flesh was dried up on his bones, what was there to decay?"

"It must be a sign from heaven," others hastened to add, and their opinion was adopted at once without protest. For it was pointed out, too, that if the decomposition had been natural, as in the case of every dead sinner, it would have been apparent later, after a lapse of at least twenty-four hours, but this premature corruption "was in excess of nature," and so the finger of God was evident. It was meant for a sign. This conclusion seemed irresistible.

Gentle Father Iosif, the librarian, a great favourite of the dead man's, tried to reply to some of the evil speakers that "this is not held everywhere alike," and that the incorruptibility of the bodies of the just was not a dogma of the Orthodox Church, but only an opinion, and that even in the most Orthodox regions, at Athos for instance, they were not greatly confounded by the smell of corruption, and there the chief sign of the glorification of the saved was not bodily incorruptibility, but the colour of the bones when the bodies have lain many years in the earth and have decayed in it. "And if the bones are yellow as wax, that is the great sign that the Lord has glorified the dead saint, if they are not yellow but black, it shows that God has not deemed him worthy of such glory—that is the belief in Athos, a great place, where the Orthodox doctrine has been preserved from of old, unbroken and in its greatest purity," said Father Iosif in conclusion.

But the meek Father's words had little effect and even provoked a mocking retort. "That's all pedantry and innovation, no use listening to it," the monks decided. "We stick to the old doctrine, there are all sorts of innovations nowadays, are we to follow them all?" added others.

"We have had as many holy fathers as they had. There they are among the Turks, they have forgotten everything. Their doctrine has long been impure and they have no bells even," the most sneering added.

Father Iosif walked away grieving the more since he had put forward his own opinion with little confidence as though scarcely believing in it himself. He foresaw with distress that something very unseemly was beginning and that there were positive signs of disobedience. Little by little, all the sensible monks were reduced to silence like Father Iosif. And so it came to pass that all who loved the elder and had accepted with devout obedience the institution of the eldership were all at once terribly cast down and glanced timidly in one another's faces, when they met. Those who were hostile to the institution of elders, as a novelty, held up their heads proudly. "There was no smell of corruption from the late elder Varsonofy, but a sweet fragrance," they recalled malignantly. "But he gained that glory not because he was an elder, but because he was a holy man."

And this was followed by a shower of criticism and even blame of Father Zossima. "His teaching was false; he taught that life is a great joy and not a vale of tears," said some of the more unreasonable. "He followed the fashionable belief, he did not recognise material fire in hell," others, still more unreasonable, added. "He was not strict in fasting, allowed himself sweet things, ate cherry jam with his tea, ladies used to send it to him. Is it for a monk of strict rule to drink tea?" could be heard among some of the envious. "He sat in pride," the most malignant declared vindictively; "he considered himself a saint and he took it as his due when people knelt before him." "He abused the sacrament of confession," the fiercest opponents of the institution of elders added in a malicious whisper. And among these were some of the oldest monks, strictest in their devotion, genuine ascetics, who had kept silent during the life of the deceased elder, but now suddenly unsealed their lips. And this was terrible, for their words had great influence on young monks who were not yet firm in their convictions. The monk from Obdorsk heard all this attentively, heaving deep sighs and nodding his head. "Yes, clearly Father Ferapont was right in his judgment yesterday," and at that moment Father Ferapont himself made his appearance, as though on purpose to increase the confusion.

I have mentioned already that he rarely left his wooden cell by the

apiary. He was seldom even seen at church and they overlooked this neglect on the ground of his craziness, and did not keep him to the rules binding on all the rest. But if the whole truth is to be told, they hardly had a
choice about it. For it would have been discreditable to insist on burdening with the common regulations so great an ascetic, who prayed day and
night (he even dropped asleep on his knees). If they had insisted, the monks
would have said "he is holier than all of us and he follows a rule harder
than ours. And if he does not go to church, it's because he knows when he
ought to; he has his own rule." It was to avoid the chance of these sinful
murmurs Father Ferapont was left in peace.

As every one was aware, Father Ferapont particularly disliked Father
Zossima. And now the news had reached him in his hut that "God's judgment is not the same as man's," and that something had happened which
was "in excess of nature." It may well be supposed that among the first to
run to him with the news was the monk from Obdorsk, who had visited
him the evening before and left his cell terror-stricken.

I have mentioned above, that though Father Païssy, standing firm and immovable reading the Gospel over the coffin, could not hear nor see what
was passing outside the cell, he gauged most of it correctly in his heart, for
he knew the men surrounding him, well. He was not shaken by it, but
awaited what would come next without fear, watching with penetration and
insight for the outcome of the general excitement.

Suddenly an extraordinary uproar in the passage in open defiance of
decorum burst on his ears. The door was flung open and Father Ferapont
appeared in the doorway. Behind him there could be seen accompanying
him a crowd of monks, together with many people from the town. They did
not, however, enter the cell, but stood at the bottom of the steps, waiting
to see what Father Ferapont would say or do. For they felt with a certain
awe, in spite of their audacity, that he had not come for nothing. Standing
in the doorway, Father Ferapont raised his arms, and under his right arm
the keen inquisitive little eyes of the monk from Obdorsk peeped in. He
alone, in his intense curiosity, could not resist running up the steps after
Father Ferapont. The others, on the contrary, pressed further back in sudden alarm when the door was noisily flung open. Holding his hands aloft,
Father Ferapont suddenly roared:

"Casting out I cast out!" and, turning in all directions, he began at once
making the sign of the cross at each of the four walls and four corners of
the cell in succession. All who accompanied Father Ferapont immediately
understood his action. For they knew he always did this wherever he went,
and that he would not sit down or say a word, till he had driven out the evil
spirits.

"Satan, go hence! Satan, go hence!" he repeated at each sign of the
cross. "Casting out I cast out," he roared again.

He was wearing his coarse gown girt with a rope. His bare chest, covered with grey hair, could be seen under his hempen shirt. His feet were
bare. As soon as he began waving his arms, the cruel irons he wore under
his gown could be heard clanking.

Father Païssy paused in his reading, stepped forward and stood before him waiting.

"What have you come for, worthy Father? Why do you offend against good order? Why do you disturb the peace of the flock?" he said at last, looking sternly at him.

"What have I come for? You ask why? What is your faith?" shouted Father Ferapont crazily. "I've come here to drive out your visitors, the unclean devils. I've come to see how many have gathered here while I have been away. I want to sweep them out with a birch broom."

"You cast out the evil spirit, but perhaps you are serving him yourself," Father Païssy went on fearlessly. "And who can say of himself 'I am holy.' Can you, Father?"

"I am unclean not holy. I would not sit in an arm-chair and would not have them bow down to me as an idol," thundered Father Ferapont. "Nowadays folk destroy the true faith. The dead man, your saint," he turned to the crowd, pointing with his finger to the coffin, "did not believe in devils. He gave medicine to keep off the devils. And so they have become as common as spiders in the corners. And now he has begun to stink himself. In that we see a great sign from God."

The incident he referred to was this. One of the monks was haunted in his dreams and, later on, in waking moments, by visions of evil spirits. When in the utmost terror he confided this to Father Zossima, the elder had advised continual prayer and rigid fasting. But when that was of no use, he advised him, while persisting in prayer and fasting, to take a special medicine. Many persons were shocked at the time and wagged their heads as they talked over it—and most of all Father Ferapont, to whom some of the censorious had hastened to report this "extraordinary" counsel on the part of the elder.

"Go away, Father!" said Father Païssy, in a commanding voice, "it's not for man to judge but for God. Perhaps we see here a 'sign' which neither you, nor I, nor any one of us is able to comprehend. Go, Father, and do not trouble the flock!" he repeated impressively.

"He did not keep the fasts according to the rule and therefore the sign has come. That is clear and it's a sin to hide it," the fanatic, carried away by a zeal that outstripped his reason, would not be quieted. "He was seduced by sweetmeats, ladies brought them to him in their pockets, he sipped tea, he worshipped his belly, filling it with sweet things and his mind with haughty thought. . . . And for this he is put to shame. . . ."

"You speak lightly, Father." Father Païssy too raised his voice. "I admire your fasting and severities, but you speak lightly like some frivolous youth, fickle and childish. Go away, Father, I command you!" Father Païssy thundered in conclusion.

"I will go," said Ferapont, seeming somewhat taken aback, but still as bitter. "You learned men! You are so clever you look down upon my humbleness. I came hither with little learning and here I have forgotten what I did know, God himself has preserved me in my weakness from your subtlety."

Father Païssy stood over him, waiting resolutely. Father Ferapont paused and, suddenly leaning his cheek on his hand despondently, pronounced in a sing-song voice, looking at the coffin of the dead elder:

"To-morrow they will sing over him 'Our Helper and Defender'—a splendid anthem—and over me when I die all they'll sing will be 'What earthly joy'—a little canticle,"* he added with tearful regret. "You are proud and puffed up, this is a vain place!" he shouted suddenly like a madman, and with a wave of his hand he turned quickly and quickly descended the steps. The crowd awaiting him below wavered; some followed him at once and some lingered, for the cell was still open, and Father Païssy, following Father Ferapont on to the steps, stood watching him. But the excited old fanatic was not completely silenced. Walking twenty steps away, he suddenly turned towards the setting sun, raised both his arms and, as though some one had cut him down, fell to the ground with a loud scream.

"My God has conquered! Christ has conquered the setting sun!" he shouted frantically, stretching up his hands to the sun, and falling face downwards on the ground, he sobbed like a little child, shaken by his tears and spreading out his arms on the ground. Then all rushed up to him; there were exclamations and sympathetic sobs . . . a kind of frenzy seemed to take possession of them all.

"This is the one who is a saint! This is the one who is a holy man!" some cried aloud, losing their fear. "This is he who should be an elder," others added malignantly.

"He wouldn't be an elder . . . he would refuse . . . he wouldn't serve a cursed innovation . . . he wouldn't imitate their foolery," other voices chimed in at once. And it is hard to say how far they might have gone, but at that moment the bell rang summoning them to service. All began crossing themselves at once. Father Ferapont, too, got up and crossing himself went back to his cell without looking round, still uttering exclamations which were utterly incoherent. A few followed him, but the greater number dispersed, hastening to service. Father Païssy let Father Iosif read in his place and went down. The frantic outcries of bigots could not shake him, but his heart was suddenly filled with melancholy for some special reason and he felt that. He stood still and suddenly wondered, "Why am I sad even to dejection?" and immediately grasped with surprise that his sudden sadness was due to a very small and special cause. In the crowd thronging at the entrance to the cell, he had noticed Alyosha and he remembered that he had felt at once a pang at heart on seeing him. "Can that boy mean so much to my heart now?" he asked himself, wondering.

At that moment Alyosha passed him, hurrying away, but not in the direction of the church. Their eyes met. Alyosha quickly turned away his

---

*When a monk's body is carried out from the cell to the church and from the church to the graveyard, the canticle "What earthly joy . . ." is sung. If the deceased was a priest as well as a monk the canticle "Our Helper and Defender" is sung instead (Dostoevsky's note).

eyes and dropped them to the ground, and from the boy's look alone, Father Païssy guessed what a great change was taking place in him at that moment.

"Have you, too, fallen into temptation?" cried Father Païssy. "Can you be with those of little faith?" he added mournfully.

Alyosha stood still and gazed vaguely at Father Païssy, but quickly turned his eyes away again and again looked on the ground. He stood sideways and did not turn his face to Father Païssy, who watched him attentively.

"Where are you hastening? The bell calls to service," he asked again, but again Alyosha gave no answer.

"Are you leaving the hermitage? What, without asking leave, without asking a blessing?"

Alyosha suddenly gave a wry smile, cast a strange, very strange, look at the Father to whom his former guide, the former sovereign of his heart and mind, his beloved elder, had confided him as he lay dying. And suddenly, still without speaking, waved his hand, as though not caring even to be respectful, and with rapid steps walked towards the gates away from the hermitage.

"You will come back again!" murmured Father Païssy, looking after him with sorrowful surprise.

2

A CRITICAL MOMENT

FATHER PAÏSSY, of course, was not wrong when he decided that his "dear boy" would come back again. Perhaps indeed, to some extent, he penetrated with insight into the true meaning of Alyosha's spiritual condition. Yet I must frankly own that it would be very difficult for me to give a clear account of that strange, vague moment in the life of the young hero I love so much. To Father Païssy's sorrowful question, "Are you too with those of little faith?" I could of course confidently answer for Alyosha no, he is not with those of little faith. Quite the contrary. Indeed, all his trouble came from the fact that he was of great faith. But still the trouble was there and was so agonising that even long afterwards Alyosha thought of that sorrowful day as one of the bitterest and most fatal days of his life. If the question is asked: "Could all his grief and disturbance have been only due to the fact that his elder's body had shown signs of premature decomposition instead of at once performing miracles?" I must answer without beating about the bush, "Yes, it certainly was." I would only beg the reader not to be in too great a hurry to laugh at my young hero's pure

heart. I am far from intending to apologise for him or to justify his innocent faith on the ground of his youth, or the little progress he had made in
his studies, or any such reason. I must declare, on the contrary, that I have
genuine respect for the qualities of his heart. No doubt a youth who received impressions cautiously, whose love was lukewarm, and whose mind
was too prudent for his age and so of little value, such a young man might,
I admit, have avoided what happened to my hero. But in some cases it is
really more creditable to be carried away by an emotion, however unreasonable, which springs from a great love, than to be unmoved. And this is
even truer in youth, for a young man who is always sensible is to be suspected and is of little worth—that's my opinion!

"But," reasonable people will exclaim perhaps, "every young man cannot believe in such a superstition and your hero is no model for others."

To this I reply again, yes! my hero had faith, a faith holy and steadfast,
but still I am not going to apologise for him.

Though I declared above, and perhaps too hastily, that I should not explain or justify my hero, I see that some explanation is necessary for the
understanding of the rest of my story. Let me say then, it was not a question of miracles. There was no frivolous and impatient expectation of miracles in his mind. And Alyosha needed no miracles at the time, for the
triumph of some preconceived idea—oh no, not at all—what he saw before all was one figure—the figure of his beloved elder, the figure of that
holy man whom he revered with such adoration. The fact is that all the
love that lay concealed in his pure young heart for everyone and everything had, for the past year, been concentrated—and perhaps wrongly
so—on one being, his beloved elder. It is true that being had for so long
been accepted by him as his ideal, that all his young strength and energy
could not but turn towards that ideal, even to the forgetting at the moment
"of every one and everything." He remembered afterwards how, on that
terrible day, he had entirely forgotten his brother Dmitri, about whom he
had been so anxious and troubled the day before; he had forgotten too to
take the two hundred roubles to Ilusha's father, though he had so warmly
intended to do so the preceding evening. But again it was not miracles he
needed but only "the higher justice" which had been in his belief outraged
by the blow that had so suddenly and cruelly wounded his heart. And what
does it signify that this "justice" looked for by Alyosha inevitably took the
shape of miracles to be wrought immediately by the ashes of his adored
teacher? Why, every one in the monastery cherished the same thought and
the same hope, even those whose intellects Alyosha revered, Father Païssy
himself, for instance. And so Alyosha, untroubled by doubts, clothed his
dreams too in the same form as all the rest. And a whole year of life in the
monastery had formed the habit of this expectation in his heart. But it was
justice, justice, he thirsted for, not simply miracles.

And now the man who should, he believed, have been exalted above
every one in the whole world, that man, instead of receiving the glory that
was his due, was suddenly degraded and dishonoured! What for? Who had
judged him? Who could have decreed this? Those were the questions that

wrung his inexperienced and virginal heart. He could not endure without
mortification, without resentment even, that the holiest of holy men should
have been exposed to the jeering and spiteful mockery of the frivolous
crowd so inferior to him. Even had there been no miracles, had there been
nothing marvellous to justify his hopes, why this indignity, why this humiliation, why this premature decay, "in excess of nature," as the spiteful monks
said? Why this "sign from heaven," which they so triumphantly acclaimed
in company with Father Ferapont, and why did they believe they had gained
the right to acclaim it? Where is the finger of Providence? Why did Providence hide its face "at the most critical moment" (so Alyosha thought it),
as though voluntarily submitting to the blind, dumb, pitiless laws of nature?

That was why Alyosha's heart was bleeding, and, of course, as I have
said already, the sting of it all was that the man he loved above everything
on earth should be put to shame and humiliated! This murmuring may
have been shallow and unreasonable in my hero, but I repeat again for the
third time—and am prepared to admit that it might be difficult to defend
my feeling—I am glad that my hero showed himself not too reasonable at
that moment, for any man of sense will always come back to reason in time,
but, if love does not gain the upper hand in a boy's heart at such an exceptional moment, when will it? I will not, however, omit to mention something strange, which came for a time to the surface of Alyosha's mind at
this fatal and obscure moment. This new something was the harassing impression left by the conversation with Ivan, which now persistently haunted
Alyosha's mind. At this moment it haunted him. Oh, it was not that something of the fundamental, elemental, so to speak, faith of his soul had been
shaken. He loved his God and believed in Him steadfastly, though he was
suddenly murmuring against Him. Yet a vague but tormenting and evil impression left by his conversation with Ivan the day before, suddenly revived again now in his soul and seemed forcing its way to the surface of his
consciousness.

It had begun to get dusk when Rakitin, crossing the pine copse from
the hermitage to the monastery, suddenly noticed Alyosha, lying face
downwards on the ground under a tree, not moving and apparently asleep.
He went up and called him by his name.

"You here, Alexey? Can you have . . ." he began wondering but broke
off. He had meant to say, "Can you have come to this?"

Alyosha did not look at him, but from a slight movement Rakitin at
once saw that he heard and understood him.

"What's the matter?" he went on; but the surprise in his face gradually
passed into a smile that became more and more ironical.

"I say, I've been looking for you for the last two hours. You suddenly
disappeared. What are you about? What foolery is this? You might just
look at me. . . ."

Alyosha raised his head, sat up and leaned his back against the tree. He
was not crying, but there was a look of suffering and irritability in his face.
He did not look at Rakitin, however, but looked away to one side of him.

"Do you know your face is quite changed? There's none of your famous mildness to be seen in it. Are you angry with some one? Have they been ill-treating you?"

"Let me alone," said Alyosha suddenly, with a weary gesture of his hand, still looking away from him.

"Oho! So that's how we are feeling! So you can shout at people like other mortals. That is a come-down from the angels. I say, Alyosha, you have surprised me, do you hear? I mean it. It's long since I've been surprised at anything here. I always took you for an educated man. . . ."

Alyosha at last looked at him, but vaguely, as though scarcely understanding what he said.

"Can you really be so upset simply because your old man has begun to stink? You don't mean to say you seriously believed that he was going to work miracles?" exclaimed Rakitin, genuinely surprised again.

"I believed, I believe, I want to believe, and I will believe, what more do you want?" cried Alyosha irritably.

"Nothing at all, my boy. Damn it all, why no schoolboy of thirteen believes in that now. But there . . . So now you are in a temper with your God, you are rebelling against Him; He hasn't given promotion, He hasn't bestowed the order of merit! Eh, you are a set!"

Alyosha gazed a long while with his eyes half closed at Rakitin, and there was a sudden gleam in his eyes . . . but not of anger with Rakitin.

"I am not rebelling against my God; I simply 'don't accept His world.' " Alyosha suddenly smiled a forced smile.

"How do you mean, you don't accept the world?" Rakitin thought a moment over his answer. "What idiocy is this?"

Alyosha did not answer.

"Come, enough nonsense, now to business. Have you had anything to eat to-day?"

"I don't remember . . . I think I have."

"You need keeping up, to judge by your face. It makes one sorry to look at you. You didn't sleep all night either, I hear, you had a meeting in there. And then all this bobbery afterwards. Most likely you've had nothing to eat but a mouthful of holy bread. I've got some sausage in my pockets; I've brought it from the town in case of need, only you won't eat sausage. . . ."

"Give me some."

"I say! You are going it! Why, it's a regular mutiny, with barricades! Well, my boy, we must make the most of it. Come to my place . . . I shouldn't mind a drop of vodka myself, I am tired to death. Vodka is going too far for you, I suppose . . . or would you like some?"

"Give me some vodka too."

"Hullo! You surprise me, brother!" Rakitin looked at him in amazement. "Well, one way or another, vodka or sausage, that is a jolly fine chance and mustn't be missed. Come along."

Alyosha got up in silence and followed Rakitin.

"If your little brother Ivan could see this—wouldn't he be surprised! By the way, your brother Ivan set off to Moscow this morning, did you know?"

"Yes," answered Alyosha listlessly, and suddenly the image of his brother Dmitri rose before his mind. But only for a minute, and though it reminded him of something that must not be put off for a moment, some duty, some terrible obligation, even that reminder made no impression on him, did not reach his heart and instantly faded out of his mind and was forgotten. But, a long while afterwards, Alyosha remembered this.

"Your brother Ivan declared once that I was a 'liberal booby with no talents whatever.' Once you, too, could not resist letting me know I was 'dishonourable.' Well! I should like to see what your talents and sense of honour will do for you now." This phrase Rakitin finished to himself in a whisper.

"Listen!" he said aloud, "let's go by the path beyond the monastery straight to the town. H'm! I ought to go to Madame Hohlakov's by the way. Only fancy, I've written to tell her everything that happened, and would you believe it, she answered me instantly in pencil (the lady has a passion for writing notes) that 'she would never have expected *such conduct* from a man of such a reverend character as Father Zossima.' That was her very word: 'conduct.' She is angry too. Eh, you are a set! Stay!" he cried suddenly again. He suddenly stopped and taking Alyosha by the shoulder made him stop too.

"Do you know, Alyosha," he peeped inquisitively in his eyes, absorbed in a sudden new thought which had dawned on him, and though he was laughing outwardly he was evidently afraid to utter that new idea aloud, so difficult he still found it to believe in the strange and unexpected mood in which he now saw Alyosha. "Alyosha, do you know where we had better go?" he brought out at last timidly, and insinuatingly.

"I don't care . . . where you like."

"Let's go to Grushenka, eh? Will you come?" pronounced Rakitin at last, trembling with timid suspense.

"Let's go to Grushenka," Alyosha answered calmly, at once, and this prompt and calm agreement was such a surprise to Rakitin that he almost started back.

"Well! I say!" he cried in amazement, but seizing Alyosha firmly by the arm he led him along the path still dreading that he would change his mind.

They walked along in silence, Rakitin was positively afraid to talk.

"And how glad she will be, how delighted," he muttered, but lapsed into silence again. And indeed it was not to please Grushenka he was taking Alyosha to her. He was a practical person and never undertook anything without a prospect of gain for himself. His object in this case was twofold, first a revengeful desire to see "the downfall of the righteous," and Alyosha's fall "from the saints to the sinners," over which he was already gloating in his imagination, and in the second place he had in view a certain material gain for himself, of which more will be said later.

"So the critical moment has come," he thought to himself with spiteful glee, "and we shall catch it on the hop, for it's just what we want."

3

AN ONION

GRUSHENKA lived in the busiest part of the town, near the cathedral square, in a small wooden lodge in the courtyard belonging to the house of the widow Morozov. The house was a large stone building of two storeys, old and very ugly. The widow led a secluded life with her two unmarried nieces, who were also elderly women. She had no need to let her lodge, but every one knew that she had taken in Grushenka as a lodger, four years before, solely to please her kinsman, the merchant Samsonov, who was known to be the girl's protector. It was said that the jealous old man's object in placing his "favourite" with the widow Morozov was that the old woman should keep a sharp eye on her new lodger's conduct. But this sharp eye soon proved to be unnecessary, and in the end the widow Morozov seldom met Grushenka and did not worry her by looking after her in any way. It is true that four years had passed since the old man had brought the slim, delicate, shy, timid, dreamy, and sad girl of eighteen from the chief town of the province, and much had happened since then. Little was known of the girl's history in the town and that little was vague. Nothing more had been learnt during the last four years, even after many persons had become interested in the beautiful young woman into whom Agrafena Alexandrovna had meanwhile developed. There were rumours that she had been at seventeen betrayed by some one, some sort of officer, and immediately afterwards abandoned by him. The officer had gone away and afterwards married, while Grushenka had been left in poverty and disgrace. It was said, however, that though Grushenka had been raised from destitution by the old man, Samsonov, she came of a respectable family belonging to the clerical class, that she was the daughter of a deacon or something of the sort.

And now after four years the sensitive, injured and pathetic little orphan had become a plump, rosy beauty of the Russian type, a woman of bold and determined character, proud and insolent. She had a good head for business, was acquisitive, saving and careful, and by fair means or foul had succeeded, it was said, in amassing a little fortune. There was only one point on which all were agreed. Grushenka was not easily to be approached and except her aged protector there had not been one man who could boast of her favours during those four years. It was a positive fact, for there had been a good many, especially during the last two years, who had attempted to obtain those favours. But all their efforts had been in vain and some of these suitors had been forced to beat an undignified and even comic retreat, owing to the firm and ironical resistance they met from the strong-willed young person. It was known too that the young person had, especially of late, been given to what is called "speculation," and that she had shown marked abilities in that direction, so that many people began to say that she was no better than a Jew. It was not that she lent money on interest, but it was known, for instance, that she had for some time past, in partnership with old Karamazov, actually invested in the purchase of bad debts for a trifle, a tenth of their nominal value, and afterwards had made out of them ten times their value.

The old widower Samsonov, a man of large fortune, was stingy and merciless. He tyrannised over his grown-up sons, but, for the last year during which he had been ill and lost the use of his swollen legs, he had fallen greatly under the influence of his protégée, whom he had at first kept strictly and in humble surroundings "on Lenten fare" as the wits said at the time. But Grushenka had succeeded in emancipating herself, while she established in him a boundless belief in her fidelity. The old man, now long since dead, had had a large business in his day and was also a noteworthy character, miserly and hard as flint. Though Grushenka's hold upon him was so strong that he could not live without her (it had been so especially for the last two years), he did not settle any considerable fortune on her and would not have been moved to do so, if she had threatened to leave him. But he had presented her with a small sum, and even that was a surprise to every one when it became known.

"You are a wench with brains," he said to her, when he gave her eight thousand roubles, "and you must look after yourself, but let me tell you that except your yearly allowance as before, you'll get nothing more from me to the day of my death, and I'll leave you nothing in my will either."

And he kept his word; he died and left everything to his sons, whom, with their wives and children, he had treated all his life as servants. Grushenka was not even mentioned in his will. All this became known afterwards. He helped Grushenka with his advice to increase her capital and put business in her way.

When Fyodor Pavlovitch, who first came into contact with Grushenka over a piece of speculation, ended to his own surprise by falling madly in love with her, old Samsonov, gravely ill as he was, was immensely amused. It is remarkable that throughout their whole acquaintance Grushenka was absolutely and spontaneously open with the old man, and he seems to have been the only person in the world with whom she was so. Of late, when Dmitri too had come on the scene with his love, the old man left off laughing. On the contrary, he once gave Grushenka a stern and earnest piece of advice.

"If you have to choose between the two, father or son, you'd better choose the old man, if only you make sure the old scoundrel will marry you and settle some fortune on you beforehand. But don't keep on with the captain, you'll get no good out of that."

These were the very words of the old profligate, who felt already that his death was not far off and who actually died five months later.

I will note, too, in passing that although many in our town knew of the grotesque and monstrous rivalry of the Karamazovs, father and son, the object of which was Grushenka, scarcely any one understood what really underlay her attitude to both of them. Even Grushenka's two servants (after the catastrophe of which we will speak later) testified in court that she received Dmitri Fyodorovitch simply from fear because "he threatened to murder her." These servants were an old cook, invalidish and almost deaf, who came from Grushenka's old home, and her granddaughter, a smart young girl of twenty, who performed the duties of a maid. Grushenka lived very economically and her surroundings were anything but luxurious. Her lodge consisted of three rooms furnished with mahogany furniture in the fashion of 1820, belonging to her landlady.

It was quite dark when Rakitin and Alyosha entered her rooms, yet they were not lighted up. Grushenka was lying down in her drawing-room on the big, hard, clumsy sofa, with a mahogany back. The sofa was covered with shabby and ragged leather. Under her head she had two white down pillows taken from her bed. She was lying stretched out motionless on her back with her hands behind her head. She was dressed as though expecting some one, in a black silk dress, with a dainty lace fichu on her head, which was very becoming. Over her shoulders was thrown a lace shawl pinned with a massive gold brooch. She certainly was expecting some one. She lay as though impatient and weary, her face rather pale and her lips and eyes hot, restlessly tapping the arm of the sofa with the tip of her right foot. The appearance of Rakitin and Alyosha caused a slight excitement. From the hall they could hear Grushenka leap up from the sofa and cry out in a frightened voice, "Who's there?" But the maid met the visitors and at once called back to her mistress.

"It's not he, it's nothing, only other visitors."

"What can be the matter?" muttered Rakitin, leading Alyosha into the drawing-room.

Grushenka was standing by the sofa as though still alarmed. A thick coil of her dark brown hair escaped from its lace covering and fell on her right shoulder, but she did not notice it and did not put it back till she had gazed at her visitors and recognised them.

"Ah, it's you, Rakitin? You quite frightened me. Whom have you brought? Who is this with you? Good heavens, you have brought him!" she exclaimed, recognising Alyosha.

"Do send for candles!" said Rakitin, with the free-and-easy air of a most intimate friend, who is privileged to give orders in the house.

"Candles . . . of course, candles . . . Fenya, fetch him a candle. . . . Well, you have chosen a moment to bring him!" she exclaimed again, nodding towards Alyosha and turning to the looking-glass she began quickly fastening up her hair with both hands. She seemed displeased.

"Haven't I managed to please you?" asked Rakitin, instantly almost offended.

"You frightened me, Rakitin, that's what it is." Grushenka turned with a smile to Alyosha. "Don't be afraid of me, my dear Alyosha, you can't think how glad I am to see you, my unexpected visitor. But you frightened me, Rakitin, I thought it was Mitya breaking in. You see, I deceived him just now, I made him promise to believe me and I told him a lie. I told him that I was going to spend the evening with my old man, Kuzma Kuzmitch, and should be there till late counting up his money. I always spend one whole evening a week with him making up his accounts. We lock ourselves in and he counts on the reckoning beads while I sit and put things down in the book. I am the only person he trusts. Mitya believes that I am there, but I came back and have been sitting locked in here, expecting some news. How was it Fenya let you in? Fenya, Fenya run out to the gate, open it and look about whether the captain is to be seen! Perhaps he is hiding and spying, I am dreadfully frightened."

"There's no one there, Agrafena Alexandrovna, I've just looked out, I keep running to peep through the crack, I am in fear and trembling myself."

"Are the shutters fastened, Fenya? And we must draw the curtains— that's better!" She drew the heavy curtains herself. "He'd rush in at once if he saw a light. I am afraid of your brother Mitya to-day, Alyosha."

Grushenka spoke aloud, and, though she was alarmed, she seemed very happy about something.

"Why are you so afraid of Mitya to-day?" inquired Rakitin. "I should have thought you were not timid with him, you'd twist him round your little finger."

"I tell you, I am expecting news, priceless news, so I don't want Mitya at all. And he didn't believe, I feel he didn't, that I should stay at Kuzma Kuzmitch's. He must be in his ambush now, behind Fyodor Pavlovitch's, in the garden, watching for me. And if he's there, he won't come here, so much the better! But I really have been to Kuzma Kuzmitch's, Mitya escorted me there. I told him I should stay there till midnight, and I asked him to be sure to come at midnight to fetch me home. He went away and I sat ten minutes with Kuzma Kuzmitch and came back here again. Ugh, I was afraid, I ran for fear of meeting him."

"And why are you so dressed up? What a curious cap you've got on!"

"How curious you are yourself, Rakitin! I tell you, I am expecting a message. If the message comes, I shall fly, I shall gallop away and you will see no more of me. That's why I am dressed up, so as to be ready."

"And where are you flying to?"

"If you know too much, you'll get old too soon."

"Upon my word! You are highly delighted . . . I've never seen you like this before. You are dressed up as if you were going to a ball." Rakitin looked her up and down.

"Much you know about balls."

"And do you know much about them?"

"I have seen a ball. The year before last, Kuzma Kuzmitch's son was married and I looked on from the gallery. Do you suppose I want to be talking to you, Rakitin, while a prince like this is standing here. Such a visitor! Alyosha, my dear boy, I gaze at you and can't believe my eyes. Good heavens, can you have come here to see me! To tell you the truth I never had a thought of seeing you and I didn't think that you would ever come and see me. Though this is not the moment now, I am awfully glad to see you. Sit down on the sofa, here, that's right, my bright young moon. I really can't take it in even now. . . . Eh, Rakitin, if only you had brought him yesterday or the day before! But I am glad as it is! Perhaps it's better he has come now, at such a moment, and not the day before yesterday."

She gaily sat down beside Alyosha on the sofa, looking at him with positive delight. And she really was glad, she was not lying when she said so. Her eyes glowed, her lips laughed, but it was a good-natured merry laugh. Alyosha had not expected to see such a kind expression in her face. . . . He had hardly met her till the day before, he had formed an alarming idea of her, and had been horribly distressed the day before by the spiteful and treacherous trick she had played on Katerina Ivanovna. He was greatly surprised to find her now altogether different from what he had expected. And, crushed as he was by his own sorrow, his eyes involuntarily rested on her with attention. Her whole manner seemed changed for the better since yesterday, there was scarcely any trace of that mawkish sweetness in her speech, of that voluptuous softness in her movements. Everything was simple and good-natured, her gestures were rapid, direct, confiding, but she was greatly excited.

"Dear me, how everything comes together to-day," she chattered on again. "And why I am so glad to see you, Alyosha, I couldn't say myself! If you ask me, I couldn't tell you."

"Come, don't you know why you're glad?" said Rakitin, grinning. "You used to be always pestering me to bring him, you'd some object, I suppose."

"I had a different object once, but now that's over, this is not the moment. I say, I want you to have something nice. I am so good-natured now. You sit down, too, Rakitin, why are you standing? You've sat down already? There's no fear of Rakitin's forgetting to look after himself. Look, Alyosha, he's sitting there opposite us, so offended that I didn't ask him to sit down before you. Ugh, Rakitin is such a one to take offence!" laughed Grushenka. "Don't be angry, Rakitin, I'm kind to-day. Why are you so depressed, Alyosha, are you afraid of me?" she peeped into his eyes with merry mockery.

"He's sad. The promotion has not been given," boomed Rakitin.

"What promotion?"

"His elder stinks."

"What? You are talking some nonsense, you want to say something nasty. Be quiet, you stupid! Let me sit on your knee, Alyosha, like this." She suddenly skipped forward and jumped, laughing, on his knee, like a nestling kitten, with her right arm about his neck. "I'll cheer you up, my pious boy. Yes, really, will you let me sit on your knee, you won't be angry? If you tell me, I'll get off?"

Alyosha did not speak. He sat afraid to move, he heard her words, "If you tell me, I'll get off," but he did not answer. But there was nothing in his heart such as Rakitin, for instance, watching him malignantly from his corner, might have expected or fancied. The great grief in his heart swallowed up every sensation that might have been aroused, and, if only he could have thought clearly at that moment, he would have realised that he had now the strongest armour to protect him from every lust and temptation. Yet in spite of the vague irresponsiveness of his spiritual condition and the sorrow that overwhelmed him, he could not help wondering at a new and strange sensation in his heart. This woman, this "dreadful" woman, had no terror for him now, none of that terror that had stirred in his soul at any passing thought of woman. On the contrary, this woman, dreaded above all women, sitting now on his knee, holding him in her arms, aroused in him now a quite different, unexpected, peculiar feeling, a feeling of the intensest and purest interest without a trace of fear, of his former terror. That was what instinctively surprised him.

"You've talked nonsense enough," cried Rakitin, "you'd much better give us some champagne. You owe it me, you know you do!"

"Yes, I really do. Do you know, Alyosha, I promised him champagne on the top of everything, if he'd bring you? I'll have some too! Fenya, Fenya, bring us the bottle Mitya left! Look sharp! Though I am so stingy, I'll stand a bottle, not for you, Rakitin, you're a toadstool, but he is a falcon! And though my heart is full of something very different, so be it, I'll drink with you. I long for some dissipation."

"But what is the matter with you? And what is this message may I ask, or is it a secret?" Rakitin put in inquisitively, doing his best to pretend not to notice the snubs that were being continually aimed at him.

"Ech, it's not a secret, and you know it, too," Grushenka said, in a voice suddenly anxious, turning her head towards Rakitin, and drawing a little away from Alyosha, though she still sat on his knee with her arm round his neck. "My officer is coming, Rakitin, my officer is coming."

"I heard he was coming, but is he so near?"

"He is at Mokroe now, he'll send a messenger from there, so he wrote. I got a letter from him to-day. I am expecting the messenger every minute."

"You don't say so! Why at Mokroe?"

"That's a long story, I've told you enough."

"Mitya'll be up to something now—I say! Does he know or doesn't he?"

"He know! Of course he doesn't. If he knew, there would be murder. But I am not afraid of that now, I am not afraid of his knife. Be quiet, Rakitin, don't remind me of Dmitri Fyodorovitch, he has bruised my heart. And I don't want to think of that at this moment. I can think of Alyosha here, I can look at Alyosha . . . smile at me, dear, cheer up, smile at my foolishness, at my pleasure. . . . Ah, he's smiling, he's smiling! How kindly he looks at me! And you know, Alyosha, I've been thinking all this time you were angry with me, because of the day before yesterday, because of that young lady. I was a cur, that's the truth. . . . But it's a good thing it happened so. It was a horrid thing, but a good thing too." Grushenka smiled dreamily, and a little cruel line showed in her smile. "Mitya told me that she screamed out that I 'ought to be flogged.' I did insult her dreadfully. She sent for me, she wanted to make a conquest of me, to win me over with her chocolate. . . . No, it's a good thing it did end like that." She smiled again. "But I am still afraid of your being angry."

"Yes, that's really true," Rakitin put in suddenly with genuine surprise. "Alyosha, she is really afraid of a chicken like you."

"He is a chicken to you, Rakitin ... because you've no conscience, that's what it is! You see, I love him with all my soul, that's how it is! Alyosha, do you believe I love you with all my soul?"

"Ah, you shameless woman! She is making you a declaration, Alexey!"

"Well, what of it, I love him!"

"And what about your officer? And the priceless message from Mokroe?"

"That is quite different."

"That's a woman's way of looking at it!"

"Don't you make me angry, Rakitin." Grushenka caught him up hotly. "This is quite different. I love Alyosha in a different way. It's true, Alyosha, I had sly designs on you before. For I am a horrid, violent creature. But at other times I've looked upon you, Alyosha, as my conscience. I've kept thinking 'how any one like that must despise a nasty thing like me.' I thought that the day before yesterday, as I ran home from the young lady's. I have thought of you a long time in that way, Alyosha, and Mitya knows, I've talked to him about it. Mitya understands. Would you believe it, I sometimes look at you and feel ashamed, utterly ashamed of myself. . . . And how, and since when, I began to think about you like that, I can't say, I don't remember. . . ."

Fenya came in and put a tray with an uncorked bottle and three glasses of champagne on the table.

"Here's the champagne!" cried Rakitin. "You're excited, Agrafena Alexandrovna, and not yourself. When you've had a glass of champagne, you'll be ready to dance. Eh, they can't even do that properly," he added, looking at the bottle. "The old woman's poured it out in the kitchen, and the bottle's been brought in warm and without a cork. Well, let me have some, anyway."

He went up to the table, took a glass, emptied it at one gulp and poured himself out another.

"One doesn't often stumble upon champagne," he said, licking his lips. "Now, Alyosha, take a glass, show what you can do! What shall we drink to? The gates of paradise? Take a glass, Grushenka, you drink to the gates of paradise, too."

"What gates of paradise?"

She took a glass, Alyosha took his, tasted it and put it back.

"No, I'd better not," he smiled gently.

"And you bragged!" cried Rakitin.

"Well, if so, I won't either," chimed in Grushenka, "I really don't want any. You can drink the whole bottle alone, Rakitin. If Alyosha has some, I will."

"What touching sentimentality!" said Rakitin tauntingly, "and she's sitting on his knee, too! He's got something to grieve over, but what's the matter with you? He is rebelling against his God and ready to eat sausage. . . ."

"How so?"

"His elder died to-day, Father Zossima, the saint."

"So Father Zossima is dead," cried Grushenka. "Good God, I did not know!" She crossed herself devoutly. "Goodness, what have I been doing, sitting on his knee like this at such a moment!" She started up as though in dismay, instantly slipped off his knee and sat down on the sofa.

Alyosha bent a long wondering look upon her and a light seemed to dawn in his face.

"Rakitin," he said suddenly, in a firm and loud voice; "don't taunt me with having rebelled against God. I don't want to feel angry with you, so you must be kinder, too. I've lost a treasure such as you have never had, and you cannot judge me now. You had much better look at her—do you see how she has pity on me? I came here to find a wicked soul—I felt drawn to evil because I was base and evil myself, and I've found a true sister, I have found a treasure—a loving heart. She had pity on me just now. . . . Agrafena Alexandrovna, I am speaking of you. You've raised my soul from the depths."

Alyosha's lips were quivering and he caught his breath.

"She has saved you, it seems," laughed Rakitin spitefully. "And she meant to get you in her clutches, do you realise that?"

"Stay, Rakitin." Grushenka jumped up. "Hush, both of you. Now I'll tell you all about it. Hush, Alyosha, your words make me ashamed, for I am bad and not good—that's what I am. And you hush, Rakitin, because you are telling lies. I had the low idea of trying to get him in my clutches, but now you are lying, now it's all different. And don't let me hear anything more from you, Rakitin."

All this Grushenka said with extreme emotion.

"They are both crazy," said Rakitin, looking at them with amazement. "I feel as though I were in a madhouse. They're both getting so feeble they'll begin crying in a minute."

"I shall begin to cry, I shall," repeated Grushenka. "He called me his sister and I shall never forget that. Only let me tell you, Rakitin, though I am bad, I did give away an onion."

"An onion? Hang it all, you really are crazy."

Rakitin wondered at their enthusiasm. He was aggrieved and annoyed, though he might have reflected that each of them was just passing through a spiritual crisis such as does not come often in a lifetime. But though Rakitin was very sensitive about everything that concerned himself, he was very obtuse as regards the feelings and sensations of others—partly from his youth and inexperience, partly from his intense egoism.

"You see, Alyosha," Grushenka turned to him with a nervous laugh. "I was boasting when I told Rakitin I had given away an onion, but it's not to boast I tell you about it. It's only a story, but it's a nice story. I used to hear it when I was a child from Matryona, my cook, who is still with me. It's like this. Once upon a time there was a peasant woman and a very wicked woman she was. And she died and did not leave a single good deed behind. The devils caught her and plunged her into the lake of fire. So her guardian angel stood and wondered what good deed of hers he could remember to tell to God; 'she once pulled up an onion in her garden,' said he, 'and gave it to a beggar woman.' And God answered: 'You take that onion then, hold it out to her in the lake, and let her take hold and be pulled out. And if you can pull her out of the lake, let her come to Paradise, but if the onion breaks, then the woman must stay where she is.' The angel ran to the woman and held out the onion to her; 'Come,' said he, 'catch hold and I'll pull you out.' And he began cautiously pulling her out. He had just pulled her right out, when the other sinners in the lake, seeing how she was being drawn out, began catching hold of her so as to be pulled out with her. But she was a very wicked woman and she began kicking them. 'I'm to be pulled out, not you. It's my onion, not yours.' As soon as she said that, the onion broke. And the woman fell into the lake and she is burning there to this day. So the angel wept and went away.[1] So that's the story, Alyosha; I know it by heart, for I am that wicked woman myself. I boasted to Rakitin that I had given away an onion, but to you I'll say: 'I've done nothing but give away one onion all my life, that's the only good deed I've done.' So don't praise me, Alyosha, don't think me good, I am bad, I am a wicked woman and you make me ashamed if you praise me. Eh, I must confess everything. Listen, Alyosha. I was so anxious to get hold of you that I promised Rakitin twenty-five roubles if he would bring you to me. Stay, Rakitin, wait!"

She went with rapid steps to the table, opened a drawer, pulled out a purse and took from it a twenty-five rouble note.

"What nonsense! What nonsense!" cried Rakitin, disconcerted.

"Take it. Rakitin, I owe it you, there's no fear of your refusing it, you asked for it yourself." And she threw the note to him.

"Likely I should refuse it," boomed Rakitin, obviously abashed, but carrying off his confusion with a swagger. "That will come in very handy; fools are made for wise men's profit."

"And now hold your tongue, Rakitin, what I am going to say now is not for your ears. Sit down in that corner and keep quiet. You don't like us, so hold your tongue."

"What should I like you for?" Rakitin snarled, not concealing his ill-humour. He put the twenty-five rouble note in his pocket and he felt ashamed at Alyosha's seeing it. He had reckoned on receiving his payment later, without Alyosha's knowing of it, and now, feeling ashamed, he lost his temper. Till that moment he had thought it discreet not to contradict Grushenka too flatly in spite of her snubbing, since he had something to get out of her. But now he, too, was angry:

"One loves people for some reason, but what have either of you done for me?"

"You should love people without a reason, as Alyosha does."

"How does he love you? How has he shown it, that you make such a fuss about it?"

Grushenka was standing in the middle of the room; she spoke with heat and there were hysterical notes in her voice.

"Hush, Rakitin, you know nothing about us! And don't dare to speak to me like that again. How dare you be so familiar? Sit in that corner and be quiet, as though you were my footman. And now, Alyosha, I'll tell you

the whole truth, that you may see what a wretch I am! I am not talking to
Rakitin, but to you. I wanted to ruin you, Alyosha, that's the holy truth; I
quite meant to. I wanted to so much, that I bribed Rakitin to bring you. And
why did I want to do such a thing? You knew nothing about it, Alyosha,
you turned away from me, if you passed me, you dropped your eyes. And
I've looked at you a hundred times before to-day, I began asking every
one about you. Your face haunted my heart. 'He despises me,' I thought,
'he won't even look at me.' And I felt it so much at last that I wondered at
myself for being so frightened of a boy. I'll get him in my clutches and laugh
at him. I was full of spite and anger. Would you believe it, nobody here
dares talk or think of coming to Agrafena Alexandrovna with any evil purpose. Old Kuzma is the only man I have anything to do with here, I was
bound and sold to him, Satan brought us together, but there has been no
one else. But looking at you, I thought, I'll get him in my clutches and laugh
at him. You see what a spiteful cur I am, and you called me your sister! And
now that man who wronged me has come; I sit here waiting for a message
from him. And do you know what that man has been to me? Five years
ago, when Kuzma brought me here, I used to shut myself up, that no one
might have sight or sound of me. I was a silly slip of a girl; I used to sit here
sobbing, I used to lie awake all night, thinking, 'Where is he now, the man
who wronged me? He is laughing at me with another woman, most likely.
If only I could see him, if I could meet him again, I'd pay him out, I'd pay
him out!' At night I used to lie sobbing into my pillow in the dark, and I
used to brood over it, I used to tear my heart on purpose and gloat over
my anger. 'I'll pay him out, I'll pay him out!' That's what I used to cry out
in the dark. And when I suddenly thought that I should really do nothing
to him, and that he was laughing at me then, or perhaps had utterly forgotten me, I would fling myself on the floor, melt into helpless tears, and lie
there shaking till dawn. In the morning I would get up more spiteful than
a dog, ready to tear the whole world to pieces. And then what do you
think? I began saving money, I became hard-hearted, grew stout—grew
wiser, would you say? No, no one in the whole world sees it, no one knows
it, but when night comes on, I sometimes lie as I did five years ago, when I
was a silly girl, clenching my teeth and crying all night, thinking: 'I'll pay
him out, I'll pay him out!' Do you hear? Well then, now you understand
me. A month ago a letter came to me—he was coming, he was a widower,
he wanted to see me. It took my breath away, then I suddenly thought: 'If
he comes and whistles to call me, I shall creep back to him like a beaten
dog.' I couldn't believe myself. Am I so abject? Shall I run to him or not?
And I've been in such a rage with myself all this month that I am worse
than I was five years ago. Do you see now, Alyosha, what a violent, vindictive creature I am? I have shown you the whole truth! I played with Mitya
to keep me from running to that other. Hush, Rakitin, it's not for you
to judge me, I am not speaking to you. Before you came in, I was lying
here waiting, brooding, deciding my whole future life and you can never
know what was in my heart. Yes, Alyosha, tell your young lady not to be
angry with me for what happened the day before yesterday. . . . Nobody in

the whole world knows what I am going through now, and no one ever can know. . . . For perhaps I shall take a knife with me to-day. I can't make up my mind. . . ."

And at this "tragic" phrase Grushenka broke down, hid her face in her hands, flung herself on the sofa pillows, and sobbed like a little child.

Alyosha got up and went to Rakitin.

"Misha," he said, "don't be angry. She wounded you, but don't be angry. You heard what she said just now? You mustn't ask too much of human endurance, one must be merciful."

Alyosha said this at the instinctive prompting of his heart. He felt obliged to speak and he turned to Rakitin. If Rakitin had not been there, he would have spoken to the air. But Rakitin looked at him ironically and Alyosha stopped short.

"You were so primed up with your elder's teaching last night that now you have to let it off on me, Alexey, man of God!" said Rakitin, with a smile of hatred.

"Don't laugh, Rakitin, don't smile, don't talk of the dead—he was better than any one in the world!" cried Alyosha, with tears in his voice. "I didn't speak to you as a judge but as the lowest of the judged. What am I beside her? I came here seeking my ruin, and said to myself, 'what does it matter?' in my cowardliness, but she, after five years in torment, as soon as any one says a word from the heart to her—it makes her forget everything, forgive everything, in her tears! The man who has wronged her has come back, he sends for her and she forgives him everything, and hastens joyfully to meet him and she won't take a knife with her. She won't! No, I am not like that. I don't know whether you are Misha, but I am not like that. It's a lesson to me. . . . She is more loving than we. . . . Have you heard her speak before of what she has just told us? No, you haven't; if you had, you'd have understood her long ago . . . and the person insulted the day before yesterday must forgive her, too! She will, when she knows . . . and she shall know. . . . This soul is not yet at peace with itself, one must be tender with it . . . there may be a treasure in that soul. . . ."

Alyosha stopped, because he caught his breath. In spite of his ill-humour Rakitin looked at him with astonishment. He had never expected such a tirade from the gentle Alyosha.

"She's found some one to plead her cause! Why, are you in love with her? Agrafena Alexandrovna, our monk's really in love with you, you've made a conquest!" he cried, with a coarse laugh.

Grushenka lifted her head from the pillow and looked at Alyosha with a tender smile shining on her tear-stained face.

"Let him alone, Alyosha, my cherub, you see what he is, he is not a person for you to speak to. Mihail Ospovitch," she turned to Rakitin, "I meant to beg your pardon for being rude to you, but now I don't want to. Alyosha, come to me, sit down here." She beckoned to him with a happy smile. "That's right, sit here. Tell me," she took him by the hand and peeped into his face, smiling, "tell me, do I love that man or not? the man who wronged me, do I love him or not? Before you came, I lay here in the dark, asking my heart whether I loved him. Decide for me, Alyosha, the time has come, it shall be as you say. Am I to forgive him or not?"

"But you have forgiven him already," said Alyosha, smiling.

"Yes, I really have forgiven him," Grushenka murmured thoughtfully. "What an abject heart! To my abject heart!" She snatched up a glass from the table, emptied it at a gulp, lifted it in the air and flung it on the floor. The glass broke with a crash. A little cruel line came into her smile.

"Perhaps I haven't forgiven him, though," she said, with a sort of menace in her voice, and she dropped her eyes to the ground as though she were talking to herself. "Perhaps my heart is only getting ready to forgive. I shall struggle with my heart. You see, Alyosha, I've grown to love my tears in these five years.... Perhaps I only love my resentment, not him...."

"Well, I shouldn't care to be in his shoes," hissed Rakitin.

"Well, you won't be, Rakitin, you'll never be in his shoes. You shall black my shoes, Rakitin, that's the place you are fit for. You'll never get a woman like me ... and he won't either, perhaps...."

"Won't he? Then why are you dressed up like that?" said Rakitin, with a venomous sneer.

"Don't taunt me with dressing up, Rakitin, you don't know all that is in my heart! If I choose to tear off my finery, I'll tear it off at once, this minute," she cried in a resonant voice. "You don't know what that finery is for, Rakitin! Perhaps I shall see him and say: 'Have you ever seen me look like this before?' He left me a thin, consumptive cry-baby of seventeen. I'll sit by him, fascinate him and work him up. 'Do you see what I am like now?' I'll say to him; 'well, and that's enough for you, my dear sir, there's many a slip twixt the cup and the lip!' That may be what the finery is for, Rakitin." Grushenka finished with a malicious laugh. "I'm violent and resentful, Alyosha, I'll tear off my finery, I'll destroy my beauty, I'll scorch my face, slash it with a knife, and turn beggar. If I choose, I won't go anywhere now to see any one. If I choose, I'll send Kuzma back all he has ever given me, to-morrow, and all his money and I'll go out charing for the rest of my life. You think I wouldn't do it, Rakitin, that I would not dare to do it? I would, I would, I could do it directly, only don't exasperate me ... and I'll send him about his business, I'll snap my fingers in his face, he shall never see me again!"

She uttered the last words in an hysterical scream, but broke down again, hid her face in her hands, buried it in the pillow and shook with sobs.

Rakitin got up.

"It's time we were off," he said, "it's late, we shall be shut out of the monastery."

Grushenka leapt up from her place.

"Surely you don't want to go, Alyosha!" she cried, in mournful surprise. "What are you doing to me? You've stirred up my feeling, tortured me, and now you'll leave me to face this night alone!"

"He can hardly spend the night with you! Though if he wants to, let him! I'll go alone," Rakitin scoffed jeeringly.

"Hush, evil tongue!" Grushenka cried angrily at him; "you never said such words to me as he has come to say."

"What has he said to you so special?" asked Rakitin irritably.

"I can't say, I don't know. I don't know what he said to me, it went straight to my heart; he has wrung my heart. . . . He is the first, the only one who has pitied me, that's what it is. Why did you not come before, you angel?" She fell on her knees before him as though in a sudden frenzy. "I've been waiting all my life for some one like you, I knew that some one like you would come and forgive me. I believed that, nasty as I am, some one would really love me, not only with a shameful love!"

"What have I done to you?" answered Alyosha bending over her with a tender smile, and gently taking her by the hands; "I only gave you an onion, nothing but a tiny little onion, that was all!"

He was moved to tears himself as he said it. At that moment there was a sudden noise in the passage, some one came into the hall. Grushenka jumped up seeming greatly alarmed. Fenya ran noisily into the room, crying out:

"Mistress, mistress darling, a messenger has galloped up," she cried, breathless and joyful. "A carriage from Mokroe for you, Timofey the driver, with three horses, they are just putting in fresh horses. . . . A letter, here's the letter, mistress."

A letter was in her hand and she waved it in the air all the while she talked. Grushenka snatched the letter from her and carried it to the candle. It was only a note, a few lines. She read it in one instant.

"He has sent for me," she cried, her face white and distorted, with a wan smile; "he whistles! Crawl back, little dog!"

But only for one instant she stood as though hesitating; suddenly the blood rushed to her head and sent a glow to her cheeks.

"I will go," she cried; "five years of my life! Good-bye! Good-bye, Alyosha, my fate is sealed. Go, go, leave me all of you, don't let me see you again! Grushenka is flying to a new life. . . . Don't you remember evil against me either, Rakitin. I may be going to my death! Ugh! I feel as though I were drunk!"

She suddenly left them and ran into her bedroom.

"Well, she has no thoughts for us now!" grumbled Rakitin. "Let's go, or we may hear that feminine shriek again. I am sick of all these tears and cries."

Alyosha mechanically let himself be led out. In the yard stood a covered cart. Horses were being taken out of the shafts, men were running to and fro with a lantern. Three fresh horses were being led in at the open gate. But when Alyosha and Rakitin reached the bottom of the steps, Grushenka's bedroom window was suddenly opened and she called in a ringing voice after Alyosha:

"Alyosha, give my greetings to your brother Mitya and tell him not to remember evil against me, though I have brought him misery. And tell him too in my words: 'Grushenka has fallen to a scoundrel, and not to you, noble heart.' And add, too, that Grushenka loved him only one hour, only one short hour she loved him—so let him remember that hour all his life—say, 'Grushenka tells you to!' "

She ended in a voice full of sobs. The window was shut with a slam.

"Hm, hm!" growled Rakitin, laughing, "she murders your brother Mitya and then tells him to remember it all his life! What ferocity!"

Alyosha made no reply, he seemed not to have heard. He walked fast beside Rakitin as though in a terrible hurry. He was lost in thought and moved mechanically, Rakitin felt a sudden twinge as though he had been touched on an open wound. He had expected something quite different by bringing Grushenka and Alyosha together. Something very different from what he had hoped for had happened.

"He is a Pole, that officer of hers," he began again, restraining himself; "and indeed he is not an officer at all now. He served in the customs in Siberia, somewhere on the Chinese frontier, some puny little beggar of a Pole, I expect. Lost his job, they say. He's heard now that Grushenka's saved a little money, so he's turned up again—that's the explanation of the mystery."

Again Alyosha seemed not to hear. Rakitin could not control himself.

"Well, so you've saved the sinner?" he laughed spitefully. "Have you turned the Magdalene into the true path? Driven out the seven devils,* eh? So you see the miracles you were looking out for just now have come to pass!"

"Hush, Rakitin," Alyosha answered, with an aching heart.

"So you despise me now for those twenty-five roubles? I've sold my friend, you think. But you are not Christ, you know, and I am not Judas."

"Oh, Rakitin, I assure you I'd forgotten about it," cried Alyosha, "you remind me of it yourself. . . ."

But this was the last straw for Rakitin.

"Damnation take you all and each of you!" he cried suddenly, "why the devil did I take you up? I don't want to know you from this time forward. Go alone, there's your road!"

And he turned abruptly into another street, leaving Alyosha alone in the dark. Alyosha came out of the town and walked across the fields to the monastery.

---

*See the Bible, Mark 16:9, Luke 8:2.

4

CANA OF GALILEE

IT was very late, according to the monastery ideas, when Alyosha returned to the hermitage; the door-keeper let him in by a special entrance. It had struck nine o'clock—the hour of rest and repose after a day of such agitation for all. Alyosha timidly opened the door and went into the elder's cell where his coffin was now standing. There was no one in the cell but Father Païssy, reading the Gospel in solitude over the coffin, and the young novice Porfiry, who, exhausted by the previous night's conversation and the disturbing incidents of the day, was sleeping the deep sound sleep of youth on the floor of the other room. Though Father Païssy heard Alyosha come in, he did not even look in his direction. Alyosha turned to the right from the door to the corner, fell on his knees and began to pray.

His soul was overflowing but with mingled feelings; no single sensation stood out distinctly, on the contrary, one drove out another in a slow, continual rotation. But there was a sweetness in his heart and, strange to say, Alyosha was not surprised at it. Again he saw that coffin before him, the hidden dead figure so precious to him, but the weeping and poignant grief of the morning was no longer aching in his soul. As soon as he came in, he fell down before the coffin as before a holy shrine, but joy, joy was glowing in his mind and in his heart. The one window of the cell was open, the air was fresh and cool. "So the smell must have become stronger, if they opened the window," thought Alyosha. But even this thought of the smell of corruption, which had seemed to him so awful and humiliating a few hours before, no longer made him feel miserable or indignant. He began quietly praying, but he soon felt that he was praying almost mechanically. Fragments of thought floated through his soul, flashed like stars and went out again at once, to be succeeded by others. But yet there was reigning in his soul a sense of the wholeness of things—something steadfast and comforting—and he was aware of it himself. Sometimes he began praying ardently, he longed to pour out his thankfulness and love. . . .

But when he had begun to pray, he passed suddenly to something else, and sank into thought, forgetting both the prayer and what had interrupted it. He began listening to what Father Païssy was reading, but worn out with exhaustion he gradually began to doze.

"And the third day there was a marriage in Cana of Galilee;" read

Father Païssy. *"And the mother of Jesus was there; And both Jesus was called, and his disciples, to the marriage."**

"Marriage? What's that.... A marriage!" floated whirling through Alyosha's mind. "There is happiness for her, too.... She has gone to the feast.... No, she has not taken the knife.... That was only a tragic phrase.... Well ... tragic phrases should be forgiven, they must be. Tragic phrases comfort the heart.... Without them, sorrow would be too heavy for men to bear. Rakitin has gone off to the back-alley. As long as Rakitin broods over his wrongs, he will always go off to the back-alley.... But the high road.... The road is wide and straight and bright as crystal, and the sun is at the end of it.... Ah! ... What's being read? ..."

"And when they wanted wine, the mother of Jesus saith unto him; 'They have no wine' " ... Alyosha heard.

"Ah, yes, I was missing that, and I didn't want to miss it, I love that passage: it's Cana of Galilee, the first miracle.... Ah, that miracle! Ah, that sweet miracle! It was not men's grief, but their joy Christ visited, He worked His first miracle to help men's gladness.... 'He who loves men loves their gladness, too.' ... *He* was always repeating that, it was one of his leading ideas.... 'There's no living without joy,' Mitya says.... Yes, Mitya.... 'Everything that is true and good is always full of forgiveness,' he used to say that, too...."

"Jesus saith unto her, Woman, what has it to do with thee or me? Mine hour is not yet come.

His mother saith unto the servants: Whatsoever he saith unto you, do it...."

"Do it.... Gladness, the gladness of some poor, very poor, people.... Of course they were poor, since they hadn't wine enough even at a wedding.... The historians write that, in those days, the people living about the Lake of Genesareth† were the poorest that can possibly be imagined ... and another great heart, that other great being, His Mother, knew that He had come not only to make His great terrible sacrifice. She knew that His heart was open even to the simple, art-less merry-making of some obscure and unlearned people, who had warmly bidden Him to their poor wedding. 'Mine hour is not yet come,' He said, with a soft smile (He must have smiled gently to her). And indeed was it to make wine abundant at poor weddings He had come down to earth? And yet He went and did as she asked Him.... Ah, he is reading again...."

"Jesus saith unto them. Fill the waterpots with water. And they filled them up to the brim.

And he saith unto them, Draw out now and bear unto the Governor of the feast. And they bare it.

When the ruler of the feast had tasted the water that was made wine, and knew not whence it was; [but the servants which drew the water knew] the governor of the feast called the bridegroom,

---

*Father Païssy begins quoting a passage from John 2:1–10.
†That is, the Sea of Galilee, in northern Israel.

And saith unto him: Every man at the beginning doth set forth good wine; and when men have well drunk, that which is worse; but thou hast kept the good wine until now."

"But what's this, what's this? Why is the room growing wider? ... Ah, yes. ... It's the marriage, the wedding ... yes, of course. Here are the guests, here are the young couple sitting, and the merry crowd and. ... Where is the wise governor of the feast? But who is this? Who? Again the walls are receding ... who is getting up there from the great table? What! ... He here, too? But he's in the coffin ... but he's here, too. He has stood up, he sees me, he is coming here. ... God! ..."

Yes, he came up to him, to him, he, the little, thin old man, with tiny wrinkles on his face, joyful and laughing softly. There was no coffin now, and he was in the same dress as he had worn yesterday sitting with them, when the visitors had gathered about him. His face was uncovered, his eyes were shining. How was this then, he, too, had been called to the feast. He, too, at the marriage of Cana in Galilee. ...

"Yes, my dear, I am called, too, called and bidden," he heard a soft voice saying over him. "Why have you hidden yourself here, out of sight? You come and join us too."

It was his voice, the voice of Father Zossima. And it must be he, since he called him.

The elder raised Alyosha by the hand and he rose from his knees.

"We are rejoicing," the little, thin old man went on. "We are drinking the new wine, the wine of new, great gladness; do you see how many guests? Here are the bride and bridegroom, here is the wise governor of the feast, he is tasting the new wine. Why do you wonder at me? I gave an onion to a beggar, so I, too, am here. And many here have given only an onion each— only one little onion. ... What are all our deeds? And you, my gentle one, you, my kind boy, you too have known how to give a famished woman an onion to-day. Begin your work, dear one, begin it, gentle one! ... Do you see our Son, do you see Him?"

"I am afraid ... I dare not look," whispered Alyosha.

"Do you fear Him. He is terrible in His greatness, awful in His sublimity, but infinitely merciful. He has made Himself like unto us from love and rejoices with us. He is changing the water into wine that the gladness of the guests may not be cut short. He is expecting new guests, He is calling new ones unceasingly for ever and ever. ... There they are bringing new wine. Do you see they are bringing the vessels. ..."

Something glowed in Alyosha's heart, something filled it till it ached, tears of rapture rose from his soul. ... He stretched out his hands, uttered a cry and waked up.

Again the coffin, the open window, and the soft, solemn, distinct reading of the Gospel. But Alyosha did not listen to the reading. It was strange, he had fallen asleep on his knees, but now he was on his feet, and suddenly, as though thrown forward, with three firm rapid steps he went right up to the coffin. His shoulder brushed against Father Païssy without his noticing it. Father Païssy raised his eyes for an instant from his book, but looked away again at once, seeing that something strange was happening to the boy. Alyosha gazed for half a minute at the coffin, at the covered, motionless dead man that lay in the coffin, with the ikon on his breast and the peaked cap with the octangular cross, on his head. He had only just been hearing his voice, and that voice was still ringing in his ears. He was listening, still expecting other words, but suddenly he turned sharply and went out of the cell.

He did not stop on the steps either, but went quickly down; his soul, overflowing with rapture, yearned for freedom, space, openness. The vault of heaven, full of soft, shining stars, stretched vast and fathomless above him. The Milky Way ran in two pale streams from the zenith to the horizon. The fresh, motionless, still night enfolded the earth. The white towers and golden domes of the cathedral gleamed out against the sapphire sky. The gorgeous autumn flowers, in the beds round the house, were slumbering till morning. The silence of earth seemed to melt into the silence of the heavens. The mystery of earth was one with the mystery of the stars. . . .

Alyosha stood, gazed, and suddenly threw himself down on the earth. He did not know why he embraced it. He could not have told why he longed so irresistibly to kiss it, to kiss it all. But he kissed it weeping, sobbing and watering it with his tears, and vowed passionately to love it, to love it for ever and ever. "Water the earth with the tears of your joy and love those tears," echoed in his soul.

What was he weeping over?

Oh! in his rapture he was weeping even over those stars, which were shining to him from the abyss of space, and "he was not ashamed of that ecstasy." There seemed to be threads from all those innumerable worlds of God, linking his soul to them, and it was trembling all over "in contact with other worlds." He longed to forgive every one and for everything, and to beg forgiveness. Oh, not for himself, but for all men, for all and for everything. "And others are praying for me too," echoed again in his soul. But with every instant he felt clearly and, as it were, tangibly, that something firm and unshakable as that vault of heaven had entered into his soul. It was as though some idea had seized the sovereignty of his mind— and it was for all his life and for ever and ever. He had fallen on the earth a weak boy, but he rose up a resolute champion, and he knew and felt it suddenly at the very moment of his ecstasy. And never, never, all his life long, could Alyosha forget that minute.

"Some one visited my soul in that hour," he used to say afterwards, with implicit faith in his words.

Within three days he left the monastery in accordance with the words of his elder, who had bidden him "sojourn in the world."

BOOK EIGHT

MITYA

1

KUZMA SAMSONOV

BUT Dmitri, to whom Grushenka, flying away to a new life, had left her last greetings, bidding him remember the hour of her love for ever, knew nothing of what had happened to her, and was at that moment in a condition of feverish agitation and activity. For the last two days he had been in such an inconceivable state of mind that he might easily have fallen ill with brain fever, as he said himself afterwards. Alyosha had not been able to find him the morning before, and Ivan had not succeeded in meeting him at the tavern on the same day. The people at his lodgings, by his orders, concealed his movements.

He had spent those two days literally rushing in all directions, "struggling with his destiny and trying to save himself," as he expressed it himself afterwards, and for some hours he even made a dash out of the town on urgent business, terrible as it was to him to lose sight of Grushenka for a moment. All this was explained afterwards in detail, and confirmed by documentary evidence; but for the present we will only note the most essential incidents of those two terrible days immediately preceding the awful catastrophe, that broke so suddenly upon him.

Though Grushenka had, it is true, loved him for an hour, genuinely and sincerely, yet she tortured him sometimes cruelly and mercilessly. The worst of it was that he could never tell what she meant to do. To prevail upon her by force or kindness was also impossible: she would yield to nothing. She would only have become angry and turned away from him altogether, he knew that well already. He suspected, quite correctly, that she, too, was passing through an inward struggle, and was in a state of extraordinary indecision, that she was making up her mind to something, and unable to determine upon it. And so, not without good reason, he divined, with a sinking heart, that at moments she must simply hate him and his passion. And so, perhaps, it was, but what was distressing Grushenka he did not understand. For him the whole tormenting question lay between him and Fyodor Pavlovitch.

Here, we must note, by the way, one certain fact: he was firmly persuaded that Fyodor Pavlovitch would offer, or perhaps had offered, Grushenka lawful wedlock, and did not for a moment believe that the old voluptuary hoped to gain his object for three thousand roubles. Mitya had reached this conclusion from his knowledge of Grushenka and her character. That was how it was that he could believe at times that all Grushenka's uneasiness rose from not knowing which of them to choose, which was most to her advantage.

Strange to say, during those days it never occurred to him to think of the approaching return of the "officer," that is, of the man who had been such a fatal influence in Grushenka's life, and whose arrival she was expecting with such emotion and dread. It is true that of late Grushenka had been very silent about it. Yet he was perfectly aware of a letter she had received a month ago from her seducer, and had heard of it from her own lips. He partly knew, too, what the letter contained. In a moment of spite Grushenka had shown him that letter, but to her astonishment he attached hardly any consequence to it. It would be hard to say why this was. Perhaps, weighed down by all the hideous horror of his struggle with his own father for this woman, he was incapable of imagining any danger more terrible, at any rate for the time. He simply did not believe in a suitor who suddenly turned up again after five years' disappearance, still less in his speedy arrival. Moreover, in the "officer's" first letter which had been shown to Mitya, the possibility of his new rival's visit was very vaguely suggested. The letter was very indefinite, high-flown, and full of sentimentality. It must be noted that Grushenka had concealed from him the last lines of the letter, in which his return was alluded to more definitely. He had, besides, noticed at that moment, he remembered afterwards, a certain involuntary proud contempt for this missive from Siberia on Grushenka's face. Grushenka told him nothing of what had passed later between her and this rival; so that by degrees he had completely forgotten the officer's existence.

He felt that whatever might come later, whatever turn things might take, his final conflict with Fyodor Pavlovitch was close upon him, and must be decided before anything else. With a sinking heart he was expecting every moment Grushenka's decision, always believing that it would come suddenly, on the impulse of the moment. All of a sudden she would say to him: "Take me, I'm yours for ever," and it would all be over. He would seize her and bear her away at once to the ends of the earth. Oh, then he would bear her away at once, as far, far away as possible; to the furthest end of Russia, if not of the earth, then he would marry her, and settle down with her incognito, so that no one would know anything about them, there, here, or anywhere. Then, oh then, a new life would begin at once!

Of this different, reformed and "virtuous" life ("it must, it must be virtuous") he dreamed feverishly at every moment. He thirsted for that reformation and renewal. The filthy morass, in which he had sunk of his own free will, was too revolting to him, and, like very many men in such cases, he put faith above all in change of place. If only it were not for these people, if only it were not for these circumstances, if only he could fly away from this accursed place—he would be altogether regenerated, would enter on a new path. That was what he believed in, and for what he was yearning.

But all this could only be on condition of the first, the *happy* solution of the question. There was another possibility, a different and awful ending. Suddenly she might say to him; "Go away. I have just come to terms with Fyodor Pavlovitch. I am going to marry him and don't want you"—and then ... but then.... But Mitya did not know what would happen then. Up to the last hour he didn't know. That must be said to his credit. He had no definite intentions, had planned no crime. He was simply watching and spying in agony, while he prepared himself for the first, happy solution of his destiny. He drove away any other idea, in fact. But for that ending a quite different anxiety arose, a new, incidental, but yet fatal and insoluble difficulty presented itself.

If she were to say to him: "I'm yours; take me away," how could he take her away? Where had he the means, the money to do it? It was just at this time that all sources of revenue from Fyodor Pavlovitch, doles which had gone on without interruption for so many years, ceased. Grushenka had money, of course, but with regard to this Mitya suddenly evinced extraordinary pride; he wanted to carry her away and begin the new life with her himself, at his own expense, not at hers. He could not conceive of taking her money, and the very idea caused him a pang of intense repulsion. I won't enlarge on this fact or analyse it here, but confine myself to remarking that this was his attitude at the moment. All this may have arisen indirectly and unconsciously from the secret stings of his conscience for the money of Katerina Ivanovna that he had dishonestly appropriated. "I've been a scoundrel to one of them, and I shall be a scoundrel again to the other directly," was his feeling then, as he explained after: "and when Grushenka knows, she won't care for such a scoundrel."

Where then was he to get the means, where was he to get the fateful money? Without it, all would be lost and nothing could be done, "and only because I hadn't the money. Oh, the shame of it!"

To anticipate things: he did, perhaps, know where to get the money, knew, perhaps, where it lay at that moment. I will say no more of this here, as it will all be clear later. But his chief trouble, I must explain however obscurely, lay in the fact that to have the sum he knew of, to *have the right* to take it, he must first restore Katerina Ivanovna's three thousand—if not, "I'm a common pick-pocket, I'm a scoundrel, and I don't want to begin a new life as a scoundrel," Mitya decided. And so he made up his mind to move heaven and earth to return Katerina Ivanovna that three thousand, and that *first of all.* The final stage of this decision, so to say, had been reached only during the last hours, that is, after his last interview with Alyosha, two days before, on the high-road, on the evening when Grushenka had insulted Katerina Ivanovna, and Mitya, after hearing Alyosha's account of it, had admitted that he was a scoundrel, and told him to tell Katerina Ivanovna so, if it could be any comfort to her. After parting from his brother on that night, he had felt in his frenzy that it would be better "to murder and rob some one than fail to pay my debt to Katya. I'd rather every one thought me a robber and a murderer, I'd rather go to Siberia than that Katya should have the right to say that I deceived her and stole her money, and used her money to run away with Grushenka and begin a new life! That I can't do!" So Mitya decided, grinding his teeth, and he might well fancy at times that his brain would give away. But meanwhile he went on struggling. . . .

Strange to say, though one would have supposed there was nothing left for him but despair—for what chance had he, with nothing in the world, to raise such a sum?—yet to the very end he persisted in hoping that he would get that three thousand, that the money would somehow come to him, of itself, as though it might drop from heaven. That is just how it is with people who, like Dmitri, have never had anything to do with money, except to squander what had come to them by inheritance without any effort of their own, and have no notion how money is obtained. A whirl of the most fantastic notions took possession of his brain immediately after he had parted with Alyosha two days before, and threw his thoughts into a tangle of confusion. This is how it was he pitched first on a perfectly wild enterprise. And perhaps to men of that kind in such circumstances the most impossible, fantastic schemes occur first, and seem most practical.

He suddenly determined to go to Samsonov, the merchant who was Grushenka's protector, and to propose a "scheme" to him, and by means of it to obtain from him at once the whole of the sum required. Of the commercial value of his scheme he had no doubt, not the slightest, and was only uncertain how Samsonov would look upon his freak, supposing he were to consider it from any but the commercial point of view. Though Mitya knew the merchant by sight, he was not acquainted with him and had never spoken a word to him. But for some unknown reason he had long entertained the conviction that the old reprobate, who was lying at death's door, would perhaps not at all object now to Grushenka's securing a respectable position, and marrying a man "to be depended upon." And he believed not only that he would not object, but that this was what he desired, and, if opportunity arose, that he would be ready to help. From some rumour, or perhaps from some stray words of Grushenka's, he had gathered further that the old man would perhaps prefer him to Fyodor Pavlovitch for Grushenka.

Possibly many of the readers of my novel will feel that in reckoning on such assistance, and being ready to take his bride, so to speak, from the hands of her protector, Dmitri showed great coarseness and want of delicacy. I will only observe that Mitya looked upon Grushenka's past as something completely over. He looked on that past with infinite pity and resolved with all the fervour of his passion that when once Grushenka told him she loved him and would marry him, it would mean the beginning of a new Grushenka and a new Dmitri, free from every vice. They would forgive one another and would begin their lives afresh. As for Kuzma Samsonov, Dmitri looked upon him as a man who had exercised a fateful influence in that remote past of Grushenka's, though she had never loved him, and who was now himself a thing of the past, completely done with, and, so to say, non-existent. Besides, Mitya hardly looked upon him as a man at all, for it was known to every one in the town that he was only a shattered wreck, whose relations with Grushenka had changed their character and were now simply paternal, and that this had been so for a long time.

In any case there was much simplicity on Mitya's part in all this, for, in spite of all his vices, he was a very simple-hearted man. It was an instance of this simplicity that Mitya was seriously persuaded that, being on the eve of his departure for the next world, old Kuzma must sincerely repent of his past relations with Grushenka, and that she had no more devoted friend and protector in the world than this, now harmless, old man.

After his conversation with Alyosha, at the cross-roads, he hardly slept all night, and, at ten o'clock next morning, he was at the house of Samsonov and telling the servant to announce him. It was a very large and gloomy old house, of two storeys, with a lodge and out-houses. In the lower storey lived Samsonov's two married sons with their families, his old sister, and his unmarried daughter. In the lodge lived two of his clerks, one of whom also had a large family. Both the lodge and the lower storey were overcrowded, but the old man kept the upper floor to himself, and would not even let the daughter live there with him, though she waited upon him, and in spite of her asthma was obliged at certain fixed hours, and at any time he might call her, to run upstairs to him from below.

This upper floor contained a number of large rooms kept purely for show, furnished in the old-fashioned merchant style, with long, monotonous rows of clumsy mahogany chairs along the walls, with glass chandeliers under shades, and gloomy mirrors on the walls. All these rooms were entirely empty and unused, for the old man kept to one room, a small, remote bedroom, where he was waited upon by an old servant with a kerchief on her head, and by a lad, who used to sit on the locker in the passage. Owing to his swollen legs, the old man could hardly walk at all, and was only rarely lifted from his leather arm-chair, when the old woman supporting him led him up and down the room once or twice. He was morose and taciturn even with this old woman.

When he was informed of the arrival of the "captain," he at once refused to see him. But Mitya persisted and sent his name up again. Samsonov questioned the lad minutely: What he looked like? Whether he was drunk? Was he going to make a row? The answer he received was: that he was sober, but wouldn't go away. The old man again refused to see him. Then Mitya, who had foreseen this, and purposely brought pencil and paper with him, wrote clearly on the piece of paper the words: "On most important business closely concerning Agrafena Alexandrovna," and sent it up to the old man.

After thinking a little Samsonov told the lad to take the visitor to the drawing-room, and sent the old woman downstairs with a summons to his younger son to come upstairs to him at once. This younger son, a man over six foot and of exceptional physical strength, who was closely shaven and dressed in the European style, though his father still wore a kaftan and a beard, came at once without a comment. All the family trembled before the father. The old man had sent for this giant, not because he was afraid of the "captain" (he was by no means of a timorous temper), but in order to have a witness in case of any emergency. Supported by his son and the servant-lad, he waddled at last into the drawing-room. It may be assumed that he felt considerable curiosity. The drawing-room in which Mitya was awaiting him was a vast, dreary room that laid a weight of depression on the heart. It had a double row of windows, a gallery, marbled walls, and three immense chandeliers with glass lustres covered with shades.

Mitya was sitting on a little chair at the entrance, awaiting his fate with nervous impatience. When the old man appeared at the opposite door, seventy feet away, Mitya jumped up at once, and with his long, military stride walked to meet him. Mitya was well dressed, in a frock-coat, buttoned up, with a round hat and black gloves in his hands, just as he had been three days before at the elder's, at the family meeting with his father and brothers. The old man waited for him, standing dignified and unbending, and Mitya felt at once that he had looked him through and through as he advanced. Mitya was greatly impressed, too, with Samsonov's immensely swollen face. His lower lip, which had always been thick, hung down now, looking like a bun. He bowed to his guest in dignified silence, motioned him to a low chair by the sofa, and, leaning on his son's arm he began lowering himself on to the sofa opposite, groaning painfully, so that Mitya, seeing his painful exertions, immediately felt remorseful and sensitively conscious of his insignificance in the presence of the dignified person he had ventured to disturb.

"What is it you want of me, sir?" said the old man, deliberately, distinctly, severely, but courteously, when he was at last seated.

Mitya started, leapt up, but sat down again. Then he began at once speaking with loud, nervous haste, gesticulating, and in a positive frenzy. He was unmistakably a man driven into a corner, on the brink of ruin, catching at the last straw, ready to sink if he failed. Old Samsonov probably grasped all this in an instant, though his face remained cold and immovable as a statue's.

"Most honoured sir, Kuzma Kuzmitch, you have no doubt heard, more than once, of my disputes with my father, Fyodor Pavlovitch Karamazov, who robbed me of my inheritance from my mother . . . seeing the whole town is gossiping about it . . . for here every one's gossiping of what they shouldn't . . . and besides, it might have reached you through Grushenka . . . I beg your pardon, through Agrafena Alexandrovna . . . Agrafena Alexandrovna, the lady for whom I have the highest respect and esteem. . . ."

So Mitya began, and broke down at the first sentence. We will not reproduce his speech word for word, but will only summarise the gist of it. Three months ago, he said, he had of express intention (Mitya purposely used these words instead of "intentionally") consulted a lawyer in the chief town of the province, "a distinguished lawyer, Kuzma Kuzmitch, Pavel Pavlovitch Korneplodov. You have perhaps heard of him? A man of vast intellect, the mind of a statesman . . . he knows you, too . . . spoke of you in the highest terms . . ." Mitya broke down again. But these breaks did not deter him. He leapt instantly over the gaps, and struggled on and on.

This Korneplodov, after questioning him minutely, and inspecting the documents he was able to bring (Mitya alluded somewhat vaguely to these documents, and slurred over the subject with special haste) reported that they certainly might take proceedings concerning the village of Tchermashnya, which ought, he said, to have come to him, Mitya, from his mother, and so checkmate the old villain, his father . . . "because every door was not closed and justice might still find a loophole." In fact, he might reckon on an additional sum of six or even seven thousand roubles from Fyodor

Pavlovitch, as Tchermashnya was worth, at least twenty-five thousand, he might say twenty-eight thousand, in fact, "thirty, thirty, Kuzma Kuzmitch, and, would you believe it, I didn't get seventeen from that heartless man!" So he, Mitya, had thrown the business up, for the time, knowing nothing about the law, but on coming here was struck dumb by a cross-claim made upon him (here Mitya went adrift again, and again took a flying leap forward), "so will not you, excellent and honoured Kuzma Kuzmitch, be willing to take up all my claims against that unnatural monster, and pay me a sum down of only three thousand? . . . You see, you cannot, in any case, lose over it. On my honour, my honour, I swear that. Quite the contrary, you may make six or seven thousand instead of three. . . ." Above all, he wanted this concluded that very day.

"I'll do the business with you at a notary's, or whatever it is . . . in fact, I'm ready to do anything. . . . I'll hand over all the deeds . . . whatever you want, sign anything . . . and we could draw up the agreement at once . . . and if it were possible, if it were only possible, that very morning. . . . You could pay me that three thousand, for there isn't a capitalist in this town to compare with you, and so would save me from . . . would save me, in fact . . . for a good, I might say an honourable, action. . . . For I cherish the most honourable feelings for a certain person, whom you know well, and care for as a father. I would not have come, indeed, if it had not been as a father. And, indeed, it's a struggle of three in this business, for it's fate—that's a fearful thing, Kuzma Kuzmitch! A tragedy, Kuzma Kuzmitch, a tragedy! And as you've dropped out long ago, it's a tug-of-war between two. I'm expressing it awkwardly, perhaps, but I'm not a literary man. You see, I'm on the one side, and that monster on the other. So you must choose. It's either I or the monster. It all lies in your hands—the fate of three lives, and the happiness of two. . . . Excuse me, I'm making a mess of it, but you understand . . . I see from your venerable eyes that you understand . . . and if you don't understand, I'm done for . . . so you see!"

Mitya broke off his clumsy speech with that, "so you see!" and jumping up from his seat, awaited the answer to his foolish proposal. At the last phrase he had suddenly become hopelessly aware that it had all fallen flat, above all, that he had been talking utter nonsense.

"How strange it is! On the way here it seemed all right, and now it's nothing but nonsense." The idea suddenly dawned on his despairing mind.

All the while he had been talking, the old man sat motionless, watching him with an icy expression in his eyes. After keeping him for a moment in suspense, Kuzma Kuzmitch pronounced at last, in the most positive and chilling tone:

"Excuse me, we don't undertake such business."

Mitya suddenly felt his legs growing weak under him.

"What am I to do now, Kuzma Kuzmitch?" he muttered, with a pale smile. "I suppose it's all up with me—what do you think?"

"Excuse me. . . ."

Mitya remained standing, staring motionless. He suddenly noticed a movement in the old man's face. He started.

"You see, sir, business of that sort's not in our line," said the old man slowly. "There's the court, and the lawyers—it's a perfect misery. But if you like, there is a man here you might apply to."

"Good heavens! Who is it? You're my salvation, Kuzma Kuzmitch," faltered Mitya.

"He doesn't live here, and he's not here just now. He is a peasant, he does business in timber. His name is Lyagavy. He's been haggling with Fyodor Pavlovitch for the last year, over your copse at Tchermashnya. They can't agree on the price, maybe you've heard? Now he's come back again and is staying with the priest at Ilyinskoe, about twelve versts from the Volovya station. He wrote to me, too, about the business of the copse, asking my advice. Fyodor Pavlovitch means to go and see him, himself. So if you were to be beforehand with Fyodor Pavlovitch and to make Lyagavy the offer you've made me, he might possibly. . . ."

"A brilliant idea!" Mitya interrupted ecstatically. "He's the very man, it would just suit him. He's haggling with him for it, being asked too much, and here he would have all the documents entitling him to the property itself. Ha-ha-ha!"

And Mitya suddenly went off into his short, wooden laugh, startling Samsonov.

"How can I thank you, Kuzma Kuzmitch?" cried Mitya effusively.

"Don't mention it," said Samsonov, inclining his head.

"But you don't know, you've saved me. Oh, it was a true presentiment brought me to you. . . . So now to this priest!"

"No need of thanks."

"I'll make haste and fly there. I'm afraid I've overtaxed your strength. I shall never forget it. It's a Russian says that, Kuzma Kuzmitch, a R-r-russian!"

"To be sure!"

Mitya seized his hand to press it, but there was a malignant gleam in the old man's eye. Mitya drew back his hand, but at once blamed himself for his mistrustfulness.

"It's because he's tired," he thought.

"For her sake! For her sake, Kuzma Kuzmitch! You understand that it's for her," he cried, his voice ringing through the room. He bowed, turned sharply round, and with the same long stride walked to the door without looking back. He was trembling with delight.

"Everything was on the verge of ruin and my guardian angel saved me," was the thought in his mind. And if such a business man as Samsonov (a most worthy old man, and what dignity!) had suggested this course, then . . . then success was assured. He would fly off immediately. "I will be back before night, I shall be back at night and the thing is done. Could the old man have been laughing at me?" exclaimed Mitya, as he strode towards his lodging. He could, of course, imagine nothing but that the advice was practical "from such a business man" with an understanding of the business, with an understanding of this Lyagavy (curious surname!). Or—the old man was laughing at him.

Alas! the second alternative was the correct one. Long afterwards, when the catastrophe had happened, old Samsonov himself confessed, laughing, that he had made a fool of the "captain." He was a cold, spiteful and sarcastic man, liable to violent antipathies. Whether it was the "captain's" excited face, or the foolish conviction of the "rake and spendthrift," that he, Samsonov, could be taken in by such a cock-and-bull story as his scheme, or jealousy over Grushenka, in whose name this "scapegrace" had rushed in on him with such a tale to get money—which worked on the old man I can't tell. But, at the instant when Mitya stood before him, feeling his legs grow weak under him, and frantically exclaiming that he was ruined, at the moment the old man looked at him with intense spite, and resolved to make a laughing-stock of him. When Mitya had gone, Kuzma Kuzmitch, white with rage, turned to his son and bade him see to it that that beggar be never seen again, and never admitted even into the yard, or else he'd . . .

He did not utter his threat. But even his son, who often saw him enraged, trembled with fear. For a whole hour afterwards, the old man was shaking with anger, and by evening he was worse, and sent for the doctor.

2

LYAGAVY

So he must drive at full speed, and he had not the money for horses. He had forty kopecks, and that was all, all that was left after so many years of prosperity! But he had at home an old silver watch which had long ceased to go. He snatched it up and carried it to a Jewish watchmaker who had a shop in the market-place. The Jew gave him six roubles for it.

"And I didn't expect that," cried Mitya, ecstatically. (He was still in a state of ecstasy.) He seized his six roubles and ran home. At home he borrowed three roubles from the people of the house, who loved him so much that they were pleased to give it him, though it was all they had. Mitya in his excitement told them on the spot that his fate would be decided that day, and he described, in desperate haste, the whole scheme he had put before Samsonov, the latter's decision, his own hopes for the future, and so on. These people had been told many of their lodger's secrets before, and so looked upon him as a gentleman who was not at all proud, and almost one of themselves. Having thus collected nine roubles Mitya sent for posting-horses to take him to the Volovya station. This was how the fact came to be remembered and established that "at midday, on the day

before the event, Mitya had not a farthing, and that he had sold his watch
to get money and had borrowed three roubles from his landlords, all in the
presence of witnesses."

I note this fact, later on it will be apparent why I do so.

Though he was radiant with the joyful anticipation that he would at last
solve all his difficulties, yet, as he drew near Volovya station, he trembled
at the thought of what Grushenka might be doing in his absence. What if
she made up her mind to-day to go to Fyodor Pavlovitch? This was why he
had gone off without telling her and why he left orders with his landlady
not to let out where he had gone, if any one came to inquire for him.

"I must, I must get back to-night," he repeated, as he was jolted along
in the cart, "and I daresay I shall have to bring this Lyagavy back here . . .
to draw up the deed." So mused Mitya, with a throbbing heart, but alas! his
dreams were not fated to be carried out.

To begin with, he was late, taking a short cut from Volovya station
which turned out to be eighteen versts instead of twelve. Secondly, he did
not find the priest at home at Ilyinskoe; he had gone off to a neighbouring
village. While Mitya, setting off there with the same exhausted horses, was
looking for him, it was almost dark.

The priest, a shy and amiable looking little man, informed him at once
that, though Lyagavy had been staying with him at first, he was now at
Suhoy Possyolok, that he was staying the night in the forester's cottage, as
he was buying timber there too. At Mitya's urgent request that he would
take him to Lyagavy at once, and by so doing "save him, so to speak," the
priest agreed, after some demur, to conduct him to Suhoy Possyolok; his
curiosity was obviously aroused. But, unluckily, he advised their going on
foot, as it would not be "much over" a verst. Mitya, of course, agreed, and
marched off with his yard-long strides, so that the poor priest almost ran
after him. He was a very cautious man, though not old.

Mitya at once began talking to him, too, of his plans, nervously and excitedly asking advice in regard to Lyagavy, and talking all the way. He
turned off Mitya's questions with: "I don't know. Ah, I can't say. How can
I tell?" and so on. When Mitya began to speak of his quarrel with his father over his inheritance, the priest was positively alarmed, as he was in
some way dependent on Fyodor Pavlovitch. He inquired, however, with
surprise, why he called the peasant-trader Gorstkin, Lyagavy, and oblig-
ingly explained to Mitya that, though the man's name really was Lyagavy,
he was never called so, as he would be grievously offended at the name,
and that he must be sure to call him Gorstkin, "or you'll do nothing with
him; he won't even listen to you," said the priest in conclusion.

Mitya was somewhat surprised for a moment, and explained that that
was what Samsonov had called him. On hearing this fact, the priest
dropped the subject, though he would have done well to put into words his
doubt whether, if Samsonov had sent him to that peasant, calling him Lyagavy, there was not something wrong about it, and he was turning him into
ridicule. But Mitya had no time to pause over such trifles. He hurried,
striding along, and only when he reached Suhoy Possyolok he realised that

they had come not one verst, nor one and a half, but at least three. This annoyed him, but he controlled himself.

They went into the hut. The forester lived in one half of the hut, and Gorstkin was lodging in the other, the better room the other side of the passage. They went into that room and lighted a tallow candle. The hut was extremely overheated. On the table there was a samovar that had gone out, a tray with cups, an empty rum bottle, a bottle of vodka partly full, and some half eaten crusts of wheaten bread. The visitor himself lay stretched at full length on the bench, with his coat crushed up under his head for a pillow, snoring heavily. Mitya stood in perplexity.

"Of course I must wake him. My business is too important. I've come in such haste. I'm in a hurry to get back to-day," he said in great agitation. But the priest and the forester stood in silence, not giving their opinion. Mitya went up and began trying to wake him himself; he tried vigorously, but the sleeper did not wake.

"He's drunk," Mitya decided. "Good Lord! What am I to do? What am I to do?" And, terribly impatient, he began pulling him by the arms, by the legs, shaking his head, lifting him up and making him sit on the bench. Yet, after prolonged exertions, he could only succeed in getting the drunken man to utter absurd grunts, and violent, but inarticulate oaths.

"No, you'd better wait a little," the priest pronounced at last, "for he's obviously not in a fit state."

"He's been drinking the whole day," the forester chimed in.

"Good Heavens!" cried Mitya. "If only you knew how important it is to me and how desperate I am!"

"No, you'd better wait till morning," the priest repeated.

"Till morning? Mercy! that's impossible!"

And in his despair he was on the point of attacking the sleeping man again, but stopped short at once, realising the uselessness of his efforts. The priest said nothing, the sleepy forester looked gloomy.

"What terrible tragedies real life contrives for people," said Mitya, in complete despair. The perspiration was streaming down his face. The priest seized the moment to put before him, very reasonably, that even if he succeeded in wakening the man, he would still be drunk and incapable of conversation. "And your business is important," he said, "so you'd certainly better put it off till morning." With a gesture of despair Mitya agreed.

"Father, I will stay here with a light, and seize the favourable moment. As soon as he wakes I'll begin. I'll pay you for the light," he said to the forester, "for the night's lodging, too; you'll remember Dmitri Karamazov. Only, father I don't know what we're to do with you. Where will you sleep?"

"No, I'm going home. I'll take his horse and get home," he said, indicating the forester. "And now I'll say good-bye. I wish you all success."

So it was settled. The priest rode off on the forester's horse, delighted to escape, though he shook his head uneasily, wondering whether he ought not next day to inform his benefactor Fyodor Pavlovitch of this curious incident, "or he may in an unlucky hour hear of it, be angry, and withdraw his favour."

The forester, scratching himself, went back to his room without a word, and Mitya sat on the bench to "catch the favourable moment," as he expressed it. Profound dejection clung about his soul like a heavy mist. A profound, intense dejection! He sat thinking, but could reach no conclusion. The candle burnt dimly, a cricket chirped; it became insufferably close in the overheated room. He suddenly pictured the garden, the path behind the garden, the door of his father's house mysteriously opening and Grushenka running in. He leapt up from the bench.

"It's a tragedy!" he said, grinding his teeth. Mechanically he went up to the sleeping man and looked in his face. He was a lean, middle-aged peasant, with a very long face, flaxen curls, and a long, thin, reddish beard, wearing a blue cotton shirt and a black waistcoat, from the pocket of which peeped the chain of a silver watch. Mitya looked at his face with intense hatred, and for some unknown reason his curly hair particularly irritated him.

What was insufferably humiliating was, that, after leaving things of such importance and making such sacrifices, he, Mitya, utterly worn out, should with business of such urgency be standing over this dolt on whom his whole fate depended, while he snored as though there were nothing the matter, as though he'd dropped from another planet.

"Oh, the irony of fate!" cried Mitya, and, quite losing his head, he fell again to rousing the tipsy peasant. He roused him with a sort of ferocity, pulled him, pushed him, even beat him; but after five minutes of vain exertions, he returned to his bench in helpless despair, and sat down.

"Stupid! Stupid!" cried Mitya. "And how dishonourable it all is!" something made him add. His head began to ache horribly. Should he fling it up and go away altogether?" he wondered. "No, wait till to-morrow now. I'll stay on purpose. What else did I come for? Besides, I've no means of going. How am I to get away from here now? Oh, the idiocy of it!"

But his head ached more and more. He sat without moving, and unconsciously dozed off and fell asleep as he sat. He seemed to have slept two hours or more. He was waked up by his head aching so unbearably that he could have screamed. There was a hammering in his temples, and the top of his head ached. It was a long time before he could wake up fully and understand what had happened to him.

At last he realised that the room was full of charcoal fumes from the stove, and that he might die of suffocation. And the drunken peasant still lay snoring. The candle guttered and was about to go out. Mitya cried out, and ran staggering across the passage into the forester's room. The forester waked up at once, but hearing that the other room was full of fumes, to Mitya's surprise and annoyance, accepted the fact with strange unconcern, though he did go to see to it.

"But he's dead, he's dead! and . . . what am I to do then?" cried Mitya frantically.

They threw open the doors, opened a window and the chimney. Mitya brought a pail of water from the passage. First he wetted his own head, then, finding a rag of some sort, dipped it into the water, and put it on Lyagavy's head. The forester still treated the matter contemptuously, and when he opened the window said grumpily:

"It'll be all right, now."

He went back to sleep, leaving Mitya a lighted lantern. Mitya fussed about the drunken peasant for half an hour, wetting his head, and gravely resolved not to sleep all night. But he was so worn out that when he sat down for a moment to take breath, he closed his eyes, unconsciously stretched himself full length on the bench and slept like the dead.

It was dreadfully late when he waked. It was somewhere about nine o'clock. The sun was shining brightly in the two little windows of the hut. The curly-headed peasant was sitting on the bench and had his coat on. He had another samovar and another bottle in front of him. Yesterday's bottle had already been finished, and the new one was more than half empty. Mitya jumped up and saw at once that the cursed peasant was drunk again, hopelessly and incurably. He stared at him for a moment with wide opened eyes. The peasant was silently and slyly watching him, with insulting composure, and even a sort of comtemptuous condescension, so Mitya fancied. He rushed up to him.

"Excuse me, you see. . . . I . . . you've most likely heard from the forester here in the hut. I'm Lieutenant Dmitri Karamazov, the son of the old Karamazov whose copse you are buying."

"That's a lie!" said the peasant, calmly and confidently.

"A lie? You know Fyodor Pavlovitch?"

"I don't know any of your Fyodor Pavlovitches," said the peasant, speaking thickly.

"You're bargaining with him for the copse, for the copse. Do wake up, and collect yourself. Father Pavel of Ilyinskoe brought me here. You wrote to Samsonov, and he has sent me to you," Mitya gasped breathlessly.

"You're l—lying!" Lyagavy blurted out again. Mitya's legs went cold.

"For mercy's sake! It isn't a joke! You're drunk, perhaps. Yet you can speak and understand . . . or else . . . I understand nothing!"

"You're a painter!"

"For mercy's sake! I'm Karamazov, Dmitri Karamazov. I have an offer to make you, an advantageous offer . . . very advantageous offer, concerning the copse!"

The peasant stroked his beard importantly.

"No, you've contracted for the job and turned out a scamp. You're a scoundrel!"

"I assure you you're mistaken," cried Mitya, wringing his hands in despair. The peasant still stroked his beard, and suddenly screwed up his eyes cunningly.

"No, you show me this: you tell me the law that allows roguery. D'you hear? You're a scoundel! Do you understand that?"

Mitya stepped back gloomily, and suddenly "something seemed to hit him on the head," as he said afterwards. In an instant a light seemed to dawn in his mind, "a light was kindled and I grasped it all." He stood, stupefied, wondering how he, after all a man of intelligence, could have yielded to such folly, have been led into such an adventure, and have kept it up for almost twenty-four hours, fussing round this Lyagavy, wetting his head.

"Why, the man's drunk, dead drunk, and he'll go on drinking now for a week; what's the use of waiting here? And what if Samsonov sent me here on purpose? What if she? . . . Oh God, what have I done?"

The peasant sat watching him and grinning. Another time Mitya might have killed the fool in a fury, but now he felt as weak as a child. He went quietly to the bench, took up his overcoat, put it on without a word, and went out of the hut. He did not find the forester in the next room; there was no one there. He took fifty kopecks in small change out of his pocket and put them on the table for his night's lodging, the candle, and the trouble he had given. Coming out of the hut he saw nothing but forest all round. He walked at hazard, not knowing which way to turn out of the hut, to the right or to the left. Hurrying there the evening before with the priest, he had not noticed the road. He had no revengeful feeling for anybody, even for Samsonov, in his heart. He strode along a narrow forest path, aimless, dazed, without heeding where he was going. A child could have knocked him down, so weak was he in body and soul. He got out of the forest some- how, however, and a vista of fields, bare after the harvest, stretched as far as the eye could see.

"What despair! What death all round!" he repeated striding on and on.

He was saved by meeting an old merchant who was being driven across country in a hired trap. When he overtook him, Mitya asked the way, and it turned out that the old merchant, too, was going to Volovya. After some discussion Mitya got into the trap. Three hours later they arrived. At Volovya, Mitya at once ordered posting-horses to drive to the town, and suddenly realised that he was appallingly hungry. While the horses were be- ing harnessed, an omelette was prepared for him. He ate it all in an instant, ate a huge hunk of bread, ate a sausage, and swallowed three glasses of vodka. After eating, his spirits and his heart grew lighter. He flew towards the town, urged on the driver, and suddenly made a new and "unalterable" plan to procure that "accursed money" before evening. "And to think, only to think that a man's life should be ruined for the sake of that paltry three thousand!" he cried, contemptuously. "I'll settle it today." And if it had not been for the thought of Grushenka and of what might have happened to her, which never left him, he would perhaps have become quite cheerful again. . . . But the thought of her was stabbing him to the heart every mo- ment, like a sharp knife.

At last they arrived, and Mitya at once ran to Grushenka.

3

GOLD-MINES

THIS was the visit of Mitya of which Grushenka had spoken to Rakitin with such horror. She was just then expecting the "message," and was much relieved that Mitya had not been to see her that day or the day before. She hoped that "please God he won't come till I'm gone away," and he suddenly burst in on her. The rest we know already. To get him off her hands she suggested at once that he should walk with her to Samsonov's, where she said she absolutely must go "to settle his accounts," and when Mitya accompanied her at once, she said good-bye to him at the gate, making him promise to come at twelve o'clock to take her home again. Mitya, too, was delighted at this arrangement. If she was sitting at Samsonov's she could not be going to Fyodor Pavlovitch's, "if only she's not lying," he added at once. But he thought she was not lying from what he saw.

He was that sort of jealous man who, in the absence of the beloved woman, at once invents all sorts of awful fancies of what may be happening to her, and how she may be betraying him, but, when shaken, heartbroken, convinced of her faithlessness, he runs back to her; at the first glance at her face, her gay, laughing, affectionate face, he revives at once, lays aside all suspicion and with joyful shame abuses himself for his jealousy.

After leaving Grushenka at the gate he rushed home. Oh, he had so much still to do that day! But a load had been lifted from his heart, anyway.

"Now I must only make haste and find out from Smerdyakov whether anything happened there last night, whether, by any chance, she went to Fyodor Pavlovitch; ough!" floated through his mind.

Before he had time to reach his lodging, jealousy had surged up again in his restless heart.

Jealousy! "Othello was not jealous, he was trustful," observed Pushkin.[1] And that remark alone is enough to show the deep insight of our great poet. Othello's soul was shattered and his whole outlook clouded simply because *his ideal was destroyed*. But Othello did not begin hiding, spying, peeping. He was trustful. On the contrary, he had to be led up, pushed on, excited with great difficulty before he could entertain the idea of deceit. The truly jealous man is not like that. It is impossible to picture to oneself the shame and moral degradation to which the jealous man can descend without a qualm of conscience. And yet it's not as though the jealous were all vulgar and base souls. On the contrary, a man of lofty feelings, whose love is pure and full of self-sacrifice, may yet hide under tables, bribe the vilest people, and be familiar with the lowest ignominy of spying and eavesdropping.

Othello was incapable of making up his mind to faithlessness—not incapable of forgiving it, but of making up his mind to it—though his soul was as innocent and free from malice as a babe's. It is not so with the really jealous man. It is hard to imagine what some jealous men can make up their mind to and overlook, and what they can forgive! The jealous are the readiest of all to forgive, and all women know it. The jealous man can forgive extraordinarily quickly (though, of course, after a violent scene), and he is able to forgive infidelity almost conclusively proved, the very kisses and embraces he has seen, if only he can somehow be convinced that it has all been "for the last time," and that his rival will vanish from that day forward, will depart to the ends of the earth, or that he himself will carry her away somewhere, where that dreaded rival will not get near her. Of course the reconciliation is only for an hour. For, even if the rival did disappear next day, he would invent another one and would be jealous of him. And one might wonder what there was in a love that had to be so watched over, what a love could be worth that needed such strenuous guarding. But that the jealous will never understand. And yet among them are men of noble hearts. It is remarkable, too, that those very men of noble hearts, standing hidden in some cupboard, listening and spying, never feel the stings of conscience at that moment, anyway, though they understand clearly enough with their "noble hearts" the shameful depths to which they have voluntarily sunk.

At the sight of Grushenka, Mitya's jealousy vanished, and for an instant he became trustful and generous, and positively despised himself for his evil feelings. But that only proved that, in his love for that woman, there was an element of something far higher than he himself imagined, that it was not only a sensual passion, not only the "curve of her body," of which he had talked to Alyosha. But, as soon as Grushenka had gone, Mitya began to suspect her of all the low cunning of faithlessness, and he felt no sting of conscience at it.

And so jealousy surged up in him again. He had, in any case, to make haste. The first thing to be done was to get hold of at least a small, temporary loan of money. The nine roubles had almost all gone on his expedition. And, as we all know, one can't take a step without money. But he had thought over in the cart where he could get a loan. He had a brace of fine duelling pistols in a case, which he had not pawned till then because he prized them above all his possessions.

In the "Metropolis" tavern he had some time since made acquaintance with a young official and had learnt that this very opulent bachelor was passionately fond of weapons. He used to buy pistols, revolvers, daggers, hang them on his wall and show them to acquaintances. He prided himself on them, and was quite a specialist on the mechanism of the revolver. Mitya, without stopping to think, went straight to him, and offered to pawn his pistols to him for ten roubles. The official, delighted, began trying to persuade him to sell them outright. But Mitya would not consent, so the young man gave him ten roubles, protesting that nothing would induce him to take interest. They parted friends.

Mitya was in haste; he rushed towards Fyodor Pavlovitch's by the back way, to his arbour, to get hold of Smerdyakov as soon as possible. In this way the fact was established that three or four hours before a certain event, of which I shall speak later on, Mitya had not a farthing, and pawned for ten roubles a possession he valued, though, three hours later, he was in possession of thousands. ... But I am anticipating. From Marya Kondratyevna (the woman living near Fyodor Pavlovitch's) he learned the very disturbing fact of Smerdyakov's illness. He heard the story of his fall in the cellar, his fit, the doctor's visit, Fyodor Pavlovitch's anxiety; he heard with interest, too, that his brother Ivan had set off that morning for Moscow.

"Then he must have driven through Volovya before me," thought Dmitri, but he was terribly distressed about Smerdyakov. "What will happen now? Who'll keep watch for me? Who'll bring me word?" he thought. He began greedily questioning the women whether they had seen anything the evening before. They quite understood what he was trying to find out, and completely reassured him. No one had been there. Ivan Fyodorovitch had been there the night; everything had been perfectly as usual. Mitya grew thoughtful. He would certainly have to keep watch to-day, but where? Here or at Samsonov's gate? He decided that he must be on the look-out both here and there, and meanwhile ... meanwhile. ... The difficulty was that he had to carry out the new plan that he had made on the journey back. He was sure of its success, but he must not delay acting upon it. Mitya resolved to sacrifice an hour to it: "in an hour I shall know everything, I shall settle everything, and then, then, first of all to Samsonov's. I'll inquire whether Grushenka's there and instantly be back here again, stay till eleven, and then to Samsonov's again to bring her home." This was what he decided.

He flew home, washed, combed his hair, brushed his clothes, dressed, and went to Madame Hohlakov's. Alas! he had built his hopes on her. He had resolved to borrow three thousand from that lady. And what was more, he felt suddenly convinced that she would not refuse to lend it to him. It may be wondered why, if he felt so certain, he had not gone to her at first, one of his own sort, so to speak, instead of to Samsonov, a man he did not know, who was not of his own class, and to whom he hardly knew how to speak.

But the fact was that he had never known Madame Hohlakov well, and had seen nothing of her for the last month, and that he knew she could not endure him. She had detested him from the first because he was engaged to Katerina Ivanovna, while she had, for some reason, suddenly conceived the desire that Katerina Ivanovna should throw him over, and marry the "charming, chivalrously refined Ivan, who had such excellent manners." Mitya's manners she detested. Mitya positively laughed at her, and had once said about her that she was just as lively and at her ease as she was uncultivated. But that morning in the cart a brilliant idea had struck him: "If she is so anxious I should not marry Katerina Ivanovna (and he knew she was positively hysterical upon the subject) why should she refuse me now that three thousand, just to enable me to leave Katya and get away

from her for ever. These spoilt fine ladies, if they set their hearts on anything will spare no expense to satisfy their caprice. Besides, she's so rich,"
Mitya argued.

As for his "plan" it was just the same as before; it consisted of the offer
of his rights to Tchermashnya—but not with a commercial object, as it had
been with Samsonov, not trying to allure the lady with the possibility of
making a profit of six or seven thousand—but simply as a security for the
debt. As he worked out this new idea, Mitya was enchanted with it, but so
it always was with him in all his undertakings, in all his sudden decisions.
He gave himself up to every new idea with passionate enthusiasm. Yet,
when he mounted the steps of Madame Hohlakov's house he felt a shiver
of fear run down his spine. At that moment he saw fully, as a mathematical
certainty, that this was his last hope, that if this broke down, nothing else
was left him in the world but to "rob and murder some one for the three
thousand." It was half-past seven when he rang at the bell.

At first fortune seemed to smile upon him. As soon as he was announced
he was received with extraordinary rapidity. "As though she were waiting
for me," thought Mitya, and as soon as he had been led to the drawing-
room, the lady of the house herself ran in, and declared at once that she was
expecting him.

"I was expecting you! I was expecting you! Though I'd no reason to
suppose you would come to see me, as you will admit yourself. Yet, I did
expect you. You may marvel at my instinct, Dmitri Fyodorovitch, but I was
convinced all the morning that you would come."

"That is certainly wonderful, Madame," observed Mitya sitting down
limply, "but I have come to you on a matter of great importance. . . . On a
matter of supreme importance for me that is, Madame . . . for me alone . . .
and I hasten . . ."

"I know you've come on most important business, Dmitri Fyodorovitch;
it's not a case of presentiment, no reactionary harking back to the miraculous (have you heard about Father Zossima?). This is a case of mathematics: you couldn't help coming, after all that has passed with Katerina
Ivanovna; you couldn't, you couldn't, that's a mathematical certainty."

"The realism of actual life, Madame, that's what it is. But allow me to
explain. . . ."

"Realism indeed, Dmitri Fyodorovitch. I'm all for realism now. I've
seen too much of miracles. You've heard that Father Zossima is dead?"

"No, Madame, it's the first time I've heard of it." Mitya was a little surprised. The image of Alyosha rose to his mind.

"Last night, and only imagine . . ."

"Madame," said Mitya, "I can imagine nothing except that I'm in a desperate position, and that if you don't help me, everything will come to
grief, and I first of all. Excuse me, for the triviality of the expression, but
I'm in a fever. . . ."

"I know, I know that you're in a fever. You could hardly fail to be, and
whatever you may say to me, I know beforehand. I have long been thinking over your destiny, Dmitri Fyodorovitch, I am watching over it and

studying it. . . . Oh, believe me, I'm an experienced doctor of the soul, Dmitri Fyodorovitch."

"Madame, if you are an experienced doctor, I'm certainly an experienced patient," said Mitya, with an effort to be polite, "and I feel that if you are watching over my destiny in this way, you will come to my help in my ruin, and so allow me, at least to explain to you the plan with which I have ventured to come to you . . . and what I am hoping of you. . . . I have come, Madame. . . ."

"Don't explain it. It's of secondary importance. But as for help, you're not the first I have helped, Dmitri Fyodorovitch. You have most likely heard of my cousin, Madame Belmesov. Her husband was ruined, 'had come to grief,' as you characteristically express it, Dmitri Fyodorovitch. I recommended him to take to horse-breeding, and now he's doing well. Have you any idea of horse-breeding, Dmitri Fyodorovitch?"

"Not the faintest, Madame; ah, Madame, not the faintest!" cried Mitya, in nervous impatience, positively starting from his seat. "I simply implore you, Madame, to listen to me. Only give me two minutes of free speech that I may just explain to you everything, the whole plan with which I have come. Besides I am short of time. I'm in a fearful hurry." Mitya cried hysterically, feeling that she was just going to begin talking again, and hoping to cut her short. "I have come in despair . . . in the last gasp of despair, to beg you to lend me the sum of three thousand, a loan, but on safe, most safe security, Madame, with the most trustworthy guarantees! Only let me explain. . . ."

"You must tell me all that afterwards, afterwards!" Madame Hohlakov with a gesture demanded silence in her turn, "and whatever you may tell me, I know it all beforehand; I've told you so already. You ask for a certain sum, for three thousand, but I can give you more, immeasurably more, I will save you, Dmitri Fyodorovitch, but you must listen to me."

Mitya started from his seat again.

"Madame, will you really be so good!" he cried, with a strong feeling. "Good God, you've saved me! You have saved a man from a violent death, from a bullet. . . . My eternal gratitude. . . ."

"I will give you more, infinitely more than three thousand!" cried Madame Hohlakov, looking with a radiant smile at Mitya's ecstasy.

"Infinitely? But I don't need so much. I only need that fatal three thousand, and on my part I can give security for that sum with infinite gratitude, and I propose a plan which . . ."

"Enough, Dmitri Fyodorovitch, it's said and done." Madame Hohlakov cut him short, with the modest triumph of beneficence: "I have promised to save you, and I will save you. I will save you as I did Belmesov. What do you think of the gold-mines, Dmitri Fyodorovitch?"

"Of the gold-mines, Madame? I have never thought anything about them."

"But I have thought of them for you. Thought of them over and over again. I have been watching you for the last month. I've watched you a hundred times as you've walked past, saying to myself: that's a man of

energy who ought to be at the gold-mines. I've studied your gait and come
to the conclusion: that's a man who would find gold."

"From my gait, Madame?" said Mitya, smiling.

"Yes, from your gait. You surely don't deny that character can be told
from the gait, Dmitri Fyodorovitch? Science supports the idea. I'm all for
science and realism now. After all this business with Father Zossima, which
has so upset me, from this very day I'm a realist and I want to devote myself to practical usefulness. I'm cured. 'Enough!' as Turgenev says."[2]

"But, Madame, the three thousand you so generously promised to lend
me . . ."

"It is yours, Dmitri Fyodorovitch," Madame Hohlakov cut in at once.
"The money is as good as in your pocket, not three thousand, but three
million, Dmitri Fyodorovitch, in less than no time. I'll make you a present
of the idea: you shall find gold-mines, make millions, return and become a
leading man, and wake us up and lead us to better things. Are we to leave
it all to the Jews? You will found institutions and enterprises of all sorts.
You will help the poor, and they will bless you. This is the age of railways,
Dmitri Fyodorovitch. You'll become famous and indispensable to the Department of Finance, which is so badly off at present. The depreciation of
the rouble keeps me awake at night, Dmitri Fyodorovitch; people don't
know that side of me. . . ."

"Madame, Madame!" Dmitri interrupted with an uneasy presentiment.
"I shall indeed, perhaps, follow your advice, your wise advice, Madame. . . .
I shall perhaps set off . . . to the gold-mines. . . . I'll come and see you
again about it . . . many times, indeed . . . but now, that three thousand you
so generously . . . oh, that would set me free, and if you could to-day . . .
you see, I haven't a minute, a minute to lose to-day. . . ."

"Enough, Dmitri Fyodorovitch, enough!" Madame Hohlakov interrupted emphatically. "The question is, will you go to the gold-mines or not;
have you quite made up your mind? Answer yes or no."

"I will go, Madame, afterwards. . . . I'll go where you like . . . but now . . ."

"Wait!" cried Madame Hohlakov. And jumping up and running to a
handsome bureau with numerous little drawers, she began pulling out one
drawer after another, looking for something with desperate haste.

"The three thousand," thought Mitya, his heart almost stopping, "and at
the instant . . . without any papers or formalities . . . that's doing things in
gentlemanly style! She's a splendid woman, if only she didn't talk so much!"

"Here!" cried Madame Hohlakov, running back joyfully to Mitya,
"here is what I was looking for!"

It was a tiny silver ikon on a cord, such as is sometimes worn next the
skin with a cross.

"This is from Kiev, Dmitri Fyodorovitch," she went on reverently,
"from the relics of the Holy Martyr, Varvara.* Let me put it on your neck
myself, and with it dedicate you to a new life, to a new career."

*Russian name of Saint Barbara, fourth-century virgin and martyr.

And she actually put the cord round his neck, and began arranging it. In extreme embarrassment, Mitya bent down and helped her, and at last he got it under his neck-tie and collar through his shirt to his chest.

"Now you can set off," Madame Hohlakov pronounced, sitting down triumphantly in her place again.

"Madame, I am so touched. I don't know how to thank you, indeed . . . for such kindness, but . . . If only you knew how precious time is to me. . . . That sum of money, for which I shall be indebted to your generosity. . . . Oh, Madame, since you are so kind, so touchingly generous to me (Mitya exclaimed impulsively) then let me reveal to you . . . though, of course, you've known it a long time . . . that I love somebody here. . . . I have been false to Katya . . . Katerina Ivanovna I should say. . . . Oh, I've behaved inhumanly, dishonourably to her, but I fell in love here with another woman . . . a woman whom you, Madame, perhaps, despise, for you know everything already, but whom I cannot leave on any account, and therefore that three thousand now. . . ."

"Leave everything, Dmitri Fyodorovitch," Madame Hohlakov interrupted in the most decisive tone. "Leave everything, especially women. Gold-mines are your goal, and there's no place for women there. Afterwards, when you come back rich and famous, you will find the girl of your heart in the highest society. That will be a modern girl, a girl of education and advanced ideas. By that time the dawning woman question will have gained ground, and the new woman will have appeared."

"Madame, that's not the point, not at all. . . ." Mitya clasped his hands in entreaty.

"Yes, it is, Dmitri Fyodorovitch, just what you need; the very thing you're yearning for, though you don't realise it yourself. I am not at all opposed to the present woman movement, Dmitri Fyodorovitch. The development of woman, and even the political emancipation of woman in the near future—that's my ideal. I've a daughter myself, Dmitri Fyodorovitch, people don't know that side of me. I wrote a letter to the author, Shtchedrin, on that subject. He has taught me so much, so much about the vocation of woman. So last year I sent him an anonymous letter of two lines: 'I kiss and embrace you, my teacher, for the modern woman. Persevere.' And I signed myself, 'a Mother.' I thought of signing myself 'a contemporary Mother,' and hesitated, but I stuck to the simple 'Mother'; there's more moral beauty in that, Dmitri Fyodorovitch. And the word 'contemporary' might have reminded him of *The Contemporary*[3]—a painful recollection owing to the censorship. . . . Good Heavens, what is the matter!"

"Madame!" cried Mitya, jumping up at last, clasping his hands before her in helpless entreaty. "You will make me weep if you delay what you have so generously . . ."

"Oh, do weep, Dmitri Fyodorovitch, do weep! That's a noble feeling . . . such a path lies open before you! Tears will ease your heart, and later on you will return rejoicing. You will hasten to me from Siberia on purpose to share your joy with me. . . ."

"But allow me, too!" Mitya cried suddenly. "For the last time I entreat you, tell me, can I have the sum you promised me to-day, if not, when may I come for it?"

"What sum, Dmitri Fyodorovitch?"

"The three thousand you promised me . . . that you so generously . . ."

"Three thousand? Roubles? Oh, no, I haven't got three thousand," Madame Hohlakov announced with serene amazement. Mitya was stupefied.

"Why, you said just now . . . you said . . . you said it was as good as in my hands. . . ."

"Oh, no, you misunderstood me, Dmitri Fyodorovitch. In that case you misunderstood me. I was talking of the gold-mines. It's true I promised you more, infinitely more than three thousand, I remember it all now, but I was referring to the gold-mines."

"But the money? The three thousand?" Mitya exclaimed, awkwardly.

"Oh, if you meant money, I haven't any. I haven't a penny, Dmitri Fyodorovitch. I'm quarrelling with my steward about it, and I've just borrowed five hundred roubles from Miüsov, myself. No, no, I've no money. And, do you know, Dmitri Fyodorovitch, if I had, I wouldn't give it to you. In the first place I never lend money. Lending money means losing friends. And I wouldn't give it to you particularly. I wouldn't give it you, because I like you and want to save you, for all you need is the gold-mines, the gold-mines, the gold-mines!"

"Oh, the devil!" roared Mitya, and with all his might brought his fist down on the table.

"Aie! Aie!" cried Madame Hohlakov, alarmed, and she flew to the other end of the drawing-room.

Mitya spat on the ground, and strode rapidly out of the room, out of the house, into the street, into the darkness! He walked like one possessed, and beating himself on the breast, on the spot where he had struck himself two days previously, before Alyosha, the last time he saw him in the dark, on the road. What those blows upon his breast signified, *on that spot,* and what he meant by it—that was, for the time, a secret which was known to no one in the world, and had not been told even to Alyosha. But that secret meant for him more than disgrace; it meant ruin, suicide. So he had determined, if he did not get hold of the three thousand that would pay his debt to Katerina Ivanovna, and so remove from his breast, from *that spot on his breast,* the shame he carried upon it, that weighed on his conscience. All this will be fully explained to the reader later on, but now that his last hope had vanished, this man, so strong in appearance, burst out crying like a little child a few steps from the Hohlakovs' house. He walked on, and not knowing what he was doing, wiped away his tears with his fist. In this way he reached the square, and suddenly became aware that he had stumbled against something. He heard a piercing wail from an old woman whom he had almost knocked down.

"Good Lord, you've nearly killed me! Why don't you look where you're going, scapegrace?"

"Why, it's you!" cried Mitya, recognising the old woman in the dark. It was the old servant who waited on Samsonov, whom Mitya had particularly noticed the day before.

"And who are you, my good sir?" said the old woman in quite a different voice. "I don't know you in the dark."

"You live at Kuzma Kuzmitch's. You're the servant there?"

"Just so, sir, I was only running out to Prohoritch's. . . . But I don't know you now."

"Tell me, my good woman, is Agrafena Alexandrovna there now?" said Mitya, beside himself with suspense. "I saw her to the house some time ago."

"She has been there, sir. She stayed a little while, and went off again."

"What? Went away?" cried Mitya. "When did she go?"

"Why, as soon as she came. She only stayed a minute. She only told Kuzma Kuzmitch a tale that made him laugh, and then she ran away."

"You're lying, damn you!" roared Mitya.

"Aie! Aie!" shrieked the old woman, but Mitya had vanished.

He ran with all his might to the house where Grushenka lived. At the moment he reached it, Grushenka was on her way to Mokroe. It was not more than a quarter of an hour after her departure.

Fenya was sitting with her grandmother, the old cook, Matryona, in the kitchen when "the captain" ran in. Fenya uttered a piercing shriek on seeing him.

"You scream?" roared Mitya, "where is she?"

But without giving the terror-stricken Fenya time to utter a word, he fell all of a heap at her feet.

"Fenya, for Christ's sake, tell me, where is she?"

"I don't know. Dmitri Fyodorovitch, my dear, I don't know. You may kill me but I can't tell you." Fenya swore and protested. "You went out with her yourself not long ago. . . ."

"She came back!"

"Indeed she didn't. By God I swear she didn't come back."

"You're lying!" shouted Mitya. "From your terror I know where she is."

He rushed away. Fenya in her fright was glad she had got off so easily. But she knew very well that it was only that he was in such haste, or she might not have fared so well. But as he ran, he surprised both Fenya and old Matryona by an unexpected action. On the table stood a brass mortar, with a pestle in it, a small brass pestle, not much more than six inches long. Mitya already had opened the door with one hand when, with the other, he snatched up the pestle, and thrust it in his side pocket.

"Oh Lord! He's going to murder some one!" cried Fenya, flinging up her hands.

4

IN THE DARK

WHERE was he running? "Where could she be except at Fyodor Pavlovitch's? She must have run straight to him from Samsonov's, that was clear now. The whole intrigue, the whole deceit was evident." . . . It all rushed whirling through his mind. He did not run to Marya Kondratyevna's. "There was no need to go there . . . not the slightest need . . . he must raise no alarm . . . they would run and tell directly. . . . Marya Kondratyevna was clearly in the plot, Smerdyakov too, he too, all had been bought over!"

He formed another plan of action: he ran a long way round Fyodor Pavlovitch's house, crossing the lane, running down Dmitrovsky Street, then over the little bridge, and so came straight to the deserted alley at the back, which was empty and uninhabited, with, on one side the hurdle fence of a neighbour's kitchen-garden, on the other, the strong high fence, that ran all round Fyodor Pavlovitch's garden. Here he chose a spot, apparently the very place, where, according to the tradition, he knew Lizaveta had once climbed over it: "If she could climb over it," the thought, God knows why, occurred to him, "surely I can." He did in fact jump up, and instantly contrived to catch hold of the top of the fence. Then he vigorously pulled himself up and sat astride on it. Close by, in the garden stood the bathhouse, but from the fence he could see the lighted window of the house too.

"Yes, the old man's bedroom is lighted up. She's there!" and he leapt from the fence into the garden. Though he knew Grigory was ill and very likely Smerdyakov, too, and that there was no one to hear him, he instinctively hid himself, stood still, and began to listen. But there was dead silence on all sides and, as though of design, complete stillness, not the slightest breath of wind.

"And naught but the whispering silence," the line for some reason rose to his mind. "If only no one heard me jump over the fence! I think not." Standing still for a minute, he walked softly over the grass in the garden, avoiding the trees and shrubs. He walked slowly, creeping stealthily at every step, listening to his own footsteps. It took him five minutes to reach the lighted window. He remembered that just under the window there were several thick and high bushes of elder and white beam. The door from the house into the garden, on the left-hand side, was shut; he had carefully looked purposely to see, in passing. At last he reached the bushes and hid behind them. He held his breath. "I must wait now," he thought, "to reassure them, in case they heard my footsteps and are listening. . . . If only I don't cough or sneeze."

He waited two minutes. His heart was beating violently, and, at moments, he could scarcely breathe. "No, this throbbing at my heart won't stop," he thought. "I can't wait any longer." He was standing behind a bush in the shadow. The light of the window fell on the front part of the bush.

"How red the white beam berries are!" he murmured, not knowing why. Softly and noiselessly, step by step, he approached the window, and raised himself on tiptoe. All Fyodor Pavlovitch's bedroom lay open before him. It was not a large room, and was divided in two parts by a red screen, "Chinese," as Fyodor Pavlovitch used to call it. The word "Chinese" flashed into Mitya's mind, "and behind the screen, is Grushenka," thought Mitya. He began watching Fyodor Pavlovitch, who was wearing his new striped-silk dressing-gown, which Mitya had never seen, and a silk cord with tassels round the waist. A clean, dandified shirt of fine linen with gold studs peeped out under the collar of the dressing-gown. On his head Fyodor Pavlovitch had the same red bandage which Alyosha had seen.

"He has got himself up," thought Mitya.

His father was standing near the window, apparently lost in thought. Suddenly he jerked up his head, listened a moment, and, hearing nothing, went up to the table, poured out half a glass of brandy from a decanter, and drank it off. Then he uttered a deep sigh, again stood still a moment, walked carelessly up to the looking-glass on the wall, with his right hand raised the red bandage on his forehead a little, and began examining his bruises and scars, which had not yet disappeared.

"He's alone," thought Mitya, "in all probability he's alone."

Fyodor Pavlovitch moved away from the looking-glass, turned suddenly to the window and looked out. Mitya instantly slipped away into the shadow.

"She may be there behind the screen. Perhaps she's asleep by now," he thought, with a pang at his heart. Fyodor Pavlovitch moved away from the window. "He's looking for her out of the window, so she's not there. Why should he stare out into the dark? He's wild with impatience. . . ." Mitya slipped back at once, and fell to gazing in at the window again. The old man was sitting down at the table, apparently disappointed. At last he put his elbow on the table, and laid his right cheek against his hand. Mitya watched him eagerly.

"He's alone, he's alone!" he repeated again. "If she were here, his face would be different."

Strange to say, a queer, irrational vexation rose up in his heart that she was not here. "It's not that she's not here," he explained to himself, immediately, "but that I can't tell for certain whether she is or not." Mitya remembered afterwards that his mind was, at that moment, exceptionally clear, that he took in everything to the slightest detail, and missed no point. But a feeling of misery, the misery of uncertainty and indecision was growing in his heart with every instant, "Is she here or not?" The angry doubt filled his heart, and suddenly, making up his mind, he put out his hand and softly knocked on the window frame. He knocked the signal the old man had agreed upon with Smerdyakov, twice slowly and then three times more quickly, the signal that meant "Grushenka is here!"

The old man started, jerked up his head, and, jumping up quickly, ran to the window. Mitya slipped away into the shadow. Fyodor Pavlovitch opened the window and thrust his whole head out.

"Grushenka, is it you? Is it you?" he said, in a sort of trembling half-whisper. "Where are you, my angel, where are you?" He was fearfully agitated and breathless.

"He's alone," Mitya decided.

"Where are you?" cried the old man again; and he thrust his head out further, thrust it out to the shoulders, gazing in all directions, right and left. "Come here, I've a little present for you. Come, I'll show you. . . ."

"He means the three thousand," thought Mitya.

"But where are you? Are you at the door? I'll open it directly."

And the old man almost climbed out of the window, peering out to the right, where there was a door into the garden, trying to see into the darkness. In another second he would certainly have run out to open the door without waiting for Grushenka's answer.

Mitya looked at him from the side without stirring. The old man's profile that he loathed so, his pendant Adam's apple, his hooked nose, his lips that smiled in greedy expectation, were all brightly lighted up by the slanting lamplight falling on the left from the room. A horrible fury of hatred suddenly surged up in Mitya's heart, "There he was, his rival, the man who had tormented him, had ruined his life!" It was a rush of that sudden, furious, revengeful anger of which he had spoken, as though foreseeing it, to Alyosha, four days ago in the arbour, when, in answer to Alyosha's question, "How can you say you'll kill our father?" "I don't know, I don't know," he had said then. "Perhaps I shall not kill him, perhaps I shall. I'm afraid he'll suddenly be so loathsome to me at that moment. I hate his double chin, his nose, his eyes, his shameless grin, I feel a personal repulsion. That's what I'm afraid of, that's what may be too much for me. . . ." This personal repulsion was growing unendurable. Mitya was beside himself, he suddenly pulled the brass pestle out of his pocket.

"God was watching over me then," Mitya himself said afterwards. At that very moment Grigory waked up on his bed of sickness. Earlier in the evening he had undergone the treatment which Smerdyakov had described to Ivan. He had rubbed himself all over with vodka mixed with a secret very strong decoction, had drunk what was left of the mixture while his wife repeated a "certain prayer" over him, after which he had gone to bed. Marfa Ignatyevna had tasted the stuff, too, and, being unused to strong drink, slept like the dead beside her husband.

But Grigory waked up in the night, quite suddenly, and, after a moment's reflection, though he immediately felt a sharp pain in his back, he sat up in bed. Then he deliberated again, got up and dressed hurriedly. Perhaps his conscience was uneasy at the thought of sleeping while the house was unguarded "in such perilous times." Smerdyakov, exhausted by his fit, lay motionless in the next room. Marfa Ignatyevna did not stir. "The stuff's been too much for the woman," Grigory thought, glancing at her, and groaning, he went out on the steps. No doubt he only intended to look out from the steps for he was hardly able to walk, the pain in his back and his right leg was intolerable. But he suddenly remembered that he had not locked the little gate into the garden that evening. He was the most punctual and precise of men, a man who adhered to an unchangeable routine, and habits that lasted for years. Limping and writhing with pain he went down the steps and towards the garden. Yes, the gate stood wide open. Mechanically he stepped into the garden. Perhaps he fancied something, perhaps caught some sound, and, glancing to the left he saw his master's window open. No one was looking out of it then.

"What's it open for? It's not summer now," thought Grigory, and suddenly, at that very instant he caught a glimpse of something extraordinary before him in the garden. Forty paces in front of him a man seemed to be running in the dark, a sort of shadow was moving very fast.

"Good Lord!" cried Grigory beside himself, and forgetting the pain in his back, he hurried to intercept the running figure. He took a short cut, evidently he knew the garden better; the flying figure went towards the bath-house, ran behind it and rushed to the garden fence. Grigory followed, not losing sight of him, and ran, forgetting everything. He reached the fence at the very moment the man was climbing over it. Grigory cried out, beside himself, pounced on him, and clutched his leg in his two hands.

Yes, his foreboding had not deceived him. He recognised him, it was he, the "monster," the "parricide."

"Parricide!" the old man shouted so that the whole neighbourhood could hear, but he had not time to shout more, he fell at once, as though struck by lightning.

Mitya jumped back into the garden and bent over the fallen man. In Mitya's hands was a brass pestle, and he flung it mechanically in the grass. The pestle fell two faces from Grigory, not in the grass but on the path, in a most conspicuous place. For some seconds he examined the prostrate figure before him. The old man's head was covered with blood. Mitya put out his hand and began feeling it. He remembered afterwards clearly, that he had been awfully anxious to make sure whether he had broken the old man's skull, or simply stunned him with the pestle. But the blood was flowing horribly; and in a moment Mitya's fingers were drenched with the hot stream. He remembered taking out of his pocket the clean white handkerchief with which he had provided himself for his visit to Madame Hohlakov, and putting it to the old man's head, senselessly trying to wipe the blood from his face and temples. But the handkerchief was instantly soaked with blood.

"Good heavens! what am I doing it for?" thought Mitya, suddenly pulling himself together. "If I have broken his skull, how can I find out now? And what difference does it make now?" he added, hopelessly. "If I've killed him, I've killed him. . . . You've come to grief, old man, so there you must lie!" he said aloud. And suddenly, turning to the fence, he vaulted over it into the lane and fell to running—the handkerchief soaked with blood he held, crushed up, in his right fist, and, as he ran, he thrust it into the back pocket of his coat. He ran headlong, and the few passersby who met him in the dark, in the streets, remembered afterwards that they had met a man running that night. He flew back again to the widow Morozov's house.

Immediately after he had left it, that evening, Fenya had rushed to the chief porter, Nazar Ivanovitch, and besought him, for Christ's sake, "not to let the captain in again to-day or to-morrow." Nazar Ivanovitch promised, but went upstairs to his mistress who had suddenly sent for him, and meeting his nephew, a boy of twenty, who had recently come from the country, on the way up told him to take his place, but forgot to mention "the captain." Mitya, running up to the gate, knocked. The lad instantly recognised him, for Mitya had more than once tipped him. Opening the gate at once, he let him in, and hastened to inform him with a good-humoured smile that "Agrafena Alexandrovna is not at home now, you know."

"Where is she then, Prohor?" asked Mitya, stopping short.

"She set off this evening, some two hours ago, with Timofey, to Mokroe."

"What for?" cried Mitya.

"That I can't say. To see some officer. Some one invited her and horses were sent to fetch her."

Mitya left him, and ran like a madman to Fenya.

5

A SUDDEN RESOLUTION

SHE was sitting in the kitchen with her grandmother; they were both just goint to bed. Relying on Nazar Ivanovitch, they had not locked themselves in. Mitya ran in, pounced on Fenya and seized her by the throat.

"Speak at once! Where is she? With whom is she now, at Mokroe?" he roared furiously.

Both the women squealed.

"Aie! I'll tell you. Aie, Dmitri Fyodorovitch, darling, I'll tell you everything directly, I won't hide anything," gabbed Fenya, frightened to death; "she's gone to Mokroe, to her officer."

"What officer?" roared Mitya.

"To her officer, the same one she used to know, the one who threw her over five years ago," cackled Fenya, as fast as she could speak.

Mitya withdrew the hands with which he was squeezing her throat. He stood facing her, pale as death, unable to utter a word, but his eyes showed that he realised it all, all, from the first word, and guessed the whole position. Poor Fenya was not in a condition at that moment to observe whether he understood or not. She remained sitting on the trunk as she had been when he ran into the room, trembling all over, holding her hands out before her as though trying to defend herself. She seemed to have grown rigid in that position. Her wide-opened, scared eyes were fixed immovably upon him. And to make matters worse, both his hands were smeared with blood. On the way, as he ran, he must have touched his forehead with them, wiping off the perspiration, so that on his forehead and his right cheek were blood-stained patches. Fenya was on the verge of hysterics. The old cook had jumped up and was staring at him like a mad woman, almost unconscious with terror.

Mitya stood for a moment, then mechanically sank on to a chair next to Fenya. He sat, not reflecting but, as it were, terror-stricken, benumbed. Yet everything was clear as day: that officer, he knew about him, he knew everything perfectly, he had known it from Grushenka herself, had known that a letter had come from him a month before. So that for a month, for a whole month this had been going on in secret from him, till the very arrival of this new man, and he had never thought of him! But how could he, how could he not have thought of him? Why was it he had forgotten this officer, like that, forgotten him as soon as he heard of him? That was the question that faced him like some monstrous thing. And he looked at this monstrous thing with horror, growing cold with horror.

But suddenly, as gently and mildly as a gentle and affectionate child, he began speaking to Fenya as though he had utterly forgotten how he had scared and hurt her just now. He fell to questioning Fenya with an extreme preciseness, astonishing in his position, and though the girl looked wildly at his blood-stained hands, she, too, with wonderful readiness and rapidity, answered every question as though eager to put the whole truth and nothing but the truth before him. Little by little, even with a sort of enjoyment, she began explaining every detail, not wanting to torment him, but, as it were, eager to be of the utmost service to him. She described the whole of that day, in great detail, the visit of Rakitin and Alyosha, how she, Fenya, had stood on the watch, how the mistress had set off, and how she had called out of the window to Alyosha to give him, Mitya, her greetings, and to tell him "to remember for ever how she had loved him for an hour."

Hearing of the message, Mitya suddenly smiled, and there was a flush of colour on his pale cheeks. At the same moment Fenya said to him, not a bit afraid now to be inquisitive:

"Look at your hands, Dmitri Fyodorovitch. They're all over blood!"

"Yes," answered Mitya mechanically. He looked carelessly at his hands and at once forgot them and Fenya's question.

He sank into silence again. Twenty minutes had passed since he had run in. His first horror was over, but evidently some new fixed determination had taken possession of him. He suddenly stood up, smiling dreamily.

"What has happened to you, sir?" said Fenya, pointing to his hands again. She spoke compassionately, as though she felt very near to him now in his grief. Mitya looked at his hands again.

"That's blood, Fenya," he said, looking at her with a strange expression. "That's human blood, and, my God! why was it shed? but . . . Fenya . . . there's a fence here" (he looked at her as though setting her a riddle) "a high fence, and terrible to look at. But, at dawn to-morrow, when the sun rises, Mitya will leap over that fence. . . . You don't understand what fence, Fenya, and, never mind. . . . You'll hear to-morrow and understand . . . and now, good-bye. I won't stand in her way. I'll step aside, I know how to step aside. Live, my joy. . . . You loved me for an hour, remember Mityenka Karamazov so for ever. . . . She always used to call me Mityenka, do you remember?"

And with those words he went suddenly out of the kitchen. Fenya was almost more frightened at this sudden departure than she had been when he ran in and attacked her.

Just ten minutes later Dmitri went in to Pyotr Ilyitch Perhotin, the young official with whom he had pawned his pistols. It was by now half-past eight, and Pyotr Ilyitch had finished his evening tea, and had just put his coat on again to go to the "Metropolis" to play billiards. Mitya caught him coming out.

Seeing him with his face all smeared with blood, the young man uttered a cry of surprise.

"Good Heavens! What is the matter?"

"I've come for my pistols," said Mitya, "and brought you the money. And thanks very much. I'm in a hurry, Pyotr Ilyitch, please make haste."

Pyotr Ilyitch grew more and more surprised; he suddenly caught sight of a bundle of bank-notes in Mitya's hand, and what was more, he had walked in holding the notes as no one walks in and no one carries money: he had them in his right hand, and held them outstretched as if to show them. Perhotin's servant-boy, who met Mitya in the passage, said afterwards that he walked into the passage in the same way, with the money outstretched in his hand, so he must have been carrying them like that even in the street. They were all rainbow-coloured hundred-rouble notes, and the fingers holding them were covered with blood.

When Pyotr Ilyitch was questioned later on as to the sum of money, he said that it was difficult to judge at a glance, but that it might have been two thousand, or perhaps three, but it was a big, "fat" bundle. "Dmitri Fyodorovitch," so he testified afterwards, "seemed unlike himself, too; not drunk, but, as it were, exalted, lost to everything, but at the same time, as it were, absorbed, as though pondering and searching for something and unable to come to a decision. He was in great haste, answered abruptly and very strangely, and at moments seemed not at all dejected but quite cheerful."

"But what *is* the matter with you? What's wrong?" cried Pyotr Ilyitch, looking wildly at his guest. "How is it that you're all covered with blood? Have you had a fall? Look at yourself!"

He took him by the elbow and led him to the glass.

Seeing his blood-stained face, Mitya started and scowled wrathfully.

"Damnation! That's the last straw," he muttered angrily, hurriedly changing the notes from his right hand to the left, and impulsively jerked the handkerchief out of his pocket. But the handkerchief turned out to be soaked with blood, too (it was the handkerchief he had used to wipe Grigory's face). There was scarcely a white spot on it, and it had not merely begun to dry, but had stiffened into a crumpled ball and could not be pulled apart. Mitya threw it angrily on the floor.

"Oh, damn it!" he said. "Haven't you a rag of some sort . . . to wipe my face?"

"So you're only stained, not wounded? You'd better wash," said Pyotr Ilyitch. "Here's a wash-stand. I'll pour you out some water."

"A wash-stand? That's all right . . . but where am I to put this?"

With the strangest perplexity he indicated his bundle of hundred-rouble notes, looking inquiringly at Pyotr Ilyitch as though it were for him to decide what he, Mitya, was to do with his own money.

"In your pocket, or on the table here. They won't be lost."

"In my pocket? Yes, in my pocket. All right. . . . But, I say, that's all nonsense," he cried, as though suddenly coming out of his absorption. "Look here, let's first settle that business of the pistols. Give them back to me. Here's your money . . . because I am in great need of them . . . and I haven't a minute, a minute to spare."

And taking the topmost note from the bundle he held it out to Pyotr Ilyitch.

"But I shan't have change enough. Haven't you less?"

"No," said Mitya, looking again at the bundle, and as though not trusting his own words he turned over two or three of the topmost ones.

"No, they're all alike," he added, and again he looked inquiringly at Pyotr Ilyitch.

"How have you grown so rich?" the latter asked. "Wait, I'll send my boy to Plotnikov's, they close late—to see if they won't change it. Here, Misha!" he called into the passage.

"To Plotnikov's shop—first rate!" cried Mitya, as though struck by an idea. "Misha," he turned to the boy as he came in, "look here, run to Plotnikov's and tell them that Dmitri Fyodorovitch sends his greetings, and will be there directly. . . . But listen, listen, tell them to have champagne, three dozen bottles ready before I come, and packed as it was to take to Mokroe. I took four dozen with me then," he added (suddenly addressing Pyotr Ilyitch); "they know all about it, don't you trouble, Misha," he turned again to the boy. "Stay, listen; tell them to put in cheese, Strasburg pies, smoked fish, ham, caviare, and everything, everything they've got, up to a hundred roubles, or a hundred and twenty as before. . . . But wait: don't let them forget dessert, sweets, pears, watermelons, two or three or four—no, one melon's enough, and chocolate, candy, toffee, fondants; in fact, everything I took to Mokroe before, three hundred roubles' worth with the champagne . . . let it be just the same again. And remember, Misha, if you are called Misha. . . . His name is Misha, isn't it?" He turned to Pyotr Ilyitch again.

"Wait a minute," Pyotr Ilyitch intervened, listening and watching him uneasily, "you'd better go yourself and tell them. He'll muddle it."

"He will, I see he will! Eh, Misha! Why, I was going to kiss you for the commission. . . . If you don't make a mistake, there's ten roubles for you, run along, make haste. . . . Champagne's the chief thing, let them bring up champagne. And brandy, too, and red and white wine, and all I had then. . . . They know what I had then."

"But listen!" Pyotr Ilyitch interrupted with some impatience. "I say, let him simply run and change the money and tell them not to close, and you go and tell them. . . . Give him your note. Be off, Misha! Put your best leg forward!"

Pyotr Ilyitch seemed to hurry Misha off on purpose, because the boy remained standing with his mouth and eyes wide open, apparently understanding little of Mitya's orders, gazing up with amazement and terror at his blood-stained face and the trembling blood-stained fingers that held the notes.

"Well, now come and wash," said Pyotr Ilyitch, sternly. "Put the money on the table or else in your pocket. . . . That's right, come along. But take off your coat."

And beginning to help him off with his coat, he cried out again:

"Look, your coat's covered with blood, too!"

"That . . . it's not the coat. It's only a little here on the sleeve. . . . And that's only here where the handkerchief lay. It must have soaked through. I must have sat on the handkerchief at Fenya's, and the blood's come through," Mitya explained at once with a childlike unconsciousness that was astounding. Pyotr Ilyitch listened, frowning.

"Well, you must have been up to something; you must have been fighting with some one," he muttered.

They began to wash. Pyotr Ilyitch held the jug and poured out the water. Mitya, in desperate haste, scarcely soaped his hands (they were trembling, and Pyotr Ilyitch remembered it afterwards). But the young official insisted on his soaping them thoroughly and rubbing them more. He seemed to exercise more and more sway over Mitya, as time went on. It may be noted in passing that he was a young man of sturdy character.

"Look, you haven't got your nails clean. Now rub your face; here, on your temples, by your ear. . . . Will you go in that shirt? Where are you going? Look, all the cuff of your right sleeve is covered with blood."

"Yes, it's all bloody," observed Mitya, looking at the cuff of his shirt.

"Then change your shirt."

"I haven't time. You see I'll . . ." Mitya went on with the same confiding ingenuousness, drying his face and hands on the towel, and putting on his coat. "I'll turn it up at the wrist. It won't be seen under the coat. . . . You see!"

"Tell me now, what game have you been up to? Have you been fighting with some one? In the tavern again, as before? Have you been beating that captain again?" Pyotr Ilyitch asked him reproachfully. "Whom have you been beating now . . . or killing, perhaps?"

"Nonsense!" said Mitya.

"Why 'nonsense'?"

"Don't worry," said Mitya, and he suddenly laughed. "I smashed an old woman in the market-place just now."

"Smashed? An old woman?"

"An old man!" cried Mitya, looking Pyotr Ilyitch straight in the face, laughing, and shouting at him as though he were deaf.

"Confound it! An old woman, an old man. . . . Have you killed some one?"

"We made it up. We had a row—and made it up. In a place I know of. We parted friends. A fool. . . . He's forgiven me. . . . He's sure to have forgiven me by now . . . if he had got up, he wouldn't have forgiven me"— Mitya suddenly winked—"only, damn him, you know, I say, Pyotr Ilyitch, damn him! Don't worry about him! I don't want to just now!" Mitya snapped out, resolutely.

"Whatever do you want to go picking quarrels with every one for? . . . Just as you did with that captain over some nonsense. . . . You've been fighting and now you're rushing off on the spree—that's you all over! Three dozen champagne—what do you want all that for?"

"Bravo! Now give me the pistols. Upon my honour I've no time now. I should like to have a chat with you, my dear boy, but I haven't the time. And there's no need, it's too late for talking. Where's my money? Where have I put it?" he cried, thrusting his hands into his pockets.

"You put it on the table . . . yourself. . . . Here it is. Had you forgotten? Money's like dirt or water to you, it seems. Here are your pistols. It's an odd thing, at six o'clock you pledged them for ten roubles, and now you've got thousands. Two or three I should say."

"Three, you bet," laughed Mitya, stuffing the notes into the side pocket of his trousers.

"You'll lose it like that. Have you found a gold-mine?"

"The mines? The gold-mines?" Mitya shouted at the top of his voice and went off in a roar of laughter. "Would you like to go to the mines, Perhotin? There's a lady here who'll stump up three thousand for you, if only you'll go. She did it for me, she's so awfully fond of gold-mines. Do you know Madame Hohlakov?"

"I don't know her, but I've heard of her and seen her. Did she really give you three thousand? Did she really?" said Pyotr Ilyitch, eyeing him dubiously.

"As soon as the sun rises to-morrow, as soon as Phœbus, ever young, flees upwards, praising and glorifying God, you go to her, this Madame Hohlakov and ask her whether she did stump up that three thousand or not. Try and find out."

"I don't know on what terms you are . . . since you say it so positively, I suppose she did give it to you. You've got the money in your hand, but instead of going to Siberia you're spending it all. . . . Where are you really off to now, eh?"

"To Mokroe."

"To Mokroe? But it's night!"

"Once the lad had all, now the lad has naught," cried Mitya suddenly.

"How 'naught'? You say that with all those thousands!"

"I'm not talking about thousands. Damn thousands! I'm talking of the female character.

> 'Fickle is the heart of woman
> Treacherous and full of vices;'*

I agree with Ulysses. That's what he says."

"I don't understand you!"

"Am I drunk?"

"Not drunk, but worse."

"I'm drunk in spirit, Pyotr Ilyitch, drunk in spirit! But that's enough!"

"What are you doing, loading the pistol?"

"I'm loading the pistol."

Unfastening the pistol-case, Mitya actually opened the powder horn, and carefully sprinkled and rammed in the charge. Then he took the bullet and before inserting it, held it in two fingers in front of the candle.

"Why are you looking at the bullet?" asked Pyotr Ilyitch, watching him with uneasy curiosity.

"Oh, a fancy. Why, if you meant to put that bullet in your brain, would you look at it or not?"

"Why look at it?"

"It's going into my brain, so it's interesting to look and see what it's like. But that's foolishness, a moment's foolishness. Now that's done," he added, putting in the bullet and driving it home with the ramrod. "Pyotr Ilyitch, my dear fellow, that's nonsense, all nonsense, and if only you knew what nonsense! Give me a little piece of paper now."

"Here's some paper."

"No, a clean new piece, writing paper. That's right."

And taking a pen from the table, Mitya rapidly wrote two lines, folded the paper in four, and thrust it in his waistcoat pocket. He put the pistols in the case, locked it up, and kept it in his hand. Then he looked at Pyotr Ilyitch with a slow, thoughtful smile.

"Now, let's go," he said.

"Where are we going? No, wait a minute. . . . Are you thinking of putting that bullet in your brain, perhaps?" Pyotr Ilyitch asked uneasily.

"I was fooling about the bullet! I want to live. I love life! You may be sure of that. I love golden-haired Phœbus and his warm light. . . . Dear Pyotr Ilyitch, do you know how to step aside?"

"What do you mean by 'stepping aside'?"

"Making way. Making way for a dear creature, and for one I hate. And to let the one I hate become dear—that's what making way means? And to say to them: God bless you, go your way, pass on, while I . . ."

---

*Quotation from Tyutchev's translation of Schiller's "The Victory Celebration" (1803); the words are spoken by Ulysses.

"While you?"

"That's enough, let's go."

"Upon my word, I'll tell some one to prevent your going there," said Pyotr Ilyitch, looking at him. "What are you going to Mokroe for, now?"

"There's a woman there, a woman. That's enough for you. You shut up."

"Listen, though you're such a savage I've always liked you. . . . I feel anxious."

"Thanks, old fellow. I'm a savage you say. Savages, savages! That's what I'm always saying. Savages! Why, here's Misha! I was forgetting him."

Misha ran in, post haste, with a handful of notes in change, and reported that every one was in a bustle at the Plotnikovs'; "They're carrying down the bottles, and the fish, and the tea; it will all be ready directly." Mitya seized ten roubles and handed it to Pyotr Ilyitch, then tossed another ten-rouble note to Misha.

"Don't dare to do such a thing!" cried Pyotr Ilyitch. "I won't have it in my house, it's a bad, demoralising habit. Put your money away. Here, put it here, why waste it? It would come in handy to-morrow, and I daresay you'll be coming to me to borrow ten roubles again. Why do you keep putting the notes in your side pocket? Ah, you'll lose them!"

"I say, my dear fellow, let's go to Mokroe together."

"What should I go for?"

"I say, let's open a bottle at once, and drink to life! I want to drink, and especially to drink with you. I've never drunk with you, have I?"

"Very well, we can go to the 'Metropolis.' I was just going there."

"I haven't time for that. Let's drink at the Plotnikovs', in the back room. Shall I ask you a riddle?"

"Ask away."

Mitya took the piece of paper out of his waistcoat pocket, unfolded it and showed it. In a large, distinct hand was written:

"I punish myself for my whole life, my whole life I punish!"

"I certainly will speak to some one, I'll go at once," said Pyotr Ilyitch, after reading the paper.

"You won't have time, dear boy, come and have a drink. March!"

Plotnikovs' shop was at the corner of the street, next door but one to Pyotr Ilyitch's. It was the largest grocery shop in our town, and by no means a bad one, belonging to some rich merchants. They kept everything that could be got in a Petersburg shop, groceries of all sorts, wines "bottled by the brothers Eliseyev," fruits, cigars, tea, coffee, sugar, and so on. There were three shop-assistants and two errand boys always employed. Though our part of the country had grown poorer, the landowners had gone away, and trade had got worse, yet the grocery stores flourished as before, every year with increasing prosperity; there were plenty of purchasers for their goods.

They were awaiting Mitya with impatience in the shop. They had vivid recollections of how he had bought, three or four weeks ago, wine and goods of all sorts to the value of several hundred roubles, paid for in cash (they would never have let him have anything on credit, of course). They remembered that then, as now, he had had a bundle of hundred-rouble notes in his hand, and had scattered them at random, without bargaining, without reflecting, or caring to reflect what use so much wine and provisions would be to him. The story was told all over the town that, driving off then with Grushenka to Mokroe he had "spent three thousand in one night and the following day, and had come back from the spree without a penny." He had picked up a whole troop of gipsies (encamped in our neighbourhood at the time), who for two days got money without stint out of him while he was drunk, and drank expensive wine without stint. People used to tell, laughing at Mitya, how he had given champagne to grimy-handed peasants, and feasted the village women and girls on sweets and Strasburg pies. Though to laugh at Mitya to his face was rather a risky proceeding, there was much laughter behind his back, especially in the tavern, at his own ingenuous public avowal that all he had got out of Grushenka by this "escapade" was "permission to kiss her foot, and that was the utmost she had allowed him."

By the time Mitya and Pyotr Ilyitch reached the shop, they found a cart with three horses harnessed abreast with bells, and with Andrey, the driver, ready waiting for Mitya at the entrance. In the shop they had almost entirely finished packing one box of provisions, and were only waiting for Mitya's arrival to nail it down and put it in the cart. Pyotr Ilyitch was astounded.

"Where did this cart come from in such a hurry?" he asked Mitya.

"I met Andrey as I ran to you, and told him to drive straight here to the shop. There's no time to lose. Last time I drove with Timofey, but Timofey now has gone on before me with the witch. Shall we be very late, Andrey?"

"They'll only get there an hour at most before us, not even that maybe. I got Timofey ready to start, I know how he'll go. Their pace won't be ours, Dmitri Fyodorovitch. How could it be? They won't get there an hour earlier!" Andrey, a lanky, red-haired, middle-aged driver, wearing a full-skirted coat, and with a kaftan on his arm, replied warmly.

"Fifty roubles for vodka if we're only an hour behind them."

"I warrant the time, Dmitri Fyodorovitch. Ech, they won't be half an hour before us, let alone an hour."

Though Mitya bustled about seeing after things, he gave his orders strangely, as it were disconnectedly, and inconsecutively. He began a sentence and forgot the end of it. Pyotr Ilyitch found himself obliged to come to the rescue.

"Four hundred roubles' worth, not less than four hundred roubles' worth, just as it was then," commanded Mitya. "Four dozen champagne, not a bottle less."

"What do you want with so much? What's it for? Stay!" cried Pyotr Ilyitch. "What's this box? What's in it? Surely there isn't four hundred roubles' worth here?"

The officious shopmen began explaining with oily politeness that the first box contained only half a dozen bottles of champagne, and only "the most indispensable articles" such as savouries, sweets, toffee, &c. But the main part of the goods ordered would be packed and sent off, as on the previous occasion, in a special cart, also with three horses, travelling at full speed, so that it would arrive not more than an hour later than Dmitri Fyodorovitch himself.

"Not more than an hour! Not more than an hour! And put in more toffee and fondants. The girls there are so fond of it," Mitya insisted hotly.

"The fondants are alright. But what do you want with four dozen of champagne? One would be enough," said Pyotr Ilyitch, almost angry. He began bargaining, asking for a bill of the goods, and refused to be satisfied. But he only succeeded in saving a hundred roubles. In the end it was agreed that only three hundred roubles' worth should be sent.

"Well, you may go to the devil!" cried Pyotr Ilyitch, on second thoughts. "What's it to do with me? Throw away your money, since it's cost you nothing."

"This way, my economist, this way, don't be angry." Mitya drew him into a room at the back of the shop. "They'll give us a bottle here directly. We'll taste it. Ech, Pyotr Ilyitch, come along with me, for you're a nice fellow, the sort I like."

Mitya sat down on a wicker chair, before a little table, covered with a dirty dinner napkin. Pyotr Ilyitch sat down opposite, and the champagne soon appeared, and oysters were suggested to the gentlemen. "First-class oysters, the last lot in."

"Hang the oysters. I don't eat them. And we don't need anything," cried Pyotr Ilyitch, almost angrily.

"There's no time for oysters," said Mitya. "And I'm not hungry. Do you know, friend," he said suddenly, with feeling, "I never have liked all this disorder."

"Who does like it? Three dozen of champagne for peasants, upon my word, that's enough to make any one angry!"

"That's not what I mean. I'm talking of a higher order. There's no order in me, no higher order. But . . . that's all over. There's no need to grieve about it. It's too late, damn it! My whole life has been disorder, and one must set it in order. Is that a pun, eh?"

"You're raving, not making puns!"

> " 'Glory be to God in Heaven,
>   Glory be to God in me' . . .

"That verse came from my heart once, it's not a verse but a tear. . . . I made it myself . . . not while I was pulling the captain's beard, though. . . ."

"Why do you bring him in all of a sudden?"

"Why do I bring him in? Foolery! All things come to an end; all things are made equal. That's the long and the short of it."

"You know, I keep thinking of your pistols."

"That's all foolery, too! Drink, and don't be fanciful. I love life. I've loved life too much, shamefully much. Enough! Let's drink to life, dear boy, I propose the toast. Why am I pleased with myself? I'm a scoundrel, but I'm satisfied with myself. And yet I'm tortured by the thought that I'm a scoundrel, but satisfied with myself. I bless the creation. I'm ready to bless God and His creation directly, but . . . I must kill one noxious insect for fear it should crawl and spoil life for others. . . . Let us drink to life, dear brother. What can be more precious than life? Nothing! To life, and to one queen of queens."

"Let's drink to life and to your queen, too, if you like."

They drank a glass each. Although Mitya was excited and expansive, yet he was melancholy, too. It was as though some heavy, overwhelming anxiety were weighing upon him.

"Misha . . . here's your Misha come! Misha, come here, my boy, drink this glass to Phœbus; the golden-haired, of to-morrow morn. . . ."

"What are you giving it to him for?" cried Pyotr Ilyitch, irritably.

"Yes, yes, yes, let me! I want to!"

"E—ech!"

Misha emptied the glass, bowed, and ran out.

"He'll remember it afterwards," Mitya remarked. "Woman, I love woman! What is woman? The queen of creation! My heart is sad, my heart is sad, Pyotr Ilyitch. Do you remember Hamlet? 'I am very sorry, good Horatio! Alas, poor Yorick!'* Perhaps that's me, Yorick? Yes, I'm Yorick now, and a skull afterwards."

Pyotr Ilyitch listened in silence. Mitya, too, was silent for awhile.

"What dog's that you've got here?" he asked the shopman, casually, noticing a pretty little lap-dog with dark eyes, sitting in the corner.

"It belongs to Varvara Alexyevna, the mistress," answered the clerk. "She brought it and forgot it here. It must be taken back to her."

"I saw one like it . . . in the regiment . . ." murmured Mitya dreamily, "only that one had its hind leg broken. . . . By the way, Pyotr Ilyitch, I wanted to ask you: have you ever stolen anything in your life?"

"What a question!"

"Oh, I didn't mean anything. From somebody's pocket, you know. I don't mean government money, every one steals that, and no doubt you do, too. . . ."

"You go to the devil."

"I'm talking of other peoples' money. Stealing straight out of a pocket? Out of a purse, eh?"

"I stole twenty kopecks from my mother when I was nine years old. I took it off the table on the sly, and held it tight in my hand."

"Well, and what happened?"

"Oh, nothing. I kept it three days, then I felt ashamed, confessed and gave it back."

"And what then?"

"Naturally I was whipped. But why do you ask? Have you stolen something?"

"I have," said Mitya winking slyly.

"What have you stolen?" inquired Pyotr Ilyitch curiously.

---

*Dmitri is recalling Shakespeare's *Hamlet* (act 5, scene 1).

"I stole twenty kopecks from my mother when I was nine years old, and gave it back three days after."

As he said this, Mitya suddenly got up.

"Dmitri Fyodorovitch, won't you come now?" called Andrey from the door of the shop.

"Are you ready? We'll come!" Mitya started. "A few more last words and . . . Andrey, a glass of vodka at starting. Give him some brandy as well! That box" (the one with the pistols) "put under my seat. Good-bye, Pyotr Ilyitch, don't remember evil against me."

"But you're coming back to-morrow?"

"Of course."

"Will you settle the little bill now?" cried the clerk, springing forward.

"Oh yes, the bill. Of course."

He pulled the bundle of notes out of his pocket again, picked out three hundred roubles, threw them on the counter, and ran hurriedly out of the shop. Every one followed him out, bowing and wishing him good luck. Andrey, coughing from the brandy he had just swallowed, jumped up on the box. But Mitya was only just taking his seat when suddenly, to his surprise, he saw Fenya before him. She ran up panting, clasped her hands before him with a cry, and plumped down at his feet.

"Dmitri Fyodorovitch, dear good Dmitri Fyodorovitch, don't harm my mistress. And it was I told you all about it. . . . And don't murder him, he came first, he's hers! He'll marry Agrafena Alexandrovna now. That's why he's come back from Siberia. Dmitri Fyodorovitch, dear, don't take a fellow creature's life!"

"Tut—tut—tut! That's it, is it? So you're off there to make trouble!" muttered Pyotr Ilyitch. "Now, it's all clear, as clear as daylight. Dmitri Fyodorovitch, give me your pistols at once if you mean to behave like a man," he shouted aloud to Mitya. "Do you hear, Dmitri?"

"The pistols? Wait a bit, brother, I'll throw them into the pool on the road," answered Mitya. "Fenya, get up, don't kneel to me. Mitya won't hurt any one, the silly fool won't hurt any one again. But I say, Fenya," he shouted, after having taken his seat. "I hurt you just now, so forgive me and have pity on me, forgive a scoundrel. . . . But it doesn't matter if you don't. It's all the same now. Now then, Andrey, look alive, fly along full speed!"

Andrey whipped up the horses, and the bells began ringing.

"Good-bye, Pyotr Ilyitch! My last tear is for you! . . ."

"He's not drunk, but he keeps babbling like a lunatic," Pyotr Ilyitch thought as he watched him go. He had half a mind to stay and see the cart packed with the remaining wines and provisions, knowing that they would deceive and defraud Mitya. But, suddenly feeling vexed with himself, he turned away with a curse and went to the tavern to play billiards.

"He's a fool, though he's a good fellow," he muttered as he went. "I've heard of that officer, Grushenka's former flame. Well, if he has turned up. . . . Ech, those pistols! Damn it all! I'm not his nurse! Let them do what they like! Besides, it'll all come to nothing. They're a set of brawlers, that's all. They'll drink and fight, fight and make friends again. They are not men who do anything real. What does he mean by 'I'm stepping aside, I'm punishing myself?' It'll come to nothing! He's shouted such phrases a thousand times, drunk, in the taverns. But now he's not drunk. 'Drunk in spirit'—they're fond of fine phrases, the villains. Am I his nurse? He must have been fighting, his face was all over blood. With whom? I shall find out at the 'Metropolis.' And his handkerchief was soaked in blood. . . . It's still lying on my floor. . . . Hang it!"

He reached the tavern in a bad humour and at once made up a game. The game cheered him. He played a second game, and suddenly began telling one of his partners that Dmitri Karamazov had come in for some cash again—something like three thousand roubles, and had gone to Mokroe again to spend it with Grushenka. . . . This news roused singular interest in his listeners. They all spoke of it, not laughing, but with a strange gravity. They left off playing.

"Three thousand? But where can he have got three thousand?"

Questions were asked. The story of Madame Hohlakov's present was received with scepticism.

"Hasn't he robbed his old father, that's the question?"

"Three thousand! There's something odd about it."

"He boasted aloud that he would kill his father; we all heard him, here. And it was three thousand he talked about. . . ."

Pyotr Ilyitch listened. All at once he became short and dry in his answers. He said not a word about the blood on Mitya's face and hands, though he had meant to speak of it at first.

They began a third game, and by degree the talk about Mitya died away. But by the end of the third game, Pyotr Ilyitch felt no more desire for billiards; he laid down the cue, and without having supper as he had intended, he walked out of the tavern. When he reached the market-place he stood still in perplexity, wondering at himself. He realised that what he wanted was to go to Fyodor Pavlovitch's and find out if anything had happened there, "On account of some stupid nonsense—as it's sure to turn out—am I going to wake up the household and make a scandal? Fooh! damn it, is it my business to look after them?"

In a very bad humour he went straight home, and suddenly remembered Fenya. "Damn it all! I ought to have questioned her just now," he thought with vexation, "I should have heard everything." And the desire to speak to her, and so find out, became so pressing and importunate that when he was half-way home he turned abruptly and went towards the house where Grushenka lodged. Going up to the gate he knocked. The sound of the knock in the silence of the night sobered him and made him feel annoyed. And no one answered him; every one in the house was asleep.

"And I shall be making a fuss!" he thought, with a feeling of positive discomfort. But instead of going away altogether, he fell to knocking again with all his might, filling the street with clamour.

"Not coming? Well, I will knock them up, I will!" he muttered at each knock, fuming at himself, but at the same time he redoubled his knocks on the gate.

6

"I AM COMING, TOO!"

B UT Dmitri Fyodorovitch was speeding along the road. It was a little more than twenty versts to Mokroe, but Andrey's three horses galloped at such a pace that the distance might be covered in an hour and a quarter. The swift motion revived Mitya. The air was fresh and cool, there were big stars shining in the sky. It was the very night, and perhaps the very hour, in which Alyosha fell on the earth, and rapturously swore to love it for ever and ever.

All was confusion, confusion, in Mitya's soul but although many things were goading his heart, at that moment his whole being was yearning for her, his queen, to whom he was flying to look on her for the last time. One thing I can say for certain; his heart did not waver for one instant. I shall perhaps not be believed when I say that this jealous lover felt not the slightest jealousy of this new rival, who seemed to have sprung out of the earth. If any other had appeared on the scene, he would have been jealous at once, and would perhaps have stained his fierce hands with blood again. But as he flew through the night, he felt no envy, no hostility even, for the man who had been her first lover. . . . It is true he had not yet seen him.

"Here there was no room for dispute: it was her right and his; this was her first love which, after five years, she had not forgotten; so she had loved him only for those five years, and I, how do I come in? What right have I? Step aside, Mitya, and make way! What am I now? Now everything is over apart from the officer—even if he had not appeared, everything would be over. . . ."

These words would roughly have expressed his feelings, if he had been capable of reasoning. But he could not reason at that moment. His present plan of action had arisen without reasoning. At Fenya's first words, it had sprung from feeling, and been adopted in a flash, with all its consequences. And yet, in spite of his resolution, there was confusion in his soul, an agonising confusion: his resolution did not give him peace. There was so much behind that tortured him. And it seemed strange to him, at moments, to think that he had written his own sentence of death with pen and paper: "I punish myself," and the paper was lying there in his pocket, ready; the pistol was loaded; he had already resolved how, next morning, he would meet the first warm ray of "golden-haired Phœbus."

And yet he could not be quit of the past, of all that he had left behind and that tortured him. He felt that miserably, and the thought of it sank into his heart with despair. There was one moment when he felt an impulse to stop Andrey, to jump out of the cart, to pull out his loaded pistol, and to make an end of everything without waiting for the dawn. But that moment flew by like a spark. The horses galloped on, "devouring space," and as he drew near his goal, again the thought of her, of her alone, took more and more complete possession of his soul, chasing away the fearful images that had been haunting it. Oh, how he longed to look upon her, if only for a moment, if only from a distance!

"She's now with *him*," he thought, "now I shall see what she looks like with him, her first love, and that's all I want." Never had this woman, who was such a fateful influence in his life, aroused such love in his breast, such new and unknown feeling, surprising even to himself, a feeling tender to devoutness, to self-effacement before her! "I will efface myself!" he said, in a rush of almost hysterical ecstasy.

They had been galloping nearly an hour. Mitya was silent, and though Andrey was, as a rule, a talkative peasant, he did not utter a word, either. He seemed afraid to talk, he only whipped up smartly his three lean, but mettlesome, bay horses. Suddenly Mitya cried out in horrible anxiety:

"Andrey! What if they're asleep?"

This thought fell upon him like a blow. It had not occurred to him before.

"It may well be that they're gone to bed, by now, Dmitri Fyodorovitch."

Mitya frowned as though in pain. Yes, indeed . . . he was rushing there . . . with such feelings . . . while they were asleep . . . she was asleep, perhaps, there too. . . . An angry feeling surged up in his heart.

"Drive on, Andrey! Whip them up! Look alive!" he cried, beside himself.

"But maybe they're not in bed!" Andrey went on after a pause. "Timofey said there were a lot of them there. . . ."

"At the station?"

"Not at the posting-station, but at Plastunovs', at the inn, where they let out horses, too."

"I know. So you say there are a lot of them? How's that? Who are they?" cried Mitya, greatly dismayed at this unexpected news.

"Well, Timofey was saying they're all gentlefolk. Two from our town—who they are I can't say—and there are two others, strangers, maybe more besides. I didn't ask particularly. They've set to playing cards, so Timofey said."

"Cards?"

"So, maybe they're not in bed if they're at cards. It's most likely not more than eleven."

"Quicker, Andrey! Quicker!" Mitya cried again, nervously.

"May I ask you something, sir?" said Andrey, after a pause. "Only I'm afraid of angering you, sir."

"What is it?"

"Why, Fenya threw herself at your feet just now, and begged you not to harm her mistress, and some one else, too . . . so you see, sir . . . It's I am taking you there . . . forgive me, sir, it's my conscience . . . maybe it's stupid of me to speak of it. . . ."

Mitya suddenly seized him by the shoulders from behind.

"Are you a driver?" he asked frantically.

"Yes, sir. . . ."

"Then you know that one has to make way. What would you say to a driver who wouldn't make way for any one, but would just drive on and crush people? No, a driver mustn't run over people. One can't run over a man. One can't spoil people's lives. And if you have spoilt a life—punish yourself . . . if only you've spoilt, if only you've ruined any one's life—punish yourself and go away."

These phrases burst from Mitya almost hysterically. Though Andrey was surprised at him, he kept up the conversation.

"That's right, Dmitri Fyodorovitch, you're quite right, one mustn't crush or torment a man, or any kind of creature, for every creature is created by God. Take a horse, for instance, for some folks, even among us drivers, drive anyhow. Nothing will restrain them, they just force it along."

"To hell?" Mitya interrupted, and went off into his abrupt, short laugh. "Andrey, simple soul," he seized him by the shoulders again, "tell me, will Dmitri Fyodorovitch Karamazov go to hell, or not, what do you think?"

"I don't know, darling, it depends on you, for you are . . . you see, sir, when the Son of God was nailed on the Cross and died, He went straight down to hell from the Cross, and set free all sinners that were in agony. And the devil groaned, because he thought that he would get no more sinners in hell. And God said to him, then, 'Don't groan, for you shall have all the mighty of the earth, the rulers, the chief judges, and the rich men, and shall be filled up as you have been in all the ages till I come again.' Those were His very words. . . ."

"A peasant legend! Capital! Whip up the left, Andrey!"

"So you see, sir, who it is hell's for," said Andrey, whipping up the left horse, "but you're like a little child . . . that's how we look on you . . . and though you're hasty-tempered, sir, yet God will forgive you for your kind heart."

"And you, do you forgive me, Andrey?"

"What should I forgive you for, sir? You've never done me any harm."

"No, for every one, for every one, you here alone, on the road, will you forgive me for every one? Speak, simple peasant heart!"

"Oh, sir! I feel afraid of driving you, your talk is so strange."

But Mitya did not hear. He was frantically praying and muttering to himself.

"Lord, receive me, with all my lawlessness, and do not condemn me. Let me pass by Thy judgment . . . do not condemn me, for I have condemned myself, do not condemn me, for I love Thee, O Lord. I am a wretch, but I love Thee. If Thou sendest me to hell, I shall love Thee there, and from there I shall cry out that I love Thee for ever and ever. . . . But let me love to the end. . . . Here and now for just five hours . . . till the first light of Thy day . . . for I love the queen of my soul . . . I love her and I cannot help loving her. Thou seest my whole heart. . . . I shall gallop up, I shall fall before her and say, 'You are right to pass on and leave me. Farewell and forget your victim . . . never fret yourself about me!' "

"Mokroe!" cried Andrey, pointing ahead with his whip.

Through the pale darkness of the night loomed a solid black mass of buildings, flung down, as it were, in the vast plain. The village of Mokroe numbered two thousand inhabitants, but at that hour all were asleep, and only here and there a few lights still twinkled.

"Drive on, Andrey, I come!" Mitya exclaimed, feverishly.

"They're not asleep," said Andrey again, pointing with his whip to the Plastunovs' inn, which was at the entrance to the village. The six windows, looking on the street, were all brightly lighted up.

"They're not asleep," Mitya repeated, joyously, "Quicker, Andrey! Gallop! Drive up with a dash! Set the bells ringing! Let all know that I have come. I'm coming! I'm coming, too!"

Andrey lashed his exhausted team into a gallop, drove with a dash and pulled up his steaming, panting horses at the high flight of steps.

Mitya jumped out of the cart just as the innkeeper, on his way to bed, peeped out from the steps curious to see who had arrived.

"Trifon Borissovitch, is that you?"

The innkeeper bent down, looked intently, ran down the steps, and rushed up to the guest with obsequious delight.

"Dmitri Fyodorovitch, your honour! Do I see you again?"

Trifon Borissovitch was a thick-set, healthy peasant, of middle height, with a rather fat face. His expression was severe and uncompromising, especially with the peasants of Mokroe, but he had the power of assuming the most obsequious countenance, when he had an inkling that it was to his interest. He dressed in Russian style, with a shirt buttoning down on one side, and a full-skirted coat. He had saved a good sum of money, but was for ever dreaming of improving his position. More than half the peasants were in his clutches, every one in the neighbourhood was in debt to him. From the neighbouring landowners he bought and rented lands which were worked by the peasants, in payment of debts which they could never shake off. He was a widower, with four grown-up daughters. One of them was already a widow and lived in the inn with her two children, his grandchildren, and worked for him like a charwoman. Another of his daughters was married to a petty official and in one of the rooms of the inn, on the wall could be seen, among the family photographs, a miniature photograph of this official in uniform and official epaulettes. The two younger daughters used to wear fashionable blue or green dresses, fitting tight at the back, and with trains a yard long, on Church holidays or when they went to pay visits. But next morning they would get up at dawn, as usual, sweep out the rooms with a birch broom, empty the slops, and clean up after lodgers.

In spite of the thousands of roubles he had saved, Trifon Borissovitch was very fond of emptying the pockets of a drunken guest, and, remembering that not a month ago he had, in twenty-four hours, made two if not three hundred roubles out of Dmitri, when he had come on his escapade with Grushenka, he met him now with eager welcome, scenting his prey the moment Mitya drove up to the steps.

"Dmitri Fyodorovitch, dear sir, we see you once more!"

"Stay, Trifon Borissovitch," began Mitya, "first and foremost, where is she?"

"Agrafena Alexandrovna?" The innkeeper understood at once, looking sharply into Mitya's face. "She's here, too. . . ."

"With whom? With whom?"

"Some strangers. One is an official gentleman, a Pole, to judge from his speech. He sent the horses for her from here; and there's another with him, a friend of his, or a fellow traveller, there's no telling. They're dressed like civilians."

"Well, are they feasting? Have they money?"

"Poor sort of a feast! Nothing to boast of, Dmitri Fyodorovitch."

"Nothing to boast of? And who are the others?"

"They're two gentlemen from the town. . . . They've come back from Tcherny, and are putting up here. One's quite a young gentleman, a relative of Mr. Miüsov, he must be, but I've forgotten his name . . . and I expect you know the other, too, a gentleman called Maximov. He's been on a pilgrimage, so he says, to the monastery in the town. He's travelling with this young relation of Mr. Miüsov."

"Is that all?"

"Yes."

"Stay, listen, Trifon Borissovitch. Tell me the chief thing: What of her? How is she?"

"Oh, she's only just come. She's sitting with them."

"Is she cheerful? Is she laughing?"

"No, I think she's not laughing much. She's sitting quite dull. She's combing the young gentleman's hair."

"The Pole—the officer?"

"He's not young, and he's not an officer, either. Not him, sir. It's the young gentleman that's M. Miüsov's relation . . . I've forgotten his name."

"Kalganov?"

"That's it, Kalganov!"

"All right. I'll see for myself. Are they playing cards?"

"They have been playing, but they've left off. They've been drinking tea, the official gentleman asked for liqueurs."

"Stay, Trifon Borissovitch, stay, my good soul, I'll see for myself. Now answer one more question: are the gipsies here?"

"You can't have the gipsies now, Dmitri Fyodorovitch. The authorities have sent them away. But we've Jews that play the cymbals and the fiddle in the village, so one might send for them. They'd come."

"Send for them. Certainly send for them!" cried Mitya. "And you can get the girls together as you did then, Marya especially, Stepanida, too, and Arina. Two hundred roubles for a chorus!"

"Oh, for a sum like that I can get all the village together, though by now they're asleep. Are the peasants here worth such kindness, Dmitri Fyodorovitch, or the girls either? To spend a sum like that on such coarseness and rudeness! What's the good of giving a peasant a cigar to smoke, the stinking ruffian! And the girls are all lousy. Besides, I'll get my daughters up for nothing, let alone a sum like that. They've only just gone to bed, I'll give them a kick and set them singing for you. You gave the peasants champagne to drink the other day, e-ech!"

For all his pretended compassion for Mitya, Trifon Borissovitch had hidden half a dozen bottles of champagne on the last occasion, and had picked up a hundred-rouble note under the table, and it had remained in his clutches.

"Trifon Borissovitch, I sent more than one thousand flying last time I was here. Do you remember?"

"You did send it flying. I may well remember. You must have left three thousand behind you."

"Well, I've come to do the same again, do you see?"

And he pulled out his roll of notes, and held them up before the innkeeper's nose.

"Now, listen and remember. In an hour's time the wine will arrive, savouries, pies, and sweets—bring them all up at once. That box Andrey has got is to be brought up at once, too. Open it, and hand champagne immediately. And the girls, we must have the girls, Marya especially."

He turned to the cart and pulled out the box of pistols.

"Here, Andrey, let's settle. Here's fifteen roubles for the drive, and fifty for vodka . . . for your readiness, for your love. . . . Remember Karamazov!"

"I'm afraid, sir," faltered Andrey. "Give me five roubles extra, but more I won't take. Trifon Borissovitch, bear witness. Forgive my foolish words. . . ."

"What are you afraid of?" asked Mitya, scanning him. "Well, go to the devil, if that's it!" he cried, flinging him five roubles. "Now, Trifon Borissovitch, take me up quietly and let me first get a look at them, so that they don't see me. Where are they? In the blue room?"

Trifon Borissovitch looked apprehensively at Mitya, but at once obediently did his bidding. Leading him into the passage, he went himself into the first large room, adjoining that in which the visitors were sitting, and took the light away. Then he stealthily led Mitya in, and put him in a corner in the dark, whence he could freely watch the company without being seen. But Mitya did not look long, and, indeed, he could not see them, he saw her, his heart throbbed violently, and all was dark before his eyes.

She was sitting sideways to the table in a low chair, and beside her, on the sofa, was the pretty youth, Kalganov. She was holding his hand and seemed to be laughing, while he, seeming vexed and not looking at her, was saying something in a loud voice to Maximov, who sat the other side of the table, facing Grushenka. Maximov was laughing violently at something. On the sofa sat *he,* and on a chair by the sofa there was another stranger. The one on the sofa was lolling backwards, smoking a pipe, and Mitya had an impression of a stoutish broad-faced short little man, who was apparently angry about something. His friend, the other stranger, struck Mitya as extraordinarily tall, but he could make out nothing more.

He caught his breath. He could not bear it for a minute, he put the pistol case on a chest, and with a throbbing heart he walked, feeling cold all over, straight into the blue room to face the company.

"Aie!" shrieked Grushenka, the first to notice him.

7

THE FIRST AND RIGHTFUL LOVER

WITH his long, rapid strides, Mitya walked straight up to the table.

"Gentlemen," he said in a loud voice, almost shouting, yet stammering at every word, "I . . . I'm all right! Don't be afraid!" he exclaimed, "I—there's nothing the matter," he turned suddenly to Grushenka, who had shrunk back in her chair towards Kalganov, and clasped his hand tightly. "I . . . I'm coming, too. I'm here till morning. Gentlemen, may I stay with you till morning? Only till morning, for the last time, in this same room?"

So he finished, turning to the fat little man, with the pipe, sitting on the sofa. The latter removed his pipe from his lips with dignity and observed severely:

"*Panie*,[4] we're here in private. There are other rooms."

"Why, it's you, Dmitri Fyodorovitch! What do you mean?" answered Kalganov suddenly. "Sit down with us. How are you?"

"Delighted to see you, dear . . . and precious fellow, I always thought a lot of you." Mitya responded, joyfully and eagerly, at once holding out his hand across the table.

"Aie! How tight you squeeze! You've quite broken my fingers," laughed Kalganov.

"He always squeezes like that, always," Grushenka put in gaily, with a timid smile, seeming suddenly convinced from Mitya's face that he was not going to make a scene. She was watching him with intense curiosity and still some uneasiness. She was impressed by something about him, and indeed the last she expected of him was that he would come in and speak like this at such a moment.

"Good evening," Maximov ventured blandly, on the left. Mitya rushed up to him, too.

"Good evening. You're here, too! How glad I am to find you here, too! Gentlemen, gentlemen, I . . ." (He addressed the Polish gentleman with the pipe again, evidently taking him for the most important person present.) "I flew here. . . . I wanted to spend my last day, my last hour in this

room, in this very room . . . where I, too, adored . . . my queen. . . . Forgive
me, *panie*," he cried wildly, "I flew here and vowed. . . . Oh, don't be afraid,
it's my last night! Let's drink to our good understanding. They'll bring the
wine at once. . . . I brought this with me." (Something made him pull out
his bundle of notes.) "Allow me, *panie*! I want to have music, singing, a
revel, as we had before. But the worm, the unnecessary worm, will crawl
away, and there'll be no more of him. I will commemorate my day of joy
and my last night."

He was almost choking. There was so much, so much he wanted to say,
but strange exclamations were all that came from his lips. The Pole gazed
fixedly at him, at the bundle of notes in his hand; looked at Grushenka,
and was in evident perplexity.

"If my suverin lady is permitting . . ." he was beginning.

"What does 'suverin' mean? 'Sovereign,' I suppose?" interrupted
Grushenka, "I can't help laughing at you, the way you talk. Sit down,
Mitya, what are you talking about? Don't frighten us, please. You won't
frighten us, will you? If you won't, I am glad to see you . . ."

"Me, me frighten you?" cried Mitya, flinging up his hands. "Oh, pass me
by, go your way, I won't hinder you!. . . ."

And suddenly he surprised them all, and no doubt himself as well, by
flinging himself on a chair, and bursting into tears, turning his head away
to the opposite wall, while his arms clasped the back of the chair tight, as
though embracing it.

"Come, come, what a fellow you are!" cried Grushenka reproachfully.
"That's just how he comes to see me—he begins talking, and I can't make
out what he means. He cried like that once before, and now he's crying
again! It's shameful! Why are you crying? *As though you had anything to
cry for!*" she added enigmatically, emphasising each word with some irritability.

". . . I'm not crying. . . . Well, good evening!" he instantly turned round
in his chair, and suddenly laughed, not his abrupt, wooden laugh, but a
long, quivering, inaudible nervous laugh.

"Well, there you are again. . . . Come, cheer up, cheer up?" Grushenka
said to him persuasively. "I'm very glad you've come, very glad, Mitya, do
you hear, I'm very glad? I want him to stay here with us," she said peremptorily, addressing the whole company, though her words were obviously
meant for the man sitting on the sofa. "I wish it, I wish it! And if he goes
away I shall go, too!" she added with flashing eyes.

"What my queen commands is law!" pronounced the Pole, gallantly
kissing Grushenka's hand. "I beg you, *panie,* to join our company," he
added politely, addressing Mitya.

Mitya was jumping up with the obvious intention of delivering another
tirade, but the words did not come.

"Let's drink, *panie*," he blurted out instead of making a speech. Every
one laughed.

"Good Heavens! I thought he was going to begin again!" Grushenka
exclaimed nervously. "Do you hear, Mitya," she went on insistently, "don't

prance about, but it's nice you've brought the champagne. I want some myself, and I can't bear liqueurs. And best of all, you've come yourself. We were fearfully dull here. . . . You've come for a spree again, I suppose? But put your money in your pocket. Where did you get such a lot?"

Mitya had been, all this time, holding in his hand the crumpled bundle of notes on which the eyes of all, especially of the Poles, were fixed. In confusion he thrust them hurriedly into his pocket. He flushed. At that moment the innkeeper brought in an uncorked bottle of champagne, and glasses on a tray. Mitya snatched up the bottle, but he was so bewildered that he did not know what to do with it. Kalganov took it from him and poured out the champagne.

"Another! Another bottle!" Mitya cried to the innkeeper, and, forgetting to clink glasses with the Pole whom he had so solemnly invited to drink to their good understanding, he drank off his glass without waiting for any one else. His whole countenance suddenly changed. The solemn and tragic expression with which he had entered vanished completely, and a look of something childlike came into his face. He seemed to have become suddenly gentle and subdued. He looked shyly and happily at every one, with a continual nervous little laugh, and the blissful expression of a dog who had done wrong, been punished, and forgiven. He seemed to have forgotten everything, and was looking round at every one with a childlike smile of delight. He looked at Grushenka, laughing, continually, and bringing his chair close up to her. By degrees he had gained some idea of the two Poles, though he had formed no definite conception of them yet.

The Pole on the sofa struck him by his dignified demeanour and his Polish accent; and, above all, by his pipe. "Well, what of it? It's a good thing he's smoking a pipe," he reflected. The Pole's puffy, middle-aged face, with its tiny nose and two very thin, pointed, dyed and impudent-looking moustaches, had not so far roused the faintest doubts in Mitya. He was not even particularly struck by the Pole's absurd wig made in Siberia, with lovelocks foolishly combed forward over the temples. "I suppose it's all right since he wears a wig," he went on, musing blissfully. The other, younger Pole, who was staring insolently and defiantly at the company and listening to the conversation with silent contempt, still only impressed Mitya by his great height, which was in striking contrast to the Pole on the sofa. "If he stood up he'd be six foot three." The thought flitted through Mitya's mind. It occurred to him, too, that this Pole must be the friend of the other, as it were, a "bodyguard," and no doubt the big Pole was at the disposal of the little Pole with the pipe. But this all seemed to Mitya perfectly right and not to be questioned. In his mood of doglike submissiveness all feeling of rivalry had died away.

Grushenka's mood and the enigmatic tone of some of her words he completely failed to grasp. All he understood, with thrilling heart, was that she was kind to him, that she had forgiven him, and made him sit by her. He was beside himself with delight, watching her sip her glass of champagne. The silence of the company seemed somehow to strike him, however, and he looked round at every one with expectant eyes.

"Why are we sitting here though, gentlemen? Why don't you begin doing something?" his smiling eyes seemed to ask.

"He keeps talking nonsense, and we were all laughing." Kalganov began suddenly, as though divining his thought, and pointing to Maximov.

Mitya immediately stared at Kalganov and then at Maximov.

"He's talking nonsense?" he laughed, his short, wooden laugh, seemingly suddenly delighted at something—"ha, ha!"

"Yes. Would you believe it, he will have it that all our cavalry officers in the 'twenties married Polish women. That's awful rot, isn't it?"

"Polish women?" repeated Mitya, perfectly ecstatic.

Kalganov was well aware of Mitya's attitude to Grushenka, and he guessed about the Pole, too, but that did not so much interest him, perhaps did not interest him at all; what he was interested in, was Maximov. He had come here with Maximov by chance, and he met the Poles here at the inn for the first time in his life. Grushenka he knew before, and had once been with some one to see her; but she had not taken to him. But here she looked at him very affectionately: before Mitya's arrival, she had been making much of him, but he seemed somehow to be unmoved by it. He was a boy, not over twenty, dressed like a dandy, with a very charming fair-skinned face, and splendid thick, fair hair. From his fair face looked out beautiful pale blue eyes, with an intelligent and sometimes even deep expression, beyond his age indeed, although the young man sometimes looked and talked quite like a child, and was not at all ashamed of it, even when he was aware of it himself. As a rule he was very wilful, even capricious, though always friendly. Sometimes there was something fixed and obstinate in his expression. He would look at you and listen, seeming all the while to be persistently dreaming over something else. Often he was listless and lazy, at other times he would grow excited, sometimes, apparently, over the most trivial matters.

"Only imagine, I've been taking him about with me for the last four days," he went on, indolently drawling his words, quite naturally though, without the slightest affectation. "Ever since your brother, do you remember, shoved him off the carriage and sent him flying. That made me take an interest in him at the time, and I took him into the country, but he keeps talking such rot I'm ashamed to be with him. I'm taking him back."

"The gentleman has not seen Polish ladies, and says what is impossible," the Pole with the pipe observed to Maximov.

He spoke Russian fairly well, much better, anyway, than he pretended. If he used Russian words, he always distorted them into a Polish form.

"But I was married to a Polish lady myself," tittered Maximov.

"But did you serve in the cavalry? You were talking about the cavalry. Were you a cavalry officer!" put in Kalganov at once.

"Was he a cavalry officer indeed? Ha, ha!" cried Mitya, listening eagerly, and turning his inquiring eyes to each as he spoke, as though there were no knowing what he might hear from each.

"No, you see," Maximov turned to him. "What I mean is that those pretty Polish ladies . . . when they danced the mazurka with our Uhlans . . . when one of them dances a mazurka with a Uhlan she jumps on his knee like a kitten . . . a little white one . . . and the *pan*-father and *pan*-mother look on and allow it. . . . They allow it . . . and next day the Uhlan comes and offers her his hand. . . . That's how it is . . . offers her his hand, he—he!" Maximov ended, tittering.

"The *pan* is a *lajdak*!"* The tall Pole on the chair growled suddenly and crossed one leg over the other. Mitya's eye was caught by his huge greased boot, with its thick, dirty sole. The dress of both the Poles looked rather greasy.

"Well, now it's *lajdak*! What's he scolding about?" said Grushenka, suddenly vexed.

"*Pani* Agrippina,† what the gentleman saw in Poland were servant girls, and not ladies of good birth," the Pole with the pipe observed to Grushenka.

"You can reckon on that," the tall Pole snapped contemptuously.

"What next! Let him talk! People talk, why hinder them? It makes it cheerful," Grushenka said crossly.

"I'm not hindering them, *pani*," said the Pole in the wig, with a long look at Grushenka, and relapsing into dignified silence he sucked his pipe again.

"No, no. The Polish gentleman spoke the truth." Kalganov got excited again, as though it were a question of vast import.

"He's never been in Poland, so how can he talk about it? I suppose you weren't married in Poland, were you?"

"No, in the Province of Smolensk. Only, a Uhlan had brought her to Russia before that, my future wife, with her mamma and her aunt, and another female relation with a grown-up son. He brought her straight from Poland and gave her up to me. He was a lieutenant in our regiment, a very nice young man. At first he meant to marry her himself. But he didn't marry her, because she turned out to be lame."

"So you married a lame woman?" cried Kalganov.

"Yes. They both deceived me a little bit at the time, and concealed it. I thought she was hopping; she kept hopping . . . I thought it was for fun."

"So pleased she was going to marry you!" yelled Kalganov, in a ringing, childish voice.

"Yes, so pleased. But it turned out to be quite a different cause. Afterwards, when we were married, after the wedding, that very evening, she confessed, and very touchingly asked forgiveness. 'I once jumped over a puddle when I was a child,' she said, 'and injured my leg.' He—he!"

Kalganov went off into the most childish laughter, almost falling on the sofa. Grushenka, too, laughed. Mitya was at the pinnacle of happiness.

"Do you know, that's the truth, he's not lying now," exclaimed Kalganov, turning to Mitya; "and do you know, he's been married twice; it's his

*Scoundrel (Polish).
†Agrippina is the Polish form of Agrafena.

first wife he's talking about. But his second wife, do you know, ran away, and is alive now."

"Is it possible?" said Mitya, turning quickly to Maximov with an expression of the utmost astonishment.

"Yes. She did run away. I've had that unpleasant experience," Maximov modestly assented, "with a *monsieur*. And what was worse, she'd had all my little property transferred to her beforehand. 'You're an educated man,' she said to me. 'You can always get your living.' She settled my business with that. A venerable bishop once said to me: 'One of your wives was lame, but the other was too light-footed.' He-he!"

"Listen, listen!" cried Kalganov, bubbling over, "if he's telling lies—and he often is—he's only doing it to amuse us all. There's no harm in that, is there? You know, I sometimes like him. He's awfully low, but it's natural to him, eh? Don't you think so? Some people are low from self-interest, but he's simply so, from nature. Only fancy, he claims (he was arguing about it all the way yesterday) that Gogol wrote *Dead Souls* about him. Do you remember, there's a landowner called Maximov in it, whom Nozdryov thrashed.* He was charged, do you remember, 'for inflicting bodily injury with rods on the landowner Maximov in a drunken condition.' Would you believe it, he claims that he was that Maximov and that he was beaten! Now can it be so? Tchitchikov made his journey, at the very latest, at the beginning of the twenties, so that the dates don't fit. He couldn't have been thrashed then, he couldn't, could he?"

It was difficult to imagine what Kalganov was excited about, but his excitement was genuine. Mitya followed his lead without protest.

"Well, but if they did thrash him!" he cried, laughing.

"It's not that they thrashed me exactly, but what I mean is . . ." put in Maximov.

"What do you mean? Either they thrashed you or they didn't."

"What o'clock is it, *panie*?" the Pole, with the pipe, asked his tall friend, with a bored expression. The other shrugged his shoulders in reply. Neither of them had a watch.

"Why not talk? Let other people talk. Mustn't other people talk because you're bored?" Grushenka flew at him with evident intention of finding fault. Something seemed for the first time to flash upon Mitya's mind. This time the Pole answered with unmistakable irritability.

"*Pani,* I didn't oppose it. I didn't say anything."

"All right then. Come, tell us your story," Grushenka cried to Maximov. "Why are you all silent?"

"There's nothing to tell, it's all so foolish," answered Maximov at once, with evident satisfaction, mincing a little. "Besides, all that's by way of allegory in Gogol, for he's made all the names have a meaning. Nozdryov was really called Nosov, and Kuvshinikov had quite a different name, he

---

*Reference to an episode in part 1, chapter 4 of Gogol's comic masterpiece (1842).

was called Shkvornev. Fenardi really was called Fenardi, only he wasn't an Italian but a Russian, and Mamsel Fenardi was a pretty girl with her pretty little legs in tights, and she had a little short skirt with spangles, and she kept turning round and round, only not for four hours but for four minutes only, and she bewitched every one. . . ."

"But what were you beaten for?" cried Kalganov.

"For Piron!" answered Maximov.

"What Piron?" cried Mitya.

"The famous French writer, Piron. We were all drinking then, a big party of us, in a tavern at that very fair. They'd invited me, and first of all I began quoting epigrams. 'Is that you, Boileau?* What a funny get-up!' and Boileau answers that he's going to a masquerade, that is to the baths, he-he! And they took it to themselves, so I made haste to repeat another, very sarcastic, well known to all educated people:

> 'Yes, Sappho and Phaon are we!
> But one grief is weighing on me.
> You don't know your way to the sea!'†

They were still more offended and began abusing me in the most unseemly way for it. And as ill-luck would have it, to set things right, I began telling a very cultivated anecdote about Piron, how he was not accepted into the French Academy, and to revenge himself wrote his own epitaph:

> 'Ci-gît Piron qui ne fut rien
> Pas même, académicien.'‡

They seized me and thrashed me."

"But what for? What for?"

"For my education. People can thrash a man for anything," Maximov concluded, briefly and sententiously.

"Eh, that's enough! That's all stupid, I don't want to listen. I thought it would be amusing," Grushenka cut them short, suddenly.

Mitya started, and at once left off laughing. The tall Pole rose upon his feet, and with the haughty air of a man, bored and out of his element, began pacing from corner to corner of the room, his hands behind his back.

"Ah, he can't sit still," said Grushenka, looking at him contemptuously.

---

*From Russian fabulist I. A. Krylov's "Epigram on a translation of the poem 'L'art poétique'" (1814).

†Modified quotation from Russian poet Konstantin Batyushkov's epigram on the woman poet A. P. Bunin, titled "A Madrigal to the New Sappho" (1809). According to legend, Sappho, a lyric poet of ancient Greece, died by throwing herself into the sea.

‡Here lies Piron who was nothing / Not even an academician (French).

Mitya began to feel anxious. He noticed besides, that the Pole on the sofa was looking at him with an irritable expression.

"*Panie!*" cried Mitya, "let's drink! and the other *pan,* too! Let us drink."

In a flash he had pulled three glasses towards him, and filled them with champagne.

"To Poland, *panovie,* I drink to your Poland!" cried Mitya.

"I shall be delighted, *panie,*" said the Pole on the sofa, with dignity and affable condescension, and he took his glass.

"And the other *pan*, what's his name? Drink, most illustrious, take your glass!" Mitya urged.

"Pan Vrublevsky," put in the Pole on the sofa.

Pan Vrublevsky came up to the table, swaying as he walked.

"To Poland, *panovie!*" cried Mitya, raising his glass. "Hurrah!"

All three drank. Mitya seized the bottle and again poured out three glasses.

"Now to Russia, *panovie,* and let us be brothers!"[5]

"Pour out some for us," said Grushenka; "I'll drink to Russia, too!"

"So will I," said Kalganov.

"And I would, too . . . to Russia, the old grandmother!" tittered Maximov.

"All! All!" cried Mitya. "Trifon Borissovitch, some more bottles!"

The other three bottles Mitya had brought with him were put on the table. Mitya filled the glasses.

"To Russia! Hurrah!" he shouted again. All drank the toast except the Poles, and Grushenka tossed off her whole glass at once. The Poles did not touch theirs.

"How's this, *panovie*?" cried Mitya, "won't you drink it?"

Pan Vrublevsky took the glass, raised it, and said with a resonant voice: "To Russia as she was before 1772."

"Come, that's better!" cried the other Pole, and they both emptied their glasses at once.

"You're fools, you *panovie,*" broke suddenly from Mitya.

"*Panie!*" shouted both the Poles, menacingly, setting on Mitya like a couple of cocks. Pan Vrublevsky was specially furious.

"Can one help loving one's own country?" he shouted.

"Be silent! Don't quarrel! I won't have any quarrelling!" cried Grushenka imperiously, and she stamped her foot on the floor. Her face glowed, her eyes were shining. The effects of the glass she had just drunk were apparent. Mitya was terribly alarmed.

"*Panovie,* forgive me! It was my fault, I'm sorry. Vrublevsky, *panie* Vrublevsky, I'm sorry."

"Hold your tongue, you, anyway! Sit down, you stupid!" Grushenka scolded with angry annoyance.

Every one sat down, all were silent, looking at one another.

"Gentlemen, I was the cause of it all," Mitya began again, unable to make anything of Grushenka's words. "Come, why are we sitting here? What shall we do . . . to amuse ourselves again?"

"Ach, it's certainly anything but amusing!" Kalganov mumbled lazily.

"Let's play faro again, as we did just now," Maximov tittered suddenly.

"Faro? Splendid!" cried Mitya. "If only the *panovie* . . ."

"It's lite, *panovie*," the Pole on the sofa responded, as it were unwillingly.

"That's true," assented Pan Vrublevsky.

"Lite? What do you mean by 'lite'?" asked Grushenka.

"Late, *pani!* 'a late hour' I mean," the Pole on the sofa explained.

"It's always late with them. They can never do anything!" Grushenka almost shrieked in her anger. "They're dull themselves, so they want others to be dull. Before you came, Mitya, they were just as silent and kept turning up their noses at me."

"My goddess!" cried the Pole on the sofa, "I see you're not well-disposed to me, that's why I'm gloomy. I'm ready, *panie*," added he, addressing Mitya.

"Begin, *panie*," Mitya assented, pulling his notes out of his pocket, and laying two hundred-rouble notes on the table. "I want to lose a lot to you. Take your cards. Make the bank."

"We'll have cards from the landlord, *panie*," said the little Pole, gravely and emphatically.

"That's much the best way," chimed in Pan Vrublevsky.

"From the landlord? Very good, I understand, let's get them from him. Cards!" Mitya shouted to the landlord.

The landlord brought in a new, unopened pack, and informed Mitya that the girls were getting ready, and that the Jews with the cymbals would most likely be here soon; but the cart with the provisions had not yet arrived, Mitya jumped up from the table and ran into the next room to give orders, but only three girls had arrived, and Marya was not there yet. And he did not know himself what orders to give and why he had run out. He only told them to take out of the box the presents for the girls, the sweets, the toffee and the fondants. "And vodka for Andrey, vodka for Andrey!" he cried in haste. "I was rude to Andrey!"

Suddenly Maximov, who had followed him out, touched him on the shoulder.

"Give me five roubles," he whispered to Mitya. "I'll stake something at faro, too, he-he!"

"Capital! Splendid! Take ten, here!"

Again he took all the notes out of his pocket and picked out one for ten roubles. "And if you lose that, come again, come again."

"Very good," Maximov whispered joyfully, and he ran back again. Mitya too, returned, apologising for having kept them waiting. The Poles had already sat down, and opened the pack. They looked much more amiable, almost cordial. The Pole on the sofa had lighted another pipe and was preparing to throw. He wore an air of solemnity.

"To your places, gentlemen," cried Pan Vrublevsky.

"No, I'm not going to play any more," observed Kalganov, "I've lost fifty roubles to them just now."

"The *pan* had no luck, perhaps he'll be lucky this time," the Pole on the sofa observed in his direction.

"How much in the bank? To correspond?" asked Mitya.

"That's according, *panie,* maybe a hundred, maybe two hundred, as much as you will stake."

"A million!" laughed Mitya.

"The Pan Captain has heard of Pan Podvysotsky, perhaps?"

"What Podvysotsky?"

"In Warsaw there was a bank and any one comes and stakes against it. Podvysotsky comes, sees a thousand gold pieces, stakes against the bank. The banker says, '*Panie* Podvysotsky, are you laying down the gold, or must we trust to your honour?' 'To my honour, *panie,*' says Podvysotsky. 'So much the better.' The banker throws the dice. Podvysotsky wins. 'Take it, *panie,*' says the banker, and pulling out the drawer he gives him a million. 'Take it, *panie,* this is your gain.' There was a million in the bank. 'I didn't know that,' says Podvysotsky. '*Panie* Podvysotsky,' said the banker, 'you pledged your honour and we pledged ours.' Podvysotsky took the million."

"That's not true," said Kalganov.

"*Panie* Kalganov, in gentlemanly society one doesn't say such things."

"As if a Polish gambler would give away a million!" cried Mitya, but checked himself at once. "Forgive me, *panie,* it's my fault again, he would, he would give away a million, for honour, for Polish honour. You see how I talk Polish, ha-ha! Here, I stake ten roubles, the knave leads."

"And I put a rouble on the queen, the queen of hearts, the pretty little *panienotchka,** he-he!" laughed Maximov, pulling out his queen, and, as though trying to conceal it from every one, he moved right up and crossed himself hurriedly under the table. Mitya won. The rouble won, too.

"A corner!" cried Mitya.

"I'll bet another rouble, a 'single' stake," Maximov muttered gleefully, hugely delighted at having won a rouble.

"Lost!" shouted Mitya. "A 'double' on the seven!"

The seven too was trumped.

"Stop!" cried Kalganov suddenly.

"Double! Double!" Mitya doubled his stakes, and each time he doubled the stake, the card he doubled was trumped by the Poles. The rouble stakes kept winning.

"On the double!" shouted Mitya, furiously.

"You've lost two hundred, *panie.* Will you stake another hundred?" the Pole on the sofa inquired.

"What? Lost two hundred already? Then another two hundred! All doubles!"

And pulling his money out of his pocket, Mitya was about to fling two hundred roubles on the queen, but Kalganov covered it with his hand.

"That's enough!" he shouted in his ringing voice.

"What's the matter?" Mitya stared at him.

"That's enough! I don't want you to play any more. Don't!"

_____

*Russian diminutive of *pani* (see note 4, book eight).

"Why?"

"Because I don't. Hang it, come away. That's why. I won't let you go on playing."

Mitya gazed at him in astonishment.

"Give it up, Mitya. He may be right. You've lost a lot as it is," said Grushenka, with a curious note in her voice. Both the Poles rose from their seats with a deeply offended air.

"Are you joking, *panie*?" said the short man, looking severely at Kalganov.

"How dare you!" Pan Vrublevsky, too, growled at Kalganov.

"Don't dare to shout like that," cried Grushenka. "Ah, you turkey cocks!"

Mitya looked at each of them in turn. But something in Grushenka's face suddenly struck him, and at the same instant something new flashed into his mind—a strange new thought!

"*Pani* Agrippina," the little Pole was beginning, crimson with anger, when Mitya suddenly went up to him and slapped him on the shoulder.

"Most illustrious, two words with you."

"What do you want?"

"In the next room, I've two words to say to you, something pleasant, very pleasant. You'll be glad to hear it."

The little *pan* was taken aback and looked apprehensively at Mitya. He agreed at once, however, on condition that Pan Vrublevsky went with them.

"The body-guard? Let him come, and I want him, too. I must have him!" cried Mitya. "March, *panovie*!"

"Where are you going?" asked Grushenka, anxiously.

"We'll be back in one moment," answered Mitya.

There was a sort of boldness, a sudden confidence shining in his eyes. His face had looked very different when he entered the room an hour before.

He led the Poles, not into the large room where the chorus of girls was assembling and the table was being laid, but into the bedroom on the right, where the trunks and packages were kept, and there were two large beds, with pyramids of cotton pillows on each. There was a lighted candle on a small deal table in the corner. The small man and Mitya sat down to this table, facing each other, while the huge Vrublevsky stood beside them, his hands behind his back. The Poles looked severe but were evidently inquisitive.

"What can I do for you, *panie*?" lisped the little Pole.

"Well, look here, *panie*, I won't keep you long. There's money for you," he pulled out his notes. "Would you like three thousand? Take it and go your way."

The Pole gazed, open-eyed at Mitya, with a searching look.

"Three thousand, *panie*?" He exchanged glances with Vrublevsky.

"Three, *panovie*, three! Listen, *panie*, I see you're a sensible man. Take three thousand and go to the devil, and Vrublevsky with you—d'you hear? But, at once, this very minute, and for ever. You understand that, *panie,* for ever. Here's the door, you go out of it. What have you got there, a great coat, a fur coat? I'll bring it out to you. They'll get the horses out directly, and then—good-bye, *panie!*"

Mitya awaited an answer with assurance. He had no doubts. An expression of extraordinary resolution passed over the Pole's face.

"And the money, *panie*?"

"The money, *panie*? Five hundred roubles I'll give you this moment for the journey, and as a first instalment, and two thousand five hundred to-morrow, in the town—I swear on my honour, I'll get it, I'll get it at any cost!" cried Mitya.

The Poles exchanged glances again. The short man's face looked more forbidding.

"Seven hundred, seven hundred, not five hundred, at once, this minute, cash down!!" Mitya added, feeling something wrong. "What's the matter, *panie*? Don't you trust me? I can't give you the whole three thousand straight off. If I give it, you may come back to her to-morrow. . . . Besides, I haven't the three thousand with me. I've got it at home in the town," faltered Mitya, his spirit sinking at every word he uttered. "Upon my word, the money's there, hidden."

In an instant an extraordinary sense of personal dignity showed itself in the little man's face.

"What next?" he asked ironically. "For shame!" and he spat on the floor. Pan Vrublevsky spat too.

"You do that, *panie,*" said Mitya, recognising with despair that all was over, "because you hope to make more out of Grushenka? You're a couple of capons, that's what you are?"

"This is a mortal insult!" The little Pole turned as red as a crab, and he went out of the room, briskly, as though unwilling to hear another word. Vrublevsky swung out after him, and Mitya followed, confused and crestfallen. He was afraid of Grushenka, afraid that the *pan* would at once raise an outcry. And so indeed he did. The Pole walked into the room and threw himself in a theatrical attitude before Grushenka.

"*Pani* Agrippina, I have received a mortal insult!" he exclaimed. But Grushenka suddenly lost all patience, as though they had wounded her in the tenderest spot.

"Speak Russian! Speak Russian!" she cried, "not another word of Polish! You used to talk Russian. You can't have forgotten it in five years."

She was red with passion.

"*Pani* Agrippina . . ."

"My name's Agrafena, Grushenka, speak Russian or I won't listen!"

The Pole gasped with offended dignity, and quickly and pompously delivered himself in broken Russian:

"*Pani* Agrafena, I came here to forget the past and forgive it, to forget all that has happened till to-day. . . ."

"Forgive? Came here to forgive me?" Grushenka cut him short, jumping up from her seat.

"Just so, *pani*, I'm not pusillanimous, I'm magnanimous. But I was astounded when I saw your lovers. Pan Mitya offered me three thousand, in the other room, to depart. I spat in the *pan*'s face."

"What? He offered you money for me?" cried Grushenka, hysterically. "Is it true, Mitya? How dare you? Am I for sale?"

"Panie, panie!" yelled Mitya, "she's pure and shining, and I have never been her lover! That's a lie. . . ."

"How dare you defend me to him?" shrieked Grushenka. "It wasn't virtue kept me pure, and it wasn't that I was afraid of Kuzma, but that I might hold up my head when I met him, and tell him he's a scoundrel. And did he actually refuse the money?"

"He took it! He took it!" cried Mitya; "only he wanted to get the whole three thousand at once, and I could only give him seven hundred straight off."

"I see: he heard I had money, and came here to marry me!"

"Pani Agrippina!" cried the little Pole. "I'm—a knight, I'm—a nobleman, and not a *lajdak*. I came here to make you my wife and I find you a different woman, perverse and shameless."

"Oh, go back where you came from! I'll tell them to turn you out and you'll be turned out," cried Grushenka, furious. "I've been a fool, a fool, to have been miserable these five years! And it wasn't for his sake, it was my anger made me miserable. And this isn't he at all! Was he like this? It might be his father! Where did you get your wig from? He was a falcon, but this is a gander. He used to laugh and sing to me. . . . And I've been crying for five years, damned fool, abject, shameless I was!"

She sank back in her low chair and hid her face in her hands. At that instant the chorus of Mokroe girls began singing in the room on the left—a rollicking dance song.

"A regular Sodom!" Vrublevsky roared suddenly. "Landlord, send the shameless hussies away!"

The landlord, who had been for some time past inquisitively peeping in at the door, hearing shouts and guessing that his guests were quarrelling, at once entered the room.

"What are you shouting for? D'you want to split your throat?" he said, addressing Vrublevsky, with surprising rudeness.

"Animal!" bellowed Pan Vrublevsky.

"Animal? And what sort of cards were you playing with just now? I gave you a pack and you hid it. You played with marked cards! I could send you to Siberia for playing with false cards, d'you know that, for it's just the same as false bank-notes. . . ."

And going up to the sofa he thrust his fingers between the sofa back and the cushion, and pulled out an unopened pack of cards.

"Here's my pack unopened!"

He held it up and showed it to all in the room. "From where I stood I saw him slip my pack away, and put his in place of it—you're a cheat and not a gentleman!"

"And I twice saw the *pan* change a card!" cried Kalganov.

"How shameful! How shameful!" exclaimed Grushenka, clasping her hands, and blushing for genuine shame. "Good Lord, he's come to that!"

"I thought so, too!" said Mitya. But before he had uttered the words, Vrublevsky, with a confused and infuriated face, shook his fist at Grushenka, shouting:

"You low harlot!"

Mitya flew at him at once, clutched him in both hands, lifted him in the air, and in one instant had carried him into the room on the right, from which they had just come.

"I've laid him on the floor, there," he announced, returning at once, gasping with excitement. "He's struggling, the scoundrel! But he won't come back, no fear of that! . . ."

He closed one half of the folding doors, and holding the other ajar called out to the little Pole:

"Most illustrious, will you be pleased to retire as well?"

"My dear Dmitri Fyodorovitch," said Trifon Borissovitch, "make them give you back the money you lost. It's as good as stolen from you."

"I don't want my fifty roubles back," Kalganov declared suddenly.

"I don't want my two hundred, either," cried Mitya, "I wouldn't take it for anything! Let him keep it as a consolation."

"Bravo, Mitya! You're a trump, Mitya!" cried Grushenka, and there was a note of fierce anger in the exclamation.

The little *pan,* crimson with fury, but still mindful of his dignity, was making for the door, but he stopped short and said suddenly, addressing Grushenka:

"*Pani,* if you want to come with me, come. If not, good-bye."

And swelling with indignation and importance he went to the door. This was a man of character: he had so good an opinion of himself that after all that had passed, he still expected that she would marry him. Mitya slammed the door after him.

"Lock it," said Kalganov. But the key clicked on the other side, they had locked it from within.

"That's capital!" exclaimed Grushenka relentlessly. "Serve them right!"

8

DELIRIUM

WHAT followed was almost an orgy, a feast to which all were welcomed. Grushenka was the first to call for wine.

"I want to drink. I want to be quite drunk, as we were before. Do you remember, Mitya, do you remember how we made friends here last time!"

Mitya himself was almost delirious, feeling that his happiness was at hand. But Grushenka was continually sending him away from her:

"Go and enjoy yourself. Tell them to dance, to make merry, 'let the stove and cottage dance';* as we had it last time," she kept exclaiming. She was tremendously excited. And Mitya hastened to obey her. The chorus were in the next room. The room in which they had been sitting till that moment was too small, and was divided in two by cotton curtains, behind which was a huge bed with a puffy feather mattress and a pyramid of cotton pillows. In the four rooms for visitors there were beds. Grushenka settled herself just at the door. Mitya set an easy chair for her. She had sat in the same place to watch the dancing and singing "the time before," when they had made merry there. All the girls who had come had been there then; the Jewish band with fiddles and zithers had come, too, and at last the long expected cart had arrived with the wines and provisions.

Mitya bustled about. All sorts of people began coming into the room to look on, peasants and their women, who had been roused from sleep and attracted by the hopes of another marvelous entertainment such as they had enjoyed a month before. Mitya remembered their faces, greeting and embracing every one he knew. He uncorked bottles and poured out wine for every one who presented himself. Only the girls were very eager for the champagne. The men preferred rum, brandy, and, above all, hot punch. Mitya had chocolate made for all the girls, and ordered that three samovars should be kept boiling all night to provide tea and punch for every one to help himself.

An absurd chaotic confusion followed, but Mitya was in his natural element, and the more foolish it became, the more his spirits rose. If the peasants had asked him for money at that moment, he would have pulled out his notes and given them away right and left. This was probably why the landlord, Trifon Borissovitch, kept hovering about Mitya to protect him. He seemed to have given up all idea of going to bed that night,

---

*Quotation from a popular Russian dance song.

though he drank little, only one glass of punch, and kept a sharp look-out on Mitya's interests after his own fashion. He intervened in the nick of time, civilly and obsequiously persuading Mitya not to give away "cigars and Rhine wine," and, above all, money to the peasants as he had done before. He was very indignant, too, at the peasant girls drinking liqueur, and eating sweets.

"They're a lousy lot, Dmitri Fyodorovitch," he said. "I'd give them a kick, every one of them, and they'd take it as an honour—that's all they're worth!"

Mitya remembered Andrey again, and ordered punch to be sent out to him. "I was rude to him just now," he repeated with a sinking, softened voice. Kalganov did not want to drink, and at first did not care for the girls' singing; but after he had drunk a couple of glasses of champagne he became extraordinarily lively, strolling about the room, laughing and praising the music and the songs, admiring every one and everything. Maximov, blissfully drunk, never left his side. Grushenka, too, was beginning to get drunk. Pointing to Kalganov, she said to Mitya:

"What a dear, charming boy he is!"

And Mitya, delighted, ran to kiss Kalganov and Maximov. Oh, great were his hopes! She had said nothing yet, and seemed, indeed, purposely to refrain from speaking. But she looked at him from time to time with caressing and passionate eyes. At last she suddenly gripped his hand and drew him vigorously to her. She was sitting at the moment in the low chair by the door.

"How was it you came just now, eh? How you walked in! . . . I *was* frightened. So you wanted to give me up to him, did you? Did you really want to?"

"I didn't want to spoil your happiness!" Mitya faltered blissfully. But she did not need his answer.

"Well, go and enjoy yourself. . . ." she sent him away once more. "Don't cry, I'll call you back again."

He would run away, and she listened to the singing and looked at the dancing, though her eyes followed him wherever he went. But in another quarter of an hour she would call him once more and again he would run back to her.

"Come, sit beside me, tell me, how did you hear about me, and my coming here yesterday? From whom did you first hear it?"

And Mitya began telling her all about it, disconnectedly, incoherently, feverishly. He spoke strangely, often frowning, and stopping abruptly.

"What are you frowning at?" she asked.

"Nothing. . . . I left a man ill there. I'd give ten years of my life for him to get well, to know he was all right!"

"Well, never mind, if he's ill. So you meant to shoot yourself tomorrow! What a silly boy! What for? I like such reckless fellows as you," she lisped, with a rather halting tongue. "So you would go any length for me, eh? Did you really mean to shoot yourself to-morrow, you stupid? No, wait a little. To-morrow I may have something to say to you. . . . I won't say it to-day, but to-morrow. You'd like it to be to-day? No, I don't want to to-day. Come, go along now, go and amuse yourself."

Once, however, she called him, as it were, puzzled and uneasy.

"Why are you sad? I see you're sad. . . . Yes, I see it," she added, looking intently into his eyes. "Though you keep kissing the peasants and shouting, I see something. No, be merry. I'm merry; you be merry, too. . . . I love somebody here. Guess who it is. Ah, look, my boy has fallen asleep, poor dear, he's drunk."

She meant Kalganov. He was, in fact, drunk, and had dropped asleep for a moment, sitting on the sofa. But he was not merely drowsy from drink; he felt suddenly dejected, or, as he said, "bored." He was intensely depressed by the girls' songs, which, as the drinking went on, gradually became coarse and more reckless. And the dances were as bad. Two girls dressed up as bears, and a lively girl, called Stepanida, with a stick in her hand, acted the part of keeper, and began to "show them."

"Look alive, Marya, or you'll get the stick!"

The bears rolled on the ground at last in the most unseemly fashion, amid roars of laughter from the closely packed crowd of men and women.

"Well, let them! Let them!" said Grushenka sententiously, with an ecstatic expression on her face. "When they do get a day to enjoy themselves, why shouldn't folks be happy?"

Kalganov looked as though he had been besmirched with dirt.

"It's swinish, all this peasant foolery," he murmured, moving away; "it's the games they play when it's light all night in summer."

He particularly disliked one "new" song to a jaunty dance-tune.[6] It described how a gentleman came and tried his luck with the girls, to see whether they would love him:

> "The master came to try the girls;
>   Would they love him, would they not?"

But the girls could not love the master:

> "He would beat me cruelly
>   And such love won't do for me."

Then a gipsy comes along and he, too, tries:

> "The gipsy came to try the girls:
>   Would they love him, would they not?"

But they couldn't love the gipsy either:

> "He would be a thief, I fear,
>   And would cause me many a tear."

And many more men come to try their luck, among them a soldier:

> "The soldier came to try the girls:
>   Would they love him, would they not?"

But the soldier is rejected with contempt, in two indecent lines, sung with absolute frankness and producing a furore in the audience. The song ends with a merchant:

> "The merchant came to try the girls:
>   Would they love him; would they not?"

And it appears that he wins their love because:

> "The merchant will make gold for me
>   And his queen I'll gladly be."

Kalganov was positively indignant:

"That's just a song of yesterday," he said aloud. "Who writes such things for them? They might just as well have had a railway man or a Jew come to try his luck with the girls; they'd have carried all before them."

And, almost as though it were a personal affront, he declared, on the spot, that he was bored, sat down on the sofa and immediately fell asleep. His pretty little face looked rather pale, as it fell back on the sofa cushion.

"Look how pretty he is," said Grushenka, taking Mitya up to him. "I was combing his hair just now; his hair's like flax, and so thick. . . ."

And, bending over him tenderly, she kissed his forehead. Kalganov instantly opened his eyes, looked at her, stood up, and with the most anxious air inquired where was Maximov.

"So that's who it is you want." Grushenka laughed. "Stay with me a minute. Mitya, run and find his Maximov."

Maximov, it appeared, could not tear himself away from the girls, only running away from time to time to pour himself out a glass of liqueur. He had drunk two cups of chocolate. His face was red, and his nose was crimson; his eyes were moist, and mawkishly sweet. He ran up and announced that he was going to dance the "sabotière."*

"They taught me all those well-bred, aristocratic dances when I was little. . . ."

"Go, go with him, Mitya, and I'll watch from here how he dances," said Grushenka.

"No, no, I'm coming to look on, too," exclaimed Kalganov, brushing aside in the most naïve way Grushenka's offer to sit with him. They all went to look on. Maximov danced his dance. But it roused no great admiration in any one but Mitya. It consisted of nothing but skipping and hopping, kicking up the feet, and at every skip Maximov slapped the upturned sole of his foot. Kalganov did not like it at all, but Mitya kissed the dancer.

---

*A peasant clog dance (*sabot* is French for "clog").

"Thanks. You're tired perhaps? What are you looking for here? Would you like some sweets? A cigar, perhaps?"

"A cigarette."

"Don't you want a drink?"

"I'll just have a liqueur. . . . Have you any chocolates?"

"Yes, there's a heap of them on the table there. Choose one, my dear soul!"

"I like one with vanilla . . . for old people. He-he!"

"No, brother, we've none of that special sort."

"I say," the old man bent down to whisper in Mitya's ear. "That girl there, little Marya, he-he! How would it be if you were to help me make friends with her?"

"So that's what you're after! No, brother, that won't do!"

"I'd do no harm to any one," Maximov muttered disconsolately.

"Oh, all right, all right. They only come here to dance and sing, you know, brother. But damn it all, wait a bit! . . . Eat and drink and be merry, meanwhile. Don't you want money?"

"Later on perhaps," smiled Maximov.

"All right, all right. . . ."

Mitya's head was burning. He went outside to the wooden balcony which ran round the whole building on the inner side, overlooking the courtyard. The fresh air revived him. He stood alone in a dark corner, and suddenly clutched his head in both hands. His scattered thoughts came together; his sensations blended into a whole and threw a sudden light into his mind. A fearful and terrible light! "If I'm to shoot myself, why not now?" passed through his mind. "Why not go for the pistols, bring them here, and here, in this dark, dirty corner, make an end?" Almost a minute he stood, undecided. A few hours earlier, when he had been dashing here, he was pursued by disgrace, by the theft he had committed, and that blood, that blood! . . . But yet it was easier for him then. Then everything was over: he had lost her, given her up. She was gone for him—oh, then his death sentence had been easier for him; at least it had seemed necessary, inevitable, for what had he to stay on earth for?

But now? Was it the same as then? Now one phantom, one terror at least was at an end: that first, rightful lover, that fateful figure had vanished, leaving no trace. The terrible phantom had turned into something so small, so comic; it had been carried into the bedroom and locked in. It would never return. She was ashamed, and from her eyes he could see now whom she loved. Now he had everything to make life happy . . . but he could not go on living, he could not; oh, damnation! "Oh, God! restore to life the man I knocked down at the fence! Let this fearful cup pass from me!* Lord, thou hast wrought miracles for such sinners as me! But what, what if the old man's alive? Oh, then the shame of the other disgrace I would wipe away. I would restore the stolen money. I'd give it back; I'd get

*See Matthew 26:39.

it somehow. . . . No trace of that shame will remain except in my heart for ever! But no, no; oh, impossible cowardly dreams! Oh, damnation!"

Yet there was a ray of light and hope in his darkness. He jumped up and ran back to the room—to her, to her, his queen for ever! Was not one moment of her love worth all the rest of life, even in the agonies of disgrace? This wild question clutched at his heart. "To her, to her alone, to see her, to hear her, to think of nothing, to forget everything, if only for that night, for an hour, for a moment!" Just as he turned from the balcony into the passage, he came upon the landlord, Trifon Borissovitch. He thought he looked gloomy and worried, and fancied he had come to find him.

"What is it, Trifon Borissovitch? are you looking for me?"

"No, sir." The landlord seemed disconcerted. "Why should I be looking for you? Where have you been?"

"Why do you look so glum? You're not angry, are you? Wait a bit, you shall soon get to bed. . . . What's the time?"

"It'll be three o'clock. Past three, it must be."

"We'll leave off soon. We'll leave off."

"Don't mention it; it doesn't matter. Keep it up as long as you like. . . ."

"What's the matter with him?" Mitya wondered for an instant, and he ran back to the room where the girls were dancing. But she was not there. She was not in the blue room either; there was no one but Kalganov asleep on the sofa. Mitya peeped behind the curtain—she was there. She was sitting in the corner, on a trunk. Bent forward, with her head and arms on the bed close by, she was crying bitterly, doing her utmost to stifle her sobs that she might not be heard. Seeing Mitya, she beckoned him to her, and when he ran to her, she grasped his hand tightly.

"Mitya, Mitya, I loved him, you know. How I have loved him these five years, all that time! Did I love him or only my own anger? No, him, him! It's a lie that it was my anger I loved and not him. Mitya, I was only seventeen then; he was so kind to me, so merry; he used to sing to me. . . . Or so it seemed to a silly girl like me. . . . And now, O Lord, it's not the same man. Even his face is not the same; he's different altogether. I shouldn't have known him. I drove here with Timofey, and all the way I was thinking how I should meet him, what I should say to him, how we should look at one another. My soul was faint, and all of a sudden it was just as though he had emptied a pail of dirty water over me. He talked to me like a schoolmaster, all so grave and learned; he met me so solemnly that I was struck dumb. I couldn't get a word in. At first I thought he was ashamed to talk before his great big Pole. I sat staring at him and wondering why I couldn't say a word to him now. It must have been his wife that ruined him; you know he threw me up to get married. She must have changed him like that. Mitya, how shameful it is! Oh, Mitya, I'm ashamed, I'm ashamed for all my life. Curse it, curse it, curse those five years!"

And again she burst into tears, but clung tight to Mitya's hand and did not let it go.

"Mitya, darling, stay, don't go away. I want to say one word to you," she whispered, and suddenly raised her face to him. "Listen, tell me who it is

I love? I love one man here. Who is that man? That's what you must tell me."

A smile lighted up her face that was swollen with weeping, and her eyes shone in the half darkness.

"A falcon flew in, and my heart sank. 'Fool! that's the man you love!' That was what my heart whispered to me at once. You came in and all grew bright. What's he afraid of? I wondered. For you were frightened; you couldn't speak. It's not them he's afraid of—could you be frightened of any one? It's me he's afraid of, I thought, only me. So Fenya told you, you little stupid, how I called to Alyosha out of the window that I'd loved Mityenka for one hour, and that I was going now to love . . . another. Mitya, Mitya, how could I be such a fool as to think I could love any one after you? Do you forgive me, Mitya? Do you forgive me or not? Do you love me? Do you love me?" She jumped up and held him with both hands on his shoulders. Mitya, dumb with rapture, gazed into her eyes, at her face, at her smile, and suddenly clasped her tightly in his arms and then kissed her passionately.

"You will forgive me for having tormented you? It was through spite I tormented you all. It was for spite I drove the old man out of his mind. . . . Do you remember how you drank at my house one day and broke the wine-glass? I remembered that and I broke a glass to-day and drank 'to my vile heart.' Mitya, my falcon, why don't you kiss me? He kissed me once, and now he draws back and looks and listens. Why listen to me? Kiss me, kiss me hard, that's right. If you love, well then love! I'll be your slave now, your slave for the rest of my life. It's sweet to be a slave. Kiss me! Beat me, ill-treat me, do what you will with me. . . . And I do deserve to suffer. Stay, wait, afterwards, I won't have that . . ." she suddenly thrust him away. "Go along, Mitya, I'll come and have some wine, I want to be drunk, I'm going to get drunk and dance; I must, I must!" She tore herself away from him and disappeared behind the curtain. Mitya followed like a drunken man.

"Yes, come what may—whatever may happen now, for one minute I'd give the whole world," he thought. Grushenka did, in fact, toss off a whole glass of champagne at one gulp, and became at once very tipsy. She sat down in the same chair as before, with a blissful smile on her face. Her cheeks were glowing, her lips were burning, her flashing eyes were moist; there was passionate appeal in her eyes. Even Kalganov felt a stir at the heart and went up to her.

"Did you feel how I kissed you when you were asleep just now?" she said thickly. "I'm drunk now, that's what it is. . . . And aren't you drunk? And why isn't Mitya drinking? Why don't you drink, Mitya? I'm drunk, and you don't drink. . . ."

"I am drunk! I'm drunk as it is . . . drunk with you . . . and now I'll be drunk with wine, too."

He drank off another glass, and—he thought it strange himself—that glass made him completely drunk. He was suddenly drunk, although till that moment he had been quite sober, he remembered that. From that moment everything whirled about him, as though he were delirious. He walked, laughed, talked to everybody, without knowing what he was doing. Only one persistent burning sensation made itself felt continually, "like a red-hot coal in his heart," he said afterwards. He went up to her, sat beside her, gazed at her, listened to her. . . . She became very talkative, kept calling every one to her, and beckoned to different girls out of the chorus. When the girl came up, she either kissed her, or made the sign of the cross over her. In another minute she might have cried. She was greatly amused by the "little old man," as she called Maximov. He ran up every minute to kiss her hands, "each little finger," and finally he danced another dance to an old song, which he sang himself. He danced with special vigour to the refrain:

> "The little pig says—umph! umph! umph!
> The little calf says—moo, moo, moo,
> The little duck says—quack, quack, quack,
> The little goose says—ga, ga, ga.
> The hen goes strutting through the porch
> Troo-roo-roo-roo-roo, she'll say
> Troo-roo-roo-roo-roo—she'll say!"*

"Give him something, Mitya," said Grushenka. "Give him a present, he's poor, you know. Ah, the poor, the insulted. . . . Do you know, Mitya, I shall go into a nunnery. No, I really shall one day. Alyosha said something to me to-day that I shall remember all my life. . . . Yes. . . . But to-day let us dance. To-morrow to the nunnery, but to-day we'll dance. I want to play to-day, good people, and what of it? God will forgive us. If I were God, I'd forgive every one: 'My dear sinners, from this day forth I forgive you.' I'm going to beg forgiveness: 'Forgive me, good people, a silly wench.' I'm a beast, that's what I am. But I want to pray. I gave a little onion. Wicked as I've been, I want to pray. Mitya, let them dance, don't stop them. Every one in the world is good. Every one—even the worst of them. The world's a nice place. Though we're bad the world's all right. We're good and bad, good and bad. . . . Come tell me, I've something to ask you; come here every one, and I'll ask you: Why am I so good? You know I am good, I'm very good. . . . Come, why am I so good?"

So Grushenka babbled on, getting more and more drunk. At last she announced that she was going to dance, too. She got up from her chair, staggering. "Mitya, don't give me any more wine—if I ask you, don't give it to me. Wine doesn't give peace. Everything's going round, the stove, and everything. I want to dance. Let every one see how I dance . . . let them see how beautifully I dance. . . ."

She really meant it. She pulled a white cambric handkerchief out of her pocket, and took it by one corner in her right hand, to wave it in the dance. Mitya ran to and fro, the girls were quiet, and got ready to break into

---

*From a Russian folksong.

a dancing song at the first signal. Maximov, hearing that Grushenka
wanted to dance, squealed with delight, and ran skipping about in front of
her, humming:

> "With legs so slim and sides so trim
> And its little tail curled tight."*

But Grushenka waved her handkerchief at him and drove him away.

"Sh-h! Mitya, why don't they come? Let every one come . . . to look on.
Call them in, too, that were locked in. . . . Why did you lock them in? Tell
them I'm going to dance. Let them look on, too. . . ."

Mitya walked with a drunken swagger to the locked door, and began
knocking to the Poles with his fist.

"Hi, you . . . Podvysotskys! Come, she's going to dance. She calls you."

"Lajdak!" one of the Poles shouted in reply.

"You're a *lajdak* yourself! You're a little scoundrel, that's what you are."

"Leave off laughing at Poland," said Kalganov sententiously. He too
was drunk.

"Be quiet, boy! If I call him a scoundrel, it doesn't mean that I called all
Poland so. One *lajdak* doesn't make a Poland. Be quiet, my pretty boy, eat
a sweetmeat."

"Ach, what fellows! As though they were not men. Why won't they make
friends?" said Grushenka, and went forward to dance. The chorus broke
into "Ah, my porch, my new porch!"† Grushenka flung back her head, half
opened her lips, smiled, waved her handkerchief, and suddenly, with a violent lurch, stood still in the middle of the room, looking bewildered.

"I'm weak. . . ." she said in an exhausted voice. "Forgive me. . . . I'm
weak, I can't. . . . I'm sorry."

She bowed to the chorus, and then began bowing in all directions.

"I'm sorry. . . . Forgive me. . . ."

"The lady's been drinking. The pretty lady has been drinking," voices
were heard saying.

"The lady's drunk too much," Maximov explained to the girls, giggling.

"Mitya, lead me away . . . take me," said Grushenka helplessly. Mitya
pounced on her, snatched her up in his arms, and carried the precious burden through the curtains.

"Well, now I'll go," thought Kalganov, and walking out of the blue
room, he closed the two halves of the door after him. But the orgy in the
larger room went on and grew louder and louder. Mitya laid Grushenka
on the bed and kissed her on the lips.

"Don't touch me. . . ." she faltered, in an imploring voice. "Don't touch

---

*From a Russian folksong.

†According to Victor Terras (*A Karamazov Companion*; see "For Further Reading"), this is a line from a popular folksong, about a peasant girl in love who
dares to oppose her father.

me, till I'm yours. . . . I've told you I'm yours, but don't touch me . . . spare me. . . . With them here, with them close, you mustn't. He's here. It's nasty here. . . ."

"I'll obey you! I won't think of it . . . I worship you!" muttered Mitya. "Yes, it's nasty here, it's abominable."

And still holding her in his arms, he sank on his knees by the bedside.

"I know, though you're a brute, you're generous," Grushenka articulated with difficulty. "It must be honourable . . . it shall be honourable for the future . . . and let us be honest, let us be good, not brutes, but good . . . take me away, take me far away, do you hear? I don't want it to be here, but far, far away. . . ."

"Oh, yes, yes, it must be!" said Mitya, pressing her in his arms. "I'll take you and we'll fly away. . . . Oh, I'd give my whole life for one year only to know about that blood!"

"What blood?" asked Grushenka, bewildered.

"Nothing," muttered Mitya, through his teeth. "Grusha, you wanted to be honest, but I'm a thief. But I've stolen money from Katya. . . . Disgrace, a disgrace!"

"From Katya, from that young lady? No, you didn't steal it. Give it her back, take it from me. . . . Why make a fuss? Now everything of mine is yours. What does money matter? We shall waste it anyway. . . . Folks like us are bound to waste money. But we'd better go and work the land. I want to dig the earth with my own hands. We must work, do you hear? Alyosha said so. I won't be your mistress, I'll be faithful to you, I'll be your slave, I'll work for you. We'll go to the young lady and bow down to her together, so that she may forgive us, and then we'll go away. And if she won't forgive us, we'll go, anyway. Take her her money and love me. . . . Don't love her. . . . Don't love her any more. If you love her, I shall strangle her. . . . I'll put out both her eyes with a needle. . . ."

"I love you. I love only you. I'll love you in Siberia. . . ."

"Why Siberia? Never mind, Siberia if you like. I don't care . . . we'll work . . . there's snow in Siberia. . . . I love driving in the snow . . . and must have bells. . . . Do you hear, there's a bell ringing? Where is that bell ringing? There are people coming. . . . Now it's stopped."

She closed her eyes, exhausted, and suddenly fell asleep for an instant. There had certainly been the sound of a bell in the distance, but the ringing had ceased. Mitya let his head sink on her breast. He did not notice that the bell had ceased ringing, nor did he notice that the songs had ceased, and that instead of singing and drunken clamour there was absolute stillness in the house. Grushenka opened her eyes.

"What's the matter? Was I asleep? Yes . . . a bell . . . I've been asleep and dreamt I was driving over the snow with bells, and I dozed. I was with some one I loved, with you. And far, far away. I was holding you and kissing you, nestling close to you. I was cold, and the snow glistened. . . . You know how the snow glistens at night when the moon shines. It was as though I was not on earth. I woke up, and my dear one is close to me. How sweet that is. . . ."

"Close to you," murmured Mitya, kissing her dress, her bosom, her hands. And suddenly he had a strange fancy: it seemed to him that she was looking straight before her, not at him, not into his face, but over his head, with an intent, almost uncanny fixity. An expression of wonder, almost of alarm, came suddenly into her face.

"Mitya, who is that looking at us?" she whispered.

Mitya turned, and saw that some one had, in fact, parted the curtains and seemed to be watching them. And not one person alone, it seemed.

He jumped up and walked quickly to the intruder.

"Here, come to us, come here," said a voice, speaking not loudly, but firmly and peremptorily.

Mitya passed to the other side of the curtain and stood stock still. The room was filled with people, but not those who had been there before. An instantaneous shiver ran down his back, and he shuddered. He recognised all those people instantly. That tall, stout old man in the overcoat and forage cap with a cockade—was the police captain, Mihail Makarovitch. And that "consumptive-looking" trim dandy, "who always has such polished boots"— that was the deputy prosecutor. "He has a chronometer worth four hundred roubles; he showed it to me." And that small young man in spectacles. . . . Mitya forgot his surname though he knew him, had seen him: he was the "investigating lawyer," from the "school of jurisprudence,"* who had only lately come to the town. And this man—the inspector of police, Mavriky Mavrikyevitch, a man he knew well. And those fellows with the brass plates on, why are they here? And those other two . . . peasants. . . . And there at the door Kalganov with Trifon Borissovitch. . . .

"Gentlemen! What's this for, gentlemen?" began Mitya, but suddenly, as though beside himself, not knowing what he was doing, he cried aloud, at the top of his voice:

"I un-der-stand!"

The young man in spectacles moved forward suddenly, and stepping up to Mitya, began with dignity, though hurriedly:

"We have to make . . . in brief, I beg you to come this way, this way to the sofa. . . . It is absolutely imperative that you should give an explanation."

"The old man!" cried Mitya frantically. "The old man and his blood! . . . I understand."

And he sank, almost fell, on a chair close by, as though he had been mown down by a scythe.

"You understand? He understands it! Monster and parricide! Your father's blood cries out against you!" the old captain of police roared suddenly, stepping up to Mitya.

He was beside himself, crimson in the face and quivering all over.

"This is impossible!" cried the small young man. "Mihail Makarovitch, Mihail Makarovitch, this won't do! . . . I beg you'll allow me to speak. I should never have expected such behaviour from you . . ."

---

*The Imperial Law School in St. Petersburg.

"This is delirium, gentlemen, raving delirium," cried the captain of police; "look at him: drunk, at this time of night, in the company of a disreputable woman, with the blood of his father on his hands. . . . It's delirium! . . ."

"I beg you most earnestly, dear Mihail Makarovitch, to restrain your feelings," the prosecutor said in a rapid whisper to the old police captain, "or I shall be forced to resort to . . ."

But the little lawyer did not allow him to finish. He turned to Mitya, and delivered himself in a loud, firm, dignified voice:

"Ex-Lieutenant Karamazov, it is my duty to inform you that you are charged with the murder of your father, Fyodor Pavlovitch Karamazov, perpetrated this night. . . ."

He said something more, and the prosecutor, too, put in something, but though Mitya heard them he did not understand them. He stared at them all with wild eyes.

BOOK NINE

THE PRELIMINARY INVESTIGATION

1

THE BEGINNING OF PERHOTIN'S OFFICIAL CAREER

Pʏᴏᴛʀ Iʟʏɪᴛᴄʜ Pᴇʀʜᴏᴛɪɴ, whom we left knocking at the strong locked gates of the widow Morozov's house, ended, of course, by making himself heard. Fenya, who was still excited by the fright she had had two hours before, and too much "upset" to go to bed, was almost frightened into hysterics on hearing the furious knocking at the gate. Though she had herself seen him drive away, she fancied that it must be Dmitri Fyodorovitch knocking again, no one else could knock so savagely. She ran to the house-porter, who had already waked up and gone out to the gate, and began imploring him not to open it. But having questioned Pyotr Ilyitch, and learned that he wanted to see Fenya on very "important business," the man made up his mind at last to open. Pyotr Ilyitch was admitted into Fenya's kitchen but the girl begged him to allow the house-porter to be present, "because of her misgivings." He began questioning her and at once learnt the most vital fact, that is, that when Dmitri Fyodorovitch had run out to look for Grushenka, he had snatched up a pestle from the mortar, and that when he returned, the pestle was not with him and his hands were smeared with blood.

"And the blood was simply flowing, dripping from him, dripping!" Fenya kept exclaiming. This horrible detail was simply the product of her disordered imagination. But although not "dripping," Pyotr Ilyitch had himself seen those hands stained with blood, and had helped to wash them. Moreover, the question he had to decide was not how soon the blood had dried, but where Dmitri Fyodorovitch had run with the pestle, or rather, whether it really was to Fyodor Pavlovitch's, and how he could satisfactorily ascertain. Pyotr Ilyitch persisted in returning to this point, and though he found out nothing conclusive, yet he carried away a conviction that Dmitri Fyodorovitch could have gone nowhere but to his father's house, and that therefore something must have happened there.

"And when he came back," Fenya added with excitement, "I told him the whole story, and then I began asking him, 'Why have you got blood on your hands, Dmitri Fyodorovitch?' and he answered that that was human blood, and that he had just killed some one. He confessed it all to me, and suddenly ran off like a madman? I sat down and began thinking, where's he run off to now like a madman? He'll go to Mokroe, I thought, and kill my mistress there. I ran out to beg him not to kill her. I was running to his lodgings, but I looked at Plotinkov's shop, and saw him just setting off, and there was no blood on his hands then." (Fenya had noticed this and remembered it.)

Fenya's old grandmother confirmed her evidence as far as she was capable. After asking some further questions, Pyotr Ilyitch left the house, even more upset and uneasy than he had been when he entered it.

The most direct and the easiest thing for him to do would have been to go straight to Fyodor Pavlovitch's, to find out whether anything had happened there, and if so, what; and only to go to the police captain, as Pyotr Ilyitch firmly intended doing, when he had satisfied himself of the fact. But the night was dark, Fyodor Pavlovitch's gates were strong, and he would have to knock again. His acquaintance with Fyodor Pavlovitch was of the slightest, and what if, after he had been knocking, they opened to him, and nothing had happened, and Fyodor Pavlovitch in his jeering way would go telling the story all over the town, how a stranger, called Perhotin, had broken in upon him at midnight to ask if any one had killed him. It would make a scandal. And scandal was what Pyotr Ilyitch dreaded more than anything in the world.

Yet the feeling that possessed him was so strong, that though he stamped his foot angrily and swore at himself, he set off again, not to Fyodor Pavlovitch's but to Madame Hohlakov's. He decided that if she denied having just given Dmitri Fyodorovitch three thousand roubles, he would go straight to the police captain, but if she admitted having given him the money, he would go home and let the matter rest till next morning.

It is, of course, perfectly evident that there was even more likelihood of causing scandal by going at eleven o'clock at night to a fashionable lady, a complete stranger, and perhaps rousing her from her bed to ask her an amazing question, than by going to Fyodor Pavlovitch. But that is just how it is, sometimes, especially in cases like the present one, with the decisions of the most precise and phlegmatic people. Pyotr Ilyitch was by no means phlegmatic at that moment. He remembered all his life how a haunting uneasiness gradually gained possession of him, growing more and more painful and driving him on, against his will. Yet he kept cursing himself, of course, all the way for going to this lady, but "I will get to the bottom of it, I will!" he repeated for the tenth time, grinding his teeth, and he carried out his intention.

It was exactly eleven o'clock when he entered Madame Hohlakov's house. He was admitted into the yard pretty quickly, but, in response to his inquiry whether the lady was still up, the porter could give no answer, except that she was usually in bed by that time.

"Ask at the top of the stairs. If the lady wants to receive you, she'll receive you. If she won't, she won't."

Pyotr Ilyitch went up, but did not find things so easy here. The footman was unwilling to take in his name, but finally called a maid. Pyotr Ilyitch politely but insistently begged her to inform her lady that an official, living in the town, called Perhotin, had called on particular business, and that, if it were not of the greatest importance, he would not have ventured to come. "Tell her in those words, in those words exactly," he asked the girl.

She went away. He remained waiting in the entry. Madame Hohlakov herself was already in her bedroom, though not yet asleep. She had felt upset ever since Mitya's visit, and had a presentiment that she would not get through the night without the sick headache which always, with her, followed such excitement. She was surprised on hearing the announcement from the maid. She irritably declined to see him, however, though the unexpected visit at such an hour, of an "official living in the town," who was a total stranger, roused her feminine curiosity intensely. But this time Pyotr Ilyitch was as obstinate as a mule. He begged the maid most earnestly to take another message in these very words.

"That he had come on business of the greatest importance, and that Madame Hohlakov might have cause to regret it later, if she refused to see him now."

"I plunged headlong," he described it afterwards.

The maid, gazing at him in amazement, went to take his message again. Madame Hohlakov was impressed. She thought a little, asked what he looked like, and learned that he was "very well dressed, young and so polite." We may note, parenthetically, that Pyotr Ilyitch was a rather good-looking young man, and well aware of the fact. Madame Hohlakov made up her mind to see him. She was in her dressing-gown and slippers, but she flung a black shawl over her shoulders. "The official" was asked to walk into the drawing-room, the very room in which Mitya had been received shortly before. The lady came to meet her visitor, with a sternly inquiring countenance, and, without asking him to sit down, began at once with the question:

"What do you want?"

"I have ventured to disturb you, Madame, on a matter concerning our common acquaintance, Dmitri Fyodorovitch Karamazov," Perhotin began.

But he had hardly uttered the name, when the lady's face showed signs of acute irritation. She almost shrieked, and interrupted him in a fury:

"How much longer am I to be worried by that awful man?" she cried hysterically. "How dare you, sir, how could you venture to disturb a lady who is a stranger to you, in her own house at such an hour! . . . And to force yourself upon her to talk of a man who came here, to this very drawing-room, only three hours ago, to murder me, and went stamping out of the room, as no one would go out of a decent house. Let me tell you, sir, that I shall lodge a complaint against you, that I will not let it pass. Kindly leave me at once . . . I am a mother. . . . I . . . I . . . ."

"Murder! then he tried to murder you, too?"

"Why, has he killed somebody else?" Madame Hohlakov asked impulsively.

"If you would kindly listen, Madame, for half a moment, I'll explain it all in a couple of words," answered Perhotin, firmly. "At five o'clock this afternoon Dmitri Fyodorovitch borrowed ten roubles from me, and I know for a fact he had no money. Yet at nine o'clock, he came to see me with a bundle of hundred-rouble notes in his hand, about two or three thousand roubles. His hands and face were all covered with blood, and he looked liked a madman. When I asked him where he had got so much money, he answered that he had just received it from you, that you had given him a sum of three thousand to go to the gold-mines. . . ."

Madame Hohlakov's face assumed an expression of intense and painful excitement.

"Good God! He must have killed his old father!" she cried, clasping her hands. "I have never given him money, never! Oh, run, run! . . . Don't say another word! Save the old man . . . run to his father . . . run!"

"Excuse me, Madame, then you did not give him money? You remember for a fact that you did not give him any money?"

"No, I didn't, I didn't! I refused to give it him, for he could not appreciate it. He ran out in a fury, stamping. He rushed at me, but I slipped away. . . . And let me tell you, as I wish to hide nothing from you now, that he positively spat at me. Can you fancy that! But why are we standing? Ah, sit down. . . . Excuse me, I . . . or better run, run, you must run and save the poor old man from an awful death!"

"But if he has killed him already?"

"Ah, good heavens, yes! Then what are we to do now? What do you think we must do now?"

Meantime she had made Pyotr Ilyitch sit down and sat down herself, facing him. Briefly, but fairly clearly, Pyotr Ilyitch told her the history of the affair, that part of it at least which he had himself witnessed. He described, too, his visit to Fenya, and told her about the pestle. All these details produced an overwhelming effect on the distracted lady, who kept uttering shrieks, and covering her face with her hands. . . .

"Would you believe it, I foresaw all this! I have that special faculty, whatever I imagine comes to pass. And how often I've looked at that awful man and always thought, that man will end by murdering me. And now it's happened . . . that is, if he hasn't murdered me, but only his own father, it's only because the finger of God preserved me, and what's more, he was ashamed to murder me because, on this very place, I put the holy ikon from the relics of the holy martyr, Saint Varvara, on his neck. . . . And to think how near I was to death at that minute, I went close up to him and he stretched out his neck to me! . . . Do you know, Pyotr Ilyitch (I think you said your name was Pyotr Ilyitch), I don't believe in miracles, but that ikon and this unmistakable miracle with me now—that shakes me, and I'm ready to believe in anything you like. Have you heard about Father Zossima? . . . But I don't know what I'm saying . . . and only fancy, with the ikon on his neck he spat at me. . . . He only spat, it's true, he didn't murder me and . . . he dashed away! but what shall we do, what must we do now? What do you think?"

Pyotr Ilyitch got up, and announced that he was going straight to the police captain, to tell him all about it, and leave him to do what he thought fit.

"Oh, he's an excellent man, excellent! Mihail Makarovitch, I know him. Of course, he's the person to go to. How practical you are, Pyotr Ilyitch! How well you've thought of everything! I should never have thought of it in your place!"

"Especially as I know the police captain very well, too," observed Pyotr Ilyitch, who still continued to stand, and was obviously anxious to escape as quickly as possible from the impulsive lady, who would not let him say good-bye and go away.

"And be sure, be sure," she prattled on, "to come back and tell me what you see there, and what you find out . . . what comes to light . . . how they'll try him . . . and what he's condemned to . . . Tell me, we have no capital punishment, have we? But be sure to come, even if it's at three o'clock at night, at four, at half-past four. . . . Tell them to wake me, to wake me, to shake me, if I don't get up. . . . But, good heavens, I shan't sleep! But wait, hadn't I better come with you?"

"N—no. But if you would write three lines with your own hand, stating that you did not give Dmitri Fyodorovitch money, it might, perhaps, be of use . . . in case it's needed. . . ."

"To be sure!" Madame Hohlakov skipped, delighted, to her bureau. "And you know I'm simply struck, amazed at your resourcefulness, your good sense in such affairs. Are you in the service here? I'm delighted to think that you're in the service here!"

And still speaking, she scribbled on half a sheet of notepaper the following lines:

"I've never in my life lent to that unhappy man, Dmitri Fyodorovitch Karamazov (for, in spite of all, he is unhappy) three thousand roubles to-day. I've never given him money, never! That I swear by all that's holy!

"K. HOHLAKOV."

"Here's the note!" she turned quickly to Pyotr Ilyitch. "Go, save him. It's a noble deed on your part!"

And she made the sign of the cross three times over him. She ran out to accompany him to the passage.

"How grateful I am to you! You can't think how grateful I am to you for having come to me, first. How is it I haven't met you before? I shall feel flattered at seeing you at my house in the future. How delightful it is that you are living here! . . . Such precision! Such practical ability! . . . They must appreciate you, they must understand you. If there's anything I can do, believe me . . . oh, I love young people! I'm in love with young people! The younger generation are the one prop of our suffering country. Her one hope. . . . Oh, go, go!"

But Pyotr Ilyitch had already run away or she would not have let him go so soon. Yet Madame Hohlakov had made a rather agreeable impression on him, which had somewhat softened his anxiety at being drawn into such an unpleasant affair. Tastes differ, as we all know. "She's by no means so elderly," he thought, feeling pleased, "on the contrary I should have taken her for her daughter."

As for Madame Hohlakov she was simply enchanted by the young man. "Such sense! such exactness! in so young a man! in our day! and all that with such manners and appearance! People say the young people of to-day are no good for anything, but here's an example!" etc., etc. So she simply forgot this "dreadful affair," and it was only as she was getting into bed, that, suddenly recalling "how near death she had been" she exclaimed: "Ah, it is awful, awful!"

But she fell at once into a sound, sweet sleep.

I would not, however, have dwelt on such trivial and irrelevant details, if this eccentric meeting of the young official with the by no means elderly widow, had not subsequently turned out to be the foundation of the whole career of that practical and precise young man. His story is remembered to this day with amazement in our town, and I shall perhaps have something to say about it, when I have finished my long history of the Brothers Karamazov.

2

THE ALARM

OUR police captain, Mihail Makarovitch Makarov, a retired lieutenant-colonel, was a widower and an excellent man. He had only come to us three years previously, but had won general esteem, chiefly because he "knew how to keep society together." He was never without visitors, and could not have got on without them. Some one or other was always dining with him; he never sat down to table without guests. He gave regular dinners, too, on all sorts of occasions, sometimes most surprising ones. Though the fare was not *recherché,* it was abundant. The fish pies were excellent, and the wine made up in quantity for what it lacked in quality.

The first room his guests entered was a well-fitted billiard-room, with pictures of English race-horses, in black frames on the walls, an essential decoration, as we all know, for a bachelor's billiard-room. There was card-playing every evening at his house, if only at one table. But at frequent intervals, all the society of our town, with the mammas and young ladies, assembled at his house to dance. Though Mihail Makarovitch was a widower, he did not live alone. His widowed daughter lived with him, with her two unmarried daughters, grown-up girls, who had finished their education. They were of agreeable appearance and lively character, and though every one knew they would have no dowry, they attracted all the young men of fashion to their grandfather's house.

Mihail Makarovitch was by no means very efficient in his work, though he performed his duties no worse than many others. To speak plainly, he was a man of rather narrow education. His understanding of the limits of his administrative power could not always be relied upon. It was not so much that he failed to grasp certain reforms enacted during the present reign, as that he made conspicuous blunders in his interpretation of them. This was not from any special lack of intelligence, but from carelessness, for he was always in too great a hurry to go into the subject.

"I have the heart of a soldier rather than of a civilian," he used to say of himself. He had not even formed a definite idea of the fundamental principles of the reforms connected with the emancipation of the serfs, and only picked it up, so to speak, from year to year, involuntarily increasing his knowledge by practice. And yet he was himself a landowner. Pyotr Ilyitch knew for certain that he would meet some of Mihail Makarovitch's visitors there that evening, but he didn't know which. As it happened, at that moment the prosecutor, and Varvinsky, our district doctor, a young man, who had only just come to us from Petersburg after taking a brilliant degree at the Academy of Medicine, were playing whist at the police captain's. Ippolit Kirillovitch, the prosecutor (he was really the deputy prosecutor, but we always called him the prosecutor) was rather a peculiar man, of about five and thirty, inclined to be consumptive, and married to a fat and childless woman. He was vain and irritable, though he had a good intellect, and even a kind heart. It seemed that all that was wrong with him was that he had a better opinion of himself than his ability warranted. And that made him seem constantly uneasy. He had, moreover, certain higher, even artistic, leanings, towards psychology, for instance, a special study of the human heart, a special knowledge of the criminal and his crime. He cherished a grievance on this ground, considering that he had been passed over in the service, and being firmly persuaded that in higher spheres he had not been properly appreciated, and had enemies. In gloomy moments he even threatened to give up his post, and practise as a barrister in criminal cases. The unexpected Karamazov case agitated him profoundly: "It was a case that might well be talked about all over Russia." But I am anticipating.

Nikolay Parfenovitch Nelyudov, the young investigating lawyer, who had only come from Petersburg two months before, was sitting in the next room with the young ladies. People talked about it afterwards and wondered that all the gentlemen should, as though intentionally, on the evening of "the crime" have been gathered together at the house of the executive authority. Yet it was perfectly simple and happened quite naturally.

Ippolit Kirillovitch's wife had had toothache for the last two days, and he was obliged to go out to escape from her groans. The doctor, from the very nature of his being, could not spend an evening except at cards. Nikolay Parfenovitch Nelyudov had been intending for three days past to drop in that evening at Mihail Makarovitch's, so to speak casually, so as slyly to startle the eldest grand-daughter, Olga Mihailovna, by showing that he knew her secret, that he knew it was her birthday, and that she was trying to conceal it on purpose, so as not to be obliged to give a dance. He anticipated a great deal of merriment, many playful jests about her age, and her being afraid to reveal it, about his knowing her secret and telling every-body, and so on. The charming young man was a great adept at such teas-ing; the ladies had christened him "the naughty man," and he seemed to be delighted at the name. He was extremely well bred, however, of good fam-ily, education and feelings, and, though leading a life of pleasure, his sallies were always innocent and in good taste. He was short and delicate look-ing. On his white, slender, little fingers he always wore a number of big, glittering rings. When he was engaged in his official duties, he always be-came extraordinarily grave, as though realising his position and the sanc-tity of the obligations laid upon him. He had a special gift for mystifying murderers and other criminals of the peasant class during interrogation, and if he did not win their respect, he certainly succeeded in arousing their wonder.

Pyotr Ilyitch was simply dumbfounded when he went into the police captain's. He saw instantly that every one knew. They had positively thrown down their cards, all were standing up and talking. Even Nikolay Parfenovitch had left the young ladies and ran in, looking strenuous and ready for action. Pyotr Ilyitch was met with the astounding news that old Fyodor Pavlovitch really had been murdered that evening in his own house, murdered and robbed. The news had only just reached them in the following manner.

Marfa Ignatyevna, the wife of old Grigory, who had been knocked senseless near the fence, was sleeping soundly in her bed and might well have slept till morning after the draught she had taken. But, all of a sudden she waked up, no doubt roused by a fearful epileptic scream from Smerdyakov, who was lying in the next room unconscious. That scream al-ways preceded his fits, and always terrified and upset Marfa Ignatyevna. She could never get accustomed to it. She jumped up and ran half-awake to Smerdyakov's room. But it was dark there, and she could only hear the in-valid beginning to gasp and struggle. Then Marfa Ignatyevna herself screamed out and was going to call her husband, but suddenly realised that when she had got up, he was not beside her in bed. She ran back to the bed-stead and began groping with her hands, but the bed was really empty. Then he must have gone out—where? She ran to the steps and timidly called him. She got no answer, of course, but she caught the sound of groans far away in the garden in the darkness. She listened. The groans were repeated, and it was evident they came from the garden.

"Good Lord! Just as it was with Lizaveta Smerdyashtchaya!" she thought distractedly. She went timidly down the steps and saw that the gate into the garden was open.

"He must be out there, poor dear," she thought. She went up to the gate and all at once she distinctly heard Grigory calling her by name, "Marfa! Marfa!" in a weak, moaning, dreadful voice.

"Lord, preserve us from harm!" Marfa Ignatyevna murmured, and ran towards the voice, and that was how she found Grigory. But she found him not by the fence where he had been knocked down, but about twenty paces off. It appeared later, that he had crawled away on coming to himself, and probably had been a long time getting so far, losing consciousness several times. She noticed at once that he was covered with blood, and screamed at the top of her voice. Grigory was muttering incoherently:

"He has murdered . . . his father murdered, . . . Why scream, silly . . . run . . . fetch some one. . . ."

But Marfa continued screaming, and seeing that her master's window was open and that there was a candle alight in the window, she ran there and began calling Fyodor Pavlovitch. But peeping in at the window, she saw a fearful sight. Her master was lying on his back, motionless, on the floor. His light-coloured dressing-gown and white shirt were soaked with blood. The candle on the table brightly lighted up the blood and the motionless dead face of Fyodor Pavlovitch. Terror-stricken, Marfa rushed away from the window, ran out of the garden, drew the bolt of the big gate, and ran headlong by the back way to the neighbour, Marya Kondratyevna. Both mother and daughter were asleep, but they waked up at Marfa's desperate and persistent screaming and knocking at the shutter. Marfa, shrieking and screaming incoherently, managed to tell them the main fact, and to beg for assistance. It happened that Foma had come back from his wanderings and was staying the night with them. They got him up immediately and all three ran to the scene of the crime. On the way, Marya Kondratyevna remembered that at about eight o'clock she heard a dreadful scream from their garden, and this was no doubt Grigory's scream, "Parricide!" uttered when he caught hold of Mitya's leg.

"Some one person screamed out and then was silent," Marya Kondratyevna explained as she ran. Running to the place where Grigory lay, the two women with the help of Foma carried him to the lodge. They lighted a candle and saw that Smerdyakov was no better, that he was writhing in convulsions, his eyes fixed in a squint, and that foam was flowing from his lips. They moistened Grigory's forehead with water mixed with vinegar, and the water revived him at once. He asked immediately:

"Is the master murdered?"

Then Foma and both the women ran to the house and saw this time that not only the window, but also the door into the garden was wide open, though Fyodor Pavlovitch had for the last week locked himself in every night and did not allow even Grigory to come in on any pretext. Seeing that door open, they were afraid to go in to Fyodor Pavlovitch "for fear anything should happen afterwards." And when they returned to Grigory, the old man told them to go straight to the police captain. Marya Kondratyevna ran there and gave the alarm to the whole party at the police captain's. She arrived only five minutes before Pyotr Ilyitch, so that his story came, not as his own surmise and theory, but as the direct confirmation, by a witness, of the theory held by all, as to the identity of the criminal (a theory he had in the bottom of his heart refused to believe till that moment).

It was resolved to act with energy. The deputy police inspector of the town was commissioned to take four witnesses, to enter Fyodor Pavlovitch's house and there to open an inquiry on the spot, according to the regular forms, which I will not go into here. The district doctor, a zealous man, new to his work, almost insisted on accompanying the police captain, the prosecutor, and the investigating lawyer.

I will note briefly that Fyodor Pavlovitch was found to be quite dead, with his skull battered in. But with what? Most likely with the same weapon with which Grigory had been attacked later. And immediately that weapon was found, Grigory, to whom all possible medical assistance was at once given, described in a weak and breaking voice how he had been knocked down. They began looking with a lantern by the fence and found the brass pestle dropped in a most conspicuous place on the garden path. There were no signs of disturbance in the room where Fyodor Pavlovitch was lying. But by the bed, behind the screen, they picked up from the floor a big and thick envelope with the inscription: "A present of three thousand roubles for my angel Grushenka, if she is willing to come." And below had been added by Fyodor Pavlovitch, "For my little chicken." There were three seals of red sealing-wax on the envelope, but it had been torn open and was empty: the money had been removed. They found also on the floor a piece of narrow pink ribbon, with which the envelope had been tied up.

One piece of Pyotr Ilyitch's evidence made a great impression on the prosecutor and the investigating magistrate, namely, his idea that Dmitri Fyodorovitch would shoot himself before daybreak, that he had resolved to do so, had spoken of it to Pyotr Ilyitch, had taken the pistols, loaded them before him, written a letter, put it in his pocket, etc. When Pyotr Ilyitch, though still unwilling to believe in it, threatened to tell some one so as to prevent the suicide, Mitya had answered grinning: "You'll be too late." So they must make haste to Mokroe to find the criminal, before he really did shoot himself.

"That's clear, that's clear!" repeated the prosecutor in great excitement. "That's just the way with mad fellows like that: 'I shall kill myself tomorrow, so I'll make merry till I die!'"

The story of how he had bought the wine and provisions excited the prosecutor more than ever.

"Do you remember the fellow that murdered a merchant called Olsufyev, gentlemen? He stole fifteen hundred, went at once to have his hair curled, and then, without even hiding the money, carrying it almost in his hand in the same way, he went off to the girls."

All were delayed, however, by the inquiry, the search, and the formalities, etc., in the house of Fyodor Pavlovitch. It all took time and so, two hours before starting, they sent on ahead to Mokroe the officer of the rural police, Mavriky Mavrikyevitch Schmertsov, who had arrived in the town the morning before to get his pay. He was instructed to avoid raising the alarm when he reached Mokroe, but to keep constant watch over the "criminal" till the arrival of the proper authorities, to procure also witnesses for the arrest, police constables, and so on. Mavriky Mavrikyevitch did as he was told, preserving his incognito, and giving no one but his old acquaintance, Trifon Borissovitch, the slightest hint of his secret business. He had spoken to him just before Mitya met the landlord in the balcony, looking for him in the dark, and noticed at once a change in Trifon Borissovitch's face and voice. So neither Mitya nor any one else knew that he was being watched. The box with the pistols had been carried off by Trifon Borissovitch and put in a suitable place. Only after four o'clock, almost at sunrise, all the officials, the police captain, the prosecutor, the investigating lawyer, drove up in two carriages, each drawn by three horses. The doctor remained at Fyodor Pavlovitch's to make a post-mortem next day on the body. But he was particularly interested in the condition of the servant, Smerdyakov.

"Such violent and protracted epileptic fits, recurring continually for twenty-four hours, are rarely to be met with, and are of interest to science," he declared enthusiastically to his companions, and, as they left, they laughingly congratulated him on his find. The prosecutor and the investigating lawyer distinctly remembered the doctor's saying that Smerdyakov could not outlive the night.

After these long, but, I think, necessary explanations, we will return to that moment of our tale at which we broke off.

3

THE SUFFERINGS OF A SOUL.
THE FIRST ORDEAL

A ND SO Mitya sat looking wildly at the people round him, not understanding what was said to him. Suddenly he got up, flung up his hands and shouted aloud:

"I'm not guilty! I'm not guilty of that blood! I'm not guilty of my father's blood. . . . I meant to kill him. But I'm not guilty. Not I."

But he had hardly said this, before Grushenka rushed from behind the curtain and flung herself at the police captain's feet.

"It was my fault! Mine! My wickedness!" she cried, in a heartrending voice, bathed in tears, stretching out her clasped hands towards them. "He did it through me. I tortured him and drove him to it. I tortured that poor old man that's dead, too, in my wickedness, and brought him to this! It's my fault, mine first, mine most, my fault!"

"Yes, it's your fault! You're the chief criminal! You fury! You harlot! You're the most to blame" shouted the police captain, threatening her with his hand. But he was quickly and resolutely suppressed. The prosecutor positively seized hold of him.

"This is absolutely irregular, Mihail Makarovitch!" he cried. "You are positively hindering the inquiry. . . . You're ruining the case. . . ." he almost gasped.

"Follow the regular course! Follow the regular course!" cried Nikolay Parfenovitch, fearfully excited too, "otherwise it's absolutely impossible! . . ."

"Judge us together!" Grushenka cried frantically, still kneeling. "Punish us together. I will go with him now, if it's to death!"

"Grusha, my life, my blood, my holy one!" Mitya fell on his knees beside her and held her tight in his arms. "Don't believe her," he cried, "she's not guilty of anything, of any blood, of anything!"

He remembered afterwards that he was forcibly dragged away from her by several men, and that she was led out, and that when he recovered himself he was sitting at the table. Beside him and behind him stood the men with metal plates. Facing him on the other side of the table sat Nikolay Parfenovitch, the investigating lawyer. He kept persuading him to drink a little water out of a glass that stood on the table.

"That will refresh you, that will calm you. Be calm, don't be frightened," he added, extremely politely. Mitya (he remembered it afterwards) became suddenly intensely interested in his big rings, one with an amethyst, and another with a transparent bright yellow stone, of great brilliance. And long afterwards he remembered with wonder how those rings had riveted his attention through all those terrible hours of interrogation, so that he was utterly unable to tear himself away from them and dismiss them, as things that had nothing to do with his position. On Mitya's left side, in the place where Maximov had been sitting at the beginning of the evening, the prosecutor was now seated and on Mitya's right hand, where Grushenka had been, was a rosy-cheeked young man in a sort of shabby hunting jacket, with ink and paper before him. This was the secretary of the investigating lawyer, who had brought him with him. The police captain was now standing by the window at the other end of the room, beside Kalganov, who was sitting there.

"Drink some water," said the investigating lawyer softly, for the tenth time.

"I have drunk it, gentlemen, I have . . . but . . . come, gentlemen, crush me, punish me, decide my fate!" cried Mitya, staring with terribly fixed wide-open eyes at the investigating lawyer.

"So you positively declare that you are not guilty of the death of your father, Fyodor Pavlovitch?" asked the investigating lawyer, softly but insistently.

"I am not guilty. I am guilty of the blood of another old man, but not of my father's. And I weep for it! I killed, I killed the old man and knocked him down. . . . But it's hard to have to answer for that murder with another, a terrible murder of which I am not guilty. . . . It's a terrible accusation, gentlemen, a knockdown blow. But who has killed my father, who has killed him? Who can have killed him if I didn't? It's marvellous, extraordinary, impossible."

"Yes, who can have killed him?" the investigating lawyer was beginning, but Ippolit Kirillovitch, the prosecutor, glancing at him, addressed Mitya.

"You need not worry yourself about the old servant, Grigory Vassilye-vitch. He is alive, he has recovered, and in spite of the terrible blows in-flicted, according to his own and your evidence, by you, there seems no doubt that he will live, so the doctor says, at least."

"Alive? He's alive?" cried Mitya, flinging up his hands. His face beamed. "Lord, I thank Thee for the miracle Thou hast wrought for me, a sinner and evildoer. That's an answer to my prayer. I've been praying all night." And he crossed himself three times. He was almost breathless.

"So from this Grigory we have received such important evidence con-cerning you, that . . ." the prosecutor would have continued, but Mitya suddenly jumped up from his chair.

"One minute, gentlemen, for God's sake, one minute; I will run to her——"

"Excuse me, at this moment it's quite impossible," Nikolay Parfen-ovitch almost shrieked. He, too, leapt to his feet. Mitya was seized by the men with the metal plates, but he sat down on his own accord. . . .

"Gentlemen, what a pity! I wanted to see her for one minute only; I wanted to tell her that it has been washed away, it has gone, that blood that was weighing on my heart all night, and that I am not a murderer now! Gentlemen, she is my betrothed!" he said ecstatically and reverently, look-ing round at them all. "Oh, thank you, gentlemen! Oh, in one minute you have given me new life, new heart! . . . That old man used to carry me in his arms, gentlemen. He used to wash me in the tub when I was a baby three years old, abandoned by every one, he was like a father to me! . . ."

"And so you . . ." the investigating lawyer began.

"Allow me, gentlemen, allow me one minute more," interposed Mitya, putting his elbows on the table and covering his face with his hands. "Let me have a moment to think, let me breathe, gentlemen. All this is horribly upsetting, horribly. A man is not a drum, gentlemen!"

"Drink a little more water," murmured Nikolay Parfenovitch. Mitya took his hands from his face and laughed. His eyes were confident. He seemed completely transformed in a moment. His whole bearing was changed; he was once more the equal of these men, with all of whom he was acquainted, as though they had all met the day before, when nothing had happened, at some social gathering. We may note in passing that, on his first arrival, Mitya had been made very welcome at the police captain's, but later, during the last month especially, Mitya had hardly called at all, and when the police captain met him, in the street, for instance, Mitya no-ticed that he frowned and only bowed out of politeness. His acquaintance with the prosecutor was less intimate, though he sometimes paid his wife, a nervous and fanciful lady, visits of politeness, without quite knowing why, and she always received him graciously and had, for some reason, taken an interest in him up to the last. He had not had time to get to know the investigating lawyer, though he had met him and talked to him twice, each time about the fair sex.

"You're a most skilful lawyer, I see, Nikolay Parfenovitch," cried Mitya, laughing gaily, "but I can help you now. Oh, gentlemen, I feel like a new man, and don't be offended at my addressing you so simply and directly. I'm rather drunk, too, I'll tell you that frankly. I believe I've had the honour and pleasure of meeting you, Nikolay Parfenovitch, at my kinsman Miüsov's. Gentlemen, gentlemen, I don't pretend to be on equal terms with you. I understand, of course, in what character I am sitting before you. Oh, of course, there's a horrible suspicion . . . hanging over me . . . if Grigory has given evidence. . . . A horrible suspicion! It's awful, awful, I understand that! But to business, gentlemen, I am ready, and we will make an end of it in one moment; for, listen, listen, gentlemen! Since I know I'm innocent, we can put an end to it in a minute. Can't we? Can't we?"

Mitya spoke much and quickly, nervously and effusively, as though he positively took his listeners to be his best friends.

"So, for the present, we will write that you absolutely deny the charge brought against you," said Nikolay Parfenovitch, impressively, and bending down to the secretary he dictated to him in an undertone what to write.

"Write it down? You want to write that down? Well, write it; I consent, I give my full consent, gentlemen, only . . . do you see. . . . Stay, stay, write this. Of disorderly conduct I am guilty, of violence on a poor old man I am guilty. And there is something else at the bottom of my heart, of which I am guilty, too—but that you need not write down (he turned suddenly to the secretary); that's my personal life, gentlemen, that doesn't concern you, the bottom of my heart, that's to say. . . . But of the murder of my old father I'm not guilty. That's a wild idea. It's quite a wild idea! . . . I will prove you that and you'll be convinced directly. . . . You will laugh, gentlemen. You'll laugh yourselves at your suspicion! . . ."

"Be calm, Dmitri Fyodorovitch," said the investigating lawyer, evidently trying to allay Mitya's excitement by his own composure. "Before we go on with our inquiry, I should like, if you will consent to answer, to hear you confirm the statement that you disliked your father, Fyodor Pavlovitch, that you were involved in continual disputes with him. Here at least, a quarter of an hour ago, you exclaimed that you wanted to kill him: 'I didn't kill him,' you said, 'but I wanted to kill him'?"

"Did I exclaim that? Ach, that may be so, gentlemen! Yes, unhappily, I did want to kill him . . . many times I wanted to . . . unhappily, unhappily!"

"You wanted to. Would you consent to explain what motives precisely led you to such a sentiment of hatred for your parent?"

"What is there to explain, gentlemen?" Mitya shrugged his shoulders sullenly, looking down. "I have never concealed my feelings. All the town knows about it—every one knows in the tavern. Only lately I declared them in Father Zossima's cell. . . . And the very same day, in the evening I beat my father. I nearly killed him, and I swore I'd come again and kill him, before witnesses. . . . Oh, a thousand witnesses! I've been shouting it aloud for the last month, any one can tell you that! . . . The fact stares you in the face, it speaks for itself, it cries aloud, but, feelings, gentlemen, feelings are another matter. You see, gentlemen (Mitya frowned), it seems to me that about feelings you've no right to question me. I know that you are bound by your office, I quite understand that, but that's my affair, my private, intimate affair, yet . . . since I haven't concealed my feelings in the past . . . in the tavern, for instance, I've talked to every one, so . . . so I won't make a secret of it now. You see, I understand, gentlemen, that there are terrible facts against me in this business. I told every one that I'd kill him, and now, all of a sudden, he's been killed. So it must have been me! Ha, ha! I can make allowances for you, gentlemen, I can quite make allowances. I'm struck all of a heap myself, for who can have murdered him, if not I? That's what it comes to, isn't it? If not I, who can it be, who? Gentlemen, I want to know, I insist on knowing!" he exclaimed suddenly. "Where was he murdered? How was he murdered? How, and with what? Tell me," he asked quickly, looking at the two lawyers.

"We found him in his study, lying on his back on the floor, with his head battered in," said the prosecutor.

"That's horrible!" Mitya shuddered and, putting his elbows on the table, hid his face in his right hand.

"We will continue," interposed Nikolay Parfenovitch. "So what was it that impelled you to this sentiment of hatred? You have asserted in public, I believe, that it was based upon jealousy?"

"Well, yes, jealousy. And not only jealousy."

"Disputes about money?"

"Yes, about money, too."

"There was a dispute about three thousand roubles, I think, which you claimed as part of your inheritance?"

"Three thousand! More, more," cried Mitya hotly; "more than six thousand, more than ten, perhaps. I told every one so, shouted it at them. But I made up my mind to let it go at three thousand. I was desperately in need of that three thousand . . . so the bundle of notes for three thousand that I knew he kept under his pillow, ready for Grushenka, I considered as simply stolen from me. Yes, gentlemen, I looked upon it as mine, as my own property. . . ."

The prosecutor looked significantly at the investigating lawyer, and had time to wink at him on the sly.

"We will return to that subject later," said the lawyer promptly. "You will allow us to note that point and write it down; that you looked upon that money as your own property?"

"Write it down, by all means. I know that's another fact that tells against me, but I'm not afraid of facts and I tell them against myself. Do you hear? Do you know, gentlemen, you take me for a different sort of man from what I am," he added, suddenly, gloomy and dejected. "You have to deal with a man of honour, a man of the highest honour; above all—don't lose sight of it—a man who's done a lot of nasty things, but has always been, and still is, honourable at bottom, in his inner being. I don't know how to express it. That's just what's made me wretched all my life, that I yearned to be honourable, that I was, so to say, a martyr to a sense of honour, seeking for it with a lantern, with the lantern of Diogenes[1] and yet, all my life I've been doing filthy things like all of us, gentlemen . . . that is like me alone. That was a mistake, like me alone, me alone! . . . Gentlemen, my head aches. . . ." His brows contracted with pain. "You see, gentlemen, I couldn't bear the look of him, there was something in him ignoble, impudent, trampling on everything sacred, something sneering and irreverent, loathsome, loathsome. But now that he's dead, I feel differently."

"How do you mean?"

"I don't feel differently, but I wish I hadn't hated him so."

"You feel penitent?"

"No, not penitent, don't write that. I'm not much good myself, I'm not very beautiful, so I had no right to consider him repulsive. That's what I mean. Write that down, if you like."

Saying this Mitya became very mournful. He had grown more and more gloomy as the inquiry continued.

At that moment another unexpected scene followed. Though Grushenka had been removed, she had not been taken far away, only into the room next but one from the blue room, in which the examination was proceeding. It was a little room with one window, next beyond the large room in which they had danced and feasted so lavishly. She was sitting there with no one by her but Maximov, who was terribly depressed, terribly scared, and clung to her side, as though for security. At their door stood one of the peasants with a metal plate on his breast. Grushenka was crying, and suddenly her grief was too much for her, she jumped up, flung up her arms, and with a loud wail of sorrow, rushed out of the room to him, to her Mitya, and so unexpectedly that they had not time to stop her. Mitya, hearing her cry, trembled, jumped up, and with a yell rushed impetuously to meet her, not knowing what he was doing. But they were not allowed to come together, though they saw one another. He was seized by the arms. He struggled, and tried to tear himself away. It took three or four men to hold him. She was seized too, and he saw her stretching out her arms to him, crying aloud as they carried her away. When the scene was over, he came to himself again, sitting in the same place as before, opposite the investigating lawyer, and crying out to them:

"What do you want with her? Why do you torment her? She's done nothing, nothing! . . ."

The lawyers tried to soothe him. About ten minutes passed like this. At last Mihail Makarovitch, who had been absent, came hurriedly into the room, and said in a loud and excited voice to the prosecutor:

"She's been removed, she's downstairs. Will you allow me to say one word to this unhappy man, gentlemen? In your presence, gentlemen, in your presence."

"By all means, Mihail Makarovitch," answered the investigating lawyer. "In the present case we have nothing against it."

"Listen, Dmitri Fyodorovitch, my dear fellow," began the police captain, and there was a look of warm, almost fatherly, feeling for the luckless prisoner on his excited face. "I took your Agrafena Alexandrovna downstairs myself, and confided her to the care of the landlord's daughters, and that old fellow Maximov is with her all the time. And I soothed her, do you hear? I soothed and calmed her. I impressed on her that you have to clear yourself, so she mustn't hinder you, must not depress you, or you may lose your head and say the wrong thing in your evidence. In fact, I talked to her and she understood. She's a sensible girl, my boy, a good-hearted girl, she would have kissed my old hands, begging help for you. She sent me herself, to tell you not to worry about her. And I must go, my dear fellow, I must go and tell her that you are calm and comforted about her. And so you must be calm, do you understand? I was unfair to her; she is a Christian soul, gentlemen, yes, I tell you, she's a gentle soul, and not to blame for anything. So what am I to tell her, Dmitri Fyodorovitch, will you sit quiet or not?"

The good-natured police captain said a great deal that was irregular, but Grushenka's suffering, a fellow creature's suffering, touched his good-natured heart, and tears stood in his eyes. Mitya jumped up and rushed towards him.

"Forgive me, gentlemen, oh, allow me, allow me!" he cried. "You've the heart of an angel, an angel, Mihail Makarovitch, I thank you for her. I will, I will be calm, cheerful, in fact. Tell her, in the kindness of your heart, that I am cheerful, quite cheerful, that I shall be laughing in a minute, knowing that she has a guardian angel like you. I shall have done with all this directly, and as soon as I'm free, I'll be with her, she'll see, let her wait. Gentlemen," he said, turning to the two lawyers, "now I'll open my whole soul to you; I'll pour out everything. We'll finish this off directly, finish it off gaily. We shall laugh at it in the end, shan't we? But, gentlemen, that woman is the queen of my heart. Oh, let me tell you that. That one thing I'll tell you now. . . . I see I'm with honourable men. She is my light, she is my holy one, and if only you knew! Did you hear her cry, 'I'll go to death with you'? And what have I, a penniless beggar, done for her? Why such love for me? How can a clumsy, ugly brute like me, with my ugly face, deserve such love, that she is ready to go to exile with me? And how she fell down at your feet for my sake, just now! . . . and yet she's proud and has done nothing! How can I help adoring her, how can I help crying out and rushing to her as I did just now? Gentlemen, forgive me! But now, now I am comforted."

And he sank back in his chair and covering his face with his hands, burst into tears. But they were happy tears. He recovered himself instantly. The old police captain seemed much pleased, and the lawyers also. They felt that the examination was passing into a new phase. When the police captain went out, Mitya was positively gay.

"Now, gentlemen, I am at your disposal, entirely at your disposal. And if it were not for all these trivial details, we should understand one another in a minute. I'm at those details again. I'm at your disposal, gentlemen, but I declare that we must have mutual confidence, you in me and I in you, or there'll be no end to it. I speak in your interests. To business, gentlemen, to business, and don't rummage in my soul; don't tease me with trifles, but only ask me about facts and what matters, and I will satisfy you at once. And damn the details!"

So spoke Mitya. The interrogation began again.

4

THE SECOND ORDEAL

"Y ou don't know how you encourage us, Dmitri Fyodorovitch, by your readiness to answer," said Nikolay Parfenovitch, with an animated air, and obvious satisfaction beaming in his very prominent, short-sighted, light grey eyes, from which he had removed his spectacles a moment before. "And you have made a very just remark about the mutual confidence, without which it is sometimes positively impossible to get on in cases of such importance, if the suspected party really hopes and desires to defend himself and is in a position to do so. We, on our side, will do everything in our power, and you can see for yourself how we are conducting the case. You approve, Ippolit Kirillovitch?" He turned to the prosecutor.

"Oh, undoubtedly," replied the prosecutor. His tone was somewhat cold, compared with Nikolay Parfenovitch's impulsiveness.

I will note once for all that Nikolay Parfenovitch, who had but lately arrived among us, had from the first felt marked respect for Ippolit Kirillovitch, our prosecutor, and had become almost his bosom friend. He was almost the only person who put implicit faith in Ippolit Kirillovitch's extraordinary talents as a psychologist and orator and in the justice of his grievance. He had heard of him in Petersburg. On the other hand, young Nikolay Parfenovitch was the only person in the whole world whom our "unappreciated" prosecutor genuinely liked. On their way to Mokroe they had time to come to an understanding about the present case. And now as they sat at the table, the sharp-witted junior caught and interpreted every indication on his senior colleague's face, at half a word, at a glance, or at a wink.

"Gentlemen, only let me tell my own story and don't interrupt me with trivial questions and I'll tell you everything in a moment," said Mitya excitedly.

"Excellent! Thank you. But before we proceed to listen to your communication, will you allow me to inquire as to another little fact of great interest to us. I mean the ten roubles you borrowed yesterday at about five o'clock on the security of your pistols, from your friend, Pyotr Ilyitch Perhotin."

"I pledged them, gentlemen. I pledged them for ten roubles. What more? That's all about it. As soon as I got back to town I pledged them."

"You got back to town? Then had you been out of town?"

"Yes, I went a journey of forty versts into the country. Didn't you know?"

The prosecutor and Nikolay Parfenovitch exchanged glances.

"Well, how would it be if you began your story with a systematic description of all you did yesterday, from the morning onwards? Allow us, for instance, to inquire why you were absent from the town, and just when you left and when you came back—all those facts."

"You should have asked me like that from the beginning," cried Mitya, laughing aloud, "and, if you like, we won't begin from yesterday, but from the morning of the day before; then you'll understand how, why, and where I went. I went the day before yesterday, gentlemen, to a merchant of the town, called Samsonov, to borrow three thousand roubles from him on safe security. It was a pressing matter, gentlemen, it was a sudden necessity."

"Allow me to interrupt you," the prosecutor put in politely. "Why were you in such pressing need for just that sum, three thousand?"

"Oh, gentlemen, you needn't go into details, how, when and why, and why just so much money, and not so much, and all that rigmarole. Why, it'll run to three volumes, and then you'll want an epilogue!"

Mitya said all this with the good-natured but impatient familiarity of a man who is anxious to tell the whole truth and is full of the best intentions.

"Gentlemen!"—he corrected himself hurriedly—"don't be vexed with me for my restiveness, I beg you again. Believe me once more, I feel the greatest respect for you and understand the true position of affairs. Don't think I'm drunk. I'm quite sober now. And, besides, being drunk would be no hindrance. It's with me, you know, like the saying: 'When he is sober, he is a fool; when he is drunk, he is a wise man.' Ha, ha! But I see, gentlemen, it's not the proper thing to make jokes to you, till we've had our explanation, I mean. And I've my own dignity to keep up, too. I quite understand the difference for the moment. I am, after all, in the position of a criminal, and so, far from being on equal terms with you. And it's your business to watch me. I can't expect you to pat me on the head for what I did to Grigory, for one can't break old men's heads with impunity. I suppose you'll put me away from him for six months, or a year perhaps, in a house of correction. I don't know what the punishment is—but it will be without loss of the rights of my rank, without loss of my rank, won't it? So you see, gentlemen, I understand the distinction between us. . . . But you must see that you could puzzle God Himself with such questions. 'How did you step? Where did you step? When did you step? And on what did you step?' I shall get mixed up, if you go on like this, and you will put it all down against me. And what will that lead to? To nothing! And even if it's nonsense I'm talking now, let me finish, and you, gentlemen, being men of honour and refinement, will forgive me! I'll finish by asking you, gentlemen, to drop that conventional method of questioning. I mean, beginning from some miserable trifle, how I got up, what I had for breakfast, how I spat, and where I spat, and so distracting the attention of the criminal, suddenly stun him with an overwhelming question, 'Whom did you murder? Whom did you rob?' Ha, ha! That's your regulation method, that's where all your cunning comes in. You can put peasants off their guard like that, but not me. I know the tricks. I've been in the service, too. Ha, ha, ha! You're not angry, gentlemen? You forgive my impertinence?" he cried, looking at them with a good-nature that was almost surprising. "It's only Mitya Karamazov, you know, so you can overlook it. It would be inexcusable in a sensible man; but you can forgive it in Mitya. Ha, ha!"

Nikolay Parfenovitch listened, and laughed too. Though the prosecutor did not laugh, he kept his eyes fixed keenly on Mitya, as though anxious not to miss the least syllable, the slightest movement, the smallest twitch of any feature of his face.

"That's how we have treated you from the beginning," said Nikolay Parfenovitch, still laughing. "We haven't tried to put you out by asking how you got up in the morning and what you had for breakfast. We began, indeed, with questions of the greatest importance."

"I understand. I saw it and appreciated it, and I appreciate still more your present kindness to me, an unprecedented kindness, worthy of your noble hearts. We three here are gentlemen, and let everything be on the footing of mutual confidence between educated, well-bred people, who have the common bond of noble birth and honour. In any case, allow me to look upon you as my best friends at this moment of my life, at this moment when my honour is assailed. That's no offence to you, gentlemen, is it?"

"On the contrary. You've expressed all that so well, Dmitri Fyodorovitch," Nikolay Parfenovitch answered with dignified approbation.

"And enough of those trivial questions, gentlemen, all those tricky questions!" cried Mitya enthusiastically. "Or there's simply no knowing where we shall get to! Is there?"

"I will follow your sensible advice entirely," the prosecutor interposed, addressing Mitya. "But I don't withdraw my question, however, It is now vitally important for us to know exactly why you needed that sum, I mean precisely three thousand."

"Why I needed it? . . . Oh, for one thing and another. . . . Well, it was to pay a debt."

"A debt to whom?"

"That I absolutely refuse to answer, gentlemen. Not because I couldn't, or because I shouldn't dare, or because it would be damaging, for it's all a paltry matter and absolutely trifling, but—I won't, because it's a matter of principle: that's my private life, and I won't allow any intrusion into my private life. That's my principle. Your question has no bearing on the case, and whatever has nothing to do with the case is my private affair. I wanted to pay a debt. I wanted to pay a debt of honour, but to whom I won't say."

"Allow me to make a note of that," said the prosecutor.

"By all means. Write down that I won't say, that I won't. Write that I should think it dishonourable to say. Ech! you can write it; you've nothing else to do with your time."

"Allow me to caution you, sir, and to remind you once more, if you are unaware of it," the prosecutor began, with a peculiar and stern impressiveness, "that you have a perfect right not to answer the questions put to you now, and we on our side, have no right to extort an answer from you, if you decline to give it for one reason or another. That is entirely a matter for your personal decision. But it is our duty, on the other hand, in such cases as the present, to explain and set before you the degree of injury you will be doing yourself by refusing to give this or that piece of evidence. After which I will beg you to continue."

"Gentlemen, I'm not angry . . . I . . ." Mitya muttered in a rather disconcerted tone. "Well, gentlemen, you see, that Samsonov to whom I went then. . . ."

We will, of course, not reproduce his account of what is known to the reader already. Mitya was impatiently anxious not to omit the slightest detail. At the same time he was in a hurry to get it over. But as he gave his evidence it was written down, and therefore they had continually to pull him up. Mitya disliked this, but submitted; got angry, though still good-humouredly. He did, it is true, exclaim, from time to time, "Gentlemen, that's enough to make an angel out of patience!" Or, "Gentlemen, it's no good your irritating me."

But even though he exclaimed he still preserved for a time his genially expansive mood. So he told them how Samsonov had made a fool of him two days before. (He had completely realised by now that he had been fooled.) The sale of his watch for six roubles to obtain money for the journey was something new to the lawyers. They were at once greatly interested, and even, to Mitya's intense indignation, thought it necessary to write the fact down as a secondary confirmation of the circumstance that he had hardly a farthing in his pocket at the time. Little by little Mitya began to grow surly. Then, after describing his journey to see Lyagavy, the night spent in the stifling hut, and so on, he came to his return to the town. Here he began, without being particularly urged, to give a minute account of the agonies of jealousy he endured on Grushenka's account.

He was heard with silent attention. They inquired particularly into the circumstance of his having a place of ambush in Marya Kondratyevna's house at the back of Fyodor Pavlovitch's garden to keep watch on Grushenka, and of Smerdyakov's bringing him information. They laid particular stress on this, and noted it down. Of his jealousy he spoke warmly and at length, and though inwardly ashamed at exposing his most intimate feelings, so to speak, to "public ignominy," he evidently overcame his shame in order to tell the truth. The frigid severity with which the investigating lawyer, and still more the prosecutor, stared intently at him as he told his story, disconcerted him at last considerably.

"That boy, Nikolay Parfenovitch, to whom I was talking nonsense about women only a few days ago, and that sickly prosecutor are not worth my telling this to," he reflected mournfully. "It's ignominious. 'Be patient, humble, hold thy peace.' "* He wound up his reflections with that line. But he pulled himself together to go on again. When he came to telling of his visit to Madame Hohlakov, he regained his spirits and even wished to tell a little anecdote of that lady which had nothing to do with the case. But the investigating lawyer stopped him, and civilly suggested that he should

---

*From Tyutchev's poem "Silence."

pass on to "more essential matters." At last, when he described his despair
and told them how, when he left Madame Hohlakov's he thought that he'd
"get three thousand if he had to murder some one to do it," they stopped
him again and noted down that he had "meant to murder some one."
Mitya let them write it without protest. At last he reached the point in his
story when he learned that Grushenka had deceived him and had returned from Samsonov's as soon as he left her there, though she had said
that she would stay there till midnight.

"If I didn't kill Fenya then, gentlemen, it was only because I hadn't
time," broke from him suddenly at that point in his story. That, too, was
carefully written down. Mitya waited gloomily, and was beginning to tell
how he ran into his father's garden when the investigating lawyer suddenly stopped him, and opening the big portfolio that lay on the sofa beside him he brought out the brass pestle.

"Do you recognise this object?" he asked, showing it to Mitya.

"Oh, yes," he laughed gloomily. "Of course I recognise it. Let me have a
look at it. . . . Damn it, never mind!"

"You have forgotten to mention it," observed the investigating lawyer.

"Hang it all, I shouldn't have concealed it from you. Do you suppose I
could have managed without it? It simply escaped my memory."

"Be so good as to tell us precisely how you came to arm yourself
with it."

"Certainly I will be so good, gentlemen."

And Mitya described how he took the pestle and ran.

"But what object had you in view in arming yourself with such a
weapon?"

"What object? No object. I just picked it up and ran off."

"What for, if you had no object?"

Mitya's wrath flared up. He looked intently at "the boy" and smiled
gloomily and malignantly. He was feeling more and more ashamed at having told "such people" the story of his jealousy so sincerely and spontaneously.

"Bother the pestle!" broke from him suddenly.

"But still . . ."

"Oh, to keep off dogs. . . . Oh, because it was dark. . . . In case anything
turned up."

"But have you ever on previous occasions taken a weapon with you
when you went out, since you're afraid of the dark?"

"Ugh! damn it all, gentlemen! There's positively no talking to you!"
cried Mitya, exasperated beyond endurance, and turning to the secretary,
crimson with anger, he said quickly, with a note of fury in his voice:

"Write down at once . . . at once . . . 'that I snatched up the pestle to go
and kill my father . . . Fyodor Pavlovitch . . . by hitting him on the head
with it!' Well, now are you satisfied, gentlemen? Are your minds relieved?" he said, glaring defiantly at the lawyers.

"We quite understand that you made that statement just now through
exasperation with us and the questions we put to you, which you consider

trivial, though they are, in fact, essential," the prosecutor remarked drily in reply.

"Well, upon my word, gentlemen! Yes, I took the pestle. . . . What does one pick things up for at such moments? I don't know what for. I snatched it up and ran—that's all. For to me, gentlemen, *passons,* or I declare I won't tell you any more."

He sat with his elbows on the table and his head in his hand. He sat sideways to them and gazed at the wall, struggling against a feeling of nausea. He had, in fact, an awful inclination to get up and declare that he wouldn't say another word, "not if you hang me for it."

"You see, gentlemen," he said at last, with difficulty controlling himself, "you see. I listen to you and am haunted by a dream. . . . It's a dream I have sometimes, you know. . . . I often dream it—it's always the same . . . that some one is hunting me, some one I'm awfully afraid of . . . that he's hunting me in the dark, in the night . . . tracking me, and I hide somewhere from him, behind a door or cupboard, hide in a degrading way, and the worst of it is, he always knows where I am, but he pretends not to know where I am on purpose, to prolong my agony, to enjoy my terror. . . . That's just what you're doing now. It's just like that!"

"Is that the sort of thing you dream about?" inquired the prosecutor.

"Yes, it is. Don't you want to write it down?" said Mitya, with a distorted smile.

"No; no need to write it down. But still you do have curious dreams."

"It's not a question of dreams now, gentlemen—this is realism, this is real life! I'm a wolf and you're the hunters. Well, hunt him down!"

"You are wrong to make such comparisons. . . ." began Nikolay Parfenovitch, with extraordinary softness.

"No, I'm not wrong, not at all!" Mitya flared up again, though his outburst of wrath had obviously relieved his heart. He grew more good-humoured at every word. "You may not trust a criminal or a man on trial tortured by your questions, but an honourable man, the honourable impulses of the heart (I say that boldly!)—no! That you must believe you have no right indeed . . . but—

> 'Be silent, heart,
> Be patient, humble, hold thy peace.'

"Well, shall I go on?" he broke off gloomily.

"If you'll be so kind," answered Nikolay Parfenovitch.

5

THE THIRD ORDEAL

THOUGH Mitya spoke sullenly, it was evident that he was trying more than ever not to forget or miss a single detail of his story. He told them how he had leapt over the fence into his father's garden; how he had gone up to the window; told them all that had passed under the window. Clearly, precisely, distinctly, he described the feelings that troubled him during those moments in the garden when he longed so terribly to know whether Grushenka was with his father or not. But, strange to say, both the lawyers listened now with a sort of awful reserve, looked coldly at him, asked few questions. Mitya could gather nothing from their faces.

"They're angry and offended," he thought. "Well, bother them!"

When he described how he made up his mind at last to make the "signal" to his father that Grushenka had come, so that he should open the window, the lawyers paid no attention to the word "signal," as though they entirely failed to grasp the meaning of the word in this connection: so much so, that Mitya noticed it. Coming at last to the moment when, seeing his father peering out of the window, his hatred flared up and he pulled the pestle out of his pocket, he suddenly, as though of design, stopped short. He sat gazing at the wall and was aware that their eyes were fixed upon him.

"Well?" said the investigating lawyer. "You pulled out the weapon and . . . and what happened then?"

"Then? Why, then I murdered him . . . hit him on the head and cracked his skull. . . . I suppose that's your story. That's it!"

His eyes suddenly flashed. All his smothered wrath suddenly flamed up with extraordinary violence in his soul.

"Our story?" repeated Nikolay Parfenovitch. "Well—and yours?"

Mitya dropped his eyes and was a long time silent.

"My story, gentlemen? Well, it was like this," he began softly. "Whether it was some one's tears, or my mother prayed to God, or a good angel kissed me at that instant, I don't know. But the devil was conquered. I rushed from the window and ran to the fence. My father was alarmed and, for the first time, he saw me then, cried out, and sprang back from the window. I remember that very well. I ran across the garden to the fence . . . and there Grigory caught me, when I was sitting on the fence."

At that point he raised his eyes at last and looked at his listeners. They seemed to be staring at him with perfectly unruffled attention. A sort of paroxysm of indignation seized on Mitya's soul.

"Why, you're laughing at me at this moment, gentlemen!" he broke off suddenly.

"What makes you think that?" observed Nikolay Parfenovitch.

"You don't believe one word—that's why! I understand, of course, that I have come to the vital point. The old man's lying there now with his skull broken, while I—after dramatically describing how I wanted to kill him, and how I snatched up the pestle—I suddenly run away from the window. A romance! Poetry! As though one could believe a fellow on his word. Ha, ha! You are scoffers, gentlemen!"

And he swung round on his chair so that it creaked.

"And did you notice," asked the prosecutor suddenly, as though not observing Mitya's excitement, "did you notice when you ran away from the window, whether the door into the garden was open?"

"No, it was not open."

"It was not?"

"It was shut. And who could open it? Bah! the door. Wait a bit!" he seemed suddenly to bethink himself, and almost with a start:

"Why, did you find the door open?"

"Yes, it was open."

"Why, who could have opened it if you did not open it yourselves?" cried Mitya, greatly astonished.

"The door stood open, and your father's murderer undoubtedly went in at that door, and, having accomplished the crime, went out again by the same door," the prosecutor pronounced deliberately, as though chiselling out each word separately. "That is perfectly clear. The murder was committed in the room and *not through the window*; that is absolutely certain from the examination that has been made, from the position of the body, and everything. There can be no doubt of that circumstance."

Mitya was absolutely dumbfounded.

"But that's utterly impossible!" he cried, completely at a loss. "I . . . I didn't go in. . . . I tell you positively, definitely, the door was shut the whole time I was in the garden, and when I ran out of the garden. I only stood at the window and saw him through the window. That's all, that's all . . . I remember to the last minute. And if I didn't remember, it would be just the same. I know it, for no one knew the signals except Smerdyakov, and me, and the dead man. And he wouldn't have opened the door to any one in the world without the signals."

"Signals? What signals?" asked the prosecutor, with greedy, almost hysterical, curiosity. He instantly lost all trace of his reserve and dignity. He asked the question with a sort of cringing timidity. He scented an important fact of which he had known nothing, and was already filled with dread that Mitya might be unwilling to disclose it.

"So you didn't know!" Mitya winked at him with a malicious and mocking smile. "What if I won't tell you? From whom could you find out? No one knew about the signals except my father, Smerdyakov, and me: that was all. Heaven knew, too, but it won't tell you. But it's an interesting fact. There's no knowing what you might build on it. Ha, ha! Take comfort, gentlemen, I'll reveal it. You've some foolish idea in your hearts. You don't know the man you have to deal with! You have to do with a prisoner who gives evidence against himself, to his own damage! Yes, for I'm a man of honour and you—are not."

The prosecutor swallowed this without a murmur. He was trembling with impatience to hear the new fact. Minutely and diffusely Mitya told them everything about the signals invented by Fyodor Pavlovitch for Smerdyakov. He told them exactly what every tap on the window meant, tapped the signals on the table, and when Nikolay Parfenovitch said that he supposed he, Mitya, had tapped the signal "Grushenka has come," when he tapped to his father, he answered precisely that he had tapped that signal, that "Grushenka had come."

"So now you can build up your tower," Mitya broke off, and again turned away from them contemptuously.

"So no one knew of the signals but your dead father, you, and the valet Smerdyakov? And no one else?" Nikolay Parfenovitch inquired once more.

"Yes. The valet Smerdyakov, and heaven. Write down about heaven. That may be of use. Besides, you will need God yourselves."

And they had already, of course, begun writing it down. But while they wrote, the prosecutor said suddenly, as though pitching on a new idea:

"But if Smerdyakov also knew of these signals and you absolutely deny all responsibility for the death of your father, was it not he, perhaps, who knocked the signal agreed upon, induced your father to open to him, and then . . . committed the crime?"

Mitya turned upon him a look of profound irony and intense hatred. His silent stare lasted so long that it made the prosecutor blink.

"You've caught the fox again," commented Mitya at last; "you've got the beast by the tail. Ha, ha! I see through you, Mr. Prosecutor. You thought, of course, that I should jump at that, catch at your prompting, and shout with all my might, 'Aie, it's Smerdyakov; he's the murderer.' Confess that's what you thought. Confess, and I'll go on."

But the prosecutor did not confess. He held his tongue and waited.

"You're mistaken. I'm not going to shout 'it's Smerdyakov,' " said Mitya.

"And you don't even suspect him?"

"Why, do you suspect him?"

"He is suspected, too."

Mitya fixed his eyes on the floor.

"Joking apart," he brought out gloomily. "Listen. From the very beginning, almost from the moment when I ran out to you from behind the curtain, I've had the thought of Smerdyakov in my mind. I've been sitting here, shouting that I'm innocent and thinking all the time 'Smerdyakov!' I can't get Smerdyakov out of my head. In fact, I, too, thought of Smerdyakov just now; but only for a second. Almost at once I thought, 'No, it's not Smerdyakov.' It's not his doing, gentlemen."

"In that case is there anybody else you suspect?" Nikolay Parfenovitch inquired cautiously.

"I don't know any one it could be, whether it's the hand of Heaven or of Satan, but . . . not Smerdyakov," Mitya jerked out with decision.

"But what makes you affirm so confidently and emphatically that it's not he?"

"From my conviction—my impression. Because Smerdyakov is a man of the most abject character and a coward. He's not a coward, he's the epitome of all the cowardice in the world walking on two legs. He has the heart of a chicken. When he talked to me, he was always trembling for fear I should kill him, though I never raised my hand against him. He fell at my feet and blubbered; he has kissed these very boots, literally, beseeching me 'not to frighten him.' Do you hear? 'Not to frighten him.' What a thing to say! Why, I offered him money. He's a puling chicken—sickly, epileptic, weak-minded—a child of eight could thrash him. He has no character worth talking about. It's not Smerdyakov, gentlemen. He doesn't care for money; he wouldn't take my presents. Besides, what motive had he for murdering the old man? Why, he's very likely his son, you know—his natural son. Do you know that?"

"We have heard that legend. But you are your father's son, too, you know; yet you yourself told every one you meant to murder him."

"That's a thrust! And a nasty, mean one, too! I'm not afraid! Oh, gentlemen, isn't it too base of you to say that to my face? It's base, because I told you that myself. I not only wanted to murder him, but I might have done it. And, what's more, I went out of my way to tell you of my own accord that I nearly murdered him. But, you see, I didn't murder him; you see, my guardian angel saved me—that's what you've not taken into account. And that's why it's so base of you. For I didn't kill him, I didn't kill him! Do you hear, I did not kill him."

He was almost choking. He had not been so moved before during the whole interrogation.

"And what has he told you, gentlemen—Smerdyakov, I mean?" he added suddenly, after a pause. "May I ask that question?"

"You may ask any question," the prosecutor replied with frigid severity, "any question relating to the facts of the case, and we are, I repeat, bound to answer every inquiry you make. We found the servant Smerdyakov, concerning whom you inquire, lying unconscious in his bed, in an epileptic fit of extreme severity, that had recurred, possibly, ten times. The doctor who was with us told us, after seeing him, that he may possibly not outlive the night."

"Well, if that's so, the devil must have killed him," broke suddenly from Mitya, as though until that moment he had been asking himself: "Was it Smerdyakov or not?"

"We will come back to this later," Nikolay Parfenovitch decided. "Now, wouldn't you like to continue your statement?"

Mitya asked for a rest. His request was courteously granted. After resting, he went on with his story. But he was evidently depressed. He was exhausted, mortified and morally shaken. To make things worse the prosecutor exasperated him, as though intentionally, by vexatious interruptions about "trifling points." Scarcely had Mitya described how, sitting on the wall, he had struck Grigory on the head with the pestle, while the old man had hold of his left leg, and how he had then jumped down to look at him, when the prosecutor stopped him to ask him to describe exactly how he was sitting on the wall, Mitya was surprised.

"Oh, I was sitting like this, astride, one leg on one side of the wall and one on the other."

"And the pestle?"

"The pestle was in my hand."

"Not in your pocket? Do you remember that precisely? Was it a violent blow you gave him?"

"It must have been a violent one. But why do you ask?"

"Would you mind sitting on the chair just as you sat on the wall then and showing us just how you moved your arm, and in what direction?"

"You're making fun of me, aren't you?" asked Mitya, looking haughtily at the speaker; but the latter did not flinch.

Mitya turned abruptly, sat astride on his chair, and swung his arm.

"This was how I struck him! That's how I knocked him down! What more do you want?"

"Thank you. May I trouble you now to explain why you jumped down, with what object, and what you had in view?"

"Oh, hang it! . . . . I jumped down to look at the man I'd hurt . . . I don't know what for!"

"Though you were so excited and were running away?"

"Yes, though I was excited and running away."

"You wanted to help him?"

"Help! . . . Yes, perhaps I did want to help him. . . . I don't remember."

"You don't remember? Then you didn't quite know what you were doing?"

"Not at all. I remember everything—every detail. I jumped down to look at him, and wiped his face with my handkerchief."

"We have seen your handkerchief. Did you hope to restore him to consciousness?"

"I don't know whether I hoped it. I simply wanted to make sure whether he was alive or not."

"Ah! You wanted to be sure? Well, what then?"

"I'm not a doctor. I couldn't decide. I ran away thinking I'd killed him. And now he's recovered."

"Excellent," commented the prosecutor. "Thank you. That's all I wanted. Kindly proceed."

Alas! it never entered Mitya's head to tell them, though he remembered it, that he had jumped back from pity, and standing over the prostrate figure had even uttered some words of regret:

"You've come to grief, old man—there's no help for it. Well, there you must lie."

The prosecutor could only draw one conclusion: that the man had jumped back "at such a moment and in such excitement simply with the object of ascertaining whether the *only* witness of his crime were dead; that he must therefore have been a man of great strength, coolness, decision and foresight even at such a moment," . . . and so on. The prosecutor was satisfied: "I've provoked the nervous fellow by 'trifles' and he has said more than he meant to."

With painful effort Mitya went on. But this time he was pulled up immediately by Nikolay Parfenovitch.

"How came you to run to the servant, Fedosya Markovna, with your hands so covered with blood, and, as it appears, your face too?"

"Why, I didn't notice the blood at all at the time," answered Mitya.

"That's quite likely. It does happen sometimes." The prosecutor exchanged glances with Nikolay Parfenovitch.

"I simply didn't notice. You're quite right there, prosecutor," Mitya assented suddenly.

Next came the account of Mitya's sudden determination to "step aside" and make way for their happiness. But he could not make up his mind to open his heart to them as before, and tell them about "the queen of his soul." He disliked speaking of her before these chilly persons "who were fastening on him like bugs." And so in response to their reiterated questions he answered briefly and abruptly:

"Well, I made up my mind to kill myself. What had I left to live for? That question stared me in the face. Her first rightful lover had come back, the man who wronged her but who'd hurried back to offer his love, after five years and atone for the wrong with marriage. . . . So I knew it was all over for me. . . . And behind me disgrace, and that blood—Grigory's. . . . What had I to live for? So I went to redeem the pistols I had pledged, to load them and put a bullet in my brain to-morrow."

"And a grand feast the night before?"

"Yes, a grand feast the night before. Damn it all, gentlemen! Do make haste and finish it. I meant to shoot myself not far from here, beyond the village, and I'd planned to do it at five o'clock in the morning. And I had a note in my pocket already. I wrote it at Perhotin's when I loaded my pistols. Here's the letter. Read it! It's not for you I tell it," he added contemptuously. He took it from his waistcoat pocket and flung it on the table. The lawyers read it with curiosity, and, as is usual, added it to the papers connected with the case.

"And you didn't even think of washing your hands at Perhotin's? You were not afraid then of arousing suspicion?"

"What suspicion? Suspicion or not, I should have galloped here just the same, and shot myself at five o'clock, and you wouldn't have been in time to do anything. If it hadn't been for what's happened to my father, you would have known nothing about it, and wouldn't have come here. Oh, it's the devil's doing. It was the devil murdered father, it was through the devil that you found it out so soon. How did you manage to get here so quick? It's marvellous, a dream!"

"Mr. Perhotin informed us that when you came to him, you held in your hands . . . your blood-stained hands . . . your money . . . a lot of money . . . a bundle of hundred-rouble notes, and that his servant boy saw it too."

"That's true, gentlemen. I remember it was so."

"Now, there's one little point presents itself. Can you inform us," Nikolay Parfenovitch began, with extreme gentleness, "where did you get so much money all of a sudden, when it appears from the facts, from the reckoning of time, that you had not been home?"

The prosecutor's brows contracted at the question being asked so plainly, but he did not interrupt Nikolay Parfenovitch.

"No, I didn't go home," answered Mitya, apparently perfectly composed, but looking at the floor.

"Allow me then to repeat my question," Nikolay Parfenovitch went on as though creeping up to the subject. "Where were you able to procure such a sum all at once, when, by your own confession, at five o'clock the same day you . . ."

"I was in want of ten roubles and pledged my pistols, with Perhotin, and then went to Madame Hohlakov to borrow three thousand which she wouldn't give me, and so on, and all the rest of it," Mitya interrupted sharply. "Yes, gentlemen, I was in want of it, and suddenly thousands turned up, eh? Do you know, gentlemen, you're both afraid now 'what if he won't tell us where he got it?' That's just how it is. I'm not going to tell you, gentlemen. You've guessed right. You'll never know," said Mitya, chipping out each word with extraordinary determination. The lawyers were silent for a moment.

"You must understand, Mr. Karamazov, that it is of vital importance for us to know," said Nikolay Parfenovitch, softly and suavely.

"I understand; but still I won't tell you."

The prosecutor, too, intervened, and again reminded him that the prisoner was at liberty to refuse to answer questions, if he thought it to his interest, and so on. But in view of the damage he might do himself by his silence, especially in a case of such importance as . . .

"And so on, gentlemen, and so on. Enough! I've heard that rigmarole before," Mitya interrupted again. "I can see for myself how important it is, and that this is the vital point, and still I won't say."

"What is it to us? It's not our business, but yours. You are doing yourself harm," observed Nikolay Parfenovitch nervously.

"You see, gentlemen, joking apart"—Mitya lifted his eyes and looked firmly at them both—"I had an inkling from the first that we should come to loggerheads at this point. But at first when I began to give my evidence, it was all still far away and misty; it was all floating, and I was so simple that I began with the supposition of mutual confidence existing between us. Now I can see for myself that such confidence is out of the question, for in any case we were bound to come to this cursed stumbling-block. And now we've come to it! It's impossible and there's an end of it! But I don't blame you. You can't believe it all simply on my word. I understand that, of course."

He relapsed into gloomy silence.

"Couldn't you, without abandoning your resolution to be silent about the chief point, could you not, at the same time, give us some slight hint as to the nature of the motives which are strong enough to induce you to refuse to answer, at a crisis so full of danger to you?"

Mitya smiled mournfully, almost dreamily.

"I'm much more good-natured than you think, gentlemen. I'll tell you the reason why and give you that hint, though you don't deserve it. I won't speak of that, gentlemen, because it would be a stain on my honour. The answer to the question where I got the money would expose me to far greater disgrace than the murder and robbing of my father, if I had murdered and robbed him. That's why I can't tell you. I can't for fear of disgrace. What, gentlemen, are you going to write that down?"

"Yes, we'll write it down," lisped Nikolay Parfenovitch.

"You ought not to write that down about 'disgrace.' I only told you that in the goodness of my heart. I needn't have told you. I made you a present of it, so to speak, and you pounce upon it at once. Oh, well, write—write what you like," he concluded, with scornful disgust. "I'm not afraid of you and I can still hold up my head before you."

"And can't you tell us the nature of that disgrace?" Nikolay Parfenovitch hazarded.

The prosecutor frowned darkly.

"No, no, *c'est fini,** don't trouble yourselves. It's not worth while soiling one's hands. I have soiled myself enough through you as it is. You're not worth it—no one is . . . Enough, gentlemen. I'm not going on."

This was said too peremptorily. Nikolay Parfenovitch did not insist further, but from Ippolit Kirillovitch's eyes he saw that he had not given up hope.

"Can you not, at least, tell us what sum you had in your hands when you went into Mr. Perhotin's—how many roubles exactly?"

"I can't tell you that."

"You spoke to Mr. Perhotin, I believe, of having received three thousand from Madame Hohlakov."

"Perhaps I did. Enough, gentlemen. I won't say how much I had."

"Will you be so good then as to tell us how you came here and what you have done since you arrived?"

"Oh! you might ask the people here about that. But I'll tell you if you like."

He proceeded to do so, but we won't repeat his story. He told it drily and curtly. Of the raptures of his love he said nothing, but told them that he abandoned his determination to shoot himself, owing to "new factors in the case." He told the story without going into motives or details. And this time the lawyers did not worry him much. It was obvious that there was no essential point of interest to them here.

"We shall verify all that. We will come back to it during the examination of the witnesses, which will, of course, take place in your presence," said Nikolay Parfenovitch in conclusion. "And now allow me to request you to lay on the table everything in your possession, especially all the money you still have about you."

---

*"That's finished" or "that's all" (French).

"My money, gentlemen? Certainly. I understand that that is necessary. I'm surprised, indeed, that you haven't inquired about it before. It's true I couldn't get away anywhere. I'm sitting here where I can be seen. But here's my money—count it—take it. That's all, I think."

He turned it all out of his pockets; even the small change—two pieces of twenty kopecks—he pulled out of his waistcoat pocket. They counted the money, which amounted to eight hundred and thirty-six roubles, and forty kopecks.

"And is that all?" asked the investigating lawyer.

"Yes."

"You stated just now in your evidence that you spent three hundred roubles at Plotnikovs'. You gave Perhotin ten, your driver twenty, here you lost two hundred, then . . ."

Nikolay Parfenovitch reckoned it all up. Mitya helped him readily. They recollected every farthing and included it in the reckoning. Nikolay Parfenovitch hurriedly added up the total.

"With this eight hundred you must have had about fifteen hundred at first?"

"I suppose so," snapped Mitya.

"How is it they all assert there was much more?"

"Let them assert it."

"But you asserted it yourself."

"Yes, I did, too."

"We will compare all this with the evidence of other persons not yet examined. Don't be anxious about your money. It will be properly taken care of and be at your disposal at the conclusion of . . . what is beginning . . . if it appears, or so to speak, is proved that you have undisputed right to it. Well, and now . . ."

Nikolay Parfenovitch suddenly got up, and informed Mitya firmly that it was his duty and obligation to conduct a minute and thorough search "of your clothes and everything else. . . ."

"By all means, gentlemen. I'll turn out all my pockets, if you like."

And he did, in fact, begin turning out his pockets.

"It will be necessary to take off your clothes, too."

"What! Undress! Ugh! Damn it! Won't you search me as I am? Can't you?"

"It's utterly impossible, Dmitri Fyodorovitch. You must take off your clothes."

"As you like," Mitya submitted gloomily; "only, please not here, but behind the curtains. Who will search them?"

"Behind the curtains, of course."

Nikolay Parfenovitch bent his head in assent. His small face wore an expression of peculiar solemnity.

6

THE PROSECUTOR CATCHES MITYA

SOMETHING utterly unexpected and amazing to Mitya followed. He could never, even a minute before, have conceived that any one could behave like that to him, Mitya Karamazov. What was worst of all, there was something humiliating in it, and on their side something "supercilious and scornful." It was nothing to take off his coat, but he was asked to undress further, or rather not asked but "commanded," he quite understood that. From pride and contempt he submitted without a word. Several peasants accompanied the lawyers and remained on the same side of the curtain. "To be ready if force is required," thought Mitya, "and perhaps for some other reason, too."

"Well, must I take off my shirt, too?" he asked sharply, but Nikolay Parfenovitch did not answer. He was busily engaged with the prosecutor in examining the coat, the trousers, the waistcoat and the cap; and it was evident that they were both much interested in the scrutiny. "They make no bones about it," thought Mitya, "they don't keep up the most elementary politeness."

"I ask you for the second time—need I take off my shirt or not?" he said, still more sharply and irritably.

"Don't trouble yourself. We will tell you what to do," Nikolay Parfenovitch said, and his voice was positively peremptory, or so it seemed to Mitya.

Meantime a consultation was going on in undertones between the lawyers. There turned out to be on the coat, especially on the left side at the back, a huge patch of blood, dry, and still stiff. There were bloodstains on the trousers, too. Nikolay Parfenovitch, moreover, in the presence of the peasant witnesses, passed his fingers along the collar, the cuffs, and all the seams of the coat and trousers, obviously looking for something— money, of course. He didn't even hide from Mitya his suspicion that he was capable of sewing money up in his clothes.

"He treats me not as an officer but as a thief," Mitya muttered to himself. They communicated their ideas to one another with amazing frankness. The secretary, for instance, who was also behind the curtain, fussing about and listening, called Nikolay Parfenovitch's attention to the cap, which they were also fingering.

"You remember Gridyenko, the copying-clerk," observed the secretary. "Last summer he received the wages of the whole office, and pretended to have lost the money when he was drunk. And where was it found? Why, in

441

just such pipings in his cap. The hundred-rouble notes were screwed up in little rolls and sewed in the piping."

Both the lawyers remembered Gridyenko's case perfectly, and so laid aside Mitya's cap, and decided that all his clothes must be more thoroughly examined later.

"Excuse me," cried Nikolay Parfenovitch, suddenly, noticing that the right cuff of Mitya's shirt was turned in, and covered with blood, "excuse me, what's that, blood?"

"Yes," Mitya jerked out.

"That is, what blood . . . and why is the cuff turned in?"

Mitya told him how he had got the sleeve stained with blood looking after Grigory, and had turned it inside when he was washing his hands at Perhotin's.

"You must take off your shirt, too. That's very important as material evidence."

Mitya flushed red and flew into a rage.

"What, am I to stay naked?" he shouted.

"Don't disturb yourself. We will arrange something. And meanwhile take off your socks."

"You're not joking? Is that really necessary?" Mitya's eyes flashed.

"We are in no mood for joking," answered Nikolay Parfenovitch sternly.

"Well, if I must . . ." muttered Mitya, and sitting down on the bed, he took off his socks. He felt unbearably awkward. All were clothed, while he was naked, and strange to say, when he was undressed he felt somehow guilty in their presence, and was almost ready to believe himself that he was inferior to them, and that now they had a perfect right to despise him.

"When all are undressed, one is somehow not ashamed, but when one's the only one undressed and everybody is looking, it's degrading," he kept repeating to himself, again and again. "It's like a dream, I've sometimes dreamed of being in such degrading positions." It was a misery to him to take off his socks. They were very dirty, and so were his underclothes, and now everyone could see it. And what was worse, he disliked his feet. All his life he had thought both his big toes hideous. He particularly loathed the coarse, flat, crooked nail on the right one, and now they would all see it. Feeling intolerably ashamed made him, at once and intentionally, rougher. He pulled off his shirt, himself.

"Would you like to look anywhere else if you're not ashamed to?"

"No, there's no need to, at present."

"Well, am I to stay naked like this?" he added savagely.

"Yes, that can't be helped for the time. . . . Kindly sit down here for a while. You can wrap yourself in a quilt from the bed, and I . . . I'll see to all this."

All the things were shown to the witnesses. The report of the search was drawn up, and at last Nikolay Parfenovitch went out, and the clothes were carried out after him. Ippolit Kirillovitch went out, too. Mitya was left alone with the peasants, who stood in silence, never taking their eyes off him. Mitya wrapped himself up in the quilt. He felt cold. His bare feet stuck out, and he couldn't pull the quilt over so as to cover them. Nikolay Parfenovitch seemed to be gone a long time, "an insufferable time." "He thinks of me as a puppy;" thought Mitya, gnashing his teeth. "That rotten prosecutor has gone, too, contemptuous no doubt, it disgusts him to see me naked!"

Mitya imagined, however, that his clothes would be examined and returned to him. But what was his indignation when Nikolay Parfenovitch came back with quite different clothes, brought in behind him by a peasant.

"Here are clothes for you," he observed airily, seeming well satisfied with the success of his mission. "Mr. Kalganov has kindly provided these for this unusual emergency, as well as a clean shirt. Luckily he had them all in his trunk. You can keep your own socks and underclothes."

Mitya flew into a passion.

"I won't have other people's clothes!" he shouted menacingly, "give me my own!"

"It's impossible!"

"Give me my own. Damn Kalganov and his clothes, too!"

It was a long time before they could persuade him. But they succeeded somehow in quieting him down. They impressed upon him that his clothes, being stained with blood, must be "included with the other material evidence," and that they "had not even the right to let him have them now . . . taking into consideration the possible outcome of the case." Mitya at last understood this. He subsided into gloomy silence and hurriedly dressed himself. He merely observed, as he put them on, that the clothes were much better than his old ones, and that he disliked "gaining by the change." The coat was, besides, "ridiculously narrow. Am I to be dressed up like a fool . . . for your amusement?"

They urged upon him again that he was exaggerating, that Kalganov was only a little taller, so that only the trousers might be a little too long. But the coat turned out to be really tight in the shoulders.

"Damn it all! I can hardly button it," Mitya grumbled. "Be so good as to tell Mr. Kalganov from me that I didn't ask for his clothes, and it's not my doing that they've dressed me up like a clown."

"He quite understands that, and is sorry . . . I mean, not sorry to lend you his clothes, but sorry about all this business," mumbled Nikolay Parfenovitch.

"Confound his sorrow! Well, where now, or am I to go on sitting here?"

He was asked to go back to the "other room." Mitya went in, scowling with anger, and trying to avoid looking at any one. Dressed in another man's clothes he felt himself disgraced, even in the eyes of the peasants, and of Trifon Borissovitch, whose face appeared, for some reason, in the doorway, and vanished immediately, "He's come to look at me dressed up," thought Mitya. He sat down on the same chair as before. He had an absurd nightmarish feeling, as though he were out of his mind.

"Well, what now? Are you going to flog me? That's all that's left for you," he said, clenching his teeth and addressing the prosecutor. He would not turn to Nikolay Parfenovitch, as though he disdained to speak to him.

"He looked too closely at my socks, and turned them inside out on purpose to show every one how dirty they were—the scoundrel!"

"Well, now we must proceed to the examination of witnesses," observed Nikolay Parfenovitch, as though in reply to Mitya's question.

"Yes," said the prosecutor thoughtfully, as though reflecting on something.

"We've done what we could in your interest, Dmitri Fyodorovitch," Nikolay Parfenovitch went on, "but having received from you such an uncompromising refusal to explain to us the source from which you obtained the money found upon you, we are, at the present moment . . ."

"What is the stone in your ring?" Mitya interrupted suddenly, as though awakening from a reverie. He pointed to one of the three large rings adorning Nikolay Parfenovitch's right hand.

"Ring?" repeated Nikolay Parfenovitch with surprise.

"Yes, that one . . . on your middle finger, with the little veins in it, what stone is that?" Mitya persisted, like a peevish child.

"That's a smoky topaz," said Nikolay Parfenovitch, smiling. "Would you like to look at it? I'll take it off. . . ."

"No, don't take it off," cried Mitya furiously, suddenly waking up, and angry with himself. "Don't take it off . . . there's no need. . . . Damn it. . . . Gentlemen, you've sullied my heart! Can you suppose that I would conceal it from you, if I really had killed my father, that I would shuffle, lie, and hide myself? No, that's not like Dmitri Karamazov, that he couldn't do, and if I were guilty, I swear I shouldn't have waited for your coming, or for the sunrise as I meant at first, but should have killed myself before this, without waiting for the dawn! I know that about myself now. I couldn't have learnt so much in twenty years as I've found out in this accursed night! . . . And should I have been like this on this night, and at this moment, sitting with you, could I have talked like this, could I have moved like this, could I have looked at you and at the world like this, if I had really been the murderer of my father, when the very thought of having accidentally killed Grigory gave me no peace all night—not from fear—oh, not simply from fear of your punishment! The disgrace of it! And you expect me to be open with such scoffers as you, who see nothing and believe in nothing, blind moles and scoffers, and to tell you another nasty thing I've done, another disgrace, even if that would save me from your accusation! No, better Siberia! The man who opened the door to my father and went in at that door, he killed him, he robbed him. Who was he—I'm racking my brains and can't think who. But I can tell you it was not Dmitri Karamazov, and that's all I can tell you, and that's enough, enough, leave me alone. . . . Exile me, punish me, but don't bother me any more. I'll say no more. Call your witnesses!"

Mitya uttered his sudden monologue as though he were determined to be absolutely silent for the future. The prosecutor watched him the whole time and only when he had ceased speaking, observed, as though it were the most ordinary thing, with the most frigid and composed air:

"Oh, about the open door of which you spoke just now, we may as well inform you, by the way, now, of a very interesting piece of evidence of the greatest importance both to you and to us, that has been given us by Grigory, the old man you wounded. On his recovery, he clearly and emphatically stated, in reply to our questions, that when, on coming out to the steps, and hearing a noise in the garden, he made up his mind to go into it through the little gate which stood open, before he noticed you running, as you have told us already, in the dark from the open window where you saw your father, he, Grigory, glanced to the left, and, while noticing the open window, observed at the same time, much nearer to him, the door, standing wide open—that door which you have stated to have been shut the whole time you were in the garden. I will not conceal from you that Grigory himself confidently affirms and bears witness that you must have run from that door, though, of course, he did not see you do so with his own eyes, since he only noticed you first some distance away in the garden, running towards the fence."

Mitya had leapt up from his chair half way through this speech.

"Nonsense!" he yelled, in a sudden frenzy, "it's a bare-faced lie. He couldn't have seen the door open because it was shut. He's lying!"

"I consider it my duty to repeat that he is firm in his statement. He does not waver. He adheres to it. We've cross-examined him several times."

"Precisely. I have cross-examined him several times," Nikolay Parfenovitch confirmed warmly.

"It's false, false! It's either an attempt to slander me, or the hallucination of a madman," Mitya still shouted. "He's simply raving, from loss of blood, from the wound. He must have fancied it when he came to. . . . He's raving."

"Yes, but he noticed the open door, not when he came to after his injuries, but before that, as soon as he went into the garden from the lodge."

"But it's false, it's false! It can't be so! He's slandering me from spite. . . . He couldn't have seen it . . . I didn't come from the door," gasped Mitya.

The prosecutor turned to Nikolay Parfenovitch and said to him impressively:

"Confront him with it."

"Do you recognise this object?"

Nikolay Parfenovitch laid upon the table a large and thick official envelope, on which three seals still remained intact. The envelope was empty, and slit open at one end. Mitya stared at it with open eyes.

"It . . . it must be that envelope of my father's, the envelope that contained the three thousand roubles . . . and if there's inscribed on it, allow me 'for my little chicken' . . . yes—three thousand!" he shouted, "do you see, three thousand, do you see?"

"Of course, we see. But we didn't find the money in it. It was empty, and lying on the floor by the bed, behind the screen."

For some seconds Mitya stood as though thunderstruck.

"Gentlemen, it's Smerdyakov!" he shouted suddenly, at the top of his voice. "It's he who's murdered him! He's robbed him! No one else knew where the old man hid the envelope. It's Smerdyakov, that's clear, now!"

"But you, too, knew of the envelope and that it was under the pillow."

"I never knew it. I've never seen it. This is the first time I've looked at it. I've only heard of it from Smerdyakov. . . . He was the only one who knew where the old man kept it hidden, I didn't know. . . ." Mitya was completely breathless.

"But you told us yourself that the envelope was under your deceased father's pillow. You especially stated that it was under the pillow, so you must have known it."

"We've got it written down," confirmed Nikolay Parfenovitch.

"Nonsense! It's absurd! I'd no idea it was under the pillow. And perhaps it wasn't under the pillow at all. . . . It was just a chance guess that it was under the pillow. What does Smerdyakov say? Have you asked him where it was? What does Smerdyakov say? that's the chief point. . . . And I went out of my way to tell lies against myself. . . . I told you without thinking that it was under the pillow, and now you . . . Oh, you know how one says the wrong thing, without meaning it. No one knew but Smerdyakov, only Smerdyakov, and no one else. . . . He didn't even tell me where it was! But it's his doing, his doing; there's no doubt about it, he murdered him, that's as clear as daylight now," Mitya exclaimed more and more frantically, repeating himself incoherently, and growing more and more exasperated and excited. "You must understand that, and arrest him at once. . . . He must have killed him while I was running away and while Grigory was unconscious, that's clear now. . . . He gave the signal and father opened to him . . . for no one but he knew the signal, and without the signal father would never have opened the door. . . ."

"But you're again forgetting the circumstances," the prosecutor observed, still speaking with the same restraint, though with a note of triumph, "that there was no need to give the signal if the door already stood open when you were there, while you were in the garden. . . ."

"The door, the door," muttered Mitya, and he stared speechless at the prosecutor. He sank back helpless in his chair. All were silent.

"Yes, the door! . . . It's a nightmare! God is against me!" he exclaimed, staring before him in complete stupefaction.

"Come, you see," the prosecutor went on with dignity, "and you can judge for yourself, Dmitri Fyodorovitch. On the one hand we have the evidence of the open door from which you ran out, a fact which overwhelms you and us. On the other side your incomprehensible, persistent, and, so to speak, obdurate silence with regard to the source from which you obtained the money which was so suddenly seen in your hands, when only three hours earlier, on your own showing, you pledged your pistols for the sake of ten roubles! In view of all these facts, judge for yourself. What are we to believe, and what can we depend upon? And don't accuse us of being 'frigid, cynical, scoffing people,' who are incapable of believing in the generous impulses of your heart. . . . Try to enter into our position. . . ."

Mitya was indescribably agitated. He turned pale.

"Very well!" he exclaimed suddenly, "I will tell you my secret. I'll tell

you where I got the money! . . . I'll reveal my shame, that I may not have
to blame myself or you hereafter."

"And believe me, Dmitri Fyodorovitch," put in Nikolay Parfenovitch,
in a voice of almost pathetic delight, "that every sincere and complete confession on your part at this moment may, later on, have an immense influence in your favour, and may, indeed, moreover . . ."

But the prosecutor gave him a slight shove under the table, and he
checked himself in time. Mitya, it is true, had not heard him.

7

MITYA'S GREAT SECRET.
RECEIVED WITH HISSES

"GENTLEMEN," he began, still in the same agitation, "I want to make a
full confession: that money was *my own*."

The lawyers' faces lengthened. That was not at all what they expected.

"How do you mean?" faltered Nikolay Parfenovitch, "when at five
o'clock on the same day, from your own confession . . ."

"Damn five o'clock on the same day and my own confession. That's
nothing to do with it now! That money was my own, my own, that is, stolen
by me . . . not mine, I mean, but stolen by me, and it was fifteen hundred
roubles, and I had it on me all the time, all the time. . . ."

"But where did you get it?"

"I took it off my neck, gentlemen, off this very neck . . . it was here,
round my neck, sewn up in a rag, and I'd had it round my neck a long time,
it's a month since I put it round my neck . . . to my shame and disgrace!"

"And from whom did you . . . appropriate it?"

"You mean, 'steal it'? Speak out plainly now. Yes, I consider that I practically stole it, but, if you prefer, I 'appropriated it.' I consider I stole it.
And last night I stole it finally."

"Last night? But you said that it's a month since you . . . obtained
it? . . ."

"Yes. But not from my father. Not from my father, don't be uneasy. I
didn't steal it from my father, but from her. Let me tell you without interrupting. It's hard to do, you know. You see, a month ago, I was sent for by
Katerina Ivanovna, formerly my betrothed. Do you know her?"

"Yes, of course."

"I know you know her. She's a noble creature, noblest of the noble. But she has hated me ever so long, oh, ever so long . . . and hated me with good reason, good reason!"

"Katerina Ivanovna!" Nikolay Parfenovitch exclaimed with wonder. The prosecutor, too, stared.

"Oh, don't take her name in vain! I'm a scoundrel to bring her into it. Yes, I've seen that she hated me . . . a long while. . . . From the very first, even that evening at my lodging . . . but enough, enough. You're unworthy even to know of that. No need of that at all. . . . I need only tell you that she sent for me a month ago, gave me three thousand roubles to send to her sister and another relation in Moscow (as though she couldn't have sent it off herself!), and I . . . it was just at that fatal moment in my life when I . . . Well, in fact, when I'd just come to love another, *her*, she's sitting down below now, Grushenka. I carried her off here to Mokroe then, and wasted here in two days half that damned three thousand, but the other half I kept on me. Well, I've kept that other half, that fifteen hundred like a locket round my neck, but yesterday I undid it, and spent it. What's left of it, eight hundred roubles, is in your hands now, Nikolay Parfenovitch. That's the change out of the fifteen hundred I had yesterday."

"Excuse me. How's that? Why, when you were here a month ago you spent three thousand, not fifteen hundred, everybody knows that."

"Who knows it? Who counted the money? Did I let any one count it?"

"Why, you told every one yourself that you'd spent exactly three thousand."

"It's true, I did. I told the whole town so, and the whole town said so. And here, at Mokroe, too, every one reckoned it was three thousand. Yet I didn't spend three thousand, but fifteen hundred. And the other fifteen hundred I sewed into a little bag. That's how it was, gentlemen. That's where I got that money yesterday. . . ."

"This is almost miraculous," murmured Nikolay Parfenovitch.

"Allow me to inquire," observed the prosecutor at last, "have you informed any one whatever of this circumstance before, I mean that you had fifteen hundred left about you a month ago?"

"I told no one."

"That's strange. Do you mean absolutely no one?"

"Absolutely no one. No one and nobody."

"What was your reason for this reticence? What was your motive for making such a secret of it? To be more precise: You have told us at last your secret, in your words, so 'disgraceful,' though in reality—that is, of course, comparatively speaking—this action, that is, the appropriation of three thousand roubles belonging to some one else, and, of course, only for a time is, in my view at least, only an act of the greatest recklessness and not so disgraceful, when one takes into consideration your character. . . . Even admitting that it was an action in the highest degree discreditable, still, discreditable is not 'disgraceful. . . .' Many people have already guessed, during this last month, about the three thousand of Katerina Ivanovna's, that you have spent, and I had heard the legend myself, apart from your confession. . . . Mihail Makarovitch, for instance, had heard it, too, so that indeed, it was scarcely a legend, but the gossip of the whole town. There are indications, too, if I am not mistaken, that you confessed this yourself to some one, I mean that the money was Katerina Ivanovna's, and so, it's extremely surprising to me that hitherto, that is, up to the present moment, you have made such an extraordinary secret of the fifteen hundred you say you put by, apparently connecting a feeling of positive horror with that secret. . . . It's not easy to believe that it could cost you such distress to confess such a secret. . . . You cried out, just now, that Siberia would be better than confessing it. . . ."

The prosecutor ceased speaking. He was provoked. He did not conceal his vexation, which was almost anger, and gave vent to all his accumulated spleen, without choosing words, disconnectedly and incoherently.

"It's not the fifteen hundred that's the disgrace, but that I put it apart from the rest of the three thousand," said Mitya firmly.

"Why," smiled the prosecutor irritably. "What is there disgraceful, to your thinking, in your having set aside half of the three thousand you had discreditably, if you prefer, 'disgracefully,' appropriated? Your taking the three thousand is more important than what you did with it. And by the way, why did you do that—why did you set apart that half, for what purpose, for what object did you do it? Can you explain that to us?"

"Oh, gentlemen, the purpose is the whole point!" cried Mitya. "I put it aside because I was vile, that is, because I was calculating, and to be calculating in such a case is vile . . . and that vileness has been going on a whole month."

"It's incomprehensible."

"I wonder at you. But I'll make it clearer. Perhaps it really is incomprehensible. You see, attend to what I say. I appropriate three thousand entrusted to my honour, I spent it on a spree, say I spend it all, and next morning I go to her and say, 'Katya, I've done wrong, I've squandered your three thousand,' well, is that right? No, it's not right—it's dishonest and cowardly, I'm a beast, with no more self-control than a beast, that's so, isn't it? But still I'm not a thief? Not a downright thief, you'll admit! I squandered it, but I didn't steal it. Now a second, rather more favourable alternative: follow me carefully, or I may get confused again—my head's going round—and so, for the second alternative: I spend here only fifteen hundred out of the three thousand, that is, only half. Next day I go and take that half to her: 'Katya, take this fifteen hundred from me, I'm a low beast, and an untrustworthy scoundrel, for I've wasted half the money, and I shall waste this, too, so keep me from temptation!' Well, what of that alternative? I should be a beast and a scoundrel, and whatever you like; but not a thief, not altogether a thief, or I should not have brought back what was left, but have kept that, too. She would see at once that since I brought back half, I should pay back what I'd spent, that I should never give up trying to, that I should work to get it and pay it back. So in that case I should be a scoundrel, but not a thief, you may say what you like, not a thief!"

"I admit that there is a certain distinction," said the prosecutor, with a cold smile. "But it's strange that you see such a vital difference."

"Yes, I see a vital difference! Every man may be a scoundrel, and perhaps every man is a scoundrel, but not every one can be a thief, it takes an arch-scoundrel to be that. Oh, of course, I don't know how to make these fine distinctions . . . but a thief is lower than a scoundrel, that's my conviction. Listen, I carry the money about me a whole month, I may make up my mind to give it back to-morrow, and I'm a scoundrel no longer, but I cannot make up my mind, you see, though I'm making up my mind every day, and every day spurring myself on to do it, and yet for a whole month I can't bring myself to it, you see. Is that right to your thinking, is that right?"

"Certainly, that's not right, that I can quite understand, and that I don't dispute," answered the prosecutor with reserve. "And let us give up all discussions of these subtleties and distinctions, and, if you will be so kind, get back to the point. And the point is, that you have still not told us, although we've asked you, why, in the first place, you halved the money, squandering one half and hiding the other? For what purpose exactly did you hide it, what did you mean to do with that fifteen hundred? I insist upon that question, Dmitri Fyodorovitch."

"Yes, of course!" cried Mitya, striking himself on the forehead; "forgive me, I'm worrying you, and am not explaining the chief point, or you'd understand in a minute, for it's just the motive of it that's the disgrace! You see, it was all to do with the old man, my dear father. He was always pestering Agrafena Alexandrovna, and I was jealous; I thought then that she was hesitating between me and him. So I kept thinking every day, suppose she were to make up her mind all of a sudden, suppose she were to leave off tormenting me, and were suddenly to say to me, 'I love you, not him; take me to the other end of the world.' And I'd only forty kopecks; how could I take her away, what could I do? Why, I'd be lost. You see, I didn't know her then, I didn't understand her, I thought she wanted money, and that she wouldn't forgive my poverty. And so I fiendishly counted out the half of that three thousand, sewed it up, calculating on it, sewed it up before I was drunk, and after I had sewn it up, I went off to get drunk on the rest. Yes, that was base. Do you understand now?"

Both the lawyers laughed aloud.

"I should have called it sensible and moral on your part not to have squandered it all," chuckled Nikolay Parfenovitch, "for after all what does it amount to?"

"Why, that I stole it, that's what it amounts to! Oh, God, you horrify me by not understanding! Every day that I had that fifteen hundred sewn up round my neck, every day and every hour I said to myself, 'you're a thief! you're a thief!' Yes, that's why I've been so savage all this month, that's why I fought in the tavern, that's why I attacked my father, it was because I felt I was a thief. I couldn't make up my mind, I didn't dare even to tell Alyosha, my brother, about that fifteen hundred: I felt I was such a scoundrel and such a pickpocket. But, do you know, while I carried it I said to myself at the same time every hour: 'No, Dmitri Fyodorovitch, you may yet not be a thief.' Why? Because I might go next day and pay back that fifteen hundred to

Katya. And only yesterday I made up my mind to tear my amulet off my neck, on my way from Fenya's to Perhotin. I hadn't been able till that moment to bring myself to it. And it was only when I tore it off that I became a downright thief, a thief and a dishonest man for the rest of my life. Why? Because, with that I destroyed, too, my dream of going to Katya and saying, 'I'm a scoundrel, but not a thief!' Do you understand now? Do you understand?"

"What was it made you decide to do it yesterday?" Nikolay Parfenovitch interrupted.

"Why? It's absurd to ask. Because I had condemned myself to die at five o'clock this morning, here, at dawn. I thought it made no difference whether I died a thief or a man of honour. But I see it's not so, it turns out that it does make a difference. Believe me, gentlemen, what has tortured me most during this night has not been the thought that I'd killed the old servant, and that I was in danger of Siberia just when my love was being rewarded, and Heaven was open to me again. Oh, that did torture me, but not in the same way; not so much as the damned consciousness that I had torn that damned money off my breast at last and spent it, and had become a downright thief! Oh, gentlemen, I tell you again, with a bleeding heart, I have learnt a great deal this night. I have learnt that it's not only impossible to live a scoundrel, but impossible to die a scoundrel. . . . No, gentlemen, one must die honest. . . ."

Mitya was pale. His face had a haggard and exhausted look, in spite of his being intensely excited.

"I am beginning to understand you, Dmitri Fyodorovitch," the prosecutor said slowly, in a soft and almost compassionate tone. "But all this, if you'll excuse my saying so, is a matter of nerves, in my opinion . . . your overwrought nerves, that's what it is. And why, for instance, should you not have saved yourself such misery for almost a month, by going and returning that fifteen hundred to the lady who had entrusted it to you? And why could you not have explained things to her, and in view of your position, which you describe as being so awful, why could you not have had recourse to the plan which would so naturally have occurred to one's mind, that is, after honourably confessing your errors to her, why could you not have asked her to lend you the sum needed for your expenses, which, with her generous heart, she would certainly not have refused you in your distress, especially if it had been with some guarantee, or even on the security you offered to the merchant Samsonov, and to Madame Hohlakov. I suppose you still regard that security as of value?"

Mitya suddenly crimsoned.

"Surely you don't think me such an out and out scoundrel as that? You can't be speaking in earnest?" he said, with indignation, looking the prosecutor straight in the face, and seeming unable to believe his ears.

"I assure you I'm in earnest. . . . Why do you imagine I'm not serious?" It was the prosecutor's turn to be surprised.

"Oh, how base that would have been! Gentlemen, do you know, you are torturing me! Let me tell you everything, so be it. I'll confess all my infernal wickedness, but to put you to shame, and you'll be surprised yourself at the depth of ignominy to which a medley of human passions can sink. You must know that I already had that plan myself, that plan you spoke of, just now, prosecutor! Yes, gentlemen, I, too, have had that thought in my mind all this current month, so that I was on the point of deciding to go to Katya—I was mean enough for that. But to go to her, to tell her of my treachery, and for that very treachery, to carry it out, for the expenses of that treachery, to beg for money from her, Katya (to beg, do you hear, to beg), and to go straight from her to run away with the other, the rival, who hated and insulted her—to think of it! You must be mad, prosecutor!"

"Mad I am not, but I did speak in haste, without thinking . . . of that feminine jealousy . . . if there could be jealousy in this case, as you assert . . . yes, perhaps there is something of the kind," said the prosecutor, smiling.

"But that would have been so infamous!" Mitya brought his fist down on the table fiercely. "That would have been filthy beyond everything! Yes, do you know that she might have given me that money, yes, and she would have given it too; she'd have given it to satisfy her vengeance, to show her contempt for me, for hers is an infernal nature, too, and she's a woman of great wrath. I'd have taken the money, too, oh, I should have taken it; I should have taken it, and then, for the rest of my life . . . oh, God! Forgive me, gentlemen, I'm making such an outcry because I've had that thought in my mind so lately, only the day before yesterday, that night when I was having all that bother with Lyagavy, and afterwards yesterday, all day yesterday, I remember, till that happened. . . ."

"Till what happened?" put in Nikolay Parfenovitch inquisitively, but Mitya did not hear it.

"I have made you an awful confession," Mitya said gloomily in conclusion. "You must appreciate it, and what's more, you must respect it, for if not, if that leaves your souls untouched, then you've simply no respect for me, gentlemen, I tell you that, and I shall die of shame at having confessed it to men like you! Oh, I shall shoot myself! Yes, I see, I see already that you don't believe me. What, you want to write that down, too?" he cried in dismay.

"Yes, what you said just now," said Nikolay Parfenovitch, looking at him in surprise, "that is, that up to the last hour you were still contemplating going to Katerina Ivanovna to beg that sum from her. . . . I assure you, that's a very important piece of evidence for us, Dmitri Fyodorovitch, I mean for the whole case . . . and particularly for you, particularly important for you."

"Have mercy, gentlemen!" Mitya flung up his hands, "Don't write that, anyway; have some shame. Here I've torn my heart asunder before you, and you seize the opportunity and are fingering the wounds in both halves. . . . Oh, my God!"

In despair he hid his face in his hands.

"Don't worry yourself so, Dmitri Fyodorovitch," observed the prosecutor, "everything that is written down will be read over to you afterwards, and what you don't agree to we'll alter as you like. But now I'll ask you one little question for the second time. Has no one, absolutely no one, heard from you of that money you sewed up? That, I must tell you, is almost impossible to believe."

"No one, no one, I told you so before, or you've not understood anything! Let me alone!"

"Very well, this matter is bound to be explained, and there's plenty of time for it, but meantime, consider; we have perhaps a dozen witnesses that you yourself spread it abroad, and even shouted almost everywhere about the three thousand you'd spent here; three thousand, not fifteen hundred. And now, too, when you got hold of the money you had yesterday, you gave many people to understand that you had brought three thousand with you."

"You've got not dozens, but hundreds of witnesses, two hundred witnesses, two hundred have heard it, thousands have heard it!" cried Mitya.

"Well, you see, all bear witness to it. And the word *all* means something."

"It means nothing. I talked rot, and every one began repeating it."

"But what need had you to 'talk rot,' as you call it?"

"The devil knows. From bravado perhaps . . . at having wasted so much money. . . . To try and forget that money I had sewn up, perhaps . . . yes, that was why . . . damn it . . . how often will you ask me that question? Well, I told a fib, and that was the end of it, once I'd said it, I didn't care to correct it. What does a man tell lies for sometimes?"

"That's very difficult to decide, Dmitri Fyodorovitch, what makes a man tell lies," observed the prosecutor impressively.

"Tell me, though, was that 'amulet,' as you call it, on your neck, a big thing?"

"No, not big."

"How big, for instance?"

"If you fold a hundred rouble note in half, that would be the size."

"You'd better show us the remains of it. You must have them somewhere."

"Damnation, what nonsense! I don't know where they are."

"But excuse me: where and when did you take it off your neck? According to your own evidence you didn't go home."

"When I was going from Fenya's to Perhotin's, on the way I tore it off my neck and took out the money."

"In the dark?"

"What should I want a light for? I did it with my fingers in one minute."

"Without scissors, in the street?"

"In the market-place I think it was. Why scissors? It was an old rag. It was torn in a minute."

"Where did you put it afterwards?"

"I dropped it there."

"Where was it, exactly?"

"In the market-place, in the market-place! The devil knows whereabouts. What do you want to know for?"

"That's extremely important, Dmitri Fyodorovitch. It would be material evidence in your favour. How is it you don't understand that? Who helped you to sew it up a month ago?"

"No one helped me. I did it myself."

"Can you sew?"

"A soldier has to know how to sew. No knowledge was needed to do that."

"Where did you get the material, that is, the rag in which you sewed the money?"

"Are you laughing at me?"

"Not at all. And we are in no mood for laughing, Dmitri Fyodorovitch."

"I don't know where I got the rag from—somewhere I suppose."

"I should have thought you couldn't have forgotten it?"

"Upon my word, I don't remember. I might have torn a bit off my linen."

"That's very interesting. We might find in your lodgings to-morrow the shirt or whatever it is from which you tore the rag. What sort of rag was it, cloth or linen?"

"Goodness only knows what it was. Wait a bit. . . . I believe I didn't tear it off anything. It was a bit of calico. . . . I believe I sewed it up in a cap of my landlady's."

"In your landlady's cap?"

"Yes, I took it from her."

"How did you get it?"

"You see, I remember once taking a cap for a rag, perhaps to wipe my pen on. I took it without asking, because it was a worthless rag. I tore it up, and I took the notes and sewed them up in it. I believe it was in that very rag I sewed it. An old piece of calico, washed a thousand times."

"And you remember that for certain now?"

"I don't know whether for certain. I think it was in the cap. But, hang it, what does it matter?"

"In that case your landlady will remember that the thing was lost?"

"No, she won't, she didn't miss it. It was an old rag, I tell you, an old rag not worth a farthing."

"And where did you get the needle and thread?"

"I'll stop now. I won't say any more. Enough of it!" said Mitya, losing his temper at last.

"It's strange that you should have so completely forgotten where you threw the pieces in the market-place."

"Give orders for the market-place to be swept to-morrow, and perhaps you'll find it," said Mitya sneering. "Enough, gentlemen, enough!" he decided, in an exhausted voice. "I see you don't believe me! Not for a moment! It's my fault, not yours. I ought not to have been so ready. Why, why did I degrade myself by confessing my secret to you? It's a joke to you. I see that from your eyes. You led me on to it, prosecutor! Sing a hymn of triumph if you can. . . . Damn you, you torturers!"

He bent his head, and hid his face in his hands. The lawyers were silent.

A minute later he raised his head and looked at them almost vacantly. His face expressed now complete, hopeless despair, and he sat mute and passive as though hardly conscious of what was happening. In the meantime they had to finish what they were about. They had immediately to begin examining the witnesses. It was by now eight o'clock in the morning. The lights had been extinguished long ago. Mihail Makarovitch and Kalganov, who had been continually in and out of the room all the while the interrogation had been going on, had now both gone out again. The lawyers, too, looked very tired. It was a wretched morning, the whole sky was over-cast, and the rain streamed down in bucketfuls. Mitya gazed blankly out of the window.

"May I look out of the window?" he asked Nikolay Parfenovitch, suddenly.

"Oh, as much as you like," the latter replied.

Mitya got up and went to the window. The rain lashed against the little greenish panes of the window. He could see the muddy road just below the window, and further away, in the rainy mist, a row of poor, black, dismal huts, looking even blacker and poorer in the rain. Mitya thought of "Phœbus the golden-haired," and how he had meant to shoot himself at his first ray. "Perhaps it would be even better on a morning like this," he thought with a smile, and suddenly, flinging his hand downwards, he turned to his "torturers."

"Gentlemen," he cried, "I see that I am lost! But she? Tell me about her, I beseech you. Surely she need not be ruined with me? She's innocent, you know, she was out of her mind when she cried last night 'it's all my fault!' She's done nothing, nothing! I've been grieving over her all night as I sat with you. . . . Can't you, won't you tell me what you are going to do with her now?"

"You can set your mind quite at rest on that score, Dmitri Fyodorovitch," the prosecutor answered at once, with evident alacrity. "We have, so far, no grounds for interfering with the lady in whom you are so interested. I trust that it may be the same in the later development of the case. . . . On the contrary, we'll do everything that lies in our power in that matter. Set your mind completely at rest."

"Gentlemen, I thank you. I knew that you were honest, straightforward people in spite of everything. You've taken a load off my heart. . . . Well, what are we to do now? I'm ready."

"Well, we ought to make haste. We must pass to examining the witnesses without delay. That must be done in your presence and therefore . . ."

"Shouldn't we have some tea first?" interposed Nikolay Parfenovitch, "I think we've deserved it!"

They decided that if tea were ready downstairs (Mihail Makarovitch had, no doubt, gone down to get some) they would have a glass and then "go on and on," putting off their proper breakfast until a more favourable opportunity. Tea really was ready below, and was soon brought up. Mitya at first refused the glass that Nikolay Parfenovitch politely offered him, but afterwards he asked for it himself and drank it greedily. He looked surprisingly exhausted. It might have been supposed from his herculean strength that one night of carousing, even accompanied by the most violent emotions, could have had little effect on him. But he felt that he could hardly hold his head up, and from time to time all the objects about him seemed heaving and dancing before his eyes. "A little more and I shall begin raving," he said to himself.

8

THE EVIDENCE OF THE WITNESSES. THE BABE

THE examination of the witnesses began. But we will not continue our story in such detail as before. And so we will not dwell on how Nikolay Parfenovitch impressed on every witness called that he must give his evidence in accordance with truth and conscience, and that he would afterwards have to repeat his evidence on oath, how every witness was called upon to sign the protocol of his evidence, and so on. We will only note that the point principally insisted upon in the examination was the question of the three thousand roubles, that is, was the sum spent here, at Mokroe, by Mitya on the first occasion, a month before, three thousand or fifteen hundred? And again had he spent three thousand or fifteen hundred yesterday? Alas, all the evidence given by every one turned out to be against Mitya. There was not one in his favour, and some witnesses introduced new, almost crushing facts, in contradiction of his, Mitya's, story.

The first witness examined was Trifon Borissovitch. He was not in the least abashed as he stood before the lawyers. He had, on the contrary, an air of stern and severe indignation with the accused, which gave him an appearance of truthfulness and personal dignity. He spoke little, and with reserve, waited to be questioned, answered precisely and deliberately. Firmly and unhesitatingly he bore witness that the sum spent a month before could not have been less than three thousand, that all the peasants about here would testify that they had heard the sum of three thousand mentioned by Dmitri Fyodorovitch himself. "What a lot of money he flung away on the gipsy girls alone. He wasted a thousand, I daresay, on them alone."

"I don't believe I gave them five hundred," was Mitya's gloomy comment on this. "It's a pity I didn't count the money at the time, but I was drunk. . . ."

Mitya was sitting sideways with his back to the curtains. He listened gloomily, with a melancholy and exhausted air, as though he would say:

"Oh, say what you like. It makes no difference now."

"More than a thousand went on them, Dmitri Fyodorovitch," retorted Trifon Borissovitch firmly. "You flung it about at random and they picked it up. They were a rascally, thievish lot, horse-stealers, they've been driven away from here, or maybe they'd bear witness themselves how much they got from you. I saw the sum in your hands, myself—count it I didn't, you didn't let me, that's true enough—but by the look of it I should say it was far more than fifteen hundred ... fifteen hundred, indeed! We've seen money too. We can judge of amount ..."

As for the sum spent yesterday he asserted that Dmitri Fyodorovitch had told him, as soon as he arrived, that he had brought three thousand with him.

"Come now, is that so, Trifon Borissovitch?" replied Mitya. "Surely I didn't declare so positively that I'd brought three thousand?"

"You did say so, Dmitri Fyodorovitch. You said it before Andrey. Andrey himself is still here. Send for him. And in the hall, when you were treating the chorus, you shouted straight out that you would leave your sixth thousand here—that is with what you spent before, we must understand. Stepan and Semyon heard it, and Pyotr Fomitch Kalganov, too, was standing beside you at the time. Maybe he'd remember it. . . ."

The evidence as to the "sixth" thousand made an extraordinary impression on the two lawyers. They were delighted with this new mode of reckoning, three and three made six, three thousand then and three now made six, that was clear.

They questioned all the peasants suggested by Trifon Borissovitch, Stepan and Semyon, the driver Andrey, and Kalganov. The peasants and the driver unhesitatingly confirmed Trifon Borissovitch's evidence. They noted down, with particular care, Andrey's account of the conversation he had had with Mitya on the road: "'Where,' says he, 'am I, Dmitri Fyodorovitch, going, to Heaven or to Hell, and shall I be forgiven in the next world or not?'"

The psychological Ippolit Kirillovitch heard this with a subtle smile, and ended by recommending that these remarks as to where Dmitri Fyodorovitch would go should be "included in the case."

Kalganov, when called, came in reluctantly, frowning and ill-humoured, and he spoke to the lawyers as though he had never met them before in his life, though they were acquaintances whom he had been meeting every day for a long time past. He began by saying that "he knew nothing about it and didn't want to." But it appeared that he had heard of the "sixth" thousand, and he admitted that he had been standing close by at the moment. As far as he could see he "didn't know" how much money Mitya had in his hands. He affirmed that the Poles had cheated at cards. In reply to reiterated questions he stated that, after the Poles had been turned out, Mitya's position with Agrafena Alexandrovna had certainly improved, and that she had said that she loved him. He spoke of Agrafena Alexandrovna with reserve and respect, as though she had been a lady of the best society, and did not once allow himself to call her Grushenka. In spite of the young man's obvious repugnance at giving evidence, Ippolit Kirillovitch examined him at great length, and only from him learnt all the details of what made up Mitya's "romance," so to say, on that night. Mitya did not once pull Kalganov up. At last they let the young man go, and he left the room with unconcealed indignation.

The Poles, too, were examined. Though they had gone to bed in their room, they had not slept all night, and on the arrival of the police officers they hastily dressed and got ready, realising that they would certainly be sent for. They gave their evidence with dignity, though not without some uneasiness. The little Pole turned out to be a retired official of the twelfth class,* who had served in Siberia as a veterinary surgeon. His name was Mussyalovitch. Pan Vrublevsky turned out to be an uncertificated dentist. Although Nikolay Parfenovitch asked them questions on entering the room they both addressed their answers to Mihail Makarovitch, who was standing on one side, taking him in their ignorance for the most important person and in command, and addressed him at every word as "Pan Colonel." Only after several reproofs from Mihail Makarovitch himself, they grasped that they had to address their answers only to Nikolay Parfenovitch. It turned out that they could speak Russian quite correctly except for their accent in some words. Of his relations with Grushenka, past and present, Pan Mussyalovitch spoke proudly and warmly, so that Mitya was roused at once and declared that he would not allow the "scoundrel" to speak like that in his presence! Pan Mussyalovitch at once called attention to the word "scoundrel," and begged that it should be put down in the protocol. Mitya fumed with rage.

"He's a scoundrel! A scoundrel! You can put that down. And put down, too, that, in spite of the protocol I still declare that he's a scoundrel!" he cried.

Though Nikolay Parfenovitch did insert this in the protocol, he showed the most praiseworthy tact and management. After sternly reprimanding Mitya, he cut short all further inquiry into the romantic aspect of the case, and hastened to pass to what was essential. One piece of evidence given by the Poles roused special interest in the lawyers: that was how, in that very room, Mitya had tried to buy off Pan Mussyalovitch, and had offered him three thousand roubles to resign his claims, seven hundred roubles down, and the remaining two thousand three hundred "to be paid next day in the town." He had sworn at the time that he had not the whole sum with him at Mokroe, but that his money was in the town. Mitya observed hotly that he had not said that he would be sure to pay him the remainder next day in the town. But Pan Vrublevsky confirmed the statement, and

*In the Table of Ranks, a bureaucratic hierarchy and system of promotion established by Czar Peter I in 1722, the twelfth rank was close to the lowest of the fourteen imperial civil service grades.

Mitya, after thinking for a moment admitted, frowning, that it must have been as the Poles stated, that he had been excited at the time, and might indeed have said so.

The prosecutor positively pounced on this piece of evidence. It seemed to establish for the prosecution (and they did, in fact, base this deduction on it) that half, or a part of, the three thousand that had come into Mitya's hands might really have been left somewhere hidden in the town, or even, perhaps, somewhere here, in Mokroe. This would explain the circumstance, so baffling for the prosecution, that only eight hundred roubles were to be found in Mitya's hands. This circumstance had been the one piece of evidence which, insignificant as it was, had hitherto told, to some extent, in Mitya's favour. Now this one piece of evidence in his favour had broken down. In answer to the prosecutor's inquiry, where he would have got the remaining two thousand three hundred roubles, since he himself had denied having more than fifteen hundred, Mitya confidently replied that he had meant to offer the "little chap," not money, but a formal deed of conveyance of his rights to the village of Tchermashnya, those rights which he had already offered to Samsonov and Madame Hohlakov. The prosecutor positively smiled at the "innocence of this subterfuge."

"And you imagine he would have accepted such a deed as a substitute for two thousand three hundred roubles in cash?"

"He certainly would have accepted it," Mitya declared warmly. "Why look here, he might have grabbed not two thousand, but four or six, for it. He would have put his lawyers, Poles and Jews, onto the job, and might have got, not three thousand, but the whole property out of the old man."

The evidence of Pan Mussyalovitch was, of course, entered into the protocol in the fullest detail. Then they let the Poles go. The incident of the cheating at cards was hardly touched upon. Nikolay Parfenovitch was too well pleased with them, as it was, and did not want to worry them with trifles, moreover, it was nothing but a foolish, drunken quarrel over cards. There had been drinking and disorder enough, that night. . . . So the two hundred roubles remained in the pockets of the Poles.

Then old Maximov was summoned. He came in timidly, approached with little steps, looking very dishevelled and depressed. He had, all this time, taken refuge below with Grushenka, sitting dumbly beside her, and "now and then he'd begin blubbering over her and wiping his eyes with a blue check handkerchief," as Mihail Makarovitch described afterwards. So that she, herself, began trying to pacify and comfort him. The old man at once confessed that he had done wrong, that he had borrowed "ten roubles in my poverty," from Dmitri Fyodorovitch, and that he was ready to pay it back. To Nikolay Parfenovitch's direct question, had he noticed how much money Dmitri Fyodorovitch held in his hand, as he must have been able to see the sum better than any one when he took the note from him, Maximov, in the most positive manner, declared that there was twenty thousand.

"Have you seen ever as much as twenty thousand before, then?" inquired Nikolay Parfenovitch, with a smile.

"To be sure I have, not twenty, but seven, when my wife mortgaged my little property. She'd only let me look at it from a distance, boasting of it to me. It was a very thick bundle, all rainbow-coloured notes. And Dmitri Fyodorovitch's were all rainbow-coloured. . . ."

He was not kept long. At last it was Grushenka's turn. Nikolay Parfenovitch was obviously apprehensive of the effect her appearance might have on Mitya, and he muttered a few words of admonition to him, but Mitya bowed his head in silence, giving him to understand "that he would not make a scene." Mihail Makarovitch, himself, led Grushenka in. She entered with a stern and gloomy face, that looked almost composed, and sat down quietly on the chair offered her by Nikolay Parfenovitch. She was very pale, she seemed to be cold, and wrapped herself closely in her magnificent black shawl. She was suffering from a slight feverish chill—the first symptom of the long illness which followed that night. Her grave air, her direct earnest look and quiet manner made a very favourable impression on every one. Nikolay Parfenovitch was even a little bit "fascinated." He admitted himself, when talking about it afterwards, that only then had he seen "how handsome the woman was," for, though he had seen her several times before, he had always looked upon her as something of a "provincial hetaira." "She has the manners of the best society," he said enthusiastically, gossiping about her in a circle of ladies. But this was received with positive indignation by the ladies, who immediately called him a "naughty man," to his great satisfaction.

As she entered the room, Grushenka only glanced for an instant at Mitya, who looked at her uneasily. But her face reassured him at once. After the first inevitable inquiries and warnings, Nikolay Parfenovitch asked her, hesitating a little, but preserving the most courteous manner, on what terms she was with the retired lieutenant, Dmitri Fyodorovitch Karamazov. To this Grushenka firmly and quietly replied:

"He was an acquaintance. He came to see me as an acquaintance during the last month." To further inquisitive questions she answered plainly and with complete frankness, that, though "at times" she had thought him attractive, she had not loved him, but had won his heart as well as his old father's "in my nasty spite," that she had seen that Mitya was very jealous of Fyodor Pavlovitch and every one else; but that had only amused her. She had never meant to go to Fyodor Pavlovitch, she had simply been laughing at him.

"I had no thoughts for either of them all this last month. I was expecting another man who had wronged me. But I think," she said in conclusion, "that there's no need for you to inquire about that, nor for me to answer you, for that's my own affair."

Nikolay Parfenovitch immediately acted upon this hint. He again dismissed the "romantic" aspect of the case and passed to the serious one, that is, to the question of most importance, concerning the three thousand roubles. Grushenka confirmed the statement that three thousand roubles had certainly been spent on the first carousal at Mokroe, and, though she had not counted the money herself, she had heard that it was three thousand from Dmitri Fyodorovitch's own lips.

"Did he tell you that alone, or before some one else, or did you only hear him speak of it to others in your presence?" the prosecutor inquired immediately.

To which Grushenka replied that she had heard him say so before other people, and had heard him say so when they were alone.

"Did he say it to you alone once, or several times?" inquired the prosecutor, and learned that he had told Grushenka so several times.

Ippolit Kirillovitch was very well satisfied with this piece of evidence. Further examination elicited that Grushenka knew, too, where that money had come from, and that Dmitri Fyodorovitch had got it from Katerina Ivanovna.

"And did you never, once, hear that the money spent a month ago was not three thousand, but less, and that Dmitri Fyodorovitch had saved half that sum for his own use?"

"No, I never heard that," answered Grushenka.

It was explained further that Mitya had, on the contrary, often told her that he hadn't a farthing.

"He was always expecting to get some from his father," said Grushenka in conclusion.

"Did he never say before you . . . casually, or in a moment of irritation," Nikolay Parfenovitch put in suddenly, "that he intended to make an attempt on his father's life?"

"Ach, he did say so," sighed Grushenka.

"Once or several times?"

"He mentioned it several times, always in anger."

"And did you believe he would do it?"

"No, I never believed it," she answered firmly. "I had faith in his noble heart."

"Gentlemen, allow me," cried Mitya suddenly, "allow me to say one word to Agrafena Alexandrovna, in your presence."

"You can speak," Nikolay Parfenovitch assented.

"Agrafena Alexandrovna!" Mitya got up from his chair, "have faith in God and in me. I am not guilty of my father's murder!"

Having uttered these words Mitya sat down again on his chair. Grushenka stood up and crossed herself devoutly before the ikon.

"Thanks be to Thee, O Lord," she said, in a voice thrilled with emotion, and still standing, she turned to Nikolay Parfenovitch and added:

"As he has spoken now, believe it! I know him. He'll say anything as a joke or from obstinacy, but he'll never deceive you against his conscience. He's telling the whole truth, you may believe it."

"Thanks, Agrafena Alexandrovna, you've given me fresh courage," Mitya responded in a quivering voice.

As to the money spent the previous day, she declared that she did not know what sum it was, but had heard him tell several people that he had three thousand with him. And to the question where he got the money, she said that he had told her that he had "stolen" it from Katerina Ivanovna, and that she had replied to that that he hadn't stolen it, and that he must pay the money back next day. On the prosecutor's asking her emphatically whether the money he said he had stolen from Katerina Ivanovna was what he had spent yesterday, or what he had squandered here a month ago, she declared that he meant the money spent a month ago, and that that was how she understood him.

Grushenka was at last released, and Nikolay Parfenovitch informed her impulsively that she might at once return to the town and that if he could be of any assistance to her, with horses for example, or if she would care for an escort he . . . would, be . . .

"I thank you sincerely," said Grushenka, bowing to him, "I'm going with this old gentleman, I am driving him back to town with me, and meanwhile, if you'll allow me, I'll wait below to hear what you decide about Dmitri Fyodorovitch."

She went out, Mitya was calm, and even looked more cheerful, but only for a moment. He felt more and more oppressed by a strange physical weakness. His eyes were closing with fatigue. The examination of the witnesses was, at last, over. They proceeded to a final revision of the protocol. Mitya got up, moved from his chair to the corner by the curtain, lay down on a large chest covered with a rug, and instantly fell asleep.

He had a strange dream, utterly out of keeping with the place and the time.

He was driving somewhere in the steppes, where he had been stationed long ago, and a peasant was driving him in a cart with a pair of horses, through snow and sleet. He was cold, it was early in November, and the snow was falling in big wet flakes, melting as soon as it touched the earth. And the peasant drove him smartly, he had a fair, long beard. He was not an old man, somewhere about fifty, and he had on a grey peasant's smock. Not far off was a village, he could see the black huts, and half the huts were burnt down, there were only the charred beams sticking up. And as they drove in, there were peasant women drawn up along the road, a lot of women, a whole row, all thin and wan, with their faces a sort of brownish colour, especially one at the edge, a tall, bony woman, who looked forty, but might have been only twenty, with a long thin face. And in her arms was a little baby crying. And her breasts seemed so dried up that there was not a drop of milk in them. And the child cried and cried, and held out its little bare arms, with its little fists blue from cold.

"Why are they crying? Why are they crying?" Mitya asked, as they dashed gaily by.

"It's the babe," answered the driver, "the babe weeping."

And Mitya was struck by his saying, in his peasant way, "the babe," and he liked the peasant's calling it a "babe." There seemed more pity in it.

"But why is it weeping?" Mitya persisted stupidly, "why are its little arms bare? Why don't they wrap it up?"

"The babe's cold, its little clothes are frozen and don't warm it."

"But why is it? Why?" foolish Mitya still persisted.

"Why, they're poor people, burnt out. They've no bread. They're begging because they've been burnt out."

"No, no," Mitya, as it were, still did not understand. "Tell me why it is those poor mothers stand there? Why are people poor? Why is the babe poor? Why is the steppe barren? Why don't they hug each other and kiss? Why don't they sing songs of joy? Why are they so dark from black misery? Why don't they feed the babe?"

And he felt that, though his questions were unreasonable and senseless, yet he wanted to ask just that, and he had to ask it just in that way. And he felt that a passion of pity, such as he had never known before, was rising in his heart, that he wanted to cry, that he wanted to do something for them all, so that the babe should weep no more, so that the dark-faced, dried-up mother should not weep, that no one should shed tears again from that moment, and he wanted to do it at once, at once, regardless of all obstacles, with all the recklessness of the Karamazovs.

"And I'm coming with you. I won't leave you now for the rest of my life, I'm coming with you," he heard close beside him Grushenka's tender voice, thrilling with emotion. And his heart glowed, and he struggled forward towards the light, and he longed to live, to live, to go on and on, towards the new, beckoning light, and to hasten, hasten, now, at once!

"What! Where?" he exclaimed opening his eyes, and sitting up on the chest, as though he had revived from a swoon, smiling brightly. Nikolay Parfenovitch was standing over him, suggesting that he should hear the protocol read aloud and sign it. Mitya guessed that he had been asleep an hour or more, but he did not hear Nikolay Parfenovitch. He was suddenly struck by the fact that there was a pillow under his head, which hadn't been there when he had leant back, exhausted, on the chest.

"Who put that pillow under my head? Who was so kind?" he cried, with a sort of ecstatic gratitude, and tears in his voice, as though some great kindness had been shown him.

He never found out who this kind man was, perhaps one of the peasant witnesses, or Nikolay Parfenovitch's little secretary had compassionately thought to put a pillow under his head, but his whole soul was quivering with tears. He went to the table and said that he would sign whatever they liked.

"I've had a good dream, gentlemen," he said in a strange voice, with a new light, as of joy, in his face.

9

THEY CARRY MITYA AWAY

WHEN the protocol had been signed, Nikolay Parfenovitch turned solemnly to the prisoner and read him the "Committal," setting forth, that in such a year, on such a day, in such a place, the investigating lawyer of such-and-such a district court, having examined so-and-so (to wit, Mitya) accused of this and of that (all the charges were carefully written out) and having considered that the accused, not pleading guilty to the charges made against him had brought forward nothing in his defence, while the witnesses, so-and-so, and so-and-so, and the circumstances such-and-such testify against him, acting in accordance with such-and-such articles of the Statute Book, and so on, has ruled, that, in order to preclude such-and-such (Mitya) from all means of evading pursuit and judgment he be detained in such-and-such a prison, which he hereby notifies to the accused and communicates a copy of this same "Committal" to the deputy prosecutor, and so on, and so on.

In brief, Mitya was informed that he was, from that moment, a prisoner, and that he would be driven at once to the town, and there shut up in a very unpleasant place. Mitya listened attentively, and only shrugged his shoulders.

"Well, gentlemen, I don't blame you. I'm ready. . . . I understand that there's nothing else for you to do."

Nikolay Parfenovitch informed him gently that he would be escorted at once by the rural police officer, Mavriky Mavrikyevitch, who happened to be on the spot. . . .

"Stay," Mitya interrupted, suddenly, and impelled by uncontrollable feeling he pronounced, addressing all in the room:

"Gentlemen, we're all cruel, we're all monsters, we all make men weep, and mothers, and babes at the breast, but of all, let it be settled here, now, of all I am the lowest reptile! I've sworn to amend, and every day I've done the same filthy things. I understand now that such men as I need a blow, a blow of destiny to catch them as with a noose, and bind them by a force from without. Never, never should I have risen of myself! But the thunderbolt has fallen.* I accept the torture of accusation, and my public shame, I want to suffer and by suffering I shall be purified. Perhaps I shall be purified, gentlemen? But listen, for the last time, I am not guilty of my father's blood.

---

*Allusion to the Russian proverb "Until the thunder strikes, the peasant will not cross himself."

I accept my punishment, not because I killed him, but because I meant to kill him, and perhaps I really might have killed him. Still I mean to fight it out with you, I warn you of that. I'll fight it out with you to the end, and then God will decide. Good-bye, gentlemen, don't be vexed with me for having shouted at you during the examination. Oh, I was still such a fool then. . . . In another minute I shall be a prisoner, but now, for the last time, as a free man, Dmitri Karamazov offers you his hand. Saying good-bye to you, I say it to all men."

His voice quivered and he stretched out his hand, but Nikolay Parfenovitch, who happened to stand nearest to him, with a sudden, almost nervous movement, hid his hands behind his back. Mitya instantly noticed this, and started. He let his outstretched hand fall at once.

"The preliminary inquiry is not yet over," Nikolay Parfenovitch faltered, somewhat embarrassed. "We will continue it in the town, and I, for my part, of course, am ready to wish you all success . . . in your defence. . . . As a matter of fact, Dmitri Fyodorovitch, I've always been disposed to regard you as, so to speak, more unfortunate than guilty. All of us here, if I may make bold to speak for all, we are all ready to recognise that you are, at bottom, a young man of honour, but, alas, one who has been carried away by certain passions to a somewhat excessive degree. . . ."

Nikolay Parfenovitch's little figure was positively majestic by the time he had finished speaking. It struck Mitya that in another minute this "boy" would take his arm, lead him to another corner, and renew their conversation about "girls." But many quite irrelevant and inappropriate thoughts sometimes occur even to a prisoner when he is being led out to execution.

"Gentlemen, you are good, you are humane, may I see *her* to say 'good-bye' for the last time?" asked Mitya.

"Certainly, but considering . . . in fact, now it's impossible except in the presence of . . ."

"Oh, well, if it must be so, it must!"

Grushenka was brought in, but the farewell was brief, and of few words, and did not at all satisfy Nikolay Parfenovitch. Grushenka made a deep bow to Mitya.

"I have told you I am yours, and I will be yours. I will follow you for ever, wherever they may send you. Farewell; you are guiltless, though you've been your own undoing."

Her lips quivered, tears flowed from her eyes.

"Forgive me, Grusha, for my love, for ruining you, too, with my love."

Mitya would have said something more, but he broke off and went out. He was at once surrounded by men who kept a constant watch on him. At the bottom of the steps to which he had driven up with such a dash the day before with Andrey's three horses, two carts stood in readiness. Mavriky Mavrikyevitch, a sturdy, thick-set man with a wrinkled face, was annoyed about something, some sudden irregularity. He was shouting angrily. He asked Mitya to get into the cart with somewhat excessive surliness.

"When I stood him drinks in the tavern, the man had quite a different face," thought Mitya, as he got in. At the gates there was a crowd of people, peasants, women and drivers. Trifon Borissovitch came down the steps too. All stared at Mitya.

"Forgive me at parting, good people!" Mitya shouted suddenly from the cart.

"Forgive us too!" he heard two or three voices.

"Good-bye to you, too, Trifon Borissovitch!"

But Trifon Borissovitch did not even turn round. He was, perhaps, too busy. He, too, was shouting and fussing about something. It appeared that everything was not yet ready in the second cart, in which two constables were to accompany Mavriky Mavrikyevitch. The peasant who had been ordered to drive the second cart was pulling on his smock, stoutly maintaining that it was not his turn to go, but Akim's. But Akim was not to be seen. They ran to look for him. The peasant persisted and besought them to wait.

"You see what our peasants are, Mavriky Mavrikyevitch. They've no shame!" exclaimed Trifon Borissovitch. "Akim gave you twenty-five kopecks the day before yesterday. You've drunk it all and now you cry out. I'm simply surprised at your good-nature, with our low peasants, Mavriky Mavrikyevitch, that's all I can say."

"But what do we want a second cart for?" Mitya put in. "Let's start with the one, Mavriky Mavrikyevitch. I won't be unruly, I won't run away from you, old fellow. What do we want an escort for?"

"I'll trouble you, sir, to learn how to speak to me if you've never been taught. I'm not 'old fellow' to you, and you can keep your advice for another time!" Mavriky Mavrikyevitch snapped out savagely, as though glad to vent his wrath.

Mitya was reduced to silence. He flushed all over. A moment later he felt suddenly very cold. The rain had ceased, but the dull sky was still overcast with clouds, and a keen wind was blowing straight in his face.

"I've taken a chill," thought Mitya, twitching his shoulders.

At last Mavriky Mavrikyevitch, too, got into the cart, sat down heavily, and, as though without noticing it, squeezed Mitya into the corner. It is true that he was out of humour and greatly disliked the task that had been laid upon him.

"Good-bye, Trifon Borissovitch!" Mitya shouted again, and felt himself, that he had not called out this time from good-nature, but involuntarily, from resentment.

But Trifon Borissovitch stood proudly, with both hands behind his back, and staring straight at Mitya with a stern and angry face, he made no reply.

"Good-bye, Dmitri Fyodorovitch, good-bye!" he heard all at once the voice of Kalganov, who had suddenly darted out. Running up to the cart he held out his hand to Mitya. He had no cap on.

Mitya had time to seize and press his hand.

"Good-bye, dear fellow! I shan't forget your generosity," he cried warmly.

But the cart moved and their hands parted. The bell began ringing and Mitya was driven off.

Kalganov ran back, sat down in a corner, bent his head, hid his face in his hands, and burst out crying. For a long while he sat like that, crying as though he were a little boy instead of a young man of twenty. Oh, he believed almost without doubt in Mitya's guilt.

"What are these people? What can men be after this?" he exclaimed incoherently, in bitter despondency, almost despair. At that moment he had no desire to live.

"Is it worth it? Is it worth it?" exclaimed the boy in his grief.

PART FOUR

BOOK TEN

THE BOYS

1

KOLYA KRASSOTKIN

IT was the beginning of November. There had been a hard frost, eleven degrees Réaumur, without snow, but a little dry snow had fallen on the frozen ground during the night, and a keen dry wind was lifting and blowing it along the dreary streets of our town, especially about the market-place. It was a dull morning, but the snow had ceased.

Not far from the market-place, close to Plotnikov's shop, there stood a small house, very clean both without and within. It belonged to Madame Krassotkin, the widow of a former provincial secretary, who had been dead for fourteen years. His widow, still a nice-looking woman of thirty-two, was living in her neat little house on her private means. She lived in respectable seclusion; she was of a soft but fairly cheerful disposition. She was about eighteen at the time of her husband's death; she had been married only a year and had just borne him a son. From the day of his death she had devoted herself heart and soul to the bringing up of her precious treasure, her boy Kolya. Though she had loved him passionately those fourteen years, he had caused her far more suffering than happiness. She had been trembling and fainting with terror almost every day, afraid he would fall ill, would catch cold, do something naughty, climb on a chair and fall off it, and so on and so on. When Kolya began going to school, the mother devoted herself to studying all the sciences with him so as to help him, and go through his lessons with him. She hastened to make the acquaintance of the teachers and their wives, even made up to Kolya's schoolfellows, and fawned upon them in the hope of thus saving Kolya from being teased, laughed at, or beaten by them. She went so far that the boys actually began to mock at him on her account, and taunt him with being a "mother's darling."

But the boy could take his own part. He was a resolute boy, "tremendously strong," as was rumoured in his class, and soon proved to be the fact; he was agile, strong-willed, and of an audacious and enterprising temper. He was good at lessons, and there was a rumour in the school that he could beat the teacher, Dardanelov, at arithmetic and universal history. Though he looked down upon every one, he was a good comrade and not supercilious. He accepted his schoolfellow's respect as his due, but was friendly with them. Above all, he knew where to draw the line. He could restrain himself on occasion, and in his relations with the teachers he never overstepped that last mystic limit beyond which a prank became an unpardonable breach of discipline. But he was as fond of mischief on every possible occasion as the smallest boy in the school, and not so much for the sake of mischief as for creating a sensation, inventing something, doing something effective and conspicuous. He was extremely vain. He knew how to make even his mother give way to him; he was almost despotic in his control of her. She gave way to him, oh, she had given way to him for years. The one thought unendurable to her was that her boy had no great love for her. She was always fancying that Kolya was "unfeeling" to her, and at times, dissolving into hysterical tears, she used to reproach him with his coldness. The boy disliked this, and the more demonstrations of feeling were demanded of him the more he seemed intentionally to avoid them. Yet it was not intentional on his part but instinctive—it was his character. His mother was mistaken; he was very fond of her. He only disliked "sheepish sentimentality," as he expressed it in his school-boy language.

There was a bookcase in the house containing a few books that had been his father's. Kolya was fond of reading, and had read several of them by himself. His mother did not mind that and only wondered sometimes at seeing the boy stand for hours by the bookcase poring over a book instead of going to play. And in that way Kolya read some things unsuitable for his age.

Though the boy, as a rule, knew where to draw the line in his mischief, he had of late begun to play pranks that caused his mother serious alarm. It is true there was nothing vicious in what he did, but a wild, mad recklessness.

It happened that July, during the summer holidays, that the mother and son went to another district, forty-five miles away, to spend a week with a distant relation, whose husband was an official at the railway station (the very station, the nearest one to our town, from which a month later Ivan Fyodorovitch Karamazov set off for Moscow). There Kolya began by carefully investigating every detail connected with the railway, knowing that he could impress his schoolfellows when he got home with his newly acquired knowledge. But there happened to be some other boys in the place with whom he soon made friends. Some of them were living at the station, others in the neighbourhood; there were six or seven of them, all between twelve and fifteen, and two of them came from our town. The boys played together, and on the fourth or fifth day of Kolya's stay at the station, a mad bet was made by the foolish boys. Kolya, who was almost the youngest of the party and rather looked down upon by the others in consequence, was moved by vanity or by reckless bravado to bet them two roubles that he would lie down between the rails at night when the eleven o'clock train was due, and would lie there without moving while the train rolled over him at full speed. It is true they made a preliminary investigation, from which it appeared that it was possible to lie so flat between the rails that the train could pass over without touching, but to lie there was no joke! Kolya maintained stoutly that he would. At first they laughed at him, called him a little liar, a braggart, but that only egged him on. What piqued him most was that these boys of fifteen turned up their noses at him too superciliously, and were at first disposed to treat him as "a small boy," not fit to associate with them, and that was an unendurable insult.

And so it was resolved to go in the evening, half a mile from the station, so that the train might have time to get up full speed after leaving the station. The boys assembled. It was a pitch dark night without a moon. At the time fixed, Kolya lay down between the rails. The five others who had taken the bet waited among the bushes below the embankment, their hearts beating with suspense, which was followed by alarm and remorse. At last they heard in the distance the rumble of the train leaving the station. Two red lights gleamed out of the darkness; the monster roared as it approached.

"Run, run away from the rails," the boys cried to Kolya from the bushes, breathless with terror. But it was too late: the train darted up and flew past. The boys rushed to Kolya. He lay without moving. They began pulling at him, lifting him up. He suddenly got up and walked away without a word. Then he explained that he had lain there as though he were insensible to frighten them, but the fact was that he really had lost consciousness, as he confessed long after to his mother. In this way his reputation as "a desperate character," was established for ever. He returned home to the station as white as a sheet. Next day he had a slight attack of nervous fever, but he was in high spirits and well pleased with himself. The incident did not become known at once, but when they came back to the town it penetrated to the school and even reached the ears of the masters. But then Kolya's mother hastened to entreat the masters on her boy's behalf, and in the end Dardanelov, a respected and influential teacher, exerted himself in his favour, and the affair was ignored.

Dardanelov was a middle-aged bachelor, who had been passionately in love with Madame Krassotkin for many years past, and had once already, about a year previously, ventured, trembling with fear and the delicacy of his sentiments, to offer her most respectfully his hand in marriage. But she refused him resolutely, feeling that to accept him would be an act of treachery to her son, though Dardanelov had, to judge from certain mysterious symptoms, reason for believing that he was not an object of aversion to the charming but too chaste and tenderhearted widow. Kolya's mad prank seemed to have broken the ice, and Dardanelov was rewarded for his intercession by a suggestion of hope. The suggestion, it is true, was a faint one, but then Dardanelov was such a paragon of purity and delicacy that it was enough for the time being to make him perfectly happy. He was fond of the boy, though he would have felt it beneath him to try and win him over, and was severe and strict with him in class. Kolya, too, kept him at a respectful distance. He learned his lessons perfectly; he was second in his class, was reserved with Dardanelov, and the whole class firmly believed that Kolya was so good at universal history that he could "beat" even Dardanelov. Kolya did indeed ask him the question, "Who founded Troy?" to which Dardanelov had made a very vague reply, referring to the movements and migrations of races, to the remoteness of the period, to the mythical legends. But the question, "Who had founded Troy?" that is, what individuals, he could not answer, and even for some reason regarded the question as idle and frivolous. But the boys remained convinced that Dardanelov did not know who founded Troy. Kolya had read of the founders of Troy in Smaragdov, whose history was among the books in his father's bookcase. In the end all the boys became interested in the question, who it was that had founded Troy, but Krassotkin would not tell his secret, and his reputation for knowledge remained unshaken.

After the incident on the railway a certain change came over Kolya's attitude to his mother. When Anna Fyodorovna (Madame Krassotkin) heard of her son's exploit, she almost went out of her mind with horror. She had such terrible attacks of hysterics, lasting with intervals for several days that Kolya, seriously alarmed at last, promised on his honour that such pranks should never be repeated. He swore on his knees before the holy image, and swore by the memory of his father, at Madame Krassotkin's instance, and the "manly" Kolya burst into tears like a boy of six. And all that day the mother and son were constantly rushing into each other's arms sobbing. Next day Kolya woke up as "unfeeling" as before, but he had become more silent, more modest, sterner, and more thoughtful.

Six weeks later, it is true, he got into another scrape, which even brought his name to the ears of our Justice of the Peace, but it was a scrape of quite another kind, amusing, foolish, and he did not, as it turned out, take the leading part in it, but was only implicated in it. But of this later. His mother still fretted and trembled, but the more uneasy she became, the greater were the hopes of Dardanelov. It must be noted that Kolya understood and divined what was in Dardanelov's heart and, of course, despised him profoundly for his "feelings"; he had in the past been so tactless as to show this contempt before his mother, hinting vaguely that he knew what Dardanelov was after. But from the time of the railway incident his behaviour in this respect also was changed; he did not allow himself the remotest allusion to the subject and began to speak more respectfully of Dardanelov before his mother, which the sensitive woman at once appreciated with boundless gratitude. But at the slightest mention of Dardanelov by a visitor in Kolya's presence, she would flush as pink as a rose. At such moments Kolya would either stare out of the window scowling, or would investigate the state of his boots, or would shout angrily for "Perezvon,"* the big, shaggy, mangy dog, which he had picked up a month before, brought home, and kept for some reason secretly indoors, not showing him to any of his schoolfellows. He bullied him frightfully, teaching him all sorts of tricks, so that the poor dog howled for him whenever he was absent at school, and when he came in, whined with delight, rushed about as if he were crazy, begged, lay down on the ground pretending to be dead, and so on; in fact, showed all the tricks he had taught him, not at the word of command, but simply from the zeal of his excited and grateful heart.

---

*The name is also the Russian word meaning "chime" or "ringing"; it refers moreover to "chain ringing or the ringing of each bell in turn" in the Russian Orthodox church.

I have forgotten, by the way, to mention that Kolya Krassotkin was the boy stabbed with a penknife by the boy already known to the reader as the son of Captain Snegiryov. Ilusha had been defending his father when the schoolboys jeered at him, shouting the nickname "wisp of tow."

2

CHILDREN

AND so on that frosty, snowy, and windy day in November, Kolya Krassotkin was sitting at home. It was Sunday and there was no school. It had just struck eleven, and he particularly wanted to go out "on very urgent business," but he was left alone in charge of the house, for it so happened that all its elder inmates were absent owing to a sudden and singular event. Madame Krassotkin had let two little rooms, separated from the rest of the house by a passage, to a doctor's wife with her two small children. This lady was the same age as Anna Fyodorovna, and a great friend of hers. Her husband, the doctor, had taken his departure twelve months before, going first to Orenburg and then to Tashkend, and for the last six months she had not heard a word from him. Had it not been for her friendship with Madame Krassotkin, which was some consolation to the forsaken lady, she would certainly have completely dissolved away in tears. And now, to add to her misfortunes, Katerina, her only servant, was suddenly moved the evening before to announce, to her mistress's amazement, that she proposed to bring a child into the world before morning. It seemed almost miraculous to every one that no one had noticed the probability of it before. The astounded doctor's wife decided to move Katerina while there was still time to an establishment in the town kept by a midwife for such emergencies. As she set great store by her servant, she promptly carried out this plan and remained there looking after her. By the morning all Madame Krassotkin's friendly sympathy and energy were called upon to render assistance and appeal to some one for help in the case.

So both the ladies were absent from home, the Krassotkin's servant, Agafya, had gone out to the market, and Kolya was thus left for a time to protect and look after "the kids," that is, the son and daughter of the doctor's wife, who were left alone. Kolya was not afraid of taking care of the house, besides he had Perezvon, who had been told to lie flat, without moving, under the bench in the hall. Every time Kolya, walking to and fro through the rooms, came into the hall, the dog shook his head and gave two loud and insinuating taps on the floor with his tail, but alas! the whistle did not sound to release him. Kolya looked sternly at the luckless dog, who relapsed again into obedient rigidity. The one thing that troubled Kolya was "the kids." He looked, of course, with the utmost scorn on Katerina's unexpected adventure, but he was very fond of the bereaved "kiddies," and had already taken them a picture book. Nastya, the elder, a girl of eight, could read, and Kostya, the boy, aged seven, was very fond of being read to by her. Krassotkin could, of course, have provided more diverting entertainment for them. He could have made them stand side by side and played soldiers with them, or send them hiding all over the house. He had done so more than once before and was not above doing it, so much so that a report once spread at school that Krassotkin played horses with the little lodgers at home, prancing with his head on one side like a race-horse. But Krassotkin haughtily parried this thrust, pointing out that to play horses with boys of one's own age, boys of thirteen, would certainly be disgraceful "at this date," but that he did it for the sake of "the kids" because he liked them, and no one had a right to call him to account for his feelings. The two "kids" adored him.

But on this occasion he was in no mood for games. He had very important business of his own before him, something almost mysterious. Meanwhile time was passing and Agafya, with whom he could have left the children, would not come back from market. He had several times already crossed the passage, opened the door of the lodgers' room and looked anxiously at the kids who were sitting over the book, as he had bidden them. Every time he opened the door they grinned at him, hoping he would come in and would do something delightful and amusing. But Kolya was bothered and did not go in.

At last it struck eleven and he made up his mind, once for all, that if that "damned" Agafya did not come back within ten minutes he should go out without waiting for her, making the kids "promise," of course, to be brave when he was away, not to be naughty, not to cry from fright. With this idea he put on his wadded winter overcoat with its catskin fur collar, slung his satchel round his shoulder, and, regardless of his mother's constantly reiterated entreaties that he would always put on goloshes in such cold weather, he looked at them contemptuously as he crossed the hall and went out with only his boots on. Perezvon, seeing him in his outdoor clothes, began tapping vigorously on the floor with his tail, nervously. Twitching all over, he even uttered a plaintive whine. But Kolya, seeing his dog's passionate excitement, decided that it was a breach of discipline, kept him for another minute under the bench, and only when he had opened the door into the passage he whistled for him. The dog leapt up like a mad creature and rushed before him rapturously.

Kolya opened the door to peep at the kids. They were both sitting as before at the table, not reading but warmly disputing about something. The children often argued together about various exciting problems of life, and Nastya, being the elder, always got the best of it. If Kostya did not agree with her, he almost always appealed to Kolya Krassotkin, and his verdict was regarded as infallible by both of them. This time the kids' discussion rather interested Krassotkin, and he stood still in the passage to listen. The children saw he was listening and that made them dispute with even greater energy.

"I shall never, never believe," Nastya prattled, "that the old women find babies among the cabbages in the kitchen garden. It's winter now and there are no cabbages, and so the old woman couldn't have taken Katerina a daughter."

Kolya whistled to himself.

"Or perhaps they do bring babies from somewhere, but only to those who are married."

Kostya stared at Nastya and listened, pondering profoundly.

"Nastya, how silly you are," he said at last, firmly and calmly. "How can Katerina have a baby when she isn't married?"

Nastya was exasperated.

"You know nothing about it," she snapped irritably. "Perhaps she has a husband, only he is in prison, so now she's got a baby."

"But is her husband in prison?" the matter-of-fact Kostya inquired gravely.

"Or, I tell you what," Nastya interrupted impulsively, completely rejecting and forgetting her first hypothesis. "She hasn't a husband, you are right there, but she wants to be married, and so she's been thinking of getting married, and thinking and thinking of it till now she's got it, that is, not a husband but a baby."

"Well, perhaps so," Kostya agreed, entirely vanquished. "But you didn't say so before. So how could I tell?"

"Come, kiddies," said Kolya, stepping into the room. "You're terrible people, I see."

"And Perezvon with you!" grinned Kostya, and began snapping his fingers and calling Perezvon.

"I am in a difficulty, kids," Krassotkin began solemnly, "and you must help me. Agafya must have broken her leg, since she has not turned up till now, that's certain. I must go out. Will you let me go?"

The children looked anxiously at one another. Their smiling faces showed signs of uneasiness, but they did not yet fully grasp what was expected of them.

"You won't be naughty while I am gone? You won't climb on the cupboard and break your legs? You won't be frightened alone and cry?"

A look of profound despondency came into the children's faces.

"And I could show you something as a reward, a little copper cannon which can be fired with real gunpowder."

The children's faces instantly brightened. "Show us the cannon," said Kostya, beaming all over.

Krassotkin put his hand in his satchel, and pulling out a little bronze cannon stood it on the table.

"Ah, you are bound to ask that! Look, it's on wheels." He rolled the toy along on the table. "And it can be fired off, too. It can be loaded with shot and fired off."

"And it could kill any one?"

"It can kill any one; you've only got to aim at anybody," and Krassotkin explained where the powder had to be put, where the shot should be rolled in, showed a tiny hole like a touch hole, and told them that it kicked when it was fired.

The children listened with intense interest. What particularly struck their imagination was that the cannon kicked.

"And have you got any powder?" Nastya inquired.

"Yes."

"Show us the powder, too," she drawled with a smile of entreaty.

Krassotkin dived again into his satchel and pulled out a small flask containing a little real gunpowder. He had some shot, too, in a screw of paper. He even uncorked the flask and shook a little powder into the palm of his hand.

"One has to be careful there's no fire about, or it would blow up and kill us all," Krassotkin warned them sensationally.

The children gazed at the powder with an awe-striken alarm that only intensified their enjoyment. But Kostya liked the shot better.

"And does the shot burn?" he inquired.

"No, it doesn't."

"Give me a little shot," he asked in an imploring voice.

"I'll give you a little shot; here, take it, but don't show it to your mother till I come back, or she'll be sure to think it's gunpowder, and will die of fright and give you a thrashing."

"Mother never does whip us," Nastya observed at once.

"I know, I only said it to finish the sentence. And don't you ever deceive your mother except just this once, until I come back. And so, kiddies, can I go out? You won't be frightened and cry when I'm gone?"

"We sha—all cry," drawled Kostya, on the verge of tears already.

"We shall cry, we shall be sure to cry," Nastya chimed in with timid haste.

"Oh, children, children, how fraught with peril are your years!* There's no help for it, chickens, I shall have to stay with you I don't know how long. And time is passing, time is passing, oogh!"

"Tell Perezvon to pretend to be dead!" Kostya begged.

"There's no help for it, we must have recourse to Perezvon. *Ici,*† Perezvon." And Kolya began giving orders to the dog, who performed all his tricks.

He was a rough-haired dog, of medium size, with a coat of a sort of lilac-grey colour. He was blind in his right eye, and his left ear was torn. He

---

*Start of "The Cock, the Tom-Cat and the Little Mouse" (1802), a fable in verse by I. I. Dmitriyev.
†Here (French).

whined and jumped, stood and walked on his hind legs, lay on his back with his paws in the air, rigid as though he were dead. While this last performance was going on, the door was opened and Agafya, Madame Krassotkin's servant, a stout woman of forty, marked with smallpox, appeared in the doorway. She had come back from market and had a bag full of provisions in her hand. Holding up the bag of provisions in her left hand she stood still to watch the dog. Though Kolya had been so anxious for her return, he did not cut short the performance, and after keeping Perezvon dead for the usual time, at last he whistled to him. The dog jumped up and began bounding about in his joy at having done his duty.

"Only think, a dog!" Agafya observed sententiously.

"Why are you late, female?" asked Krassotkin sternly.

"Female, indeed! Go on with you, you brat."

"Brat?"

"Yes, a brat. What is it to you if I'm late; if I'm late, you may be sure I have good reason," muttered Agafya, busying herself about the stove, without a trace of anger or displeasure in her voice. She seemed quite pleased, in fact, to enjoy a skirmish with her merry young master.

"Listen, you frivolous old woman," Krassotkin began, getting up from the sofa, "can you swear by all you hold sacred in the world and something else besides, that you will watch vigilantly over the kids in my absence? I am going out."

"And what am I going to swear for?" laughed Agafya. "I shall look after them without that."

"No, you must swear on your eternal salvation. Else I shan't go."

"Well, don't then. What does it matter to me? It's cold out; stay at home."

"Kids," Kolya turned to the children, "this woman will stay with you till I come back or till your mother comes, for she ought to have been back long ago. She will give you some lunch, too. You'll give them something, Agafya, won't you?"

"That I can do."

"Good-bye, chickens, I go with my heart at rest. And you, granny," he added gravely, in an undertone, as he passed Agafya, "I hope you'll spare their tender years and not tell them any of your old woman's nonsense about Katerina. *Ici*, Perezvon!"

"Get along with you!" retorted Agafya, really angry this time. "Ridiculous boy! You want a whipping for saying such things, that's what you want!"

3

THE SCHOOLBOY

B UT Kolya did not hear her. At last he could go out. As he went out
at the gate he looked round him, shrugged up his shoulders, and
saying "It is freezing," went straight along the street and turned off
to the right towards the market-place. When he reached the last house but
one before the market-place he stopped at the gate, pulled a whistle out of
his pocket, and whistled with all his might as though giving a signal. He had
not to wait more than a minute before a rosy-cheeked boy of about eleven,
wearing a warm, neat, and even stylish coat, darted out to meet him. This
was Smurov, a boy in the preparatory class (two classes below Kolya Krassotkin), son of a well-to-do official. Apparently he was forbidden by his
parents to associate with Krassotkin, who was well known to be a desperately naughty boy, so Smurov was obviously slipping out on the sly. He
was—if the reader has not forgotten—one of the group of boys who two
months before had thrown stones at Ilusha. He was the one who told
Alyosha Karamazov about Ilusha.

"I've been waiting for you for the last hour, Krassotkin," said Smurov
stolidly, and the boys strode towards the market-place.

"I am late," answered Krassotkin. "I was detained by circumstances.
You won't be thrashed for coming with me?"

"Come, I say, I'm never thrashed! And you've got Perezvon with you?"

"Yes."

"You're taking him, too?"

"Yes."

"Ah! if it were only Zhutchka!"

"That's impossible. Zhutchka's non-existent. Zhutchka is lost in the
mists of obscurity."

"Ah! couldn't we do this?" Smurov suddenly stood still. "You see
Ilusha says that Zhutchka was a shaggy, greyish, smoky-looking dog
like Perezvon. Couldn't you tell him this is Zhutchka, and he might
believe you?"

"Boy, shun a lie, that's one thing; even with a good object—that's another. Above all, I hope you've said nothing about my coming."

"Heaven forbid! I know what I am about. But you won't comfort him
with Perezvon," said Smurov, with a sigh. "You know his father, the captain, 'the wisp of tow,' told us that he was going to bring him a real mastiff
pup, with a black nose, to-day. He thinks that would comfort Ilusha; but I
doubt it."

"And how is Ilusha?"

"Ah, he is bad, very bad! I believe he's in consumption: he is quite conscious, but his breathing! His breathing's gone wrong. The other day he asked to have his boots on to be led round the room. He tried to walk, but he couldn't stand. 'Ah, I told you before, father,' he said, 'that those boots were no good. I could never walk properly in them.' He fancied it was his boots that made him stagger, but it was simply weakness, really. He won't live another week. Herzenstube is looking after him. Now they are rich again—they've got heaps of money."

"They are rogues."

"Who are rogues?"

"Doctors and the whole crew of quacks collectively, and also, of course, individually. I don't believe in medicine. It's a useless institution. I mean to go into all that. But what's that sentimentality you've got up there? The whole class seems to be there every day?"

"Not the whole class: it's only ten of our fellows who go to see him every day. There's nothing in that."

"What I don't understand in all this is the part that Alexey Karamazov is taking in it. His brother's going to be tried to-morrow or next day for such a crime, and yet he has so much time to spend on sentimentality with boys."

"There's no sentimentality about it. You are going yourself now to make it up with Ilusha."

"Make it up with him? What an absurd expression! But I allow no one to analyse my actions."

"And how pleased Ilusha will be to see you! He has no idea that you are coming. Why was it, why was it you wouldn't come all this time?" Smurov cried with sudden warmth.

"My dear boy, that's my business, not yours. I am going of myself because I choose to, but you've all been hauled there by Alexey Karamazov— there's a difference, you know. And how do you know? I may not be going to make it up at all. It's a stupid expression."

"It's not Karamazov at all; it's not his doing. Our fellows began going there of themselves. Of course, they went with Karamazov at first. And there's been nothing of that sort—no silliness. First one went, and then another. His father was awfully pleased to see us. You know he will simply go out of his mind if Ilusha dies. He sees that Ilusha's dying. And he seems so glad we've made it up with Ilusha. Ilusha asked after you, that was all. He just asks and says no more. His father will go out of his mind or hang himself. He behaved like a madman before. You know he is a very decent man. We made a mistake then. It's all the fault of that murderer who beat him then."

"Karamazov's a riddle to me all the same. I might have made his acquaintance long ago, but I like to have a proper pride in some cases. Besides, I have a theory about him which I must work out and verify."

Kolya subsided into dignified silence. Smurov, too, was silent. Smurov, of course, worshipped Krassotkin and never dreamed of putting himself on a level with him. Now he was tremendously interested at Kolya's saying that he was "going of himself" to see Ilusha. He felt that there must be some mystery in Kolya's suddenly taking it into his head to go to him that day. They crossed the market-place, in which at that hour were many loaded waggons from the country and a great number of live fowls. The market women were selling rolls, cottons and threads, etc., in their booths. These Sunday markets were naïvely called "fairs" in the town, and there were many such fairs in the year.

Perezvon ran about in the wildest spirits, sniffling about first one side, then the other. When he met other dogs they zealously smelt each other over according to the rules of canine etiquette.

"I like to watch such realistic scenes, Smurov," said Kolya suddenly. "Have you noticed how dogs sniff at one another when they meet? It seems to be a law of their nature."

"Yes; it's a funny habit."

"No, it's not funny; you are wrong there. There's nothing funny in nature, however funny it may seem to man with his prejudices. If dogs could reason and criticise us they'd be sure to find just as much that would be funny to them, if not far more, in the social relations of men, their masters—far more, indeed. I repeat that, because I am convinced that there is far more foolishness among us. That's Rakitin's idea—a remarkable idea. I am a Socialist, Smurov."

"And what is a Socialist?" asked Smurov.

"That's when all are equal and all have property in common, there are no marriages, and every one has any religion and laws he likes best, and all the rest of it. You are not old enough to understand that yet. It's cold, though."

"Yes, twelve degrees of frost. Father just looked at the thermometer."

"Have you noticed, Smurov, that in the middle of winter we don't feel so cold even when there are fifteen or eighteen degrees of frost as we do now, in the beginning of winter, when there is a sudden frost of twelve degrees, especially when there is not much snow. It's because people are not used to it. Everything is habit with men, everything even in their social and political relations. Habit is the great motive-power. What a funny-looking peasant!"

Kolya pointed to a tall peasant, with a good-natured countenance, in a long sheepskin coat, who was standing by his waggon, clapping together his hands, in their shapeless leather gloves, to warm them. His long fair beard was all white with frost.

"That peasant's beard's frozen," Kolya cried in a loud provocative voice as he passed him.

"Lots of people's beards are frozen," the peasant replied, calmly and sententiously.

"Don't provoke him," observed Smurov.

"It's all right; he won't be cross; he's a nice fellow. Good-bye, Matvey."

"Good-bye."

"Is your name Matvey?"

"Yes. Didn't you know?"

"No, I didn't. It was a guess."

"You don't say so! You are a schoolboy, I suppose?"

"Yes."

"You get whipped, I expect?"

"Nothing to speak of—sometimes."

"Does it hurt?"

"Well, yes, it does."

"Ech, what a life!" The peasant heaved a sigh from the bottom of his heart.

"Good-bye, Matvey."

"Good-bye. You are a nice chap, that you are."

The boys went on.

"That was a nice peasant," Kolya observed to Smurov. "I like talking to the peasants, and am always glad to do them justice."

"Why did you tell a lie, pretending we are thrashed?" asked Smurov.

"I had to say that to please him."

"How do you mean?"

"You know, Smurov, I don't like being asked the same thing twice. I like people to understand at the first word. Some things can't be explained. According to a peasant's notions, schoolboys are whipped, and must be whipped. What would a schoolboy be, if he were not whipped? And if I were to tell him we are not, he'd be disappointed. But you don't understand that. One has to know how to talk to the peasants."

"Only don't tease them, please, or you'll get into another scrape as you did about that goose."

"So you're afraid?"

"Don't laugh, Kolya. Of course, I'm afraid. My father would be awfully cross. I am strictly forbidden to go out with you."

"Don't be uneasy, nothing will happen this time. Hullo, Natasha!" he shouted to a market woman in one of the booths.

"Call me Natasha! What next! My name is Marya," the middle-aged market woman shouted at him.

"I am so glad it's Marya. Good-bye!"

"Ah, you young rascal! A brat like you to carry on so!"

"I'm in a hurry. I can't stay now. You shall tell me next Sunday." Kolya waved his hand at her, as though she had attacked him and not he her.

"I've nothing to tell you next Sunday. You set upon me, you impudent young monkey. I didn't say anything," bawled Marya. "You want a whipping, that's what you want, you saucy jackanapes!"

There was a roar of laughter among the other market women round her. Suddenly a man in a violent rage darted out from the arcade of shops close by. He was a young man, not a native of the town, with dark, curly hair and a long, pale face, marked with smallpox. He wore a long blue coat and a peaked cap, and looked like a merchant's clerk. He was in a state of stupid excitement and brandished his fist at Kolya.

"I know you," he cried angrily, "I know you!"

Kolya stared at him. He could not recall when he could have had a row with the man. But he had been in so many rows in the street that he could hardly remember them all.

"Do you?" he asked sarcastically.

"I know you! I know you!" the man repeated idiotically.

"So much the better for you. Well, it's time I was going. Good-bye!"

"You are at your saucy pranks again?" cried the man. "You are at your saucy pranks again? I know, you are at it again!"

"It's not your business, brother, if I am at my saucy pranks again," said Kolya, standing still and scanning him.

"Not my business?"

"No; it's not your business."

"Whose then? Whose then? Whose then?"

"It's Trifon Nikititch's business, not yours."

"What Trifon Nikititch?" asked the youth, staring with loutish amazement at Kolya, but still angry as ever.

Kolya scanned him gravely.

"Have you been to the Church of the Ascension?" he suddenly asked him, with stern emphasis.

"What Church of Ascension? What for? No, I haven't," said the young man, somewhat taken aback.

"Do you know Sabaneyev?" Kolya went on even more emphatically and even more severely.

"What Sabaneyev? No, I don't know him."

"Well, then you can go to the devil," said Kolya, cutting short the conversation, and turning sharply to the right he strode quickly on his way as though he disdained further conversation with a dolt who did not even know Sabaneyev.

"Stop, heigh! What Sabaneyev?" the young man recovered from his momentary stupefaction and was as excited as before. "What did he say?" He turned to the market woman with a silly stare.

The women laughed.

"You can never tell what he's after," said one of them.

"What Sabaneyev is it he's talking about?" the young man repeated, still furious and brandishing his right arm.

"It must be a Sabaneyev who worked for the Kuzmitchovs, that's who it must be," one of the women suggested.

The young man stared at her wildly.

"For the Kuzmitchovs?" repeated another woman. "But his name wasn't Trifon. His name's Kuzma, not Trifon; but the boy said Trifon Nikititch, so it can't be the same."

"His name is not Trifon and not Sabaneyev, it's Tchizhov," put in suddenly a third woman, who had hitherto been silent, listening gravely. "Alexey Ivanitch is his name. Tchizhov, Alexey Ivanitch."

"Not a doubt about it, it's Tchizhov," a fourth woman emphatically confirmed the statement.

The bewildered youth gazed from one to another.

"But what did he ask for, what did he ask for, good people?" he cried almost in desperation. "'Do you know Sabaneyev?' says he. And who the devil's to know who is Sabaneyev?"

"You're a senseless fellow. I tell you it's not Sabaneyev, but Tchizhov, Alexey Ivanitch Tchizhov, that's who it is!" one of the women shouted at him impressively.

"What Tchizhov? Who is he? Tell me, if you know."

"That tall, snivelling fellow who used to sit in the market in the summer."

"And what's your Tchizhov to do with me, good people, eh?"

"How can I tell what he's to do with you?" put in another. "You ought to know yourself what you want with him, if you make such a clamour about him. He spoke to you, he did not speak to us, you stupid. Don't you really know him?"

"Know whom?"

"Tchizhov."

"The devil take Tchizhov and you with him. I'll give him a hiding, that I will. He was laughing at me!"

"Will give Tchizhov a hiding! More likely he will give you one. You are a fool, that's what you are!"

"Not Tchizhov, not Tchizhov, you spiteful, mischievous woman. I'll give the boy a hiding. Catch him, catch him, he was laughing at me!"

The women guffawed. But Kolya was by now a long way off, marching along with a triumphant air. Smurov walked beside him, looking round at the shouting group far behind. He, too, was in high spirits, though he was still afraid of getting into some scrape in Kolya's company.

"What Sabaneyev did you mean?" he asked Kolya, foreseeing what his answer would be.

"How do I know? Now there'll be a hubbub among them all day. I like to stir up fools in every class of society. There's another blockhead, that peasant there. You know, they say 'there's no one stupider than a stupid Frenchman,' but a stupid Russian shows it in his face just as much. Can't you see it all over his face that he is a fool, that peasant?"

"Let him alone, Kolya. Let's go on."

"Nothing could stop me, now I am once off. Hay, good morning, peasant!"

A sturdy-looking peasant, with a round, simple face, and grizzled beard, who was walking by, raised his head and looked at the boy. He seemed not quite sober.

"Good morning, if you are not laughing at me," he said deliberately in reply.

"And if I am?" laughed Kolya.

"Well, a joke's a joke. Laugh away. I don't mind. There's no harm in a joke."

"I beg your pardon, brother, it was a joke."

"Well, God forgive you!"

"Do you forgive me, too?"

"I quite forgive you. Go along."

"I say, you seem a clever peasant."

"Cleverer than you," the peasant answered unexpectedly with the same gravity.

"I doubt it," said Kolya, somewhat taken aback.

"It's true though."

"Perhaps it is."

"It is, brother."

"Good-bye, peasant!"

"Good-bye!"

"There are all sorts of peasants," Kolya observed to Smurov, after a brief silence. "How could I tell I had hit on a clever one. I am always ready to recognise intelligence in the peasantry."

In the distance the cathedral clock struck half-past eleven. The boys made haste and they walked as far as Captain Snegiryov's lodging, a considerable distance, quickly and almost in silence. Twenty paces from the house Kolya stopped and told Smurov to go on ahead and ask Karamazov to come out to him.

"One must sniff round a bit first," he observed to Smurov.

"Why ask him to come out?" Smurov protested. "You go in; they will be awfully glad to see you. What's the sense of making friends in the frost out here?"

"I know why I want to see him out here in the frost," Kolya cut him short in the despotic tone he was fond of adopting with "small boys," and Smurov ran to do his bidding.

4

THE LOST DOG

KOLYA leaned against the fence with an air of dignity, waiting for Alyosha to appear. Yes, he had long wanted to meet him. He had heard a great deal about him from the boys, but hitherto he had always maintained an appearance of disdainful indifference when he was mentioned, and he had even "criticised" what he heard about Alyosha. But secretly he had a great longing to make his acquaintance; there was something sympathetic and attractive in all he was told about Alyosha. So the present moment was important: to begin with, he had to show himself at his best, to show his independence. "Or, he'll think of me as thirteen and take me for a boy, like the rest of them. And what are these boys to him? I shall ask him when I get to know him. It's a pity I am so short, though. Tuzikov is younger than I am, yet he is half a head taller. But I have a clever face. I am not good-looking. I know I'm hideous, but I've a clever face. I mustn't talk too freely; if I fall into his arms all at once, he may think . . . Tfoo! how horrible if he should think! . . ."

Such were the thoughts that excited Kolya while he was doing his utmost to assume the most independent air. What distressed him most was his being so short; he did not mind so much his "hideous" face, as being so short. On the wall in a corner at home he had the year before made a pencil mark to show his height, and every two months since, he anxiously measured himself against it to see how much he had gained. But, alas! he grew very slowly, and this sometimes reduced him almost to despair. His face was in reality by no means "hideous"; on the contrary, it was rather attractive, with a fair, pale skin, freckled. His small, lively grey eyes had a fearless look, and often glowed with feeling. He had rather high cheekbones; small, very red, but very thick, lips; his nose was small and unmistakably turned up. "I've a regular pug nose, a regular pug nose," Kolya used to mutter to himself when he looked in the looking-glass, and he always left it with indignation. "But perhaps I haven't got a clever face?" he sometimes thought, doubtful even of that. But it must not be supposed that his mind was preoccupied with his face and his height. On the contrary, however bitter the moments before the looking-glass were to him, he quickly forgot them, and forgot them for a long time, "abandoning himself entirely to ideas and to real life," as he formulated it to himself.

Alyosha came out quickly and hastened up to Kolya. Before he reached him, Kolya could see that he looked delighted. "Can he be so glad to see me?" Kolya wondered, feeling pleased. We may note here, in passing, that Alyosha's appearance had undergone a complete change since we saw him last. He had abandoned his cassock and was wearing now a well-cut coat, a soft, round hat, and his hair had been cropped short. All this was very becoming to him, and he looked quite handsome. His charming face always had a good-humoured expression; but there was a gentleness and serenity in his good-humour. To Kolya's surprise, Alyosha came out to him just as he was, without an overcoat. He had evidently come in haste. He held out his hand to Kolya at once.

"Here you are at last! How anxious we've been to see you!"

"There were reasons which you shall know directly. Anyway, I am glad to make your acquaintance. I've long been hoping for an opportunity, and have heard a great deal about you," Kolya muttered, a little breathless.

"We should have met anyway. I've heard a great deal about you, too; but you've been a long time coming here."

"Tell me, how are things going?"

"Ilusha is very ill. He is certainly dying."

"How awful! You must admit that medicine is a fraud, Karamazov," cried Kolya warmly.

"Ilusha has mentioned you often, very often, even in his sleep, in delirium, you know. One can see that you used to be very, very dear to him . . . before the incident . . . with the knife . . . There there's another reason. . . . Tell me, is that your dog?"

"Yes, Perezvon."

"Not Zhutchka?"* Alyosha looked at Kolya with eyes full of pity. "Is she lost for ever?"

"I know you would all like it to be Zhutchka. I've heard all about it." Kolya smiled mysteriously. "Listen, Karamazov, I'll tell you all about it. That's what I came for; that's what I asked you to come out here for, to explain the whole episode to you before we go in," he began with animation. "You see, Karamazov, Ilusha came into the preparatory class last spring. Well, you know what our preparatory class is—a lot of small boys. They began teasing Ilusha at once. I am two classes higher up, and, of course, I only look on at them from a distance. I saw the boy was weak and small, but he wouldn't give in to them; he fought with them. I saw he was proud, and his eyes were full of fire. I like children like that. And they teased him all the more. The worst of it was he was horribly dressed at the time, his breeches were too small for him, and there were holes in his boots. They worried him about it; they jeered at him. That I can't stand. I stood up for him at once, and gave it to them hot. I beat them, but they adore me, do you know, Karamazov?" Kolya boasted impulsively; "but I am always fond of children. I've two chickens on my hands at home now—that's what detained me to-day. So they left off beating Ilusha and I took him under my protection. I saw the boy was proud. I tell you that, the boy was proud; but in the end he became slavishly devoted to me: he did my slightest bidding, obeyed me as though I were God, tried to copy me. In the intervals between the classes he used to run to me at once, and I'd go about with him. On Sundays, too. They always laugh when an older boy makes friends with a younger one like that; but that's a prejudice. If it's my fancy, that's enough. I am teaching him, developing him. Why shouldn't I develop him if I like him? Here you, Karamazov, have taken up with all these nestlings. I see you want to influence the younger generation—to develop them, to be of use to them, and I assure you this trait in your character, which I knew by hearsay, attracted me more than anything. Let us get to the point, though. I noticed that there was a sort of softness and sentimentality coming over the boy, and you know I have a positive hatred of this sheepish sentimentality, and I have had it from a baby. There were contradictions in him, too: he was proud, but he was slavishly devoted to me, and yet all at once his eyes would flash and he'd refuse to agree with me; he'd argue, fly into a rage. I used sometimes to propound certain ideas; I could see that it was not so much that he disagreed with the ideas, but that he was simply rebelling against me, because I was cool in responding to his endearments. And so, in order to train him properly, the tenderer he was, the colder I became. I did it on purpose: that was my idea. My object was to form his character, to lick him into shape, to make a man of him . . . and besides . . . no doubt, you understand me at a word. Suddenly I noticed for three days in succession he was downcast and dejected, not because of my coldness,

---

*In Russia, a common name for a male or female dog.

but for something else, something more important. I wondered what the tragedy was. I have pumped him and found out that he had somehow got to know Smerdyakov, who was footman to your late father—it was before his death, of course—and he taught the little fool a silly trick—that is, a brutal, nasty trick. He told him to take a piece of bread, to stick a pin in it, and throw it to one of those hungry dogs who snap up anything without biting it, and then to watch and see what would happen. So they prepared a piece of bread like that and threw it to Zhutchka, that shaggy dog there's been such a fuss about. The people of the house it belonged to never fed it at all, though it barked all day. (Do you like that stupid barking, Karamazov? I can't stand it.) So it rushed at the bread, swallowed it, and began to squeal; it turned round and round and ran away, squealing as it ran out of sight. That was Ilusha's own account of it. He confessed it to me, and cried bitterly. He hugged me, shaking all over. He kept on repeating 'He ran away squealing': the sight of that haunted him. He was tormented by remorse, I could see that. I took it seriously. I determined to give him a lesson for other things as well. So I must confess I wasn't quite straightforward, and pretended to be more indignant perhaps than I was. 'You've done a nasty thing,' I said, 'you are a scoundrel. I won't tell of it, of course, but I shall have nothing more to do with you for a time. I'll think it over and let you know through Smurov (that's the boy who's just come with me; he's always ready to do anything for me) whether I will have anything to do with you in the future or whether I give you up for good as a scoundrel.' He was tremendously upset. I must own I felt I'd gone too far as I spoke, but there was no help for it. I did what I thought best at the time. A day or two after, I sent Smurov to tell him that I would not speak to him again. That's what we call it when two schoolfellows refuse to have anything more to do with one another. Secretly I only meant to send him to Coventry for a few days and then, if I saw signs of repentance, to hold out my hand to him again. That was my intention. But what do you think happened? He heard Smurov's message, his eyes flashed. 'Tell Krassotkin from me,' he cried, 'that I will throw bread with pins to all the dogs—all—all of them!' 'So he's going in for a little temper. We must smoke it out of him.' And I began to treat him with contempt; whenever I met him I turned away or smiled sarcastically. And just then that affair with his father happened. You remember? You must realise that he was fearfully worked up by what had happened already. The boys, seeing I'd given him up, set on him and taunted him, shouting, 'Wisp of tow, wisp of tow!' And he had soon regular skirmishes with them, which I am very sorry for. They seem to have given him one very bad beating. One day he flew at them all as they were coming out of school. I stood a few yards off, looking on. And, I swear, I don't remember that I laughed; it was quite the other way, I felt awfully sorry for him, in another minute I would have run up to take his part. But he suddenly met my eyes. I don't know what he fancied; but he pulled out a penknife, rushed at me, and struck at my thigh, here in my right leg. I didn't move. I don't mind owning I am plucky sometimes, Karamazov. I simply looked at him contemptuously, as though to say, 'this is how you repay all my kindness! Do it again, if you like, I'm at your service.' But he didn't stab me again; he broke down, he was frightened at what he had done, he threw away the knife, burst out crying, and ran away. I did not sneak on him, of course, and I made them all keep quiet, so it shouldn't come to the ears of the masters. I didn't even tell my mother till it had healed up. And the wound was a mere scratch. And then I heard that the same day he'd been throwing stones and had bitten your finger—but you understand now what a state he was in! Well, it can't be helped: it was stupid of me not to come and forgive him—that is, to make it up with him—when he was taken ill. I am sorry for it now. But I had a special reason. So now I've told you all about it . . . but I'm afraid it was stupid of me."

"Oh, what a pity," exclaimed Alyosha, with feeling, "that I didn't know before what terms you were on with him, or I'd have come to you long ago to beg you to go to him with me. Would you believe it, when he was feverish he talked about you in delirium. I didn't know how much you were to him! And you've really not succeeded in finding that dog? His father and the boys have been hunting all over the town for it. Would you believe it, since he's been ill, I've three times heard him repeat with tears, 'It's because I killed Zhutchka, father, that I am ill now. God is punishing me for it.' He can't get that idea out of his head. And if the dog were found and proved to be alive, one might almost fancy the joy would cure him. We have all rested our hopes on you."

"Tell me, what made you hope that I should be the one to find him?" Kolya asked, with great curiosity. "Why did you reckon on me rather than any one else?"

"There was a report that you were looking for the dog, and that you would bring it when you'd found it. Smurov said something of the sort. We've all been trying to persuade Ilusha that the dog is alive, that it's been seen. The boys brought him a live hare: he just looked at it, with a faint smile, and asked them to set it free in the fields. And so we did. His father has just this moment come back, bringing him a mastiff pup, hoping to comfort him with that; but I think it only makes it worse."

"Tell me, Karamazov, what sort of man is the father? I know him, but what do you make of him—a mountebank, a buffoon?"

"Oh, no; there are people of deep feeling who have been somehow crushed. Buffoonery in them is a form of resentful irony against those to whom they daren't speak the truth, from having been for years humiliated and intimidated by them. Believe me, Krassotkin, that sort of buffoonery is sometimes tragic in the extreme. His whole life now is centered in Ilusha, and if Ilusha dies, he will either go mad with grief, or kill himself. I feel almost certain of that when I look at him now."

"I understand you, Karamazov. I see you understand human nature," Kolya added, with feeling.

"And as soon as I saw you with a dog, I thought it was Zhutchka you were bringing."

"Wait a bit, Karamazov, perhaps we shall find it yet; but this is

Perezvon. I'll let him go in now and perhaps it will amuse Ilusha more than the mastiff pup. Wait a bit, Karamazov, you will know something in a minute. But, I say, I am keeping you here!" Kolya cried suddenly. "You've no overcoat on in this bitter cold. You see what an egoist I am. Oh, we are all egoists, Karamazov!"

"Don't trouble; it is cold, but I don't often catch cold. Let us go in though, and, by the way, what is your name? I know you are called Kolya, but what else?"

"Nikolay—Nikolay Ivanovitch Krassotkin, or, as they say in official documents 'Krassotkin son.' " Kolya laughed for some reason, but added suddenly, "Of course I hate my name Nikolay."

"Why so?"

"It's so trivial, so ordinary."

"You are thirteen?" asked Alyosha.

"No, fourteen—that is, I shall be fourteen very soon, in a fortnight. I'll confess one weakness of mine, Karamazov, just to you, since it's our first meeting, so that you may understand my character at once. I hate being asked my age, more than that . . . and in fact . . . there's a libellous story going about me, that last week I played robbers with the preparatory boys. It's a fact that I did play with them, but it's a perfect libel to say I did it for my own amusement. I have reasons for believing that you've heard the story; but I wasn't playing for my own amusement, it was for the sake of the children, because they couldn't think of anything to do by themselves. But they've always got some silly tale. This is an awful town for gossip, I can tell you."

"But what if you had been playing for your own amusement, what's the harm?"

"Come, I say, for my own amusement! You don't play horses, do you?"

"But you must look at it like this," said Alyosha, smiling. "Grown-up people go to the theatre and there the adventures of all sorts of heroes are represented—sometimes there are robbers and battles, too—and isn't that just the same thing, in a different form, of course? And young people's games of soldiers or robbers in their play-time are also art in its first stage. You know, they spring from the growing artistic instincts of the young. And sometimes these games are much better than performances in the theatre, the only difference is that people go there to look at actors, while in these games the young people are the actors themselves. But that's only natural."

"You think so? Is that your idea?" Kolya looked at him intently. "Oh, you know, that's rather an interesting view. When I go home, I'll think it over. I'll admit I thought I might learn something from you. I've come to learn of you, Karamazov," Kolya concluded, in a voice full of spontaneous feeling.

"And I of you," said Alyosha, smiling and pressing his hand.

Kolya was much pleased with Alyosha. What struck him most was that he treated him exactly like an equal and that he talked to him just as if he were "quite grown up."

"I'll show you something directly, Karamazov; it's a theatrical performance, too," he said, laughing nervously. "That's why I've come."

"Let us go first to the people of the house, on the left. All the boys leave
their coats in there, because the room is small and hot."

"Oh, I'm only coming in for a minute. I'll keep on my overcoat.
Perezvon will stay here in the passage and be dead. *Ici*, Perezvon, lie down
and be dead! You see how he's dead. I'll go in first and explore, then I'll
whistle to him when I think fit, and you'll see, he'll dash in like mad. Only
Smurov must not forget to open the door at the moment. I'll arrange it all
and you'll see something."

5

BY ILUSHA'S BEDSIDE

THE room inhabited by the family of the retired captain Snegiryov is
already familiar to the reader. It was close and crowded at that moment with a number of visitors. Several boys were sitting with
Ilusha and, though all of them like Smurov were prepared to deny that it
was Alyosha who had brought them and reconciled them with Ilusha, it
was really the fact. All the art he had used had been to take them, one by
one, to Ilusha, without "sheepish sentimentality," appearing to do so casually and without design. It was a great consolation to Ilusha in his suffering.
He was greatly touched by seeing the almost tender affection and sympathy
shown him by these boys, who had been his enemies. Krassotkin was the
only one missing and his absence was a heavy load on Ilusha's heart. Perhaps
the bitterest of all his bitter memories was his stabbing Krassotkin, who had
been his one friend and protector. Clever little Smurov, who was the first to
make it up with Ilusha, thought it was so. But when Smurov hinted to Krassotkin that Alyosha wanted to come and see him about something, the latter
cut him short, bidding Smurov tell "Karamazov" at once that he knew best
what to do, that he wanted no one's advice, and that, if he went to see Ilusha,
he would choose his own time for he had "his own reasons."

That was a fortnight before this Sunday. That was why Alyosha had not
been to see him, as he had meant to. But though he waited, he sent Smurov
to him twice again. Both times Krassotkin met him with a curt, impatient
refusal, sending Alyosha a message not to bother him any more, that if he
came himself, he, Krassotkin, would not go to Ilusha at all. Up to the very
last day, Smurov did not know that Kolya meant to go to Ilusha that morning, and only the evening before, as he parted from Smurov, Kolya

abruptly told him to wait at home for him next morning, for he would go with him to the Snegiryovs, but warned him on no account to say he was coming, as he wanted to drop in casually. Smurov obeyed. Smurov's fancy that Kolya would bring back the lost dog was based on the words Kolya had dropped that "they must be asses not to find the dog, if it was alive." When Smurov, waiting for an opportunity, timidly hinted at his guess about the dog, Krassotkin fled into a violent rage. "I'm not such an ass as to go hunting about the town for other people's dogs when I've got a dog of my own! And how can you imagine a dog could be alive after swallowing a pin? Sheepish sentimentality, that's what it is!"

For the last fortnight Ilusha had not left his little bed under the ikons in the corner. He had not been to school since the day he met Alyosha and bit his finger. He was taken ill the same day, though for a month afterwards he was sometimes able to get up and walk about the room and passage. But latterly he had become so weak that he could not move without help from his father. His father was terribly concerned about him. He even gave up drinking and was almost crazy with terror that his boy would die. And often, especially after leading him round the room on his arm and putting him back to bed, he would run to a dark corner in the passage and, leaning his head against the wall, he would break into paroxysms of violent weeping, stifling his sobs that they might not be heard by Ilusha.

Returning to the room, he would usually begin doing something to amuse and comfort his precious boy, he would tell him stories, funny anecdotes, or would mimic comic people he had happened to meet, even imitate the howls and cries of animals. But Ilusha could not bear to see his father fooling and playing the buffoon. Though the boy tried not to show how he disliked it, he saw with an aching heart that his father was an object of contempt, and he was continually haunted by the memory of the "wisp of tow" and that "terrible day."

Nina, Ilusha's gentle, crippled sister, did not like her father's buffoonery either (Varvara had been gone for some time past to Petersburg to study at the University). But the half imbecile mother was greatly diverted and laughed heartily when her husband began capering about or performing something. It was the only way she could be amused, all the rest of the time she was grumbling and complaining that now every one had forgotten her, that no one treated her with respect, that she was slighted and so on. But during the last few days she had completely changed. She began looking constantly at Ilusha's bed in the corner and seemed lost in thought. She was more silent, quieter, and, if she cried, she cried quietly so as not to be heard. The captain noticed the change in her with mournful perplexity. The boys' visits at first only angered her, but later on their merry shouts and stories began to divert her, and at last she liked them so much that, if the boys had given up coming, she would have felt dreary without them. When the children told a story or played a game, she laughed and clapped her hands. She called some of them to her and kissed them. She was particularly fond of Smurov.

As for the captain, the presence in his room of the children, who came

to cheer up Ilusha, filled his heart from the first with ecstatic joy. He even
hoped that Ilusha would now get over his depression, and that that would
hasten his recovery. In spite of his alarm about Ilusha, he had not, till lately,
felt one minute's doubt of his boy's ultimate recovery.

He met his little visitors with homage, waited upon them hand and foot,
he was ready to be their horse and even began letting them ride on his
back, but Ilusha did not like the game and it was given up. He began buying
little things for them, gingerbread and nuts, gave them tea and cut them
sandwiches. It must be noted that all this time he had plenty of money. He
had taken the two hundred roubles from Katerina Ivanovna just as
Alyosha had predicted he would. And afterwards Katerina Ivanovna,
learning more about their circumstances and Ilusha's illness, visited them
herself, made the acquaintance of the family and succeeded in fascinating
the half imbecile mother. Since then she had been lavish in helping them,
and the captain, terror-stricken at the thought that his boy might be dying,
forgot his pride and humbly accepted her assistance.

All this time Doctor Herzenstube, who was called in by Katerina
Ivanovna, came punctually every other day, but little was gained by his visits and he dosed the invalid mercilessly. But on that Sunday morning a
new doctor was expected, who had come from Moscow, where he had a
great reputation. Katerina Ivanovna had sent for him from Moscow at
great expense, not expressly for Ilusha, but for another object of which
more will be said in its place hereafter. But, as he had come, she had asked
him to see Ilusha as well, and the captain had been told to expect him. He
hadn't the slightest idea that Kolya Krassotkin was coming, though he had
long wished for a visit from the boy for whom Ilusha was fretting.

At the moment when Krassotkin opened the door and came into the
room, the captain and all the boys were round Ilusha's bed, looking at a
tiny mastiff pup, which had only been born the day before, though the captain had bespoken it a week ago to comfort and amuse Ilusha, who was
still fretting over the lost and probably dead Zhutchka. Ilusha, who had
heard three days before that he was to be presented with a puppy, not an
ordinary puppy, but a pedigree mastiff (a very important point, of course),
tried from delicacy of feeling to pretend that he was pleased. But his father and the boys could not help seeing that the puppy only served to recall to his little heart the thought of the unhappy dog he had killed. The
puppy lay beside him feebly moving and he, smiling sadly, stroked it with
his thin, pale, wasted hand. Clearly he liked the puppy, but . . . it wasn't
Zhutchka; if he could have had Zhutchka and the puppy, too, then he
would have been completely happy.

"Krassotkin!" cried one of the boys suddenly. He was the first to see
him come in.

Krassotkin's entrance made a general sensation, the boys moved away
and stood on each side of the bed, so that he could get a full view of Ilusha.
The captain ran eagerly to meet Kolya.

"Please come in . . . you are welcome!" he said hurriedly. "Ilusha, Mr.
Krassotkin has come to see you!"

But Krassotkin, shaking hands with him hurriedly, instantly showed his complete knowledge of the manners of good society. He turned first to the captain's wife sitting in her armchair, who was very ill-humoured at the moment, and was grumbling that the boys stood between her and Ilusha's bed and did not let her see the new puppy. With the greatest courtesy he made her a bow, scraping his foot and then turning to Nina, he made her, as the only other lady present, a similar bow. This polite behaviour made an extremely favourable impression on the deranged lady.

"There, you can see at once he is a young man that has been well brought up," she commented aloud, throwing up her hands; "but as for our other visitors they come in one on the top of another."

"How do you mean, mamma, one on the top of another, how is that?" muttered the captain affectionately, though a little anxious on her account.

"That's how they ride in. They get on each other's shoulders in the passage and prance in like that on a respectable family. Strange sort of visitors!"

"But who's come in like that, mamma?"

"Why, that boy came in riding on that one's back and this one on that one's."

Kolya was already by Ilusha's bedside. The sick boy turned visibly paler. He raised himself in the bed and looked intently at Kolya. Kolya had not seen his little friend for two months, and he was overwhelmed at the sight of him. He had never imagined that he would see such a wasted, yellow face, such enormous, feverishly glowing eyes and such thin little hands. He saw, with grieved surprise, Ilusha's rapid, hard breathing and dry lips. He stepped close to him, held out his hand, and almost overwhelmed, he said:

"Well, old man . . . how are you?" But his voice failed him, he couldn't achieve an appearance of ease; his face suddenly twitched and the corners of his mouth quivered. Ilusha smiled a pitiful little smile, still unable to utter a word. Something moved Kolya to raise his hand and pass it over Ilusha's hair.

"Never mind!" he murmured softly to him to cheer him up, or perhaps not knowing why he said it. For a minute they were silent again.

"Hullo, so you've got a new puppy?" Kolya said suddenly, in a most callous voice.

"Ye-es," answered Ilusha in a long whisper, gasping for breath.

"A black nose, that means he'll be fierce, a good house-dog," Kolya observed gravely and stolidly, as if the only thing he cared about was the puppy and its black nose. But in reality he still had to do his utmost to control his feelings not to burst out crying like a child, and do what he would he could not control it. "When it grows up, you'll have to keep it on the chain, I'm sure."

"He'll be a huge dog!" cried one of the boys.

"Of course he will," "a mastiff," "large," "like this," "as big as a calf," shouted several voices.

"As big as a calf, as a real calf," chimed in the captain. "I got one like that on purpose, one of the fiercest breed, and his parents are huge and very fierce, they stand as high as this from the floor. . . . Sit down here, on Ilusha's bed, or here on the bench. You are welcome, we've been hoping to see you a long time. . . . You were so kind as to come with Alexey Fyodorovitch?"

Krassotkin sat on the edge of the bed, at Ilusha's feet. Though he had perhaps prepared a free-and-easy opening for the conversation on his way, now he completely lost the thread of it.

"No . . . I came with Perezvon. I've got a dog now, called Perezvon. A Slavonic name. He's out there . . . if I whistle, he'll run in. I've brought a dog too," he said, addressing Ilusha all at once. "Do you remember Zhutchka, old man?" he suddenly fired the question at him.

Ilusha's little face quivered. He looked with an agonised expression at Kolya. Alyosha, standing at the door, frowned and signed to Kolya not to speak of Zhutchka, but he did not or would not notice.

"Where . . . is Zhutchka?" Ilusha asked in a broken voice.

"Oh, well, my boy, your Zhutchka's lost and done for!"

Ilusha did not speak, but he fixed an intent gaze once more on Kolya. Alyosha, catching Kolya's eye, signed to him vigorously again, but he turned away his eyes pretending not to have noticed.

"It must have run away and died somewhere. It must have died after a meal like that," Kolya pronounced pitilessly, though he seemed a little breathless. "But I've got a dog, Perezvon. . . . A Slavonic name. . . . I've brought him to show you."

"I don't want him!" said Ilusha suddenly.

"No, no, you really must see him . . . it will amuse you. I brought him on purpose. . . . He's the same sort of shaggy dog. . . . You allow me to call in my dog, Madame?" he suddenly addressed Madame Snegiryov, with inexplicable excitement in his manner.

"I don't want him, I don't want him!" cried Ilusha, with a mournful break in his voice. There was a reproachful light in his eyes.

"You'd better," the captain started up from the chest by the wall on which he had just sat down, "you'd better . . . another time," he muttered, but Kolya could not be restrained. He hurriedly shouted to Smurov, "Open the door," and as soon as it was open, he blew his whistle. Perezvon dashed headlong into the room.

"Jump, Perezvon, beg! Beg!" shouted Kolya, jumping up, and the dog stood erect on its hind legs by Ilusha's bedside. What followed was a surprise to every one: Ilusha started, lurched violently forward, bent over Perezvon and gazed at him, faint with suspense.

"It's . . . Zhutchka!" he cried suddenly, in a voice breaking with joy and suffering.

"And who did you think it was?" Krassotkin shouted with all his might, in a ringing, happy voice, and bending down he seized the dog and lifted him up to Ilusha.

"Look, old man, you see, blind of one eye and the left ear is torn, just the marks you described to me. It was by that I found him. I found him directly. He did not belong to any one!" he explained, turning quickly to the captain, to his wife, to Alyosha and then again to Ilusha. "He used to live in the Fedotovs' back yard. Though he made his home there, they did not feed him. He was a stray dog that had run away from the village . . . I found him. . . . You see, old man, he couldn't have swallowed what you gave him. If he had, he must have died, he must have! So he must have spat it out, since he is alive. You did not see him do it. But the pin pricked his tongue, that is why he squealed. He ran away squealing and you thought he'd swallowed it. He might well squeal, because the skin of dogs' mouths is so tender . . . tenderer than in men, much tenderer!" Kolya cried impetuously, his face glowing and radiant with delight. Ilusha could not speak. White as a sheet, he gazed open-mouthed at Kolya, with his great eyes almost starting out of his head. And if Krassotkin, who had no suspicion of it, had known what a disastrous and fatal effect such a moment might have on the sick child's health, nothing would have induced him to play such a trick on him. But Alyosha was perhaps the only person in the room who realised it. As for the captain he behaved like a small child.

"Zhutchka! It's Zhutchka!" he cried in a blissful voice. "Ilusha, this is Zhutchka, your Zhutchka! Mamma, this is Zhutchka!" He was almost weeping.

"And I never guessed!" cried Smurov regretfully. "Bravo, Krassotkin, I said he'd find the dog and here he's found him."

"Here he's found him!" another boy repeated gleefully.

"Krassotkin's a brick!" cried a third voice.

"He's a brick, he's a brick!" cried the other boys, and they began clapping.

"Wait, wait," Krassotkin did his utmost to shout above them all. "I'll tell you how it happened, that's the whole point. I found him, I took him home and hid him at once. I kept him locked up at home and did not show him to any one till to-day. Only Smurov had known for the last fortnight, but I assured him this dog was called Perezvon and he did not guess. And meanwhile I taught the dog all sorts of tricks. You should only see all the things he can do! I trained him so as to bring you a well-trained dog, in good condition, old man, so as to be able to say to you, 'See, old man, what a fine dog your Zhutchka is now!' Haven't you a bit of meat, he'll show you a trick that will make you die with laughing. A piece of meat, haven't you got any?"

The captain ran across the passage to the landlady, where their cooking was done. Not to lose precious time, Kolya, in desperate haste, shouted to Perezvon "dead!" And the dog immediately turned round and lay on his back with its four paws in the air. The boys laughed, Ilusha looked on with the same suffering smile, but the person most delighted with the dog's performance was "mamma." She laughed at the dog and began snapping her fingers and calling it, "Perezvon, Perezvon!"

"Nothing will make him get up, nothing!" Kolya cried triumphantly, proud of his success. "He won't move for all the shouting in the world, but if I call to him, he'll jump up in a minute. *Ici,* Perezvon!" The dog leapt up and bounded about, whining with delight. The captain ran back with a piece of cooked beef.

"Is it hot?" Kolya inquired hurriedly, with a businesslike air, taking the meat. "Dogs don't like hot things. No, it's all right. Look, everybody, look, Ilusha, look, old man; why aren't you looking? He does not look at him, now I've brought him."

The new trick consisted in making the dog stand motionless with his nose out and putting a tempting morsel of meat just on his nose. The luckless dog had to stand without moving, with the meat on his nose, as long as his master chose to keep him, without a movement, perhaps for half an hour. But he kept Perezvon only for a brief moment.

"Paid for!" cried Kolya, and the meat passed in a flash from the dog's nose to his mouth. The audience, of course, expressed enthusiasm and surprise.

"Can you really have put off coming all this time simply to train the dog?" exclaimed Alyosha, with an involuntary note of reproach in his voice.

"Simply for that!" answered Kolya, with perfect simplicity. "I wanted to show him in all his glory."

"Perezvon! Perezvon," called Ilusha suddenly, snapping his thin fingers and beckoning to the dog.

"What is it? Let him jump up on the bed! *Ici,* Perezvon!" Kolya slapped the bed and Perezvon darted up by Ilusha. The boy threw both arms round his head and Perezvon instantly licked his cheek. Ilusha crept close to him, stretched himself out in bed and hid his face in the dog's shaggy coat.

"Dear, dear!" kept exclaiming the captain. Kolya sat down again on the edge of the bed.

"Ilusha, I can show you another trick. I've brought you a little cannon. You remember, I told you about it before and you said how much you'd like to see it. Well, here, I've brought it to you."

And Kolya hurriedly pulled out of his satchel the little bronze cannon. He hurried, because he was happy himself. Another time he would have waited till the sensation made by Perezvon had passed off, now he hurried on regardless of all consideration. "You are all happy now," he felt, "so here's something to make you happier!" He was perfectly enchanted himself.

"I've been coveting this thing for a long while; it's for you, old man, it's for you. It belonged to Morozov, it was no use to him, he had it from his brother. I swopped a book from father's bookcase for it, 'A Kinsman of Mahomet or Salutary Folly,' a scandalous book published in Moscow a hundred years ago, before they had any censorship. And Morozov has a taste for such things. He was grateful to me, too. . . ."

Kolya held the cannon in his hand so that all could see and admire it. Ilusha raised himself, and, with his right arm still round the dog, he gazed enchanted at the toy. The sensation was even greater, when Kolya announced that he had gunpowder too, and that it could be fired off at once "if it won't alarm the ladies." "Mamma" immediately asked to look at the toy closer and her request was granted. She was much pleased with the little bronze cannon on wheels and began rolling it to and fro on her lap. She readily gave permission for the cannon to be fired, without any idea of what she had been asked. Kolya showed the powder and the shot. The captain, as a military man, undertook to load it, putting in a minute quantity of powder. He asked that the shot might be put off till another time. The cannon was put on the floor, aiming towards an empty part of the room, three grains of powder were thrust into the touch hole and a match was put to it. A magnificent explosion followed. Mamma was startled, but at once laughed with delight. The boys gazed in speechless triumph. But the captain, looking at Ilusha, was more enchanted than any of them. Kolya picked up the cannon and immediately presented it to Ilusha, together with the powder and the shot.

"I got it for you, for you! I've been keeping it for you a long time," he repeated once more in his delight.

"Oh, give it to me! No, give me the cannon!" Mamma began begging like a little child. Her face showed a piteous fear that she would not get it. Kolya was disconcerted. The captain fidgeted uneasily.

"Mamma, mamma," he ran to her, "the cannon's yours, of course, but let Ilusha have it, because it's a present to him, but it's just as good as yours. Ilusha will always let you play with it, it shall belong to both of you, both of you."

"No, I don't want it to belong to both of us, I want it to be mine altogether, not Ilusha's," persisted mamma, on the point of tears.

"Take it, mother, here, keep it!" Ilusha cried. "Krassotkin, may I give it to my mother?" he turned to Krassotkin with an imploring face, as though he were afraid he might be offended at his giving his present to some one else.

"Of course, you may," Krassotkin assented heartily, and, taking the cannon from Ilusha, he handed it himself to mamma with a polite bow. She was so touched that she cried.

"Ilusha, darling, he's the one who loves his mamma!" she said tenderly, and at once began wheeling the cannon to and fro on her lap.

"Mamma, let me kiss your hand." The captain darted up to her at once and did so.

"And I never saw such a charming fellow as this nice boy," said the grateful lady, pointing to Krassotkin.

"And I'll bring you as much powder as you like, Ilusha. We make the powder ourselves now. Borovikov found out how it's made—twenty-four parts of saltpetre, ten of sulphur and six of birchwood charcoal. It's all pounded together, mixed into a paste with water and rubbed through a tammy sieve—that's how it's done."

"Smurov told me about your powder, only father says it's not real gunpowder," responded Ilusha.

"Not real?" Kolya flushed. "It burns. I don't know, of course."

"No, I didn't mean that," put in the captain with a guilty face. "I only said that real powder is not made like that, but that's nothing, it can be made so."

"I don't know, you know best. We lighted some in a pomatum pot, it burned splendidly, it all burnt away leaving only a tiny ash. But that was only the paste, and if you rub it through . . . but of course you know best, I don't know. . . . And Bulkin's father thrashed him on account of our powder, did you hear?" he turned to Ilusha.

"Yes," answered Ilusha. He listened to Kolya with immense interest and enjoyment.

"We had prepared a whole bottle of it and he used to keep it under his bed. His father saw it. He said it might explode, and thrashed him on the spot. He was going to make a complaint against me to the masters. He is not allowed to go about with me now, no one is allowed to go about with me now. Smurov is not allowed to either, I've got a bad name with every one. They say I'm a 'desperate character,'" Kolya smiled scornfully. "It all began from what happened on the railway."

"Ah, we've heard of that exploit of yours, too," cried the captain. "How could you lie still on the line? Is it possible you weren't the least afraid, lying there under the train? Weren't you frightened?"

The captain was abject in his flattery of Kolya.

"N-not particularly," answered Kolya carelessly. "What's blasted my reputation more than anything here was that cursed goose," he said, turning again to Ilusha. But though he assumed an unconcerned air as he talked, he still could not control himself and was continually missing the note he tried to keep up.

"Ah! I heard about the goose!" Ilusha laughed, beaming all over. "They told me, but I didn't understand. Did they really take you to the court?"

"The most stupid, trivial affair, they made a mountain of a mole-hill as they always do," Kolya began carelessly. "I was walking through the market-place here one day, just when they'd driven in the geese. I stopped and looked at them. All at once a fellow, who is an errand boy at Plotnikov's, now looked at me and said, 'What are you looking at the geese for?' I looked at him, he was a stupid, moon-faced fellow of twenty. I am always on the side of the peasantry, you know. I like talking to the peasants. . . . We've dropped behind the peasants—that's an axiom. I believe you are laughing, Karamazov?"

"No, heaven forbid, I am listening," said Alyosha with a most good-natured air, and the sensitive Kolya was immediately reassured.

"My theory, Karamazov, is clear and simple," he hurried on again, looking pleased. "I believe in the people and am always glad to give them their due, but I am not for spoiling them, that is a *sine qua non**. . . . But I was telling you about the goose. So I turned to the fool and answered, 'I am wondering what the goose thinks about.' He looked at me quite stupidly, 'And what does the goose think about?' he asked. 'Do you see that cart

---

*Essential condition.

full of oats?' I said. 'The oats are dropping out of the sack, and the goose has put its neck right under the wheel to gobble them up—do you see?' 'I see that quite well,' he said. 'Well,' said I, 'if that cart were to move on a little, would it break the goose's neck or not?' 'It'd be sure to break it,' and he grinned all over his face, highly delighted. 'Come on then,' said I, 'let's try.' 'Let's,' he said. And it did not take us long to arrange: he stood at the bridle without being noticed, and I stood on one side to direct the goose. And the owner wasn't looking, he was talking to some one, so I had nothing to do, the goose thrust its head in after the oats of itself, under the cart, just under the wheel. I winked at the lad, he tugged at the bridle, and crack! The goose's neck was broken in half. And, as luck would have it, all the peasants saw us at that moment and they kicked up a shindy at once. 'You did that on purpose!' 'No, not on purpose.' 'Yes, you did, on purpose!' Well, they shouted, 'Take him to the justice of the peace!' They took me, too. 'You were there, too,' they said, 'you helped, you're known all over the market!' And, for some reason, I really am known all over the market," Kolya added conceitedly. "We all went off to the justice's, they brought the goose, too. The fellow was crying in a great funk, simply blubbering like a woman. And the farmer kept shouting that you could kill any number of geese like that. Well, of course, there were witnesses. The justice of the peace settled it in a minute, that the farmer was to be paid a rouble for the goose, and the fellow to have the goose. And he was warned not to play such pranks again. And the fellow kept blubbering like a woman, 'It wasn't me,' he said, 'it was he egged me on,' and he pointed to me. I answered with the utmost composure that I hadn't egged him on, that I simply stated the general proposition, had spoken hypothetically. The justice of the peace smiled and was vexed with himself at once for having smiled. 'I'll complain to your masters of you, so that for the future you mayn't waste your time on such general propositions, instead of sitting at your books and learning your lessons.' He didn't complain to the masters, that was a joke, but the matter was noised abroad and came to the ears of the masters. Their ears are long, you know! The classical master, Kolbasnikov, was particularly shocked about it, but Dardanelov got me off again. But Kolbasnikov is savage with every one now like a green ass. Did you know, Ilusha, he is just married, got a dowry of a thousand roubles, and his bride's a regular fright of the first rank and the last degree. The third class fellows wrote an epigram on it.

> 'Astounding news has reached the class
> Kolbasnikov has been an ass.'

And so on, awfully funny, I'll bring it to you later on. I say nothing against Dardanelov, he is a learned man, there's no doubt about it. I respect men like that and it's not because he stood up for me."

"But you took him down about the founders of Troy!" Smurov put in suddenly, unmistakably proud of Krassotkin at such a moment. He was particularly pleased with the story of the goose.

"Did you really take him down?" the captain inquired, in a flattering way. "On the question who founded Troy? We heard of it, Ilusha told me about it at the time."

"He knows everything, father, he knows more than any of us!" put in Ilusha; "he only pretends to be like that, but really he is top in every subject. . . ."

Ilusha looked at Kolya with infinite happiness.

"Oh, that's all nonsense about Troy, a trivial matter. I consider this an unimportant question," said Kolya with haughty humility. He had by now completely recovered his dignity, though he was still a little uneasy. He felt that he was greatly excited and that he had talked about the goose, for instance, with too little reserve, while Alyosha had looked serious and had not said a word all the time. And the vain boy began by degrees to have a rankling fear that Alyosha was silent because he despised him, and thought he was showing off before him. If he dared to think anything like that Kolya would . . .

"I regard the question as quite a trivial one," he rapped out again, proudly.

"And I know who founded Troy," a boy, who had not spoken before, said suddenly, to the surprise of every one. He was silent and seemed to be shy. He was a pretty boy of about eleven, called Kartashov. He was sitting near the door. Kolya looked at him with dignified amazement.

The fact was that the identity of the founders of Troy had become a secret for the whole school, a secret which could only be discovered by reading Smaragdov, and no one had Smaragdov but Kolya. One day when Kolya's back was turned, Kartashov hastily opened Smaragdov, which lay among Kolya's books, and immediately lighted on the passage relating to the foundation of Troy. This was a good time ago, but he felt uneasy and could not bring himself to announce publicly that he, too, knew who had founded Troy, afraid of what might happen and of Krassotkin's somehow putting him to shame over it. But now he couldn't resist saying it. For weeks he had been longing to.

"Well, who did found it?" asked Kolya, turning to him with haughty superciliousness. He saw from his face that he really did know and at once made up his mind how to take it. There was, so to speak, a discordant note in the general harmony.

"Troy was founded by Teucer, Dardanus, Ilius and Tros," the boy rapped out at once, and in the same instant he blushed, blushed so, that it was painful to look at him. But the boys stared at him, stared at him for a whole minute, and then all the staring eyes turned at once and were fastened upon Kolya, who was still scanning the audacious boy with disdainful composure.

"In what sense did they found it?" he deigned to comment at last. "And what is meant by founding a city or a state? What did they do—did they go and each lay a brick, do you suppose?"

There was laughter. The offending boy turned from pink to crimson. He was silent and on the point of tears. Kolya held him so for a minute.

"Before you talk of a historical event like the foundation of a nationality, you must first understand what you mean by it," he admonished him in stern incisive tones. "But I attach no consequence to these old wives' tales and I don't think much of universal history in general," he added carelessly, addressing the company generally.

"Universal history?" the captain inquired, looking almost scared.

"Yes, universal history! It's the study of the successive follies of mankind and nothing more. The only subjects I respect are mathematics and natural science," said Kolya. He was showing off and he stole a glance at Alyosha, his was the only opinion he was afraid of there. But Alyosha was still silent and still serious as before. If Alyosha had said a word it would have stopped him, but Alyosha was silent and "it might be the silence of contempt" and that finally irritated Kolya.

"The classical languages, too . . . they are simply madness, nothing more. You seem to disagree with me again, Karamazov?"

"I don't agree," said Alyosha, with a faint smile.

"The study of the classics, if you ask my opinion, is simply a police measure, that's simply why it has been introduced into our schools." By degrees Kolya began to get breathless again. "Latin and Greek were introduced because they are a bore and because they stupefy the intellect. It was dull before, so what could they do to make things duller? It was senseless enough before, so what could they do to make it more senseless? So they thought of Greek and Latin. That's my opinion, I hope I shall never change it," Kolya finished abruptly. His cheeks were flushed.

"That's true," assented Smurov suddenly, in a ringing tone of conviction. He had listened attentively.

"And yet he is first in Latin himself," cried one of the group of boys suddenly.

"Yes, father, he says that and yet he is first in Latin," echoed Ilusha.

"What of it?" Kolya thought fit to defend himself, though the praise was very sweet to him. "I am fagging away at Latin, because I have to, because I promised my mother to pass my examination, and I think that whatever you do, it's worth doing it well. But in my soul I have a profound contempt for the classics and all that fraud. . . . You don't agree, Karamazov?"

"Why 'fraud'?" Alyosha smiled again.

"Well, all the classical authors have been translated into all languages, so it was not for the sake of studying the classics they introduced Latin, but solely as a police measure, to stupefy the intelligence. So what can one call it but a fraud?"

"Why, who taught you all this?" cried Alyosha, surprised at last.

"In the first place I am capable of thinking for myself without being taught. Besides, what I said just now about the classics being translated our teacher Kolbasnikov has said to the whole of the third class."

"The doctor has come!" cried Nina, who had been silent till then.

A carriage belonging to Madame Hohlakov drove up to the gate. The captain, who had been expecting the doctor all the morning, rushed headlong out to meet him. "Mamma" pulled herself together and assumed a dignified air. Alyosha went up to Ilusha and began setting his pillows straight. Nina, from her invalid chair, anxiously watched him putting the bed tidy. The boys hurriedly took leave. Some of them promised to come again in the evening. Kolya called Perezvon and the dog jumped off the bed.

"I won't go away, I won't go away," Kolya said hastily to Ilusha. "I'll wait in the passage and come back when the doctor's gone, I'll come back with Perezvon."

But by now the doctor had entered, an important looking person with long, dark whiskers and a shiny, shaven chin, wearing a bear-skin coat. As he crossed the threshold he stopped, taken aback; he probably fancied he had come to the wrong place. "How is this? Where am I?" he muttered, not removing his coat nor his peaked sealskin cap. The crowd, the poverty of the room, the washing hanging on a line in the corner, puzzled him. The captain, bent double, was bowing low before him.

"It's here, sir, here, sir," he muttered cringingly; "it's here, you've come right, you were coming to us . . ."

"Sne-gi-ryov?" the doctor said loudly and pompously. "Mr. Snegiryov— is that you?"

"That's me, sir!"

"Ah!"

The doctor looked round the room with a squeamish air once more and threw off his coat, displaying to all eyes the grand decoration at his neck. The captain caught the fur coat in the air, and the doctor took off his cap.

"Where is the patient?" he asked emphatically.

6

PRECOCITY

"WHAT do you think the doctor will say to him?" Kolya asked quickly. "What a repulsive mug though, hasn't he? I can't endure medicine!"

"Ilusha is dying. I think that's certain," answered Alyosha mournfully.

"They are rogues! Medicine's a fraud! I am glad to have made your acquaintance though, Karamazov. I wanted to know you for a long time. I am only sorry we meet in such sad circumstances."

Kolya had a great inclination to say something even warmer and more demonstrative, but he felt ill at ease. Alyosha noticed this, smiled, and pressed his hand.

"I've long learned to respect you as a rare person," Kolya muttered again, faltering and uncertain. "I have heard you are a mystic and have been in the monastery. I know you are a mystic but . . . that hasn't put me off. Contact with real life will cure you. . . . It's always so with characters like yours."

"What do you mean by mystic? Cure me of what?" Alyosha was rather astonished.

"Oh, God and all the rest of it."

"What, don't you believe in God?"

"Oh, I've nothing against God. Of course, God is only a hypothesis, but . . . I admit that He is needed . . . for the order of the universe and all that . . . and that if there were no God He would have to be invented," added Kolya, beginning to blush. He suddenly fancied that Alyosha might think he was trying to show off his knowledge and to prove that he was "grown up." "I haven't the slightest desire to show off my knowledge to him," Kolya thought indignantly. And all of a sudden he felt horribly annoyed.

"I must confess I can't endure entering on such discussions," he said with a final air. "It's possible for one who doesn't believe in God to love mankind, don't you think so? Voltaire didn't believe in God and loved mankind?" ("I am at it again," he thought to himself.)

"Voltaire believed in God, though not very much, I think, and I don't think he loved mankind very much either," said Alyosha quietly, gently, and quite naturally, as though he were talking to some one of his own age, or even older. Kolya was particularly struck by Alyosha's apparent diffidence about his opinion of Voltaire. He seemed to be leaving the question for him, little Kolya, to settle.

"Have you read Voltaire?" Alyosha finished.

"No, not to say read. . . . But I've read *Candide** in the Russian translation . . . in an absurd, grotesque, old translation. . . . (At it again! again!)"

"And did you understand it?"

"Oh, yes, everything. . . . That is . . . Why do you suppose I shouldn't understand it? There's a lot of nastiness in it, of course. . . . Of course I can understand that it's a philosophical novel and written to advocate an idea. . . ." Kolya was getting mixed by now. "I am a Socialist, Karamazov, I am an incurable Socialist," he announced suddenly, apropos of nothing.

"A Socialist?" laughed Alyosha. "But when have you had time to become one? Why, I thought you are only thirteen?"

Kolya winced.

"In the first place I am not thirteen, but fourteen, fourteen in a fortnight," he flushed angrily, "and in the second place I am at a complete loss to understand what my age has to do with it? The question is what are my convictions, not what is my age, isn't it?"

"When you are older, you'll understand for yourself the influence of age on convictions. I fancied, too, that you were not expressing your own

---

*Philosophical satire (1759) by Voltaire.

ideas," Alyosha answered serenely and modestly, but Kolya interrupted him hotly:

"Come, you want obedience and mysticism. You must admit that the Christian religion, for instance, has only been of use to the rich and the powerful to keep the lower classes in slavery, that's so, isn't it?"

"Ah, I know where you read that, and I am sure some one told you so!" cried Alyosha.

"I say, what makes you think I read it? And certainly no one told me so. I can think for myself. . . . I am not opposed to Christ, if you like. He was a most humane person, and if He were alive to-day, He would be found in the ranks of the revolutionists, and would perhaps play a conspicuous part. . . . There's no doubt about that."

"Oh, where, where did you get that from? What fool have you made friends with?" exclaimed Alyosha.

"Come, the truth will out! It has so chanced that I have often talked to Mr. Rakitin, of course, but . . . old Byelinsky[1] said that, too, so they say."

"Byelinsky? I don't remember. He hasn't written that anywhere."

"If he didn't write it, they say he said it. I heard that from a . . . but never mind."

"And have you read Byelinsky?"

"Well, no . . . I haven't read all of him, but . . . I read the passage about Tatyana, why she didn't go off with Onyegin."*

"Didn't go off with Onyegin? Surely you don't . . . understand that already?"

"Why, you seem to take me for little Smurov," said Kolya, with a grin of irritation. "But please don't suppose I'm such a revolutionist. I often disagree with Mr. Rakitin. Though I mention Tatyana, I am not at all for the emancipation of women. I acknowledge that women are a subject race and must obey. *Les femmes tricottent,*† as Napoleon said." Kolya, for some reason, smiled, "And on that question at least I am quite of one mind with that pseudo-great man. I think, too, that to leave one's own country and fly to America is mean, worse than mean—silly. Why go to America when one may be of great service to humanity here? Now especially. There's a perfect mass of fruitful activity open to us. That's what I answered."

"What do you mean? Answered whom? Has some one suggested your going to America already?"

"I must own, they've been at me to go, but I declined. That's between ourselves, of course, Karamazov; do you hear, not a word to any one. I say this only to you. I am not at all anxious to fall into the clutches of the secret police and take lessons at the Chain bridge,

> 'Long will you remember
> The house at the Chain bridge.'[2]

---

*Characters that appear in Pushkin's novel *Eugene Onegin* (1824–1830).
†The women knit (French).

Do you remember? It's splendid. Why are you laughing? You don't suppose I am fibbing, do you?" ("What if he should find out that I've only that one number of *The Bell*[3] in father's bookcase, and haven't read any more of it?" Kolya thought with a shudder.)

"Oh, no, I am not laughing and don't suppose for a moment that you are lying. No, indeed, I can't suppose so, for all this alas! is perfectly true. But tell me, have you read Pushkin, Onyegin, for instance? . . . You spoke just now of Tatyana."

"No, I haven't read it yet, but I want to read it. I have no prejudices, Karamazov; I want to hear both sides. What makes you ask?"

"Oh, nothing."

"Tell me, Karamazov, have you an awful contempt for me?" Kolya rapped out suddenly and drew himself up before Alyosha, as though he were on drill. "Be so kind as to tell me, without beating about the bush."

"I have a contempt for you?" Alyosha looked at him wondering. "What for? I am only sad that a charming nature such as yours should be perverted by all this crude nonsense before you have begun life."

"Don't be anxious about my nature," Kolya interrupted, not without complacency. "But it's true that I am stupidly sensitive, crudely sensitive. You smiled just now, and I fancied you seemed to . . ."

"Oh, my smile meant something quite different. I'll tell you why I smiled. Not long ago I read the criticism made by a German who had lived in Russia, on our students and schoolboys of to-day. 'Show a Russian schoolboy,' he writes, 'a map of the stars, which he knows nothing about, and he will give you back the map next day with corrections on it.' No knowledge and unbounded conceit—that's what the German meant to say about the Russian schoolboy."

"Yes, that's perfectly right," Kolya laughed suddenly, "exactly so! Bravo the German. But he did not see the good side, what do you think? Conceit may be, that comes from youth, that will be corrected if need be, but, on the other hand, there is an independent spirit almost from childhood, boldness of thought and conviction, and not the spirit of these sausage makers, grovelling before authority. . . . But the German was right all the same. Bravo the German. But Germans want strangling all the same. Though they are so good at science and learning they must be strangled."

"Strangled, what for?" smiled Alyosha.

"Well, perhaps I am talking nonsense, I agree. I am awfully childish sometimes, and when I am pleased about anything I can't restrain myself and am ready to talk any stuff. But, I say, we are chattering away here about nothing, and that doctor has been a long time in there. But perhaps he's examining the mamma and that poor crippled Nina. I liked that Nina, you know. She whispered to me suddenly as I was coming away, 'Why didn't you come before?' And in such a voice, so reproachfully! I think she is awfully nice and pathetic."

"Yes, yes! Well, you'll be coming often, you will see what she is like. It would do you a great deal of good to know people like that, to learn to value a great deal which you will find out from knowing these people,"

Alyosha observed warmly. "That would have more effect on you than anything."

"Oh, how I regret and blame myself for not having come sooner!"
Kolya exclaimed, with bitter feeling.

"Yes, it's a great pity. You saw for yourself how delighted the poor child
was to see you. And how he fretted for you to come!"

"Don't tell me! You make it worse! But it serves me right. What kept
me from coming was my conceit, my egoistic vanity, and the beastly wilful-
ness, which I never can get rid of, though I've been struggling with it all my
life. I see that now. I am a beast in lots of ways, Karamazov!"

"No, you have a charming nature, though it's been distorted, and I
quite understand why you have had such an influence on this generous,
morbidly sensitive boy," Alyosha answered warmly.

"And you say that to me!" cried Kolya; "and would you believe it, I
thought—I've thought several times since I've been here—that you despised me! If only you knew how I prize your opinion!"

"But are you really so sensitive? At your age! Would you believe it, just
now, when you were telling your story, I thought, as I watched you, that
you must be very sensitive!"

"You thought so? What an eye you've got, I say! I bet that was when
I was talking about the goose. That was just when I was fancying you had
a great contempt for me for being in such a hurry to show off, and for a
moment I quite hated you for it, and began talking like a fool. Then I
fancied—just now, here—when I said that if there were no God He
would have to be invented, that I was in too great a hurry to display my
knowledge, especially as I got that phrase out of a book. But I swear I
wasn't showing off out of vanity, though I really don't know why, because
I was so pleased, yes, I believe it was because I was so pleased . . . though
it's perfectly disgraceful for any one to be gushing directly they are
pleased, I know that. But I am convinced now that you don't despise me;
it was all my imagination. Oh, Karamazov, I am profoundly unhappy. I
sometimes fancy all sorts of things, that every one is laughing at me, the
whole world, and then I feel ready to overturn the whole order of things."

"And you worry every one about you," smiled Alyosha.

"Yes, I worry every one about me, especially my mother. Karamazov,
tell me, am I very ridiculous now?"

"Don't think about that, don't think of it at all!" cried Alyosha. "And
what does ridiculous mean? Isn't every one constantly being or seeming
ridiculous? Besides, nearly all clever people now are fearfully afraid of being ridiculous, and that makes them unhappy. All I am surprised at is that
you should be feeling that so early, though I've observed it for some time
past, and not only in you. Nowadays the very children have begun to suffer
from it. It's almost a sort of insanity. The devil has taken the form of that
vanity and entered into the whole generation; it's simply the devil," added
Alyosha, without a trace of the smile that Kolya, staring at him expected to
see. "You are like every one else," said Alyosha, in conclusion, "that is, like
very many others. Only you must not be like everybody else, that's all."

"Even if every one is like that?"

"Yes, even if every one is like that. You be the only one not like it. You really are not like every one else, here you are not ashamed to confess to something bad and even ridiculous. And who will admit so much in these days? No one. And people have even ceased to feel the impulse to self-criticism. Don't be like every one else, even if you were the only one."

"Splendid! I was not mistaken in you. You know how to console one. Oh, how I have longed to know you, Karamazov. I've long been eager for this meeting. Can you really have thought about me, too? You said just now that you thought of me, too?"

"Yes, I'd heard of you and had thought of you, too . . . and if it's partly vanity that makes you ask, it doesn't matter."

"Do you know, Karamazov, our talk has been like a declaration of love," said Kolya, in a bashful and melting voice. "That's not ridiculous, is it?"

"Not at all ridiculous, and if it were, it wouldn't matter, because it's been a good thing." Alyosha smiled brightly.

"But do you know, Karamazov, you must admit that you are a little ashamed yourself, now. . . . I see it by your eyes." Kolya smiled with a sort of sly happiness.

"Why ashamed?"

"Well, why are you blushing?"

"It was you made me blush," laughed Alyosha, and he really did blush. "Oh, well, I am a little, goodness knows why, I don't know. . . ." he muttered almost embarrassed.

"Oh, how I love you and admire you at this moment just because you are rather ashamed! Because you are just like me," cried Kolya, in positive ecstasy. His cheeks glowed, his eyes beamed.

"You know, Kolya, you will be very unhappy in your life," something made Alyosha say suddenly.

"I know, I know. How you know it all beforehand!" Kolya agreed at once.

"But you will bless life on the whole, all the same."

"Just so, hurrah! You are a prophet. Oh, we shall get on together, Karamazov! Do you know, what delights me most, is that you treat me quite like an equal. But we are not equals, no, we are not, you are better! But we shall get on. Do you know, all this last month I've been saying to myself, 'either we shall be friends at once, for ever, or we shall part enemies to the grave!'"

"And saying that, of course, you loved me," Alyosha laughed gaily.

"I did. I loved you awfully. I've been loving and dreaming of you. And how do you know it all beforehand? Ah, here's the doctor. Goodness! What will he tell us? Look at his face!"

7

ILUSHA

THE doctor came out of the room again, muffled in his fur coat and with his cap on his head. His face looked almost angry and disgusted, as though he were afraid of getting dirty. He cast a cursory glance round the passage, looking sternly at Alyosha and Kolya as he did so. Alyosha waved from the door to the coachman, and the carriage that had brought the doctor drove up. The captain darted out after the doctor, and, bowing apologetically, stopped him to get the last word. The poor fellow looked utterly crushed; there was a scared look in his eyes.

"Your Excellency, your Excellency . . . is it possible?" he began, but could not go on and clasped his hands in despair. Yet he still gazed imploringly at the doctor, as though a word from him might still change the poor boy's fate.

"I can't help it, I am not God!" the doctor answered offhand, though with the customary impressiveness.

"Doctor . . . your Excellency . . . and will it be soon, soon?"

"You must be prepared for anything," said the doctor in emphatic and incisive tones, and dropping his eyes, he was about to step out to the coach.

"Your Excellency, for Christ's sake," the terror-stricken captain stopped him again. "Your Excellency! but can nothing, absolutely nothing save him now?"

"It's not in my hands now," said the doctor impatiently, "but h'm . . ." he stopped suddenly. "If you could, for instance . . . send . . . your patient . . . at once, without delay" (the words "at once, without delay," the doctor uttered with an almost wrathful sternness that made the captain start) "to Syracuse, the change to the new be-ne-ficial climatic conditions might possibly affect . . ."

"To Syracuse!" cried the captain, unable to grasp what was said.

"Syracuse is in Sicily," Kolya jerked out suddenly in explanation. The doctor looked at him.

"Sicily! your Excellency," faltered the captain, "but you've seen"—he spread out his hands, indicating his surroundings—"mamma and my family?"

"N-no, Sicily is not the place for the family, the family should go to the Caucasus in the early spring . . . your daughter must go to the Caucasus, and your wife . . . after a course of the waters in the Caucasus for her rheumatism . . . must be sent straight to Paris to the mental specialist Lepelletier; I could give you a note to him, and then . . . there might be a change. . . ."

"Doctor, doctor! But you see!" The captain flung wide his hands again despairingly, indicating the bare wooden walls of the passage.

510

"Well, that's not my business," grinned the doctor. "I have only told you the answer of medical science to your question as to possible treatment. As for the rest, to my regret . . ."

"Don't be afraid, apothecary, my dog won't bite you," Kolya rapped out loudly, noticing the doctor's rather uneasy glance at Perezvon, who was standing in the doorway. There was a wrathful note in Kolya's voice. He used the word apothecary instead of doctor on purpose, and, as he explained afterwards, "I used it to insult him."

"What's that?" The doctor flung up his head, staring with surprise at Kolya. "Who's this?" he addressed Alyosha, as though asking him to explain.

"It's Perezvon's master, don't worry about me," Kolya said incisively.

"Perezvon," repeated the doctor, perplexed.

"He hears the bell, but where it is he cannot tell. Good-bye, we shall meet in Syracuse."

"Who's this? Who's this?" The doctor flew into a terrible rage.

"He is a schoolboy, doctor, he is a mischievous boy; take no notice of him," said Alyosha, frowning and speaking quickly. "Kolya, hold your tongue!" he cried to Krassotkin. "Take no notice of him, doctor," he repeated, rather impatiently.

"He wants a thrashing, a good thrashing!" The doctor stamped in a perfect fury.

"And you know, apothecary, my Perezvon might bite!" said Kolya, turning pale, with quivering voice and flashing eyes. "*Ici*, Perezvon!"

"Kolya, if you say another word, I'll have nothing more to do with you," Alyosha cried peremptorily.

"There is only one man in the world who can command Nikolay Krassotkin—this is the man (Kolya pointed to Alyosha). I obey him, good-bye!"

He stepped forward, opened the door, and quickly went into the inner room. Perezvon flew after him. The doctor stood still for five seconds in amazement, looking at Alyosha; then, with a curse, he went out quickly to the carriage, repeating aloud, "This is . . . this is . . . I don't know what it is!" The captain darted forward to help him into the carriage. Alyosha followed Kolya into the room. He was already by Ilusha's bedside. The sick boy was holding his hand and calling for his father. A minute later the captain, too, came back.

"Father, father, come . . . we . . . ," Ilusha faltered in violent excitement, but apparently unable to go on, he flung his wasted arms round his father and Kolya, uniting them in one embrace, and hugging them as tightly as he could. The captain suddenly began to shake with dumb sobs, and Kolya's lips and chin twitched.

"Father, father! How sorry I am for you!!" Ilusha moaned bitterly.

"Ilusha . . . darling . . . the doctor said . . . you would be all right . . . we shall be happy . . . the doctor . . ." the captain began.

"Ah, father! I know what the new doctor said to you about me. . . . I saw!" cried Ilusha, and again he hugged them both with all his strength, hiding his face on his father's shoulder.

"Father, don't cry, and when I die get a good boy, another one . . . choose one of them all, a good one, call him Ilusha and love him instead of me. . . ."

"Hush, old man, you'll get well," Krassotkin cried suddenly, in a voice that sounded angry.

"But don't ever forget me, father," Ilusha went on, "come to my grave . . . and father, bury me by our big stone, where we used to go for our walk, and come to me there with Krassotkin in the evening . . . and Perezvon . . . I shall expect you. . . . Father, father!"

His voice broke. They were all three silent, still embracing. Nina was crying, quietly in her chair, and at last seeing them all crying, "mamma," too, burst into tears.

"Ilusha! Ilusha!" she exclaimed.

Krassotkin suddenly released himself from Ilusha's embrace.

"Good-bye, old man, mother expects me back to dinner," he said quickly. "What a pity I did not tell her! She will be dreadfully anxious. . . . But after dinner I'll come back to you for the whole day, for the whole evening, and I'll tell you all sorts of things, all sorts of things. And I'll bring Perezvon but now I will take him with me, because he will begin to howl when I am away and bother you. Good-bye!"

And he ran out into the passage. He didn't want to cry, but in the passage he burst into tears. Alyosha found him crying.

"Kolya, you must be sure to keep your word and come, or he will be terribly disappointed," Alyosha said emphatically.

"I will! Oh, how I curse myself for not having come before," muttered Kolya, crying, and no longer ashamed of it.

At that moment the captain flew out of the room, and at once closed the door behind him. His face looked frenzied, his lips were trembling. He stood before the two lads and flung up his arms.

"I don't want a good boy! I don't want another boy!" he muttered in a wild whisper, clenching his teeth. "If I forget thee, Jerusalem, may my tongue . . ." he broke off with a sob and sank on his knees before the wooden bench. Pressing his fists against his head, he began sobbing with absurd whimpering cries, doing his utmost that his cries should not be heard in the room.

Kolya ran out into the street.

"Good-bye, Karamazov! Will you come yourself?" he cried sharply and angrily to Alyosha.

"I will certainly come in the evening."

"What was that he said about Jerusalem. . . . What did he mean by that?"

"It's from the Bible. 'If I forget thee, Jerusalem,'* that is, if I forget all that is most precious to me, if I let anything take its place, then may . . ."

"I understand, that's enough! Mind you come! *Ici,* Perezvon!" he cried with positive ferocity to the dog, and with rapid strides he went home.

---

*See Psalm 137.

BOOK ELEVEN

IVAN

1

AT GRUSHENKA'S

ALYOSHA went towards the cathedral square to the widow Morozov's house to see Grushenka, who had sent Fenya to him early in the morning with an urgent message begging him to come. Questioning Fenya, Alyosha learned that her mistress had been particularly distressed since the previous day. During the two months that had passed since Mitya's arrest, Alyosha had called frequently at the widow Morozov's house, both from his own inclination and to take messages for Mitya. Three days after Mitya's arrest, Grushenka was taken very ill and was ill for nearly five weeks. For one whole week she was unconscious. She was very much changed—thinner and a little sallow, though she had for the past fortnight been well enough to go out. But to Alyosha her face was even more attractive than before, and he liked to meet her eyes when he went in to her. A look of firmness and intelligent purpose had developed in her face. There were signs of a spiritual transformation in her, and a steadfast, fine and humble determination that nothing could shake could be discerned in her. There was a small vertical line between her brows which gave her charming face a look of concentrated thought, almost austere at the first glance. There was scarcely a trace of her former frivolity.

It seemed strange to Alyosha, too, that in spite of the calamity that had overtaken the poor girl, betrothed to a man who had been arrested for a terrible crime, almost at the instant of their betrothal, in spite of her illness and the almost inevitable sentence hanging over Mitya, Grushenka had yet not lost her youthful cheerfulness. There was a soft light in the once proud eyes, though at times they gleamed with the old vindictive fire when she was visited by one disturbing thought stronger than ever in her heart. The object of that uneasiness was the same as ever—Katerina Ivanovna, of whom Grushenka had even raved when she lay in delirium. Alyosha knew that she was fearfully jealous of her. Yet Katerina Ivanovna had not once visited Mitya in his prison, though she might have done it whenever she liked. All this made a difficult problem for Alyosha, for he was the only person to whom Grushenka opened her heart and from whom she was continually asking advice. Sometimes he was unable to say anything.

Full of anxiety he entered her lodging. She was at home. She had returned from seeing Mitya half an hour before, and from the rapid movement with which she leapt up from her chair to meet him he saw that she had been expecting him with great impatience. A pack of cards dealt for a game of "fools" lay on the table. A bed had been made up on the leather sofa on the other side and Maximov lay, half-reclining, on it. He wore a dressing-gown and a cotton nightcap, and was evidently ill and weak, though he was smiling blissfully. When the homeless old man returned with Grushenka from Mokroe two months before, he had simply stayed on and was still staying with her. He arrived with her in rain and sleet, sat down on the sofa, drenched and scared, and gazed mutely at her with a timid, appealing smile. Grushenka, who was in terrible grief and in the first stage of fever, almost forgot his existence in all she had to do the first half-hour after her arrival. Suddenly she chanced to look at him intently: he laughed a pitiful, helpless little laugh. She called Fenya and told her to give him something to eat. All that day he sat in the same place, almost without stirring. When it got dark and the shutters were closed, Fenya asked her mistress:

"Is the gentleman going to stay the night, mistress?"

"Yes; make him a bed on the sofa," answered Grushenka.

Questioning him more in detail, Grushenka learned from him that he had literally nowhere to go, and that "Mr. Kalganov, my benefactor, told me straight that he wouldn't receive me again and gave me five roubles."

"Well, God bless you, you'd better stay then," Grushenka decided in her grief, smiling compassionately at him. Her smile wrung the old man's heart and his lips twitched with grateful tears. And so the destitute wanderer had stayed with her ever since. He did not leave the house even when she was ill. Fenya and her grandmother, the cook, did not turn him out, but went on serving him meals and making up his bed on the sofa. Grushenka had grown used to him, and coming back from seeing Mitya (whom she had begun to visit in prison before she was really well) she would sit down and begin talking to "Maximushka" about trifling matters, to keep her from thinking of her sorrow. The old man turned out to be a good story-teller on occasions, so that at last he became necessary to her. Grushenka saw scarcely any one else besides Alyosha, who did not come every day and never stayed long. Her old merchant lay seriously ill at this time, "at his last gasp" as they said in the town, and he did, in fact, die a week after Mitya's trial. Three weeks before his death, feeling the end approaching, he made his sons, their wives and children, come upstairs to him at last and bade them not leave him again. From that moment he gave strict orders to his servants not to admit Grushenka and to tell her if she came, "The master wishes you long life and happiness and tells you to forget him." But Grushenka sent almost every day to inquire after him.

"You've come at last!" she cried, flinging down the cards and joyfully greeting Alyosha, "and Maximushka's been scaring me that perhaps you wouldn't come. Ah, how I need you! Sit down to the table. What will you have—coffee?"

"Yes, please," said Alyosha, sitting down at the table. "I am very hungry."

"That's right, Fenya, Fenya, coffee," cried Grushenka. "It's been made a long time ready for you. And bring some little pies, and mind they are hot. Do you know, we've had a storm over those pies to-day. I took them to the prison for him, and would you believe it, he threw them back to me: he would not eat them. He flung one of them on the floor and stamped on it.

So I said to him: 'I shall leave them with the warder; if you don't eat them before evening, it will be that your venomous spite is enough for you!' With that I went away. We quarrelled again, would you believe it? Whenever I go we quarrel."

Grushenka said all this in one breath in her agitation. Maximov, feeling nervous, at once smiled and looked on the floor.

"What did you quarrel about this time?" asked Alyosha.

"I didn't expect it in the least. Only fancy, he is jealous of the Pole. 'Why are you keeping him?' he said. 'So you've begun keeping him.' He is jealous, jealous of me all the time, jealous eating and sleeping! He even took it into his head to be jealous of Kuzma last week."

"But he knew about the Pole before?"

"Yes, but there it is. He has known about him from the very beginning, but to-day he suddenly got up and began scolding about him. I am ashamed to repeat what he said. Silly fellow! Rakitin went in as I came out. Perhaps Rakitin is egging him on. What do you think?" she added carelessly.

"He loves you, that's what it is; he loves you so much. And now he is particularly worried."

"I should think he might be, with the trial to-morrow. And I went to him to say something about to-morrow, for I dread to think what's going to happen then. You say that he is worried, but how worried I am! And he talks about the Pole! He's too silly! He is not jealous of Maximushka yet, anyway."

"My wife was dreadfully jealous over me, too," Maximov put in his word.

"Jealous of you?" Grushenka laughed in spite of herself. "Of whom could she have been jealous?"

"Of the servant girls."

"Hold your tongue, Maximushka, I am in no laughing mood now, I feel angry. Don't ogle the pies. I shan't give you any; they are not good for you, and I won't give you any vodka either. I have to look after him, too, just as though I kept an almshouse," she laughed.

"I don't deserve your kindness. I am a worthless creature," said Maximov, with tears in his voice. "You would do better to spend your kindness on people of more use than me."

"Ech, every one is of use, Maximushka, and how can we tell who's of most use. If only that Pole didn't exist, Alyosha. He's taken it into his head to fall ill, too, to-day. I've been to see him also. And I shall send him some pies, too, on purpose. I hadn't sent him any, but Mitya accused me of it, so now I shall send some! Ah, here's Fenya with a letter! Yes, it's from the Poles—begging again!"

Pan Mussyalovitch had indeed sent an extremely long and characteristically eloquent letter in which he begged her to lend him three roubles. In the letter was enclosed a receipt for the sum, with a promise to repay it within three months, signed by Pan Vrublevsky as well. Grushenka had received many such letters, accompanied by such receipts, from her former lover during the fortnight of her convalescence. But she knew that the two Poles had been to ask after her health during her illness. The first letter Grushenka got from them was a long one, written on large notepaper and with a big family crest on the seal. It was so obscure and rhetorical that Grushenka put it down before she had read half, unable to make head or tail of it. She could not attend to letters then. The first letter was followed next day by another in which Pan Mussyalovitch begged her for a loan of two thousand roubles for a very short period. Grushenka left that letter, too, unanswered. A whole series of letters had followed—one every day— all as pompous and rhetorical, but the loan asked for, gradually diminishing, dropped to a hundred roubles, then to twenty-five, to ten, and finally Grushenka received a letter in which both the Poles begged her for only one rouble and included a receipt signed by both.

Then Grushenka suddenly felt sorry for them, and at dusk she went round herself to their lodging. She found the two Poles in great poverty, almost destitution, without food or fuel, without cigarettes, in debt to their landlady. The two hundred roubles they had carried off from Mitya at Mokroe had soon disappeared. But Grushenka was surprised at their meeting her with arrogant dignity and self-assertion, with the greatest punctilio and pompous speeches. Grushenka simply laughed, and gave her former admirer ten roubles. Then, laughing, she told Mitya of it and he was not in the least jealous. But ever since, the Poles had attached themselves to Grushenka and bombarded her daily with requests for money and she had always sent them small sums. And now that day Mitya had taken it into his head to be fearfully jealous.

"Like a fool, I went round to him just for a minute, on the way to see Mitya, for he is ill, too, my Pole," Grushenka began again with nervous haste. "I was laughing, telling Mitya about it. 'Fancy,' I said, 'my Pole had the happy thought to sing his old songs to me to the guitar. He thought I would be touched and marry him!' Mitya leapt up swearing. . . . So, there, I'll send them the pies! Fenya, is it that little girl they've sent? Here, give her three roubles and pack a dozen pies up in a paper and tell her to take them. And you, Alyosha, be sure to tell Mitya that I did send them the pies."

"I wouldn't tell him for anything," said Alyosha, smiling.

"Ech! You think he is unhappy about it. Why, he's jealous on purpose. He doesn't care," said Grushenka bitterly.

"On purpose?" queried Alyosha.

"I tell you you are silly, Alyosha. You know nothing about it, with all your cleverness. I am not offended that he is jealous of a girl like me. I would be offended if he were not jealous. I am like that. I am not offended at jealousy. I have a fierce heart, too. I can be jealous myself. Only what offends me is that he doesn't love me at all. I tell you he is jealous now on *purpose*. Am I blind? Don't I see? He began talking to me just now of that woman, of Katerina, saying she was this and that, how she had ordered a doctor from Moscow for him, to try and save him; how she had ordered the best counsel, the most learned one, too. So he loves her, if he'll praise her to my face, more shame to him! He's treated me badly himself, so he attacked me, to make out I am in fault first and to throw it all on me. 'You were with your Pole before me, so I can't be blamed for Katerina,' that's what it amounts to. He wants to throw the whole blame on me. He attacked me on purpose, on purpose, I tell you, but I'll . . ."

Grushenka could not finish saying what she would do. She hid her eyes in her handkerchief and sobbed violently.

"He doesn't love Katerina Ivanovna," said Alyosha firmly.

"Well, whether he loves her or not, I'll soon find out for myself," said Grushenka, with a menacing note in her voice, taking the handkerchief from her eyes. Her face was distorted. Alyosha saw sorrowfully that from being mild and serene, it had become sullen and spiteful.

"Enough of this foolishness," she said suddenly; "it's not for that I sent for you. Alyosha, darling, to-morrow—what will happen to-morrow? That's what worries me! And it's only me it worries! I look at every one and no one is thinking of it. No one cares about it. Are you thinking about it even? To-morrow he'll be tried, you know. Tell me, how will he be tried? You know it's the valet, the valet killed him! Good heavens! Can they condemn him in place of the valet and will no one stand up for him? They haven't troubled the valet at all, have they?"

"He's been severely cross-examined," observed Alyosha thoughtfully; "but every one came to the conclusion it was not he. Now he is lying very ill. He has been ill ever since that attack. Really ill," added Alyosha.

"Oh, dear! couldn't you go to that counsel yourself and tell him the whole thing by yourself? He's been brought from Petersburg for three thousand roubles, they say."

"We gave these three thousand together—Ivan, Katerina Ivanovna and I—but she paid two thousand for the doctor from Moscow herself. The counsel Fetyukovitch would have charged more, but the case has become known all over Russia; it's talked of in all the papers and journals. Fetyukovitch agreed to come more for the glory of the thing, because the case has become so notorious. I saw him yesterday."

"Well? Did you talk to him?" Grushenka put in eagerly.

"He listened and said nothing. He told me that he had already formed his opinion. But he promised to give my words consideration."

"Consideration! Ah, they are swindlers! They'll ruin him. And why did she send for the doctor?"

"As an expert. They want to prove that Mitya's mad and committed the murder when he didn't know what he was doing"; Alyosha smiled gently; "but Mitya won't agree to that."

"Yes; but that would be the truth if he had killed him!" cried Grushenka. "He was mad then, perfectly mad, and that was my fault, wretch that I am! But, of course, he didn't do it, he didn't do it! And they are all against him, the whole town. Even Fenya's evidence went to prove he had done it. And the people at the shop, and that official, and at the tavern, too, before, people had heard him say so! They are all, all against him, all crying out against him."

"Yes, there's a fearful accumulation of evidence," Alyosha observed grimly.

"And Grigory—Grigory Vassilyevitch—sticks to his story that the door was open, persists that he saw it—there's no shaking him. I went and talked to him myself. He's rude about it, too."

"Yes, that's perhaps the strongest evidence against him," said Alyosha.

"And as for Mitya's being mad, he certainly seems like it now," Grushenka began with a peculiarly anxious and mysterious air. "Do you know, Alyosha, I've been wanting to talk to you about it for a long time. I go to him every day and simply wonder at him. Tell me, now, what do you suppose he's always talking about? He talks and talks and I can make nothing of it. I fancied he was talking of something intellectual that I couldn't understand in my foolishness. Only he suddenly began talking to me about a babe—that is, about some child. 'Why is the babe poor?' he said. 'It's for that babe I am going to Siberia now. I am not a murderer, but I must go to Siberia!' What that meant, what babe, I couldn't tell for the life of me. Only I cried when he said it, because he said it so nicely. He cried himself, and I cried, too. He suddenly kissed me and made the sign of the cross over me. What did it mean, Alyosha, tell me? What is this babe?"

"It must be Rakitin, who's been going to see him lately," smiled Alyosha, "though . . . that's not Rakitin's doing. I didn't see Mitya yesterday. I'll see him to-day."

"No, it's not Rakitin; it's his brother Ivan Fyodorovitch upsetting him. It's his going to see him, that's what it is," Grushenka began, and suddenly broke off. Alyosha gazed at her in amazement.

"Ivan's going? Has he been to see him? Mitya told me himself that Ivan hasn't been once."

"There . . . there! What a girl I am! Blurting things out!" exclaimed Grushenka, confused and suddenly blushing. "Stay, Alyosha, hush! Since I've said so much I'll tell the whole truth—he's been to see him twice, the first time directly he arrived. He galloped here from Moscow at once, of course, before I was taken ill; and the second time was a week ago. He told Mitya not to tell you about it, under any circumstances; and not to tell any one, in fact. He came secretly."

Alyosha sat plunged in thought, considering something. The news evidently impressed him.

"Ivan doesn't talk to me of Mitya's case," he said slowly. "He's said very little to me these last two months. And whenever I go to see him, he seems vexed at my coming, so I've not been to him for the last three weeks. Hm! . . . if he was there a week ago . . . there certainly has been a change in Mitya this week."

"There has been a change," Grushenka assented quickly. "They have a secret, they have a secret! Mitya told me himself there was a secret, and such a secret that Mitya can't rest. Before then, he was cheerful—and, indeed, he is cheerful now—but when he shakes his head like that, you know, and strides about the room and keeps pulling at the hair on his right temple with his right hand, I know there is something on his mind worrying him. . . . I know! He was cheerful before, though, indeed, he is cheerful to-day."

"But you said he was worried."

"Yes, he is worried and yet cheerful. He keeps on being irritable for a minute and then cheerful and then irritable again. And you know, Alyosha, I am constantly wondering at him—with this awful thing hanging over him, he sometimes laughs at such trifles as though he were a baby himself."

"And did he really tell you not to tell me about Ivan? Did he say 'don't tell him'?"

"Yes, he told me 'don't tell him.' It's you that Mitya's most afraid of. Because it's a secret: he said himself it was a secret. Alyosha, darling, go to him and find out what their secret is and come and tell me," Grushenka besought him with sudden eagerness. "Set my mind at rest that I may know the worst that's in store for me. That's why I sent for you."

"You think it's something to do with you? If it were, he wouldn't have told you there was a secret."

"I don't know. Perhaps he wants to tell me, but doesn't dare to. He warns me. There is a secret, he tells me, but he won't tell me what it is."

"What do you think yourself?"

"What do I think? It's the end for me, that's what I think. They all three have been plotting my end, for Katerina's in it. It's all Katerina, it all comes from her. She is this and that means that I am not. He tells me that beforehand—warns me. He is planning to throw me over, that's the whole secret. They've planned it together, the three of them—Mitya, Katerina, and Ivan Fyodorovitch. Alyosha, I've been wanting to ask you a long time. A week ago he suddenly told me that Ivan was in love with Katerina, because he often goes to see her. Did he tell me the truth or not? Tell me, on your conscience, tell me the worst."

"I won't tell you a lie. Ivan is not in love with Katerina Ivanovna, I think."

"Oh, that's what I thought! He is lying to me, shameless deceiver, that's what it is! And he was jealous of me just now, so as to put the blame on me afterwards. He is stupid, he can't disguise what he is doing; he is so open, you know. . . . But I'll give it to him, I'll give it to him! 'You believe I did it,' he said. He said that to me, to me. He reproached me with that! God forgive him! You wait, I'll make it hot for Katerina at the trial! I'll just say a word then . . . I'll tell everything then!"

And again she cried bitterly.

"This I can tell you for certain, Grushenka," Alyosha said, getting up. "First, that he loves you, loves you more than any one in the world, and you only, believe me. I know. I do know. The second thing is that I don't want to worm his secret out of him, but if he'll tell me of himself to-day, I shall tell him straight out that I have promised to tell you. Then I'll come to you to-day and tell you. Only . . . I fancy . . . Katerina Ivanovna has nothing to do with it, and that the secret is about something else. That's certain. It isn't likely it's about Katerina Ivanovna, it seems to me. Good-bye for now."

Alyosha shook hands with her. Grushenka was still crying. He saw that she put little faith in his consolation, but she was better for having had her sorrow out, for having spoken of it. He was sorry to leave her in such a state of mind, but he was in haste. He had a great many things to do still.

2

THE INJURED FOOT

THE first of these things was at the house of Madame Hohlakov, and he hurried there to get it over as quickly as possible and not be too late for Mitya. Madame Hohlakov had been slightly ailing for the last three weeks: her foot had for some reason swollen up, and though she was not in bed, she lay all day half-reclining on the couch in her boudoir, in a fascinating but decorous *déshabillé*.* Alyosha had once noted with innocent amusement that, in spite of her illness, Madame Hohlakov had begun to be rather dressy—topknots, ribbons, loose wrappers, had made their appearance, and he had an inkling of the reason, though he dismissed such ideas from his mind as frivolous. During the last two months the young official, Perhotin, had become a regular visitor at the house.

Alyosha had not called for four days and he was in haste to go straight to Lise, as it was with her he had to speak, for Lise had sent a maid to him the previous day, specially asking him to come to her "about something very important," a request which, for certain reasons, had interest for Alyosha. But while the maid went to take his name in to Lise, Madame Hohlakov heard of his arrival from some one, and immediately sent to beg him to come to her "just for one minute." Alyosha reflected that it was better to accede to the mamma's request, or else she would be sending down to Lise's room every minute that he was there. Madame Hohlakov was lying on a couch. She was particularly smartly dressed and was evidently in a state of extreme nervous excitement. She greeted Alyosha with cries of rapture.

"It's ages, ages, perfect ages since I've seen you! It's a whole week—only think of it! Ah, but you were here only four days ago, on Wednesday. You have come to see Lise. I'm sure you meant to slip into her room on tiptoe, without my hearing you. My dear, dear Alexey Fyodorovitch, if you

*Negligee (French).

only knew how worried I am about her! But of that later, though that's the most important thing, of that later. Dear Alexey Fyodorovitch, I trust you implicitly with my Lise. Since the death of Father Zossima—God rest his soul! (she crossed herself)—I look upon you as a monk, though you look charming in your new suit. Where did you find such a tailor in these parts? No, no, that's not the chief thing—of that later. Forgive me for sometimes calling you Alyosha; an old woman like me may take liberties," she smiled coquettishly; "but that will do later, too. The important thing is that I shouldn't forget what is important. Please remind me of it yourself. As soon as my tongue runs away with me, you just say 'the important thing?' Ach! how do I know now what is of most importance? Ever since Lise took back her promise—her childish promise, Alexey Fyodorovitch—to marry you, you've realised, of course, that it was only the playful fancy of a sick child who had been so long confined to her chair—thank God, she can walk now! . . . that new doctor Katya sent for from Moscow for your unhappy brother, who will to-morrow . . . But why speak of to-morrow? I am ready to die at the very thought of to-morrow. Ready to die of curiosity. . . . That doctor was with us yesterday and saw Lise. . . . I paid him fifty roubles for the visit. But that's not the point, that's not the point again. You see, I'm mixing everything up. I am in such a hurry. Why am I in a hurry? I don't understand. It's awful how I seem growing unable to understand anything. Everything seems mixed up in a sort of tangle. I am afraid you are so bored you will jump up and run away, and that will be all I shall see of you. Goodness! Why are we sitting here and no coffee? Yulia, Glafira, coffee!"

Alyosha made haste to thank her, and said that he had only just had coffee.

"Where?"

"At Agrafena Alexandrovna's."

"At . . . at that woman's? Ah, it's she has brought ruin on every one. I know nothing about it though. They say she has become a saint, though it's rather late in the day. She had better have done it before. What use is it now? Hush, hush, Alexey Fyodorovitch, for I have so much to say to you that I am afraid I shall tell you nothing. This awful trial . . . I shall certainly go, I am making arrangements. I shall be carried there in my chair; besides I can sit up. I shall have people with me. And, you know, I am a witness. How shall I speak, how shall I speak? I don't know what I shall say. One has to take an oath, hasn't one?"

"Yes; but I don't think you will be able to go."

"I can sit up. Ah, you put me out; Ah! this trial, this savage act, and then they are all going to Siberia, some are getting married, and all this so quickly, so quickly, everything's changing, and at last—nothing. All grow old and have death to look forward to. Well, so be it! I am weary. This Katya, *cette charmante personne,** has disappointed all my hopes. Now she

_____

*This charming creature (French).

is going to follow one of your brothers to Siberia, and your other brother is going to follow her, and will live in the nearest town, and they will all torment one another. It drives me out of my mind. Worst of all—the publicity. The story has been told a million times over in all the papers in Moscow and Petersburg. Ah! yes, would you believe it, there's a paragraph that I was 'a dear friend' of your brother's—, I can't repeat the horrid word. Just fancy, just fancy!"

"Impossible! Where was the paragraph? What did it say?"

"I'll show you directly. I got the paper and read it yesterday. Here, in the Petersburg paper *Gossip*. The paper began coming out this year. I am awfully fond of gossip, and I take it in, and now it pays me out—this is what gossip comes to! Here it is, here, this passage. Read it."

And she handed Alyosha a sheet of newspaper which had been under her pillow.

It was not exactly that she was upset, she seemed overwhelmed, and perhaps everything really was mixed up in a tangle in her head. The paragraph was very typical, and must have been a great shock to her, but, fortunately perhaps, she was unable to keep her mind fixed on any one subject at that moment, and so might race off in a minute to something else and quite forget the newspaper.

Alyosha was well aware that the story of the terrible case had spread all over Russia. And, good heavens! what wild rumours about his brother, about the Karamazovs, and about himself he had read in the course of those two months, among other equally credible items. One paper had even stated that he had gone into a monastery and become a monk, in horror at his brother's crime. Another contradicted this, and stated that he and his elder, Father Zossima, had broken into the monastery chest and "made tracks from the monastery." The present paragraph in the paper *Gossip* was under the heading, "The Karamazov Case at Skotoprigonyevsk."* (That, alas! was the name of our little town. I had hitherto kept it concealed.) It was brief, and Madame Hohlakov was not directly mentioned in it. No names appeared, in fact. It was merely stated that the criminal, whose approaching trial was making such a sensation—retired army captain, an idle swaggerer, and reactionary bully—was continually involved in amorous intrigues, and particularly popular with certain ladies "who were pining in solitude." One such lady, a pining widow, who tried to seem young though she had a grown-up daughter, was so fascinated by him that only two hours before the crime she offered him three thousand roubles, on condition that he would elope with her to the gold-mines. But the criminal, counting on escaping punishment, had preferred to murder his father to get the three thousand, rather than go off to Siberia with the middle-aged charms of his pining lady. This playful paragraph finished, of course, with an outburst of generous indignation at the wickedness of parricide and at the lately abolished institution of serfdom. Reading it with

---

*Literally, "a place where one would drive cattle," alluding to a stockyard.

curiosity, Alyosha folded up the paper and handed it back to Madame Hohlakov.

"Well, that must be me," she hurried on again. "Of course I am meant. Scarcely more than an hour before, I suggested gold-mines to him, and here they talk of 'middle-aged charms' as though that were my motive! He writes that out of spite! God Almighty forgive him for the middle-aged charms, as I forgive him! You know it's . . . Do you know who it is? It's your friend Rakitin."

"Perhaps," said Alyosha, "though I've heard nothing about it."

"It's he, it's he! No 'perhaps' about it. You know I turned him out of the house. . . . You know all that story, don't you?"

"I know that you asked him not to visit you for the future, but why it was, I haven't heard . . . from you, at least."

"Ah, then you've heard it from him! He abuses me, I suppose, abuses me dreadfully?"

"Yes, he does; but then he abuses every one. But why you've given him up I haven't heard from him either. I meet him very seldom now, indeed. We are not friends."

"Well, then, I'll tell you all about it. There's no help for it, I'll confess, for there is one point in which I was perhaps to blame. Only a little, little point, so little that perhaps it doesn't count. You see, my dear boy"— Madame Hohlakov suddenly looked arch and a charming, though enigmatic, smile played about her lips—"you see, I suspect . . . You must forgive me, Alyosha. I am like a mother to you. . . . No, no; quite the contrary. I speak to you now, as though you were my father—mother's quite out of place. Well, it's as though I were confessing to Father Zossima, that's just it. I called you a monk just now. Well, that poor young man, your friend, Rakitin (Mercy on us! I can't be angry with him. I feel cross, but not very), that frivolous young man, would you believe it, seems to have taken it into his head to fall in love with me. I only noticed it later. At first—a month ago—he only began to come oftener to see me, almost every day; though, of course, we were acquainted before. I knew nothing about it . . . and suddenly it dawned upon me, and I began to notice things with surprise. You know, two months ago, that modest, charming, excellent young man, Pyotr Ilyitch Perhotin, who's in the service here, began to be a regular visitor at the house. You met him here ever so many times yourself. And he is an excellent, earnest young man, isn't he? He comes once every three days, not every day (though I should be glad to see him every day), and always so well dressed. Altogether, I love young people, Alyosha, talented, modest, like you, and he has almost the mind of a statesman, he talks so charmingly, and I shall certainly, certainly try and get promotion for him. He is a future diplomat. On that awful day he almost saved me from death by coming in the night. And your friend Rakitin comes in such boots, and always stretches them out on the carpet. . . . He began hinting at his feelings, in fact, and one day, as he was going, he squeezed my hand terribly hard. My foot began to swell directly after he pressed my hand like that. He had met Pyotr Ilyitch here before, and would you believe it, he is always gibing

at him, growling at him, for some reason. I simply looked at the way they
went on together and laughed inwardly. So I was sitting here alone—no, I
was laid up then. Well, I was lying here alone and suddenly Rakitin comes
in, and only fancy! brought me some verses of his own composition—a
short poem, on my bad foot: that is, he described my foot in a poem. Wait
a minute—how did it go?

'A captivating little foot.'

It began somehow like that. I can never remember poetry. I've got it here.
I'll show it to you later. But it's a charming thing—charming; and, you
know, it's not only about the foot; it had a good moral, too, a charming
idea, only I've forgotten it; in fact, it was just the thing for an album. So, of
course, I thanked him, and he was evidently flattered. I'd hardly had time
to thank him when in comes Pyotr Ilyitch, and Rakitin suddenly looked as
black as night. I could see that Pyotr Ilyitch was in the way, for Rakitin certainly wanted to say something after giving me the verses. I had a presentiment of it; but Pyotr Ilyitch came in. I showed Pyotr Ilyitch the verses
and didn't say who was the author. But I am convinced that he guessed,
though he won't own it to this day, and declares he had no idea. But he
says that on purpose. Pyotr Ilyitch began to laugh at once, and fell to criti-
cising it. 'Wretched doggerel,' he said they were, 'some divinity student
must have written them,' and with such vehemence, such vehemence!
Then, instead of laughing, your friend flew into a rage. 'Good gracious!' I
thought, 'they'll fly at each other.' 'It was I who wrote them,' said he. 'I
wrote them as a joke,' he said, 'for I think it degrading to write verses. . . .
But they are good poetry. They want to put a monument to your Pushkin
for writing about women's feet,[1] while I wrote with a moral purpose, and
you,' said he, 'are an advocate of serfdom. You've no humane ideas,' said
he. 'You have no modern, enlightened feelings, you are uninfluenced by
progress, you are a mere official,' he said, 'and you take bribes.' Then I began screaming and imploring them. And, you know, Pyotr Ilyitch is anything but a coward. He at once took up the most gentlemanly tone, looked
at him sarcastically, listened, and apologised. 'I'd no idea,' said he. 'I
shouldn't have said it, if I had known. I should have praised it. Poets are all
so irritable,' he said. In short, he laughed at him under the cover of the
most gentlemanly tone. He explained to me afterwards that it was all sarcastic. I thought he was in earnest. Only as I lay there, just as before you
now, I thought, 'would it, or would it not, be the proper thing for me to
turn Rakitin out for shouting so rudely at a visitor in my house?' And,
would you believe it, I lay here, shut my eyes, and wondered, would it be
the proper thing or not. I kept worrying and worrying, and my heart began
to beat, and I couldn't make up my mind whether to make an outcry or
not. One voice seemed to be telling me, 'speak,' and the other 'no, don't
speak.' And no sooner had the second voice said that than I cried out, and
fainted. Of course, there was a fuss. I got up suddenly and said to Rakitin,
'It's painful for me to say it, but I don't wish to see you in my house again.'

So I turned him out. Ah! Alexey Fyodorovitch, I know myself I did wrong. I was putting it on. I wasn't angry with him at all really; but I suddenly fancied—that was what did it—that it would be such a fine scene. . . . And yet, believe me, it was quite natural, for I really shed tears and cried for several days afterwards, and then suddenly, one afternoon, I forgot all about it. So it's a fortnight since he's been here, and I kept wondering whether he would come again. I wondered even yesterday, then suddenly last night came this *Gossip*. I read it and gasped. Who could have written it? He must have written it. He went home, sat down, wrote it on the spot, sent it, and they put it in. It was a fortnight ago, you see. But, Alyosha, it's awful how I keep talking and don't say what I want to say. Ah! the words come of themselves!"

"It's very important for me to be in time to see my brother to-day," Alyosha faltered.

"To be sure, to be sure! You bring it all back to me. Listen, what is an aberration?"

"What aberration?" asked Alyosha, wondering.

"In the legal sense. An aberration in which everything is pardonable. Whatever you do, you will be acquitted at once."

"What do you mean?"

"I'll tell you. This Katya . . . Ah! she is a charming, charming creature, only I never can make out who it is she is in love with. She was with me some time ago and I couldn't get anything out of her. Especially as she won't talk to me except on the surface now. She is always talking about my health and nothing else, and she takes up such a tone with me, too. I simply said to myself, 'Well, so be it. I don't care . . .', Oh, yes. I was talking of aberration. This doctor has come. You know a doctor has come? Of course you know it—the one who discovers madmen. You wrote for him. No, it wasn't you, but Katya. It's all Katya's doing. Well, you see, a man may be sitting perfectly sane and suddenly have an aberration. He may be conscious and know what he is doing and yet be in a state of aberration. And there's no doubt that Dmitri Fyodorovitch was suffering from aberration. They found out about aberration as soon as the law courts were reformed. It's all the good effect of the reformed law courts. The doctor has been here and questioned me about that evening, about the gold-mines. 'How did he seem then?' he asked me. He must have been in a state of aberration. He came in shouting, 'Money, money, three thousand! Give me three thousand!' and then went away and immediately did the murder. 'I don't want to murder him,' he said, and he suddenly went and murdered him. That's why they'll acquit him, because he struggled against it and yet he murdered him."

"But he didn't murder him," Alyosha interrupted rather sharply. He felt more and more sick with anxiety and impatience.

"Yes, I know it was that old man Grigory murdered him."

"Grigory?" cried Alyosha.

"Yes, yes; it was Grigory. He lay as Dmitri Fyodorovitch struck him down, and then got up, saw the door open, went in and killed Fyodor Pavlovitch."

"But why, why?"

"Suffering from aberration. When he recovered from the blow Dmitri Fyodorovitch gave him on the head, he was suffering from aberration: he went and committed the murder. As for his saying he didn't, he very likely doesn't remember. Only, you know, it'll be better, ever so much better, if Dmitri Fyodorovitch murdered him. And that's how it must have been, though I say it was Grigory. It certainly was Dmitri Fyodorovitch, and that's better, ever so much better! Oh, not better that a son should have killed his father, I don't defend that. Children ought to honour their parents, and yet it would be better if it were he, as you'd have nothing to cry over then, for he did it when he was unconscious or rather when he was conscious, but did not know what he was doing. Let them acquit him—that's so humane, and would show what a blessing reformed law courts are. I knew nothing about it, but they say they have been so a long time. And when I heard it yesterday, I was so struck by it that I wanted to send for you at once. And if he is acquitted, make him come straight from the law courts to dinner with me, and I'll have a party of friends, and we'll drink to the reformed law courts. I don't believe he'd be dangerous; besides, I'll invite a great many friends, so that he could always be led out if he did anything. And then he might be made a justice of the peace or something in another town, for those who have been in trouble themselves make the best judges. And, besides, who isn't suffering from aberration, nowadays?—you, I, all of us are in a state of aberration, and there are ever so many examples of it: a man sits singing a song, suddenly something annoys him, he takes a pistol and shoots the first person he comes across, and no one blames him for it. I read that lately, and all the doctors confirm it. The doctors are always confirming; they confirm anything. Why, my Lise is in a state of aberration. She made me cry again yesterday, and the day before, too, and to-day I suddenly realised that it's all due to aberration. Oh, Lise grieves me so! I believe she's quite mad. Why did she send for you? Did she send for you or did you come of yourself?"

"Yes, she sent for me, and I am just going to her." Alyosha got up resolutely.

"Oh, my dear, dear Alexey Fyodorovitch, perhaps that's what's most important," Madame Hohlakov cried, suddenly bursting into tears. "God knows I trust Lise to you with all my heart, and it's no matter her sending for you on the sly, without telling her mother. But forgive me, I can't trust my daughter so easily to your brother Ivan Fyodorovitch, though I still consider him the most chivalrous young man. But only fancy, he's been to see Lise and I knew nothing about it!"

"How? What? When?" Alyosha was exceedingly surprised. He had not sat down again and listened standing.

"I will tell you, that's perhaps why I asked you to come, for I don't know now why I did ask you to come. Well, Ivan Fyodorovitch has been to see me twice, since he came back from Moscow. First time he came as a friend to call on me, and the second time Katya was here and he came because he heard she was here. I didn't, of course, expect him to come often, knowing what a lot he has to do as it is, *vous comprenez, cette affaire et la mort terrible* *de votre papa.** But I suddenly heard he'd been here again, not to see me but to see Lise. That's six days ago now. He came, stayed five minutes, and went away. And I didn't hear of it till three days afterwards, from Glafira, so it was a great shock to me. I sent for Lise directly. She laughed. 'He thought you were asleep,' she said, 'and came in to me to ask after your health.' Of course, that's how it happened. But Lise, Lise, mercy on us, how she distresses me! Would you believe it, one night, four days ago, just after you saw her last time, and had gone away, she suddenly had a fit, screaming, shrieking, hysterics! Why is it I never have hysterics? Then, next day another fit and the same thing on the third, and yesterday too, and then yesterday that aberration. She suddenly screamed out, 'I hate Ivan Fyodorovitch. I insist on your never letting him come to the house again.' I was struck dumb at these amazing words, and answered, 'On what grounds could I refuse to see such an excellent young man, a young man of such learning too, and so unfortunate,' for all this business is a misfortune, isn't it? She suddenly burst out laughing at my words, and so rudely, you know. Well, I was pleased, I thought I had amused her and the fits would pass off, especially as I wanted to refuse to see Ivan Fyodorovitch any way on account of his strange visits without my knowledge, and meant to ask him for an explanation. But early this morning Lise waked and flew into a passion with Yulia and, would you believe it, slapped her in the face. That's monstrous, I am always polite to my servants. And an hour later she was hugging Yulia's feet and kissing them. She sent a message to me, that she wasn't coming to me at all, and would never come and see me again, and when I dragged myself down to her, she rushed to kiss me, crying, and as she kissed me, she pushed me out of the room without saying a word, so I couldn't find out what was the matter. Now, dear Alexey Fyodorovitch, I rest all my hopes on you, and, of course, my whole life is in your hands. I simply beg you to go to Lise and find out everything from her, as you alone can, and come back and tell me—me, her mother, for you understand it will be the death of me, simply the death of me, if this goes on, or else I shall run away. I can stand no more. I have patience; but I may lose patience, and then . . . then something awful will happen. Ah, dear me! At last, Pyotr Ilyitch!" cried Madame Hohlakov, beaming all over as she saw Perhotin enter the room. "You are late, you are late! Well, sit down, speak, put us out of suspense. What does the counsel say? Where are you off to, Alexey Fyodorovitch?"

"To Lise."

"Oh, yes. You won't forget, you won't forget what I asked you? It's a question of life and death!"

"Of course, I won't forget, if I can . . . but I am so late," muttered Alyosha, beating a hasty retreat.

"No, be sure, be sure to come in; don't say 'if you can.' I shall die if you don't," Madame Hohlakov called after him, but Alyosha had already left the room.

---

*You understand, this business and the terrible death of your papa (French).

3

A LITTLE DEMON

GOING in to Lise, he found her half reclining in the invalid chair, in which she had been wheeled when she was unable to walk. She did not move to meet him, but her sharp keen eyes were simply riveted on his face. There was a feverish look in her eyes, her face was pale and yellow. Alyosha was amazed at the change that had taken place in her in three days. She was positively thinner. She did not hold out her hand to him. He touched the thin, long fingers which lay motionless on her dress, then he sat down facing her, without a word.

"I know you are in a hurry to get to the prison," Lise said curtly, "and mamma's kept you there for hours, she's just been telling you about me and Yulia."

"How do you know?" asked Alyosha.

"I've been listening. Why do you stare at me? I want to listen and I do listen, there's no harm in that. I don't apologise."

"You are upset about something?"

"On the contrary, I am very happy. I've only just been reflecting for the thirtieth time what a good thing it is I refused you and shall not be your wife. You are not fit to be a husband. If I were to marry you and give you a note to take to the man I loved after you, you'd take it and be sure to give it to him and bring an answer back, too. If you were forty, you would still go on taking my love-letters for me."

She suddenly laughed.

"There is something spiteful and yet open-hearted about you," Alyosha smiled to her.

"The open-heartedness consists in my not being ashamed of myself with you. What's more, I don't want to feel ashamed with you, just with you. Alyosha, why is it I don't respect you? I am very fond of you, but I don't respect you. If I respected you, I shouldn't talk to you without shame, should I?"

"No."

"But do you believe that I am not ashamed with you?"

"No, I don't believe it."

Lise laughed nervously again; she spoke rapidly.

"I sent your brother, Dmitri Fyodorovitch, some sweets in prison. Alyosha, you know, you are quite pretty! I shall love you awfully for having so quickly allowed me not to love you."

"Why did you send for me to-day, Lise?"

"I wanted to tell you of a longing I have. I should like some one to torture me, marry me and then torture me, deceive me and go away. I don't want to be happy."

"You are in love with disorder?"

"Yes, I want disorder. I keep wanting to set fire to the house. I keep imagining how I'll creep up and set fire to the house on the sly, it must be on the sly. They'll try to put it out, but it'll go on burning. And I shall know and say nothing. Ah, what silliness! And how bored I am!"

She waved her hand with a look of repulsion.

"It's your luxurious life," said Alyosha, softly.

"Is it better then to be poor?"

"Yes, it is better."

"That's what your monk taught you. That's not true. Let me be rich and all the rest poor, I'll eat sweets and drink cream and not give any to any one else. Ach, don't speak, don't say anything," she shook her hand at him, though Alyosha had not opened his mouth. "You've told me all that before, I know it all by heart. It bores me. If I am ever poor, I shall murder somebody, and even if I am rich, I may murder some one, perhaps—why do nothing! But do you know, I should like to reap, cut the rye? I'll marry you, and you shall become a peasant, a real peasant; we'll keep a colt, shall we? Do you know Kalganov?"

"Yes."

"He is always wandering about, dreaming. He says, why live in real life, it's better to dream. One can dream the most delightful things, but real life is a bore. But he'll be married soon for all that, he's been making love to me already. Can you spin tops?"

"Yes."

"Well, he's just like a top: he wants to be wound up and set spinning and then to be lashed, lashed, lashed with a whip. If I marry him, I'll keep him spinning all his life. You are not ashamed to be with me?"

"No."

"You are awfully cross, because I don't talk about holy things. I don't want to be holy. What will they do to one in the next world for the greatest sin? You must know all about that."

"God will censure you." Alyosha was watching her steadily.

"That's just what I should like. I would go up and they would censure me and I would burst out laughing in their faces. I should dreadfully like to set fire to the house, Alyosha, to our house, you still don't believe me?"

"Why? There are children of twelve years old, who have a longing to set fire to something and they do set things on fire too. It's a sort of disease."

"That's not true, that's not true, there may be children, but that's not what I mean."

"You take evil for good; it's a passing crisis, it's the result of your illness, perhaps."

"You do despise me though! It's simply that I don't want to do good, I want to do evil, and it has nothing to do with illness."

"Why do evil?"

"So that everything might be destroyed. Ah, how nice it would be if everything were destroyed! You know, Alyosha, I sometimes think of doing a fearful lot of harm and everything bad, and I should do it for a long while on the sly and suddenly every one would find it out. Every one will stand round and point their fingers at me and I would look at them all. That would be awfully nice. Why would it be so nice, Alyosha?"

"I don't know. It's a craving to destroy something good or as you say, to set fire to something. It happens sometimes."

"I not only say it, I shall do it."

"I believe you."

"Ah, how I love you for saying you believe me. And you are not lying one little bit. But perhaps you think that I am saying all this on purpose to annoy you?"

"No, I don't think that . . . though perhaps there is a little desire to do that in it, too."

"There is a little. I never can tell lies to you," she declared, with a strange fire in her eyes.

What struck Alyosha above everything was her earnestness. There was not a trace of humour or jesting in her face now, though, in old days, fun and gaiety never deserted her even at her most "earnest" moments.

"There are moments when people love crime," said Alyosha thoughtfully.

"Yes, yes! You have uttered my thought, they love crime, every one loves crime, they love it always, not at some 'moments.' You know, it's as though people have made an agreement to lie about it and have lied about it ever since. They all declare that they hate evil, but secretly they all love it."

"And are you still reading nasty books?"

"Yes, I am. Mamma reads them and hides them under her pillow and I steal them."

"Aren't you ashamed to destroy yourself?"

"I want to destroy myself. There's a boy here, who lay down between the railway lines when the train was passing. Lucky fellow! Listen, your brother is being tried now for murdering his father and every one loves his having killed his father."

"Loves his having killed his father?"

"Yes, loves it, every one loves it! Everybody says it's so awful, but secretly they simply love it. I for one love it."

"There is some truth in what you say about every one," said Alyosha softly.

"Oh, what ideas you have!" Lise shrieked in delight. "And you a monk, too! You wouldn't believe how I respect you, Alyosha, for never telling lies. Oh, I must tell you a funny dream of mine. I sometimes dream of devils. It's night, I am in my room with a candle and suddenly there are devils all over the place, in all the corners, under the table, and they open the doors, there's a crowd of them behind the doors and they want to come and seize me. And they are just coming, just seizing me. But I suddenly cross myself and they all draw back, though they don't go away altogether, they stand at the doors and in the corners, waiting. And suddenly I have a frightful longing to revile God aloud, and so I begin, and then they come crowding back to me, delighted, and seize me again and I cross myself again and they all draw back. It's awful fun, it takes one's breath away."

"I've had the same dream, too," said Alyosha suddenly.

"Really?" cried Lise, greatly surprised. "I say, Alyosha, don't laugh, that's awfully important. Could two different people have the same dream?"

"It seems they can."

"Alyosha, I tell you, it's awfully important," Lise went on, with really excessive amazement. "It's not the dream that's important, but your having the same dream as me. You never lie to me, don't lie now: is it true? You are not laughing?"

"It's true."

Lise seemed extraordinarily impressed and for half a minute she was silent.

"Alyosha, come and see me, come and see me more often," she said suddenly, in a supplicating voice.

"I'll always come to see you, all my life," answered Alyosha firmly.

"You are the only person I can talk to, you know," Lise began again. "I talk to no one but myself and you. Only you in the whole world. And to you more readily than to myself. And I am not a bit ashamed with you, not a bit. Alyosha, why am I not ashamed with you, not a bit? Alyosha, is it true that at Easter the Jews steal a child and kill it?"

"I don't know."

"There's a book here in which I read about the trial of a Jew, who took a child of four years old and cut off the fingers from both hands, and then crucified him on the wall, hammered nails into him, and crucified him, and afterwards, when he was tried, he said that the child died soon, within four hours. That was 'soon'! He said the child moaned, kept on moaning and he stood admiring it. That's nice!"

"Nice?"

"Nice, I sometimes imagine that it was I who crucified him. He would hang there moaning and I would sit opposite him eating pineapple compote. I am awfully fond of pineapple compote. Do you like it?"

Alyosha looked at her in silence. Her pale, sallow face was suddenly contorted, her eyes burned.

"You know, when I read about that Jew I shook with sobs all night. I kept fancying how the little thing cried and moaned (a child of four years old understands, you know) and all the while the thought of pineapple compote haunted me. In the morning I wrote a letter to a certain person, begging him *particularly* to come and see me. He came and I suddenly told him all about the child and the pineapple compote. *All* about it, *all*, and said that it was nice. He laughed and said it really was nice. Then he got up and went away. He was only here five minutes. Did he despise me? Did he despise me? Tell me, tell me, Alyosha, did he despise me or not?" She sat up on the couch, with flashing eyes.

"Tell me," Alyosha asked anxiously, "did you send for that person?"

"Yes, I did."

"Did you send him a letter?"

"Yes."

"Simply to ask about that, about that child?"

"No, not about that at all. But when he came, I asked him about that at once. He answered, laughed, got up and went away."

"That person behaved honourably," Alyosha murmured.

"And did he despise me? Did he laugh at me?"

"No, for perhaps he believes in the pineapple compote himself. He is very ill now, too, Lise."

"Yes, he does believe in it," said Lise, with flashing eyes.

"He doesn't despise any one," Alyosha went on. "Only he does not believe any one. If he doesn't believe in people, of course, he does despise them."

"Then he despises me, me?"

"You, too."

"Good." Lise seemed to grind her teeth. "When he went out laughing, I felt that it was nice to be despised. The child with fingers cut off is nice and to be despised is nice. . . ."

And she laughed in Alyosha's face, a feverish malicious laugh.

"Do you know, Alyosha, do you know, I should like . . . Alyosha save me!" she suddenly jumped from the couch, rushed to him and seized him with both hands. "Save me!" she almost groaned. "Is there any one in the world I could tell what I've told you? I've told you the truth, the truth. I shall kill myself, because I loathe everything! I don't want to live, because I loathe everything! I loathe everything, everything. Alyosha, why don't you love me in the least?" she finished in a frenzy.

"But I do love you!" answered Alyosha warmly.

"And will you weep over me, will you?"

"Yes."

"Not because I won't be your wife, but simply weep for me?"

"Thank you! It's only your tears I want. Every one else may punish me and trample me under foot, every one, every one, not excepting *any one*. For I don't love any one. Do you hear, not any one! On the contrary, I hate him! Go, Alyosha, it's time you went to your brother," she tore herself away from him suddenly.

"How can I leave you like this?" said Alyosha, almost in alarm.

"Go to your brother, the prison will be shut, go, here's your hat. Give my love to Mitya, go, go!"

And she almost forcibly pushed Alyosha out of the door. He looked at her with pained surprise, when he was suddenly aware of a letter in his right hand, a tiny letter folded up tight and sealed. He glanced at it and instantly read the address "to Ivan Fyodorovitch Karamazov." He looked quickly at Lise. Her face had become almost menacing.

"Give it to him, you must give it to him!" she ordered him, trembling and beside herself. "To-day, at once, or I'll poison myself! That's why I sent for you."

And she slammed the door quickly. The bolt clicked. Alyosha put the note in his pocket and went straight downstairs, without going back to Madame Hohlakov, forgetting her, in fact. As soon as Alyosha had gone, Lise unbolted the door, opened it a little, put her finger in the crack and slammed the door with all her might, pinching her finger. Ten seconds after, releasing her finger, she walked softly, slowly to her chair, sat up straight in it and looked intently at her blackened finger and at the blood that oozed from under the nail. Her lips were quivering and she kept whispering rapidly to herself:

"I am a wretch, wretch, wretch, wretch!"

4

A HYMN AND A SECRET

I T was quite late (days are short in November) when Alyosha rang at the prison gate. It was beginning to get dusk. But Alyosha knew that he would be admitted without difficulty. Things were managed in our little town, as everywhere else. At first, of course, on the conclusion of the preliminary inquiry, relations and a few other persons could only obtain interviews with Mitya by going through certain inevitable formalities. But later, though the formalities were not relaxed, exceptions were made for some, at least, of Mitya's visitors. So much so, that sometimes the interviews with the prisoner in the room set aside for the purpose were practically tête-à-tête.

These exceptions, however, were few in number; only Grushenka, Alyosha and Rakitin were treated like this. But the captain of the police, Mihail Mihailovitch, was very favourably disposed to Grushenka. His abuse of her at Mokroe weighed on the old man's conscience, and when he learned the whole story, he completely changed his view of her. And, strange to say, though he was firmly persuaded of his guilt, yet after Mitya was once in prison, the old man came to take a more and more lenient view of him. "He was a man of good heart, perhaps," he thought, "who had come to grief from drinking and dissipation." His first horror had been succeeded by pity. As for Alyosha, the police captain was very fond of him and had known him for a long time. Rakitin, who had of late taken to coming very often to see the prisoner, was one of the most intimate acquaintances of the "police captain's young ladies," as he called them, and was always hanging about their house. He gave lessons in the house of the prison superintendent, too, who, though scrupulous in the performance of his duties, was a kind-hearted old man. Alyosha, again, had an intimate acquaintance of long standing with the superintendent, who was fond of talking to him, generally on sacred subjects. He respected Ivan Fyodorovitch, and stood in awe of his opinion, though he was a great philosopher himself; "self-taught," of course. But Alyosha had an irresistible attraction for him. During the last year the old man had taken to studying the Apocryphal Gospels,* and constantly talked over his impressions with his young friend. He used to come and see him in the monastery and discussed for hours together with him and with the monks. So even if Alyosha were late at the prison, he had only to go to the superintendent and everything was made easy. Besides, every one in the prison, down to the humblest warder, had grown used to Alyosha. The sentry, of course, did not trouble him so long as the authorities were satisfied.

When Mitya was summoned from his cell, he always went downstairs, to the place set aside for interviews. As Alyosha entered the room he came upon Rakitin, who was just taking leave of Mitya. They were both talking loudly. Mitya was laughing heartily as he saw him out, while Rakitin seemed grumbling. Rakitin did not like meeting Alyosha, especially of late. He scarcely spoke to him, and bowed to him stiffly. Seeing Alyosha enter now, he frowned and looked away, as though he were entirely absorbed in buttoning his big, warm, fur-trimmed overcoat. Then he began looking at once for his umbrella.

"I must mind not to forget my belongings," he muttered, simply to say something.

"Mind you don't forget other people's belongings," said Mitya, as a joke, and laughed at once at his own wit. Rakitin fired up instantly.

"You'd better give that advice to your own family, who've always been a slave-driving lot, and not to Rakitin," he cried, suddenly trembling with anger.

"What's the matter? I was joking," cried Mitya. "Damn it all! They are all like that," he turned to Alyosha, nodding towards Rakitin's hurriedly retreating figure. "He was sitting here, laughing and cheerful, and all at once he boils up like that. He didn't even nod to you. Have you broken with him completely? Why are you so late? I've not been simply waiting, but thirsting for you the whole morning. But never mind. We'll make up for it now."

"Why does he come here so often? Surely you are not such great friends?" asked Alyosha. He, too, nodded at the door through which Rakitin had disappeared.

"Great friends with Rakitin? No, not as much as that. Is it likely—a pig like that? He considers I am . . . a blackguard. They can't understand a joke either, that's the worst of such people. They never understand a joke, and their souls are dry, dry and flat; they remind me of prison walls when I was first brought here. But he is a clever fellow, very clever. Well, Alexey, it's all over with me now."

---

*Accounts of Christ's life not included in the New Testament and not accepted as canonical.

He sat down on the bench and made Alyosha sit down beside him.

"Yes, the trial's to-morrow. Are you so hopeless, brother?" Alyosha said, with an apprehensive feeling.

"What are you talking about?" said Mitya, looking at him rather uncertainly. "Oh, you mean the trial! Damn it all! Till now we've been talking of things that don't matter, about this trial, but I haven't said a word to you about the chief thing. Yes, the trial is to-morrow; but it wasn't the trial I meant, when I said it was all over with me. Why do you look at me so critically?"

"What do you mean, Mitya?"

"Ideas, ideas, that's all! Ethics! What is ethics?"

"Ethics?" asked Alyosha, wondering.

"Yes; is it a science?"

"Yes, there is such a science . . . but . . . I confess I can't explain to you what sort of science it is."

"Rakitin knows. Rakitin knows a lot, damn him! He's not going to be a monk. He means to go to Petersburg. There he'll go in for criticism of an elevating tendency. Who knows, he may be of use and make his own career, too. Ough! they are first-rate, these people, at making a career! Damn ethics. I am done for, Alexey, I am, you man of God! I love you more than any one. It makes my heart yearn to look at you. Who was Karl Bernard?"

"Karl Bernard?" Alyosha was surprised again.

"No, not Karl. Stay, I made a mistake. Claude Bernard.[2] What was he? Chemist or what?"

"He must be a savant," answered Alyosha; "but I confess I can't tell you much about him, either. I've heard of him as a savant, but what sort I don't know."

"Well, damn him, then! I don't know either," swore Mitya. "A scoundrel of some sort, most likely. They are all scoundrels. And Rakitin will make his way. Rakitin will get on anywhere; he is another Bernard. Ugh, these Bernards! They are all over the place."

"But what is the matter?" Alyosha asked insistently.

"He wants to write an article about me, about my case, and so begin his literary career. That's what he comes for; he said so himself. He wants to prove some theory. He wants to say 'he couldn't help murdering his father, he was corrupted by his environment,' and so on. He explained it all to me. He is going to put in a tinge of Socialism, he says. But there, damn the fellow, he can put in a tinge, if he likes, I don't care. He can't bear Ivan, he hates him. He's not fond of you, either. But I don't turn him out, for he is a clever fellow. Awfully conceited though. I said to him just now, 'the Karamazovs are not blackguards, but philosophers; for all true Russians are philosophers, and though you've studied, you are not a philosopher—you are a low fellow.' He laughed, so maliciously. And I said to him, '*de ideabus non est disputandum.*'[3] Isn't that rather good? I can set up for being a classic, you see!" Mitya laughed suddenly.

"Why is it all over with you? You said so just now?" Alyosha interposed.

"Why is it all over with me? Mm! . . . . The fact of it is . . . if you take it as a whole, I am sorry to lose God—that's why it is."

"What do you mean by 'sorry to lose God'?"

"Imagine: inside, in the nerves, in the head—that is, these nerves are there in the brain . . . (damn them!) there are sort of little tails, the little tails of those nerves, and as soon as they begin quivering . . . that is, you see, I look at something with my eyes and then they begin quivering, those little tails . . . and when they quiver, then an image appears . . . it doesn't appear at once, but an instant, a second, passes . . . and then something like a moment appears; that is, not a moment—devil take the moment!— but an image; that is, an object, or an action, damn it! That's why I see and then think, because of those tails, not at all because I've got a soul, and that I am some sort of image and likeness. All that is nonsense! Rakitin explained it all to me yesterday, brother, and it simply bowled me over. It's magnificent, Alyosha, this science! A new man's arising—that I understand. . . . And yet I am sorry to lose God!"

"Well, that's a good thing, anyway," said Alyosha.

"That I am sorry to lose God! It's chemistry, brother, chemistry! There's no help for it, your reverence, you must make way for chemistry. And Rakitin does dislike God. Ough! doesn't he dislike Him! That's the sore point with all of them. But they conceal it. They tell lies. They pretend. 'Will you preach this in your reviews?' I asked him. 'Oh, well, if I did it openly, they won't let it through,' he said. He laughed. 'But what will become of men then?' I asked him, 'without God and immortal life? All things are lawful then, they can do what they like?' 'Didn't you know?' he said laughing, 'a clever man can do what he likes,' he said. 'A clever man knows his way about, but you've put your foot in it, committing a murder, and now you are rotting in prison.' He says that to my face! A regular pig! I used to kick such people out, but now I listen to them. He talks a lot of sense, too. Writes well. He began reading me an article last week. I copied out three lines of it. Wait a minute. Here it is."

Mitya hurriedly pulled out a piece of paper from his pocket and read:

" 'In order to determine this question, it is above all essential to put one's personality in contradiction to one's reality.' Do you understand that?"

"No, I don't," said Alyosha. He looked at Mitya and listened to him with curiosity.

"I don't understand either. It's dark and obscure, but intellectual. 'Every one writes like that now,' he says, 'it's the effect of their environment.' They are afraid of the environment. He writes poetry, too, the rascal. He's written in honour of Madame Hohlakov's foot. Ha, ha, ha!"

"I've heard about it," said Alyosha.

"Have you? And have you heard the poem?"

"No."

"I've got it. Here it is. I'll read it to you. You don't know—I haven't told you—there's quite a story about it. He's a rascal! Three weeks ago he began to tease me: 'You've got yourself into a mess, like a fool, for the sake of three thousand, but I'm going to collar a hundred and fifty thousand. I am going to

marry a widow and buy a house in Petersburg.' And he told me he was
courting Madame Hohlakov. She hadn't much brains in her youth, and now
at forty she has lost what she had. 'But she's awfully sentimental,' he says;
'that's how I shall get hold of her. When I marry her, I shall take her to Petersburg and there I shall start a newspaper.' And his mouth was simply watering, the beast, not for the widow, but for the hundred and fifty thousand.
And he made me believe it. He came to see me every day. 'She is coming
round,' he declared. He was beaming with delight. And then, all of a sudden,
he was turned out of the house. Perhotin's carrying everything before him,
bravo! I could kiss the silly old noodle for turning him out of the house. And
he had written this doggerel. 'It's the first time I've soiled my hands with
writing poetry,' he said. 'It's to win her heart, so it's in a good cause. When I
get hold of the silly woman's fortune, I can be of great social utility.' They
have this social justification for every nasty thing they do! 'Anyway it's better than your Pushkin's poetry,' he said, 'for I've managed to advocate enlightenment even in that. I understand what he means about Pushkin, I
quite see that, if he really was a man of talent and only wrote about
women's feet. But wasn't Rakitin stuck up about his doggerel! The vanity
of these fellows! 'On the convalescence of the swollen foot of the object of
my affections'—he thought of that for a title. He's a waggish fellow.

> A captivating little foot,
> Though swollen and red and tender!
> The doctors come and plasters put,
> But still they cannot mend her.
>
> Yet, 'tis not for her foot I dread—
> A theme for Pushkin's muse more fit—
> It's not her foot, it is her head:
> I tremble for her loss of wit!
>
> For as her foot swells, strange to say,
> Her intellect is on the wane—
> Oh, for some remedy I pray
> That may restore both foot and brain!'

He is a pig, a regular pig, but he's very arch, the rascal! And he really has
put in a progressive idea. And wasn't he angry when she kicked him out!
He was gnashing his teeth!"

"He's taken his revenge already," said Alyosha. "He's written a paragraph about Madame Hohlakov."

And Alyosha told him briefly about the paragraph in *Gossip*.

"That's his doing, that's his doing!" Mitya assented, frowning. "That's
him! These paragraphs . . . I know . . . the insulting things that have been
written about Grushenka, for instance. . . . And about Katya, too. . . . Hm!"

He walked across the room with a harassed air.

"Brother, I cannot stay long," Alyosha said, after a pause. "To-morrow will be a great and awful day for you, the judgment of God will be accomplished . . . I am amazed at you, you walk about here, talking of I don't know what. . . ."

"No, don't be amazed at me," Mitya broke in warmly. "Am I to talk of that stinking dog? Of the murderer? We've talked enough of him. I don't want to say more of the stinking son of Stinking Lizaveta! God will kill him, you will see. Hush!"

He went up to Alyosha excitedly and kissed him. His eyes glowed.

"Rakitin wouldn't understand it," he began in a sort of exaltation; "but you, you'll understand it all. That's why I was thirsting for you. You see, there's so much I've been wanting to tell you for ever so long, here, within these peeling walls, but I haven't said a word about what matters most; the moment never seems to have come. Now I can wait no longer. I must pour out my heart to you. Brother, these last two months I've found in myself a new man. A new man has risen up in me. He was hidden in me, but would never have come to the surface, if it hadn't been for this blow from heaven. I am afraid! And what do I care if I spend twenty years in the mines, breaking out ore with a hammer? I am not a bit afraid of that—it's something else I am afraid of now: that that new man may leave me. Even there, in the mines, under ground, I may find a human heart in another convict and murderer by my side, and I may make friends with him, for even there one may live and love and suffer. One may thaw and revive a frozen heart in that convict, one may wait upon him for years, and at last bring up from the dark depths a lofty soul, a feeling, suffering creature; one may bring forth an angel, create a hero! There are so many of them, hundreds of them, and we are all to blame for them. Why was it I dreamed of that 'babe' at such a moment? 'Why is the babe so poor?' That was a sign to me at that moment. It's for the babe I'm going. Because we are all responsible for all. For all the 'babes,' for there are big children as well as little children. All are 'babes.' I go for all, because some one must go for all. I didn't kill father, but I've got to go. I accept it. It's all come to me here, here, within these peeling walls. There are numbers of them there, hundreds of them underground, with hammers in their hands. Oh, yes, we shall be in chains and there will be no freedom, but then, in our great sorrow, we shall rise again to joy, without which man cannot live nor God exist, for God gives joy: it's His privilege—a grand one. Ah, man should be dissolved in prayer! What should I be underground there without God? Rakitin's laughing! If they drive God from the earth, we shall shelter Him underground. One cannot exist in prison without God; it's even more impossible than out of prison. And then we men underground will sing from the bowels of the earth a glorious hymn to God, with Whom is joy. Hail to God and His joy! I love Him!"

Mitya was almost gasping for breath as he uttered his wild speech. He turned pale, his lips quivered, and tears rolled down his cheeks.

"Yes, life is full, there is life even underground," he began again. "You wouldn't believe, Alexey, how I want to live now, what a thirst for existence and consciousness has sprung up in me within these peeling walls. Rakitin doesn't understand that; all he cares about is building a house and letting flats. But I've been longing for you. And what is suffering? I am not afraid of it, even if it were beyond reckoning. I am not afraid of it now. I was afraid of it before. Do you know, perhaps I won't answer at the trial at all. . . . And I seem to have such strength in me now, that I think I could stand anything, any suffering, only to be able to say and to repeat to myself every moment, 'I exist.' In thousands of agonies—I exist. I'm tormented on the rack—but I exist! Though I sit alone in a pillar—I exist! I see the sun, and if I don't see the sun, I know it's there. And there's a whole life in that, in knowing that the sun is there. Alyosha, my angel, all these philosophies are the death of me. Damn them! Brother Ivan. . . ."

"What of brother Ivan?" interrupted Alyosha, but Mitya did not hear.

"You see, I never had any of these doubts before, but it was all hidden away in me. It was perhaps just because ideas I did not understand were surging up in me, that I used to drink and fight and rage. It was to stifle them in myself, to still them, to smother them. Ivan is not Rakitin, there is an idea in him. Ivan is a sphinx and is silent; he is always silent. It's God that's worrying me. That's the only thing that's worrying me. What if He doesn't exist? What if Rakitin's right—that it's an idea made up by men? Then, if He doesn't exist, man is the chief of the earth, of the universe. Magnificent! Only how is he going to be good without God? That's the question. I always come back to that. For whom is man going to love then? To whom will he be thankful? To whom will he sing the hymn? Rakitin laughs. Rakitin says that one can love humanity without God. Well, only a snivelling idiot can maintain that. I can't understand it. Life's easy for Rakitin. 'You'd better think about the extension of civic rights, or even of keeping down the price of meat. You will show your love for humanity more simply and directly by that, than by philosophy.' I answered him, 'Well, but you, without a God, are more likely to raise the price of meat, if it suits you, and make a rouble on every kopeck.' He lost his temper. But after all, what is goodness? Answer me that, Alexey. Goodness is one thing with me and another with a Chinaman, so it's a relative thing. Or isn't it? Is it not relative? A treacherous question! You won't laugh if I tell you it's kept me awake two nights. I only wonder now how people can live and think nothing about it. Vanity! Ivan has no God. He has an idea. It's beyond me. But he is silent. I believe he is a freemason. I asked him, but he is silent. I wanted to drink from the springs of his soul—he was silent. But once he did drop a word."

"What did he say?" Alyosha took it up quickly.

"I said to him, 'Then everything is lawful, if it is so?' He frowned. 'Fyodor Pavlovitch, our papa,' he said, 'was a pig, but his ideas were right enough.' That was what he dropped. That was all he said. That was going one better than Rakitin."

"Yes," Alyosha assented bitterly. "When was he with you?"

"Of that later, now I must speak of something else. I have said nothing about Ivan to you before. I put it off to the last. When my business here is over and the verdict has been given, then I'll tell you something. I'll tell you everything. We're something tremendous on hand. . . . And you shall be my judge in it. But don't begin about that now; be silent. You talk of to-morrow, of the trial; but, would you believe it, I know nothing about it."

"Have you talked to the counsel?"

"What's the use of the counsel? I told him all about it. He's a soft, city-bred rogue—a Bernard! But he doesn't believe me—not a bit of it. Only imagine, he believes I did it. I see it. 'In that case,' I asked him, 'why have you come to defend me?' Hang them all! They've got a doctor down, too, want to prove I'm mad. I won't have that! Katerina Ivanovna wants to do her 'duty' to the end, whatever the strain!" Mitya smiled bitterly. "The cat! Hard-hearted creature! She knows that I said of her at Mokroe that she was a woman of 'great wrath.' They repeated it. Yes, the facts against me have grown numerous as the sands of the sea. Grigory sticks to his point. Grigory's honest, but a fool. Many people are honest because they are fools: that's Rakitin's idea. Grigory's my enemy. And there are some peo-ple who are better as foes than friends. I mean Katerina Ivanovna. I am afraid, oh, I am afraid she will tell how she bowed to the ground after that four thousand. She'll pay it back to the last farthing. I don't want her sacri-fice; they'll put me to shame at the trial. I wonder how I can stand it. Go to her, Alyosha, ask her not to speak of that in the court, can't you? But damn it all, it doesn't matter! I shall get through somehow. I don't pity her. It's her own doing. She deserves what she gets. I shall have my own story to tell, Alexey." He smiled bitterly again. "Only . . . only Grusha, Grusha! Good Lord! Why should she have such suffering to bear?" he exclaimed suddenly, with tears. "Grusha's killing me; the thought of her's killing me, killing me. She was with me just now. . . ."

"She told me she was very much grieved by you to-day."

"I know. Confound my temper! It was jealousy. I was sorry, I kissed her as she was going. I didn't ask her forgiveness."

"Why didn't you?" exclaimed Alyosha.

Suddenly Mitya laughed almost mirthfully.

"God preserve you, my dear boy, from ever asking forgiveness for a fault from a woman you love. From one you love especially, however greatly you may have been in fault. For a woman—devil only knows what to make of a woman: I know something about them, anyway. But try acknowledging you are in fault to a woman. Say, 'I am sorry, forgive me,' and a shower of re-proaches will follow! Nothing will make her forgive you simply and directly, she'll humble you to the dust, bring forward things that have never hap-pened, recall everything, forget nothing, add something of her own, and only then forgive you. And even the best, the best of them do it. She'll scrape up all the scrapings and load them on your head. They are ready to flay you alive, I tell you, every one of them, all these angels without whom we cannot live! I tell you plainly and openly, dear boy, every decent man ought to be under some woman's thumb. That's my conviction—not conviction, but feeling. A man ought to be magnanimous, and it's no disgrace to a man! No disgrace to a hero, not even a Cæsar! But don't ever beg her pardon all the same for anything. Remember that rule given you by your brother Mitya, who's come to ruin through women. No, I'd better make it up to Grusha somehow, without begging pardon. I worship her, Alexey, worship her. Only she doesn't see it. No, she still thinks I don't love her enough. And she tortures me, tortures me with her love. The past was nothing! In the past it was only those infernal curves of hers that tortured me, but now I've taken all her soul into my soul and through her I've become a man myself. Will they marry us? If they don't, I shall die of jealousy. I imagine something every day. . . . What did she say to you about me?"

Alyosha repeated all Grushenka had said to him that day. Mitya listened, made him repeat things, and seemed pleased.

"Then she is not angry at my being jealous?" he exclaimed. "She is a regular woman! 'I've a fierce heart myself!' Ah, I love such fierce hearts, though I can't bear any one's being jealous of me. I can't endure it. We shall fight. But I shall love her, I shall love her infinitely. Will they marry us? Do they let convicts marry? That's the question. And without her I can't exist. . . ."

Mitya walked frowning across the room. It was almost dark. He suddenly seemed terribly worried.

"So there's a secret, she says, a secret? We have got up a plot against her, and Katya is mixed up in it, she thinks. No, my good Grushenka, that's not it. You are very wide of the mark, in your foolish feminine way. Alyosha, darling, well, here goes! I'll tell you our secret!"

He looked round, went close up quickly to Alyosha, who was standing before him, and whispered to him with an air of mystery, though in reality no one could hear them: the old warder was dozing in the corner, and not a word could reach the ears of the soldiers on guard.

"I will tell you all our secret," Mitya whispered hurriedly. "I meant to tell you later, for how could I decide on anything without you? You are everything to me. Though I say that Ivan is superior to us, you are my angel. It's your decision will decide it. Perhaps it's you that is superior and not Ivan. You see, it's a question of conscience, question of the higher conscience—the secret is so important that I can't settle it myself, and I've put it off till I could speak to you. But anyway it's too early to decide now, for we must wait for the verdict. As soon as the verdict is given, you shall decide my fate. Don't decide it now. I'll tell you now. You listen, but don't decide. Stand and keep quiet. I won't tell you everything. I'll only tell you the idea, without details, and you keep quiet. Not a question, not a movement. You agree? But, goodness, what shall I do with your eyes? I'm afraid your eyes will tell me your decision, even if you don't speak. Oo! I'm afraid! Alyosha, listen! Ivan suggests my *escaping*. I won't tell you the details: it's all been thought out: it can all be arranged. Hush, don't decide. I should go to America with Grusha. You know I can't live without Grusha! What if they won't let her follow me to Siberia? Do they let convicts get married? Ivan thinks not. And without Grusha what should I do there underground with a hammer? I should only smash my skull with the hammer! But on the other hand, my conscience? I should have run away from suffering. A sign has come, I reject the sign. I have a way of salvation and I turn my back on it. Ivan says that in America, 'with the good-will,' I can be of more use than underground. But what becomes of our hymn from underground? What's America? America is vanity again! And there's a lot of swindling in America, too, I expect. I should have run away from crucifixion! I tell you, you know, Alexey, because you are the only person who can understand this. There's no one else. It's folly, madness to others, all I've told you of the hymn. They'll say I'm out of my mind or a fool. I am not out of my mind and I am not a fool. Ivan understands about the hymn, too. He understands, only he doesn't answer—he doesn't speak. He doesn't believe in the hymn. Don't speak, don't speak. I see how you look! You have already decided. Don't decide, spare me! I can't live without Grusha. Wait till after the trial!"

Mitya ended beside himself. He held Alyosha with both hands on his shoulders, and his yearning, feverish eyes were fixed on his brother's.

"They don't let convicts marry, do they?" he repeated for the third time in a supplicating voice.

Alyosha listened with extreme surprise and was deeply moved.

"Tell me one thing," he said, "is Ivan very keen on it, and whose idea was it?"

"His, his, and he is very keen on it. He didn't come to see me at first, then he suddenly came a week ago and he began about it straight away. He is awfully keen on it. He doesn't ask me, but orders me to escape. He doesn't doubt of my obeying him, though I showed him all my heart as I have to you, and told him about the hymn, too. He told me he'd arrange it; he's found out about everything. But of that later. He's simply set on it. It's all a matter of money: he'll pay ten thousand for escape and give me a twenty thousand for America. And he says we can arrange a magnificent escape for ten thousand."

"And he told you on no account to tell me?" Alyosha asked again.

"To tell no one, and especially not you; on no account to tell you. He is afraid, no doubt, that you'll stand before me as my conscience. Don't tell him I told you. Don't tell him, for anything."

"You are right," Alyosha pronounced; "it's impossible to decide anything before the trial is over. After the trial you'll decide of yourself. Then you'll find that new man in yourself and he will decide."

"A new man, or a Bernard who'll decide *à la* Bernard, for I believe I'm a contemptible Bernard myself," said Mitya, with a bitter grin.

"But, brother, have you no hope then of being acquitted?"

Mitya shrugged his shoulders nervously and shook his head.

"Alyosha, darling, it's time you were going," he said, with a sudden haste. "There's the superintendent shouting in the yard. He'll be here directly. We are late; it's irregular. Embrace me quickly. Kiss me! Sign me with the cross, darling, for the cross I have to bear to-morrow."

They embraced and kissed.

"Ivan," said Mitya suddenly, "suggests my escaping; but, of course, he believes I did it."

A mournful smile came on to his lips.

"Have you asked him whether he believes it?" asked Alyosha.

"No, I haven't. I wanted to, but I couldn't. I hadn't the courage. But I saw it from his eyes. Well, good-bye!"

Once more they kissed hurriedly, and Alyosha was just going out, when Mitya suddenly called him back.

"Stand facing me! That's right!" And again he seized Alyosha, putting both hands on his shoulders. His face became suddenly quite pale, so that it was dreadfully apparent, even through the gathering darkness. His lips twitched, his eyes fastened upon Alyosha.

"Alyosha, tell me the whole truth, as you would before God. Do you believe I did it? Do you, do you in yourself, believe it? The whole truth, don't lie!" he cried desperately.

Everything seemed heaving before Alyosha, and he felt something like a stab at his heart.

"Hush! What do you mean?" he faltered helplessly.

"The whole truth, the whole, don't lie!" repeated Mitya.

"I've never for one instant believed that you were the murderer!" broke in a shaking voice from Alyosha's breast, and he raised his right hand in the air, as though calling God to witness his words.

Mitya's whole face was lighted up with bliss.

"Thank you!" he articulated slowly, as though letting a sigh escape him after fainting. "Now you have given me new life. Would you believe it, till this moment I've been afraid to ask you, you, even you. Well, go! You've given me strength for to-morrow. God bless you! Come, go along! Love Ivan!" was Mitya's last word.

Alyosha went out in tears. Such distrustfulness in Mitya, such lack of confidence even to him, to Alyosha—all this suddenly opened before Alyosha an unsuspected depth of hopeless grief and despair in the soul of his unhappy brother. Intense, infinite compassion overwhelmed him instantly. There was a poignant ache in his torn heart. "Love Ivan"—he suddenly recalled Mitya's words. And he was going to Ivan. He badly wanted to see Ivan all day. He was as much worried about Ivan as about Mitya, and more than ever now.

5

NOT YOU, NOT YOU!

O N the way to Ivan he had to pass the house where Katerina Ivanovna was living. There was light in the windows. He suddenly stopped and resolved to go in. He had not seen Katerina Ivanovna for more than a week. But now it struck him that Ivan might be with her, especially on the eve of the terrible day. Ringing, and mounting the staircase, which was dimly lighted by a Chinese lantern, he saw a man coming down, and as they met, he recognised him as his brother. So he was just coming from Katerina Ivanovna.

"Ah, it's only you," said Ivan drily. "Well, good-bye! You are going to her?"

"Yes."

"I don't advise you to; she's upset and you'll upset her more."

A door was instantly flung open above, and a voice cried suddenly:

"No, no! Alexey Fyodorovitch, have you come from him?"

"Yes, I have been with him."

"Has he sent me any message? Come up, Alyosha, and you, Ivan Fyodorovitch, you must come back, you must. Do you hear?"

There was such a peremptory note in Katya's voice that Ivan, after a moment's hesitation, made up his mind to go back with Alyosha.

"She was listening," he murmured angrily to himself, but Alyosha heard it.

"Excuse my keeping my greatcoat on," said Ivan, going into the drawing-room. "I won't sit down. I won't stay more than a minute."

"Sit down, Alexey Fyodorovitch," said Katerina Ivanovna, though she remained standing. She had changed very little during this time, but there was an ominous gleam in her dark eyes. Alyosha remembered afterwards that she had struck him as particularly handsome at that moment.

"What did he ask you to tell me?"

"Only one thing," said Alyosha, looking her straight in the face, "that you would spare yourself and say nothing at the trial of what (he was a little confused) . . . passed between you . . . at the time of your first acquaintance . . . in that town."

"Ah! that I bowed down to the ground for that money!" She broke into a bitter laugh. "Why, is he afraid for me or for himself? He asks me to spare—whom? Him or myself? Tell me, Alexey Fyodorovitch!"

Alyosha watched her intently, trying to understand her.

"Both yourself and him," he answered softly.

"I am glad to hear it," she snapped out maliciously, and she suddenly blushed.

"You don't know me yet, Alexey Fyodorovitch," she said menacingly. "And I don't know myself yet. Perhaps you'll want to trample me under foot after my examination to-morrow."

"You will give your evidence honourably," said Alyosha; "that's all that's wanted."

"Women are often dishonourable," she snarled. "Only an hour ago I was thinking I felt afraid to touch that monster . . . as though he were a reptile . . . but no, he is still a human being to me! But did he do it? Is he the murderer?" she cried, all of a sudden hysterically, turning quickly to Ivan. Alyosha saw at once that she had asked Ivan that question before, perhaps only a moment before he came in, and not for the first time, but for the hundredth, and that they had ended by quarrelling.

"I've been to see Smerdyakov. . . . It was you, you who persuaded me that he murdered his father. It's only you I believed!" she continued, still addressing Ivan. He gave her a sort of strained smile. Alyosha started at her tone. He had not suspected such familiar intimacy between them.

"Well, that's enough, anyway," Ivan cut short the conversation. "I am going. I'll come to-morrow." And turning at once, he walked out of the room and went straight downstairs.

With an imperious gesture, Katerina Ivanovna seized Alyosha by both hands.

"Follow him! Overtake him! Don't leave him alone for a minute!" she said, in a hurried whisper. "He's mad! Don't you know that he's mad? He is in a fever, nervous fever. The doctor told me so. Go, run after him. . . ."

Alyosha jumped up and ran after Ivan, who was not fifty paces ahead of him.

"What do you want?" He turned quickly on Alyosha, seeing that he was running after him. "She told you to catch me up, because I'm mad. I know it all by heart," he added irritably.

"She is mistaken, of course; but she is right that you are ill," said Alyosha. "I was looking at your face just now. You look very ill, Ivan."

Ivan walked on without stopping. Alyosha followed him.

"And do you know, Alexey Fyodorovitch, how people do go out of their mind?" Ivan asked in a voice suddenly quiet, without a trace of irritation, with a note of the simplest curiosity.

"No, I don't. I suppose there are all kinds of insanity."

"And can one observe that one's going mad oneself?"

"I imagine one can't see oneself clearly in such circumstances," Alyosha answered with surprise.

Ivan paused for half a minute.

"If you want to talk to me, please change the subject," he said suddenly.

"Oh, while I think of it, I have a letter for you," said Alyosha timidly, and he took Lise's note from his pocket and held it out to Ivan. They were just under a lamp-post. Ivan recognised the handwriting at once.

"Ah, from that little demon!" he laughed maliciously, and, without opening the envelope, he tore it into bits and threw it in the air. The bits were scattered by the wind.

"She's not sixteen yet, I believe, and already offering herself," he said contemptuously, striding along the street again.

"How do you mean, offering herself?" exclaimed Alyosha.

"As wanton women offer themselves, to be sure."

"How can you, Ivan, how can you?" Alyosha cried warmly in a grieved voice. "She is a child; you are insulting a child! She is ill; she is very ill, too. She is on the verge of insanity, too, perhaps . . . I had hoped to hear something from you . . . that would save her."

"You'll hear nothing from me. If she is a child I am not her nurse. Be quiet, Alexey. Don't go on about her. I am not even thinking about it."

They were silent again for a moment.

"She will be praying all night now to the Mother of God to show her how to act to-morrow at the trial," he said sharply and angrily again.

"You . . . you mean Katerina Ivanovna?"

"Yes. Whether she's to save Mitya or ruin him. She'll pray for light from above. She can't make up her mind for herself, you see. She has not had time to decide yet. She takes me for her nurse, too. She wants me to sing lullabys to her."

"Katerina Ivanovna loves you, brother," said Alyosha sadly.

"Perhaps; but I am not very keen on her."

"She is suffering. Why do you . . . sometimes say things to her that give her hope?" Alyosha went on, with timid reproach. "I know that you've given her hope. Forgive me for speaking to you like this," he added.

"I can't behave to her as I ought—break off altogether and tell her so straight out," said Ivan, irritably. "I must wait till sentence is passed on the murderer. If I break off with her now, she will avenge herself on me by ruining that scoundrel to-morrow at the trial, for she hates him and knows she hates him. It's all a lie—lie upon lie! As long as I don't break off with her, she goes on hoping, and she won't ruin that monster, knowing how I want to get him out of trouble. If only that damned verdict would come!"

The words "murderer" and "monster" echoed painfully in Alyosha's heart.

"But how can she ruin Mitya?" he asked, pondering on Ivan's words. "What evidence can she give that would ruin Mitya?"

"You don't know that yet. She's got a document in her hands, in Mitya's own writing, that proves conclusively that he did murder Fyodor Pavlovitch."

"That's impossible!" cried Alyosha.

"Why is it impossible? I've read it myself."

"There can't be such a document!" Alyosha repeated warmly. "There can't be, because he's not the murderer. It's not he murdered father, not he!"

Ivan suddenly stopped.

"Who is the murderer then, according to you?" he asked, with apparent coldness. There was even a supercilious note in his voice.

"You know who," Alyosha pronounced in a low, penetrating voice.

"Who? You mean the myth about that crazy idiot, the epileptic, Smerdyakov?"

Alyosha suddenly felt himself trembling all over.

"You know who," broke helplessly from him. He could scarcely breathe.

"Who? Who?" Ivan cried almost fiercely. All his restraint suddenly vanished.

"I only know one thing," Alyosha went on, still almost in a whisper, "*it wasn't you* killed father."

"Not you! What do you mean by 'not you'?" Ivan was thunderstruck.

"It was not you killed father, not you!" Alyosha repeated firmly.

The silence lasted for half a minute.

"I know I didn't. Are you raving?" said Ivan, with a pale, distorted smile. His eyes were riveted on Alyosha. They were standing again under a lamp-post.

"No, Ivan. You've told yourself several times that you are the murderer."

"When did I say so? I was in Moscow. . . . When have I said so?" Ivan faltered helplessly.

"You've said so to yourself many times, when you've been alone during these two dreadful months," Alyosha went on softly and distinctly as before. Yet he was speaking now, as it were, not of himself, not of his own will, but obeying some irresistible command. "You have accused yourself and have confessed to yourself that you are the murderer and no one else. But you didn't do it: you are mistaken: you are not the murderer. Do you hear? It was not you! God has sent me to tell you so."

They were both silent. The silence lasted a whole long minute. They were both standing still, gazing into each other's eyes. They were both pale. Suddenly Ivan began trembling all over, and clutched Alyosha's shoulder.

"You've been in my room!" he whispered hoarsely. "You've been there at night, when he came. . . . Confess . . . have you seen him, have you seen him?"

"Whom do you mean—Mitya?" Alyosha asked, bewildered.

"Not him, damn the monster!" Ivan shouted, in a frenzy. "Do you know that he visits me? How did you find out? Speak!"

"Who is *he?* I don't know whom you are talking about," Alyosha faltered, beginning to be alarmed.

"Yes, you do know . . . or how could you . . . ? It's impossible that you don't know."

Suddenly he seemed to check himself. He stood still and seemed to reflect. A strange grin contorted his lips.

"Brother," Alyosha began again, in a shaking voice, "I have said this to you, because you'll believe my word, I know that. I tell you once and for all, it's not you. You hear, once for all! God has put it into my heart to say this to you, even though it may make you hate me from this hour."

But by now Ivan had apparently regained his self-control.

"Alexey Fyodorovitch," he said, with a cold smile, "I can't endure prophets and epileptics—messengers from God especially—and you know that only too well. I break off all relations with you from this moment and probably for ever. I beg you to leave me at this turning. It's the way to your lodgings, too. You'd better be particularly careful not to come to me to-day! Do you hear?"

He turned and walked on with a firm step, not looking back.

"Brother," Alyosha called after him, "if anything happens to you to-day, turn to me before any one!"

But Ivan made no reply. Alyosha stood under the lamp-post at the cross roads, till Ivan had vanished into the darkness. Then he turned and walked slowly homewards. Both Alyosha and Ivan were living in lodgings; neither of them was willing to live in Fyodor Pavlovitch's empty house. Alyosha had a furnished room in the house of some working people. Ivan lived some distance from him. He had taken a roomy and fairly comfortable lodge attached to a fine house that belonged to a well-to-do lady, the widow of an official. But his only attendant was a deaf and rheumatic old crone who went to bed at six o'clock every evening and got up at six in the morning. Ivan had become remarkably indifferent to his comforts of late, and very fond of being alone. He did everything for himself in the one room he lived in, and rarely entered any of the other rooms in his abode.

He reached the gate of the house and had his hand on the bell, when he suddenly stopped. He felt that he was trembling all over with anger. Suddenly he let go of the bell, turned back with a curse, and walked with rapid steps in the opposite direction. He walked a mile and a half to a tiny, slanting, wooden house, almost a hut, where Marya Kondratyevna, the neighbour who used to come to Fyodor Pavlovitch's kitchen for soup and to whom Smerdyakov had once sung his songs and played on the guitar, was now lodging. She had sold their little house, and was now living here with her mother. Smerdyakov, who was ill—almost dying—had been with them ever since Fyodor Pavlovitch's death. It was to him Ivan was going now, drawn by a sudden and irresistible prompting.

6

THE FIRST INTERVIEW WITH SMERDYAKOV

THIS was the third time that Ivan had been to see Smerdyakov since his return from Moscow. The first time he had seen him and talked to him was on the first day of his arrival, then he had visited him once more, a fortnight later. But his visits had ended with that second one, so that it was now over a month since he had seen him. And he had scarcely heard anything of him.

Ivan had only returned five days after his father's death, so that he was not present at the funeral, which took place the day before he came back. The cause of his delay was that Alyosha, not knowing his Moscow address, had to apply to Katerina Ivanovna to telegraph to him, and she, not knowing his address either, telegraphed to her sister and aunt, reckoning on Ivan's going to see them as soon as he arrived in Moscow. But he did not go to them till four days after his arrival. When he got the telegram, he had, of course, set off post-haste to our town. The first to meet him was Alyosha, and Ivan was greatly surprised to find that in opposition to the general opinion of the town, he refused to entertain a suspicion against Mitya, and spoke openly of Smerdyakov as the murderer. Later on, after seeing the police captain and the prosecutor, and hearing the details of the charge and the arrest, he was still more surprised at Alyosha, and ascribed his opinion only to his exaggerated brotherly feeling and sympathy with Mitya, of whom Alyosha, as Ivan knew, was very fond.

By the way, let us say a word or two of Ivan's feeling to his brother Dmitri. He positively disliked him, at most, felt sometimes a compassion for him, and even that was mixed with great contempt, almost repugnance. Mitya's whole personality, even his appearance, was extremely unattractive to him. Ivan looked with indignation on Katerina Ivanovna's love for his brother. Yet he went to see Mitya on the first day of his arrival, and that interview, far from shaking Ivan's belief in his guilt, positively strengthened it. He found his brother agitated, nervously excited. Mitya had been talkative, but very absent-minded and incoherent. He used violent language, accused Smerdyakov, and was fearfully muddled. He talked principally about the three thousand roubles, which he said had been "stolen" from him by his father.

"The money was mine, it was my money," Mitya kept repeating. "Even if I had stolen it, I should have had the right."

He hardly contested the evidence against him, and if he tried to turn a fact to his advantage, it was in an absurd and incoherent way. He hardly seemed to wish to defend himself to Ivan or any one else. Quite the contrary, he was angry and proudly scornful of the charges against him; he was continually firing up and abusing every one. He only laughed contemptuously at Grigory's evidence about the open door, and declared that it was "the devil that opened it." But he could not bring forward any coherent explanation of the fact. He even succeeded in insulting Ivan during their first interview, telling him sharply that it was not for people who declared that "everything was lawful," to suspect and question him. Altogether he was anything but friendly with Ivan on that occasion. Immediately after that interview with Mitya, Ivan went for the first time to see Smerdyakov.

In the railway train on his way from Moscow, he kept thinking of Smerdyakov and of his last conversation with him on the evening before he went away. Many things seemed to him puzzling and suspicious. But when he gave his evidence to the investigating lawyer Ivan said nothing, for the time, of that conversation. He put that off till he had seen Smerdyakov, who was at that time in the hospital.

Doctor Herzenstube and Varvinsky, the doctor he met in the hospital, confidently asserted in reply to Ivan's persistent questions, that Smerdyakov's epileptic attack was unmistakably genuine, and were surprised indeed at Ivan asking whether he might not have been shamming on the day of the catastrophe. They gave him to understand that the attack was an exceptional one, the fits persisting and recurring several times, so that the patient's life was positively in danger, and it was only now, after they had applied remedies, that they could assert with confidence that the patient would survive. "Though it might well be," added Doctor Herzenstube, "that his reason would be impaired for a considerable period, if not permanently." On Ivan's asking impatiently whether that meant that he was now mad, they told him that this was not yet the case, in the full sense of the word, but that certain abnormalities were perceptible. Ivan decided to find out for himself what those abnormalities were.

At the hospital he was at once allowed to see the patient. Smerdyakov was lying on a truckle bed in a separate ward. There was only one other bed in the room, and in it lay a tradesman of the town, swollen with dropsy, who was obviously almost dying; he could be no hindrance to their conversation. Smerdyakov grinned uncertainly on seeing Ivan, and for the first instant seemed nervous. So at least Ivan fancied. But that was only momentary. For the rest of the time he was struck, on the contrary, by Smerdyakov's composure. From the first glance Ivan had no doubt that he was very ill. He was very weak; he spoke slowly, seeming to move his tongue with difficulty; he was much thinner and sallower. Throughout the interview, which lasted twenty minutes, he kept complaining of headache and of pain in all his limbs. His thin emasculate face seemed to have become so tiny; his hair was ruffled, and his crest of curls in front stood up in a thin tuft. But in the left eye, which was screwed up and seemed to be insinuating something, Smerdyakov showed himself unchanged. "It's always worth while speaking to a clever man." Ivan was reminded of that at once. He sat down on the stool at his feet. Smerdyakov, with painful effort, shifted his position in bed, but he was not the first to speak. He remained dumb, and did not even look much interested.

"Can you talk to me?" asked Ivan. "I won't tire you much."

"Certainly I can," mumbled Smerdyakov, in a faint voice.

"Has your honour been back long?" he added patronisingly, as though encouraging a nervous visitor.

"I only arrived to-day. . . . To see the mess you are in here."

Smerdyakov sighed.

"Why do you sigh, you knew of it all along?" Ivan blurted out.

Smerdyakov was stolidly silent for a while.

"How could I help knowing? It was clear beforehand. But how could I tell it would turn out like that?"

"What would turn out? Don't prevaricate! You've foretold you'd have a fit; on the way down to the cellar, you know. You mentioned the very spot."

"Have you said so at the examination yet?" Smerdyakov queried with composure.

Ivan felt suddenly angry.

"No, I haven't yet, but I certainly shall. You must explain a great deal to me, my man, and let me tell you, I am not going to let you play with me!"

"Why should I play with you, when I put my whole trust in you, as in God Almighty?" said Smerdyakov, with the same composure, only for a moment closing his eyes.

"In the first place," began Ivan. "I know that epileptic fits can't be foretold beforehand. I've inquired, don't try and take me in. You can't foretell the day and the hour. How was it you told me the day and the hour beforehand, and about the cellar, too? How could you tell that you would fall down the cellar stairs in a fit, if you didn't sham a fit on purpose?"

"I had to go to the cellar anyway, several times a day, indeed," Smerdyakov drawled deliberately. "I fell from the garret just in the same way a year ago. It's quite true you can't foretell the day and hour of a fit beforehand, but you can always have a presentiment of it."

"But you did foretell the day and the hour!"

"In regard to my epilepsy, sir, you had much better inquire of the doctors here. You can ask them whether it was a real fit or a sham; it's no use my saying any more about it."

"And the cellar? How could you know beforehand of the cellar?"

"You don't seem able to get over that cellar! As I was going down to the cellar, I was in terrible dread and doubt. What frightened me most was losing you and being left without defence in all the world. So I went down into the cellar thinking, 'Here, it'll come on directly, it'll strike me down directly, shall I fall?' And it was through this fear that I suddenly felt the spasm that always comes . . . and so I went flying. All that and all my previous conversation with you at the gate the evening before, when I told you how frightened I was and spoke of the cellar. I told all that to Doctor Herzenstube and Nikolay Parfenovitch, the investigating lawyer, and it's all been written down in the protocol. And the doctor here, Mr. Varvinsky, maintained to all of them that it was just the thought of it brought it on, the apprehension that I might fall. It was just then that the fit seized me. And so they've written it down, that it's just how it must have happened, simply from my fear."

As he finished, Smerdyakov drew a deep breath, as though exhausted.

"Then you have said all that in your evidence?" said Ivan, somewhat taken aback.

He had meant to frighten him with the threat of repeating their conversation, and it appeared that Smerdyakov had already reported it all himself.

"What have I to be afraid of? Let them write down the whole truth," Smerdyakov pronounced firmly.

"And have you told them every word of our conversation at the gate?"

"Not, not to say every word."

"And did you tell them that you can sham fits, as you boasted then?"

"No, I didn't tell them that either."

"Tell me now, why did you send me then to Tchermashnya?"

"I was afraid you'd go away to Moscow, Tchermashnya is nearer, anyway."

"You are lying, you suggested my going away yourself; you told me to get out of the way of trouble."

"That was simply out of affection and my sincere devotion to you, foreseeing trouble in the house, to spare you. Only I wanted to spare myself even more. That's why I told you to get out of harm's way, that you might understand that there would be trouble in the house, and would remain at home to protect your father."

"You might have said it more directly, you blockhead!" Ivan suddenly fired up.

"How could I have said it more directly then? It was simply my fear that made me speak, and you might have been angry, too. I might well have been apprehensive that Dmitri Fyodorovitch would make a scene and carry away that money, for he considered it as good as his own, but who could tell that it would end in a murder like this? I thought that he would only carry off the three thousand that lay under the master's mattress in the envelope, and you see, he's murdered him. How could you guess it either, sir?"

"But if you say yourself that it couldn't be guessed, how could I have guessed and stayed at home? You contradict yourself!" said Ivan pondering.

"You might have guessed from my sending you to Tchermashnya and not to Moscow."

"How could I guess it from that?"

Smerdyakov seemed much exhausted, and again he was silent for a minute.

"You might have guessed from the fact of my asking you not to go to Moscow, but to Tchermashnya, that I wanted to have you nearer, for Moscow's a long way off, and Dmitri Fyodorovitch, knowing you are not far off, would not be so bold. And if anything had happened, you might have come to protect me, too, for I warned you of Grigory Vassilyevitch's illness, and that I was afraid of having a fit. And when I explained those knocks to you, by means of which one could go in to the deceased, and that Dmitri Fyodorovitch knew them all through me, I thought that you would guess yourself that he would be sure to do something, and so wouldn't go to Tchermashnya even, but would stay."

"He talks very coherently," thought Ivan, "though he does mumble; what's the derangement of his faculties that Herzenstube talked of?"

"You are cunning with me, damn you," he exclaimed, getting angry.

"But I thought at the time that you quite guessed," Smerdyakov parried with the simplest air.

"If I'd guessed, I should have stayed," cried Ivan.

"Why, I thought that it was because you guessed that you went away in such a hurry, only to get out of trouble, only to run away and save yourself in your fright."

"You think that every one is as great a coward as yourself?"

"Forgive me, I thought you were like me."

"Of course, I ought to have guessed," Ivan said in agitation, "and I did guess there was some mischief brewing on your part . . . only you are lying, you are lying again," he cried, suddenly recollecting. "Do you remember how you went up to the carriage and said to me, 'it's always worth while speaking to a clever man'? So you were glad I went away, since you praised me?"

Smerdyakov sighed again and again. A trace of colour came into his face.

"If I was pleased," he articulated rather breathlessly, "it was simply because you agreed not to go to Moscow, but to Tchermashnya. For it was nearer, anyway. Only when I said these words to you, it was not by way of praise, but of reproach. You didn't understand it."

"What reproach?"

"Why, that foreseeing such a calamity you deserted your own father, and would not protect us, for I might have been taken up any time for stealing that three thousand."

"Damn you!" Ivan swore again. "Stay, did you tell the prosecutor and the investigating lawyer about those knocks?"

"I told them everything just as it was."

Ivan wondered inwardly again.

"If I thought of anything then," he began again, "it was solely of some wickedness on your part. Dmitri might kill him, but that he would steal — I did not believe that then. . . . But I was prepared for any wickedness from you. You told me yourself you could sham a fit. What did you say that for?"

"It was just through my simplicity, and I never have shammed a fit on purpose in my life. And I only said so then to boast to you. It was just foolishness. I liked you so much then, and was openhearted with you."

"My brother directly accuses you of the murder and theft."

"What else is left for him to do?" said Smerdyakov, with a bitter grin. "And who will believe him with all the proofs against him? Grigory Vassilyevitch saw the door open. What can he say after that? But never mind him! He is trembling to save himself."

He slowly ceased speaking, and suddenly, as though on reflection, added:

"And look here again. He wants to throw it on me and make out that it is the work of my hands—I've heard that already. But as to my being clever at shamming a fit: should I have told you beforehand that I could sham one, if I really had had such a design against your father? If I had been planning such a murder could I have been such a fool as to give such evidence against myself beforehand? And to his son, too! Upon my word! Is that likely? As if that could be, such a thing has never happened. No one hears this talk of ours now, except Providence itself, and if you were to tell of it to the prosecutor and Nikolay Parfenovitch you might defend me completely by doing so, for who would be likely to be such a criminal, if he is openhearted beforehand? Any one can see that."

"Well," and Ivan got up to cut short the conversation, struck by Smerdyakov's last argument. "I don't suspect you at all, and I think it's absurd indeed to suspect you. On the contrary, I am grateful to you for setting my mind at rest. Now I am going, but I'll come again. Meanwhile, good-bye. Get well. Is there anything you want?"

"I am very thankful for everything. Marfa Ignatyevna does not forget me, and provides me anything I want, according to her kindness. Good people visit me every day."

"Good-bye. But I shan't say anything of your being able to sham a fit, and I don't advise you to, either," something made Ivan say suddenly.

"I quite understand. And if you don't speak of that, I shall say nothing of that conversation of ours at the gate."

Then it happened that Ivan went out, and only when he had gone a dozen steps along the corridor, he suddenly felt that there was an insulting significance in Smerdyakov's last words. He was almost on the point of turning back, but it was only a passing impulse, and muttering, "nonsense!" he went out of the hospital.

His chief feeling was one of relief at the fact that it was not Smerdyakov, but Mitya, who had committed the murder, though he might have been expected to feel the opposite. He did not want to analyse the reason for this feeling, and even felt a positive repugnance at prying into his sensations. He felt as though he wanted to make haste to forget something. In the following days he became convinced of Mitya's guilt, as he got to know all the weight of evidence against him. There was evidence of people of no importance, Fenya and her mother, for instance, but the effect of it was almost overpowering. As to Perhotin, the people at the tavern, and at Plotnikov's shop, as well as the witnesses at Mokroe, their evidence seemed conclusive. It was the details that were so damning. The secret of the knocks impressed the lawyers almost as much as Grigory's evidence as to the open door. Grigory's wife, Marfa, in answer to Ivan's questions, declared that Smerdyakov had been lying all night the other side of the partition wall, "He was not three paces from our bed," and that although she was a sound sleeper she waked several times and heard him moaning, "He was moaning the whole time, moaning continually."

Talking to Herzenstube, and giving it as his opinion that Smerdyakov was not mad, but only rather weak, Ivan only evoked from the old man a subtle smile.

"Do you know how he spends his time now?" he asked, "learning lists of French words by heart. He has an exercise-book under his pillow with the French words written out in Russian letters for him by some one, he, he, he!"

Ivan ended by dismissing all doubts. He could not think of Dmitri without repulsion. Only one thing was strange, however. Alyosha persisted that Dmitri was not the murderer, and that "in all probability" Smerdyakov was. Ivan always felt that Alyosha's opinion meant a great deal to him, and so he was astonished at it now. Another thing that was strange was that Alyosha did not make any attempt to talk about Mitya with Ivan, that he never began on the subject and only answered his questions. This, too, struck Ivan particularly.

But he was very much preoccupied at that time with something quite apart from that. On his return from Moscow, he abandoned himself hopelessly to his mad and consuming passion for Katerina Ivanovna. This is not the time to begin to speak of this new passion of Ivan's, which left its mark on all the rest of his life: this would furnish the subject for another novel, which I may perhaps never write. But I cannot omit to mention here that when Ivan, on leaving Katerina Ivanovna with Alyosha, as I've related already, told him, "I am not keen on her," it was an absolute lie: he loved her madly, though at times he hated her so that he might have murdered her. Many causes helped to bring about this feeling. Shattered by what had happened with Mitya, she rushed on Ivan's return to meet him as her one salvation. She was hurt, insulted and humiliated in her feelings. And here the man had come back to her, who had loved her so ardently before (oh, she knew that very well), and whose heart and intellect she considered so superior to her own. But the sternly virtuous girl did not abandon herself altogether to the man she loved, in spite of the Karamazov violence of his passions and the great fascination he had for her. She was continually tormented at the same time by remorse for having deserted Mitya, and in moments of discord and violent anger (and they were numerous) she told

Ivan so plainly. This was what he had called to Alyosha "lies upon lies." There was, of course, much that was false in it, and that angered Ivan more than anything. . . . But of all this later.

He did, in fact, for a time almost forget Smerdyakov's existence, and yet, a fortnight after his first visit to him, he began to be haunted by the same strange thoughts as before. It's enough to say that he was continually asking himself, why was it that on that last night in Fyodor Pavlovitch's house he had crept out on to the stairs like a thief and listened to hear what his father was doing below. Why had he recalled that afterwards with repulsion; why, next morning, had he been suddenly so depressed on the journey; why, as he reached Moscow, had he said to himself "I am a scoundrel"? And now he almost fancied that these tormenting thoughts would make him even forget Katerina Ivanovna, so completely did they take possession of him again. It was just after fancying this, that he met Alyosha in the street. He stopped him at once, and put a question to him:

"Do you remember when Dmitri burst in after dinner and beat father, and afterwards I told you in the yard that I reserved 'the right to desire' . . . tell me, did you think then that I desired father's death or not?"

"I did think so," answered Alyosha, softly.

"It was so, too; it was not a matter of guessing. But didn't you fancy then that what I wished was just that 'one reptile should devour another'; that is, just that Dmitri should kill father, and as soon as possible . . . and that I myself was even prepared to help to bring that about?"

Alyosha turned rather pale, and looked silently into his brother's face.

"Speak!" cried Ivan, "I want above everything to know what you thought then. I want the truth, the truth!"

He drew a deep breath, looking angrily at Alyosha before his answer came.

"Forgive me, I did think that, too, at the time," whispered Alyosha, and he did not add one softening phrase.

"Thanks," snapped Ivan, and, leaving Alyosha, he went quickly on his way. From that time Alyosha noticed that Ivan began obviously to avoid him and seemed to have taken a dislike to him, so much so that Alyosha gave up going to see him. Immediately after that meeting with him, Ivan had not gone home, but went straight to Smerdyakov again.

7

THE SECOND VISIT TO SMERDYAKOV

B Y that time Smerdyakov had been discharged from the hospital. Ivan knew his new lodging, the dilapidated little wooden house, divided in two by a passage on one side of which lived Marya Kondratyevna and her mother, and on the other, Smerdyakov. No one knew on what terms he lived with them, whether as a friend or as a lodger. It was supposed afterwards that he had come to stay with them as Marya Kondratyevna's betrothed, and was living there for a time without paying for board or lodging. Both mother and daughter had the greatest respect for him and looked upon him as greatly superior to themselves.

Ivan knocked, and, on the door being opened, went into the passage. By Marya Kondratyevna's directions he went straight to the better room on the left, occupied by Smerdyakov. There was a tiled stove in the room and it was extremely hot. The walls were gay with blue paper, which was a good deal used however, and in the cracks under it cockroaches swarmed in amazing numbers, so that there was a continual rustling from them. The furniture was very scanty: two benches against each wall and two chairs by the table. The table of plain wood was covered with a cloth with pink patterns on it. There was a pot of geranium on each of the two little windows. In the corner there was a case of ikons. On the table stood a little copper samovar with many dents in it, and a tray with two cups. But Smerdyakov had finished tea and the samovar was out. He was sitting at the table on a bench. He was looking at an exercise-book and slowly writing with a pen. There was a bottle of ink by him and a flat iron candlestick, but with a composite candle. Ivan saw at once from Smerdyakov's face that he had completely recovered from his illness. His face was fresher, fuller, his hair stood up jauntily in front and was plastered down at the sides. He was sitting in a particoloured, wadded dressing-gown, rather dirty and frayed, however. He had spectacles on his nose, which Ivan had never seen him wearing before. This trifling circumstance suddenly redoubled Ivan's anger: "A creature like that and wearing spectacles!"

Smerdyakov slowly raised his head and looked intently at his visitor through his spectacles; then he slowly took them off and rose from the bench, but by no means respectfully, almost lazily, doing the least possible required by common civility. All this struck Ivan instantly, he took it all in and noted it at once—most of all the look in Smerdyakov's eyes, positively malicious, churlish and haughty. "What do you want to intrude for?" it seemed to say; "we settled everything then, why have you come again?" Ivan could scarcely control himself.

"It's hot here," he said, still standing, and unbuttoned his overcoat.

"Take off your coat," Smerdyakov conceded.

Ivan took off his coat and threw it on a bench with trembling hands. He took a chair, moved it quickly to the table and sat down. Smerdyakov managed to sit down on his bench before him.

"To begin with, are we alone?" Ivan asked sternly and impulsively. "Can they overhear us in there?"

"No one can hear anything. You've seen for yourself: there's a passage."

"Listen, my good fellow, what was that you babbled, as I was leaving the hospital, that if I said nothing about your faculty of shamming fits, you wouldn't tell the investigating lawyer all our conversation at the gate. What do you mean by *all*? What could you mean by it? Were you threatening me? Have I entered into some sort of compact with you? Do you suppose I am afraid of you?"

Ivan said this in a perfect fury, giving him to understand with obvious intention that he scorned any subterfuge or indirectness and meant to show his cards. Smerdyakov's eyes gleamed resentfully, his left eye winked and he at once gave his answer, with his habitual composure and deliberation: "You want to have everything above board, very well, you shall have it," he seemed to say.

"This is what I meant then, and this is why I said that, that you, knowing beforehand of this murder of your own parent, left him to his fate, and that people mightn't after that conclude any evil about your feelings and perhaps of something else, too—that's what I promised not to tell the authorities."

Though Smerdyakov spoke without haste and obviously controlling himself, yet there was something in his voice, determined and emphatic, resentful and insolently defiant. He stared impudently at Ivan. A mist passed before Ivan's eyes for the first moment.

"How? What? Are you out of your mind?"

"I'm perfectly in possession of all my faculties."

"Do you suppose I *knew* of the murder?" Ivan cried at last, and he brought his fist violently on the table. "What do you mean by 'something else, too'? Speak, scoundrel!"

Smerdyakov was silent and still scanned Ivan with the same insolent stare.

"Speak, you stinking rogue, what is that 'something else, too'?"

"The 'something else' I meant was that you probably too were very desirous of your parent's death."

Ivan jumped up and struck him with all his might on the shoulder, so that he fell back against the wall. In an instant his face was bathed in tears. Saying, "It's a shame, sir, to strike a sick man," he dried his eyes with a very dirty blue check handkerchief and sank into quiet weeping. A minute passed.

"That's enough! Leave off," Ivan said peremptorily, sitting down again. "Don't put me out of all patience."

Smerdyakov took the rag from his eyes. Every line of his puckered face reflected the insult he had just received.

"So you thought then, you scoundrel, that together with Dmitri I meant to kill my father?"

"I didn't know what thoughts were in your mind then," said Smerdyakov resentfully; "and so I stopped you then at the gate to sound you on that very point."

"To sound what, what?"

"Why, that very circumstance, whether you wanted your father to be murdered or not?"

What infuriated Ivan more than anything was the aggressive, insolent tone to which Smerdyakov persistently adhered.

"It was you murdered him?" he cried suddenly.

Smerdyakov smiled contemptuously.

"You know of yourself, for a fact, that it wasn't I murdered him. And I should have thought that there was no need for a sensible man to speak of it again."

"But why, why had you such a suspicion about me at the time?"

"As you know already, it was simply from fear. For I was in such a position, shaking with fear, that I suspected every one. I resolved to sound you, too, for I thought if you wanted the same as your brother, then the business was as good as settled and I should be crushed like a fly, too."

"Look here, you didn't say that a fortnight ago."

"I meant the same when I talked to you in the hospital, only I thought you'd understand without wasting words, and that being such a sensible man you wouldn't care to talk of it openly."

"What next! Come answer, answer, I insist: what was it . . . what could I have done to put such a degrading suspicion into your mean soul?"

"As for the murder, you couldn't have done that and didn't want to, but as for wanting some one else to do it, that was just what you did want."

"And how coolly, how coolly he speaks! But why should I have wanted it, what grounds had I for wanting it?"

"What grounds had you? What about the inheritance?" said Smerdyakov sarcastically, and as it were vindictively. "Why, after your parent's death there was at least forty thousand to come to each of you, and very likely more, but if Fyodor Pavlovitch got married then to that lady, Agrafena Alexandrovna, she would have had all his capital made over to her directly after the wedding, for she's plenty of sense, so that your parent would not have left you two roubles between the three of you. And were they far from a wedding, either? Not a hair's-breadth: that lady had only to lift her little finger and he would have run after her to church, with his tongue out."

Ivan restrained himself with painful effort.

"Very good," he commented at last, "you see, I haven't jumped up, I haven't knocked you down, I haven't killed you. Speak on. So, according to you, I had fixed on Dmitri to do it, I was reckoning on him?"

"How could you help reckoning on him? If he killed him, then he would lose all the rights of a nobleman, his rank and property, and would go off to exile, so his share of the inheritance would come to you and your brother Alexey Fyodorovitch, in equal parts, so you'd each have not forty, but sixty thousand each. There's not a doubt you did reckon on Dmitri Fyodorovitch."

"What I put up with from you! Listen, scoundrel, if I had reckoned on any one then, it would have been on you, not on Dmitri, and I swear I did expect some wickedness from you . . . at the time . . . I remember my impression!"

"I thought, too, for a minute, at the time, that you were reckoning on me as well," said Smerdyakov, with a sarcastic grin. "So that it was just by that more than anything you showed me what was in your mind. For if you had a foreboding about me and yet went away, you as good as said to me, 'You can murder my parent, I won't hinder you!' "

"You scoundrel! So that's how you understood it!"

"It was all that going to Tchermashnya. Why! You were meaning to go to Moscow and refused all your father's entreaties to go to Tchermashnya—and simply at a foolish word from me you consented at once! What reason had you to consent to Tchermashnya? Since you went to Tchermashnya with no reason, simply at my word, it shows that you must have expected something from me."

"No, I swear I didn't!" shouted Ivan, grinding his teeth.

"You didn't? Then you ought, as your father's son, to have had me taken to the lock-up and thrashed at once for my words then . . . or at least, to have given me a punch in the face on the spot, but you were not a bit angry, if you please, and at once in a friendly way acted on my foolish word and went away, which was utterly absurd, for you ought to have stayed to save your parent's life. How could I help drawing my conclusions?"

Ivan sat scowling, both his fists convulsively pressed on his knees.

"Yes, I am sorry I didn't punch you in the face," he said with a bitter smile. "I couldn't have taken you to the lock-up just then. Who would have believed me and what charge could I bring against you? But the punch in the face . . . oh, I'm sorry I didn't think of it. Though blows are forbidden, I should have pounded your ugly face to a jelly."

Smerdyakov looked at him almost with relish.

"In the ordinary occasions of life," he said in the same complacent and sententious tone in which he had taunted Grigory and argued with him about religion at Fyodor Pavlovitch's table, "in the ordinary occasions of life, blows on the face are forbidden nowadays by law and people have given them up, but in exceptional occasions of life people still fly to blows, not only among us but all over the world, be it even the fullest Republic of France, just as in the time of Adam and Eve, and they never will leave off, but you, even in an exceptional case, did not dare."

"What are you learning French words for?" Ivan nodded towards the exercise-book lying on the table.

"Why shouldn't I learn them so as to improve my education, supposing that I may myself chance to go some day to those happy parts of Europe."

"Listen, monster," Ivan's eyes flashed and he trembled all over. "I am not afraid of your accusations, you can say what you like about me, and if

I don't beat you to death, it's simply because I suspect you of that crime and I'll drag you to justice. I'll unmask you."

"To my thinking, you'd better keep quiet, for what can you accuse me of, considering my absolute innocence; and who would believe you? Only if you begin, I shall tell everything, too, for I must defend myself."

"Do you think I am afraid of you now?"

"If the court doesn't believe all I've said to you just now, the public will, and you will be ashamed."

"That's as much as to say 'It's always worth while speaking to a sensible man,' eh?" snarled Ivan.

"You hit the mark, indeed. And you'd better be sensible."

Ivan got up, shaking all over with indignation, put on his coat, and without replying further to Smerdyakov, without even looking at him, walked quickly out of the cottage. The cool evening air refreshed him. There was a bright moon in the sky. A nightmare of ideas and sensations filled his soul. "Shall I go at once and give information against Smerdyakov? But what information can I give? He is not guilty, anyway. On the contrary, he'll accuse me. And in fact why did I set off for Tchermashnya then? What for? What for?" Ivan asked himself. "Yes, of course, I was expecting something and he is right. . . ." And he remembered for the hundredth time how, on that last night in his father's house, he had listened on the stairs. But he remembered it now with such anguish that he stood still on the spot as though he had been stabbed. "Yes, I expected it then, that's true! I wanted the murder, I did want the murder! Did I want the murder? Did I want it? I must kill Smerdyakov! If I don't dare kill Smerdyakov now, life is not worth living!"

Ivan did not go home, but went straight to Katerina Ivanovna and alarmed her by his appearance. He was like a madman. He repeated all his conversation with Smerdyakov, every syllable of it. He couldn't be calmed, however much she tried to soothe him: he kept walking about the room, speaking strangely, disconnectedly. At last he sat down, put his elbows on the table, leaned his head on his hands and pronounced this strange sentence: "If it's not Dmitri, but Smerdyakov who's the murderer, I share his guilt, for I put him up to it. Whether I did, I don't know yet. But if he is the murderer, and not Dmitri, then, of course, I am the murderer, too."

When Katerina Ivanovna heard that, she got up from her seat without a word, went to her writing-table, opened a box standing on it, took out a sheet of paper and laid it before Ivan. This was the document of which Ivan spoke to Alyosha later on as a "conclusive proof" that Dmitri had killed his father. This was the letter written by Mitya to Katerina Ivanovna when he was drunk, on the very evening he met Alyosha at the cross roads on the way to the monastery, after the scene at Katerina Ivanovna's, when Grushenka had insulted her. Then, parting from Alyosha, Mitya had rushed to Grushenka. I don't know whether he saw her, but in the evening he was at the "Metropolis," where he got thoroughly drunk. Then he asked for pen and paper and wrote a document of weighty consequences to himself. It was a wordy, disconnected, frantic letter, a drunken letter in fact. It was like the talk of a drunken man, who, on his return home, begins with extraordinary heat telling his wife or one of his household how he has just been insulted, what a rascal had just insulted him, what a fine fellow he is on the other hand, and how he will pay that scoundrel out; and all that at great length, with great excitement and incoherence, with drunken tears and blows on the table. The letter was written on a dirty piece of ordinary paper of the cheapest kind. It had been provided by the tavern and there were figures scrawled on the back of it. There was evidently not space enough for his drunken verbosity and Mitya not only filled the margins but had written the last line right across the rest. The letter ran as follows:

"FATAL KATYA! To-morrow I will get the money and repay your three thousand and farewell, woman of great wrath, but farewell too my love! Let us make an end! To-morrow I shall try and get it from every one, and if I can't borrow it, I give you my word of honour I shall go to my father and break his skull and take the money from under the pillow, if only Ivan has gone. If I had to go to Siberia for it, I'll give you back your three thousand. And farewell. I bow down to the ground before you, for I've been a scoundrel to you. Forgive me! No, better not forgive me, you'll be happier and so shall I! Better Siberia than your love, for I love another woman and you got to know her too well to-day, so how can you forgive? I will murder the man who's robbed me! I'll leave you all and go to the East so as to see no one again. Not *her* either, for you are not my only tormentress, she is too. Farewell!

"PS.—I write my curse, but I adore you! I hear it in my heart. One string is left, and it vibrates. Better tear my heart in two! I shall kill myself, but first of all that cur. I shall tear three thousand from him and fling it to you. Though I've been a scoundrel to you, I am not a thief! You can expect three thousand. The cur keeps it under his mattress, in pink ribbon. I am not a thief, but I'll murder my thief. Katya, don't look disdainful. Dmitri is not a thief; but a murderer! He has murdered his father and ruined himself to hold his ground, rather than endure your pride. And he doesn't love you.

"PPS.—I kiss your feet, farewell! PPPS.—Katya, pray to God that some one'll give me the money. Then I shall not be steeped in gore, and if no one does—I shall! Kill me!

"Your slave and enemy,
"D. KARAMAZOV."

When Ivan read this "document," he was convinced. So then it was his brother, not Smerdyakov. And if not Smerdyakov, then not he, Ivan. This letter at once assumed in his eyes the aspect of a logical proof. There could be no longer the slightest doubt of Mitya's guilt. The suspicion never occurred to Ivan, by the way, that Mitya might have committed the murder in conjunction with Smerdyakov, and indeed such a theory did not fit in with the facts. Ivan was completely reassured. The next morning he only thought of Smerdyakov and his gibes with contempt. A few days later he positively wondered how he could have been so horribly distressed at his suspicions. He resolved to dismiss him with contempt and forget him. So passed a month. He made no further inquiry about Smerdyakov, but twice he happened to hear that he was very ill and out of his mind.

"He'll end in madness," the young doctor, Varvinsky, observed about him and Ivan remembered this. During the last week of that month Ivan himself began to feel very ill. He went to consult the Moscow doctor who had been sent for by Katerina Ivanovna just before the trial. And just at that time his relations with Katerina Ivanovna became acutely strained. They were like two enemies in love with one another. Katerina Ivanovna's "returns" to Mitya, that is, her brief but violent revulsions of feeling in his favour, drove Ivan to perfect frenzy. Strange to say, until that last scene described above, when Alyosha came from Mitya to Katerina Ivanovna, Ivan had never once, during that month, heard her express a doubt of Mitya's guilt, in spite of those "returns" that were so hateful to him. It is remarkable, too, that while he felt that he hated Mitya more and more every day, he realised that it was not on account of Katya's "returns" that he hated him, but just *because he was the murderer of his father*. He was conscious of this and fully recognised it to himself.

Nevertheless, he went to see Mitya ten days before the trial and proposed to him a plan of escape—a plan he had obviously thought over a long time. He was partly impelled to do this by a sore place still left in his heart from a phrase of Smerdyakov, that it was to his, Ivan's, advantage that his brother should be convicted, as that would increase his inheritance and Alyosha's from forty to sixty thousand roubles. He determined to sacrifice thirty thousand on arranging Mitya's escape. On his return from seeing him, he was very mournful and dispirited, he suddenly began to feel that he was anxious for Mitya's escape, not only to heal that sore place by sacrificing thirty thousand, but for another reason. "Is it because I am as much a murderer at heart?" he asked himself. Something very deep down seemed burning and rankling in his soul. His pride above all suffered cruelly all that month. But of that later. . . .

When, after his conversation with Alyosha, Ivan suddenly decided with his hand on the bell of his lodging to go to Smerdyakov, he obeyed a sudden and peculiar impulse of indignation. He suddenly remembered how Katerina Ivanovna had only just cried out to him in Alyosha's presence: "It was you, you, persuaded me of his (that is, Mitya's) guilt!" Ivan was thunderstruck when he recalled it. He had never once tried to persuade her that Mitya was the murderer, on the contrary, he had suspected himself in her presence, that time when he came back from Smerdyakov. It was *she,* she, who had produced that "document" and proved his brother's guilt. And now she suddenly exclaimed: "I've been at Smerdyakov's myself!" When had she been there? Ivan had known nothing of it. So she was not at all so sure of Mitya's guilt! And what could Smerdyakov have told her? What, what, had he said to her? His heart burned with violent anger. He could not understand how he could, half an hour before, have let those words pass and not have cried out at the moment. He let go of the bell and rushed off to Smerdyakov. "I shall kill him perhaps this time," he thought on the way.

8

THE THIRD AND LAST INTERVIEW
WITH SMERDYAKOV

WHEN he was half-way there, the keen dry wind that had been blowing early that morning rose again, and a fine dry snow began falling thickly. It did not lie on the ground, but was whirled about by the wind, and soon there was a regular snowstorm. There were scarcely any lamp-posts in the part of the town where Smerdyakov lived. Ivan strode alone in the darkness, unconscious of the storm, instinctively picking out his way. His head ached and there was a painful throbbing in his temples. He felt that his hands were twitching convulsively. Not far from Marya Kondratyevna's cottage, Ivan suddenly came upon a solitary drunken little peasant. He was wearing a coarse and patched coat, and was walking in zigzags, grumbling and swearing to himself. Then suddenly he would begin singing in a husky drunken voice:

> "Ach, Vanka's gone to Petersburg
> I won't wait till he comes back."

But he broke off every time at the second line and began swearing again; then he would begin the same song again. Ivan felt an intense hatred for him before he had thought about him at all. Suddenly he realised his presence and felt an irresistible impulse to knock him down. At that moment they met, and the peasant with a violent lurch fell full tilt against Ivan, who pushed him back furiously. The peasant went flying backwards and fell like a log on the frozen ground. He uttered one plaintive "O-oh!" and then was silent. Ivan stepped up to him. He was lying on his back, without movement or consciousness. "He will be frozen," thought Ivan, and he went on his way to Smerdyakov's.

In the passage, Marya Kondratyevna, who ran out to open the door with a candle in her hand, whispered that Smerdyakov was very ill; "it's not that he's laid up, but he seems not himself, and he even told us to take the tea away; he wouldn't have any."

"Why, does he make a row?" asked Ivan coarsely.

"Oh, dear, no, quite the contrary, he's very quiet. Only please don't talk to him too long," Marya Kondratyevna begged him. Ivan opened the door and stepped into the room.

It was overheated as before, but there were changes in the room. One of the benches at the side had been removed, and in its place had been put a large old mahogany leather sofa, on which a bed had been made up, with

565

fairly clean white pillows. Smerdyakov was sitting on the sofa, wearing the same dressing-gown. The table had been brought out in front of the sofa, so that there was hardly room to move. On the table lay a thick book in yellow cover, but Smerdyakov was not reading it. He seemed to be sitting doing nothing. He met Ivan with a slow silent gaze, and was apparently not at all surprised at his coming. There was a great change in his face; he was much thinner and sallower. His eyes were sunken and there were blue marks under them.

"Why, you really are ill?" Ivan stopped short. "I won't keep you long, I won't even take off my coat. Where can one sit down?"

He went to the other end of the table, moved up a chair and sat down on it.

"Why do you look at me without speaking? I've only come with one question, and I swear I won't go without an answer. Has the young lady, Katerina Ivanovna, been with you?"

Smerdyakov still remained silent, looking quietly at Ivan as before. Suddenly, with a motion of his hand, he turned his face away.

"What's the matter with you?" cried Ivan.

"Nothing."

"What do you mean by 'nothing'?"

"Yes, she has. It's no matter to you. Let me alone."

"No, I won't let you alone. Tell me, when was she here?"

"Why, I'd quite forgotten about her," said Smerdyakov, with a scornful smile, and turning his face to Ivan again, he stared at him with a look of frenzied hatred, the same look that he had fixed on him at their last interview, a month before.

"You seem very ill yourself, your face is sunken; you don't look like yourself," he said to Ivan.

"Never mind my health, tell me what I ask you."

"But why are your eyes so yellow? The whites are quite yellow. Are you so worried?" He smiled contemptuously and suddenly laughed outright.

"Listen, I've told you I won't go away without an answer?" Ivan cried, intensely irritated.

"Why do you keep pestering me? Why do you torment me?" said Smerdyakov, with a look of suffering.

"Damn it! I've nothing to do with you. Just answer my question and I'll go away."

"I've no answer to give you," said Smerdyakov, looking down again.

"You may be sure I'll make you answer!"

"Why are you so uneasy?" Smerdyakov stared at him, not simply with contempt, but almost with a repulsion. "Is this because the trial begins to-morrow? Nothing will happen to you, can't you believe that at last? Go home, go to bed and sleep in peace, don't be afraid of anything."

"I don't understand you. . . . What have I to be afraid of to-morrow?" Ivan articulated in astonishment, and suddenly a chill breath of fear did in fact pass over his soul. Smerdyakov measured him with his eyes.

"You don't understand?" he drawled reproachfully. "It's a strange thing a sensible man should care to play such a farce!"

Ivan looked at him speechless. The startling, incredibly supercilious tone of this man who had once been his valet, was extraordinary in itself. He had not taken such a tone even at their last interview.

"I tell you, you've nothing to be afraid of. I won't say anything about you, there's no proof against you. I say, how your hands are trembling. Why are your fingers moving like that? Go home, *you* did not murder him."

Ivan started. He remembered Alyosha.

"I know it was not I," he faltered.

"Do you?" Smerdyakov caught him up again.

Ivan jumped up and seized him by the shoulder.

"Tell me everything, you viper! Tell me everything!"

Smerdyakov was not in the least scared. He only riveted his eyes on Ivan with insane hatred.

"Well, it was you who murdered him, if that's it," he whispered furiously.

Ivan sank back on his chair, as though pondering something. He laughed malignantly.

"You mean my going away. What you talked about last time?"

"You stood before me last time and understood it all, and you understand it now."

"All I understand is that you are mad."

"Aren't you tired of it? Here we are face to face; what's the use of going on keeping up a farce to each other? Are you still trying to throw it all on me, to my face? *You* murdered him; you are the real murderer, I was only your instrument, your faithful servant, and it was following your words I did it."

"*Did* it? Why, did you murder him?" Ivan turned cold.

Something seemed to give way in his brain, and he shuddered all over with a cold shiver. Then Smerdyakov himself looked at him wonderingly; probably the genuineness of Ivan's horror struck him.

"You don't mean to say you really did not know?" he faltered mistrustfully, looking with a forced smile into his eyes. Ivan still gazed at him, and seemed unable to speak.

> Ach, Vanka's gone to Petersburg
> I won't wait till he comes back,

suddenly echoed in his head.

"Do you know, I am afraid that you are a dream, a phantom sitting before me," he muttered.

"There's no phantom here, but only us two and one other. No doubt he is here, that third, between us."

"Who is he? Who is here? What third person?" Ivan cried in alarm, looking about him, his eyes hastily searching in every corner.

"That third is God Himself, Providence. He is the third beside us now. Only don't look for him, you won't find him."

"It's a lie that you killed him!" Ivan cried madly. "You are mad, or teasing me again!"

Smerdyakov, as before, watched him curiously, with no sign of fear. He could still scarcely get over his incredulity; he still fancied that Ivan knew everything and was trying to "throw it all on him to his face."

"Wait a minute," he said at last in a weak voice, and suddenly bringing up his left leg from under the table, he began turning up his trouser leg. He was wearing long white stockings and slippers. Slowly he took off his garter and fumbled to the bottom of his stocking. Ivan gazed at him, and suddenly shuddered in a paroxysm of terror.

"He's mad!" he cried, and rapidly jumping up, he drew back, so that he knocked his back against the wall and stood up against it, stiff and straight. He looked with insane terror at Smerdyakov, who, entirely unaffected by his terror, continued fumbling in his stocking, as though he were making an effort to get hold of something with his fingers and pull it out. At last he got hold of it and began pulling it out. Ivan saw that it was a piece of paper, or perhaps a roll of papers. Smerdyakov pulled it out and laid it on the table.

"Here," he said quietly.

"What is it?" responded Ivan, trembling.

"Kindly look at it," Smerdyakov answered, still in the same low tone.

Ivan stepped up to the table, took up the roll of paper and began unfolding it, but suddenly he drew back his fingers, as though from contact with a loathsome reptile.

"Your hands keep twitching," observed Smerdyakov, and he deliberately unfolded the bundle himself. Under the wrapper were three packets of hundred-rouble notes.

"They are all here; all the three thousand roubles; you need not count them. Take them," Smerdyakov suggested to Ivan, nodding at the notes. Ivan sank back in his chair. He was as white as a handkerchief.

"You frightened me . . . with your stocking," he said, with a strange grin.

"Can you really not have known till now?" Smerdyakov asked once more.

"No, I did not know. I kept thinking of Dmitri. Brother, brother! Ach!" He suddenly clutched his head in both hands.

"Listen. Did you kill him alone? With my brother's help or without?"

"It was only with you, with your help, I killed him, and Dmitri Fyodorovitch is quite innocent."

"All right, all right. Talk about me later. Why do I keep on trembling? I can't speak properly."

"You were bold enough then. You said 'everything was lawful,' and how frightened you are now," Smerdyakov muttered in surprise. "Won't you have some lemonade? I'll ask for some at once. It's very refreshing. Only I must hide this first."

And again he motioned at the notes. He was just going to get up and call at the door to Marya Kondratyevna to make some lemonade and bring it them, but, looking for something to cover up the notes that she might not see them, he first took out his handkerchief, and as it turned out to be very dirty, took up the big yellow book that Ivan had noticed at first lying on the table, and put it over the notes. The book was "The Sayings of the Holy Father Isaac the Syrian." Ivan read it mechanically.

"I won't have any lemonade," he said. "Talk of me later. Sit down and tell me how you did it. Tell me all about it."

"You'd better take off your greatcoat, or you'll be too hot." Ivan, as though he'd only just thought of it, took off his coat, and, without getting up from his chair, threw it on the bench.

"Speak, please, speak."

He seemed calmer. He waited, feeling sure that Smerdyakov would tell him *all* about it.

"How it was done?" sighed Smerdyakov. "It was done in a most natural way, following your very words."

"Of my words later," Ivan broke in again, apparently with complete self-possession, firmly uttering his words, and not shouting as before. "Only tell me in detail how you did it. Everything, as it happened. Don't forget anything. The details, above everything, the details, I beg you."

"You'd gone away, then I fell into the cellar."

"In a fit or in a sham one?"

"A sham one, naturally. I shammed it all. I went quietly down the steps to the very bottom and lay down quietly, and as I lay down I gave a scream, and struggled, till they carried me out."

"Stay! And were you shamming all along, afterwards, and in the hospital?"

"No, not at all. Next day, in the morning, before they took me to the hospital, I had a real attack and a more violent one than I've had for years. For two days I was quite unconscious."

"All right, all right. Go on."

"They laid me on the bed. I knew I'd be the other side of the partition, for whenever I was ill, Marfa Ignatyevna used to put me there, near them. She's always been very kind to me from my birth up. At night I moaned, but quietly. I kept expecting Dmitri Fyodorovitch to come."

"Expecting him? To come to you?"

"Not to me. I expected him to come into the house, for I'd no doubt that he'd come that night, for being without me and getting no news, he'd be sure to come and climb over the fence, as he used to and do something."

"And if he hadn't come?"

"Then nothing would have happened. I should never have brought myself to it without him."

"All right, all right . . . speak more intelligibly, don't hurry; above all, don't leave anything out!"

"I expected him to kill Fyodor Pavlovitch. I thought that was certain, for I had prepared him for it . . . during the last few days. . . . He knew about the knocks, that was the chief thing. With his suspiciousness and the fury which had been growing in him all those days, he was bound to get into the house by means of those taps. That was inevitable, so I was expecting him."

"Stay," Ivan interrupted, "if he had killed him, he would have taken the money and carried it away; you must have considered that. What would you have got by it afterwards? I don't see."

"But he would never have found the money. That was only what I told him, that the money was under the mattress. But that wasn't true. It had been lying in a box. And afterwards I suggested to Fyodor Pavlovitch, as I was the only person he trusted, to hide the envelope with the notes in the corner behind the ikons, for no one would have guessed that place, especially if they came in a hurry. So that's where the envelope lay, in the corner behind the ikons. It would have been absurd to keep it under the mattress, the box, anyway, could be locked. But all believe it was under the mattress. A stupid thing to believe. So if Dmitri Fyodorovitch had committed the murder, finding nothing, he would either have run away in a hurry, afraid of every sound, as always happens with murderers, or he would have been arrested. So I could always have clambered up to the ikons and have taken away the money next morning or even that night, and it would have all been put down to Dmitri Fyodorovitch. I could reckon upon that."

"But what if he did not kill him, but only knocked him down?"

"If he did not kill him, of course, I would not have ventured to take the money, and nothing would have happened. But I calculated that he would beat him senseless, and I should have time to take it then, and then I'd make out to Fyodor Pavlovitch that it was no one but Dmitri Fyodorovitch who had taken the money after beating him."

"Stop . . . I am getting mixed. Then it was Dmitri after all who killed him, you only took the money?"

"No, he didn't kill him. Well, I might as well have told you now that he was the murderer. . . . But I don't want to lie to you now, because . . . because if you really haven't understood till now, as I see for myself, and are not pretending, so as to throw your guilt on me to my very face, you are still responsible for it all, since you knew of the murder and charged me to do it, and went away knowing all about it. And so I want to prove to your face this evening that you are the only real murderer in the whole affair, and I am not the real murderer, though I did kill him. You are the rightful murderer."

"Why, why, am I a murderer? Oh, God!" Ivan cried, unable to restrain himself at last, and forgetting that he had put off discussing himself till the end of the conversation. "You still mean that Tchermashnya? Stay, tell me, why did you want my consent, if you really took Tchermashnya for consent? How will you explain that now?"

"Assured of your consent, I should have known that you wouldn't have made an outcry over those three thousand being lost, even if I'd been suspected, instead of Dmitri Fyodorovitch, or as his accomplice; on the contrary, you would have protected me from others. . . . And when you got your inheritance you would have rewarded me when you were able, all the rest of your life. For you'd have received your inheritance through me, seeing that if he had married Agrafena Alexandrovna, you wouldn't have had a farthing."

"Ah! Then you intended to worry me all my life afterwards," snarled Ivan. "And what if I hadn't gone away then, but had informed against you?"

"What could you have informed? That I persuaded you to go to Tchermashnya? That's all nonsense. Besides, after our conversation you would either have gone away or have stayed. If you had stayed, nothing would have happened. I should have known that you didn't want it done, and should have attempted nothing. As you went away, it meant you assured me that you wouldn't dare to inform against me at the trial, and that you'd overlook my having the three thousand. And, indeed, you couldn't have prosecuted me afterwards, because then I should have told it all in the court; that is, not that I had stolen the money or killed him—I should have said that—but that you'd put me up to the theft and the murder, though I didn't consent to it. That's why I needed your consent, so that you couldn't have cornered me afterwards, for what proof could you have had? I could always have cornered you, revealing your eagerness for your father's death, and I tell you the public would all have believed it, and you would have been ashamed for the rest of your life."

"Was I so eager then, was I?" Ivan snarled again.

"To be sure you were, and by your consent you silently sanctioned my doing it." Smerdyakov looked resolutely at Ivan. He was very weak and spoke slowly and wearily, but some hidden inner force urged him on. He evidently had some design. Ivan felt that.

"Go on," he said. "Tell me what happened that night."

"What more is there to tell! I lay there and I thought I heard the master shout. And before that Grigory Vassilyevitch had suddenly got up and came out, and he suddenly gave a scream, and then all was silence and darkness. I lay there waiting, my heart beating; I couldn't bear it, I got up at last, went out. I saw the window open on the left into the garden, and I stepped to the left to listen whether he was sitting there alive, and I heard the master moving about, sighing, so I knew he was alive. Ech! I thought. I went to the window and shouted to the master, 'It's I.' And he shouted to me, 'He's been, he's been; he's run away.' He meant Dmitri Fyodorovitch had been. 'He's killed Grigory!' 'Where?' I whispered. 'There, in the corner,' he pointed. He was whispering, too. 'Wait a bit,' I said. I went to the corner of the garden to look, and there I came upon Grigory Vassilyevitch lying by the wall, covered with blood, senseless. So it's true that Dmitri Fyodorovitch has been here, was the thought that came into my head, and I determined on the spot to make an end of it, as Grigory Vassilyevitch, even if he were alive, would see nothing of it, as he lay there senseless. The only risk was that Marfa Ignatyevna might wake up. I felt that at the moment, but the longing to get it done came over me, till I could scarcely breathe. I went back to the window to the master and said, 'She's here, she's come; Agrafena Alexandrovna has come, wants to be let in.' And he started like a baby. 'Where is she?' he fairly gasped, but couldn't believe it. 'She's standing there,' said I, 'open.' He looked out of the window at me, half believing and half distrustful, but afraid to open. 'Why he is afraid of me now,' I thought. And it was funny. I bethought me to knock on the window frame those taps we'd agreed upon as a signal that Grushenka had come, in his presence, before his eyes. He didn't seem to believe my words, but as soon as he heard the taps, he ran at once to open the door. He opened it. I would have gone in, but he stood in the way to prevent me passing. 'Where is she? Where is she?' He looked at me, all of a tremble. Well, thought I, if he's so frightened of me as all that, it's a bad look-out! And my legs went weak with fright that he wouldn't let me in or would call out, or Marfa Ignatyevna would run up, or something else might happen. I don't remember now, but I must have stood pale, facing him. I whispered to him, 'Why, she's there, there, under the window, how is it you don't see her?' I said. 'Bring her then, bring her.' 'She's afraid,' said I, 'she was frightened at the noise, she's hidden in the bushes; go and call to her yourself from the study.' He ran to the window, put the candle in the window. 'Grushenka,' he cried, 'Grushenka, are you here?' Though he cried that, he didn't want to lean out of the window, he didn't want to move away from me, for he was panic-stricken; he was so frightened he didn't dare to turn his back on me. 'Why, here she is,' said I. I went up to the window and leaned right out of it. 'Here she is, she's in the bush, laughing at you, don't you see her?' He suddenly believed it: he was all of a shake—he was awfully crazy about her—and he leaned right out of the window. I snatched up that iron paper weight from his table: do you remember, weighing about three pounds. I swung it and hit him on the top of the skull with the corner of it. He didn't even cry out. He only sank down suddenly, and I hit him again and a third time. And the third time I knew I'd broken his skull. He suddenly rolled on his back, face upwards, covered with blood. I looked round. There was no blood on me, not a spot. I wiped the paper weight, put it back, went up to the ikons, took the money out of the envelope, and flung the envelope on the floor and the pink ribbon beside it. I went out into the garden all of a tremble, straight to the apple tree with a hollow in it—you know that hollow. I'd marked it long before and put a rag and a piece of paper ready in it. I wrapped all the notes in the rag and stuffed it deep down in the hole. And there it stayed for over a fortnight. I took it out later, when I came out of the hospital. I went back to my bed, lay down and thought 'if Grigory Vassilyevitch has been killed outright, it may be a bad job for me, but if he is not killed and recovers, it will be first rate, for then he'll bear witness that Dmitri Fyodorovitch has been here, and so he must have killed him and taken the money.' Then I began groaning with suspense and impatience, so as to wake Marfa Ignatyevna as soon as possible. At last she got up, and she rushed to me, but when she saw Grigory Vassilyevitch was not there, she ran out, and I heard her scream in the garden. And that set it all going and set my mind at rest."

He stopped. Ivan had listened all the time in dead silence without stirring or taking his eyes off him. As he told his story Smerdyakov glanced at him from time to time, but for the most part kept his eyes averted. When he had finished he was evidently agitated and was breathing hard. The perspiration stood out on his face. But it was impossible to tell whether it was remorse he was feeling, or what.

"Stay," cried Ivan, pondering. "What about the door? If he only opened the door to you, how could Grigory have seen it open before? For Grigory saw it before you went."

It was remarkable that Ivan spoke quite amicably, in a different tone, not angry as before, so if anyone had opened the door at that moment and peeped in at them, he would certainly have concluded that they were talking peaceably about some ordinary, though interesting subject.

"As for that door and Grigory Vassilyevitch's having seen it open, that's only his fancy," said Smerdyakov, with a wry smile. "He is not a man, I assure you, but an obstinate mule. He didn't see it, but fancied he had seen it, and there's no shaking him. It's just our luck he took that notion into his head, for they can't fail to convict Dmitri Fyodorovitch after that."

"Listen. . . ." said Ivan, beginning to seem bewildered again and making an effort to grasp something. "Listen. There are a lot of questions I want to ask you, but I forget them . . . I keep forgetting and getting mixed up. Yes. Tell me this at least, why did you open the envelope and leave it there on the floor? Why didn't you simply carry off the envelope? . . . When you were telling me, I thought you spoke about it as though it were the right thing to do . . . but why, I can't understand. . . ."

"I did that for a good reason. For if a man had known all about it, as I did for instance, if he'd seen those notes before, and perhaps had put them in that envelope himself, and had seen the envelope sealed up and addressed, with his own eyes, if such a man had done the murder, what should have made him tear open the envelope afterwards, especially in such desperate haste, since he'd know for certain the notes must be in the envelope? No, if the robber had been some one like me, he'd simply have put the envelope straight in his pocket and got away with it as fast as he could. But it'd be quite different with Dmitri Fyodorovitch. He only knew about the envelope by hearsay; he had never seen it, and if he'd found it, for instance, under the mattress, he'd have torn it open as quickly as possible to make sure the notes were in it. And he'd have thrown the envelope down, without having time to think that it would be evidence against him. Because he was not an habitual thief and had never directly stolen anything before, for he is a gentleman born, and if he did bring himself to steal, it would not be regular stealing, but simply taking what was his own, for he'd told the whole town he meant to before, and had even bragged aloud before every one that he'd go and take his property from Fyodor Pavlovitch. I didn't say that openly to the prosecutor when I was being examined, but quite the contrary, I brought him to it by a hint, as though I didn't see it myself, and as though he'd thought of it himself and I hadn't prompted him; so that Mr. Prosecutor's mouth positively watered at my suggestion."

"But can you possibly have thought of all that on the spot?" cried Ivan, overcome with astonishment. He looked at Smerdyakov again with alarm.

"Mercy on us! Could any one think of it all in such a desperate hurry? It was all thought out beforehand."

"Well . . . well, it was the devil helped you!" Ivan cried again. "No, you are not a fool, you are far cleverer than I thought. . . ."

He got up, obviously intending to walk across the room. He was in terrible distress. But as the table blocked his way, and there was hardly room to pass between the table and the wall, he only turned round where he stood and sat down again. Perhaps the impossibility of moving irritated him, as he suddenly cried out almost as furiously as before.

"Listen, you miserable, contemptible creature! Don't you understand that if I haven't killed you, it's simply because I am keeping you to answer to-morrow at the trial. God sees," Ivan raised his hand, "perhaps I, too, was guilty; perhaps I really had a secret desire for my father's . . . death, but I swear I was not as guilty as you think, and perhaps I didn't urge you on at all. No, no, I didn't urge you on! But no matter, I will give evidence against myself to-morrow, at the trial. I'm determined to! I shall tell everything, everything. But we'll make our appearance together. And whatever you may say against me at the trial, whatever evidence you give, I'll face it, I am not afraid of you. I'll confirm it all myself! But you must confess, too! You must, you must, we'll go together. That's how it shall be!"

Ivan said this solemnly and resolutely, and from his flashing eyes alone it could be seen that it would be so.

"You are ill, I see, you are quite ill. Your eyes are yellow," Smerdyakov commented, without the least irony, with apparent sympathy in fact.

"We'll go together," Ivan repeated. "And if you won't go, no matter, I'll go alone."

Smerdyakov paused as though pondering.

"There'll be nothing of the sort, and you won't go," he concluded at last positively.

"You don't understand me," Ivan exclaimed reproachfully.

"You'll be too much ashamed, if you confess it all. And, what's more, it will be no use at all, for I shall say straight out that I never said anything of the sort to you, and that you are either ill (and it looks like it, too), or that you're so sorry for your brother that you are sacrificing yourself to save him and have invented it all against me, for you've always thought no more of me than if I'd been a fly. And who will believe you, and what single proof have you got?"

"Listen, you showed me those notes just now to convince me."

Smerdyakov lifted the book off the notes and laid it on one side.

"Take that money away with you," Smerdyakov sighed.

"Of course I shall take it. But why do you give it to me, if you committed the murder for the sake of it?" Ivan looked at him with great surprise.

"I don't want it," Smerdyakov articulated in a shaking voice, with a gesture of refusal. "I did have an idea of beginning a new life with that money in Moscow or, better still, abroad. I did dream of it, chiefly because 'all things are lawful.' That was quite right what you taught me, for you talked a lot to me about that. For if there's no everlasting God, there's no such thing as virtue, and there's no need of it. You were right there. So that's how I looked at it."

"Did you come to that of yourself?" asked Ivan, with a wry smile.

"With your guidance."

"And now, I suppose, you believe in God, since you are giving back the money?"

"No, I don't believe," whispered Smerdyakov.

"Then why are you giving it back?"

"Leave off . . . that's enough!" Smerdyakov waved his hand again. "You used to say yourself that everything was lawful, so now why are you so upset, too? You even want to go and give evidence against yourself. . . . Only there'll be nothing of the sort! You won't go to give evidence," Smerdyakov decided with conviction.

"You'll see," said Ivan.

"It isn't possible. You are very clever. You are fond of money, I know that. You like to be respected, too, for you're very proud; you are far too fond of female charms, too, and you mind most of all about living in undisturbed comfort, without having to depend on any one—that's what you care most about. You won't want to spoil your life for ever by taking such a disgrace on yourself. You are like Fyodor Pavlovitch, you are more like him than any of his children; you've the same soul as he had."

"You are not a fool," said Ivan, seeming struck. The blood rushed to his face. "You are serious now!" he observed, looking suddenly at Smerdyakov with a different expression.

"It was your pride made you think I was a fool. Take the money."

Ivan took the three rolls of notes and put them in his pocket without wrapping them in anything.

"I shall show them at the court to-morrow," he said.

"Nobody will believe you, as you've plenty of money of your own; you may simply have taken it out of your cash-box and brought it to the court."

Ivan rose from his seat.

"I repeat," he said, "the only reason I haven't killed you is that I need you for to-morrow, remember that, don't forget it!"

"Well, kill me. Kill me now," Smerdyakov said, all at once looking strangely at Ivan. "You won't dare do that even!" he added, with a bitter smile. "You won't dare to do anything, you, who used to be so bold!"

"Till to-morrow," cried Ivan, and moved to go out.

"Stay a moment. . . . Show me those notes again."

Ivan took out the notes and showed them to him. Smerdyakov looked at them for ten seconds.

"Well, you can go," he said, with a wave of his hand. "Ivan Fyodorovitch!" he called after him again.

"What do you want?" Ivan turned without stopping.

"Good-bye!"

"Till to-morrow!" Ivan cried again, and he walked out of the cottage.

The snowstorm was still raging. He walked the first few steps boldly, but suddenly began staggering. "It's something physical," he thought with a grin. Something like joy was springing up in his heart. He was conscious of unbounded resolution; he would make an end of the wavering that had so tortured him of late. His determination was taken, "and now it will not be changed," he thought with relief. At that moment he stumbled against something and almost fell down. Stopping short, he made out at his feet the peasant he had knocked down, still lying senseless and motionless. The snow had almost covered his face. Ivan seized him and lifted him in his arms. Seeing a light in the little house to the right he went up, knocked at the shutters, and asked the man to whom the house belonged to help him carry the peasant to the police-station, promising him three roubles. The man got ready and came out. I won't describe in detail how Ivan succeeded in his object, bringing the peasant to the police-station and arranging for a doctor to see him at once, providing with a liberal hand for the expenses. I will only say that this business took a whole hour, but Ivan was well content with it. His mind wandered and worked incessantly.

"If I had not taken my decision so firmly for to-morrow," he reflected with satisfaction, "I should not have stayed a whole hour to look after the peasant, but should have passed by, without caring about his being frozen. I am quite capable of watching myself, by the way," he thought at the same instant, with still greater satisfaction, "although they have decided that I am going out of my mind!"

Just as he reached his own house he stopped short, asking himself suddenly hadn't he better go at once now to the prosecutor and tell him everything. He decided the question by turning back to the house. "Everything together to-morrow!" he whispered to himself, and, strange to say, almost all his gladness and self-satisfaction passed in one instant.

As he entered his own room he felt something like a touch of ice on his heart, like a recollection or, more exactly, a reminder of something agonising and revolting that was in that room now, at that moment, and had been there before. He sank wearily on his sofa. The old woman brought him a samovar; he made tea, but did not touch it. He sat on the sofa and felt giddy. He felt that he was ill and helpless. He was beginning to drop asleep, but got up uneasily and walked across the room to shake off his drowsiness. At moments he fancied he was delirious, but it was not illness that he thought of most. Sitting down again, he began looking round, as though searching for something. This happened several times. At last his eyes were fastened intently on one point. Ivan smiled, but an angry flush suffused his face. He sat a long time in his place, his head propped on both arms, though he looked sideways at the same point, at the sofa that stood against the opposite wall. There was evidently something, some object, that irritated him there, worried him and tormented him.

9

THE DEVIL. IVAN'S NIGHTMARE

I AM not a doctor, but yet I feel that the moment has come when I must inevitably give the reader some account of the nature of Ivan's illness. Anticipating events I can say at least one thing: he was at that moment on the very eve of an attack of brain fever. Though his health had long been affected, it had offered a stubborn resistance to the fever which in the end gained complete mastery over it. Though I know nothing of medicine, I venture to hazard the suggestion that he really had perhaps, by a terrible effort of will, succeeded in delaying the attack for a time, hoping, of course, to check it completely. He knew that he was unwell, but he loathed the thought of being ill at that fatal time, at the approaching crisis in his life, when he needed to have all his wits about him, to say what he had to say boldly and resolutely and "to justify himself to himself."

He had however consulted the new doctor, who had been brought from Moscow by a fantastic notion of Katerina Ivanovna's to which I have referred already. After listening to him and examining him the doctor came to the conclusion that he was actually suffering from some disorder of the brain, and was not at all surprised by an admission which Ivan had reluctantly made him. "Hallucinations are quite likely in your condition," the doctor opined, "though it would be better to verify them . . . you must take steps at once, without a moment's delay, or things will go badly with you." But Ivan did not follow this judicious advice and did not take to his bed to be nursed. "I am walking about, so I am strong enough, if I drop, it'll be different then, any one may nurse me who likes," he decided, dismissing the subject.

And so he was sitting almost conscious himself of his delirium and, as I have said already, looking persistently at some object on the sofa against the opposite wall. Some one appeared to be sitting there, though goodness knows how he had come in, for he had not been in the room when Ivan came into it, on his return from Smerdyakov. This was a person or, more accurately speaking, a Russian gentleman of a particular kind, no longer young, *qui faisait la cinquantane*,* as the French say, with rather long, still thick, dark hair, slightly streaked with grey and a small pointed beard. He was wearing a brownish reefer jacket, rather shabby, evidently made by a good tailor though, and of a fashion at least three years old, that had been discarded by smart and well-to-do people for the last two years. His linen

---

*Looking every bit fifty (French).

and his long scarf-like neck-tie were all such as are worn by people who aim at being stylish, but on closer inspection his linen was not over clean and his wide scarf was very threadbare. The visitor's check trousers were of excellent cut, but were too light in colour and too tight for the present fashion. His soft fluffy white hat was out of keeping with the season.

In brief there was every appearance of gentility on straitened means. It looked as though the gentleman belonged to that class of idle landowners who used to flourish in the times of serfdom. He had unmistakably been, at some time, in good and fashionable society, had once had good connections, had possibly preserved them indeed, but, after a gay youth, becoming gradually impoverished on the abolition of serfdom, he had sunk into the position of a poor relation of the best class, wandering from one good old friend to another and received by them for his companionable and accommodating disposition and as being, after all, a gentleman who could be asked to sit down with any one, though, of course, not in a place of honour. Such gentlemen of accommodating temper and dependent position, who can tell a story, take a hand at cards, and who have a distinct aversion for any duties that may be forced upon them, are usually solitary creatures, either bachelors or widowers. Sometimes they have children, but if so, the children are always being brought up at a distance, at some aunt's, to whom these gentlemen never allude in good society, seeming ashamed of the relationship. They gradually lose sight of their children altogether, though at intervals they receive a birthday or Christmas letter from them and sometimes even answer it.

The countenance of the unexpected visitor was not so much good-natured, as accommodating and ready to assume any amiable expression as occasion might arise. He had no watch, but he had a tortoise-shell lorgnette on a black ribbon. On the middle finger of his right hand was a massive gold ring with a cheap opal stone in it.

Ivan was angrily silent and would not begin the conversation. The visitor waited and sat exactly like a poor relation who had come down from his room to keep his host company at tea, and was discreetly silent, seeing that his host was frowning and preoccupied. But he was ready for any affable conversation as soon as his host should begin it. All at once his face expressed a sudden solicitude.

"I say," he began to Ivan, "excuse me, I only mention it to remind you. You went to Smerdyakov's to find out about Katerina Ivanovna, but you came away without finding out anything about her, you probably forgot. . . ."

"Ah, yes," broke from Ivan and his face grew gloomy with uneasiness. "Yes, I'd forgotten . . . but it doesn't matter now, never mind, till tomorrow," he muttered to himself, "and you," he added, addressing his visitor, "I should have remembered that myself in a minute, for that was just what was tormenting me! Why do you interfere, as if I should believe that you prompted me, and that I didn't remember it of myself?"

"Don't believe it then," said the gentleman, smiling amicably, "what's the good of believing against your will? Besides, proofs are no help to believing, especially material proofs. Thomas believed,* not because he saw Christ risen, but because he wanted to believe, before he saw. Look at the spiritualists, for instance. . . . I am very fond of them . . . only fancy, they imagine that they are serving the cause of religion, because the devils show them their horns from the other world. That, they say, is a material proof, so to speak, of the existence of another world. The other world and material proofs, what next! And if you come to that, does proving there's a devil prove that there's a God? I want to join an idealist society, I'll lead the opposition in it, I'll say I am a realist, but not a materialist, he-he!"

"Listen," Ivan suddenly got up from the table. "I seem to be delirious . . . I am delirious, in fact, talk any nonsense you like, I don't care! You won't drive me to fury, as you did last time. But I feel somehow ashamed . . . I want to walk about the room . . . I sometimes don't see you and don't even hear your voice as I did last time, but I always guess what you are prating, for it's I, *I myself speaking, not you.* Only I don't know whether I was dreaming last time or whether I really saw you. I'll wet a towel and put it on my head and perhaps you'll vanish into air."

Ivan went into the corner, took a towel, and did as he said, and with a wet towel on his head began walking up and down the room.

"I am so glad you treat me so familiarly," the visitor began.

"Fool," laughed Ivan, "do you suppose I should stand on ceremony with you? I am in good spirits now, though I've a pain in my forehead . . . and in the top of my head . . . only please don't talk philosophy, as you did last time. If you can't take yourself off, talk of something amusing. Talk gossip, you are a poor relation, you ought to talk gossip. What a nightmare to have! But I am not afraid of you. I'll get the better of you. I won't be taken to a mad-house!"

"*C'est charmant,*† poor relation. Yes, I am in my natural shape. For what am I on earth but a poor relation? By the way, I am listening to you and am rather surprised to find you are actually beginning to take me for something real, not simply your fancy, as you persisted in declaring last time. . . ."

"Never for one minute have I taken you for reality," Ivan cried with a sort of fury. "You are a lie, you are my illness, you are a phantom. It's only that I don't know how to destroy you and I see I must suffer for a time. You are my hallucination. You are the incarnation of myself, but only of one side of me . . . of my thoughts and feelings, but only the nastiest and stupidest of them. From that point of view you might be of interest to me, if only I had time to waste on you. . . ."

"Excuse me, excuse me, I'll catch you. When you flew out at Alyosha under the lamp-post this evening and shouted to him. 'You learnt it from *him!* How do you know that *he* visits me?' You were thinking of me then. So for one brief moment you did believe that I really exist," the gentleman laughed blandly.

---

*See John 20:25–29.
†That's charming (French).

"Yes, that was a moment of weakness . . . but I couldn't believe in you. I don't know whether I was asleep or awake last time. Perhaps I was only dreaming then and didn't see you really at all. . . ."

"And why were you so surly with Alyosha just now? He is a dear; I've treated him badly over Father Zossima."

"Don't talk of Alyosha! How dare you, you flunkey!" Ivan laughed again.

"You scold me, but you laugh—that's a good sign. But you are ever so much more polite than you were last time and I know why: that great resolution of yours. . . ."

"Don't speak of my resolution," cried Ivan, savagely.

"I understand, I understand, *c'est noble, c'est charmant*, you are going to defend your brother and to sacrifice yourself . . . *C'est chevaleresque*."*

"Hold your tongue, I'll kick you!"

"I shan't be altogether sorry, for then my object will be attained. If you kick me, you must believe in my reality, for people don't kick ghosts. Joking apart, it doesn't matter to me, scold if you like, though it's better to be a trifle more polite even to me. 'Fool, flunkey!' what words!"

"Scolding you, I scold myself," Ivan laughed again, "you are myself, myself, only with a different face. You just say what I am thinking . . . and are incapable of saying anything new!"

"If I am like you in my way of thinking, it's all to my credit," the gentleman declared, with delicacy and dignity.

"You choose out only my worst thoughts, and what's more, the stupid ones. You are stupid and vulgar. You are awfully stupid. No, I can't put up with you! What am I to do, what am I to do!" Ivan said through his clenched teeth.

"My dear friend, above all things I want to behave like a gentleman and to be recognised as such," the visitor began in an access of deprecating and simple-hearted pride, typical of a poor relation. "I am poor, but . . . I won't say very honest, but . . . it's an axiom generally accepted in society that I am a fallen angel. I certainly can't conceive how I can ever have been an angel. If I ever was, it must have been so long ago that there's no harm in forgetting it. Now I only prize the reputation of being a gentlemanly person and live as I can, trying to make myself agreeable. I love men genuinely, I've been greatly calumniated! Here when I stay with you from time to time, my life gains a kind of reality and that's what I like most of all. You see, like you, I suffer from the fantastic and so I love the realism of earth. Here, with you, everything is circumscribed, here all is formulated and geometrical, while we have nothing but indeterminate equations! I wander about here dreaming. I like dreaming. Besides, on earth I become superstitious. Please don't laugh, that's just what I like, to become superstitious. I adopt all your habits here: I've grown fond of going to the public baths, would you believe it? and I go and steam myself with merchants and priests. What I dream of is becoming incarnate once for all and irrevocably in the

---

*That's noble, that's charming. . . . That's chivalrous (French).

form of some merchant's wife weighing eighteen stone, and of believing all she believes. My ideal is to go to church and offer a candle in simple-hearted faith, upon my word it is. Then there would be an end to my sufferings. I like being doctored too; in the spring there was an outbreak of smallpox and I went and was vaccinated in a foundling hospital—if only you knew how I enjoyed myself that day. I subscribed ten roubles to the cause of the Slavs! . . . But you are not listening. Do you know, you are not at all well this evening? I know you went yesterday to that doctor . . . well, what about your health? What did the doctor say?"

"Fool!" Ivan snapped out.

"But you are clever, anyway. You are scolding again? I didn't ask out of sympathy. You needn't answer. Now rheumatism has come in again. . . ."

"Fool!" repeated Ivan.

"You keep saying the same thing; but I had such an attack of rheumatism last year that I remember it to this day."

"The devil have rheumatism!"

"Why not, if I sometimes put on fleshly form? I put on fleshly form and I take the consequences. Satan *sum et nihil humanum a me alienum puto*."*

"What, what? Satan *sum et nihil humanum* . . . that's not bad for the devil!"

"I am glad I've pleased you at last."

"But you didn't get that from me," Ivan stopped suddenly, seeming struck, "That never entered my head, that's strange."

"*C'est du nouveau, n'est ce pas?*† This time I'll act honestly and explain to you. Listen, in dreams and especially in nightmares, from indigestion or anything, a man sees sometimes such artistic visions, such complex and real actuality, such events, even a whole world of events, woven into such a plot, with such unexpected details from the most exalted matters to the last button on a cuff, as I swear Leo Tolstoy has never invented. Yet such dreams are sometimes seen not by writers, but by the most ordinary people, officials, journalists, priests. . . . The subject is a complete enigma. A statesman confessed to me, indeed, that all his best ideas came to him when he was asleep. Well, that's how it is now, though I am your hallucination, yet just as in a nightmare, I say original things which had not entered your head before. So I don't repeat your ideas, yet I am only your nightmare, nothing more."

"You are lying, your aim is to convince me you exist apart and are not my nightmare, and now you are asserting you are a dream."

"My dear fellow, I've adopted a special method to-day, I'll explain it to you afterwards. Stay, where did I break off? Oh, yes! I caught cold then, only not here but yonder."

---

*I am Satan and nothing human is alien to me (Latin). This is a play on a line from *The Self-Torturer*, a comedy by the Roman dramatist Terence (c.185–159 B.C.): *Homo sum, humani nihil a me alienum puto* (I am a human and nothing human is alien to me).

†That's something new, isn't it? (French).

"Where is yonder? Tell me, will you be here long? Can't you go away?" Ivan exclaimed almost in despair. He ceased walking to and fro, sat down on the sofa, leaned his elbows on the table again and held his head tight in both hands. He pulled the wet towel off and flung it away in vexation. It was evidently of no use.

"Your nerves are out of order," observed the gentleman, with a carelessly easy, though perfectly polite, air. "You are angry with me even for being able to catch cold, though it happened in a most natural way. I was hurrying then to a diplomatic soirée at the house of a lady of high rank in Petersburg, who was aiming at influence in the Ministry. Well, an evening suit, white tie, gloves, though I was God knows where and had to fly through space to reach your earth. . . . Of course, it took only an instant, but you know a ray of light from the sun takes full eight minutes, and fancy in an evening suit and open waistcoat. Spirits don't freeze, but when one's in fleshly form, well . . . in brief, I didn't think, and set off, and you know in those ethereal spaces, in the water that is above the firmament, there's such a frost . . . at least one can't call it frost, you can fancy, 150° below zero! You know the game the village girls play—they invite the unwary to lick an axe in thirty degrees of frost, the tongue instantly freezes to it and the dupe tears the skin off, so it bleeds. But that's only in 30°, in 150° I imagine it would be enough to put your finger on the axe and it would be the end of it . . . if only there could be an axe there."

"And can there be an axe there?" Ivan interrupted, carelessly and disdainfully. He was exerting himself to the utmost not to believe in the delusion and not to sink into complete insanity.

"An axe?" the guest interrupted in surprise.

"Yes, what would become of an axe there?" Ivan cried suddenly, with a sort of savage and insistent obstinacy.

"What would become of an axe in space? *Quelle idée!** If it were to fall to any distance, it would begin, I think, flying round the earth without knowing why, like a satellite. The astronomers would calculate the rising and the setting of the axe, *Gattzuk* would put it in his calendar,[4] that's all."

"You are stupid, awfully stupid, said Ivan peevishly. "Fib more cleverly or I won't listen. You want to get the better of me by realism, to convince me that you exist, but I don't want to believe you exist! I won't believe it!"

"But I am not fibbing, it's all the truth; the truth is unhappily hardly ever amusing: I see you persist in expecting something big of me, and perhaps something fine. That's a great pity, for I only give what I can. . . ."

"Don't talk philosophy, you ass!"

"Philosophy, indeed, when all my right side is numb and I am moaning and groaning. I've tried all the medical faculty: they can diagnose beautifully, they have the whole of your disease at their finger-tips, but they've no idea how to cure you. There was an enthusiastic little student here, 'You may die,' said he, 'but you'll know perfectly what disease you are dying of!'

---

*What an idea! (French).

And then what a way they have of sending people to specialists. 'We only diagnose,' they say, 'but go to such-and-such a specialist, he'll cure you.' The old doctor who used to cure all sorts of disease has completely disappeared, I assure you, now there are only specialists and they all advertise in the newspapers. If anything is wrong with your nose, they send you to Paris: there, they say, is a European specialist who cures noses. If you go to Paris, he'll look at your nose; I can only cure your right nostril,[5] he'll tell you, for I don't cure the left nostril, that's not my specialty, but go to Vienna, there there's a specialist who will cure your left nostril. What are you to do? I fell back on popular remedies, a German doctor advised me to rub myself with honey and salt in the bath-house. Solely to get an extra bath I went, smeared myself all over and it did me no good at all. In despair I wrote to Count Mattei in Milan. He sent me a book and some drops, bless him, and, only fancy, Hoff's malt extract cured me! I bought it by accident, drank a bottle and a half of it, and I was ready to dance, it took it away completely. I made up my mind to write to the papers to thank him, I was prompted by a feeling of gratitude, and only fancy, it led to no end of a bother: not a single paper would take my letter. 'It would be very reactionary,' they said, no one will believe it. *Le diable n'existe point.** 'You'd better remain anonymous,' they advised me. What use is a letter of thanks if it's anonymous? I laughed with the men at the newspaper office, 'it's reactionary to believe in God in our days,' I said, 'but I am the devil, so I may be believed in.' 'We quite understand that,' they said. 'Who doesn't believe in the devil? Yet it won't do, it might injure our reputation. As a joke, if you like.' But I thought as a joke it wouldn't be very witty. So it wasn't printed. And do you know, I have felt sore about it to this day. My best feelings, gratitude, for instance, are literally denied me simply from my social position."

"Philosophical reflections again?" Ivan snarled malignantly.

"God preserve me from it, but one can't help complaining sometimes. I am a slandered man. You upbraid me every moment with being stupid. One can see you are young. My dear fellow, intelligence isn't the only thing! I have naturally a kind and merry heart. 'I also write vaudevilles of all sorts.'† You seem to take me for Hlestakov grown old, but my fate is a far more serious one. Before time was, by some decree which I could never make out, I was predestined 'to deny' and yet I am genuinely good-hearted and not at all inclined to negation. 'No, you must go and deny, without denial there's no criticism and what would a journal be without a column of criticism?' Without criticism it would be nothing but one 'hosannah.' But nothing but hosannah is not enough for life, the hosannah must be tried in the crucible of doubt and so on, in the same style. But I don't meddle in that, I didn't create it, I am not answerable for it. Well, they've chosen their

---

*The devil doesn't exist at all (French).
†Spoken by Khlestakov in act 3, scene 6 of Gogol's comedy *The Government Inspector* (1836).

scapegoat, they've made me write the column of criticism and so life was made possible. We understand that comedy; I, for instance, simply ask for annihilation. No, live, I am told, for there'd be nothing without you. If everything in the universe were sensible, nothing would happen. There would be no events without you, and there must be events. So against the grain I serve to produce events and do what's irrational because I am commanded to. For all their indisputable intelligence, men take this farce as something serious, and that is their tragedy. They suffer, of course . . . but then they live, they live a real life, not a fantastic one, for suffering is life. Without suffering what would be the pleasure of it? It would be transformed into an endless church service; it would be holy, but tedious. But what about me? I suffer, but still, I don't live. I am x in an indeterminate equation. I am a sort of phantom in life who has lost all beginning and end, and who has even forgotten his own name. You are laughing—no, you are not laughing, you are angry again. You are for ever angry, all you care about is intelligence, but I repeat again that I would give away all this superstellar life, all the ranks and honours, simply to be transformed into the soul of a merchant's wife weighing eighteen stone and set candles at God's shrine."

"Then even you don't believe in God?" said Ivan, with a smile of hatred.

"What can I say—that is, if you are in earnest . . ."

"Is there a God or not?" Ivan cried with the same savage intensity.

"Ah, then you are in earnest! My dear fellow, upon my word I don't know. There! I've said it now!"

"You don't know, but you see God? No, you are not some one apart, you are myself, you are I and nothing more! You are rubbish, you are my fancy!"

"Well, if you like, I have the same philosophy as you, that would be true. *Je pense, donc je suis,** I know that for a fact, all the rest, all these worlds, God and even Satan—all that is not proved, to my mind. Does all that exist of itself, or is it only an emanation of myself, a logical development of my ego which alone has existed for ever: but I make haste to stop, for I believe you will be jumping up to beat me directly."

"You'd better tell me some anecdote!" said Ivan miserably.

"There is an anecdote precisely on our subject, or rather a legend, not an anecdote. You reproach me with unbelief, you see, you say, yet you don't believe. But, my dear fellow, I am not the only one like that. We are all in a muddle over there now and all through your science. Once there used to be atoms, five senses, four elements, and then everything hung together somehow. There were atoms in the ancient world even, but since we've learned that you've discovered the chemical molecule and protoplasm and the devil knows what, we had to lower our crest. There's a regular muddle, and, above all, superstition, scandal; there's as much scandal

*I think, therefore I am (French); French philosopher René Descartes's celebrated line from *Discourse on Method* (1637).

among us as among you, you know; a little more in fact, and spying, indeed, for we have our secret police department where private information is received. Well, this wild legend belongs to our middle ages—not yours, but ours—and no one believes it even among us, except the old ladies of eighteen stone, not your old ladies I mean, but ours. We've everything you have, I am revealing one of our secrets out of friendship for you; though it's forbidden. This legend is about Paradise. There was, they say, here on earth a thinker and philosopher. He rejected everything, 'laws, conscience, faith,'* and, above all, the future life. He died; he expected to go straight to darkness and death and he found a future life before him. He was astounded and indignant. 'This is against my principles!' he said. And he was punished for that . . . that is, you must excuse me, I am just repeating what I heard myself, it's only a legend . . . he was sentenced to walk a quadrillion kilometres in the dark (we've adopted the metric system you know) and when he had finished that quadrillion, the gates of heaven would be opened to him and he would be forgiven. . . ."

"And what tortures have you in the other world besides the quadrillion kilometres?" asked Ivan, with a strange eagerness.

"What tortures? Ah, don't ask. In old days we had all sorts, but now they have taken chiefly to moral punishments—'the stings of conscience' and all that nonsense. We got that, too, from you, from the softening of your manners. And who's the better for it? Only those who have got no conscience, for how can they be tortured by conscience when they have none? But decent people who have conscience and a sense of honour suffer for it. Reforms, when the ground has not been prepared for them, especially if they are institutions copied from abroad, do nothing but mischief! The ancient fire was better. Well, this man, who was condemned to the quadrillion kilometres, stood still, looked round and lay down across the road. 'I won't go, I refuse on principle!' Take the soul of an enlightened Russian atheist and mix it with the soul of the prophet Jonah,† who sulked for three days and nights in the belly of the whale, and you get the character of that thinker who lay across the road."

"What did he lie on there?"

"Well, I suppose there was something to lie on. You are not laughing?"

"Bravo!" cried Ivan, still with the same strange eagerness. Now he was listening with an unexpected curiosity. "Well, is he lying there now?"

"That's the point, that he isn't. He lay there almost a thousand years and then he got up and went on."

"What an ass!" cried Ivan, laughing nervously and still seeming to be pondering something intently. "Does it make any difference whether he lies there for ever or walks the quadrillion kilometres? It would take a billion years to walk it?"

---

*Repetilov's words in act 4, scene 4 of Russian poet A. S. Griboyedov's comedy *Woe from Wit* (1824).
†Reference to Jonah 1:17.

"Much more than that, I haven't got a pencil and paper or I could work it out. But he got there long ago and that's where the story begins."

"What, he got there? But how did he get the billion years to do it?"

"Why, you keep thinking of our present earth! But our present earth may have been repeated a billion times. Why, it's become extinct, been frozen; cracked, broken to bits, disintegrated into its elements, again 'the water above the firmament,' then again a comet, again a sun, again from the sun it becomes earth—and the same sequence may have been repeated endlessly and exactly the same to every detail, most unseemly and insufferably tedious. . . ."

"Well, well, what happened when he arrived?"

"Why, the moment the gates of Paradise were open and he walked in, before he had been there two seconds, by his watch, (though to my thinking his watch must have long dissolved into its elements on the way) he cried out that those two seconds were worth walking not a quadrillion kilometres but a quadrillion of quadrillions, raised to the quadrillionth power! In fact, he sang 'hosannah' and overdid it so, that some persons there of lofty ideals wouldn't shake hands with him at first—he'd become too rapidly reactionary, they said. The Russian temperament. I repeat, it's a legend. I give it for what it's worth. So that's the sort of ideas we have on such subjects even now."

"I've caught you!" Ivan cried, with an almost childish delight, as though he had succeeded in remembering something at last. "That anecdote about the quadrillion years, I made up myself! I was seventeen then, I was at the high school. I made up that anecdote and told it to a schoolfellow called Korovkin, it was at Moscow. . . . The anecdote is so characteristic that I couldn't have taken it from anywhere. I thought I'd forgotten it . . . but I've unconsciously recalled it—I recalled it myself—it was not you telling it! Thousands of things are unconsciously remembered like that even when people are being taken to execution . . . it's come back to me in a dream. You are that dream! You are a dream, not a living creature!"

"From the vehemence with which you deny my existence," laughed the gentleman, "I am convinced that you believe in me."

"Not in the slightest! I haven't a hundredth part of a grain of faith in you!"

"But you have the thousandth of a grain. Homeopathic doses perhaps are the strongest. Confess that you have faith even to the ten-thousandth of a grain."

"Not for one minute," cried Ivan furiously. "But I should like to believe in you," he added strangely.

"Aha! There's an admission! But I am good-natured. I'll come to your assistance again. Listen, it was I caught you, not you me. I told you your anecdote you'd forgotten, on purpose, so as to destroy your faith in me completely."

"You are lying. The object of your visit is to convince me of your existence!"

"Just so. But hesitation, suspense, conflict between belief and disbelief—
is sometimes such torture to a conscientious man, such as you are, that it's
better to hang oneself at once. Knowing that you are inclined to believe in
me, I administered some disbelief by telling you that anecdote. I lead you
to belief and disbelief by turns, and I have my motive in it. It's the new
method. As soon as you disbelieve in me completely, you'll begin assuring
me to my face that I am not a dream but a reality. I know you. Then I shall
have attained my object, which is an honourable one. I shall sow in you
only a tiny grain of faith and it will grow into an oak-tree—and such an
oak-tree that, sitting on it, you will long to enter the ranks of 'the hermits
in the wilderness and the saintly women,' for that is what you are secretly
longing for. You'll dine on locusts, you'll wander into the wilderness to
save your soul!"

"Then it's for the salvation of my soul you are working, is it, you
scoundrel?"

"One must do a good work sometimes. How ill-humoured you are!"

"Fool! did you ever tempt those holy men who ate locusts and prayed
seventeen years in the wilderness till they were over-grown with moss?"

"My dear fellow, I've done nothing else. One forgets the whole world
and all the worlds, and sticks to one such saint, because he is a very precious diamond. One such soul, you know, is sometimes worth a whole constellation. We have our system of reckoning, you know. The conquest is
priceless! And some of them, on my word, are not inferior to you in culture, though you won't believe it. They can contemplate such depths of belief and disbelief at the same moment that sometimes it really seems that
they are within a hair's-breadth of being 'turned upside down,' as the actor
Gorbunov says."

"Well, did you get your nose pulled?"*

"My dear fellow," observed the visitor sententiously, "it's better to get
off with your nose pulled than without a nose at all. As an afflicted marquis observed not long ago (he must have been treated by a specialist) in
confession to his spiritual father—a Jesuit. I was present, it was simply
charming. 'Give me back my nose!' he said, and he beat his breast. 'My
son,' said the priest evasively, 'all things are accomplished in accordance
with the inscrutable decrees of Providence, and what seems a misfortune
sometimes leads to extraordinary, though unapparent, benefits. If stern
destiny has deprived you of your nose, it's to your advantage that no one
can ever pull you by your nose. 'Holy father, that's no comfort,' cried the
despairing marquis. 'I'd be delighted to have my nose pulled every day of
my life, if it were only in its proper place.' 'My son,' sighs the priest, 'you
can't expect every blessing at once. This is murmuring against Providence,
who even in this has not forgotten you, for if you repine as you repined
just now, declaring you'd be glad to have your nose pulled for the rest of

---

*Literally, did you get off with a long nose made at you?; a proverbial expression
in Russia for failure (translator's note).

your life, your desire has already been fulfilled indirectly, for when you lost your nose, you were led by the nose."

"Fool, how stupid!" cried Ivan.

"My dear friend, I only wanted to amuse you. But I swear that's the genuine Jesuit casuistry and I swear that it all happened word for word as I've told you. It happened lately and gave me a great deal of trouble. The unhappy young man shot himself that very night when he got home. I was by his side till the very last moment. Those Jesuit confessionals are really my most delightful diversion at melancholy moments. Here's another incident that happened only the other day. A little blonde Norman girl of twenty—a buxom, unsophisticated beauty that would make your mouth water—comes to an old priest. She bends down and whispers her sin into the grating. 'Why, my daughter, have you fallen again already?' cries the priest. 'O Sancta Maria, what do I hear! Not the same man this time, how long is this going on? Aren't you ashamed!' *'Ah, mon père,'* answers the sinner with tears of penitence, *'ça lui fait tant de plaisir, et à moi si peu de peine!'*[6] Fancy, such an answer! I drew back. It was the cry of nature, better than innocence itself, if you like. I absolved her sin on the spot and was turning to go, but I was forced to turn back. I heard the priest at the grating making an appointment with her for the evening—though he was an old man hard as flint, he fell in an instant! It was nature, the truth of nature asserted its rights! What, you are turning up your nose again? Angry again? I don't know how to please you. . . ."

"Leave me alone, you are beating on my brain like a haunting nightmare," Ivan moaned miserably, helpless before his apparition. "I am bored with you, agonisingly and insufferably. I would give anything to be able to shake you off!"

"I repeat, moderate your expectations, don't demand of me 'everything great and noble' and you'll see how well we shall get on," said the gentleman impressively. "You are really angry with me for not having appeared to you in a red glow, with thunder and lightning, with scorched wings, but have shown myself in such a modest form. You are wounded, in the first place, in your æsthetic feelings, and, secondly, in your pride. How could such a vulgar devil visit such a great man as you! Yes, there is that romantic strain in you, that was so derided by Byelinsky. I can't help it, young man, as I got ready to come to you I did think as a joke of appearing in the figure of a retired general who had served in the Caucasus, with a star of the Lion and the Sun on my coat. But I was positively afraid of doing it, for you'd have thrashed me for daring to pin the Lion and the Sun on my coat, instead of, at least, the Polar Star or the Sirius.[7] And you keep on saying I am stupid, but, mercy on us! I make no claim to be equal to you in intelligence. Mephistopheles declared to Faust* that he desired evil, but did only good. Well, he can say what he likes, it's quite the opposite with me. I am perhaps the one man in all creation who loves the truth

---

*In Goethe's dramatic poem *Faust* (1808, 1832).

and genuinely desires good. I was there when the Word, Who died on the Cross, rose up into Heaven bearing on His bosom the soul of the penitent thief. I heard the glad shrieks of the cherubim singing and shouting hosannah and the thunderous rapture of the seraphim which shook heaven and all creation, and I swear to you by all that's sacred, I longed to join the choir and shout hosannah with them all. The word had almost escaped me, had almost broken from my lips . . . you know how susceptible and æsthetically impressionable I am. But common sense—oh, a most unhappy trait in my character—kept me in due bounds and I let the moment pass! For what would have happened, I reflected, what would have happened after my hosannah? Everything on earth would have been extinguished at once and no events could have occurred. And so, solely from a sense of duty and my social position, I was forced to suppress the good moment and to stick to my nasty task. Somebody takes all the credit of what's good for himself, and nothing but nastiness is left for me. But I don't envy the honour of a life of idle imposture, I am not ambitious. Why am I, of all creatures in the world, doomed to be cursed by all decent people and even to be kicked, for if I put on mortal form I am bound to take such consequences sometimes? I know, of course, there's a secret in it, but they won't tell me the secret for anything, for then perhaps, seeing the meaning of it, I might bawl hosannah, and the indispensable minus would disappear at once, and good sense would reign supreme throughout the whole world. And that, of course, would mean the end of everything, even of magazines and newspapers, for who would take them in? I know that at the end of all things I shall be reconciled. I, too, shall walk my quadrillion and learn the secret. But till that happens I am sulking and fulfil my destiny though it's against the grain—that is, to ruin thousands for the sake of saving one. How many souls have had to be ruined and how many honourable reputations destroyed for the sake of that one righteous man, Job, over whom they made such a fool of me in old days. Yes, till the secret is revealed, there are two sorts of truth for me—one, their truth, yonder, which I know nothing about so far and the other my own. And there's no knowing which will turn out the better. . . . Are you asleep?"

"I might well be," Ivan groaned angrily. "All my stupid ideas—outgrown, thrashed out long ago, and flung aside like a dead carcass—you present to me as something new!"

"There's no pleasing you! And I thought I should fascinate you by my literary style. That hosannah in the skies really wasn't bad, was it? And then that ironical tone *à la* Heine, eh?"*

"No, I was never such a flunkey! How then could my soul beget a flunkey like you?"

"My dear fellow, I know a most charming and attractive young Russian gentleman, a young thinker and a great lover of literature and art, the

---

*Heinrich Heine (1797–1856), German poet and essayist noted for his immense wit and irony.

author of a promising poem entitled 'The Grand Inquisitor.' I was only thinking of him!"

"I forbid you to speak of 'The Grand Inquisitor,' " cried Ivan, crimson with shame.

"And the 'Geological Cataclysm.' Do you remember? That was a poem, now!"

"Hold your tongue, or I'll kill you!"

"You'll kill me? No, excuse me, I will speak. I came to treat myself to that pleasure. Oh, I love the dreams of my ardent young friends, quivering with eagerness for life! 'There are new men,' you decided last spring, when you were meaning to come here, 'they propose to destroy everything and begin with cannibalism. Stupid fellows! they didn't ask my advice! I maintain that nothing need be destroyed, that we only need to destroy the idea of God in man, that's how we have to set to work. It's that, that we must begin with. Oh, blind race of men who have no understanding! As soon as men have all of them denied God—and I believe that period, analogous with geological periods, will come to pass—the old conception of the universe will fall of itself without cannibalism and what's more the old morality, and everything will begin anew. Men will unite to take from life all it can give, but only for joy and happiness in the present world. Man will be lifted up with a spirit of divine Titanic pride and the man-god will appear. From hour to hour extending his conquest of nature infinitely by his will and his science, man will feel such lofty joy from hour to hour in doing it that it will make up for all his old dreams of the joys of heaven. Every one will know that he is mortal and will accept death proudly and serenely like a god. His pride will teach him that it's useless for him to repine at life's being a moment, and he will love his brother without need of reward. Love will be sufficient only for a moment of life, but the very consciousness of its momentariness will intensify its fire, which now is dissipated in dreams of eternal love beyond the grave' . . . and so on and so on in the same style. Charming!"

Ivan sat with his eyes on the floor, and his hands pressed to his ears, but he began trembling all over. The voice continued.

"The question now is, my young thinker reflected, is it possible that such a period will ever come? If it does, everything is determined and humanity is settled for ever. But as, owing to man's inveterate stupidity, this cannot come about for at least a thousand years, every one who recognises the truth even now may legitimately order his life as he pleases, on the new principles. In that sense, 'all things are lawful' for him. What's more, even if this period never comes to pass, since there is anyway no God and no immortality, the new man may well become the man-god, even if he is the only one in the whole world, and promoted to his new position, he may lightheartedly overstep all the barriers of the old morality of the old slave-man, if necessary. There is no law for God. Where God stands, the place is holy. Where I stand will be at once the foremost place . . . 'all things are lawful' and that's the end of it! That's all very charming; but if you want to swindle why do you want a moral sanction for doing it? But that's our modern Russian all over. He can't bring himself to swindle without a moral sanction. He is so in love with truth. . . ."

The visitor talked, obviously carried away by his own eloquence, speaking louder and louder and looking ironically at his host. But he did not succeed in finishing; Ivan suddenly snatched a glass from the table and flung it at the orator.

"*Ah, mais c'est bête enfin,*"* cried the latter, jumping up from the sofa and shaking the drops of tea off himself. "He remembers Luther's inkstand!† He takes me for a dream and throws glasses at a dream! It's like a woman! I suspected you were only pretending to stop up your ears."

A loud, persistent knocking was suddenly heard at the window. Ivan jumped up from the sofa.

"Do you hear? You'd better open," cried the visitor; "it's your brother Alyosha with the most interesting and surprising news, I'll be bound!"

"Be silent, deceiver, I knew it was Alyosha, I felt he was coming, and of course he has not come for nothing; of course he brings 'news,' " Ivan exclaimed frantically.

"Open, open to him. There's a snowstorm and he is your brother. *Monsieur sait-il le temps qu'il fait? C'est à ne pas mettre un chien dehors.*"[8]

The knocking continued. Ivan wanted to rush to the window, but something seemed to fetter his arms and legs. He strained every effort to break his chains, but in vain. The knocking at the window grew louder and louder. At last the chains were broken and Ivan leapt up from the sofa. He looked round him wildly. Both candles had almost burnt out, the glass he had just thrown at his visitor stood before him on the table, and there was no one on the sofa opposite. The knocking on the window frame went on persistently, but it was by no means so loud as it had seemed in his dream, on the contrary, it was quite subdued.

"It was not a dream! No, I swear it was not a dream, it all happened just now!" cried Ivan. He rushed to the window and opened the movable pane.

"Alyosha, I told you not to come," he cried fiercely to his brother. "In two words, what do you want? In two words, do you hear?"

"An hour ago Smerdyakov hanged himself," Alyosha answered from the yard.

"Come round to the steps, I'll open at once," said Ivan, going to open the door to Alyosha.

---

*Ah, but that's stupid, finally (French).

†Reference to the legendary scene in which the German religious reformer Martin Luther (1483–1546) is said to have thrown his inkstand at the devil, who had come to tempt him.

10

"IT WAS HE WHO SAID THAT"

ALYOSHA coming in told Ivan that a little over an hour ago Marya Kondratyevna had run to his rooms and informed him Smerdyakov had taken his own life. "I went in to clear away the samovar and he was hanging on a nail in the wall." On Alyosha's inquiring whether she had informed the police, she answered that she had told no one, "but I flew straight to you, I've run all the way." She seemed perfectly crazy, Alyosha reported, and was shaking like a leaf. When Alyosha ran with her to the cottage, he found Smerdyakov still hanging. On the table lay a note: "I destroy my life of my own will and desire, so as to throw no blame on any one." Alyosha left the note on the table and went straight to the police captain and told him all about it. "And from him I've come straight to you," said Alyosha, in conclusion, looking intently into Ivan's face. He had not taken his eyes off him while he told his story, as though struck by something in his expression.

"Brother," he cried suddenly, "you must be terribly ill. You look and don't seem to understand what I tell you."

"It's a good thing you came," said Ivan, as though brooding, and not hearing Alyosha's exclamation. "I knew he had hanged himself."

"From whom?"

"I don't know. But I knew. Did I know? Yes, he told me. He told me so just now."

Ivan stood in the middle of the room, and still spoke in the same brooding tone, looking at the ground.

"Who is *he*?" asked Alyosha, involuntarily looking round.

"He's slipped away."

Ivan raised his head and smiled softly.

"He was afraid of you, of a dove like you. You are a 'pure cherub.'* Dmitri calls you a cherub. Cherub! . . . the thunderous rapture of the seraphim. What are seraphim? Perhaps a whole constellation. But perhaps that constellation is only a chemical molecule. There's a constellation of the Lion and the Sun. Don't you know it?"

"Brother, sit down," said Alyosha in alarm. "For goodness' sake, sit down on the sofa! You are delirious; put your head on the pillow, that's right. Would you like a wet towel on your head? Perhaps it will do you good."

"Give me the towel: it's here on the chair. I just threw it down there."

"It's not here. Don't worry yourself. I know where it is—here," said

---

*Quotation from Russian poet Mikhail Lermontov's poem "The Demon" (1841).

Alyosha, finding a clean towel folded up and unused, by Ivan's dressing-table in the other corner of the room. Ivan looked strangely at the towel: recollection seemed to come back to him for an instant.

"Stay"—he got up from the sofa—"an hour ago I took that new towel from there and wetted it. I wrapped it round my head and threw it down here. . . . How is it it's dry? There was no other."

"You put that towel on your head?" asked Alyosha.

"Yes, and walked up and down the room an hour ago. . . . Why have the candles burnt down so? What's the time?"

"Nearly twelve."

"No, no, no!" Ivan cried suddenly. "It was not a dream. He was here; he was sitting here, on that sofa. When you knocked at the window, I threw a glass at him . . . this one. Wait a minute. I was asleep last time, but this dream was not a dream. It has happened before. I have dreams now, Alyosha . . . yet they are not dreams, but reality. I walk about, talk and see . . . though I am asleep. But he was sitting here, on that sofa there. . . . He is frightfully stupid, Alyosha, frightfully stupid." Ivan laughed suddenly and began pacing about the room.

"Who is stupid? Of whom are you talking, brother?" Alyosha asked anxiously again.

"The devil! He's taken to visiting me. He's been here twice, almost three times. He taunted me with being angry at his being a simple devil and not Satan, with scorched wings, in thunder and lightning. But he is not Satan: that's a lie. He is an impostor. He is simply a devil—a paltry, trivial devil. He goes to the baths. If you undressed him, you'd be sure to find he had a tail, long and smooth like a Danish dog's, a yard long, dun colour. . . . Alyosha, you are cold. You've been in the snow. Would you like some tea? What? Is it cold? Shall I tell her to bring some? *C'est à ne pas mettre un chien dehors.* . . ."

Alyosha ran to the washing stand, wetted the towel, persuaded Ivan to sit down again, and put the wet towel round his head. He sat down beside him.

"What were you telling me just now about Lise?" Ivan began again. (He was becoming very talkative.) "I like Lise. I said something nasty about her. It was a lie. I like her . . . I am afraid for Katya to-morrow. I am more afraid of her than of anything. On account of the future. She will cast me off to-morrow and trample me under foot. She thinks that I am ruining Mitya from jealousy on her account! Yes, she thinks that! But it's not so. To-morrow the cross, but not the gallows. No, I shan't hang myself. Do you know, I can never commit suicide, Alyosha. Is it because I am base? I am not a coward. Is it from love of life? How did I know that Smerdyakov had hanged himself? Yes, it was *he* told me so."

"And you are quite convinced that there has been some one here?" asked Alyosha.

"Yes, on that sofa in the corner. You would have driven him away. You did drive him away: he disappeared when you arrived. I love your face, Alyosha. Did you know that I loved your face? And *he* is myself, Alyosha.

All that's base in me, all that's mean and contemptible. Yes, I am a romantic. He guessed it . . . though it's a libel. He is frightfully stupid; but it's to his advantage. He has cunning, animal cunning—he knew how to infuriate me. He kept taunting me with believing in him, and that was how he made me listen to him. He fooled me like a boy. He told me a great deal that was true about myself, though. I should never have owned it to myself. Do you know, Alyosha," Ivan added in an intensely earnest and confidential tone, "I should be awfully glad to think that it was *he* and not I."

"He has worn you out," said Alyosha, looking compassionately at his brother.

"He's been teasing me. And you know he does it so cleverly, so cleverly. 'Conscience! What is conscience! I make it up for myself. Why am I tormented by it? From habit. From the universal habit of mankind for the seven thousand years. So let us give it up, and we shall be gods.' It was he said that, it was he said that!"

"And not you, not you?" Alyosha could not help crying, looking frankly at his brother. "Never mind him, anyway; have done with him and forget him. And let him take with him all that you curse now, and never come back!"

"Yes, but he is spiteful. He laughed at me. He was impudent, Alyosha," Ivan said, with a shudder of offence. "But he was unfair to me, unfair to me about lots of things. He told lies about me to my face. 'Oh, you are going to perform an act of heroic virtue: to confess you murdered your father, that the valet murdered him at your instigation.' "

"Brother," Alyosha interposed, "restrain yourself. It was not you murdered him. It's not true!"

"That's what he says, he, and he knows it. 'You are going to perform an act of heroic virtue, and you don't believe in virtue; that's what tortures you and makes you angry, that's why you are so vindictive.' He said that to me about me and he knows what he says."

"It's you say that, not he," exclaimed Alyosha mournfully, "and you say it because you are ill and delirious, tormenting yourself."

"No, he knows what he says. 'You are going from pride,' he says, 'You'll stand up and say it was I killed him, and why do you writhe with horror? You are lying! I despise your opinion, I despise your horror!' He said that about me. 'And do you know you are longing for their praise—"he is a criminal, a murderer, but what a generous soul; he wanted to save his brother and he confessed." ' "That's a lie, Alyosha!" Ivan cried suddenly, with flashing eyes. "I don't want the low rabble to praise me, I swear I don't! That's a lie! That's why I threw the glass at him and it broke against his ugly face."

"Brother, calm yourself, stop!" Alyosha entreated him.

"Yes, he knows how to torment one. He's cruel," Ivan went on, unheeding. "I had an inkling from the first what he came for. 'Granting that you go through pride, still you had a hope that Smerdyakov might be convicted and sent to Siberia, and Mitya would be acquitted, while you would only be punished with *moral* condemnation' ('Do you hear?' he laughed then)—'and some people will praise you. But now Smerdyakov's dead, he has hanged himself, and who'll believe you alone? But yet you are going, you are going, you'll go all the same, you've decided to go. What are you going for now?' That's awful, Alyosha. I can't endure such questions. Who dare ask me such questions?"

"Brother," interposed Alyosha. His heart sank with terror, but he still seemed to hope to bring Ivan to reason, "how could he have told you of Smerdyakov's death before I came, when no one knew of it and there was no time for any one to know of it?"

"He told me," said Ivan firmly, refusing to admit a doubt. "It was all he did talk about, if you come to that. 'And it would be all right if you believed in virtue,' he said. 'No matter if they disbelieve you, you are going for the sake of principle. But you are a little pig like Fyodor Pavlovitch and what do you want with virtue? Why do you want to go meddling if your sacrifice is of no use to any one? Because you don't know yourself why you go! Oh, you'd give a great deal to know yourself why you go! And can you have made up your mind? You've not made up your mind. You'll sit all night deliberating whether to go or not. But you will go; you know you'll go. You know that whichever way you decide, the decision does not depend on you. You'll go because you won't dare not to go. Why won't you dare? You must guess that for yourself. That's a riddle for you!' He got up and went away. You came and he went. He called me a coward, Alyosha! *Le mot de l'énigme** is that I am a coward. 'It is not for such eagles to soar above the earth. It was he added that—he! And Smerdyakov said the same. He must be killed! Katya despises me. I've seen that for a month past. Even Lise will begin to despise me! 'You are going in order to be praised.' That's a brutal lie! And you despise me too, Alyosha. Now I am going to hate you again! And I hate the monster, too! I hate the monster! I don't want to save the monster. Let him rot in Siberia! He's begun singing a hymn! Oh, to-morrow I'll go, stand before them, and spit in their faces!"

He jumped up in a frenzy, flung off the towel, and fell to pacing up and down the room again. Alyosha recalled what he had just said. "I seem to be sleeping awake. . . . I walk, I speak, I see, but I am asleep." It seemed to be just like that now. Alyosha did not leave him. The thought passed through his mind to run for a doctor, but he was afraid to leave his brother alone: there was no one to whom he could leave him. By degrees Ivan lost consciousness completely at last. He still went on talking, talking incessantly, but quite incoherently, and even articulated his words with difficulty. Suddenly he staggered violently; but Alyosha was in time to support him. Ivan let him lead him to his bed. Alyosha undressed him somehow and put him to bed. He sat watching over him for another two hours. The sick man slept soundly, without stirring, breathing softly and evenly. Alyosha took a pillow and lay down on the sofa, without undressing.

---

*The answer to the riddle (French).

As he fell asleep he prayed for Mitya and Ivan. He began to understand Ivan's illness. "The anguish of a proud determination. An earnest conscience!" God, in Whom he disbelieved, and His truth were gaining mastery over his heart, which still refused to submit. "Yes," the thought floated through Alyosha's head as it lay on the pillow, "yes, if Smerdyakov is dead, no one will believe Ivan's evidence; but he will go and give it." Alyosha smiled softly. "God will conquer!" he thought. "He will either rise up in the light of truth, or . . . he'll perish in hate, revenging on himself and on every one his having served the cause he does not believe in," Alyosha added bitterly, and again he prayed for Ivan.

BOOK TWELVE

A JUDICIAL ERROR

1

THE FATAL DAY

AT ten o'clock in the morning of the day following the events I have described, the trial of Dmitri Karamazov began in our district court.

I hasten to emphasise the fact that I am far from esteeming myself capable of reporting all that took place at the trial in full detail, or even in the actual order of events. I imagine that to mention everything with full explanation would fill a volume, even a very large one. And so I trust I may not be reproached for confining myself to what struck me. I may have selected as of most interest what was of secondary importance, and may have omitted the most prominent and essential details. But I see I shall do better not to apologise. I will do my best and the reader will see for himself that I have done all I can.

And, to begin with, before entering the court, I will mention what surprised me most on that day. Indeed, as it appeared later, every one was surprised at it, too. We all knew that the affair had aroused great interest, that every one was burning with impatience for the trial to begin, that it had been a subject of talk, conjecture, exclamation and surmise for the last two months in local society. Every one knew, too, that the case had become known throughout Russia, but yet we had not imagined that it had aroused such burning, such intense, interest in every one, not only among ourselves, but all over Russia. This became evident at the trial this day.

Visitors had arrived not only from the chief town of our province, but from several other Russian towns, as well as from Moscow and Petersburg. Among them were lawyers, ladies, and even several distinguished personages. Every ticket of admission had been snatched up. A special place behind the table at which the three judges sat was set apart for the most distinguished and important of the men visitors; a row of armchairs had been placed there—something exceptional, which had never been allowed before. A large proportion—not less than half of the public—were ladies. There was such a large number of lawyers from all parts that they did not know where to seat them, for every ticket had long since been eagerly sought for and distributed. I saw at the end of the room, behind the platform, a special partition hurriedly put up, behind which all these lawyers were admitted, and they thought themselves lucky to have standing room there, for all chairs had been removed for the sake of space, and the crowd behind the partition stood throughout the case closely packed, shoulder to shoulder.

Some of the ladies, especially those who came from a distance, made their appearance in the gallery very smartly dressed, but the majority of the ladies were oblivious even of dress. Their faces betrayed hysterical, intense, almost morbid, curiosity. A peculiar fact—established afterwards by many observations—was that almost all the ladies, or, at least the vast majority of them, were on Mitya's side and in favour of his being acquitted. This was perhaps chiefly owing to his reputation as a conqueror of female hearts. It was known that two women rivals were to appear in the case. One of them—Katerina Ivanovna—was an object of general interest. All sorts of extraordinary tales were told about her, amazing anecdotes of her passion for Mitya, in spite of his crime. Her pride and "aristocratic connections" were particularly insisted upon (she had called upon scarcely any one in the town). People said she intended to petition the Government for leave to accompany the criminal to Siberia and to be married to him somewhere in the mines. The appearance of Grushenka in court was awaited with no less impatience. The public was looking forward with anxious curiosity to the meeting of the two rivals—the proud aristocratic girl and "the hetaira." But Grushenka was a more familiar figure to the ladies of the district than Katerina Ivanovna. They had already seen "the woman who had ruined Fyodor Pavlovitch and his unhappy son," and, all, almost without exception, wondered how father and son could be so in love with "such a very common, ordinary Russian girl, who was not even pretty."

In brief, there was a great deal of talk, I know for a fact that there were several serious family quarrels on Mitya's account in our town. Many ladies quarrelled violently with their husbands over differences of opinion about the dreadful case, and it was only natural that the husbands of these ladies, far from being favourably disposed to the prisoner, should enter the court bitterly prejudiced against him. In fact, one may say pretty certainly that the masculine, as distinguished from the feminine part of the audience were biassed against the prisoner. There were numbers of severe, frowning, even vindictive, faces. Mitya, indeed, had managed to offend many people during his stay in the town. Some of the visitors were, of course, in excellent spirits and quite unconcerned as to the fate of Mitya personally. But all were interested in the trial, and the majority of the men were certainly hoping for the conviction of the criminal, except perhaps the lawyers, who were more interested in the legal, than in the moral aspect of the case.

Everybody was excited at the presence of the celebrated lawyer, Fetyukovitch. His talent was well known, and this was not the first time he had defended notorious criminal cases in the provinces. And if he defended them, such cases became celebrated and long remembered all over Russia. There were stories, too, about our prosecutor and about the President of the Court. It was said that Ippolit Kirillovitch was in a tremor at meeting Fetyukovitch, and that they had been enemies from the beginning of their careers in Petersburg, that though our sensitive prosecutor, who always considered that he had been aggrieved by some one in Petersburg because his talents had not been properly appreciated, was keenly excited over the Karamazov case, and was even dreaming of rebuilding his flagging fortunes by means of it, Fetyukovitch, they said, was his one anxiety. But these rumours were not quite just. Our prosecutor was not one of those men who lose heart in face of danger. On the contrary, his self-confidence increased with the increase of danger. It must be noted that our prosecutor was in general too hasty and morbidly impressionable. He would put his whole soul into some case and work at it as though his whole fate and his whole fortune depended on its result. This was the subject of some ridicule in the legal world, for just by this characteristic our prosecutor had gained a wider notoriety than could have been expected from his modest position. People laughed particularly at his passion for psychology. In my opinion, they were wrong, and our prosecutor was, I believe, a character of greater depth than was generally supposed. But with his delicate health he had failed to make his mark at the outset of his career and had never made up for it later.

As for the President of our Court, I can only say that he was a humane and cultured man, who had a practical knowledge of his work and progressive views. He was rather ambitious, but did not concern himself greatly about his future career. The great aim of his life was to be a man of advanced ideas. He was, too, a man of connections and property. He felt, as we learnt afterwards, rather strongly about the Karamazov case, but from a social, not from a personal standpoint. He was interested in it as a social phenomenon, in its classification and its character as a product of our social conditions, as typical of the national character, and so on, and so on. His attitude to the personal aspect of the case, to its tragic significance and the persons involved in it, including the prisoner, was rather indifferent and abstract, as was perhaps fitting, indeed.

The court was packed and overflowing long before the judges made their appearance. Our court is the best hall in the town—spacious, lofty, and good for sound. On the right of the judges, who were on a raised platform, a table and two rows of chairs had been put ready for the jury. On the left was the place for the prisoner and the counsel for the defence. In the middle of the court, near the judges, was a table with the "material proofs." On it lay Fyodor Pavlovitch's white silk dressing-gown, stained with blood; the fatal brass pestle with which the supposed murder had been committed: Mitya's shirt, with a bloodstained sleeve; his coat, stained with blood in patches over the pocket in which he had put his handkerchief; the handkerchief itself, stiff with blood and by now quite yellow; the pistol loaded by Mitya at Perhotin's with a view to suicide, and taken from him on the sly at Mokroe by Trifon Borissovitch; the envelope in which the three thousand roubles had been put ready for Grushenka, the narrow pink ribbon with which it had been tied, and many other articles I don't remember. In the body of the hall, at some distance, came the seats for the public. But in front of the balustrade a few chairs had been placed for witnesses who remained in the court after giving their evidence.

At ten o'clock the three judges arrived—the President, one honorary justice of the peace, and one other. The prosecutor, of course, entered immediately after. The President was a short, stout, thick-set man of fifty, with a dyspeptic complexion, dark hair turning grey and cut short, and a red ribbon, of what Order I don't remember. The prosecutor struck me and the others, too, as looking particularly pale, almost green. His face seemed to have grown suddenly thinner, perhaps in a single night for I had seen him looking as usual only two days before. The President began with asking the court whether all the jury were present.

But I see I can't go on like this, partly because some things I did not hear, others I did not notice, and others I have forgotten, but most of all because, as I have said before, I have literally no time or space to mention everything that was said and done. I only know that neither side objected to very many of the jurymen. I remember the twelve jurymen—four were petty officials of the town, two were merchants, and six peasants and artisans of the town. I remember, long before the trial, questions were continually asked with some surprise, especially by ladies, "Can such a delicate, complex and psychological case be submitted for decision to petty officials and even peasants?" and "What can an official, still more a peasant, understand in such an affair?" All the four officials in the jury were, in fact, men of no consequence and of low rank. Except one who was rather younger, they were grey-headed men, little known in society, who had vegetated on a pitiful salary, and who probably had elderly, unpresentable wives and crowds of children, perhaps even without shoes and stockings. At most, they spent their leisure over cards and, of course, had never read a single book. The two merchants looked respectable, but were strangely silent and stolid. One of them was close-shaven, and was dressed in European style; the other had a small, grey beard, and wore a red ribbon with some sort of a medal upon it on his neck. There is no need to speak of the artisans and the peasants. The artisans of Skotoprigonyevsk are almost peasants, and even work on the land. Two of them also wore European dress, and, perhaps for that reason, were dirtier and more uninviting-looking than the others. So that one might well wonder, as I did as soon as I had looked at them, "what men like that could possibly make of such a case?" Yet their faces made a strangely imposing, almost menacing, impression; they were stern and frowning.

At last the President opened the case of the murder of Fyodor Pavlovitch Karamazov. I don't quite remember how he described him. The court usher was told to bring in the prisoner, and Mitya made his appearance. There was a hush through the court. One could have heard a fly. I don't know how it was with others, but Mitya made a most unfavourable impression on me. He looked an awful dandy in a brand-new frock-coat. I heard afterwards that he had ordered it in Moscow expressly for the occasion from his own tailor, who had his measure. He wore immaculate black kid gloves and exquisite linen. He walked in with his yard-long strides, looking stiffly straight in front of him, and sat down in his place with a most unperturbed air.

At the same moment the counsel for defence, the celebrated Fetyukovitch, entered, and a sort of subdued hum passed through the court. He was a tall, spare man, with long thin legs, with extremely long, thin, pale fingers, clean-shaven face, demurely brushed, rather short hair, and thin lips that were at times curved into something between a sneer and a smile. He looked about forty. His face would have been pleasant, if it had not been for his eyes, which, in themselves small and inexpressive, were set re-markably close together, with only the thin, long nose as a dividing line be-tween them. In fact, there was something strikingly bird-like about his face. He was in evening dress and white tie.

I remember the President's first questions to Mitya, about his name, his calling, and so on. Mitya answered sharply, and his voice was so unexpect-edly loud that it made the President start and look at the prisoner with surprise. Then followed a list of persons who were to take part in the proceedings—that is, of the witnesses and experts. It was a long list. Four of the witnesses were not present—Miüsov, who had given evidence at the preliminary inquiry, but was now in Paris; Madame Hohlakov and Maxi-mov, who were absent through illness; and Smerdyakov, through his sud-den death, of which an official statement from the police was presented. The news of Smerdyakov's death produced a sudden stir and whisper in the court. Many of the audience, of course, had not heard of the sudden suicide. What struck people most was Mitya's sudden outburst. As soon as the statement of Smerdyakov's death was made, he cried out aloud from his place:

"He was a dog and died like a dog!"

I remember how his counsel rushed to him, and how the President ad-dressed him, threatening to take stern measures, if such an irregularity were repeated. Mitya nodded and in a subdued voice repeated several times abruptly to his counsel, with no show of regret:

"I won't again, I won't. It escaped me. I won't do it again."

And, of course, this brief episode did him no good with the jury or the public. His character was displayed, and it spoke for itself. It was under the influence of this incident that the opening statement was read. It was rather short, but circumstantial. It only stated the chief reason why he had been arrested, why he must be tried, and so on. Yet it made a great impression on me. The clerk read it loudly and distinctly. The whole tragedy was sud-denly unfolded before us, concentrated, in bold relief, in a fatal and pitiless light. I remember how immediately after it had been read, the President asked Mitya in a loud impressive voice:

"Prisoner, do you plead guilty?"

Mitya suddenly rose from his seat.

"I plead guilty to drunkenness and dissipation," he exclaimed, again in a startling, almost frenzied voice, "to idleness and debauchery. I meant to become an honest man for good, just at the moment when I was struck down by fate. But I am not guilty of the death of that old man, my enemy and my father. No, no, I am not guilty of robbing him! I could not be. Dmitri Karamazov is a scoundrel, but not a thief."

He sat down again, visibly trembling all over. The President again briefly, but impressively admonished him to answer only what was asked, and not to go off into irrelevant exclamations. Then he ordered the case to proceed. All the witnesses were led up to take the oath. Then I saw them all together. The brothers of the prisoner were, however, allowed to give evidence without taking the oath. After an exhortation from the priest and the President, the witnesses were led away and were made to sit as far as possible apart from one another. Then they began calling them up one by one.

2

DANGEROUS WITNESSES

I DO not know whether the witnesses for the defence and for the prosecution were separated into groups by the President, and whether it was arranged to call them in certain order. But no doubt it was so. I only know that the witnesses for the prosecution were called first. I repeat I don't intend to describe all the questions step by step. Besides, my account would be to some extent superfluous, because in the speeches for the prosecution and for the defence the whole course of the evidence was brought together and set in a strong and significant light, and I took down parts of those two remarkable speeches in full, and will quote them in due course, together with one extraordinary and quite unexpected episode, which occurred before the final speeches, and undoubtedly influenced the sinister and fatal outcome of the trial.

I will only observe that from the first moments of the trial one peculiar characteristic of the case was conspicuous and observed by all, that is, the overwhelming strength of the prosecution as compared with the arguments the defence had to rely upon. Every one realised it from the first moment that the facts began to group themselves round a single point, and the whole horrible and bloody crime was gradually revealed. Every one, perhaps, felt from the first that the case was beyond dispute, that there was no doubt about it, that there could be really no discussion, and that the defence was only a matter of form, and that the prisoner was guilty, obviously and conclusively guilty. I imagine that even the ladies, who were so impatiently longing for the acquittal of the interesting prisoner, were at the same time, without exception, convinced of his guilt. What's more, I believe they would have been mortified if his guilt had not been so firmly established, as that would have lessened the effect of the closing scene of the criminal's acquittal. That he would be acquitted all the ladies, strange to say, were firmly persuaded up to the very last moment. "He is guilty, but he will be acquitted, from motives of humanity, in accordance with the new ideas, the new sentiments that had come into fashion," and so on, and so on. And that was why they had crowded into the court so impatiently. The men were more interested in the contest between the prosecutor and the famous Fetyukovitch. All were wondering and asking themselves what could even a talent like Fetyukovitch's make of such a desperate case; and so they followed his achievements, step by step, with concentrated attention.

But Fetyukovitch remained an enigma to all up to the very end, up to his speech. Persons of experience suspected that he had some design, that he was working towards some object, but it was almost impossible to guess what it was. His confidence and self-reliance were unmistakable, however. Every one noticed with pleasure, moreover, that he, after so short a stay, not more than three days, perhaps among us, had so wonderfully succeeded in mastering the case and "had studied it to a nicety." People described with relish, afterwards, how cleverly he had "taken down" all the witnesses for the prosecution, and as far as possible perplexed them and, what's more, had aspersed their reputation and so depreciated the value of their evidence. But it was supposed that he did this rather by way of sport, so to speak, for professional glory, to show nothing had been omitted of the accepted methods, for all were convinced that he could do no real good by such disparagement of the witnesses, and probably was more aware of this than any one, having some idea of his own in the background, some concealed weapon of defence, which he would suddenly reveal when the time came. But meanwhile, conscious of his strength, he seemed to be diverting himself.

So, for instance, when Grigory, Fyodor Pavlovitch's old servant, who had given the most damning piece of evidence about the open door, was examined, the counsel for the defence positively fastened upon him when his turn came to question him. It must be noted that Grigory entered the hall with a composed and almost stately air, not the least disconcerted by the majesty of the court or the vast audience listening to him. He gave evidence with as much confidence as though he had been talking with his Marfa, only perhaps more respectfully. It was impossible to make him contradict himself. The prosecutor questioned him first in detail about the family life of the Karamazovs. The family picture stood out in lurid colours. It was plain to ear and eye that the witness was guileless and impartial. In spite of his profound reverence for the memory of his deceased master, he yet bore witness that he had been unjust to Mitya and "hadn't brought up his children as he should. He'd have been devoured by lice when he was little, if it hadn't been for me," he added, describing Mitya's early childhood. "It wasn't fair either of the father to wrong his son over his mother's property, which was by right his."

In reply to the prosecutor's question what grounds he had for asserting that Fyodor Pavlovitch had wronged his son in their money relations, Grigory, to the surprise of every one, had no proof at all to bring forward, but he still persisted that the arrangement with the son was "unfair," and that he ought "to have paid him several thousand roubles more." I must note, by the way, that the prosecutor asked this question whether Fyodor

Pavlovitch had really kept back part of Mitya's inheritance with marked persistence of all the witnesses who could be asked it, not excepting Alyosha and Ivan, but he obtained no exact information from any one; all alleged that it was so, but were unable to bring forward any distinct proof. Grigory's description of the scene at the dinner-table, when Dmitri had burst in and beaten his father, threatening to come back to kill him, made a sinister impression on the court, especially as the old servant's composure in telling it, his parsimony of words and peculiar phraseology were as effective as eloquence. He observed that he was not angry with Mitya for having knocked him down and struck him on the face; he had forgiven him long ago, he said. Of the deceased Smerdyakov he observed, crossing himself, that he was a lad of ability, but stupid and afflicted, and, worse still, an infidel, and that it was Fyodor Pavlovitch and his elder son who had taught him to be so. But he defended Smerdyakov's honesty almost with warmth, and related how Smerdyakov had once found the master's money in the yard, and, instead of concealing it, had taken it to his master, who had rewarded him with a "gold piece" for it, and trusted him implicitly from that time forward. He maintained obstinately that the door into the garden had been open. But he was asked so many questions that I can't recall them all.

At last the counsel for the defence began to cross-examine him, and the first question he asked was about the envelope in which Fyodor Pavlovitch was supposed to have put three thousand roubles for "a certain person." "Have you ever seen it, you, who were for so many years in close attendance on your master?" Grigory answered that he had not seen it and had never heard of the money from any one "till everybody was talking about it." This question about the envelope Fetyukovitch put to every one who could conceivably have known of it, as persistently as the prosecutor asked his question about Dmitri's inheritance, and got the same answer from all, that no one had seen the envelope, though many had heard of it. From the beginning every one noticed Fetyukovitch's persistence on this subject.

"Now, with your permission I'll ask you a question," Fetyukovitch said, suddenly and unexpectedly. "Of what was that balsam, or, rather, decoction, made, which, as we learn from the preliminary inquiry, you used on that evening to rub your lumbago, in the hope of curing it?"

Grigory looked blankly at the questioner, and after a brief silence muttered, "there was saffron in it."

"Nothing but saffron? Don't you remember any other ingredient?"

"There was milfoil in it, too."

"And pepper perhaps?" Fetyukovitch queried.

"Yes, there was pepper, too."

"Etcetera. And all dissolved in vodka?"

"In spirit."

There was a faint sound of laughter in the court.

"You see, in spirit. After rubbing your back, I believe, you drank what was left in the bottle with a certain pious prayer, only known to your wife?"

"I did."

"Did you drink much? Roughly speaking, a wine-glass or two?"

"It might have been a tumbler-full."

"A tumbler-full, even. Perhaps a tumbler and a half?"

Grigory did not answer. He seemed to see what was meant.

"A glass and a half of neat spirit—is not at all bad, don't you think? You might see the gates of heaven open,* not only the door into the garden?"

Grigory remained silent. There was another laugh in the court. The President made a movement.

"Do you know for a fact," Fetyukovitch persisted, "whether you were awake or not when you saw the open door?"

"I was on my legs."

"That's not a proof that you were awake." (There was again laughter in the court.) "Could you have answered at that moment, if any one had asked you a question—for instance, what year it is?"

"I don't know."

"And what year is it, Anno Domini, do you know?"

Grigory stood with a perplexed face, looking straight at his tormentor. Strange to say, it appeared he really did not know what year it was.

"But perhaps you can tell me how many fingers you have on your hands?"

"I am a servant," Grigory said suddenly, in a loud and distinct voice. "If my betters think fit to make game of me, it is my duty to suffer it."

Fetyukovitch was a little taken aback, and the President intervened, reminding him that he must ask more relevant questions. Fetyukovitch bowed with dignity and said that he had no more questions to ask of the witness. The public and the jury, of course, were left with a grain of doubt in their minds as to the evidence of a man who might, while undergoing a certain cure, have seen "the gates of heaven," and who did not even know what year he was living in. But before Grigory left the box another episode occurred. The President, turning to the prisoner, asked him whether he had any comment to make on the evidence of the last witness.

"Except about the door, all he has said is true," cried Mitya, in a loud voice. "For combing the lice off me, I thank him; for forgiving my blows, I thank him. The old man has been honest all his life and as faithful to my father as seven hundred poodles."

"Prisoner, be careful in your language," the President admonished him.

"I am not a poodle," Grigory muttered.

"All right, it's I am a poodle myself," cried Mitya. "If it's an insult, I take it to myself and I beg his pardon. I was a beast and cruel to him. I was cruel to Æsop, too."

"What Æsop?" the President asked sternly again.

"Oh, Pierrot . . . my father, Fyodor Pavlovitch."

The President again and again warned Mitya impressively and very sternly to be more careful in his language.

---

*See Revelation 4:1.

"You are injuring yourself in the opinion of your judges."

The counsel for the defence was equally clever in dealing with the evidence of Rakitin. I may remark that Rakitin was one of the leading witnesses and one to whom the prosecutor attached great significance. It appeared that he knew everything; his knowledge was amazing, he had been everywhere, seen every thing, talked to everybody, knew every detail of the biography of Fyodor Pavlovitch and all the Karamazovs. Of the envelope, it is true, he had only heard from Mitya himself. But he described minutely Mitya's exploits in the "Metropolis," all his compromising doings and sayings, and told the story of Captain Snegiryov's "wisp of tow." But even Rakitin could say nothing positive about Mitya's inheritance, and confined himself to contemptuous generalities.

"Who could tell which of them was to blame, and which was in debt to the other, with their crazy Karamazov way of muddling things so that no one could make head or tail of it." He attributed the tragic crime to the habits that had become ingrained by ages of serfdom and the distressed condition of Russia, due to the lack of appropriate institutions. He was, in fact, allowed some latitude of speech. This was the first occasion on which Rakitin showed what he could do, and attracted notice. The prosecutor knew that the witness was preparing a magazine article on the case, and afterwards in his speech, as we shall see later, quoted some ideas from the article, showing that he had seen it already. The picture drawn by the witness was a gloomy and sinister one, and greatly strengthened the case for the prosecution. Altogether, Rakitin's discourse fascinated the public by its independence and the extraordinary nobility of its ideas. There were even two or three outbreaks of applause when he spoke of serfdom and the distressed condition of Russia.

But Rakitin, in his youthful ardour, made a slight blunder, of which the counsel for the defence at once adroitly took advantage. Answering certain questions about Grushenka, and carried away by the loftiness of his own sentiments and his success, of which he was, of course, conscious, he went so far as to speak somewhat contemptuously of Agrafena Alexandrovna as "the kept mistress of Samsonov." He would have given a good deal to take back his words afterwards, for Fetyukovitch caught him out over it at once. And it was all because Rakitin had not reckoned on the lawyer having been able to become so intimately acquainted with every detail in so short a time.

"Allow me to ask," began the counsel for the defence, with the most affable and even respectful smile, "you are, of course, the same Mr. Rakitin whose pamphlet, 'The Life of the Deceased Elder, Father Zossima,' published by the diocesan authorities, full of profound and religious reflections and preceded by an excellent and devout dedication to the Bishop, I have just read with such pleasure?"

"I did not write it for publication . . . it was published afterwards," muttered Rakitin, for some reason fearfully disconcerted and almost ashamed.

"Oh, that's excellent! A thinker like you can, and indeed ought to, take the widest view of every social question. Your most instructive pamphlet has been widely circulated through the patronage of the Bishop, and has been of appreciable service. . . . But this is the chief thing I should like to learn from you. You stated just now that you were very intimately acquainted with Madame Svyetlov." (It must be noted that Grushenka's surname was Svyetlov. I heard it for the first time that day, during the case.)

"I cannot answer for all my acquaintances. . . . I am a young man . . . and who can be responsible for every one he meets?" cried Rakitin, flushing all over.

"I understand, I quite understand," cried Fetyukovitch, as though he, too, were embarrassed and in haste to excuse himself. "You, like any other, might well be interested in an acquaintance with a young and beautiful woman who would readily entertain the *élite* of the youth of the neighbourhood, but . . . I only wanted to know . . . it has come to my knowledge that Madame Svyetlov was particularly anxious a couple of months ago to make the acquaintance of the younger Karamazov, Alexey Fyodorovitch, and promised you twenty-five roubles, if you would bring him to her in his monastic dress. And that actually took place on the evening of the day on which the terrible crime, which is the subject of the present investigation, was committed. You brought Alexey Karamazov to Madame Svyetlov, and did you receive the twenty-five roubles from Madame Svyetlov as a reward, that's what I wanted to hear from you?"

"It was a joke. . . . I don't see of what interest that can be to you. . . . I took it for a joke . . . meaning to give it back later. . . ."

"Then you did take . . . But you have not given it back yet . . . or have you?"

"That's of no consequence," muttered Rakitin, "I refuse to answer such questions. . . . Of course I shall give it back."

The President intervened, but Fetyukovitch declared he had no more questions to ask of the witness. Mr. Rakitin left the witness-box not absolutely without a stain upon his character. The effect left by the lofty idealism of his speech was somewhat marred, and Fetyukovitch's expression, as he watched him walk away, seemed to suggest to the public "this is a specimen of the lofty-minded persons who accuse him." I remember that this incident, too, did not pass off without an outbreak from Mitya. Enraged by the tone in which Rakitin had referred to Grushenka, he suddenly shouted "Bernard!" When, after Rakitin's cross-examination, the President asked the prisoner if he had anything to say, Mitya cried loudly:

"Since I've been arrested, he has borrowed money from me! He is a contemptible Bernard and opportunist, and he doesn't believe in God; he took the Bishop in!"

Mitya, of course, was pulled up again for the intemperance of his language, but Rakitin was done for. Captain Snegiryov's evidence was a failure, too, but from quite a different reason. He appeared in ragged and dirty clothes, muddy boots, and in spite of the vigilance and expert observation of the police officers, he turned out to be hopelessly drunk. On being asked about Mitya's attack upon him, he refused to answer.

"God bless him. Ilusha told me not to. God will make it up to me yonder."

"Who told you not to tell? Of whom are you talking?"

"Ilusha, my little son. 'Father, father, how he insulted you!' He said that at the stone. Now he is dying. . . ."

The captain suddenly began sobbing, and plumped down on his knees before the President. He was hurriedly led away amidst the laughter of the public. The effect prepared by the prosecutor did not come off at all.

Fetyukovitch went on making the most of every opportunity, and amazed people more and more by his minute knowledge of the case. Thus, for example, Trifon Borissovitch made a great impression, of course, very prejudicial to Mitya. He calculated almost on his fingers that on his first visit to Mokroe, Mitya must have spent three thousand roubles, "or very little less. Just think what he squandered on those gipsy girls alone! And as for our lousy peasants, it wasn't a case of flinging half a rouble in the street, he made them presents of twenty-five roubles each, at least, he didn't give them less. And what a lot of money was simply stolen from him! And if any one did steal, he did not leave a receipt. How could one catch the thief when he was flinging his money away all the time? Our peasants are robbers, you know; they have no care for their souls. And the way he went on with the girls, our village girls! They're completely set up since then, I tell you, they used to be poor." He recalled, in fact, every item of expense and added it all up. So the theory that only fifteen hundred had been spent and the rest had been put aside in a little bag seemed inconceivable.

"I saw three thousand as clear as a penny in his hands, I saw it with my own eyes; I should think I ought to know how to reckon money," cried Trifon Borissovitch, doing his best to satisfy "his betters."

When Fetyukovitch had to cross-examine him, he scarcely tried to refute his evidence, but began asking him about an incident at the first carousal at Mokroe, a month before the arrest, when Timofey and another peasant called Akim had picked up on the floor in the passage a hundred roubles dropped by Mitya when he was drunk, and had given them to Trifon Borissovitch, and received a rouble each from him for doing so. "Well," asked the lawyer, "did you give that hundred roubles back to Mr. Karamazov?" Trifon Borissovitch shuffled in vain. . . . He was obliged, after the peasants had been examined, to admit the finding of the hundred roubles, only adding that he had religiously returned it all to Dmitri Fyodorovitch "in perfect honesty, and it's only because his honour was in liquor at the time, he wouldn't remember it." But, as he had denied the incident of the hundred roubles till the peasants had been called to prove it, his evidence as to returning the money to Mitya was naturally regarded with great suspicion. So one of the most dangerous witnesses brought forward by the prosecution was again discredited.

The same thing happened with the Poles. They took up an attitude of pride and independence; they vociferated loudly that they had both been in the service of the Crown, and that "Pan Mitya" had offered them three thousand "to buy their honour," and that they had seen a large sum of money in his hands. Pan Mussyalovitch introduced a terrible number of

Polish words into his sentences, and seeing that this only increased his consequence in the eyes of the President and the prosecutor, grew more and
more pompous, and ended by talking in Polish altogether. But Fetyukovitch caught them, too, in his snares. Trifon Borissovitch, recalled,
was forced, in spite of his evasions, to admit that Pan Vrublevsky had sub-
stituted another pack of cards for the one he had provided, and that Pan
Mussyalovitch had cheated during the game. Kalganov confirmed this, and
both the Poles left the witness-box with damaged reputations, amidst
laughter fom the public.

Then exactly the same thing happened with almost all the most dangerous witnesses. Fetyukovitch succeeded in casting a slur on all of them, and
dismissing them with a certain derision. The lawyers and experts were lost in
admiration, and were only at a loss to understand what good purpose could
be served by it, for all, I repeat, felt that the case for the prosecution could
not be refuted, but was growing more and more tragically overwhelming.
But from the confidence of the "great magician" they saw that he was
serene, and they waited, feeling that "such a man" had not come from Petersburg for nothing, and that he was not a man to return unsuccessful.

3

THE MEDICAL EXPERTS AND
A POUND OF NUTS

THE evidence of the medical experts, too, was of little use to the prisoner. And it appeared later that Fetyukovitch had not reckoned
much upon it. The medical line of defence had only been taken up
through the insistence of Katerina Ivanovna, who had sent for a celebrated doctor from Moscow on purpose. The case for the defence could, of
course, lose nothing by it and might, with luck, gain something from it.
There was, however, an element of comedy about it, through the difference of opinion of the doctors. The medical experts were the famous doctor from Moscow, our doctor, Herzenstube, and the young doctor,
Varvinsky. The two latter appeared also as witnesses for the prosecution.

The first to be called in the capacity of expert was Doctor Herzenstube.
He was a grey and bald old man of seventy, of middle height and sturdy
build. He was much esteemed and respected by every one in the town. He
was a conscientious doctor and an excellent and pious man, a Herrnhuter
or Moravian brother,[1] I am not quite sure which. He had been living
amongst us for many years, and behaved with wonderful dignity. He was

a kind-hearted and humane man. He treated the sick poor and peasants for nothing, visited them in their slums and huts, and left money for medicine, but he was as obstinate as a mule. If once he had taken an idea into his head, there was no shaking it. Almost every one in the town was aware, by the way, that the famous doctor had, within the first two or three days of his presence among us, uttered some extremely offensive allusions to Doctor Herzenstube's qualifications. Though the Moscow doctor asked twenty-five roubles for a visit, several people in the town were glad to take advantage of his arrival, and rushed to consult him regardless of expense. All these had, of course, been previously patients of Doctor Herzenstube, and the celebrated doctor had criticised his treatment with extreme harshness. Finally, he had asked the patients as soon as he saw them, "Well, who has been cramming you with nostrums? Herzenstube? He, he!" Doctor Herzenstube, of course, heard all this, and now all the three doctors made their appearance, one after another, to be examined.

Doctor Herzenstube roundly declared that the abnormality of the prisoner's mental faculties was self-evident. Then giving his ground for this opinion, which I omit here, he added that the abnormality was not only evident in many of the prisoner's actions in the past, but was apparent even now at this very moment. When he was asked to explain how it was apparent now at this moment, the old doctor, with simple-hearted directness, pointed out that the prisoner on entering the court had "an extraordinary air, remarkable in the circumstances"; that he had "marched in like a soldier, looking straight before him, though it would have been more natural for him to look to the left where, among the public, the ladies were sitting, seeing that he was a great admirer of the fair sex and must be thinking much of what the ladies are saying of him now," the old man concluded in his peculiar language.

I must add that he spoke Russian readily, but every phrase was formed in German style, which did not, however, trouble him, for it had always been a weakness of his to believe that he spoke Russian perfectly, better indeed than Russians. And he was very fond of using Russian proverbs, always declaring that the Russian proverbs were the best and most expressive sayings in the whole world. I may remark, too, that in conversation, through absent-mindedness he often forgot the most ordinary words, which sometimes went out of his head, though he knew them perfectly. The same thing happened, though, when he spoke German, and at such times he always waved his hand before his face as though trying to catch the lost word, and no one could induce him to go on speaking till he had found the missing word. His remark that the prisoner ought to have looked at the ladies on entering roused a whisper of amusement in the audience. All our ladies were very fond of our old doctor; they knew, too, that having been all his life a bachelor and a religious man of exemplary conduct, he looked upon women as lofty creatures. And so his unexpected observation struck every one as very queer.

The Moscow doctor, being questioned in his turn, definitely and emphatically repeated that he considered the prisoner's mental condition abnormal in the highest degree. He talked at length and with erudition of "aberration" and "mania," and argued that, from all the facts collected, the prisoner had undoubtedly been in a condition of aberration for several days before his arrest, and, if the crime had been committed by him, it must, even if he were conscious of it, have been almost involuntary, as he had not the power to control the morbid impulse that possessed him.

But apart from temporary aberration, the doctor diagnosed mania, which promised, in his words, to lead to complete insanity in the future. (It must be noted that I report this in my own words, the doctor made use of very learned and professional language.) "All his actions are in contravention of common sense and logic," he continued. "Not to refer to what I have not seen, that is, the crime itself and the whole catastrophe, the day before yesterday, while he was talking to me, he had an unaccountably fixed look in his eye. He laughed unexpectedly when there was nothing to laugh at. He showed continual and inexplicable irritability, using strange words, 'Bernard!' 'Ethics!' and others equally inappropriate." But the doctor detected mania, above all, in the fact that the prisoner could not even speak of the three thousand roubles, of which he considered himself to have been cheated, without extraordinary irritation, though he could speak comparatively lightly of other misfortunes and grievances. According to all accounts, he had even in the past, whenever the subject of the three thousand roubles was touched on, flown into a perfect frenzy, and yet he was reported to be a disinterested and not a grasping man.

"As to the opinion of my learned colleague," the Moscow doctor added ironically in conclusion, "that the prisoner would, on entering the court, have naturally looked at the ladies and not straight before him, I will only say that, apart from the playfulness of this theory, it is radically unsound. For though I fully agree that the prisoner, on entering the court where his fate will be decided, would not naturally look straight before him in that fixed way, and that that may really be a sign of his abnormal mental condition, at the same time I maintain that he would naturally not look to the left at the ladies, but, on the contrary, to the right to find his legal adviser, on whose help all his hopes rest and on whose defence all his future depends." The doctor expressed his opinion positively and emphatically.

But the unexpected pronouncement of Doctor Varvinsky gave the last touch of comedy to the difference of opinion between the experts. In his opinion the prisoner was now, and had been all along, in a perfectly normal condition, and, although he certainly must have been in a nervous and exceedingly excited state before his arrest, this might have been due to several perfectly obvious causes, jealousy, anger, continual drunkenness, and so on. But this nervous condition would not involve the mental aberration of which mention had just been made. As to the question whether the prisoner should have looked to the left or to the right on entering the court, "in his modest opinion," the prisoner would naturally look straight before him on entering the court, as he had in fact done, as that was where the judges, on whom his fate depended, were sitting. So that it was just by looking straight before him that he showed his perfectly normal state of mind at the present. The young doctor concluded his "modest" testimony with some heat.

"Bravo, doctor!" cried Mitya, from his seat, "just so!"

Mitya, of course, was checked, but the young doctor's opinion had a decisive influence on the judges and on the public, and, as appeared afterwards, every one agreed with him. But Doctor Herzenstube, when called as a witness, was quite unexpectedly of use to Mitya. As an old resident in the town who had known the Karamazov family for years, he furnished some facts of great value for the prosecution, and suddenly, as though recalling something, he added:

"But the poor young man might have had a very different life, for he had a good heart both in childhood and after childhood, that I know. But the Russian proverb says, 'If a man has one head, it's good, but if another clever man comes to visit him, it would be better still, for then there will be two heads and not only one.' "

"One head is good, but two are better," the prosecutor put in impatiently. He knew the old man's habit of talking slowly and deliberately, regardless of the impression he was making and of the delay he was causing, and highly prizing his flat, dull and always gleefully complacent German wit. The old man was fond of making jokes.

"Oh, yes, that's what I say," he went on stubbornly. "One head is good, but two are much better, but he did not meet another head with wits, and his wits went. Where did they go? I've forgotten the word." He went on, passing his hand before his eyes, "Oh, yes, *spazieren*."

"Wandering?"

"Oh, yes, wandering, that's what I say. Well, his wits went wandering and fell in such a deep hole that he lost himself. And yet he was a grateful and sensitive boy. Oh, I remember him very well, a little chap so high, left neglected by his father in the back yard, when he ran about without boots on his feet, and his little breeches hanging by one button."

A note of feeling and tenderness suddenly came into the honest old man's voice. Fetyukovitch positively started, as though scenting something and caught at it instantly.

"Oh, yes, I was a young man then. . . . I was . . . well, I was forty-five then, and had only just come here. And I was so sorry for the boy then: I asked myself why shouldn't I buy him a pound of . . . a pound of what? I've forgotten what it's called. A pound of what children are very fond of, what is it, what is it?" The doctor began waving his hands again. "It grows on a tree and is gathered and given to every one. . . ."

"Apples?"

"Oh, no no. You have a dozen of apples, not a pound. . . . No, there are a lot of them, and all little. You put them in the mouth and crack."

"Nuts?"

"Quite so, nuts, I say so." The doctor repeated in the calmest way as though he had been at no loss for a word. "And I bought him a pound of nuts, for no one had ever bought the boy a pound of nuts before. And I lifted my finger and said to him, 'Boy, *Gott der Vater*.' He laughed and said,

'*Gott der Vater.*' . . . '*Gott der Sohn.*' He laughed again and lisped '*Gott der Sohn.*' '*Gott der heilige Geist.*'* Then he laughed and said as best as he could, '*Gott der heilige Geist.*' I went away, and two days after I happened to be passing, and he shouted to me of himself, 'Uncle *Gott der Vater, Gott der Sohn,*' and he had only forgotten '*Gott der heilige Geist.*' But I reminded him of it and I felt very sorry for him again. But he was taken away, and I did not see him again. Twenty-three years passed. I am sitting one morning in my study, a white-haired old man, when there walks into the room a blooming young man, whom I should never have recognised, but he held up his finger and said, laughing, '*Gott der Vater, Gott der Sohn* and *Gott der heilige Geist.* I have just arrived and have come to thank you for that pound of nuts, for no one else ever bought me a pound of nuts; you are the only one that ever did.' And then I remembered my happy youth and the poor child in the yard, without boots on his feet, and my heart was touched and I said, 'You are a grateful young man, for you have remembered all your life the pound of nuts I bought you in your childhood.' And I embraced him and blessed him. And I shed tears. He laughed, but he shed tears, too . . . for the Russian often laughs when he ought to be weeping. But he did weep; I saw it. And now, alas! . . ."

"And I am weeping now, German, I am weeping now, too, you saintly man," Mitya cried suddenly.

In any case the anecdote made a certain favourable impression on the public. But the chief sensation in Mitya's favour was created by the evidence of Katerina Ivanovna, which I will describe directly. Indeed, when the witnesses *à décharge,*† that is, called by the defence, began giving evidence, fortune seemed all at once markedly more favourable to Mitya, and what was particularly striking, this was a surprise even to the counsel for the defence. But before Katerina Ivanovna was called, Alyosha was examined, and he recalled a fact which seemed to furnish positive evidence against one important point made by the prosecution.

---

*God the Father . . . God the Son . . . God the Holy Spirit (German).
†Literally, to discharge or unload, a French juridical term.

4

FORTUNE SMILES ON MITYA

I T came quite as a surprise even to Alyosha himself. He was not required to take the oath, and I remember that both sides addressed him
very gently and sympathetically. It was evident that his reputation for
goodness had preceded him. Alyosha gave his evidence modestly and with
restraint, but his warm sympathy for his unhappy brother was unmistakable. In answer to one question, he sketched his brother's character as that
of a man, violent-tempered perhaps and carried away by his passions, but
at the same time honourable, proud and generous, capable of self-sacrifice,
if necessary. He admitted, however, that, through his passion for Grushenka
and his rivalry with his father, his brother had been of late in an intolerable position. But he repelled with indignation the suggestion that his
brother might have committed a murder for the sake of gain, though he
recognised that the three thousand roubles had become almost an obsession with Mitya; that he looked upon them as part of the inheritance he
had been cheated of by his father, and that, indifferent as he was to money
as a rule, he could not even speak of that three thousand without fury. As
for the rivalry of the two "ladies," as the prosecutor expressed it—that is,
of Grushenka and Katya—he answered evasively and was even unwilling
to answer one or two questions altogether.

"Did your brother tell you, anyway, that he intended to kill your father?" asked the prosecutor. "You can refuse to answer if you think necessary," he added.

"He did not tell me so directly," answered Alyosha.

"How so? Did he indirectly?"

"He spoke to me once of his hatred for our father and his fear that at an
extreme moment . . . at a moment of fury, he might perhaps murder him."

"And you believed him?"

"I am afraid to say that I did. But I never doubted that some higher
feeling would always save him at the fatal moment, as it has indeed saved
him, for it was not he killed my father," Alyosha said firmly, in a loud voice
that was heard throughout the court.

The prosecutor started like a warhorse at the sound of a trumpet.

"Let me assure you that I fully believe in the complete sincerity of your
conviction and do not explain it by or identify it with your affection for
your unhappy brother. Your peculiar view of the whole tragic episode is
known to us already from the preliminary investigation. I won't attempt to
conceal from you that it is highly individual and contradicts all the other
evidence collected by the prosecution. And so I think it essential to press

you to tell me what facts have led you to this conviction of your brother's innocence and of the guilt of another person against whom you gave evidence at the preliminary inquiry?"

"I only answered the questions asked me at the preliminary inquiry," replied Alyosha, slowly and calmly. "I made no accusation against Smerdyakov of myself."

"Yet you gave evidence against him?"

"I was led to do so by my brother Dmitri's words. I was told what took place at his arrest and how he had pointed to Smerdyakov before I was examined. I believe absolutely that my brother is innocent, and if he didn't commit the murder, then . . ."

"Then Smerdyakov? Why Smerdyakov? And why are you so completely persuaded of your brother's innocence?"

"I cannot help believing my brother. I know he wouldn't lie to me. I saw from his face he wasn't lying."

"Only from his face? Is that all the proof you have?"

"I have no other proof."

"And of Smerdyakov's guilt have you no proof whatever but your brother's word and the expression of his face?"

"No, I have no other proof."

The prosecutor dropped the examination at this point. The impression left by Alyosha's evidence on the public was most disappointing. There had been talk about Smerdyakov before the trial; some one had heard something, some one had pointed out something else, it was said that Alyosha had gathered together some extraordinary proofs of his brother's innocence and Smerdyakov's guilt, and after all there was nothing, no evidence except certain moral convictions so natural in a brother.

But Fetyukovitch began his cross-examination. On his asking Alyosha when it was that the prisoner had told him of his hatred for his father and that he might kill him, and whether he had heard it, for instance, at their last meeting before the catastrophe, Alyosha started as he answered, as though only just recollecting and understanding something.

"I remember one circumstance now which I'd quite forgotten myself. It wasn't clear to me at the time, but now . . ."

And, obviously only now for the first time struck by an idea, he recounted eagerly how, at his last interview with Mitya that evening under the tree, on the road to the monastery, Mitya had struck himself on the breast, "the upper part of the breast," and had repeated several times that he had a means of regaining his honour, that that means was here, here on his breast. "I thought, when he struck himself on the breast, he meant that it was in his heart," Alyosha continued, "that he might find in his heart strength to save himself from some awful disgrace which was awaiting him and which he did not dare confess even to me. I must confess I did think at the time that he was speaking of our father, and that the disgrace he was shuddering at was the thought of going to our father and doing some violence to him. Yet it was just then that he pointed to something on his breast, so that I remember the idea struck me at the time that the heart is not on that part of the breast, but below, and that he struck himself much too high, just below the neck, and kept pointing to that place. My idea seemed silly to me at the time, but he was perhaps pointing then to that little bag in which he had fifteen hundred roubles!"

"Just so," Mitya cried from his place. "That's right, Alyosha, it was the little bag I struck with my fist."

Fetyukovitch flew to him in hot haste entreating him to keep quiet, and at the same instant pounced on Alyosha. Alyosha, carried away himself by his recollection, warmly expressed his theory that this disgrace was probably just that fifteen hundred roubles on him, which he might have returned to Katerina Ivanovna as half of what he owed her, but which he had yet determined not to repay her and to use for another purpose—namely, to enable him to elope with Grushenka, if she consented.

"It is so, it must be so," exclaimed Alyosha, in sudden excitement. "My brother cried several times that half of the disgrace, half of it (he said *half* several times) he could free himself from at once, but that he was so unhappy in his weakness of will that he wouldn't do it . . . that he knew beforehand he was incapable of doing it!"

"And you clearly, confidently remember that he struck himself just on this part of the breast?" Fetyukovitch asked eagerly.

"Clearly and confidently, for I thought at the time, 'Why does he strike himself up there when the heart is lower down,' and the thought seemed stupid to me at the time . . . I remember its seeming stupid . . . it flashed through my mind. That's what brought it back to me just now. How could I have forgotten it till now! It was that little bag he meant when he said he had the means but wouldn't give back that fifteen hundred. And when he was arrested at Mokroe he cried out—I know, I was told it—that he considered it the most disgraceful act of his life that when he had the means of repaying Katerina Ivanovna half (half, note!) what he owed her, he yet could not bring himself to repay the money and preferred to remain a thief in her eyes rather than part with it. And what torture, what torture that debt has been to him!" Alyosha exclaimed in conclusion.

The prosecutor, of course, intervened. He asked Alyosha to describe once more how it had all happened, and several times insisted on the question, had the prisoner seemed to point to anything. Perhaps he had simply struck himself with his fist on the breast?

"But it was not with his fist," cried Alyosha; "he pointed with his fingers and pointed here, very high up. . . . How could I have so completely forgotten it till this moment!"

The President asked Mitya what he had to say to the last witness's evidence. Mitya confirmed it, saying that he had been pointing to the fifteen hundred roubles which were on his breast, just below the neck, and that that was, of course, the disgrace, "A disgrace I cannot deny, the most shameful act of my whole life," cried Mitya. "I might have repaid it and didn't repay it. I preferred to remain a thief in her eyes rather than give it back. And the most shameful part of it was that I knew beforehand I shouldn't give it back! You are right, Alyosha! Thanks, Alyosha!"

So Alyosha's cross-examination ended. What was important and striking about it was that one fact at least had been found, and even though this
were only one tiny bit of evidence, a mere hint at evidence, it did go some
little way towards proving that the bag had existed and had contained fifteen hundred roubles and that the prisoner had not been lying at the preliminary inquiry, when he alleged at Mokroe that those fifteen hundred
roubles were "his own." Alyosha was glad. With a flushed face he moved
away to the seat assigned to him. He kept repeating to himself: "How was
it I forgot! How could I have forgotten it! And what made it come back to
me now?"

Katerina Ivanovna was called to the witness-box. As she entered something extraordinary happened in the court. The ladies clutched their
lorgnettes and opera-glasses. There was a stir among the men: some stood
up to get a better view. Everybody alleged afterwards that Mitya had
turned "white as a sheet" on her entrance. All in black, she advanced modestly, almost timidly. It was impossible to tell from her face that she was agitated; but there was a resolute gleam in her dark and gloomy eyes. I may
remark that many people mentioned that she looked particularly handsome at that moment. She spoke softly but clearly, so that she was heard all
over the court. She expressed herself with composure, or at least tried to
appear composed. The President began his examination discreetly and
very respectfully, as though afraid to touch on "certain chords," and showing consideration for her great unhappiness. But in answer to one of the
first questions Katerina Ivanovna replied firmly that she had been formerly betrothed to the prisoner "until he left me of his own accord . . ."
she added quietly. When they asked her about the three thousand she had
entrusted to Mitya to post to her relations, she said firmly, "I didn't give
him the money simply to send it off. I felt at the time that he was in great
need of money. . . . I gave him the three thousand on the understanding
that he should post it within the month if he cared to. There was no need
for him to worry himself about that debt afterwards."

I will not repeat all the questions asked her and all her answers in detail. I will only give the substance of her evidence.

"I was firmly convinced that he would send off that sum as soon as he
got money from his father," she went on. "I have never doubted his disinterestedness and his honesty . . . his scrupulous honesty . . . in money matters. He felt quite certain that he would receive the money from his father,
and spoke to me several times about it. I knew he had a feud with his father and have always believed that he had been unfairly treated by his father. I don't remember any threat uttered by him against his father. He
certainly never uttered any such threat before me. If he had come to me at
that time, I should have at once relieved his anxiety about that unlucky
three thousand roubles, but he had given up coming to see me . . . and I
myself was put in such a position . . . that I could not invite him. . . . And I
had no right, indeed, to be exacting as to that money," she added suddenly,
and there was a ring of resolution in her voice. "I was once indebted to
him for assistance in money for more than three thousand, and I took it,

although I could not at that time foresee that I should ever be in a position to repay my debt."

There was a note of defiance in her voice. It was then Fetyukovitch began his cross-examination.

"Did that take place not here, but at the beginning of your acquaintance?" Fetyukovitch suggested cautiously, feeling his way, instantly scenting something favourable. I must mention in parenthesis that, though Fetyukovitch had been brought from Petersburg partly at the instance of Katerina Ivanovna herself, he knew nothing about the episode of the five thousand roubles given her by Mitya, and of her "bowing to the ground to him." She concealed this from him and said nothing about it, and that was strange. It may be pretty certainly assumed that she herself did not know till the very last minute whether she would speak of that episode in the court, and waited for the inspiration of the moment.

No, I can never forget those moments. She began telling her story. She told everything, the whole episode that Mitya had told Alyosha, and her bowing to the ground, and her reason. She told about her father and her going to Mitya, and did not in one word, in a single hint, suggest that Mitya had himself, through her sister, proposed they should "send him Katerina Ivanovna" to fetch the money. She generously concealed that and was not ashamed to make it appear as though she had of her own impulse run to the young officer, relying on something . . . to beg him for the money. It was something tremendous! I turned cold and trembled as I listened. The court was hushed, trying to catch each word. It was something unexampled. Even from such a self-willed and contemptuously proud girl as she was, such an extremely frank avowal, such sacrifice, such self-immolation, seemed incredible. And for what, for whom? To save the man who had deceived and insulted her and to help, in however small a degree, in saving him, by creating a strong impression in his favour. And, indeed, the figure of the young officer who, with a respectful bow to the innocent girl, handed her his last five thousand roubles—all he had in the world—was thrown into a very sympathetic and attractive light, but . . . I had a painful misgiving at heart! I felt that calumny might come of it later (and it did, in fact, it did). It was repeated all over the town afterwards with spiteful laughter that the story was perhaps not quite complete—that is, in the statement that the officer had let the young lady depart "with nothing but a respectful bow." It was hinted that something was here omitted.

"And even if nothing had been omitted, if this were the whole story," the most highly respected of our ladies maintained, "even then it's very doubtful whether it was creditable for a young girl to behave in that way, even for the sake of saving her father."

And can Katerina Ivanovna, with her intelligence, her morbid sensitiveness, have failed to understand that people would talk like that? She must have understood it, yet she made up her mind to tell everything. Of course, all these nasty little suspicions as to the truth of her story only arose afterwards and at the first moment all were deeply impressed by it. As for the judges and the lawyers, they listened in reverent, almost shame-faced silence to Katerina Ivanovna. The prosecutor did not venture upon even one question on the subject. Fetyukovitch made a low bow to her. Oh, he was almost triumphant! Much ground had been gained. For a man to give his last five thousand on a generous impulse and then for the same man to murder his father for the sake of robbing him of three thousand—the idea seemed too incongruous. Fetyukovitch felt that now the charge of theft, at least, was as good as disproved. "The case" was thrown into quite a different light. There was a wave of sympathy for Mitya. As for him. . . . I was told that once or twice, while Katerina Ivanovna was giving her evidence, he jumped up from his seat, sank back again, and hid his face in his hands. But when she had finished, he suddenly cried in a sobbing voice:

"Katya, why have you ruined me?" and his sobs were audible all over the court. But he instantly restrained himself, and cried again:

"Now I am condemned!"

Then he sat rigid in his place, with his teeth clenched and his arms across his chest. Katerina Ivanovna remained in the court and sat down in her place. She was pale and sat with her eyes cast down. Those who were sitting near her declared that for a long time she shivered all over as though in a fever. Grushenka was called.

I am approaching the sudden catastrophe which was perhaps the final cause of Mitya's ruin. For I am convinced, so is every one—all the lawyers said the same afterwards—that if the episode had not occurred, the prisoner would at least have been recommended to mercy. But of that later. A few words first about Grushenka.

She, too, was dressed entirely in black, with her magnificent black shawl on her shoulders. She walked to the witness-box with her smooth, noiseless tread, with the slightly swaying gait common in women of full figure. She looked steadily at the President, turning her eyes neither to the right nor to the left. To my thinking she looked very handsome at that moment, and not at all pale, as the ladies alleged afterwards. They declared, too, that she had a concentrated and spiteful expression. I believe that she was simply irritated and painfully conscious of the contemptuous and inquisitive eyes of our scandal-loving public. She was proud and could not stand contempt. She was one of those people who flare up, angry and eager to retaliate, at the mere suggestion of contempt. There was an element of timidity, too, of course, and inward shame at her own timidity, so it was not strange that her tone kept changing. At one moment it was angry, contemptuous and rough, and at another there was a sincere note of self-condemnation. Sometimes she spoke as though she were taking a desperate plunge; as though she felt, "I don't care what happens. I'll say it. . . ." À propos of her acquaintance with Fyodor Pavlovitch, she remarked curtly, "That's all nonsense, and was it my fault that he would pester me?" But a minute later she added, "It was all my fault. I was laughing at them both—at the old man and at him, too—and I brought both of them to this. It was all on account of me it happened."

Samsonov's name came up somehow. "That's nobody's business," she snapped at once, with a sort of insolent defiance. "He was my benefactor;

he took me when I hadn't a shoe to my foot, when my family had turned me out." The President reminded her, though very politely, that she must answer the questions directly, without going off into irrelevant details. Grushenka crimsoned and her eyes flashed.

The envelope with the notes in it she had not seen, but had only heard from "that wicked wretch" that Fyodor Pavlovitch had an envelope with notes for three thousand in it. "But that was all foolishness. I was only laughing. I wouldn't have gone to him for anything."

"To whom are you referring 'as that wicked wretch'?" inquired the prosecutor.

"The lackey, Smerdyakov, who murdered his master and hanged himself last night."

She was, of course, at once asked what ground she had for such a definite accusation; but it appeared that she, too, had no grounds for it.

"Dmitri Fyodorovitch told me so himself; you can believe him. The woman who came between us has ruined him; she is the cause of it all, let me tell you," Grushenka added. She seemed to be quivering with hatred, and there was a vindictive note in her voice. She was again asked to whom she was referring. "The young lady, Katerina Ivanovna there. She sent for me, offered me chocolate, tried to fascinate me. There's not much true shame about her, I can tell you that. . . ."

At this point the President checked her sternly, begging her to moderate her language. But the jealous woman's heart was burning, and she did not care what she did.

"When the prisoner was arrested at Mokroe," the prosecutor asked, "every one saw and heard you run out of the next room and cry out: 'It's all my fault. We'll go to Siberia together!' So you already believed him to have murdered his father?"

"I don't remember what I felt at the time," answered Grushenka. "Every one was crying out that he had killed his father, and I felt that it was my fault, that it was on my account he had murdered him. But when he said he wasn't guilty, I believed him at once, and I believe him now and always shall believe him. He is not the man to tell a lie."

Fetyukovitch began his cross-examination. I remember that among other things he asked about Rakitin and the twenty-five roubles "you paid him for bringing Alexey Fyodorovitch Karamazov to see you."

"There was nothing strange about his taking the money," sneered Grushenka, with angry contempt. "He was always coming to me for money: he used to get thirty roubles a month at least out of me, chiefly for luxuries: he had enough to keep him without my help."

"What led you to be so liberal to Mr. Rakitin?" Fetyukovitch asked, in spite of an uneasy movement on the part of the President.

"Why, he is my cousin. His mother was my mother's sister. But he's always besought me not to tell any one here of it, he is so dreadfully ashamed of me."

This fact was a complete surprise to every one; no one in the town nor in the monastery, not even Mitya, knew of it. I was told that Rakitin turned purple with shame where he sat. Grushenka had somehow heard before she came into the court that he had given evidence against Mitya, and so she was angry. The whole effect on the public, of Rakitin's speech, of his noble sentiments, of his attacks upon serfdom and the political disorder of Russia, was this time finally ruined. Fetyukovitch was satisfied: it was another godsend. Grushenka's cross-examination did not last long and, of course, there could be nothing particularly new in her evidence. She left a very disagreeable impression on the public; hundreds of contemptuous eyes were fixed upon her, as she finished giving her evidence and sat down again in the court, at a good distance from Katerina Ivanovna. Mitya was silent throughout her evidence. He sat as though turned to stone, with his eyes fixed on the ground.

Ivan was called to give evidence.

5

A SUDDEN CATASTROPHE

I MAY note that he had been called before Alyosha. But the usher of the court announced to the President that, owing to an attack of illness or some sort of fit, the witness could not appear at the moment, but was ready to give his evidence as soon as he recovered. But no one seemed to have heard it and it only came out later.

His entrance was for the first moment almost unnoticed. The principal witnesses, especially the two rival ladies, had already been questioned. Curiosity was satisfied for the time; the public was feeling almost fatigued. Several more witnesses were still to be heard, who probably had little information to give after all that had been given. Time was passing. Ivan walked up with extraordinary slowness, looking at no one, and with his head bowed, as though plunged in gloomy thought. He was irreproachably dressed, but his face made a painful impression, on me at least: there was an earthy look in it, a look like a dying man's. His eyes were lustreless; he raised them and looked slowly round the court. Alyosha jumped up from his seat and moaned "Ah!" I remember that, but it was hardly noticed.

The President began by informing him that he was a witness not on oath, that he might answer or refuse to answer, but that, of course, he must bear witness according to his conscience, and so on and so on. Ivan listened and looked at him blankly, but his face gradually relaxed into a smile, and as soon as the President, looking at him in astonishment, finished, he laughed outright.

"Well, and what else?" he asked in a loud voice.

There was a hush in the court; there was a feeling of something strange. The President showed signs of uneasiness.

"You . . . are perhaps still unwell?" he began, looking everywhere for the usher.

"Don't trouble yourself, your excellency, I am well enough and can tell you something interesting." Ivan answered with sudden calmness and respectfulness.

"You have some special communication to make?" the President went on, still mistrustfully.

Ivan looked down, waited a few seconds and, raising his head, answered, almost stammering:

"No . . . I haven't. I have nothing particular."

They began asking him questions. He answered, as it were reluctantly, with extreme brevity, with a sort of disgust which grew more and more marked, though he answered rationally. To many questions he answered that he did not know. He knew nothing of his father's money relations with Dmitri. "I wasn't interested in the subject," he added. Threats to murder his father he had heard from the prisoner. Of the money in the envelope he had heard from Smerdyakov.

"The same thing over and over again," he interrupted suddenly, with a look of weariness. "I have nothing particular to tell the court."

"I see you are unwell and understand your feelings," the President began.

He turned to the prosecutor and the counsel for the defence to invite them to examine the witness, if necessary, when Ivan suddenly asked in an exhausted voice:

"Let me go, your excellency, I feel very ill."

And with these words, without waiting for permission, he turned to walk out of the court. But after taking four steps he stood still, as though he had reached a decision, smiled slowly, and went back.

"I am like the peasant girl, your excellency . . . you know. How does it go? 'I'll stand up if I like, and I won't if I don't.' They were trying to put on her sarafan* to take her to church to be married, and she said, 'I'll stand up if I like, and I won't if I don't.' . . . It's in some book about the peasantry."

"What do you mean by that?" the President asked severely.

"Why, this," Ivan suddenly pulled out a roll of notes. "Here's the money . . . the notes that lay in that envelope" (he nodded towards the table on which lay the material evidence) "for the sake of which our father was murdered. Where shall I put them? Mr. Superintendent, take them."

The usher of the court took the whole roll and handed it to the President.

"How could this money have come into your possession if it is the same money?" the President asked wonderingly.

"I got them from Smerdyakov, from the murderer, yesterday. . . . I was

---

*A jumper-style dress worn over a shirt.

with him just before he hanged himself. It was he, not my brother, killed our father. He murdered him and I incited him to do it. . . . Who doesn't desire his father's death?"

"Are you in your right mind?" broke involuntarily from the President.

"I should think I am in my right mind . . . in the same nasty mind as all of you . . . as all these . . . ugly faces." He turned suddenly to the audience. "My father has been murdered and they pretend they are horrified," he snarled, with furious contempt. "They keep up the sham with one another. Liars! They all desire the death of their fathers. One reptile devours another. . . . If there hadn't been a murder, they'd have been angry and gone home ill-humoured. It's a spectacle they want! *Panem et circenses.** Though I am one to talk! Have you any water? Give me a drink for Christ's sake!" He suddenly clutched his head.

The usher at once approached him. Alyosha jumped up and cried, "He is ill. Don't believe him: he has brain fever." Katerina Ivanovna rose impulsively from her seat and, rigid with horror, gazed at Ivan. Mitya stood up and greedily looked at his brother and listened to him with a wild, strange smile.

"Don't disturb yourselves. I am not mad, I am only a murderer," Ivan began again. "You can't expect eloquence from a murderer," he added suddenly for some reason and laughed a queer laugh.

The prosecutor bent over to the President in obvious dismay. The two other judges communicated in agitated whispers. Fetyukovitch pricked up his ears as he listened: the hall was hushed in expectation. The President seemed suddenly to recollect himself.

"Witness, your words are incomprehensible and impossible here. Calm yourself, if you can, and tell your story . . . if you really have something to tell. How can you confirm your statement . . . if indeed you are not delirious?"

"That's just it. I have no proof. That cur Smerdyakov won't send you proofs from the other world . . . in an envelope. You think of nothing but envelopes—one is enough. I've no witnesses . . . except one, perhaps," he smiled thoughtfully.

"Who is your witness?"

"He has a tail, your excellency, and that would be irregular! *Le diable n'existe point!* Don't pay attention: he is a paltry, pitiful devil," he added suddenly. He ceased laughing and spoke, as it were, confidentially. "He is here somewhere, no doubt—under that table with the material evidence on it, perhaps. Where should he sit if not there? You see, listen to me. I told him I don't want to keep quiet, and he talked about the geological cataclysm . . . idiocy! Come, release the monster . . . he's been singing a hymn. That's because his heart is light! It's like a drunken man in the street bawling how "Vanka went to Petersburg,' and I would give a quadrillion quadrillions

---

*Bread and circuses (Latin); quotation from the tenth Satire of first-century Roman satirist Juvenal, referring to the way that Roman rulers kept the rabble in line.

for two seconds of joy. You don't know me! Oh, how stupid all this business is! Come, take me instead of him! I didn't come for nothing. . . . Why, why is everything so stupid? . . ."

And he began slowly, and as it were reflectively, looking round him again. But the court was all excitement by now. Alyosha rushed towards him, but the court usher had already seized Ivan by the arm.

"What are you about?" he cried, staring into the man's face, and suddenly seizing him by the shoulders, he flung him violently to the floor. But the police were on the spot and he was seized. He screamed furiously.* And all the time he was being removed, he yelled and screamed something incoherent.

The whole court was thrown into confusion. I don't remember everything as it happened. I was excited myself and could not follow. I only know that afterwards, when everything was quiet again and every one understood what had happened, the court usher came in for a reprimand, though he very reasonably explained that the witness had been quite well, that the doctor had seen him an hour ago, when he had a slight attack of giddiness, but that, until he had come into the court, he had talked quite consecutively, so that nothing could have been foreseen—that he had, in fact, insisted on giving evidence. But before every one had completely regained their composure and recovered from this scene, it was followed by another. Katerina Ivanovna had an attack of hysterics. She sobbed, shrieking loudly, but refused to leave the court, struggled, and besought them not to remove her. Suddenly she cried to the President:

"There is more evidence I must give at once . . . at once! Here is a document, a letter . . . take it, read it quickly, quickly! It's a letter from that monster . . . that man there, there!" she pointed to Mitya. "It was he killed his father, you will see that directly. He wrote to me how he would kill his father! But the other one is ill, he is ill, he is delirious!" she kept crying out, beside herself.

The court usher took the document she held out to the President, and she, dropping into her chair, hiding her face in her hands, began convulsively and noiselessly sobbing, shaking all over, and stifling every sound for fear she should be ejected from the court. The document she had handed up was that letter Mitya had written at the Metropolis tavern, which Ivan had spoken of as a "mathematical proof." Alas! its mathematical conclusiveness was recognised, and had it not been for that letter, Mitya might have escaped his doom or, at least, that doom would have been less terrible. It was, I repeat, difficult to notice every detail. What followed is still confused to my mind. The President must, I suppose, have at once passed on the document to the judges, the jury, and the lawyers on both sides. I only remember how they began examining the witness. On being gently asked by the President whether she had recovered sufficiently, Katerina Ivanovna exclaimed impetuously:

---

*Possible reference to the cries of those possessed by the devil in Acts 8:7.

"I am ready, I am ready! I am quite equal to answering you," she added, evidently still afraid that she would somehow be prevented from giving evidence. She was asked to explain in detail what this letter was and under what circumstances she received it.

"I received it the day before the crime was committed, but he wrote it the day before that, at the tavern—that is, two days before he committed the crime. Look, it is written on some sort of bill!" she cried breathlessly. "He hated me at the time, because he had behaved contemptibly and was running after that creature . . . and because he owed me that three thousand. . . . Oh! he was humiliated by that three thousand on account of his own meanness! This is how it happened about that three thousand. I beg you, I beseech you, to hear me. Three weeks before he murdered his father, he came to me one morning. I knew he was in want of money, and what he wanted it for. Yes, yes—to win that creature and carry her off. I knew then that he had been false to me and meant to abandon me, and it was I, I, who gave him that money, who offered it to him on the pretext of his sending it to my sister in Moscow. And as I gave it him, I looked him in the face and said that he could send it when he liked, 'in a month's time would do.' How, how could he have failed to understand that I was practically telling him to his face, 'You want money to be false to me with your creature, so here's the money for you. I give it to you myself. Take it, if you have so little honour as to take it!' I wanted to prove what he was, and what happened? He took it, he took it, and squandered it with that creature in one night. . . . But he knew, he knew that I knew all about it. I assure you he understood, too, that I gave him that money to test him, to see whether he was so lost to all sense of honour as to take it from me. I looked into his eyes and he looked into mine, and he understood it all and he took it—he carried off my money!"

"That's true, Katya," Mitya roared suddenly, "I looked into your eyes and I knew that you were dishonouring me, and yet I took your money. Despise me as a scoundrel, despise me, all of you! I've deserved it!"

"Prisoner," cried the President, "another word and I will order you to be removed."

"That money was a torment to him," Katya went on with impulsive haste. "He wanted to repay it me. He wanted to, that's true; but he needed money for that creature, too. So he murdered his father, but he didn't repay me, and went off with her to that village where he was arrested. There, again, he squandered the money he had stolen after the murder of his father. And a day before the murder he wrote me this letter. He was drunk when he wrote it. I saw it at once, at the time. He wrote it from spite, and feeling certain, positively certain, that I should never show it to any one, even if he did kill him, or else he wouldn't have written it. For he knew I shouldn't want to revenge myself and ruin him! But read it, read it attentively—more attentively, please—and you will see that he had described it all in his letter, all beforehand, how he would kill his father and where his money was kept. Look, please, don't overlook that, there's one phrase there, 'I shall kill him as soon as Ivan has gone away.' So he thought it all out beforehand how he would kill him," Katerina Ivanovna pointed out to the court with venomous and malignant triumph. Oh! it was clear she had studied every line of that letter and detected every meaning underlining it. "If he hadn't been drunk, he wouldn't have written to me; but, look, everything is written there beforehand, just as he committed the murder after. A complete programme of it!" she exclaimed frantically.

She was reckless now of all consequences to herself, though, no doubt, she had foreseen them even a month ago, for even then, perhaps, shaking with anger, she had pondered whether to show it at the trial or not. Now she had taken the fatal plunge. I remember that the letter was read aloud by the clerk, directly afterwards, I believe. It made an overwhelming impression. They asked Mitya whether he admitted having written the letter.

"It's mine, mine!" cried Mitya. "I shouldn't have written it, if I hadn't been drunk! ... We've hated each other for many things, Katya, but I swear, I swear I loved you even while I hated you, and you didn't love me!"

He sank back on his seat, wringing his hands in despair. The prosecutor and counsel for the defence began cross-examining her, chiefly to ascertain what had induced her to conceal such a document and to give her evidence in quite a different tone and spirit just before.

"Yes, yes. I was telling lies just now. I was lying against my honour and my conscience, but I wanted to save him, for he has hated and despised me so!" Katya cried madly. "Oh, he has despised me horribly, he has always despised me, and do you know, he has despised me from the very moment that I bowed down to him for that money. I saw that. . . . I felt it at once at the time, but for a long time I wouldn't believe it. How often I have read it in his eyes 'you came of yourself, though.' Oh, he didn't understand, he had no idea why I ran to him, he can suspect nothing but baseness, he judged me by himself, he thought every one was like himself!" Katya hissed furiously, in a perfect frenzy. "And he only wanted to marry me, because I'd inherited a fortune, because of that, because of that! I always suspected it was because of that! Oh, he is a brute! He was always convinced that I should be trembling with shame all my life before him, because I went to him then, and that he had a right to despise me for ever for it, and so to be superior to me—that's why he wanted to marry me! That's so, that's all so! I tried to conquer him by my love—a love that knew no bounds, I even tried to forgive his faithlessness; but he understood nothing, nothing! How could he understand indeed? He is a monster! I only received that letter the next evening: it was brought me from the tavern—and only that morning, only that morning I wanted to forgive him everything, everything—even his treachery!"

The President and the prosecutor, of course, tried to calm her. I can't help thinking that they felt ashamed of taking advantage of her hysteria and of listening to such avowals. I remember hearing them say to her, "We understand how hard it is for you; be sure we are able to feel for you," and so on, and so on. And yet they dragged the evidence out of the raving, hysterical woman. She described at last with extraordinary clearness, which is so often seen, though only for a moment, in such overwrought states, how

Ivan had been nearly driven out of his mind during the last two months trying to save "the monster and murderer," his brother.

"He tortured himself," she exclaimed, "he was always trying to minimize his brother's guilt and confessing to me that he, too, had never loved his father, and perhaps desired his death himself. Oh, he has a tender, over-tender conscience! He tormented himself with his conscience! He told me everything, everything! He came every day and talked to me as his only friend. I have the honour to be his only friend!" she cried suddenly with a sort of defiance, and her eyes flashed. "He had been twice to see Smerdyakov. One day he came to me and said, 'If it was not my brother, but Smerdyakov committed the murder (for the legend was circulating everywhere that Smerdyakov had done it), perhaps I too am guilty, for Smerdyakov knew I didn't like my father and perhaps believed that I desired my father's death. Then I brought out that letter and showed it him. He was entirely convinced that his brother had done it, and he was overwhelmed by it. He couldn't endure the thought that his own brother was a parricide! Only a week ago I saw that it was making him ill. During the last few days he has talked incoherently in my presence. I saw his mind was giving way. He walked about, raving; he was seen muttering in the streets. The doctor from Moscow, at my request, examined him the day before yesterday and told me that he was on the eve of brain fever—and all on his account, on account of this monster! And last night he learnt that Smerdyakov was dead! It was such a shock that it drove him out of his mind . . . and all through this monster, all for the sake of saving the monster!"

Oh, of course, such an outpouring, such an avowal is only possible once in a lifetime—at the hour of death, for instance, on the way to the scaffold! But it was in Katya's character, and it was such a moment in her life. It was the same impetuous Katya who had thrown herself on the mercy of a young profligate to save her father; the same Katya who had just before, in her pride and chastity, sacrificed herself and her maidenly modesty before all these people, telling of Mitya's generous conduct, in the hope of softening his fate a little. And now, again, she sacrificed herself; but this time it was for another, and perhaps only now—perhaps only at this moment—she felt and knew how dear that other was to her! She had sacrificed herself in terror for him, conceiving all of a sudden that he had ruined himself by his confession that it was he who had committed the murder, not his brother, she had sacrificed herself to save him, to save his good name, his reputation!

And yet one terrible doubt occurred to one—was she lying in her description of her former relations with Mitya?—that was the question. No, she had not intentionally slandered him when she cried that Mitya despised her for her bowing down to him! She believed it herself. She had been firmly convinced, perhaps ever since that bow, that the simple-hearted Mitya, who even then adored her, was laughing at her and despising her. She had loved him with an hysterical, "lacerated" love only from pride, from wounded pride, and that love was not like love, but more like revenge. Oh! perhaps that lacerated love would have grown into real love, perhaps Katya longed for nothing more than that, but Mitya's faithlessness had wounded her to the bottom of her heart, and her heart could not forgive him. The moment of revenge had come upon her suddenly, and all that had been accumulating so long and so painfully in the offended woman's breast burst out all at once and unexpectedly. She betrayed Mitya, but she betrayed herself, too. And no sooner had she given full expression to her feelings than the tension of course was over and she was overwhelmed with shame. Hysterics began again: she fell on the floor, sobbing and screaming. She was carried out. At that moment Grushenka, with a wail, rushed towards Mitya before they had time to prevent her.

"Mitya," she wailed, "your serpent has destroyed you! There, she has shown you what she is!" she shouted to the judges, shaking with anger. At a signal from the President they seized her and tried to remove her from the court. She wouldn't allow it. She fought and struggled to get back to Mitya. Mitya uttered a cry and struggled to get to her. He was overpowered.

Yes, I think the ladies who came to see the spectacle must have been satisfied—the show had been a varied one. Then I remember the Moscow doctor appeared on the scene. I believe the President had previously sent the court usher to arrange for medical aid for Ivan. The doctor announced to the court that the sick man was suffering from a dangerous attack of brain fever and that he must be at once removed. In answer to questions from the prosecutor and the counsel for the defence he said that the patient had come to him of his own accord the day before yesterday and that he had warned him that he had such an attack coming on, but he had not consented to be looked after. "He was certainly not in a normal state of mind: he told me himself that he saw visions when he was awake, that he met several persons in the street, who were dead, and that Satan visited him every evening," said the doctor, in conclusion. Having given his evidence, the celebrated doctor withdrew. The letter produced by Katerina Ivanovna was added to the material proofs. After some deliberation, the judges decided to proceed with the trial and to enter both the unexpected pieces of evidence (given by Ivan and Katerina Ivanovna) on the protocol.

But I will not detail the evidence of the other witnesses, who only repeated and confirmed what had been said before, though all with their characteristic peculiarities. I repeat, all was brought together in the prosecutor's speech, which I shall quote immediately. Every one was excited, every one was electrified by the late catastrophe, and all were awaiting the speeches for the prosecution and the defence with intense impatience. Fetyukovitch was obviously shaken by Katerina Ivanovna's evidence. But the prosecutor was triumphant. When all the evidence had been taken, the court was adjourned for almost an hour. I believe it was just eight o'clock when the President returned to his seat and our prosecutor, Ippolit Kirillovitch, began his speech.

6

THE PROSECUTOR'S SPEECH.
SKETCHES OF CHARACTER

IPPOLIT KIRILLOVITCH began his speech, trembling with nervousness, with cold sweat on his forehead, feeling hot and cold all over by turns. He described this himself afterwards. He regarded this speech as his *chef d'œuvre*,* the *chef d'œuvre* of his whole life, as his swan-song. He died, it is true, nine months later of rapid consumption, so that he had the right, as it turned out, to compare himself to a swan singing his last song. He had put his whole heart and all the brain he had into that speech. And poor Ippolit Kirillovitch unexpectedly revealed that at least some feeling for the public welfare and "the eternal question"† lay concealed in him. Where his speech really excelled was in its sincerity. He genuinely believed in the prisoner's guilt; he was accusing him not as an official duty only, and in calling for vengeance he quivered with a genuine passion "for the security of society." Even the ladies in the audience, though they remained hostile to Ippolit Kirillovitch, admitted that he made an extraordinary impression on them. He began in a breaking voice, but it soon gained strength and filled the court to the end of his speech. But as soon as he had finished, he almost fainted.

"Gentlemen of the jury," began the prosecutor, "this case has made a stir throughout Russia. But what is there to wonder at, what is there so peculiarly horrifying in it for us? We are so accustomed to such crimes! That's what's so horrible, that such dark deeds have ceased to horrify us. What ought to horrify us is that we are so accustomed to it, and not this or that isolated crime. What are the causes of our indifference, our lukewarm attitude to such deeds, to such signs of the times, ominous of an unenviable future? Is it our cynicism, is it the premature exhaustion of intellect and imagination in a society that is sinking into decay, in spite of its youth? Is it that our moral principles are shattered to their foundations, or is it, perhaps, a complete lack of such principles among us? I cannot answer such questions; nevertheless they are disturbing, and every citizen not only must, but ought to be harassed by them. Our newborn and still timid press has done good service to the public already, for without it we should never have heard of the horrors of unbridled violence and moral degradation which are continually made known by the press, not merely to those who

---

*Masterpiece (French).
†That is, the unanswered and unanswerable questions about life and death.

attend the new jury courts[2] established in the present reign, but to every
one. And what do we read almost daily? Of things beside which the present case grows pale, and seems almost commonplace. But what is most important is that the majority of our national crimes of violence bear witness
to a widespread evil, now so general among us that it is difficult to contend
against it.

"One day we see a brilliant young officer of high society, at the very
outset of his career, in a cowardly underhand way, without a pang of conscience, murdering an official who had once been his benefactor, and the
servant girl, to steal his own I O U and what ready money he could find on
him; 'it will come in handy for my pleasures in the fashionable world and for
my career in the future.' After murdering them, he puts pillows under the
head of each of his victims; he goes away. Next, a young hero 'decorated
for bravery' kills the mother of his chief and benefactor, like a highway-
man, and to urge his companions to join him he asserts that 'she loves him
like a son, and so will follow all his directions and take no precautions.'
Granted that he is a monster, yet I dare not say in these days that he is
unique. Another man will not commit the murder, but will feel and think
like him, and is as dishonourable in soul. In silence, alone with his conscience, he asks himself perhaps, 'What is honour, and isn't the condemnation of bloodshed a prejudice?'

"Perhaps people will cry out against me that I am morbid, hysterical,
that it is a monstrous slander, that I am exaggerating. Let them say so—
and heavens! I should be the first to rejoice if it were so! Oh, don't believe
me, think of me as morbid, but remember my words; if only a tenth, if only
a twentieth part of what I say is true—even so it's awful! Look how our
young people commit suicide, without asking themselves Hamlet's question what there is beyond,* without a sign of such a question, as though all
that relates to the soul and to what awaits us beyond the grave had long
been erased in their minds and buried under the sands. Look at our vice, at
our profligates. Fyodor Pavlovitch, the luckless victim in the present case,
was almost an innocent babe compared with many of them. And yet we all
knew him, 'he lived among us!'† . . .

"Yes, one day perhaps the leading intellects of Russia and of Europe
will study the psychology of Russian crime, for the subject is worth it. But
this study will come later, at leisure, when all the tragic topsy-turvy-dom of
to-day is further behind us, so that it's possible to examine it with more insight and more impartiality than I can do. Now we are either horrified or
pretend to be horrified, though we really gloat over the spectacle, and love
strong and eccentric sensations which tickle our cynical, pampered idleness. Or, like little children, we brush the dreadful ghosts away and hide

---

*Reference, one among many in this novel, to Shakespeare's *Hamlet* (specifically to Hamlet's "To be, or not to be" soliloquy in act 3, scene 1).
†First line of a poem by Pushkin on the Polish poet Adam Bernard Mickiewicz
(1798–1855).

our heads in the pillow so as to return to our sports and merriment as soon as they have vanished. But we must one day begin life in sober earnest, we must look at ourselves as a society; it's time we tried to grasp something of our social position, or at least to make a beginning in that direction.

"A great writer of the last epoch, comparing Russia to a swift troika galloping to an unknown goal, exclaims, 'Oh, troika, birdlike troika, who invented thee!'* and adds, in proud ecstasy, that all the peoples of the world stand aside respectfully to make way for the recklessly galloping troika to pass. That may be, they may stand aside, respectfully or no, but in my poor opinion the great writer ended his book in this way either in an access of childish and naïve optimism, or simply in fear of the censorship of the day. For if the troika were drawn by his heroes, Sobakevitch, Nozdryov, Tchitchikov, it could reach no rational goal, whoever might be driving it. And those were the heroes of an older generation, ours are worse specimens still. . . ."

At this point Ippolit Kirillovitch's speech was interrupted by applause. The liberal significance of this simile was appreciated. The applause was, it's true, of brief duration, so that the President did not think it necessary to caution the public, and only looked severely in the direction of the offenders. But Ippolit Kirillovitch was encouraged; he had never been applauded before! He had been all his life unable to get a hearing, and now he suddenly had an opportunity of securing the ear of all Russia.

"What, after all, is this Karamazov family, which has gained such an unenviable notoriety throughout Russia?" he continued. "Perhaps I am exaggerating, but it seems to me that certain fundamental features of the educated class of to-day are reflected in this family picture—only, of course, in miniature, 'like the sun in a drop of water.'† Think of that unhappy, vicious, unbridled old man, who has met with such a melancholy end, the head of a family! Beginning life of noble birth, but in a poor dependent position, through an unexpected marriage he came into a small fortune. A petty knave, a toady and buffoon, of fairly good, though undeveloped, intelligence, he was, above all, a moneylender, who grew bolder with growing prosperity. His abject and servile characteristics disappeared, his malicious and sarcastic cynicism was all that remained. On the spiritual side he was undeveloped, while his vitality was excessive. He saw nothing in life but sensual pleasure, and he brought his children up to be the same. He had no feelings for his duties as a father. He ridiculed those duties. He left his little children to the servants, and was glad to be rid of them, forgot about them completely. The old man's maxim was *après moi le deluge.*‡ He was an example of everything that is opposed to civic duty, of the most complete and malignant individualism. 'The world may burn for aught I care, so long as I am all right,' and he was all right; he was content, he was eager to

---

*This phrase appears at the conclusion of Gogol's *Dead Souls*.

†Quotation from Russian poet Gavrila Derzhavin's ode "God" (1784).

‡After me, the flood (French); attributed to Louis XV of France (1710–1774).

go on living in the same way for another twenty or thirty years. He swindled his own son and spent his money, his maternal inheritance, on trying to get his mistress from him. No, I don't intend to leave the prisoner's defence altogether to my talented colleague from Petersburg. I will speak the truth myself, I can well understand what resentment he had heaped up in his son's heart against him.

"But enough, enough of that unhappy old man; he has paid the penalty. Let us remember, however, that he was a father, and one of the typical fathers of to-day. Am I unjust, indeed, in saying that he is typical of many modern fathers? Alas! many of them only differ in not openly professing such cynicism, for they are better educated, more cultured, but their philosophy is essentially the same as his. Perhaps I am a pessimist, but you have agreed to forgive me. Let us agree beforehand, you need not believe me, but let me speak. Let me say what I have to say, and remember something of my words.

"Now for the children of this father, this head of a family. One of them is the prisoner before us, all the rest of my speech will deal with him. Of the other two I will speak only cursorily.

"The elder is one of those modern young men of brilliant education and vigorous intellect, who has lost all faith in everything. He has denied and rejected much already, like his father. We have all heard him, he was a welcome guest in local society. He never concealed his opinions, quite the contrary in fact, which justifies me in speaking rather openly of him now, of course, not as an individual, but as a member of the Karamazov family. Another personage closely connected with the case died here by his own hand last night. I mean an afflicted idiot, formerly the servant, and possibly the illegitimate son of Fyodor Pavlovitch, Smerdyakov. At the preliminary inquiry, he told me with hysterical tears how the young Ivan Karamazov had horrified him by his spiritual audacity. 'Everything in the world is lawful according to him, and nothing must be forbidden in the future—that is what he always taught me.' I believe that idiot was driven out of his mind by this theory, though, of course, the epileptic attacks from which he suffered, and this terrible catastrophe, have helped to unhinge his faculties. But he dropped one very interesting observation, which would have done credit to a more intelligent observer, and that is, indeed, why I've mentioned it, 'If there is one of the sons that is like Fyodor Pavlovitch in character, it is Ivan Fyodorovitch.'

"With that remark I conclude my sketch of his character, feeling it indelicate to continue further. Oh, I don't want to draw any further conclusions and croak like a raven over the young man's future. We've seen to-day in this court that there are still good impulses in his young heart, that family feeling has not been destroyed in him by lack of faith and cynicism, which has come to him rather by inheritance than by the exercise of independent thought.

"Then the third son. Oh, he is a devout and modest youth, who does not share his elder brother's gloomy and destructive theory of life. He has sought to cling to the 'ideas of the people,' or to what goes by that name in some circles of our intellectual classes. He clung to the monastery, and was within an ace of becoming a monk. He seems to me to have betrayed unconsciously, and so early, that timid despair which leads so many in our unhappy society, who dread cynicism and its corrupting influences, and mistakenly attribute all the mischief to European enlightenment, to return to their 'native soil,' as they say, to the bosom, so to speak, of their mother earth, like frightened children, yearning to fall asleep on the withered bosom of their decrepit mother, and to sleep there for ever, only to escape the horrors that terrify them.

"For my part I wish the excellent and gifted young man every success; I trust that his youthful idealism and impulse towards the ideas of the people may never degenerate, as often happens, on the moral side into gloomy mysticism, and on the political into blind Chauvinism—two elements which are even a greater menace to Russia than the premature decay, due to misunderstanding and gratuitous adoption of European ideas, from which his elder brother is suffering."

Two or three people clapped their hands at the mention of Chauvinism and mysticism. Ippolit Kirillovitch had been, indeed, carried away by his own eloquence. All this had little to do with the case in hand, to say nothing of its being somewhat vague, but the sickly and consumptive man was overcome by the desire to express himself once in his life. People said afterwards that he was actuated by unworthy motives in his criticism of Ivan, because the latter had on one or two occasions got the better of him in argument, and Ippolit Kirillovitch remembering it, tried now to take his revenge. But I don't know whether it was true. All this was only introductory, however, and the speech passed to more direct consideration of the case.

"But to return to the eldest son," Ippolit Kirillovitch went on. "He is the prisoner before us. We have his life and his actions, too, before us; the fatal day has come and all has been brought to the surface. While his brothers seem to stand for 'Europeanism' and 'the principles of the people,' he seems to represent Russia *as she is*. Oh, not all Russia, not all! God preserve us, if it were! Yet, here we have her, our mother Russia, the very scent and sound of her. Oh, he is spontaneous, he is a marvellous mingling of good and evil, he is a lover of culture and Schiller, yet he brawls in taverns and plucks out the beards of his boon companions. Oh, he, too, can be good and noble, but only when all goes well with him. What is more, he can be carried off his feet, positively carried off his feet by noble ideals, but only if they come of themselves, if they fall from heaven for him, if they need not be paid for. He dislikes paying for anything, but is very fond of receiving, and that's so with him in everything. Oh, give him every possible good in life (he couldn't be content with less), and put no obstacle in his way, and he will show that he, too, can be noble. He is not greedy, no, but he must have money, a great deal of money, and you will see how generously, with what scorn of filthy lucre, he will fling it all away in the reckless dissipation of one night. But if he has not money, he will show what he is ready to do to get it when he is in great need of it. But all this later, let us take events in their chronological order.

"First, we have before us a poor abandoned child, running about the back yard 'without boots on his feet,' as our worthy and esteemed fellow citizen, of foreign origin, alas! expressed it just now. I repeat it again, I yield to no one the defence of the criminal. I am here to accuse him, but to defend him also. Yes, I, too, am human; I, too, can weigh the influence of home and childhood on the character. But the boy grows up and becomes an officer; for a duel and other reckless conduct he is exiled to one of the remote frontier towns of Russia. There he led a wild life as an officer. And, of course, he needed money, money before all things, and so after prolonged disputes he came to a settlement with his father, and the last six thousand was sent him. A letter is in existence in which he practically gives up his claim to the rest and settles his conflict with his father over the inheritance on the payment of this six thousand.

"Then came his meeting with a young girl of lofty character and brilliant education. Oh, I do not venture to repeat the details; you have only just heard them. Honour, self-sacrifice were shown there, and I will be silent. The figure of the young officer, frivolous and profligate, doing homage to true nobility and a lofty ideal, was shown in a very sympathetic light before us. But the other side of the medal was unexpectedly turned to us immediately after in this very court. Again I will not venture to conjecture why it happened so, but there were causes. The same lady, bathed in tears of long-concealed indignation, alleged that he, he of all men, had despised her for her action, which, though incautious, reckless perhaps, was still dictated by lofty and generous motives. He, he, the girl's betrothed, looked at her with that smile of mockery, which was more insufferable from him than from any one. And knowing that he had already deceived her (he had deceived her, believing that she was bound to endure everything from him, even treachery), she intentionally offered him three thousand roubles, and clearly, too clearly, let him understand that she was offering him money to deceive her. 'Well, will you take it or not, are you so lost to shame?' was the dumb question in her scrutinising eyes. He looked at her, saw clearly what was in her mind (he's admitted here before you that he understood it all), appropriated that three thousand unconditionally, and squandered it in two days with the new object of his affections.

"What are we to believe then? The first legend of the young officer sacrificing his last farthing in a noble impulse of generosity and doing reverence to virtue, or this other revolting picture? As a rule, between two extremes one has to find the mean, but in the present case this is not true. The probability is that in the first case he was genuinely noble, and in the second as genuinely base. And why? Because he was of the broad Karamazov character—that's just what I am leading up to—capable of combining the most incongruous contradictions, and capable of the greatest heights and of the greatest depths. Remember the brilliant remark made by a young observer who has seen the Karamazov family at close quarters—Mr. Rakitin: 'The sense of their own degradation is as essential to these reckless, unbridled natures as the sense of their lofty generosity.' And that's true, they need continually this unnatural mixture. Two extremes at the same moment, or they are miserable and dissatisfied and their existence is incomplete. They are wide, wide as mother Russia; they include everything and put up with everything.

"By the way, gentlemen of the jury, we've just touched upon that three thousand roubles, and I will venture to anticipate things a little. Can you conceive that a man like that, on receiving that sum and in such a way, at the price of such shame, such disgrace, such utter degradation, could have been capable that very day of setting apart half that sum, that very day, and sewing it up in a little bag, and would have had the firmness of character to carry it about with him for a whole month afterwards, in spite of every temptation and his extreme need of it! Neither in drunken debauchery in taverns, nor when he was flying into the country, trying to get from God knows whom, the money so essential to him to remove the object of his affections from being tempted by his father, did he bring himself to touch that little bag! Why, if only to avoid abandoning his mistress to the rival of whom he was so jealous, he would have been certain to have opened that bag and to have stayed at home to keep watch over her, and to await the moment when she would say to him at last 'I am yours,' and to fly with her far from their fatal surroundings.

"But no, he did not touch his talisman, and what is the reason he gives for it? The chief reason, as I have just said, was that when she would say 'I am yours, take me where you will,' he might have the wherewithal to take her. But that first reason, in the prisoner's own words, was of little weight beside the second. While I have that money on me, he said, I am a scoundrel, not a thief, for I can always go to my insulted betrothed, and, laying down half the sum I have fraudulently appropriated, I can always say to her, 'You see I've squandered half your money, and shown I am a weak and immoral man, and, if you like, a scoundrel' (I use the prisoner's own expressions), 'but though I am a scoundrel, I am not a thief, for if I had been a thief, I shouldn't have brought you back this half of the money, but should have taken it as I did the other half!' A marvellous explanation! This frantic, but weak man, who could not resist the temptation of accepting the three thousand roubles at the price of such disgrace, this very man suddenly develops the most stoical firmness, and carries about a thousand roubles without daring to touch it. Does that fit in at all with the character we have analysed? No, and I venture to tell you how the real Dmitri Karamazov would have behaved in such circumstances, if he really had brought himself to put away the money.

"At the first temptation—for instance, to entertain the woman with whom he had already squandered half the money—he would have unpicked his little bag and have taken out some hundred roubles, for why should he have taken back precisely half the money, that is, fifteen hundred roubles; why not fourteen hundred? He could just as well have said then that he was not a thief, because he brought back fourteen hundred roubles. Then another time he would have unpicked it again and taken out another hundred, and then a third, and then a fourth, and before the end of the month he would have taken the last note but one, feeling that if he took back only a hundred it would answer the purpose, for a thief would have stolen it all. And then he would have looked at this last note, and have said to himself, 'It's really not worth while to give back one hundred; let's spend that, too!' That's how the real Dmitri Karamazov, as we know him, would have behaved. One cannot imagine anything more incongruous with the actual fact than this legend of the little bag. Nothing could be more inconceivable. But we shall return to that later."

After touching upon what had come out in the proceedings concerning the financial relations of father and son, and arguing again and again that it was utterly impossible, from the facts known, to determine which was in the wrong, Ippolit Kirillovitch passed to the evidence of the medical experts in reference to Mitya's fixed idea about the three thousand owing him.

7

AN HISTORICAL SURVEY

THE medical experts have striven to convince us that the prisoner is out of his mind and, in fact, a maniac. I maintain that he is in his right mind, and that if he had not been, he would have behaved more cleverly. As for his being a maniac, that I would agree with, but only in one point, that is, his fixed idea about the three thousand. Yet I think one might find a much simpler cause than his tendency to insanity. For my part I agree thoroughly with the young doctor who maintained that the prisoner's mental faculties have always been normal, and that he has only been irritable and exasperated. The object of the prisoner's continual and violent anger was not the sum itself; there was a special motive at the bottom of it. That motive is jealousy!"

Here Ippolit Kirillovitch described at length the prisoner's fatal passion for Grushenka. He began from the moment when the prisoner went to the "young person's" lodgings "to beat her"—"I use his own expression," the prosecutor explained—"but instead of beating her, he remained there, at her feet. That was the beginning of the passion. At the same time the prisoner's father was captivated by the same young person—a strange and fatal coincidence, for they both lost their hearts to her simultaneously, though both had known her before. And she inspired in both of them the most violent, characteristically Karamazov passion. We have her own confession: 'I was laughing at both of them.' Yes, the sudden desire to make a jest of them came over her, and she conquered both of them at once. The old man, who worshipped money, at once set aside three thousand roubles as a reward for one visit from her, but soon after that, he would have been happy to lay his property and his name at her feet, if only she would become his lawful wife. We have good evidence of this. As for the prisoner, the tragedy of his fate is evident; it is before us. But such was the young person's 'game.' The enchantress gave the unhappy young man no hope until the last moment, when he knelt before her, stretching out hands that were already stained with the blood of his father and rival. It was in that position that he was arrested. 'Send me to Siberia with him, I have brought him to this, I am most to blame,' the woman herself cried, in genuine remorse at the moment of his arrest.

"The talented young man, to whom I have referred already, Mr. Rakitin, characterised this heroine in brief and impressive terms: 'She was disillusioned early in life, deceived and ruined by a betrothed, who seduced and abandoned her. She was left in poverty, cursed by her respectable family, and taken under the protection of a wealthy old man, whom she still, however, considers as her benefactor. There was perhaps much that was good in her young heart, but it was embittered too early. She became prudent and saved money. She grew sarcastic and resentful against society.' After this sketch of her character it may well be understood that she might laugh at both of them simply from mischief, from malice.

"After a month of hopeless love and moral degradation, during which he betrayed his betrothed and appropriated money entrusted to his honour, the prisoner was driven almost to frenzy, almost to madness by continual jealousy—and of whom? His father! And the worst of it was that the crazy old man was alluring and enticing the object of his affection by means of that very three thousand roubles, which the son looked upon as his own property, part of his inheritance from his mother, of which his father was cheating him. Yes, I admit it was hard to bear! It might well drive a man to madness. It was not the money, but the fact that this money was used with such revolting cynicism to ruin his happiness!"

Then the prosecutor went on to describe how the idea of murdering his father had entered the prisoner's head, and illustrated his theory with facts.

"At first he only talked about it in taverns—he was talking about it all that month. Ah, he likes being always surrounded with company, and he likes to tell his companions everything, even his most diabolical and dangerous ideas; he likes to share every thought with others, and expects, for some reason, that those he confides in will meet him with perfect sympathy, enter into all his troubles and anxieties, take his part and not oppose him in anything. If not, he flies into a rage and smashes up everything in the tavern. [Then followed the anecdote about Captain Snegiryov.] Those who heard the prisoner began to think at last that he might mean more than threats, and that such a frenzy might turn threats into actions."

Here the prosecutor described the meeting of the family at the monastery, the conversations with Alyosha, and the horrible scene of violence when the prisoner had rushed into his father's house just after dinner.

"I cannot positively assert," the prosecutor continued, "that the prisoner fully intended to murder his father before that incident. Yet the idea had several times presented itself to him, and he had deliberated on it—for that we have facts, witnesses, and his own words. I confess, gentlemen of the jury," he added, "that till to-day I have been uncertain whether to attribute to the prisoner conscious premeditation. I was firmly convinced that he had pictured the fatal moment beforehand, but had only pictured it, contemplating it as a possibility. He had not definitely considered when and how he might commit the crime.

"But I was only uncertain till to-day, till that fatal document was presented to the court just now. You yourselves heard that young lady's exclamation, 'it is the plan, the programme of the murder!' That is how she defined that miserable, drunken letter of the unhappy prisoner. And, in fact, from that letter we see that the whole fact of the murder was premeditated. It was written two days before, and so we know now for a fact that, forty-eight hours before the perpetration of his terrible design, the prisoner swore that, if he could not get money next day, he would murder his father in order to take the envelope with the notes from under his pillow, as soon as Ivan had left. 'As soon as Ivan had gone away'—you hear that; so he had thought everything out, weighing every circumstance, and he carried it all out just as he had written it. The proof of premeditation is conclusive; the crime must have been committed for the sake of the money, that is stated clearly, that is written and signed. The prisoner does not deny his signature.

"I shall be told he was drunk when he wrote it. But that does not diminish the value of the letter, quite the contrary; he wrote when drunk what he had planned when sober. Had he not planned it when sober, he would not have written it when drunk. I shall be asked: Then why did he talk about it in taverns? A man who premeditates such a crime is silent and keeps it to himself. Yes, but he talked about it before he had formed a plan, when he had only the desire, only the impulse to it. Afterwards he talked less about it. On the evening he wrote that letter at the Metropolis tavern, contrary to his custom he was silent, though he had been drinking. He did not play billiards, he sat in a corner, talked to no one. He did indeed turn a shopman out of his seat, but that was done almost unconsciously, because he could never enter a tavern without making a disturbance. It is true that after he had taken the final decision, he must have felt apprehensive that he had talked too much about his design beforehand, and that this might lead to his arrest and prosecution afterwards. But there was nothing for it; he could not take his words back, but his luck had served him before, it would serve him again. He believed in his star, you know! I must confess, too, that he did a great deal to avoid the fatal catastrophe. 'To-morrow I shall try and borrow the money from every one,' as he writes in his peculiar language, 'and if they won't give it to me, there will be bloodshed.'"

Here Ippolit Kirillovitch passed to a detailed description of all Mitya's efforts to borrow the money. He described his visit to Samsonov, his journey to Lyagavy. "Harassed, jeered at, hungry, after selling his watch to pay

for the journey (though he tells us he had fifteen hundred roubles on him—
a likely story), tortured by jealousy at having left the object of his affections in the town, suspecting that she would go to Fyodor Pavlovitch in his
absence, he returned at last to the town, to find, to his joy, that she had not
been near his father. He accompanied her himself to her protector. (Strange
to say, he doesn't seem to have been jealous of Samsonov, which is psychologically interesting.) Then he hastens back to his ambush in the back
gardens, and there learns that Smerdyakov is in a fit, that the other servant
is ill—the coast is clear and he knows the 'signals'—what a temptation! Still
he resists it; he goes off to a lady who has for some time been residing in
the town, and who is highly esteemed among us, Madame Hohlakov. That
lady, who had long watched his career with compassion, gave him the most
judicious advice, to give up his dissipated life, his unseemly love-affair, the
waste of his youth and vigour in pothouse debauchery, and to set off to
Siberia to the gold-mines: 'that would be an outlet for your turbulent energies, your romantic character, your thirst for adventure.' "

After describing the result of this conversation and the moment when
the prisoner learnt that Grushenka had not remained at Samsonov's, the
sudden frenzy of the luckless man, worn out with jealousy and nervous exhaustion, at the thought that she had deceived him and was now with his
father, Ippolit Kirillovitch concluded by dwelling upon the fatal influence
of chance. "Had the maid told him that her mistress was at Mokroe with
her former lover, nothing would have happened. But she lost her head, she
could only swear and protest her ignorance, and if the prisoner did not kill
her on the spot, it was only because he flew in pursuit of his false mistress."

"But note, frantic as he was, he took with him a brass pestle. Why that?
Why not some other weapon? But since he had been contemplating his
plan and preparing himself for it for a whole month, he would snatch up
anything like a weapon that caught his eye. He had realised for a month
past that any object of the kind would serve as a weapon, so he instantly,
without hesitation, recognised that it would serve his purpose. So it was by
no means unconsciously, by no means involuntarily, that he snatched up
that fatal pestle. And then we find him in his father's garden—the coast is
clear, there are no witnesses, darkness and jealousy. The suspicion that she
was there, with him, with his rival, in his arms, and perhaps laughing at him
at that moment—took his breath away. And it was not mere suspicion, the
deception was open, obvious. She must be there, in that lighted room,
she must be behind the screen; and the unhappy man would have us believe that he stole up to the window, peeped respectfully in, and discreetly
withdrew, for fear something terrible and immoral should happen. And he
tries to persuade us of that, us, who understand his character, who know
his state of mind at the moment, and that he knew the signals by which he
could at once enter the house." At this point Ippolit Kirillovitch broke off
to discuss exhaustively the suspected connection of Smerdyakov with the
murder. He did this very circumstantially, and every one realised that, although he professed to despise that suspicion, he thought the subject of
great importance.

8

A TREATISE ON SMERDYAKOV

To begin with, what was the source of this suspicion?" (Ippolit Kirillovitch began). "The first person who cried out that Smerdyakov had committed the murder was the prisoner himself at the moment of his arrest, yet from that time to this he had not brought forward a single fact to confirm the charge, nor the faintest suggestion of a fact. The charge is confirmed by three persons only—the two brothers of the prisoner and Madame Svyetlov. The elder of these brothers expressed his suspicions only to-day, when he was undoubtedly suffering from brain fever. But we know that for the last two months he has completely shared our conviction of his brother's guilt and did not attempt to combat that idea. But of that later. The younger brother has admitted that he has not the slightest fact to support his notion of Smerdyakov's guilt, and has only been led to that conclusion from the prisoner's own words and the expression of his face. Yes, that astounding piece of evidence has been brought forward twice to-day by him. Madame Svyetlov was even more astounding. 'What the prisoner tells you, you must believe; he is not a man to tell a lie.' That is all the evidence against Smerdyakov produced by these three persons, who are all deeply concerned in the prisoner's fate. And yet the theory of Smerdyakov's guilt has been noised about, has been and is still maintained. Is it credible? Is it conceivable?"

Here Ippolit Kirillovitch thought it necessary to describe the personality of Smerdyakov, "who had cut short his life in a fit of insanity." He depicted him as a man of weak intellect, with a smattering of education, who had been thrown off his balance by philosophical ideas above his level and certain modern theories of duty, which he learnt in practice from the reckless life of his master, who was also perhaps his father—Fyodor Pavlovitch; and, theoretically, from various strange philosophical conversations with his master's elder son, Ivan Fyodorovitch, who readily indulged in this diversion, probably feeling dull or wishing to amuse himself at the valet's expense. "He spoke to me himself of his spiritual condition during the last few days at his father's house," Ippolit Kirillovitch explained; "but others too have borne witness to it—the prisoner himself, his brother, and the servant Grigory—that is, all who knew him well."

"Moreover, Smerdyakov, whose health was shaken by his attacks of epilepsy, had not the courage of a chicken. 'He fell at my feet and kissed them,' the prisoner himself has told us, before he realised how damaging such a statement was to himself. 'He is an epileptic chicken,' he declared about him in his characteristic language. And the prisoner chose him for his confidant (we have his own word for it) and he frightened him into consenting at last to act as a spy for him. In that capacity he deceived his master, revealing to the prisoner the existence of the envelope with the notes in it and the signals by means of which he could get into the house. How could he help telling him, indeed? 'He would have killed me, I could see that he would have killed me,' he said at the inquiry, trembling and shaking even before us, though his tormentor was by that time arrested and could do him no harm. 'He suspected me at every instant. In fear and trembling I hastened to tell him every secret to pacify him, that he might see that I had not deceived him and let me off alive.' Those are his own words. I wrote them down and I remember them. 'When he began shouting at me, I would fall on my knees.'

"He was naturally very honest and enjoyed the complete confidence of his master, ever since he had restored him some money he had lost. So it may be supposed that the poor fellow suffered pangs of remorse at having deceived his master, whom he loved as his benefactor. Persons severely afflicted with epilepsy are, so the most skilful doctor tells us, always prone to continual and morbid self-reproach. They worry over their 'wickedness,' they are tormented by pangs of conscience, often entirely without cause; they exaggerate and often invent all sorts of faults and crimes. And here we have a man of that type who had really been driven to wrongdoing by terror and intimidation.

"He had, besides, a strong presentiment that something terrible would be the outcome of the situation that was developing before his eyes. When Ivan Fyodorovitch was leaving for Moscow, just before the catastrophe, Smerdyakov besought him to remain, though he was too timid to tell him plainly what he feared. He confined himself to hints, but his hints were not understood.

"It must be observed that he looked on Ivan Fyodorovitch as a protector, whose presence in the house was a guarantee that no harm would come to pass. Remember the phrase in Dmitri Karamazov's drunken letter, 'I shall kill the old man, if only Ivan goes away.' So Ivan Fyodorovitch's presence seemed to every one a guarantee of peace and order in the house.

"But he went away, and within an hour of his young master's departure Smerdyakov was taken with an epileptic fit. But that's perfectly intelligible. Here I must mention that Smerdyakov, oppressed by terror and despair of a sort, had felt during those last few days that one of the fits from which he had suffered before at moments of strain, might be coming upon him again. The day and hour of such an attack cannot, of course, be foreseen, but every epileptic can feel beforehand that he is likely to have one. So the doctors tell us. And so, as soon as Ivan Fyodorovitch had driven out of the yard, Smerdyakov, depressed by his lonely and unprotected position, went to the cellar. He went down the stairs wondering if he would have a fit or not, and what if it were to come upon him at once. And that very apprehension, that very wonder, brought on the spasm in his throat that always precedes such attacks, and he fell unconscious into the cellar. And in this perfectly natural occurrence people try to detect a suspicion, a hint that he was shamming an attack *on purpose*. But, if it were on purpose, the question arises at once, what was his motive? What was he reckoning on? What was he aiming at? I say nothing about medicine: science, I am told, may go astray: the doctors were not able to discriminate between the counterfeit and the real. That may be so, but answer me one question: what motive had he for such a counterfeit? Could he, had he been plotting the murder, have desired to attract the attention of the household by having a fit just before?

"You see, gentlemen of the jury, on the night of the murder, there were five persons in Fyodor Pavlovitch's—Fyodor Pavlovitch himself (but he did not kill himself, that's evident); then his servant, Grigory, but he was almost killed himself; the third person was Grigory's wife, Marfa Ignatyevna, but it would be simply shameful to imagine her murdering her master. Two persons are left—the prisoner and Smerdyakov. But, if we are to believe the prisoner's statement that he is not the murderer, then Smerdyakov must have been, for there is no other alternative, no one else can be found. That is what accounts for the artful, astounding accusation against the unhappy idiot who committed suicide yesterday. Had a shadow of suspicion rested on any one else, had there been any sixth person, I am persuaded that even the prisoner would have been ashamed to accuse Smerdyakov, and would have accused that sixth person, for to charge Smerdyakov with that murder is perfectly absurd.

"Gentlemen, let us lay aside psychology, let us lay aside medicine, let us even lay aside logic, let us turn only to the facts and see what the facts tell us. If Smerdyakov killed him, how did he do it? Alone or with the assistance of the prisoner? Let us consider the first alternative—that he did it alone. If he had killed him it must have been with some object, for some advantage to himself. But not having a shadow of the motive that the prisoner had for the murder—hatred, jealousy, and so on—Smerdyakov could only have murdered him for the sake of gain, in order to appropriate the three thousand roubles he had seen his master put in the envelope. And yet he tells another person—and a person most closely interested, that is, the prisoner—everything about the money and the signals, where the envelope lay, what was written on it, what it was tied up with, and, above all, told him of those signals by which he could enter the house. Did he do this simply to betray himself, or to invite to the same enterprise one who would be anxious to get that envelope for himself? 'Yes,' I shall be told, 'but he betrayed it from fear.' But how do you explain this? A man who could conceive such an audacious, savage act, and carry it out, tells facts which are known to no one else in the world, and which, if he held his tongue, no one would ever have guessed!

"No, however cowardly he might be, if he had plotted such a crime, nothing would have induced him to tell any one about the envelope and the signals, for that was as good as betraying himself beforehand. He would have invented something, he would have told some lie if he had been forced to give information, but he would have been silent about that.

For, on the other hand, if he had said nothing about the money but had committed the murder and stolen the money, no one in the world could have charged him with murder for the sake of robbery, since no one but he had seen the money, no one but he knew of its existence in the house. Even if he had been accused of the murder, it could only have been thought that he had committed it from some other motive. But since no one had observed any such motive in him beforehand, and every one saw, on the contrary, that his master was fond of him and honoured him with his confidence, he would, of course, have been the last to be suspected. People would have suspected first the man who had a motive, a man who had himself declared he had such motives, who had made no secret of it; they would, in fact, have suspected the son of the murdered man, Dmitri Fyodorovitch. Had Smerdyakov killed and robbed him, and the son been accused of it, that would, of course, have suited Smerdyakov. Yet are we to believe that, though plotting the murder, he told that son, Dmitri, about the money, the envelope, and the signals? Is that logical? Is that clear?

"When the day of the murder planned by Smerdyakov came, we have him falling downstairs in a *feigned* fit—with what object? In the first place that Grigory, who had been intending to take his medicine, might put it off and remain on guard, seeing there was no one to look after the house, and, in the second place, I suppose, that his master seeing that there was no one to guard him, and in terror of a visit from his son, might redouble his vigilance and precaution. And, most of all, I suppose that he, Smerdyakov, disabled by the fit, might be carried from the kitchen, where he always slept, apart from all the rest, and where he could go in and out as he liked, to Grigory's room at the other end of the lodge, where he was always put, shut off by a screen three paces from their own bed. This was the immemorial custom established by his master and the kind-hearted Marfa Ignatyevna, whenever he had a fit. There, lying behind the screen, he would most likely, to keep up the sham, have begun groaning, and so keeping them awake all night (as Grigory and his wife testified). And all this, we are to believe, that he might more conveniently get up and murder his master!

"But I shall be told that he shammed illness on purpose that he might not be suspected and that he told the prisoner of the money and the signals to tempt him to commit the murder, and when he had murdered him and had gone away with the money making a noise, most likely, and waking people, Smerdyakov got up, am I to believe, and went in—what for? To murder his master a second time and carry off the money that had already been stolen? Gentlemen, are you laughing? I am ashamed to put forward such suggestions, but, incredible as it seems, that's just what the prisoner alleges. When he had left the house, had knocked Grigory down and raised an alarm, he tells us Smerdyakov got up, went in and murdered his master and stole the money! I won't press the point that Smerdyakov could hardly have reckoned on this beforehand, and have foreseen that the furious and exasperated son would simply come to peep in respectfully, though he knew the signals, and beat a retreat, leaving Smerdyakov his booty. Gentlemen of the jury, I put this question to you in earnest; when was the moment when Smerdyakov could have committed his crime? Name that moment, or you can't accuse him.

"But, perhaps, the fit was a real one, the sick man suddenly recovered, heard a shout, and went out. Well—what then? He looked about him and said, 'Why not go and kill the master?' And how did he know what had happened, since he had been lying unconscious till that moment? But there's a limit to these flights of fancy.

" 'Quite so,' some astute people will tell me, 'but what if they were in agreement? What if they murdered him together and shared the money— what then?' A weighty question, truly! And the facts to confirm it are astounding. One commits the murder and takes all the trouble while his accomplice lies on one side shamming a fit, apparently to arouse suspicion in every one, alarm in his master and alarm in Grigory. It would be interesting to know what motives could have induced the two accomplices to form such an insane plan.

"But perhaps it was not a case of active complicity on Smerdyakov's part, but only a passive acquiescence; perhaps Smerdyakov was intimidated and agreed not to prevent the murder, and foreseeing that he would be blamed for letting his master be murdered, without screaming for help or resisting, he may have obtained permission from Dmitri Karamazov to get out of the way by shamming a fit—'you may murder him as you like; it's nothing to me.' But as this attack of Smerdyakov's was bound to throw the household into confusion, Dmitri Karamazov could never have agreed to such a plan. I will waive that point however. Supposing that he did agree, it would still follow that Dmitri Karamazov is the murderer and the instigator, and Smerdyakov is only a passive accomplice, and not even an accomplice, but merely acquiesced against his will through terror.

"But what do we see? As soon as he is arrested the prisoner instantly throws all the blame on Smerdyakov, not accusing him of being his accomplice, but of being himself the murderer. 'He did it alone,' he says. 'He murdered and robbed him. It was the work of his hands.' Strange sort of accomplices who begin to accuse one another at once! And think of the risk for Karamazov. After committing the murder while his accomplice lay in bed, he throws the blame on the invalid, who might well have resented it and in self-preservation might well have confessed the truth. For he might well have seen that the court would at once judge how far he was responsible, and so he might well have reckoned that if he were punished it would be far less severely than the real murderer. But in that case he would have been certain to make a confession, yet he has not done so. Smerdyakov never hinted at their complicity, though the actual murderer persisted in accusing him and declaring that he had committed the crime alone.

"What's more, Smerdyakov at the inquiry volunteered the statement that it was *he* who had told the prisoner of the envelope of notes and of the signals, and that, but for him, he would have known nothing about them. If he had really been a guilty accomplice, would he so readily have made this statement at the inquiry? On the contrary, he would have tried to conceal it, to distort the facts or minimise them. But he was far from distorting or minimising them. No one but an innocent man, who had no fear of being charged with complicity, could have acted as he did. And in a fit of melancholy arising from his disease and this catastrophe he hanged himself yesterday. He left a note written in his peculiar language, 'I destroy myself of my own will and inclination so as to throw no blame on any one.' What would it have cost him to add: 'I am the murderer, not Karamazov'? But that he did not add. Did his conscience lead him to suicide and not to avowing his guilt?

"And what followed? Notes for three thousand roubles were brought into the court just now, and we were told that they were the same that lay in the envelope now on the table before us, and that the witness had received them from Smerdyakov the day before. But I need not recall the painful scene, though I will make one or two comments, selecting such trivial ones as might not be obvious at first sight to every one, and so may be overlooked. In the first place, Smerdyakov must have given back the money and hanged himself yesterday from remorse. And only yesterday he confessed his guilt to Ivan Karamazov, as the latter informs us. If it were not so, indeed, why should Ivan Fyodorovitch have kept silence till now? And so, if he has confessed, then why, I ask again, did he not avow the whole truth in the last letter he left behind, knowing that the innocent prisoner had to face this terrible ordeal the next day?

"The money alone is no proof. A week ago, quite by chance, the fact came to the knowledge of myself and two other persons in this court that Ivan Fyodorovitch had sent two five per cent. coupons of five thousand each—that is, ten thousand in all—to the chief town of the province to be changed. I only mention this to point out that any one may have money, and that it can't be proved that these notes are the same as were in Fyodor Pavlovitch's envelope.

"Ivan Karamazov, after receiving yesterday a communication of such importance from the real murderer, did not stir. Why didn't he report it at once? Why did he put it all off till morning? I think I have a right to conjecture why. His health had been giving way for a week past: he had admitted to a doctor and to his most intimate friends that he was suffering from hallucinations and seeing phantoms of the dead: he was on the eve of the attack of brain fever by which he has been stricken down to-day. In this condition he suddenly heard of Smerdyakov's death, and at once reflected, 'The man is dead, I can throw the blame on him and save my brother. I have money. I will take a roll of notes and say that Smerdyakov gave them me before his death.' You will say that was dishonourable: it's dishonourable to slander even the dead, and even to save a brother. True, but what if he slandered him unconsciously? What if, finally unhinged by the sudden news of the valet's death, he imagined it really was so? You saw the recent scene: you have seen the witness's condition. He was standing up and was speaking, but where was his mind?

"Then followed the document, the prisoner's letter written two days before the crime and containing a complete programme of the murder.

Why, then, are we looking for any other programme? The crime was committed precisely according to this programme, and by no other than the writer of it. Yes, gentlemen of the jury, it went off without a hitch! He did not run respectfully and timidly away from his father's window, though he was firmly convinced that the object of his affections was with him. No, that is absurd and unlikely! He went in and murdered him. Most likely he killed him in anger, burning with resentment, as soon as he looked on his hated rival. But having killed him, probably with one blow of the brass pestle, and having convinced himself, after careful search, that she was not there, he did not, however, forget to put his hand under the pillow and take out the envelope, the torn cover of which lies now on the table before us.

"I mention this fact that you may note one, to my thinking, very characteristic circumstance. Had he been an experienced murderer and had he committed the murder for the sake of gain only, would he have left the torn envelope on the floor as it was found, beside the corpse? Had it been Smerdyakov, for instance, murdering his master to rob him, he would have simply carried away the envelope with him, without troubling himself to open it over his victim's corpse, for he would have known for certain that the notes were in the envelope—they had been put in and sealed up in his presence—and had he taken the envelope with him, no one would ever have known of the robbery. I ask you, gentlemen, would Smerdyakov have behaved in that way? Would he have left the envelope on the floor?

"No, this was the action of a frantic murderer, a murderer who was not a thief and had never stolen before that day, who snatched the notes from under the pillow, not like a thief stealing them, but as though seizing his own property from the thief who had stolen it. For that was the idea which had become almost an insane obsession in Dmitri Karamazov in regard to that money. And pouncing upon the envelope, which he had never seen before, he tore it open to make sure whether the money was in it, and ran away with the money in his pocket, even forgetting to consider that he had left an astounding piece of evidence against himself in that torn envelope on the floor. All because it was Karamazov, not Smerdyakov, he didn't think, he didn't reflect, and how should he? He ran away; he heard behind him the servant cry out; the old man caught him, stopped him and was felled to the ground by the brass pestle.

"The prisoner, moved by pity, leapt down to look at him. Would you believe it, he tells us that he leapt down out of pity, out of compassion, to see whether he could do anything for him. Was that a moment to show compassion? No; he jumped down simply to make certain whether the only witness of his crime were dead or alive. Any other feeling, any other motive would be unnatural. Note that he took trouble over Grigory, wiped his head with his handkerchief and, convincing himself he was dead, he ran to the house of his mistress, dazed and covered with blood. How was it he never thought that he was covered with blood and would be at once detected? But the prisoner himself assures us that he did not even notice that he was covered with blood. That may be believed, that is very possible, that always happens at such moments with criminals. On one point they will show diabolical cunning, while another will escape them altogether. But he was thinking at that moment of one thing only—where was *she?* He wanted to find out at once where she was, so he ran to her lodging and learnt an unexpected and astounding piece of news—she had gone off to Mokroe to meet her first lover."

9

THE GALLOPING TROIKA.
THE END OF THE PROSECUTOR'S SPEECH

IPPOLIT KIRILLOVITCH had chosen the historical method of exposition, beloved by all nervous orators, who find in its limitations a check on their own eager rhetoric. At this moment in his speech he went off into a dissertation on Grushenka's "first lover," and brought forward several interesting thoughts on this theme.

"Karamazov, who had been frantically jealous of every one, collapsed, so to speak, and effaced himself at once before this first lover. What makes it all the more strange is that he seems to have hardly thought of this formidable rival. But he had looked upon him as a remote danger, and Karamazov always lives in the present. Possibly he regarded him as a fiction. But his wounded heart grasped instantly that the woman had been concealing this new rival and deceiving him, because he was anything but a fiction to her, because he was the one hope of her life. Grasping this instantly, he resigned himself.

"Gentlemen of the jury, I cannot help dwelling on this unexpected trait in the prisoner's character. He suddenly evinces an irresistible desire for justice, a respect for woman and a recognition of her right to love. And all this at the very moment when he had stained his hands with his father's blood for her sake! It is true that the blood he had shed was already crying out for vengeance, for, after having ruined his soul and his life in this world, he was forced to ask himself at that same instant what he was and what he could be *now* to her, to that being, dearer to him than his own soul, in comparison with that former lover who had returned penitent, with new love, to the woman he had once betrayed, with honourable offers, with the promise of a reformed and happy life. And he, luckless man, what could he give her now, what could he offer her?

"Karamazov felt all this, knew that all ways were barred to him by his crime and that he was a criminal under sentence, and not a man with life before him! This thought crushed him. And so he instantly flew to one frantic plan, which, to a man of Karamazov's character, must have appeared the one inevitable way out of his terrible position. That way out was suicide. He ran for the pistols he had left in pledge with his friend Perhotin and on the way, as he ran, he pulled out of his pocket the money, for the sake of which he had stained his hands with his father's gore. Oh, now he needed money more than ever. Karamazov would die, Karamazov would shoot himself and it should be remembered! To be sure, he was a poet and had burnt the candle at both ends all his life. 'To her, to her! and there, oh, there I will give a feast to the whole world, such as never was before, that will be remembered and talked of long after! In the midst of shouts of wild merriment, reckless gipsy songs and dances I shall raise the glass and drink to the woman I adore and her new-found happiness! And then, on the spot, at her feet, I shall dash out my brains before her and punish myself! She will remember Mitya Karamazov sometimes, she will see how Mitya loved her, she will feel for Mitya.'

"Here we see in excess a love of effect, a romantic despair and sentimentality, and the wild recklessness of the Karamazovs. Yes, but there is something else, gentlemen of the jury, something that cries out in the soul, throbs incessantly in the mind, and poisons the heart unto death—that *something* is conscience, gentlemen of the jury, its judgment, its terrible torments! The pistol will settle everything, the pistol is the only way out! But *beyond*—I don't know whether Karamazov wondered at that moment 'What lies beyond,' and whether Karamazov could, like Hamlet, wonder 'What lies beyond.' No, gentlemen of the jury, they have their Hamlets, but we still have our Karamazovs!"

Here Ippolit Kirillovitch drew a minute picture of Mitya's preparations, the scene at Perhotin's, at the shop, with the drivers. He quoted numerous words and actions, confirmed by witnesses, and the picture made a terrible impression on the audience. The guilt of this harassed and desperate man stood out clear and convincing, when the facts were brought together.

"What need had he of precaution? Two or three times he almost confessed, hinted at it, all but spoke out. (Then followed the evidence given by witnesses.) He even cried out to the peasant who drove him, 'Do you know, you are driving a murderer!' But it was impossible for him to speak out, he had to get to Mokroe and there to finish his romance. But what was awaiting the luckless man? Almost from the first minute at Mokroe he saw that his invincible rival was perhaps by no means so invincible, that the toast to their new-found happiness was not desired and would not be acceptable. But you know the facts, gentlemen of the jury, from the preliminary inquiry. Karamazov's triumph over his rival was complete and his soul passed into quite a new phase, perhaps the most terrible phase through which his soul has passed or will pass.

"One may say with certainty, gentlemen of the jury," the prosecutor continued, "that outraged nature and the criminal heart bring their own vengeance more completely than any earthly justice. What's more, justice and punishment on earth positively alleviate the punishment of nature and are, indeed, essential to the soul of the criminal at such moments, as its salvation from despair. For I cannot imagine the horror and moral suffering of Karamazov when he learnt that she loved him, that for his sake she had rejected her first lover, that she was summoning him, Mitya, to a new life, that she was promising him happiness—and when? When everything was over for him and nothing was possible!

"By the way, I will note in parenthesis a point of importance for the light it throws on the prisoner's position at the moment. This woman, this love of his, had been till the last moment, till the very instant of his arrest, a being unattainable, passionately desired by him but unattainable. Yet why did he not shoot himself then, why did he relinquish his design and even forget where his pistol was? It was just that passionate desire for love and the hope of satisfying it that restrained him. Throughout their revels he kept close to his adored mistress, who was at the banquet with him and was more charming and fascinating to him than ever—he did not leave her side, abasing himself in his homage before her.

"His passion might well, for a moment, stifle not only the fear of arrest, but even the torments of conscience. For a moment, oh, only for a moment. I can picture the state of mind of the criminal hopelessly enslaved by these influences—first, the influence of drink, of noise and excitement, of the thud of the dance and the scream of the song, and of her, flushed with wine, singing and dancing and laughing to him! Secondly, the hope in the background that the fatal end might still be far off, that not till next morning, at least, they would come and take him. So he had a few hours and that's much, very much! In a few hours one can think of many things. I imagine that he felt something like what criminals feel when they are being taken to the scaffold. They have another long, long street to pass down and at walking pace, past thousands of people. Then there will be a turning into another street and only at the end of that street the dread place of execution! I fancy that at the beginning of the journey the condemned man, sitting on his shameful cart, must feel that he has infinite life still before him. The houses recede, the cart moves on—oh, that's nothing, it's still far to the turning into the second street and he still looks boldly to right and to left at those thousands of callously curious people with their eyes fixed on him, and he still fancies that he is just such a man as they. But now the turning comes to the next street. Oh, that's nothing, nothing, there's still a whole street before him, and however many houses have been passed, he will still think there are many left. And so to the very end, to the very scaffold.

"This I imagine is how it was with Karamazov then. 'They've not had time yet,' he must have thought, 'I may still find some way out, oh, there's still time to make some plan of defence, and now, now—she is so fascinating!'

"His soul was full of confusion and dread, but he managed however, to put aside half his money and hide it somewhere—I cannot otherwise explain the disappearance of quite half of the three thousand he had just taken from his father's pillow. He had been in Mokroe more than once before, he had caroused there for two days together already, he knew the old big house with all its passages and outbuildings. I imagine that part of the money was hidden in that house, not long before the arrest, in some crevice, under some floor, in some corner, under the roof. With what object? I shall be asked. Why, the catastrophe may take place at once, of course; he hadn't yet considered how to meet it, he hadn't the time, his head was throbbing and his heart was with *her,* but money—money was indispensable in any case! With money a man is always a man. Perhaps such foresight at such a moment may strike you as unnatural? But he assures us himself that a month before, at a critical and exciting moment, he had halved his money and sewn it up in a little bag. And though that was not true, as we shall prove directly, it shows the idea was a familiar one to Karamazov, he had contemplated it. What's more, when he declared at the inquiry that he had put fifteen hundred roubles in a bag (which never existed) he may have invented that little bag on the inspiration of the moment, because he had two hours before divided his money and hidden half of it at Mokroe till morning, in case of emergency, simply not to have it on himself. Two extremes, gentlemen of the jury, remember that Karamazov can contemplate two extremes and both at once.

"We have looked in the house, but we haven't found the money. It may still be there or it may have disappeared next day and be in the prisoner's hands now. In any case he was at her side, on his knees before her, she was lying on the bed, he had his hands stretched out to her and he had so entirely forgotten everything that he did not even hear the men coming to arrest him. He hadn't time to prepare any line of defence in his mind. He was caught unawares and confronted with his judges, the arbiters of his destiny.

"Gentlemen of the jury, there are moments in the execution of our duties when it is terrible for us to face a man, terrible on his account, too! The moments of contemplating that animal fear, when the criminal sees that all is lost, but still struggles, still means to struggle, the moments when every instinct of self-preservation rises up in him at once and he looks at you with questioning and suffering eyes, studies you, your face, your thoughts, uncertain on which side you will strike, and his distracted mind frames thousands of plans in an instant, but he is still afraid to speak, afraid of giving himself away! This purgatory of the spirit, this animal thirst for self-preservation, these humiliating moments of the human soul, are awful, and sometimes arouse horror and compassion for the criminal even in the lawyer. And this was what we all witnessed then.

"At first he was thunderstruck and in his terror dropped some very compromising phrases. 'Blood! I've deserved it!' But he quickly restrained himself. He had not prepared what he was to say, what answer he was to make, he had nothing but a bare denial ready. 'I am not guilty of my father's death.' That was his fence for the moment and behind it he hoped to throw up a barricade of some sort. His first compromising exclamations he hastened to explain by declaring that he was responsible for the death of the servant Grigory only. 'Of that bloodshed I am guilty, but who has killed my father, gentlemen, who has killed him? Who can have killed him, *if not I*?' Do you hear, he asked us that, us, who had come to ask him that question! Do you hear that phrase uttered with such premature haste—'if not I'—the animal cunning, the naïveté, the Karamazov impatience of it? 'I didn't kill him and you mustn't think I did! I wanted to kill him, gentlemen, I wanted to kill him,' he hastens to admit (he was in a hurry, in a terrible hurry), 'but still I am not guilty, it is not I murdered him.' He concedes to us that he wanted to murder him, as though to say, you can see for yourselves how truthful I am, so you'll believe all the sooner that I didn't murder him. Oh, in such cases the criminal is often amazingly shallow and credulous.

"At that point one of the lawyers asked him, as it were incidentally, the most simple question, 'Wasn't it Smerdyakov killed him?' Then, as we expected, he was horribly angry at our having anticipated him and caught him unawares, before he had time to pave the way to choose and snatch the moment when it would be most natural to bring in Smerdyakov's name. He rushed at once to the other extreme, as he always does, and began to assure us that Smerdyakov could not have killed him, was not capable of it. But don't believe him, that was only his cunning; he didn't really give up the idea of Smerdyakov; on the contrary, he meant to bring him forward again; for, indeed, he had no one else to bring forward, but he would do that later, because for the moment that line was spoiled for him. He would bring him forward perhaps next day, or even a few days later, choosing an opportunity to cry out to us, 'You know I was more sceptical about Smerdyakov than you, you remember that yourselves, but now I am convinced. He killed him, he must have done!' And for the present he falls back upon a gloomy and irritable denial. Impatience and anger prompted him, however, to the most inept and incredible explanation of how he looked into his father's window and how he respectfully withdrew. The worst of it was that he was unaware of the position of affairs, of the evidence given by Grigory.

"We proceeded to search him. The search angered, but encouraged him, the whole three thousand had not been found on him, only half of it. And no doubt only at that moment of angry silence, the fiction of the little bag first occurred to him. No doubt he was conscious himself of the improbability of the story and strove painfully to make it sound more likely, to weave it into a romance that would sound plausible. In such cases the first duty, the chief task of the investigating lawyers, is to prevent the criminal being prepared, to pounce upon him unexpectedly so that he may blurt out his cherished ideas in all their simplicity, improbability and inconsistency. The criminal can only be made to speak by the sudden and apparently incidental communication of some new fact, of some circumstance of great importance in the case, of which he had no previous idea and could not have foreseen. We had such a fact in readiness—that was Grigory's evidence about the open door through which the prisoner had run out. He had completely forgotten about that door and had not even suspected that Grigory could have seen it.

"The effect of it was amazing. He leapt up and shouted to us, 'Then Smerdyakov murdered him, it was Smerdyakov!' and so betrayed the basis of the defence he was keeping back, and betrayed it in its most improbable shape, for Smerdyakov could only have committed the murder after he had knocked Grigory down and run away. When we told him that Grigory saw the door was open before he fell down, and had heard Smerdyakov behind the screen as he came out of his bedroom—Karamazov was positively crushed. My esteemed and witty colleague, Nikolay Parfenovitch, told me afterwards that he was almost moved to tears at the sight of him. And to improve matters, the prisoner hastened to tell us about the much-talked-of little bag—so be it, you shall hear this romance!

"Gentlemen of the jury, I have told you already why I consider this romance not only an absurdity, but the most improbable invention that could have been brought forward in the circumstances. If one tried for a bet to invent the most unlikely story, one could hardly find anything more incredible. The worst of such stories is that the triumphant romancers can always be put to confusion and crushed by the very details in which real life is so rich and which these unhappy and involuntary story-tellers neglect as insignificant trifles. Oh, they have no thought to spare for such details, their minds are concentrated on their grand invention as a whole and fancy any one daring to pull them up for a trifle! But that's how they are caught. The prisoner was asked the question, 'Where did you get the stuff for your little bag and who made it for you?' 'I made it myself.' 'And where did you get the linen?' The prisoner was positively offended, he thought it almost insulting to ask him such a trivial question, and would you believe it, his resentment was genuine! But they are all like that. 'I tore it off my shirt.' 'Then we shall find that shirt among your linen tomorrow, with a piece torn off.' And only fancy, gentlemen of the jury, if we really had found that torn shirt (and how could we have failed to find it in his chest of drawers or trunks?) that would have been a fact, a material fact in support of his statement! But he was incapable of that reflection. 'I don't remember, it may not have been off my shirt, I sewed it up in one of my landlady's caps.' 'What sort of a cap?' 'It was an old cotton rag of hers lying about.' 'And do you remember that clearly?' 'No, I don't.' And he was angry, very angry, and yet imagine not remembering it! At the most terrible moments of man's life, for instance when he is being led to execution, he remembers just such trifles. He will forget anything but some green roof that has flashed past him on the road, or a jackdaw on a cross—that he will remember. He concealed the making of that little bag from his household, he must have remembered his humiliating fear that some one might come in and find him needle in hand, how at the slightest sound he slipped behind the screen (there is a screen in his lodgings).

"But, gentlemen of the jury, why do I tell you all this, all these details, trifles?" cried Ippolit Kirillovitch suddenly. "Just because the prisoner still persists in these absurdities to this moment. He has not explained anything since that fatal night two months ago, he has not added one actual illuminating fact to his former fantastic statements; all those are trivialities. 'You must believe it on my honour.' Oh, he was glad to believe it, we are eager to believe it, even if only on his word of honour! Are we jackals thirsting for human blood? Show us a single fact in the prisoner's favour and we shall rejoice; but let it be a substantial, real fact, and not a conclusion drawn from the prisoner's expression by his own brother, or that when he beat himself on the breast he must have meant to point to the little bag, in the darkness, too. We shall rejoice at the new fact, we shall be the first to repudiate our charge, we shall hasten to repudiate it. But now justice cries out and we persist, we cannot repudiate anything."

Ippolit Kirillovitch passed to his final peroration. He looked as though he was in a fever, he spoke of the blood that cried for vengeance, the blood of the father murdered by his son, with the base motive of robbery! He pointed to the tragic and glaring consistency of the facts.

"And whatever you may hear from the talented and celebrated counsel for the defence," Ippolit Kirillovitch could not resist adding, "whatever eloquent and touching appeals may be made to your sensibilities, remember that at this moment you are in a temple of justice. Remember that you are the champions of our justice, the champions of our holy Russia, of her principles, her family, everything that she holds sacred! Yes, you represent Russia here at this moment, and your verdict will be heard not in this hall only but will re-echo throughout the whole of Russia, and all Russia will hear you, as her champions and her judges, and she will be encouraged or disheartened by your verdict. Do not disappoint Russia and her expectations. Our fatal troika dashes on in her headlong flight perhaps to destruction and in all Russia for long past men have stretched out imploring hands and called a halt to its furious reckless course. And if other nations stand aside from that troika that may be, not from respect, as the poet would fain believe, but simply from horror. From horror, perhaps from disgust. And well it is that they stand aside, but may be they will cease one day to do so and will form a firm wall confronting the hurrying apparition and will check the frenzied rush of our lawlessness, for the sake of their own safety, enlightenment and civilisation. Already we have heard voices of alarm from Europe, they already begin to sound. Do not tempt them! Do not heap up their growing hatred by a sentence justifying the murder of a father by his son!"

Though Ippolit Kirillovitch was genuinely moved, he wound up his speech with this rhetorical appeal—and the effect produced by him was extraordinary. When he had finished his speech, he went out hurriedly and, as I have mentioned before, almost fainted in the adjoining room. There was no applause in the court, but serious persons were pleased. The ladies were not so well satisfied, though even they were pleased with his eloquence, especially as they had no apprehensions as to the upshot of the trial and had full trust in Fetyukovitch. "He will speak at last and of course carry all before him."

Every one looked at Mitya; he sat silent through the whole of the prosecutor's speech, clenching his teeth, with his hands clasped, and his head bowed. Only from time to time he raised his head and listened, especially when Grushenka was spoken of. When the prosecutor mentioned Rakitin's opinion of her, a smile of contempt and anger passed over his face and he murmured rather audibly "the Bernards!" When Ippolit Kirillovitch described how he had questioned and tortured him at Mokroe, Mitya raised his head and listened with intense curiosity. At one point he seemed about to jump up and cry out, but controlled himself and only shrugged his shoulders disdainfully. People talked afterwards of the end of the speech, of the prosecutor's feat in examining the prisoner at Mokroe and jeered at Ippolit Kirillovitch. "The man could not resist boasting of his cleverness," they said.

The court was adjourned, but only for a short interval, a quarter of an hour or twenty minutes at most. There was a hum of conversation and exclamations in the audience. I remember some of them.

"A weighty speech," a gentleman in one group observed gravely.

"He brought in too much psychology," said another voice.

"But it was all true, the absolute truth!"

"Yes, he is first rate at it."

"He summed it all up."

"Yes, he summed us up, too," chimed in another voice. "Do you remember, at the beginning of his speech, making out we were all like Fyodor Pavlovitch."

"And at the end, too. But that was all rot."

"And obscure too."

"He was a little too much carried away."

"It's unjust, it's unjust."

"No, it was smartly done, anyway. He's had long to wait, but he's had his say, ha-ha!"

"What will the counsel for the defence say?"

In another group I heard:

"He had no business to make a thrust at the Petersburg man like that; 'appealing to your sensibilities'—do you remember?"

"Yes, that was awkward of him."

"He was in too great a hurry."

"He is a nervous man."

"We laugh, but what must the prisoner be feeling?"

"Yes, what must it be for Mitya?"

In a third group:

"What lady is that, the fat one, with the lorgnette, sitting at the end?"

"She is a general's wife, divorced, I know her."

"That's why she has the lorgnette."

"She is not good for much."

"Oh, no, she is a *piquante* little woman."

"Two places beyond her there is a little fair woman, she is prettier."

"They caught him smartly at Mokroe, didn't they, eh?"

"Oh, it was smart enough. We've heard it before, how often he has told the story at people's houses!"

"And he couldn't resist doing it now. That's vanity."

"He is a man with a grievance, he-he!"

"Yes, and quick to take offence. And there was too much rhetoric, such long sentences."

"Yes, he tries to alarm us, he kept trying to alarm us. Do you remember about the troika? Something about 'They have Hamlets, but we have, so far, only Karamazovs!' That was cleverly said!"

"That was to propitiate the liberals. He is afraid of them."

"Yes, and he is afraid of the lawyer, too."

"Yes, what will Fetyukovitch say?"

"Whatever he says, he won't get round our peasants."

"Don't you think so?"

A fourth group:

"What he said about the troika was good, that piece about the other nations."

"And that was true what he said about other nations not standing it."

"What do you mean?"

"Why, in the English Parliament a Member got up last week and speaking about the Nihilists asked the Ministry whether it was not high time to intervene, to educate this barbarous people. Ippolit was thinking of him, I know he was. He was talking about that last week."

"Not an easy job."

"Not an easy job? Why not?"

"Why, we'd shut up Kronstadt and not let them have any corn.[3] Where would they get it?"

"In America. They get it from America now."

"Nonsense!"

But the bell rang, all rushed to their places. Fetyukovitch mounted the tribune.

10

THE SPEECH FOR THE DEFENCE.
AN ARGUMENT THAT CUTS BOTH WAYS

ALL was hushed as the first words of the famous orator rang out. The eyes of the audience were fastened upon him. He began very simply and directly, with an air of conviction, but not the slightest trace of conceit. He made no attempt at eloquence, at pathos, or emotional phrases. He was like a man speaking in a circle of intimate and sympathetic friends. His voice was a fine one, sonorous and sympathetic, and there was

something genuine and simple in the very sound of it. But every one realised at once that the speaker might suddenly rise to genuine pathos and
"pierce the heart with untold power."* His language was perhaps more irregular than Ippolit Kirillovitch's, but he spoke without long phrases, and
indeed, with more precision. One thing did not please the ladies; he kept
bending forward, especially at the beginning of his speech, not exactly bowing, but as though he were about to dart at his listeners, bending his long
spine in half, as though there were a spring in the middle that enabled him
to bend at right angles.

At the beginning of his speech he spoke rather disconnectedly, without
system, one may say, dealing with facts separately, though, at the end, these
facts formed a whole. His speech might be divided into two parts, the first
consisting of criticism in refutation of the charge, sometimes malicious and
sarcastic. But in the second half he suddenly changed his tone, and even his
manner, and at once rose to pathos. The audience seemed on the look-out
for it, and quivered with enthusiasm.

He went straight to the point, and began by saying that although he
practised in Petersburg, he had more than once visited provincial towns to
defend prisoners, of whose innocence he had a conviction or at least a preconceived idea. "That is what has happened to me in the present case," he
explained. "From the very first accounts in the newspapers I was struck by
something which strongly prepossessed me in the prisoner's favour. What
interested me most was a fact which often occurs in legal practice, but rarely,
I think, in such an extreme and peculiar form as in the present case. I ought
to formulate that peculiarity only at the end of my speech, but I will do so
at the very beginning, for it is my weakness to go to work directly, not keeping my effects in reserve and economising my material. That may be im-
prudent on my part, but at least it's sincere. What I have in mind is this: there
is an overwhelming chain of evidence against the prisoner, and at the same
time not one fact that will stand criticism, if it is examined separately. As I
followed the case more closely in the papers my idea was more and more
confirmed, and I suddenly received from the prisoner's relatives a request
to undertake his defence. I at once hurried here, and here I became completely convinced. It was to break down this terrible chain of facts, and to
show that each piece of evidence taken separately was unproved and fantastic, that I undertook the case."

So Fetyukovitch began.

"Gentlemen of the jury," he suddenly protested, "I am new to this district. I have no preconceived ideas. The prisoner, a man of turbulent and unbridled temper, has not insulted me. But he has insulted perhaps hundreds
of persons in this town, and so prejudiced many people against him beforehand. Of course I recognise that the moral sentiment of local society is
justly excited against him. The prisoner is of turbulent and violent temper.

---

*From Pushkin's poem "Answer to an Anonymous Correspondent" (1830).

Yet he was received in society here; he was even welcome in the family of my talented friend, the prosecutor."

(N.B. At these words there were two or three laughs in the audience, quickly suppressed, but noticed by all. All of us knew that the prosecutor received Mitya against his will, solely because he had somehow interested his wife—a lady of the highest virtue and moral worth, but fanciful, capricious, and fond of opposing her husband, especially in trifles. Mitya's visits, however, had not been frequent.)

"Nevertheless I venture to suggest," Fetyukovitch continued, "that in spite of his independent mind and just character, my opponent may have formed a mistaken prejudice against my unfortunate client. Oh, that is so natural; the unfortunate man has only too well deserved such prejudice. Outraged morality, and still more outraged taste, is often relentless. We have, in the talented prosecutor's speech, heard a stern analysis of the prisoner's character and conduct, and his severe critical attitude to the case was evident. And, what's more, he went into psychological subtleties into which he could not have entered, if he had the least conscious and malicious prejudice against the prisoner. But there are things which are even worse, even more fatal in such cases, than the most malicious and consciously unfair attitude. It is worse if we are carried away by the artistic instinct, by the desire to create, so to speak, a romance, especially if God has endowed us with psychological insight. Before I started on my way here, I was warned in Petersburg, and was myself aware, that I should find a talented opponent whose psychological insight and subtlety had gained him peculiar renown in legal circles of recent years. But profound as psychology is, it's a knife that cuts both ways." (Laughter among the public.) "You will, of course, forgive me my comparison; I can't boast of eloquence. But I will take as an example any point in the prosecutor's speech."

"The prisoner, running away in the garden in the dark, climbed over the fence, was seized by the servant, and knocked him down with a brass pestle. Then he jumped back into the garden and spent five minutes over the man, trying to discover whether he had killed him or not. And the prosecutor refuses to believe the prisoner's statement that he ran to old Grigory out of pity. 'No,' he says, 'such sensibility is impossible at such a moment, that's unnatural; he ran to find out whether the only witness of his crime was dead or alive, and so showed that he had committed the murder, since he would not have run back for any other reason.'

"Here you have psychology; but let us take the same method and apply it to the case the other way round, and our result will be no less probable. The murderer, we are told, leapt down to find out, as a precaution, whether the witness was alive or not, yet he had left in his murdered father's study, as the prosecutor himself argues, an amazing piece of evidence in the shape of a torn envelope, with an inscription that there had been three thousand roubles in it. 'If he had carried that envelope away with him, no one in the world would have known of that envelope and of the notes in it, and that the money had been stolen by the prisoner.' Those are the prosecutor's own words. So on one side you see a complete absence of precaution, a man who has lost his head and run away in a fright, leaving that clue on the floor, and two minutes later, when he has killed another man, we are entitled to assume the most heartless and calculating foresight in him. But even admitting this was so, it is psychological subtlety, I suppose, that discerns that under certain circumstances I become as blood-thirsty and keen-sighted as a Caucasian eagle, while at the next I am as timid and blind as a mole. But if I am so bloodthirsty and cruelly calculating that when I kill a man I only run back to find out whether he is alive to witness against me, why should I spend five minutes looking after my victim at the risk of en-countering other witnesses? Why soak my handkerchief, wiping the blood off his head so that it may be evidence against me later? If he were so cold-hearted and calculating, why not hit the servant on the head again and again with the same pestle so as to kill him outright and relieve himself of all anxiety about the witness?

"Again, though he ran to see whether the witness was alive, he left an-other witness on the path, that brass pestle which he had taken from the two women, and which they could always recognise afterwards as theirs, and prove that he had taken it from them. And it is not as though he had forgotten it on the path, dropped it through carelessness or haste, no, he had flung away his weapon, for it was found fifteen paces from where Grigory lay. Why did he do so? Just because he was grieved at having killed a man, an old servant; and he flung away the pestle with a curse, as a murderous weapon. That's how it must have been, what other reason could he have had for throwing it so far? And if he was capable of feeling grief and pity at having killed a man, it shows that he was innocent of his father's mur-der. Had he murdered him, he would never have run to another victim out of pity; then he would have felt differently; his thoughts would have been centered on self-preservation. He would have had none to spare for pity, that is beyond doubt. On the contrary, he would have broken his skull in-stead of spending five minutes looking after him. There was room for pity and good-feeling just because his conscience had been clear till then. Here we have a different psychology. I have purposely resorted to this method, gentlemen of the jury, to show that you can prove anything by it. It all de-pends on who makes use of it. Psychology lures even most serious people into romancing, and quite unconsciously. I am speaking of the abuse of psychology, gentlemen."

Sounds of approval and laughter, at the expense of the prosecutor, were again audible in the court. I will not repeat the speech in detail; I will only quote some passage from it, some leading points.

11

THERE WAS NO MONEY.
THERE WAS NO ROBBERY

THERE was one point that struck every one in Fetyukovitch's speech. He flatly denied the existence of the fatal three thousand roubles, and consequently the possibility of their having been stolen.

"Gentlemen of the jury," he began. "Every new and unprejudiced observer must be struck by a characteristic peculiarity in the present case, namely, the charge of robbery, and the complete impossibility of proving that there was anything to be stolen. We are told that money was stolen—three thousand roubles—but whether those roubles ever existed, nobody knows. Consider, how have we heard of that sum, and who has seen the notes? The only person who saw them, and stated that they had been put in the envelope, was the servant, Smerdyakov. He had spoken of it to the prisoner and his brother, Ivan Fyodorovitch, before the catastrophe. Madame Svyetlov, too, had been told of it. But not one of these three persons had actually seen the notes, no one but Smerdyakov had seen them."

"Here the question arises, if it's true that they did exist, and that Smerdyakov had seen them, when did he see them for the last time? What if his master had taken the notes from under his bed and put them back in his cash-box without telling him? Note, that according to Smerdyakov's story the notes were kept under the mattress; the prisoner must have pulled them out, and yet the bed was absolutely unrumpled; that is carefully recorded in the protocol. How could the prisoner have found the notes without disturbing the bed? How could he have helped soiling with his blood-stained hands the fine and spotless linen with which the bed had been purposely made?

"But I shall be asked; what about the envelope on the floor? Yes, it's worth saying a word or two about that envelope. I was somewhat surprised just now to hear the highly talented prosecutor declare of himself—of himself, observe—that but for that envelope, but for its being left on the floor, no one in the world would have known of the existence of that envelope and the notes in it, and therefore of the prisoner's having stolen it. And so that torn scrap of paper is, by the prosecutor's own admission, the sole proof on which the charge of robbery rests, 'otherwise no one would have known of the robbery, nor perhaps even of the money.' But is the mere fact that that scrap of paper was lying on the floor a proof that there was money in it, and that that money had been stolen? Yet, it will be objected, Smerdyakov had seen the money in the envelope. But when, when had he seen it for the last time, I ask you that? I talked to Smerdyakov, and he told me that he had seen the notes two days before the catastrophe. Then why not imagine that old Fyodor Pavlovitch, locked up alone in impatient and hysterical expectation of the object of his adoration, may have whiled away the time by breaking open the envelope and taking out the notes. 'What's the use of the envelope,' he may have asked himself, 'she won't believe the notes are there, but when I show her the thirty rainbow-coloured notes in one roll, it will make more impression, you may be sure, it will make her mouth water.' And so he tears open the envelope, takes out the money, and flings the envelope on the floor, conscious of being the owner and untroubled by any fears of leaving evidence.

"Listen, gentlemen, could anything be more likely than this theory and such an action? Why is it out of the question? But if anything of the sort could have taken place, the charge of robbery falls to the ground; if there was no money, there was no theft of it. If the envelope on the floor may be taken as evidence that there had been money in it, why may I not maintain the opposite, that the envelope was on the floor because the money had been taken from it by its owner?

"But I shall be asked what became of the money if Fyodor Pavlovitch took it out of the envelope since it was not found when the police searched the house? In the first place, part of the money was found in the cash-box, and secondly, he might have taken it out that morning or the evening before to make some other use of it, to give or send it away; he may have changed his idea, his plan of action completely, without thinking it necessary to announce the fact to Smerdyakov beforehand. And if there is the barest possibility of such an explanation, how can the prisoner be so positively accused of having committed murder for the sake of robbery, and of having actually carried out that robbery? This is encroaching on the domain of romance. If it is maintained that something has been stolen, the thing must be produced, or at least its existence must be proved beyond doubt. Yet no one had ever seen these notes.

"Not long ago in Petersburg a young man of eighteen, hardly more than a boy, who carried on a small business as a costermonger, went in broad daylight into a moneychanger's shop with an axe, and with extraordinary, typical audacity killed the master of the shop and carried off fifteen hundred roubles. Five hours later he was arrested, and, except fifteen roubles he had already managed to spend, the whole sum was found on him. Moreover, the shopman, on his return to the shop after the murder, informed the police not only of the exact sum stolen, but even of the notes and gold coins of which that sum was made up, and those very notes and coins were found on the criminal. This was followed by a full and genuine confession on the part of the murderer. That's what I call evidence, gentlemen of the jury! In that case I know, I see, I touch the money, and cannot deny its existence. Is it the same in the present case? And yet it is a question of life and death.

"Yes, I shall be told, but he was carousing that night, squandering money; he was shown to have had fifteen hundred roubles—where did he get the money? But the very fact that only fifteen hundred could be found, and the other half of the sum could nowhere be discovered, shows that the money was not the same, and had never been in any envelope. By strict calculation of time it was proved at the preliminary inquiry that the prisoner ran straight from those women servants to Perhotin's without going home, and that he had been nowhere. So he had been all the time in company and therefore could not have divided the three thousand in half and hidden half in the town. It's just this consideration that has led the prosecutor to assume that the money is hidden in some crevice at Mokroe. Why not in the dungeons of the castle of Udolpho,* gentlemen? Isn't this supposition really too fantastic and too romantic? And observe, if that supposition breaks down, the whole charge of robbery is scattered to the winds, for in that case what could have become of the other fifteen hundred roubles? By what miracle could they have disappeared, since it's proved that the prisoner went nowhere else? And we are ready to ruin a man's life with such tales!

"I shall be told that he could not explain where he got the fifteen hundred that he had, and every one knew that he was without money before that night. Who knew it, pray? The prisoner has made a clear and unflinching statement of the source of that money, and if you will have it so, gentlemen of the jury, nothing can be more probable than that statement, and more consistent with the temper and spirit of the prisoner. The prosecutor is charmed with his own romance. A man of weak will, who had brought himself to take the three thousand so insultingly offered by his betrothed, could not, we are told, have set aside half and sewn it up, but would, even if he had done so, have unpicked it every two days and taken out a hundred, and so would have spent it all in a month. All this, you will remember, was put forward in a tone that brooked no contradiction. But what if the thing happened quite differently? What if you've been weaving a romance, and about quite a different kind of man? That's just it, you have invented quite a different man!

"I shall be told, perhaps, there are witnesses that he spent on one day all that three thousand given him by his betrothed a month before the catastrophe, so he could not have divided the sum in half. But who are these witnesses? The value of their evidence has been shown in court already. Besides, in another man's hand a crust always seems larger, and no one of these witnesses counted that money; that all judged simply at sight. And the witness Maximov has testified that the prisoner had twenty thousand in his hand. You see, gentlemen of the jury, psychology is a two-edged weapon. Let me turn the other edge now and see what comes of it.

"A month before the catastrophe the prisoner was entrusted by Katerina Ivanovna with three thousand roubles to send off by post. But the question is: is it true that they were entrusted to him in such an insulting and degrading way as was proclaimed just now? The first statement made by the young lady on the subject was different, perfectly different. In the

The Mysteries of Udolfo (1794), a gothic novel by English author Ann Radcliffe, was popular in early-nineteenth-century Russia.

second statement we heard only cries of resentment and revenge, cries of long-concealed hatred. And the very fact that the witness gave her first evidence incorrectly, gives us a right to conclude that her second piece of evidence may have been incorrect also. The prosecutor will not, dare not (his own words) touch on that story. So be it. I will not touch on it either, but will only venture to observe that if a lofty and high-principled person, such as that highly respected young lady unquestionably is, if such a person, I say, allows herself suddenly in court to contradict her first statement, with the obvious motive of ruining the prisoner, it is clear that this evidence has been given not impartially, not coolly. Have not we the right to assume that a revengeful woman might have exaggerated much? Yes, she may well have exaggerated, in particular, the insult and humiliation of her offering him the money. No, it was offered in such a way that it was possible to take it, especially for a man so easy-going as the prisoner above all, as he expected to receive shortly from his father the three thousand roubles that he reckoned was owing to him. It was unreflecting of him, but it was just his irresponsible want of reflection that made him so confident that his father would give him the money, that he would get it, and so could always despatch the money entrusted to him and repay the debt.

"But the prosecutor refuses to allow that he could the same day have set aside half the money and sewn it up in a little bag. That's not his character, he tells us, he couldn't have had such feelings. But yet he talked himself of the broad Karamazov nature; he cried out about the two extremes which a Karamazov can contemplate at once. Karamazov is just such a two-sided nature, fluctuating between two extremes, that even when moved by the most violent craving for riotous gaiety, he can pull himself up, if something strikes him on the other side. And on the other side is love—that new love which had flamed up in his heart, and for that love he needed money; oh, far more than for carousing with his mistress. If she were to say to him, 'I am yours, I won't have Fyodor Pavlovitch,' then he must have money to take her away. That was more important than carousing. Could a Karamazov fail to understand it? That anxiety was just what he was suffering from—what is there improbable in his laying aside that money and concealing it in case of emergency?

"But time passed, and Fyodor Pavlovitch did not give the prisoner the expected three thousand; on the contrary, the latter heard that he meant to use this sum to seduce the woman he, the prisoner, loved. 'If Fyodor Pavlovitch doesn't give the money,' he thought, 'I shall be put in the position of a thief before Katerina Ivanovna.' And then the idea presented itself to him that he would go to Katerina Ivanovna, lay before her the fifteen hundred roubles he still carried round his neck, and say, 'I am a scoundrel, but not a thief.' So here we have already a twofold reason why he should guard that sum of money as the apple of his eye, why he shouldn't unpick the little bag, and spend it a hundred at a time. Why should you deny the prisoner a sense of honour? Yes, he has a sense of honour, granted that it's misplaced, granted it's often mistaken, yet it exists and amounts to a passion, and he has proved that.

"But now the affair becomes even more complex; his jealous torments reach a climax, and those same two questions torture his fevered brain more and more: 'If I repay Katerina Ivanovna, where can I find the means to go off with Grushenka?' If he behaved wildly, drank, and made disturbances in the taverns in the course of that month, it was perhaps because he was wretched and strained beyond his powers of endurance. These two questions became so acute that they drove him at last to despair. He sent his younger brother to beg for the last time for the three thousand roubles, but without waiting for a reply, burst in himself and ended by beating the old man in the presence of witnesses. After that he had no prospect of getting it from any one; his father would not give it him after that beating.

"The same evening he struck himself on the breast, just on the upper part of the breast where the little bag was, and swore to his brother that he had the means of not being a scoundrel, but that still he would remain a scoundrel, for he foresaw that he would not use that means, that he wouldn't have the character, that he wouldn't have the will-power to do it. Why, why does the prosecutor refuse to believe the evidence of Alexey Karamazov, given so genuinely and sincerely, so spontaneously and convincingly? And why, on the contrary, does he force me to believe in money hidden in a crevice, in the dungeons of the castle of Udolpho?

"The same evening, after his talk with his brother, the prisoner wrote that fatal letter, and that letter is the chief, the most stupendous proof of the prisoner having committed robbery! 'I shall beg from every one, and if I don't get it I shall murder my father and shall take the envelope with the pink ribbon on it from under his mattress as soon as Ivan has gone.' A full programme of the murder, we are told, so it must have been he. 'It has all been done as he wrote,' cries the prosecutor.

"But in the first place, it's the letter of a drunken man and written in great irritation; secondly, he writes of the envelope from what he has heard from Smerdyakov again, for he has not seen the envelope himself; and thirdly, he wrote it indeed, but how can you prove that he did it? Did the prisoner take the envelope from under the pillow, did he find the money, did that money exist indeed? And was it to get money that the prisoner ran off, if you remember? He ran off post-haste not to steal, but to find out where she was, the woman who had crushed him. He was not running to carry out a programme, to carry out what he had written, that is, not for an act of premeditated robbery, but he ran suddenly, spontaneously, in a jealous fury. Yes! I shall be told, but when he got there and murdered him he seized the money, too. But did he murder him after all? The charge of robbery I repudiate with indignation. A man cannot be accused of robbery, if it's impossible to state accurately what he has stolen; that's an axiom. But did he murder him without robbery, did he murder him at all? Is that proved? Isn't that, too, a romance?"

12

AND THERE WAS NO MURDER EITHER

ALLOW me, gentlemen of the jury, to remind you that a man's life is at stake and that you must be careful. We have heard the prosecutor himself admit that until to-day he hesitated to accuse the prisoner of a full and conscious premeditation of the crime; he hesitated till he saw that fatal drunken letter which was produced in court to-day. 'All was done as written.' But, I repeat again, he was running to her, to seek her, solely to find out where she was. That's a fact that can't be disputed. Had she been at home, he would not have run away, but would have remained at her side, and so would not have done what he promised in the letter. He ran unexpectedly and accidentally, and by that time very likely he did not even remember his drunken letter. 'He snatched up the pestle,' they say, and you will remember how a whole edifice of psychology was built on that pestle—why he was bound to look at that pestle as a weapon, to snatch it up, and so on, and so on. A very commonplace idea occurs to me at this point: What if that pestle had not been in sight, had not been lying on the shelf from which it was snatched by the prisoner, but had been put away in a cupboard? It would not have caught the prisoner's eye, and he would have run away without a weapon, with empty hands, and then he would certainly not have killed any one. How then can I look upon the pestle as a proof of premeditation?

"Yes, but he talked in the taverns of murdering his father, and two days before, on the evening when he wrote his drunken letter, he was quiet and only quarrelled with a shopman in the tavern, because a Karamazov could not help quarrelling, forsooth! But my answer to that is, that, if he was planning such a murder in accordance with his letter, he certainly would not have quarrelled even with a shopman, and probably would not have gone into the tavern at all, because a person plotting such a crime seeks quiet and retirement, seeks to efface himself, to avoid being seen and heard, and that not from calculation, but from instinct. Gentlemen of the jury, the psychological method is a two-edged weapon, and we, too, can use it. As for all this shouting in taverns throughout the month, don't we often hear children, or drunkards coming out of taverns shout, 'I'll kill you'? but they don't murder any one. And that fatal letter—isn't that simply drunken irritability, too? Isn't that simply the shout of the brawler outside the tavern, 'I'll kill you! I'll kill the lot of you!' Why not, why could it not be that? What reason have we to call that letter 'fatal' rather than 'absurd'? Because his father has been found murdered, because a witness saw the prisoner running out of the garden with a weapon in his hand, and was knocked down by him: therefore, we are told, everything was done as he had planned in writing, and the letter was not 'absurd,' but 'fatal.'

"Now, thank God! we've come to the real point: 'since he was in the garden, he must have murdered him.' In those few words: 'since he *was*, then he *must*' lies the whole case for the prosecution. He was there, so he must have. And what if there is no *must* about it, even if he was there? Oh, I admit that the chain of evidence—the coincidences—are really suggestive. But examine all these facts separately, regardless of their connection. Why, for instance, does the prosecution refuse to admit the truth of the prisoner's statement that he ran away from his father's window? Remember the sarcasms in which the prosecutor indulged at the expense of the respectful and 'pious' sentiments which suddenly came over the murderer. But what if there were something of the sort, a feeling of religious awe, if not of filial respect? 'My mother must have been praying for me at that moment,' were the prisoner's words at the preliminary inquiry, and so he ran away as soon as he convinced himself that Madame Svyetlov was not in his father's house. 'But he could not convince himself by looking through the window,' the prosecutor objects. But why couldn't he? Why? The window opened at the signals given by the prisoner. Some word might have been uttered by Fyodor Pavlovitch, some exclamation which showed the prisoner that she was not there. Why should we assume everything as we imagine it, as we make up our minds to imagine it? A thousand things may happen in reality which elude the subtlest imagination.

" 'Yes, but Grigory saw the door open and so the prisoner certainly was in the house, therefore he killed him.' Now about that door, gentlemen of the jury. . . . Observe that we have only the statement of one witness as to that door, and he was at the time in such a condition that . . . But supposing the door was open; supposing the prisoner has lied in denying it, from an instinct of self-defence, natural in his position; supposing he did go into the house—well, what then? How does it follow that because he was there he committed the murder? He might have dashed in, run through the rooms; might have pushed his father away; might have struck him; but as soon as he had made sure Madame Svyetlov was not there, he may have run away rejoicing that she was not there and that he had not killed his father. And it was perhaps just because he had escaped from the temptation to kill his father, because he had a clear conscience and was rejoicing at not having killed him, that he was capable of a pure feeling, the feeling of pity and compassion, and leapt off the fence a minute later to the assistance of Grigory after he had, in his excitement, knocked him down.

"With terrible eloquence the prosecutor has described to us the dreadful state of the prisoner's mind at Mokroe when love again lay before him calling him to new life, while love was impossible for him because he had his father's bloodstained corpse behind him and beyond that corpse—retribution. And yet the prosecutor allowed him love, which he explained, according to his method, talking about his drunken condition, about a criminal being taken to execution, about it being still far off, and so on and so on. But again I ask, Mr. Prosecutor, have you not invented a new personality?

Is the prisoner so coarse and heartless as to be able to think at that moment of love and of dodging to escape punishment, if his hands were really stained with his father's blood? No, no no! As soon as it was made plain to him that she loved him and called him to her side, promising him new happiness, oh! then, I protest he must have felt the impulse to suicide doubled, trebled, and must have killed himself, if he had his father's murder on his conscience. Oh, no! he would not have forgotten where his pistols lay! I know the prisoner: the savage, stony heartlessness ascribed to him by the prosecutor is inconsistent with his character. He would have killed himself, that's certain. He did not kill himself just because 'his mother's prayers had saved him,' and he was innocent of his father's blood. He was troubled, he was grieving that night at Mokroe only about old Grigory and praying to God that the old man would recover, that his blow had not been fatal, and that he would not have to suffer for it. Why not accept such an interpretation of the facts? What trustworthy proof have we that the prisoner is lying?

"But we shall be told at once again, 'There is his father's corpse! If he ran away without murdering him, who did murder him?' Here, I repeat, you have the whole logic of the prosecution. Who murdered him, if not he? There's no one to put in his place.

"Gentlemen of the jury, is that really so? Is it positively, actually true that there is no one else at all? We've heard the prosecutor count on his fingers all the persons who were in that house that night. They were five in number; three of them, I agree, could not have been responsible—the murdered man himself, old Grigory, and his wife. There are left then the prisoner and Smerdyakov, and the prosecutor dramatically exclaims that the prisoner pointed to Smerdyakov because he had no one else to fix on, that had there been a sixth person, even a phantom of a sixth person, he would have abandoned the charge against Smerdyakov at once in shame and have accused the other. But, gentlemen of the jury, why may I not draw the very opposite conclusion? There are two persons—the prisoner and Smerdyakov. Why can I not say that you accuse my client, simply because you have no one else to accuse? And you have no one else only because you have determined to exclude Smerdyakov from all suspicion.

"It's true, indeed, Smerdyakov is accused only by the prisoner, his two brothers, and Madame Svyetlov. But there are others who accuse him: there are vague rumours of a question, of a suspicion, an obscure report, a feeling of expectation. Finally, we have the evidence of a combination of facts very suggestive, though, I admit, inconclusive. In the first place we have precisely on the day of the catastrophe that fit, for the genuineness of which the prosecutor, for some reason, has felt obliged to make a careful defence. Then Smerdyakov's sudden suicide on the eve of the trial. Then the equally startling evidence given in court to-day by the elder of the prisoner's brothers, who had believed in his guilt, but has to-day produced a bundle of notes and proclaimed Smerdyakov as the murderer. Oh, I fully share the court's and the prosecutor's conviction that Ivan Karamazov is suffering from brain fever, that his statement may really be a desperate effort, planned in delirium, to save his brother by throwing the guilt on the dead man. But again Smerdyakov's name is pronounced, again there is a suggestion of mystery. There is something unexplained, incomplete. And perhaps it may one day be explained. But we won't go into that now. Of that later.

"The court has resolved to go on with the trial, but, meantime, I might make a few remarks about the character-sketch of Smerdyakov drawn with subtlety and talent by the prosecutor. But while I admire his talent I cannot agree with him. I have visited Smerdyakov. I have seen him and talked to him, and he made a very different impression on me. He was weak in health, it is true; but in character, in spirit, he was by no means the weak man the prosecutor has made him out to be. I found in him no trace of the timidity on which the prosecutor so insisted. There was no simplicity about him, either. I found in him, on the contrary, an extreme mistrustfulness concealed under a mask of naïveté, and an intelligence of considerable range. The prosecutor was too simple in taking him for weak-minded. He made a very definite impression on me: I left him with the conviction that he was a distinctly spiteful creature, excessively ambitious, vindictive, and intensely envious. I made some inquiries: he resented his parentage, was ashamed of it, and would clench his teeth when he remembered that he was the son of 'stinking Lizaveta.' He was disrespectful to the servant Grigory and his wife, who had cared for him in his childhood. He cursed and jeered at Russia. He dreamed of going to France and becoming a Frenchman. He used often to say that he hadn't the means to do so. I fancy he loved no one but himself and had a strangely high opinion of himself. His conception of culture was limited to good clothes, clean shirt fronts and polished boots. Believing himself to be the illegitimate son of Fyodor Pavlovitch (there is evidence of this) he might well have resented his position, compared with that of his master's legitimate sons. They had everything, he nothing. They had all the rights, they had the inheritance, while he was only the cook. He told me himself that he had helped Fyodor Pavlovitch to put the notes in the envelope. The destination of that sum—a sum which would have made his career—must have been hateful to him. Moreover, he saw three thousand roubles in new rainbow-coloured notes. (I asked him about that on purpose.) Oh, beware of showing an ambitious and envious man a large sum of money at once! And it was the first time he had seen so much money in the hands of one man. The sight of the rainbow-coloured notes may have made a morbid impression on his imagination, but with no immediate results.

"The talented prosecutor, with extraordinary subtlety, sketched for us all the arguments for and against the hypothesis of Smerdyakov's guilt, and asked us in particular what motive he had in feigning a fit. But he may not have been feigning at all, the fit may have happened quite naturally, but it may have passed off quite naturally, and the sick man may have recovered, not completely perhaps, but still regaining consciousness, as happens with epileptics.

"The prosecutor asks at what moment could Smerdyakov have committed the murder. But it is very easy to point out that moment. He might have waked up from deep sleep (for he was only asleep—an epileptic fit is always followed by a deep sleep) at that moment when the old Grigory shouted at the top of his voice 'Parricide!' That shout in the dark and stillness may have waked Smerdyakov whose sleep may have been less sound at the moment: he might naturally have waked up an hour before.

"Getting out of bed, he goes almost unconsciously and with no definite motive towards the sound to see what's the matter. His head is still clouded with his attack, his faculties are half asleep; but, once in the garden, he walks to the lighted windows and he hears terrible news from his master, who would be, of course, glad to see him. His mind sets to work at once. He hears all the details from his frightened master, and gradually in his disordered brain there shapes itself an idea—terrible, but seductive and irresistibly logical. To kill the old man, take the three thousand, and throw all the blame on to his young master. A terrible lust of money, of booty, might seize upon him as he realised his security from detection. Oh! these sudden and irresistible impulses come so often when there is a favourable opportunity, and especially with murderers who have had no idea of committing a murder beforehand. And Smerdyakov may have gone in and carried out his plan. With what weapon? Why, with any stone picked up in the garden. But what for, with what object? Why, the three thousand which means a career for him. Oh, I am not contradicting myself—the money may have existed. And perhaps Smerdyakov alone knew where to find it, where his master kept it. And the covering of the money—the torn envelope on the floor?

"Just now, when the prosecutor was explaining his subtle theory that only an inexperienced thief like Karamazov would have left the envelope on the floor, and not one like Smerdyakov, who would have avoided leaving a piece of evidence against himself, I thought as I listened that I was hearing something very familiar, and, would you believe it, I have heard that very argument, that very conjecture, of how Karamazov would have behaved, precisely two days before, from Smerdyakov himself. What's more it struck me at the time. I fancied that there was an artificial simplicity about him; that he was in a hurry to suggest this idea to me that I might fancy it was my own. He insinuated it, as it were. Did he not insinuate the same idea at the inquiry and suggest it to the talented prosecutor?

"I shall be asked, 'what about the old woman, Grigory's wife? She heard the sick man moaning close by, all night.' Yes, she heard it, but that evidence is extremely unreliable. I knew a lady who complained bitterly that she had been kept awake all night by a dog in the yard. Yet the poor beast, it appeared, had only yelped once or twice in the night. And that's natural. If any one is asleep and hears a groan he wakes up, annoyed at being waked, but instantly falls asleep again. Two hours later, again a groan, he wakes up and falls asleep again; and the same thing again two hours later—three times altogether in the night. Next morning the sleeper wakes up and complains that some one has been groaning all night and keeping him awake. And it is bound to seem so to him: the intervals of two hours of sleep he does not remember, he only remembers the moments of waking, so he feels he has been waked up all night.

"But why, why, asks the prosecutor, did not Smerdyakov confess in his last letter? Why did his conscience prompt him to one step and not to both? But, excuse me, conscience implies penitence, and the suicide may not have felt penitence, but only despair. Despair and penitence are two very different things. Despair may be vindictive and irreconcilable, and the suicide, laying his hands on himself, may well have felt redoubled hatred for those whom he had envied all his life.

"Gentlemen of the jury, beware of a miscarriage of justice! What is there unlikely in all I have put before you just now? Find the error in my reasoning; find the impossibility, the absurdity. And if there is but a shade of possibility, but a shade of probability in my propositions, do not condemn him. And is there only a shade? I swear by all that is sacred, I fully believe in the explanation of the murder I have just put forward. What troubles me and makes me indignant is that of all the mass of facts heaped up by the prosecution against the prisoner, there is not a single one certain and irrefutable. And yet the unhappy man is to be ruined by the accumulation of these facts. Yes, the accumulated effort is awful: the blood, the blood dripping from his fingers, the blood-stained shirt, the dark night resounding with the shout 'Parricide!' and the old man falling with a broken head. And then the mass of phrases, statements, gestures, shouts! Oh! this has so much influence, it can so bias the mind; but, gentlemen of the jury, can it bias your minds? Remember, you have been given absolute power to bind and to loose,* but the greater the power, the more terrible its responsibility.

"I do not draw back one iota from what I have said just now, but suppose for one moment I agreed with the prosecution that my luckless client had stained his hands with his father's blood. This is only an hypothesis, I repeat; I never for one instant doubt of his innocence. But, so be it, I assume that my client is guilty of parricide. Even so, hear what I have to say, I have it in my heart to say something more to you, for I feel that there must be a great conflict in your hearts and minds. . . . Forgive my referring to your hearts and minds, gentlemen of the jury, but I want to be truthful and sincere to the end. Let us all be sincere!"

At this point the speech was interrupted by rather loud applause. The last words, indeed, were pronounced with a note of such sincerity that every one felt that he really might have something to say, and that what he was about to say would be of the greatest consequence. But the President, hearing the applause, in a loud voice threatened to clear the court if such an incident were repeated. Every sound was hushed and Fetyukovitch began in a voice full of feeling quite unlike the tone he had used hitherto.

---

*See Matthew 18:18.

13

A CORRUPTER OF THOUGHT

"IT'S not only the accumulation of facts that threatens my client with ruin, gentlemen of the jury," he began, "what is really damning for my client is one fact—the dead body of his father. Had it been an ordinary case of murder you would have rejected the charge in view of the triviality, the incompleteness, and the fantastic character of the evidence, if you examine each part of it separately; or, at least, you would have hesitated to ruin a man's life simply from the prejudice against him which he has, alas! only too well deserved. But it's not an ordinary case of murder, it's a case of parricide. That impresses men's minds, and to such a degree that the very triviality and incompleteness of the evidence becomes less trivial and less incomplete even to an unprejudiced mind. How can such a prisoner be acquitted? What if he committed the murder and gets off unpunished? That is what every one, almost involuntarily, instinctively, feels at heart.

"Yes, it's a fearful thing to shed a father's blood—the father who has begotten me, loved me, not spared his life for me, grieved over my illnesses from childhood up, troubled all his life for my happiness, and has lived in my joys, in my successes. To murder such a father—that's inconceivable. Gentlemen of the jury, what is a father—a real father? What is the meaning of that great word? What is the great idea in that name? We have just indicated in part what a true father is and what he ought to be. In the case in which we are now so deeply occupied and over which our hearts are aching—in the present case, the father, Fyodor Pavlovitch Karamazov, did not correspond to that conception of a father to which we have just referred. That's the misfortune. And indeed some fathers are a misfortune. Let us examine this misfortune rather more closely: we must shrink from nothing, gentlemen of the jury, considering the importance of the decision you have to make. It's our particular duty not to shrink from any idea, like children or frightened women, as the talented prosecutor happily expresses it.

"But in the course of his heated speech my esteemed opponent (and he was my opponent before I opened my lips) exclaimed several times, 'Oh, I will not yield the defence of the prisoner to the lawyer who has come down from Petersburg. I accuse, but I defend also!' He exclaimed that several times, but forgot to mention that if this terrible prisoner was for twenty-three years so grateful for a mere pound of nuts given him by the only man who had been kind to him, as a child in his father's house, might not such a man well have remembered for twenty-three years how he ran in his father's back yard, 'without boots on his feet and with his little trousers hanging by one button'—to use the expression of the kind-hearted doctor, Herzenstube?

"Oh, gentlemen of the jury, why need we look more closely at this misfortune, why repeat what we all know already? What did my client meet with when he arrived here, at his father's house, and why depict my client as a heartless egoist and monster? He is uncontrolled, he is wild and unruly—we are trying him now for that—but who is responsible for his life? Who is responsible for his having received such an unseemly bringing up, in spite of his excellent disposition and his grateful and sensitive heart? Did any one train him to be reasonable? Was he enlightened by study? Did any one love him ever so little in his childhood? My client was left to the care of Providence like a beast of the field. He thirsted perhaps to see his father after long years of separation. A thousand times perhaps he may, recalling his childhood, have driven away the loathsome phantoms that haunted his childish dreams and with all his heart he may have longed to embrace and to forgive his father! And what awaited him? He was met by cynical taunts, suspicions and wrangling about money. He heard nothing but revolting talk and vicious precepts uttered daily over the brandy, and at last he saw his father seducing his mistress from him with his own money. Oh, gentlemen of the jury, that was cruel and revolting! And that old man was always complaining of the disrespect and cruelty of his son. He slandered him in society, injured him, calumniated him, bought up his unpaid debts to get him thrown into prison.

"Gentlemen of the jury, people like my client, who are fierce, unruly, and uncontrolled on the surface, are sometimes, most frequently indeed, exceedingly tender-hearted, only they don't express it. Don't laugh, don't laugh at my idea! The talented prosecutor laughed mercilessly just now at my client loving Schiller—loving the sublime and beautiful! I should not have laughed at that in his place. Yes, such natures—oh, let me speak in defence of such natures, so often and so cruelly misunderstood—these natures often thirst for tenderness, goodness, and justice, as it were, in contrast to themselves, their unruliness, their ferocity—they thirst for it unconsciously. Passionate and fierce on the surface, they are painfully capable of loving woman, for instance, and with a spiritual and elevated love. Again do not laugh at me, this is very often the case in such natures. But they cannot hide their passions—sometimes very coarse—and that is conspicuous and is noticed, but the inner man is unseen. Their passions are quickly exhausted; but, by the side of a noble and lofty creature that seemingly coarse and rough man seeks a new life, seeks to correct himself, to be better, to become noble and honourable, 'sublime and beautiful,' however much the expression has been ridiculed.

"I said just now that I would not venture to touch upon my client's engagement. But I may say half a word. What we heard just now was not evidence, but only the scream of a frenzied and revengeful woman, and it was not for her—oh, not for her!—to reproach him with treachery, for she has betrayed him! If she had had but a little time for reflection she would not have given such evidence. Oh, do not believe her! No, my client is not a monster, as she called him!

"The Lover of Mankind on the eve of His Crucifixion said: 'I am the Good Shepherd. The good shepherd lays down his life for his sheep, so that not one of them might be lost.* Let not a man's soul be lost through us!

"I asked just now what does 'father' mean, and exclaimed that it was a great word, a precious name. But one must use words honestly, gentlemen, and I venture to call things by their right names: such a father as old Karamazov cannot be called a father and does not deserve to be. Filial love for an unworthy father is an absurdity, an impossibility. Love cannot be created from nothing: only God can create something from nothing.

" 'Fathers, provoke not your children to wrath,'† the apostle writes, from a heart glowing with love. It's not for the sake of my client that I quote these sacred words, I mention them for all fathers. Who has authorised me to preach to fathers? No one. But as a man and a citizen I make my appeal—*vivos voco*![4] We are not long on earth, we do many evil deeds and say many evil words. So let us all catch a favourable moment when we are all together to say a good word to each other. That's what I am doing: while I am in this place I take advantage of my opportunity. Not for nothing is this tribune given us by the highest authority—all Russia hears us! I am not speaking only for the fathers here present, I cry aloud to all fathers: 'Fathers, provoke not your children to wrath.' Yes, let us first fulfil Christ's injunction ourselves and only then venture to expect it of our children. Otherwise we are not fathers, but enemies of our children, and they are not our children, but our enemies, and we have made them our enemies ourselves. 'What measure ye mete it shall be measured unto you again'— it's not I who say that, it's the Gospel precept, measure to others according as they measure to you. How can we blame children if they measure us according to our measure?

"Not long ago a servant girl in Finland was suspected of having secretly given birth to a child. She was watched, and a box of which no one knew anything was found in the corner of the loft, behind some bricks. It was opened and inside was found the body of a new-born child which she had killed. In the same box were found the skeletons of two other babies which, according to her own confession, she had killed at the moment of their birth.

"Gentlemen of the jury, was she a mother to her children? She gave birth to them, indeed; but was she a mother to them? Would any one venture to give her the sacred name of mother? Let us be bold, gentlemen, let us be audacious even: it's our duty to be so at this moment and not be afraid of certain words and ideas like the Moscow women in Ostrovsky's play, who are scared at the sound of certain words.[5] No, let us prove that the progress of the last few years has touched even us, and let us say plainly,

---

*See John 10:11, 14–15.
†See Colossians 3:21.

the father is not merely he who begets the child, but he who begets it and does his duty by it.

"Oh, of course, there is the other meaning, there is the other interpretation of the word 'father,' which insists that any father, even though he be a monster, even though he be the enemy of his children, still remains my father simply because he begot me. But this is, so to say, the mystical meaning which I cannot comprehend with my intellect, but can only accept by faith, or better to say, *on faith,* like many other things which I do not understand, but which religion bids me believe. But in that case let it be kept outside the sphere of actual life. In the sphere of actual life, which has, indeed, its own rights, but also lays upon us great duties and obligations, in that sphere, if we want to be humane—Christian, in fact—we must, or ought to, act only upon convictions justified by reason and experience, which have been passed through the crucible of analysis, in a word, we must act rationally, and not as though in dream and delirium, that we may not do harm, that we may not ill-treat and ruin a man. Then it will be real Christian work, not only mystic, but rational and philanthropic. . . ."

There was violent applause at this passage from many parts of the courts, but Fetyukovitch waved his hands as though imploring them to let him finish without interruption. The court relapsed into silence at once. The orator went on.

"Do you suppose, gentlemen, that our children as they grow up and begin to reason can avoid such questions? No, they cannot, and we will not impose on them an impossible restriction. The sight of an unworthy father involuntarily suggests tormenting questions to a young creature, especially when he compares him with the excellent fathers of his companions. The conventional answer to this question is: 'He begot you, and you are his flesh and blood, and therefore you are bound to love him.' The youth involuntarily reflects: 'But did he love me when he begot me?' he asks, wondering more and more. 'Was it for my sake he begot me? He did not know me, not even my sex, at that moment, at the moment of passion, perhaps, inflamed by wine, and he has only transmitted to me a propensity to drunkenness—that's all he's done for me. . . . Why am I bound to love him, simply for begetting me when he has cared nothing for me all my life after?'

"Oh, perhaps those questions strike you as coarse and cruel, but do not expect an impossible restraint from a young mind. 'Drive nature out of the door and it will fly in at the window,'[6] and, above all, let us not be afraid of words, but decide the question according to the dictates of reason and humanity and not of mystic ideas. How shall it be decided? Why, like this. Let the son stand before his father and ask him, 'Father, tell me, why must I love you? Father, show me that I must love you,' and if that father is able to answer him and show him good reason, we have a real, normal, parental relation, not resting on mystical prejudice, but on a rational, responsible and strictly humanitarian basis. But if he does not, there's an end to the family tie. He is not a father to him, and the son has a right to look upon him as a stranger, and even an enemy. Our tribune, gentleman of the jury, ought to be a school of true and sound ideas."

(Here the orator was interrupted by irrepressible and almost frantic applause. Of course, it was not the whole audience, but a good half of it applauded. The fathers and mothers present applauded. Shrieks and exclamations were heard from the gallery, where the ladies were sitting. Handkerchiefs were waved. The President began ringing his bell with all his might. He was obviously irritated by the behaviour of the audience, but did not venture to clear the court as he had threatened. Even persons of high position, old men with stars on their breasts, sitting on specially reserved seats behind the judges, applauded the orator and waved their handkerchiefs. So that when the noise died down, the President confined himself to repeating his stern threat to clear the court, and Fetyukovitch, excited and triumphant, continued his speech.)

"Gentlemen of the jury, you remember that awful night of which so much has been said to-day, when the son got over the fence and stood face to face with the enemy and persecutor who had begotten him. I insist most emphatically it was not for money he ran to his father's house: the charge of robbery is an absurdity, as I proved before. And it was not to murder him he broke into the house, oh, no! If he had had that design he would, at least, have taken the precaution of arming himself beforehand. The brass pestle he caught up instinctively without knowing why he did it. Granted that he deceived his father by tapping at the window, granted that he made his way in—I've said already that I do not for a moment believe that legend, but let it be so, let us suppose it for a moment. Gentlemen, I swear to you by all that's holy, if it had not been his father, but an ordinary enemy, he would, after running through the rooms and satisfying himself that the woman was not there, have made off, post haste, without doing any harm to his rival. He would have struck him, pushed him away perhaps, nothing more, for he had no thought and no time to spare for that. What he wanted to know was where she was. But his father, his father! The mere sight of the father who had hated him from his childhood, had been his enemy, his persecutor, and now his unnatural rival, was enough! A feeling of hatred came over him involuntarily, irresistibly, clouding his reason. It all surged up in one moment! It was an impulse of madness and insanity, but also an impulse of nature, irresistibly and unconsciously (like everything in nature) avenging the violation of its eternal laws.

"But the prisoner even then did not murder him—I maintain that, I cry that aloud!—no, he only brandished the pestle in a burst of indignant disgust, not meaning to kill him, not knowing that he would kill him. Had he not had this fatal pestle in his hand, he would have only knocked his father down perhaps, but would not have killed him. As he ran away, he did not know whether he had killed the old man. Such a murder is not a murder. Such a murder is not a parricide. No, the murder of such a father cannot be called parricide. Such a murder can only be reckoned parricide by prejudice.

"But I appeal to you again and again from the depths of my soul; did this murder actually take place? Gentlemen of the jury, if we convict and punish him, he will say to himself: 'These people have done nothing for my bringing up, for my education, nothing to improve my lot, nothing to make me better, nothing to make me a man. These people have not given me to eat and to drink, have not visited me in prison and nakedness, and here they have sent me to penal servitude.* I am quits, I owe them nothing now, and owe no one anything for ever. They are wicked and I will be wicked. They are cruel and I will be cruel.' That is what he will say, gentlemen of the jury. And I swear, by finding him guilty you will only make it easier for him: you will ease his conscience, he will curse the blood he has shed and will not regret it. And the same time you will destroy in him the possibility of becoming a new man, for he will remain in his wickedness and blindness all his life.

"But do you want to punish him fearfully, terribly, with the most awful punishment that could be imagined, and at the same time to save him and regenerate his soul? If so, overwhelm him with your mercy! You will see, you will hear how he will tremble and be horror-struck. 'How can I endure this mercy? How can I endure so much love? Am I worthy of it?' That's what he will exclaim.

"Oh, I know, I know that heart, that wild but grateful heart, gentlemen of the jury! It will bow before your mercy; it thirsts for a great and loving action, it will melt and mount upwards. There are souls which, in their limitation, blame the whole world. But subdue such a soul with mercy, show it love, and it will cure its past, for there are many good impulses in it. Such a heart will expand and see that God is merciful and that men are good and just. He will be horror-stricken; he will be crushed by remorse and the vast obligation laid upon him henceforth. And he will not say then, 'I am quits,' but will say, 'I am guilty in the sight of all men and am more unworthy than all.' With tears of penitence and poignant, tender anguish, he will exclaim: 'Others are better than I, they wanted to save me, not to ruin me!' Oh, this act of mercy is so easy for you, for in the absence of anything like real evidence it will be too awful for you to pronounce: 'Yes, he is guilty.'

"Better acquit ten guilty men than punish one innocent man!† Do you hear, do you hear that majestic voice from the past century of our glorious history? It is not for an insignificant person like me to remind you that the Russian court does not exist for the punishment only, but also for the salvation of the criminal! Let other nations think of retribution and the letter of the law, we will cling to the spirit and the meaning—the salvation and the reformation of the lost. If this is true, if Russia and her justice are such, she may go forward with good cheer! Do not try to scare us with your frenzied troikas from which all the nations stand aside in disgust. Not a runaway troika, but the stately chariot of Russia will move calmly and majestically to its goal. In your hands is the fate of my client, in your hands is the fate of Russian justice. You will defend it, you will save it, you will prove that there are men to watch over it, that it is in good hands!"

---

*See Matthew 25:35–43.

†Paraphrase from Peter the Great's *Military Code* (1716), imagined as pronounced in his "majestic voice."

14

THE PEASANTS STAND FIRM

THIS was how Fetyukovitch concluded his speech, and the enthusiasm of the audience burst like an irresistible storm. It was out of the question to stop it: the women wept, many of the men wept too, even two important personages shed tears. The President submitted, and even postponed ringing his bell. The suppression of such an enthusiasm would be the suppression of something sacred, as the ladies cried afterwards. The orator himself was genuinely touched.

And it was at this moment that Ippolit Kirillovitch got up to make certain objections. People looked at him with hatred. "What? What's the meaning of it? He positively dares to make objections," the ladies babbled. But if the whole world of ladies, including his wife, had protested he could not have been stopped at that moment. He was pale, he was shaking with emotion, his first phrases were even unintelligible, he gasped for breath, could hardly speak clearly, lost the thread. But he soon recovered himself. Of this new speech of his I will quote only a few sentences.

". . . I am reproached with having woven a romance. But what is this defence if not one romance on the top of another? All that was lacking was poetry. Fyodor Pavlovitch, while waiting for his mistress, tears open the envelope and throws it on the floor. We are even told what he said while engaged in this strange act. Is not this a flight of fancy? And what proof have we that he had taken out the money? Who heard what he said? The weak-minded idiot, Smerdyakov, transformed into a Byronic hero, avenging society for his illegitimate birth—isn't this a romance in the Byronic style? And the son who breaks into his father's house and murders him without murdering him is not even a romance—this is a sphinx setting us a riddle which he cannot solve himself. If he murdered him, he murdered him, and what's the meaning of his murdering him without having murdered him—who can make head or tail of this?

"Then we are admonished that our tribune is a tribune of true and sound ideas and from this tribune of 'sound ideas' is heard a solemn declaration that to call the murder of a father 'parricide' is nothing but a prejudice! But if parricide is a prejudice, and if every child is to ask his father why he is to love him, what will become of us? What will become of the foundations of society? What will become of the family? Parricide, it appears, is only a bogey of Moscow merchants' wives. The most precious, the most sacred guarantees for the destiny and future of Russian justice are presented to us in a perverted and frivolous form, simply to attain an object—to obtain the justification of something which cannot be justified.

'Oh, crush him by mercy,' cries the counsel for the defence; but that's all the criminal wants, and to-morrow it will be seen how much he is crushed. And is not the counsel for the defence too modest in asking only for the acquittal of the prisoner? Why not found a charity in the honour of the parricide to commemorate his exploit among future generations? Religion and the Gospel are corrected—that's all mysticism, we are told, and ours is the only true Christianity which has been subjected to the analysis of reason and common sense. And so they set up before us a false semblance of Christ! 'What measure ye mete so it shall be meted unto you again,' cries the counsel for the defence, and instantly deduces that Christ teaches us to measure as it is measured to us—and this from the tribune of truth and sound sense! We peep into the Gospel only on the eve of making speeches, in order to dazzle the audience by our acquaintance with what is, anyway, a rather original composition, which may be of use to produce a certain effect—all to serve the purpose! But what Christ commands us is something very different: He bids us beware of doing this, because the wicked world does this, but we ought to forgive and to turn the other cheek, and not to measure to our persecutors as they measure to us. This is what our God has taught us and not that to forbid children to murder their fathers is a prejudice. And we will not from the tribune of truth and good sense correct the Gospel of our Lord, Whom the counsel for the defence deigns to call only 'the crucified lover of humanity,' in opposition to all orthodox Russia, which calls to Him, 'For Thou art our God!'"

At this the President intervened and checked the overzealous speaker, begging him not to exaggerate, not to overstep the bounds, and so on, as presidents always do in such cases. The audience, too, was uneasy. The public was restless: there were even exclamations of indignation. Fetyukovitch did not so much as reply; he only mounted the tribune to lay his hand on his heart and, with an offended voice, utter a few words full of dignity. He only touched again, lightly and ironically, on "romancing" and "psychology," and in an appropriate place quoted, "Jupiter, you are angry, therefore you are wrong," which provoked a burst of approving laughter in the audience, for Ippolit Kirillovitch was by no means like Jupiter. Then, à propos of the accusation that he was teaching the young generation to murder their fathers, Fetyukovitch observed, with great dignity, that he would not even answer. As for the prosecutor's charge of uttering unorthodox opinions, Fetyukovitch hinted that it was a personal insinuation and that he had expected in this court to be secure from accusations "damaging to my reputation as a citizen and a loyal subject." But at these words the President pulled him up, too, and Fetyukovitch concluded his speech with a bow, amid a hum of approbation in the court. And Ippolit Kirillovitch was, in the opinion of our ladies, "crushed for good."

Then the prisoner was allowed to speak. Mitya stood up, but said very little. He was fearfully exhausted, physically and mentally. The look of strength and independence with which he had entered in the morning had almost disappeared. He seemed as though he had passed through an experience that day, which had taught him for the rest of his life something very important he had not understood till then. His voice was weak, he did not shout as before. In his words there was a new note of humility, defeat and submission.

"What am I to say, gentlemen of the jury? The hour of judgment has come for me, I feel the hand of God upon me! The end has come to an erring man! But, before God, I repeat to you, I am innocent of my father's blood! For the last time I repeat, it wasn't I killed him! I was erring, but I loved what is good. Every instant I strove to reform, but I lived like a wild beast. I thank the prosecutor, he told me many things about myself that I did not know; but it's not true that I killed my father, the prosecutor is mistaken. I thank my counsel, too. I cried listening to him; but it's not true that I killed my father, and he needn't have supposed it. And don't believe the doctors. I am perfectly sane, only my heart is heavy. If you spare me, if you let me go, I will pray for you. I will be a better man. I give you my word before God I will! And if you will condemn me, I'll break my sword over my head myself[7] and kiss the pieces. But spare me, do not rob me of my God! I know myself, I shall rebel! My heart is heavy, gentlemen . . . spare me!"

He almost fell back in his place: his voice broke: he could hardly articulate the last phrase. Then the judges proceeded to put the questions and began to ask both sides to formulate their conclusions. But I will not describe the details. At last the jury rose to retire for consultation. The President was very tired, and so his last charge to the jury was rather feeble. "Be impartial, don't be influenced by the eloquence of the defence, but yet weigh the arguments. Remember that there is a great responsibility laid upon you," and so on and so on.

The jury withdrew and the court adjourned. People could get up, move about, exchange their accumulated impressions, refresh themselves at the buffet. It was very late, almost one o'clock in the night, but nobody went away: the strain was so great that no one could think of repose. All waited with sinking hearts; though that is, perhaps, too much to say, for the ladies were only in a state of hysterical impatience and their hearts were untroubled. An acquittal, they thought, was inevitable. They all prepared themselves for a dramatic moment of general enthusiasm. I must own there were many among the men, too, who were convinced that an acquittal was inevitable. Some were pleased, others frowned, while some were simply dejected, not wanting him to be acquitted. Fetyukovitch himself was confident of his success. He was surrounded by people congratulating him and fawning upon him.

"There are," he said to one group, as I was told afterwards, "there are invisible threads which bind the counsel for the defence with the jury. One feels during one's speech if they are being formed. I was aware of them. They exist. Our cause is won. Set your mind at rest."

"What will our peasants say now?" said one stout, cross-looking, pockmarked gentleman, a landowner of the neighbourhood, approaching a group of gentlemen engaged in conversation.

"But they are not all peasants. There are four government clerks among them."

"Yes, there are clerks," said a member of the district council, joining the group.

"And do you know that Nazaryev, the merchant with the medal, a juryman?"

"What of him?"

"He is a man with brains."

"But he never speaks."

"He is no great talker, but so much the better. There's no need for the Petersburg man to teach him: he could teach all Petersburg himself. He's the father of twelve children. Think of that!"

"Upon my word, you don't suppose they won't acquit him?" one of our young officials exclaimed in another group.

"They'll acquit him for certain," said a resolute voice.

"It would be shameful, disgraceful, not to acquit him!" cried the official. "Suppose he did murder him—there are fathers and fathers! And, besides, he was in such a frenzy.... He really may have done nothing but swing the pestle in the air, and so knocked the old man down. But it was a pity they dragged the valet in. That was simply an absurd theory! If I'd been in Fetyukovitch's place, I should simply have said straight out: 'He murdered him; but he is not guilty, hang it all!'"

"That's what he did, only without saying, 'Hang it all!'"

"No, Mihail Semyonovitch, he almost said that, too," put in a third voice.

"Why, gentlemen, in Lent an actress was acquitted in our town who had cut the throat of her lover's lawful wife."[8]

"Oh, but she did not finish cutting it."

"That makes no difference. She began cutting it."

"What did you think of what he said about children? Splendid, wasn't it?"

"Splendid!"

"And about mysticism, too!"

"Oh, drop mysticism, do!" cried some one else; "think of Ippolit and his fate from this day forth. His wife will scratch his eyes out to-morrow for Mitya's sake."

"Is she here?"

"What an idea! If she'd been here she'd have scratched them out in court. She is at home with toothache. He, he, he!"

"He, he, he!"

In a third group:

"I daresay they will acquit Mityenka, after all."

"I should not be surprised if he turns the 'Metropolis' upside down tomorrow. He will be drinking for ten days!"

"Oh, the devil!"

"The devil's bound to have a hand in it. Where should he be if not here?"

"Well, gentlemen, I admit it was eloquent. But still it's not the thing to break your father's head with a pestle! Oh what are we coming to?"

"The chariot! Do you remember the chariot?"

"Yes; he turned a cart into a chariot!"

"And to-morrow he will turn a chariot into a cart, just to suit his purpose."

"What cunning chaps there are nowadays. Is there any justice to be had in Russia?"

But the bell rang. The jury deliberated for exactly an hour, neither more nor less. A profound silence reigned in the court as soon as the public had taken their seats. I remember how the jurymen walked into the court. At last! I won't repeat the questions in order, and, indeed, I have forgotten them. I remember only the answer to the President's first and chief question: "Did the prisoner commit the murder for the sake of robbery and with premeditation?" (I don't remember the exact words.) There was a complete hush. The foreman of the jury, the youngest of the clerks, pronounced, in a clear, loud voice, amidst the deathlike stillness of the court:

"Yes, guilty!"

And the same answer was repeated to every question: "Yes, guilty!" and without the slightest extenuating comment. This no one had expected; almost every one had reckoned upon a recommendation to mercy, at least. The deathlike silence in the court was not broken—all seemed petrified: those who desired his conviction as well as those who had been eager for his acquittal. But that was only for the first instant, and it was followed by a fearful hubbub. Many of the men in the audience were pleased. Some were rubbing their hands with no attempt to conceal their joy. Those who disagreed with the verdict seemed crushed, shrugged their shoulders, whispered, but still seemed unable to realise this. But how shall I describe the state the ladies were in? I thought they would create a riot. At first they could scarcely believe their ears. Then suddenly the whole court rang with exclamations: "What's the meaning of it? What next?" They leapt up from their places. They seemed to fancy that it might be at once reconsidered and reversed. At that instant Mitya suddenly stood up and cried in a heartrending voice, stretching his hands out before him:

"I swear by God and the dreadful Day of Judgment I am not guilty of my father's blood! Katya, I forgive you! Brothers, friends, have pity on the other woman!"

He could not go on, and broke into a terrible sobbing wail that was heard all over the court in a strange, unnatural voice unlike his own. From the furthest corner at the back of the gallery came a piercing shriek—it was Grushenka. She had succeeded in begging admittance to the court again before the beginning of the lawyers' speeches. Mitya was taken away. The passing of the sentence was deferred till next day. The whole court was in a hubbub but I did not wait to hear. I only remember a few exclamations I heard on the steps as I went out.

"He'll have a twenty years' trip to the mines!"

"Not less."

"Well, our peasants have stood firm."

"And have done for our Mitya."

EPILOGUE

1

PLANS FOR MITYA'S ESCAPE

VERY early, at nine o'clock in the morning, five days after the trial, Alyosha went to Katerina Ivanovna's to talk over a matter of great importance to both of them, and to give her a message. She sat and talked to him in the very room in which she had once received Grushenka. In the next room Ivan Fyodorovitch lay unconscious in a high fever. Katerina Ivanovna had immediately after the scene at the trial ordered the sick and unconscious man to be carried to her house, disregarding the inevitable gossip and general disapproval of the public. One of the two relations who lived with her had departed to Moscow immediately after the scene at the court, the other remained. But if both had gone away, Katerina Ivanovna would have adhered to her resolution, and would have gone on nursing the sick man and sitting by him day and night. Varvinsky and Herzenstube were attending him. The famous doctor had gone back to Moscow, refusing to give an opinion as to the probable end of the illness. Though the doctors encouraged Katerina Ivanovna and Alyosha, it was evident that they could not give them positive hopes of recovery.

Alyosha came to see his sick brother twice a day. But this time he had specially urgent business, and he foresaw how difficult it would be to approach the subject, yet he was in great haste. He had another engagement that could not be put off for that same morning, and there was need of haste.

They had been talking for a quarter of an hour. Katerina Ivanovna was pale and terribly fatigued, yet at the same time in a state of hysterical excitement. She had a presentiment of the reason why Alyosha had come to her.

"Don't worry about his decision," she said, with confident emphasis to Alyosha. "One way or another he is bound to come to it. He must escape. That unhappy man, that hero of honour and principle—not he, not Dmitri Fyodorovitch, but the man lying the other side of that door, who has sacrificed himself for his brother," Katya added, with flashing eyes, "told me the whole plan of escape long ago. You know he has already entered into negotiations. . . . I've told you something already. . . . You see, it will probably come off at the third *étape* from here, when the party of prisoners is being taken to Siberia. Oh, it's a long way off yet. Ivan Fyodorovitch has already visited the superintendent of the third *étape*. But we don't know yet who will be in charge of the party, and it's impossible to find that out so long beforehand. To-morrow perhaps I will show you in detail the whole plan which Ivan Fyodorovitch left me on the eve of the trial in case of need. . . . That was when—do you remember?—you found us quarrelling. He had just gone downstairs, but seeing you I made him come back; do you remember? Do you know what we were quarrelling about then?"

"No, I don't," said Alyosha.

"Of course he did not tell you. It was about that plan of escape. He had told me the main idea three days before, and we began quarrelling about it at once and quarrelled for three days. We quarrelled because when he told me that, if Dmitri Fyodorovitch were convicted he would escape abroad with that creature, I felt furious at once—I can't tell you why, I don't know myself why. . . . Oh, of course, I was furious then about that creature, and that she, too, should go abroad with Dmitri!" Katerina Ivanovna exclaimed suddenly, her lips quivering with anger. "As soon as Ivan Fyodorovitch saw that I was furious about that woman, he instantly imagined I was jealous of Dmitri, and that I still loved Dmitri. That is how our first quarrel began. I would not give an explanation, I could not ask forgiveness. I could not bear to think that such a man could suspect me of still loving that . . . and when I myself had told him long before that I did not love Dmitri, that I loved no one but him! It was only resentment against that creature that made me angry with him. Three days later, on the evening you came, he brought me a sealed envelope, which I was to open at once, if anything happened to him. Oh, he foresaw his illness! He told me that the envelope contained the details of the escape, and that if he died or was taken dangerously ill, I was to save Mitya alone. Then he left me money, nearly ten thousand—those notes to which the prosecutor referred in his speech, having learnt from some one that he had sent them to be changed. I was tremendously impressed to find that Ivan Fyodorovitch had not given up his idea of saving his brother, and was confiding this plan of escape to me, though he was still jealous of me and still convinced that I loved Mitya. Oh, that was a sacrifice; No, you cannot understand the greatness of such self-sacrifice, Alexey Fyodorovitch. I wanted to fall at his feet in reverence, but I thought at once that he would take it only for my joy at the thought of Mitya's being saved (and he certainly would have imagined that!), and I was so exasperated at the mere possibility of such an unjust thought on his part that I lost my temper again, and instead of kissing his feet, flew into a fury again! Oh, I am unhappy! It's my character, my awful, unhappy character! Oh, you will see, I shall end by driving him, too, to abandon me for another with whom he can get on better, like Dmitri. But . . . no, I could not bear it, I should kill myself. And when you came in then, and when I called to you and told him to come back, I was so enraged by the look of contempt and hatred he turned on me that—do you remember?—I cried out to you that it was he, he alone who had persuaded me that his brother Dmitri was a murderer! I said that malicious thing on purpose to wound him again. He had never, never persuaded me that his brother was a murderer. On the contrary, it was I who persuaded him! Oh, my vile temper was the cause of everything! I paved the way to that hideous scene at the trial. He wanted to show me that he was an honourable man, and that, even if I loved his brother, he would not ruin him for revenge or jealousy. So he came to the court . . . I am the cause of it all, I alone am to blame!"

Katya never had made such confessions to Alyosha before, and he felt that she was now at that stage of unbearable suffering when even the proudest heart painfully crushes its pride and falls vanquished by grief. Oh, Alyosha knew another terrible reason of her present misery, though she had carefully concealed it from him during those days since the trial; it would have been for some reason too painful to him if she had been brought so low as to speak to him now about that. She was suffering for her "treachery" at the trial, and Alyosha felt that her conscience was impelling her to confess it to him, to him, Alyosha, with tears and cries and hysterical writhings on the floor. But he dreaded that moment and longed to spare her. It made the commission on which he had come even more difficult. He spoke of Mitya again.

"It's all right, it's all right, don't be anxious about him!" she began again, sharply and stubbornly. "All that is only momentary, I know him, I know his heart only too well. You may be sure he will consent to escape. It's not as though it would be immediately; he will have time to make up his mind to it. Ivan Fyodorovitch will be well by that time and will manage it all himself, so that I shall have nothing to do with it. Don't be anxious; he will consent to run away. He has agreed already: do you suppose he would give up that creature? And they won't let her go to him, so he is bound to escape. It's you he's most afraid of, he is afraid you won't approve of his escape on moral grounds. But you must generously *allow* it, if your sanction is so necessary," Katya added viciously. She paused and smiled.

"He talks about some hymn," she went on again, "some cross he has to bear, some duty; I remember Ivan Fyodorovitch told me a great deal about it, and if you knew how he talked!" Katya cried suddenly, with feeling she could not repress, "if you knew how he loved that wretched man at the moment he told me, and how he hated him, perhaps, at the same moment. And I heard his story and his tears with sneering disdain. Brute! Yes, I am a brute. I am responsible for his fever. But that man in prison is incapable of suffering," Katya concluded irritably. "Can such a man suffer? Men like him never suffer!"

There was a note of hatred and contemptuous repulsion in her words. And yet it was she who had betrayed him. "Perhaps because she feels how she's wronged him she hates him at moments," Alyosha thought to himself. He hoped that it was only "at moments." In Katya's last words he detected a challenging note, but he did not take it up.

"I sent for you this morning to make you promise to persuade him yourself. Or do you, too, consider that to escape would be dishonourable, cowardly, or something . . . unchristian, perhaps?" Katya added, even more defiantly.

"Oh, no. I'll tell him everything," muttered Alyosha. "He asks you to come and see him to-day," he blurted out suddenly, looking her steadily in the face. She started, and drew back a little from him on the sofa.

"Me? Can that be?" she faltered, turning pale.

"It can and ought to be!" Alyosha began emphatically, growing more animated. "He needs you particularly just now. I would not have opened the subject and worried you, if it were not necessary. He is ill, he is beside himself, he keeps asking for you. It is not to be reconciled with you that he wants you, but only that you would go and show yourself at his door. So much has happened to him since that day. He realises that he has injured you beyond all reckoning. He does not ask your forgiveness; 'it's impossible to forgive me,' he says himself, but only that you would show yourself in his doorway."

"It's so sudden. . . ." faltered Katya. "I had a presentiment all these days that you would come with that message. I knew he would ask me to come. It's impossible!"

"Let it be impossible, but do it. Only think, he realises for the first time how he has wounded you, the first time in his life; he had never grasped it before so fully. He said, 'if she refuses to come I shall be unhappy all my life.' Do you hear? Though he is condemned to penal servitude for twenty years, he is still planning to be happy—is not that piteous? Think—you must visit him; though he is ruined, he is innocent," broke like a challenge from Alyosha. "His hands are clean, there is no blood on them! For the sake of his infinite sufferings in the future visit him now. Go, greet him on his way into the darkness—stand at his door, that is all. . . . You ought to do it, you ought to!" Alyosha concluded, laying immense stress on the word "ought."

"I ought to . . . but I cannot. . . ." Katya moaned. "He will look at me. . . . I can't."

"Your eyes ought to meet. How will you live all your life, if you don't make up your mind to do it now?"

"Better suffer all my life."

"You ought to go, you ought to go," Alyosha repeated with merciless emphasis.

"But why to-day, why at once? . . . I can't leave our patient. . . ."

"You can for a moment. It will only be a moment. If you don't come, he will be in delirium by to-night. I would not tell you a lie; have pity on him!"

"Have pity on *me!*" Katya said, with bitter reproach, and she burst into tears.

"Then you will come," said Alyosha firmly, seeing her tears. "I'll go and tell him you will come directly."

"No, don't tell him so on any account," cried Katya in alarm. "I will come, but don't tell him beforehand, for perhaps I may go, but not go in . . . I don't know yet. . . ."

Her voice failed her. She gasped for breath. Alyosha got up to go.

"And what if I meet any one?" she said suddenly, in a low voice, turning white again.

"That's just why you must go now, to avoid meeting any one. There will be no one there, I can tell you that for certain. We will expect you," he concluded emphatically, and went out of the room.

2

FOR A MOMENT THE LIE BECOMES TRUTH

HE hurried to the hospital where Mitya was lying now. The day after his fate was determined, Mitya had fallen ill with nervous fever, and was sent to the prison division of the town hospital. But at the request of several persons (Alyosha, Madame Hohlakov, Lise, etc.), Doctor Varvinsky had put Mitya not with other prisoners, but in a separate little room, the one where Smerdyakov had been. It is true that there was a sentinel at the other end of the corridor, and there was a grating over the window, so that Varvinsky could be at ease about the indulgence he had shown, which was not quite legal, indeed; but he was a kind-hearted and compassionate young man. He knew how hard it would be for a man like Mitya to pass at once so suddenly into the society of robbers and murderers, and that he must get used to it by degrees. The visits of relations and friends were informally sanctioned by the doctor and overseer, and even by the police captain. But only Alyosha and Grushenka had visited Mitya. Rakitin had tried to force his way in twice, but Mitya persistently begged Varvinsky not to admit him.

Alyosha found him sitting on his bed in a hospital dressing-gown, rather feverish, with a towel, soaked in vinegar and water, on his head. He looked at Alyosha as he came in with an undefined expression, but there was a shade of something like dread discernible in it. He had become terribly preoccupied since the trial; sometimes he would be silent for half an hour together, and seemed to be pondering something heavily and painfully, oblivious of everything about him. If he roused himself from his brooding and began to talk, he always spoke with a kind of abruptness and never of what he really wanted to say. He looked sometimes with a face of suffering at his brother. He seemed to be more at ease with Grushenka than with Alyosha. It is true, he scarcely spoke to her at all, but as soon as she came in, his whole face lighted up with joy.

Alyosha sat down beside him on the bed in silence. This time Mitya was waiting for Alyosha in suspense, but he did not dare ask him a question. He felt it almost unthinkable that Katya would consent to come, and at the same time he felt that if she did not come, something inconceivable would happen.

Alyosha understood his feelings.

"Trifon Borissovitch," Mitya began nervously, "has pulled his whole inn to pieces, I am told. He's taken up the flooring, pulled apart the planks, split up all the gallery, I am told. He is seeking treasure all the time—the fifteen hundred roubles which the prosecutor said I'd hidden there. He began playing these tricks, they say, as soon as he got home. Serve him right, the swindler! The guard here told me yesterday; he comes from there."

"Listen," began Alyosha. "She will come, but I don't know when. Perhaps to-day, perhaps in a few days, that I can't tell. But she will come, she will, that's certain."

Mitya started, would have said something, but was silent. The news had a tremendous effect on him. It was evident that he would have liked terribly to know what had been said, but he was again afraid to ask. Something cruel and contemptuous from Katya would have cut him like a knife at that moment.

"This was what she said among other things; that I must be sure to set your conscience at rest about escaping. If Ivan is not well by then she will see to it all herself."

"You've spoken of that already," Mitya observed musingly.

"And you have repeated it to Grusha," observed Alyosha.

"Yes," Mitya admitted. "She won't come this morning." He looked timidly at his brother. "She won't come till the evening. When I told her yesterday that Katya was taking measures, she was silent, but she set her mouth. She only whispered, 'Let her!' She understood that it was important. I did not dare to try her further. She understands now, I think, that Katya no longer cares for me, but loves Ivan."

"Does she?" broke from Alyosha.

"Perhaps she does not. Only she is not coming this morning," Mitya hastened to explain again; "I asked her to do something for me. You know, Ivan is superior to all of us. He ought to live, not us. He will recover."

"Would you believe it, though Katya is alarmed about him, she scarcely doubts of his recovery," said Alyosha.

"That means that she is convinced he will die. It's because she is frightened she's so sure he will get well."

"Ivan has a strong constitution, and I, too, believe there's every hope that he will get well," Alyosha observed anxiously.

"Yes, he will get well. But she is convinced that he will die. She has a great deal of sorrow to bear. . . ." A silence followed. A grave anxiety was fretting Mitya.

"Alyosha, I love Grusha terribly," he said suddenly in a shaking voice, full of tears.

"They won't let her go out there to you," Alyosha put in at once.

"And there is something else I wanted to tell you," Mitya went on, with a sudden ring in his voice. "If they beat me on the way or out there, I won't submit to it. I shall kill some one, and shall be shot for it. And this will be going on for twenty years! They speak to me rudely as it is. I've been lying here all night, passing judgment on myself. I am not ready! I am not able to resign myself. I wanted to sing a 'hymn'; but if a guard speaks to me, I have not the strength to bear it. For Grusha I would bear anything . . . anything except blows. . . . But she won't be allowed to come there."

Alyosha smiled gently.

"Listen, brother, once for all," he said. "This is what I think about it. And you know that I would not tell you a lie. Listen: you are not ready, and such a cross is not for you. What's more, you don't need such a martyr's cross when you are not ready for it. If you had murdered our father, it would grieve me that you should reject your punishment. But you are innocent, and such a cross is too much for you. You wanted to make yourself another man by suffering. I say, only remember that other man always, all your life and wherever you go; and that will be enough for you. Your refusal of that great cross will only serve to make you feel all your life an even greater duty, and that constant feeling will do more to make you a new man, perhaps, than if you went there. For there you would not endure it and would repine, and perhaps at last would say: 'I am quits.' The lawyer was right about that. Such heavy burdens are not for all men. For some they are impossible. These are my thoughts about it, if you want them so much. If other men would have to answer for your escape, officers or soldiers, then I would not have 'allowed' you," smiled Alyosha. "But they declare—the superintendent of that *étape* told Ivan himself—that if it's well managed there will be no great inquiry, and that they can get off easily. Of course, bribing is dishonest even in such a case, but I can't undertake to judge about it, because if Ivan and Katya commissioned me to act for you, I know I should go and give bribes. I must tell you the truth. And so I can't judge of your own action. But let me assure you that I shall never condemn you. And it would be a strange thing if I could judge you in this. Now I think I've gone into everything."

"But I do condemn myself!" cried Mitya. "I shall escape, that was settled apart from you; could Mitya Karamazov do anything but run away? But I shall condemn myself, and I will pray for my sin for ever. That's how the Jesuits talk, isn't it? Just as we are doing?"

"Yes," Alyosha smiled gently.

"I love you for always telling the whole truth and never hiding anything," cried Mitya, with a joyful laugh. "So I've caught my Alyosha being Jesuitical. I must kiss you for that. Now listen to the rest; I'll open the other side of my heart to you. This is what I planned and decided. If I run away, even with money and a passport, and even to America, I should be cheered up by the thought that I am not running away for pleasure, not for happiness, but to another exile as bad, perhaps, as Siberia. It is as bad, Alyosha, it is! I hate that America, damn it, already. Even though Grusha will be with me. Just look at her; is she an American? She is Russian, Russian to the marrow of her bones; she will be homesick for the mother country, and I shall see every hour that she is suffering for my sake, that she has taken up that cross for me. And what harm has she done? And how shall I, too, put up with the rabble out there, though they may be better than I, every one of them. I hate that America already! And though they may be wonderful at machinery, every one of them, damn them, they are not of my soul. I love Russia, Alyosha, I love the Russian God, though I am a scoundrel myself. I shall choke there!" he exclaimed, his eyes suddenly flashing. His voice was trembling with tears. "So this is what I've decided, Alyosha, listen," he began again, mastering his emotion. "As soon as I arrive there with Grusha,

we will set to work at once on the land, in solitude, somewhere very remote, with wild bears. There must be some remote parts even there. I am
told there are still Redskins there, somewhere, on the edge of the horizon.
So to the country of the *Last of the Mohicans*,* and there we'll tackle the
grammar at once, Grusha and I. Work and grammar—that's how we'll spend
three years. And by that time we shall speak English like any Englishman.
And as soon as we've learnt it—good-bye to America! We'll run here to
Russia as American citizens. Don't be uneasy—we would not come to this
little town. We'd hide somewhere, a long way off, in the north or in the
south. I shall be changed by that time, and she will, too, in America. The
doctors shall make me some sort of wart on my face—what's the use of their
being so mechanical!—or else I'll put out one eye, let my beard grow a
yard, and I shall turn grey, fretting for Russia. I daresay they won't recognise us. And if they do, let them send us to Siberia—I don't care. It will
show it's our fate. We'll work on the land here, too, somewhere in the wilds,
and I'll make up as an American all my life. But we shall die on our own
soil. That's my plan, and it shan't be altered. Do you approve?"

"Yes," said Alyosha, not wanting to contradict him. Mitya paused for a
minute and said suddenly:

"And how they worked it up at the trial! Didn't they work it up!"

"If they had not, you would have been convicted just the same," said
Alyosha, with a sigh.

"Yes, people are sick of me here! God bless them, but it's hard," Mitya
moaned miserably. Again there was silence for a minute.

"Alyosha, put me out of my misery at once!" he exclaimed suddenly.
"Tell me, is she coming now, or not? Tell me? What did she say? How did
she say it?"

"She said she would come, but I don't know whether she will come to-
day. It's hard for her, you know," Alyosha looked timidly at his brother.

"I should think it is hard for her! Alyosha, it will drive me out of my
mind. Grusha keeps looking at me. She understands. My God, calm my
heart: what is it I want? I want Katya! Do I understand what I want? It's
the headstrong, evil Karamazov spirit! No, I am not fit for suffering. I am a
scoundrel, that's all one can say."

"Here she is!" cried Alyosha.

At that instant Katya appeared in the doorway. For a moment she
stood still, gazing at Mitya with a dazed expression. He leapt impulsively
to his feet, and a scared look came into his face. He turned pale, but a timid,
pleading smile appeared on his lips at once, and with an irresistible impulse he held out both hands to Katya. Seeing it, she flew impetuously to
him. She seized him by the hands, and almost by force made him sit down
on the bed. She sat down beside him, and still keeping his hands pressed
them violently. Several times they both strove to speak, but stopped short

---

*Novel (1826) by American author James Fenimore Cooper, which was very
popular in Russia; Dostoevsky owned a French translation.

and again gazed speechless with a strange smile, their eyes fastened on one another. So passed two minutes.

"Have you forgiven me?" Mitya faltered at last, and at the same moment turning to Alyosha, his face working with joy, he cried, "Do you hear what I am asking, do you hear?"

"That's what I loved you for, that you are generous at heart!" broke from Katya. "My forgiveness is no good to you, nor yours to me; whether you forgive me or not, you will always be a sore place in my heart, and I in yours—so it must be. . . ." She stopped to take breath. "What have I come for?" she began again with nervous haste: "to embrace your feet, to press your hands like this, till it hurts—you remember how in Moscow I used to squeeze them—to tell you again that you are my god, my joy, to tell you that I love you madly," she moaned in anguish, and suddenly pressed his hand greedily to her lips. Tears streamed from her eyes. Alyosha stood speechless and confounded; he had never expected what he was seeing.

"Love is over, Mitya!" Katya began again, "but the past is painfully dear to me. Know that will always be so. But now let what might have been come true for one minute," she faltered, with a drawn smile, looking into his face joyfully again. "You love another woman, and I love another man, and yet I shall love you for ever, and you will love me; do you know that? Do you hear? Love me, love me all your life!" she cried, with a quiver almost of menace, in her voice.

"I shall love you, and . . . do you know, Katya," Mitya began, drawing a deep breath at each word, "do you know, five days ago, that same evening, I loved you. . . . When you fell down and were carried out . . . All my life! So it will be, so it will always be. . . ."

So they murmured to one another frantic words, almost meaningless, perhaps not even true, but at that moment it was all true, and they both believed what they said implicitly.

"Katya," cried Mitya suddenly, "do you believe I murdered him? I know you don't believe it now, but then . . . when you gave evidence. . . . Surely, surely you did not believe it!"

"I did not believe it even then. I've never believed it. I hated you, and for a moment I persuaded myself. While I was giving evidence I persuaded myself and believed it, but when I'd finished speaking I left off believing it at once. Don't doubt that! I have forgotten that I came here to punish myself," she said, with a new expression in her voice, quite unlike the loving tones of a moment before.

"Woman, yours is a heavy burden," broke, as it were, involuntarily from Mitya.

"Let me go," she whispered. "I'll come again. It's more than I can bear now."

She was getting up from her place, but suddenly uttered a loud scream and staggered back, Grushenka walked suddenly and noiselessly into the room. No one had expected her. Katya moved swiftly to the door, but when she reached Grushenka, she stopped suddenly, turned as white as chalk and moaned softly, almost in a whisper:

"Forgive me!"

Grushenka stared at her and, pausing for an instant, in a vindictive, venomous voice, answered:

"We are full of hatred, my girl, you and I! We are both full of hatred! As though we could forgive one another! Save him, and I'll worship you all my life."

"You won't forgive her!" cried Mitya, with frantic reproach.

"Don't be anxious, I'll save him for you!" Katya whispered rapidly, and she ran out of the room.

"And you could refuse to forgive her when she begged your forgiveness herself?" Mitya exclaimed bitterly again.

"Mitya, don't dare to blame her; you have no right to!" Alyosha cried hotly.

"Her proud lips spoke, not her heart," Grushenka brought out in a tone of disgust. "If she saves you I'll forgive her everything. . . ."

She stopped speaking, as though suppressing something. She could not yet recover herself. She had come in, as appeared afterwards, accidentally, with no suspicion of what she would meet.

"Alyosha, run after her!" Mitya cried to his brother; "tell her . . . I don't know . . . don't let her go away like this!"

"I'll come to you again at nightfall," said Alyosha, and he ran after Katya. He overtook her outside the hospital grounds. She was walking fast, but as soon as Alyosha caught her up she said quickly:

"No, before that woman I can't punish myself! I asked her forgiveness because I wanted to punish myself to the bitter end. She would not forgive me. . . . I like her for that!" she added, in an unnatural voice, and her eyes flashed with fierce resentment.

"My brother did not expect this in the least," muttered Alyosha. "He was sure she would not come. . . ."

"No doubt. Let us leave that," she snapped. "Listen: I can't go with you to the funeral now. I've sent them flowers. I think they still have money. If necessary, tell them I'll never abandon them. . . . Now leave me, leave me, please. You are late as it is—the bells are ringing for the service. . . . Leave me, please!"

3

ILUSHA'S FUNERAL.
THE SPEECH AT THE STONE

H E really was late. They had waited for him and had already decided to bear the pretty flower-decked little coffin to the church without him. It was the coffin of poor little Ilusha. He had died two days after Mitya was sentenced. At the gate of the house Alyosha was met by the shouts of the boys, Ilusha's schoolfellows. They had all been impatiently expecting him and were glad that he had come at last. There were about twelve of them, they all had their school-bags, or satchels on their shoulders. "Father will cry, be with father," Ilusha had told them as he lay dying, and the boys remembered it. Kolya Krassotkin was the foremost of them.

"How glad I am you've come, Karamazov!" he cried, holding out his hand to Alyosha. "It's awful here. It's really horrible to see it. Snegiryov is not drunk, we know for a fact he's had nothing to drink to-day, but he seems as if he were drunk . . . I am always manly, but this is awful Karamazov, if I am not keeping you, one question before you go in?"

"What is it, Kolya?" said Alyosha.

"Is your brother innocent or guilty? Was it he killed your father or was it the valet? As you say, so it will be. I haven't slept for the last four nights for thinking of it."

"The valet killed him, my brother is innocent," answered Alyosha.

"That's what I said," cried Smurov.

"So he will perish an innocent victim!" exclaimed Kolya; "though he is ruined he is happy! I could envy him!"

"What do you mean? How can you? Why?" cried Alyosha surprised.

"Oh, if I, too, could sacrifice myself some day for truth!" said Kolya with enthusiasm.

"But not in such a cause, not with such disgrace and such horror!" said Alyosha.

"Of course . . . I should like to die for all humanity, and as for disgrace, I don't care about that—our names may perish, I respect your brother!"

"And so do I!" the boy, who had once declared that he knew who had founded Troy, cried suddenly and unexpectedly and he blushed up to his ears like a peony as he had done on that occasion.

Alyosha went into the room. Ilusha lay with his hands folded and his eyes closed in a blue coffin with a white frill round it. His thin face was hardly changed at all, and strange to say there was no smell of decay from the corpse. The expression of his face was serious and, as it were, thoughtful. His hands, crossed over his breast, looked particularly beautiful, as though chiselled in marble. There were flowers in his hands and the coffin, inside and out, was decked with flowers, which had been sent early in the morning by Lise Hohlakov. But there were flowers too from Katerina Ivanovna, and when Alyosha opened the door, the captain had a bunch in his trembling hands and was strewing them again over his dear boy. He scarcely glanced at Alyosha when he came in, and he would not look at any one, even at his crazy weeping wife, "mamma," who kept trying to stand on her crippled legs to get a nearer look at her dead boy. Nina had been pushed in her chair by the boys close up to the coffin. She sat with her head pressed to it and she too was no doubt quietly weeping. Snegiryov's face looked eager, yet bewildered and exasperated. There was something crazy about his gestures and the words that broke from him. "Old man, dear old man!" he exclaimed every minute, gazing at Ilusha. It was his habit to call Ilusha "old man," as a term of affection when he was alive.

"Father, give me a flower, too; take that white one out of his hand and give it me," the crazy mother begged, whimpering. Either because the little white rose in Ilusha's hand had caught her fancy or that she wanted one from his hand to keep in memory of him, she moved restlessly, stretching out her hands for the flower.

"I won't give it to any one, I won't give you anything," Snegiryov cried callously. "They are his flowers, not yours! Everything is his, nothing is yours!"

"Father, give mother a flower!" said Nina, lifting her face wet with tears.

"I won't give away anything and to her less than any one! She didn't love Ilusha. She took away his little cannon and he gave it to her," the captain broke into loud sobs at the thought of how Ilusha had given up his cannon to his mother. The poor, crazy creature was bathed in noiseless tears, hiding her face in her hands.

The boys, seeing that the father would not leave the coffin and that it was time to carry it out, stood round it in a close circle and began to lift it up.

"I don't want him to be buried in the churchyard," Snegiryov wailed suddenly; "I'll bury him by the stone, by our stone! Ilusha told me to. I won't let him be carried out!"

He had been saying for the last three days that he would bury him by the stone, but Alyosha, Krassotkin, the landlady, her sister and all the boys interfered.

"What an idea, bury him by an unholy stone, as though he had hanged himself," the old landlady said sternly. "There in the churchyard the ground has been crossed. He'll be prayed for there. One can hear the singing in church and the deacon reads so plainly and verbally that it will reach him every time just as though it were read over his grave."

At last the captain made a gesture of despair as though to say, "Take him where you will." The boys raised the coffin, but as they passed the mother, they stopped for a moment and lowered it that she might say good-bye to Ilusha. But on seeing that precious little face, which for the last three days she had only looked at from a distance, she trembled all over and her grey head began twitching spasmodically over the coffin.

"Mother, make the sign of the cross over him, give him your blessing, kiss him," Nina cried to her. But her head still twitched like an automaton and with a face contorted with bitter grief she began, without a word, beating her breast with her fist. They carried the coffin past her. Nina pressed her lips to her brother's for the last time as they bore the coffin by her. As Alyosha went out of the house he begged the landlady to look after those who were left behind, but she interrupted him before he had finished.

"To be sure, I'll stay with them, we are Christians, too." The old woman wept as she said it.

They had not far to carry the coffin to the church, not more than three hundred paces. It was a still clear day, with a slight frost. The church bells were still ringing. Snegiryov ran fussing and distracted after the coffin, in his short old summer overcoat, with his head bare and his soft, old, wide-brimmed hat in his hand. He seemed in a state of bewildered anxiety. At one minute he stretched out his hand to support the head of the coffin and only hindered the bearers, at another he ran alongside and tried to find a place for himself there. A flower fell on the snow and he rushed to pick it up as though everything in the world depended on the loss of that flower.

"And the crust of bread, we've forgotten the crust!" he cried suddenly in dismay. But the boys reminded him at once that he had taken the crust of bread already and that it was in his pocket. He instantly pulled it out and was reassured.

"Ilusha told me to, Ilusha," he explained at once to Alyosha. "I was sitting by him one night and he suddenly told me: 'Father, when my grave is filled up crumble a piece of bread on it so that the sparrows may fly down, I shall hear and it will cheer me up not to be lying alone.'"

"That's a good thing," said Alyosha, "we must often take some."

"Every day, every day!" said the captain quickly, seeming cheered at the thought.

They reached the church at last and set the coffin in the middle of it. The boys surrounded it and remained reverently standing so, all through the service. It was an old and rather poor church. Many of the ikons were without settings but such churches are the best for praying in. During the mass Snegiryov became somewhat calmer, though at times he had outbursts of the same unconscious and, as it were, incoherent anxiety. At one moment he went up to the coffin to set straight the cover or the wreath, when a candle fell out of the candlestick he rushed to replace it and was a fearful time fumbling over it, then he subsided and stood quietly by the coffin with a look of blank uneasiness and perplexity. After the Epistle he suddenly whispered to Alyosha, who was standing beside him, that the Epistle had not been read properly but did not explain what he meant. During the prayer, "Like the Cherubim," he joined in the singing but did not go on to the end. Falling on his knees, he pressed his forehead to the stone floor and lay so for a long while.

At last came the funeral service itself and candles were distributed. The distracted father began fussing about again, but the touching and impressive funeral prayers moved and roused his soul. He seemed suddenly to shrink together and broke into rapid, short sobs, which he tried at first to smother, but at last he sobbed aloud. When they began taking leave of the dead and closing the coffin, he flung his arms about, as though he would not allow them to cover Ilusha, and began greedily and persistently kissing his dead boy on the lips. At last they succeeded in persuading him to come away from the step, but suddenly he impulsively stretched out his hand and snatched a few flowers from the coffin. He looked at them and a new idea seemed to dawn upon him, so that he apparently forgot his grief for a minute. Gradually he seemed to sink into brooding and did not resist when the coffin was lifted up and carried to the grave. It was an expensive one in the churchyard close to the church, Katerina Ivanovna had paid for it. After the customary rites the grave-diggers lowered the coffin. Snegiryov with his flowers in his hands bent down so low over the open grave that the boys caught hold of his coat in alarm and pulled him back. He did not seem to understand fully what was happening. When they began filling up the grave, he suddenly pointed anxiously at the falling earth and began trying to say something, but no one could make out what he meant, and he stopped suddenly. Then he was reminded that he must crumble the bread and he was awfully excited, snatched up the bread and began pulling it to pieces and flinging the morsels on the grave.

"Come, fly down, birds, fly down, sparrows!" he muttered anxiously.

One of the boys observed that it was awkward for him to crumble the bread with the flowers in his hands and suggested he should give them to some one to hold for a time. But he would not do this and seemed indeed suddenly alarmed for his flowers, as though they wanted to take them from him altogether. And after looking at the grave and, as it were, satisfying himself that everything had been done and the bread had been crumbled, he suddenly, to the surprise of every one, turned, quite composedly even, and made his way homewards. But his steps became more and more hurried, he almost ran. The boys and Alyosha kept up with him.

"The flowers are for mamma, the flowers are for mamma! I was unkind to mamma," he began exclaiming suddenly.

Some one called to him to put on his hat as it was cold. But he flung the hat in the snow as though he were angry and kept repeating, "I won't have the hat, I won't have the hat." Smurov picked it up and carried it after him. All the boys were crying, and Kolya and the boy who discovered about Troy most of all. Though Smurov, with the captain's hat in his hand, was crying bitterly too, he managed, as he ran, to snatch up a piece of red brick that lay on the snow of the path, to fling it at the flock of sparrows that was flying by. He missed them, of course, and went on crying as he ran. Half way, Snegiryov suddenly stopped, stood still for half a minute, as though struck by something, and suddenly turning back to the church, ran towards the deserted grave. But the boys instantly overtook him and caught hold of him on all sides. Then he fell helpless on the snow as though he had been knocked down, and struggling, sobbing, and wailing, he began crying out, "Ilusha, old man, dear old man!" Alyosha and Kolya tried to make him get up, soothing and persuading him.

"Captain, give over, a brave man must show fortitude," muttered Kolya.

"You'll spoil the flowers," said Alyosha, "and mamma is expecting them, she is sitting crying because you would not give her any before. Ilusha's little bed is still there. . . ."

"Yes, yes, mamma!" Snegiryov suddenly recollected, "they'll take away the bed, they'll take it away," he added as though alarmed that they really would. He jumped up and ran homewards again. But it was not far off and they all arrived together. Snegiryov opened the door hurriedly and called to his wife with whom he had so cruelly quarrelled just before:

"Mamma, poor crippled darling, Ilusha has sent you these flowers," he cried, holding out to her a little bunch of flowers that had been frozen and broken while he was struggling in the snow. But at that instant he saw in the corner, by the little bed, Ilusha's little boots, which the landlady had put tidily side by side. Seeing the old, patched, rusty-looking, stiff boots he flung up his hands and rushed to them, fell on his knees, snatched up one boot and, pressing his lips to it, began kissing it greedily, crying, "Ilusha, old man, dear old man, where are your little feet?"

"Where have you taken him away? Where have you taken him?" the lunatic cried in a heartrending voice. Nina, too, broke into sobs. Kolya ran out of the room, the boys followed him. At last Alyosha too went out.

"Let them weep," he said to Kolya, "it's no use trying to comfort them just now. Let us wait a minute and then go back."

"No, it's no use, it's awful," Kolya assented. "Do you know, Karamazov," he dropped his voice so that no one could hear them, "I feel dreadfully sad, and if it were only possible to bring him back, I'd give anything in the world to do it."

"Ah, so would I," said Alyosha.

"What do you think, Karamazov, had we better come back here tonight? He'll be drunk, you know."

"Perhaps he will. Let us come together, you and I, that will be enough, to spend an hour with them, with the mother and Nina. If we all come together we shall remind them of everything again," Alyosha suggested.

"The landlady is laying the table for them now—there'll be a funeral dinner or something, the priest is coming; shall we go back to it, Karamazov?"

"Of course," said Alyosha.

"It's all so strange, Karamazov, such sorrow and then pancakes after it, it all seems so unnatural in our religion."

"They are going to have salmon, too," the boy who had discovered about Troy observed in a loud voice.

"I beg you most earnestly, Kartashov, not to interrupt again with your idiotic remarks, especially when one is not talking to you and doesn't care to know whether you exist or not!" Kolya snapped out irritably. The boy flushed crimson but did not dare to reply.

Meantime they were strolling slowly along the path and suddenly Smurov exclaimed:

"There's Ilusha's stone, under which they wanted to bury him."

They all stood still by the big stone. Alyosha looked and the whole picture of what Snegiryov had described to him that day, how Ilusha, weeping and hugging his father, had cried, "Father, father, how he insulted you," rose at once before his imagination. A sudden impulse seemed to come into his soul. With a serious and earnest expression he looked from one to another of the bright, pleasant faces of Ilusha's school-fellows, and suddenly said to them:

"Boys, I should like to say one word to you, here at this place."

The boys stood round him and at once bent attentive and expectant eyes upon him.

"Boys, we shall soon part. I shall be for some time with my two brothers, of whom one is going to Siberia and the other is lying at death's door. But soon I shall leave this town, perhaps for a long time, so we shall part. Let us make a compact, here, at Ilusha's stone that we will never forget Ilusha and one another. And whatever happens to us later in life, if we don't meet for twenty years afterwards, let us always remember how we buried the poor boy at whom we once threw stones, do you remember, by the bridge? and afterwards we all grew so fond of him. He was a fine boy, a kind-hearted, brave boy, he felt for his father's honour and resented the cruel insult to him and stood up for him. And so in the first place, we will remember him, boys, all our lives. And even if we are occupied with most important things, if we attain to honour or fall into great misfortune—still let us remember how good it was once here, when we were all together, united by a good and kind feeling which made us, for the time we were loving that poor boy, better perhaps than we are. My little doves—let me call you so, for you are very like them, those pretty blue birds, at this minute as I look at your good dear faces. My dear children, perhaps you won't understand what I am saying to you, because I often speak very unintelligibly, but you'll remember it all the same and will agree with my words sometime. You must know that there is nothing higher and stronger and more wholesome and good for life in the future than some good memory, especially a memory of childhood, of home. People talk to you a great deal about your education, but some good, sacred memory, preserved from childhood, is perhaps the best education. If a man carries many such memories with him into life, he is safe to the end of his days, and if one has only one good memory left in one's heart, even that may sometime be the means of saving us. Perhaps we may even grow wicked later on, may be unable to refrain from a bad action, may laugh at men's tears and at those people who say as Kolya did just now, 'I want to suffer for all men,' and may even jeer spitefully at such people. But however bad we may become—which God forbid—yet, when we recall how we buried Ilusha, how we loved him in his last days, and how we have been talking like friends all together, at this stone, the cruellest and most mocking of us—if we do become so—will not dare to laugh inwardly at having been kind and good at this moment! What's more, perhaps, that one memory may keep him from great evil and he will reflect and say, 'Yes, I was good and brave and honest then!' Let him laugh to himself, that's no matter, a man often laughs at what's good and kind. That's only from thoughtlessness. But I assure you, boys, that as he laughs he will say at once in his heart, 'No, I do wrong to laugh, for that's not a thing to laugh at.' "

"That will be so, I understand you, Karamazov!" cried Kolya, with flashing eyes.

The boys were excited and they, too, wanted to say something, but they restrained themselves, looking with intentness and emotion at the speaker.

"I say this in case we become bad," Alyosha went on, "but there's no reason why we should become bad, is there, boys? Let us be, first and above all, kind, then honest and then let us never forget each other! I say that again. I give you my word for my part that I'll never forget one of you. Every face looking at me now I shall remember even for thirty years. Just now Kolya said to Kartashov that we did not care to know whether he exists or not. But I cannot forget that Kartashov exists and that he is not blushing now as he did when he discovered the founders of Troy, but is looking at me with his jolly, kind, dear little eyes. Boys, my dear boys, let us all be generous and brave like Ilusha, clever, brave and generous like Kolya (though he will be ever so much cleverer when he is grown up), and let us all be as modest, as clever and sweet as Kartashov. But why am I talking about those two! You are all dear to me, boys, from this day forth, I have a place in my heart for you all, and I beg you to keep a place in your hearts for me! Well, and who has united us in this kind, good feeling which we shall remember and intend to remember all our lives? Who, if not Ilusha, the good boy, the dear boy, precious to us for ever! Let us never forget him. May his memory live for ever in our hearts from this time forth!"[1]

"Yes, yes, for ever, for ever!" the boys cried in their ringing voices, with softened faces.

"Let us remember his face and his clothes and his poor little boots, his coffin and his unhappy, sinful father, and how boldly he stood up for him alone against the whole school."

"We will remember, we will remember," cried the boys. "He was brave, he was good!"

"Ah, how I loved him!" exclaimed Kolya.

"Ah, children, ah, dear friends, don't be afraid of life! How good life is when one does something good and just!"

"Yes, yes," the boys repeated enthusiastically.

"Karamazov, we love you!" a voice, probably Kartashov's, cried impulsively.

"We love you, we love you!" they all caught it up. There were tears in the eyes of many of them.

"Hurrah for Karamazov!" Kolya shouted ecstatically.

"And may the dear boy's memory live for ever!" Alyosha added again with feeling.

"For ever!" the boys chimed in again.

"Karamazov," cried Kolya, "can it be true what's taught us in religion, that we shall all rise again from the dead and shall live and see each other again, all, Ilusha too?"

"Certainly we shall all rise again, certainly we shall see each other and shall tell each other with joy and gladness all that has happened!" Alyosha answered, half laughing, half enthusiastic.

"Ah, how splendid it will be!" broke from Kolya.

"Well, now we will finish talking and go to his funeral dinner. Don't be put out at our eating pancakes—it's a very old custom and there's something nice in that!" laughed Alyosha. "Well, let us go! And now we go hand in hand."

"And always so, all our lives hand in hand! Hurrah for Karamazov!" Kolya cried once more rapturously and once more the boys took up his exclamation:

"Hurrah for Karamazov!"

Endnotes

1. (p. 3) Dedicated to Anna Grigorievna Dostoevsky: Anna Grigorievna Snitkina, Dostoevsky's second wife, was a stenographer to whom Dostoevsky dictated his novel *The Gambler* in 1866; they married the following year.

Book One: The History of a Family

1. (p. 17) *"Lord, now lettest Thou Thy servant depart in peace"*: Saint Simeon's prayer, spoken when he first beheld the Christ child, continues: "According to thy word: for mine eyes have seen thy salvation" (see the Bible, Luke 2:29–30, King James Version). It had been revealed to Saint Simeon that he would not die until he had seen the Lord Christ.

2. (p. 23) *a subject which was being debated everywhere at the time—the position of the ecclesiastical courts:* Russia's Judicial Reform Act of 1864, which addressed the principle of equality in civil law, spurred wide debates about whether the ecclesiastical courts, which operated by canon law, also needed to be reformed or even eliminated altogether; Dostoevsky often entered into such debates.

3. (p. 30) *"J'ai vu l'ombre d'un cocher qui avec l'ombre d'une brosse frottait l'ombre d'une carosse"*: "I saw the shadow of a coachman who with the shadow of a brush was cleaning the shadow of a coach" (French); the quotation is from a parody by French writer Charles Perrault (1628–1703) of book 6 of Virgil's *Aeneid*, in which Aeneas descends into the underworld.

4. (p. 32) *the calamities which overtook Russia—the Tatars, civil war, the interruption of relations with the East after the destruction of Constantinople:* The Tatars, of Turkish and Mongol origin, dominated Russia from 1237 to 1480. Constantinople (now Istanbul), the capital of the Eastern Roman Empire, was captured by the Ottoman Turks in 1453. Following the cruel reign of Ivan the Terrible, there was a period of civil war that ended in 1613, when the Russian nobles elected Michael Romanov as czar.

5. (p. 32) *one of the great "ascetics," as they called him, Païssy Velitchkovsky:* Païssy Velichkovsky (1722–1794) was a Russian Orthodox elder who traveled to monasteries throughout Russia; he also visited Mount Athos in northern Greece, a center of Eastern Orthodox monastic life. Dostoevsky owned a copy of Velichkovsky's translation of the homilies of the seventh-century monk Saint Isaac the Syrian, which influence Father Zossima's exhortations on hell and eternal love.

Book Two: An Unfortunate Gathering

1. (p. 46) *" 'Mr. Ispravnik,' said I, 'be our Napravnik' "*: This is a pun on the Russian word *ispravnik* (police captain), which suggests "rectifier" or "corrector," and E. F. Nápravnik (1839–1916), the Czech-born composer and conductor at the Mariinsky Opera Theatre in St. Petersburg, whose name suggests "conductor" or "director."

2. (p. 47) *"I'm like the philosopher, Diderot, your reverence. Did you ever hear . . . how Diderot went to see the Metropolitan Platon, in the time of the Empress Catherine?"*: Denis Diderot, the French philosopher, author, and founder of the *Encyclopédie* (1751–1772), visited Russia for five months in 1733 at the invitation of Catherine the Great. Pyotr Yegorovich Levshin (1737–1812), known as the Metropolitan Platon of Moscow, was a renowned Russian prelate and church leader; he adopted the name Platon when he became a monk.

3. (p. 47) *"Princess Dashkov was his godmother, and Potyomkin his godfather"*: Princess Yekaterina Romanovna Dashkova (1744–1810) was a friend of Catherine and helped her ascend to the throne during the Palace Revolt of 1762. Grigory Potyomkin (1739–1791) was a Russian statesman and military leader; as a favorite of Catherine, he was influential in state affairs.

4. (p. 54) *"After Alexey, the man of God?"*: Dostoevsky modeled Alyosha in part on Saint Alexis (died c.412), the patron saint of hermits and beggars. According to legend, Saint Alexis was born to wealthy Roman parents, but he left home and wandered to Greece, where he lived as a pauper and spent his days in prayer; eventually Alexis returned to Rome to live as a hermit on his family's estate. Like Saint Alexis, Alyosha is sometimes referred to as a "man of God."

5. (p. 64) *"The purest Ultramontanism!"*: The reference is to a movement favoring the absolute supremacy of the Pope over the Roman Catholic Church; originating in the fifteenth century in Italy, "across the mountains" (the Latin roots of the word) from French opponents of the movement, it was still a powerful force in Dostoevsky's time.

6. (p. 72) *"they are both out of Schiller's* Robbers, *and so I am the reigning Count von Moor!"*: German writer Friedrich Schiller (1759–1805) influenced Dostoevsky greatly, and there are many references to him in this novel. His *Sturm und Drang* drama *The Robbers* (1781) also concerns the relationship of a father, Count von Moor, to his sons.

Book Three: The Sensualists

1. (p. 104) *"he came to me like the golden fish to the silly old fishermen in the fable!"*: The reference is to Pushkin's "The Tale of the Fisherman and the Fish" (1833), which was inspired by a Grimm's fairy tale.

2. (p. 123) *There is a remarkable picture by the painter Kramskoy, called "Contemplation"*: The famous Russian portraitist Ivan Nikolayevich

Kramskoy (1837–1887) painted many of his eminent contemporaries, including Tolstoy, and he made a drawing of the dead Dostoevsky before his funeral in 1881. Kramskoy's *The Contemplator* (also known as *The Meditator*) was painted in 1876 and first exhibited in 1878.

3. (p. 129) *"There's a set of de Sades for you!":* The sexual excesses and cruelty of French writer and novelist Marquis de Sade (1740–1814) gave birth to the word "sadism."

4. (p. 131) "Il y a du Piron là dedans": "There's something of Piron in him" (French). French epigrammatist and playwright Alexis Piron (1689–1773) was refused entry into L'Académie Française (the French Academy), a literary society established in the early seventeenth century, because of a pornographic ode he had written early in his career.

5. (p. 131) *"There's something of Mephistopheles about him, or rather of 'The hero of our time.' . . . Arbenin, or what's his name?":* The hero of Mikhail Lermontov's novel *A Hero of Our Time* (1840) is actually Pechorin; Arbenin is the hero of Lermontov's play *Masquerade* (1835).

6. (p. 148) *"It's a regular discovery of the four continents of the world, that is, of the five!":* In the nineteenth century, only five continents were acknowledged: Europe, Asia, Africa, America, and Australia.

Book Four: Lacerations

1. (p. 188) *"Mr. Tchernomazov":* Arina Petrovna uses the Russian form of "black" instead of the Turkish *kara* (black or dark), from which the name Karamazov stems.

Book Five: Pro and Contra

1. (p. 206) *"I feel like Famusov in the last scene of* Sorrow from Wit": The final act of the well-known satire on Russian society *Woe from Wit* (or *Misfortune from Intelligence*), by Russian poet and dramatist A. S. Griboyedov (1795–1829), takes place on a staircase; Famusov, Tchatsky, and Sofya are characters in the play. The play was censored and not published until 1833, but it was copied and privately circulated earlier.

2. (p. 208) *On her and on me!:* According to a May 22, 1879, letter from Dostoevsky to N. A. Lyubimov, the editor of the *Russian Herald* (where *The Brothers Karamazov* first appeared), this is an original Russian song, composed by merchant clerks of the Third Guild, that Dostoevsky had heard in Moscow and written down forty years earlier. Dostoevsky said that the song appeared in print for the first time in his novel.

3. (p. 217) "S'il n'existait pas Dieu, il faudrait l'inventer": "If God did not exist, it would be necessary to invent him" (French), a quotation

from the verse epistle "To the Author of a New Book on the Three Imposters" (1769), by Voltaire.

4. (p. 219) *"John the Merciful... began breathing into his mouth, which was putrid and loathsome from some awful disease":* The reference is to Saint John the Merciful, patriarch of Alexandria (611–619); but the story Ivan tells is from French author Gustave Flaubert's "The Legend of St. Julien, the Hospitalier," a short story in *Trois Contes* (*Three Tales*; 1877), in which Julien (changed to John by Ivan) is a father murderer. Turgenev's translation of Flaubert's work also appeared in 1877.

5. (pp. 223–224) *"A well-educated, cultured gentleman and his wife beat their own child with a birch-rod.... There was a little girl of five who was ... subjected to every possible torture ... and ... her mother did this":* These two stories are based on actual court cases. Dostoevsky discussed the first, the Kroneberg case, and V. D. Spassovich, the defense attorney in that case, at length in *A Writer's Diary* (1876). Spassovich may be a model for Fetyukovitch in this novel (see p. 519) though Dostoevsky denied it.

6. (p. 224) *"I have only just read it in some collection of Russian antiquities. I've forgotten the name":* The article "Memoirs of a Serf" appeared in the *Russian Herald* (1877, no. 9).

7. (p. 229) *"one such poem (of course, from the Greek), 'The Wanderings of Our Lady through Hell,' with descriptions as bold as Dante's.... 'Thou are just, O Lord, in this judgment' ":* The Journey of the Mother of God Through the Torments was a twelfth-century apocryphal legend translated from a Byzantine source, which was well known in Russia and published several times in various journals.

8. (p. 229) *"And just then there appeared in the north of Germany a terrible new heresy":* The reference is to the Reformation, a religious revolution of the sixteenth century that resulted in the split between Roman Catholicism and Protestantism; the movement was led in Germany by religious reformer Martin Luther.

9. (p. 230) *"in the splendid* auto da fé *the wicked heretics were burnt":* This is a paraphrase from A. I. Polezhayev's poem "Coriolanus" (1857). An *auto da fé* (from the Spanish for "act of faith") was a judgment of the Inquisition that led to the public burning of heretics.

10. (p. 238) *"Just eight centuries ago, we took from him what Thou didst reject with scorn":* Pope Stephen II assumed secular power in A.D. 755, eight centuries before the mid-sixteenth century of the Grand Inquisitor. Pepin the Short, king of the Franks, turned the territories of the duchy of Rome over to Stephen, thereby laying the basis for the Papal States and founding the Pope's temporal power.

11. (p. 242) *"I fancy that even among the Masons there's something of the same mystery at the bottom":* The Masons, or Freemasons, were a secret brotherhood that reputedly originated in medieval England (though the first organized lodge dates from 1717) and spread throughout the world. In the eighteenth century, the Russian Orthodox and Roman Catholic Churches deemed the society heretical.

12. (p. 244) *"Come, go now to your Pater Seraphicus"*: Pater Seraphicus (Latin for "Angelic Father"), from the final scene of Goethe's *Faust* (part 2), is an epithet used in connection with Saint Francis of Assisi and, here, Father Zossima. In Goethe's work, Pater Seraphicus is an anchorite who guides the souls of stillborn boys toward divine bliss.

Book Six: The Russian Monk

1. (p. 267) *I had a book of Scripture history . . . called "A Hundred and Four Stories from the Old and New Testament"*: This collection of Bible stories, translated from the German, is one that Dostoevsky learned to read from as a child.
2. (p. 268) *In the land of Uz, there lived a man*: This passage begins the biblical book of Job, from which Zossima begins to paraphrase from memory in the subsequent narration.
3. (p. 270) *Mary of Egypt*: According to legend, Mary (344–421?) spent seventeen years as a prostitute in Alexandria and traveled to Jerusalem to continue her trade, but when she felt a secret force prevent her from entering the church three times, she repented and subsequently spent forty-seven years alone in the desert. She is a saint in the Russian Orthodox Church.
4. (p. 271) *"once a bear came to a great saint, . . . and . . . walked away meekly and obediently, doing no harm"*: The bear episode is taken from the *Life of St. Sergius of Radonezh*. Saint Sergius (1314–1392) was a Russian monk and an important figure in the history of the Russian Orthodox Church; he founded the famous Troitze-Sergievki monastery in the forest of Radonezh, near Moscow in 1340.
5. (pp. 297–298) *woe to the suicides! . . . I believe that we may pray even for them*: Zossima is consistent with his own teaching of loving everything when he includes the suicides, who were denied both burial and a memorial service in the Russian Orthodox Church because of the enormity of the sin of self-slaughter.

Book Seven: Alyosha

1. (pp. 322–323) *"Once upon a time there was a peasant woman. . . . So the angel wept and went away"*: In a letter to N. A. Lyubimov (September 16, 1879). Dostoevsky calls this story, which he heard from a peasant woman, a "gem" that he is the first to publish.

Book Eight: Mitya

1. (p. 349) *"Othello was not jealous, he was trustful," observed Pushkin*: This comment on Shakespeare's *Othello* is in Pushkin's *Table-Talk*

(published after his death), the title of which he kept in English as a reference to English writer William Hazlitt's *Table Talk* (1821).

2. (p. 354) *" 'Enough!' as Turgenev says"*: Turgenev's novella *Enough: A Fragment from the Notes of a Deceased Artist* (1865) was his "farewell" to literature, though he continued to write for nearly two decades until his death in 1883. Dostoevsky caricatured Turgenev and ridiculed his ideas in his novel *The Demons*. Their relationship was difficult and turbulent, but ultimately respectful.

3. (p. 355) *"the author, Shtchedrin. . . . And the word 'contemporary' might have reminded him of* The Contemporary": In this passage Dostoevsky continues his parody of his adversary, N. Shtchedrin (pseudonym of Mikhail Saltykov, 1826–1889), a Russian journalist, novelist, and satirist. *The Contemporary* was a literary-political journal founded in 1836 by Pushkin and edited for a time by Shtchedrin; it represented the censored revolutionary democratic voices of the time and was closed down by the authorities in 1866.

4. (p. 381) "Panie": In Polish, *pan* (plural *panowie*) means "sir" or "gentleman," and *pani* refers to "lady" or "mistress." Dostoevsky used many Polish sentences and phrases in this part of the original text, sometimes giving Russian translations, especially when the sense would not be clear to Russians.

5. (p. 388) *"To Poland,* panovie, *I drink to your Poland! . . . Now to Russia,* panovie, *and let us be brothers!"*: Russia, Prussia, and Austria partitioned Poland in 1772, which heightened Polish nationalism and led to the Polish uprising of 1863. The toast is conciliatory on Dmitri's part, but Pan Vrublevsky refuses to join in the toast to Russia.

6. (p. 397) *one "new" song to a jaunty dance-tune:* In his November 16, 1879, letter to N. A. Lyubimov, Dostoevsky says that he copied down the song as "a real example of contemporary compositions."

Book Nine: The Preliminary Investigation

1. (p. 423) *"with the lantern of Diogenes"*: Legend has it that the Greek philosopher and cynic Diogenes (404–323? B.C.), who practiced self-control and rigid abstinence and had contempt for all riches, honor, and ambition, went about with a lantern in the daytime "looking for an honest man."

Book Ten: The Boys

1. (p. 506) *"old Byelinsky"*: The reference is to Vissarion Belinsky (1811–1848), a very influential radical and liberal literary critic who promoted Dostoevsky in his early career. In *A Writer's Diary*, Dostoevsky reports on his conversations with Belinsky.

2. (p. 506) *"Long will you remember/The house at the Chain bridge"*: This is a quotation from a radical satire by Russian poet D. D. Minayev, which appeared in 1861 and was familiar to most of Dostoevsky's readers. The headquarters of the czarist secret police were near the Chain Bridge (now renamed the Pestal Bridge) across the Neva River in St. Petersburg.

3. (p. 507) *"What if he should find out that I've only that one number of* The Bell": *The Bell* (1857–1867) was a revolutionary newspaper published by Russian political writer and expatriate Aleksandr Herzen; it was smuggled into Russia, where it was widely read. A sequel to Minayev's satire appeared there.

Book Eleven: Ivan

1. (p. 526) *"They want to put a monument to your Pushkin for writing about women's feet":* Reference to the poetry of Aleksandr Pushkin (1799–1837). Dostoevsky's speech on Pushkin at the monument's unveiling on June 6, 1880, the year before his death, produced a "tempest of ecstasy" in the audience. According to his wife, Dostoevsky returned that night to the monument and bowed down to the ground before it.

2. (p. 537) *"Claude Bernard":* Bernard (1813–1878) was a French physiologist and pathologist whose important book, *Introduction to Experimental Medicine*, lays out the basic principles of scientific research; the book appeared in Russian translation in 1866 and was read by Dostoevsky.

3. (p. 537) "de ideabus non est disputandum": "There is no disputing ideas" (Latin), Mitya's variation on the Latin aphorism *de gustibus non est disputandum* (there is no disputing tastes).

4. (p. 582) *"Gattzuk would put it in his calendar":* A. A. Gattzuk (1832–1891) published the yearly *Religious Calendar* (1876–1890) and the Moscow periodical *A. Gattzuk's Gazette*.

5. (p. 583) *"I can only cure your right nostril":* Dostoevsky may be echoing Voltaire, in whose philosophical novel *Zadig* (1747) the doctor can only cure the right eye.

6. (p. 588) "Ah mon père, . . . ça lui fait tant de plaisir, et à moi si peu de peine!": "Ah, Father, it gives him so much pleasure and me so little pain" (French). An often-quoted French epigram that begins "Tendre Gaussin . . ." is thought, therefore, to have been originally inspired by the famous French actress J. C. Gaussin (1722–1767).

7. (p. 588) *"I did think . . . of appearing in the figure of a retired general who had served in the Caucasus, with a star of the Lion and the Sun on my coat . . . instead of, at least, the Polar Star or the Sirius":* The "star of the Lion and the Sun" was a Persian decoration sometimes awarded to Russian civil servants who served in the Caucasus, a mountainous region of southwestern Russia. The Royal Order of the Polar Star was the name of a Swedish decoration for civil service and also of a radical literary almanac. The Sirius, another decoration, also

refers to the hero of Voltaire's novella *Micromégas* (1752), who lives on Sirius. The politically conservative devil is needling Ivan about his radicalism.

8. (p. 591) "Monsieur sait-il le temps qu'il fait? C'est à ne pas mettre un chien dehors": "Does the gentleman know what the weather is? You wouldn't put a dog out in it" (French). This line is part of a joke about a servant who, when asked to deliver a note, hesitates to go; it ends with the master answering: "But, Baptiste, you are not a dog."

Book Twelve: A Judicial Error

1. (p. 611) *a Herrnhuter or Moravian brother:* The Herrnhuter were members of a Protestant religious and social movement that arose in 1722 in the town of Herrnhut in Saxony, in southeastern Germany; missionary work subsequently spread it worldwide, including throughout Russia. Herrnhuter doctrines were in part derived from the Bohemian Moravian Brethren, a religious sect from the mid-fifteenth century, originally inspired by the Protestant reformer Jan Hus, who was burned as a heretic in 1415; later the movement's orientation focused on the concrete life circumstances of people.

2. (p. 632) *"new jury courts":* The Russian judicial reforms of 1864 introduced jury trials that were open to the public; newspapers printed transcriptions of the speeches delivered by the prosecution and the defense.

3. (p. 657) *"we'd shut up Kronstadt and not let them have any corn":* Kronshtadt, located on the island of Kotlin in the Gulf of Finland, was one of Russia's main ports and the naval base guarding the entry to St. Petersburg.

4. (p. 674) vivos voco: "I call the living" (Latin). This was the motto of Herzen's revolutionary journal *The Bell* (see note 3, book 10); it derives from Schiller's epigraph to his poem "Song of the Bell" (1798).

5. (p. 674) *"like the Moscow women in Ostrovsky's play, who are scared at the sound of certain words":* In Russian dramatist A. N. Ostrovsky's play *Hard Days* (1863), two merchants' wives speak of their fear of biblical words like "metal" and "brimstone" (act 2, scene 2).

6. (p. 675) *"Drive nature out of the door and it will fly in at the window":* The quotation comes from a Russian translation by author and historian N. M. Karamzin of French poet Jean de La Fontaine's fable "Chatte metamorphosée en femme" (The Cat Changed into a Woman), from *Fables* (1668–1694; book 2, poem 18).

7. (p. 680) *"I'll break my sword over my head myself":* In a ceremony known as a "civil execution," a sword was broken over the head of a man condemned to death. Dostoevsky suffered the trauma of such a condemnation and near execution on December 22, 1849, and described it in a letter to his brother, Mikhail, that same day (*Complete Letters: Vol. 1, 1832–1859*, pp. 178–182; see "For Further Reading").

8. (p. 681) *"an actress was acquitted in our town who had cut the throat of her lover's lawful wife":* This refers to the actual case of the actress A. V. Kairova, which Dostoevsky wrote about in the May 1876 issue of *A Writer's Diary.*

Epilogue

1. (p. 701) *"May his memory live for ever in our hearts from this time forth!":* At the end Alyosha speaks to the children about memory and specifically their memory of each other; but here there is also a reference to a prayer from the end of the Orthodox funeral service, "Memory Eternal," which refers to God's memory. They have just sung it at Ilusha's funeral. Memories of goodness and good deeds are very important to Dostoevsky and are a critical component of every conversion experience in the novel.

Inspired by The Brothers Karamazov

Theater

Inspired by Hollywood's disastrous 1958 adaptation of *The Brothers Karamazov*, starring Yul Brynner and William Shatner, a precocious high school student from New Jersey hired local actors to star in his own eight-millimeter version of Dostoevsky's classic. The student, Christopher Durang, would grow up to become the renowned playwright; the film, replete with Catholic monks' robes borrowed from school, became what Durang affectionately referred to as his "crackpot movie." Later, at the Yale School of Drama, Durang showed his zany film to budding playwright Albert Innaurato (*Gemini*, 1977; *Passione*, 1980). Inspired anew, the two penned a stage adaptation of *The Brothers Karamazov* (1973), giving translator Constance Garnett the lead role. They announced, on flyers posted around the Yale campus, that this role would be played by none other than esteemed actress Dame Edith Evans. However, at actual performances a cross-dressing Innaurato managed the part of the famous translator. In the play, Garnett's lunacy is matched only by her imperious self-regard. As she struggles with Dostoevsky's tome, she joins a party of characters, both fictional and historical (including diarist Anaïs Nin)—all of them somewhat absurd. The result is a gentle parody of the greater part of the Western canon.

The play captured the attention of theater professor Howard Stein, who encouraged Durang and Innaurato to expand and rework it. The resulting new version, titled *The Idiots Karamazov* (referencing another of Dostoevsky's novels, *The Idiot*, as well as the play's general absurdity), premiered at the Yale Repertory Theater in 1974 and starred Meryl Streep as Constance Garnett. *The Idiots Karamazov* successfully launched the careers of both Durang and Innaurato. Durang went on to write some of the twentieth century's funniest theater, in plays such as the Obie-winning *Sister Mary Ignatius Explains It All for You* (1979) and an ensemble of six one-act parodies titled *Durang Durang* (1994).

Dance

The dramatic power of dance to evoke the complicated relationships of Dostoevsky's characters is evidenced in Russian choreographer Boris Eifman's two-act ballet *The Karamazovs* (1995). The work, set to the music of Sergei Rachmaninoff, Modest Mussorgsky, and Richard Wagner, is characterized by simple, stylized movements and theatrical sweeps of light—red for Russia's debased sensualists and white for Alyosha's spiritual quest. The cast, streamlined from the novel, consists of the three legitimate Karamazovs, Ivan, Alexey, and Dmitri; their father, Fyodor; Katerina Ivanovna; and Grushenka (Agrafena Alexandrovna). In the striking second act, Ivan and Alexey transmogrify, respectively, into the Grand Inquisitor and Jesus, who wrestle each other to the ground in the ballet's memorable climax.

Choreographer Kim Brandstrup ambitiously reinterprets Dostoevsky with his dance piece *Brothers* (2002). Expanding his 2001 work, *Elegy*, which sketched the love triangle of *The Idiot*, Brandstrup's *Brothers* blends plot elements and characters from three Dostoevsky novels: *The House of the Dead*, *The Idiot*, and *The Brothers Karamazov*. The interweaving plotlines allow for the shared passions of the characters: thwarted love, cruelty, and haunting, intense longing. The swirling dancers—six brothers plus their female counterparts—are set against the drab monochrome of the backdrops, meant to symbolize Russia's peasantry and penal servitude. Each of the three acts corresponds to a novel, and the result is a challenging, nonlinear meditation on the weight of human suffering. *Brothers* features the design talents of Craig Givens and Tina MacHugh, and is set to composer Jonathan Stone's mournful score.

Literature

With a titular reference to Dostoevsky's epic, David James Duncan's *The Brothers K* (1992) offers an American analogue: an affectionate history of a working-class family filled with soul-searching, 1960s pop culture, and an abundance of baseball. The book revolves around the four brothers (and two twin sisters) of Papa Chance, a retired minor-league pitcher who spends his days in a sawmill. Set in the small town of Camas, Washington (not to mention Vietnam, India, and Canada), *The Brothers K* carries Dostoevsky's metaphysical dialogue into twentieth-century America, as the brothers, especially Kincaid Chance, try to puzzle out the meaning of religion and faith.

Comments & Questions

In this section, we aim to provide the reader with an array of perspectives on the text, as well as questions that challenge those perspectives. The commentary has been culled from sources as diverse as reviews contemporaneous with the work, letters written by the author, literary criticism of later generations, and appreciations written throughout the work's history. Following the commentary, a series of questions seeks to filter Fyodor Dostoevsky's The Brothers Karamazov *through a variety of points of view and bring about a richer understanding of this enduring work.*

Comments

FRIEDRICH NIETZSCHE

Dostoevsky [is] the only psychologist, incidentally, from whom I had something to learn; he ranks among the most beautiful strokes of fortune in my life.

—from *Twilight of the Idols* (1888)

JOSEPH CONRAD

I do hope you are not too disgusted with me for not thanking you for the "Karamazov" before. It was very good of you to remember me; and of course I was extremely interested. But it's an impossible lump of valuable matter. It's terrifically bad and impressive and exasperating. Moreover, I don't know what D[ostoevsky] stands for or reveals, but I do know that he is too Russian for me. It sounds to me like some fierce mouthings from prehistoric ages. I understand the Russians have just 'discovered' him. I wish them joy.

—from a letter to Edward Garnett (May 27, 1912)

THE NATION

In boldness of conception ["The Brothers Karamazoff"] might very well rank as the author's masterpiece. Its mere length is impressive; nearly half a million words, one should say, and that but a fragment. But unfortunately the execution fell far short of the plan. Dostoievsky's worst faults show here in exaggerated form. The book is ill-jointed and fearfully verbose. Its analysis of character degenerates too frequently into psychological acrobatics. . . . One might as well be frank and admit that Dostoievsky in this book frequently loses himself in the meshes of his own word spinning. The personality of his men and women is in danger of being diluted in the verbal flow. The search of the interplay of motive can be carried to the point of subtlety where character disappears and only the shifting impulses of the moment remain. There are in "The Brothers Karamazoff" pages of extraordinary depth and poignancy. There is one scene which, for pathos, it would be very hard to match in modern fiction. But of the book as a whole, it must be said that it exemplifies Dostoievsky's common fault in choosing to be the chronicler of the soul instead of its historian.

—July 11, 1912

MAURICE LAZAR
Dostoevsky's last and unquestionably finest work, *The Brothers Karamazov*, . . . is incomplete, actually one-third as long as he had intended it to be. He died before he could finish the book. Nevertheless it is a compactly-formed material as the work now stands, and superior to his other novels not because his outlines are more constrained, his movement more co-ordinate, and the actual writing of a more intensive quality, but because here he defines his own conception of spiritual beauty in a distinctive fashion not to be found in his other books.

He offers us the history of a family,—and what a family! Each figure in this domestic (?) group embodies conflicting phases of his great idea. Fyodor Karamazov, the father, is a sensualist of the lowest type imaginable. His three sons are Dimitri, Ivan, and Alyosha. There is also another (illegitimate) son, Smerdyakov, an epileptic.

Dimitri Karamazov inherits his father's passion for wine, women, and song, but the son's pursuit of this tame and conventional item is tempered by frequent lapses, by periods of misgiving. The second son is a materialist and a cynic. He changes his mind after a severe illness, and his materialistic beliefs are all but supplanted by intense spiritual curiosity. The third and youngest son is an idealist, lovable and loving. Here again we have Dostoevsky's discordant elements conveyed in terms of human characterizations. The plot of the story is as formless as life itself, for it is with life, not with plots, that Dostoevsky deals.

—from *Little Review* (July 1914)

ROBERT LYND
Dostoevsky's visible world was a world of sensationalism. He may in the last analysis be a great mystic or a great psychologist; but he almost always reveals his genius on a stage crowded with people who behave like the men and women one reads about in the police news. There are more murders and attempted murders in his books than in those of any other great novelist. His people more nearly resemble madmen and wild beasts than normal human beings.

He releases them from most of the ordinary inhibitions. He is fascinated by the loss of self-control—by the disturbance and excitement which this produces, often in the most respectable circles. He is beyond all his rivals the novelist of "scenes." His characters get drunk, or go mad with jealousy, or fall in epileptic fits, or rave hysterically. If Dostoevsky had had less vision he would have been Strindberg. If his vision had been æsthetic and sensual, he might have been D'Annunzio.

Like them, he is a novelist of torture. Turgenev found in his work something Sadistic, because of the intensity with which he dwells on cruelty and pain. Certainly the lust of cruelty—the lust of destruction for destruction's sake—is the most conspicuous of the deadly sins in Dostoevsky's men and women.

—from *Old and New Masters* (1919)

EDWIN MUIR
Dostoyevsky wrote of the unconscious as if it were conscious: that is in reality the reason why his characters seem "pathological," while they are only visualized more clearly than any other figures in imaginative literature.

This capacity to "experience two opposite feelings at one and the same time" is at the centre of Dostoyevsky's art, religion and psychology; and his whole work is the demonstration of a sort of unconscious theology within us, a sort of religion working in the subconscious minds of men like an ineluctable process, and demanding an end, a solution, a poise, a harmony: Absolute Value or God.

—from *Latitudes* (1924)

Questions

1. Should we make anything out of the fact that Father Zossima's corpse stinks?

2. Do you agree that if there is no God, everything is permitted?

3. Do you think that the Soviet Union as it was under Stalin would have had the Grand Inquisitor's approval?

4. Can the theory of love that emerges from the novel be concisely formulated in ordinary language? Do you believe that this notion of love is achievable by actual humans, or is it a utopian standard by which we can only measure ourselves?

5. Which of the brothers Karamazov do you find most sympathetic? Why? Could you, if you worked at it, love them equally and non-judgmentally? If not, are you a failure?

6. If *The Brothers Karamazov* was originally intended as the first part of a trilogy, what might Dostoevsky have intended for the latter two installments? Do you think Alyosha would grow into a version of his father, Fyodor Karamazov, or would he more resemble Father Zossima?

For Further Reading

Biography

Dostoevsky, Fyodor. *Complete Letters: Vol. 1, 1832–1859*. Edited and translated by David Lowe and Ronald Meyer. Ann Arbor, MI: Ardis, 1988.

———. *Complete Letters: Vol. 2, 1860–1867*. Edited and translated by David Lowe. Ann Arbor, MI: Ardis, 1989.

Frank, Joseph. *Dostoevsky: The Seeds of Revolt, 1821–1849*. Princeton, NJ: Princeton University Press, 1976.

———. *Dostoevsky: The Years of Ordeal, 1850–1859*. Princeton, NJ: Princeton University Press, 1983.

———. *Dostoevsky: The Stir of Liberation, 1860–1865*. Princeton, NJ: Princeton University Press, 1986.

———. *Dostoevsky: The Miraculous Years, 1865–1871*. Princeton, NJ: Princeton University Press, 1995.

———. *Dostoevsky: The Mantle of the Prophet, 1871–1881*. Princeton, NJ: Princeton University Press, 2002. The last volume of Frank's brilliant, definitive five-volume biography. The summa of all previous biographies and known facts about Dostoevsky, and indispensable reading for all Dostoevsky scholars. This volume contains an outstanding, book-by-book analysis of *The Brothers Karamazov*.

Criticism

Bakhtin, Mikhail. *Problems of Dostoevsky's Poetics*. Edited and translated by Caryl Emerson, with an introduction by Wayne C. Booth. Minneapolis: University of Minnesota Press, 1984. A significant and revolutionary twentieth-century contribution to Dostoevsky studies and to the poetics of the novel as a whole.

Belknap, Robert L. *The Genesis of "The Brothers Karamazov": The Aesthetics, Ideology, and Psychology of Text Making*. Evanston, IL: Northwestern University Press, 1990. A learned and fascinating study of how Dostoevsky incorporated and transformed his sources, readings, interests, and experiences to create *The Brothers Karamazov*.

———. *The Structure of "The Brothers Karamazov."* Evanston, IL: Northwestern University Press, 1989. A fine close, critical analysis of the structure of the novel and how its parts form a whole.

Berdiaev, Nikolai. *Dostoevsky*. Translated by Donald Attwater. New York: Meridian Books, 1957. A masterful study by a religious philosopher of Dostoevsky's ideas about freedom, evil, love, revolution, socialism, and Russia.

Gide, André. *Dostoevsky*. 1925. Westport, CT: Greenwood Publishing Group, 1979. An intensely personal, sympathetic, and engaging reading.

Girard, René. *Resurrection from the Underground: Feodor Dostoevsky.* Edited and translated by James G. Williams. New York: Crossroads Publishing Company, 1997. Focuses on mimetic desire and the "underground" of envy, shame, and sadomasochism in Dostoevsky's works.

Holquist, Michael. *Dostoevsky and the Novel.* Princeton, NJ: Princeton University Press, 1977. A provocative questioning of Dostoevsky's place in the theories of the novel of Georg Lukács and René Girard and his fit with Sigmund Freud's theses on fathers and sons.

Ivanov, V. I. *Freedom and the Tragic Life: A Study in Dostoevsky.* Wolfeboro, NH: Longwood Academic, 1989. A compelling, poetic reading of the tragic, mythological, and theological aspects of *The Brothers Karamazov* by a major Russian symbolist poet, critic, and philosopher.

Jackson, Robert Louis. *Dialogues with Dostoevsky: The Overwhelming Questions.* Stanford, CA: Stanford University Press, 1993. A set of essays that create a multivoiced dialogue linking Dostoevsky to Chateaubriand, Sade, Turgenev, Chekhov, Gogol, Tolstoy, Shakespeare, Nietzsche, Ivanov, and Bakhtin.

———, ed. *Dostoevsky: New Perspectives.* Englewood Cliffs, NJ: Prentice-Hall, 1984. Contains four essays on *The Brothers Karamazov* by Victor Terras, Valentina A. Vetlovskaya, Robert L. Belknap, and Jacques Catteau.

Rozanov, V. V. *Dostoevsky and the Legend of the Grand Inquisitor.* Translated by Spencer E. Roberts. Ithaca, NY: Cornell University Press, 1972. An influential early study, published in 1891 by an eccentric Russian writer and thinker.

Shestov, Lev. *Dostoevsky, Tolstoy, and Nietzsche.* Athens: Ohio University Press, 1969. An eloquent though controversial view of Dostoevsky.

Steiner, George. *Tolstoy or Dostoevsky: An Essay in the Old Criticism.* Chicago, IL: University of Chicago Press, 1959. A brilliantly wide-ranging and learned essay in poetic and philosophic criticism.

Straus, Nina Pelikan. *Dostoevsky and the Woman Question: Rereadings at the End of a Century.* New York: St. Martin's Press, 1994. A forceful and original feminist perspective on Dostoevsky's novels and female figures.

Terras, Victor. *A Karamazov Companion: Commentary on the Genesis, Language, and Style of Dostoevsky's Novel.* Madison: University of Wisconsin Press, 1981. A significant, highly intelligent, and deeply erudite commentary on the novel.

Thompson, Diane Oenning. *"The Brothers Karamazov" and the Poetics of Memory.* Cambridge and New York: Cambridge University Press, 1991. Focuses on memory as a subject and a principle of aesthetic and artistic composition in *The Brothers Karamazov.*

Wasiolek, Edward. *Dostoevsky: The Major Fiction.* Cambridge: M.I.T. Press, 1964. Illuminating, close, critical readings of the great novels.

———. *"The Brothers Karamazov" and the Critics.* Belmont, CA: Wadsworth Publishing Company, 1967. Contains Sigmund Freud's essay "Dostoevsky and Parricide" and essays by Ernest Simmons, Eliseo Vivas, Albert Camus, D. H. Lawrence, Philip Rahv, Mark Kanzer, Ralph Matlaw, and Wasiolek.

Look for the following titles, available now from
BARNES & NOBLE CLASSICS

Visit your local bookstore for these and more fine titles.
Or to order online go to: WWW.BN.COM/CLASSICS

Adventures of Huckleberry Finn	Mark Twain	1-59308-112-X	$6.95
The Adventures of Tom Sawyer	Mark Twain	1-59308-139-1	$6.95
The Aeneid	Vergil	1-59308-237-1	$10.95
Aesop's Fables		1-59308-062-X	$8.95
The Age of Innocence	Edith Wharton	1-59308-143-X	$8.95
Alice's Adventures in Wonderland and Through the Looking-Glass	Lewis Carroll	1-59308-015-8	$7.95
Anna Karenina	Leo Tolstoy	1-59308-027-1	$9.95
The Arabian Nights	Anonymous	1-59308-281-9	$11.95
The Art of War	Sun Tzu	1-59308-017-4	$9.95
The Autobiography of an Ex-Colored Man and Other Writings	James Weldon Johnson	1-59308-289-4	$5.95
The Awakening and Selected Short Fiction	Kate Chopin	1-59308-113-8	$6.95
Billy Budd and The Piazza Tales	Herman Melville	1-59308-253-3	$7.95
The Brothers Karamazov	Fyodor Dostoevsky	1-59308-045-X	$12.95
The Call of the Wild and White Fang	Jack London	1-59308-200-2	$6.95
Candide	Voltaire	1-59308-028-X	$7.95
The Canterbury Tales	Geoffrey Chaucer	1-59308-080-8	$10.95
A Christmas Carol, The Chimes and The Cricket on the Hearth	Charles Dickens	1-59308-033-6	$7.95
The Collected Oscar Wilde		1-59308-310-6	$11.95
The Collected Poems of Emily Dickinson		1-59308-050-6	$7.95
The Complete Sherlock Holmes, Vol. I	Sir Arthur Conan Doyle	1-59308-034-4	$10.95
The Complete Sherlock Holmes, Vol. II	Sir Arthur Conan Doyle	1-59308-040-9	$10.95
Confessions	Saint Augustine	1-59308-259-2	$6.95
The Count of Monte Cristo	Alexandre Dumas	1-59308-151-0	$10.95
Don Quixote	Miguel de Cervantes	1-59308-046-8	$10.95
Dracula	Bram Stoker	1-59308-114-6	$8.95
Emma	Jane Austen	1-59308-152-9	$6.95
Essays and Poems by Ralph Waldo Emerson		1-59308-076-X	$12.95
The Essential Tales and Poems of Edgar Allan Poe		1-59308-064-6	$10.95
Ethan Frome and Selected Stories	Edith Wharton	1-59308-090-5	$7.95
Fairy Tales	Hans Christian Andersen	1-59308-260-6	$9.95
Founding America: Documents from the Revolution to the Bill of Rights	Jefferson, et al.	1-59308-230-4	$13.95
Frankenstein	Mary Shelley	1-59308-115-4	$6.95
Great American Short Stories: From Hawthorne to Hemingway	Various	1-59308-086-7	$11.95
The Great Escapes: Four Slave Narratives	Various	1-59308-294-0	$6.95
Great Expectations	Charles Dickens	1-59308-116-2	$7.95
Grimm's Fairy Tales	Jacob and Wilhelm Grimm	1-59308-056-5	$10.95
Gulliver's Travels	Jonathan Swift	1-59308-132-4	$7.95
Heart of Darkness and Selected Short Fiction	Joseph Conrad	1-59308-123-5	$7.95
The Idiot	Fyodor Dostoevsky	1-59308-058-1	$10.95
The Importance of Being Earnest and Four Other Plays	Oscar Wilde	1-59308-059-X	$9.95
The Inferno	Dante Alighieri	1-59308-051-4	$10.95
Jane Eyre	Charlotte Brontë	1-59308-117-0	$7.95

(continued)

Jude the Obscure	Thomas Hardy	1-59308-035-2	$8.95
The Jungle	Upton Sinclair	1-59308-118-9	$9.95
The Last of the Mohicans	James Fenimore Cooper	1-59308-137-5	$9.95
Les Liaisons Dangereuses	Pierre Choderlos de Laclos	1-59308-240-1	$9.95
Little Women	Louisa May Alcott	1-59308-108-1	$7.95
Lost Illusions	Honoré de Balzac	1-59308-315-7	$11.95
Main Street	Sinclair Lewis	1-59308-386-6	$10.95
Mansfield Park	Jane Austen	1-59308-154-5	$6.95
The Metamorphosis and Other Stories	Franz Kafka	1-59308-029-8	$9.95
Moby-Dick	Herman Melville	1-59308-018-2	$11.95
My Ántonia	Willa Cather	1-59308-202-9	$6.95
Narrative of Sojourner Truth		1-59308-293-2	$7.95
The Odyssey	Homer	1-59308-009-3	$9.95
Oliver Twist	Charles Dickens	1-59308-206-1	$6.95
The Origin of Species	Charles Darwin	1-59308-077-8	$10.95
Paradise Lost	John Milton	1-59308-095-6	$9.95
Persuasion	Jane Austen	1-59308-130-8	$5.95
The Picture of Dorian Gray	Oscar Wilde	1-59308-025-5	$6.95
A Portrait of the Artist as a Young Man and Dubliners	James Joyce	1-59308-031-X	$8.95
Pride and Prejudice	Jane Austen	1-59308-201-0	$6.95
The Prince and Other Writings	Niccolò Machiavelli	1-59308-060-3	$5.95
The Red Badge of Courage and Selected Short Fiction	Stephen Crane	1-59308-119-7	$6.95
Republic	Plato	1-59308-097-2	$8.95
Robinson Crusoe	Daniel Defoe	1-59308-360-2	$6.95
The Scarlet Letter	Nathaniel Hawthorne	1-59308-207-X	$6.95
The Secret Agent	Joseph Conrad	1-59308-305-X	$8.95
Selected Stories of O. Henry		1-59308-042-5	$9.95
Sense and Sensibility	Jane Austen	1-59308-125-1	$5.95
Siddhartha	Hermann Hesse	1-59308-379-3	$8.95
The Souls of Black Folk	W. E. B. Du Bois	1-59308-014-X	$8.95
The Strange Case of Dr. Jekyll and Mr. Hyde and Other Stories	Robert Louis Stevenson	1-59308-131-6	$6.95
A Tale of Two Cities	Charles Dickens	1-59308-138-3	$6.95
Three Theban Plays	Sophocles	1-59308-235-5	$8.95
Thus Spoke Zarathustra	Friedrich Nietzsche	1-59308-278-9	$9.95
The Time Machine and The Invisible Man	H. G. Wells	1-59308-388-2	$7.95
Treasure Island	Robert Louis Stevenson	1-59308-247-9	$6.95
The Turn of the Screw, The Aspern Papers and Two Stories	Henry James	1-59308-043-3	$5.95
Uncle Tom's Cabin	Harriet Beecher Stowe	1-59308-121-9	$7.95
Vanity Fair	William Makepeace Thackeray	1-59308-071-9	$8.95
Walden and Civil Disobedience	Henry David Thoreau	1-59308-208-8	$8.95
The War of the Worlds	H. G. Wells	1-59308-362-9	$6.95
Ward No. 6 and Other Stories	Anton Chekhov	1-59308-003-4	$8.95
Wuthering Heights	Emily Brontë	1-59308-128-6	$5.95

BARNES & NOBLE CLASSICS

If you are an educator and would like to receive an
Examination or Desk Copy of a Barnes & Noble Classics edition,
please refer to Academic Resources on our website at
WWW.BN.COM/CLASSICS
or contact us at
BNCLASSICS@BN.COM

All prices are subject to change.